Selected Works of Joseph Conrad

Selected Works of
Joseph Conrad

INCLUDING THE NOVELS

Lord Jim, Nostromo,
& The Secret Agent

AND THE SHORT STORIES

Youth, Typhoon,
Heart of Darkness,
The End of the Tether &
The Shadow-Line

Wordsworth Editions

In loving memory of
MICHAEL TRAYLER
the founder of Wordsworth Editions

2

Readers who are interested in other titles from
Wordsworth Editions are invited to visit our website at
www.wordsworth-editions.com

For our latest list and a full mail-order service, contact
Bibliophile Books, 5 Datapoint, South Crescent, London E16 4TL
TEL: +44 (0)20 7474 2474 FAX: +44 (0)20 7474 8589
ORDERS: orders@bibliophilebooks.com
WEBSITE: www.bibliophilebooks.com

This edition published 2005 by Wordsworth Editions Limited
8B East Street, Ware, Hertfordshire SG12 9HJ

ISBN   978 1 84022 061 2

Text © Wordsworth Editions Limited 2005

Typeset in Great Britain by Antony Gray
Printed and bound by Clays Ltd, St Ives plc

CONTENTS

NOVELS

Lord Jim – 1900   7

Nostromo – 1904   245

The Secret Agent – 1907   577

SHORT STORIES

The Lagoon – 1896   769

An Outpost of Progress – 1896   781

Karain: A Memory – 1897   801

Youth: A Narrative – 1898   833

Amy Foster – 1901   859

Typhoon – 1901   883

Falk – 1901   947

Heart of Darkness – 1902   1003

The End of the Tether – 1902   1071

An Anarchist (*A Desperate Tale*) – 1906   1171

The Informer (*An Ironic Tale*) – 1906   1189

Il Conde (*A Pathetic Tale*) – 1906   1209

The Secret Sharer – 1910   1223

Prince Roman – 1911   1257

The Shadow-Line: A Confession – 1915   1275

The Tale – 1917   1357

LORD JIM

Lord Jim

A Tale

A novel by

JOSEPH CONRAD

first published in 1900

*It is certain my Conviction gains infinitely
the moment another soul will believe in it.*

NOVALIS, *Fragmente*

To

MR AND MRS G. F. W. HOPE

with grateful affection

after many years of friendship

Author's Note to the 1917 Edition

When this novel first appeared in book form a notion got about that I had been bolted away with. Some reviewers maintained that the work starting as a short story had got beyond the writer's control. One or two discovered internal evidence of the fact, which seemed to amuse them. They pointed out the limitations of the narrative form. They argued that no man could have been expected to talk all that time, and other men to listen so long. It was not, they said, very credible.

After thinking it over for something like sixteen years I am not so sure about that. Men have been known, both in the tropics and in the temperate zone, to sit up half the night 'swapping yarns'. This, however, is but one yarn, yet with interruptions affording some measure of relief; and in regard to the listeners' endurance, the postulate must be accepted that the story *was* interesting. It is the necessary preliminary assumption. If I hadn't believed that it *was* interesting I could never have begun to write it. As to the mere physical possibility we all know that some speeches in Parliament have taken nearer six than three hours in delivery; whereas all that part of the book which is Marlow's narrative can be read through aloud, I should say, in less than three hours. Besides – though I have kept strictly all such insignificant details out of the tale – we may presume that there must have been refreshments on that night, a glass of mineral water of some sort to help the narrator on.

But, seriously, the truth of the matter is that my first thought was of a short story, concerned only with the pilgrim-ship episode; nothing more. And that was a legitimate conception. After writing a few pages, however, I became for some reason discontented and I laid them aside for a time. I didn't take them out of the drawer till the late Mr William Blackwood suggested I should give something again to his magazine.

It was only then that I perceived that the pilgrim-ship episode was a good starting-point for a free and wandering tale; that it was an event, too, which could conceivably colour the whole 'sentiment of existence' in a simple and sensitive character. But all these preliminary moods and stirrings of spirit were rather obscure at the time, and they do not appear clearer to me now after the lapse of so many years.

The few pages I had laid aside were not without their weight in the choice of subject. But the whole was rewritten deliberately. When I sat down to it I knew it would be a long book, though I didn't foresee that it would spread itself over thirteen numbers of *Maga*.

I have been asked at times whether this was not the book of mine I liked best. I am a great foe to favouritism in public life, in private life, and even in the delicate relationship of an author to his works. As a matter of principle I will have no favourites; but I don't go so far as to feel grieved and annoyed by the preference some people give to my Lord Jim. I won't even say that I 'fail to understand . . . ' No! But once I had occasion to be puzzled and surprised.

A friend of mine returning from Italy had talked with a lady there who did not like the book. I regretted that, of course, but what surprised me was the ground of her dislike. 'You know,' she said, 'it is all so morbid.'

The pronouncement gave me food for an hour's anxious thought. Finally I arrived at the conclusion that, making due allowances for the subject itself being rather foreign to women's normal sensibilities, the lady could not have been an Italian. I wonder whether she was European at all? In any case, no Latin temperament would have perceived anything morbid in the acute consciousness of lost honour. Such a consciousness may be wrong, or it may be right, or it may be condemned as artificial; and, perhaps, my Jim is not a type of wide commonness. But I can safely assure my readers that he is not the product of coldly perverted thinking. He's not a figure of Northern Mists either. One sunny morning in the commonplace surroundings of an Eastern roadstead, I saw his form pass by – appealing – significant – under a cloud – perfectly silent. Which is as it should be. It was for me, with all the sympathy of which I was capable, to seek fit words for his meaning. He was 'one of us'.

JOSEPH CONRAD
June 1917

Chapter I

He was an inch, perhaps two, under six feet, powerfully built, and he advanced straight at you with a slight stoop of the shoulders, head forward, and a fixed from-under stare which made you think of a charging bull. His voice was deep, loud, and his manner displayed a kind of dogged self-assertion which had nothing aggressive in it. It seemed a necessity, and it was directed apparently as much at himself as at anybody else. He was spotlessly neat, apparelled in immaculate white from shoes to hat, and in the various Eastern ports where he got his living as ship-chandler's water-clerk he was very popular.

A water-clerk need not pass an examination in anything under the sun, but he must have Ability in the abstract and demonstrate it practically. His work consists in racing under sail, steam, or oars against other water-clerks for any ship about to anchor, greeting her captain cheerily, forcing upon him a card – the business card of the ship-chandler – and on his first visit on shore piloting him firmly but without ostentation to a vast, cavern-like shop which is full of things that are eaten and drunk on board ship; where you can get everything to make her seaworthy and beautiful, from a set of chain-hooks for her cable to a book of gold-leaf for the carvings of her stern; and where her commander is received like a brother by a ship-chandler he has never seen before. There is a cool parlour, easy-chairs, bottles, cigars, writing implements, a copy of harbour regulations, and a warmth of welcome that melts the salt of a three months' passage out of a seaman's heart. The connection thus begun is kept up, as long as the ship remains in harbour, by the daily visits of the water-clerk. To the captain he is faithful like a friend and attentive like a son, with the patience of Job, the unselfish devotion of a woman, and the jollity of a boon companion. Later on the bill is sent in. It is a beautiful and humane occupation. Therefore good water-clerks are scarce. When a water-clerk who possesses Ability in the abstract has also the advantage of having been brought up to the sea, he is worth to his employer a lot of money and some humouring. Jim had always good wages and as much humouring as would have bought the fidelity of a fiend. Nevertheless, with black ingratitude he would throw up the job suddenly and depart. To his employers the reasons he gave were obviously inadequate. They said 'Confounded fool!' as soon as his back was turned. This was their criticism on his exquisite sensibility.

To the white men in the waterside business and to the captains of ships he was just Jim – nothing more. He had, of course, another name, but he was anxious that it should not be pronounced. His incognito, which had as many holes as a sieve, was not meant to hide a personality but a fact. When the fact broke through the incognito he would leave suddenly the seaport where he happened to be at the time and go to another – generally farther east. He kept to seaports because he was a seaman in exile from the sea, and had Ability in the abstract, which is good for no other work but that of a water-clerk. He retreated in good order towards the rising sun, and the fact followed him casually but inevitably. Thus in the course of years he was known successively in Bombay, in Calcutta, in Rangoon, in Penang, in Batavia – and in each of these halting-places was just Jim the water-clerk. Afterwards, when his keen perception of the Intolerable drove him away for good from seaports and white men, even into the virgin forest, the Malays of the jungle village, where he had elected to conceal his deplorable faculty, added a word to the monosyllable of his incognito. They called him Tuan Jim: as one might say – Lord Jim.

Originally he came from a parsonage. Many commanders of fine merchant-ships come from these abodes of piety and peace. Jim's father possessed such certain knowledge of the Unknowable as made for the righteousness of people in cottages without disturbing the ease of mind of those whom an unerring Providence enables to live in mansions. The little church on a hill had the mossy greyness of a rock seen through a ragged screen of leaves. It had stood there for centuries, but the trees around probably remembered the laying of the first stone. Below, the red front of the rectory gleamed with a warm tint in the midst of grass-plots, flower-beds, and fir trees, with an orchard at the back, a paved stable-yard to the left, and the sloping glass of greenhouses tacked along a wall of bricks. The living had belonged to the family for generations; but Jim was one of five sons, and when after a course of light holiday literature his vocation for the sea had declared itself, he was sent at once to a 'training-ship for officers of the mercantile marine.'

He learned there a little trigonometry and how to cross top-gallant yards. He was generally liked. He had the third place in navigation and pulled stroke in the first cutter. Having a steady head with an excellent physique, he was very smart aloft. His station was in the fore-top, and often from there he looked down, with the contempt of a man destined to shine in the midst of dangers, at the peaceful multitude of roofs cut in two by the brown tide of the stream, while scattered on the outskirts of the surrounding plain the factory chimneys rose perpendicular against a grimy sky, each slender like a pencil, and belching out smoke like a volcano. He could see the big ships departing, the broad-beamed ferries constantly on the move, the little boats floating far below his feet, with the hazy splendour of the sea in the distance, and the hope of a stirring life in the world of adventure.

On the lower deck in the babel of two hundred voices he would forget himself, and beforehand live in his mind the sea-life of light literature. He saw himself saving people from sinking ships, cutting away masts in a hurricane, swimming through a surf with a line; or as a lonely castaway, barefooted and half naked, walking on uncovered reefs in search of shellfish to stave off starvation. He confronted savages on tropical shores, quelled mutinies on the high seas, and in a small boat upon the ocean kept up the hearts of despairing men – always an example of devotion to duty, and as unflinching as a hero in a book.

'Something's up. Come along.'

He leaped to his feet. The boys were streaming up the ladders. Above could be heard a great scurrying about and shouting, and when he got through the hatchway he stood still – as if confounded.

It was the dusk of a winter's day. The gale had freshened since noon, stopping the traffic on the river, and now blew with the strength of a hurricane in fitful bursts that boomed like salvoes of great guns firing over the ocean. The rain slanted in sheets that flicked and subsided, and between whiles Jim had threatening glimpses of the tumbling tide, the small craft jumbled and tossing along the shore, the motionless buildings in the driving mist, the broad ferry-boats pitching ponderously at anchor, the vast landing-stages heaving up and down and smothered in sprays. The next gust seemed to blow all this away. The air was full of flying water. There was a fierce purpose in the gale, a furious earnestness in the screech of the wind, in the brutal tumult of earth and sky, that seemed directed at him, and made him hold his breath in awe. He stood still. It seemed to him he was whirled around.

He was jostled. 'Man the cutter!' Boys rushed past him. A coaster running in for shelter had crashed through a schooner at anchor, and one of the ship's instructors had seen the accident. A mob of boys clambered on the rails, clustered round the davits. 'Collision. Just ahead of us. Mr Symons saw it.' A push made him stagger against the mizzen-mast, and he caught hold of a rope. The old training-ship chained to her moorings quivered all over, bowing gently head to wind, and with her scanty rigging humming in a deep bass the breathless song of her youth at sea. 'Lower away!' He saw the boat, manned, drop swiftly below the rail, and rushed after her. He heard a splash. 'Let go; clear the falls!' He leaned over. The river alongside seethed in frothy streaks. The cutter could be seen in the falling darkness under the spell of tide and wind, that for a moment held her bound, and tossing abreast of the ship. A yelling voice in her reached him faintly: 'Keep stroke, you young whelps, if you want to save anybody! Keep stroke!' And suddenly she lifted high her bow, and, leaping with raised oars over a wave, broke the spell cast upon her by the wind and tide.

Jim felt his shoulder gripped firmly. 'Too late, youngster.' The captain of the ship laid a restraining hand on that boy, who seemed on the point of leaping overboard, and Jim looked up with the pain of conscious defeat in his eyes. The captain smiled sympathetically. 'Better luck next time. This will teach you to be smart.'

A shrill cheer greeted the cutter. She came dancing back half full of water, and with two exhausted men washing about on her bottom boards. The tumult and the menace of wind and sea now appeared very contemptible to Jim, increasing the regret of his awe at their inefficient menace. Now he knew what to think of it. It seemed to him he cared nothing for the gale. He could affront greater perils. He would do so – better than anybody. Not a particle of fear was left. Nevertheless he brooded apart that evening while the bowman of the cutter – a boy with a face like a girl's and big grey eyes – was the hero of the lower deck. Eager questioners crowded round him. He narrated: 'I just saw his head bobbing, and I dashed my boat-hook in the water. It caught in his breeches and I nearly went overboard, as I thought I would, only old Symons let go the tiller and grabbed my legs – the boat nearly swamped. Old Symons is a fine old chap. I don't mind a bit him being grumpy with us. He swore at me all the time he held my leg, but that was only his way of telling me to stick to the boat-hook. Old Symons is awfully excitable – isn't he? No – not the little fair chap – the other, the big one with a beard. When we pulled him in he groaned, 'Oh, my leg! oh, my leg!' and turned up his eyes. Fancy such a big chap fainting like a girl. Would any of you fellows faint for a jab with a boat-hook? – I wouldn't. It went into his leg so far.' He showed the boat-hook, which he had carried below for the purpose, and produced a sensation. 'No, silly! It was not his flesh that held him – his breeches did. Lots of blood, of course.'

Jim thought it a pitiful display of vanity. The gale had ministered to a heroism as spurious as its own pretence of terror. He felt angry with the brutal tumult of earth and sky for taking him unawares and checking unfairly a generous readiness for narrow escapes. Otherwise he was rather glad he had not gone into the cutter, since a lower achievement had served the turn. He had enlarged his knowledge more than those who had done the work. When all men flinched, then – he felt sure – he alone would know how to deal with the spurious menace of wind and seas. He knew what to think of it. Seen dispassionately, it seemed contemptible. He could detect no trace of emotion in himself, and the final effect of a staggering event was that, unnoticed and apart from the noisy crowd of boys, he exulted with fresh certitude in his avidity for adventure, and in a sense of many-sided courage.

Chapter 2

After two years of training he went to sea, and entering the regions so well known to his imagination, found them strangely barren of adventure. He made many voyages. He knew the magic monotony of existence between sky and water: he had to bear the criticism of men, the exactions of the sea, and the prosaic severity of the daily task that gives bread – but whose only reward is in the perfect love of the work. This reward eluded him. Yet he could not go back, because there is nothing more enticing, disenchanting, and enslaving than the life at sea. Besides, his prospects were good. He was gentlemanly, steady, tractable, with a thorough knowledge of his duties; and in time, when very young, he became chief mate of a fine ship, without ever having been tested by those events of the sea that show in the light of day the inner worth of a man, the edge of his temper, and the fibre of his stuff; that reveal the quality of his resistance and the secret truth of his pretences, not only to others but also to himself.

[Only once in all that time he had again the glimpse of the earnestness in the anger of the sea. That truth is not so often made apparent as people might think. There are many shades in the danger of adventures and gales, and it is only now and then that there appears on the face of facts a sinister violence of intention – that indefinable something which forces it upon the mind and the heart of a man, that this complication of accidents or these elemental furies are coming at him with a purpose of malice, with a strength beyond control, with an unbridled cruelty that means to tear out of him his hope and his fear, the pain of his fatigue and his longing for rest: which means to smash, to destroy, to annihilate all he had seen, known, loved, enjoyed, or hated; all that is priceless and necessary – the sunshine, the memories, the future – which means to sweep the whole precious world utterly away from his sight by the simple and appalling act of taking his life.]

Jim, disabled by a falling spar at the beginning of a week of which his Scottish captain used to say afterwards: 'Man! it's a perfect meeracle to me how she lived through it!', spent many days stretched on his back, dazed, battered, hopeless, and tormented as if at the bottom of an abyss of unrest. He did not care what the end would be, and in his lucid moments over-valued his indifference. The danger, when not seen, has the imperfect vagueness of human thought. The fear grows shadowy; and Imagination, the enemy of men, the father of all terrors, unstimulated, sinks to rest in the dullness of exhausted emotion. Jim saw nothing but the disorder of his tossed cabin. He lay there battened down in the midst of a small devastation, and felt secretly glad he had not to go on deck. But now and again an uncontrollable rush of anguish would grip him bodily, make him gasp and writhe under the blankets, and then the unintelligent brutality of an existence liable to the agony of such sensations filled him with a despairing desire to escape at any cost. Then fine weather returned, and he thought no more about it.

His lameness, however, persisted, and when the ship arrived at an Eastern port he had to go to the hospital. His recovery was slow, and he was left behind.

There were only two other patients in the white men's ward: the purser of a gunboat, who had broken his leg falling down a hatchway; and a kind of railway contractor from a neighbouring province, afflicted by some mysterious tropical disease, who held the doctor for an ass, and indulged in secret debaucheries of patent medicine which his Tamil servant used to smuggle in with unwearied devotion. They told each other the story of their lives, played cards a little, or, yawning and in pyjamas, lounged through the day in easy-chairs without saying a word. The hospital stood on a hill, and a gentle breeze entering through the windows, always flung wide open, brought into the bare room the softness of the sky, the languor of the earth, the bewitching breath of the Eastern waters. There were perfumes in it, suggestions of infinite repose, the gift of endless dreams. Jim looked every day over the thickets of gardens, beyond the roofs of the town, over the fronds of palms growing on the shore, at that roadstead which is a thoroughfare to the East – at the roadstead dotted by garlanded islets, lighted by festal sunshine, its ships like toys, its brilliant activity resembling a holiday pageant, with the eternal serenity of the Eastern sky overhead and the smiling peace of the Eastern seas possessing the space as far as the horizon.

Directly he could walk without a stick, he descended into the town to look for some opportunity to get home. Nothing offered just then, and, while waiting, he associated naturally with the men of his calling in the port. These were of two kinds. Some, very few and seen there but seldom, led mysterious lives, had preserved an undefaced energy with the temper of buccaneers and the eyes of dreamers. They appeared to live in a crazy maze of plans, hopes, dangers, enterprises, ahead of civilisation, in the dark places of the sea; and their death was the only event of their fantastic existence that seemed to have a reasonable certitude of achievement. The majority were men who, like himself, thrown there by some accident, had remained as officers of country ships. They had now a horror of the home service, with its harder conditions, severer view of duty, and the hazard of stormy oceans. They were attuned to the eternal peace of Eastern sky and sea. They loved short passages, good deck-chairs, large native crews, and the distinction of being white. They shuddered at the thought of hard work, and led precariously easy lives, always on the verge of dismissal, always on the verge of engagement, serving Chinamen, Arabs, half-castes – would have served the devil himself had he made it easy enough. They talked everlastingly of turns of luck: how So-and-so got charge of a boat on the coast of China – a soft thing; how this one had an easy billet in Japan somewhere, and that one was doing well in the Siamese navy; and in all they said – in their actions, in their looks, in their persons – could be detected the soft spot, the place of decay, the determination to lounge safely through existence.

To Jim that gossiping crowd, viewed as seamen, seemed at first more unsubstantial than so many shadows. But at length he found a fascination in the sight of those men, in their appearance of doing so well on such a small allowance of danger and toil. In time, beside the original disdain there grew up slowly another sentiment; and suddenly, giving up the idea of going home, he took a berth as chief mate of the *Patna*.

The *Patna* was a local steamer as old as the hills, lean like a greyhound, and eaten up with rust worse than a condemned water-tank. She was owned by a Chinaman, chartered by an Arab, and commanded by a sort of renegade New South Wales German, very anxious to curse publicly his native country, but who, apparently on the strength of Bismarck's victorious policy, brutalised all those he was not afraid of, and wore a 'blood-and-iron' air, combined with a purple nose and a red moustache. After she had been painted outside and whitewashed inside, eight hundred pilgrims (more or less) were driven on board of her as she lay with steam up alongside a wooden jetty.

They streamed aboard over three gangways, they streamed in urged by faith and the hope of paradise, they streamed in with a continuous tramp and shuffle of bare feet, without a word, a murmur, or a look back; and when clear of confining rails spread on all sides over the deck, flowed forward and aft, overflowed down the yawning hatchways, filled the inner recesses of the ship – like water filling a cistern, like water flowing into crevices and crannies, like water rising silently even with the rim. Eight hundred men and women with faith and hopes, with affections and memories, they had collected there, coming from north and south and from the outskirts of the East, after treading the jungle paths, descending the rivers, coasting in *praus* along the shallows, crossing in small canoes from island to island, passing through suffering, meeting strange sights, beset by strange fears, upheld by one desire. They came from solitary huts in the wilderness, from populous *campongs*, from villages by the sea. At the call of an idea they had left their forests, their clearings, the protection of their rulers, their prosperity, their poverty, the surroundings of their youth and the graves of their fathers. They came covered with dust, with sweat, with grime, with rags – the strong men at the head of family parties, the lean old men pressing forward without hope of return; young boys with fearless eyes glancing curiously, shy little girls with tumbled long hair; the timid women muffled up and clasping to their breasts, wrapped in loose ends of soiled head-cloths, their sleeping babies, the unconscious pilgrims of an exacting belief.

'Look at dese cattle,' said the German skipper to his new chief mate.

An Arab, the leader of that pious voyage, came last. He walked slowly aboard, handsome and grave in his white gown and large turban. A string of servants followed, loaded with his luggage; the *Patna* cast off and backed away from the wharf.

She was headed between two small islets, crossed obliquely the anchoring-ground of sailing-ships, swung through half a circle in the shadow of a hill, then ranged close to a ledge of foaming reefs. The Arab, standing up aft, recited aloud the prayer of travellers by sea. He invoked the favour of the Most High upon that journey, implored His blessing on men's toil and on the secret purposes of their hearts; the steamer pounded in the dusk the calm water of the Strait; and far astern of the pilgrim ship a screw-pile lighthouse, planted by unbelievers on a treacherous shoal, seemed to wink at her its eye of flame, as if in derision of her errand of faith.

She cleared the Strait, crossed the bay, continued on her way through the 'One-degree' passage. She held on straight for the Red Sea under a serene sky, under a sky scorching and unclouded, enveloped in a fulgor of sunshine that killed all thought, oppressed the heart, withered all impulses of strength and energy. And under the sinister splendour of that sky the sea, blue and profound, remained still, without a stir, without a ripple, without a wrinkle – viscous, stagnant, dead. The *Patna*, with a slight hiss, passed over that plain luminous and smooth, unrolled a black ribbon of smoke across the sky, left behind her on the water a white ribbon of foam that vanished at once, like the phantom of a track drawn upon a lifeless sea by the phantom of a steamer.

Every morning the sun, as if keeping pace in his revolutions with the progress of the pilgrimage, emerged with a silent burst of light exactly at the same distance astern of the ship, caught up with her at noon, pouring the concentrated fire of his rays on the pious purposes of the men, glided past on his descent, and sank mysteriously into the sea evening after evening, preserving the same distance ahead of her advancing bows. The five whites on board lived amidships, isolated from the human cargo. The awnings covered the deck with a white roof from stem to stern, and a faint hum, a low murmur of sad voices, alone revealed the presence of a crowd of people upon the great blaze of the ocean. Such were the days, still, hot, heavy, disappearing one by one into the past, as if falling into an abyss for ever open in the wake of the ship; and the ship, lonely under a wisp of smoke, held on her steadfast way black and smouldering in a luminous immensity, as if scorched by a flame flicked at her from a heaven without pity.

The nights descended on her like a benediction.

Chapter 3

A marvellous stillness pervaded the world, and the stars, together with the serenity of their rays, seemed to shed upon the earth the assurance of everlasting security. The young moon, recurved, and shining low in the west, was like a slender shaving thrown up from a bar of gold, and the Arabian Sea, smooth and cool to the eye like a sheet of ice, extended its perfect level to the perfect circle of a dark horizon. The propeller turned without a check, as though its beat had been part of the scheme of a safe universe; and on each side of the *Patna* two deep folds of water, permanent and sombre on the unwrinkled shimmer, enclosed within their straight and diverging ridges a few white swirls of foam bursting in a low hiss, a few wavelets, a few ripples, a few undulations that, left behind, agitated the surface of the sea for an instant after the passage of the ship, subsided splashing gently, calmed down at last into the circular stillness of water and sky with the black speck of the moving hull remaining everlastingly in its centre.

Jim on the bridge was penetrated by the great certitude of unbounded safety and peace that could be read on the silent aspect of nature like the certitude of fostering love upon the placid tenderness of a mother's face. Below the roof of awnings, surrendered to the wisdom of white men and to their courage, trusting the power of their unbelief and the iron shell of their fire-ship, the pilgrims of an exacting faith slept on mats, on blankets, on bare planks, on every deck, in all the dark corners, wrapped in dyed cloths, muffled in soiled rags, with their heads resting on small bundles, with their faces pressed to bent forearms: the men, the women, the children; the old with the young, the decrepit with the lusty – all equal before sleep, death's brother.

A draught of air, fanned from forward by the speed of the ship, passed steadily through the long gloom between the high bulwarks, swept over the rows of prone bodies; a few dim flames in globe-lamps were hung short here and there under the ridge-poles, and in the blurred circles of light thrown down and trembling slightly to the unceasing vibration of the ship appeared a chin upturned, two closed eyelids, a dark hand with silver rings, a meagre limb draped in a torn covering, a head bent back, a naked foot, a throat bared and stretched as if offering itself to the knife. The well-to-do had made for their families shelters with heavy boxes and dusty mats; the poor reposed side by side with all they had on earth tied up in a rag under their heads; the lone old men slept, with drawn-up legs, upon their prayer-carpets, with their hands over their ears and one elbow on each side of the face; a father, his shoulders up and his knees under his forehead, dozed dejectedly by a boy who slept on his back with tousled hair and one arm commandingly extended; a woman covered from head to foot, like a corpse, with a piece of white sheeting, had a naked child in the hollow of each arm; the Arab's belongings, piled right aft, made a heavy mound of broken outlines, with a cargo-lamp swung above, and a great confusion of vague forms behind: gleams of paunchy brass pots, the foot-rest of a deck-chair, blades of spears, the straight scabbard of an old sword leaning against a heap of pillows, the spout of a tin coffee-pot. The patent log on the taffrail periodically rang a single tinkling stroke for every mile traversed on an errand of faith. Above the mass of sleepers a faint and patient sigh at times floated, the exhalation of a troubled dream; and short metallic clangs bursting out suddenly in the depths of the ship, the harsh scrape of a shovel, the violent slam of a furnace-door, exploded brutally, as if the men handling the mysterious things below had their breasts full of fierce anger: while the slim high hull of the steamer went on evenly ahead, without a sway of her bare masts, cleaving continuously the great calm of the waters under the inaccessible serenity of the sky.

Jim paced athwart, and his footsteps in the vast silence were loud to his own ears, as if echoed by the watchful stars: his eyes roaming about the line of the horizon, seemed to gaze hungrily into the unattainable, and did not see the shadow of the coming event. The only shadow on the sea was the shadow of the black smoke pouring heavily from the funnel its immense streamer, whose end was constantly dissolving in the air. Two Malays, silent and almost motionless, steered, one on each side of the wheel, whose brass rim shone fragmentarily in the oval of light thrown out by the binnacle. Now and then a hand, with black fingers alternately letting go and catching hold of revolving spokes, appeared in the illumined part; the links of wheel-chains ground heavily in the grooves of the barrel. Jim would glance at the compass, would glance around the unattainable horizon, would stretch himself till his joints cracked with a leisurely twist of the body, in the very excess of well-being; and, as if made audacious by the invincible aspect of the peace, he felt he cared for nothing that could happen to him to the end of his days. From time to time he glanced idly at a chart pegged out with four drawing-pins on a low three-legged table abaft the steering-gear case. The sheet of paper portraying the depths of the sea presented a shiny surface under the light of a bull's-eye lamp lashed to a stanchion, a surface as level and smooth as the glimmering surface of the waters. Parallel rulers with a pair of dividers reposed on it; the ship's position at last noon was marked with a small black cross, and the straight pencil-line drawn firmly as far as Perim figured the course of the ship – the path of souls towards the holy place, the promise of salvation, the reward of eternal life – while the pencil with its sharp end touching the Somali coast lay round and still like a naked ship's spar floating in the pool of a sheltered dock. 'How steady she goes,' thought Jim with wonder, with something like gratitude for this high peace of sea and sky. At such times his thoughts would be full of valorous deeds: he loved these dreams and the success of his imaginary achievements. They were the best parts of life, its secret truth, its hidden reality. They had a gorgeous virility, the charm of vagueness, they passed before him with a heroic tread; they carried his soul away with them and made it drunk with the divine philtre of an unbounded confidence in itself. There was nothing he could not face. He was so pleased with the idea that he smiled, keeping perfunctorily his eyes ahead; and when he happened to glance back he saw the white streak of the wake drawn as straight by the ship's keel upon the sea as the black line drawn by the pencil upon the chart.

The ash-buckets racketed, clanking up and down the stokehold ventilators, and this tin-pot clatter warned him the end of his watch was near. He sighed with content, with regret as well at having to part from that serenity which fostered the adventurous freedom of his thoughts. He was a little sleepy, too, and felt a pleasurable languor running through every limb as though all the blood in his body had turned to warm milk. His skipper had come up noiselessly, in pyjamas and with his sleeping-jacket flung wide open. Red of face, only half awake, the left eye partly closed, the right staring stupid and glassy, he hung his big head over the chart and scratched his ribs sleepily. There was something obscene in the sight of his naked flesh. His bared breast glistened soft and greasy as though he had sweated out his fat in his sleep. He pronounced a professional remark in a voice harsh and dead, resembling the rasping sound of a wood-file on the edge of a plank; the fold of his double chin hung like a bag triced up close under the hinge of his jaw. Jim started, and his answer was full of deference; but the odious and fleshy figure, as though seen for the first time in a revealing moment, fixed itself in his memory for ever as the incarnation of everything vile and base that lurks in the world we love: in our own hearts we trust for our salvation in the men that surround us, in the sights that fill our eyes, in the sounds that fill our ears, and in the air that fills our lungs.

The thin gold shaving of the moon floating slowly downwards had lost itself on the darkened surface of the waters, and the eternity beyond the sky seemed to come down nearer to the earth, with the augmented glitter of the stars, with the more profound sombreness in the lustre of the half-transparent dome covering the flat disk of an opaque sea. The ship moved so smoothly that her onward motion was imperceptible to the senses of men, as though she had been a crowded planet speeding through the dark spaces of ether behind the swarm of suns, in the appalling and calm solitudes awaiting the breath of future creations. 'Hot is no name for it down below,' said a voice.

Jim smiled without looking round. The skipper presented an unmoved breadth of back: it was the renegade's trick to appear pointedly unaware of your existence unless it suited his purpose to turn at you with a devouring glare before he let loose a torrent of foamy, abusive jargon that came like a gush from a sewer. Now he emitted only a sulky grunt; the second engineer at the head of the bridge-ladder, kneading with damp palms a dirty sweat-rag, unabashed, continued the tale of his complaints. The sailors had a good time of it up here, and what was the use of them in the world he would be blowed if he could see. The poor devils of engineers had to get the ship along anyhow, and they could very well do the rest too; by gosh they – 'Shut up,' growled the German stolidly. 'Oh, yes! Shut up – and when anything goes wrong you fly to us, don't you?' went on the other. He was more than half cooked, he expected; but anyway, now, he did not mind how much he sinned, because these last three days he had passed through a fine course of training for the place where the bad boys go when they die – b'gosh, he had – besides being made jolly well deaf by the blasted racket below. The durned, compound, surface-condensing, rotten scrap-heap rattled and banged down there like an old deck-winch, only more so; and what made him risk his life every night and day that God made amongst the refuse of a breaking-up yard flying round at fifty-seven revolutions, was more than *he* could tell. He must have been born reckless, b'gosh. He . . . 'Where did you get drink?' enquired the German, very savage, but motionless in the light of the binnacle, like a clumsy effigy of a man cut out of a block of fat. Jim went on smiling at the retreating horizon; his heart was full of generous impulses, and his thought was contemplating his own superiority. 'Drink!' repeated the engineer with amiable scorn: he was hanging on with both hands to the rail, a shadowy figure with flexible legs. 'Not from you, captain. You're far too mean, b'gosh. You would let a good man die sooner than give him a drop of schnapps. That's what you Germans call economy. Penny wise, pound foolish.' He became sentimental. The chief had given him a four-finger nip about ten o'clock – 'only one, s'elp me!' – good old chief; but as to getting the old fraud out of his bunk – a five-ton crane couldn't do it. Not it. Not tonight anyhow. He was sleeping sweetly like a little child, with a bottle of prime brandy under his pillow. From the thick throat of the commander of the *Patna* came a low rumble, on which the sound of the word *Schwein* fluttered high and low like a capricious feather in a faint stir of air. He and the chief engineer had been cronies for a good few years – serving the same jovial, crafty, old Chinaman, with horn-rimmed goggles and strings of red silk plaited into the venerable grey hairs of his pigtail. The quayside opinion in the *Patna's* home-port was that these two in the way of brazen peculation 'had done together pretty well everything you can think of.' Outwardly they were badly matched: one dull-eyed, malevolent, and of soft fleshy curves; the other lean, all hollows, with a head long and bony like the head of an old horse, with sunken cheeks, with sunken temples, with an indifferent glazed glance of sunken eyes. He had been stranded out East somewhere – in Canton, in Shanghai, or perhaps in Yokohama; he probably did not care to remember himself the exact locality, nor yet the cause of his shipwreck. He had been, in mercy to his youth, kicked quietly out of his ship twenty years ago or more, and it might have been so much worse for him that the memory of the episode had in it hardly a trace of misfortune. Then, steam navigation expanding in these seas and men of his craft being scarce at first, he had 'got on' after a sort. He was eager to let strangers know in a dismal mumble that he was 'an old stager out here'. When he moved a skeleton seemed to sway loose in his clothes; his walk was mere wandering, and he was given to wander thus around the engine-room skylight, smoking, without relish, doctored tobacco in a brass bowl at the end of a cherrywood stem four feet long, with the imbecile gravity of a thinker evolving a system of philosophy from the hazy glimpse of a truth. He was usually anything but free with his private store of liquor; but on that night he had departed from his principles, so that his second, a weak-headed child of Wapping, what with the unexpectedness of the treat and the strength of the stuff, had become very happy, cheeky, and talkative. The fury of the New South Wales German was extreme; he puffed like an exhaust-pipe, and Jim, faintly amused by the scene, was impatient for the time when he could get below: the last ten minutes of the watch were irritating like a gun that hangs fire; those men did not belong to the world of heroic adventure; they weren't bad chaps though. Even the skipper himself . . . His gorge rose at the mass of panting flesh from which issued gurgling mutters, a cloudy trickle of filthy expressions; but he was too pleasurably languid to dislike actively this or any other thing. The quality of these men did not matter; he rubbed shoulders with them, but they could not touch him; he shared the air they breathed, but he was different . . . Would the skipper go for the engineer? . . . The life was easy and he was too sure of himself – too sure of himself to . . . The line dividing his meditation from a surreptitious doze on his feet was thinner than a thread in a spider's web.

The second engineer was coming by easy transitions to the considerations of his finances and of his courage.

'Who's drunk? I? No, no, captain! That won't do. You ought to know by this time the chief ain't free-hearted enough to make a sparrow drunk, b'gosh. I've never been the worse for liquor in my life; the stuff ain't made yet that would make *me* drunk. I could drink liquid fire against your whisky peg for peg, b'gosh, and keep as cool as a cucumber. If I thought I was drunk I would jump overboard – do away with myself, b'gosh. I would! Straight! And I won't go off the bridge. Where do you expect me to take the air on a night like this, eh? On deck amongst that vermin down there? Likely – ain't it! And I am not afraid of anything you can do.'

The German lifted two heavy fists to heaven and shook them a little without a word.

'I don't know what fear is,' pursued the engineer, with the enthusiasm of sincere conviction. 'I am not afraid of doing all the bloomin' work in this rotten hooker, b'gosh! And a jolly good thing for you that there are some of us about the world that aren't afraid of their lives, or where would you be – you and this old thing here with her plates like brown paper – brown paper, s'elp me? It's all very fine for you – you get a power of pieces out of her one way and another; but what about me – what do I get? A measly hundred and fifty dollars a month and find yourself. I wish to ask you respectfully – respectfully, mind – who wouldn't chuck a dratted job like this? 'Tain't safe, s'elp me, it ain't! Only I am one of them fearless fellows . . . '

He let go the rail and made ample gestures as if demonstrating in the air the shape and extent of his valour; his thin voice darted in prolonged squeaks upon the sea, he tiptoed back and forth for the better emphasis of utterance, and suddenly pitched down head-first as though he had been clubbed from behind. He said 'Damn!' as he tumbled; an instant of silence followed upon his screeching: Jim and the skipper staggered forward by common accord, and catching themselves up, stood very stiff and still gazing, amazed, at the undisturbed level of the sea. Then they looked upwards at the stars.

What had happened? The wheezy thump of the engines went on. Had the earth been checked in her course? They could not understand; and suddenly the calm sea, the sky without a cloud, appeared formidably insecure in their immobility, as if poised on the brow of yawning destruction. The engineer rebounded vertically full length and collapsed again into a vague heap. This heap said: 'What's that?' in the muffled accents of profound grief. A faint noise as of thunder infinitely remote, less than a sound, hardly more than a vibration, passed slowly, and the ship quivered in response, as if the thunder had growled deep in the water. The eyes of the two Malays at the wheel glittered towards the white men, but their dark hands remained closed on the spokes. The sharp hull driving on its way seemed to rise a few inches in succession through its whole length, as though it had become pliable, and settled down again rigidly to its work of cleaving the smooth surface of the sea. Its quivering stopped, and the faint noise of thunder ceased all at once, as though the ship had steamed across a narrow belt of vibrating water and of humming air.

Chapter 4

A month or so afterwards, when Jim, in answer to pointed questions, tried to tell honestly the truth of this experience, he said, speaking of the ship: 'She went over whatever it was as easy as a snake crawling over a stick.' The illustration was good: the questions were aiming at facts, and the official inquiry was being held in the police court of an Eastern port. He stood elevated in the witness-box, with burning cheeks in a cool lofty room: the big framework of punkahs moved gently to and fro high above his head, and from below many eyes were looking at him out of dark faces, out of white faces, out of red faces, out of faces attentive, spellbound, as if all these people sitting in orderly rows upon narrow benches had been enslaved by the fascination of his voice. It was very loud, it rang startling in his own ears, it was the only sound audible in the world, for the terribly distinct questions that extorted his answers seemed to shape themselves in anguish and pain within his breast – came to him poignant and silent like the terrible questioning of one's conscience. Outside the court the sun blazed – within was the wind of great punkahs that made you shiver, the shame that made you burn, the attentive eyes whose glance stabbed. The face of the presiding magistrate, clean shaved and impassible, looked at him deadly pale between the red faces of the two nautical assessors. The light of a broad window under the ceiling fell from above on the heads and shoulders of the three men, and they were fiercely distinct in the half-light of the big court-room where the audience seemed composed of staring shadows. They wanted facts. Facts! They demanded facts from him, as if facts could explain anything!

'After you had concluded you had collided with something floating awash, say a waterlogged wreck, you were ordered by your captain to go forward and ascertain if there was any damage done. Did you think it likely from the force of the blow?' asked the assessor sitting to the left. He had a thin horseshoe beard, salient cheek-bones and with both elbows on the desk clasped his rugged hands before his face, looking at Jim with thoughtful blue eyes; the other, a heavy, scornful man, thrown back in his seat, his left arm extended full length, drummed delicately with his fingertips on a blotting-pad: in the middle the magistrate upright in the roomy armchair, his head inclined slightly on the shoulder, had his arms crossed on his breast and a few flowers in a glass vase by the side of his inkstand.

'I did not,' said Jim. 'I was told to call no one and to make no noise for fear of creating a panic. I thought the precaution reasonable. I took one of the lamps that were hung under the awnings and went forward. After opening the forepeak hatch I heard splashing there. I lowered then the lamp the whole drift of its lanyard, and saw that the forepeak was more than half full of water already. I knew then there must be a big hole below the water-line.' He paused.

'Yes,' said the big assessor, with a dreamy smile at the blotting pad; his fingers played incessantly, touching the paper without noise.

'I did not think of danger just then. I might have been a little startled; all this happened in such a quiet way and so very suddenly. I knew there was no other bulkhead in the ship but the collision bulkhead separating the forepeak from the forehold. I went back to tell the captain. I came upon the second engineer getting up at the foot of the bridge-ladder: he seemed dazed, and told me he thought his left arm was broken; he had slipped on the top step when getting down while I was forward. He exclaimed, "My God! That rotten bulkhead'll give way in a minute, and the damned thing will go down under us like a lump of lead." He pushed me away with his right arm and ran before me up the ladder, shouting as he climbed. His left arm hung by his side. I followed up in time to see the captain rush at him and knock him down flat on his back. He did not strike him again: he stood bending over and speaking angrily but quite low. I fancy he was asking him why the devil he didn't go and stop the engines, instead of making a row about it on deck. I heard him say, "Get up! Run! Fly!" He swore also. The engineer slid down the starboard ladder and bolted round the skylight to the engine-room companion which was on the port-side. He moaned as he ran . . .'

He spoke slowly; he remembered swiftly and with extreme vividness; he could have reproduced like an echo the moaning of the engineer for the better information of these men who wanted facts. After his first feeling of revolt he had come round to the view that only a meticulous precision of statement would bring out the true horror behind the appalling face of things. The facts those men were so eager to know had been visible, tangible, open to the senses, occupying their place in space and time, requiring for their existence a fourteen-hundred-ton steamer and twenty-seven minutes by the watch; they made a whole that had features, shades of expression, a complicated aspect that could be remembered by the eye, and something else besides, something invisible, a directing spirit of perdition that dwelt within, like a malevolent soul in a detestable body. He was anxious to make this clear. This had not been a common affair, everything in it had been of the utmost importance, and fortunately he remembered everything. He wanted to go on talking for truth's sake, perhaps for his own sake also; and while his utterance was deliberate, his mind positively flew round and round the serried circle of facts that had surged up all about him to cut him off from the rest of his kind: it was like a creature that, finding itself imprisoned within an enclosure of high stakes, dashes round and round, distracted in the night, trying to find a weak spot, a crevice, a place to scale, some opening through which it may squeeze itself and escape. This awful activity of mind made him hesitate at times in his speech . . .

'The captain kept on moving here and there on the bridge; he seemed calm enough, only he stumbled several times; and once as I stood speaking to him he walked right into me as though he had been stone-blind. He made no definite answer to what I had to tell. He mumbled to himself; all I heard of it were a few words that sounded like "confounded steam!" and "infernal steam!" – something about steam. I thought . . .'

He was becoming irrelevant; a question to the point cut short his speech, like a pang of pain, and he felt extremely discouraged and weary. He was coming to that, he was coming to that – and now, checked brutally, he had to answer by yes or no. He answered truthfully by a curt 'Yes, I did;' and fair of face, big of frame, with young, gloomy eyes, he held his shoulders upright above the box while his soul writhed within him. He was made to answer another question so much to the point and so useless, then waited again. His mouth was tastelessly dry, as though he had been eating dust, then salt and bitter as after a drink of sea-water. He wiped his damp forehead, passed his tongue over parched lips, felt a shiver run down his back. The big assessor had dropped his eyelids, and drummed on without a sound, careless and mournful; the eyes of the other above the sunburnt, clasped fingers seemed to glow with kindliness; the magistrate swayed forward; his pale face hovered near the flowers, and then dropping sideways over the arm of his chair, he rested his temple in the palm of his hand. The wind of the punkahs eddied down on the heads, on the dark-faced natives wound about in voluminous draperies, on the Europeans sitting together very hot and in drill suits that seemed to fit them as close as their skins, and holding their round pith hats on their knees; while gliding along the walls the court peons, buttoned tight in long white coats, flitted rapidly to and fro, running on bare toes, red-sashed, red turban on head, as noiseless as ghosts, and on the alert like so many retrievers.

Jim's eyes, wandering in the intervals of his answers, rested upon a white man who sat apart from the others, with his face worn and clouded, but with quiet eyes that glanced straight, interested and clear. Jim answered another question and was tempted to cry out, 'What's the good of this! what's the good!' He tapped with his foot slightly, bit his lip, and looked away over the heads. He met the eyes of the white man. The glance directed at him was not the fascinated stare of the others. It was an act of intelligent volition. Jim between two questions forgot himself so far as to find leisure for a thought. This fellow – ran the thought – looks at me as though he could see somebody or something past my shoulder. He had come across that man before – in the street perhaps. He was positive he had never spoken to him. For days, for many days, he had spoken to no one, but had held silent, incoherent, and endless converse with himself, like a prisoner alone in his cell or like a wayfarer lost in a wilderness. At present he was answering questions that did not matter though they had a purpose, but he doubted whether he would ever again speak out as long as he lived. The sound of his own truthful statements confirmed his deliberate opinion that speech was of no use to him any longer. That man there seemed to be aware of his hopeless difficulty. Jim looked at him, then turned away resolutely, as after a final parting.

And later on, many times, in distant parts of the world, Marlow showed himself willing to remember Jim, to remember him at length, in detail and audibly.

Perhaps it would be after dinner, on a veranda draped in motionless foliage and crowned with flowers, in the deep dusk speckled by fiery cigar-ends. The elongated bulk of each cane-chair harboured a silent listener. Now and then a small red glow would move abruptly, and expanding light up the fingers of a languid hand, part of a face in profound repose, or flash a crimson gleam into a pair of pensive eyes overshadowed by a fragment of an unruffled forehead; and with the very first word uttered Marlow's body, extended at rest in the seat, would become very still, as though his spirit had winged its way back into the lapse of time and were speaking through his lips from the past.

Chapter 5

'Oh, yes. I attended the inquiry,' he would say, 'and to this day I haven't left off wondering why I went. I am willing to believe each of us has a guardian angel, if you fellows will concede to me that each of us has a familiar devil as well. I want you to own up, because I don't like to feel exceptional in any way, and I know I have him – the devil, I mean. I haven't seen him, of course, but I go upon circumstantial evidence. He is there right enough, and, being malicious, he lets me in for that kind of thing. What kind of thing, you ask? Why, the inquiry thing, the yellow-dog thing – you wouldn't think a mangy, native tyke would be allowed to trip up people in the veranda of a magistrate's court, would you? – the kind of thing that by devious, unexpected, truly diabolical ways causes me to run up against men with soft spots, with hard spots, with hidden plague spots, by Jove! and loosens their tongues at the sight of me for their infernal confidences; as though, forsooth, I had no confidences to make myself, as though – God help me! – I didn't have enough confidential information about myself to harrow my own soul till the end of my appointed time. And what I have done to be thus favoured I want to know. I declare I am as full of my own concerns as the next man, and I have as much memory as the average pilgrim in this valley, so you see I am not particularly fit to be a receptacle of confessions. Then why? Can't tell – unless it be to make time pass away after dinner. Charley, my dear chap, your dinner was extremely good, and in consequence these men here look upon a quiet rubber as a tumultuous occupation. They wallow in your good chairs and think to themselves, "Hang exertion. Let that Marlow talk."

'Talk! So be it. And it's easy enough to talk of Master Jim, after a good spread, two hundred feet above the sea-level, with a box of decent cigars handy, on a blessed evening of freshness and starlight that would make the best of us forget we are only on sufferance here and got to pick our way in cross lights, watching every precious minute and every irremediable step, trusting we shall manage yet to go out decently in the end – but not so sure of it after all – and with dashed little help to expect from those we touch elbows with right and left. Of course there are men here and there to whom the whole of life is like an after-dinner hour with a cigar; easy, pleasant, empty, perhaps enlivened by some fable of strife to be forgotten before the end is told – before the end is told – even if there happens to be any end to it.

'My eyes met his for the first time at that inquiry. You must know that everybody connected in any way with the sea was there, because the affair had been notorious for days, ever since that mysterious cable message came from Aden to start us all cackling. I say mysterious, because it was so in a sense though it contained a naked fact, about as naked and ugly as a fact can well be. The whole waterside talked of nothing else. First thing in the morning as I was dressing in my stateroom, I would hear through the bulkhead my Parsee *dubash* jabbering about the *Patna* with the steward, while he drank a cup of tea, by favour, in the pantry. No sooner on shore I would meet some acquaintance, and the first remark would be, "Did you ever hear of anything to beat this?" and according to his kind the man would smile cynically, or look sad, or let out a swear or two. Complete strangers would accost each other familiarly, just for the sake of easing their minds on the subject: every confounded loafer in the town came in for a harvest of drinks over this affair: you heard of it in the harbour office, at every ship-broker's, at your agent's, from whites, from natives, from half-castes, from the very boatmen squatting half-naked on the stone steps as you went up – by Jove! There was some indignation, not a few jokes, and no end of discussions as to what had become of them, you know. This went on for a couple of weeks or more, and the opinion that whatever was mysterious in this would turn out to be tragic as well, began to prevail, when one fine morning, as I was standing in the shade by the steps of the harbour office, I perceived four men walking towards me along the quay. I wondered for a while where that queer lot had sprung from, and suddenly, I may say, I shouted to myself, "Here they are!"

'There they were, sure enough, three of them as large as life, and one much larger of girth than any living man has a right to be, just landed with a good breakfast inside of them from an outward-bound Dale Line steamer that had come in about an hour after sunrise. There could be no mistake; I spotted the jolly skipper of the *Patna* at the first glance: the fattest man in the whole blessed tropical belt clear round that good old earth of ours. Moreover, nine months or so before, I had come across him in Samarang. His steamer was loading in the Roads, and he was abusing the tyrannical institutions of the German Empire, and soaking himself in beer all day long and day after day in De Jongh's back-shop, till De Jongh, who charged a guilder for every bottle without as much as the quiver of an eyelid, would beckon me aside, and, with his little leathery face all puckered up, declare confidentially, "Business is business, but this man, captain, he make me very sick. Tfui!"

'I was looking at him from the shade. He was hurrying on a little in advance, and the sunlight beating on him brought out his bulk in a startling way. He made me think of a trained baby elephant walking on hind-legs. He was extravagantly gorgeous too – got up in a soiled sleeping-suit, bright green and deep orange vertical stripes, with a pair of ragged straw slippers on his bare feet, and somebody's cast-off pith hat, very dirty and two sizes too small for him, tied up with a manila rope-yarn on the top of his big head.

You understand a man like that hasn't the ghost of a chance when it comes to borrowing clothes. Very well. On he came in hot haste, without a look right or left, passed within three feet of me, and in the innocence of his heart went on pelting upstairs in the harbour office to make his deposition, or report, or whatever you like to call it.

'It appears he addressed himself in the first instance to the principal shipping-master. Archie Ruthvel had just come in, and, as his story goes, was about to begin his arduous day by giving a dressing-down to his chief clerk. Some of you might have known him – an obliging little Portuguese half-caste with a miserable skinny neck, and always on the hop to get something from the shipmasters in the way of eatables – a piece of salt pork, a bag of biscuits, a few potatoes, or what not. One voyage, I recollect, I tipped him a live sheep out of the remnant of my sea-stock: not that I wanted him to do anything for me – he couldn't, you know – but because his childlike belief in the sacred right to perquisites quite touched my heart. It was so strong as to be almost beautiful. The race – the two races rather – and the climate . . . However, never mind. I know where I have a friend for life.

'Well, Ruthvel says he was giving him a severe lecture – on official morality, I suppose – when he heard a kind of subdued commotion at his back, and turning his head he saw, in his own words, something round and enormous, resembling a sixteen-hundredweight sugar-hogshead wrapped in striped flannelette, up-ended in the middle of the large floor space in the office. He declares he was so taken aback that for quite an appreciable time he did not realise the thing was alive, and sat still wondering for what purpose and by what means that object had been transported in front of his desk. The archway from the anteroom was crowded with punkah-pullers, sweepers, police peons, the coxswain and crew of the harbour steam-launch, all craning their necks and almost climbing on each other's backs. Quite a riot. By that time the fellow had managed to tug and jerk his hat clear of his head, and advanced with slight bows at Ruthvel, who told me the sight was so discomposing that for some time he listened quite unable to make out what that apparition wanted. It spoke in a voice harsh and lugubrious but intrepid, and little by little it dawned upon Archie that this was a development of the *Patna* case. He says that as soon as he understood who it was before him he felt quite unwell – Archie is so sympathetic and easily upset – but pulled himself together and shouted: "Stop! I can't listen to you. You must go to the Master Attendant. I can't possibly listen to you. Captain Elliot is the man you want to see. This way, this way." He jumped up, ran round that long counter, pulled, shoved: the other let him, surprised but obedient at first, and only at the door of the private office some sort of animal instinct made him hang back and snort like a frightened bullock. "Look here! what's up? Let go! Look here!" Archie flung open the door without knocking. "The master of the *Patna*, sir," he shouts. "Go in, captain." He saw the old man lift his head from some writings so sharp that his nosenippers fell off, banged the door to, and fled to his desk, where he had some papers waiting for his signature: but he says the row that burst out in there was so awful that he couldn't collect his senses sufficiently to remember the spelling of his own name. Archie's the most sensitive shipping-master in the two hemispheres. He declares he felt as though he had thrown a man to a hungry lion. No doubt the noise was great. I heard it down below, and I have every reason to believe it was heard clear across the Esplanade as far as the bandstand. Old father Elliot had a great stock of words and could shout – and didn't mind who he shouted at either. He would have shouted at the Viceroy himself. As he used to tell me: "I am as high as I can get; my pension is safe. I've a few pounds laid by, and if they don't like my notions of duty I would just as soon go home as not. I am an old man, and I have always spoken my mind. All I care for now is to see my girls married before I die." He was a little crazy on that point. His three daughters were awfully nice, though they resembled him amazingly, and on the mornings he woke up with a gloomy view of their matrimonial prospects the office would read it in his eye and tremble, because, they said, he was sure to have somebody for breakfast. However, that morning he did not eat the renegade, but, if I may be allowed to carry on the metaphor, chewed him up very small, so to speak, and – ah! ejected him again.

'Thus in a very few moments I saw his monstrous bulk descend in haste and stand still on the outer steps. He had stopped close to me for the purpose of profound meditation: his large purple cheeks quivered. He was biting his thumb, and after a while noticed me with a sidelong vexed look. The other three chaps that had landed with him made a little group waiting at some distance. There was a sallow-faced, mean little chap with his arm in a sling, and a long individual in a blue flannel coat, as dry as a chip and no stouter than a broomstick, with drooping grey moustaches, who looked about him with an air of jaunty imbecility. The third was an upstanding, broad-shouldered youth, with his hands in his pockets, turning his back on the other two who appeared to be talking together earnestly. He stared across the empty Esplanade. A ramshackle gharry, all dust and venetian blinds, pulled up short opposite the group, and the driver, throwing up his right foot over his knee, gave himself up to the critical examination of his toes. The young chap, making no movement, not even stirring his head, just stared into the sunshine. This was my first view of Jim. He looked as unconcerned and unapproachable as only the young can look. There he stood, clean-limbed, clean-faced, firm on his feet, as promising a boy as the sun ever shone on; and, looking at him, knowing all he knew and a little more too, I was angry as though I had detected him trying to get something out of me by false pretences. He had no business to look so sound. I thought to myself – Well, if this sort can go wrong like that . . . and I felt as though I could fling down my hat and dance on it from sheer mortification, as I once saw the skipper of an Italian barque do because his duffer of a mate got into a mess with his anchors when making a flying moor in a roadstead full of ships. I asked myself, seeing him there apparently so much at ease – Is he silly? is he callous? He seemed ready to start whistling a tune. And note, I did not care a rap about the behaviour of the other two. Their persons somehow fitted the tale that was public property, and was going to be the subject of an official inquiry. "That old mad rogue upstairs called me a hound," said the captain of the *Patna*. I can't tell whether he recognised me – I rather think he did; but at any rate our glances met. He glared – I smiled; hound was the very mildest epithet that had reached me through the open window. "Did he?" I said from some strange inability to hold my tongue. He nodded, bit his thumb again, swore under his breath: then lifting his head and looking at me with sullen and passionate impudence – "Bah! the Pacific is big, my friend. You damned Englishmen can do your worst; I know where there's plenty room for a man like me: I am well aguaindt in Apia, in Honolulu, in . . . " He paused reflectively, while without effort I could depict to myself the sort of people he was "aguaindt" with in those places. I won't make a secret of it that I had been "aguaindt" with not a few of that sort myself. There are times when a man must act as though life were equally sweet in any company. I've known such a time, and, what's more, I shan't now pretend to pull a long face over my necessity, because a good many of that bad company from want of moral – moral – what shall I say? – posture, or from some other equally profound cause, were twice as instructive and twenty times more amusing than the usual respectable thief of commerce you fellows ask to sit at your table without any real necessity – from habit, from cowardice, from good nature, from a hundred sneaking and inadequate reasons.

"'You Englishmen are all rogues," went on my patriotic Flensborg or Stettin Australian, I really don't recollect now what decent little port on the shores of the Baltic was defiled by being the nest of that precious bird. "What are you to shout? Eh? You tell me? You are no better than other people, and that old rogue he make Gottam fuss with me." His thick carcass trembled on its legs that were like a pair of pillars; it trembled from head to foot. "That's what you English always make – make a tam' fuss – for any little thing, because I was not born in your tam' country. Take away my certificate. Take it. I don't want the certificate. A man like me don't want your *verfluchte* certificate. I shpit on it." He spat. "I vill an American citizen begome," he cried, fretting and fuming and shuffling his feet as if to free his ankles from some invisible and mysterious grasp that would not let him get away from that spot. He made himself so warm that the top of his bullet head positively smoked. Nothing mysterious prevented me from going away: curiosity is the most obvious of sentiments, and it held me there to see the effect of a full information upon that young fellow who, hands in pockets, and turning his back upon the sidewalk, gazed across the grass-plots of the Esplanade at the yellow portico of the Malabar Hotel with the air of a man about to go for a walk as soon as his friend is ready. That's how he looked, and it was odious. I waited to see him overwhelmed, confounded, pierced through and through, squirming like an impaled beetle – and I was half afraid to see it too – if you understand what I mean. Nothing more awful than to watch a man who has been found out, not in a crime but in a more than criminal weakness. The commonest sort of fortitude prevents us from becoming criminals in a legal sense; it is from weakness unknown, but perhaps suspected, as in some parts of the world you suspect a deadly snake in every bush – from weakness that may lie hidden, watched or unwatched, prayed against or manfully scorned, repressed or maybe ignored more than half a lifetime, not one of us is safe. We are snared into doing things for which we get called names, and things for which we get hanged, and yet the spirit may well survive – survive the condemnations, survive the halter, by Jove! And there are things – they look small enough sometimes too – by which some of us are totally and completely undone. I watched the youngster there. I liked his appearance; I knew his appearance; he came from the right place; he was one of us. He stood there for all the parentage of his kind, for men and women by no means clever or amusing, but whose very existence is based upon honest faith, and upon the instinct of courage. I don't mean military courage, or civil courage, or any special kind of courage. I mean just that inborn ability to look temptations straight in the face – a readiness unintellectual enough, goodness knows, but without pose – a power of resistance, don't you see, ungracious if you like, but priceless – an unthinking and blessed stiffness before the outward and inward terrors, before the might of nature, and the seductive corruption of men – backed by a faith invulnerable to the strength of facts, to the contagion of example, to the solicitation of ideas. Hang ideas! They are tramps, vagabonds, knocking at the back-door of your mind, each taking a little of your substance, each carrying away some crumb of that belief in a few simple notions you must cling to if you want to live decently and would like to die easy!

'This has nothing to do with Jim, directly; only he was outwardly so typical of that good, stupid kind we like to feel marching right and left of us in life, of the kind that is not disturbed by the vagaries of intelligence and the perversions of – of nerves, let us say. He was the kind of fellow you would, on the strength of his looks, leave in charge of the deck – figuratively and professionally speaking. I say I would, and I ought to know. Haven't I turned out youngsters enough in my time, for the service of the Red Rag, to the craft of the sea, to the craft whose whole secret could be expressed in one short sentence, and yet must be driven afresh every day into young heads till it becomes the component part of every waking thought – till it is present in every dream of their young sleep! The sea has been good to me, but when I remember all these boys that passed through my hands, some grown up now and some drowned by this time, but all good stuff for the sea, I don't think I have done badly by it either. Were I to go home tomorrow, I bet that before two days passed over my head some sunburnt young chief mate would overtake me at some dock gateway or other, and a fresh deep voice speaking above my hat would ask: "Don't you remember me, sir? Why! little So-and-so. Such and such a ship. It was my first voyage." And I would remember a bewildered little shaver, no higher than the back of this chair, with a mother and perhaps a big sister on the quay, very quiet but too upset to wave their handkerchiefs at the ship that glides out gently between the pier-heads: or perhaps some decent middle-aged father who had come early with his boy to see him off, and stays all the morning because he is interested in the windlass apparently, and stays too long, and has got to scramble ashore at last with no time at all to say goodbye. The mud pilot on the poop sings out to me in a drawl: "Hold her with the check line for a moment, Mister Mate. There's a gentleman wants to get shore . . . Up with you, sir. Nearly got carried off to Talcahuano, didn't you? Now's your time; easy does it . . . All right. Slack away again forward there." The tugs, smoking like the pit of perdition, get hold and churn the old river into fury; the gentleman ashore is dusting his knees – the benevolent steward has shied his umbrella after him. All very proper. He has offered his bit of sacrifice to the sea, and now he may go home pretending he thinks nothing of it; and the little willing victim shall be very seasick before next morning. By and by, when he has learned all the little mysteries and the one great secret of the craft, he shall be fit to live or die as the sea may decree; and the man who had taken a hand in this fool game, in which the sea wins every toss, will be pleased to have his back slapped by a heavy young hand, and to hear a cheery sea-puppy voice: "Do you remember me, sir? The little So-and-so."

'I tell you this is good; it tells you that once in your life at least you had gone the right way to work. I have been thus slapped, and I have winced, for the slap was heavy, and I have glowed all day long and gone to bed feeling less lonely in the world by virtue of that hearty thump. Don't I remember the little So-and-so's! I tell you I ought to know the right kind of looks. I would have trusted the deck to that youngster on the strength of a single glance, and gone to sleep with both eyes – and, by Jove! it wouldn't have been safe. He looked as genuine as a new sovereign, but there was some infernal alloy in his metal. How much? The least thing – the least drop of something rare and accursed; the least drop! – but he made you – standing there with his don't-care-hang air – he made you wonder whether perchance he were nothing more rare than brass.

'I couldn't believe it. I tell you I wanted to see him squirm for the honour of the craft. The other two no-account chaps spotted their captain, and began to move slowly towards us. They chatted together as they strolled, and I did not care any more than if they had not been visible to the naked eye. They grinned at each other – might have been exchanging jokes, for all I know. I saw that with one of them it was the case of a broken arm; and as to the long individual with grey moustaches he was the chief engineer, and in various ways a pretty notorious personality. They were nobodies. They approached. The skipper gazed in an inanimate way between his feet: he seemed to be swollen to an unnatural size by some awful disease, by the mysterious action of an unknown poison. He lifted his head, saw the two before him waiting, opened his mouth with an extraordinary, sneering contortion of his puffed face – to speak to them, I suppose – and then a thought seemed to strike him. His thick, purplish lips came together without a sound, he went off in a resolute waddle to the gharry and began to jerk at the door-handle with such a blind brutality of impatience that I expected to see the whole concern overturned on its side, pony and all. The driver, shaken out of his meditation over the sole of his foot, displayed at once all the signs of intense terror, and held with both hands, looking round from his box at this vast carcass forcing its way into his conveyance. The little machine shook and rocked tumultuously, and the crimson nape of that lowered neck, the size of those straining thighs, the immense heaving of that dingy, striped green-and-orange back, the whole burrowing effort of that gaudy and sordid mass troubled one's sense of probability with a droll and fearsome effect, like one of those grotesque and distinct visions that scare and fascinate one in a fever. He disappeared. I half expected the roof to split in two, the little box on wheels to burst open in the manner of a ripe cotton-pod – but it only sank with a click of flattened springs, and suddenly one venetian blind rattled down. His shoulders reappeared, jammed in the small opening; his head hung out, distended and tossing like a captive balloon, perspiring, furious, spluttering. He reached for the gharry-wallah with vicious flourishes of a fist as dumpy and red as a lump of raw meat. He roared at him to be off, to go on. Where? Into the Pacific, perhaps. The driver lashed; the pony snorted, reared once, and darted off at a gallop. Where? To Apia? to Honolulu? He had 6,000 miles of tropical belt to disport himself in, and I did not hear the precise address. A snorting pony snatched him into "*Ewigkeit*" in the twinkling of an eye, and I never saw him again; and, what's more, I don't know of anybody that ever had a glimpse of him after he departed from my knowledge sitting inside a ramshackle little gharry that fled round the corner in a white smother of dust. He departed, disappeared, vanished, absconded; and absurdly enough it looked as though he had taken that gharry with him, for never again did I come across a sorrel pony with a slit ear and a lackadaisical Tamil driver afflicted by a sore foot. The Pacific is indeed big; but whether he found a place for a display of his talents in it or not, the fact remains he had flown into space like a witch on a broomstick. The little chap with his arm in a sling started to run after the carriage, bleating, "Captain! I say, captain! I sa-a-ay!" – but after a few steps stopped short, hung his head, and walked back slowly. At the sharp rattle of the wheels the young fellow spun round where he stood. He made no other movement, no gesture, no sign, and remained facing in the new direction after the gharry had swung out of sight.

'All this happened in much less time than it takes to tell, since I am trying to interpret for you into slow speech the instantaneous effect of visual impressions. Next moment the half-caste clerk, sent by Archie to look a little after the poor castaways of the *Patna*, came upon the scene. He ran out eager and bareheaded, looking right and left, and very full of his mission. It was doomed to be a failure as far as the principal person was concerned, but he approached the others with fussy importance, and, almost immediately, found himself involved in a violent altercation with the chap that carried his arm in a sling and who turned out to be extremely anxious for a row. He wasn't going to be ordered about – "not he, b'gosh." He wouldn't be terrified with a pack of lies by a cocky half-bred little quill-driver. He was not going to be bullied by "no object of that sort," if the story were true "ever so!" He bawled his wish, his desire, his determination to go to bed. "If you weren't a God-forsaken Portuguee," I heard him yell, "you would know that the hospital is the right place for me." He pushed the fist of his sound arm under the other's nose; a crowd began to collect; the half-caste, flustered, but doing his best to appear dignified, tried to explain his intentions. I went away without waiting to see the end.

'But it so happened that I had a man in the hospital at the time, and going there to see about him the day before the opening of the inquiry, I saw in the white men's ward that little chap tossing on his back, with his arm in splints, and quite light-headed. To my great surprise the other one, the long individual with drooping white moustache, had also found his way there. I remembered I had seen him slinking away during the quarrel, in a half prance, half shuffle, and trying very hard not to look scared. He was no stranger to the port, it seems, and in his distress was able to make tracks straight for Mariani's billiard-room and grog-shop near the bazaar. That unspeakable vagabond, Mariani, who had known the man and had ministered to his vices in one or two other places, kissed the ground, in a manner of speaking, before him, and shut him up with a supply of bottles in an upstairs room of his infamous hovel. It appears he was under some hazy apprehension as to his personal safety, and wished to be concealed. However, Mariani told me a long time after (when he came on board one day to dun my steward for the price of some cigars) that he would have done more for him without asking any questions, from gratitude for some unholy favour received very many years ago – as far as I could make out. He thumped twice his brawny chest, rolled enormous black and white eyes glistening with tears: "Antonio never forget – Antonio never forget!" What was the precise nature of the immoral obligation I never learned, but be it what it may, he had every facility given him to remain under lock and key, with a chair, a table, a mattress in a corner, and a litter of fallen plaster on the floor, in an irrational state of funk, and keeping up his pecker with such tonics as Mariani dispensed. This lasted till the evening of the third day, when, after letting out a few horrible screams, he found himself compelled to seek safety in flight from a legion of centipedes. He burst the door open, made one leap for dear life down the crazy little stairway, landed bodily on

Mariani's stomach, picked himself up, and bolted like a rabbit into the streets.
The police plucked him off a garbage-heap in the early morning. At first he
had a notion they were carrying him off to be hanged, and fought for liberty
like a hero, but when I sat down by his bed he had been very quiet for two
days. His lean bronzed head, with white moustaches, looked fine and calm on
the pillow, like the head of a war-worn soldier with a childlike soul, had it not
been for a hint of spectral alarm that lurked in the blank glitter of his glance,
resembling a nondescript form of a terror crouching silently behind a pane of
glass. He was so extremely calm, that I began to indulge in the eccentric hope
of hearing something explanatory of the famous affair from his point of view.
Why I longed to go grubbing into the deplorable details of an occurrence
which, after all, concerned me no more than as a member of an obscure body
of men held together by a community of inglorious toil and by fidelity to a
certain standard of conduct, I can't explain. You may call it an unhealthy
curiosity if you like; but I have a distinct notion I wished to find something.
Perhaps, unconsciously, I hoped I would find that something, some profound
and redeeming cause, some merciful explanation, some convincing shadow
of an excuse. I see well enough now that I hoped for the impossible – for
the laying of what is the most obstinate ghost of man's creation, of the
uneasy doubt uprising like a mist, secret and gnawing like a worm, and
more chilling than the certitude of death – the doubt of the sovereign
power enthroned in a fixed standard of conduct. It is the hardest thing to
stumble against; it is the thing that breeds yelling panics and good little
quiet villainies; it's the true shadow of calamity. Did I believe in a miracle?
and why did I desire it so ardently? Was it for my own sake that I wished to
find some shadow of an excuse for that young fellow whom I had never seen
before, but whose appearance alone added a touch of personal concern to
the thoughts suggested by the knowledge of his weakness – made it a thing
of mystery and terror – like a hint of a destructive fate ready for us all
whose youth – in its day – had resembled his youth? I fear that such was the
secret motive of my prying. I was, and no mistake, looking for a miracle.
The only thing that at this distance of time strikes me as miraculous is the
extent of my imbecility. I positively hoped to obtain from that battered and
shady invalid some exorcism against the ghost of doubt. I must have been
pretty desperate too, for, without a loss of time, after a few indifferent and
friendly sentences which he answered with languid readiness, just as any
decent sick man would do, I produced the word *Patna* wrapped up in a
delicate question as in a wisp of floss silk. I was delicate selfishly; I did not
want to startle him; I had no solicitude for him; I was not furious with him
and sorry for him: his experience was of no importance, his redemption
would have had no point for me. He had grown old in minor iniquities, and
could no longer inspire aversion or pity. He repeated *Patna?* interrogatively,
seemed to make a short effort of memory and said: "Quite right. I am an
old stager out here. I saw her go down." I made ready to vent my

indignation at such a stupid lie, when he added smoothly, "She was full of reptiles."

'This made me pause. What did he mean? The unsteady phantom of terror behind his glassy eyes seemed to stand still and look into mine wistfully. "They turned me out of my bunk in the middle watch to look at her sinking," he pursued in a reflective tone. His voice sounded alarmingly strong all at once. I was sorry for my folly. There was no snowy-winged coif of a nursing sister to be seen flitting in the perspective of the ward; but away in the middle of a long row of empty iron bedsteads an accident case from some ship in the Roads sat up brown and gaunt with a white bandage set rakishly on the forehead. Suddenly my interesting invalid shot out an arm thin like a tentacle and clawed my shoulder. "Only my eyes were good enough to see. I am famous for my eyesight. That's why they called me, I expect. None of them was quick enough to see her go, but they saw that she was gone right enough, and sang out together – like this." . . . A wolfish howl searched the very recesses of my soul. "Oh! make 'im dry up," whined the accident case irritably. "You don't believe me, I suppose," went on the other, with an air of ineffable conceit. "I tell you there are no such eyes as mine this side of the Persian Gulf. Look under the bed."

'Of course I stooped instantly. I defy anybody not to have done so. "What can you see?" he asked. "Nothing," I said, feeling awfully ashamed of myself. He scrutinised my face with wild and withering contempt. "Just so," he said, "but if I were to look I could see – there's no eyes like mine, I tell you." Again he clawed, pulling at me downwards in his eagerness to relieve himself by a confidential communication. "Millions of pink toads. There's no eyes like mine. Millions of pink toads. It's worse than seeing a ship sink. I could look at sinking ships and smoke my pipe all day long. Why don't they give me back my pipe? I would get a smoke while I watched these toads. The ship was full of them. They've got to be watched, you know." He winked facetiously. The perspiration dripped on him off my head, my drill coat clung to my wet back; the afternoon breeze swept impetuously over the row of bedsteads, the stiff folds of curtains stirred perpendicularly, rattling on brass rods, the covers of empty beds blew about noiselessly near the bare floor all along the line, and I shivered to the very marrow. The soft wind of the tropics played in that naked ward as bleak as a winter's gale in an old barn at home. "Don't you let him start his hollering, mister," hailed from afar the accident case in a distressed angry shout that came ringing between the walls like a quavering call down a tunnel. The clawing hand hauled at my shoulder; he leered at me knowingly. "The ship was full of them, you know, and we had to clear out on the strict Q.T.," he whispered with extreme rapidity. "All pink. All pink – as big as mastiffs, with an eye on the top of the head and claws all round their ugly mouths. Ough! Ough!" Quick jerks as of galvanic shocks disclosed under the flat coverlet the outlines of meagre and agitated legs; he let go my shoulder and reached after something in the air;

his body trembled tensely like a released harp-string; and while I looked down, the spectral horror in him broke through his glassy gaze. Instantly his face of an old soldier, with its noble and calm outlines, became decomposed before my eyes by the corruption of stealthy cunning, of an abominable caution and of desperate fear. He restrained a cry – "Ssh! what are they doing now down there?" he asked, pointing to the floor with fantastic precautions of voice and gesture, whose meaning, borne upon my mind in a lurid flash, made me very sick of my cleverness. "They are all asleep," I answered, watching him narrowly. That was it. That's what he wanted to hear; these were the exact words that could calm him. He drew a long breath. "Ssh! Quiet, steady. I am an old stager out here. I know them brutes. Bash in the head of the first that stirs. There's too many of them, and she won't swim more than ten minutes." He panted again. "Hurry up," he yelled suddenly, and went on in a steady scream: "They are all awake – millions of them. They are trampling on me! Wait! Oh, wait! I'll smash them in heaps like flies. Wait for me! Help! H–e–lp!" An interminable and sustained howl completed my discomfiture. I saw in the distance the accident case raise deplorably both his hands to his bandaged head; a dresser, aproned to the shin, showed himself in the vista of the ward, as if seen in the small end of a telescope. I confessed myself fairly routed, and without more ado, stepping out through one of the long windows, escaped into the outside gallery. The howl pursued me like a vengeance. I turned into a deserted landing, and suddenly all became very still and quiet around me, and I descended the bare and shiny staircase in a silence that enabled me to compose my distracted thoughts. Down below I met one of the resident surgeons who was crossing the courtyard and stopped me. "Been to see your man, captain? I think we may let him go tomorrow. These fools have no notion of taking care of themselves, though. I say, we've got the chief engineer of that pilgrim ship here. A curious case. DTs of the worst kind. He has been drinking hard in that Greek's or Italian's grog-shop for three days. What can you expect? Four bottles of that kind of brandy a day, I am told. Wonderful, if true. Sheeted with boiler-iron inside, I should think. The head, ah! the head, of course, gone, but the curious part is there's some sort of method in his raving. I am trying to find out. Most unusual – that thread of logic in such a delirium. Traditionally he ought to see snakes, but he doesn't. Good old tradition's at a discount nowadays. Eh! His – er – visions are batrachian. Ha! ha! No, seriously, I never remember being so interested in a case of jimjams before. He ought to be dead, don't you know, after such a festive experiment. Oh! he is a tough object. Four-and-twenty years of the tropics too. You ought really to take a peep at him. Noble-looking old boozer. Most extraordinary man I ever met – medically, of course. Won't you?"

'I had been all along exhibiting the usual polite signs of interest, but now assuming an air of regret I murmured of want of time, and shook hands in a hurry. "I say," he cried after me, "he can't attend that inquiry. Is his evidence material, you think?"

' "Not in the least," I called back from the gateway.'

Chapter 6

'The authorities were evidently of the same opinion. The inquiry was not adjourned. It was held on the appointed day to satisfy the law, and it was well attended because of its human interest, no doubt. There was no incertitude as to facts – as to the one material fact, I mean. How the *Patna* came by her hurt it was impossible to find out; the court did not expect to find out; and in the whole audience there was not a man who cared. Yet, as I've told you, all the sailors in the port attended, and the waterside business was fully represented. Whether they knew it or not, the interest that drew them there was purely psychological – the expectation of some essential disclosure as to the strength, the power, the horror, of human emotions. Naturally nothing of the kind could be disclosed. The examination of the only man able and willing to face it was beating futilely round the well-known fact, and the play of questions upon it was as instructive as the tapping with a hammer on an iron box, were the object to find out what's inside. However, an official inquiry could not be any other thing. Its object was not the fundamental why, but the superficial how, of this affair.

'The young chap could have told them, and, though that very thing was the thing that interested the audience, the questions put to him necessarily led him away from what to me, for instance, would have been the only truth worth knowing. You can't expect the constituted authorities to inquire into the state of a man's soul – or is it only of his liver? Their business was to come down upon the consequences, and frankly, a casual police magistrate and two nautical assessors are not much good for anything else. I don't mean to imply these fellows were stupid. The magistrate was very patient. One of the assessors was a sailing-ship skipper with a reddish beard, and of a pious disposition. Brierly was the other. Big Brierly. Some of you must have heard of Big Brierly – the captain of the crack ship of the Blue Star line. That's the man.

'He seemed consumedly bored by the honour thrust upon him. He had never in his life made a mistake, never had an accident, never a mishap, never a check in his steady rise, and he seemed to be one of those lucky fellows who know nothing of indecision, much less of self-mistrust. At thirty-two he had one of the best commands going in the Eastern trade – and, what's more, he thought a lot of what he had. There was nothing like it in the world, and I suppose if you had asked him point-blank he would have confessed that in his opinion there was not such another commander. The choice had fallen upon the right man. The rest of mankind that did not command the sixteen-knot steel steamer *Ossa* were rather poor creatures. He had saved lives at sea, had rescued ships in distress, had a gold chronometer presented to him by the underwriters, and a pair of binoculars with a suitable inscription from some foreign Government, in commemoration of these services. He was acutely aware of his merits and of his rewards. I liked him well enough, though some I know – meek, friendly men at that – couldn't stand him at any price. I haven't the slightest doubt he considered himself vastly my superior – indeed, had you been Emperor of East and West, you could not have ignored your inferiority in his presence – but I couldn't get up any real sentiment of offence. He did not despise me for anything I could help, for anything I was – don't you know? I was a negligible quantity simply because I was not *the* fortunate man of the earth, not Montague Brierly in command of the *Ossa*, not the owner of an inscribed gold chronometer and of silver-mounted binoculars testifying to the excellence of my seamanship and to my indomitable pluck; not possessed of an acute sense of my merits and of my rewards, besides the love and worship of a black retriever, the most wonderful of its kind – for never was such a man loved thus by such a dog. No doubt, to have all this forced upon you was exasperating enough; but when I reflected that I was associated in these fatal disadvantages with twelve hundred millions of other more or less human beings, I found I could bear my share of his good-natured and contemptuous pity for the sake of something indefinite and attractive in the man. I have never defined to myself this attraction, but there were moments when I envied him. The sting of life could do no more to his complacent soul than the scratch of a pin to the smooth face of a rock. This was enviable. As I looked at him flanking on one side the unassuming pale-faced magistrate who presided at the inquiry, his self-satisfaction presented to me and to the world a surface as hard as granite. He committed suicide very soon after.

'No wonder Jim's case bored him, and while I thought with something akin to fear of the immensity of his contempt for the young man under examination, he was probably holding silent inquiry into his own case. The verdict must have been of unmitigated guilt, and he took the secret of the evidence with him in that leap into the sea. If I understand anything of men, the matter was no doubt of the gravest import, one of those trifles that awaken ideas – start into life some thought with which a man unused to such companionship finds it impossible to live. I am in a position to know that it wasn't money, and it wasn't drink, and it wasn't woman. He jumped overboard at sea barely a week after the end of the inquiry, and less than three days after leaving port on his outward passage; as though on that exact spot in the midst of waters he had suddenly perceived the gates of the other world flung open wide for his reception.

'Yet it was not a sudden impulse. His grey-headed mate, a first-rate sailor and a nice old chap with strangers, but in his relations with his commander the surliest chief officer I've ever seen, would tell the story with tears in his eyes. It appears that when he came on deck in the morning Brierly had been writing in the chart-room. "It was ten minutes to four," he said, "and the middle watch was not relieved yet of course. He heard my voice on the bridge speaking to the second mate, and called me in. I was loath to go, and that's the truth, Captain Marlow – I couldn't stand poor Captain Brierly, I tell you with shame; we never know what a man is made of. He had been promoted over too many heads, not counting my own, and he had a damnable trick of making you feel small, nothing but by the way he said 'Good-morning.' I never addressed him, sir, but on matters of duty, and then it was as much as I could do to keep a civil tongue in my head." (He flattered himself there. I often wondered how Brierly could put up with his manners for more than half a voyage.) "I've a wife and children," he went on, "and I had ten years in the Company, always expecting the next command – more fool I. Says he, just like this: 'Come in here, Mr Jones,' in that swagger voice of his – 'Come in here, Mr Jones.' In I went. 'We'll lay down her position,' he says, stooping over the chart, a pair of dividers in hand. By the standing orders, the officer going off duty would have done that at the end of his watch. However, I said nothing, and looked on while he marked off the ship's position with a tiny cross and wrote the date and time. I can see him this moment writing his neat figures: seventeen, eight, four a.m. The year would be written in red ink at the top of the chart. He never used his charts more than a year, Captain Brierly didn't. I've the chart now. When he had done he stands looking down at the mark he had made and smiling to himself, then looks up at me. 'Thirty-two miles more as she goes,' says he, 'and then we shall be clear, and you may alter the course twenty degrees to the southward.'

' "We were passing to the north of the Hector Bank that voyage. I said, 'All right, sir,' wondering what he was fussing about, since I had to call him before altering the course anyhow. Just then eight bells were struck: we came out on the bridge, and the second mate before going off mentions in the usual way – 'Seventy-one on the log.' Captain Brierly looks at the compass and then all round. It was dark and clear, and all the stars were out as plain as on a frosty night in high latitudes. Suddenly he says with a sort of a little sigh: 'I am going aft, and shall set the log at zero for you myself, so that there can be no mistake. Thirty-two miles more on this course and then you are safe. Let's see – the correction on the log is six per cent additive; say, then, thirty by the dial to run, and you may come twenty degrees to starboard at once. No use losing any distance – is there?' I had never heard him talk so much at a stretch, and to no purpose as it seemed to me. I said nothing. He went down the ladder, and the dog, that was always at his heels whenever he moved, night or day, sliding nose first, after him. I heard his boot-heels tap,

tap on the after-deck, then he stopped and spoke to the dog – 'Go back, Rover. On the bridge, boy! Go on – get.' Then he calls out to me from the dark, 'Shut that dog up in the chart-room, Mr Jones – will you?'

' "This was the last time I heard his voice, Captain Marlow. These are the last words he spoke in the hearing of any living human being, sir." At this point the old chap's voice got quite unsteady. "He was afraid the poor brute would jump after him, don't you see?" he pursued with a quaver. "Yes, Captain Marlow. He set the log for me; he – would you believe it? – he put a drop of oil in it too. There was the oil-feeder where he left it near by. The boatswain's mate got the hose along aft to wash down at half-past five; by and by he knocks off and runs up on the bridge – 'Will you please come aft, Mr Jones,' he says. 'There's a funny thing. I don't like to touch it.' It was Captain Brierly's gold chronometer watch carefully hung under the rail by its chain.

' "As soon as my eyes fell on it something struck me, and I knew, sir. My legs got soft under me. It was as if I had seen him go over; and I could tell how far behind he was left too. The taffrail-log marked eighteen miles and three-quarters, and four iron belaying-pins were missing round the mainmast. Put them in his pockets to help him down, I suppose; but, Lord! what's four iron pins to a powerful man like Captain Brierly. Maybe his confidence in himself was just shook a bit at the last. That's the only sign of fluster he gave in his whole life, I should think; but I am ready to answer for him, that once over he did not try to swim a stroke, the same as he would have had pluck enough to keep up all day long on the bare chance had he fallen overboard accidentally. Yes, sir. He was second to none – if he said so himself, as I heard him once. He had written two letters in the middle watch, one to the Company and the other to me. He gave me a lot of instructions as to the passage – I had been in the trade before he was out of his time – and no end of hints as to my conduct with our people in Shanghai, so that I should keep the command of the *Ossa*. He wrote like a father would to a favourite son, Captain Marlow, and I was five-and-twenty years his senior and had tasted salt water before he was fairly breeched. In his letter to the owners – it was left open for me to see – he said that he had always done his duty by them – up to that moment – and even now he was not betraying their confidence, since he was leaving the ship to as competent a seaman as could be found – meaning me, sir, meaning me! He told them that if the last act of his life didn't take away all his credit with them, they would give weight to my faithful service and to his warm recommendation, when about to fill the vacancy by his death. And much more like this, sir. I couldn't believe my eyes. It made me feel queer all over," went on the old chap in great perturbation, and squashing something in the corner of his eye with the end of a thumb as broad as a spatula. "You would think, sir, he had jumped overboard only to give an unlucky man a last show to get on. What with the shock of him going in this awful rash way, and thinking myself a made man by that chance, I was nearly off my chump for a week. But no fear. The captain of the *Pelion* was shifted into the *Ossa* – came aboard in Shanghai – a little popinjay, sir, in a grey check suit, with his hair parted in the middle. 'Aw – I am – aw – your new captain, mister – mister – aw – Jones.' He was drowned in scent – fairly stunk with it, Captain Marlow. I dare say it was the look I gave him that made him stammer. He mumbled something about my natural disappointment – I had better know at once that his chief officer got the promotion to the *Pelion* – he had nothing to do with it, of course – supposed the office knew best – sorry . . . Says I, 'Don't you mind old Jones, sir; damn his soul, he's used to it.' I could see directly I had shocked his delicate ear, and while we sat at our first tiffin together he began to find fault in a nasty manner with this and that in the ship. I never heard such a voice out of a Punch and Judy show. I set my teeth hard, and glued my eyes to my plate, and held my peace as long as I could; but at last I had to say something: up he jumps tiptoeing, ruffling all his pretty plumes, like a little fighting cock. 'You'll find you have a different person to deal with than the late Captain Brierly.' 'I've found it,' says I, very glum, but pretending to be mighty busy with my steak. 'You are an old ruffian, Mr – aw – Jones; and what's more, you are known for an old ruffian in the employ,' he squeaks at me. The damned bottle-washers stood about listening with their mouths stretched from ear to ear. 'I may be a hard case,' answers I, 'but I ain't so far gone as to put up with the sight of you sitting in Captain Brierly's chair.' With that I lay down my knife and fork. 'You would like to sit in it yourself – that's where the shoe pinches,' he sneers. I left the saloon, got my rags together, and was on the quay with all my dunnage about my feet before the stevedores had turned to again. Yes. Adrift – on shore – after ten years' service – and with a poor woman and four children six thousand miles off depending on my half-pay for every mouthful they ate. Yes, sir! I chucked it rather than hear Captain Brierly abused. He left me his night-glasses – here they are; and he wished me to take care of the dog – here he is. Hallo, Rover, poor boy. Where's the captain, Rover?" The dog looked up at us with mournful yellow eyes, gave one desolate bark, and crept under the table.

'All this was taking place, more than two years afterwards, on board that nautical ruin the *Fire-Queen* this Jones had got charge of – quite by a funny accident, too – from Matherson – mad Matherson they generally called him – the same who used to hang out in Haï-phong, you know, before the occupation days. The old chap snuffled on: ' "Ay, sir, Captain Brierly will be remembered here, if there's no other place on earth. I wrote fully to his father and did not get a word in reply – neither Thank you, nor Go to the devil! – nothing! Perhaps they did not want to know."

'The sight of that watery-eyed old Jones mopping his bald head with a red cotton handkerchief, the sorrowing yelp of the dog, the squalor of that fly-brown cuddy which was the only shrine of his memory, threw a veil of inexpressibly mean pathos over Brierly's remembered figure, the post-humous revenge of fate for that belief in his own splendour which had almost cheated his life of its legitimate terrors. Almost! Perhaps wholly. Who can tell what flattering view he had induced himself to take of his own suicide?

' "Why did he commit the rash act, Captain Marlow – can you think?" asked Jones, pressing his palms together. "Why? It beats me! Why?" He slapped his low and wrinkled forehead. "If he had been poor and old and in debt – and never a show – or else mad. But he wasn't of the kind that goes mad, not he. You trust me. What a mate don't know about his skipper isn't worth knowing. Young, healthy, well off, no cares . . . I sit here sometimes thinking, thinking, till my head fairly begins to buzz. There was some reason."

' "You may depend on it, Captain Jones," said I, "it wasn't anything that would have disturbed much either of us two," I said; and then, as if a light had been flashed into the muddle of his brain, poor old Jones found a last word of amazing profundity. He blew his nose, nodding at me dolefully: "Ay, ay! neither you nor I, sir, had ever thought so much of ourselves."

'Of course the recollection of my last conversation with Brierly is tinged with the knowledge of his end that followed so close upon it. I spoke with him for the last time during the progress of the inquiry. It was after the first adjournment, and he came up with me in the street. He was in a state of irritation, which I noticed with surprise, his usual behaviour when he condescended to converse being perfectly cool, with a trace of amused tolerance, as if the existence of his interlocutor had been a rather good joke. "They caught me for that inquiry, you see," he began, and for a while enlarged complainingly upon the inconveniences of daily attendance in court. "And goodness knows how long it will last. Three days, I suppose." I heard him out in silence; in my then opinion it was a way as good as another of putting on side. "What's the use of it? It is the stupidest set-out you can imagine," he pursued, hotly. I remarked that there was no option. He interrupted me with a sort of pent-up violence. "I feel like a fool all the time." I looked up at him. This was going very far – for Brierly – when talking of Brierly. He stopped short, and seizing the lapel of my coat, gave it a slight tug. "Why are we tormenting that young chap?" he asked. This question chimed in so well to the tolling of a certain thought of mine that, with the image of the absconding renegade in my eye, I answered at once, "Hanged if I know, unless it be that he lets you." I was astonished to see him fall into line, so to speak, with that utterance, which ought to have been tolerably cryptic. He said angrily, "Why, yes. Can't he see that wretched skipper of his has cleared out? What does he expect to happen? Nothing can save him. He's done for." We walked on in silence a few steps. "Why eat all that dirt?" he exclaimed, with an oriental energy of expression – about the only sort of energy you can find a trace of east of the fiftieth meridian. I wondered greatly at the direction of his thoughts, but now I strongly suspect it was strictly in character: at bottom poor Brierly must have been thinking of himself. I pointed out to him that the skipper of the *Patna* was known to have feathered his nest pretty well, and could procure almost anywhere the means of getting away. With Jim it was otherwise: the Government was keeping him in the Sailors' Home for the time being, and probably he hadn't a penny in his pocket to bless himself with. It costs some money to run away. "Does it? Not always," he said, with a bitter laugh, and to some further remark of mine – "Well, then, let him creep twenty feet underground and stay there! By heavens! *I* would." I don't know why his tone provoked me, and I said, "There is a kind of courage in facing it out as he does, knowing very well that if he went away nobody would trouble to run after him." "Courage be hanged!" growled Brierly. "That sort of courage is of no use to keep a man straight, and I don't care a snap for such courage. If you were to say it was a kind of cowardice now – of softness. I tell you what, I will put up two hundred rupees if you put up another hundred and undertake to make the beggar clear out early tomorrow morning. The fellow's a gentleman if he ain't fit to be touched – he will understand. He must! This infernal publicity is too shocking: there he sits while all these confounded natives, serangs, lascars, quartermasters, are giving evidence that's enough to burn a man to ashes with shame. This is abominable. Why, Marlow, don't you think, don't you feel, that this is abominable; don't you now – come – as a seaman? If he went away all this would stop at once." Brierly said those words with a most unusual animation, and made as if to reach after his pocket-book. I restrained him, and declared coldly that the cowardice of these four men did not seem to me a matter of such great importance. "And you call yourself a seaman, I suppose," he pronounced, angrily. I said that's what I called myself, and I hoped I was too. He heard me out, and made a gesture with his big arm that seemed to deprive me of my individuality, to push me away into the crowd. "The worst of it," he said, "is that all you fellows have no sense of dignity; you don't think enough of what you are supposed to be."

'We had been walking slowly meantime, and now stopped opposite the harbour office, in sight of the very spot from which the immense captain of the *Patna* had vanished as utterly as a tiny feather blown away in a hurricane. I smiled. Brierly went on: "This is a disgrace. We've got all kinds amongst us – some anointed scoundrels in the lot; but, hang it, we must preserve professional decency or we become no better than so many tinkers going about loose. We are trusted. Do you understand? – trusted! Frankly, I don't care a snap for all the pilgrims that ever came out of Asia, but a decent man would not have behaved like this to a full cargo of old rags in bales. We aren't an organised body of men, and the only thing that holds us together is just the name for that kind of decency. Such an affair destroys one's confidence. A man may go pretty near through his whole sea-life without any call to show a stiff upper lip. But when the call comes . . . Aha! . . . If I . . . "

'He broke off, and in a changed tone, "I'll give you two hundred rupees now, Marlow, and you just talk to that chap. Confound him! I wish he had never come out here. Fact is, I rather think some of my people know his. The old man's a parson, and I remember now I met him once when staying with my cousin in Essex last year. If I am not mistaken, the old chap seemed rather to fancy his sailor son. Horrible. I can't do it myself – but you . . . ."

'Thus, apropos of Jim, I had a glimpse of the real Brierly a few days before he committed his reality and his sham together to the keeping of the sea. Of course I declined to meddle. The tone of this last "but you" (poor Brierly couldn't help it), that seemed to imply I was no more noticeable than an insect, caused me to look at the proposal with indignation, and on account of that provocation, or for some other reason, I became positive in my mind that the inquiry was a severe punishment to that Jim, and that his facing it – practically of his own free will – was a redeeming feature in his abominable case. I hadn't been so sure of it before. Brierly went off in a huff. At the time his state of mind was more of a mystery to me than it is now.

'Next day, coming into court late, I sat by myself. Of course I could not forget the conversations I had with Brierly, and now I had them both under my eyes. The demeanour of one suggested gloomy impudence and of the other a contemptuous boredom; yet one attitude might not have been truer than the other, and I was aware that one was not true. Brierly was not bored – he was exasperated; and if so, then Jim might not have been impudent. According to my theory he was not. I imagined he was hopeless. Then it was that our glances met. They met, and the look he gave me was discouraging of any intention I might have had to speak to him. Upon either hypothesis – insolence or despair – I felt I could be of no use to him. This was the second day of the proceedings. Very soon after that exchange of glances the inquiry was adjourned again to the next day. The white men began to troop out at once. Jim had been told to stand down some time before, and was able to leave amongst the first. I saw his broad shoulders and his head outlined in the light of the door, and while I made my way slowly out talking with someone – some stranger who had addressed me casually – I could see him from within the courtroom resting both elbows on the balustrade of the veranda and turning his back on the small stream of people trickling down the few steps. There was a murmur of voices and a shuffle of boots.

'The next case was that of assault and battery committed upon a money-lender, I believe; and the defendant – a venerable villager with a straight white beard – sat on a mat just outside the door with his sons, daughters, sons-in-law, their wives, and, I should think, half the population of his village besides, squatting or standing around him. A slim dark woman, with part of her back and one black shoulder bared, and with a thin gold ring in her nose, suddenly began to talk in a high-pitched, shrewish tone. The man with me instinctively looked up at her. We were then just through the door, passing behind Jim's burly back.

'Whether those villagers had brought the yellow dog with them, I don't know. Anyhow, a dog was there, weaving himself in and out amongst people's legs in that mute stealthy way native dogs have, and my companion stumbled over him. The dog leaped away without a sound; the man, raising his voice a little, said with a slow laugh: "Look at that wretched cur," and directly afterwards we became separated by a lot of people pushing in. I stood back for a moment against the wall while the stranger managed to get down the steps and disappeared. I saw Jim spin round. He made a step forward and barred my way. We were alone; he glared at me with an air of stubborn resolution. I became aware I was being held up, so to speak, as if in a wood. The veranda was empty by then, the noise and movement in court had ceased: a great silence fell upon the building, in which, somewhere far within, an oriental voice began to whine abjectly. The dog, in the very act of trying to sneak in at the door, sat down hurriedly to hunt for fleas.

' "Did you speak to me?" asked Jim very low, and bending forward, not so much towards me but at me, if you know what I mean. I said "No" at once. Something in the sound of that quiet tone of his warned me to be on my defence. I watched him. It was very much like a meeting in a wood, only more uncertain in its issue, since he could possibly want neither my money nor my life – nothing that I could simply give up or defend with a clear conscience. "You say you didn't," he said, very sombre. "But I heard." "Some mistake," I protested, utterly at a loss, and never taking my eyes off him. To watch his face was like watching a darkening sky before a clap of thunder, shade upon shade imperceptibly coming on, the gloom growing mysteriously intense in the calm of maturing violence.

' "As far as I know, I haven't opened my lips in your hearing," I affirmed with perfect truth. I was getting a little angry, too, at the absurdity of this encounter. It strikes me now I have never in my life been so near a beating – I mean it literally; a beating with fists. I suppose I had some hazy prescience of that eventuality being in the air. Not that he was actively threatening me. On the contrary, he was strangely passive – don't you know? but he was lowering, and, though not exceptionally big, he looked generally fit to demolish a wall. The most reassuring symptom I noticed was a kind of slow and ponderous hesitation, which I took as a tribute to the evident sincerity of my manner and of my tone. We faced each other. In the court the assault case was proceeding. I caught the words: "Well – buffalo – stick – in the greatness of my fear . . . '

' "What did you mean by staring at me all the morning?" said Jim at last. He looked up and looked down again. "Did you expect us all to sit with downcast eyes out of regard for your susceptibilities?" I retorted sharply. I was not going to submit meekly to any of his nonsense. He raised his eyes again, and this time continued to look me straight in the face. "No. That's all right," he pronounced with an air of deliberating with himself upon the truth of this statement – "that's all right. I am going through with that. Only" – and there he spoke a little faster – "I won't let any man call me names outside this court. There was a fellow with you. You spoke to him – oh, yes – I know; 'tis all very fine. You spoke to him, but you meant me to hear . . . "

'I assured him he was under some extraordinary delusion. I had no conception how it came about. "You thought I would be afraid to resent this," he said, with just a faint tinge of bitterness. I was interested enough to discern the slightest shades of expression, but I was not in the least enlightened; yet I don't know what in these words, or perhaps just the intonation of that phrase, induced me suddenly to make all possible allowances for him. I ceased to be annoyed at my unexpected predicament. It was some mistake on his part; he was blundering and I had an intuition that the blunder was of an odious, of an unfortunate nature. I was anxious to end this scene on grounds of decency, just as one is anxious to cut short some unprovoked and abominable confidence. The funniest part was, that in the midst of all these considerations of the higher order I was conscious of a certain trepidation as to the possibility – nay, likelihood – of this encounter ending in some disreputable brawl which could not possibly be explained, and would make me ridiculous. I did not hanker after a three days' celebrity as the man who got a black eye or something of the sort from the mate of the *Patna*. He, in all probability, did not care what he did, or at any rate would be fully justified in his own eyes. It took no magician to see he was amazingly angry about something, for all his quiet and even torpid demeanour. I don't deny I was extremely desirous to pacify him at all costs, had I only known what to do. But I didn't know, as you may well imagine. It was blackness without a single gleam. We confronted each other in silence. He hung fire for about fifteen seconds, then made a step nearer, and I made ready to ward off a blow, though I don't think I moved a muscle. "If you were as big as two men and as strong as six," he said very softly, "I would tell you what I think of you. You . . . " "Stop!" I exclaimed. This checked him for a second. "Before you tell me what you think of me," I went on, quickly, "will you kindly tell me what it is I've said or done?" During the pause that ensued he surveyed me with indignation, while I made supernatural efforts of memory, in which I was hindered by the oriental voice within the court-room expostulating with impassioned volubility against the charge of falsehood. Then we spoke almost together. "I will soon show you I am not," he said, in a tone suggestive of a crisis. "I declare I don't know," I protested earnestly at the same time. He tried to crush me by the scorn of his glance. "Now that you see I am not afraid you try to crawl out of it," he said. "Who's a cur now – hey?" Then, at last, I understood.

'He had been scanning my features as though looking for a place where he would plant his fist. "I will allow no man . . . " he mumbled, threateningly. It was, indeed, a hideous mistake; he had given himself away utterly. I can't give you an idea how shocked I was. I suppose he saw some reflection of my feelings in my face, because his expression changed just a little. "Good God!" I stammered, "you don't think I . . . " "But I am sure I've heard," he persisted, raising his voice for the first time since the beginning of this deplorable scene. Then with a shade of disdain he added, "It wasn't you, then? Very well; I'll find the other." "Don't be a fool," I cried in exasperation; "it wasn't that at all." "I've heard," he said again with an unshaken and sombre perseverance.

'There may be those who could have laughed at his pertinacity. I didn't. Oh, I didn't! There had never been a man so mercilessly shown up by his own natural impulse. A single word had stripped him of his discretion – of that discretion which is more necessary to the decencies of our inner being than clothing is to the decorum of our body. "Don't be a fool," I repeated. "But the other man said it, you don't deny that?" he pronounced distinctly, and looking in my face without flinching. "No, I don't deny," said I, returning his gaze. At last his eyes followed downwards the direction of my pointing finger. He appeared at first uncomprehending, then confounded, and at last amazed and scared as though a dog had been a monster and he had never seen a dog before. "Nobody dreamt of insulting you," I said.

'He contemplated the wretched animal, that moved no more than an effigy: it sat with ears pricked and its sharp muzzle pointed into the doorway, and suddenly snapped at a fly like a piece of mechanism.

'I looked at him. The red of his fair, sunburnt complexion deepened suddenly under the down of his cheeks, invaded his forehead, spread to the roots of his curly hair. His ears became intensely crimson, and even the clear blue of his eyes was darkened many shades by the rush of blood to his head. His lips pouted a little, trembling as though he had been on the point of bursting into tears. I perceived he was incapable of pronouncing a word from the excess of his humiliation. From disappointment too – who knows? Perhaps he looked forward to that hammering he was going to give me for rehabilitation, for appeasement? Who can tell what relief he expected from this chance of a row? He was naïve enough to expect anything; but he had given himself away for nothing in this case. He had been frank with himself – let alone with me – in the wild hope of arriving in that way at some effective refutation, and the stars had been ironically unpropitious. He made an inarticulate noise in his throat like a man imperfectly stunned by a blow on the head. It was pitiful.

'I didn't catch up again with him till well outside the gate. I had even to trot a bit at the last, but when, out of breath at his elbow, I taxed him with running away, he said, "Never!" and at once turned at bay. I explained I never meant to say he was running away from *me*. "From no man – from not a single man on earth," he affirmed with a stubborn mien. I forbore to point out the one obvious exception which would hold good for the bravest of us; I thought he would find out by himself very soon. He looked at me patiently while I was thinking of something to say, but I could find nothing on the spur of the moment, and he began to walk on. I kept up, and anxious not to lose him, I said hurriedly that I couldn't think of leaving him under a false impression of my – of my – I stammered. The stupidity of the phrase appalled me while I was trying to finish it, but the power of sentences has nothing to do with their sense or the logic of their construction. My idiotic mumble seemed to please him. He cut it short by saying, with courteous placidity that argued an immense power of self-control or else a wonderful elasticity of spirits – "Altogether my mistake." I marvelled greatly at this expression: he might have been alluding to some trifling occurrence. Hadn't he understood its deplorable meaning? "You may well forgive me," he continued, and went on a little moodily, "All these staring people in court seemed such fools that – that it might have been as I supposed."

'This opened suddenly a new view of him to my wonder. I looked at him curiously and met his unabashed and impenetrable eyes. "I can't put up with this kind of thing," he said, very simply, "and I don't mean to. In court it's different; I've got to stand that – and I can do it too."

'I don't pretend I understood him. The views he let me have of himself were like those glimpses through the shifting rents in a thick fog – bits of vivid and vanishing detail, giving no connected idea of the general aspect of a country. They fed one's curiosity without satisfying it; they were no good for purposes of orientation. Upon the whole he was misleading. That's how I summed him up to myself after he left in the evening. I had been staying at the Malabar House for a few days, and on my pressing invitation he dined with me there.'

Chapter 7

'An outward-bound mail-boat had come in that afternoon, and the big dining-room of the hotel was more than half full of people with a hundred pounds round-the-world tickets in their pockets. There were married couples looking domesticated and bored with each other in the midst of their travels; there were small parties and large parties, and lone individuals dining solemnly or feasting boisterously, but all thinking, conversing, joking, or scowling as was their wont at home; and just as intelligently receptive of new impressions as their trunks upstairs. Henceforth they would be labelled as having passed this and that place and so would be their luggage. They would cherish this distinction of their persons, and preserve the gummed tickets on their portmanteaux as documentary evidence, as the only permanent trace of their improving enterprise. The dark-faced servants tripped without noise over the vast and polished floor; now and then a girl's laugh would be heard, as innocent and empty as her mind, or, in a sudden hush of crockery, a few words in an affected drawl from some wit embroidering for the benefit of a grinning tableful the last funny story of shipboard scandal. Two nomadic old maids, dressed up to kill, worked acrimoniously through the bill of fare, whispering to each other with faded lips, wooden-faced and bizarre, like two sumptuous scarecrows. A little wine opened Jim's heart and loosened his tongue. His appetite was good, too, I noticed. He seemed to have buried somewhere the opening episode of our acquaintance. It was like a thing of which there would be no more question in this world. And all the time I had before me these blue, boyish eyes looking straight into mine, this young face, these capable shoulders, the open bronzed forehead with a white line under the roots of clustering fair hair, this appearance appealing at sight to all my sympathies: this frank aspect, the artless smile, the youthful seriousness. He was of the right sort; he was one of us. He talked soberly, with a sort of composed unreserve, and with a quiet bearing that might have been the outcome of manly self-control, of impudence, of callousness, of a colossal unconsciousness, of a gigantic deception. Who can tell! From our tone we might have been discussing a third person, a football match, last year's weather. My mind floated in a sea of conjectures till the turn of the conversation enabled me, without being offensive, to remark that, upon the whole, this inquiry must have been pretty trying to him. He darted his arm across the tablecloth, and clutching my hand by the side of my plate, glared fixedly. I *was* startled. "It must be awfully hard," I stammered, confused by the display of speechless feeling. "It is – hell," he burst out in a muffled voice.

'This movement and these words caused two well-groomed male globe-trotters at a neighbouring table to look up in alarm from their ice-pudding. I rose, and we passed into the front gallery for coffee and cigars.

'On little octagon tables candles burned in glass globes; clumps of stiff-leaved plants separated sets of cosy wicker chairs; and between the pairs of columns, whose reddish shafts caught in a long row the sheen from the tall windows, the night, glittering and sombre, seemed to hang like a splendid drapery. The riding lights of ships winked afar like setting stars, and the hills across the roadstead resembled rounded black masses of arrested thunder-clouds.

' "I couldn't clear out," Jim began. "The skipper did – that's all very well for him. I couldn't, and I wouldn't. They all got out of it in one way or another, but it wouldn't do for me."

'I listened with concentrated attention, not daring to stir in my chair; I wanted to know – and to this day I don't know, I can only guess. He would be confident and depressed all in the same breath, as if some conviction of innate blamelessness had checked the truth writhing within him at every turn. He began by saying, in the tone in which a man would admit his inability to jump a twenty-foot wall, that he could never go home now; and this declaration recalled to my mind what Brierly had said, that "the old parson in Essex seemed to fancy his sailor son not a little."

'I can't tell you whether Jim knew he was especially "fancied", but the tone of his references to "my dad" was calculated to give me a notion that the good old rural dean was about the finest man that ever had been worried by the cares of a large family since the beginning of the world. This, though never stated, was implied with an anxiety that there should be no mistake about it, which was really very true and charming, but added a poignant sense of lives far off to the other elements of the story. "He has seen it all in the home papers by this time," said Jim. "I can never face the poor old chap." I did not dare to lift my eyes at this till I heard him add, "I could never explain. He wouldn't understand." Then I looked up. He was smoking reflectively, and after a moment, rousing himself, began to talk again. He discovered at once a desire that I should not confound him with his partners in – in crime, let us call it. He was not one of them; he was altogether of another sort. I gave no sign of dissent. I had no intention, for the sake of barren truth, to rob him of the smallest particle of any saving grace that would come in his way. I didn't know how much of it he believed himself. I didn't know what he was playing up to – if he was playing up to anything at all – and I suspect he did not know either; for it is my belief no man ever understands quite his own artful dodges to escape from the grim shadow of self-knowledge. I made no sound all the time he was wondering what he had better do after "that stupid inquiry was over."

'Apparently he shared Brierly's contemptuous opinion of these proceedings ordained by law. He would not know where to turn, he confessed, clearly thinking aloud rather than talking to me. Certificate gone, career broken, no money to get away, no work that he could obtain as far as he could see. At home he could perhaps get something; but it meant going to his people for help, and that he would not do. He saw nothing for it but ship before the mast – could get perhaps a quartermaster's billet in some steamer. Would do for a quartermaster . . . "Do you think you would?" I asked pitilessly. He jumped up, and going to the stone balustrade looked out into the night. In a moment he was back, towering above my chair with his youthful face clouded yet by the pain of a conquered emotion. He had understood very well I did not doubt his ability to steer a ship. In a voice that quavered a bit he asked me, Why did I say that? I had been "no end kind" to him. I had not even laughed at him when – here he began to mumble – "that mistake, you know – made a confounded ass of myself." I broke in by saying rather warmly that for me such a mistake was not a matter to laugh at. He sat down and drank deliberately some coffee, emptying the small cup to the last drop. "That does not mean I admit for a moment the cap fitted," he declared, distinctly. "No?" I said. "No," he affirmed with quiet decision. "Do you know what *you* would have done? Do you? And you don't think yourself" . . . he gulped something . . . "you don't think yourself a – a – cur?"

'And with this – upon my honour! – he looked up at me inquisitively. It was a question it appears – a bona fide question! However, he didn't wait for an answer. Before I could recover he went on, with his eyes straight before him, as if reading off something written on the body of the night. "It is all in being ready. I wasn't; not – not then. I don't want to excuse myself; but I would like to explain – I would like somebody to understand – somebody – one person at least! You! Why not you?"

'It was solemn, and a little ridiculous, too, as they always are, those struggles of an individual trying to save from the fire his idea of what his moral identity should be, this precious notion of a convention, only one of the rules of the game, nothing more, but all the same so terribly effective by its assumption of unlimited power over natural instincts, by the awful penalties of its failure. He began his story quietly enough. On board that Dale Line steamer that had picked up these four floating in a boat upon the discreet sunset glow of the sea, they had been after the first day looked askance upon. The fat skipper told some story, the others had been silent, and at first it had been accepted. You don't cross-examine poor castaways you had the good luck to save, if not from cruel death, then at least from cruel suffering. Afterwards, with time to think it over, it might have struck the officers of the *Avondale* that there was "something fishy" in the affair; but of course they would keep their doubts to themselves. They had picked up the captain, the mate, and two engineers of the steamer *Patna* sunk at sea, and that, very properly, was enough for them. I did not ask Jim about the nature of his feelings during the ten days he spent on board. From the way he narrated that part I was at liberty to infer he was partly stunned by the discovery he had made – the discovery about himself – and no doubt was at work trying to explain it away to the only man who was capable of appreciating all its tremendous magnitude. You must understand he did not try to minimise its importance. Of that I am sure; and therein lies his distinction. As to what sensations he experienced when he got ashore and heard the unforeseen conclusion of the tale in which he had taken such a pitiful part, he told me nothing of them, and it is difficult to imagine. I wonder whether he felt the ground cut from under his feet? I wonder? But no doubt he managed to get a fresh foothold very soon. He was ashore a whole fortnight waiting in the Sailors' Home, and as there were six or seven men staying there at the time, I had heard of him a little. Their languid opinion seemed to be that in addition to his other shortcomings, he was a sulky brute. He had passed these days on the veranda, buried in a long-chair, and coming out of his place of sepulture only at meal-times or late at night, when he wandered on the quays all by himself, detached from his surroundings, irresolute and silent, like a ghost without a home to haunt. "I don't think I've spoken three words to a living soul in all that time," he said, making me very sorry for him; and directly he added, "One of these fellows would have been sure to blurt out something I had made up my mind not to put up with, and I didn't want a row. No! Not then. I was too – too . . . I had no heart for it." "So that bulkhead held out after all," I remarked, cheerfully. "Yes," he murmured, "it held. And yet I swear to you I felt it bulge under my hand." "It's extraordinary what strains old iron will stand sometimes," I said. Thrown back in his seat, his legs stiffly out and arms hanging down, he nodded slightly several times. You could not conceive a sadder spectacle. Suddenly he lifted his head; he sat up; he slapped his thigh. "Ah! what a chance missed! My God! what a chance missed!" he blazed out, but the ring of the last "missed" resembled a cry wrung out by pain.

'He was silent again with a still, far-away look of fierce yearning after that missed distinction, with his nostril for an instant dilated, sniffing the intoxicating breath of that wasted opportunity. If you think I was either surprised or shocked you do me an injustice in more ways than one! Ah, he was an imaginative beggar! He would give himself away; he would give himself up. I could see in his glance darted into the night all his inner being carried on, projected headlong into the fanciful realm of recklessly heroic aspirations. He had no leisure to regret what he had lost, he was so wholly and naturally concerned for what he had failed to obtain. He was very far away from me who watched him across three feet of space. With every instant he was penetrating deeper into the impossible world of romantic achievements. He got to the heart of it at last! A strange look of beatitude overspread his features, his eyes sparkled in the light of the candle burning between us; he positively smiled! He had penetrated to the very heart – to the very heart. It was an ecstatic smile that your faces – or mine either – will never wear, my dear boys. I whisked him back by saying, "If you had stuck to the ship, you mean!"'

'He turned upon me, his eyes suddenly amazed and full of pain, with a bewildered, startled, suffering face, as though he had tumbled down from a star. Neither you nor I will ever look like this on any man. He shuddered profoundly, as if a cold fingertip had touched his heart. Last of all he sighed.

'I was not in a merciful mood. He provoked one by his contradictory indiscretions. "It is unfortunate you didn't know beforehand!" I said with every unkind intention; but the perfidious shaft fell harmless – dropped at his feet like a spent arrow, as it were, and he did not think of picking it up. Perhaps he had not even seen it. Presently, lolling at ease, he said, "Dash it all! I tell you it bulged. I was holding up my lamp along the angle-iron in the lower deck when a flake of rust as big as the palm of my hand fell off the plate, all of itself." He passed his hand over his forehead. "The thing stirred and jumped off like something alive while I was looking at it." "That made you feel pretty bad," I observed, casually. "Do you suppose," he said, "that I was thinking of myself, with a hundred and sixty people at my back, all fast asleep in that fore-'tween-deck alone – and more of them aft; more on the deck – sleeping – knowing nothing about it – three times as many as there were boats for, even if there had been time? expected to see the iron open out as I stood there and the rush of water going over them as they lay . . . What could I do – what?"

'I can easily picture him to myself in the peopled gloom of the cavernous place, with the light of the bulk-lamp falling on a small portion of the bulkhead that had the weight of the ocean on the other side, and the breathing of unconscious sleepers in his ears. I can see him glaring at the iron, startled by the falling rust, overburdened by the knowledge of an imminent death. This, I gathered, was the second time he had been sent forward by that skipper of his, who, I rather think, wanted to keep him away from the bridge. He told me that his first impulse was to shout and straight away make all those people leap out of sleep into terror; but such an overwhelming sense of his helplessness came over him that he was not able to produce a sound. This is, I suppose, what people mean by the tongue cleaving to the roof of the mouth. "Too dry," was the concise expression he used in reference to this state. Without a sound, then, he scrambled out on deck through the number one hatch. A wind-sail rigged down there swung against him accidentally, and he remembered that the light touch of the canvas on his face nearly knocked him off the hatchway ladder.

'He confessed that his knees wobbled a good deal as he stood on the foredeck looking at another sleeping crowd. The engines having been stopped by that time, the steam was blowing off. Its deep rumble made the whole night vibrate like a bass string. The ship trembled to it.

'He saw here and there a head lifted off a mat, a vague form uprise in sitting posture, listen sleepily for a moment, sink down again into the billowy confusion of boxes, steam-winches, ventilators. He was aware all these people did not know enough to take intelligent notice of that strange noise. The ship of iron, the men with white faces, all the sights, all the sounds, everything on board to that ignorant and pious multitude was strange alike, and as trustworthy as it would for ever remain incomprehensible. It occurred to him that the fact was fortunate. The idea of it was simply terrible.

'You must remember he believed, as any other man would have done in his place, that the ship would go down at any moment; the bulging, rust-eaten plates that kept back the ocean, fatally must give way, all at once like an undermined dam, and let in a sudden and overwhelming flood. He stood still looking at these recumbent bodies, a doomed man aware of his fate, surveying the silent company of the dead. They *were* dead! Nothing could save them! There were boats enough for half of them perhaps, but there was no time. No time! No time! It did not seem worthwhile to open his lips, to stir hand or foot. Before he could shout three words, or make three steps, he would be floundering in a sea whitened awfully by the desperate struggles of human beings, clamorous with the distress of cries for help. There was no help. He imagined what would happen perfectly; he went through it all motionless by the hatchway with the lamp in his hand – he went through it to the very last harrowing detail. I think he went through it again while he was telling me these things he could not tell the court.

' "I saw as clearly as I see you now that there was nothing I could do. It seemed to take all the life out of my limbs. I thought I might just as well stand where I was and wait. I did not think I had many seconds . . . " Suddenly the steam ceased blowing off. The noise, he remarked, had been distracting, but the silence at once became intolerably oppressive.

' "I thought I would choke before I got drowned," he said.

'He protested he did not think of saving himself. The only distinct thought formed, vanishing, and re-forming in his brain, was: eight hundred people and seven boats; eight hundred people and seven boats.

' "Somebody was speaking aloud inside my head," he said a little wildly. "Eight hundred people and seven boats – and no time! Just think of it." He leaned towards me across the little table, and I tried to avoid his stare. "Do you think I was afraid of death?" he asked in a voice very fierce and low. He brought down his open hand with a bang that made the coffee-cups dance. "I am ready to swear I was not – I was not . . . By God – no!" He hitched himself upright and crossed his arms; his chin fell on his breast.

'The soft clashes of crockery reached us faintly through the high windows. There was a burst of voices, and several men came out in high good-humour into the gallery. They were exchanging jocular reminiscences of the donkeys in Cairo. A pale anxious youth stepping softly on long legs was being chaffed by a strutting and rubicund globe-trotter about his purchases in the bazaar. "No, really – do you think I've been done to that extent?" he enquired very earnest and deliberate. The band moved away, dropping into chairs as they went; matches flared, illuminating for a second faces without the ghost of an expression and the flat glaze of white shirt-fronts; the hum of many conversations animated with the ardour of feasting sounded to me absurd and infinitely remote.

' "Some of the crew were sleeping on the number one hatch within reach of my arm," began Jim again.

'You must know they kept Kalashee watch in that ship, all hands sleeping through the night, and only the reliefs of quartermasters and look-out men being called. He was tempted to grip and shake the shoulder of the nearest lascar, but he didn't. Something held his arms down along his sides. He was not afraid – oh no! only he just couldn't – that's all. He was not afraid of death perhaps, but I'll tell you what, he was afraid of the emergency. His confounded imagination had evoked for him all the horrors of panic, the trampling rush, the pitiful screams, boats swamped – all the appalling incidents of a disaster at sea he had ever heard of. He might have been resigned to die, but I suspect he wanted to die without added terrors, quietly, in a sort of peaceful trance. A certain readiness to perish is not so very rare, but it is seldom that you meet men whose souls, steeled in the impenetrable armour of resolution, are ready to fight a losing battle to the last, the desire of peace waxes stronger as hope declines, till at last it conquers the very desire of life. Which of us here has not observed this, or maybe experienced something of that feeling in his own person – this extreme weariness of emotions, the vanity of effort, the yearning for rest? Those striving with unreasonable forces know it well – the shipwrecked castaways in boats, wanderers lost in a desert, men battling against the unthinking might of nature, or the stupid brutality of crowds.'

Chapter 8

'How long he stood stock-still by the hatch expecting every moment to feel the ship dip under his feet and the rush of water to take him at the back and toss him like a chip, I cannot say. Not very long – two minutes perhaps. A couple of men he could not make out began to converse drowsily, and also, he could not tell where, he detected a curious noise of shuffling feet. Above these faint sounds there was that awful stillness preceding a catastrophe, that trying silence of the moment before the crash; then it came into his head perhaps he would have time to rush along and cut all the lanyards of the gripes, so that the boats would float off as the ship went down.

'The *Patna* had a long bridge, and all the boats were up there, four on one side and three on the other – the smallest of them on the port side and nearly abreast of the steering gear. He assured me, with evident anxiety to be believed, that he had been most careful to keep them ready for instant service. He knew his duty. I dare say he was a good enough mate as far as that went. "I always believed in being prepared for the worst," he commented, staring anxiously in my face. I nodded my approval of the sound principle, averting my eyes before the subtle unsoundness of the man.

'He started unsteadily to run. He had to step over legs, avoid stumbling against the heads. Suddenly someone caught hold of his coat from below, and a distressed voice spoke under his elbow. The light of the lamp he carried in his right hand fell upon an upturned dark face whose eyes entreated him together with a voice. He had picked up enough of the language to understand the word water, repeated several times in a tone of insistence, of prayer, almost of despair. He gave a jerk to get away, and felt an arm embrace his leg.

' "The beggar clung to me like a drowning man," he said impressively. "Water, water! What water did he mean? What did he know? As calmly as I could I ordered him to let go. He was stopping me, time was pressing, other men began to stir; I wanted time – time to cut the boats adrift. He got hold of my hand now, and I felt that he would begin to shout. It flashed upon me it was enough to start a panic, and I hauled off with my free arm and slung the lamp in his face. The glass jingled, the light went out, but the blow made him let go, and I ran off – I wanted to get at the boats; I wanted to get at the boats. He leaped after me from behind. I turned on him. He would not keep quiet; he tried to shout; I had half throttled him before I made out what he wanted. He wanted some water – water to drink; they were on strict allowance, you know, and he had with him a young boy I had noticed several times. His child was sick – and thirsty. He had caught sight of me as I passed by, and was begging for a little water. That's all. We were under the bridge, in the dark. He kept on snatching at my wrists; there was no getting rid of him. I dashed into my berth, grabbed my water-bottle, and thrust it into his hands. He vanished. I didn't find out till then how much I was in want of a drink myself." He leaned on one elbow with a hand over his eyes.

'I felt a creepy sensation all down my backbone; there was something peculiar in all this. The fingers of the hand that shaded his brow trembled slightly. He broke the short silence.

' "These things happen only once to a man and . . . Ah! well! When I got on the bridge at last the beggars were getting one of the boats off the chocks. A boat! I was running up the ladder when a heavy blow fell on my shoulder, just missing my head. It didn't stop me, and the chief engineer – they had got him out of his bunk by then – raised the boat-stretcher again. Somehow I had no mind to be surprised at anything. All this seemed natural – and awful – and awful. I dodged that miserable maniac, lifted him off the deck as though he had been a little child, and he started whispering in my arms: 'Don't! don't! I thought you were one of them niggers.' I flung him away, he skidded along the bridge and knocked the legs from under the little chap – the second. The skipper, busy about the boat, looked round and came at me head down, growling like a wild beast. I flinched no more than a stone. I was as solid standing there as this," he tapped lightly with his knuckles the wall beside his chair. "It was as though I had heard it all, seen it all, gone through it all twenty times already. I wasn't afraid of them. I drew back my fist and he stopped short, muttering: "Ah! it's you. Lend a hand quick." ' '

' "That's what he said. Quick! As if anybody could be quick enough. 'Aren't you going to do something?' I asked. 'Yes. Clear out,' he snarled over his shoulder.

' "I don't think I understood then what he meant. The other two had picked themselves up by that time, and they rushed together to the boat. They tramped, they wheezed, they shoved, they cursed the boat, the ship, each other – cursed me. All in mutters. I didn't move, I didn't speak. I watched the slant of the ship. She was as still as if landed on the blocks in a dry dock – only she was like this." He held up his hand, palm under, the tips of the fingers inclined downwards. "Like this," he repeated. "I could see the line of the horizon before me, as clear as a bell, above her stem-head; I could see the water far off there black and sparkling, and still – still as a pond, deadly still, more still than ever sea was before – more still than I could bear to look at. Have you watched a ship floating head down, checked in sinking by a sheet of old iron too rotten to stand being shored up? Have you? Oh, yes, shored up! I thought of that – I thought of every mortal thing; but can you shore up a bulkhead in five minutes – or in fifty for that matter? Where was I going to get men that would go down below? And the timber – the timber! Would you have had the courage to swing the maul for the first blow if you had seen that bulkhead? Don't say you would: you had not seen it; nobody would. Hang it – to do a thing like that you must believe there is a chance, one in a thousand, at least, some ghost of a chance; and you would not have believed. Nobody would have believed. You think me a cur for standing there, but what would you have done? What! You can't tell – nobody can tell. One must have time to turn round. What would you have me do? Where was the kindness in making crazy with fright all those people I could not save single-handed – that nothing could save? Look here! As true as I sit on this chair before you . . . "

'He drew quick breaths at every few words and shot quick glances at my face, as though in his anguish he were watchful of the effect. He was not speaking to me, he was only speaking before me, in a dispute with an invisible personality, an antagonistic and inseparable partner of his existence – another possessor of his soul. These were issues beyond the competency of a court of inquiry: it was a subtle and momentous quarrel as to the true essence of life, and did not want a judge. He wanted an ally, a helper, an accomplice. I felt the risk I ran of being circumvented, blinded, decoyed, bullied, perhaps, into taking a definite part in a dispute impossible of decision if one had to be fair to all the phantoms in possession – to the reputable that had its claims and to the disreputable that had its exigencies. I can't explain to you who haven't seen him and who hear his words only at second hand the mixed nature of my feelings. It seemed to me I was being made to comprehend the Inconceivable – and I know of nothing to compare with the discomfort of such a sensation. I was made to look at the convention that lurks in all truth and on the essential sincerity of falsehood. He appealed to all sides at once – to the side turned perpetually to the light of day, and to that side of us, which like the other hemisphere of the moon, exists stealthily in perpetual darkness, with only a fearful ashy light falling at times on the edge. He swayed me. I own to it, I own up. The occasion was obscure, insignificant – what you will: a lost youngster, one in a million – but then he was one of us; an incident as completely devoid of importance as the flooding of an ant-heap, and yet the mystery of his attitude got hold of me as though he had been an individual in the forefront of his kind, as if the obscure truth involved were momentous enough to affect mankind's conception of itself . . . '

Marlow paused to put new life into his expiring cheroot, seemed to forget all about the story, and abruptly began again.

'My fault of course. One has no business really to get interested. It's a weakness of mine. His was of another kind. My weakness consists in not having a discriminating eye for the incidental – for the externals – no eye for the hod of the rag-picker or the fine linen of the next man. Next man – that's it. I have met so many men,' he pursued, with momentary sadness – 'met them, too, with a certain – certain – impact, let us say; like this fellow, for instance – and in each case all I could see was merely the human being. A confounded democratic quality of vision which may be better than total blindness, but had been of no advantage to me, I can assure you. Men expect one to take into account their fine linen. But I never could get up any enthusiasm about these things. Oh! it's a failing; it's a failing; and then comes a soft evening; a lot of men too indolent for whist – and a story . . .'

He paused again to wait for an encouraging remark, perhaps, but nobody spoke; only the host, as if reluctantly performing a duty, murmured: 'You are so subtle, Marlow.'

'Who? I?' said Marlow in a low voice. 'Oh, no! But *he* was; and try as I may for the success of this yarn I am missing innumerable shades – they were so fine, so difficult to render in colourless words. Because he complicated matters by being so simple, too – the simplest poor devil! . . . By Jove! he was amazing. There he sat telling me that just as I saw him before my eyes he wouldn't be afraid to face anything – and believing in it, too. I tell you it was fabulously innocent and it was enormous, enormous! I watched him covertly, just as though I had suspected him of an intention to take a jolly good rise out of me. He was confident that, on the square, "on the square, mind!" there was nothing he couldn't meet. Ever since he had been "so high" – "quite a little chap," he had been preparing himself for all the difficulties that can beset one on land and water. He confessed proudly to this kind of foresight. He had been elaborating dangers and defences, expecting the worst, rehearsing his best. He must have led a most exalted existence. Can you fancy it? A succession of adventures, so much glory, such a victorious progress! and the deep sense of his sagacity crowning every day of his inner life. He forgot himself, his eyes shone; and with every word my heart, searched by the light of his absurdity, was growing heavier in my breast. I had no mind to laugh, and lest I should smile I made for myself a stolid face. He gave signs of irritation.

' "It is always the unexpected that happens," I said in a propitiatory tone. My obtuseness provoked him into a contemptuous "Pshaw!" I suppose he meant that the unexpected couldn't touch him; nothing less than the unconceivable itself could get over his perfect state of preparation. He had been taken unawares – and he whispered to himself a malediction upon the waters and the firmament, upon the ship, upon the men. Everything had betrayed him! He had been tricked into that sort of high-minded resignation which prevented him lifting as much as his little finger, while these others who had a very clear perception of the actual necessity were tumbling against each other and sweating desperately over that boat business. Something had gone wrong there at the last moment. It appears that in their flurry they had contrived in some mysterious way to get the sliding bolt of the foremost boat-chock jammed tight, and forthwith had gone out of the remnants of their minds over the deadly nature of that accident. It must have been a pretty sight, the fierce industry of these beggars toiling on a motionless ship that floated quietly in the silence of a world asleep, fighting against time for the freeing of that boat, grovelling on all fours, standing up in despair, tugging, pushing, snarling at each other venomously, ready to kill, ready to weep, and only kept from flying at each other's throats by the fear of death that stood silent behind them like an inflexible and cold-eyed taskmaster. Oh, yes! It must have been a pretty sight. He saw it all, he could talk about it with scorn and bitterness; he had a minute knowledge of it by means of some sixth sense, I conclude, because he swore to me he had remained apart without a glance at them and at the boat – without one single glance. And I believe him. I should think he was too busy watching the threatening slant of the ship, the suspended menace discovered in the midst of the most perfect security – fascinated by the sword hanging by a hair over his imaginative head.

'Nothing in the world moved before his eyes, and he could depict to himself without hindrance the sudden swing upwards of the dark skyline, the sudden tilt up of the vast plain of the sea, the swift still rise, the brutal fling, the grasp of the abyss, the struggle without hope, the starlight closing over his head for ever like the vault of a tomb – the revolt of his young life – the black end. He could! By Jove! who couldn't? And you must remember he was a finished artist in that peculiar way, he was a gifted poor devil with the faculty of swift and forestalling vision. The sights it showed him had turned him into cold stone from the soles of his feet to the nape of his neck; but there was a hot dance of thoughts in his head, a dance of lame, blind, mute thoughts – a whirl of awful cripples. Didn't I tell you he confessed himself before me as though I had the power to bind and to loose? He burrowed deep, deep, in the hope of my absolution, which would have been of no good to him. This was one of those cases which no solemn deception can palliate, which no man can help; where his very Maker seems to abandon a sinner to his own devices.

'He stood on the starboard side of the bridge, as far as he could get from the struggle for the boat, which went on with the agitation of madness and the stealthiness of a conspiracy. The two Malays had meantime remained holding to the wheel. Just picture to yourselves the actors in that, thank God! unique, episode of the sea, four beside themselves with fierce and secret exertions, and three looking on in complete immobility, above the awnings covering the profound ignorance of hundreds of human beings, with their weariness, with their dreams, with their hopes, arrested, held by an invisible hand on the brink of annihilation. For that they were so, makes no doubt to me, given the state of the ship, this was the deadliest possible description of accident that could happen. These beggars by the boat had every reason to go distracted with funk. Frankly, had I been there I would not have given as much as a counterfeit farthing for the ship's chance to keep above water to the end of each successive second. And still she floated!

These sleeping pilgrims were destined to accomplish their whole pilgrimage to the bitterness of some other end. It was as if the Omnipotence whose mercy they confessed had needed their humble testimony on earth for a while longer, and had looked down to make a sign, "Thou shalt not!" to the ocean. Their escape would trouble me as a prodigiously inexplicable event, did I not know how tough old iron can be – as tough sometimes as the spirit of some men we meet now and then, worn to a shadow and breasting the weight of life. Not in the least wonder of these twenty minutes, to my mind, is the behaviour of the two helmsmen. They were amongst the native batch of all sorts brought over from Aden to give evidence at the inquiry. One of them, labouring under intense bashfulness, was very young, and with his smooth, yellow, cheery countenance looked even younger than he was. I remember perfectly Brierly asking, through the interpreter, what he thought of it at the time, and the interpreter, after a short colloquy, turning to the court with an important air: "He says he thought nothing."

'The other with patient blinking eyes, a blue cotton handkerchief, faded with much washing, bound with a smart twist over a lot of grey wisps, his face shrunk into grim hollows, his brown skin made darker by a mesh of wrinkles, explained that he had a knowledge of some evil thing befalling the ship, but there had been no order; he could not remember an order; why should he leave the helm? To some further questions he jerked back his spare shoulders, and declared it never came into his mind then that the white men were about to leave the ship through fear of death. He did not believe it now. There might have been secret reasons. He wagged his old chin knowingly. Aha! secret reasons. He was a man of great experience, and he wanted *that* white *tuan* to know – he turned towards Brierly, who didn't raise his head – that he had acquired a knowledge of many things by serving white men on the sea for a great number of years – and, suddenly, with shaky excitement he poured upon our spellbound attention a lot of queer-sounding names, names of dead-and-gone skippers, names of forgotten country ships, names of familiar and distorted sound, as if the hand of dumb time had been at work on them for ages. They stopped him at last. A silence fell upon the court – a silence that remained unbroken for at least a minute, and passed gently into a deep murmur. This episode was *the* sensation of the second day's proceedings – affecting all the audience, affecting everybody except Jim, who was sitting moodily at the end of the first bench, and never looked up at this extraordinary and damning witness that seemed possessed of some mysterious theory of defence.

'So these two lascars stuck to the helm of that ship without steerage-way, where death would have found them if such had been their destiny. The whites did not give them half a glance, had probably forgotten their existence. Assuredly Jim did not remember it. He remembered he could do nothing; he could do nothing, now he was alone. There was nothing to do but to sink with the ship. No use making a disturbance about it. Was there? He waited upstanding, without a sound, stiffened in the idea of some sort of heroic discretion. The first engineer ran cautiously across the bridge to tug at his sleeve.

' "Come and help! For God's sake, come and help!"

'He ran back to the boat on the points of his toes, and returned directly to worry at his sleeve, begging and cursing at the same time.

' "I believe he would have kissed my hands," said Jim, savagely, "and, next moment, he starts foaming and whispering in my face, 'If I had the time I would like to crack your skull for you.' I pushed him away. Suddenly he caught hold of me round the neck. Damn him! I hit him. I hit out without looking. 'Won't you save your own life – you infernal coward?' he sobs. Coward! He called me an infernal coward! Ha! ha! ha! ha! He called me – ha! ha! ha! . . . "

'He had thrown himself back and was shaking with laughter. I had never in my life heard anything so bitter as that noise. It fell like a blight on all the merriment about donkeys, pyramids, bazaars, or what not. Along the whole dim length of the gallery the voices dropped, the pale blotches of faces turned our way with one accord, and the silence became so profound that the clear tinkle of a teaspoon falling on the tessellated floor of the veranda rang out like a tiny and silvery scream.

' "You mustn't laugh like this, with all these people about," I remonstrated. "It isn't nice for them, you know."

'He gave no sign of having heard at first, but after a while, with a stare that, missing me altogether, seemed to probe the heart of some awful vision, he muttered carelessly: "Oh! they'll think I am drunk."

'And after that you would have thought from his appearance he would never make a sound again. But no fear! He could no more stop telling now than he could have stopped living by the mere exertion of his will.'

Chapter 9

' "I was saying to myself, 'Sink – curse you! Sink!' " These were the words with which he began again. He wanted it over. He was severely left alone, and he formulated in his head this address to the ship in a tone of imprecation, while at the same time he enjoyed the privilege of witnessing scenes – as far as I can judge – of low comedy. They were still at that bolt. The skipper was ordering, "Get under and try to lift," and the others naturally shirked. You understand that to be squeezed flat under the keel of a boat wasn't a desirable position to be caught in if the ship went down suddenly. "Why don't you – you're the

strongest?" whined the little engineer. "Gott-for-dam! I am too thick,"
spluttered the skipper in despair. It was funny enough to make angels weep.
They stood idle for a moment, and suddenly the chief engineer rushed
again at Jim.

' "Come and help, man! Are you mad to throw your only chance away?
Come and help, man! Man! Look there – look!"

'And at last Jim looked astern where the other pointed with maniacal
insistence. He saw a silent black squall which had eaten up already one-third
of the sky. You know how these squalls come up there about that time of the
year. First you see a darkening of the horizon – no more; then a cloud rises
opaque like a wall. A straight edge of vapour lined with sickly whitish gleams
flies up from the south-west, swallowing the stars in whole constellations; its
shadow flies over the waters, and confounds sea and sky into one abyss of
obscurity. And all is still. No thunder, no wind, no sound; not a flicker of
lightning. Then in the tenebrous immensity a livid arch appears; a swell or
two like undulations of the very darkness run past, and suddenly, wind and
rain strike together with a peculiar impetuosity as if they had burst through
something solid. Such a cloud had come up while they weren't looking.
They had just noticed it, and were perfectly justified in surmising that if in
absolute stillness there was some chance for the ship to keep afloat a few
minutes longer, the least disturbance of the sea would make an end of her
instantly. Her first nod to the swell that precedes the burst of such a squall
would be also her last, would become a plunge, would, so to speak, be
prolonged into a long dive, down, down to the bottom. Hence these new
capers of their fright, these new antics in which they displayed their extreme
aversion to die.

' "It was black, black," pursued Jim with moody steadiness. "It had sneaked
upon us from behind. The infernal thing! I suppose there had been at the
back of my head some hope yet. I don't know. But that was all over anyhow.
It maddened me to see myself caught like this. I was angry, as though I had
been trapped. I *was* trapped! The night was hot, too, I remember. Not a
breath of air."

'He remembered so well that, gasping in the chair, he seemed to sweat
and choke before my eyes. No doubt it maddened him; it knocked him over
afresh – in a manner of speaking – but it made him also remember that
important purpose which had sent him rushing on that bridge only to slip
clean out of his mind. He had intended to cut the lifeboats clear of the ship.
He whipped out his knife and went to work slashing as though he had seen
nothing, had heard nothing, had known of no one on board. They thought
him hopelessly wrong-headed and crazy, but dared not protest noisily against
this useless loss of time. When he had done he returned to the very same
spot from which he had started. The chief was there, ready with a clutch at
him to whisper close to his head, scathingly, as though he wanted to bite his
ear: "You silly fool! do you think you'll get the ghost of a show when all that

lot of brutes is in the water? Why, they will batter your head for you from these boats."

'He wrung his hands, ignored, at Jim's elbow. The skipper kept up a nervous shuffle in one place and mumbled, "Hammer! hammer! *Mein Gott!* Get a hammer."

'The little engineer whimpered like a child, but broken arm and all, he turned out the least craven of the lot as it seems, and, actually, mustered enough pluck to run an errand to the engine-room. No trifle, it must be owned in fairness to him. Jim told me he darted desperate looks like a cornered man, gave one low wail, and dashed off. He was back instantly clambering, hammer in hand, and without a pause flung himself at the bolt. The others gave up Jim at once and ran off to assist. He heard the tap, tap of the hammer, the sound of the released chock falling over. The boat was clear. Only then he turned to look – only then. But he kept his distance – he kept his distance. He wanted me to know he had kept his distance; that there was nothing in common between him and these men – who had the hammer. Nothing whatever. It is more than probable he thought himself cut off from them by a space that could not be traversed, by an obstacle that could not be overcome, by a chasm without bottom. He was as far as he could get from them – the whole breadth of the ship.

'His feet were glued to that remote spot and his eyes to their indistinct group bowed together and swaying strangely in the common torment of fear. A hand-lamp lashed to a stanchion above a little table rigged up on the bridge – the *Patna* had no chart-room amidships – threw a light on their labouring shoulders, on their arched and bobbing backs. They pushed at the bow of the boat; they pushed out into the night; they pushed, and would no more look back at him. They had given him up as if indeed he had been too far, too hopelessly separated from themselves, to be worth an appealing word, a glance, or a sign. They had no leisure to look back upon his passive heroism, to feel the sting of his abstention. The boat was heavy; they pushed at the bow with no breath to spare for an encouraging word: but the turmoil of terror that had scattered their self-control, like chaff before the wind, converted their desperate exertions into a bit of fooling, upon my word fit for knockabout clowns in a farce. They pushed with their hands, with their heads, they pushed for dear life with all the weight of their bodies, they pushed with all the might of their souls – only no sooner had they succeeded in canting the stem clear of the davit than they would leave off like one man and start a wild scramble into her. As a natural consequence the boat would swing in abruptly, driving them back, helpless and jostling against each other. They would stand nonplussed for a while, exchanging in fierce whispers all the infamous names they could call to mind, and go at it again. Three times this occurred. He described it to me with morose thoughtfulness. He hadn't lost a single movement of that comic business. "I loathed them. I hated them. I had to look at all that," he said without emphasis, turning upon me a sombrely watchful glance. "Was ever there anyone so shamefully tried!"

'He took his head in his hands for a moment, like a man driven to distraction by some unspeakable outrage. These were things he could not explain to the court – and not even to me; but I would have been little fitted for the reception of his confidences had I not been able at times to understand the pauses between the words. In this assault upon his fortitude there was the jeering intention of a spiteful and vile vengeance; there was an element of burlesque in his ordeal – a degradation of funny grimaces in the approach of death or dishonour.

'He related facts which I have not forgotten, but at this distance of time I couldn't recall his very words: I only remember that he managed wonderfully to convey the brooding rancour of his mind into the bare recital of events. Twice, he told me, he shut his eyes in the certitude that the end was upon him already, and twice he had to open them again. Each time he noted the darkening of the great stillness. The shadow of the silent cloud had fallen upon the ship from the zenith, and seemed to have extinguished every sound of her teeming life. He could no longer hear the voices under the awnings. He told me that each time he closed his eyes a flash of thought showed him that crowd of bodies, laid out for death, as plain as daylight. When he opened them, it was to see the dim struggle of four men fighting like mad with a stubborn boat. "They would fall back before it time after time, stand swearing at each other, and suddenly make another rush in a bunch . . . Enough to make you die laughing," he commented with downcast eyes; then raising them for a moment to my face with a dismal smile, "I ought to have a merry life of it, by God! for I shall see that funny sight a good many times yet before I die." His eyes fell again. "See and hear . . . See and hear," he repeated twice, at long intervals, filled by vacant staring.

'He roused himself.

' "I made up my mind to keep my eyes shut," he said, "and I couldn't. I couldn't, and I don't care who knows it. Let them go through that kind of thing before they talk. Just let them – and do better – that's all. The second time my eyelids flew open and my mouth too. I had felt the ship move. She just dipped her bows – and lifted them gently – and slow! everlastingly slow; and ever so little. She hadn't done that much for days. The cloud had raced ahead, and this first swell seemed to travel upon a sea of lead. There was no life in that stir. It managed, though, to knock over something in my head. What would you have done? You are sure of yourself – aren't you? What would you do if you felt now – this minute – the house here move, just move a little under your chair. Leap! By heavens! you would take one spring from where you sit and land in that clump of bushes yonder."

'He flung his arm out at the night beyond the stone balustrade. I held my peace. He looked at me very steadily, very severe. There could be no mistake: I was being bullied now, and it behoved me to make no sign lest by a gesture or a word I should be drawn into a fatal admission about myself which would have had some bearing on the case. I was not disposed to take any risk of that sort. Don't forget I had him before me, and really he was too much like one of us not to be dangerous. But if you want to know I don't mind telling you that I did, with a rapid glance, estimate the distance to the mass of denser blackness in the middle of the grass-plot before the veranda. He exaggerated. I would have landed short by several feet – and that's the only thing of which I am fairly certain.

'The last moment had come, as he thought, and he did not move. His feet remained glued to the planks if his thoughts were knocking loose in his head. It was at this moment, too, that he saw one of the men around the boat step backwards suddenly, clutch at the air with raised arms, totter and collapse. He didn't exactly fall, he only slid gently into a sitting posture, all hunched up and with his shoulders propped against the side of the engine-room skylight. "That was the donkey-man. A haggard, white-faced chap with a ragged moustache. Acted third engineer," he explained.

' "Dead," I said. We had heard something of that in court.

' "So they say," he pronounced with sombre indifference. "Of course I never knew. Weak heart. The man had been complaining of being out of sorts for some time before. Excitement. Over-exertion. Devil only knows. Ha! ha! ha! It was easy to see he did not want to die either. Droll, isn't it? May I be shot if he hadn't been fooled into killing himself! Fooled – neither more nor less. Fooled into it, by heavens! just as I . . . Ah! If he had only kept still; if he had only told them to go to the devil when they came to rush him out of his bunk because the ship was sinking! If he had only stood by with his hands in his pockets and called them names!"

'He got up, shook his fist, glared at me, and sat down.

' "A chance missed, eh?" I murmured.

' "Why don't you laugh?" he said. "A joke hatched in hell. Weak heart! . . . I wish sometimes mine had been."

'This irritated me. "Do you?" I exclaimed with deep, rooted irony. "Yes! Can't *you* understand?" he cried. "I don't know what more you could wish for," I said angrily. He gave me an utterly uncomprehending glance. This shaft had also gone wide of the mark, and he was not the man to bother about stray arrows. Upon my word, he was too unsuspecting; he was not fair game. I was glad that my missile had been thrown away – that he had not even heard the twang of the bow.

'Of course he could not know at the time the man was dead. The next minute – his last on board – was crowded with a tumult of events and sensations which beat about him like the sea upon a rock. I use the simile advisedly, because from his relation I am forced to believe he had preserved through it all a strange illusion of passiveness, as though he had not acted but had suffered himself to be handled by the infernal powers who had selected him for the victim of their practical joke. The first thing that came to him was the grinding surge of the heavy davits swinging out at last – a jar which seemed to enter his body from the deck through the soles of his feet, and travel up his spine to the crown of his head. Then, the squall being very near now, another and heavier swell lifted the passive hull in a threatening heave that checked his breath, while his brain and his heart together were pierced as with daggers by panic-stricken screams. "Let go! For God's sake, let go! Let go! She's going." Following upon that the boat-falls ripped through the blocks, and a lot of men began to talk in startled tones under the awnings. "When these beggars did break out, their yelps were enough to wake the dead," he said. Next, after the splashing shock of the boat literally dropped in the water, came the hollow noises of stamping and tumbling in her, mingled with confused shouts: "Unhook! Unhook! Shove! Unhook! Shove for your life! Here's the squall down on us . . . " He heard, high above his head, the faint muttering of the wind; he heard below his feet a cry of pain. A lost voice alongside started cursing a swivel hook. The ship began to buzz fore and aft like a disturbed hive, and, as quietly as he was telling me all of this – because just then he was very quiet in attitude, in face, in voice – he went on to say without the slightest warning as it were, "I stumbled over his legs."

'This was the first I heard of his having moved at all. I could not restrain a grunt of surprise. Something had started him off at last, but of the exact moment, of the cause that tore him out of his immobility, he knew no more than the uprooted tree knows of the wind that laid it low. All this had come to him; the sounds, the sights, the legs of the dead man – by Jove! The infernal joke was being crammed devilishly down his throat, but – look you – he was not going to admit of any sort of swallowing motion in his gullet. It's extraordinary how he could cast upon you the spirit of his illusion. I listened as if to a tale of black magic at work upon a corpse.

' "He went over sideways, very gently, and this is the last thing I remember seeing on board," he continued. "I did not care what he did. It looked as though he were picking himself up: I thought he was picking himself up, of course: I expected him to bolt past me over the rail and drop into the boat after the others. I could hear them knocking about, down there, and a voice as if crying up a shaft called out, 'George!' Then three voices together raised a yell. They came to me separately: one bleated, another screamed, one howled. Ough!"

'He shivered a little, and I beheld him rise slowly as if a steady hand from above had been pulling him out of the chair by his hair. Up, slowly – to his full height, and when his knees had locked stiff the hand let him go, and he swayed a little on his feet. There was a suggestion of awful stillness in his face, in his movements, in his very voice when he said, "They shouted" – and involuntarily I pricked up my ears for the ghost of that shout that would be heard directly through the false effect of silence. "There were eight hundred people in that ship," he said, impaling me to the back of my seat with an awful blank stare. "Eight hundred living people, and they were yelling after the one dead man to come down and be saved. 'Jump, George! Jump! Oh, jump!' I stood by with my hand on the davit. I was very quiet. It had come over pitch dark. You could see neither sky nor sea. I heard the boat alongside go bump, bump, and not another sound down there for a while, but the ship under me was full of talking noises. Suddenly the skipper howled, '*Mein Gott!* The squall! The squall! Shove off!' With the first hiss of rain, and the first gust of wind, they screamed, 'Jump, George! We'll catch you! Jump!' The ship began a slow plunge; the rain swept over her like a broken sea; my cap flew off my head; my breath was driven back into my throat. I heard as if I had been on the top of a tower another wild screech, 'Geo–o–o–orge! Oh, jump!' She was going down, down, head first under me . . . "

'He raised his hand deliberately to his face, and made picking motions with his fingers as though he had been bothered with cobwebs, and afterwards he looked into the open palm for quite half a second before he blurted out: "I had jumped . . . " He checked himself, averted his gaze . . . "It seems," he added.

'His clear blue eyes turned to me with a piteous stare, and looking at him standing before me, dumbfounded and hurt, I was oppressed by a sad sense of resigned wisdom, mingled with the amused and profound pity of an old man helpless before a childish disaster.

' "Looks like it," I muttered.

' "I knew nothing about it till I looked up," he explained, hastily. And that's possible, too. You had to listen to him as you would to a small boy in trouble. He didn't know. It had happened somehow. It would never happen again. He had landed partly on somebody and fallen across a thwart. He felt as though all his ribs on his left side must be broken; then he rolled over, and saw vaguely the ship he had deserted uprising above him, with the red side-light glowing large in the rain like a fire on the brow of a hill seen through a mist. "She seemed higher than a wall; she loomed like a cliff over the boat . . . I wished I could die," he cried. "There was no going back. It was as if I had jumped into a well – into an everlasting deep hole . . . " '

Chapter 10

'He locked his fingers together and tore them apart. Nothing could be more true: he had indeed jumped into an everlasting deep hole. He had tumbled from a height he could never scale again. By that time the boat had gone driving forward past the bows. It was too dark just then for them to see each other, and, moreover, they were blinded and half drowned with rain. He told me it was like being swept by a flood through a cavern. They turned their backs to the squall; the skipper, it seems, got an oar over the stern to keep the boat before it, and for two or three minutes the end of the world had come through a deluge in a pitchy blackness. The sea hissed "like twenty thousand kettles." That's his simile, not mine. I fancy there was not much wind after the first gust, and he himself had admitted at the inquiry that the sea never got up that night to any extent. He crouched down in the bows and stole a furtive glance back. He saw just one yellow gleam of the masthead light high up and blurred like a last star ready to dissolve. "It terrified me to see it still there," he said. That's what he said. What terrified him was the thought that the drowning was not over yet. No doubt he wanted to be done with that abomination as quickly as possible. Nobody in the boat made a sound. In the dark she seemed to fly, but of course she could not have had much way. Then the shower swept ahead, and the great, distracting, hissing noise followed the rain into the distance and died out. There was nothing to be heard then but the slight wash about the boat's sides. Somebody's teeth were chattering violently. A hand touched his back. A faint voice said, "You there?" Another cried out, shakily, "She's gone!" and they all stood up together to look astern. They saw no lights. All was black. A thin cold drizzle was driving into their faces. The boat lurched slightly. The teeth chattered faster, stopped, and began again twice before the man could master his shiver sufficiently to say, "Ju-ju-st in ti-ti-me . . . Brrrr." He recognised the voice of the chief engineer saying surlily, "I saw her go down. I happened to turn my head." The wind had dropped almost completely.

'They watched in the dark with their heads half turned to windward as if expecting to hear cries. At first he was thankful the night had covered up the scene before his eyes, and then to know of it and yet to have seen and heard nothing appeared somehow the culminating point of an awful misfortune. "Strange, isn't it?" he murmured, interrupting himself in his disjointed narrative.

'It did not seem so strange to me. He must have had an unconscious conviction that the reality could not be half as bad, not half as anguishing, appalling, and vengeful as the created terror of his imagination. I believe that, in this first moment, his heart was wrung with all the suffering, that his soul knew the accumulated savour of all the fear, all the horror, all the despair of eight hundred human beings pounced upon in the night by a sudden and violent death, else why should he have said, "It seemed to me that I must jump out of that accursed boat and swim back to see – half a mile – more – any distance – to the very spot . . . "? Why this impulse? Do you see the significance? Why back to the very spot? Why not drown alongside – if he meant drowning? why back to the very spot, to see – as if his imagination had to be soothed by the assurance that all was over before death could bring relief? I defy any one of you to offer another explanation. It was one of those bizarre and exciting glimpses through the fog. It was an extraordinary disclosure. He let it out as the most natural thing one could say.

He fought down that impulse and then he became conscious of the silence. He mentioned this to me. A silence of the sea, of the sky, merged into one indefinite immensity still as death around these saved, palpitating lives. "You might have heard a pin drop in the boat," he said with a queer contraction of his lips, like a man trying to master his sensibilities while relating some extremely moving fact. A silence! God alone, who had willed him as he was, knows what he made of it in his heart. "I didn't think any spot on earth could be so still," he said. "You couldn't distinguish the sea from the sky; there was nothing to see and nothing to hear. Not a glimmer, not a shape, not a sound. You could have believed that every bit of dry land had gone to the bottom, that every man on earth but I and these beggars in the boat had got drowned." He leaned over the table with his knuckles propped amongst coffee- cups, liqueur-glasses, cigar-ends. "I seemed to believe it. Everything was gone and – all was over . . . " he fetched a deep sigh . . . "with me." '

Marlow sat up abruptly and flung away his cheroot with force. It made a darting red tail like a toy rocket fired through the drapery of creepers. Nobody stirred.

'Hey, what do you think of it?' he cried with sudden animation. 'Wasn't he true to himself, wasn't he? His saved life was over for want of ground under his feet, for want of sight for his eyes, for want of voices in his ears. Annihilation – hey! And all the time it was only a clouded sky, a sea that did not break, the air that did not stir. Only a night; only a silence.

'It lasted for a while, and then they were suddenly and unanimously moved to make a noise over their escape. "I knew from the first she would go." "Not a minute too soon." "A narrow squeak, b'gosh!" He said nothing, but the breeze that had dropped came back, a gentle draught freshened steadily, and the sea joined its murmuring voice to this talkative reaction succeeding the dumb moments of awe. She was gone! She was gone! Not a doubt of it. Nobody could have helped. They repeated the same words over and over again as though they couldn't stop themselves. Never doubted she would go. The lights were gone. No mistake. The lights were gone. Couldn't expect anything else. She had to go . . . He noticed that they talked as though they had left behind them nothing but an empty ship. They concluded she would not have been long when she once started. It seemed to cause them some sort of satisfaction. They assured each other that she couldn't have been long about it – "Just shot down like a flat-iron." The chief engineer declared that the masthead light at the moment of sinking seemed to drop "like a lighted match you throw down." At this the second laughed hysterically. "I am g–g–glad, I am gla–a–a–d." His teeth went on "like an electric rattle," said Jim, "and all at once he began to cry. He wept and blubbered like a child, catching his breath and sobbing, 'Oh, dear! oh, dear! oh, dear!' He would be quiet for a while and start suddenly, 'Oh, my poor arm! oh, my poor a–a–a–arm!' I felt I could knock him down. Some of them sat in the stern-sheets. I could just make out their shapes. Voices came to me, mumble, mumble, grunt, grunt. All this seemed very hard to bear. I was cold, too. And I could do nothing. I thought that if I moved I would have to go over the side and . . . "

'His hand groped stealthily, came in contact with a liqueur-glass, and was withdrawn suddenly as if it had touched a red-hot coal. I pushed the bottle slightly. "Won't you have some more?" I asked. He looked at me angrily. "Don't you think I can tell you what there is to tell without screwing myself up?" he asked. The squad of globe-trotters had gone to bed. We were alone but for a vague white form erect in the shadow, that, being looked at, cringed forward, hesitated, backed away silently. It was getting late, but I did not hurry my guest.

'In the midst of his forlorn state he heard his companions begin to abuse someone. "What kept you from jumping, you lunatic?" said a scolding voice. The chief engineer left the stern-sheets, and could be heard clambering forward as if with hostile intentions against "the greatest idiot that ever was." The skipper shouted with rasping effort offensive epithets from where he sat at the oars. He lifted his head at that uproar, and heard the name "George," while a hand in the dark struck him on the breast. "What have you got to say for yourself, you fool?" queried somebody, with a sort of virtuous fury. "They were after me," he said. "They were abusing me – abusing me . . . by the name of George."

'He paused to stare, tried to smile, turned his eyes away and went on. "That little second puts his head right under my nose, 'Why, it's that blasted mate!' 'What!' howls the skipper from the other end of the boat. 'No!' shrieks the chief. And he, too, stopped to look at my face."

'The wind had left the boat suddenly. The rain began to fall again, and the soft, uninterrupted, a little mysterious sound with which the sea receives a shower arose on all sides in the night. "They were too taken aback to say anything more at first," he narrated steadily, "and what could I have to say to them?" He faltered for a moment, and made an effort to go on. "They called me horrible names." His voice, sinking to a whisper, now and then would leap up suddenly, hardened by the passion of scorn, as though he had been talking of secret abominations. "Never mind what they called me," he said, grimly. "I could hear hate in their voices. A good thing too. They could not forgive me for being in that boat. They hated it. It made them mad . . . " He laughed short . . . "But it kept me from – Look! I was sitting with my arms crossed, on the gunwale! . . . " He perched himself smartly on the edge of the table and crossed his arms . . . "Like this – see? One little tilt backwards and I would have been gone – after the others. One little tilt – the least bit – the least bit." He frowned, and tapping his forehead with the tip of his middle finger, "It was there all the time," he said, impressively. "All the time – that notion. And the rain – cold, thick, cold as melted snow – colder – on my thin cotton clothes – I'll never be so cold again in my life, I know. And the sky was black, too – all black. Not a star, not a light anywhere. Nothing outside that confounded boat and those two yapping before me like a couple of mean mongrels at a tree'd thief. Yap! yap! What you doing here? You're a fine sort! Too much of a bloomin' gentleman to put his hand to it. Come out of your trance, did you? To sneak in? Did you? Yap! yap! You ain't fit to live! Yap! yap! Two of them together trying to out-bark each other. The other would bay from the stern through rain – couldn't see him – couldn't make out – some of his filthy jargon. Yap! yap! Bow-ow-ow-ow-ow! Yap! yap! It was sweet to hear them; it kept me alive, I tell you. It has saved my life. At it they went, as if trying to drive me overboard with the noise! . . . I wonder you had pluck enough to jump. You ain't wanted here. If I had known who it was, I would have tipped you over – you skunk. What have you done with the other? Where did you get the pluck to jump – you coward? What's to prevent us three from firing you overboard? . . . They were out of breath; the shower passed away upon the sea. Then nothing. There was nothing round the boat, not even a sound. Wanted to see me overboard, did they? Upon my soul! I think they would have had their wish if they had only kept quiet. Fire me overboard! Would they? 'Try,' I said. 'I would for twopence.' 'Too good for you,' they screeched together. It was so dark that it was only when one or the other of them moved that I was quite sure of seeing him. By heavens! I only wish they had tried."

'I couldn't help exclaiming, "What an extraordinary affair!"'

' "Not bad – eh?" he said, as if in some sort astounded. "They pretended to think I had done away with that donkey-man for some reason or other. Why should I? And how the devil was I to know? Didn't I get somehow into that boat? into that boat – I . . . " The muscles round his lips contracted into an unconscious grimace that tore through the mask of his usual expression – something violent, short-lived and illuminating like a twist of lightning that admits the eye for an instant into the secret convolutions of a cloud. "I did. I was plainly there with them – wasn't I? Isn't it awful a man should be driven to do a thing like that – and be responsible? What did I know about their George they were howling after? I remembered I had seen him curled up on the deck. 'Murdering coward!' the chief kept on calling me. He didn't seem able to remember any other two words. I didn't care, only his noise began to worry me. 'Shut up,' I said. At that he collected himself for a confounded screech. 'You killed him. You killed him.' 'No,' I shouted, 'but I will kill you directly.' I jumped up, and he fell backwards over a thwart with an awful loud thump. I don't know why. Too dark. Tried to step back, I suppose. I stood still facing aft, and the wretched little second began to whine, 'You ain't going to hit a chap with a broken arm – and you call yourself a gentleman, too.' I heard a heavy tramp – one – two – and wheezy grunting. The other beast was coming at me, clattering his oar over the stern. I saw him moving, big, big – as you see a man in a mist, in a dream. 'Come on,' I cried. I would have tumbled him over like a bale of shakings. He stopped, muttered to himself, and went back. Perhaps he had heard the wind. I didn't. It was the last heavy gust we had. He went back to his oar. I was sorry. I would have tried to – to . . . "

'He opened and closed his curved fingers, and his hands had an eager and cruel flutter. "Steady, steady," I murmured.

' "Eh? What? I am not excited," he remonstrated, awfully hurt, and with a convulsive jerk of his elbow knocked over the cognac-bottle. I started forward, scraping my chair. He bounced off the table as if a mine had been exploded behind his back, and half turned before he alighted, crouching on his feet to show me a startled pair of eyes and a face white about the nostrils. A look of intense annoyance succeeded. "Awfully sorry. How clumsy of me!" he mumbled very vexed, while the pungent odour of spilt alcohol enveloped us suddenly with an atmosphere of a low drinking-bout in the cool, pure darkness of the night. The lights had been put out in the dining-hall; our candle glimmered solitary in the long gallery, and the columns had turned black from pediment to capital. On the vivid stars the high corner of the Harbour Office stood out distinct across the Esplanade, as though the sombre pile had glided nearer to see and hear.

'He assumed an air of indifference.

' "I dare say I am less calm now than I was then. I was ready for anything. These were trifles . . . "

' "You had a lively time of it in that boat," I remarked.

' "I was ready," he repeated. "After the ship's lights had gone, anything might have happened in that boat – anything in the world – and the world no wiser. I felt this, and I was pleased. It was just dark enough, too. We were like men walled up quick in a roomy grave. No concern with anything on earth. Nobody to pass an opinion. Nothing mattered." For the third time during this conversation he laughed harshly, but there was no one about to suspect him of being only drunk. "No fear, no law, no sounds, no eyes – not even our own, till – till sunrise at least."

'I was struck by the suggestive truth of his words. There is something peculiar in a small boat upon the wide sea. Over the lives borne from under the shadow of death there seems to fall the shadow of madness. When your ship fails you, your whole world seems to fail you; the world that made you, restrained you, taken care of you. It is as if the souls of men floating on an abyss and in touch with immensity had been set free for any excess of heroism, absurdity, or abomination. Of course, as with belief, thought, love, hate, conviction, or even the visual aspect of material things, there are as many shipwrecks as there are men, and in this one there was something abject which made the isolation more complete – there was a villainy of circumstances that cut these men off more completely from the rest of mankind, whose ideal of conduct had never undergone the trial of a fiendish and appalling joke. They were exasperated with him for being a half-hearted shirker: he focused on them his hatred of the whole thing; he would have liked to take a signal revenge for the abhorrent opportunity they had put in his way. Trust a boat on the high seas to bring out the Irrational that lurks at the bottom of every thought, sentiment, sensation, emotion. It was part of the burlesque meanness pervading that particular disaster at sea that they did not come to blows. It was all threats, all a terribly effective feint, a sham from beginning to end, planned by the tremendous disdain of the Dark Powers whose real terrors, always on the verge of triumph, are perpetually foiled by the steadfastness of men. I asked, after waiting for a while, "Well, what happened?" A futile question. I knew too much already to hope for the grace of a single uplifting touch, for the favour of hinted madness, of shadowed horror. "Nothing," he said. "I meant business, but they meant noise only. Nothing happened."

'And the rising sun found him just as he had jumped up first in the bows of the boat. What a persistence of readiness! He had been holding the tiller in his hand, too, all the night. They had dropped the rudder overboard while attempting to ship it, and I suppose the tiller got kicked forward somehow while they were rushing up and down that boat trying to do all sorts of things at once so as to get clear of the side. It was a long heavy piece of hardwood, and apparently he had been clutching it for six hours or so. If you don't call that being ready! Can you imagine him, silent and on his feet half the night, his face to the gusts of rain, staring at sombre forms, watchful of vague movements, straining his ears to catch rare low murmurs in the stern-sheets! Firmness of courage or effort of fear? What do you think? And the endurance is undeniable, too. Six hours more or less on the defensive; six hours of alert immobility while the boat drove slowly or floated arrested according to the caprice of the wind; while the sea, calmed, slept at last; while the clouds passed above his head; while the sky, from an immensity lustreless and black, diminished to a sombre and lustrous vault, scintillated with a greater brilliance, faded to the east, paled at the zenith; while the dark shapes blotting the low stars astern got outlines, relief; became shoulders, heads, faces, features – confronted him with dreary stares, had dishevelled hair, torn clothes, blinked red eyelids at the white dawn. "They looked as though they had been knocking about drunk in gutters for a week," he described graphically; and then he muttered something about the sunrise being of a kind that foretells a calm day. You know that sailor habit of referring to the weather in every connection. And on my side his few mumbled words were enough to make me see the lower limb of the sun clearing the line of the horizon, the tremble of a vast ripple running over all the visible expanse of the sea, as if the waters had shuddered, giving birth to the globe of light, while the last puff of the breeze would stir the air in a sigh of relief.

' "They sat in the stern shoulder to shoulder, with the skipper in the middle, like three dirty owls, and stared at me," I heard him say with an intention of hate that distilled a corrosive virtue into the commonplace words like a drop of powerful poison falling into a glass of water; but my thoughts dwelt upon that sunrise. I could imagine under the pellucid emptiness of the sky these four men imprisoned in the solitude of the sea, the lonely sun, regardless of the speck of life, ascending the clear curve of the heaven as if to gaze ardently from a greater height at his own splendour reflected in the still ocean. "They called out to me from aft," said Jim, "as though we had been chums together. I heard them. They were begging me to be sensible and drop that 'blooming piece of wood.' Why *would* I carry on so? They hadn't done me any harm – had they? There had been no harm . . . No harm!"

'His face crimsoned as though he could not get rid of the air in his lungs.

' "No harm!" he burst out. "I leave it to you. You can understand. Can't you? You see it – don't you? No harm! Oh, yes, I know very well – I jumped. Certainly. I jumped! I told you I jumped; but I tell you they were too much for any man. It was their doing as plainly as if they had reached up with a boat-hook and pulled me over. Can't you see it? You must see it. Come. Speak – straight out.'

'His uneasy eyes fastened upon mine, questioned, begged, challenged, entreated. For the life of me I couldn't help murmuring, "You've been tried." "More than is fair," he caught up, swiftly. "I wasn't given half a chance – with a gang like that. And now they were friendly – oh, so damnably friendly! Chums, shipmates. All in the same boat. Make the best of it. They hadn't meant anything. They didn't care a hang for George. George had gone back to his berth for something at the last moment and got caught. The man was a manifest fool. Very sad, of course . . . Their eyes looked at me; their lips moved; they wagged their heads at the other end of the boat – three of them; they beckoned – to me. Why not? Hadn't I jumped? I said nothing. There are no words for the sort of things I wanted to say. If I had opened my lips just then I would have simply howled like an animal. I was asking myself when I would wake up. They urged me aloud to come aft and hear quietly what the skipper had to say. We were sure to be picked up before the evening – right in the track of all the Canal traffic; there was smoke to the north-west now.

' "It gave me an awful shock to see this faint, faint blur, this low trail of brown mist through which you could see the boundary of sea and sky. I called out to them that I could hear very well where I was. The skipper started swearing, as hoarse as a crow. He wasn't going to talk at the top of his voice for *my* accommodation. 'Are you afraid they will hear you on shore?' I asked. He glared as if he would have liked to claw me to pieces. The chief engineer advised him to humour me. He said I wasn't right in my head yet. The other rose astern, like a thick pillar of flesh – and talked – talked . . . "

'Jim remained thoughtful. "Well?" I said. "What did I care what story they agreed to make up?" he cried, recklessly. "They could tell what they jolly well liked. It was their business. I knew the story. Nothing they could make people believe would alter it for me. I let him talk, argue – talk, argue.

He went on and on and on. Suddenly I felt my legs give way under me. I was sick, tired – tired to death. I let fall the tiller, turned my back on them, and sat down on the foremost thwart. I had enough. They called to me to know if I understood – wasn't it true, every word of it? It was true, by God! after their fashion. I did not turn my head. I heard them palavering together. 'The silly ass won't say anything.' 'Oh, he understands well enough.' 'Let him be; he will be all right.' 'What can he do?' What could I do? Weren't we all in the same boat? I tried to be deaf. The smoke had disappeared to the northward. It was a dead calm. They had a drink from the water-breaker, and I drank, too. Afterwards they made a great business of spreading the boat-sail over the gunwales. Would I keep a look-out? They crept under, out of my sight, thank God! I felt weary, weary, done up, as if I hadn't had one hour's sleep since the day I was born. I couldn't see the water for the glitter of the sunshine. From time to time one of them would creep out, stand up to take a look all round, and get under again. I could hear spells of snoring below the sail. Some of them could sleep. One of them at least. I couldn't! All was light, light, and the boat seemed to be falling through it. Now and then I would feel quite surprised to find myself sitting on a thwart . . . "

'He began to walk with measured steps to and fro before my chair, one hand in his trousers-pocket, his head bent thoughtfully, and his right arm at long intervals raised for a gesture that seemed to put out of his way an invisible intruder.

' "I suppose you think I was going mad," he began in a changed tone. "And well you may, if you remember I had lost my cap. The sun crept all the way from east to west over my bare head, but that day I could not come to any harm, I suppose. The sun could not make me mad . . . " His right arm put aside the idea of madness . . . "Neither could it kill me . . . " Again his arm repulsed a shadow . . . "*That* rested with me."

' "Did it?" I said, inexpressibly amazed at this new turn, and I looked at him with the same sort of feeling I might be fairly conceived to experience had he, after spinning round on his heel, presented an altogether new face.

' "I didn't get brain fever, I did not drop dead either," he went on. "I didn't bother myself at all about the sun over my head. I was thinking as coolly as any man that ever sat thinking in the shade. That greasy beast of a skipper poked his big cropped head from under the canvas and screwed his fishy eyes up at me. '*Donnerwetter!* you will die,' he growled, and drew in like a turtle. I had seen him. I had heard him. He didn't interrupt me. I was thinking just then that I wouldn't."

'He tried to sound my thought with an attentive glance dropped on me in passing. "Do you mean to say you had been deliberating with yourself whether you would die?" I asked in as impenetrable a tone as I could command. He nodded without stopping. "Yes, it had come to that as I sat there alone," he said. He passed on a few steps to the imaginary end of his beat, and when he flung round to come back both his hands were thrust deep into his pockets. He stopped short in front of my chair and looked down. "Don't you believe it?" he enquired with tense curiosity. I was moved to make a solemn declaration of my readiness to believe implicitly anything he thought fit to tell me.'

Chapter 11

'He heard me out with his head on one side, and I had another glimpse through the rent in the mist in which he moved and had his being. The dim candle spluttered within the ball of glass, and that was all I had to see him by; at his back was the dark night with the clear stars, whose distant glitter disposed in retreating planes lured the eyes into the depths of a greater darkness; and yet a mysterious light seemed to show me his boyish head, as if in that moment the youth within him had, for a moment, gleamed and expired. "You are an awful good sort to listen like this," he said. "It does me good. You don't know what it is to me. You don't . . . " words seemed to fail him. It was a distinct glimpse. He was a youngster of the sort you like to see about you; of the sort you like to imagine yourself to have been; of the sort whose appearance claims the fellowship of these illusions you had thought gone out, extinct, cold, and which, as if rekindled at the approach of another flame, give a flutter deep, deep down somewhere, give a flutter of light . . . of heat! . . . Yes; I had a glimpse of him then . . . and it was not the last of that kind . . . "You don't know what it is for a fellow in my position to be believed – make a clean breast of it to an elder man. It is so difficult – so awfully unfair – so hard to understand."

'The mists were closing again. I don't know how old I appeared to him – and how much wiser. Not half as old as I felt just then; not half as uselessly wise as I knew myself to be. Surely in no other craft as in that of the sea do the hearts of those already launched to sink or swim go out so much to the youth on the brink, looking with shining eyes upon that glitter of the vast surface which is only a reflection of his own glances full of fire. There is such magnificent vagueness in the expectations that had driven each of us to sea, such a glorious indefiniteness, such a beautiful greed of adventures that are their own and only reward! What we get – well, we won't talk of that; but can one of us restrain a smile? In no other kind of life is the illusion more wide of reality – in no other is the beginning *all* illusion – the disenchantment more swift – the subjugation more complete. Hadn't we all commenced with the same desire, ended with the same knowledge, carried the memory of the same cherished glamour through the sordid days of imprecation? What wonder that when some heavy prod gets home the bond is found to be close; that besides the fellowship of the craft there is felt the strength of a wider feeling – the feeling that binds a man to a child? He was there before me, believing that age and wisdom can find a remedy against the pain of truth, giving me a glimpse of himself as a young fellow in a scrape that is the very devil of a scrape, the sort of scrape grey beards wag at solemnly while they hide a smile. And he had been deliberating upon death – confound him! He had found *that* to meditate about because he thought he had saved his life, while all its glamour had gone with the ship in the night. What more natural! It was tragic enough and funny enough in all conscience to call aloud for compassion, and in what was I better than the rest of us to refuse him my pity? And even as I looked at him the mists rolled into the rent, and his voice spoke: "I was so lost, you know. It was the sort of thing one does not expect to happen to one. It was not like a fight, for instance."

' "It was not," I admitted. He appeared changed, as if he had suddenly matured.

' "One couldn't be sure," he muttered.

' "Ah! You were not sure," I said, and was placated by the sound of a faint sigh that passed between us like the flight of a bird in the night.

' "Well, I wasn't," he said courageously. "It was something like that wretched story they made up. It was not a lie – but it wasn't truth all the same. It was something . . . One knows a downright lie. There was not the thickness of a sheet of paper between the right and wrong of this affair."

' "How much more did you want?" I asked; but I think I spoke so low that he did not catch what I said. He had advanced his argument as though life had been a network of paths separated by chasms. His voice sounded reasonable.

' "Suppose I had not – I mean to say, suppose I had stuck to the ship? Well. How much longer? Say a minute – half a minute. Come. In thirty seconds, as it seemed certain then, I would have been overboard; and do you think I would not have laid hold of the first thing that came in my way – oar, life-buoy, grating – anything? Wouldn't you?"

' "And be saved," I interjected.

' "I would have meant to be," he retorted. "And that's more than I meant when I" . . . he shivered as if about to swallow some nauseous drug . . . "jumped," he pronounced with a convulsive effort, whose stress, as if propagated by the waves of the air, made my body stir a little in the chair. He fixed me with lowering eyes. "Don't you believe me?" he cried. "I swear! . . . Confound it! You got me here to talk, and . . . You must! . . . You said you would believe." "Of course I do," I protested in a matter-of-fact tone which produced a calming effect. "Forgive me," he said. "Of course I wouldn't have talked to you about all this if you had not been a gentleman. I ought to have known . . . I am – I am – a gentleman, too . . . " "Yes, yes," I said, hastily. He was looking me squarely in the face and withdrew his gaze slowly. "Now you understand why I didn't after all . . . didn't go out in that way. I wasn't going to be frightened at what I had done. And, anyhow, if I had stuck to the ship I would have done my best to be saved. Men have been known to float for hours – in the open sea – and be picked up not much the worse for it. I might have lasted it out better than many others. There's nothing the matter with *my* heart." He withdrew his right fist from his pocket, and the blow he struck on his chest resounded like a muffled detonation in the night.

' "No," I said. He meditated, with his legs slightly apart and his chin sunk. "A hair's breadth," he muttered. "Not the breadth of a hair between this and that. And at the time . . . "

' "It is difficult to see a hair at midnight," I put in, a little viciously I fear. Don't you see what I mean by the solidarity of the craft? I was aggrieved against him, as though he had cheated me – me! – of a splendid opportunity to keep up the illusion of my beginnings, as though he had robbed our common life of the last spark of its glamour. "And so you cleared out – at once."

' "Jumped," he corrected me incisively. "Jumped – mind!" he repeated, and I wondered at the evident but obscure intention. "Well, yes! Perhaps I could not see then. But I had plenty of time and any amount of light in that boat. And I could think, too. Nobody would know, of course, but this did not make it any easier for me. You've got to believe that, too. I did not want all this talk . . . No . . . Yes . . . I won't lie . . . I wanted it: it is the very thing I wanted – there. Do you think you or anybody could have made me if I . . . I am – I am not afraid to tell. And I wasn't afraid to think either. I looked it in the face. I wasn't going to run away. At first – at night, if it hadn't been for these fellows I might have . . . No! by heavens! I was not going to give them that satisfaction. They had done enough. They made up a story, and believed it for all I know. But I knew the truth, and I would live it down – alone, with myself. I wasn't going to give in to such a beastly unfair thing. What did it prove after all? I was confoundedly cut up. Sick of life – to tell you the truth; but what would have been the good to shirk it – in – in – that way? That was not the way. I believe – I believe it would have – it would have ended – nothing."

'He had been walking up and down, but with the last word he turned short at me.

' "What do *you* believe?" he asked with violence. A pause ensued, and suddenly I felt myself overcome by a profound and hopeless fatigue, as though his voice had startled me out of a dream of wandering through empty spaces whose immensity had harassed my soul and exhausted my body.

' " . . . Would have ended nothing," he muttered over me obstinately, after a little while. "No! the proper thing was to face it out – alone for myself – wait for another chance – find out . . . " '

Chapter 12

'All around everything was still as far as the ear could reach. The mist of his feelings shifted between us, as if disturbed by his struggles, and in the rifts of the immaterial veil he would appear to my staring eyes distinct of form and pregnant with appeal like a symbolic figure in a picture. The chill air of the night seemed to lie on my limbs as heavy as a slab of marble.

' "I see," I murmured, more to prove to myself that I could break my state of numbness than for any other reason.

' "The *Avondale* picked us up just before sunset," he remarked, moodily. "Steamed right straight for us. We had only to sit and wait."

'After a long interval, he said, "They told their story." And again there was that oppressive silence. "Then only I knew what it was I made up my mind to," he added.

' "You said nothing," I whispered.

' "What could I say?" he asked, in the same low tone . . . "Shock slight. Stopped the ship. Ascertained the damage. Took measures to get the boats out without creating a panic. As the first boat was lowered ship went down in a squall. Sank like lead . . . What could be more clear" . . . he hung his head . . . "and more awful?" His lips quivered while he looked straight into my eyes. "I had jumped – hadn't I?," he asked dismayed. "That's what I had to live down. The story didn't matter." . . . He clasped his hands for an instant, glanced right and left into the gloom: "It was like cheating the dead," he stammered.

' "And there were no dead," I said.

'He went away from me at this. That is the only way I can describe it. In a moment I saw his back close to the balustrade. He stood there for some time, as if admiring the purity and the peace of the night. Some flowering shrub in the garden below spread its powerful scent through the damp air. He returned to me with hasty steps.

' "And that did not matter," he said, as stubbornly as you please.

' "Perhaps not," I admitted. I began to have a notion he was too much for me. After all, what did I know?

' "Dead or not dead, I could not get clear," he said. "I had to live; hadn't I?"

' "Well, yes – if you take it in that way," I mumbled.

' "I was glad, of course," he threw out carelessly with his mind fixed on something else. "The exposure," he pronounced, slowly, and lifted his head. "Do you know what was my first thought when I heard? I was relieved. I was relieved to learn that those shouts – did I tell you I heard shouts? No? Well, I did. Shouts for help . . . blown along with the drizzle. Imagination I suppose. And yet I can hardly . . . How stupid . . . The others did not. I asked them afterwards. They all said No. No? And I was hearing them even then! I might have known – but I didn't think – I only listened. Very faint screams – day after day. Then that little half-caste chap here came up and spoke to me. 'The *Patna* . . . French gunboat . . . towed successfully to Aden . . . Investigation . . . Marine Office . . . Sailors' Home . . . arrangements made for your board and lodging.' I walked along with him, and I enjoyed the silence. So there had been no shouting. Imagination. I had to believe him. I could hear nothing any more. I wonder how long I could have stood it. It was getting worse, too . . . I mean – louder."

'He fell into thought.

' "And I had heard nothing! Well – so be it. But the lights! The lights did go! We did not see them. They were not there. If they had been, I would have swam back – I would have gone back and shouted alongside – I would have begged them to take me on board . . . I would have had my chance . . . You doubt me? . . . How do you know how I felt? . . . What right have you to doubt? . . . I very nearly did it as it was – do you understand?" His voice fell. "There was not a glimmer – not a glimmer," he protested, mournfully. "Don't you understand that if there had been, you would not have seen me here? You see me – and you doubt."

'I shook my head negatively. This question of the lights being lost sight of when the boat could not have been more than a quarter of a mile from the ship was a matter for much discussion. Jim stuck to it that there was nothing to be seen after the first shower had cleared away; and the others had affirmed the same thing to the officers of the *Avondale*. Of course people shook their heads and smiled. One old skipper who sat near me in court tickled my ear with his white beard to murmur, "Of course they would lie." As a matter of fact nobody lied; not even the chief engineer with his story of the masthead light dropping like a match you throw down. Not consciously, at least. A man with his liver in such a state might very well have seen a floating spark in the corner of his eye when stealing a hurried glance over his shoulder. They had seen no light of any sort though they were well within range, and they could only explain this in one way: the ship had gone down. It was obvious and comforting. The foreseen fact coming so swiftly had justified their haste. No wonder they did not cast about for any other explanation. Yet the true one was very simple, and as soon as Brierly suggested it the court ceased to bother about the question. If you remember, the ship had been stopped and was lying with her head on the course steered through the night, with her stern canted high and her bows brought low down in the water through the filling of the fore-compartment. Being thus out of trim, when the squall struck her a little on the quarter, she swung head to wind as sharply as though she had been at anchor. By this change in her position all her lights were in a very few moments shut off from the boat to leeward. It may very well be that, had they been seen, they would have had the effect of a mute appeal – that their glimmer lost in the darkness of the cloud would have had the mysterious power of the human glance that can awaken the feelings of remorse and pity. It would have said, "I am here – still here" . . . and what more can the eye of the most forsaken of human beings say? But she turned her back on them as if in disdain of their fate: she had swung round, burdened, to glare stubbornly at the new danger of the open sea which she so strangely survived to end her days in a breaking-up yard, as if it had been her recorded fate to die obscurely under the blows of many hammers. What were the various ends their destiny provided for the pilgrims I am unable to say; but the immediate future brought, at about nine o'clock next morning, a French gunboat homeward bound from Réunion. The report of her commander was public property. He had swept a little out of his course to ascertain what was the matter with that steamer floating dangerously by the head upon a still and hazy sea. There was an ensign, union down, flying at her main gaff (the serang had the sense to make a signal of distress at daylight); but the cooks were preparing the food in the cooking-boxes forward as usual. The decks were packed as close as a sheep-pen: there were people perched all along the rails, jammed on the bridge in a solid mass; hundreds of eyes stared, and not a sound was heard when the gunboat ranged abreast, as if all that multitude of lips had been sealed by a spell.

'The Frenchman hailed, could get no intelligible reply, and after ascertaining through his binoculars that the crowd on deck did not look plague-stricken, decided to send a boat. Two officers came aboard, listened to the serang, tried to talk with the Arab, couldn't make head or tail of it: but of course the nature of the emergency was obvious enough. They were also very much struck by discovering a white man dead and curled up peacefully on the bridge. "Fort intrigués par ce cadavre," as I was informed a long time after by an elderly French lieutenant whom I came across one afternoon in Sydney, by the merest chance, in a sort of café, and who remembered the affair perfectly. Indeed this affair, I may notice in passing, had an extraordinary power of defying the shortness of memories and the length of time: it seemed to live, with a sort of uncanny vitality, in the minds of men, on the tips of their tongues. I've had the questionable pleasure of meeting it often, years afterwards, thousands of miles away, emerging from the remotest possible talk, coming to the surface of the most distant allusions. Has it not turned up tonight between us? And I am the only seaman here. I am the only one to whom it is a memory. And yet it has made its way out! But if two men who, unknown to each other, knew of this affair met accidentally on any spot of this earth, the thing would pop up between them as sure as fate, before they parted. I had never seen that Frenchman before, and at the end of an hour we had done with each other for life: he did not seem particularly talkative either; he was a quiet, massive chap in a creased uniform sitting drowsily over a tumbler half-full of some dark liquid. His shoulder-straps were a bit tarnished, his clean-shaved cheeks were large and sallow; he looked like a man who would be given to taking snuff – don't you know? I won't say he did; but the habit would have fitted that kind of man. It all began by his handing me a number of *Home News*, which I didn't want, across the marble table. I said, "Merci." We exchanged a few apparently innocent remarks, and suddenly, before I knew how it had come about, we were in the midst of it, and he was telling me how much they had been "intrigued by that corpse". It turned out he had been one of the boarding officers.

'In the establishment where we sat one could get a variety of foreign drinks which were kept for the visiting naval officers, and he took a sip of the dark medical-looking stuff, which probably was nothing more nasty than *cassis à l'eau*, and glancing with one eye into the tumbler, shook his head slightly. "Impossible de comprendre – vous concevez," he said, with a curious mixture of unconcern and thoughtfulness. I could very easily conceive how impossible it had been for them to understand. Nobody in the gunboat knew enough English to get hold of the story as told by the serang. There was a good deal of noise, too, round the two officers. "They crowded upon us. There was a circle round that dead man (*autour de ce mort*)," he described. "One had to attend to the most pressing. These people were beginning to agitate themselves – *Parbleu!* A mob like that – don't you see?" he interjected with philosophic indulgence. As to the bulkhead, he had advised his commander that the safest thing was to leave it alone, it was so villainous to look at. They got two hawsers on board promptly (*en toute hâte*) and took the *Patna* in tow – stern foremost at that – which, under the circumstances, was not so foolish, since the rudder was too much out of the water to be of any great use for steering, and this manoeuvre eased the strain on the bulkhead, whose state, he expounded with stolid glibness, demanded the greatest care (*exigeait les plus grands ménagements*). I could not help thinking that my new acquaintance must have had a voice in most of these arrangements: he looked a reliable officer, no longer very active, and he was seamanlike, too, in a way, though as he sat there, with his thick fingers clasped lightly on his stomach, he reminded you of one of those snuffy, quiet village priests, into whose ears are poured the sins, the sufferings, the remorse of peasant generations, on whose faces the placid and simple expression is like a veil thrown over the mystery of pain and distress. He ought to have had a threadbare black *soutane* buttoned smoothly up to his ample chin, instead of a frock-coat with shoulder-straps and brass buttons. His broad bosom heaved regularly while he went on telling me that it had been the very devil of a job, as doubtless (*sans doute*) I could figure to myself in my quality of a seaman (*en votre qualité de marin*). At the end of the period he inclined his body slightly towards me, and, pursing his shaved lips, allowed the air to escape with a gentle hiss. "Luckily," he continued, "the sea was level like this table, and there was no more wind than there is here." . . . The place struck me as indeed intolerably stuffy, and very hot; my face burned as though I had been young enough to be embarrassed and blushing. They had directed their course, he pursued, to the nearest English port "naturellement," where their responsibility ceased, "Dieu merci." . . . He blew out his flat cheeks a little . . . "Because, mind you (*notez bien*), all the time of towing we had two quartermasters stationed with axes by the hawsers, to cut us clear of our tow in case she . . . " He fluttered downwards his heavy eyelids, making his meaning as plain as possible . . . "What would you! One does what one can (*on fait ce qu'on peut*)," and for a moment he managed to invest his ponderous immobility with an air of resignation. "Two quartermasters – thirty hours – always there. Two!" he repeated, lifting up his right hand a little, and exhibiting two fingers. This was absolutely the first gesture I saw him make. It gave me the opportunity to "note" a starred scar on the back of his hand – effect of a gunshot clearly; and, as if my sight had been made more acute by this discovery, I perceived also the seam of an old wound, beginning a little below the temple and going out of sight under the short grey hair at the side of his head – the graze of a spear or the cut of a sabre. He clasped his hands on his stomach again. "I remained on board that – that – my memory is going (*s'en va*). Ah! *Patt-nà. C'est bien ça. Patt-nà. Merci.* It is droll how one forgets. I stayed on that ship thirty hours . . . "

' "You did!" I exclaimed. Still gazing at his hands, he pursed his lips a little, but this time made no hissing sound. "It was judged proper," he said, lifting his eyebrows dispassionately, "that one of the officers should remain to keep an eye open (*pour ouvrir l'œil*)" . . . he sighed idly . . . "and for communicating by signals with the towing ship – do you see? – and so on. For the rest, it was my opinion, too. We made our boats ready to drop over – and I also on that ship took measures . . . *Enfin*! One has done one's possible. It was a delicate position. Thirty hours. They prepared me some food. As for the wine – go and whistle for it – not a drop." In some extraordinary way, without any marked change in his inert attitude and in the placid expression of his face, he managed to convey the idea of profound disgust. "I – you know – when it comes to eating without my glass of wine – I am nowhere."

'I was afraid he would enlarge upon the grievance, for though he didn't stir a limb or twitch a feature, he made one aware how much he was irritated by the recollection. But he seemed to forget all about it. They delivered their charge to the "port authorities," as he expressed it. He was struck by the calmness with which it had been received. "One might have thought they had such a droll find (*drôle de trouvaille*) brought them every day. You are extraordinary – you others," he commented, with his back propped against the wall, and looking himself as incapable of an emotional display as a sack of meal. There happened to be a man-of-war and an Indian Marine steamer in the harbour at the time, and he did not conceal his admiration of the efficient manner in which the boats of these two ships cleared the *Patna* of her passengers. Indeed his torpid demeanour concealed nothing: it had that mysterious, almost miraculous, power of producing striking effects by means impossible of detection which is the last word of the highest art. "Twenty-five minutes – watch in hand – twenty-five, no more." . . . He unclasped and clasped again his fingers without removing his hands from his stomach, and made it infinitely more effective than if he had thrown up his arms to heaven in amazement . . . "All that lot (*tout ce monde*) on shore – with their little affairs – nobody left but a guard of seamen (*marins de l'État*) and that interesting corpse (*cet intéressant cadavre*). Twenty-five minutes." . . . With downcast eyes and his head tilted slightly on one side he seemed to roll knowingly on his tongue the savour of a smart bit of work. He persuaded one without any further demonstration that his approval was eminently worth having, and resuming his hardly interrupted immobility, he went on to inform me that, being under orders to make the best of their way to Toulon, they left in two hours' time, "so that (*de sorte que*) there are many things in this incident of my life (*dans cet épisode de ma vie*) which have remained obscure." '

Chapter 13

'After these words, and without a change of attitude, he, so to speak, submitted himself passively to a state of silence. I kept him company; and suddenly, but not abruptly, as if the appointed time had arrived for his moderate and husky voice to come out of his immobility, he pronounced, "*Mon Dieu!* how the time passes!" Nothing could have been more commonplace than this remark; but its utterance coincided for me with a moment of vision. It's extraordinary how we go through life with eyes half shut, with dull ears, with dormant thoughts. Perhaps it's just as well; and it may be that it is this very dullness that makes life to the incalculable majority so supportable and so welcome. Nevertheless, there can be but few of us who had never known one of these rare moments of awakening when we see, hear, understand ever so much – everything – in a flash – before we fall back again into our agreeable somnolence. I raised my eyes when he spoke, and I saw him as though I had never seen him before. I saw his chin sunk on his breast, the clumsy folds of his coat, his clasped hands, his motionless pose, so curiously suggestive of his having been simply left there. Time had passed indeed: it had overtaken him and gone ahead. It had left him hopelessly behind with a few poor gifts; the iron-grey hair, the heavy fatigue of the tanned face, two scars, a pair of tarnished shoulder-straps; one of those steady, reliable men who are the raw material of great reputations, one of those uncounted lives that are buried without drums and trumpets under the foundations of monumental successes. "I am now third lieutenant of the *Victorieuse*" (she was the flagship of the French Pacific squadron at the time), he said, detaching his shoulders from the wall a couple of inches to introduce himself. I bowed slightly on my side of the table, and told him I commanded a merchant vessel at present anchored in Rushcutter's Bay. He had "remarked" her – a pretty little craft. He was very civil about it in his impassive way. I even fancy he went the length of tilting his head in compliment as he repeated, breathing visibly the while, "Ah, yes. A little craft painted black – very pretty – very pretty (*très coquet*)." After a time he twisted his body slowly to face the glass door on our right. "A dull town (*triste ville*)," he observed, staring into the street. It was a brilliant day; a southerly buster was raging, and we could see the passers-by, men and women, buffeted by the wind on the sidewalks, the sunlit fronts of the houses across the road blurred by the tall whirls of dust. "I descended on shore," he said, "to stretch my legs a little, but . . . " He didn't finish, and sank into the depths of his repose. "Pray – tell me," he began, coming up ponderously, "what was there at the bottom of this affair – precisely (*au juste*)? It is curious. That dead man, for instance – and so on."

' "There were living men, too," I said; "much more curious."

' "No doubt, no doubt," he agreed half audibly, then, as if after mature consideration, murmured, "Evidently." I made no difficulty in communicating to him what had interested me most in this affair. It seemed as though he had a right to know: hadn't he spent thirty hours on board the *Patna* – had he not taken the succession, so to speak, had he not done "his possible"? He listened to me, looking more priestlike than ever, and with what – probably on account of his downcast eyes – had the appearance of devout concentration. Once or twice he elevated his eyebrows (but without raising his eyelids), as one would say, "The devil!" Once he calmly exclaimed, "Ah, bah!" under his breath, and when I had finished he pursed his lips in a deliberate way and emitted a sort of sorrowful whistle.

'In anyone else it might have been evidence of boredom, a sign of indifference; but he, in his occult way, managed to make his immobility appear profoundly responsive, and as full of valuable thoughts as an egg is of meat. What he said at last was nothing more than a "very interesting," pronounced politely, and not much above a whisper. Before I got over my disappointment he added, but as if speaking to himself, "That's it. That *is* it." His chin seemed to sink lower on his breast, his body to weigh heavier on his seat. I was about to ask him what he meant when a sort of preparatory tremor passed over his whole person, as a faint ripple may be seen upon stagnant water even before the wind is felt. "And so that poor young man ran away along with the others," he said, with grave tranquillity.

'I don't know what made me smile: it is the only genuine smile of mine I can remember in connection with Jim's affair. But somehow this simple statement of the matter sounded funny in French . . . "S'est enfui avec les autres," had said the lieutenant. And suddenly I began to admire the discrimination of the man. He had made out the point at once: he did get hold of the only thing I cared about. I felt as though I were taking professional opinion on the case. His imperturbable and mature calmness was that of an expert in possession of the facts, and to whom one's perplexities are mere child's play. "Ah! The young, the young," he said, indulgently. "And after all, one does not die of it." "Die of what?" I asked, swiftly. "Of being afraid." He elucidated his meaning and sipped his drink.

'I perceived that the three last fingers of his wounded hand were stiff and could not move independently of each other, so that he took up his tumbler with an ungainly clutch. "One is always afraid. One may talk, but . . . " He put down the glass awkwardly . . . "The fear, the fear – look you – it is always there." . . . He touched his breast near a brass button on the very spot where Jim had given a thump to his own when protesting that there was nothing the matter with his heart. I suppose I made some sign of dissent, because he insisted, "Yes! yes! One talks, one talks; this is all very fine; but at the end of the reckoning one is no cleverer than the next man – and no more brave. Brave! This is always to be seen. I have rolled my hump (*roulé ma bosse*)," he said, using the slang expression with imperturbable seriousness, "in all parts of the world; I have known brave men – famous ones! *Allez*!" . . . He drank carelessly . . . "Brave – you conceive – in the Service – one has got to be – the trade demands it (*le métier veut ça*). Is it not so?" he appealed to me reasonably. "*Eh bien*! Each of them – I say each of them, if he were an honest man – *bien entendu* – would confess that there is a point – there is a point – for the best of us – there is somewhere a point when you let go everything (*vous lâchez tout*). And you have got to live with that truth – do you see? Given a certain combination of circumstances, fear is sure to come. Abominable funk (*un trac épouvantable*). And even for those who do not believe this truth there is fear all the same – the fear of themselves. Absolutely so. Trust me. Yes. Yes . . . At my age one knows what one is talking about – *que diable*!" . . . He had delivered himself of all this as immovably as though he had been the mouthpiece of abstract wisdom, but at this point he heightened the effect of detachment by beginning to twirl his thumbs slowly. "It's evident – *parbleu*!" he continued; "for, make up your mind as much as you like, even a simple headache or a fit of indigestion (*un dérangement d'estomac*) is enough to . . . Take me, for instance – I have made my proofs. *Eh bien*! I, who am speaking to you, once . . . "

'He drained his glass and returned to his twirling. "No, no; one does not die of it," he pronounced, finally, and when I found he did not mean to proceed with the personal anecdote, I was extremely disappointed; the more so as it was not the sort of story, you know, one could very well press him for. I sat silent, and he too, as if nothing could please him better. Even his thumbs were still now. Suddenly his lips began to move. "That is so," he resumed, placidly. "Man is born a coward (*L'homme est né poltron*). It is a difficulty – *parbleu*! It would be too easy otherwise. But habit – habit – necessity – do you see? – the

eye of others – *voilà*. One puts up with it. And then the example of others who
are no better than yourself, and yet make good countenance . . . "

'His voice ceased.

' "That young man – you will observe – had none of these inducements –
at least at the moment," I remarked.

'He raised his eyebrows forgivingly: "I don't say; I don't say. The young
man in question might have had the best dispositions – the best dispositions,"
he repeated, wheezing a little.

' "I am glad to see you taking a lenient view," I said. "His own feeling in
that matter was – ah! – hopeful, and . . . "

'The shuffle of his feet under the table interrupted me. He drew up his
heavy eyelids. Drew up, I say – no other expression can describe the steady
deliberation of the act – and at last was disclosed completely to me. I was
confronted by two narrow grey circlets, like two tiny steel rings around the
profound blackness of the pupils. The sharp glance, coming from that massive
body, gave a notion of extreme efficiency, like a razor-edge on a battle-axe.
"Pardon," he said, punctiliously. His right hand went up, and he swayed
forward. "Allow me . . . I contended that one may get on knowing very well
that one's courage does not come of itself (*ne vient pas tout seul*). There's
nothing much in that to get upset about. One truth the more ought not to
make life impossible . . . But the honour – the honour, monsieur! . . . The
honour . . . that is real – that is! And what life may be worth when" . . . he got
on his feet with a ponderous impetuosity, as a startled ox might scramble up
from the grass . . . "when the honour is gone – *ah ça! par exemple* – I can
offer no opinion. I can offer no opinion – because – monsieur – I know
nothing of it."

'I had risen, too, and, trying to throw infinite politeness into our attitudes,
we faced each other mutely, like two china dogs on a mantelpiece. Hang the
fellow! he had pricked the bubble. The blight of futility that lies in wait for
men's speeches had fallen upon our conversation, and made it a thing of
empty sounds. "Very well," I said, with a disconcerted smile, "but couldn't it
reduce itself to not being found out?" He made as if to retort readily, but
when he spoke he changed his mind. "This, monsieur, is too fine for me –
much above me – I don't think about it." He bowed heavily over his cap,
which he held before him by the peak, between the thumb and the forefinger
of his rounded hand. I bowed, too. We bowed together: we scraped our feet
at each other with much ceremony, while a dirty specimen of a waiter looked
on critically, as though he had paid for the performance. "Serviteur," said the
Frenchman. Another scrape. "Monsieur" . . . "Monsieur." . . . The glass door
swung behind his burly back. I saw the southerly buster get hold of him and
drive him down wind with his hand to his head, his shoulders braced, and the
tails of his coat blown hard against his legs.

'I sat down again alone and discouraged – discouraged about Jim's case. If
you wonder that after more than three years it had preserved its actuality, you

must know that I had seen him only very lately. I had come straight from Samarang, where I had loaded a cargo for Sydney; an utterly uninteresting bit of business – what Charley here would call one of my rational transactions – and in Samarang I had seen something of Jim. He was then working for De Jongh, on my recommendation. Water-clerk. "My representative afloat," as De Jongh called him. You can't imagine a mode of life more barren of consolation, less capable of being invested with a spark of glamour – unless it be the business of an insurance canvasser. Little Bob Stanton – Charley here knew him well – had gone through that experience. The same who got drowned afterwards trying to save a lady's-maid in the *Sephora* disaster. A case of collision on a hazy morning off the Spanish coast, you may remember. All the passengers had been packed tidily into the boats and shoved clear of the ship when Bob sheered alongside again and scrambled back on deck to fetch that girl. How she had been left behind I can't make out; anyhow, she had gone completely crazy – wouldn't leave the ship – held to the rail like grim death. The wrestling-match could be seen plainly from the boats; but poor Bob was the shortest chief mate in the merchant service, and the woman stood five feet ten in her shoes and was as strong as a horse, I've been told. So it went on, pull devil, pull baker, the wretched girl screaming all the time, and Bob letting out a yell now and then to warn his boat to keep well clear of the ship. One of the hands told me, hiding a smile at the recollection, "It was for all the world, sir, like a naughty youngster fighting with his mother." The same old chap said that "At the last we could see that Mr Stanton had given up hauling at the gal, and just stood by looking at her, watchful like. We thought afterwards he must've been reckoning that, maybe, the rush of water would tear her away from the rail by and by and give him a show to save her. We daren't come alongside for our life; and after a bit the old ship went down all on a sudden with a lurch to starboard – plop. The suck in was something awful. We never saw anything alive or dead come up." Poor Bob's spell of shore-life had been one of the complications of a love affair, I believe. He fondly hoped he had done with the sea for ever, and made sure he had got hold of all the bliss on earth, but it came to canvassing in the end. Some cousin of his in Liverpool put him up to it. He used to tell us his experiences in that line. He made us laugh till we cried, and, not altogether displeased at the effect, undersized and bearded to the waist like a gnome, he would tiptoe amongst us and say, "It's all very well for you beggars to laugh, but my immortal soul was shrivelled down to the size of a parched pea after a week of that work." I don't know how Jim's soul accommodated itself to the new conditions of his life – I was kept too busy in getting him something to do that would keep body and soul together – but I am pretty certain his adventurous fancy was suffering all the pangs of starvation. It had certainly nothing to feed upon in this new calling. It was distressing to see him at it, though he tackled it with a stubborn serenity for which I must give him full credit. I kept my eye on his shabby plodding with a sort of notion that it was

a punishment for the heroics of his fancy – an expiation for his craving after
more glamour than he could carry. He had loved too well to imagine himself
a glorious racehorse, and now he was condemned to toil without honour like
a costermonger's donkey. He did it very well. He shut himself in, put his
head down, said never a word. Very well; very well indeed – except for
certain fantastic and violent outbreaks, on the deplorable occasions when
the irrepressible *Patna* case cropped up. Unfortunately that scandal of the
Eastern seas would not die out. And this is the reason why I could never feel
I had done with Jim for good.

'I sat thinking of him after the French lieutenant had left, not, however,
in connection with De Jongh's cool and gloomy back-shop, where we had
hurriedly shaken hands not very long ago, but as I had seen him years
before in the last flickers of the candle, alone with me in the long gallery of
the Malabar House, with the chill and the darkness of the night at his back.
The respectable sword of his country's law was suspended over his head.
Tomorrow – or was it today? (midnight had slipped by long before we
parted) – the marble-faced police magistrate, after distributing fines and
terms of imprisonment in the assault-and-battery case, would take up the
awful weapon and smite his bowed neck. Our communion in the night was
uncommonly like a last vigil with a condemned man. He was guilty, too.
He was guilty – as I had told myself repeatedly, guilty and done for;
nevertheless, I wished to spare him the mere detail of a formal execution. I
don't pretend to explain the reasons of my desire – I don't think I could; but
if you haven't got a sort of notion by this time, then I must have been very
obscure in my narrative, or you too sleepy to seize upon the sense of my
words. I don't defend my morality. There was no morality in he impulse
which induced me to lay before him Brierly's plan of evasion – I may call it –
in all its primitive simplicity. There were the rupees – absolutely ready in
my pocket and very much at his service. Oh! a loan; a loan of course – and if
an introduction to a man (in Rangoon) who could put some work in his
way . . . why! with the greatest pleasure. I had pen, ink, and paper in my
room on the first floor. And even while I was speaking I was impatient to
begin the letter: day, month, year, 2.30 a.m . . . for the sake of our old
friendship I ask you to put some work in the way of Mr James So-and-so, in
whom, etc., etc . . . I was even ready to write in that strain about him. If he
had not enlisted my sympathies he had done better for himself – he had gone
to the very fount and origin of that sentiment, he had reached the secret
sensibility of my egoism. I am concealing nothing from you, because were I
to do so my action would appear more unintelligible than any man's action
has the right to be, and – in the second place – tomorrow you shall forget my
sincerity along with the other lessons of the past. In this transaction, to
speak grossly and precisely, I was the irreproachable man; but the subtle
intentions of my immorality were defeated by the moral simplicity of the
criminal. No doubt he was selfish, too, but his selfishness had a higher

origin, a more lofty aim. I discovered that, say what I would, he was eager to go through the ceremony of execution; and I didn't say much, for I felt that in argument his youth would tell against me heavily: he believed where I had already ceased to doubt. There was something fine in the wildness of his unexpressed, hardly formulated hope. "Clear out! Couldn't think of it," he said, with a shake of the head. "I make you an offer for which I neither demand nor expect any sort of gratitude," I said; "you shall repay the money when convenient, and . . . " "Awfully good of you," he muttered without looking up. I watched him narrowly: the future must have appeared horribly uncertain to him; but he did not falter, as though indeed there had been nothing wrong with his heart. I felt angry – not for the first time that night. "The whole wretched business," I said, "is bitter enough, I should think, for a man of your kind . . . " "It is, it is," he whispered twice, with his eyes fixed on the floor. It was heart-rending. He towered above the light, and I could see the down on his cheek, the colour mantling warm under the smooth skin of his face. Believe me or not, I say it was outrageously heart-rending. It provoked me to brutality. "Yes," I said; "and allow me to confess that I am totally unable to imagine what advantage you can expect from this licking of the dregs." "Advantage!" he murmured out of his stillness. "I am dashed if I do," I said, enraged. "I've been trying to tell you all there is in it," he went on, slowly, as if meditating something unanswerable. "But after all, it is *my* trouble." I opened my mouth to retort, and discovered suddenly that I'd lost all confidence in myself; and it was as if he, too, had given me up, for he mumbled like a man thinking half aloud. "Went away . . . went into hospitals . . . Not one of them would face it . . . They! . . . " He moved his hand slightly to imply disdain. "But I've got to get over this thing, and I mustn't shirk any of it or . . . I won't shirk any of it." He was silent. He gazed as though he had been haunted. His unconscious face reflected the passing expressions of scorn, of despair, of resolution – reflected them in turn, as a magic mirror would reflect the gliding passage of unearthly shapes. He lived surrounded by deceitful ghosts, by austere shades. "Oh! nonsense, my dear fellow," I began. He had a movement of impatience. "You don't seem to understand," he said incisively; then looking at me without a wink, "I may have jumped, but I don't run away." "I meant no offence," I said; and added stupidly, "Better men than you have found it expedient to run, at times." He coloured all over, while in my confusion I half-choked myself with my own tongue. "Perhaps so," he said at last; "I am not good enough; I can't afford it. I am bound to fight this thing down – I am fighting it *now*." I got out of my chair and felt stiff all over. The silence was embarrassing, and to put an end to it I imagined nothing better but to remark, "I had no idea it was so late," in an airy tone . . . "I dare say you have had enough of this," he said, brusquely: "and to tell you the truth" – he began to look round for his hat – "so have I."

'Well! he had refused this unique offer. He had struck aside my helping hand; he was ready to go now, and beyond the balustrade the night seemed to wait for him very still, as though he had been marked down for its prey. I heard his voice. "Ah! here it is." He had found his hat. For a few seconds we hung in the wind. "What will you do after – after . . . ?" I asked very low. "Go to the dogs as likely as not," he answered in a gruff mutter. I had recovered my wits in a measure, and judged best to take it lightly. "Pray remember," I said, "that I should like very much to see you again before you go." "I don't know what's to prevent you. The damned thing won't make me invisible," he said with intense bitterness – "no such luck." And then at the moment of taking leave he treated me to a ghastly muddle of dubious stammers and movements, to an awful display of hesitations. God forgive him – me! He had taken it into his fanciful head that I was likely to make some difficulty as to shaking hands. It was too awful for words. I believe I shouted suddenly at him as you would bellow to a man you saw about to walk over a cliff; I remember our voices being raised, the appearance of a miserable grin on his face, a crushing clutch on my hand, a nervous laugh. The candle spluttered out, and the thing was over at last, with a groan that floated up to me in the dark. He got himself away somehow. The night swallowed his form. He was a horrible bungler. Horrible. I heard the quick crunch-crunch of the gravel under his boots. He was running. Absolutely running, with nowhere to go to. And he was not yet four-and-twenty.'

Chapter 14

'I slept little, hurried over my breakfast, and after a slight hesitation gave up my early morning visit to my ship. It was really very wrong of me, because, though my chief mate was an excellent man all round, he was the victim of such black imaginings that if he did not get a letter from his wife at the expected time he would go quite distracted with rage and jealousy, lose all grip on the work, quarrel with all hands, and either weep in his cabin or develop such a ferocity of temper as all but drove the crew to the verge of mutiny. The thing had always seemed inexplicable to me: they had been married thirteen years; I had a glimpse of her once, and, honestly, I couldn't conceive a man abandoned enough to plunge into sin for the sake of such an unattractive person. I don't know whether I have not done wrong by refraining from putting that view before poor Selvin: the man made a little hell on earth for himself, and I also suffered indirectly, but some sort of, no doubt, false delicacy prevented me. The marital relations of seamen would make an interesting subject, and I could tell you instances . . . However, this is not the place, not the time, and we are concerned with Jim – who was unmarried. If his imaginative conscience or his pride; if all the extravagant ghosts and austere shades that were the disastrous familiars of his youth would not let him run away from the block, I, who of course can't be suspected of such familiars, was irresistibly impelled to go and see his head roll off. I wended my way towards the court. I didn't hope to be very much impressed or edified, or interested or even frightened – though, as long as there is any life before one, a jolly good fright now and then is a salutary discipline. But neither did I expect to be so awfully depressed. The bitterness of his punishment was in its chill and mean atmosphere. The real significance of crime is in its being a breach of faith with the community of mankind, and from that point of view he was no mean traitor, but his execution was a hole-and-corner affair. There was no high scaffolding, no scarlet cloth (did they have scarlet cloth on Tower Hill? They should have had), no awestricken multitude to be horrified at his guilt and be moved to tears at his fate – no air of sombre retribution. There was, as I walked along, the clear sunshine, a brilliance too passionate to be consoling, the streets were full of jumbled bits of colour like a damaged kaleidoscope: yellow, green, blue, dazzling white, the brown nudity of an undraped shoulder, a bullock-cart with a red canopy, a company of native infantry in a drab body with dark heads marching in dusty laced boots, a native policeman in a sombre uniform of scanty cut and belted in patent leather, who looked up at me with orientally pitiful eyes as though his migrating spirit were suffering exceedingly from that unforeseen – what d'ye call 'em? – avatar – incarnation. Under the shade of a lonely tree in the courtyard, the villagers connected with the assault case sat in a picturesque group, looking like a chromo-lithograph of a camp in a book of Eastern travel. One missed the obligatory thread of smoke in the foreground and the pack-animals grazing. A blank yellow wall rose behind overtopping the tree, reflecting the glare. The court-room was sombre, seemed more vast. High up in the dim space the punkahs were swaying to and fro, to and fro. Here and there a draped figure, dwarfed by the bare walls, remained without stirring amongst the rows of empty benches, as if absorbed in pious meditation. The plaintiff, who had been beaten, an obese chocolate-coloured man with shaved head, one fat breast bare and a bright yellow caste-mark above the bridge of his nose, sat in pompous immobility: only his eyes glittered, rolling in the gloom, and the nostrils dilated and collapsed violently as he breathed. Brierly dropped into his seat looking done up, as though he had spent the night in sprinting on a cinder-track. The pious sailing-ship skipper appeared excited and made uneasy movements, as if restraining with difficulty an impulse to stand up and exhort us earnestly to prayer and repentance. The head of the magistrate, delicately pale under the neatly arranged hair, resembled the head of a hopeless invalid after he had been washed and brushed and propped up in bed. He moved aside the vase of flowers – a bunch of purple with a few pink blossoms on long stalks – and seizing in both hands a long sheet of bluish paper, ran his eye over it, propped his forearms on the edge of the desk and began to read aloud in an even, distinct, and careless voice.

'By Jove! For all my foolishness about scaffolds and heads rolling off – I assure you it was infinitely worse than a beheading. A heavy sense of finality brooded over all this, unrelieved by the hope of rest and safety following the fall of the axe. These proceedings had all the cold vengefulness of a death sentence, had all the cruelty of a sentence of exile. This is how I looked at it that morning – and even now I seem to see an undeniable vestige of truth in that exaggerated view of a common occurrence. You may imagine how strongly I felt this at the time. Perhaps it is for that reason that I could not bring myself to admit the finality. The thing was always with me, I was always eager to take opinion on it, as though it had not been practically settled: individual opinion – international opinion – by Jove! That Frenchman's, for instance. His own country's pronouncement was uttered in the passionless and definite phraseology a machine would use, if machines could speak. The head of the magistrate was half hidden by the paper, his brow was like alabaster.

'There were several questions before the court. The first as to whether the ship was in every respect fit and seaworthy for the voyage. The court found she was not. The next point, I remember, was, whether up to the time of the accident the ship had been navigated with proper and seamanlike care. They said Yes to that, goodness knows why, and then they declared that there was no evidence to show the exact cause of the accident. A floating derelict, probably. I myself remember that a Norwegian barque bound out with a cargo of pitch-pine had been given up as missing about that time, and it was just the sort of craft that would capsize in a squall and float bottom up for months – a kind of maritime ghoul on the prowl to kill ships in the dark. Such wandering corpses are common enough in the North Atlantic, which is haunted by all the terrors of the sea – fogs, icebergs, dead ships bent upon mischief, and long sinister gales that fasten upon one like a vampire till all the strength and the spirit and even hope are gone, and one feels like the empty shell of a man. But there – in those seas – the incident was rare enough to resemble a special arrangement of a malevolent providence, which, unless it had for its object the killing of a donkey-man and the bringing of worse than death upon Jim, appeared an utterly aimless piece of devilry. This view occurring to me took off my attention. For a time I was aware of the magistrate's voice as a sound merely; but in a moment it shaped itself into distinct words . . . "in utter disregard of their plain duty," it said. The next sentence escaped me somehow, and then . . . "abandoning in the moment of danger the lives and property confided to their charge" . . . went on the voice evenly, and stopped. A pair of eyes under the white forehead shot darkly a glance above the edge of the paper. I looked for Jim hurriedly, as though I had expected him to disappear. He was very still – but he was there. He sat pink and fair and extremely attentive. "Therefore, . . . " began the voice emphatically. He stared with parted lips, hanging upon the words of the man behind the desk. These came out into the stillness wafted on the wind made by the punkahs, and I, watching for their effect upon him, caught only fragments of official language ... "The Court ... Gustav So-and-so ... master ... native of Germany ... James So-and-so ... mate ... certificates cancelled." A silence fell. The magistrate had dropped the paper, and leaning sideways on the arm of his chair, began to talk with Brierly easily. People started to move out; others were pushing in, and I also made for the door. Outside I stood still, and when Jim passed on his way to the gate, I caught at his arm and detained him. The look he gave discomposed me, as though I had been responsible for his state: he looked at me as if I had been the embodied evil of life. "It's all over," I stammered. "Yes," he said, thickly. "And now let no man ... " He jerked his arm out of my grasp. I watched his back as he went away. It was a long street, and he remained in sight for some time. He walked rather slow, and straddling his legs a little, as if he had found it difficult to keep a straight line. Just before I lost him I fancied he staggered a bit.

' "Man overboard," said a deep voice behind me. Turning round, I saw a fellow I knew slightly, a West Australian; Chester was his name. He, too, had been looking after Jim. He was a man with an immense girth of chest, a rugged, clean-shaved face of mahogany colour, and two blunt tufts of iron-grey, thick wiry hairs on his upper lip. He had been pearler, wrecker, trader, whaler, too, I believe; in his own words – anything and everything a man may be at sea, but a pirate. The Pacific, north and south, was his proper hunting-ground; but he had wandered so far afield looking for a cheap steamer to buy. Lately he had discovered – so he said – a guano island somewhere, but its approaches were dangerous, and the anchorage, such as it was, could not be considered safe, to say the least of it. "As good as a gold-mine," he would exclaim. "Right bang in the middle of the Walpole Reefs, and if it's true enough that you can get no holding-ground anywhere in less than forty fathom, then what of that? There are the hurricanes, too. But it's a first-rate thing. As good as a gold-mine – better! Yet there's not a fool of them that will see it. I can't get a skipper or a shipowner to go near the place. So I made up my mind to cart the blessed stuff myself." ... This was what he required a steamer for, and I knew he was just then negotiating enthusiastically with a Parsee firm for an old, brig-rigged sea-anachronism of ninety horsepower. We had met and spoken together several times. He looked knowingly after Jim. "Take it to heart?" he asked, scornfully. "Very much," I said. "Then he's no good," he opined. "What's all the to-do about? A bit of ass's skin. That never yet made a man. You must see things exactly as they are – if you don't, you may just as well give in at once. You will never do anything in this world. Look at me. I made it a practice never to take anything to heart." "Yes," I said, "you see things as they are." "I wish I could see my partner coming along, that's what I wish to see," he said. "Know my partner?

Old Robinson. Yes; *the* Robinson. Don't *you* know? The notorious Robinson. The man who smuggled more opium and bagged more seals in his time than any loose Johnny now alive. They say he used to board the sealing-schooners up Alaska way when the fog was so thick that the Lord God, He alone, could tell one man from another. Holy-Terror Robinson. That's the man. He is with me in that guano thing. The best chance he ever came across in his life." He put his lips to my ear. "Cannibal? – well, they used to give him the name years and years ago. You remember the story? A shipwreck on the west side of Stewart Island; that's right; seven of them got ashore, and it seems they did not get on very well together. Some men are too cantankerous for anything – don't know how to make the best of a bad job – don't see things as they are – as they *are*, my boy! And then what's the consequence? Obvious! Trouble, trouble; as likely as not a knock on the head; and serve 'em right, too. That sort is the most useful when it's dead. The story goes that a boat of Her Majesty's ship *Wolverine* found him kneeling on the kelp, naked as the day he was born, and chanting some psalm-tune or other; light snow was falling at the time. He waited till the boat was an oar's length from the shore, and then up and away. They chased him for an hour up and down the boulders, till a marine flung a stone that took him behind the ear providentially and knocked him senseless. Alone? Of course. But that's like that tale of sealing-schooners; the Lord God knows the right and the wrong of that story. The cutter did not investigate much. They wrapped him in a boat-cloak and took him off as quick as they could, with a dark night coming on, the weather threatening, and the ship firing recall guns every five minutes. Three weeks afterwards he was as well as ever. He didn't allow any fuss that was made on shore to upset him; he just shut his lips tight, and let people screech. It was bad enough to have lost his ship, and all he was worth besides, without paying attention to the hard names they called him. That's the man for me." He lifted his arm for a signal to someone down the street. "He's got a little money, so I had to let him into my thing. Had to! It would have been sinful to throw away such a find, and I was cleaned out myself. It cut me to the quick, but I could see the matter just as it was, and if I *must* share – thinks I – with any man, then give me Robinson. I left him at breakfast in the hotel to come to court, because I've an idea ... Ah! Good-morning, Captain Robinson ... Friend of mine, Captain Robinson."

'An emaciated patriarch in a suit of white drill, a solah topi with a green-lined rim on a head trembling with age, joined us after crossing the street in a trotting shuffle, and stood propped with both hands on the handle of an umbrella. A white beard with amber streaks hung lumpily down to his waist. He blinked his creased eyelids at me in a bewildered way. "How do you do? how do you do?" he piped, amiably, and tottered. "A little deaf," said Chester aside. "Did you drag him over six thousand miles to get a cheap steamer?" I asked. "I would have taken him twice round the world as soon as look at him," said Chester with immense energy. "The steamer will be the making of us, my lad. Is it my fault that every skipper and shipowner in the whole of blessed Australasia turns out a blamed fool? Once I talked for three hours to a man in Auckland. 'Send a ship,' I said, 'send a ship. I'll give you half of the first cargo for yourself, free gratis for nothing – just to make a good start.' Says he, 'I wouldn't do it if there was no other place on earth to send a ship to.' Perfect ass, of course. Rocks, currents, no anchorage, sheer cliff to lay to, no insurance company would take the risk, didn't see how he could get loaded under three years. Ass! I nearly went on my knees to him. 'But look at the thing as it is,' says I. 'Damn rocks and hurricanes. Look at it as it is. There's guano there, Queensland sugar-planters would fight for – fight for on the quay, I tell you.' . . . What can you do with a fool? . . . 'That's one of your little jokes, Chester,' he says . . . Joke! I could have wept. Ask Captain Robinson here . . . And there was another shipowning fellow – a fat chap in a white waistcoat in Wellington, who seemed to think I was up to some swindle or other. 'I don't know what sort of fool you're looking for,' he says, 'but I am busy just now. Good-morning.' I longed to take him in my two hands and smash him through the window of his own office. But I didn't. I was as mild as a curate. 'Think of it,' says I. '*Do* think it over. I'll call tomorrow.' He grunted something about being 'out all day.' On the stairs I felt ready to beat my head against the wall from vexation. Captain Robinson here can tell you. It was awful to think of all that lovely stuff lying waste under the sun – stuff that would send the sugar-cane shooting sky-high. The making of Queensland! The making of Queensland! And in Brisbane, where I went to have a last try, they gave me the name of a lunatic. Idiots! The only sensible man I came across was the cabman who drove me about. A broken-down swell he was, I fancy. Hey! Captain Robinson! You remember I told you about my cabby in Brisbane – don't you? The chap had a wonderful eye for things. He saw it all in a jiffy. It was a real pleasure to talk with him. One evening after a devil of a day amongst shipowners I felt so bad that, says I, 'I must get drunk. Come along; I must get drunk, or I'll go mad.' 'I am your man' he says; 'go ahead.' I don't know what I would have done without him. Hey! Captain Robinson."

'He poked the ribs of his partner. "He! he! he!" laughed the Ancient, looked aimlessly down the street, then peered at me doubtfully with sad, dim pupils . . . "He! he! he!" . . . He leaned heavier on the umbrella, and dropped his gaze on the ground. I needn't tell you I had tried to get away several times, but Chester had foiled every attempt by simply catching hold of my coat. "One minute. I've a notion." "What's your infernal notion?" I exploded at last. "If you think I am going in with you . . . " "No, no, my boy. Too late, if you wanted ever so much. We've got a steamer." "You've got the ghost of a steamer," I said. "Good enough for a start – there's no superior nonsense about us. Is there, Captain Robinson?" "No! no! no!" croaked the old man without lifting his eyes, and the senile tremble of his head became almost fierce with determination. "I understand you know that young chap," said Chester, with a nod at the street from which Jim had disappeared long ago. "He's been having grub with you in the Malabar last night – so I was told."

'I said that was true, and after remarking that he, too, liked to live well and in style, only that, for the present, he had to be saving of every penny – "none too many for the business! Isn't that so, Captain Robinson?" – he squared his shoulders and stroked his dumpy moustache, while the notorious Robinson, coughing at his side, clung more than ever to the handle of the umbrella, and seemed ready to subside passively into a heap of old bones. "You see, the old chap has all the money," whispered Chester, confidentially. "I've been cleaned out trying to engineer the dratted thing. But wait a bit, wait a bit. The good time is coming." . . . He seemed suddenly astonished at the signs of impatience I gave. "Oh, crakee!" he cried; "I am telling you of the biggest thing that ever was, and you . . . " "I have an appointment," I pleaded mildly. "What of that?" he asked with genuine surprise; "let it wait." "That's exactly what I am doing now," I remarked; "hadn't you better tell me what it is you want?" "Buy twenty hotels like that," he growled to himself; "and every joker boarding in them, too – twenty times over." He lifted his head smartly. "I want that young chap." "I don't understand," I said. "He's no good, is he?" said Chester, crisply. "I know nothing about it," I protested. "Why, you told me yourself he was taking it to heart," argued Chester. "Well, in my opinion a chap who . . . Anyhow, he can't be much good; but then you see I am on the look-out for somebody, and I've just got a thing that will suit him. I'll give him a job on my island." He nodded significantly. "I'm going to dump forty coolies there – if I've got to steal 'em. Somebody must work the stuff. Oh! I mean to act square: wooden shed, corrugated-iron roof – I know a man in Hobart who will take my bill at six months for the materials. I do. Honour bright. Then there's the water-supply. I'll have to fly round and get somebody to trust me for half a dozen second-hand iron tanks. Catch rain-water, hey? Let him take charge. Make him supreme boss over the coolies. Good idea, isn't it? What do you say?" "There are whole years when not a drop of rain falls on Walpole," I said, too amazed to laugh. He bit his lip and seemed bothered. "Oh, well, I will fix up something for them – or land a supply. Hang it all! That's not the question."

'I said nothing. I had a rapid vision of Jim perched on a shadowless rock, up to his knees in guano, with the screams of sea-birds in his ears, the incandescent ball of the sun above his head; the empty sky and the empty ocean all a-quiver, simmering together in the heat as far as the eye could reach. "I wouldn't advise my worst enemy . . . " I began. "What's the matter with you?" cried Chester; "I mean to give him a good screw – that is, as soon as the thing is set going, of course. It's as easy as falling off a log. Simply nothing to do; two six-shooters in his belt . . . Surely he wouldn't be afraid of anything forty coolies could do – with two six-shooters and he the only armed man, too! It's much better than it looks. I want you to help me to talk him over." "No!" I shouted. Old Robinson lifted his bleared eyes dismally for a moment, Chester looked at me with infinite contempt. "So you wouldn't advise him?" he uttered, slowly. "Certainly not," I answered, as indignant as though he had requested me to help murder somebody; "moreover, I am sure he wouldn't. He is badly cut up, but he isn't mad as far as I know. "He is no earthly good for anything," Chester mused aloud. "He would just have done for me. If you only could see a thing as it is, you would see it's the very thing for him. And besides . . . Why! it's the most splendid, sure chance . . . " He got angry suddenly. "I must have a man. There! . . . " He stamped his foot and smiled unpleasantly. "Anyhow, I could guarantee the island wouldn't sink under him – and I believe he is a bit particular on that point." "Good-morning," I said, curtly. He looked at me as though I had been an incomprehensible fool . . . "Must be moving, Captain Robinson," he yelled suddenly into the old man's ear. "These Parsee Johnnies are waiting for us to clinch the bargain." He took his partner under the arm with a firm grip, swung him round, and, unexpectedly, leered at me over his shoulder. "I was trying to do him a kindness," he asserted, with an air and tone that made my blood boil. "Thank you for nothing – in his name," I rejoined. "Oh! you are devilish smart," he sneered; "but you are like the rest of them. Too much in the clouds. See what *you* will do with him." "I don't know that I want to do anything with him." "Don't you?" he spluttered; his grey moustache bristled with anger, and by his side the notorious Robinson, propped on the umbrella, stood with his back to me, as patient and still as a worn-out cab-horse. "I haven't found a guano island," I said. "It's my belief you wouldn't know one if you were led right up to it by the hand," he riposted quickly; "and in this world you've got to see a thing first, before you can make use of it. Got to see it through and through at that, neither more nor less." "And get others to see it, too," I insinuated, with a glance at the bowed back by his side. Chester snorted at me. "His eyes are right enough – don't you worry. He ain't a puppy." "Oh, dear, no!" I said. "Come along, Captain Robinson," he shouted, with a sort of bullying deference under the rim of the old man's hat; the Holy Terror gave a submissive little jump. The ghost of a steamer was waiting for them, Fortune on that fair isle! They made a curious pair of Argonauts. Chester strode on leisurely, well set up, portly, and of conquering mien; the other, long, wasted, drooping, and hooked to his arm, shuffled his withered shanks with desperate haste.'

Chapter 15

'I did not start in search of Jim at once, only because I had really an appointment which I could not neglect. Then, as ill-luck would have it, in my agent's office I was fastened upon by a fellow fresh from Madagascar with a little scheme for a wonderful piece of business. It had something to do with cattle and cartridges and a Prince Ravonalo something; but the pivot of the whole affair was the stupidity of some admiral – Admiral Pierre, I think. Everything turned on that, and the chap couldn't find words strong enough to express his confidence. He had globular eyes starting out of his head with a fishy glitter, bumps on his forehead, and wore his long hair brushed back without a parting. He had a favourite phrase which he kept on repeating triumphantly: "The minimum of risk with the maximum of profit is my motto. What?" He made my head ache, spoiled my tiffin, but got his own out of me all right; and as soon as I had shaken him off, I made straight for the waterside. I caught sight of Jim leaning over the parapet of the quay. Three native boatmen quarrelling over five annas were making an awful row at his elbow. He didn't hear me come up, but spun round as if the slight contact of my finger had released a catch. "I was looking," he stammered. I don't remember what I said, not much anyhow, but he made no difficulty in following me to the hotel.

He followed me as manageable as a little child, with an obedient air, with no sort of manifestation, rather as though he had been waiting for me there to come along and carry him off. I need not have been so surprised as I was at his tractability. On all the round earth, which to some seems so big and that others affect to consider as rather smaller than a mustard-seed, he had no place where he could – what shall I say? – where he could withdraw. That's it! Withdraw – be alone with his loneliness. He walked by my side very calm, glancing here and there, and once turned his head to look after a Sidiboy fireman in a cutaway coat and yellowish trousers, whose black face had silky gleams like a lump of anthracite coal. I doubt, however, whether he saw anything, or even remained all the time aware of my companionship, because if I had not edged him to the left here, or pulled him to the right there, I believe he would have gone straight before him in any direction till stopped by a wall or some other obstacle. I steered him into my bedroom, and sat down at once to write letters. This was the only place in the world (unless, perhaps, the Walpole Reef – but that was not so handy) where he could have it out with himself without being bothered by the rest of the universe. The damned thing – as he had expressed it – had not made him invisible, but I behaved exactly as though he were. No sooner in my chair I bent over my writing-desk like a medieval scribe, and, but for the movement of the hand holding the pen, remained anxiously quiet. I can't say I was frightened; but I certainly kept as still as if there had been something dangerous in the room, that at the first hint of a movement on my part would be provoked to pounce upon me. There was not much in the room – you know how these bedrooms are – a sort of four-poster bedstead under a mosquito-net, two or three chairs, the table I was writing at, a bare floor. A glass door opened on an upstairs veranda, and he stood with his face to it, having a hard time with all possible privacy. Dusk fell; I lit a candle with the greatest economy of movement and as much prudence as though it were an illegal proceeding. There is no doubt that he had a very hard time of it, and so had I, even to the point, I must own, of wishing him to the devil, or on Walpole Reef at least. It occurred to me once or twice that, after all, Chester was, perhaps, the man to deal effectively with such a disaster. That strange idealist had found a practical use for it at once – unerringly, as it were. It was enough to make one suspect that, maybe, he really could see the true aspect of things that appeared mysterious or utterly hopeless to less imaginative persons. I wrote and wrote; I liquidated all the arrears of my correspondence, and then went on writing to people who had no reason whatever to expect from me a gossipy letter about nothing at all. At times I stole a sidelong glance. He was rooted to the spot, but convulsive shudders ran down his back; his shoulders would heave suddenly. He was fighting, he was fighting – mostly for his breath, as it seemed. The massive shadows, cast all one way from the straight flame of the candle, seemed possessed of gloomy consciousness; the immobility of the furniture had to my furtive eye an air of attention. I was becoming fanciful in the midst of my industrious scribbling; and though, when the scratching of my pen stopped for a moment, there was complete silence and stillness in the room, I suffered from that profound disturbance and confusion of thought which is caused by a violent and menacing uproar – of a heavy gale at sea, for instance. Some of you may know what I mean – that mingled anxiety, distress, and irritation with a sort of craven feeling creeping in – not pleasant to acknowledge, but which gives a quiet special merit to one's endurance. I don't claim any merit for standing the stress of Jim's emotions; I could take refuge in the letters; I could have written to strangers if necessary. Suddenly, as I was taking up a fresh sheet of notepaper, I heard a low sound, the first sound that, since we had been shut up together, had come to my ears in the dim stillness of the room. I remained with my head down, with my hand arrested. Those who have kept vigil by a sick-bed have heard such faint sounds in the stillness of the night watches, sounds wrung from a racked body, from a weary soul. He pushed the glass door with such force that all the panes rang: he stepped out, and I held my breath, straining my ears without knowing what else I expected to hear. He was really taking too much to heart an empty formality which to Chester's rigorous criticism seemed unworthy of the notice of a man who could see things as they were. An empty formality; a piece of parchment. Well, well. As to the inaccessible guano deposit, that was another story altogether. One could intelligibly break one's heart over that. A feeble burst of many voices mingled with the tinkle of silver and glass floated up from the dining-room below; through the open door the outer edge of the light from my candle fell on his back faintly; beyond all was black; he stood on the brink of a vast obscurity, like a lonely figure by the shore of a sombre and hopeless ocean. There was the Walpole Reef in it – to be sure – a speck in the dark void, a straw for the drowning man. My compassion for him took the shape of the thought that I wouldn't have liked his people to see him at that moment. I found it trying myself. His back was no longer shaken by his gasps; he stood straight as an arrow, faintly visible and still; and the meaning of this stillness sank to the bottom of my soul like lead into the water, and made it so heavy that for a second I wished heartily that the only course left open for me were to pay for his funeral. Even the law had done with him. To bury him would have been such an easy kindness! It would have been so much in accordance with the wisdom of life, which consists in putting out of sight all the reminders of our folly, of our weakness, of our mortality; all that makes against our efficiency – the memory of our failures, the hints of our undying fears, the bodies of our dead friends. Perhaps he did take it too much to heart. And if so then – Chester's offer . . . At this point I took up a fresh sheet and began to write resolutely. There was nothing but myself between him and the dark ocean. I had a sense of responsibility. If I spoke, would that motionless and suffering youth leap into the obscurity – clutch at the straw? I found out how difficult it may be sometimes to make a sound. There is a weird power in a spoken word. And why the devil not? I was asking myself persistently while I drove on with my writing. All at once, on the blank page, under the very point of the pen, the two figures of Chester and his antique partner, very distinct and complete, would dodge into view with stride and gestures, as if reproduced in the field of some optical toy. I would watch them for a while. No! They were too phantasmal and extravagant to enter into anyone's fate. And a word carries far – very far – deals destruction through time as the bullets go flying through space. I said nothing; and he, out there with his back to the light, as if bound and gagged by all the invisible foes of man, made no stir and made no sound.'

Chapter 16

'The time was coming when I should see him loved, trusted, admired, with a legend of strength and prowess forming round his name as though he had been the stuff of a hero. It's true – I assure you; as true as I'm sitting here talking about him in vain. He, on his side, had that faculty of beholding at a hint the face of his desire and the shape of his dream, without which the earth would know no lover and no adventurer. He captured much honour and an Arcadian happiness (I won't say anything about innocence) in the bush, and it was as good to him as the honour and the Arcadian happiness of the streets to another man. Felicity, felicity – how shall I say it? – is quaffed out of a golden cup in every latitude: the flavour is with you – with you alone, and you can make it as intoxicating as you please. He was of the sort that would drink deep, as you may guess from what went before. I found him, if not exactly intoxicated, then at least flushed with the elixir at his lips. He had not obtained it at once. There had been, as you know, a period of probation amongst infernal ship-chandlers, during which he had suffered and I had worried about – about – my trust – you may call it. I don't know that I am completely reassured now, after beholding him in all his brilliance. That was my last view of him – in a strong light, dominating, and yet in complete accord with his surroundings – with the life of the forests and with the life of men. I own that I was impressed, but I must admit to myself that after all this is not the lasting impression. He was protected by his isolation, alone of his own superior kind, in close touch with Nature, that keeps faith on such easy terms with her lovers. But I cannot fix before my eye the image of his safety. I shall always remember him as seen through the open door of my room, taking, perhaps, too much to heart the mere consequences of his failure. I am pleased, of course, that some good – and even some splendour – came out of my endeavours; but at times it seems to me it would have been better for my peace of mind if I had not stood between him and Chester's confoundedly generous offer. I wonder what his exuberant imagination would have made of Walpole islet – that most hopelessly forsaken crumb of dry land on the face of the waters. It is not likely I would ever have heard, for I must tell you that Chester, after calling at some Australian port to patch up his brig-rigged sea-anachronism, steamed out into the Pacific with a crew of twenty-two hands all told, and the only news having a possible bearing upon the mystery of his fate was the news of a hurricane which is supposed to have swept in its course over the Walpole shoals, a month or so afterwards. Not a vestige of the Argonauts ever turned up; not a sound came out of the waste. Finis! The Pacific is the most discreet of live, hot-tempered oceans: the chilly Antarctic can keep a secret, too, but more in the manner of a grave.

'And there is a sense of blessed finality in such discretion, which is what we all more or less sincerely are ready to admit – for what else is it that makes the idea of death supportable? End! Finis! the potent word that exorcises from the house of life the haunting shadow of fate. This is what – notwithstanding the testimony of my eyes and his own earnest assurances – I miss when I look back upon Jim's success. While there's life there is hope, truly; but there is fear, too. I don't mean to say that I regret my action, nor will I pretend that I can't sleep o' nights in consequence; still the idea obtrudes itself that he made so much of his disgrace while it is the guilt alone that matters. He was not – if I may say so – clear to me. He was not clear. And there is a suspicion he was not clear to himself either. There were his fine sensibilities, his fine feelings, his fine longings – a sort of sublimated, idealised selfishness. He was – if you allow me to say so – very fine; very fine – and very unfortunate. A little coarser nature would not have borne the strain; it would have had to come to terms with itself – with a sigh, with a grunt, or even with a guffaw; a still coarser one would have remained invulnerably ignorant and completely uninteresting.

'But he was too interesting or too unfortunate to be thrown to the dogs, or even to Chester. I felt this while I sat with my face over the paper and he fought and gasped, struggling for his breath in that terribly stealthy way, in my room; I felt it when he rushed out on the veranda as if to fling himself over – and didn't; I felt it more and more all the time he remained outside, faintly lighted on the background of night, as if standing on the shore of a sombre and hopeless sea.

'An abrupt heavy rumble made me lift my head. The noise seemed to roll away, and suddenly a searching and violent glare fell on the blind face of the night. The sustained and dazzling flickers seemed to last for an unconscionable time. The growl of the thunder increased steadily while I looked at him, distinct and black, planted solidly upon the shores of a sea of light. At the moment of greatest brilliance the darkness leaped back with a culminating crash, and he vanished before my dazzled eyes as utterly as though he had been blown to atoms. A blustering sigh passed; furious hands seemed to tear at the shrubs, shake the tops of the trees below, slam doors, break windowpanes, all along the front of the building. He stepped in, closing the door behind him, and found me bending over the table: my sudden anxiety as to what he would say was very great, and akin to a fright. "May I have a cigarette?" he asked. I gave a push to the box without raising my head. "I want – want – tobacco," he muttered. I became extremely buoyant. "Just a moment," I grunted, pleasantly. He took a few steps here and there. "That's over," I heard him say. A single distant clap of thunder came from the sea like a gun of distress. "The monsoon breaks up early this year," he remarked, conversationally, somewhere behind me. This encouraged me to turn round, which I did as soon as I had finished addressing the last envelope. He was smoking greedily in the middle of the room, and though he heard the stir I made, he remained with his back to me for a time.

' "Come – I carried it off pretty well," he said, wheeling suddenly. "Something's paid off – not much. I wonder what's to come." His face did not show any emotion, only it appeared a little darkened and swollen, as though he had been holding his breath. He smiled reluctantly as it were, and went on while I gazed up at him mutely . . . "Thank you, though – your room – jolly convenient – for a chap – badly hipped." . . . The rain pattered and swished in the garden; a water-pipe (it must have had a hole in it) performed just outside the window a parody of blubbering woe with funny sobs and gurgling lamentations, interrupted by jerky spasms of silence . . . "A bit of shelter," he mumbled and ceased.

'A flash of faded lightning darted in through the black framework of the windows and ebbed out without any noise. I was thinking how I had best approach him (I did not want to be flung off again) when he gave a little laugh. "No better than a vagabond now" . . . the end of the cigarette smouldered between his fingers . . . "without a single – single . . . " he pronounced slowly; "and yet . . . " He paused; the rain fell with redoubled violence. "Someday one's bound to come upon some sort of chance to get it all back again. Must!" he whispered, distinctly, glaring at my boots.

'I did not even know what it was he wished so much to regain, what it was he had so terribly missed. It might have been so much that it was impossible to say. A piece of ass's skin, according to Chester . . . He looked up at me inquisitively. "Perhaps. If life's long enough," I muttered through my teeth with unreasonable animosity. "Don't reckon too much on it."

' "Jove! I feel as if nothing could ever touch me," he said in a tone of sombre conviction. "If this business couldn't knock me over, then there's no fear of there being not enough time to – climb out, and . . . " He looked upwards.

'It struck me that it is from such as he that the great army of waifs and strays is recruited, the army that marches down, down into all the gutters of the earth. As soon as he left my room, that "bit of shelter," he would take his place in the ranks, and begin the journey towards the bottomless pit. I at least had no illusions; but it was I, too, who a moment ago had been so sure of the power of words, and now was afraid to speak, in the same way one dares not move for fear of losing a slippery hold. It is when we try to grapple with another man's intimate need that we perceive how incomprehensible, wavering, and misty are the beings that share with us the sight of the stars and the warmth of the sun. It is as if loneliness were a hard and absolute condition of existence; the envelope of flesh and blood on which our eyes are fixed melts before the outstretched hand, and there remains only the capricious, unconsolable, and elusive spirit that no eye can follow, no hand can grasp. It was the fear of losing him that kept me silent, for it was borne upon me suddenly and with unaccountable force that should I let him dip away into the darkness I would never forgive myself.

' "Well. Thanks – once more. You've been – er – uncommonly – really there's no word to . . . Uncommonly! I don't know why, I am sure. I am afraid I don't feel as grateful as I would if the whole thing hadn't been so brutally sprung on me. Because at bottom . . . you, yourself . . . " He stuttered.

' "Possibly," I struck in. He frowned.

' "All the same, one is responsible." He watched me like a hawk. ' "And that's true, too," I said.

' "Well. I've gone with it to the end, and I don't intend to let any man cast it in my teeth without – without – resenting." He clenched his fist.

' "There's yourself," I said with a smile – mirthless enough, God knows – but he looked at me menacingly. "That's my business," he said. An air of indomitable resolution came and went upon his face like a vain and passing shadow. Next moment he looked a dear good boy in trouble, as before. He flung away the cigarette. "Goodbye," he said, with the sudden haste of a man who had lingered too long in view of a pressing bit of work waiting for him; and then for a second or so he made not the slightest movement. The downpour fell with the heavy uninterrupted rush of a sweeping flood, with a sound of unchecked overwhelming fury that called to one's mind the images of collapsing bridges, of uprooted trees, of undermined mountains. No man could breast the colossal and headlong stream that seemed to break and swirl against the dim stillness in which we were precariously sheltered as if on an island. The perforated pipe gurgled, choked, spat, and splashed in odious ridicule of a swimmer fighting for his life. "It is raining," I remonstrated, "and I . . . " "Rain or shine," he began, brusquely, checked himself, and walked to the window. "Perfect deluge," he muttered after a while: he leaned his forehead on the glass. "It's dark, too."

' "Yes, it is very dark," I said.

'He pivoted on his heels, crossed the room, and had actually opened the door leading into the corridor before I leaped up from my chair. "Wait," I cried, "I want you to . . . " "I can't dine with you again tonight," he flung at me, with one leg out of the room already. "I haven't the slightest intention to ask you," I shouted. At this he drew back his foot, but remained mistrustfully in the very doorway. I lost no time in entreating him earnestly not to be absurd; to come in and shut the door.'

Chapter 17

'He came in at last; but I believe it was mostly the rain that did it; it was falling just then with a devastating violence which quieted down gradually while we talked. His manner was very sober and set; his bearing was that of a naturally taciturn man possessed by an idea. My talk was of the material aspect of his position; it had the sole aim of saving him from the degradation, ruin, and despair that out there close so swiftly upon a friendless, homeless man; I pleaded with him to accept my help; I argued reasonably: and every time I looked up at that absorbed smooth face, so grave and youthful, I had a disturbing sense of being no help but rather an obstacle to some mysterious, inexplicable, impalpable striving of his wounded spirit.

' "I suppose you intend to eat and drink and to sleep under shelter in the usual way," I remember saying with irritation. "You say you won't touch the money that is due to you." . . . He came as near as his sort can to making a gesture of horror. (There were three weeks and five days' pay owing him as mate of the *Patna*.) "Well, that's too little to matter anyhow; but what will you do tomorrow? Where will you turn? You must live . . ." "That isn't the thing," was the comment that escaped him under his breath. I ignored it, and went on combating what I assumed to be the scruples of an exaggerated delicacy. "On every conceivable ground," I concluded, "you must let me help you." "You can't," he said very simply and gently, and holding fast to some deep idea which I could detect shimmering like a pool of water in the dark, but which I despaired of ever approaching near enough to fathom. I surveyed his well-proportioned bulk. "At any rate," I said, "I am able to help what I can see of you. I don't pretend to do more." He shook his head sceptically without looking at me. I got very warm. "But I can," I insisted. "I can do even more. I *am* doing more. I am trusting you . . ." "The money . . ." he began. "Upon my word you deserve being told to go to the devil," I cried, forcing the note of indignation. He was startled, smiled, and I pressed my attack home. "It isn't a question of money at all. You are too superficial," I said (and at the same time I was thinking to myself: Well, here goes! And perhaps he is after all). "Look at the letter I want you to take. I am writing to a man of whom I've never asked a favour, and I am writing about you in terms that one only ventures to use when speaking of an intimate friend. I make myself unreservedly responsible for you. That's what I am doing. And really if you will only reflect a little what that means . . ."

'He lifted his head. The rain had passed away: only the water-pipe went on shedding tears with an absurd drip-drip outside the window. It was very quiet in the room, whose shadows huddled together in corners, away from the still flame of the candle flaring upright in the shape of a dagger; his face after a while seemed suffused by a reflection of a soft light as if the dawn had broken already.

' "Jove!" he gasped out. "It is noble of you!"

'Had he suddenly put out his tongue at me in derision, I could not have felt more humiliated. I thought to myself: Serve me right for a sneaking humbug . . . His eyes shone straight into my face, but I perceived it was not a mocking brightness. All at once he sprang into jerky agitation, like one of those flat wooden figures that are worked by a string. His arms went up, then came down with a slap. He became another man altogether. "And I had never seen," he shouted; then suddenly bit his lip and frowned. "What a bally ass I've been," he said very slow in an awed tone . . . "You are a brick," he cried next in a muffled voice. He snatched my hand as though he had just then seen it for the first time, and dropped it at once. "Why! this is what I – you – I . . . " he stammered, and then with a return of his old stolid, I may say mulish, manner he began heavily, "I would be a brute now if I . . . " and then his voice seemed to break. "That's all right," I said. I was almost alarmed by this display of feeling, through which pierced a strange elation. I had pulled the string accidentally as it were; I did not fully understand the working of the toy. "I must go now," he said. "Jove! You *have* helped me. Can't sit still. The very thing . . . " He looked at me with puzzled admiration. "The very thing . . . "

'Of course it was the thing. It was ten to one that I had saved him from starvation – of that peculiar sort that is almost invariably associated with drink. This was all. I had not a single illusion on that score, but looking at him, I allowed myself to wonder at the nature of the one he had, within the last three minutes, so evidently taken into his bosom. I had forced into his hands the means to carry on decently the serious business of life, to get food, drink, and shelter of the customary kind while his wounded spirit, like a bird with a broken wing, might hop and flutter into some hole to die quietly of inanition there. This is what I had thrust upon him: a definitely small thing; and – behold! – by the manner of its reception it loomed in the dim light of the candle like a big, indistinct, perhaps a dangerous shadow. "You don't mind me not saying anything appropriate," he burst out. "There isn't anything one could say. Last night already you had done me no end of good. Listening to me – you know. I give you my word I've thought more than once the top of my head would fly off . . . " He darted – positively darted – here and there, rammed his hands into his pockets, jerked them out again, flung his cap on his head. I had no idea it was in him to be so airily brisk. I thought of a dry leaf imprisoned in an eddy of wind, while a mysterious apprehension, a load of indefinite doubt, weighed me down in my chair. He stood stock-still, as if struck motionless by a discovery. "You have given me

confidence," he declared, soberly. "Oh! for God's sake, my dear fellow –
don't!" I entreated, as though he had hurt me. "All right. I'll shut up now
and henceforth. Can't prevent me thinking, though . . . Never mind! . . . I'll
show yet . . . " He went to the door in a hurry, paused with his head down,
and came back, stepping deliberately. "I always thought that if a fellow could
begin with a clean slate . . . And now you . . . in a measure . . . yes . . . clean
slate." I waved my hand, and he marched out without looking back; the sound
of his footfalls died out gradually behind the closed door – the unhesitating
tread of a man walking in broad daylight.

'But as to me, left alone with the solitary candle, I remained strangely
unenlightened. I was no longer young enough to behold at every turn the
magnificence that besets our insignificant footsteps in good and in evil. I
smiled to think that, after all, it was yet he, of us two, who had the light. And
I felt sad. A clean slate, did he say? As if the initial word of each our destiny
were not graven in imperishable characters upon the face of a rock.'

Chapter 18

'Six months afterwards my friend (he was a cynical, more than middle-aged
bachelor, with a reputation for eccentricity, and owned a rice-mill) wrote to
me, and judging, from the warmth of my recommendation, that I would like
to hear, enlarged a little upon Jim's perfections. These were apparently of a
quiet and effective sort. "Not having been able so far to find more in my heart
than a resigned toleration for any individual of my kind, I have lived till now
alone in a house that even in this steaming climate could be considered as too
big for one man. I have had him to live with me for some time past. It seems I
haven't made a mistake." It seemed to me on reading this letter that my friend
had found in his heart more than tolerance for Jim – that there were the
beginnings of active liking. Of course he stated his grounds in a characteristic
way. For one thing, Jim kept his freshness in the climate. Had he been a girl –
my friend wrote – one could have said he was blooming – blooming modestly –
like a violet, not like some of these blatant tropical flowers. He had been in
the house for six weeks, and had not as yet attempted to slap him on the back,
or address him as "old boy," or try to make him feel a superannuated fossil.
He had nothing of the exasperating young man's chatter. He was good-
tempered, had not much to say for himself, was not clever by any means,
thank goodness – wrote my friend. It appeared, however, that Jim was clever
enough to be quietly appreciative of his wit, while, on the other hand, he
amused him by his naïveness. "The dew is yet on him, and since I had the

bright idea of giving him a room in the house and having him at meals I feel less withered myself. The other day he took it into his head to cross the room with no other purpose but to open a door for me; and I felt more in touch with mankind than I had been for years. Ridiculous, isn't it? Of course I guess there is something – some awful little scrape – which you know all about – but if I am sure that it is terribly heinous, I fancy one could manage to forgive it. For my part, I declare I am unable to imagine him guilty of anything much worse than robbing an orchard. Is *it* much worse? Perhaps you ought to have told me; but it is such a long time since we both turned saints that you may have forgotten we, too, had sinned in our time? It may be that someday I shall have to ask you, and then I shall expect to be told. I don't care to question him myself till I have some idea what it is. Moreover, it's too soon as yet. Let him open the door a few times more for me . . . " Thus my friend. I was trebly pleased – at Jim's shaping so well, at the tone of the letter, at my own cleverness. Evidently I had known what I was doing. I had read characters aright, and so on. And what if something unexpected and wonderful were to come of it? That evening, reposing in a deck-chair under the shade of my own poop awning (it was in Hong Kong harbour), I laid on Jim's behalf the first stone of a castle in Spain.

'I made a trip to the northward, and when I returned I found another letter from my friend waiting for me. It was the first envelope I tore open. "There are no spoons missing as far as I know," ran the first line; "I haven't been interested enough to enquire. He is gone, leaving on the breakfast-table a formal little note of apology, which is either silly or heartless. Probably both – and it's all one to me. Allow me to say, lest you should have some more mysterious young men in reserve, that I have shut up shop, definitely and for ever. This is the last eccentricity I shall be guilty of. Do not imagine for a moment that I care a hang; but he is very much regretted at tennis-parties, and for my own sake I've told a plausible lie at the club . . . " I flung the letter aside and started looking through the batch on my table, till I came upon Jim's handwriting. Would you believe it? One chance in a hundred! But it is always that hundredth chance! That little second engineer of the *Patna* had turned up in a more or less destitute state, and got a temporary job of looking after the machinery of the mill. "I couldn't stand the familiarity of the little beast," Jim wrote from a seaport seven hundred miles south of the place where he should have been in clover. "I am now for the time with Egström & Blake, ship-chandlers, as their – well – runner, to call the thing by its right name. For reference I gave them your name, which they know of course, and if you could write a word in my favour it would be a permanent employment." I was utterly crushed under the ruins of my castle, but of course I wrote as desired. Before the end of the year my new charter took me that way, and I had an opportunity of seeing him.

'He was still with Egström & Blake, and we met in what they called "our parlour" opening out of the store. He had that moment come in from boarding a ship, and confronted me head down, ready for a tussle. "What have you got to say for yourself?" I began as soon as we had shaken hands. "What I wrote you – nothing more," he said stubbornly. "Did the fellow blab – or what?" I asked. He looked up at me with a troubled smile. "Oh, no! He didn't. He made it a kind of confidential business between us. He was most damnably mysterious whenever I came over to the mill; he would wink at me in a respectful manner – as much as to say, "We know what we know." Infernally fawning and familiar – and that sort of thing." He threw himself into a chair and stared down his legs. "One day we happened to be alone and the fellow had the cheek to say, 'Well, Mr James' – I was called Mr James there as if I had been the son – 'here we are together once more. This is better than the old ship – ain't it?' . . . Wasn't it appalling, eh? I looked at him, and he put on a knowing air. 'Don't you be uneasy, sir,' he says. 'I know a gentleman when I see one, and I know how a gentleman feels. I hope, though, you will be keeping me on this job. I had a hard time of it, too, along of that rotten old *Patna* racket.' Jove! It was awful. I don't know what I should have said or done if I had not just then heard Mr Denver calling me in the passage. It was tiffin-time, and we walked together across the yard and through the garden to the bungalow. He began to chaff me in his kindly way . . . I believe he liked me . . . "

'Jim was silent for a while.

' "I know he liked me. That's what made it so hard. Such a splendid man! That morning he slipped his hand under my arm . . . He, too, was familiar with me." He burst into a short laugh, and dropped his chin on his breast. "Pah! When I remembered how that mean little beast had been talking to me," he began suddenly in a vibrating voice, "I couldn't bear to think of myself . . . I suppose you know . . . " I nodded . . . "More like a father," he cried; his voice sank. "I would have had to tell him. I couldn't let it go on – could I?" "Well?" I murmured, after waiting a while. "I preferred to go," he said, slowly; "this thing must be buried."

'We could hear in the shop Blake upbraiding Egström in an abusive, strained voice. They had been associated for many years, and every day from the moment the doors were opened to the last minute before closing, Blake, a little man with sleek, jetty hair and unhappy, beady eyes, could be heard rowing his partner incessantly with a sort of scathing and plaintive fury. The sound of that everlasting scolding was part of the place like the other fixtures; even strangers would very soon come to disregard it completely unless it be perhaps to mutter, "Nuisance," or to get up suddenly and shut the door of the "parlour". Egström himself, a rawboned, heavy Scandinavian, with a busy manner and immense blond whiskers, went on directing his people, checking parcels, making out bills or writing letters at a stand-up desk in the shop, and comported himself in that clatter exactly as though he had been stone-deaf. Now and again he would emit a bothered perfunctory, "Sssh," which neither produced nor was expected to produce the slightest effect. "They are very

decent to me here," said Jim. "Blake's a little cad, but Egström's all right."
He stood up quickly, and walking with measured steps to a tripod telescope
standing in the window and pointed at the roadstead, he applied his eye to
it. "There's that ship which had been becalmed outside all the morning. It
has got a breeze now and is coming in," he remarked, patiently; "I must go
and board." We shook hands in silence, and he turned to go. "Jim!" I cried.
He looked round with his hand on the lock. "You – you have thrown away
something like a fortune." He came back to me all the way from the door.
"Such a splendid old chap," he said. "How could I? How could I?" His lips
twitched. "*Here* it does not matter." "Oh! you – you" I began, and had to
cast about for a suitable word, but before I became aware that there was no
name that would just do, he was gone. I heard outside Egström's deep
gentle voice saying cheerily, "That's the *Sarah W. Granger*, Jimmy. You
must manage to be first aboard;" and directly Blake struck in, screaming
after the manner of an outraged cockatoo, "Tell the captain we've got some
of his mail here. That'll fetch him. D'ye hear, Mister What's-your-name?"
And there was Jim answering Egström with something boyish in his tone.
"All right. I'll make a race of it." He seemed to take refuge in the boat-
sailing part of that sorry business.

"I did not see him again that trip, but on my next (I had a six months'
charter) I went up to the store. Ten yards away from the door Blake's scolding
met my ears, and when I came in he gave me a glance of utter wretchedness;
Egström, all smiles, advanced, extending a large bony hand. "Glad to see you,
captain . . . Ssssh . . . Been thinking you were about due back here. What
did you say, sir? . . . Ssssh . . . Oh! him! He has left us. Come into the
parlour." . . . After the slam of the door Blake's strained voice became faint, as
the voice of one scolding desperately in a wilderness . . . "Put us to a great
inconvenience, too. Used us badly, I must say . . . " "Where's he gone to? Do
you know?" I asked. "No. It's no use asking either," said Egström, standing
bewhiskered and obliging before me with his arms hanging down his sides
clumsily and a thin silver watch-chain looped very low on a rucked-up blue
serge waistcoat. "A man like that don't go anywhere in particular." I was too
concerned at the news to ask for the explanation of that pronouncement, and
he went on. "He left – let's see – the very day a steamer with returning pilgrims
from the Red Sea put in here with two blades of her propeller gone. Three
weeks ago now." "Wasn't there something said about the *Patna* case?" I asked,
fearing the worst. He gave a start, and looked at me as if I had been a sorcerer.
"Why, yes! How do you know? Some of them were talking about it here.
There was a captain or two, the manager of Vanlo's engineering shop at the
harbour, two or three others, and myself. Jim was in here, too, having a
sandwich and a glass of beer; when we are busy – you see, captain – there's no
time for a proper tiffin. He was standing by this table eating sandwiches, and
the rest of us were round the telescope watching that steamer come in; and by
and by Vanlo's manager began to talk about the chief of the *Patna*; he had

done some repairs for him once, and from that he went on to tell us what an old ruin she was, and the money that had been made out of her. He came to mention her last voyage, and then we all struck in. Some said one thing and some another – not much – what you or any other man might say; and there was some laughing. Captain O'Brien of the *Sarah W. Granger*, a large, noisy old man with a stick – he was sitting listening to us in this armchair here – he let drive suddenly with his stick at the floor, and roars out, 'Skunks!' . . . Made us all jump. Vanlo's manager winks at us and asks, 'What's the matter, Captain O'Brien?' 'Matter! matter!' the old man began to shout; 'what are you Injuns laughing at? It's no laughing matter. It's a disgrace to human natur' – that's what it is. I would despise being seen in the same room with one of those men. Yes, sir!' He seemed to catch my eye like, and I had to speak out of civility. 'Skunks!' says I, 'of course, Captain O'Brien, and I wouldn't care to have them here myself, so you're quite safe in this room, Captain O'Brien. Have a little something cool to drink.' 'Damn your drink, Egström,' says he, with a twinkle in his eye; 'when I want a drink I will shout for it. I am going to quit. It stinks here now.' At this all the others burst out laughing, and out they go after the old man. And then, sir, that blasted Jim he puts down the sandwich he had in his hand and walks round the table to me; there was his glass of beer poured out quite full. 'I'm off,' he says just like this. 'It isn't half-past one yet' says I; 'you might snatch a smoke first.' I thought he meant it was time for him to go down to his work. When I understood what he was up to, my arms fell – so! Can't get a man like that every day, you know, sir; a regular devil for sailing a boat; ready to go out miles to sea to meet ships in any sort of weather. More than once a captain would come in here full of it, and the first thing he would say would be, 'That's a reckless sort of a lunatic you've got for a water-clerk, Egström. I was feeling my way in at daylight under short canvas when there comes flying out of the mist right under my forefoot a boat half under water, sprays going over the masthead, two frightened niggers on the bottom boards, a yelling fiend at the tiller. Hey! hey! Ship ahoy! ahoy! Captain! Hey! hey! Egström & Blake's man first to speak to you! Hey! hey! Egström & Blake! Hallo! hey! whoop! Kick the niggers – out reefs – a squall on at the time – shoots ahead whooping and yelling to me to make sail and he would give me a lead in – more like a demon than a man. Never saw a boat handled like that in all my life. Couldn't have been drunk – was he? Such a quiet, soft-spoken chap, too – blushed like a girl when he came on board . . . I tell you, Captain Marlow, nobody had a chance against us with a strange ship when Jim was out. The other ship-chandlers just kept their old customers, and . . . "

'Egström appeared overcome with emotion.

' "Why, sir – it seemed as though he wouldn't mind going a hundred miles out to sea in an old shoe to nab a ship for the firm. If the business had been his own and all to make yet, he couldn't have done more in that way. And now . . . all at once . . . like this! Thinks I to myself: 'Oho! a rise in the screw – that's the trouble – is it? All right' says I, 'no need of all that fuss with me, Jimmy. Just mention your figure. Anything in reason.' He looks at me as if he wanted to swallow something that stuck in his throat. 'I can't stop with you.' 'What's that blooming joke?' I asks. He shakes his head, and I could see in his eye he was as good as gone already, sir. So I turned to him and slanged him till all was blue. 'What is it you're running away from?' I asks. 'Who has been getting at you? What scared you? You haven't as much sense as a rat; they don't clear out from a good ship. Where do you expect to get a better berth? – you this and you that.' I made him look sick, I can tell you. 'This business ain't going to sink,' says I. He gave a big jump. 'Goodbye,' he says, nodding at me like a lord; 'you ain't half a bad chap, Egström. I give you my word that if you knew my reasons you wouldn't care to keep me.' 'That's the biggest lie you ever told in your life,' says I; 'I know my own mind.' He made me so mad that I had to laugh. 'Can't you really stop long enough to drink this glass of beer here, you funny beggar, you?' I don't know what came over him; he didn't seem able to find the door; something comical, I can tell you, captain. I drank the beer myself. 'Well, if you're in such a hurry, here's luck to you in your own drink,' says I; 'only, you mark my words, if you keep up this game you'll very soon find that the earth ain't big enough to hold you – that's all.' He gave me one black look, and out he rushed with a face fit to scare little children."

'Egström snorted bitterly, and combed one auburn whisker with knotty fingers. "Haven't been able to get a man that was any good since. It's nothing but worry, worry, worry in business. And where might you have come across him, captain, if it's fair to ask?"

' "He was the mate of the *Patna* that voyage," I said, feeling that I owed some explanation. For a time Egström remained very still, with his fingers plunged in the hair at the side of his face, and then exploded. "And who the devil cares about that?" "I dare say no one," I began . . . "And what the devil is he – anyhow – for to go on like this?" He stuffed suddenly his left whisker into his mouth and stood amazed. "Jee!" he exclaimed, "I told him the earth wouldn't be big enough to hold his caper." '

Chapter 19

'I have told you these two episodes at length to show his manner of dealing with himself under the new conditions of his life. There were many others of the sort, more than I could count on the fingers of my two hands.

'They were all equally tinged by a high-minded absurdity of intention which made their futility profound and touching. To fling away your daily bread so as to get your hands free for a grapple with a ghost may be an act of prosaic heroism. Men had done it before (though we who have lived know full well that it is not the haunted soul but the hungry body that makes an outcast), and men who had eaten and meant to eat every day had applauded the creditable folly. He was indeed unfortunate, for all his recklessness could not carry him out from under the shadow. There was always a doubt of his courage. The truth seems to be that it is impossible to lay the ghost of a fact. You can face it or shirk it – and I have come across a man or two who could wink at their familiar shades. Obviously Jim was not of the winking sort; but what I could never make up my mind about was whether his line of conduct amounted to shirking his ghost or to facing him out.

'I strained my mental eyesight only to discover that, as with the complexion of all our actions, the shade of difference was so delicate that it was impossible to say. It might have been flight and it might have been a mode of combat. To the common mind he became known as a rolling stone, because this was the funniest part; he did after a time become perfectly known, and even notorious, within the circle of his wanderings (which had a diameter of, say, three thousand miles), in the same way as an eccentric character is known to a whole countryside. For instance, in Bangkok, where he found employment with Yucker Brothers, charterers and teak merchants, it was almost pathetic to see him go about in sunshine hugging his secret, which was known to the very up-country logs on the river. Schomberg, the keeper of the hotel where he boarded, a hirsute Alsatian of manly bearing and an irrepressible retailer of all the scandalous gossip of the place, would, with both elbows on the table, impart an adorned version of the story to any guest who cared to imbibe knowledge along with the more costly liquors. "And, mind you, the nicest fellow you could meet," would be his generous conclusion; "quite superior." It says a lot for the casual crowd that frequented Schomberg's establishment that Jim managed to hang out in Bangkok for a whole six months. I remarked that people, perfect strangers, took to him as one takes to a nice child. His manner was reserved, but it was as though his personal appearance, his hair, his eyes, his smile, made friends for him wherever he went. And, of course, he was no fool. I heard Siegmund Yucker (native of Switzerland), a gentle creature ravaged by a cruel dyspepsia, and so frightfully lame that his head swung through a quarter of a circle at every step he took, declare appreciatively that for one so young he was "of great gabasidy," as though it had been a mere question of cubic contents. "Why not send him up country?" I suggested anxiously. (Yucker Brothers had concessions and teak forests in the interior.) "If he has capacity, as you say, he will soon get hold of the work. And physically he is very fit. His health is always excellent." "Ach! It's a great ting in dis goundry to be vree vrom tispepshia," sighed poor Yucker enviously, casting a stealthy glance at the pit of his ruined stomach. I left him drumming pensively on his desk and muttering, *Es ist ein Idee. Es ist ein Idee.* Unfortunately, that very evening an unpleasant affair took place in the hotel.

'I don't know that I blame Jim very much, but it was a truly regrettable incident. It belonged to the lamentable species of bar-room scuffles, and the other party to it was a cross-eyed Dane of sorts whose visiting card recited under his misbegotten name: first lieutenant in the Royal Siamese Navy. The fellow, of course, was utterly hopeless at billiards, but did not like to be beaten, I suppose. He had had enough to drink to turn nasty after the sixth game, and make some scornful remark at Jim's expense. Most of the people there didn't hear what was said, and those who had heard seemed to have had all precise recollection scared out of them by the appalling nature of the consequences that immediately ensued. It was very lucky for the Dane that he could swim, because the room opened on a veranda and the Menam flowed below very wide and black. A boat-load of Chinamen, bound, as likely as not, on some thieving expedition, fished out the officer of the King of Siam, and Jim turned up at about midnight on board my ship without a hat. "Everybody in the room seemed to know," he said, gasping yet from the contest, as it were. He was rather sorry, on general principles, for what had happened, though in this case there had been, he said, "no option." But what dismayed him was to find the nature of his burden as well known to everybody as though he had gone about all that time carrying it on his shoulders. Naturally after this he couldn't remain in the place. He was universally condemned for the brutal violence, so unbecoming a man in his delicate position; some maintained he had been disgracefully drunk at the time; others criticised his want of tact. Even Schomberg was very much annoyed. "He is a very nice young man," he said, argumentatively, to me, "but the lieutenant is a first-rate fellow, too. He dines every night at my table d'hôte, you know. And there's a billiard-cue broken. I can't allow that. First thing this morning I went over with my apologies to the lieutenant, and I think I've made it all right for myself; but only think, captain, if everybody started such games! Why, the man might have been drowned! And here I can't run out into the next street and buy a new cue. I've got to write to Europe for them. No, no! A temper like that won't do!" . . . He was extremely sore on the subject.

'This was the worst incident of all in his – his retreat. Nobody could deplore it more than myself; for if, as somebody said hearing him mentioned, "Oh, yes! I know. He has knocked about a good deal out here," yet he had somehow avoided being battered and chipped in the process. This last affair, however, made me seriously uneasy, because if his exquisite sensibilities were to go the length of involving him in pot-house shindies, he would lose his name of an inoffensive, if aggravating fool, and acquire that of a common loafer. For all my confidence in him I could not help reflecting that in such cases from the name to the thing itself is but a step. I suppose you will understand that by that time I could not think of washing my hands of him. I took him away from Bangkok in my ship, and we had a longish passage. It was pitiful to see how he shrank within himself. A seaman, even if a mere passenger, takes an interest in a ship, and looks at the sea-life around him with the critical enjoyment of a painter, for instance, looking at another man's work. In every sense of the expression he is "on deck," but my Jim, for the most part, skulked down below as though he had been a stowaway. He infected me so that I avoided speaking on professional matters, such as would suggest themselves naturally to two sailors during a passage. For whole days we did not exchange a word; I felt extremely unwilling to give orders to my officers in his presence. Often, when alone with him on deck or in the cabin, we didn't know what to do with our eyes.

'I placed him with De Jongh, as you know, glad enough to dispose of him in any way, yet persuaded that his position was now growing intolerable. He had lost some of that elasticity which had enabled him to rebound back into his uncompromising position after every overthrow. One day, coming ashore, I saw him standing on the quay; the water of the roadstead and the sea in the offing made one smooth ascending plane, and the outermost ships at anchor seemed to ride motionless in the sky. He was waiting for his boat, which was being loaded at our feet with packages of small stores for some vessel ready to leave. After exchanging greetings, we remained silent – side by side. "Jove!" he said, suddenly, "this is killing work."

'He smiled at me; I must say he generally could manage a smile. I made no reply. I knew very well he was not alluding to his duties; he had an easy time of it with De Jongh. Nevertheless, as soon as he had spoken I became completely convinced that the work was killing. I did not even look at him. "Would you like," said I, "to leave this part of the world altogether; try California or the West Coast? I'll see what I can do . . . " He interrupted me a little scornfully. "What difference would it make?" . . . I felt at once convinced that he was right. It would make no difference; it was not relief he wanted; I seemed to perceive dimly that what he wanted, what he was, as it were, waiting for, was something not easy to define – something in the nature of an opportunity. I had given him many opportunities, but they had been merely opportunities to earn his bread. Yet what more could any man do. The position struck me as hopeless, and poor Brierly's saying recurred to me: "Let him creep twenty feet underground and stay there." Better that, I thought, than this waiting above ground for the impossible. Yet one could not be sure even of that. There and then, before his boat was three oars' lengths away from the quay, I had made up my mind to go and consult Stein in the evening.

'This Stein was a wealthy and respected merchant. His "house" (because it was a house, Stein & Co., and there was some sort of partner who, as Stein said, "looked after the Moluccas") had a large inter-island business, with a lot of trading posts established in the most out-of-the-way places for collecting the produce. His wealth and his respectability were not exactly the reasons why I was anxious to seek his advice. I desired to confide my difficulty to him because he was one of the most trustworthy men I had ever known. The gentle light of a simple unwearied, as it were, and intelligent good-nature illumined his long hairless face. It had deep downward folds, and was pale as of a man who had always led a sedentary life – which was indeed very far from being the case. His hair was thin, and brushed back from a massive and lofty forehead. One fancied that at twenty he must have looked very much like what he was now at threescore. It was a student's face; only the eyebrows nearly all white, thick and bushy, together with the resolute searching glance that came from under them, were not in accord with his, I may say, learned appearance. He was tall and loose-jointed; his slight stoop, together with an innocent smile, made him appear benevolently ready to lend you his ear; his long arms with pale big hands had rare deliberate gestures of a pointing out, demonstrating kind. I speak of him at length, because under this exterior, and in conjunction with an upright and indulgent nature, this man possessed an intrepidity of spirit and a physical courage that could have been called reckless had it not been like a natural function of the body – say good digestion, for instance – completely unconscious of itself. It is sometimes said of a man that he carries his life in his hand. Such a saying would have been inadequate if applied to him; during the early part of his existence in the East he had been playing ball with it. All this was in the past, but I knew the story of his life and the origin of his fortune. He was also a naturalist of some distinction, or perhaps I should say a learned collector. Entomology was his special study. His collection of *Buprestidae* and *Longicornes* – beetles all – horrible miniature monsters, looking malevolent in death and immobility, and his cabinet of butterflies, beautiful and hovering under the glass of cases of lifeless wings, had spread his fame far over the earth. The name of this merchant, adventurer, sometime adviser of a Malay sultan (to whom he never alluded otherwise than as "my poor Mohammed Bonso"), had, on account of a few bushels of dead insects, become known to learned persons in Europe, who could have had no conception, and certainly would not have cared to know anything, of his life or character. I, who knew, considered him an eminently suitable person to receive my confidences about Jim's difficulties as well as my own.'

Chapter 20

'Late in the evening I entered his study, after traversing an imposing but empty dining-room very dimly lit. The house was silent. I was preceded by an elderly grim Javanese servant in a sort of livery of white jacket and yellow sarong, who, after throwing the door open, exclaimed low: "Oh, master!" and stepping aside, vanished in a mysterious way as though he had been a ghost only momentarily embodied for that particular service. Stein turned round with the chair, and in the same movement his spectacles seemed to get pushed up on his forehead. He welcomed me in his quiet and humorous voice. Only one corner of the vast room, the corner in which stood his writing-desk, was strongly lighted by a shaded reading-lamp, and the rest of the spacious apartment melted into shapeless gloom like a cavern. Narrow shelves filled with dark boxes of uniform shape and colour ran round the walls, not from floor to ceiling, but in a sombre belt about four feet broad. Catacombs of beetles. Wooden tablets were hung above at irregular intervals. The light reached one of them, and the word *Coleoptera* written in gold letters glittered mysteriously upon a vast dimness. The glass cases containing the collection of butterflies were ranged in three long rows upon slender-legged little tables. One of these cases had been removed from its place and stood on the desk, which was bestrewn with oblong slips of paper blackened with minute handwriting.

' "So you see me – so," he said. His hand hovered over the case where a butterfly in solitary grandeur spread out dark bronze wings, seven inches or more across, with exquisite white veinings and a gorgeous border of yellow spots. "Only one specimen like this they have in *your* London, and then – no more. To my small native town this my collection I shall bequeath. Something of me. The best."

'He bent forward in the chair and gazed intently, his chin over the front of the case. I stood at his back. "Marvellous," he whispered, and seemed to forget my presence. His history was curious. He had been born in Bavaria, and when a youth of twenty-two had taken an active part in the revolutionary movement of 1848. Heavily compromised, he managed to make his escape, and at first found a refuge with a poor republican watchmaker in Trieste. From there he made his way to Tripoli with a stock of cheap watches to hawk about – not a very great opening truly, but it turned out lucky enough because it was there he came upon a Dutch traveller – a rather famous man, I believe, but I don't remember his name. It was that naturalist who, engaging him as a sort of assistant, took him to the East. They travelled in the Archipelago together and separately, collecting insects and birds, for four years or more. Then the naturalist went home, and Stein, having no home to go to, remained with an old trader he had come across in his journeys in the interior of Celebes – if Celebes may be said to have an interior. This old Scotsman, the only white man allowed to reside in the country at the time, was a privileged friend of the chief ruler of Wajo States, who was a woman. I often heard Stein relate how that chap, who was slightly paralysed on one side, had introduced him to the native court a short time before another stroke carried him off. He was a heavy man with a patriarchal white beard, and of imposing stature. He came into the council-hall where all the rajahs, pangerans, and headmen were assembled, with the queen, a fat wrinkled woman (very free in her speech, Stein said), reclining on a high couch under a canopy. He dragged his leg, thumping with his stick, and grasped Stein's arm, leading him right up to the couch. "Look, queen, and you rajahs, this is my son," he proclaimed in a stentorian voice. "I have traded with your fathers, and when I die he shall trade with you and your sons."

'By means of this simple formality Stein inherited the Scotsman's privileged position and all his stock-in-trade, together with a fortified house on the banks of the only navigable river in the country. Shortly afterwards the old queen, who was so free in her speech, died, and the country became disturbed by various pretenders to the throne. Stein joined the party of a younger son, the one of whom thirty years later he never spoke otherwise but as "my poor Mohammed Bonso." They both became the heroes of innumerable exploits; they had wonderful adventures, and once stood a siege in the Scotsman's house for a month, with only a score of followers against a whole army. I believe the natives talk of that war to this day. Meantime, it seems, Stein never failed to annex on his own account every butterfly or beetle he could lay hands on. After some eight years of war, negotiations, false truces, sudden outbreaks, reconciliation, treachery, and so on, and just as peace seemed at last permanently established, his "poor Mohammed Bonso" was assassinated at the gate of his own royal residence while dismounting in the highest spirits on his return from a successful deer-hunt. This event rendered Stein's position extremely insecure, but he would have stayed perhaps had it not been that a short time afterwards he lost Mohammed's sister ("my dear wife the princess," he used to say solemnly), by whom he had had a daughter – mother and child both dying within three days of each other from some infectious fever. He left the country, which this loss had made unbearable to him. Thus ended the first and adventurous part of his existence. What followed was so different that, but for the reality of sorrow which remained with him, this strange part must have resembled a dream. He had a little money; he started life afresh, and in the course of years acquired a considerable fortune. At first he had travelled a good deal amongst the islands, but age had stolen upon him, and of late he seldom left his spacious house three miles out of town, with an extensive garden, and surrounded by stables, offices, and bamboo cottages for his servants and dependants, of whom he had many. He drove in his buggy every morning to town, where he had an office with white and Chinese clerks. He owned a small fleet of schooners and native craft, and dealt in island produce on a large scale. For the rest he lived solitary, but not misanthropic, with his books and his collection, classing and arranging specimens, corresponding with entomologists in Europe, writing up a descriptive catalogue of his treasures. Such was the history of the man whom I had come to consult upon Jim's case without any definite hope. Simply to hear what he would have to say would have been a relief. I was very anxious, but I respected the intense, almost passionate, absorption with which he looked at a butterfly, as though on the bronze sheen of these frail wings, in the white tracings, in the gorgeous markings, he could see other things, an image of something as perishable and defying destruction as these delicate and lifeless tissues displaying a splendour unmarred by death.

' "Marvellous!" he repeated, looking up at me. "Look! The beauty – but that is nothing – look at the accuracy, the harmony. And so fragile! And so strong! And so exact! This is Nature – the balance of colossal forces. Every star is so – and every blade of grass stands *so* – and the mighty Kosmos in perfect equilibrium produces – this. This wonder; this masterpiece of Nature – the great artist."

' "Never heard an entomologist go on like this," I observed, cheerfully. "Masterpiece! And what of man?"

' "Man is amazing, but he is not a masterpiece," he said, keeping his eyes fixed on the glass case. "Perhaps the artist was a little mad. Eh? What do you think? Sometimes it seems to me that man is come where he is not wanted, where there is no place for him; for if not, why should he want all the place? Why should he run about here and there making a great noise about himself, talking about the stars, disturbing the blades of grass? . . . "

' "Catching butterflies," I chimed in.

'He smiled, threw himself back in his chair, and stretched his legs. "Sit down," he said. "I captured this rare specimen myself one very fine morning. And I had a very big emotion. You don't know what it is for a collector to capture such a rare specimen. You can't know."

'I smiled at my ease in a rocking-chair. His eyes seemed to look far beyond the wall at which they stared; and he narrated how, one night, a messenger arrived from his "poor Mohammed," requiring his presence at the "residenz" – as he called it – which was distant some nine or ten miles by a bridle-path over a cultivated plain, with patches of forest here and there. Early in the morning he started from his fortified house, after embracing his little Emma, and leaving the "princess," his wife, in command. He described how she came with him as far as the gate, walking with one hand on the neck of his horse; she had on a white jacket, gold pins in her hair, and a brown leather belt over her left shoulder with a revolver in it. "She talked as women will talk," he said, "telling me to be careful, and to try to get back before dark, and what a great wickedness it was for me to go alone. We were at war, and the country was not safe; my men were putting up bullet-proof shutters to the house and loading their rifles, and she begged me to have no fear for her. She could defend the house against anybody till I returned. And I laughed with pleasure a little. I liked to see her so brave and young and strong. I, too, was young then. At the gate she caught hold of my hand and gave it one squeeze and fell back. I made my horse stand still outside till I heard the bars of the gate put up behind me. There was a great enemy of mine, a great noble – and a great rascal, too – roaming with a band in the neighbourhood. I cantered for four or five miles; there had been rain in the night, but the mists had gone up, up – and the face of the earth was clean; it lay smiling to me, so fresh and innocent – like a little child. Suddenly somebody fires a volley – twenty shots at least it seemed to me. I hear bullets sing in my ear, and my hat jumps to the back of my head. It was a little intrigue, you understand. They got my poor Mohammed to send for me and then laid that ambush. I see it all in a minute, and I think: This wants a little management. My pony snort, jump, and stand, and I fall slowly forward with my head on his mane. He begins to walk, and with one eye I could see over his neck a faint cloud of smoke hanging in front of a clump of bamboos to my left. I think: Aha! my friends, why you not wait long enough before you shoot? This is not yet *gelungen*. Oh, no! I get hold of my revolver with my right hand – quiet – quiet. After all, there were only seven of these rascals. They get up from the grass and start running with their sarongs tucked up, waving spears above their heads and yelling to each other to look out and catch the horse, because I was dead. I let them come as close as the door here, and then bang, bang, bang – take aim each time, too. One more shot I fire at a man's back, but I miss. Too far already. And then I sit alone on my horse with the clean earth smiling at me, and there are the bodies of three men lying on the ground. One was curled up like a dog, another on his back had an arm over his eyes as if to keep off the sun, and the third man he draws up his leg very slowly and makes it with one kick straight again. I watch him very carefully from my horse, but there is no more – *bleibt ganz ruhig* – keep still, so. And as I looked at his face for some sign of life I observed something like a faint shadow pass over his forehead. It was the shadow of this butterfly. Look at the form of the wing. This species fly high with a strong flight. I raised my eyes and I saw him fluttering away. I think: Can it be possible? And then I lost him. I dismounted and went on very slow, leading my horse and holding my revolver with one hand and my eyes darting up and down and right and left, everywhere! At last I saw him sitting on a small heap of dirt ten feet away. At once my heart began to beat quick. I let go my horse, keep my revolver in one hand, and with the other snatch my soft felt hat off my head. One step. Steady. Another step. Flop! I got him! When I got up I shook like a leaf with excitement, and when I opened these beautiful wings and made sure what a rare and so extraordinary perfect specimen I had, my head went round and my legs became so weak with emotion that I had to sit on the ground. I had greatly desired to possess myself of a specimen of that species when collecting for the professor. I took long journeys and underwent great privations; I had dreamed of him in my sleep, and here suddenly I had him in my fingers – for myself! In the words of the poet' (he pronounced it 'boet'):

' "So halt' ich's endlich denn in meinen Händen,
        Und nenn' es in gewissem Sinne mein."

'He gave to the last word the emphasis of a suddenly lowered voice, and withdrew his eyes slowly from my face. He began to charge a long-stemmed pipe busily and in silence, then, pausing with his thumb on the orifice of the bowl, looked again at me significantly.

' "Yes, my good friend. On that day I had nothing to desire; I had greatly annoyed my principal enemy; I was young, strong; I had friendship, I had the love" (he said "lof") "of woman, a child I had, to make my heart very full – and even what I had once dreamed in my sleep had come into my hand, too!"

'He struck a match, which flared violently. His thoughtful placid face twitched once.

' "Friend, wife, child," he said, slowly, gazing at the small flame – "phoo!" The match was blown out. He sighed and turned again to the glass case. The frail and beautiful wings quivered faintly, as if his breath had for an instant called back to life that gorgeous object of his dreams.

' "The work," he began, suddenly, pointing to the scattered slips, and in his usual gentle and cheery tone, "is making great progress. I have been this rare specimen describing . . . *Na!* And what is your good news?"

' "To tell you the truth, Stein," I said with an effort that surprised me, "I came here to describe a specimen . . . "

' "Butterfly?" he asked, with an unbelieving and humorous eagerness.

' "Nothing so perfect," I answered, feeling suddenly dispirited with all sorts of doubts. "A man!"

' "*Ach so!*" he murmured, and his smiling countenance, turned to me, became grave. Then after looking at me for a while he said slowly, "Well – I am a man, too."

'Here you have him as he was; he knew how to be so generously encouraging as to make a scrupulous man hesitate on the brink of confidence; but if I did hesitate it was not for long.

'He heard me out, sitting with crossed legs. Sometimes his head would disappear completely in a great eruption of smoke, and a sympathetic growl would come out from the cloud. When I finished he uncrossed his legs, laid down his pipe, leaned forward towards me earnestly with his elbows on the arms of his chair, the tips of his fingers together.

' "I understand very well. He is romantic."

'He had diagnosed the case for me, and at first I was quite startled to find how simple it was; and indeed our conference resembled so much a medical consultation – Stein, of learned aspect, sitting in an armchair before his desk; I, anxious, in another, facing him, but a little to one side – that it seemed natural to ask: "What's good for it?"

'He lifted up a long forefinger.

' "There is only one remedy! One thing alone can us from being ourselves cure!" The finger came down on the desk with a smart rap. The case which he had made to look so simple before became if possible still simpler – and altogether hopeless. There was a pause. "Yes," said I, "strictly speaking, the question is not how to get cured, but how to live."

'He approved with his head, a little sadly as it seemed. "*Ja! ja!* In general, adapting the words of your great poet: That is the question . . ." He went on nodding sympathetically . . . "How to be! *Ach!* How to be!"

'He stood up with the tips of his fingers resting on the desk. "We want in so many different ways to be," he began again. "This magnificent butterfly finds a little heap of dirt and sits still on it; but man he will never on his heap of mud keep still. He want to be so, and again he want to be so . . . " He moved his hand up, then down . . . "He wants to be a saint, and he wants to be a devil – and every time he shuts his eyes he sees himself as a very fine fellow – so fine as he can never be . . . In a dream . . . "

'He lowered the glass lid, the automatic lock clicked sharply, and taking up the case in both hands he bore it religiously away to its place, passing out of the bright circle of the lamp into the ring of fainter light – into shapeless dusk at last. It had an odd effect – as if these few steps had carried him out of this concrete and perplexed world. His tall form, as though robbed of its substance, hovered noiselessly over invisible things with stooping and in-definite movements; his voice, heard in that remoteness where he could be glimpsed mysteriously busy with immaterial cares, was no longer incisive, seemed to roll voluminous and grave – mellowed by distance.

' "And because you not always can keep your eyes shut there comes the real trouble – the heart pain – the world pain. I tell you, my friend, it is not good for you to find you cannot make your dream come true, for the reason that you not strong enough are, or not clever enough. *Ja!* . . . And all the time you are such a fine fellow, too! *Wie? Was? Gott in Himmel!* How can that be? Ha! ha! ha!"

'The shadow prowling amongst the graves of butterflies laughed boister-ously.

' "Yes! Very funny this terrible thing is. A man that is born falls into a dream like a man who falls into the sea. If he tries to climb out into the air as inexperienced people endeavour to do, he drowns – *nicht wahr?* . . . No! I tell you! The way is to the destructive element submit yourself, and with the exertions of your hands and feet in the water make the deep, deep sea keep you up. So if you ask me – how to be?"

'His voice leaped up extraordinarily strong, as though away there in the dusk he had been inspired by some whisper of knowledge. "I will tell you! For that, too, there is only one way."

'With a hasty swish-swish of his slippers he loomed up in the ring of faint light, and suddenly appeared in the bright circle of the lamp. His extended hand aimed at my breast like a pistol; his deep-set eyes seemed to pierce through me, but his twitching lips uttered no word, and the austere exaltation of a certitude seen in the dusk vanished from his face. The hand that had been pointing at my breast fell, and by and by, coming a step nearer, he laid it gently on my shoulder. There were things, he said mournfully, that perhaps could never be told, only he had lived so much alone that sometimes he forgot – he forgot. The light had destroyed the assurance which had inspired him in the distant shadows. He sat down and, with both elbows on the desk, rubbed his forehead. "And yet it is true – it is true. In the destructive element immerse." . . . He spoke in a subdued tone, without looking at me, one hand on each side of his face. "That was the way. To follow the dream, and again to follow the dream – and so – *ewig* – *usque ad finem* . . . " The whisper of his conviction seemed to open before me a vast and uncertain expanse, as of a crepuscular horizon on a plain at dawn – or was it, perchance, at the coming of the night? One had not the courage to decide; but it was a charming and deceptive light, throwing the impalpable poesy of its dimness over pitfalls – over graves. His life had begun in sacrifice in enthusiasm for generous ideas; he had travelled very far, on various ways, on strange paths, and whatever he followed it had been without faltering, and therefore without shame and without regret. In so far he was right. That was the way no doubt. Yet for all that the great plain on which men wander amongst graves and pitfalls remained very desolate under the impalpable poesy of its crepuscular light, overshadowed in the centre, circled with a bright edge as if surrounded by an abyss full of flames. When at last I broke the silence it was to express the opinion that no one could be more romantic than himself.

'He shook his head slowly, and afterwards looked at me with a patient and enquiring glance. It was a shame, he said. There we were sitting and talking like two boys, instead of putting our heads together to find something practical – a practical remedy – for the evil – for the great evil – he repeated, with a humorous and indulgent smile. For all that, our talk did not grow more practical. We avoided pronouncing Jim's name as though we had tried to keep flesh and blood out of our discussion, or he were nothing but an erring spirit, a suffering and nameless shade. "*Na!*" said Stein, rising. "Tonight you sleep here, and in the morning we shall do something practical – practical . . . " He lit a two-branched candlestick and led the way. We passed through empty dark rooms, escorted by gleams from the lights Stein carried. They glided along the waxed floors, sweeping here and there over the polished surface of the table, leaped upon a fragmentary curve of a piece of furniture, or flashed perpendicularly in and out of distant mirrors, while the forms of two men and the flicker of two flames could be seen for a moment stealing silently across the depths of a crystalline void. He walked slowly a pace in advance with stooping courtesy, there was a profound, as it were a listening, quietude on his face; the long flaxen locks mixed with white threads were scattered thinly upon his slightly bowed neck.

' "He is romantic – romantic," he repeated. "And that is very bad – very bad . . . Very good, too," he added. "But *is he?*" I queried.

' "*Gewiss*," he said, and stood still holding up the candelabrum, but without looking at me. "Evident! What is it that by inward pain makes him know himself? What is it that for you and me makes him – exist?"

'At that moment it was difficult to believe in Jim's existence – starting from a country parsonage, blurred by crowds of men as by clouds of dust, silenced by the clashing claims of life and death in a material world – but his imperishable reality came to me with a convincing, with an irresistible force! I saw it vividly, as though in our progress through the lofty silent rooms amongst fleeting gleams of light and the sudden revelations of human figures stealing with flickering flames within unfathomable and pellucid depths, we had approached nearer to absolute Truth, which, like Beauty itself, floats elusive, obscure, half submerged, in the silent still waters of mystery. "Perhaps he is," I admitted with a slight laugh, whose unexpectedly loud reverberation made me lower my voice directly; "but I am sure you are." With his head dropping on his breast and the light held high he began to walk again. "Well – I exist, too," he said.

'He preceded me. My eyes followed his movements, but what I did see was not the head of the firm, the welcome guest at afternoon receptions, the correspondent of learned societies, the entertainer of stray naturalists; I saw only the reality of his destiny, which he had known how to follow with unfaltering footsteps, that life begun in humble surroundings, rich in generous enthusiasms, in friendship, love, war – in all the exalted elements of romance. At the door of my room he faced me. "Yes," I said, as though carrying on a discussion, "and amongst other things you dreamed foolishly of a certain butterfly; but when one fine morning your dream came in your way you did not let the splendid opportunity escape. Did you? Whereas he . . ." Stein lifted his hand. "And do you know how many opportunities I let escape; how many dreams I had lost that had come in my way?" He shook his head regretfully. "It seems to me that some would have been very fine – if I had made them come true. Do you know how many? Perhaps I myself don't know." "Whether his were fine or not," I said, "he knows of one which he certainly did not catch." "Everybody knows of one or two like that," said Stein; "and that is the trouble – the great trouble . . . "

'He shook hands on the threshold, peered into my room under his raised arm. "Sleep well. And tomorrow we must do something practical – practical . . . "

'Though his own room was beyond mine I saw him return the way he came. He was going back to his butterflies.'

Chapter 21

'I don't suppose any of you had ever heard of Patusan?' Marlow resumed, after a silence occupied in the careful lighting of a cigar. 'It does not matter; there's many a heavenly body in the lot crowding upon us of a night that mankind had never heard of, it being outside the sphere of its activities and of no earthly importance to anybody but to the astronomers who are paid to talk learnedly about its composition, weight, path – the irregularities of its conduct, the aberrations of its light – a sort of scientific scandal-mongering. Thus with Patusan. It was referred to knowingly in the inner government circles in Batavia, especially as to its irregularities and aberrations, and it was known by name to some few, very few, in the mercantile world. Nobody, however, had been there, and I suspect no one desired to go there in person, just as an astronomer, I should fancy, would strongly object to being transported into a distant heavenly body, where, parted from his earthly emoluments, he would be bewildered by the view of an unfamiliar heavens. However, neither heavenly bodies nor astronomers have anything to do with Patusan. It was Jim who went there. I only meant you to understand that had Stein arranged to send him into a star of the fifth magnitude the change could not have been greater. He left his earthly failings behind him and that sort of reputation he had, and there was a totally new set of conditions for his imaginative faculty to work upon. Entirely new, entirely remarkable. And he got hold of them in a remarkable way.

'Stein was the man who knew more about Patusan than anybody else. More than was known in the government circles, I suspect. I have no doubt he had been there, either in his butterfly-hunting days or later on, when he tried in his incorrigible way to season with a pinch of romance the fattening dishes of his commercial kitchen. There were very few places in the Archipelago he had not seen in the original dusk of their being, before light (and even electric light) had been carried into them for the sake of better morality and – and – well – the greater profit, too. It was at breakfast of the morning following our talk about Jim that he mentioned the place, after I had quoted poor Brierly's remark: "Let him creep twenty feet underground and stay there." He looked up at me with interested attention, as though I had been a rare insect. "This could be done, too," he remarked, sipping his coffee. "Bury him in some sort," I explained. "One doesn't like to do it of course, but it would be the best thing, seeing what he is." "Yes; he is young," Stein mused. "The youngest human being now in existence," I affirmed. "*Schön.*

There's Patusan," he went on in the same tone . . . "And the woman is dead now," he added incomprehensibly.

'Of course I don't know that story; I can only guess that once before Patusan had been used as a grave for some sin, transgression, or misfortune. It is impossible to suspect Stein. The only woman that had ever existed for him was the Malay girl he called "my wife the princess," or, more rarely in moments of expansion, "the mother of my Emma." Who was the woman he had mentioned in connection with Patusan I can't say; but from his allusions I understand she had been an educated and very good-looking Dutch-Malay girl, with a tragic or perhaps only a pitiful history, whose most painful part no doubt was her marriage with a Malacca Portuguese who had been clerk in some commercial house in the Dutch colonies. I gathered from Stein that this man was an unsatisfactory person in more ways than one, all being more or less indefinite and offensive. It was solely for his wife's sake that Stein had appointed him manager of Stein & Co.'s trading post in Patusan; but commercially the arrangement was not a success, at any rate for the firm, and now the woman had died, Stein was disposed to try another agent there. The Portuguese, whose name was Cornelius, considered himself a very deserving but ill-used person, entitled by his abilities to a better position. This man Jim would have to relieve. "But I don't think he will go away from the place," remarked Stein. "That has nothing to do with me. It was only for the sake of the woman that I . . . But as I think there is a daughter left, I shall let him, if he likes to stay, keep the old house."

'Patusan is a remote district of a native-ruled state, and the chief settlement bears the same name. At a point on the river about forty miles from the sea, where the first houses come into view, there can be seen rising above the level of the forests the summits of two steep hills very close together, and separated by what looks like a deep fissure, the cleavage of some mighty stroke. As a matter of fact, the valley between is nothing but a narrow ravine; the appearance from the settlement is of one irregularly conical hill split in two, and with the two halves leaning slightly apart. On the third day after the full, the moon, as seen from the open space in front of Jim's house (he had a very fine house in the native style when I visited him), rose exactly behind these hills, its diffused light at first throwing the two masses into intensely black relief, and then the nearly perfect disk, glowing ruddily, appeared, gliding upwards between the sides of the chasm, till it floated away above the summits, as if escaping from a yawning grave in gentle triumph. "Wonderful effect," said Jim by my side. "Worth seeing. Is it not?"

'And this question was put with a note of personal pride that made me smile, as though he had had a hand in regulating that unique spectacle. He had regulated so many things in Patusan! Things that would have appeared as much beyond his control as the motions of the moon and the stars.

'It was inconceivable. That was the distinctive quality of the part into which Stein and I had tumbled him unwittingly, with no other notion than to get him out of the way; out of his own way, be it understood. That was our main purpose, though, I own, I might have had another motive which had influenced me a little. I was about to go home for a time; and it may be I desired, more than I was aware of myself, to dispose of him – to dispose of him, you understand – before I left. I was going home, and he had come to me from there, with his miserable trouble and his shadowy claim, like a man panting under a burden in a mist. I cannot say I had ever seen him distinctly – not even to this day, after I had my last view of him; but it seemed to me that the less I understood the more I was bound to him in the name of that doubt which is the inseparable part of our knowledge. I did not know so much more about myself. And then, I repeat, I was going home – to that home distant enough for all its hearthstones to be like one hearthstone, by which the humblest of us has the right to sit. We wander in our thousands over the face of the earth, the illustrious and the obscure, earning beyond the seas our fame, our money, or only a crust of bread; but it seems to me that for each of us going home must be like going to render an account. We return to face our superiors, our kindred, our friends – those whom we obey, and those whom we love; but even they who have neither, the most free, lonely, irresponsible, and bereft of ties – even those for whom home holds no dear face, no familiar voice even they have to meet the spirit that dwells within the land, under its sky, in its air, in its valleys, and on its rises, in its fields, in its waters and its trees – a mute friend, judge, and inspirer. Say what you like, to get its joy, to breathe its peace, to face its truth, one must return with a clear consciousness. All this may seem to you sheer sentimentalism; and indeed very few of us have the will or the capacity to look consciously under the surface of familiar emotions. There are the girls we love, the men we look up to, the tenderness, the friendships, the opportunities, the pleasures! But the fact remains that you must touch your reward with clean hands, lest it turn to dead leaves, to thorns, in your grasp. I think it is the lonely, without a fireside or an affection they may call their own, those who return not to a dwelling but to the land itself, to meet its disembodied, eternal, and unchangeable spirit – it is those who understand best its severity, its saving power, the grace of its secular right to our fidelity, to our obedience. Yes! few of us understand, but we all feel it though, and I say all without exception, because those who do not feel do not count. Each blade of grass has its spot on earth whence it draws its life, its strength; and so is man rooted to the land from which he draws his faith together with his life. I don't know how much Jim understood; but I know he felt, he felt confusedly but powerfully, the demand of some such truth or some such illusion – I don't care how you call it, there is so little difference, and the difference means so little. The thing is that in virtue of his feeling he mattered. He would never go home now. Not he. Never. Had he been capable of picturesque manifestations he would have shuddered at the thought and made you shudder, too. But he was not of that sort, though he was expressive enough in his way. Before the idea of going home he would grow desperately stiff and immovable, with lowered chin and pouted lips, and with those candid blue eyes of his glowering darkly under a frown, as if before something unbearable, as if before something revolting. There was imagination in that hard skull of his, over which the thick clustering hair fitted like a cap. As to me, I have no imagination (I would be more certain about him today, if I had), and I do not mean to imply that I figured to myself the spirit of the land uprising above the white cliffs of Dover, to ask me what I – returning with no bones broken, so to speak – had done with my very young brother. I could not make such a mistake. I knew very well he was of those about whom there is no enquiry; I had seen better men go out, disappear, vanish utterly, without provoking a sound of curiosity or sorrow. The spirit of the land, as becomes the ruler of great enterprises, is careless of innumerable lives. Woe to the stragglers! We exist only in so far as we hang together. He had straggled in a way; he had not hung on; but he was aware of it with an intensity that made him touching, just as a man's more intense life makes his death more touching than the death of a tree. I happened to be handy, and I happened to be touched. That's all there is to it. I was concerned as to the way he would go out. It would have hurt me if, for instance, he had taken to drink. The earth is so small that I was afraid of, someday, being waylaid by a blear-eyed, swollen-faced, besmirched loafer, with no soles to his canvas shoes, and with a flutter of rags about the elbows, who, on the strength of old acquaintance, would ask for a loan of five dollars. You know the awful jaunty bearing of these scarecrows coming to you from a decent past, the rasping careless voice, the half-averted impudent glances – those meetings more trying to a man who believes in the solidarity of our lives than the sight of an impenitent deathbed to a priest. That, to tell you the truth, was the only danger I could see for him and for me; but I also mistrusted my want of imagination. It might even come to something worse, in some way it was beyond my powers of fancy to foresee. He wouldn't let me forget how imaginative he was, and your imaginative people swing farther in any direction, as if given a longer scope of cable in the uneasy anchorage of life. They do. They take to drink, too. It may be I was belittling him by such a fear. How could I tell? Even Stein could say no more than that he was romantic. I only knew he was one of us. And what business had he to be romantic? I am telling you so much about my own instinctive feelings and bemused reflections because there remains so little to be told of him. He existed for me, and after all it is only through me that he exists for you. I've led him out by the hand; I have paraded him before you. Were my commonplace fears unjust? I won't say – not even now. You may be able to tell better, since the proverb has it that the onlookers see most of the game. At any rate, they were superfluous. He did not go out, not at all; on the contrary, he came on wonderfully, came on straight as a die and in excellent form, which showed that he could stay as well as spurt. I ought to be delighted, for it is a victory in which I had taken my part; but I am not so pleased as I would have expected to be. I ask myself whether his rush had really carried him out of that mist in which he loomed interesting if not very big, with floating outlines – a straggler yearning inconsolably for his humble place in the ranks. And besides, the last word is not said – probably shall never be said. Are not our lives too short for that full utterance which through all our stammerings is of course our only and abiding intention? I have given up expecting those last words, whose ring, if they could only be pronounced, would shake both heaven and earth. There is never time to say our last word – the last word of our love, of our desire, faith, remorse, submission, revolt. The heaven and the earth must not be shaken, I suppose – at least, not by us who know so many truths about either. My last words about Jim shall be few. I affirm he had achieved greatness; but the thing would be dwarfed in the telling, or rather in the hearing. Frankly, it is not my words that I mistrust but your minds. I could be eloquent were I not afraid you fellows had starved your imaginations to feed your bodies. I do not mean to be offensive; it is respectable to have no illusions – and safe – and profitable – and dull. Yet you, too, in your time must have known the intensity of life, that light of glamour created in the shock of trifles, as amazing as the glow of sparks struck from a cold stone – and as short-lived, alas!'

Chapter 22

'The conquest of love, honour, men's confidence – the pride of it, the power of it, are fit materials for a heroic tale; only our minds are struck by the externals of such a success, and to Jim's success there were no externals. Thirty miles of forest shut it off from the sight of an indifferent world, and the noise of the white surf along the coast overpowered the voice of fame. The stream of civilisation, as if divided on a headland a hundred miles north of Patusan, branches east and south-east, leaving its plains and valleys, its old trees and its old mankind, neglected and isolated, such as an insignificant and crumbling islet between the two branches of a mighty, devouring stream. You find the name of the country pretty often in collections of old voyages. The seventeenth-century traders went there for pepper, because the passion for pepper seemed to burn like a flame of love in the breast of Dutch and English adventurers about the time of James the First. Where wouldn't they go for pepper! For a bag of pepper they would cut each other's throats without hesitation, and would forswear their souls, of which they were so careful otherwise: the bizarre obstinacy of that desire made them defy death in a thousand shapes; the unknown seas, the loathsome and strange diseases;

wounds, captivity, hunger, pestilence, and despair. It made them great! By heavens! it made them heroic; and it made them pathetic, too, in their craving for trade with the inflexible death levying its toll on young and old. It seems impossible to believe that mere greed could hold men to such a steadfastness of purpose, to such a blind persistence in endeavour and sacrifice. And indeed those who adventured their persons and lives risked all they had for a slender reward. They left their bones to lie bleaching on distant shores, so that wealth might flow to the living at home. To us, their less tried successors, they appear magnified, not as agents of trade but as instruments of a recorded destiny, pushing out into the unknown in obedience to an inward voice, to an impulse beating in the blood, to a dream of the future. They were wonderful; and it must be owned they were ready for the wonderful. They recorded it complacently in their sufferings, in the aspect of the seas, in the customs of strange nations, in the glory of splendid rulers.

'In Patusan they had found lots of pepper, and had been impressed by the magnificence and the wisdom of the Sultan; but somehow, after a century of chequered intercourse, the country seems to drop gradually out of the trade. Perhaps the pepper had given out. Be it as it may, nobody cares for it now; the glory has departed, the Sultan is an imbecile youth with two thumbs on his left hand and an uncertain and beggarly revenue extorted from a miserable population and stolen from him by his many uncles.

'This of course I have from Stein. He gave me their names and a short sketch of the life and character of each. He was as full of information about native states as an official report, but infinitely more amusing. He *had* to know. He traded in so many, and in some districts – as in Patusan, for instance – his firm was the only one to have an agency by special permit from the Dutch authorities. The Government trusted his discretion, and it was understood that he took all the risks. The men he employed understood that, too, but he made it worth their while apparently. He was perfectly frank with me over the breakfast-table in the morning. As far as he was aware (the last news was thirteen months old, he stated precisely), utter insecurity for life and property was the normal condition. There were in Patusan antagonistic forces, and one of them was Rajah Allang, the worst of the Sultan's uncles, the governor of the river, who did the extorting and the stealing, and ground down to the point of extinction the country-born Malays, who, utterly defenceless, had not even the resource of emigrating – "for indeed," as Stein remarked, "where could they go, and how could they get away?" No doubt they did not even desire to get away. The world (which is circumscribed by lofty impassable mountains) has been given into the hand of the high-born, and *this* Rajah they knew: he was of their own royal house. I had the pleasure of meeting the gentleman later on. He was a dirty, little, used-up old man with evil eyes and a weak mouth, who swallowed an opium pill every two hours, and in defiance of common decency wore his hair uncovered and falling in wild stringy locks about his wizened grimy face. When giving audience he would clamber upon a sort of narrow stage erected in a hall like a ruinous barn with a rotten bamboo floor, through the cracks of which you could see twelve or fifteen feet below the heaps of refuse and garbage of all kinds lying under the house. That is where and how he received us when, accompanied by Jim, I paid him a visit of ceremony. There were about forty people in the room, and perhaps three times as many in the great courtyard below. There was constant movement, coming and going, pushing and murmuring, at our backs. A few youths in gay silks glared from the distance; the majority, slaves and humble dependants, were half naked, in ragged sarongs, dirty with ashes and mud-stains. I had never seen Jim look so grave, so self-possessed, in an impenetrable, impressive way. In the midst of these dark-faced men, his stalwart figure in white apparel, the gleaming clusters of his fair hair, seemed to catch all the sunshine that trickled through the cracks in the closed shutters of that dim hall, with its walls of mats and a roof of thatch. He appeared like a creature not only of another kind but of another essence. Had they not seen him come up in a canoe they might have thought he had descended upon them from the clouds. He did, however, come in a crazy dug-out, sitting (very still and with his knees together, for fear of overturning the thing) – sitting on a tin box – which I had lent him – nursing on his lap a revolver of the Navy pattern – presented by me on parting – which, through an interposition of Providence, or through some wrong-headed notion, that was just like him, or else from sheer instinctive sagacity, he had decided to carry unloaded. That's how he ascended the Patusan river. Nothing could have been more prosaic and more unsafe, more extravagantly casual, more lonely. Strange, this fatality that would cast the complexion of a flight upon all his acts, of impulsive unreflecting desertion – of a jump into the unknown.

'It is precisely the casualness of it that strikes me most. Neither Stein nor I had a clear conception of what might be on the other side when we, metaphorically speaking, took him up and hove him over the wall with scant ceremony. At the moment I merely wished to achieve his disappearance. Stein characteristically enough had a sentimental motive. He had a notion of paying off (in kind, I suppose) the old debt he had never forgotten. Indeed he had been all his life especially friendly to anybody from the British Isles. His late benefactor, it is true, was a Scot – even to the length of being called Alexander M'Neil – and Jim came from a long way south of the Tweed; but at the distance of six or seven thousand miles Great Britain, though never diminished, looks foreshortened enough even to its own children to rob such details of their importance. Stein was excusable, and his hinted intentions were so generous that I begged him most earnestly to keep them secret for a time. I felt that no consideration of personal advantage should be allowed to influence Jim; that not even the risk of such influence should be run. We had to deal with another sort of reality. He wanted a refuge, and a refuge at the cost of danger should be offered him – nothing more.

'Upon every other point I was perfectly frank with him, and I even (as I believed at the time) exaggerated the danger of the undertaking. As a matter of fact I did not do it justice; his first day in Patusan was nearly his last – would have been his last if he had not been so reckless or so hard on himself and had condescended to load that revolver. I remember, as I unfolded our precious scheme for his retreat, how his stubborn but weary resignation was gradually replaced by surprise, interest, wonder, and by boyish eagerness. This was a chance he had been dreaming of. He couldn't think how he merited that I . . . He would be shot if he could see to what he owed . . . And it was Stein, Stein the merchant, who . . . but of course it was me he had to . . . I cut him short. He was not articulate, and his gratitude caused me inexplicable pain. I told him that if he owed this chance to anyone especially, it was to an old Scot of whom he had never heard, who had died many years ago, of whom little was remembered besides a roaring voice and a rough sort of honesty. There was really no one to receive his thanks. Stein was passing on to a young man the help he had received in his own young days, and I had done no more than to mention his name. Upon this he coloured, and, twisting a bit of paper in his fingers, he remarked bashfully that I had always trusted him.

'I admitted that such was the case, and added after a pause that I wished he had been able to follow my example. "You think I don't?" he asked uneasily, and remarked in a mutter that one had to get some sort of show first; then brightening up, and in a loud voice, he protested he would give me no occasion to regret my confidence, which – which . . .

' "Do not misapprehend," I interrupted. "It is not in your power to make me regret anything." There would be no regrets; but if there were, it would be altogether my own affair: on the other hand, I wished him to understand clearly that this arrangement, this – this – experiment, was his own doing; he was responsible for it and no one else. "Why! Why," he stammered, "this is the very thing that I . . . " I begged him not to be dense, and he looked more puzzled than ever. He was in a fair way to make life intolerable to himself . . . "Do you think so?" he asked, disturbed; but in a moment added confidently, "I was going on, though. Was I not?" It was impossible to be angry with him: I could not help a smile, and told him that in the old days people who went on like this were on the way of becoming hermits in a wilderness. "Hermits be hanged!" he commented with engaging impulsiveness. Of course he didn't mind a wilderness . . . I was glad of it, I said. That was where he would be going to. He would find it lively enough, I ventured to promise. "Yes, yes," he said, keenly. He had shown a desire, I continued inflexibly, to go out and shut the door after him . . . "Did I?" he interrupted in a strange access of gloom that seemed to envelop him from head to foot like the shadow of a passing cloud. He was wonderfully expressive after all. Wonderfully! "Did I?" he repeated, bitterly. "You can't say I made much noise about it. And I can keep it up, too – only, confound it! you show me a door." . . . "Very well. Pass on," I struck in. I could make him a solemn promise that it would be shut behind him with a vengeance. His fate, whatever it was, would be ignored, because the country, for all its rotten state, was not judged ripe for interference. Once he got in, it would be for the outside world as though he had never existed. He would have nothing but the soles of his two feet to stand upon, and he would have first to find his ground at that. "Never existed – that's it, by Jove!" he murmured to himself. His eyes, fastened upon my lips, sparkled. If he had thoroughly understood the conditions, I concluded, he had better jump into the first gharry he could see and drive on to Stein's house for his final instructions. He flung out of the room before I had fairly finished speaking.'

Chapter 23

'He did not return till next morning. He had been kept to dinner and for the night. There never had been such a wonderful man as Mr Stein. He had in his pocket a letter for Cornelius ("the Johnnie who's going to get the sack," he explained with a momentary drop in his elation), and he exhibited with glee a silver ring, such as natives use, worn down very thin and showing faint traces of chasing.

'This was his introduction to an old chap called Doramin – one of the principal men out there – a big pot – who had been Mr Stein's friend in that country where he had all these adventures. Mr Stein called him "war-comrade." War-comrade was good. Wasn't it? And didn't Mr Stein speak English wonderfully well? Said he had learned it in Celebes – of all places! That was awfully funny. Was it not? He did speak with an accent – a twang – did I notice? That chap Doramin had given him the ring. They had exchanged presents when they parted for the last time. Sort of promising eternal friendship. He called it fine – did I not? They had to make a dash for dear life out of the country when that Mohammed – Mohammed – What's-his-name had been killed. I knew the story, of course. Seemed a beastly shame, didn't it? . . .

'He ran on like this, forgetting his plate, with a knife and fork in hand (he had found me at tiffin), slightly flushed, and with his eyes darkened many shades, which was with him a sign of excitement. The ring was a sort of credential – ("It's like something you read of in books," he threw in appreciatively) and Doramin would do his best for him. Mr Stein had been the means of saving that chap's life on some occasion; purely by accident, Mr Stein had said, but he – Jim – had his own opinion about that. Mr Stein was just the man to look out for such accidents. No matter. Accident or purpose, this would serve his turn immensely. Hoped to goodness the jolly old beggar had not gone off the hooks meantime. Mr Stein could not tell. There had been no news for more than a year; they were kicking up no end of an all-fired row amongst themselves, and the river was closed. Jolly awkward, this; but, no fear; he would manage to find a crack to get in.

'He impressed, almost frightened, me with his elated rattle. He was voluble like a youngster on the eve of a long holiday with a prospect of delightful scrapes, and such an attitude of mind in a grown man and in this connection had in it something phenomenal, a little mad, dangerous, unsafe. I was on the point of entreating him to take things seriously when he dropped his knife and fork (he had begun eating, or rather swallowing food, as it were, unconsciously), and began a search all round his plate. The ring! The ring! Where the devil . . . Ah! Here it was . . . He closed his big hand on it, and tried all his pockets one after another. Jove! wouldn't do to lose the thing. He meditated gravely over his fist. Had it! Would hang the bally affair round his neck! And he proceeded to do this immediately, producing a string (which looked like a bit of a cotton shoe-lace) for the purpose. There! That would do the trick! It would be the deuce if . . . He seemed to catch sight of my face for the first time, and it steadied him a little. I probably didn't realise, he said with a naïve gravity, how much importance he attached to that token. It meant a friend; and it is a good thing to have a friend. He knew something about that. He nodded at me expressively, but before my disclaiming gesture he leaned his head on his hand and for a while sat silent, playing thoughtfully with the bread-crumbs on the cloth . . . "Slam the door – that was jolly well put," he cried, and jumping up, began to pace the room, reminding me by the set of the shoulders, the turn of his head, the headlong and uneven stride, of that night when he had paced thus, confessing, explaining – what you will – but, in the last instance, living – living before me, under his own little cloud, with all his unconscious subtlety which could draw consolation from the very source of sorrow. It was the same mood, the same and different, like a fickle companion that today guiding you on the true path, with the same eyes, the same step, the same impulse, tomorrow will lead you hopelessly astray. His tread was assured, his straying, darkened eyes seemed to search the room for something. One of his footfalls somehow sounded louder than the other – the fault of his boots probably – and gave a curious impression of an invisible halt in his gait. One of his hands was rammed deep into his trousers-pocket, the other waved suddenly above his head. "Slam the door!" he shouted. "I've been waiting for that. I'll show yet . . . I'll . . . I'm ready for any confounded thing . . . I've been dreaming of it . . . Jove! Get out of this. Jove! This is luck at last . . . You wait. I'll . . . "

'He tossed his head fearlessly, and I confess that for the first and last time in our acquaintance I perceived myself unexpectedly to be thoroughly sick of him. Why these vapourings? He was stumping about the room flourishing his arms absurdly, and now and then feeling on his breast for the ring under his clothes. Where was the sense of such exaltation in a man appointed to be a trading-clerk, and in a place where there was no trade – at that? Why hurl defiance at the universe? This was not a proper frame of mind to approach any undertaking; an improper frame of mind not only for him, I said, but for any man. He stood still over me. Did I think so? he asked, by no means subdued, and with a smile in which I seemed to detect something insolent. But then I am twenty years his senior. Youth *is* insolent; it is its right – its necessity; it has got to assert itself, and all assertion in this world of doubts is a defiance, is an insolence. He went off into a far corner, and coming back, he, figuratively speaking, turned to rend me. I spoke like that because I – even I, who had been no end kind to him – even I remembered – remembered – against him – what – what had happened. And what about others – the – the – world? Where's the wonder he wanted to get out, meant to get out, meant to stay out – by heavens! And I talked about proper frames of mind!

' "It is not I or the world who remember," I shouted. "It is you – you, who remember."

'He did not flinch, and went on with heat, "Forget everything, everybody, everybody." . . . His voice fell . . . "But you," he added.

' "Yes – me, too – if it would help," I said, also in a low tone. After this we remained silent and languid for a time as if exhausted. Then he began again, composedly, and told me that Mr Stein had instructed him to wait for a month or so, to see whether it was possible for him to remain, before he began building a new house for himself, so as to avoid "vain expense." He did make use of funny expressions – Stein did. "Vain expense" was good . . . Remain? Why! of course. He would hang on. Let him get in – that's all; he would answer for it; he would remain. Never get out. It was easy enough to remain.

' "Don't be foolhardy," I said, rendered uneasy by his threatening tone. "If you only live long enough you will want to come back."

' "Come back to what?" he asked, absently, with his eyes fixed upon the face of a clock on the wall.

'I was silent for a while. "Is it to be never, then?" I said. "Never," he repeated, dreamily, without looking at me, and then flew into sudden activity. "Jove! Two o'clock, and I sail at four!"

'It was true. A brigantine of Stein's was leaving for the westward that afternoon, and he had been instructed to take his passage in her, only no orders to delay the sailing had been given. I suppose Stein forgot. He made a rush to get his things while I went aboard my ship, where he promised to call on his way to the outer roadster. He turned up accordingly in a great hurry and with a small leather valise in his hand. This wouldn't do, and I offered him an old tin trunk of mine supposed to be watertight, or at least damp-tight. He effected the transfer by the simple process of shooting out the contents of his valise as you would empty a sack of wheat. I saw three books in the tumble; two small, in dark covers, and a thick green-and-gold volume – a half-crown complete Shakespeare. "You read this?" I asked. "Yes. Best thing to cheer up a fellow," he said hastily. I was struck by this appreciation, but there was no time for Shakespearian talk. A heavy revolver and two small boxes of cartridges were lying on the cuddy-table. "Pray take this," I said. "It may help you to remain." No sooner were these words out of my mouth than I perceived what grim meaning they could bear. "May help you to get in," I corrected myself remorsefully. He, however, was not troubled by obscure meanings; he thanked me effusively and bolted out, calling Goodbye over his shoulder. I heard his voice through the ship's side urging his boatmen to give way, and looking out of the stern-port I saw the boat rounding under the counter. He sat in her leaning forward, exciting his men with voice and gestures; and as he had kept the revolver in his hand and seemed to be presenting it at their heads, I shall never forget the scared faces of the four Javanese, and the frantic swing of their stroke which snatched that vision from under my eyes. Then turning away, the first thing I saw were the two boxes of cartridges on the cuddy-table. He had forgotten to take them.

'I ordered my gig manned at once; but Jim's rowers, under the impression that their lives hung on a thread while they had that madman in the boat, made such excellent time that before I had traversed half the distance between the two vessels I caught sight of him clambering over the rail, and of his box being passed up. All the brigantine's canvas was loose, her mainsail was set, and the windlass was just beginning to clink as I stepped upon her deck: her master, a dapper little half-caste of forty or so, in a blue flannel suit, with lively eyes, his round face the colour of lemon-peel, and with a thin little black moustache drooping on each side of his thick, dark lips, came forward smirking. He turned out, notwithstanding his self-satisfied and cheery exterior, to be of a careworn temperament. In answer to a remark of mine (while Jim had gone below for a moment) he said, "Oh, yes. Patusan." He was going to carry the gentleman to the mouth of the river, but would "never ascend." His flowing English seemed to be derived from a dictionary compiled by a lunatic. Had Mr Stein desired him to "ascend," he would have "reverentially" – (I think he wanted to say respectfully – but devil only knows) – "reverentially made objects for the safety of properties." If disregarded, he would have presented "resignation to quit." Twelve months ago he had made his last voyage there, and though Mr Cornelius "propitiated many offertories" to Mr Rajah Allang and the "principal populations," on conditions which made the trade "a snare and ashes in the mouth," yet his ship had been fired upon from the woods by "irresponsive parties" all the way down the river; which causing his crew "from exposure to limb to remain silent in hidings," the brigantine was nearly stranded on a sandbank at the bar, where she "would have been perishable beyond the act of man." The angry disgust at the recollection, the pride of his fluency, to which he turned an attentive ear, struggled for the possession of his broad simple face. He scowled and beamed at me, and watched with satisfaction the undeniable effect of his phraseology. Dark frowns ran swiftly over the placid sea, and the brigantine, with her fore-topsail to the mast and her mainboom amidships, seemed bewildered amongst the cat's-paws. He told me further, gnashing his teeth, that the Rajah was a "laughable hyena" (can't imagine how he got hold of hyenas); while somebody else was many times falser than the "weapons of a crocodile." Keeping one eye on the movements of his crew forward, he let loose his volubility – comparing the place to a "cage of beasts made ravenous by long impenitence." I fancy he meant impunity. He had no intention, he cried, to "exhibit himself to be made attached purposefully to robbery." The long-drawn wails, giving the time for the pull of the men catting the anchor, came to an end, and he lowered his voice. "Plenty too much enough of Patusan," he concluded, with energy.

'I heard afterwards he had been so indiscreet as to get himself tied up by the neck with a rattan halter to a post planted in the middle of a mud-hole before the Rajah's house. He spent the best part of a day and a whole night in that unwholesome situation, but there is every reason to believe the thing had been meant as a sort of joke. He brooded for a while over that horrid memory, I suppose, and then addressed in a quarrelsome tone the man coming aft to the helm. When he turned to me again it was to speak judicially, without passion. He would take the gentleman to the mouth of the river at Batu Kring (Patusan town "being situated internally," he remarked, "thirty miles"). But in his eyes, he continued – a tone of bored, weary conviction replacing his previous voluble delivery – the gentleman was already "in the similitude of a corpse." "What? What do you say?" I asked. He assumed a startlingly ferocious demeanour, and imitated to perfection the act of stabbing from behind. "Already like the body of one deported," he explained, with the insufferably conceited air of his kind after what they imagine a display of cleverness. Behind him I perceived Jim smiling silently at me, and with a raised hand checking the exclamation on my lips.

'Then, while the half-caste, bursting with importance, shouted his orders, while the yards swung creaking and the heavy boom came surging over, Jim and I, alone as it were, to leeward of the mainsail, clasped each other's hands and exchanged the last hurried words. My heart was freed from that dull resentment which had existed side by side with interest in his fate. The absurd chatter of the half-caste had given more reality to the miserable dangers of his path than Stein's careful statements. On that occasion the sort of formality that had been present in our intercourse vanished from our speech; I believe I called him "dear boy," and he tacked on the words "old man" to some half-uttered expression of gratitude, as though his risk set off against my years had made us more equal in age and in feeling. There was a moment of real and profound intimacy, unexpected and short-lived like a glimpse of some everlasting, of some saving truth. He exerted himself to soothe me as though he had been the more mature of the two. "All right, all right," he said, rapidly, and with feeling. "I promise to take care of myself.

Yes; I won't take any risks. Not a single blessed risk. Of course not. I mean to hang out. Don't you worry. Jove! I feel as if nothing could touch me. Why! this is luck from the word Go. I wouldn't spoil such a magnificent chance!" . . . A magnificent chance! Well, it *was* magnificent, but chances are what men make them, and how was I to know? As he had said, even I – even I remembered – his – his misfortunes against him. It was true. And the best thing for him was to go.

'My gig had dropped in the wake of the brigantine, and I saw him aft detached upon the light of the westering sun, raising his cap high above his head. I heard an indistinct shout, "You – shall – hear – of – me." Of me, or from me, I don't know which. I think it must have been *of* me. My eyes were too dazzled by the glitter of the sea below his feet to see him clearly; I am fated never to see him clearly; but I can assure you no man could have appeared less "in the similitude of a corpse," as that half-caste croaker had put it. I could see the little wretch's face, the shape and colour of a ripe pumpkin, poked out somewhere under Jim's elbow. He, too, raised his arm as if for a downward thrust. *Absit omen!*'

Chapter 24

'The coast of Patusan (I saw it nearly two years afterwards) is straight and sombre, and faces a misty ocean. Red trails are seen like cataracts of rust streaming under the dark-green foliage of bushes and creepers clothing the low cliffs. Swampy plains open out at the mouth of rivers, with a view of jagged blue peaks beyond the vast forests. In the offing a chain of islands, dark, crumbling shapes, stand out in the everlasting sunlit haze like the remnants of a wall breached by the sea.

'There is a village of fisher-folk at the mouth of the Batu Kring branch of the estuary. The river, which had been closed so long, was open then, and Stein's little schooner, in which I had my passage, worked her way up in three tides without being exposed to a fusillade from "irresponsive parties." Such a state of affairs belonged already to ancient history, if I could believe the elderly headman of the fishing village, who came on board to act as a sort of pilot. He talked to me (the second white man he had ever seen) with confidence, and most of his talk was about the first white man he had ever seen. He called him Tuan Jim, and the tone of his references was made remarkable by a strange mixture of familiarity and awe. They, in the village, were under that lord's special protection, which showed that Jim bore no grudge. If he had warned me that I would hear of him it was perfectly true. I was hearing of him. There was already a story that the tide had turned two hours before its time to help him on his journey up the river. The talkative old man himself had steered the canoe and had marvelled at the phenomenon. Moreover, all the glory was in his family. His son and his son-in-law had paddled; but they were only youths without experience, who did not notice the speed of the canoe till he pointed out to them the amazing fact.

'Jim's coming to that fishing village was a blessing; but to them, as to many of us, the blessing came heralded by terrors. So many generations had been released since the last white man had visited the river that the very tradition had been lost. The appearance of the being that descended upon them and demanded inflexibly to be taken up to Patusan was discomposing; his insistence was alarming; his generosity more than suspicious. It was an unheard-of request. There was no precedent. What would the Rajah say to this? What would he do to them? The best part of the night was spent in consultation; but the immediate risk from the anger of that strange man seemed so great that at last a cranky dug-out was got ready. The women shrieked with grief as it put off. A fearless old hag cursed the stranger.

'He sat in it, as I've told you, on his tin box, nursing the unloaded revolver on his lap. He sat with precaution – than which there is nothing more fatiguing – and thus entered the land he was destined to fill with the fame of his virtues, from the blue peaks inland to the white ribbon of surf on the coast. At the first bend he lost sight of the sea with its labouring waves for ever rising, sinking, and vanishing to rise again – the very image of struggling mankind – and faced the immovable forests rooted deep in the soil, soaring towards the sunshine, everlasting in the shadowy might of their tradition, like life itself. And his opportunity sat veiled by his side like an Eastern bride waiting to be uncovered by the hand of the master. He, too, was the heir of a shadowy and mighty tradition! He told me, however, that he had never in his life felt so depressed and tired as in that canoe. All the movement he dared to allow himself was to reach, as it were by stealth, after the shell of half a coconut floating between his shoes, and bail some of the water out with a carefully restrained action. He discovered how hard the lid of a block-tin case was to sit upon. He had heroic health; but several times during that journey he experienced fits of giddiness, and between whiles he speculated hazily as to the size of the blister the sun was raising on his back. For amusement he tried by looking ahead to decide whether the muddy object he saw lying on the water's edge was a log of wood or an alligator. Only very soon he had to give that up. No fun in it. Always alligator. One of them flopped into the river and all but capsized the canoe. But this excitement was over directly. Then in a long empty reach he was very grateful to a troop of monkeys who came right down on the bank and made an insulting hullabaloo on his passage. Such was the way in which he was approaching greatness as genuine as any man ever achieved. Principally, he longed for sunset; and meantime his three paddlers were preparing to put into execution their plan of delivering him up to the Rajah.

' "I suppose I must have been stupid with fatigue, or perhaps I did doze off for a time," he said. The first thing he knew was his canoe coming to the bank. He became instantaneously aware of the forest having been left behind, of the first houses being visible higher up, of a stockade on his left, and of his boatmen leaping out together upon a low point of land and taking to their heels. Instinctively he leaped out after them. At first he thought himself deserted for some inconceivable reason, but he heard excited shouts, a gate swung open, and a lot of people poured out, making towards him. At the same time a boat full of armed men appeared on the river and came alongside his empty canoe, thus shutting off his retreat.

' "I was too startled to be quite cool – don't you know? and if that revolver had been loaded I would have shot somebody – perhaps two, three bodies, and that would have been the end of me. But it wasn't . . . " "Why not?" I asked. "Well, I couldn't fight the whole population, and I wasn't coming to them as if I were afraid of my life," he said, with just a faint hint of his stubborn sulkiness in the glance he gave me. I refrained from pointing out to him that they could not have known the chambers were actually empty. He had to satisfy himself in his own way . . . "Anyhow it wasn't," he repeated, good-humouredly, "and so I just stood still and asked them what was the matter. That seemed to strike them dumb. I saw some of these thieves going off with my box. That long-legged old scoundrel Kassim (I'll show him to you tomorrow) ran out fussing to me about the Rajah wanting to see me. I said, 'All right'; I, too, wanted to see the Rajah, and I simply walked in through the gate and – and – here I am." He laughed, and then with unexpected emphasis, "And do you know what's the best in it?" he asked. "I'll tell you. It's the knowledge that had I been wiped out it is this place that would have been the loser."

'He spoke thus to me before his house on that evening I've mentioned – after we had watched the moon float away above the chasm between the hills like an ascending spirit out of a grave; its sheen descended, cold and pale, like the ghost of dead sunlight. There is something haunting in the light of the moon; it has all the dispassionateness of a disembodied soul, and something of its inconceivable mystery. It is to our sunshine, which – say what you like – is all we have to live by, what the echo is to the sound: misleading and confusing whether the note be mocking or sad. It robs all forms of matter – which, after all, is our domain – of their substance, and gives a sinister reality to shadows alone. And the shadows were very real around us, but Jim by my side looked very stalwart, as though nothing – not even the occult power of moonlight – could rob him of his reality in my eyes. Perhaps, indeed, nothing could touch him since he had survived the assault of the dark powers. All was silent, all was still; even on the river the moonbeams slept as on a pool. It was the moment of high water, a moment of immobility that accentuated the utter isolation of this lost corner of the earth. The houses crowding along the wide shining sweep without ripple or glitter, stepping into the water in a line of jostling, vague, grey, silvery forms mingled with black masses of shadow, were like a spectral herd of shapeless creatures pressing forward to drink in a spectral and lifeless stream. Here and there a red gleam twinkled within the bamboo walls, warm, like a living spark, significant of human affections, of shelter, of repose.

'He confessed to me that he often watched these tiny warm gleams go out one by one, that he loved to see people go to sleep under his eyes, confident in the security of tomorrow. "Peaceful here, eh?" he asked. He was not eloquent, but there was a deep meaning in the words that followed. "Look at these houses; there's not one where I am not trusted. Jove! I told you I would hang on. Ask any man, woman, or child . . . " He paused. "Well, I am all right anyhow."

'I observed quickly that he had found that out in the end. I had been sure of it, I added. He shook his head. "Were you?" He pressed my arm lightly above the elbow. "Well, then – you were right."

'There was elation and pride, there was awe almost, in that low exclamation. "Jove!" he cried, "only think what it is to me." Again he pressed my arm. "And you asked me whether I thought of leaving. Good God! I! Want to leave! Especially now after what you told me of Mr Stein's . . . Leave! Why! That's what I was afraid of. It would have been – it would have been harder than dying. No – on my word. Don't laugh. I must feel – every day, every time I open my eyes – that I am trusted – that nobody has a right – don't you know? Leave! For where? What for? To get what?"

'I had told him (indeed it was the main object of my visit) that it was Stein's intention to present him at once with the house and the stock of trading goods, on certain easy conditions which would make the transaction perfectly regular and valid. He began to snort and plunge at first. "Confound your delicacy!" I shouted. "It isn't Stein at all. It's giving you what you had made for yourself. And in any case keep your remarks for M'Neil – when you meet him in the other world. I hope it won't happen soon . . . " He had to give in to my arguments, because all his conquests, the trust, the fame, the friendships, the love – all these things that made him master had made him a captive, too. He looked with an owner's eye at the peace of the evening, at the river, at the houses, at the everlasting life of the forests, at the life of the old mankind, at the secrets of the land, at the pride of his own heart: but it was they that possessed him and made him their own to the innermost thought, to the slightest stir of blood, to his last breath.

'It was something to be proud of. I, too, was proud – for him, if not so certain of the fabulous value of the bargain. It was wonderful. It was not so much of his fearlessness that I thought. It is strange how little account I took of it: as if it had been something too conventional to be at the root of the matter. No. I was more struck by the other gifts he had displayed. He had proved his grasp of the unfamiliar situation, his intellectual alertness in that field of thought. There was his readiness, too! Amazing. And all this had come to him in a manner like keen scent to a well-bred hound. He was not eloquent, but there was a dignity in this constitutional reticence, there was a high seriousness in his stammerings. He had still his old trick of stubborn blushing. Now and then, though, a word, a sentence, would escape him that showed how deeply, how solemnly, he felt about that work which had given him the certitude of rehabilitation. That is why he seemed to love the land and the people with a sort of fierce egoism, with a contemptuous tenderness.'

Chapter 25

' "This is where I was prisoner for three days," he murmured to me (it was on the occasion of our visit to the Rajah), while we were making our way slowly through a kind of awestruck riot of dependants across Tunku Allang's courtyard. "Filthy place, isn't it? And I couldn't get anything to eat either, unless I made a row about it, and then it was only a small plate of rice and a fried fish not much bigger than a stickleback – confound them! Jove! *I've* been hungry prowling inside this stinking enclosure with some of these vagabonds shoving their mugs right under my nose. I had given up that famous revolver of yours at the first demand. Glad to get rid of the bally thing. Look like a fool walking about with an empty shooting-iron in my hand." At that moment we came into the presence, and he became unflinchingly grave and complimentary with his late captor. Oh! magnificent! I want to laugh when I think of it. But I was impressed, too. The old disreputable Tunku Allang could not help showing his fear (he was no hero, for all the tales of his hot youth he was fond of telling); and at the same time there was a wistful confidence in his manner towards his late prisoner. Note! Even where he would be most hated he was still trusted. Jim – as far as I could follow the conversation – was improving the occasion by the delivery of a lecture. Some poor villagers had been waylaid and robbed while on their way to Doramin's house with a few pieces of gum or beeswax which they wished to exchange for rice. "It was Doramin who was a thief," burst out the Rajah. A shaking fury seemed to enter that old frail body. He writhed weirdly on his mat, gesticulating with his hands and feet, tossing the tangled strings of his mop – an impotent incarnation of rage. There were staring eyes and dropping jaws all around us. Jim began to speak. Resolutely, coolly, and for some time he enlarged upon the text that no man should be prevented from getting his food and his children's food honestly. The other sat like a tailor at his board, one palm on each knee, his head low, and fixing Jim through the grey hair that fell over his very eyes. When Jim had done there was a great stillness. Nobody seemed to breathe even; no one made a sound till the old Rajah sighed faintly, and looking up, with a toss of his head, said quickly, "You hear, my people! No more of these little games." This decree was received in profound silence. A rather heavy man, evidently in a position of confidence, with intelligent eyes, a bony, broad, very dark face, and a cheerily officious manner (I learned later on he was the executioner), presented to us two cups of coffee on a brass tray, which he took from the hands of an inferior attendant. "You needn't drink," muttered Jim very rapidly. I didn't perceive the meaning at first, and only looked at him. He took a good sip and sat composedly, holding the saucer in his left hand. In a moment I felt excessively annoyed. "Why the devil," I whispered, smiling at him amiably, "do you expose me to such a stupid risk?" I drank, of course, there was nothing for it, while he gave no sign, and almost immediately afterwards we took our leave. While we were going down the courtyard to our boat, escorted by the intelligent and cheery executioner, Jim said he was very sorry. It was the barest chance, of course. Personally he thought nothing of poison. The remotest chance. He was – he assured me – considered to be infinitely more useful than dangerous, and so . . . "But the Rajah is afraid of you abominably. Anybody can see that," I argued, with, I own, a certain peevishness, and all the time watching anxiously for the first twist of some sort of ghastly colic. I was awfully disgusted. "If I am to do any good here and preserve my position," he said, taking his seat by my side in the boat, "I must stand the risk: I take it once every month, at least. Many people trust me to do that – for them. Afraid of me! That's just it. Most likely he is afraid of me because I am not afraid of his coffee." Then showing me a place on the north front of the stockade where the pointed tops of several stakes were broken, "This is where I leaped over on my third day in Patusan. They haven't put new stakes there yet. Good leap, eh?" A moment later we passed the mouth of a muddy creek. "This is my second leap. I had a bit of a run and took this one flying, but fell short. Thought I would leave my skin there. Lost my shoes struggling. And all the time I was thinking to myself how beastly it would be to get a jab with a bally long spear while sticking in the mud like this. I remember how sick I felt wriggling in that slime. I mean really sick – as if I had bitten something rotten."

'That's how it was – and the opportunity ran by his side, leaped over the gap, floundered in the mud . . . still veiled. The unexpectedness of his coming was the only thing, you understand, that saved him from being at once dispatched with krises and flung into the river. They had him, but it was like getting hold of an apparition, a wraith, a portent. What did it mean? What to do with it? Was it too late to conciliate him? Hadn't he better be killed without more delay? But what would happen then? Wretched old Allang went nearly mad with apprehension and through the difficulty of making up his mind. Several times the council was broken up, and the advisers made a break helter-skelter for the door and out on to the veranda. One – it is said – even jumped down to the ground – fifteen feet, I should judge – and broke his leg. The royal governor of Patusan had bizarre mannerisms, and one of them was to introduce boastful rhapsodies into every arduous discussion, when, getting gradually excited, he would end by flying off his perch with a kris in his hand. But, barring such interruptions, the deliberations upon Jim's fate went on night and day.

'Meanwhile he wandered about the courtyard, shunned by some, glared at by others, but watched by all, and practically at the mercy of the first casual ragamuffin with a chopper, in there. He took possession of a small tumbledown shed to sleep in; the effluvia of filth and rotten matter incommoded him greatly: it seems he had not lost his appetite though, because – he told me – he had been hungry all the blessed time. Now and again "some fussy ass" deputed from the council-room would come out running to him, and in honeyed tones would administer amazing interrogatories: "Were the Dutch coming to take the country? Would the white man like to go back down the river? What was the object of coming to such a miserable country? The Rajah wanted to know whether the white man could repair a watch? They did actually bring out to him a nickel clock of New England make, and out of sheer unbearable boredom he busied himself in trying to get the alarum to work. It was apparently when thus occupied in his shed that the true perception of his extreme peril dawned upon him. He had dropped the thing – he says – "like a hot potato," and walked out hastily, without the slightest idea of what he would, or indeed could do. He only knew that the position was intolerable. He strolled aimlessly beyond a sort of ramshackle little granary on posts, and his eyes fell on the broken stakes of the palisade; and then – he says – at once, without any mental process as it were, without any stir of emotion, he set about his escape as if executing a plan matured for a month. He walked off carelessly to give himself a good run, and when he faced about there was some dignitary, with two spearmen in attendance, close at his elbow ready with a question. He started off "from under his very nose," went over "like a bird," and landed on the other side with a fall that jarred all his bones and seemed to split his head. He picked himself up instantly. He never thought of anything at the time; all he could remember – he said – was a great yell; the first houses of Patusan were before him four hundred yards away; he saw the creek, and as it were mechanically put on more pace. The earth seemed fairly to fly backwards under his feet. He took off from the last dry spot, felt himself flying through the air, felt himself, without any shock, planted upright in an extremely soft and sticky mudbank. It was only when he tried to move his legs and found he couldn't that, in his own words, "he came to himself." He began to think of the "bally long spears." As a matter of fact, considering that the people inside the stockade had to run to the gate, then get down to the landing-place, get into boats, and pull round a point of land, he had more advance than he imagined. Besides, it being low water, the creek was without water – you couldn't call it dry – and practically he was safe for a time from everything but a very long shot perhaps. The higher firm ground was about six feet in front of him. "I thought I would have to die there all the same," he said. He reached and grabbed desperately with his hands, and only succeeded in gathering a horrible cold shiny heap of slime against his breast – up to his very chin. It seemed to him he was burying himself alive, and then he struck out madly, scattering the mud with his fists. It fell on his head, on his face, over his eyes, into his mouth. He told me that he remembered suddenly the courtyard, as you remember a place where you had been very happy years ago. He longed – so he said – to be back there again, mending the clock. Mending the clock – that was the idea. He made efforts, tremendous sobbing, gasping efforts, efforts that seemed to burst his eyeballs in their sockets and make him blind, and culminating into one mighty supreme effort in the darkness to crack the earth asunder, to throw it off his limbs – and he felt himself creeping feebly up the bank. He lay full length on the firm ground and saw the light, the sky. Then as a sort of happy thought the notion came to him that he would go to sleep. He will have it that he *did* actually go to sleep: that he slept – perhaps for a minute, perhaps for twenty seconds, or only for one second, but he recollects distinctly the violent convulsive start of awakening. He remained lying still for a while, and then he arose muddy from head to foot and stood there, thinking he was alone of his kind for hundreds of miles, alone, with no help, no sympathy, no pity to expect from anyone, like a hunted animal. The first houses were not more than twenty yards from him; and it was the desperate screaming of a frightened woman trying to carry off a child that started him again. He pelted straight on in his socks, be-plastered with filth out of all semblance to a human being. He traversed more than half the length of the settlement. The nimbler women fled right and left, the men just dropped whatever they had in their hands, and remained petrified with dropping jaws. He was a flying terror. He says he noticed the little children trying to run for life, falling on their little stomachs and kicking. He swerved between two houses up a slope, clambered in desperation over a barricade of felled trees (there wasn't a week without some fight in Patusan at that time), burst through a fence into a maize-patch, where a scared boy flung a stick at him, blundered upon a path, and ran all at once into the arms of several startled men. He just had breath enough to gasp out, "Doramin! Doramin!" He remembers being half-carried, half-rushed to the top of the slope, and in a vast enclosure with palms and fruit-trees being run up to a large man sitting massively in a chair in the midst of the greatest possible commotion and excitement. He fumbled in mud and clothes to produce the ring, and, finding himself suddenly on his back, wondered who had knocked him down. They had simply let him go – don't you know? – but he couldn't stand. At the foot of the slope random shots were fired, and above the roofs of the settlement there rose a dull roar of amazement. But he was safe. Doramin's people were barricading the gate and pouring water down his throat; Doramin's old wife, full of business and commiseration, was issuing shrill orders to her girls. "The old woman," he said, softly, "made a to-do over me as if I had been her own son. They put me into an immense bed – her state bed – and she ran in and out wiping her eyes to give me pats on the back. I must have been a pitiful object. I just lay there like a log for I don't know how long."

'He seemed to have a great liking for Doramin's old wife. She on her side had taken a motherly fancy to him. She had a round, nut-brown, soft face, all fine wrinkles, large, bright red lips (she chewed betel assiduously), and screwed-up, winking, benevolent eyes. She was constantly in movement, scolding busily and ordering unceasingly a troop of young women with clear brown faces and big grave eyes, her daughters, her servants, her slave-girls. You know how it is in these households: it's generally impossible to tell the difference. She was very spare, and even her ample outer garment, fastened in front with jewelled clasps, had somehow a skimpy effect. Her dark bare feet were thrust into yellow straw slippers of Chinese make. I have seen her myself flitting about with her extremely thick, long, grey hair falling about her shoulders. She uttered homely shrewd sayings, was of noble birth, and was eccentric and arbitrary. In the afternoon she would sit in a very roomy armchair opposite her husband, gazing steadily through a wide opening in the wall which gave an extensive view of the settlement and the river.

'She invariably tucked up her feet under her, but old Doramin sat squarely, sat imposingly as a mountain sits on a plain. He was only of the *nakhoda* or merchant class, but the respect shown to him and the dignity of his bearing were very striking. He was the chief of the second power in Patusan. The immigrants from Celebes (about sixty families that, with dependants and so on, could muster some two hundred men "wearing the kris") had elected him years ago for their head. The men of that race are intelligent, enterprising, revengeful, but with a more frank courage than the other Malays, and restless under oppression. They formed the party opposed to the Rajah. Of course the quarrels were for trade. This was the primary cause of faction fights, of the sudden outbreaks that would fill this or that part of the settlement with smoke, flame, the noise of shots and shrieks. Villages were burnt, men were dragged into the Rajah's stockade to be killed or tortured for the crime of trading with anybody else but himself. Only a day or two before Jim's arrival several heads of households in the very fishing village that was afterwards taken under his especial protection had been driven over the cliffs by a party of the Rajah's spearmen, on suspicion of having been collecting edible birds' nests for a Celebes trader. Rajah Allang pretended to be the only trader in his country, and the penalty for the breach of the monopoly was death; but his idea of trading was indistinguishable from the commonest forms of robbery. His cruelty and rapacity had no other bounds than his cowardice, and he was afraid of the organised power of the Celebes men, only – till Jim came – he was not afraid enough to keep quiet. He struck at them through his subjects, and thought himself pathetically in the right. The situation was complicated by a wandering stranger, an Arab half-breed, who, I believe, on purely religious grounds, had incited the tribes in the interior (the bush-folk, as Jim himself called them) to rise, and had established himself in a fortified camp on the summit of one of the twin hills. He hung over the town of Patusan like a hawk over a poultry yard, but he devastated the open country. Whole villages, deserted, rotted on their blackened posts over the banks of clear streams, dropping piecemeal into the water the grass of their walls, the leaves of their roofs, with a curious effect of natural decay as if they had been a form of vegetation stricken by a blight at its very root. The two parties in Patusan were not sure which one this partisan most desired to plunder. The Rajah intrigued with him feebly. Some of the Bugis settlers, weary with endless insecurity, were half inclined to call him in. The younger spirits amongst them, chaffing, advised to "get Sherif Ali with his wild men and drive the Rajah Allang out of the country." Doramin restrained them with difficulty. He was growing old, and, though his influence had not diminished, the situation was getting beyond him. This was the state of affairs when Jim, bolting from the Rajah's stockade, appeared before the chief of the Bugis, produced the ring, and was received in a manner of speaking, into the heart of the community.'

Chapter 26

'Doramin was one of the most remarkable men of his race I had ever seen. His bulk for a Malay was immense, but he did not look merely fat, he looked imposing, monumental. This motionless body, clad in rich stuffs, coloured silks, gold embroideries; this huge head, enfolded in a red-and-gold headkerchief; the flat, big, round face, wrinkled, furrowed, with two semicircular heavy folds starting on each side of wide, fierce nostrils, and enclosing a thick-lipped mouth; the throat like a bull; the vast corrugated brow overhanging the staring proud eyes – made a whole that, once seen, can never be forgotten. His impassive repose (he seldom stirred a limb when once he sat down) was like a display of dignity. He was never known to raise his voice. It was a hoarse and powerful murmur, slightly veiled as if heard from a distance. When he walked, two short, sturdy young fellows, naked to the waist, in white sarongs and with black skull-caps on the backs of their heads, sustained his elbows; they would ease him down and stand behind his chair till he wanted to rise, when he would turn his head slowly, as if with difficulty, to the right and to the left, and then they would catch him under his armpits and help him up. For all that, there was nothing of a cripple about him: on the contrary, all his ponderous movements were like manifestations of a mighty deliberate force. It was generally believed he consulted his wife as to public affairs; but nobody, as far as I know, had ever heard them exchange a single word. When they sat in state by the wide opening it was in silence. They could see below them in the declining light the vast expanse of the forest country, a dark sleeping sea of sombre green undulating as far as the violet and purple range of mountains; the shining sinuosity of the river like an immense letter S of beaten silver; the brown ribbon of houses following the sweep of both banks, overtopped by the twin hills uprising above the nearer tree-tops. They were wonderfully contrasted: she, light, delicate, spare, quick, a little witch-like, with a touch of motherly fussiness in her repose; he, facing her, immense and heavy, like a figure of a man roughly fashioned of stone, with something magnanimous and ruthless in his immobility. The son of these old people was a most distinguished youth.

'They had him late in life. Perhaps he was not really so young as he looked. Four- or five-and-twenty is not so young when a man is already father of a family at eighteen. When he entered the large room, lined and carpeted with fine mats, and with a high ceiling of white sheeting, where the couple sat in state surrounded by a most deferential retinue, he would make his way straight to Doramin, to kiss his hand – which the other abandoned to him majestically – and then would step across to stand by his mother's chair. I suppose I may say they idolised him, but I never caught them giving him an overt glance. Those, it is true, were public functions. The room was generally thronged. The solemn formality of greetings and leave-takings, the profound respect expressed in gestures, on the faces, in the low whispers, is simply indescribable. "It's well worth seeing," Jim had assured me while we were crossing the river, on our way back. "They are like people in a book, aren't they?" he said triumphantly. "And Dain Waris – their son – is the best friend (barring you) I ever had. What Mr Stein would call a good 'war-comrade.' I was in luck. Jove! I was in luck when I tumbled amongst them at my last gasp." He meditated with bowed head, then rousing himself he added: "Of course I didn't go to sleep over it, but . . . " He paused again. "It seemed to come to me," he murmured. "All at once I saw what I had to do . . . "

'There was no doubt that it had come to him; and *it* had come through the war, too, as is natural, since this power that came to him was the power to make peace. It is in this sense alone that might so often *is* right. You must not think he had seen his way at once. When he arrived the Bugis community was in a most critical position. "They were all afraid," he said to me – "each man afraid for himself; while I could see as plain as possible that they must do something at once, if they did not want to go under one after another, what between the Rajah and that vagabond Sherif." But to see that was nothing. When he got his idea he had to drive it into reluctant minds, through the bulwarks of fear, of selfishness. He drove it in at last. And that was nothing. He had to devise the means. He devised them – an audacious plan; and his task was only half done. He had to inspire with his own confidence a lot of people who had hidden and absurd reasons to hang back; he had to conciliate imbecile jealousies, and argue away all sorts of senseless mistrusts. Without the weight of Doramin's authority, and his son's fiery enthusiasm, he would have failed. Dain Waris, the distinguished youth, was the first to believe in him; theirs was one of those strange, profound, rare friendships between brown and white, in which the very difference of race seems to draw two human beings closer by some mystic element of sympathy. Of Dain Waris, his own people said with pride that he knew how to fight like a white man. This was true; he had that sort of courage – the courage in the open, I may say – but he had also a European mind. You meet them sometimes like that, and are surprised to discover unexpectedly a familiar turn of thought, an unobscured vision, a tenacity of purpose, a touch of altruism. Of small stature, but admirably well proportioned, Dain Waris had a proud carriage, a polished, easy bearing, a temperament like a clear flame. His dusky face, with big black eyes, was in action expressive, and in repose thoughtful. He was of a silent disposition; a firm glance, an ironic smile, a courteous deliberation of manner seemed to hint at great reserves of intelligence and power. Such beings open to the Western eye, so often concerned with mere surfaces, the hidden possibilities of races and lands over which hangs the mystery of unrecorded ages. He not only trusted Jim, he understood him, I firmly believe. I speak of him because he had captivated me. His – if I may say so – his caustic placidity, and at the same time, his intelligent sympathy with Jim's aspirations, appealed to me. I seemed to behold the very origin of friendship. If Jim took the lead, the other had captivated his leader. In fact, Jim the leader was a captive in every sense. The land, the people, the friendship, the love, were like the jealous guardians of his body. Every day added a link to the fetters of that strange freedom. I felt convinced of it, as from day to day I learned more of the story.

'The story! Haven't I heard the story? I've heard it on the march, in camp (he made me scour the country after invisible game); I've listened to a good part of it on one of the twin summits, after climbing the last hundred feet or so on my hands and knees. Our escort (we had volunteer followers from village to village) has camped meantime on a bit of level ground half-way up the slope, and in the still breathless evening the smell of wood-smoke reached our nostrils from below with the penetrating delicacy of some choice scent. Voices also ascended, wonderful in their distinct and immaterial clearness. Jim sat on the trunk of a felled tree, and pulling out his pipe began to smoke. A new growth of grass and bushes was springing up; there were traces of an earthwork under a mass of thorny twigs. "It all started from here," he said, after a long and meditative silence. On the other hill, two hundred yards across a sombre precipice, I saw a line of high blackened stakes, showing here and there ruinously – the remnants of Sherif Ali's impregnable camp.

'But it had been taken, though. That had been his idea. He had mounted Doramin's old ordnance on the top of that hill; two rusty iron seven-pounders, a lot of small brass cannon – currency cannon. But if the brass guns represent wealth, they can also, when crammed recklessly to the muzzle, send a solid shot to some little distance. The thing was to get them up there. He showed me where he had fastened the cables, explained how he had improvised a rude capstan out of a hollowed log turning upon a pointed stake, indicated with the bowl of his pipe the outline of the earthwork. The last hundred feet of the ascent had been the most difficult. He had made himself responsible for success on his own head. He had induced the war party to work hard all night. Big fires lighted at intervals blazed all down the slope, "but up here," he explained, "the hoisting gang had to fly around in the dark." From the top he saw men moving on the hillside like ants at work. He himself on that night had kept on rushing down and climbing up like a squirrel, directing, encouraging, watching all along the line. Old Doramin had himself carried up the hill in his armchair. They put him down on the level place upon the slope, and he sat there in the light of one of the big fires – "amazing old chap – real old chieftain," said Jim, "with his little fierce eyes – a pair of immense flintlock pistols on his knees. Magnificent things, ebony, silver-mounted, with beautiful locks and a calibre like an old blunderbuss. A present from Stein, it seems – in exchange for that ring, you know. Used to belong to good old M'Neil. God only knows how *he* came by them. There he sat, moving neither hand nor foot, a flame of dry brushwood behind him, and lots of people rushing about, shouting and pulling round him – the most solemn, imposing old chap you can imagine. *He* wouldn't have had much chance if Sherif Ali had let his infernal crew loose at us and stampeded my lot. Eh? Anyhow he had come up there to die if anything went wrong. No mistake! Jove! It thrilled me to see him there – like a rock. But the Sherif must have thought us mad, and never troubled to come and see how we got on. Nobody believed it could be done. Why! I think the very chaps who pulled and shoved and sweated over it did not believe it could be done! Upon my word I don't think they did . . ."

'He stood erect, the smouldering brier-wood in his clutch, with a smile on his lips and a sparkle in his boyish eyes. I sat on the stump of a tree at his feet, and below us stretched the land, the great expanse of the forests, sombre under the sunshine, rolling like a sea, with glints of winding rivers, the grey spots of villages, and here and there a clearing, like an islet of light amongst the dark waves of continuous tree-tops. A brooding gloom lay over this vast and monotonous landscape; the light fell on it as if into an abyss. The land devoured the sunshine; only far off, along the coast, the empty ocean, smooth and polished within the faint haze, seemed to rise up to the sky in a wall of steel.

'And there I was with him, high in the sunshine on the top of that historic hill of his. He dominated the forest, the secular gloom, the old mankind. He was like a figure set up on a pedestal, to represent in his persistent youth the power, and perhaps the virtues, of races that never grow old, that have emerged from the gloom. I don't know why he should always have appeared to me symbolic. Perhaps this is the real cause of my interest in his fate. I don't know whether it was exactly fair to him to remember the incident which had given a new direction to his life, but at that very moment I remembered very distinctly. It was like a shadow in the light.'

Chapter 27

'Already the legend had gifted him with supernatural powers. Yes, it was said, there had been many ropes cunningly disposed, and a strange contrivance that turned by the efforts of many men, and each gun went up tearing slowly through the bushes, like a wild pig rooting its way in the undergrowth, but . . . and the wisest shook their heads. There was something occult in all this, no doubt; for what is the strength of ropes and of men's arms? There is a rebellious soul in things which must be overcome by powerful charms and incantations. Thus old Sura – a very respectable householder of Patusan – with whom I had a quiet chat one evening. However, Sura was a professional sorcerer also, who attended all the rice sowings and reapings for miles around for the purpose of subduing the stubborn soul of things. This occupation he seemed to think a most arduous one, and perhaps the souls of things are more stubborn than the souls of men. As to the simple folk of outlying villages, they believed and said (as the most natural thing in the world) that Jim had carried the guns up the hill on his back – two at a time.

'This would make Jim stamp his foot in vexation and exclaim with an exasperated little laugh: "What can you do with such silly beggars? They will sit up half the night talking bally rot, and the greater the lie the more they seem to like it." You could trace the subtle influence of his surroundings in this irritation. It was part of his captivity. The earnestness of his denials was amusing, and at last I said: "My dear fellow, you don't suppose *I* believe this." He looked at me quite startled. "Well, no! I suppose not," he said, and burst into a Homeric peal of laughter. "Well, anyhow the guns were there, and went off together at sunrise. Jove! You should have seen the splinters fly," he cried. By his side Dain Waris, listening with a quiet smile, dropped his eyelids and shuffled his feet a little. It appears that the success in mounting the guns had given Jim's people such a feeling of confidence that he ventured to leave the battery under charge of two elderly Bugis who had seen some fighting in their day, and went to join Dain Waris and the storming party who were concealed in the ravine. In the small hours they began creeping up, and when two-thirds of the way up, lay in the wet grass waiting for the appearance of the sun, which was the agreed signal. He told me with what impatient anguishing emotion he watched the swift coming of the dawn; how, heated with the work and the climbing, he felt the cold dew chilling his very bones; how afraid he was he would begin to shiver and shake like a leaf before the time came for the advance. "It was the slowest half-hour in my life," he declared. Gradually the silent stockade came out on the sky above him. Men scattered all down the slope were crouching amongst the dark stones and dripping bushes. Dain Waris was lying flattened by his side. "We looked at each other," Jim said, resting a gentle hand on his friend's shoulder. "He smiled at me as cheery as you please, and I dared not stir my lips for fear I would break out into a shivering fit. 'Pon my word, it's true! I had been streaming with perspiration when we took cover – so you may imagine . . . " He declared, and I believe him, that he had no fears as to the result. He was only anxious as to his ability to repress these shivers. He didn't bother about the result. He was bound to get to the top of that hill and stay there, whatever might happen. There could be no going back for him. Those people had trusted him implicitly. Him alone! His bare word . . .

'I remember how, at this point, he paused with his eyes fixed upon me. "As far as he knew, they never had an occasion to regret it yet," he said. "Never. He hoped to God they never would. Meantime – worse luck! – they had got into the habit of taking his word for anything and everything. I could have no idea! Why! Only the other day an old fool he had never seen in his life came from some village miles away to find out if he should divorce his wife. Fact. Solemn word. That's the sort of thing . . . He wouldn't have believed it. Would I? Squatted on the veranda chewing betel-nut, sighing and spitting all over the place for more than an hour, and as glum as an undertaker before he came out with that dashed conundrum. That's the kind of thing that isn't so funny as it looks. What was a fellow to say? – Good wife? – Yes. Good wife – old though; started a confounded long story about some brass pots. Been living together for fifteen years – twenty years – could not tell. A long, long time. Good wife. Beat her a little – not much – just a little, when she was young. Had to – for the sake of his honour. Suddenly in her old age she goes and lends three brass pots to her sister's son's wife, and begins to abuse him every day in a loud voice. His enemies jeered at him; his face was utterly blackened. Pots totally lost. Awfully cut up about it. Impossible to fathom a story like that; told him to go home, and promised to come along myself and settle it all. It's all very well to grin, but it was the dashedest nuisance! A day's journey through the forest, another day lost in coaxing a lot of silly villagers to get at the rights of the affair. There was the making of a sanguinary shindy in the thing. Every bally idiot took sides with one family or the other, and one half of the village was ready to go for the other half with anything that came handy. Honour bright! No joke! . . . Instead of attending to their bally crops. Got him the infernal pots back of course – and pacified all hands. No trouble to settle it. Of course not. Could settle the deadliest quarrel in the country by crooking his little finger. The trouble was to get at the truth of anything. Was not sure to this day whether he had been fair to all parties. It worried him. And the talk! Jove! There didn't seem to be any head or tail to it. Rather storm a twenty-foot-high old stockade any day. Much! Child's play to that other job. Wouldn't take so long either. Well, yes; a funny set-out, upon the whole – the fool looked old enough to be his grandfather. But from another point of view it was no joke. His word decided everything – ever since the smashing of Sherif Ali. An awful responsibility," he repeated. "No, really – joking apart, had it been three lives instead of three rotten brass pots it would have been the same . . . "

'Thus he illustrated the moral effect of his victory in war. It was in truth immense. It had led him from strife to peace, and through death into the innermost life of the people; but the gloom of the land spread out under the sunshine preserved its appearance of inscrutable, of secular repose. The sound of his fresh young voice – it's extraordinary how very few signs of wear he showed – floated lightly, and passed away over the unchanged face of the forests like the sound of the big guns on that cold dewy morning when he had no other concern on earth but the proper control of the chills in his body. With the first slant of sun-rays along these immovable tree-tops the summit of one hill wreathed itself, with heavy reports, in white clouds of smoke, and the other burst into an amazing noise of yells, war-cries, shouts of anger, of surprise, of dismay. Jim and Dain Waris were the first to lay their hands on the stakes. The popular story has it that Jim with a touch of one finger had thrown down the gate. He was, of course, anxious to disclaim this achievement. The whole stockade – he would insist on explaining to you – was a poor affair (Sherif Ali trusted mainly to the inaccessible position); and, anyway, the thing had been already knocked to pieces and only hung together by a miracle. He put his shoulder to it like a little fool and went in head over heels. Jove! If it hadn't been for Dain Waris, a pock-marked tattooed vagabond would have pinned him with his spear to a baulk of timber like one of Stein's beetles. The third man in, it seems, had been Tamb' Itam, Jim's own servant. This was a Malay from the north, a stranger who had wandered into Patusan, and had been forcibly detained by Rajah Allang as paddler of one of the state boats. He had made a bolt of it at the first opportunity, and finding a precarious refuge (but very little to eat) amongst the Bugis settlers, had attached himself to Jim's person. His complexion was very dark, his face flat, his eyes prominent and injected with bile. There was something excessive, almost fanatical, in his devotion to his "white lord." He was inseparable from Jim like a morose shadow. On state occasions he would tread on his master's heels, one hand on the haft of his kris, keeping the common people at a distance by his truculent brooding glances. Jim had made him the headman of his establishment, and all Patusan respected and courted him as a person of much influence. At the taking of the stockade he had distinguished himself greatly by the methodical ferocity of his fighting. The storming-party had come on so quick – Jim said – that notwithstanding the panic of the garrison, there was a "hot five minutes hand-to-hand inside that stockade, till some bally ass set fire to the shelters of boughs and dry grass, and we all had to clear out for dear life."

'The rout, it seems, had been complete. Doramin, waiting immovably in his chair on the hillside, with the smoke of the guns spreading slowly above his big head, received the news with a deep grunt. When informed that his son was safe and leading the pursuit, he, without another sound, made a mighty effort to rise; his attendants hurried to his help, and, held up reverently, he shuffled with great dignity into a bit of shade where he laid himself down to sleep covered entirely with a piece of white sheeting. In Patusan the excitement was intense. Jim told me that from the hill, turning his back on the stockade with its embers, black ashes, and half-consumed corpses, he could see time after time the open spaces between the houses on both sides of the stream fill suddenly with a seething rush of people and get empty in a moment. His ears caught feebly from below the tremendous din of gongs and drums; the wild shouts of the crowd reached him in bursts of faint roaring. A lot of streamers made a flutter as of little white, red, yellow birds amongst the brown ridges of roofs. "You must have enjoyed it," I murmured, feeling the stir of sympathetic emotion.

' "It was . . . it was immense! Immense!" he cried aloud, flinging his arms open. The sudden movement startled me as though I had seen him bare the secrets of his breast to the sunshine, to the brooding forests, to the steely sea. Below us the town reposed in easy curves upon the banks of a stream whose current seemed to sleep. "Immense!" he repeated for a third time, speaking in a whisper, for himself alone.

'Immense! No doubt it was immense; the seal of success upon his words, the conquered ground for the soles of his feet, the blind trust of men, the belief in himself snatched from the fire, the solitude of his achievement. All this, as I've warned you, gets dwarfed in the telling. I can't with mere words convey to you the impression of his total and utter isolation. I know, of course, he was in every sense alone of his kind there, but the unsuspected qualities of his nature had brought him in such close touch with his surroundings that this isolation seemed only the effect of his power. His loneliness added to his stature. There was nothing within sight to compare him with, as though he had been one of those exceptional men who can be only measured by the greatness of their fame; and his fame, remember, was the greatest thing around for many a day's journey. You would have to paddle, pole, or track a long weary way through the jungle before you passed beyond the reach of its voice. Its voice was not the trumpeting of the disreputable goddess we all know – not blatant – not brazen. It took its tone from the stillness and gloom of the land without a past, where his word was the one truth of every passing day. It shared something of the nature of that silence through which it accompanied you into unexplored depths, heard continuously by your side, penetrating, far-reaching – tinged with wonder and mystery on the lips of whispering men.'

Chapter 28

'The defeated Sherif Ali fled the country without making another stand, and when the miserable hunted villagers began to crawl out of the jungle back to their rotting houses, it was Jim who, in consultation with Dain Waris, appointed the headmen. Thus he became the virtual ruler of the land. As to old Tunku Allang, his fears at first had known no bounds. It is said that at the intelligence of the successful storming of the hill he flung himself, face down, on the bamboo floor of his audience-hall, and lay motionless for a whole night and a whole day, uttering stifled sounds of such an appalling nature that no man dared approach his prostrate form nearer than a spear's length. Already he could see himself driven ignominiously out of Patusan, wandering abandoned, stripped, without opium, without his women, without his followers, a fair game for the first comer to kill. After Sherif Ali his turn would come, and who could resist an attack led by such a devil? And indeed he owed his life and such authority as he still possessed at the time of my visit to Jim's idea of what was fair alone. The Bugis had been extremely anxious to pay off old scores, and the impassive old Doramin cherished the hope of yet seeing his son ruler of Patusan. During one of our interviews he deliberately allowed me to get a glimpse of this secret ambition. Nothing could be finer in its way than the dignified wariness of his approaches. He himself – he began by declaring – had used his strength in his younger days, but now he had grown old and tired . . . With his imposing bulk and haughty little eyes darting sagacious, inquisitive glances, he reminded one irresistibly of a cunning old elephant; the slow rise and fall of his vast breast went on, powerful and regular, like the heave of a calm sea. He, too, as he protested, had an unbounded confidence in Tuan Jim's wisdom. If he could only obtain a promise! One word would be enough! . . . His breathing silences, the low rumblings of his voice, recalled the last efforts of a spent thunderstorm.

'I tried to put the subject aside. It was difficult, for there could be no question that Jim had the power; in his new sphere there did not seem to be anything that was not his to hold or to give. But that, I repeat, was nothing in comparison with the notion, which occurred to me, while I listened with a show of attention, that he seemed to have come very near at last to mastering his fate. Doramin was anxious about the future of the country, and I was struck by the turn he gave to the argument. The land remains where God had put it; but white men – he said – they come to us and in a little while they go. They go away. Those they leave behind do not know when to look for their return. They go to their own land, to their people, and so this white man, too, would . . . I don't know what induced me to commit myself at this point by a vigorous "No. no." The whole extent of this indiscretion became apparent when Doramin, turning full upon me his face, whose expression, fixed in rugged deep folds, remained unalterable, like a huge brown mask, said that this was good news indeed, reflectively; and then wanted to know why.

'His little, motherly witch of a wife sat on my other hand, with her head covered and her feet tucked up, gazing through the great shutter-hole. I could only see a straying lock of grey hair, a high cheek-bone, the slight masticating motion of the sharp chin. Without removing her eyes from the vast prospect of forests stretching as far as the hills, she asked me in a pitying voice why was it that he so young had wandered from his home, coming so far, through so many dangers? Had he no household there, no kinsmen in his own country? Had he no old mother, who would always remember his face? . . .

'I was completely unprepared for this. I could only mutter and shake my head vaguely. Afterwards I am perfectly aware I cut a very poor figure trying to extricate myself out of this difficulty. From that moment, however, the old *nakhoda* became taciturn. He was not very pleased I fear, and evidently I had given him food for thought. Strangely enough, on the evening of that very day (which was my last in Patusan) I was once more confronted with the same question, with the unanswerable why of Jim's fate. And this brings me to the story of his love.

'I suppose you think it is a story that you can imagine for yourselves. We have heard so many such stories, and the majority of us don't believe them to be stories of love at all. For the most part we look upon them as stories of opportunities: episodes of passion at best, or perhaps only of youth and temptation, doomed to forgetfulness in the end, even if they pass through the reality of tenderness and regret. This view mostly is right, and perhaps in this case, too . . . Yet I don't know. To tell this story is by no means so easy as it should be – were the ordinary standpoint adequate. Apparently it is a story very much like the others; for me, however, there is visible in its background the melancholy figure of a woman, the shadow of a cruel wisdom buried in a lonely grave, looking on wistfully, helplessly, with sealed lips. The grave itself, as I came upon it during an early morning stroll, was a rather shapeless brown mound, with an inlaid neat border of white lumps of coral at the base, and enclosed within a circular fence made of split saplings, with the bark left on. A garland of leaves and flowers was woven about the heads of the slender posts – and the flowers were fresh.

'Thus, whether the shadow is of my imagination or not, I can at all events point out the significant fact of an unforgotten grave. When I tell you besides that Jim with his own hands had worked at the rustic fence, you will perceive directly the difference, the individual side of the story. There is in his espousal of memory and affection belonging to another human being something characteristic of his seriousness. He had a conscience, and it was a romantic conscience. Through her whole life the wife of the unspeakable Cornelius had no other companion, confidant, and friend but her daughter. How the poor woman had come to marry the awful Malacca Portuguese – after the separation from the father of her girl – and how that separation had been brought about, whether by death, which can be sometimes merciful, or by the merciless pressure of conventions, is a mystery to me. From the little which Stein (who knew so many stories) had let drop in my hearing, I am convinced that she was no ordinary woman. Her own father had been a white; a high official; one of the brilliantly endowed men who are not dull enough to nurse a success, and whose careers so often end under a cloud. I suppose she, too, must have lacked the saving dullness – and her career ended in Patusan. Our common fate . . . for where is the man – I mean a real sentient man – who does not remember vaguely having been deserted in the fullness of possession by someone or something more precious than life? . . . our common fate fastens upon the women with a peculiar cruelty. It does not punish like a master, but inflicts lingering torment, as if to gratify a secret, unappeasable spite. One would think that, appointed to rule on earth, it seeks to revenge itself upon the beings that come nearest to rising above the trammels of earthly caution; for it is only women who manage to put at times into their love an element just palpable enough to give one a fright – an extraterrestrial touch. I ask myself with wonder – how the world can look to them – whether it has the shape and substance *we* know, the air *we* breathe! Sometimes I fancy it must be a region of unreasonable sublimities seething with the excitement of their adventurous souls, lighted by the glory of all possible risks and renunciations. However, I suspect there are very few women in the world, though of course I am aware of the multitudes of mankind and of the equality of sexes in point of numbers – that is. But I am sure that the mother was as much of a woman as the daughter seemed to be. I cannot help picturing to myself these two, at first the young woman and the child, then the old woman and the young girl, the awful sameness and the swift passage of time, the barrier of forest, the solitude and the turmoil round these two lonely lives, and every word spoken between them penetrated with sad meaning. There must have been confidences, not so much of fact, I suppose, as of innermost feelings – regrets – fears – warnings, no doubt: warnings that the younger did not fully understand till the elder was dead – and Jim came along. Then I am sure she understood much – not everything – the fear mostly, it seems. Jim called her by a word that means precious, in the sense of a precious gem – jewel. Pretty, isn't it? But he was capable of anything. He was equal to his fortune, as he – after all – must have been equal to his misfortune. Jewel he called her; and he would say this as he might have said "Jane," don't you know – with a marital, homelike, peaceful effect. I heard the name for the first time ten minutes after I had landed in his courtyard, when, after nearly shaking my arm off, he darted up the steps and began to make a joyous, boyish disturbance at the door under the heavy eaves. "Jewel! O Jewel! Quick! Here's a friend come" . . . and suddenly peering at me in the dim veranda, he mumbled earnestly, "You know – this – no confounded nonsense about it – can't tell you how much I owe to her – and so – you understand – I – exactly as if . . ." His hurried, anxious whispers were cut short by the flitting of a white form within the house, a faint exclamation, and a childlike but energetic little face with delicate features and a profound, attentive glance peeped out of the inner gloom, like a bird out of the recess of a nest. I was struck by the name, of course; but it was not till later on that I connected it with an astonishing rumour that had met me on my journey, at a little place on the coast about 230 miles south of Patusan river. Stein's schooner, in which I had my passage, put in there, to collect some produce, and going ashore, I found to my great surprise that the wretched locality could boast of a third-class deputy-assistant resident, a big, fat, greasy, blinking fellow of mixed descent, with turned-out, shiny lips. I found him lying extended on his back in a cane chair, odiously unbuttoned, with a large green leaf of some sort on the top of his steaming head, and another in his hand which he used lazily as a fan . . . Going to Patusan? Oh, yes. Stein's Trading Company. He knew. Had a permission. No business of his. It was not so bad there now, he remarked negligently, and, he went on drawling, "There's some sort of white vagabond had got in there, I hear . . . Eh? What you say? Friend of yours? So! . . . Then it was true there was one of these *vordamte* – What was he up to? Found his way in, the rascal. Eh? I had not been sure. Patusan – they cut throats there – no business of ours." He interrupted himself to groan. "Phoo! Almighty! The heat! The heat! Well, then, there might be something in the story, too, after all, and . . ." He shut one of his beastly glassy eyes (the eyelid went on quivering), while he leered at me atrociously with the other. "Look here," says he, mysteriously, "if – do you understand? – if he has really got hold of something fairly good – none of your bits of green glass – understand? – I am a government official – you tell the rascal . . . Eh? What? Friend of yours?" . . . He continued wallowing calmly in the chair . . . "You said so; that's just it; and I am pleased to give you the hint. I suppose you, too, would like to get something out of it? Don't interrupt. You just tell him I've heard the tale, but to my government I have made no report. Not yet. See? Why make a report? Eh? Tell him to come to me if they let him get alive out of the country. He had better look out for himself. Eh? I promise to ask no questions. On the quiet – you understand? You, too – you shall get something from me. Small commission for the trouble. Don't interrupt. I am a government official, and make no report. That's business. Understand? I know some good people that will buy anything worth having, and can give him more money than the scoundrel ever saw in his life. I know his sort." He fixed me steadfastly with both his eyes open, while I stood over him utterly amazed, and asking myself whether he was mad or drunk. He perspired, puffed, moaning feebly, and scratching himself with such horrible composure that I could not bear the sight long enough to find out. Next day, talking casually with the people of the little native court of the place, I discovered that a story was travelling slowly down the coast about a mysterious white man in Patusan who had got hold of an extraordinary gem – namely, an emerald of an enormous size, and altogether priceless. The emerald seems to appeal more to the Eastern imagination than any other precious stone. The white man had obtained it, I was told, partly by the exercise of his wonderful strength and partly by cunning, from the ruler of a distant country, whence he had fled instantly arriving in Patusan in utmost distress, but frightening the people by his extreme ferocity, which nothing seemed able to subdue. Most of my informants were of the opinion that the stone was probably unlucky – like the famous stone of the Sultan of Succadana, which in the old times had brought wars and untold calamities upon that country. Perhaps it was the same stone – one couldn't say. Indeed the story of a fabulously large emerald is as old as the arrival of the first white men in the Archipelago; and the belief in it is so persistent that less than forty years ago there had been an official Dutch inquiry into the truth of it. Such a jewel – it was explained to me by the old fellow from whom I heard most of this amazing Jim-myth – a sort of scribe to the wretched little Rajah of the place; such a jewel, he said, cocking his poor purblind eyes up at me (he was sitting on the cabin floor out of respect), is best preserved by being concealed about the person of a woman. Yet it is not every woman that would do. She must be young – he sighed deeply – and insensible to the seductions of love. He shook his head sceptically. But such a woman seemed to be actually in existence. He had been told of a tall girl, whom the white man treated with great respect and care, and who never went forth from the house unattended. People said the white man could be seen with her almost any day; they walked side by side openly, he holding her arm under his – pressed to his side – thus – in a most extraordinary way. This might be a lie, he conceded, for it was indeed a strange thing for anyone to do: on the other hand, there could be no doubt she wore the white man's jewel concealed upon her bosom.'

Chapter 29

'This was the theory of Jim's marital evening walks. I made a third on more than one occasion, unpleasantly aware every time of Cornelius, who nursed the aggrieved sense of his legal paternity, slinking in the neighbourhood with that peculiar twist of his mouth as if he were perpetually on the point of gnashing his teeth. But do you notice how, three hundred miles beyond the end of telegraph cables and mail-boat lines, the haggard utilitarian lies of our civilisation wither and die, to be replaced by pure exercises of imagination, that have the futility, often the charm, and sometimes the deep hidden truthfulness, of works of art? Romance had singled Jim for its own – and that was the true part of the story, which otherwise was all wrong. He did not hide his jewel. In fact, he was extremely proud of it.

'It comes to me now that I had, on the whole, seen very little of her. What I remember best is the even, olive pallor of her complexion, and the intense blue-black gleams of her hair flowing abundantly from under a small crimson cap she wore far back on her shapely head. Her movements were free, assured, and she blushed a dusky red. While Jim and I were talking, she would come and go with rapid glances at us, leaving on her passage an impression of grace and charm and a distinct suggestion of watchfulness. Her manner presented a curious combination of shyness and audacity. Every pretty smile was succeeded swiftly by a look of silent, repressed anxiety, as if put to flight by the recollection of some abiding danger. At times she would sit down with us and, with her soft cheek dimpled by the knuckles of her little hand, she would listen to our talk; her big clear eyes would remain fastened on our lips, as though each pronounced word had a visible shape. Her mother had taught her to read and write; she had learned a good bit of English from Jim, and she spoke it most amusingly, with his own clipping, boyish intonation. Her tenderness hovered over him like a flutter of wings. She lived so completely in his contemplation that she had acquired something of his outward aspect, something that recalled him in her movements, in the way she stretched her arm, turned her head, directed her glances. Her vigilant affection had an intensity that made it almost perceptible to the senses; it seemed actually to exist in the ambient matter of space, to envelop him like a peculiar fragrance, to dwell in the sunshine like a tremulous, subdued, and impassioned note. I suppose you think that I, too, am romantic, but it is a mistake. I am relating to you the sober impressions of a bit of youth, of a strange uneasy romance that had come in my way. I observed with interest the work of his – well – good fortune. He was jealously loved, but why she should be jealous, and of what, I could not tell. The land, the people, the forests were her accomplices, guarding him with vigilant accord, with an air of seclusion, of mystery, of invincible possession. There was no appeal, as it were; he was imprisoned within the very freedom of his power, and she, though ready to make a footstool of her head for his feet, guarded her conquest inflexibly – as though he were hard to keep. The very Tamb' Itam, marching on our journeys upon the heels of his white lord, with his head thrown back, truculent and be-weaponed like a janissary, with kris, chopper, and lance (besides carrying Jim's gun); even Tamb' Itam allowed himself to put on the airs of uncompromising guardianship, like a surly devoted jailer ready to lay down his life for his captive. On the evenings when we sat up late his silent, indistinct form would pass and repass under the veranda, with noiseless footsteps, or lifting my head I would unexpectedly make him out standing rigidly erect in the shadow. As a general rule he would vanish after a time, without a sound; but when we rose he would spring up close to us as if from the ground, ready for any orders Jim might wish to give. The girl, too, I believe, never went to sleep till we had separated for the night. More than once I saw her and Jim through the window of my room come out together quietly and lean on the rough balustrade – two white forms very close, his arm about her waist, her head on his shoulder. Their soft murmurs reached me, penetrating, tender, with a calm sad note in the stillness of the night, like a self-communion of one being carried on in two tones. Later on, tossing on my bed under the mosquito net, I was sure to hear slight creakings, faint breathing, a throat cleared cautiously – and I would know that Tamb' Itam was still on the prowl. Though he had (by the favour of the white lord) a house in the compound, had "taken wife," and had lately been blessed with a child, I believe that, during my stay at all events, he slept on the veranda every night. It was very difficult to make this faithful and grim retainer talk. Even Jim himself was answered in jerky short sentences, under protest as it were. Talking, he seemed to imply, was no business of his. The longest speech I heard him volunteer was one morning when, suddenly extending his hand towards the courtyard, he pointed at Cornelius and said, "Here comes the Nazarene." I don't think he was addressing me, though I stood at his side; his object seemed rather to awaken the indignant attention of the universe. Some muttered allusions, which followed, to dogs and the smell of roast meat, struck me as singularly felicitous. The courtyard, a large square space, was one torrid blaze of sunshine, and, bathed in intense light, Cornelius was creeping across in full view with an inexpressible effect of stealthiness, of dark and secret slinking. He reminded one of everything that is unsavoury. His slow laborious walk resembled the creeping of a repulsive beetle, the legs alone moving with horrid industry while the body glided evenly. I suppose he made straight enough for the place where he wanted to get to, but his progress with one shoulder carried forward seemed oblique. He was often seen circling slowly amongst the sheds, as if following a scent; passing before the veranda with upward stealthy glances; disappearing without haste round the corner of some hut. That he seemed free of the place demonstrated Jim's absurd carelessness or else his infinite disdain, for Cornelius had played a very dubious part (to say the least of it) in a certain episode which might have ended fatally for Jim. As a matter of fact, it had redounded to his glory. But everything redounded to his glory, and it was the irony of his good fortune that he, who had been too careful of it once, seemed to bear a charmed life.

'You must know he had left Doramin's place very soon after his arrival – much too soon, in fact, for his safety, and of course a long time before the war. In this he was actuated by a sense of duty; he had to look after Stein's business, he said. Hadn't he? To that end, with an utter disregard of his personal safety, he crossed the river and took up his quarters with Cornelius. How the latter had managed to exist through the troubled times I can't say. As Stein's agent, after all, he must have had Doramin's protection in a measure; and in one way or another he had managed to wriggle through all the deadly complications, while I have no doubt that his conduct, whatever line he was forced to take, was marked by that abjectness which was like the stamp of the man. That was his characteristic; he was fundamentally and outwardly abject, as other men are markedly of a generous, distinguished, or venerable appearance. It was the element of his nature which permeated all his acts and passions and emotions; he raged abjectly, smiled abjectly, was abjectly sad; his civilities and his indignations were alike abject. I am sure his love would have been the most abject of sentiments – but can one imagine a loathsome insect in love? And his loathsomeness, too, was abject, so that a simply disgusting person would have appeared noble by his side. He has his place neither in the background nor in the foreground of the story; he is simply seen skulking on its outskirts, enigmatical and unclean, tainting the fragrance of its youth and of its naïveness.

'His position in any case could not have been other than extremely miserable, yet it may very well be that he found some advantages in it. Jim told me he had been received at first with an abject display of the most amicable sentiments. "The fellow apparently couldn't contain himself for joy," said Jim with disgust. "He flew at me every morning to shake both my hands – confound him! but I could never tell whether there would be any breakfast. If I got three meals in two days I considered myself jolly lucky, and he made me sign a chit for ten dollars every week. Said he was sure Mr Stein did not mean him to keep me for nothing. Well – he kept me on nothing as near as possible. Put it down to the unsettled state of the country, and made as if to tear his hair out, begging my pardon twenty times a day, so that I had at last to entreat him not to worry. It made me sick. Half the roof of his house had fallen in, and the whole place had a mangy look, with wisps of dry grass sticking out and the corners of broken mats flapping on every wall. He did his best to make out that Mr Stein owed him money on the last three years' trading, but his books were all torn, and some were missing. He tried to hint it was his late wife's fault. Disgusting scoundrel! At last I had to forbid him to mention his late wife at all. It made Jewel cry. I couldn't discover what became of all the trade-goods; there was nothing in the store but rats, having a high old time amongst a litter of brown paper and old sacking. I was assured on every hand that he had a lot of money buried somewhere, but of course could get nothing out of him. It was the most miserable existence I led there in that wretched house. I tried to do my duty by Stein, but I had also other matters to think of. When I escaped to Doramin old Tunku Allang got frightened and returned all my things. It was done in a roundabout way, and with no end of mystery, through a Chinaman who keeps a small shop here; but as soon as I left the Bugis quarter and went to live with Cornelius it began to be said openly that the Rajah had made up his mind to have me killed before long. Pleasant, wasn't it? And I couldn't see what there was to prevent him if he really *had* made up his mind. The worst of it was, I couldn't help feeling I wasn't doing any good either for Stein or for myself. Oh! it was beastly – the whole six weeks of it." '

Chapter 30

'He told me further that he didn't know what made him hang on – but of course we may guess. He sympathised deeply with the defenceless girl, at the mercy of that "mean, cowardly scoundrel." It appears Cornelius led her an awful life, stopping only short of actual ill-usage, for which he had not the pluck, I suppose. He insisted upon her calling him father – "and with respect, too – with respect," he would scream, shaking a little yellow fist in her face. "I am a respectable man, and what are you? Tell me – what are you? You think I am going to bring up somebody else's child and not to be treated with respect? You ought to be glad I let you. Come – say, Yes, father . . . No? . . . You wait a bit." Thereupon he would begin to abuse the dead woman, till the girl would run off with her hands to her head. He pursued her, dashing in and out and round the house and amongst the sheds, would drive her into some corner where she would fall on her knees stopping her ears, and then he would stand at a distance and declaim filthy denunciations at her back for half an hour at a stretch. "Your mother was a devil, a deceitful devil – and you, too, are a devil," he would shriek in a final outburst, pick up a bit of dry earth or a handful of mud (there was plenty of mud around the house), and fling it into her hair.

Sometimes, though, she would hold out full of scorn, confronting him in silence, her face sombre and contracted, and only now and then uttering a word or two that would make the other jump and writhe with the sting. Jim told me these scenes were terrible. It was indeed a strange thing to come upon in a wilderness. The endlessness of such a subtly cruel situation was appalling – if you think of it. The respectable Cornelius (Inchi 'Nelyus the Malays called him, with a grimace that meant many things) was a much disappointed man. I don't know what he had expected would be done for him in consideration of his marriage; but evidently the liberty to steal, and embezzle, and appropriate to himself for many years and in any way that suited him best, the goods of Stein's Trading Company (Stein kept the supply up unfalteringly as long as he could get his skippers to take it there) did not seem to him a fair equivalent for the sacrifice of his honourable name. Jim would have enjoyed exceedingly thrashing Cornelius within an inch of his life; on the other hand, the scenes were of so painful a character, so abominable, that his impulse would be to get out of earshot, in order to spare the girl's feelings. They left her agitated, speechless, clutching her bosom now and then with a stony, desperate face, and then Jim would lounge up and say unhappily, "Now – come – really – what's the use – you must try to eat a bit," or give some such mark of sympathy. Cornelius would keep on slinking through the doorways, across the veranda and back again, as mute as a fish, and with malevolent, mistrustful, underhand glances. "I can stop his game," Jim said to her once. "Just say the word." And do you know what she answered? She said – Jim told me impressively – that if she had not been sure he was intensely wretched himself, she would have found the courage to kill him with her own hands. "Just fancy that! The poor devil of a girl, almost a child, being driven to talk like that," he exclaimed in horror. It seemed impossible to save her not only from that mean rascal but even from herself! It wasn't that he pitied her so much, he affirmed; it was more than pity; it was as if he had something on his conscience, while that life went on. To leave the house would have appeared a base desertion. He had understood at last that there was nothing to expect from a longer stay, neither accounts nor money, nor truth of any sort, but he stayed on, exasperating Cornelius to the verge, I won't say of insanity, but almost of courage. Meantime he felt all sorts of dangers gathering obscurely about him. Doramin had sent over twice a trusty servant to tell him seriously that he could do nothing for his safety unless he would recross the river again and live amongst the Bugis as at first. People of every condition used to call often in the dead of night, in order to disclose to him plots for his assassination. He was to be poisoned. He was to be stabbed in the bath-house. Arrangements were being made to have him shot from a boat on the river. Each of these informants professed himself to be his very good friend. It was enough – he told me – to spoil a fellow's rest for ever. Something of the kind was extremely possible – nay, probable – but the lying warnings gave him only the sense of deadly scheming going on all around him, on all sides, in the dark. Nothing more calculated to shake the best of nerve. Finally, one night, Cornelius himself, with a great apparatus of alarm and secrecy, unfolded in solemn wheedling tones a little plan wherein for one hundred dollars – or even for eighty; let's say eighty – he, Cornelius, would procure a trustworthy man to smuggle Jim out of the river, all safe. There was nothing else for it now – if Jim cared a pin for his life. What's eighty dollars? A trifle. An insignificant sum. While he, Cornelius, who had to remain behind, was absolutely courting death by his proof of devotion to Mr Stein's young friend. The sight of his abject grimacing was – Jim told me – very hard to bear: he clutched at his hair, beat his breast, rocked himself to and fro with his hands pressed to his stomach, and actually pretended to shed tears. "Your blood be on your own head," he squeaked at last, and rushed out. It is a curious question how far Cornelius was sincere in that performance. Jim confessed to me that he did not sleep a wink after the fellow had gone. He lay on his back on a thin mat spread over the bamboo flooring, trying idly to make out the bare rafters, and listening to the rustlings in the torn thatch. A star suddenly twinkled through a hole in the roof. His brain was in a whirl; but, nevertheless, it was on that very night that he matured his plan for overcoming Sherif Ali. It had been the thought of all the moments he could spare from the hopeless investigation into Stein's affairs, but the notion – he says – came to him then all at once. He could see, as it were, the guns mounted on the top of the hill. He got very hot and excited lying there; sleep was out of the question more than ever. He jumped up, and went out barefooted on the veranda. Walking silently, he came upon the girl, motionless against the wall, as if on the watch. In his then state of mind it did not surprise him to see her up, nor yet to hear her ask in an anxious whisper where Cornelius could be. He simply said he did not know. She moaned a little, and peered into the *campong*. Everything was very quiet. He was possessed by his new idea, and so full of it that he could not help telling the girl all about it at once. She listened, clapped her hands lightly, whispered softly her admiration, but was evidently on the alert all the time. It seems he had been used to make a confidant of her all along – and that she on her part could and did give him a lot of useful hints as to Patusan affairs there is no doubt. He assured me more than once that he had never found himself the worse for her advice. At any rate, he was proceeding to explain his plan fully to her there and then, when she pressed his arm once, and vanished from his side. Then Cornelius appeared from somewhere, and, perceiving Jim, ducked sideways, as though he had been shot at, and afterwards stood very still in the dusk. At last he came forward prudently, like a suspicious cat. "There were some fishermen there – with fish," he said in a shaky voice. "To sell fish – you understand." . . . It must have been then two o'clock in the morning – a likely time for anybody to hawk fish about!

'Jim, however, let the statement pass, and did not give it a single thought.

Other matters occupied his mind, and besides he had neither seen nor heard anything. He contented himself by saying, "Oh!" absently, got a drink of water out of a pitcher standing there, and leaving Cornelius a prey to some inexplicable emotion – that made him embrace with both arms the worm-eaten rail of the veranda as if his legs had failed – went in again and lay down on his mat to think. By and by he heard stealthy footsteps. They stopped. A voice whispered tremulously through the wall, "Are you asleep?" "No! What is it?" he answered, briskly, and there was an abrupt movement outside, and then all was still, as if the whisperer had been startled. Extremely annoyed at this, Jim came out impetuously, and Cornelius with a faint shriek fled along the veranda as far as the steps, where he hung on to the broken banister. Very puzzled, Jim called out to him from the distance to know what the devil he meant. "Have you given your consideration to what I spoke to you about?" asked Cornelius, pronouncing the words with difficulty, like a man in the cold fit of a fever. "No!" shouted Jim in a passion. "I did not, and I don't intend to. I am going to live here, in Patusan." "You shall d-d-die h-h-here," answered Cornelius, still shaking violently, and in a sort of expiring voice. The whole performance was so absurd and provoking that Jim didn't know whether he ought to be amused or angry. "Not till I have seen you tucked away, you bet," he called out, exasperated yet ready to laugh. Half seriously (being excited with his own thoughts, you know) he went on shouting, "Nothing can touch me! You can do your damnedest." Somehow the shadowy Cornelius far off there seemed to be the hateful embodiment of all the annoyances and difficulties he had found in his path. He let himself go – his nerves had been overwrought for days – and called him many pretty names – swindler, liar, sorry rascal: in fact, carried on in an extraordinary way. He admits he passed all bounds, that he was quite beside himself – defied all Patusan to scare him away – declared he would make them all dance to his own tune yet, and so on, in a menacing, boasting strain. Perfectly bombastic and ridiculous, he said. His ears burned at the bare recollection. Must have been off his chump in some way . . . The girl, who was sitting with us, nodded her little head at me quickly, frowned faintly, and said, "I heard him," with childlike solemnity. He laughed and blushed. What stopped him at last, he said, was the silence, the complete deathlike silence, of the indistinct figure far over there, that seemed to hang collapsed, doubled over the rail in a weird immobility. He came to his senses, and ceasing suddenly, wondered greatly at himself. He watched for a while. Not a stir, not a sound. "Exactly as if the chap had died while I had been making all that noise," he said. He was so ashamed of himself that he went indoors in a hurry without another word, and flung himself down again. The row seemed to have done him good, though, because he went to sleep for the rest of the night like a baby. Hadn't slept like that for weeks. "But *I* didn't sleep," struck in the girl, one elbow on the table and nursing her cheek. "I watched." Her big eyes flashed, rolling a little, and then she fixed them on my face intently.'

Chapter 31

'You may imagine with what interest I listened. All these details were perceived to have some significance twenty-four hours later. In the morning Cornelius made no allusion to the events of the night. "I suppose you will come back to my poor house," he muttered, surlily, slinking up just as Jim was entering the canoe to go over to Doramin's *campong*. Jim only nodded, without looking at him. "You find it good fun, no doubt," muttered the other in a sour tone. Jim spent the day with the old *nakhoda*, preaching the necessity of vigorous action to the principal men of the Bugis community, who had been summoned for a big talk. He remembered with pleasure how very eloquent and persuasive he had been. "I managed to put some backbone into them that time, and no mistake," he said. Sherif Ali's last raid had swept the outskirts of the settlement, and some women belonging to the town had been carried off to the stockade. Sherif Ali's emissaries had been seen in the market-place the day before, strutting about haughtily in white cloaks, and boasting of the Rajah's friendship for their master. One of them stood forward in the shade of a tree, and, leaning on the long barrel of a rifle, exhorted the people to prayer and repentance, advising them to kill all the strangers in their midst, some of whom, he said, were infidels and others even worse – children of Satan in the guise of Moslems. It was reported that several of the Rajah's people amongst the listeners had loudly expressed their approbation. The terror amongst the common people was intense. Jim, immensely pleased with his day's work, crossed the river again before sunset.

'As he had got the Bugis irretrievably committed to action, and had made himself responsible for success on his own head, he was so elated that in the lightness of his heart he absolutely tried to be civil with Cornelius. But Cornelius became wildly jovial in response, and it was almost more than he could stand, he says, to hear his little squeaks of false laughter, to see him wriggle and blink, and suddenly catch hold of his chin and crouch low over the table with a distracted stare. The girl did not show herself, and Jim retired early. When he rose to say good-night, Cornelius jumped up, knocking his chair over, and ducked out of sight as if to pick up something he had dropped. His good-night came huskily from under the table. Jim was amazed to see him emerge with a dropping jaw, and staring, stupidly frightened eyes. He clutched the edge of the table. "What's the matter? Are you unwell?" asked Jim. "Yes, yes, yes. A great colic in my stomach," says the other; and it is Jim's opinion that it was perfectly true. If so, it was, in view of his contemplated action, an abject sign of a still imperfect callousness for which he must be given all due credit.

'Be it as it may, Jim's slumbers were disturbed by a dream of heavens like brass resounding with a great voice, which called upon him to Awake! Awake! so loud that, notwithstanding his desperate determination to sleep on, he did wake up in reality. The glare of a red spluttering conflagration going on in mid-air fell on his eyes. Coils of black thick smoke curved round the head of some apparition, some unearthly being, all in white, with a severe, drawn, anxious face. After a second or so he recognised the girl. She was holding a dammar torch at arm's length aloft, and in a persistent, urgent monotone she was repeating, "Get up! Get up! Get up!"

'Suddenly he leaped to his feet; at once she put into his hand a revolver, his own revolver, which had been hanging on a nail, but loaded this time. He gripped it in silence, bewildered, blinking in the light. He wondered what he could do for her.

'She asked rapidly and very low, "Can you face four men with this?" He laughed while narrating this part at the recollection of his polite alacrity. It seems he made a great display of it. "Certainly – of course – certainly – command me." He was not properly awake, and had a notion of being very civil in these extraordinary circumstances, of showing his unquestioning, devoted readiness. She left the room, and he followed her; in the passage they disturbed an old hag who did the casual cooking of the household, though she was so decrepit as to be hardly able to understand human speech. She got up and hobbled behind them, mumbling toothlessly. On the veranda a hammock of sailcloth, belonging to Cornelius, swayed lightly to the touch of Jim's elbow. It was empty.

'The Patusan establishment, like all the posts of Stein's Trading Company, had originally consisted of four buildings. Two of them were represented by two heaps of sticks, broken bamboos, rotten thatch, over which the four corner-posts of hardwood leaned sadly at different angles: the principal storeroom, however, stood yet, facing the agent's house. It was an oblong hut, built of mud and clay: it had at one end a wide door of stout planking, which so far had not come off the hinges, and in one of the side walls there was a square aperture, a sort of window, with three wooden bars. Before descending the few steps the girl turned her face over her shoulder and said quickly: "You were to be set upon while you slept." Jim tells me he experienced a sense of deception. It was the old story. He was weary of these attempts upon his life. He had had his fill of these alarms. He was sick of them. He assured me he was angry with the girl for deceiving him. He had followed her under the impression that it was she who wanted his help, and now he had half a mind to turn on his heel and go back in disgust. "Do you know," he commented, profoundly, "I rather think I was not quite myself for whole weeks on end about that time." "Oh, yes. You were, though," I couldn't help contradicting.

'But she moved on swiftly, and he followed her into the courtyard. All its fences had fallen in a long time ago; the neighbours' buffaloes would pace in the morning across the open space, snorting profoundly, without haste; the very jungle was invading it already. Jim and the girl stopped in the rank grass. The light in which they stood made a dense blackness all round, and only above their heads there was an opulent glitter of stars. He told me it was a beautiful night – quite cool, with a little stir of breeze from the river. It seems he noticed its friendly beauty. Remember this is a love-story I am telling you now. A lovely night that seemed to breathe on them a soft caress. The flame of the torch streamed now and then with a fluttering noise like a flag, and for a time this was the only sound. "They are in the storeroom waiting," whispered the girl; "they are waiting for the signal." "Who's to give it?" he asked. She shook the torch, which blazed up after a shower of sparks. "Only you have been sleeping so restlessly," she continued in a murmur. "I watched your sleep, too." "You!" he exclaimed craning his neck to look about him. "You think I watched on this night only!" she said, with a sort of despairing indignation.

'He says it was as if he had received a blow on the chest. He gasped. He thought he had been an awful brute somehow, and he felt remorseful, touched, happy, elated. This, let me remind you again, is a love story; you can see it by the imbecility, not a repulsive imbecility, the exalted imbecility of these proceedings, this station in torchlight, as if they had come there on purpose to have it out for the edification of concealed murderers. If Sherif Ali's emissaries had been possessed – as Jim remarked – of a pennyworth of spunk, this was the time to make a rush. His heart was thumping – not with fear – but he seemed to hear the grass rustle, and he stepped smartly out of the light. Something dark, imperfectly seen, flitted rapidly out of sight. He called out in a strong voice, "Cornelius! O Cornelius!" A profound silence succeeded: his voice did not seem to have carried twenty feet. Again the girl was by his side. "Fly!" she said. The old woman was coming up; her broken figure hovered in crippled little jumps on the edge of the light; they heard her mumbling, and a light, moaning sigh. "Fly!" repeated the girl, excitedly. "They are frightened now – this light – the voices. They know you are awake now – they know you are big, strong, fearless . . . " "If I am all that," he began, but she interrupted him. "Yes – tonight! But what of tomorrow night? Of the next night? Of the night after – of all the many, many nights? Can I be always watching?" A sobbing catch of her breath affected him beyond the power of words.

'He told me that he had never felt so small, so powerless – and as to courage, what was the good of it? he thought. He was so helpless that even flight seemed of no use; and though she kept on whispering, "Go to Doramin, go to Doramin," with feverish insistence, he realised that for him there was no refuge from that loneliness which centupled all his dangers except – in her. "I thought," he said to me, "that if I went away from her it would be the end of everything somehow." Only as they couldn't stop there for ever in the middle of that courtyard, he made up his mind to go and look into the storehouse. He let her follow him without thinking of any protest, as if they had been indissolubly united. "I am fearless – am I?" he muttered through his teeth. She restrained his arm. "Wait till you hear my voice," she said, and, torch in hand, ran lightly round the corner. He remained alone in the darkness, his face to the door: not a sound, not a breath came from the other side. The old hag let out a dreary groan somewhere behind his back. He heard a high-pitched almost screaming call from the girl. "Now! Push!" He pushed violently; the door swung with a creak and a clatter, disclosing to his intense astonishment the low dungeon-like interior illuminated by a lurid, wavering glare. A turmoil of smoke eddied down upon an empty wooden crate in the middle of the floor, a litter of rags and straw tried to soar, but only stirred feebly in the draught. She had thrust the light through the bars of the window. He saw her bare round arm extended and rigid, holding up the torch with the steadiness of an iron bracket. A conical ragged heap of old mats cumbered a distant corner almost to the ceiling, and that was all.

'He explained to me that he was bitterly disappointed at this. His fortitude had been tried by so many warnings, he had been for weeks surrounded by so many hints of danger, that he wanted the relief of some reality, of something tangible that he could meet. "It would have cleared the air for a couple of hours at least, if you know what I mean," he said to me. "Jove! I had been living for days with a stone on my chest." Now at last he had thought he would get hold of something, and – nothing! Not a trace, not a sign of anybody. He had raised his weapon as the door flew open, but now his arm fell. "Fire! Defend yourself," the girl outside cried in an agonising voice. She, being in the dark and with her arm thrust in to the shoulder through the small hole, couldn't see what was going on, and she dared not withdraw the torch now to run round. "There's nobody here!" yelled Jim, contemptuously, but his impulse to burst into a resentful exasperated laugh died without a sound: he had perceived in the very act of turning away that he was exchanging glances with a pair of eyes in the heap of mats. He saw a shifting gleam of whites. "Come out!" he cried in a fury, a little doubtful, and a dark-faced head, a head without a body, shaped itself in the rubbish, a strangely detached head, that looked at him with a steady scowl. Next moment the whole mound stirred, and with a low grunt a man emerged swiftly, and bounded towards Jim. Behind him the mats as it were jumped and flew, his right arm was raised with a crooked elbow, and the dull blade of a kris protruded from his fist held off, a little above his head. A cloth wound tight round his loins seemed dazzlingly white on his bronze skin; his naked body glistened as if wet.

'Jim noted all this. He told me he was experiencing a feeling of unutterable relief, of vengeful elation. He held his shot, he says, deliberately. He held it for the tenth part of a second, for three strides of the man – an unconscionable time. He held it for the pleasure of saying to himself: That's a dead man! He was absolutely positive and certain. He let him come on because it did not matter. A dead man, anyhow. He noticed the dilated nostrils, the wide eyes, the intent, eager stillness of the face, and then he fired.

'The explosion in that confined space was stunning. He stepped back a pace. He saw the man jerk his head up, fling his arms forward, and drop the kris. He ascertained afterwards that he had shot him through the mouth, a little upwards, the bullet coming out high at the back of the skull. With the impetus of his rush the man drove straight on, his face suddenly gaping disfigured, with his hands open before him gropingly, as though blinded, and landed with terrific violence on his forehead, just short of Jim's bare toes. Jim says he didn't lose the smallest detail of all this. He found himself calm, appeased, without rancour, without uneasiness, as if the death of that man had atoned for everything. The place was getting very full of sooty smoke from the torch, in which the unswaying flame burned blood-red without a flicker. He walked in resolutely, striding over the dead body, and covered with his revolver another naked figure outlined vaguely at the other end. As he was about to pull the trigger, the man threw away with force a short heavy spear, and squatted submissively on his hams, his back to the wall and his clasped hands between his legs. "You want your life?" Jim said. The other made no sound. "How many more of you?" asked Jim again. "Two more, *tuan*," said the man very softly, looking with big fascinated eyes into the muzzle of the revolver. Accordingly two more crawled from under the mats, holding out ostentatiously their empty hands.'

Chapter 32

'Jim took up an advantageous position and shepherded them out in a bunch through the doorway: all that time the torch had remained vertical in the grip of a little hand, without so much as a tremble. The three men obeyed him, perfectly mute, moving automatically. He ranged them in a row. "Link arms!" he ordered. They did so. "The first who withdraws his arm or turns his head is a dead man," he said. "March!" They stepped out together, rigidly; he followed, and at the side the girl, in a trailing white gown, her black hair falling as low as her waist, bore the light. Erect and swaying, she seemed to glide without touching the earth; the only sound was the silky swish and rustle of the long grass. "Stop!" cried Jim.

'The river-bank was steep; a great freshness ascended, the light fell on the edge of smooth dark water frothing without a ripple; right and left the shapes of the houses ran together below the sharp outlines of the roofs.

"Take my greetings to Sherif Ali – till I come myself," said Jim. Not one head of the three budged. "Jump!" he thundered. The three splashes made one splash, a shower flew up, black heads bobbed convulsively, and disappeared; but a great blowing and spluttering went on, growing faint, for they were diving industriously, in great fear of a parting shot. Jim turned to the girl, who had been a silent and attentive observer. His heart seemed suddenly to grow too big for his breast and choke him in the hollow of his throat. This probably made him speechless for so long, and after returning his gaze she flung the burning torch with a wide sweep of the arm into the river. The ruddy fiery glare, taking a long flight through the night, sank with a vicious hiss, and the calm soft starlight descended upon them, unchecked.

'He did not tell me what it was he said when at last he recovered his voice. I don't suppose he could be very eloquent. The world was still, the night breathed on them, one of those nights that seem created for the sheltering of tenderness, and there are moments when our souls, as if freed from their dark envelope, glow with an exquisite sensibility that makes certain silences more lucid than speeches. As to the girl, he told me, "She broke down a bit. Excitement – don't you know. Reaction. Deucedly tired she must have been – and all that kind of thing. And – and – hang it all – she was fond of me, don't you see . . . I, too . . . didn't know, of course . . . never entered my head . . . "

'There he got up and began to walk about in some agitation. "I – I love her dearly. More than I could tell. Of course one cannot tell. You take a different view of your actions when you come to understand, when you are *made* to understand every day that your existence is necessary – you see, absolutely necessary – to another person. I am made to feel that. Wonderful. But only try to think what her life had been. It is too extravagantly awful! Isn't it? And me finding her here like this – as you may go out for a stroll and come suddenly upon somebody drowning in a lonely dark place. Jove! No time to lose. Well, it is a trust, too . . . I believe I am equal to it . . . "

'I must tell you the girl had left us to ourselves some time before. He slapped his chest. "Yes! I feel that, but believe I am equal to all my luck!" He had the gift of finding a special meaning in everything that happened to him. This was the view he took of his love-affair; it was idyllic, a little solemn, and also true, since his belief had all the unshakable seriousness of youth. Some time after, on another occasion, he said to me, "I've been only two years here, and now, upon my word, I can't conceive being able to live anywhere else. The very thought of the world outside is enough to give me a fright; because, don't you see," he continued, with downcast eyes watching the action of his boot busied in squashing thoroughly a tiny bit of dried mud (we were strolling on the river-bank) – "because I have not forgotten why I came here. Not yet!"

'I refrained from looking at him, but I think I heard a short sigh; we took a turn or two in silence. "Upon my soul and conscience," he began again, "if such a thing can be forgotten, then I think I have a right to dismiss it from my mind. Ask any man here" . . . his voice changed. "Is it not strange," he went on in a gentle, almost yearning tone, "that all these people, all these people who would do anything for me, can never be made to understand? Never! If you disbelieve me I could not call them up. It seems hard, somehow. I am stupid, am I not? What more can I want? If you ask them who is brave – who is true – who is just – who is it they would trust with their lives? – they would say, Tuan Jim. And yet they can never know the real, real truth . . . "

'That's what he said to me on my last day with him. I did not let a murmur escape me: I felt he was going to say more, and come nearer to the root of the matter. The sun, whose concentrated glare dwarfs the earth into a restless mote of dust, had sunk behind the forest, and the diffused light from an opal sky seemed to cast upon a world without shadows and without brilliance the illusion of a calm and pensive greatness. I don't know why, listening to him, I should have noted so distinctly the gradual darkening of the river, of the air; the irresistible slow work of the night settling silently on all the visible forms, effacing the outlines, burying the shapes deeper and deeper, like a steady fall of impalpable black dust.

' "Jove!" he began, abruptly, "there are days when a fellow is too absurd for anything; only I know I can tell you what I like. I talk about being done with it – with the bally thing at the back of my head . . . Forgetting . . . Hang me if I know! I can think of it quietly. After all, what has it proved? Nothing. I suppose you don't think so . . . "

'I made a protesting murmur.

' "No matter," he said. "I am satisfied . . . nearly. I've got to look only at the face of the first man that comes along, to regain my confidence. They can't be made to understand what is going on in me. What of that? Come! I haven't done so badly."

' "Not so badly," I said.

' "But all the same, you wouldn't like to have me aboard your own ship – hey?"

' "Confound you!" I cried. "Stop this."

' "Aha! You see," he cried, crowing, as it were, over me placidly. "Only," he went on, "you just try to tell this to any of them here. They would think you a fool, a liar, or worse. And so I can stand it. I've done a thing or two for them, but this is what they have done for me."

' "My dear chap," I cried, "you shall always remain for them an insoluble mystery." Thereupon we were silent.

' "Mystery," he repeated, before looking up. "Well, then let me always remain here."

'After the sun had set, the darkness seemed to drive upon us, borne in every faint puff of the breeze. In the middle of a hedged path I saw the arrested, gaunt, watchful, and apparently one-legged silhouette of Tamb' Itam; and across the dusky space my eye detected something white moving to and fro behind the supports of the roof. As soon as Jim, with Tamb' Itam at his heels, had started upon his evening rounds, I went up to the house alone, and, unexpectedly, found myself waylaid by the girl, who had been clearly waiting for this opportunity.

'It is hard to tell you what it was precisely she wanted to wrest from me. Obviously it would be something very simple – the simplest impossibility in the world; as, for instance, the exact description of the form of a cloud. She wanted an assurance, a statement, a promise, an explanation – I don't know how to call it: the thing has no name. It was dark under the projecting roof, and all I could see were the flowing lines of her gown, the pale small oval of her face, with the white flash of her teeth, and, turned towards me, the big sombre orbits of her eyes, where there seemed to be a faint stir, such as you may fancy you can detect when you plunge your gaze to the bottom of an immensely deep well. What is it that moves there? you ask yourself. Is it a blind monster or only a lost gleam from the universe? It occurred to me – don't laugh – that all things being dissimilar, she was more inscrutable in her childish ignorance than the Sphinx propounding childish riddles to wayfarers. She had been carried off to Patusan before her eyes were open. She had grown up there; she had seen nothing, she had known nothing, she had no conception of anything. I ask myself whether she were sure that anything else existed. What notions she may have formed of the outside world is to me inconceivable: all that she knew of its inhabitants were a betrayed woman and a sinister pantaloon. Her lover also came to her from there, gifted with irresistible seductions; but what would become of her if he should return to these inconceivable regions that seemed always to claim back their own? Her mother had warned her of this with tears before she died . . .

'She had caught hold of my arm firmly, and as soon as I had stopped she had withdrawn her hand in haste. She was audacious and shrinking. She feared nothing, but she was checked by the profound incertitude and the extreme strangeness – a brave person groping in the dark. I belonged to this Unknown that might claim Jim for its own at any moment. I was, as it were, in the secret of its nature and of its intentions – the confidant of a threatening mystery; armed with its power perhaps! I believe she supposed I could with a word whisk Jim away out of her very arms; it is my sober conviction she went through agonies of apprehension during my long talks with Jim; through a real and intolerable anguish that might have conceivably driven her into plotting my murder, had the fierceness of her soul been equal to the tremendous situation it had created. This is my impression, and it is all I can give you. The whole thing dawned gradually upon me, and as it got clearer and clearer I was overwhelmed by a slow incredulous amazement. She made me believe her, but there is no word that on my lips could render the effect of the headlong and vehement whisper, of the soft passionate tones, of the sudden breathless pause and the appealing movement of the white arms extended swiftly. They fell; the ghostly figure swayed like a slender tree in the wind, the pale oval of the face drooped; it was impossible to distinguish her features, the darkness of the eyes was unfathomable; two wide sleeves uprose in the dark like unfolding wings, and she stood silent, holding her head in her hands.'

Chapter 33

'I was immensely touched: her youth, her ignorance, her pretty beauty, which had the simple charm and the delicate vigour of a wild-flower, her pathetic pleading, her helplessness, appealed to me with almost the strength of her own unreasonable and natural fear. She feared the unknown as we all do, and her ignorance made the unknown infinitely vast. I stood for it, for myself, for you fellows, for all the world that neither cared for Jim nor needed him in the least. I would have been ready enough to answer for the indifference of the teeming earth but for the reflection that he, too, belonged to this mysterious unknown of her fears, and that, however much I stood for, I did not stand for him. This made me hesitate. A murmur of hopeless pain unsealed my lips. I began by protesting that I at least had come with no intention to take Jim away.

'Why did I come, then? After a slight movement she was as still as a marble statue in the night. I tried to explain briefly: friendship, business; if I had any wish in the matter it was rather to see him stay . . . "They always leave us," she murmured. The breath of sad wisdom from the grave which her piety wreathed with flowers seemed to pass in a faint sigh . . . Nothing, I said, could separate Jim from her.

'It is my firm conviction now; it was my conviction at the time; it was the only possible conclusion from the facts of the case. It was not made more certain by her whispering in a tone in which one speaks to oneself, "He swore this to me." "Did you ask him?" I said.

'She made a step nearer. "No. Never!" She had asked him only to go away. It was that night on the river-bank, after he had killed the man – after she had flung the torch in the water because he was looking at her so. There was too much light, and the danger was over then – for a little time – for a little time. He said then he would not abandon her to Cornelius. She had insisted. She wanted him to leave her. He said that he could not – that it was impossible. He trembled while he said this. She had felt him tremble . . . One does not require much imagination to see the scene, almost to hear their whispers. She was afraid for him, too. I believe that then she saw in him only a predestined victim of dangers which she understood better than himself. Though by nothing but his mere presence he had mastered her heart, had filled all her thoughts, and had possessed himself of all her affections, she underestimated his chances of success. It is obvious that at about that time everybody was inclined to underestimate his chances. Strictly speaking he didn't seem to have any. I know this was Cornelius's view. He confessed that much to me in extenuation of the shady part he had played in Sherif Ali's plot to do away with the infidel. Even Sherif Ali himself, as it seems certain now, had nothing but contempt for the white man. Jim was to be murdered mainly on religious grounds, I believe. A simple act of piety (and so far infinitely meritorious), but otherwise without much importance. In the last part of this opinion Cornelius concurred. "Honourable sir," he argued abjectly on the only occasion he managed to have me to himself – "Honourable sir, how was I to know? Who was he? What could he do to make people believe him? What did Mr Stein mean sending a boy like that to talk big to an old servant? I was ready to save him for eighty dollars. Only eighty dollars. Why didn't the fool go? Was I to get stabbed myself for the sake of a stranger?" He grovelled in spirit before me, with his body doubled up insinuatingly and his hands hovering about my knees, as though he were ready to embrace my legs. "What's eighty dollars? An insignificant sum to give a defenceless old man ruined for life by a deceased she-devil." Here he wept. But I anticipate. I didn't that night chance upon Cornelius till I had had it out with the girl.

'She was unselfish when she urged Jim to leave her, and even to leave the country. It was his danger that was foremost in her thoughts – even if she wanted to save herself, too – perhaps unconsciously: but then look at the warning she had, look at the lesson that could be drawn from every moment of the recently ended life in which all her memories were centred. She fell at his feet – she told me so – there by the river, in the discreet light of stars which showed nothing except great masses of silent shadows, indefinite open spaces, and trembling faintly upon the broad stream made it appear as wide as the sea. He had lifted her up. He lifted her up, and then she would struggle no more. Of course not. Strong arms, a tender voice, a stalwart shoulder to rest her poor lonely little head upon. The need – the infinite need – of all this for the aching heart, for the bewildered mind; the promptings of youth – the necessity of the moment. What would you have? One understands – unless one is incapable of understanding anything under the sun. And so she was content to be lifted up – and held. "You know – Jove! this is serious – no nonsense in it!" as Jim had whispered hurriedly with a troubled concerned face on the threshold of his house. I don't know so much about nonsense, but there was nothing light-hearted in their romance: they came together under the shadow of a life's disaster, like knight and maiden meeting to exchange vows amongst haunted ruins. The starlight was good enough for that story, a light so faint and remote that it cannot resolve shadows into shapes, and show the other shore of a stream. I did look upon the stream that night and from the very place; it rolled silent and as black as Styx: the next day I went away, but I am not likely to forget what it was she wanted to be saved from when she entreated him to leave her while there was time. She told me what it was, calmed – she was now too passionately interested for mere excitement – in a voice as quiet in the obscurity as her white half-lost figure. She told me, "I didn't want to die weeping." I thought I had not heard aright.

' "You did not want to die weeping?" I repeated after her. "Like my mother," she added readily. The outlines of her white shape did not stir in the least. "My mother had wept bitterly before she died," she explained. An inconceivable calmness seemed to have risen from the ground around us, imperceptibly, like the still rise of a flood in the night, obliterating the familiar landmarks of emotions. There came upon me, as though I had felt myself losing my footing in the midst of waters, a sudden dread, the dread of the unknown depths. She went on explaining that, during the last moments, being alone with her mother, she had to leave the side of the couch to go and set her back against the door, in order to keep Cornelius out. He desired to get in, and kept on drumming with both fists, only desisting now and again to shout huskily: "Let me in! Let me in! Let me in!" In a far corner upon a few mats the moribund woman, already speechless and unable to lift her arm, rolled her head over, and with a feeble movement of her hand seemed to command – "No! No!" and the obedient daughter, setting her shoulders with all her strength against the door, was looking on. "The tears fell from her eyes – and then she died," concluded the girl in an imperturbable monotone, which more than anything else, more than the white statuesque immobility of her person, more than mere words could do, troubled my mind profoundly with the passive, irremediable horror of the scene. It had the power to drive me out of my conception of existence, out of that shelter each of us makes for himself to creep under in moments of danger, as a tortoise withdraws within its shell. For a moment I had a view of a world that seemed to wear a vast and dismal aspect of disorder, while, in truth, thanks to our unwearied efforts, it is as sunny an arrangement of small conveniences as the mind of man can conceive. But still – it was only a moment: I went back into my shell directly. One *must* – don't you know? – though I seemed to have lost all my words in the chaos of dark thoughts I had contemplated for a second or two beyond the pale. These came back, too, very soon, for words also belong to the sheltering conception of light and order which is our refuge. I had them ready at my disposal before she whispered softly: "He swore he would never leave me, when we stood there alone! He swore to me!" . . . "And is it possible that you – you! do not believe him?" I asked, sincerely reproachful, genuinely shocked. Why couldn't she believe? Wherefore this craving for incertitude, this clinging to fear, as if incertitude and fear had been the safeguards of her love? It was monstrous. She should have made for herself a shelter of inexpugnable peace out of that honest affection. She had not the knowledge – not the skill perhaps. The night had come on apace; it had grown pitch-dark where we were, so that without stirring she had faded like the intangible form of a wistful and perverse spirit. And suddenly I heard her quiet whisper again: "Other men had sworn the same thing." It was like a meditative comment on some thoughts full of sadness, of awe. And she added, still lower if possible: "My father did." She paused the time to draw an inaudible breath. Her father, too . . . These were the things she knew! At once I said: "Ah! but he is not like that." This, it seemed, she did not intend to dispute; but after a time the strange still whisper wandering dreamily in the air stole into my ears. "Why is he different? Is he better? Is he . . . " "Upon my word of honour," I broke in, "I believe he is." We subdued our tones to a mysterious pitch. Amongst the huts of Jim's workmen (they were mostly liberated slaves from the Sherif's stockade) somebody started a shrill, drawling song. Across the river a big fire (at Doramin's, I think) made a glowing ball, completely isolated in the night. "Is he more true?" she murmured. "Yes," I said. "More true than any other man?" she repeated in lingering accents. "Nobody here," I said, "would dream of doubting his word – nobody would dare – except you."

'I think she made a movement at this. "More brave?" she went on in a changed tone. "Fear shall never drive him away from you," I said a little nervously. The song stopped short on a shrill note, and was succeeded by several voices talking in the distance. Jim's voice, too. I was struck by her silence. "What has he been telling you? He has been telling you something?" I asked. There was no answer. "What is it he told you?" I insisted.

' "Do you think I can tell you? How am I to know? How am I to understand?" she cried at last. There was a stir. I believe she was wringing her hands. "There is something he can never forget."

' "So much the better for you," I said, gloomily.

' "What is it? What is it?" She put an extraordinary force of appeal into her supplicating tone. "He says he had been afraid. How can I believe this? Am I a mad woman to believe this? You all remember something! You all go back to it. What is it? You tell me! What is this thing? Is it alive? – is it dead? I hate it. It is cruel. Has it got a face and a voice – this calamity? Will he see it – will he hear it? In his sleep perhaps when he cannot see me – and then arise and go. Ah! I shall never forgive him. My mother had forgiven – but I, never! Will it be a sign – a call?"

'It was a wonderful experience. She mistrusted his very slumbers – and she seemed to think I could tell her why! Thus a poor mortal seduced by the charm of an apparition might have tried to wring from another ghost the tremendous secret of the claim the other world holds over a disembodied soul astray amongst the passions of this earth. The very ground on which I stood seemed to melt under my feet. And it was so simple, too; but if the spirits evoked by our fears and our unrest have ever to vouch for each other's constancy before the forlorn magicians that we are, then I – I alone of us dwellers in the flesh – have shuddered in the hopeless chill of such a task. A sign, a call! How telling in its expression was her ignorance. A few words! How she came to know them, how she came to pronounce them, I can't imagine. Women find their inspiration in the stress of moments that for us are merely awful, absurd, or futile. To discover that she had a voice at all was enough to strike awe into the heart. Had a spurned stone cried out in pain it could not have appeared a greater and more pitiful miracle. These few sounds wandering in the dark had made their two benighted lives tragic to my mind. It was impossible to make her understand. I chafed silently at my impotence. And Jim, too – poor devil! Who would need him? Who would remember him? He had what he wanted. His very existence probably had been forgotten by this time. They had mastered their fates. They were tragic.

'Her immobility before me was clearly expectant, and my part was to speak for my brother from the realm of forgetful shades. I was deeply moved at my responsibility and at her distress. I would have given anything for the power to soothe her frail soul, tormenting itself in its invincible ignorance like a small bird beating about the cruel wires of a cage. Nothing easier than to say, Have no fear! Nothing more difficult. How does one kill fear, I wonder? How do you shoot a spectre through the heart, slash off its spectral head, take it by its spectral throat? It is an enterprise you rush into while you dream, and are glad to make your escape with wet hair and every limb shaking. The bullet is not run, the blade not forged, the man not born; even the winged words of truth drop at your feet like lumps of lead. You require for such a desperate encounter an enchanted and poisoned shaft dipped in a lie too subtle to be found on earth. An enterprise for a dream, my masters!

'I began my exorcism with a heavy heart, with a sort of sullen anger in it, too. Jim's voice, suddenly raised with a stern intonation, carried across the courtyard, reproving the carelessness of some dumb sinner by the riverside. Nothing – I said, speaking in a distinct murmur – there could be nothing, in that unknown world she fancied so eager to rob her of her happiness, there was nothing neither living nor dead, there was no face, no voice, no power, that could tear Jim from her side. I drew breath and she whispered softly, "He told me so." "He told you the truth," I said. "Nothing," she sighed out, and abruptly turned upon me with a barely audible intensity of tone: "Why did you come to us from out there? He speaks of you too often. You make me afraid. Do you – do you want him?" A sort of stealthy fierceness had crept into our hurried mutters. "I shall never come again," I said, bitterly. "And I don't want him. No one wants him." "No one?" she repeated in a tone of doubt. "No one," I affirmed, feeling myself swayed by some strange excitement. "You think him strong, wise, courageous, great – why not believe him to be true, too? I shall go tomorrow – and that is the end. You shall never be troubled by a voice from there again. This world you don't know is too big to miss him. You understand? Too big. You've got his heart in your hand. You must feel that. You must know that." "Yes, I know that," she breathed out, hard and still, as a statue might whisper.

'I felt I had done nothing. And what is it that I had wished to do? I am not sure now. At the time I was animated by an inexplicable ardour, as if before some great and necessary task – the influence of the moment upon my mental and emotional state. There are in all our lives such moments, such influences, coming from the outside, as it were, irresistible, incomprehensible – as if brought about by the mysterious conjunctions of the planets. She owned, as I had put it to her, his heart. She had that and everything else – if she could only believe it. What I had to tell her was that in the whole world there was no one who ever would need his heart, his mind, his hand. It was a common fate, and yet it seemed an awful thing to say of any man. She listened without a word, and her stillness now was like the protest of an invincible unbelief. What need she care for the world beyond the forests? I asked. From all the multitudes that peopled the vastness of that unknown there would come, I assured her, as long as he lived, neither a call nor a sign for him. Never. I was carried away. Never! Never! I remember with wonder the sort of dogged fierceness I displayed. I had the illusion of having got the spectre by the throat at last. Indeed the whole real thing has left behind the detailed and amazing impression of a dream. Why should she fear? She knew him to be strong, true, wise, brave. He was all that. Certainly. He was more. He was great – invincible – and the world did not want him, it had forgotten him, it would not even know him.

'I stopped; the silence over Patusan was profound, and the feeble dry sound of a paddle striking the side of a canoe somewhere in the middle of the river seemed to make it infinite. "Why?" she murmured. I felt that sort of rage one feels during a hard tussle. The spectre was trying to slip out of my grasp. "Why?" she repeated louder; "tell me!" And as I remained confounded, she stamped with her foot like a spoilt child. "Why? Speak." "You want to know?" I asked in a fury. "Yes!" she cried. "Because he is not good enough," I said, brutally. During the moment's pause I noticed the fire on the other shore blaze up, dilating the circle of its glow like an amazed stare, and contract suddenly to a red pin-point. I only knew how close to me she had been when I felt the clutch of her fingers on my forearm. Without raising her voice, she threw into it an infinity of scathing contempt, bitterness, and despair.

' "This is the very thing he said . . . You lie!"

'The last two words she cried at me in the native dialect. "Hear me out!" I entreated: she caught her breath tremulously, flung my arm away. "Nobody, nobody is good enough," I began with the greatest earnestness. I could hear the sobbing labour of her breath frightfully quickened. I hung my head. What was the use? Footsteps were approaching; I slipped away without another word . . . '

Chapter 34

Marlow swung his legs out, got up quickly, and staggered a little, as though he had been set down after a rush through space. He leaned his back against the balustrade and faced a disordered array of long cane-chairs. The bodies prone in them seemed startled out of their torpor by his movement. One or two sat up as if alarmed; here and there a cigar glowed yet; Marlow looked at them all with the eyes of a man returning from the excessive remoteness of a dream. A throat was cleared; a calm voice encouraged negligently, 'Well?'

'Nothing,' said Marlow with a slight start. 'He had told her – that's all. She did not believe him – nothing more. As to myself, I do not know whether it be just, proper, decent for me to rejoice or to be sorry. For my part, I cannot say what I believed – indeed I don't know to this day, and never shall probably. But what did the poor devil believe himself? Truth shall prevail – don't you know *Magna est veritas et* . . . Yes, when it gets a chance. There is a law, no doubt – and likewise a law regulates your luck in the throwing of dice. It is not Justice the servant of men, but accident, hazard, Fortune – the ally of patient Time – that holds an even and scrupulous balance. Both of us had said the very same thing. Did we both speak the truth – or did one of us – or neither? . . .'

Marlow paused, crossed his arms on his breast, and in a changed tone: 'She said we lied. Poor soul. Well – let's leave it to chance, whose ally is Time, that cannot be hurried, and whose enemy is Death, that will not wait. I had retreated – a little cowed, I must own. I had tried a fall with fear itself and got thrown – of course. I had only succeeded in adding to her anguish the hint of some mysterious collusion, of an inexplicable and incomprehensible conspiracy to keep her for ever in the dark. And it had come easily, naturally, unavoidably, by his act, by her own act! It was as though I had been shown the working of the implacable destiny of which we are the victims – and the tools. It was appalling to think of the girl whom I had left standing there motionless; Jim's footsteps had a fateful sound as he tramped by, without seeing me, in his heavy laced boots. "What? No lights!" he said in a loud surprised voice. "What are you doing in the dark – you two?" Next moment he caught sight of her, I suppose. "Hallo, girl!" he cried, cheerily. "Hallo, boy!" she answered at once, with amazing pluck.

'This was their usual greeting to each other, and the bit of swagger she would put into her rather high but sweet voice was very droll, pretty, and childlike. It delighted Jim greatly. This was the last occasion on which I heard them exchange this familiar hail, and it struck a chill into my heart.

There was the high sweet voice, the pretty effort, the swagger; but it all seemed to die out prematurely, and the playful call sounded like a moan. It was too confoundedly awful. "What have you done with Marlow?" Jim was asking; and then, "Gone down – has he? Funny I didn't meet him . . . You there Marlow?"

'I didn't answer. I wasn't going in – not yet at any rate. I really couldn't. While he was calling me I was engaged in making my escape through a little gate leading out upon a stretch of newly cleared ground. No; I couldn't face them yet. I walked hastily with lowered head along a trodden path. The ground rose gently, the few big trees had been felled, the undergrowth had been cut down and the grass fired. He had a mind to try a coffee-plantation there. The big hill, rearing its double summit coal-black in the clear yellow glow of the rising moon, seemed to cast its shadow upon the ground prepared for that experiment. He was going to try so many experiments; I had admired his energy, his enterprise, and his shrewdness. Nothing on earth seemed less real now than his plans, his energy, and his enthusiasm; and raising my eyes, I saw part of the moon glittering through the bushes at the bottom of the chasm. For a moment it looked as though the smooth disk, falling from its place in the sky upon the earth, had rolled to the bottom of that precipice: its ascending movement was like a leisurely rebound; it disengaged itself from the tangle of twigs; the bare contorted limb of some tree, growing on the slope, made a black crack right across its face. It threw its level rays afar as if from a cavern, and in this mournful eclipse-like light the stumps of felled trees uprose very dark, the heavy shadows fell at my feet on all sides, my own moving shadow, and across my path the shadow of the solitary grave perpetually garlanded with flowers. In the darkened moonlight the interlaced blossoms took on shapes foreign to one's memory and colours indefinable to the eye, as though they had been special flowers gathered by no man, grown not in this world, and destined for the use of the dead alone. Their powerful scent hung in the warm air, making it thick and heavy like the fumes of incense. The lumps of white coral shone round the dark mound like a chaplet of bleached skulls, and everything around was so quiet that when I stood still all sound and all movements in the world seemed to come to an end.

'It was a great peace, as if the earth had been one grave, and for a time I stood there thinking mostly of the living who, buried in remote places out of the knowledge of mankind, still are fated to share in its tragic or grotesque miseries. In its noble struggles, too – who knows? The human heart is vast enough to contain all the world. It is valiant enough to bear the burden, but where is the courage that would cast it off?

'I suppose I must have fallen into a sentimental mood; I only know that I stood there long enough for the sense of utter solitude to get hold of me so completely that all I had lately seen, all I had heard, and the very human speech itself, seemed to have passed away out of existence, living only for a while longer in my memory, as though I had been the last of mankind. It was a strange and melancholy illusion, evolved half-consciously like all our illusions, which I suspect only to be visions of remote unattainable truth, seen dimly. This was, indeed, one of the lost, forgotten, unknown places of the earth; I had looked under its obscure surface; and I felt that when tomorrow I had left it for ever, it would slip out of existence, to live only in my memory till I myself passed into oblivion. I have that feeling about me now; perhaps it is that feeling which had incited me to tell you the story, to try to hand over to you, as it were, its very existence, its reality – the truth disclosed in a moment of illusion.

'Cornelius broke upon it. He bolted out, vermin-like, from the long grass growing in a depression of the ground. I believe his house was rotting somewhere near by, though I've never seen it, not having been far enough in that direction. He ran towards me upon the path; his feet, shod in dirty white shoes, twinkled on the dark earth; he pulled himself up, and began to whine and cringe under a tall stove-pipe hat. His dried-up little carcass was swallowed up, totally lost, in a suit of black broadcloth. That was his costume for holidays and ceremonies, and it reminded me that this was the fourth Sunday I had spent in Patusan. All the time of my stay I had been vaguely aware of his desire to confide in me, if he only could get me all to himself. He hung about with an eager craving look on his sour yellow little face; but his timidity had kept him back as much as my natural reluctance to have anything to do with such an unsavoury creature. He would have succeeded, nevertheless, had he not been so ready to slink off as soon as you looked at him. He would slink off before Jim's severe gaze, before my own, which I tried to make indifferent, even before Tamb' Itam's surly, superior glance. He was perpetually slinking away; whenever seen he was seen moving off deviously, his face over his shoulder, with either a mistrustful snarl or a woebegone, piteous, mute aspect, but no assumed expression could conceal this innate irremediable abjectness of his nature, any more than an arrangement of clothing can conceal some monstrous deformity of the body.

'I don't know whether it was the demoralisation of my utter defeat in my encounter with a spectre of fear less than an hour ago, but I let him capture me without even a show of resistance. I was doomed to be the recipient of confidences, and to be confronted with unanswerable questions. It was trying; but the contempt, the unreasoned contempt, the man's appearance provoked, made it easier to bear. He couldn't possibly matter. Nothing mattered, since I had made up my mind that Jim, for whom alone I cared, had at last mastered his fate. He had told me he was satisfied . . . nearly. This is going further than most of us dare. I – who have the right to think myself good enough – dare not. Neither does any of you here, I suppose? . . . '

Marlow paused, as if expecting an answer. Nobody spoke.

'Quite right,' he began again. 'Let no soul know, since the truth can be wrung out of us only by some cruel, little, awful catastrophe. But he is one of us, and he could say he was satisfied . . . nearly. Just fancy this! Nearly satisfied. One could almost envy him his catastrophe. Nearly satisfied. After this nothing could matter. It did not matter who suspected him, who trusted him, who loved him, who hated him – especially as it was Cornelius who hated him.

'Yet after all this was a kind of recognition. You shall judge of a man by his foes as well as by his friends, and this enemy of Jim was such as no decent man would be ashamed to own, without, however, making too much of him. This was the view Jim took, and in which I shared; but Jim disregarded him on general grounds. "My dear Marlow," he said, "I feel that if I go straight nothing can touch me. Indeed I do. Now you have been long enough here to have a good look round – and, frankly, don't you think I am pretty safe? It all depends upon me, and, by Jove! I have lots of confidence in myself. The worst thing he could do would be to kill me, I suppose. I don't think for a moment he would. He couldn't, you know – not if I were myself to hand him a loaded rifle for the purpose, and then turn my back on him. That's the sort of thing he is. And suppose he would – suppose he could? Well – what of that? I didn't come here flying for my life – did I? I came here to set my back against the wall, and I am going to stay here . . .

' "Till you are *quite* satisfied," I struck in.

'We were sitting at the time under the roof in the stern of his boat; twenty paddles flashed like one, ten on a side, striking the water with a single splash, while behind our backs Tamb' Itam dipped silently right and left, and stared right down the river, attentive to keep the long canoes in the greatest strength of the current. Jim bowed his head, and our last talk seemed to flicker out for good. He was seeing me off as far as the mouth of the river. The schooner had left the day before, working down and drifting on the ebb, while I had prolonged my stay overnight. And now he was seeing me off.

'Jim had been a little angry with me for mentioning Cornelius at all. I had not, in truth, said much. The man was too insignificant to be dangerous, though he was as full of hate as he could hold. He had called me "honourable sir" at every second sentence, and had whined at my elbow as he followed me from the grave of his "late wife" to the gate of Jim's compound. He declared himself the most unhappy of men, a victim, crushed like a worm; he entreated me to look at him. I wouldn't turn my head to do so; but I could see out of the corner of my eye his obsequious shadow gliding after mine, while the moon, suspended on our right hand, seemed to gloat serenely upon the spectacle. He tried to explain – as I've told you – his share in the events of the memorable night. It was a matter of expediency. How could he know who was going to get the upper hand? "I would have saved him, honourable sir! I would have saved him for eighty dollars," he protested in dulcet tones, keeping a pace behind me. "He had saved himself," I said, "and he has forgiven you." I heard a sort of tittering, and turned upon him; at once he appeared ready to take to his heels. "What are you laughing at?" I asked, standing still. "Don't be deceived, honourable sir!" he shrieked, seemingly losing all control over his feelings. "*He* save himself! He knows nothing, honourable sir – nothing whatever. Who is he? What does he want here – the big thief? What does he want here? He throws dust into everybody's eyes; he throws dust into your eyes, honourable sir; but he can't throw dust into my eyes. He is a big fool, honourable sir." I laughed contemptuously, and, turning on my heel, began to walk on again. He ran up to my elbows and whispered forcibly, "He's no more than a little child here – like a little child – a little child." Of course I didn't take the slightest notice, and seeing the time pressed, because we were approaching the bamboo fence that glittered over the blackened ground of the clearing, he came to the point. He commenced by being abjectly lachrymose. His great misfortunes had affected his head. He hoped I would kindly forget what nothing but his troubles made him say. He didn't mean anything by it; only the honourable sir did not know what it was to be ruined, broken down, trampled upon. After this introduction he approached the matter near his heart, but in such a rambling, ejaculatory, craven fashion, that for a long time I couldn't make out what he was driving at. He wanted me to intercede with Jim in his favour. It seemed, too, to be some sort of money affair. I heard time and again the words, "Moderate provision – suitable present." He seemed to be claiming value for something, and he even went the length of saying with some warmth that life was not worth having if a man were to be robbed of everything. I did not breathe a word, of course, but neither did I stop my ears. The gist of the affair, which became clear to me gradually, was in this, that he regarded himself as entitled to some money in exchange for the girl. He had brought her up. Somebody else's child. Great troubles and pains – old man now – suitable present. If the honourable sir would say a word . . . I stood still to look at him with curiosity, and fearful lest I should think him extortionate, I suppose, he hastily brought himself to make a concession. In consideration of a "suitable present" given at once, he would, he declared, be willing to undertake the charge of the girl, "without any other provision – when the time came for the gentleman to go home." His little yellow face, all crumpled as though it had been squeezed together, expressed the most anxious, eager avarice. His voice whined coaxingly, "No more trouble – natural guardian – a sum of money . . ."

'I stood there and marvelled. That kind of thing, with him, was evidently a vocation. I discovered suddenly in his cringing attitude a sort of assurance, as though he had been all his life dealing in certitudes. He must have thought I was dispassionately considering his proposal, because he became as sweet as honey. "Every gentleman made a provision when the time came to go home," he began, insinuatingly. I slammed the little gate. "In this case, Mr Cornelius," I said, "the time shall never come." He took a few seconds to gather this in. "What!" he fairly squealed. "Why," I continued from my side of the gate, "haven't you heard him say to himself? He will never go home." "Oh! this is too much," he shouted. He would not address me as "honourable sir" any more. He was very still for a time, and then without a trace of humility began very low: "Never go – ah! He – he – he comes here devil knows from where – comes here – devil knows why – to trample on me till I die – ah – trample" (he stamped softly with both feet), "trample like this – nobody knows why – till I die . . . " His voice became quite extinct; he was bothered by a little cough; he came up close to the fence and told me, dropping into a confidential and piteous tone, that he would *not* be trampled upon. "Patience – patience," he muttered, striking his breast. I had done laughing at him, but unexpectedly he treated me to a wild cracked burst of it. "Ha! ha! ha! We shall see! We shall see! What! Steal from me? Steal from me everything! Everything! Everything!" His head drooped on one shoulder, his hands were hanging before him lightly clasped. One would have thought he had cherished the girl with surpassing love, that his spirit had been crushed and his heart broken by the most cruel of spoliations. Suddenly he lifted his head and shot out an infamous word. "Like her mother – she is like her deceitful mother. Exactly. In her face, too. In her face. The devil!" He leaned his forehead against the fence, and in that position uttered threats and horrible blasphemies in Portuguese in very weak ejaculations, mingled with miserable plaints and groans, coming out with a heave of the shoulders as though he had been overtaken by a deadly fit of sickness. It was an inexpressibly grotesque and vile performance, and I hastened away. He tried to shout something after me. Some disparagement of Jim, I believe – not too loud though, we were too near the house. All I heard distinctly was, "No more than a little child – a little child." '

Chapter 35

'But next morning, at the first bend of the river shutting off the houses of Patusan, all this dropped out of my sight bodily, with its colour, its design, and its meaning, like a picture created by fancy on a canvas, upon which, after long contemplation, you turn your back for the last time. It remains in the memory motionless, unfaded, with its life arrested, in an unchanging light. There are the ambitions, the fears, the hate, the hopes, and they remain in my mind just as I had seen them – intense and as if for ever suspended in their expression. I had turned away from the picture and was going back to the world where events move, men change, light flickers, life flows in a clear stream, no matter whether over mud or over stones. I wasn't going to dive into it; I would have enough to do to keep my head above the surface. But as to what I was leaving behind, I cannot imagine any alteration.

The immense and magnanimous Doramin and his little motherly witch of a wife, gazing together upon the land and nursing secretly their dreams of parental ambition; Tunju Allang, wizened and greatly perplexed; Dain Waris, intelligent and brave, with his faith in Jim, with his firm glance and his ironic friendliness; the girl, absorbed in her frightened, suspicious adoration; Tamb' Itam, surly and faithful; Cornelius, leaning his forehead against the fence under the moonlight – I am certain of them. They exist as if under an enchanter's wand. But the figure round which all these are grouped – that one lives, and I am not certain of him. No magician's wand can immobilise him under my eyes. He is one of us.

'Jim, as I've told you, accompanied me on the first stage of my journey back to the world he had renounced, and the way at times seemed to lead through the very heart of untouched wilderness. The empty reaches sparkled under the high sun; between the high walls of vegetation the heat drowsed upon the water, and the boat, impelled vigorously, cut her way through the air that seemed to have settled dense and warm under the shelter of lofty trees.

'The shadow of the impending separation had already put an immense space between us, and when we spoke it was with an effort, as if to force our low voices across a vast and increasing distance. The boat fairly flew; we sweltered side by side in the stagnant superheated air; the smell of mud, of marsh, the primeval smell of fecund earth, seemed to sting our faces; till suddenly at a bend it was as if a great hand far away had lifted a heavy curtain, had flung open an immense portal. The light itself seemed to stir, the sky above our heads widened, a far-off murmur reached our ears, a freshness enveloped us, filled our lungs, quickened our thoughts, our blood, our regrets – and, straight ahead, the forests sank down against the dark-blue ridge of the sea.

'I breathed deeply, I revelled in the vastness of the opened horizon, in the different atmosphere that seemed to vibrate with a toil of life, with the energy of an impeccable world. This sky and this sea were open to me. The girl was right – there was a sign, a call in them – something to which I responded with every fibre of my being. I let my eyes roam through space, like a man released from bonds who stretches his cramped limbs, runs, leaps, responds to the inspiring elation of freedom. "This is glorious!" I cried, and then I looked at the sinner by my side. He sat with his head sunk on his breast and said, "Yes," without raising his eyes, as if afraid to see writ large on the clear sky of the offing the reproach of his romantic conscience.

'I remember the smallest details of that afternoon. We landed on a bit of white beach. It was backed by a low cliff wooded on the brow, draped in creepers to the very foot. Below us the plain of the sea, of a serene and intense blue, stretched with a slight upward tilt to the thread-like horizon drawn at the height of our eyes. Great waves of glitter blew lightly along the pitted dark surface, as swift as feathers chased by the breeze. A chain of islands sat broken and massive facing the wide estuary, displayed in a sheet of pale glassy water reflecting faithfully the contour of the shore. High in the colourless sunshine a solitary bird, all black, hovered, dropping and soaring above the same spot with a slight rocking motion of the wings. A ragged, sooty bunch of flimsy mat hovels was perched over its own inverted image upon a crooked multitude of high piles the colour of ebony. A tiny black canoe put off from amongst them with two tiny men, all black, who toiled exceedingly, striking down at the pale water: and the canoe seemed to slide painfully on a mirror. This bunch of miserable hovels was the fishing village that boasted of the white lord's especial protection, and the two men crossing over were the old headman and his son-in-law. They landed and walked up to us on the white sand, lean, dark-brown as if dried in smoke, with ashy patches on the skin of their naked shoulders and breasts. Their heads were bound in dirty but carefully folded handkerchiefs, and the old man began at once to state a complaint, voluble, stretching a lank arm, screwing up at Jim his old bleared eyes confidently. The Rajah's people would not leave them alone; there had been some trouble about a lot of turtles' eggs his people had collected on the islets there – and leaning at arm's length upon his paddle, he pointed with a brown skinny hand over the sea. Jim listened for a time without looking up, and at last told him gently to wait. He would hear him by and by. They withdrew obediently to some little distance, and sat on their heels, with their paddles lying before them on the sand; the silvery gleams in their eyes followed our movements patiently; and the immensity of the outspread sea, the stillness of the coast, passing north and south beyond the limits of my vision, made up one colossal Presence watching us four dwarfs isolated on a strip of glistening sand.

' "The trouble is," remarked Jim, moodily, "that for generations these beggars of fishermen in that village there had been considered as the Rajah's personal slaves – and the old rip can't get it into his head that . . . "

'He paused. "That you have changed all that," I said.

' "Yes. I've changed all that," he muttered in a gloomy voice.

' "You have had your opportunity," I pursued.

' "Had I?" he said. "Well, yes. I suppose so. Yes. I have got back my confidence in myself – a good name – yet sometimes I wish . . . No! I shall hold what I've got. Can't expect anything more." He flung his arm out towards the sea. "Not out there anyhow." He stamped his foot upon the sand. "This is my limit, because nothing less will do."

'We continued pacing the beach. "Yes, I've changed all that," he went on, with a sidelong glance at the two patient squatting fishermen; "but only try to think what it would be if I went away. Jove! can't you see it? Hell loose. No! Tomorrow I shall go and take my chance of drinking that silly old Tunku Allang's coffee, and I shall make no end of fuss over these rotten turtles' eggs. No. I can't say – enough. Never. I must go on, go on for ever holding up my end, to feel sure that nothing can touch me. I must stick to their belief in me to feel safe and to – to" . . . He cast about for a word, seemed to look for it on the sea ... "to keep in touch with" ... His voice sank suddenly to a murmur ... "with those whom, perhaps, I shall never see any more. With – with – you, for instance."

'I was profoundly humbled by his words. "For God's sake," I said, "don't set me up, my dear fellow; just look to yourself." I felt a gratitude, an affection, for that straggler whose eyes had singled me out, keeping my place in the ranks of an insignificant multitude. How little that was to boast of, after all! I turned my burning face away; under the low sun, glowing, darkened and crimson, like an ember snatched from the fire, the sea lay outspread, offering all its immense stillness to the approach of the fiery orb. Twice he was going to speak, but checked himself: at last, as if he had found a formula: "I shall be faithful," he said, quietly. "I shall be faithful," he repeated, without looking at me, but for the first time letting his eyes wander upon the waters, whose blueness had changed to a gloomy purple under the fires of sunset. Ah! he was romantic, romantic. I recalled some words of Stein's ... "In the destructive element immerse! ... To follow the dream, and again to follow the dream – and so – always – *usque ad finem* ..." He was romantic, but none the less true. Who could tell what forms, what visions, what faces, what forgiveness he could see in the glow of the west! ... A small boat, leaving the schooner, moved slowly, with a regular beat of two oars, towards the sandbank to take me off. "And then there's Jewel," he said, out of the great silence of earth, sky, and sea, which had mastered my very thoughts so that his voice made me start. "There's Jewel." "Yes," I murmured. "I need not tell you what she is to me," he pursued. "You've seen. In time she will come to understand ..." "I hope so," I interrupted. "She trusts me, too," he mused, and then changed his tone. "When shall we meet next, I wonder?" he said.

' "Never – unless you come out," I answered, avoiding his glance. He didn't seem to be surprised; he kept very quiet for a while.

' "Goodbye, then," he said, after a pause. "Perhaps it's just as well."

'We shook hands, and I walked to the boat, which waited with her nose on the beach. The schooner, her mainsail set and jib-sheet to windward, curvetted on the purple sea; there was a rosy tinge on her sails. "Will you be going home again soon?" asked Jim, just as I swung my leg over the gunwale. "In a year or so if I live," I said. The forefoot grated on the sand, the boat floated, the wet oars flashed and dipped once, twice. Jim, at the water's edge, raised his voice. "Tell them ..." he began. I signed to the men to cease rowing, and waited in wonder. Tell who? The half-submerged sun faced him; I could see its red gleam in his eyes that looked dumbly at me ... "No – nothing," he said, and with a slight wave of his hand motioned the boat away. I did not look again at the shore till I had clambered on board the schooner.

'By that time the sun had set. The twilight lay over the east, and the coast, turned black, extended infinitely its sombre wall that seemed the very stronghold of the night; the western horizon was one great blaze of gold and crimson in which a big detached cloud floated dark and still, casting a slaty shadow on the water beneath, and I saw Jim on the beach watching the schooner fall off and gather headway.

'The two half-naked fishermen had risen as soon as I had gone; they were no doubt pouring the plaint of their trifling, miserable, oppressed lives into the ears of the white lord, and no doubt he was listening to it, making it his own, for was it not a part of his luck – the luck "from the word Go" – the luck to which he had assured me he was so completely equal? They, too, I should think, were in luck, and I was sure their pertinacity would be equal to it. Their dark-skinned bodies vanished on the dark background long before I had lost sight of their protector. He was white from head to foot, and remained persistently visible with the stronghold of the night at his back, the sea at his feet, the opportunity by his side – still veiled. What do you say? Was it still veiled? I don't know. For me that white figure in the stillness of coast and sea seemed to stand at the heart of a vast enigma. The twilight was ebbing fast from the sky above his head, the strip of sand had sunk already under his feet, he himself appeared no bigger than a child – then only a speck, a tiny white speck, that seemed to catch all the light left in a darkened world . . . And, suddenly, I lost him . . . '

Chapter 36

With these words Marlow had ended his narrative, and his audience had broken up forthwith, under his abstract, pensive gaze. Men drifted off the veranda in pairs or alone without loss of time, without offering a remark, as if the last image of that incomplete story, its incompleteness itself, and the very tone of the speaker, had made discussion vain and comment impossible. Each of them seemed to carry away his own impression, to carry it away with him like a secret; but there was only one man of all these listeners who was ever to hear the last word of the story. It came to him at home, more than two years later, and it came contained in a thick packet addressed in Marlow's upright and angular handwriting.

The privileged man opened the packet, looked in, then, laying it down, went to the window. His rooms were in the highest flat of a lofty building, and his glance could travel afar beyond the clear panes of glass, as though he were looking out of the lantern of a lighthouse. The slopes of the roofs glistened, the dark broken ridges succeeded each other without end like sombre, uncrested waves, and from the depths of the town under his feet ascended a confused and unceasing mutter. The spires of churches, numerous, scattered haphazard, uprose like beacons on a maze of shoals without a channel; the driving rain mingled with the falling dusk of a winter's evening; and the booming of a big clock on a tower striking the hour, rolled past in voluminous, austere bursts of sound, with a shrill vibrating cry at the core. He drew the heavy curtains.

The light of his shaded reading-lamp slept like a sheltered pool, his footfalls made no sound on the carpet, his wandering days were over. No more horizons as boundless as hope, no more twilights within the forests as solemn as temples, in the hot quest of the Ever-undiscovered Country over the hill, across the stream, beyond the wave. The hour was striking! No more! No more! – but the opened packet under the lamp brought back the sounds, the visions, the very savour of the past – a multitude of fading faces, a tumult of low voices, dying away upon the shores of distant seas under a passionate and unconsoling sunshine. He sighed and sat down to read.

At first he saw three distinct enclosures. A good many pages closely blackened and pinned together; a loose square sheet of greyish paper with a few words traced in a handwriting he had never seen before, and an explanatory letter from Marlow. From this last fell another letter, yellowed by time and frayed on the folds. He picked it up and, laying it aside, turned to Marlow's message, ran swiftly over the opening lines, and, checking himself, thereafter read on deliberately, like one approaching with slow feet and alert eyes the glimpse of an undiscovered country.

' . . . I don't suppose you've forgotten,' went on the letter. 'You alone have showed an interest in him that survived the telling of his story, though I remember well you would not admit he had mastered his fate. You prophesied for him the disaster of weariness and of disgust with acquired honour, with the self-appointed task, with the love sprung from pity and youth. You had said you knew so well "that kind of thing", its illusory satisfaction, its unavoidable deception. You said also – I call to mind – that "giving your life up to them" (*them* meaning all of mankind with skins brown, yellow, or black in colour) "was like selling your soul to a brute." You contended that "that kind of thing" was only endurable and enduring when based on a firm conviction in the truth of ideas racially our own, in whose name are established the order, the morality of an ethical progress. "We want its strength at our backs," you had said. "We want a belief in its necessity and its justice, to make a worthy and conscious sacrifice of our lives. Without it the sacrifice is only forgetfulness, the way of offering is no better than the way to perdition." In other words, you maintained that we must fight in the ranks or our lives don't count. Possibly! You ought to know – be it said without malice – you who have rushed into one or two places single-handed and came out cleverly, without singeing your wings. The point, however, is that of all mankind Jim had no dealings but with himself, and the question is whether at the last he had not confessed to a faith mightier than the laws of order and progress.

'I affirm nothing. Perhaps you may pronounce – after you've read. There is much truth – after all – in the common expression "under a cloud." It is impossible to see him clearly – especially as it is through the eyes of others that we take our last look at him. I have no hesitation in imparting to you all I know of the last episode that, as he used to say, had "come to him." One wonders whether this was perhaps that supreme opportunity, that last and satisfying test for which I had always suspected him to be waiting, before he could frame a message to the impeccable world. You remember that when I was leaving him for the last time he had asked whether I would be going home soon, and suddenly cried after me: "Tell them!" . . . I had waited – curious I'll own, and hopeful, too – only to hear him shout, "No – nothing." That was all then – and there shall be nothing more; there shall be no message, unless such as each of us can interpret for himself from the language of facts, that are so often more enigmatic than the craftiest arrangement of words. He made, it is true, one more attempt to deliver himself; but that, too, failed, as you may perceive if you look at the sheet of greyish foolscap enclosed here. He had tried to write; do you notice the commonplace hand? It is headed: "The Fort, Patusan." I suppose he had carried out his intention of making out of his house a place of defence. It was an excellent plan: a deep ditch, an earth wall topped by a palisade, and at the angles guns mounted on platforms to sweep each side of the square. Doramin had agreed to furnish him the guns; and so each man of his party would know there was a place of safety, upon which every faithful partisan could rally in case of some sudden danger. All this showed his judicious foresight, his faith in the future. What he called "my own people" – the liberated captives of the Sherif – were to make a distinct quarter of Patusan, with their huts and little plots of ground under the walls of the stronghold. Within he would be an invincible host in himself. "The Fort, Patusan." No date, as you observe. What is a number and a name to a day of days? It is also impossible to say whom he had in his mind when he seized the pen: Stein – myself – the world at large – or was this only the aimless startled cry of a solitary man confronted by his fate? "An awful thing has happened," he wrote before he flung the pen down for the first time; look at the ink blot resembling the head of an arrow under these words. After a while he had tried again, scrawling heavily, as if with a hand of lead, another line. "I must now at once . . . " The pen had spluttered, and that time he gave it up. There's nothing more; he had seen a broad gulf that neither eye nor voice could span. I can understand this. He was overwhelmed by the inexplicable; he was overwhelmed by his own personality – the gift of that destiny which he had done his best to master.

'I send you also an old letter – a very old letter. It was found carefully preserved in his writing-case. It is from his father, and by the date you can see he must have received it a few days before he joined the *Patna*. Thus it must be the last letter he ever had from home. He had treasured it all these years. The good old parson fancied his sailor-son. I've looked in at a sentence here and there. There is nothing in it except just affection. He tells his "dear James" that the last long letter from him was very "honest and entertaining". He would not have him "judge men harshly or hastily". There are four pages of it, easy morality and family news. Tom had "taken orders". Carrie's husband had "money losses". The old chap goes on equably trusting Providence and the established order of the universe, but alive to its small dangers and its small mercies. One can almost see him, grey-haired and serene in the inviolable shelter of his book-lined, faded, and comfortable study, where for forty years he had conscientiously gone over and over again the round of his little thoughts about faith and virtue, about the conduct of life and the only proper manner of dying; where he had written so many sermons, where he sits talking to his boy over there, on the other side of the earth. But what of the distance? Virtue is one all over the world, and there is only one faith, one conceivable conduct of life, one manner of dying. He hopes his "dear James" will never forget that "who once gives way to temptation, in the very instant hazards his total depravity and everlasting ruin. Therefore resolve fixedly never, through any possible motives, to do anything which you believe to be wrong." There is also some news of a favourite dog; and a pony, "which all you boys used to ride", had gone blind from old age and had to be shot. The old chap invokes Heaven's blessing; the mother and all the girls then at home send their love . . . No, there is nothing much in that yellow frayed letter fluttering out of his cherishing grasp after so many years. It was never answered, but who can say what converse he may have held with all these placid, colourless forms of men and women peopling that quiet corner of the world as free of danger or strife as a tomb, and breathing equably the air of undisturbed rectitude. It seems amazing that he should belong to it, he to whom so many things "had come". Nothing ever came to them; they would never be taken unawares, and never be called upon to grapple with fate. Here they all are, evoked by the mild gossip of the father, all these brothers and sisters, bone of his bone and flesh of his flesh, gazing with clear unconscious eyes, while I seem to see him, returned at last, no longer a mere white speck at the heart of an immense mystery, but of full stature, standing disregarded amongst their untroubled shapes, with a stern and romantic aspect, but always mute, dark – under a cloud.

'The story of the last events you shall find in the few pages enclosed here. You must admit that it is romantic beyond the wildest dreams of his boyhood, and yet there is to my mind a sort of profound and terrifying logic in it, as if it were our imagination alone that could set loose upon us the might of an overwhelming destiny. The imprudence of our thoughts recoils upon our heads; who toys with the sword shall perish by the sword. This astounding adventure, of which the most astounding part is that it is true, comes on as an unavoidable consequence. Something of the sort had to happen. You repeat this to yourself while you marvel that such a thing could happen in the year of grace before last. But it has happened – and there is no disputing its logic.

'I put it down here for you as though I had been an eyewitness. My information was fragmentary, but I've fitted the pieces together, and there is enough of them to make an intelligible picture. I wonder how he would have related it himself. He has confided so much in me that at times it seems as though he must come in presently and tell the story in his own words, in his careless yet feeling voice, with his offhand manner, a little puzzled, a little bothered, a little hurt, but now and then by a word or a phrase giving one of these glimpses of his very own self that were never any good for purposes of orientation. It's difficult to believe he will never come. I shall never hear his voice again, nor shall I see his smooth tan-and-pink face with a white line on the forehead, and the youthful eyes darkened by excitement to a profound, unfathomable blue.'

Chapter 37

'It all begins with a remarkable exploit of a man called Brown, who stole with complete success a Spanish schooner out of a small bay near Zamboanga. Till I discovered the fellow my information was incomplete, but most unexpectedly I did come upon him a few hours before he gave up his arrogant ghost. Fortunately he was willing and able to talk between the choking fits of asthma, and his racked body writhed with malicious exultation at the bare thought of Jim. He exulted thus at the idea that he had "paid out the stuck-up beggar after all." He gloated over his action. I had to bear the sunken glare of his fierce crow-footed eyes if I wanted to know; and so I bore it, reflecting how much certain forms of evil are akin to madness, derived from intense egoism, inflamed by resistance, tearing the soul to pieces, and giving factitious vigour to the body. The story also reveals unsuspected depths of cunning in the wretched Cornelius, whose abject and intense hate acts like a subtle inspiration, pointing out an unerring way towards revenge. ' "I could see directly I set my eyes on him what sort of a fool he was," gasped the dying Brown. "He a man! Hell! He was a hollow sham. As if he couldn't have said straight out: 'Hands off my plunder!' blast him! That would have been like a man! Rot his superior soul! He had me there – but he hadn't devil enough in him to make an end of me. Not he! A thing like that letting me off as if I wasn't worth a kick! . . . " Brown struggled desperately for breath . . . "Fraud . . . Letting me off . . . And so I did make an end of him after all . . . " He choked again . . . "I expect this thing'll kill me, but I shall die easy now. You . . . you hear . . . I don't know your name – I would give you a five-pound note if – if I had it – for the news – or my name's not Brown . . . " He grinned horribly . . . "Gentleman Brown."

'He said all these things in profound gasps, staring at me with his yellow eyes out of a long, ravaged brown face; he jerked his left arm; a pepper-and-salt matted beard hung almost into his lap; a dirty ragged blanket covered his legs. I had found him out in Bangkok through that busybody Schomberg, the hotel-keeper, who had, confidentially, directed me where to look. It appears that a sort of loafing, fuddled vagabond – a white man living amongst the natives with a Siamese woman – had considered it a great privilege to give a shelter to the last days of the famous Gentleman Brown. While he was talking to me in the wretched hovel, and, as it were, fighting for every minute of his life, the Siamese woman, with big bare legs and a stupid coarse face, sat in a dark corner chewing betel stolidly. Now and then she would get up for the purpose of shooing a chicken away from the door. The whole hut shook when she walked. An ugly yellow child, naked and pot-bellied like a little heathen god, stood at the foot of the couch, finger in mouth, lost in a profound and calm contemplation of the dying man.

'He talked feverishly; but in the middle of a word, perhaps, an invisible hand would take him by the throat, and he would look at me dumbly with an expression of doubt and anguish. He seemed to fear that I would get tired of waiting and go away, leaving him with his tale untold, with his exultation unexpressed. He died during the night, I believe, but by that time I had nothing more to learn.

'So much as to Brown, for the present.

'Eight months before this, coming into Samarang, I went as usual to see Stein. On the garden side of the house a Malay on the veranda greeted me shyly, and I remembered that I had seen him in Patusan, in Jim's house, amongst other Bugis men who used to come in the evening to talk interminably over their war reminiscences and to discuss State affairs. Jim had pointed him out to me once as a respectable petty trader owning a small seagoing native craft, who had showed himself "one of the best at the taking of the stockade." I was not very surprised to see him, since any Patusan trader venturing as far as Samarang would naturally find his way to Stein's house. I returned his greeting and passed on. At the door of Stein's room I came upon another Malay in whom I recognised Tamb' Itam.

'I asked him at once what he was doing there; it occurred to me that Jim might have come on a visit. I own I was pleased and excited at the thought. Tamb' Itam looked as if he did not know what to say. "Is Tuan Jim inside?" I asked, impatiently. "No," he mumbled, hanging his head for a moment, and then with sudden earnestness, "He would not fight. He would not fight," he repeated twice. As he seemed unable to say anything else, I pushed him aside and went in.

'Stein, tall and stooping, stood alone in the middle of the room between the rows of butterfly cases. "*Ach!* is it you, my friend?" he said, sadly, peering through his glasses. A drab sack-coat of alpaca hung, unbuttoned, down to his knees. He had a Panama hat on his head, and there were deep furrows on his pale cheeks. "What's the matter now?" I asked, nervously. "There's Tamb' Itam there . . . " "Come and see the girl. Come and see the girl. She is here," he said, with a half-hearted show of activity. I tried to detain him, but with gentle obstinacy he would take no notice of my eager questions. "She is here, she is here," he repeated, in great perturbation. "They came here two days ago. An old man like me, a stranger – *sehen Sie* – cannot do much . . . Come this way . . . Young hearts are unforgiving . . . " I could see he was in utmost distress . . . "The strength of life in them, the cruel strength of life . . . " He mumbled, leading me round the house; I followed him, lost in dismal and angry conjectures. At the door of the drawing-room he barred my way. "He loved her very much?" he said, interrogatively, and I only nodded, feeling so bitterly disappointed that I would not trust myself to speak. "Very frightful," he murmured. "She can't understand me. I am only a strange old man. Perhaps you . . . she knows you. Talk to her. We can't leave it like this. Tell her to forgive him. It was very frightful." "No doubt," I said, exasperated at being in the dark; "but have *you* forgiven him?" He looked at me queerly. "You shall hear," he said, and opening the door, absolutely pushed me in.

'You know Stein's big house and the two immense reception-rooms, uninhabited and uninhabitable, clean, full of solitude and of shining things that look as if never beheld by the eye of man? They are cool on the hottest days, and you enter them as you would a scrubbed cave underground. I passed through one, and in the other I saw the girl sitting at the end of a big mahogany table, on which she rested her head, the face hidden in her arms. The waxed floor reflected her dimly as though it had been a sheet of frozen water. The rattan screens were down, and through the strange greenish gloom made by the foliage of the trees outside, a strong wind blew in gusts, swaying the long draperies of windows and doorways. Her white figure seemed shaped in snow; the pendent crystals of a great chandelier clicked above her head like glittering icicles. She looked up and watched my approach. I was chilled as if these vast apartments had been the cold abode of despair.

'She recognised me at once, and as soon as I had stopped, looking down at her: "He has left me," she said, quietly; "you always leave us – for your own ends." Her face was set. All the heat of life seemed withdrawn within some inaccessible spot in her breast. "It would have been easy to die with him," she went on, and made a slight weary gesture as if giving up the incomprehensible. "He would not! It was like a blindness – and yet it was I who was speaking to him; it was I who stood before his eyes; it was at me that he looked all the time! Ah! you are hard, treacherous, without truth, without compassion. What makes you so wicked? Or is it that you are all mad?"

'I took her hand; it did not respond, and when I dropped it, it hung down to the floor. That indifference, more awful than tears, cries, and reproaches, seemed to defy time and consolation. You felt that nothing you could say would reach the seat of the still and benumbing pain.

'Stein had said, "You shall hear." I did hear. I heard it all, listening with amazement, with awe, to the tones of her inflexible weariness. She could not grasp the real sense of what she was telling me, and her resentment filled me with pity for her – for him, too. I stood rooted to the spot after she had finished. Leaning on her arm, she stared with hard eyes, and the wind passed in gusts, the crystals kept on clicking in the greenish gloom. She went on whispering to herself: "And yet he was looking at me! He could see my face, hear my voice, hear my grief! When I used to sit at his feet, with my cheek against his knee and his hand on my head, the curse of cruelty and madness was already within him, waiting for the day. The day came! . . . and before the sun had set he could not see me any more – he was made blind and deaf and without pity, as you all are. He shall have no tears from me. Never, never. Not one tear. I will not! He went away from me as if I had been worse than death. He fled as if driven by some accursed thing he had heard or seen in his sleep . . . "

'Her steady eyes seemed to strain after the shape of a man torn out of her arms by the strength of a dream. She made no sign to my silent bow. I was glad to escape.

'I saw her once again, the same afternoon. On leaving her I had gone in search of Stein, whom I could not find indoors; and I wandered out, pursued by distressful thoughts, into the gardens, those famous gardens of Stein, in which you can find every plant and tree of tropical lowlands. I followed the course of the canalised stream, and sat for a long time on a shaded bench near the ornamental pond, where some waterfowl with clipped wings were diving and splashing noisily. The branches of casuarina trees behind me swayed lightly, incessantly, reminding me of the soughing of fir trees at home.

'This mournful and restless sound was a fit accompaniment to my meditations. She had said he had been driven away from her by a dream – and there was no answer one could make her – there seemed to be no forgiveness for such a transgression. And yet is not mankind itself, pushing on its blind way, driven by a dream of its greatness and its power upon the dark paths of excessive cruelty and of excessive devotion? And what is the pursuit of truth, after all?

'When I rose to get back to the house I caught sight of Stein's drab coat through a gap in the foliage, and very soon at a turn of the path I came upon him walking with the girl. Her little hand rested on his forearm, and under the broad, flat rim of his Panama hat he bent over her, grey-haired, paternal, with compassionate and chivalrous deference. I stood aside, but they stopped, facing me. His gaze was bent on the ground at his feet; the girl, erect and slight on his arm, stared sombrely beyond my shoulder with black, clear, motionless eyes. "*Schrecklich*!" he murmured. "Terrible! Terrible! What can one do?" He seemed to be appealing to me, but her youth, the length of days suspended over her head, appealed to me more; and suddenly, even as I realised that nothing could be said, I found myself pleading his cause for her sake. "You must forgive him," I concluded, and my own voice seemed to me muffled, lost in an irresponsive deaf immensity. "We all want to be forgiven," I added after a while.

' "What have I done?" she asked with her lips only.

' "You always mistrusted him," I said.

' "He was like the others," she pronounced slowly.

' "Not like the others," I protested, but she continued evenly, without any feeling: "He was false." And suddenly Stein broke in. "No! no! no! My poor child! . . . " He patted her hand lying passively on his sleeve. "No! no! Not false! True! true! true!" He tried to look into her stone face. "You don't understand. *Ach!* Why you do not understand? . . . Terrible!" he said to me. "Someday she *shall* understand."

' "Will *you* explain?" I asked, looking hard at him. They moved on.

'I watched them. Her gown trailed on the path, her black hair fell loose. She walked upright and light by the side of the tall man, whose long shapeless coat hung in perpendicular folds from the stooping shoulders, whose feet moved slowly. They disappeared beyond that spinney (you may remember) where sixteen different kinds of bamboo grow together, all distinguishable to the learned eye. For my part, I was fascinated by the exquisite grace and beauty of that fluted grove, crowned with pointed leaves and feathery heads, the lightness, the vigour, the charm as distinct as a voice of the unperplexed luxuriating life. I remember staying to look at it for a long time, as one would linger within reach of a consoling whisper. The sky was pearly grey. It was one of those overcast days so rare in the tropics in which memories crowd upon one, memories of other shores, of other faces.

'I drove back to town the same afternoon, taking with me Tamb' Itam and the other Malay, in whose seagoing craft they had escaped in the bewilderment, fear, and gloom of the disaster. The shock of it seemed to have changed their natures. It had turned her passion into stone, and it made the surly taciturn Tamb' Itam almost loquacious. His surliness, too, was subdued into puzzled humility, as though he had seen the failure of a potent charm in a supreme moment. The Bugis trader, a shy hesitating man, was very clear in the little he had to say. Both were evidently overawed by a sense of deep inexpressible wonder, by the touch of an inscrutable mystery.'

There with Marlow's signature the letter proper ended. The privileged reader screwed up his lamp, and solitary above the billowy roofs of the town, like a lighthouse-keeper above the sea, he turned to the pages of the story.

Chapter 38

'It all begins, as I've told you, with the man called Brown,' ran the opening sentence of Marlow's narrative. 'You who have knocked about the Western Pacific must have heard of him. He was the show ruffian on the Australian coast – not that he was often to be seen there, but because he was always trotted out in the stories of lawless life a visitor from home is treated to; and the mildest of these stories which were told about him from Cape York to Eden Bay was more than enough to hang a man if told in the right place. They never failed to let you know, too, that he was supposed to be the son of a baronet. Be it as it may, it is certain he had deserted from a home ship in the early gold-digging days, and in a few years became talked about as the terror of this or that group of islands in Polynesia. He would kidnap natives, he would strip some lonely white trader to the very pyjamas he stood in, and after he had robbed the poor devil, he would as likely as not invite him to fight a duel with shotguns on the beach – which would have been fair enough as these things go, if the other man hadn't been by that time already half-dead with fright. Brown was a latter-day buccaneer, sorry enough, like his more celebrated prototypes, but what distinguished him from his contemporary brother ruffians, like Bully Hayes or the mellifluous Pease, or that perfumed, Dundreary-whiskered, dandified scoundrel known as Dirty Dick, was the arrogant temper of his misdeeds and a vehement scorn for mankind at large and for his victims in particular. The others were merely vulgar and greedy brutes, but he seemed moved by some complex intention. He would rob a man as if only to demonstrate his poor opinion of the creature, and he would bring to the shooting or maiming of some quiet, unoffending stranger a savage and vengeful earnestness fit to terrify the most reckless of desperadoes. In the days of his greatest glory he owned an armed barque, manned by a mixed crew of Kanakas and runaway whalers, and boasted, I don't know with what truth, of being financed on the quiet by a most respectable firm of copra merchants. Later on he ran off – it was reported – with the wife of a missionary, a very young girl from Clapham way, who had married the mild, flat-footed fellow in a moment of enthusiasm, and, suddenly transplanted to Melanesia, lost her bearings somehow. It was a dark story. She was ill at the time he carried her off, and died on board his ship. It is said – as the most wonderful part of the tale – that over her body he gave way to an outburst of sombre and violent grief. His luck left him, too, very soon after. He lost his ship on some rocks off Malaita and disappeared for a time as though he had gone down with her. He is heard of next at Nuka-Hiva, where he bought an old French schooner out of Government service. What creditable enterprise he might have had in view when he made that purchase I can't say, but it is evident that what with High Commissioners, consuls, men-of-war, and international control, the South Seas were getting too hot to hold gentlemen of his kidney. Clearly he must have shifted the scene of his operations farther west, because a year later he plays an incredibly audacious, but not a very profitable part, in a serio-comic business in Manila Bay, in which a peculating governor and an absconding treasurer are the principal figures; thereafter he seems to have hung around the Philippines in his rotten schooner, battling with an adverse fortune, till at last, running his appointed course, he sails into Jim's history, a blind accomplice of the Dark Powers.

'His tale goes that when a Spanish patrol cutter captured him he was simply trying to run a few guns for the insurgents. If so, then I can't understand what he was doing off the south coast of Mindanao. My belief, however, is that he was blackmailing the native villages along the coast. The principal thing is that the cutter, throwing a guard on board, made him sail in company towards Zamboanga. On the way, for some reason or other, both vessels had to call at one of these new Spanish settlements – which never came to anything in the end – where there was not only a civil official in charge on shore, but a good stout coasting schooner lying at anchor in the little bay; and this craft, in every way much better than his own, Brown made up his mind to steal.

'He was down on his luck – as he told me himself. The world he had bullied for twenty years with fierce, aggressive disdain, had yielded him nothing in the way of material advantage except a small bag of silver dollars, which was concealed in his cabin so that "the devil himself couldn't smell it out." And that was all – absolutely all. He was tired of his life, and not afraid of death. But this man, who would stake his existence on a whim with a bitter and jeering recklessness, stood in mortal fear of imprisonment. He had an unreasoning cold-sweat, nerve-shaking, blood-to-water-turning sort of horror at the bare possibility of being locked up – the sort of terror a superstitious man would feel at the thought of being embraced by a spectre. Therefore the civil official who came on board to make a preliminary investigation into the capture, investigated arduously all day long, and only went ashore after dark, muffled up in a cloak, and taking great care not to let Brown's little all clink in its bag. Afterwards, being a man of his word, he contrived (the very next evening, I believe) to send off the Government cutter on some urgent bit of special service. As her commander could not spare a prize crew, he contented himself by taking away before he left all the sails of Brown's schooner to the very last rag, and took good care to tow his two boats on to the beach a couple of miles off.

'But in Brown's crew there was a Solomon Islander, kidnapped in his youth and devoted to Brown, who was the best man of the whole gang. That fellow swam off to the coaster – five hundred yards or so – with the end of a warp made up of all the running gear unrove for the purpose. The water was smooth and the bay dark, "like the inside of a cow", as Brown described it. The Solomon Islander clambered over the bulwarks with the end of the rope in his teeth. The crew of the coaster – all Tagals – were ashore having a jollification in the native village. The two shipkeepers left on board woke up suddenly and saw the devil. It had glittering eyes and leaped quick as lightning about the deck. They fell on their knees, paralysed with fear, crossing themselves and mumbling prayers. With a long knife he found in the caboose the Solomon Islander, without interrupting their orisons, stabbed first one, then the other; with the same knife he set to sawing patiently at the coir cable till suddenly it parted under the blade with a splash. Then in the silence of the bay he let out a cautious shout, and Brown's gang, who meantime had been peering and straining their hopeful ears in the darkness, began to pull gently at their end of the warp. In less then five minutes the two schooners came together with a slight shock and a creak of spars.

'Brown's crowd transferred themselves without losing an instant, taking with them their firearms and a large supply of ammunition. They were sixteen in all: two runaway bluejackets, a lanky deserter from a Yankee man-of-war, a couple of simple, blond Scandinavians, a mulatto of sorts, one bland Chinaman who cooked – and the rest of the nondescript spawn of the South Seas. None of them cared; Brown bent them to his will, and Brown, indifferent to gallows, was running away from the spectre of a Spanish prison. He didn't give them the time to tranship enough provisions; the weather was calm, the air was charged with dew, and when they cast off the ropes and set sail to a faint offshore draught there was no flutter in the damp canvas; their old schooner seemed to detach itself gently from the stolen craft and slip away silently, together with the black mass of the coast, into the night.

'They got clear away. Brown related to me in detail their passage down the Straits of Macassar. It is a harrowing and desperate story. They were short of food and water; they boarded several native craft and got a little from each. With a stolen ship Brown did not dare to put into any port, of course. He had no money to buy anything, no papers to show, and no lie plausible enough to get him out again. An Arab barque, under the Dutch flag, surprised one night at anchor off Poulo Laut, yielded a little dirty rice, a bunch of bananas, and a cask of water; three days of squally misty weather from the north-east shot the schooner across the Java Sea. The yellow muddy waves drenched that collection of hungry ruffians. They sighted mail-boats moving on their appointed routes; passed well-found home ships with rusty iron sides anchored in the shallow sea waiting for a change of weather or the turn of the tide; an English gunboat, white and trim, with two slim masts crossed their bows one day in the distance; and on another occasion a Dutch corvette, black and heavily sparred, loomed upon their quarter, steaming dead slow in the mist. They slipped through unseen or disregarded, a wan, sallow-faced band of utter outcasts, enraged with hunger and hunted by fear. Brown's idea was to make for Madagascar, where he expected, on grounds not altogether illusory, to sell the schooner in Tamatave, and no questions asked, or perhaps obtain some more or less forged papers for her. Yet before he could face the long passage across the Indian Ocean food was wanted – water, too.

'Perhaps he had heard of Patusan – or perhaps he just only happened to see the name written in small letters on the chart – probably that of a largish village up a river in a native state, perfectly defenceless, far from the beaten tracks of the sea and from the ends of submarine cables. He had done that kind of thing before – in the way of business; and this now was an absolute necessity, a question of life and death – or rather of liberty. Of liberty! He was sure to get provisions – bullocks – rice – sweet-potatoes. The sorry gang licked their chops. A cargo of produce for the schooner perhaps could be extorted – and, who knows? – some real ringing coined money! Some of these chiefs and village headmen can be made to part freely. He told me he would have roasted their toes rather than be balked. I believe him. His men believed him too. They didn't cheer aloud, being a dumb pack, but made ready wolfishly.

'Luck served him as to weather. A few days of calm would have brought unmentionable horrors on board that schooner, but with the help of land and sea breezes, in less than a week after clearing the Sunda Straits, he anchored off the Batu Kring mouth within a pistol-shot of the fishing village.

'Fourteen of them packed into the schooner's long-boat (which was big, having been used for cargo-work) and started up the river, while two remained in charge of the schooner with food enough to keep starvation off for ten days. The tide and wind helped, and early one afternoon the big white boat under a ragged sail shouldered its way before the sea breeze into Patusan Reach, manned by fourteen assorted scarecrows glaring hungrily ahead, and fingering the breech-blocks of cheap rifles. Brown calculated upon the terrifying surprise of his appearance. They sailed in with the last of the flood; the Rajah's stockade gave no sign; the first houses on both sides of the stream seemed deserted. A few canoes were seen up the reach in full flight. Brown was astonished at the size of the place. A profound silence reigned. The wind dropped between the houses; two oars were got out and the boat held on upstream, the idea being to effect a lodgment in the centre of the town before the inhabitants could think of resistance.

'It seems, however, that the headman of the fishing village at Batu Kring had managed to send off a timely warning. When the long-boat came abreast of the mosque (which Doramin had built: a structure with gables and roof finials of carved coral) the open space before it was full of people. A shout went up, and was followed by a clash of gongs all up the river. From a point above two little brass six-pounders were discharged, and the round-shot came skipping down the empty reach, spirting glittering jets of water in the sunshine. In front of the mosque a shouting lot of men began firing in volleys that whipped athwart the current of the river; an irregular, rolling fusillade was opened on the boat from both banks, and Brown's men replied with a wild, rapid fire. The oars had been got in.

'The turn of the tide at high water comes on very quick in that river, and the boat in midstream, nearly hidden in smoke, began to drift back stern foremost. Along both shores the smoke thickened also, lying below the roofs in a level streak as you may see a long cloud cutting the slope of a mountain. A tumult of war-cries, the vibrating clang of gongs, the deep snoring of drums, yells of rage, crashes of volley-firing, made an awful din, in which Brown sat confounded but steady at the tiller, working himself into a fury of hate and rage against those people who dared to defend themselves. Two of his men had been wounded, and he saw his retreat cut off below the town by some boats that had put off from Tunku Allang's stockade. There were six of them full of men. While he was thus beset he perceived the entrance of the narrow creek (the same which Jim had jumped at low water). It was then brim full. Steering the long-boat in, they landed, and, to make a long story short, they established themselves on a little knoll about nine hundred yards from the stockade, which, in fact, they commanded from that position. The slopes of the knoll were bare, but there were a few trees on the summit. They went to work cutting these down for a breastwork, and were fairly entrenched before dark; meantime the Rajah's boats remained in the river with curious neutrality. When the sun set the glare of many brushwood blazes lighted on the river-front, and between the double line of houses on the land side threw into black relief the roofs, the groups of slender palms, the heavy clumps of fruit trees. Brown ordered the grass round his position to be fired; a low ring of thin flames under the slow, ascending smoke wriggled rapidly down the slopes of the knoll; here and there a dry bush caught with a tall, vicious roar. The conflagration made a clear zone of fire for the rifles of the small party, and expired smouldering on the edge of the forests and along the muddy bank of the creek. A strip of jungle luxuriating in a damp hollow between the knoll and the Rajah's stockade stopped it on that side with a great crackling and detonations of bursting bamboo stems. The sky was sombre, velvety, and swarming with stars. The blackened ground smoked quietly with low creeping wisps, till a little breeze came on and blew everything away. Brown expected an attack to be delivered as soon as the tide had flowed enough again to enable the war-boats which had cut off his retreat to enter the creek. At any rate he was sure there would be an attempt to carry off his long-boat, which lay below the hill, a dark high lump on the feeble sheen of a wet mud-flat. But no move of any sort was made by the boats in the river. Over the stockade and the Rajah's buildings Brown saw their lights on the water. They seemed to be anchored across the stream. Other lights afloat were moving in the reach, crossing and recrossing from side to side. There were also lights twinkling motionless upon the long wall of houses up the reach, as far as the bend, and more still beyond, others isolated inland. The loom of the big fires disclosed buildings, roofs, black piles as far as he could see. It was an immense place. The fourteen desperate invaders lying flat behind the felled trees raised their chins to look over at the stir of that town that seemed to extend up-river for miles and swarm with thousands of angry men. They did not speak to each other. Now and then they would hear a loud yell, or a single shot rang out, fired very far somewhere. But round their position everything was still, dark, silent. They seemed to be forgotten, as if the excitement keeping awake all the population had nothing to do with them, as if they had been dead already.'

Chapter 39

'All the events of that night have a great importance, since they brought about a situation which remained unchanged till Jim's return: Jim had been away in the interior for more than a week, and it was Dain Waris who had directed the first repulse. That brave and intelligent youth ("who knew how to fight after the manner of white men") wished to settle the business offhand, but his people were too much for him. He had not Jim's racial prestige and the reputation of invincible, supernatural power. He was not the visible tangible incarnation of unfailing truth and of unfailing victory. Beloved, trusted, and admired as he was, he was still one of *them*, while Jim was one of *us*. Moreover, the white man, a tower of strength in himself, was invulnerable, while Dain Waris could be killed. Those unexpressed thoughts guided the opinions of the chief men of the town, who elected to assemble in Jim's fort for deliberation upon the emergency, as if expecting to find wisdom and courage in the dwelling of the absent white man. The shooting of Brown's ruffians was so far good, or lucky, that there had been half a dozen casualties amongst the defenders. The wounded were lying on the veranda tended by their womenfolk. The women and children from the lower part of the town had been sent into the fort at the first alarm. There Jewel was in command, very efficient and high-spirited, obeyed by Jim's "own people", who, quitting in a body their little settlement under the stockade, had gone in to form the garrison. The refugees crowded round her; and through the whole affair, to the very disastrous last, she showed an extraordinary martial ardour. It was to her that Dain Waris had gone at once at the first intelligence of danger, for you must know that Jim was the only one in Patusan who possessed a store of gunpowder. Stein, with whom he had kept up intimate relations by letters, had obtained from the Dutch Government a special authorisation to export five hundred kegs of it to Patusan. The powder-magazine was a small hut of rough logs covered entirely with earth, and in Jim's absence the girl had the key. In the council, held at eleven o'clock in the evening in Jim's dining-room, she backed up Waris's advice for immediate and vigorous action. I am told that she stood up by the side of Jim's empty chair at the head of the long table and made a warlike impassioned speech, which for the moment extorted murmurs of approbation from the assembled headmen. Old Doramin, who had not showed himself outside his own gate for more than a year, had been brought across with great difficulty. He was, of course, the chief man there. The temper of the council was very unforgiving, and the old man's word would have been decisive; but it is my opinion that, well aware of his son's fiery courage, he dared not pronounce the word. More dilatory counsels prevailed. A certain Haji Saman pointed out at great length that "these tyrannical and ferocious men had delivered themselves to a certain death in any case. They would stand fast on their hill and starve, or they would try to regain their boat and be shot from ambushes across the creek, or they would break and fly into the forest and perish singly there." He argued that by the use of proper stratagems these evil-minded strangers could be destroyed without the risk of a battle, and his words had a great weight, especially with the Patusan men proper. What unsettled the minds of the townsfolk was the failure of the Rajah's boats to act at the decisive moment. It was the diplomatic Kassim who represented the Rajah at the council. He spoke very little, listened smilingly, very friendly and impenetrable. During the sitting messengers kept arriving every few minutes almost, with reports of the invaders' proceedings. Wild and exaggerated rumours were flying: there was a large ship at the mouth of the river with big guns and many more men – some white, others with black skins and of bloodthirsty appearance. They were coming with many more boats to exterminate every living thing. A sense of near, incomprehensible danger affected the common people. At one moment there was a panic in the courtyard amongst the women; shrieking; a rush; children crying – Haji Saman went out to quiet them. Then a fort sentry fired at something moving on the river, and nearly killed a villager bringing in his womenfolk in a canoe together with the best of his domestic utensils and a dozen fowls. This caused more confusion. Meantime the palaver inside Jim's house went on in the presence of the girl. Doramin sat fierce-faced, heavy, looking at the speakers in turn, and breathing slow like a bull. He didn't speak till the last, after Kassim had declared that the Rajah's boats would be called in because the men were required to defend his master's stockade. Dain Waris in his father's presence would offer no opinion, though the girl entreated him in Jim's name to speak out. She offered him Jim's own men in her anxiety to have these intruders driven out at once. He only shook his head, after a glance or two at Doramin. Finally, when the council broke up it had been decided that the houses nearest the creek should be strongly occupied to obtain the command of the enemy's boat. The boat itself was not to be interfered with openly, so that the robbers on the hill should be tempted to embark, when a well-directed fire would kill most of them, no doubt. To cut off the escape of those who might survive, and to prevent more of them coming up, Dain Waris was ordered by Doramin to take an armed party of Bugis down the river to a certain spot ten miles below Patusan, and there form a camp on the shore and blockade the stream with the canoes. I don't believe for a moment that Doramin feared the arrival of fresh forces. My opinion is, that his conduct was guided solely by his wish to keep his son out of harm's way. To prevent a rush being made into the town the construction of a stockade was to be commenced at daylight at the end of the street on the left bank. The old *nakhoda* declared his intention to command there himself. A distribution of powder, bullets, and percussion caps was made immediately under the girl's supervision. Several messengers were to be dispatched in different directions after Jim, whose exact whereabouts were unknown. These men started at dawn, but before that time Kassim had managed to open communications with the besieged Brown.

'That accomplished diplomatist and confidant of the Rajah, on leaving the fort to go back to his master, took into his boat Cornelius, whom he found slinking mutely amongst the people in the courtyard. Kassim had a little plan of his own and wanted him for an interpreter. Thus it came about that towards morning Brown, reflecting upon the desperate nature of his position, heard from the marshy overgrown hollow an amicable, quavering, strained voice crying – in English – for permission to come up, under a promise of personal safety and on a very important errand. He was overjoyed. If he was spoken to he was no longer a hunted wild beast. These friendly sounds took off at once the awful stress of vigilant watchfulness as of so many blind men not knowing whence the deathblow might come. He pretended a great reluctance. The voice declared itself "a white man. A poor, ruined, old man who had been living here for years." A mist, wet and chilly, lay on the slopes of the hill, and after some more shouting from one to the other, Brown called out, "Come on, then, but alone, mind!" As a matter of fact – he told me, writhing with rage at the recollection of his helplessness – it made no difference. They couldn't see more than a few yards before them, and no treachery could make their position worse. By and by Cornelius, in his weekday attire of a ragged dirty shirt and pants, barefooted, with a broken-rimmed pith hat on his head, was made out vaguely, sidling up to the defences, hesitating, stopping to listen in a peering posture. "Come along! You are safe," yelled Brown, while his men stared. All their hopes of life became suddenly centred in that dilapidated, mean newcomer, who in profound silence clambered clumsily over a felled tree-trunk, and shivering, with his sour mistrustful face, looked about at the knot of bearded, anxious, sleepless desperadoes.

'Half an hour's confidential talk with Cornelius opened Brown's eyes as to the home affairs of Patusan. He was on the alert at once. There were possibilities, immense possibilities; but before he would talk over Cornelius's proposals he demanded that some food should be sent up as a guarantee of good faith. Cornelius went off, creeping sluggishly down the hill on the side of the Rajah's palace, and after some delay a few of Tunku Allang's men came up, bringing a scanty supply of rice, chillies, and dried fish. This was immeasurably better than nothing. Later on Cornelius returned accompanying Kassim, who stepped out with an air of perfect good-humoured trustfulness, in sandals, and muffled up from neck to ankles in dark-blue sheeting. He shook hands with Brown discreetly, and the three drew aside for a conference. Brown's men, recovering their confidence, were slapping each other on the back, and cast knowing glances at their captain while they busied themselves with preparations for cooking.

'Kassim disliked Doramin and his Bugis very much, but he hated the new order of things still more. It had occurred to him that these whites, together with the Rajah's followers, could attack and defeat the Bugis before Jim's return. Then, he reasoned, general defection of the townsfolk was sure to follow, and the reign of the white man who protected poor people would be over. Afterwards the new allies could be dealt with. They would have no friends. The fellow was perfectly able to perceive the difference of character, and had seen enough of white men to know that these newcomers were outcasts, men without country. Brown preserved a stern and inscrutable demeanour. When he first heard Cornelius's voice demanding admittance, it brought merely the hope of a loophole for escape. In less than an hour other thoughts were seething in his head. Urged by an extreme necessity, he had come there to steal food, a few tons of rubber or gum maybe, perhaps a handful of dollars, and had found himself enmeshed by deadly dangers. Now in consequence of these overtures from Kassim he began to think of stealing the whole country. Some confounded fellow had apparently accomplished something of the kind – single-handed at that. Couldn't have done it very well though. Perhaps they could work together – squeeze everything dry and then go out quietly. In the course of his negotiations with Kassim he became aware that he was supposed to have a big ship with plenty of men outside. Kassim begged him earnestly to have this big ship with his many guns and men brought up the river without delay for the Rajah's service. Brown professed himself willing, and on this basis the negotiation was carried on with mutual distrust. Three times in the course of the morning the courteous and active Kassim went down to consult the Rajah and came up busily with his long stride. Brown, while bargaining, had a sort of grim enjoyment in thinking of his wretched schooner, with nothing but a heap of dirt in her hold, that stood for an armed ship, and a Chinaman and a lame ex-beachcomber of Levuka on board, who represented all his many men. In the afternoon he obtained further doles of food, a promise of some money, and a supply of mats for his men to make shelters for themselves. They lay down and snored, protected from the burning sunshine; but Brown, sitting fully exposed on one of the felled trees, feasted his eyes upon the view of the town and the river. There was much loot here. Cornelius, who had made himself at home in the camp, talked at his elbow, pointing out the localities, imparting advice, giving his own version of Jim's character, and commenting in his own fashion upon the events of the last three years. Brown, who, apparently indifferent and gazing away, listened with attention to every word, could not make out clearly what sort of man this Jim could be. "What's his name? Jim! Jim! That's not enough for a man's name." "They call him," said Cornelius, scornfully, "Tuan Jim here. As you may say Lord Jim." "What is he? Where does he come from?" enquired Brown. "What sort of man is he? Is he an Englishman?" "Yes, yes! he's an Englishman. I am an Englishman, too. From Malacca. He is a fool. All you have to do is to kill him and then you are king here. Everything belongs to him," explained Cornelius. "It strikes me he may be made to share with somebody before very long," commented Brown half aloud. "No, no. The proper way is to kill him the first chance you get, and then you can do what you like," Cornelius would insist earnestly. "I have lived for many years here, and I am giving you a friend's advice."

'In such converse and in gloating over the view of Patusan, which he had determined in his mind should become his prey, Brown whiled away most of the afternoon, his men, meantime, resting. On that day Dain Waris's fleet of canoes stole one by one under the shore farthest from the creek, and went down to close the river against his retreat. Of this Brown was not aware, and Kassim, who came up the knoll an hour before sunset, took good care not to enlighten him. He wanted the white man's ship to come up the river, and this news, he feared, would be discouraging. He was very pressing with Brown to send the "order", offering at the same time a trusty messenger, who for greater secrecy (as he explained) would make his way by land to the mouth of the river and deliver the "order" on board. After some reflection Brown judged it expedient to tear a page out of his pocket-book, on which he simply wrote: "We are getting on. Big job. Detain the man." The stolid youth selected by Kassim for that service performed it faithfully, and was rewarded by being suddenly tipped, head first, into the schooner's empty hold by the ex-beachcomber and the Chinaman, who thereupon hastened to put on the hatches. What became of him afterwards Brown did not say.'

Chapter 40

'Brown's object was to gain time by fooling with Kassim's diplomacy. For doing a real stroke of business he could not help thinking the white man was the person to work with. He could not imagine such a chap (who must be confoundedly clever after all to get hold of the natives like that) refusing a help that would do away with the necessity for slow, cautious, risky cheating, that imposed itself as the only possible line of conduct for a single-handed man. He, Brown, would offer him the power. No man could hesitate. Everything was in coming to a clear understanding. Of course they would share. The idea of there being a fort – all ready to his hand – a real fort, with artillery (he knew this from Cornelius), excited him. Let him only once get in and . . . He would impose modest conditions. Not too low, though. The man was no fool, it seemed. They would work like brothers till . . . till the time came for a quarrel and a shot that would settle all accounts. With grim impatience of plunder he wished himself to be talking with the man now. The land already seemed to be his to tear to pieces, squeeze, and throw away. Meantime Kassim had to be fooled for the sake of food first – and for a second string. But the principal thing was to get something to eat from day to day. Besides, he was not averse to begin fighting on that Rajah's account, and teach a lesson to those people who had received him with shots. The lust of battle was upon him.

'I am sorry that I can't give you this part of the story, which of course I have mainly from Brown, in Brown's own words. There was in the broken, violent speech of that man, unveiling before me his thoughts with the very hand of Death upon his throat, an undisguised ruthlessness of purpose, a strange vengeful attitude towards his own past, and a blind belief in the righteousness of his will against all mankind. Something of that feeling which could induce the leader of a horde of wandering cutthroats to call himself proudly the Scourge of God. No doubt the natural senseless ferocity which is the basis of such a character was exasperated by failure, ill-luck, and the recent privations, as well as by the desperate position in which he found himself; but what was most remarkable of all was this, that while he planned treacherous alliances, had already settled in his own mind the fate of the white man, and intrigued in an overbearing, offhand manner with Kassim, one could perceive that what he had really desired, almost in spite of himself, was to play havoc with that jungle town which had defied him, to see it strewn over with corpses and enveloped in flames. Listening to his pitiless, panting voice, I could imagine how he must have looked at it from the hillock, peopling it with images of murder and rapine. The part nearest to the creek wore an abandoned aspect, though as a matter of fact every house concealed a few armed men on the alert. Suddenly beyond the stretch of waste ground, interspersed with small patches of low dense bush, excavations, heaps of rubbish, with trodden paths between, a man, solitary and looking very small, strolled out into the deserted opening of the street between the shut-up, dark, lifeless buildings at the end. Perhaps one of the inhabitants, who had fled to the other bank of the river, coming back for some object of domestic use. Evidently he supposed himself quite safe at that distance from the hill on the other side of the creek. A light stockade, set up hastily, was just round the turn of the street, full of his friends. He moved leisurely. Brown saw him, and instantly called to his side the Yankee deserter, who acted as a sort of second in command. This lanky, loose-jointed fellow came forward, wooden-faced, trailing his rifle lazily. When he understood what was wanted from him a homicidal and conceited smile uncovered his teeth, making two deep folds down his sallow, leathery cheeks. He prided himself on being a dead shot. He dropped on one knee, and taking aim from a steady rest through the unlopped branches of a felled tree, fired, and at once stood up to look. The man, far away, turned his head to the report, made another step forward, seemed to hesitate, and abruptly got down on his hands and knees. In the silence that fell upon the sharp crack of the rifle, the dead shot, keeping his eyes fixed upon the quarry, guessed that "that there coon's health would never be a source of anxiety to his friends any more." The man's limbs were seen to move rapidly under his body in an endeavour to run on all fours. In that empty space arose a multitudinous shout of dismay and surprise. The man sank flat, face down, and moved no more. "That showed them what we could do," said Brown to me. "Struck the fear of sudden death into them. That was what we wanted. They were two hundred to one, and this gave them something to think over for the night. Not one of them had an idea of such a long shot before. That beggar belonging to the Rajah scouted downhill with his eyes hanging out of his head."

'As he was telling me this he tried with a shaking hand to wipe the thin foam on his blue lips. "Two hundred to one. Two hundred to one . . . strike terror . . . terror, terror, I tell you . . ." His own eyes were starting out of their sockets. He fell back, clawing the air with skinny fingers, sat up again, bowed and hairy, glared at me sideways like some man-beast of folklore, with open mouth in his miserable and awful agony before he got his speech back after that fit. There are sights one never forgets.

'Furthermore, to draw the enemy's fire and locate such parties as might have been hiding in the bushes along the creek, Brown ordered the Solomon Islander to go down to the boat and bring an oar, as you send a spaniel after a stick into the water. This failed, and the fellow came back without a single shot having been fired at him from anywhere. "There's nobody," opined some of the men. "It is onnatural," remarked the Yankee. Kassim had gone, by that time, very much impressed, pleased, too, and also uneasy. Pursuing his tortuous policy, he had dispatched a message to Dain Waris warning him to look out for the white men's ship, which, he had had information, was about to come up the river. He minimised its strength and exhorted him to oppose its passage. This double-dealing answered his purpose, which was to keep the Bugis forces divided and to weaken them by fighting. On the other hand, he had in the course of that day sent word to the assembled Bugis chiefs in town, assuring them that he was trying to induce the invaders to retire; his messages to the fort asked earnestly for powder for the Rajah's men. It was a long time since Tunku Allang had had ammunition for the score or so of old muskets rusting in their arm-racks in the audience-hall. The open intercourse between the hill and the palace unsettled all the minds. It was already time for men to take sides, it began to be said. There would soon be much bloodshed, and thereafter great trouble for many people. The social fabric of orderly, peaceful life, when every man was sure of tomorrow, the edifice raised by Jim's hands, seemed on that evening ready to collapse into a ruin reeking with blood. The poorer folk were already taking to the bush or flying up the river. A good many of the upper class judged it necessary to go and pay their court to the Rajah. The Rajah's youths jostled them rudely. Old Tunku Allang, almost out of his mind with fear and indecision, either kept a sullen silence or abused them violently for daring to come with empty hands: they departed very much frightened; only old Doramin kept his countrymen together and pursued his tactics inflexibly. Enthroned in a big chair behind the improvised stockade, he issued his orders in a deep veiled rumble, unmoved, like a deaf man, in the flying rumours.

'Dusk fell, hiding first the body of the dead man, which had been left lying with arms outstretched as if nailed to the ground, and then the revolving sphere of the night rolled smoothly over Patusan and came to a rest, showering the glitter of countless worlds upon the earth. Again, in the exposed part of the town big fires blazed along the only street, revealing from distance to distance upon their glares the falling straight lines of roofs, the fragments of wattled walls jumbled in confusion, here and there a whole hut elevated in the glow upon the vertical black stripes of a group of high piles; and all this line of dwellings, revealed in patches by the swaying flames, seemed to flicker tortuously away up-river into the gloom at the heart of the land. A great silence, in which the looms of successive fires played without noise, extended into the darkness at the foot of the hill; but the other bank of the river, all dark save for a solitary bonfire at the river-front before the fort, sent out into the air an increasing tremor that might have been the stamping of a multitude of feet, the hum of many voices, or the fall of an immensely distant waterfall. It was then, Brown confessed to me, while, turning his back on his men, he sat looking at it all, that notwithstanding his disdain, his ruthless faith in himself, a feeling came over him that at last he had run his head against a stone wall. Had his boat been afloat at the time, he believed he would have tried to steal away, taking his chances of a long chase down the river and of starvation at sea. It was very doubtful whether he would have succeeded in getting away. However, he didn't try this. For another moment he had a passing thought of trying to rush the town, but he perceived very well that in the end he would find himself in the lighted street, where they would be shot down like dogs from the houses. They were two hundred to one – he thought, while his men, huddling round two heaps of smouldering embers, munched the last of the bananas and roasted the few yams they owed to Kassim's diplomacy. Cornelius sat amongst them dozing sulkily.

'Then one of the whites remembered that some tobacco had been left in the boat, and, encouraged by the impunity of the Solomon Islander, said he would go to fetch it. At this all the others shook off their despondency. Brown, applied to, said, "Go and be d—d to you," scornfully. He didn't think there was any danger in going to the creek in the dark. The man threw a leg over the tree-trunk and disappeared. A moment later he was heard clambering into the boat and then clambering out. "I've got it," he cried. A flash and a report at the very foot of the hill followed. "I am hit," yelled the man. "Look out, look out – I am hit," and instantly all the rifles went off. The hill squirted fire and noise into the night like a little volcano, and when Brown and the Yankee with curses and cuffs stopped the panic-stricken firing, a profound, weary groan floated up from the creek, succeeded by a plaint whose heart-rending sadness was like some poison turning the blood cold in the veins. Then a strong voice pronounced several distinct incomprehensible words somewhere beyond the creek. "Let no one fire," shouted Brown. "What does it mean?" . . . "Do you hear on the hill? Do you hear? Do you hear?" repeated the voice three times. Cornelius translated, and then prompted the answer. "Speak," cried Brown, "we hear." Then the voice, declaiming in the sonorous inflated tone of a herald, and shifting continually on the edge of the vague wasteland, proclaimed that between the men of the Bugis nation living in Patusan and the white men on the hill and those with them, there would be no faith, no compassion, no speech, no peace. A bush rustled; a haphazard volley rang out. "Dam' foolishness," muttered the Yankee, vexedly grounding the butt. Cornelius translated. The wounded man below the hill, after crying out twice, "Take me up! take me up!" went on complaining in moans. While he had kept on the blackened earth of the slope and afterwards crouching in the boat, he had been safe enough. It seems that in his joy at finding tobacco he forgot himself and jumped out on her off-side, as it were. The white boat, lying high and dry, showed him up; the creek was no more than seven yards wide in that place, and there happened to be a man crouching in the bush on the other bank.

'He was a Bugis of Tondano only lately come to Patusan, and a relation of the man shot in the afternoon. That famous long shot had indeed appalled the beholders. The man in utter security had been struck down, in full view of his friends, dropping with a joke on his lips, and they seemed to see in the act an atrocity which had stirred a bitter rage. That relation of his, Si-Lapa by name, was then with Doramin in the stockade only a few feet away. You who know these chaps must admit that the fellow showed an unusual pluck by volunteering to carry the message, alone, in the dark. Creeping across the open ground, he had deviated to the left and found himself opposite the boat. He was startled when Brown's man shouted. He came to a sitting position with his gun to his shoulder, and when the other jumped out, exposing himself, he pulled the trigger and lodged three jagged slugs point-blank into the poor wretch's stomach. Then, lying flat on his face, he gave himself up for dead, while a thin hail of lead chopped and swished the bushes close on his right hand; afterwards he delivered his speech shouting, bent double, dodging all the time in cover. With the last word he leaped sideways, lay close for a while, and afterwards got back to the houses unharmed, having achieved on that night such a renown as his children will not willingly allow to die.

'And on the hill the forlorn band let the two little heaps of embers go out under their bowed heads. They sat dejected on the ground with compressed lips and downcast eyes, listening to their comrade below. He was a strong man and died hard, with moans now loud, now sinking to a strange confidential note of pain. Sometimes he shrieked, and again, after a period of silence, he could be heard muttering deliriously a long and unintelligible complaint. Never for a moment did he cease.

' "What's the good" Brown had said unmoved once, seeing the Yankee, who had been swearing under his breath, prepare to go down. "That's so," assented the deserter, reluctantly desisting. "There's no encouragement for wounded men here. Only his noise is calculated to make all the others think too much of the hereafter, cap'n." "Water!" cried the wounded man in an extraordinarily clear vigorous voice, and then went off moaning feebly. "Ay, water. Water will do it," muttered the other to himself, resignedly. "Plenty by and by. The tide is flowing."

'At last the tide flowed, silencing the plaint and the cries of pain, and the dawn was near when Brown, sitting with his chin in the palm of his hand before Patusan, as one might stare at the unscalable side of a mountain, heard the brief ringing bark of a brass six-pounder far away in town somewhere. "What's this?" he asked of Cornelius, who hung about him. Cornelius listened. A muffled roaring shout rolled down-river over the town; a big drum began to throb, and others responded, pulsating and droning. Tiny scattered lights began to twinkle in the dark half of the town, while the part lighted by the loom of fires hummed with a deep and prolonged murmur. "He has come," said Cornelius. "What? Already? Are you sure?" Brown asked. "Yes! yes! Sure. Listen to the noise." "What are they making that row about?" pursued Brown. "For joy," snorted Cornelius; "he is a very great man, but all the same, he knows no more than a child, and so they make a great noise to please him, because they know no better." "Look here," said Brown, "how is one to get at him?" "He shall come to talk to you," Cornelius declared. "What do you mean? Come down here strolling as it were?" Cornelius nodded vigorously in the dark. "Yes. He will come straight here and talk to you. He is just like a fool. You shall see what a fool he is." Brown was incredulous. "You shall see; you shall see," repeated Cornelius. "He is not afraid – not afraid of anything. He will come and order you to leave his people alone. Everybody must leave his people alone. He is like a little child. He will come to you straight." Alas! he knew Jim well – that "mean little skunk", as Brown called him to me. "Yes, certainly," he pursued with ardour, "and then, captain, you tell that tall man with a gun to shoot him. Just you kill him, and you shall frighten everybody so much that you can do anything you like with them afterwards – get what you like – go away when you like. Ha! ha! ha! Fine . . . " He almost danced with impatience and eagerness; and Brown, looking over his shoulder at him, could see, shown up by the pitiless dawn, his men drenched with dew, sitting amongst the cold ashes and the litter of the camp, haggard, cowed, and in rags.'

Chapter 41

To the very last moment, till the full day came upon them with a spring, the fires of the west bank blazed bright and clear; and then Brown saw in a knot of coloured figures motionless between the advanced houses a man in European clothes, in a helmet, all white. "That's him; look! look!" Cornelius said excitedly. All Brown's men had sprung up and crowded at his back with lustreless eyes. The group of vivid colours and dark faces with the white figure in the midst were observing the knoll. Brown could see naked arms being raised to shade the eyes and other brown arms pointing. What should he do? He looked around, and the forests that faced him on all sides walled the cockpit of an unequal contest. He looked once more at his men. A contempt, a weariness, the desire of life, the wish to try for one more chance – for some other grave – struggled in his breast. From the outline the figure presented it seemed to him that the white man there, backed up by all the power of the land, was examining his position through binoculars. Brown jumped up on the log, throwing his arms up, the palms outwards. The coloured group closed round the white man, and fell back twice before he got clear of them, walking slowly alone. Brown remained standing on the log till Jim, appearing and disappearing between the patches of thorny scrub, had nearly reached the creek; then Brown jumped off and went down to meet him on his side.

'They met, I should think, not very far from the place, perhaps on the very spot, where Jim took the second desperate leap of his life – the leap that landed him into the life of Patusan, into the trust, the love, the confidence of the people. They faced each other across the creek, and with steady eyes tried to understand each other before they opened their lips. Their antagonism must have been expressed in their glances; I know that Brown hated Jim at first sight. Whatever hopes he might have had vanished at once. This was not the man he had expected to see. He hated him for this – and in a checked flannel shirt with sleeves cut off at the elbows, grey-bearded, with a sunken, sun-blackened face – he cursed in his heart the other's youth and assurance, his clear eyes and his untroubled bearing. That fellow had got in a long way before him! He did not look like a man who would be willing to give anything for assistance. He had all the advantages on his side – possession, security, power; he was on the side of an overwhelming force! He was not hungry and desperate, and he did not seem in the least afraid. And there was something in the very neatness of Jim's clothes, from the white helmet to the canvas leggings and the pipe-clayed shoes, which in Brown's sombre irritated eyes seemed to belong to things he had in the very shaping of his life contemned and flouted.

' "Who are you?" asked Jim at last, speaking in his usual voice. "My name's Brown," answered the other, loudly, "Captain Brown. What's yours?" and Jim after a little pause went on quietly, as if he had not heard: "What made you come here?" "You want to know?" said Brown, bitterly. "It's easy to tell. Hunger. And what made you?"

' "The fellow started at this," said Brown, relating to me the opening of this strange conversation between those two men separated only by the muddy bed of a creek, but standing on the opposite poles of that conception of life which includes all mankind – "The fellow started at this and got very red in the face. Too big to be questioned, I suppose. I told him that if he looked upon me as a dead man with whom you may take liberties, he himself was not a whit better off really. I had a fellow up there who had a bead drawn on him all the time, and only waited for a sign from me. There was nothing to be shocked at in this. He had come down of his own free will. 'Let us agree," said I, 'that we are both dead men, and let us talk on that basis, as equals. We are all equal before death,' I said. I admitted I was there like a rat in a trap, but we had been driven to it, and even a trapped rat can give a bite. He caught me up in a moment. 'Not if you don't go near the trap till the rat is dead.' I told him that sort of game was good enough for these native friends of his, but I would have thought him too white to serve even a rat so. Yes, I had wanted to talk with him. Not to beg for my life, though. My fellows were – well – what they were – men like himself, anyhow. All we wanted from him was to come on in the devil's name and have it out. 'God d—n it,' said I, while he stood there as still as a wooden post, 'you don't want to come out here every day with your glasses to count how many of us are left on our feet. Come. Either bring your infernal crowd along or let us go out and starve in the open sea, by God! You have been white once, for all your tall talk of this being your own people and you being one with them. Are you? And what the devil do you get for it; what is it you've found here that is so d—d precious? Hey? You don't want us to come down here perhaps – do you? You are two hundred to one. You don't want us to come down into the open. Ah! I promise you we shall give you some sport before you've done. You talk about me making a cowardly set upon unoffending people. What's that to me that they are unoffending when I am starving for next to no offence? But I am not a coward. Don't you be one. Bring them along or, by all the fiends, we shall yet manage to send half your unoffending town to heaven with us in smoke!' "

'He was terrible – relating this to me – this tortured skeleton of a man drawn up together with his face over his knees, upon a miserable bed in that wretched hovel, and lifting his head to look at me with malignant triumph.

' "That's what I told him – I knew what to say," he began again, feebly at first, but working himself up with incredible speed into a fiery utterance of his scorn. " 'We aren't going into the forest to wander like a string of living skeletons dropping one after another for ants to go to work upon us before we are fairly dead. Oh, no!' . . . 'You don't deserve a better fate,' he said. 'And what do you deserve,' I shouted at him, 'you that I find skulking here with your mouth full of your responsibility, of innocent lives, of your infernal duty? What do you know more of me than I know of you? I came here for food. D'ye hear? – food to fill our bellies. And what did *you* come for? What did you ask for when you came here? We don't ask you for anything but to give us a fight or a clear road to go back whence we came . . . ' 'I would fight with you now,' says he, pulling at his little moustache. 'And I would let you shoot me, and welcome,' I said. 'This is as good a jumping-off place for me as another. I am sick of my infernal luck. But it would be too easy. There are my men in the same boat – and, by God, I am not the sort to jump out of trouble and leave them in a d—d lurch,' I said. He stood thinking for a while and then wanted to know what I had done ('out there', he says, tossing his head downstream) to be hazed about so. 'Have we met to tell each other the story of our lives?' I asked him. 'Suppose you begin. No? Well, I am sure I don't want to hear. Keep it to yourself. I know it is no better than mine. I've lived – and so did you though you talk as if you were one of those people that should have wings so as to go about without touching the dirty earth. Well – it is dirty. I haven't got any wings. I am here because I was afraid once in my life. Want to know what of? Of a prison. That scares me, and you may know it – if it's any good to you. I won't ask you what scared you into this infernal hole, where you seem to have found pretty pickings. That's your luck and this is mine – the privilege to beg for the favour of being shot quickly, or else kicked out to go free and starve in my own way.' " . . .

'His debilitated body shook with an exultation so vehement, so assured, and so malicious that it seemed to have driven off the death waiting for him in that hut. The corpse of his mad self-love uprose from rags and destitution as from the dark horrors of a tomb. It is impossible to say how much he lied to Jim then, how much he lied to me now – and to himself always. Vanity plays lurid tricks with our memory, and the truth of every passion wants some pretence to make it live. Standing at the gate of the other world in the guise of a beggar, he had slapped this world's face, he had spat on it, he had thrown upon it an immensity of scorn and revolt at the bottom of his misdeeds. He had overcome them all – men, women, savages, traders, ruffians, missionaries – and Jim – that beefy-faced beggar. I did not begrudge him this triumph *in articulo mortis*, this almost posthumous illusion of having trampled all the earth under his feet. While he was boasting to me, in his sordid and repulsive agony, I couldn't help thinking of the chuckling talk relating to the time of his greatest splendour when, during a year or more, Gentleman Brown's ship was to be seen, for many days on end, hovering off an islet befringed with green upon azure, with the dark dot of the mission-house on a white beach; while Gentleman Brown, ashore, was casting his spells over a romantic girl for whom Melanesia had been too much, and giving hopes of a remarkable conversion to her husband. The poor man, sometime or other, had been heard to express the intention of winning "Captain Brown to a better way of life." . . . "Bag Gentleman Brown for Glory" – as a leery-eyed loafer expressed it once – "just to let them see up above what a Western Pacific trading skipper looks like." And this was the man, too, who had run off with a dying woman, and had shed tears over her body. "Carried on like a big baby," his then mate was never tired of telling, "and where the fun came in may I be kicked to death by diseased Kanakas if *I* know. Why, gents! she was too far gone when he brought her aboard to know him; she just lay there on her back in his bunk staring at the beam with awful shining eyes – and then she died. Dam' bad sort of fever, I guess . . . " I remembered all these stories while, wiping his matted lump of a beard with a livid hand, he was telling me from his noisome couch how he got round, got in, got home, on that confounded, immaculate, don't-you-touch-me sort of fellow. He admitted that he couldn't be scared, but there was a way, "as broad as a turnpike, to get in and shake his twopenny soul around and inside out and upside down – by God!" '

Chapter 42

'I don't think he could do more than perhaps look upon that straight path.
He seemed to have been puzzled by what he saw, for he interrupted himself
in his narrative more than once to exclaim, "He nearly slipped from me
there. I could not make him out. Who was he?" And after glaring at me
wildly he would go on, jubilating and sneering. To me the conversation of
these two across the creek appears now as the deadliest kind of duel on
which Fate looked on with her cold-eyed knowledge of the end. No, he
didn't turn Jim's soul inside out, but I am much mistaken if the spirit so
utterly out of his reach had not been made to taste to the full the bitterness
of that contest. These were the emissaries with whom the world he had
renounced was pursuing him in his retreat. White men from "out there"
where he did not think himself good enough to live. This was all that came
to him – a menace, a shock, a danger to his work. I suppose it is this sad,
half-resentful, half-resigned feeling, piercing through the few words Jim
said now and then, that puzzled Brown so much in the reading of his
character. Some great men owe most of their greatness to the ability of
detecting in those they destine for their tools the exact quality of strength
that matters for their work, and Brown, as though he had been really great,
had a satanic gift of finding out the best and the weakest spot in his victims.
He admitted to me that Jim wasn't of the sort that can be got over by
truckling, and accordingly he took care to show himself as a man confronting without dismay ill-luck, censure, and disaster. The smuggling of a
few guns was no great crime, he pointed out. As to coming to Patusan, who
had the right to say he hadn't come to beg? The infernal people here let
loose at him from both banks without staying to ask questions. He made the
point brazenly, for, in truth, Dain Waris's energetic action had prevented
the greatest calamities; because Brown told me distinctly that, perceiving the
size of the place, he had resolved instantly in his mind that as soon as he had
gained a footing he would set fire right and left, and begin by shooting down
everything living in sight, in order to cow and terrify the population. The
disproportion of forces was so great that this was the only way giving him
the slightest chance of attaining his ends – he argued in a fit of coughing.
But he didn't tell Jim this. As to the hardships and starvation they had gone
through, these had been very real; it was enough to look at his band. He
made, at the sound of a shrill whistle, all his men appear standing in a row on
the logs in full view, so that Jim could see them. For the killing of the man, it

had been done – well, it had – but was not this war, bloody war – in a corner? and the fellow had been killed cleanly, shot through the chest, not like that poor devil of his lying now in the creek. They had to listen to him dying for six hours, with his entrails torn with slugs. At any rate this was a life for a life . . . And all this was said with the weariness, with the recklessness of a man spurred on and on by ill-luck till he cares not where he runs. When he asked Jim, with a sort of brusque despairing frankness, whether he himself – straight now – didn't understand that when "it came to saving one's life in the dark, one didn't care who else went – three, thirty, three hundred people" – it was as if a demon had been whispering advice in his ear. "I made him wince," boasted Brown to me. "He very soon left off coming the righteous over me. He just stood there with nothing to say, and looking as black as thunder – not at me – on the ground." He asked Jim whether he had nothing fishy in his life to remember that he was so damnedly hard upon a man trying to get out of a deadly hole by the first means that came to hand – and so on, and so on. And there ran through the rough talk a vein of subtle reference to their common blood, an assumption of common experience; a sickening suggestion of common guilt, of secret knowledge that was like a bond of their minds and of their hearts.

'At last Brown threw himself down full length and watched Jim out of the corners of his eyes. Jim on his side of the creek stood thinking and switching his leg. The houses in view were silent, as if a pestilence had swept them clean of every breath of life; but many invisible eyes were turned, from within, upon the two men with the creek between them, a stranded white boat, and the body of the third man half sunk in the mud. On the river canoes were moving again, for Patusan was recovering its belief in the stability of earthly institutions since the return of the white lord. The right bank, the platforms of the houses, the rafts moored along the shores, even the roofs of bathing-huts, were covered with people that, far away out of earshot and almost out of sight, were straining their eyes towards the knoll beyond the Rajah's stockade. Within the wide irregular ring of forests broken in two places by the sheen of the river there was a silence. "Will you promise to leave the coast?" Jim asked. Brown lifted and let fall his hand, giving everything up as it were – accepting the inevitable. "And surrender your arms?" Jim went on. Brown sat up and glared across. "Surrender our arms! Not till you come to take them out of our stiff hands. You think I am gone crazy with funk? Oh, no! That and the rags I stand in is all I have got in the world, besides a few more breechloaders on board; and I expect to sell the lot in Madagascar, if I ever get so far – begging my way from ship to ship."

'Jim said nothing to this. At last, throwing away the switch he held in his hand, he said, as if speaking to himself, "I don't know whether I have the power." . . . "You don't know! And you wanted me just now to give up my arms! That's good, too," cried Brown. "Suppose they say one thing to you, and do the other thing to me." He calmed down markedly. "I dare say you have the power, or what's the meaning of all this talk?" he continued. "What did you come down here for? To pass the time of day?"

' "Very well," said Jim, lifting his head suddenly after a long silence. "You shall have a clear road or else a clear fight." He turned on his heel and walked away.

'Brown got up at once, but he did not go up the hill till he had seen Jim disappear between the first houses. He never set his eyes on him again. On his way back he met Cornelius slouching down with his head between his shoulders. He stopped before Brown. "Why didn't you kill him?" he demanded in a sour, discontented voice. "Because I could do better than that," Brown said with an amused smile. "Never! never!" protested Cornelius with energy. "Couldn't. I have lived here for many years." Brown looked up at him curiously. There were many sides to the life of that place in arms against him; things he would never find out. Cornelius slunk past dejectedly in the direction of the river. He was now leaving his new friends; he accepted the disappointing course of events with a sulky obstinacy which seemed to draw more together his little yellow old face; and as he went down he glanced askant here and there, never giving up his fixed idea.

'Henceforth events move fast without a check, flowing from the very hearts of men like a stream from a dark source, and we see Jim amongst them, mostly through Tamb' Itam's eyes. The girl's eyes had watched him too, but her life is too much entwined with his: there is her passion, her wonder, her anger, and, above all, her fear and her unforgiving love. Of the faithful servant, uncomprehending as the rest of them, it is the fidelity alone that comes into play; a fidelity and a belief in his lord so strong that even amazement is subdued to a sort of saddened acceptance of a mysterious failure. He has eyes only for one figure, and through all the mazes of bewilderment he preserves his air of guardianship, of obedience, of care.

'His master came back from his talk with the white men, walking slowly towards the stockade in the street. Everybody was rejoiced to see him return, for while he was away every man had been afraid not only of him being killed, but also of what would come after. Jim went into one of the houses, where old Doramin had retired, and remained alone for a long time with the head of the Bugis settlers. No doubt he discussed the course to follow with him then, but no man was present at the conversation. Only Tamb' Itam, keeping as close to the door as he could, heard his master say: "Yes. I shall let all the people know that such is my wish; but I spoke to you, O Doramin, before all the others, and alone; for you know my heart as well as I know yours and its greatest desire. And you know well also that I have no thought but for the people's good." Then his master, lifting the sheeting in the doorway, went out, and he, Tamb' Itam, had a glimpse of old Doramin within, sitting in the chair with his hands on his knees, and looking between his feet. Afterwards he followed his master to the fort, where all the principal Bugis and Patusan inhabitants had been summoned for a talk. Tamb' Itam himself hoped there would be some fighting. "What was it but the taking of another hill?" he exclaimed regretfully. However, in the town many hoped that the rapacious strangers would be induced, by the sight of so many brave men ready to fight, to go away. It would be a good thing if they went away. Since Jim's arrival had been made known before daylight by the gun fired from the fort and the beating of a big drum there, the fear that had hung over Patusan had broken and subsided like a wave on a rock, leaving the seething foam of excitement, curiosity, and endless speculation. Half of the population had been ousted out of their homes for purposes of defence, and were living in the street on the left side of the river, crowding round the fort, and in momentary expectation of seeing their abandoned dwellings on the threatened bank burst into flames. The general anxiety was to see the matter settled quickly. Food, through Jewel's care, had been served out to the refugees. Nobody knew what their white man would do. Some remarked that it was worse than in Sherif Ali's war. Then many people did not care; now everybody had something to lose. The movements of canoes passing to and fro between the two parts of the town were watched with interest. A couple of Bugis war-boats lay anchored in the middle of the stream to protect the river, and a thread of smoke stood at the bow of each; the men in them were cooking their midday rice when Jim, after his interviews with Brown and Doramin, crossed the river and entered by the water-gate of his fort. The people inside crowded round him so that he could hardly make his way to the house. They had not seen him before, because on his arrival during the night he had only exchanged a few words with the girl, who had come down to the landing-stage for the purpose, and had then gone on at once to join the chiefs and the fighting men on the other bank. People shouted greetings after him. One old woman raised a laugh by pushing her way to the front madly and enjoining him in a scolding voice to see to it that her two sons, who were with Doramin, did not come to harm at the hands of the robbers. Several of the bystanders tried to pull her away, but she struggled and cried: "Let me go. What is this, O Moslems? This laughter is unseemly. Are they not cruel, bloodthirsty robbers bent on killing?" "Let her be," said Jim, and as a silence fell suddenly, he said slowly, "Everybody shall be safe." He entered the house before the great sigh, and the loud murmurs of satisfaction, had died out.

'There's no doubt his mind was made up that Brown should have his way clear back to the sea. His fate, revolted, was forcing his hand. He had for the first time to affirm his will in the face of outspoken opposition. "There was much talk, and at first my master was silent," Tamb' Itam said. "Darkness came, and then I lit the candles on the long table. The chiefs sat on each side, and the lady remained by my master's right hand."

'When he began to speak the unaccustomed difficulty seemed only to fix his resolve more immovably. The white men were now waiting for his answer on the hill. Their chief had spoken to him in the language of his own people, making clear many things difficult to explain in any other speech. They were erring men whom suffering had made blind to right and wrong. It is true that lives had been lost already, but why lose more? He declared to his hearers, the assembled heads of the people, that their welfare was his welfare, their losses his losses, their mourning his mourning. He looked round at the grave listening faces and told them to remember that they had fought and worked side by side. They knew his courage . . . Here a murmur interrupted him . . . And that he had never deceived them. For many years they had dwelt together. He loved the land and the people living in it with a very great love. He was ready to answer with his life for any harm that should come to them if the white men with beards were allowed to retire. They were evil-doers, but their destiny had been evil, too. Had he ever advised them ill? Had his words ever brought suffering to the people? he asked. He believed that it would be best to let these whites and their followers go with their lives. It would be a small gift. "I whom you have tried and found always true ask you to let them go." He turned to Doramin. The old *nakhoda* made no movement. "Then," said Jim, "call in Dain Waris, your son, my friend, for in this business I shall not lead." '

Chapter 43

'Tamb' Itam behind his chair was thunderstruck. The declaration produced an immense sensation. "Let them go because this is best in my knowledge which has never deceived you," Jim insisted. There was a silence. In the darkness of the courtyard could be heard the subdued whispering, shuffling noise of many people. Doramin raised his heavy head and said that there was no more reading of hearts than touching the sky with the hand, but – he consented. The others gave their opinion in turn: "It is best," "Let them go," and so on. But most of them simply said that they "believed Tuan Jim".

'In this simple form of assent to his will lies the whole gist of the situation; their creed, his truth; and the testimony to that faithfulness which made him in his own eyes the equal of the impeccable men who never fall out of the ranks. Stein's words, "Romantic! – Romantic!" seem to ring over those distances that will never give him up now to a world indifferent to his failing and his virtues, and to that ardent and clinging affection that refuses him the dole of tears in the bewilderment of a great grief and of eternal separation. From the moment the sheer truthfulness of his last three years of life carries the day against the ignorance, the fear, and the anger of men, he appears no longer to me as I saw him last – a white speck catching all the dim light left upon a sombre coast and the darkened sea – but greater and more pitiful in the loneliness of his soul, that remains even for her who loved him best a cruel and insoluble mystery.

'It is evident that he did not mistrust Brown; there was no reason to doubt the story, whose truth seemed warranted by the rough frankness, by a sort of virile sincerity in accepting the morality and the consequences of his acts. But Jim did not know the almost inconceivable egotism of the man which made him, when resisted and foiled in his will, mad with the indignant and revengeful rage of a thwarted autocrat. But if Jim did not mistrust Brown, he was evidently anxious that some misunderstanding should not occur, ending perhaps in collision and bloodshed. It was for this reason that directly the Malay chiefs had gone he asked Jewel to get him something to eat, as he was going out of the fort to take command in the town. On her remonstrating against this on the score of his fatigue, he said that something might happen for which he would never forgive himself. "I am responsible for every life in the land," he said. He was moody at first; she served him with her own hands, taking the plates and dishes (of the dinner-service presented him by Stein) from Tamb' Itam. He brightened up after a while; told her she would be again in command of the fort for another night. "There's no sleep for us, old girl," he said, "while our people are in danger." Later on he said jokingly that she was the best man of them all. "If you and Dain Waris had done what you wanted, not one of these poor devils would be alive today." "Are they very bad?" she asked, leaning over his chair. "Men act badly sometimes without being much worse than others," he said after some hesitation.

'Tamb' Itam followed his master to the landing-stage outside the fort. The night was clear, but without a moon, and the middle of the river was dark, while the water under each bank reflected the light of many fires "as on a night of Ramadan," Tamb' Itam said. War-boats drifted silently in the dark lane or, anchored, floated motionless with a loud ripple. That night there was much paddling in a canoe and walking at his master's heels for Tamb' Itam: up and down the street they tramped, where the fires were burning, inland on the outskirts of the town where small parties of men kept guard in the fields. Tuan Jim gave his orders and was obeyed. Last of all they went to the Rajah's stockade, which a detachment of Jim's people manned on that night. The old Rajah had fled early in the morning with most of his women to a small house he had near a jungle village on a tributary stream. Kassim, left behind, had attended the council with his air of diligent activity to explain away the diplomacy of the day before. He was considerably cold-shouldered, but managed to preserve his smiling, quiet alertness, and professed himself highly delighted when Jim told him sternly that he proposed to occupy the stockade on that night with his own men. After the council broke up he was heard outside accosting this and that departing chief, and speaking in a loud, gratified tone of the Rajah's property being protected in the Rajah's absence.

'About ten or so Jim's men marched in. The stockade commanded the mouth of the creek, and Jim meant to remain there till Brown had passed below. A small fire was lit on the flat, grassy point outside the wall of stakes, and Tamb' Itam placed a little folding-stool for his master. Jim told him to try and sleep. Tamb' Itam got a mat and lay down a little way off; but he could not sleep, though he knew he had to go on an important journey before the night was out. His master walked to and fro before the fire with bowed head and with his hands behind his back. His face was sad. Whenever his master approached him Tamb' Itam pretended to sleep, not wishing his master to know he had been watched. At last his master stood still, looking down on him as he lay, and said softly: "It is time."

'Tamb' Itam arose directly and made his preparations. His mission was to go down the river, preceding Brown's boat by an hour or more, to tell Dain Waris finally and formally that the whites were to be allowed to pass out unmolested. Jim would not trust anybody else with that service. Before starting Tamb' Itam, more as a matter of form (since his position about Jim made him perfectly known), asked for a token. "Because, Tuan," he said, "the message is important, and these are thy very words I carry." His master first put his hand into one pocket, then into another, and finally took off his forefinger Stein's silver ring, which he habitually wore, and gave it to Tamb' Itam. When Tamb' Itam left on his mission, Brown's camp on the knoll was dark but for a single small glow shining through the branches of one of the trees the white men had cut down.

'Early in the evening Brown had received from Jim a folded piece of paper on which was written: "You get the clear road. Start as soon as your boat floats on the morning tide. Let your men be careful. The bushes on both sides of the creek and the stockade at the mouth are full of well-armed men. You would have no chance, but I don't believe you want bloodshed." Brown read it, tore the paper into small pieces, and, turning to Cornelius, who had brought it, said jeeringly, "Goodbye, my excellent friend." Cornelius had been in the fort, and had been sneaking around Jim's house during the afternoon. Jim chose him to carry the note because he could speak English, was known to Brown, and was not likely to be shot by some nervous mistake of one of the men as a Malay, approaching in the dusk, perhaps might have been.

'Cornelius didn't go away after delivering the paper. Brown was sitting up over a tiny fire; all the others were lying down. "I could tell you something you would like to know," Cornelius mumbled crossly. Brown paid no attention. "You did not kill him," went on the other, "and what do you get for it? You might have had money from the Rajah, besides the loot of all the Bugis houses, and now you get nothing." "You had better clear out from here," growled Brown, without even looking at him. But Cornelius let himself drop by his side and began to whisper very fast, touching his elbow from time to time. What he had to say made Brown sit up at first, with a curse. He had simply informed him of Dain Waris's armed party down the river. At first Brown saw himself completely sold and betrayed, but a moment's reflection convinced him that there could be no treachery intended. He said nothing, and after a while Cornelius remarked, in a tone of complete indifference, that there was another way out of the river which he knew very well. "A good thing to know, too," said Brown, pricking up his ears; and Cornelius began to talk of what went on in town and repeated all that had been said in council, gossiping in an even undertone at Brown's ear as you talk amongst sleeping men you do not wish to wake. "He thinks he has made me harmless, does he?" mumbled Brown very low . . . "Yes. He is a fool. A little child. He came here and robbed me," droned on Cornelius, "and he made all the people believe him. But if something happened that they did not believe him any more, where would he be? And the Bugis Dain who is waiting for you down the river there, captain, is the very man who chased you up here when you first came." Brown observed nonchalantly that it would be just as well to avoid him, and with the same detached, musing air Cornelius declared himself acquainted with a backwater broad enough to take Brown's boat past Waris's camp. "You will have to be quiet," he said as an afterthought, "for in one place we pass close behind his camp. Very close. They are camped ashore with their boat hauled up." "Oh, we know how to be as quiet as mice; never fear," said Brown. Cornelius stipulated that in case he were to pilot Brown out, his canoe should be towed. "I'll have to get back quick," he explained.

'It was two hours before the dawn when word was passed to the stockade from outlying watchers that the white robbers were coming down to their boat. In a very short time every armed man from one end of Patusan to the other was on the alert, yet the banks of the river remained so silent that but for the fires burning with sudden blurred flares the town might have been asleep as if in peace-time. A heavy mist lay very low on the water, making a sort of illusive grey light that showed nothing. When Brown's long-boat glided out of the creek into the river, Jim was standing on the low point of land before the Rajah's stockade – on the very spot where for the first time he put his foot on Patusan shore. A shadow loomed up, moving in the greyness, solitary, very bulky, and yet constantly eluding the eye. A murmur of low talking came out of it. Brown at the tiller heard Jim speak calmly: "A clear road. You had better trust to the current while the fog lasts; but this will lift presently." "Yes, presently we shall see clear," replied Brown.

'The thirty or forty men standing with muskets at ready outside the stockade held their breath. The Bugis owner of the prau, whom I saw on Stein's veranda, and who was amongst them, told me that the boat, shaving the low point close, seemed for a moment to grow big and hang over it like a mountain. "If you think it worth your while to wait a day outside," called out Jim, "I'll try to send you down something – bullock, some yams – what I can." The shadow went on moving. "Yes. Do," said a voice, blank and muffled out of the fog. Not one of the many attentive listeners understood what the words meant; and then Brown and his men in their boat floated away, fading spectrally without the slightest sound.

'Thus Brown, invisible in the mist, goes out of Patusan elbow to elbow with Cornelius in the stern-sheets of the long-boat. "Perhaps you shall get a small bullock," said Cornelius. "Oh, yes. Bullock. Yam. You'll get it if *he* said so. He always speaks the truth. He stole everything I had. I suppose you like a small bullock better than the loot of many houses." "I would advise you to hold your tongue, or somebody here may fling you overboard into this damned fog," said Brown. The boat seemed to be standing still; nothing could be seen, not even the river alongside, only the water-dust flew and trickled, condensed, down their beards and faces. It was weird, Brown told me. Every individual man of them felt as though he were adrift alone in a boat, haunted by an almost imperceptible suspicion of sighing, muttering ghosts. "Throw me out, would you? But I would know where I was," mumbled Cornelius, surlily. "I've lived many years here." "Not long enough to see through a fog like this," Brown said, lolling back with his arm swinging to and fro on the useless tiller. "Yes. Long enough for that," snarled Cornelius. "That's very useful," commented Brown. "Am I to believe you could find that backway you spoke of blindfold, like this?" Cornelius grunted. "Are you too tired to row?" he asked after a silence. "No, by God!" shouted Brown suddenly. "Out with your oars there." There was a great knocking in the fog, which after a while settled into a regular grind of invisible sweeps against invisible thole-pins. Otherwise nothing was changed, and but for the slight splash of a dipped blade it was like rowing a balloon car in a cloud, said Brown. Thereafter Cornelius did not open his lips except to ask querulously for somebody to bail out his canoe, which was towing behind the long-boat. Gradually the fog whitened and became luminous ahead. To the left Brown saw a darkness as though he had been looking at the back of the departing night. All at once a big bough covered with leaves appeared above his head, and ends of twigs, dripping and still, curved slenderly close alongside. Cornelius, without a word, took the tiller from his hand.'

Chapter 44

'I don't think they spoke together again. The boat entered a narrow by-channel, where it was pushed by the oar-blades set into crumbling banks, and there was a gloom as if enormous black wings had been outspread above the mist that filled its depth to the summits of the trees. The branches overhead showered big drops through the gloomy fog. At a mutter from

Cornelius, Brown ordered his men to load. "I'll give you a chance to get even with them before we're done, you dismal cripples, you," he said to his gang. "Mind you don't throw it away – you hounds." Low growls answered that speech. Cornelius showed much fussy concern for the safety of his canoe.

'Meantime Tamb' Itam had reached the end of his journey. The fog had delayed him a little, but he had paddled steadily, keeping in touch with the south bank. By and by daylight came like a glow in a ground-glass globe. The shores made on each side of the river a dark smudge, in which one could detect hints of columnar forms and shadows of twisted branches high up. The mist was still thick on the water, but a good watch was being kept, for as Tamb' Itam approached the camp the figures of two men emerged out of the white vapour, and voices spoke to him boisterously. He answered, and presently a canoe lay alongside, and he exchanged news with the paddlers. All was well. The trouble was over. Then the men in the canoe let go their grip on the side of his dug-out and incontinently fell out of sight. He pursued his way till he heard voices coming to him quietly over the water, and saw, under the now lifting, swirling mist, the glow of many little fires burning on a sandy stretch, backed by lofty thin timber and bushes. There again a look-out was kept, for he was challenged. He shouted his name as the two last sweeps of his paddle ran his canoe up on the strand. It was a big camp. Men crouched in many knots under a subdued murmur of early morning talk. Many thin threads of smoke curled slowly on the white mist. Little shelters, elevated above the ground, had been built for the chiefs. Muskets were stacked in small pyramids, and long spears were stuck singly into the sand near the fires.

'Tamb' Itam, assuming an air of importance, demanded to be led to Dain Waris. He found the friend of his white lord lying on a raised couch made of bamboo, and sheltered by a sort of shed of sticks covered with mats. Dain Waris was awake, and a bright fire was burning before his sleeping-place, which resembled a rude shrine. The only son of Nakhoda Doramin answered his greeting kindly. Tamb' Itam began by handing him the ring which vouched for the truth of the messenger's words. Dain Waris, reclining on his elbow, bade him speak and tell all the news. Beginning with the consecrated formula: "The news is good," Tamb' Itam delivered Jim's own words. The white men, departing with the consent of all the chiefs, were to be allowed to pass down the river. In answer to a question or two Tamb' Itam then reported the proceedings of the last council. Dain Waris listened attentively to the end, toying with the ring which ultimately he slipped on the forefinger of his right hand. After hearing all he had to say he dismissed Tamb' Itam to have food and rest. Orders for the return in the afternoon were given immediately. Afterwards Dain Waris lay down again, open-eyed, while his personal attendants were preparing his food at the fire, by which Tamb' Itam also sat talking to the men who lounged up to hear the latest intelligence from the town. The sun was eating up the mist. A good watch was kept upon the reach of the main stream where the boat of the whites was expected to appear every moment.

'It was then that Brown took his revenge upon the world which, after twenty years of contemptuous and reckless bullying, refused him the tribute of a common robber's success. It was an act of cold-blooded ferocity, and it consoled him on his deathbed like a memory of an indomitable defiance. Stealthily he landed his men on the other side of the island opposite to the Bugis camp, and led them across. After a short but quite silent scuffle, Cornelius, who had tried to slink away at the moment of landing, resigned himself to show the way where the undergrowth was most sparse. Brown held both his skinny hands together behind his back in the grip of one vast fist, and now and then impelled him forward with a fierce push. Cornelius remained as mute as a fish, abject but faithful to his purpose, whose accomplishment loomed before him dimly. At the edge of the patch of forest Brown's men spread themselves out in cover and waited. The camp was plain from end to end before their eyes, and no one looked their way. Nobody even dreamed that the white men could have any knowledge of the narrow channel at the back of the island. When he judged the moment come, Brown yelled: "Let them have it," and fourteen shots rang out like one.

'Tamb' Itam told me the surprise was so great that, except for those who fell dead or wounded, not a soul of them moved for quite an appreciable time after the first discharge. Then a man screamed, and after that scream a great yell of amazement and fear went up from all the throats. A blind panic drove these men in a surging swaying mob to and fro along the shore like a herd of cattle afraid of the water. Some few jumped into the river then, but most of them did so only after the last discharge. Three times Brown's men fired into the ruck, Brown, the only one in view, cursing and yelling: "Aim low! aim low!"

'Tamb' Itam says that, as for him, he understood at the first volley what had happened. Though untouched he fell down and lay as if dead, but with his eyes open. At the sound of the first shots Dain Waris, reclining on the couch, jumped up and ran out upon the open shore, just in time to receive a bullet in his forehead at the second discharge. Tamb' Itam saw him fling his arms wide open before he fell. Then, he says, a great fear came upon him – not before. The white men retired as they had come – unseen.

'Thus Brown balanced his account with the evil fortune. Notice that even in this awful outbreak there is a superiority as of a man who carries right – the abstract thing – within the envelope of his common desires. It was not a vulgar and treacherous massacre; it was a lesson, a retribution – a demonstration of some obscure and awful attribute of our nature which, I am afraid, is not so very far under the surface as we like to think.

'Afterwards the whites depart unseen by Tamb' Itam, and seem to vanish from before men's eyes altogether; and the schooner, too, vanishes after the manner of stolen goods. But a story is told of a white long-boat picked up a month later in the Indian Ocean by a cargo-steamer. Two parched, yellow, glassy-eyed, whispering skeletons in her recognised the authority of a third, who declared that his name was Brown. His schooner, he reported, bound south with a cargo of Java sugar, had sprung a bad leak and sank under his feet. He and his companions were the survivors of a crew of six. The two died on board the steamer which rescued them. Brown lived to be seen by me, and I can testify that he had played his part to the last.

'It seems, however, that in going away they had neglected to cast off Cornelius's canoe. Cornelius himself Brown had let go at the beginning of the shooting, with a kick for a parting benediction. Tamb' Itam, after arising from amongst the dead, saw the Nazarene running up and down the shore amongst the corpses and the expiring fires. He uttered little cries. Suddenly he rushed to the water, and made frantic efforts to get one of the Bugis boats into the water. "Afterwards, till he had seen me," related Tamb' Itam, "he stood looking at the heavy canoe and scratching his head." "What became of him?" I asked. Tamb' Itam, staring at me, made an expressive gesture with his right arm. "Twice I struck, *tuan*," he said. "When he beheld me approaching he cast himself violently on the ground and made a great outcry, kicking. He screeched like a frightened hen till he felt the point; then he was still, and lay staring at me while his life went out of his eyes."

'This done, Tamb' Itam did not tarry. He understood the importance of being the first with the awful news at the fort. There were, of course, many survivors of Dain Waris's party; but in the extremity of panic some had swum across the river, others had bolted into the bush. The fact is that they did not know really who struck that blow – whether more white robbers were not coming, whether they had not already got hold of the whole land. They imagined themselves to be the victims of a vast treachery, and utterly doomed to destruction. It is said that some small parties did not come in till three days afterwards. However, a few tried to make their way back to Patusan at once, and one of the canoes that were patrolling the river that morning was in sight of the camp at the very moment of the attack. It is true that at first the men in her leaped overboard and swam to the opposite bank,· but afterwards they returned to their boat and started fearfully upstream. Of these Tamb' Itam had an hour's advance.'

Chapter 45

'When Tamb' Itam, paddling madly, came into the town-reach, the women, thronging the platforms before the houses, were looking out for the return of Dain Waris's little fleet of boats. The town had a festive air; here and there men, still with spears or guns in their hands, could be seen moving or standing on the shore in groups. Chinamen's shops had been opened early; but the market-place was empty, and a sentry, still posted at the corner of the fort, made out Tamb' Itam, and shouted to those within. The gate was wide open. Tamb' Itam jumped ashore and ran in headlong. The first person he met was the girl coming down from the house.

'Tamb' Itam, disordered, panting, with trembling lips and wild eyes, stood for a time before her as if a sudden spell had been laid on him. Then he broke out very quickly: "They have killed Dain Waris and many more." She clapped her hands, and her first words were, "Shut the gates." Most of the fortmen had gone back to their houses, but Tamb' Itam hurried on the few who remained for their turn of duty within. The girl stood in the middle of the courtyard while the others ran about. "Doramin," she cried despairingly, as Tamb' Itam passed her. Next time he went by he answered her thought rapidly, "Yes. But we have all the powder in Patusan." She caught him by the arm, and, pointing at the house, "Call him out," she whispered, trembling.

'Tamb' Itam ran up the steps. His master was sleeping. "It is I, Tamb' Itam," he cried at the door, "with tidings that cannot wait." He saw Jim turn over on the pillow and open his eyes, and he burst out at once: "This, *tuan*, is a day of evil, an accursed day." His master raised himself on his elbow to listen just as Dain Waris had done. And then Tamb' Itam began his tale, trying to relate the story in order, calling Dain Waris Panglima, and saying: "The Panglima then called out to the chief of his own boatmen: 'Give Tamb' Itam something to eat,' " – when his master put his feet to the ground and looked at him with such a discomposed face that the words remained in his throat.

' "Speak out," said Jim. "Is he dead?" "May you live long," cried Tamb' Itam. "It was a most cruel treachery. He ran out at the first shots and fell." . . . His master walked to the window and with his fist struck at the shutter. The room was made light; and then in a steady voice, but speaking fast, he began to give him orders to assemble a fleet of boats for immediate pursuit, go to this man, to the other – send messengers; and as he talked he sat down on the bed, stooping to lace his boots hurriedly, and suddenly looked up. "Why do you stand here?" he asked very red-faced. "Waste no time." Tamb' Itam did not move. "Forgive me, *tuan*, but . . . but," he began to stammer. "What?" cried his master aloud, looking terrible, leaning forward with his hands gripping the edge of the bed. "It is not safe for thy servant to go out amongst the people," said Tamb' Itam, after hesitating a moment.

'Then Jim understood. He had retreated from one world, for a small matter of an impulsive jump, and now the other, the work of his own hands, had fallen in ruins upon his head. It was not safe for his servant to go out amongst his own people! I believe that in that very moment he had decided to defy the disaster in the only way it occurred to him such a disaster could be defied; but all I know is that, without a word, he came out of his room and sat before the long table, at the head of which he was accustomed to regulate the affairs of his world, proclaiming daily the truth that surely lived in his heart. The dark powers should not rob him twice of his peace. He sat like a stone figure. Tamb' Itam, deferential, hinted at preparations for defence. The girl he loved came in and spoke to him, but he made a sign with his hand, and she was awed by the dumb appeal for silence in it. She went out on the veranda and sat on the threshold, as if to guard him with her body from dangers outside.

'What thoughts passed through his head – what memories? Who can tell? Everything was gone, and he who had been once unfaithful to his trust had lost again all men's confidence. It was then, I believe, he tried to write – to somebody – and gave it up. Loneliness was closing on him. People had trusted him with their lives – only for that; and yet they could never, as he had said, never be made to understand him. Those without did not hear him make a sound. Later, towards the evening, he came to the door and called for Tamb' Itam. "Well?" he asked. "There is much weeping. Much anger, too," said Tamb' Itam. Jim looked up at him. "You know," he murmured. "Yes, *tuan*," said Tamb' Itam. "Thy servant does know, and the gates are closed. We shall have to fight." "Fight! What for?" he asked. "For our lives." "I have no life," he said. Tamb' Itam heard a cry from the girl at the door. "Who knows?" said Tamb' Itam. "By audacity and cunning we may even escape. There is much fear in men's hearts, too." He went out, thinking vaguely of boats and of open sea, leaving Jim and the girl together.

'I haven't the heart to set down here such glimpses as she has given me of the hour or more she had passed in there wrestling with him for the possession of her happiness. Whether he had any hope – what he expected, what he imagined – it is impossible to say. He was inflexible, and with the growing loneliness of his obstinacy his spirit seemed to rise above the ruins of his existence. She cried "Fight!" into his ear. She could not understand. There was nothing to fight for. He was going to prove his power in another way and conquer the fatal destiny itself. He come out into the courtyard, and behind him, with streaming hair, wild of face, breathless, she staggered out and leaned on the side of the doorway. "Open the gates," he ordered. Afterwards, turning to those of his men who were inside, he gave them leave to depart to their homes. "For how long, *tuan?*" asked one of them timidly. "For all life," he said, in a sombre tone.

'A hush had fallen upon the town after the outburst of wailing and lamentation that had swept over the river, like a gust of wind from the opened abode of sorrow. But rumours flew in whispers, filling the hearts with consternation and horrible doubts. The robbers were coming back, bringing many others with them, in a great ship, and there would be no refuge in the land for anyone. A sense of utter insecurity as during an earthquake pervaded the minds of men, who whispered their suspicions, looking at each other as if in the presence of some awful portent.

'The sun was sinking towards the forests when Dain Waris's body was brought into Doramin's *campong*. Four men carried it in, covered decently with a white sheet which the old mother had sent out down to the gate to meet her son on his return. They laid him at Doramin's feet, and the old man sat still for a long time, one hand on each knee, looking down. The fronds of palms swayed gently, and the foliage of fruit trees stirred above his head. Every single man of his people was there, fully armed, when the old *nakhoda* at last raised his eyes. He moved them slowly over the crowd, as if seeking for a missing face. Again his chin sank on his breast. The whispers of many men mingled with the slight rustling of the leaves.

'The Malay who had brought Tamb' Itam and the girl to Samarang was there, too. "Not so angry as many," he said to me, but struck with a great awe and wonder at the "suddenness of men's fate, which hangs over their heads like a cloud charged with thunder." He told me that when Dain Waris's body was uncovered at a sign of Doramin's, he whom they often called the white lord's friend was disclosed lying unchanged with his eyelids a little open as if about to wake. Doramin leaned forward a little more, like one looking for something fallen on the ground. His eyes searched the body from its feet to its head, for the wound maybe. It was in the forehead and small; and there was no word spoken while one of the bystanders, stooping, took off the silver ring from the cold stiff hand. In silence he held it up before Doramin. A murmur of dismay and horror ran through the crowd at the sight of that familiar token. The old *nakhoda* stared at it, and suddenly let out one great fierce cry, deep from the chest, a roar of pain and fury, as mighty as the bellow of a wounded bull, bringing great fear into men's hearts, by the magnitude of his anger and his sorrow that could be plainly discerned without words. There was a great stillness afterwards for a space, while the body was being borne aside by four men. They laid it down under a tree, and on the instant, with one long shriek, all the women of the household began to wail together; they mourned with shrill cries; the sun was setting, and in the intervals of screamed lamentations the high singsong voices of two old men intoning the Koran chanted alone.

'About this time Jim, leaning on a gun-carriage, looked at the river, and turned his back on the house; and the girl, in the doorway, panting as if she had run herself to a standstill, was looking at him across the yard. Tamb' Itam stood not far from his master, waiting patiently for what might happen. All at once Jim, who seemed to be lost in quiet thought, turned to him and said: "Time to finish this."

' "*Tuan?*" said Tamb' Itam, advancing with alacrity. He did not know what his master meant, but as soon as Jim made a movement the girl started, too, and walked down into the open space. It seems that no one else of the people of the house was in sight. She tottered slightly, and about half-way down called out to Jim, who had apparently resumed his peaceful contemplation of the river. He turned round, setting his back against the gun. "Will you fight?" she cried. "There is nothing to fight for," he said; "nothing is lost." Saying this he made a step towards her. "Will you fly?" she cried again. "There is no escape," he said, stopping short, and she stood still also, silent, devouring him with her eyes. "And you shall go?" she said, slowly. He bent his head. "Ah!" she exclaimed, peering at him as it were, "you are mad or false. Do you remember the night I prayed you to leave me, and you said that you could not? That it was impossible! Impossible! Do you remember you said you would never leave me? Why? I asked you for no promise. You promised unasked – remember." "Enough, poor girl," he said. "I should not be worth having."

'Tamb' Itam said that while they were talking she would laugh loud and senselessly like one under the visitation of God. His master put his hands to his head. He was fully dressed as for everday, but without a hat. She stopped laughing suddenly. "For the last time," she cried, menacingly, "will you defend yourself?" "Nothing can touch me," he said in a last flicker of superb egoism. Tamb' Itam saw her lean forward where she stood, open her arms, and run at him swiftly. She flung herself upon his breast and clasped him round the neck.

' "Ah! but I shall hold thee thus," she cried . . . "Thou art mine!"

'She sobbed on his shoulder. The sky over Patusan was blood-red, immense, streaming like an open vein. An enormous sun nestled crimson amongst the tree-tops, and the forest below had a black and forbidding face.

'Tamb' Itam tells me that on that evening the aspect of the heavens was angry and frightful. I may well believe it, for I know that on that very day a cyclone passed within sixty miles of the coast, though there was hardly more than a languid stir of air in the place.

'Suddenly Tamb' Itam saw Jim catch her arms, trying to unclasp her hands. She hung on them with her head fallen back; her hair touched the ground. "Come here!" his master called, and Tamb' Itam helped to ease her down. It was difficult to separate her fingers. Jim, bending over her, looked earnestly upon her face, and all at once ran to the landing-stage. Tamb' Itam followed him, but turning his head, he saw that she had struggled up to her feet. She ran after them a few steps, then fell down heavily on her knees. *"Tuan! Tuan!"* called Tamb' Itam, "look back"; but Jim was already in a canoe, standing up paddle in hand. He did not look back. Tamb' Itam had just time to scramble in after him when the canoe floated clear. The girl was then on her knees, with clasped hands, at the water-gate. She remained thus for a time in a supplicating attitude before she sprang up. "You are false!" she screamed out after Jim. "Forgive me," he cried. "Never! Never!" she called back.

'Tamb' Itam took the paddle from Jim's hands, it being unseemly that he should sit while his lord paddled. When they reached the other shore his master forbade him to come any farther; but Tamb' Itam did follow him at a distance, walking up the slope to Doramin's *campong*.

'It was beginning to grow dark. Torches twinkled here and there. Those they met seemed awestruck, and stood aside hastily to let Jim pass. The wailing of women came from above. The courtyard was full of armed Bugis with their followers, and of Patusan people.

'I do not know what this gathering really meant. Were these preparations for war, or for vengeance, or to repulse a threatened invasion? Many days elapsed before the people had ceased to look out, quaking, for the return of the white men with long beards and in rags, whose exact relation to their own white man they could never understand. Even for those simple minds poor Jim remains under a cloud.

'Doramin, alone, immense and desolate, sat in his armchair with the pair of flintlock pistols on his knees, faced by an armed throng. When Jim appeared, at somebody's exclamation, all the heads turned round together, and then the mass opened right and left, and he walked up a lane of averted glances. Whispers followed him; murmurs: "He has worked all the evil." "He hath a charm." . . . He heard them – perhaps!

'When he came up into the light of torches the wailing of the women ceased suddenly. Doramin did not lift his head, and Jim stood silent before him for a time. Then he looked to the left, and moved in that direction with measured steps. Dain Waris's mother crouched at the head of the body, and the grey dishevelled hair concealed her face. Jim came up slowly, looked at his dead friend, lifting the sheet, then dropped it without a word. Slowly he walked back.

' "He came! He came!" was running from lip to lip, making a murmur to which he moved. "He hath taken it upon his own head," a voice said aloud. He heard this and turned to the crowd. "Yes. Upon my head." A few people recoiled. Jim waited awhile before Doramin, and then said gently: "I am come in sorrow." He waited again. "I am come ready and unarmed," he repeated.

'The unwieldly old man, lowering his big forehead like an ox under a yoke, made an effort to rise, clutching at the flintlock pistols on his knees. From his throat came gurgling, choking, inhuman sounds, and his two attendants helped him from behind. People remarked that the ring which he had dropped on his lap fell and rolled against the foot of the white man, and that poor Jim glanced down at the talisman that had opened for him the door of fame, love, and success within the wall of forests fringed with white foam, within the coast that under the western sun looks like the very stronghold of the night. Doramin, struggling to keep his feet, made with his two supporters a swaying, tottering group; his little eyes stared with an expression of mad pain, of rage, with a ferocious glitter, which the by-standers noticed; and then, while Jim stood stiffened and with bared head in the light of torches, looking him straight in the face, he clung heavily with his left arm round the neck of a bowed youth, and lifting deliberately his right, shot his son's friend through the chest.

'The crowd, which had fallen apart behind Jim as soon as Doramin had raised his hand, rushed tumultuously forward after the shot. They say that the white man sent right and left at all those faces a proud and unflinching glance. Then with his hand over his lips he fell forward, dead.

'And that's the end. He passes away under a cloud, inscrutable at heart, forgotten, unforgiven, and excessively romantic. Not in the wildest days of his boyish visions could he have seen the alluring shape of such an extraordinary success! For it may very well be that in the short moment of his last proud and unflinching glance, he had beheld the face of that opportunity which, like an Eastern bride, had come veiled to his side.

'But we can see him, an obscure conqueror of fame, tearing himself out of the arms of a jealous love at the sign, at the call of his exalted egoism. He goes away from a living woman to celebrate his pitiless wedding with a shadowy ideal of conduct. Is he satisfied – quite, now, I wonder? We ought to know. He is one of us – and have I not stood up once, like an evoked ghost, to answer for his eternal constancy? Was I so very wrong after all? Now he is no more, there are days when the reality of his existence comes to me with an immense, with an overwhelming force; and yet upon my honour there are moments, too, when he passes from my eyes like a disembodied spirit astray amongst the passions of this earth, ready to surrender himself faithfully to the claim of his own world of shades.

'Who knows? He is gone, inscrutable at heart, and the poor girl is leading a sort of soundless, inert life in Stein's house. Stein has aged greatly of late. He feels it himself, and says often that he is "preparing to leave all this; preparing to leave . . . " while he waves his hand sadly at his butterflies.'

September 1899 – *July* 1900

NOSTROMO

A Tale of the Seaboard

Nostromo

A Tale of the Seaboard

A novel by

JOSEPH CONRAD

first published in 1904

So foul a sky clears not without a storm.
SHAKESPEARE, *King John*, 4, 2, 108

To
JOHN GALSWORTHY

Author's Note

Nostromo is the most anxiously meditated of the longer novels which belong to the period following upon the publication of the *Typhoon* volume of short stories.

I don't mean to say that I became then conscious of any impending change in my mentality and in my attitude towards the tasks of my writing life. And perhaps there was never any change, except in that mysterious, extraneous thing which has nothing to do with the theories of art; a subtle change in the nature of the inspiration; a phenomenon for which I can not in any way be held responsible. What, however, did cause me some concern was that after finishing the last story of the *Typhoon* volume it seemed somehow that there was nothing more in the world to write about.

This so strangely negative but disturbing mood lasted some little time; and then, as with many of my longer stories, the first hint for *Nostromo* came to me in the shape of a vagrant anecdote completely destitute of valuable details.

As a matter of fact in 1875 or '76, when very young, in the West Indies or rather in the Gulf of Mexico, for my contacts with land were short, few, and fleeting, I heard the story of some man who was supposed to have stolen single-handed a whole lighter-full of silver, somewhere on the Tierra Firme seaboard during the troubles of a revolution.

On the face of it this was something of a feat. But I heard no details, and having no particular interest in crime *qua* crime I was not likely to keep that one in my mind. And I forgot it till twenty-six or seven years afterwards I came upon the very thing in a shabby volume picked up outside a second-hand bookshop. It was the life story of an American seaman written by himself with the assistance of a journalist. In the course of his wanderings that American sailor worked for some months on board a schooner, the master and owner of which was the thief of whom I had heard in my very young days. I have no doubt of that because there could hardly have been two exploits of that peculiar kind in the same part of the world and both connected with a South American revolution.

The fellow had actually managed to steal a lighter with silver, and this, it seems, only because he was implicitly trusted by his employers, who must have been singularly poor judges of character. In the sailor's story he is represented as an unmitigated rascal, a small cheat, stupidly ferocious, morose, of mean appearance, and altogether unworthy of the greatness this opportunity had thrust upon him. What was interesting was that he would boast of it openly.

He used to say: 'People think I make a lot of money in this schooner of mine. But that is nothing. I don't care for that. Now and then I go away quietly and lift a bar of silver. I must get rich slowly – you understand.'

There was also another curious point about the man. Once in the course of some quarrel the sailor threatened him: 'What's to prevent me reporting ashore what you have told me about that silver?'

The cynical ruffian was not alarmed in the least. He actually laughed. 'You fool, if you dare talk like that on shore about me you will get a knife stuck in your back. Every man, woman, and child in that port is my friend. And who's to prove the lighter wasn't sunk? I didn't show you where the silver is hidden. Did I? So you know nothing. And suppose I lied? Eh?'

Ultimately the sailor, disgusted with the sordid meanness of that impenitent thief, deserted from the schooner. The whole episode takes about three pages of his autobiography. Nothing to speak of; but as I looked them over, the curious confirmation of the few casual words heard in my early youth evoked the memories of that distant time when everything was so fresh, so surprising, so venturesome, so interesting; bits of strange coasts under the stars, shadows of hills in the sunshine, men's passions in the dusk, gossip half-forgotten, faces grown dim . . . Perhaps, perhaps, there still was in the world something to write about. Yet I did not see anything at first in the mere story. A rascal steals a large parcel of a valuable commodity – so people say. It's either true or untrue; and in any case it has no value in itself. To invent a circumstantial account of the robbery did not appeal to me, because my talents not running that way I did not think that the game was worth the candle. It was only when it dawned upon me that the purloiner of the treasure need not necessarily be a confirmed rogue, that he could be even a man of character, an actor and possibly a victim in the changing scenes of a revolution, it was only then that I had the first vision of a twilight country which was to become the province of Sulaco, with its high shadowy Sierra and its misty Campo for mute witnesses of events flowing from the passions of men short-sighted in good and evil.

Such are in very truth the obscure origins of *Nostromo* – the book. From that moment, I suppose, it had to be. Yet even then I hesitated, as if warned by the instinct of self-preservation from venturing on a distant and toilsome journey into a land full of intrigues and revolutions. But it had to be done.

It took the best part of the years 1903–4 to do; with many intervals of renewed hesitation, lest I should lose myself in the ever-enlarging vistas opening before me as I progressed deeper in my knowledge of the country. Often, also, when I had thought myself to a standstill over the tangled-up affairs of the Republic, I would, figuratively speaking, pack my bag, rush away from Sulaco for a change of air and write a few pages of the *Mirror of the Sea*. But generally, as I've said before, my sojourn on the continent of Latin America, famed for its hospitality, lasted for about two years. On my return I found (speaking somewhat in the style of Captain Gulliver) my family all well, my wife heartily glad to learn that the fuss was all over, and our small boy considerably grown during my absence.

My principal authority for the history of Costaguana is, of course, my venerated friend, the late Don José Avellanos, Minister to the Courts of England and Spain, etc., etc., in his impartial and eloquent *History of Fifty Years of Misrule*. That work was never published – the reader will discover why – and I am in fact the only person in the world possessed of its contents. I have mastered them in not a few hours of earnest meditation, and I hope that my accuracy will be trusted. In justice to myself, and to allay the fears of prospective readers, I beg to point out that the few historical allusions are never dragged in for the sake of parading my unique erudition, but that each of them is closely related to actuality; either throwing a light on the nature of current events or affecting directly the fortunes of the people of whom I speak.

As to their own histories I have tried to set them down, Aristocracy and People, men and women, Latin and Anglo-Saxon, bandit and politician, with as cool a hand as was possible in the heat and clash of my own conflicting emotions. And after all this is also the story of their conflicts. It is for the reader to say how far they are deserving of interest in their actions and in the secret purposes of their hearts revealed in the bitter necessities of the time. I confess that, for me, that time is the time of firm friendships and unforgotten hospitalities. And in my gratitude I must mention here Mrs Gould, 'the first lady of Sulaco', whom we may safely leave to the secret devotion of Dr Monygham, and Charles Gould, the Idealist-creator of Material Interests whom we must leave to his Mine – from which there is no escape in this world.

About Nostromo, the second of the two racially and socially contrasted men, both captured by the silver of the San Tomé Mine, I feel bound to say something more.

I did not hesitate to make that central figure an Italian. First of all the thing is perfectly credible: Italians were swarming into the Occidental Province at the time, as anybody who will read further can see; and secondly, there was no one who could stand so well by the side of Giorgio Viola the Garibaldino, the Idealist of the old, humanitarian revolutions. For myself I needed there a Man of the People as free as possible from his class-conventions and all settled modes of thinking. This is not a side snarl at conventions. My reasons were not moral but artistic. Had he been an Anglo-Saxon he would have tried to get into local politics. But Nostromo does not aspire to be a leader in a personal game. He does not want to raise himself above the mass. He is content to feel himself a power – within the People.

But mainly Nostromo is what he is because I received the inspiration for him in my early days from a Mediterranean sailor. Those who have read certain pages of mine will see at once what I mean when I say that Dominic, the padrone of the *Tremolino*, might under given circumstances have been a Nostromo. At any rate Dominic would have understood the younger man perfectly – if scornfully. He and I were engaged together in a rather absurd adventure, but the absurdity does not matter. It is a real satisfaction to think that in my very young days there must, after all, have been something in me worthy to command that man's half-bitter fidelity, his half-ironic devotion. Many of Nostromo's speeches I have heard first in Dominic's voice. His hand on the tiller and his fearless eyes roaming the horizon from within the monkish hood shadowing his face, he would utter the usual exordium of his remorseless wisdom: 'Vous autres gentilhommes!' in a caustic tone that hangs on my ear yet. Like Nostromo! 'You hombres finos!' Very much like Nostromo. But Dominic the Corsican nursed a certain pride of ancestry from which my Nostromo is free; for Nostromo's lineage had to be more ancient still. He is a man with the weight of countless generations behind him and no parentage to boast of . . . Like the People.

In his firm grip on the earth he inherits, in his improvidence and generosity, in his lavishness with his gifts, in his manly vanity, in the obscure sense of his greatness and in his faithful devotion with something despairing as well as desperate in its impulses, he is a Man of the People, their very own unenvious force, disdaining to lead but ruling from within. Years afterwards, grown older as the famous Captain Fidanza, with a stake in the country, going about his many affairs followed by respectful glances in the modernised streets of Sulaco, calling on the widow of the *cargador*, attending the Lodge, listening in unmoved silence to anarchist speeches at the meeting, the enigmatical patron of the new revolutionary agitation, the trusted, the wealthy comrade Fidanza with the knowledge of his moral ruin locked up in his breast, he remains essentially a Man of the People. In his mingled love and scorn of life and in the bewildered conviction of having been betrayed, of dying betrayed he hardly knows by what or by whom, he is still of the People, their undoubted Great Man – with a private history of his own.

One more figure of those stirring times I would like to mention: and that is Antonia Avellanos – the 'beautiful Antonia'. Whether she is a possible variation of Latin-American girlhood I wouldn't dare to affirm. But, for me, she *is*. Always a little in the background by the side of her father (my venerated friend) I hope she has yet relief enough to make intelligible what I am going to say. Of all the people who had seen with me the birth of the Occidental Republic, she is the only one who has kept in my memory the aspect of continued life. Antonia the Aristocrat and Nostromo the Man of the People are the artisans of the New Era, the true creators of the New State; he by his legendary and daring feat, she, like a woman, simply by the force of what she is: the only being capable of inspiring a sincere passion in the heart of a trifler.

If anything could induce me to revisit Sulaco (I should hate to see all these changes) it would be Antonia. And the true reason for that – why not be frank about it? – the true reason is that I have modelled her on my first love. How we, a band of tallish schoolboys, the chums of her two brothers, how we used to look up to that girl just out of the schoolroom herself, as the standard-bearer of a faith to which we all were born but which she alone knew how to hold aloft with an unflinching hope! She had perhaps more glow and less serenity in her soul than Antonia, but she was an uncompromising Puritan of patriotism with no taint of the slightest worldliness in her thoughts. I was not the only one in love with her; but it was I who had to hear oftenest her scathing criticism of my levities – very much like poor Decoud – or stand the brunt of her austere, unanswerable invective. She did not quite understand – but never mind. That afternoon when I came in, a shrinking yet defiant sinner, to say the final goodbye I received a hand-squeeze that made my heart leap and saw a tear that took my breath away. She was softened at the last as though she had suddenly perceived (we were such children still!) that I was really going away for good, going very far away – even as far as Sulaco, lying unknown, hidden from our eyes in the darkness of the Placid Gulf.

That's why I long sometimes for another glimpse of the 'beautiful Antonia' (or can it be the Other?) moving in the dimness of the great cathedral, saying a short prayer at the tomb of the first and last Cardinal-Archbishop of Sulaco, standing absorbed in filial devotion before the monument of Don José Avellanos, and, with a lingering, tender, faithful glance at the medallion-memorial to Martin Decoud, going out serenely into the sunshine of the Plaza with her upright carriage and her white head; a relic of the past disregarded by men awaiting impatiently the Dawns of other New Eras, the coming of more Revolutions.

But this is the idlest of dreams; for I did understand perfectly well at the time that the moment the breath left the body of the Magnificent Capataz, the Man of the People, freed at last from the toils of love and wealth, there was nothing more for me to do in Sulaco.

JOSEPH CONRAD
October 1917

NOSTROMO: PART FIRST

The Silver of the Mine

Chapter 1

In the time OF Spanish rule, and for many years afterwards, the town of
Sulaco – the luxuriant beauty of the orange gardens bears witness to its
antiquity – had never been commercially anything more important than a
coasting port with a fairly large local trade in ox-hides and indigo. The
clumsy deep-sea galleons of the conquerors that, needing a brisk gale to
move at all, would lie becalmed, where your modern ship built on clipper
lines forges ahead by the mere flapping of her sails, had been barred out of
Sulaco by the prevailing calms of its vast gulf. Some harbours of the earth are
made difficult of access by the treachery of sunken rocks and the tempests of
their shores. Sulaco had found an inviolable sanctuary from the temptations
of a trading world in the solemn hush of the deep Golfo Placido as if within
an enormous semicircular and unroofed temple open to the ocean, with its
walls of lofty mountains hung with the mourning draperies of cloud.

On one side of this broad curve in the straight seaboard of the Republic of
Costaguana, the last spur of the coast range forms an insignificant cape
whose name is Punta Mala. From the middle of the gulf the point of the land
itself is not visible at all; but the shoulder of a steep hill at the back can be
made out faintly like a shadow on the sky.

On the other side, what seems to be an isolated patch of blue mist floats
lightly on the glare of the horizon. This is the peninsula of Azuera, a wild
chaos of sharp rocks and stony levels cut about by vertical ravines. It lies far
out to sea like a rough head of stone stretched from a green-clad coast at the
end of a slender neck of sand covered with thickets of thorny scrub. Utterly
waterless, for the rainfall runs off at once on all sides into the sea, it has not
soil enough – it is said – to grow a single blade of grass, as if it were blighted
by a curse. The poor, associating by an obscure instinct of consolation the
ideas of evil and wealth, will tell you that it is deadly because of its forbidden
treasures. The common folk of the neighbourhood, peóns of the estancias,
vaqueros of the seaboard plains, tame Indians coming miles to market with a
bundle of sugar-cane or a basket of maize worth about threepence, are well
aware that heaps of shining gold lie in the gloom of the deep precipices
cleaving the stony levels of Azuera. Tradition has it that many adventurers
of olden time had perished in the search. The story goes also that within
men's memory two wandering sailors – Americanos, perhaps, but gringos of
some sort for certain – talked over a gambling, good-for-nothing mozo, and
the three stole a donkey to carry for them a bundle of dry sticks, a water-skin,

and provisions enough to last a few days. Thus accompanied, and with revolvers at their belts, they had started to chop their way with machetes through the thorny scrub on the neck of the peninsula.

On the second evening an upright spiral of smoke (it could only have been from their campfire) was seen for the first time within memory of man standing up faintly upon the sky above a razor-backed ridge on the stony head. The crew of a coasting schooner, lying becalmed three miles off the shore, stared at it with amazement till dark. A Negro fisherman, living in a lonely hut in a little bay near by, had seen the start and was on the lookout for some sign. He called to his wife just as the sun was about to set. They had watched the strange portent with envy, incredulity, and awe.

The impious adventurers gave no other sign. The sailors, the Indian, and the stolen burro were never seen again. As to the mozo, a Sulaco man – his wife paid for some masses, and the poor four-footed beast, being without sin, had been probably permitted to die; but the two gringos, spectral and alive, are believed to be dwelling to this day amongst the rocks, under the fatal spell of their success. Their souls cannot tear themselves away from their bodies mounting guard over the discovered treasure. They are now rich and hungry and thirsty – a strange theory of tenacious gringo ghosts suffering in their starved and parched flesh of defiant heretics, where a Christian would have renounced and been released.

These, then, are the legendary inhabitants of Azuera guarding its forbidden wealth; and the shadow on the sky on one side with the round patch of blue haze blurring the bright skirt of the horizon on the other, mark the two outermost points of the bend which bears the name of Golfo Placido, because never a strong wind had been known to blow upon its waters.

On crossing the imaginary line drawn from Punta Mala to Azuera the ships from Europe bound to Sulaco lose at once the strong breezes of the ocean. They become the prey of capricious airs that play with them for thirty hours at a stretch sometimes. Before them the head of the calm gulf is filled on most days of the year by a great body of motionless and opaque clouds. On the rare clear mornings another shadow is cast upon the sweep of the gulf. The dawn breaks high behind the towering and serrated wall of the Cordillera, a clear-cut vision of dark peaks rearing their steep slopes on a lofty pedestal of forest rising from the very edge of the shore. Amongst them the white head of Higuerota rises majestically upon the blue. Bare clusters of enormous rocks sprinkle with tiny black dots the smooth dome of snow.

Then, as the midday sun withdraws from the gulf the shadow of the mountains, the clouds begin to roll out of the lower valleys. They swathe in sombre tatters the naked crags of precipices above the wooded slopes, hide the peaks, smoke in stormy trails across the snows of Higuerota. The Cordillera is gone from you as if it had dissolved itself into great piles of grey and black vapours that travel out slowly to seaward and vanish into thin air all along the front before the blazing heat of the day. The wasting edge of the cloud-bank always strives for, but seldom wins, the middle of the gulf. The sun – as the sailors say – is eating it up. Unless perchance a sombre thunder-head breaks away from the main body to career all over the gulf till it escapes into the offing beyond Azuera, where it bursts suddenly into flame and crashes like a sinister pirate-ship of the air, hove-to above the horizon, engaging the sea.

At night the body of clouds advancing higher up the sky smothers the whole quiet gulf below with an impenetrable darkness, in which the sound of the falling showers can be heard beginning and ceasing abruptly – now here, now there. Indeed, these cloudy nights are proverbial with the seamen along the whole west coast of a great continent. Sky, land, and sea disappear together out of the world when the Placido – as the saying is – goes to sleep under its black poncho. The few stars left below the seaward frown of the vault shine feebly as into the mouth of a black cavern. In its vastness your ship floats unseen under your feet, her sails flutter invisible above your head. The eye of God Himself – they add with grim profanity – could not find out what work a man's hand is doing in there; and you would be free to call the devil to your aid with impunity if even his malice were not defeated by such a blind darkness.

The shores on the gulf are steep-to all round; three uninhabited islets basking in the sunshine just outside the cloud veil, and opposite the entrance to the harbour of Sulaco, bear the name of 'The Isabels.'

There is the Great Isabel; the Little Isabel, which is round; and Hermosa, which is the smallest.

That last is no more than a foot high, and about seven paces across, a mere flat top of a grey rock which smokes like a hot cinder after a shower, and where no man would care to venture a naked sole before sunset. On the Little Isabel an old ragged palm, with a thick bulging trunk rough with spines, a very witch amongst palm trees, rustles a dismal bunch of dead leaves above the coarse sand. The Great Isabel has a spring of fresh water issuing from the overgrown side of a ravine. Resembling an emerald green wedge of land a mile long, and laid flat upon the sea, it bears two forest trees standing close together, with a wide spread of shade at the foot of their smooth trunks. A ravine extending the whole length of the island is full of bushes; and presenting a deep tangled cleft on the high side spreads itself out on the other into a shallow depression abutting on a small strip of sandy shore.

From that low end of the Great Isabel the eye plunges through an opening two miles away, as abrupt as if chopped with an axe out of the regular sweep of the coast, right into the harbour of Sulaco. It is an oblong, lake-like piece of water. On one side the short wooded spurs and valleys of the Cordillera come down at right angles to the very strand; on the other the open view of the great Sulaco plain passes into the opal mystery of great distances overhung by dry haze. The town of Sulaco itself – tops of walls, a great cupola, gleams of white miradors in a vast grove of orange trees – lies between the mountains and the plain, at some little distance from its harbour and out of the direct line of sight from the sea.

Chapter 2

The only sign of commercial activity within the harbour, visible from the beach of the Great Isabel, is the square blunt end of the wooden jetty which the Oceanic Steam Navigation Company (the OSN of familiar speech) had thrown over the shallow part of the bay soon after they had resolved to make of Sulaco one of their ports of call for the Republic of Costaguana. The State possesses several harbours on its long seaboard, but except Cayta, an important place, all are either small and inconvenient inlets in an iron-bound coast – like Esmeralda, for instance, sixty miles to the south – or else mere open roadsteads exposed to the winds and fretted by the surf.

Perhaps the very atmospheric conditions which had kept away the merchant fleets of bygone ages induced the OSN Company to violate the sanctuary of peace sheltering the calm existence of Sulaco. The variable airs sporting lightly with the vast semicircle of waters within the head of Azuera could not baffle the steam power of their excellent fleet. Year after year the black hulls of their ships had gone up and down the coast, in and out, past Azuera, past the Isabels, past Punta Mala – disregarding everything but the tyranny of time. Their names, the names of all mythology, became the household words of a coast that had never been ruled by the gods of Olympus. The *Juno* was known only for her comfortable cabins amidships, the *Saturn* for the geniality of her captain and the painted and gilt luxuriousness of her saloon, whereas the *Ganymede* was fitted out mainly for cattle transport, and to be avoided by coastwise passengers. The humblest Indian in the obscurest village on the coast was familiar with the *Cerberus*, a little black puffer without charm or living accommodation to speak of, whose mission was to creep inshore along the wooded beaches close to mighty ugly rocks, stopping obligingly before every cluster of huts to collect produce, down to three-pound parcels of india rubber bound in a wrapper of dry grass.

And as they seldom failed to account for the smallest package, rarely lost a bullock, and had never drowned a single passenger, the name of the OSN stood very high for trustworthiness. People declared that under the Company's care their lives and property were safer on the water than in their own houses on shore.

The OSN's superintendent in Sulaco for the whole Costaguana section of the service was very proud of his Company's standing. He resumed it in a saying which was very often on his lips, 'We never make mistakes.' To the Company's officers it took the form of a severe injunction, 'We must make no mistakes. I'll have no mistakes here, no matter what Smith may do at his end.'

Smith, on whom he had never set eyes in his life, was the other superintendent of the service, quartered some fifteen hundred miles away from Sulaco. 'Don't talk to me of your Smith.'

Then, calming down suddenly, he would dismiss the subject with studied negligence.

'Smith knows no more of this continent than a baby.'

'Our excellent Señor Mitchell' for the business and official world of Sulaco, 'Fussy Joe' for the commanders of the Company's ships, Captain Joseph Mitchell prided himself on his profound knowledge of men and things in the country – cosas de Costaguana. Amongst these last he accounted as most unfavourable to the orderly working of his Company the frequent changes of government brought about by revolutions of the military type.

The political atmosphere of the Republic was generally stormy in these days. The fugitive patriots of the defeated party had the knack of turning up again on the coast with half a steamer's load of small arms and ammunition. Such resourcefulness Captain Mitchell considered as perfectly wonderful in view of their utter destitution at the time of flight. He had observed that 'they never seemed to have enough change about them to pay for their passage ticket out of the country.' And he could speak with knowledge; for on a memorable occasion he had been called upon to save the life of a dictator, together with the lives of a few Sulaco officials – the political chief, the director of the customs, and the head of police – belonging to an overturned government. Poor Señor Ribiera (such was the dictator's name) had come pelting eighty miles over mountain tracks after the lost battle of Socorro, in the hope of outdistancing the fatal news – which, of course, he could not manage to do on a lame mule. The animal, moreover, expired under him at the end of the Alameda, where the military band plays sometimes in the evenings between the revolutions. 'Sir,' Captain Mitchell would pursue with portentous gravity, 'the ill-timed end of that mule attracted attention to the unfortunate rider. His features were recognised by several deserters from the Dictatorial army amongst the rascally mob already engaged in smashing the windows of the Intendencia.'

Early on the morning of that day the local authorities of Sulaco had fled for refuge to the OSN Company's offices, a strong building near the shore end of the jetty, leaving the town to the mercies of a revolutionary rabble; and as the Dictator was execrated by the populace on account of the severe recruitment law his necessities had compelled him to enforce during the struggle, he stood a good chance of being torn to pieces. Providentially, Nostromo – invaluable fellow – with some Italian workmen, imported to work upon the National Central Railway, was at hand, and managed to snatch him away – for the time at least. Ultimately, Captain Mitchell succeeded in taking everybody off in his own gig to one of the Company's steamers – it was the *Minerva* – just then, as luck would have it, entering the harbour.

He had to lower these gentlemen at the end of a rope out of a hole in the wall at the back, while the mob which, pouring out of the town, had spread itself all along the shore, howled and foamed at the foot of the building in front. He had to hurry them then the whole length of the jetty; it had been a desperate dash, neck or nothing – and again it was Nostromo, a fellow in a thousand, who, at the head, this time, of the Company's body of lightermen, held the jetty against the rushes of the rabble, thus giving the fugitives time to reach the gig lying ready for them at the other end with the Company's flag at the stern. Sticks, stones, shots flew; knives, too, were thrown. Captain Mitchell exhibited willingly the long cicatrice of a cut over his left ear and temple, made by a razor-blade fastened to a stick – a weapon, he explained, very much in favour with the 'worst kind of nigger out here.'

Captain Mitchell was a thick, elderly man, wearing high, pointed collars and short side-whiskers, partial to white waistcoats, and really very communicative under his air of pompous reserve.

'These gentlemen,' he would say, staring with great solemnity, 'had to run like rabbits, sir. I ran like a rabbit myself. Certain forms of death are – er – distasteful to a – a – er – respectable man. They would have pounded me to death, too. A crazy mob, sir, does not discriminate. Under providence we owed our preservation to my Capataz de Cargadores, as they called him in the town, a man who, when I discovered his value, sir, was just the bos'n of an Italian ship, a big Genoese ship, one of the few European ships that ever came to Sulaco with a general cargo before the building of the National Central. He left her on account of some very respectable friends he made here, his own countrymen, but also, I suppose, to better himself. Sir, I am a pretty good judge of character. I engaged him to be the foreman of our lightermen, and caretaker of our jetty. That's all that he was. But without him Señor Ribiera would have been a dead man. This Nostromo, sir, a man absolutely above reproach, became the terror of all the thieves in the town. We were infested, infested, overrun, sir, here at that time by ladrónes and matreros, thieves and murderers from the whole province. On this occasion they had been flocking into Sulaco for a week past. They had scented the end, sir. Fifty per cent of that murdering mob were professional bandits from the Campo, sir, but there wasn't one that hadn't heard of Nostromo. As to the town léperos, sir, the sight of his black whiskers and white teeth was enough for them. They quailed before him, sir. That's what the force of character will do for you.'

It could very well be said that it was Nostromo alone who saved the lives of these gentlemen. Captain Mitchell, on his part, never left them till he had seen them collapse, panting, terrified, and exasperated, but safe, on the luxuriant velvet sofas in the first-class saloon of the *Minerva*. To the very last he had been careful to address the ex-Dictator as 'Your Excellency'.

'Sir, I could do no other. The man was down – ghastly, livid, one mass of scratches.'

The *Minerva* never let go her anchor that call. The superintendent ordered her out of the harbour at once. No cargo could be landed, of course, and the passengers for Sulaco naturally refused to go ashore. They could hear the firing and see plainly the fight going on at the edge of the water. The repulsed mob devoted its energies to an attack upon the Custom House, a dreary, unfinished-looking structure with many windows two hundred yards away from the OSN Offices, and the only other building near the harbour. Captain Mitchell, after directing the commander of the *Minerva* to land 'these gentlemen' in the first port of call outside Costaguana, went back in his gig to see what could be done for the protection of the Company's property. That and the property of the railway were preserved by the European residents; that is, by Captain Mitchell himself and the staff of engineers building the road, aided by the Italian and Basque workmen who rallied faithfully round their English chiefs. The Company's lightermen, too, natives of the Republic, behaved very well under their Capataz. An outcast lot of very mixed blood, mainly Negroes, everlastingly at feud with the other customers of low grog shops in the town, they embraced with delight this opportunity to settle their personal scores under such favourable auspices. There was not one of them that had not, at sometime or other, looked with terror at Nostromo's revolver poked very close at his face, or been otherwise daunted by Nostromo's resolution. He was 'much of a man', their Capataz was, they said, too scornful in his temper ever to utter abuse, a tireless taskmaster, and the more to be feared because of his aloofness. And behold! there he was that day, at their head, condescending to make jocular remarks to this man or the other.

Such leadership was inspiriting, and in truth all the harm the mob managed to achieve was to set fire to one – only one – stack of railway-sleepers, which, being creosoted, burned well. The main attack on the railway yards, on the OSN Offices, and especially on the Custom House, whose strong room, it was well known, contained a large treasure in silver ingots, failed completely. Even the little hotel kept by old Giorgio, standing alone halfway between the harbour and the town, escaped looting and destruction, not by a miracle, but because with the safes in view they had neglected it at first, and afterwards found no leisure to stop. Nostromo, with his Cargadores, was pressing them too hard then.

Chapter 3

It might have been said that there he was only protecting his own. From the first he had been admitted to live in the intimacy of the family of the hotel-keeper who was a countryman of his. Old Giorgio Viola, a Genoese with a shaggy white leonine head – often called simply 'the Garibaldino' (as Mohammedans are called after their prophet) – was, to use Captain Mitchell's own words, the 'respectable married friend' by whose advice Nostromo had left his ship to try for a run of shore luck in Costaguana.

The old man, full of scorn for the populace, as your austere republican so often is, had disregarded the preliminary sounds of trouble. He went on that day as usual pottering about the 'casa' in his slippers, muttering angrily to himself his contempt of the non-political nature of the riot, and shrugging his shoulders. In the end he was taken unawares by the out-rush of the rabble. It was too late then to remove his family, and, indeed, where could he have run to with the portly Signora Teresa and two little girls on that great plain? So, barricading every opening, the old man sat down sternly in the middle of the darkened café with an old shotgun on his knees. His wife sat on another chair by his side, muttering pious invocations to all the saints of the calendar.

The old republican did not believe in saints, or in prayers, or in what he called 'priest's religion'. Liberty and Garibaldi were his divinities, but he tolerated 'superstition' in women, preserving in these matters a lofty and silent attitude.

His two girls, the eldest fourteen, and the other two years younger, crouched on the sanded floor, on each side of the Signora Teresa, with their heads on their mother's lap, both scared, but each in her own way, the dark-haired Linda indignant and angry, the fair Giselle, the younger, bewildered and resigned. The padrona removed her arms, which embraced her daughters, for a moment to cross herself and wring her hands hurriedly. She moaned a little louder.

'Oh! Gian' Battista, why art thou not here? Oh! why art thou not here?'

She was not then invoking the saint himself, but calling upon Nostromo, whose patron he was. And Giorgio, motionless on the chair by her side, would be provoked by these reproachful and distracted appeals.

'Peace, woman! Where's the sense of it? There's his duty,' he murmured in the dark; and she would retort, panting – 'Eh! I have no patience. Duty! What of the woman who has been like a mother to him? I bent my knee to him this morning, don't you go out, Gian' Battista – stop in the house, Battistino – look at those two little innocent children!'

Mrs Viola was an Italian, too, a native of Spezzia, and though considerably younger than her husband, already middle-aged. She had a handsome face, whose complexion had turned yellow because the climate of Sulaco did not suit her at all. Her voice was a rich contralto. When, with her arms folded tight under her ample bosom, she scolded the squat, thick-legged China girls handling linen, plucking fowls, pounding corn in wooden mortars amongst the mud outbuildings at the back of the house, she could bring out such an impassioned, vibrating, sepulchral note that the chained watchdog bolted into his kennel with a great rattle. Luis, a cinnamon-coloured mulatto with a sprouting moustache and thick, dark lips, would stop sweeping the café with a broom of palm-leaves to let a gentle shudder run down his spine. His languishing almond eyes would remain closed for a long time.

This was the staff of the Casa Viola, but all these people had fled early that morning at the first sounds of the riot, preferring to hide on the plain rather than trust themselves in the house; a preference for which they were in no way to blame, since, whether true or not, it was generally believed in the town that the Garibaldino had some money buried under the clay floor of the kitchen. The dog, an irritable, shaggy brute, barked violently and whined plaintively in turns at the back, running in and out of his kennel as rage or fear prompted him.

Bursts of great shouting rose and died away, like wild gusts of wind on the plain round the barricaded house; the fitful popping of shots grew louder above the yelling. Sometimes there were intervals of unaccountable stillness outside, and nothing could have been more gaily peaceful than the narrow bright lines of sunlight from the cracks in the shutters, ruled straight across the café over the disarranged chairs and tables to the wall opposite. Old Giorgio had chosen that bare, whitewashed room for a retreat. It had only one window, and its only door swung out upon the track of thick dust fenced by aloe hedges between the harbour and the town, where clumsy carts used to creak along behind slow yokes of oxen guided by boys on horseback.

In a pause of stillness Giorgio cocked his gun. The ominous sound wrung a low moan from the rigid figure of the woman sitting by his side. A sudden outbreak of defiant yelling quite near the house sank all at once to a confused murmur of growls. Somebody ran along; the loud catching of his breath was heard for an instant passing the door; there were hoarse mutters and footsteps near the wall; a shoulder rubbed against the shutter, effacing the bright lines of sunshine pencilled across the whole breadth of the room. Signora Teresa's arms thrown about the kneeling forms of her daughters embraced them closer with a convulsive pressure.

The mob, driven away from the Custom House, had broken up into several bands, retreating across the plain in the direction of the town. The subdued crash of irregular volleys fired in the distance was answered by faint yells far away. In the intervals the single shots rang feebly, and the low, long, white building blinded in every window seemed to be the centre of a turmoil widening in a great circle about its closed-up silence. But the cautious movements and whispers of a routed party seeking a momentary shelter behind the wall made the darkness of the room, striped by threads of quiet sunlight, alight with evil, stealthy sounds. The Violas had them in their ears as though invisible ghosts hovering about their chairs had consulted in mutters as to the advisability of setting fire to this foreigner's casa.

It was trying to the nerves. Old Viola had risen slowly, gun in hand, irresolute, for he did not see how he could prevent them. Already voices could be heard talking at the back. Signora Teresa was beside herself with terror.

'Ah! the traitor! the traitor!' she mumbled, almost inaudibly. 'Now we are going to be burnt; and I bent my knee to him. No! he must run at the heels of his English.'

She seemed to think that Nostromo's mere presence in the house would have made it perfectly safe. So far, she, too, was under the spell of that reputation the Capataz de Cargadores had made for himself by the water-side, along the railway line, with the English and with the populace of Sulaco. To his face, and even against her husband, she invariably affected to laugh it to scorn, sometimes good-naturedly, more often with a curious bitterness. But then women are unreasonable in their opinions, as Giorgio used to remark calmly on fitting occasions. On this occasion, with his gun held at ready before him, he stooped down to his wife's head, and, keeping his eyes steadfastly on the barricaded door, he breathed out into her ear that Nostromo would have been powerless to help. What could two men shut up in a house do against twenty or more bent upon setting fire to the roof? Gian' Battista was thinking of the casa all the time, he was sure.

'He think of the casa! He!' gasped Signora Viola, crazily. She struck her breast with her open hands. 'I know him. He thinks of nobody but himself.'

A discharge of firearms near by made her throw her head back and close her eyes. Old Giorgio set his teeth hard under his white moustache, and his eyes began to roll fiercely. Several bullets struck the end of the wall together; pieces of plaster could be heard falling outside; a voice screamed 'Here they come!' and after a moment of uneasy silence there was a rush of running feet along the front.

Then the tension of old Giorgio's attitude relaxed, and a smile of contemptuous relief came upon his lips of an old fighter with a leonine face. These were not a people striving for justice, but thieves. Even to defend his life against them was a sort of degradation for a man who had been one of Garibaldi's immortal thousand in the conquest of Sicily. He had an immense scorn for this outbreak of scoundrels and léperos, who did not know the meaning of the word 'liberty'.

He grounded his old gun, and, turning his head, glanced at the coloured lithograph of Garibaldi in a black frame on the white wall; a thread of strong sunshine cut it perpendicularly. His eyes, accustomed to the luminous twilight, made out the high colouring of the face, the red of the shirt, the outlines of the square shoulders, the black patch of the Bersagliere hat with cock's feathers curling over the crown. An immortal hero! This was your liberty; it gave you not only life, but immortality as well!

For that one man his fanaticism had suffered no diminution. In the moment of relief from the apprehension of the greatest danger, perhaps, his family had been exposed to in all their wanderings, he had turned to the picture of his old chief, first and only, then laid his hand on his wife's shoulder.

The children kneeling on the floor had not moved. Signora Teresa opened her eyes a little, as though he had awakened her from a very deep and dreamless slumber. Before he had time in his deliberate way to say a reassuring word she jumped up, with the children clinging to her, one on each side, gasped for breath, and let out a hoarse shriek.

It was simultaneous with the bang of a violent blow struck on the outside of the shutter. They could hear suddenly the snorting of a horse, the restive tramping of hoofs on the narrow, hard path in front of the house; the toe of a boot struck at the shutter again; a spur jingled at every blow, and an excited voice shouted, 'Hola! hola, in there!'

Chapter 4

All the morning Nostromo had kept his eye from afar on the Casa Viola, even in the thick of the hottest scrimmage near the Custom House. 'If I see smoke rising over there,' he thought to himself, 'they are lost.' Directly the mob had broken he pressed with a small band of Italian workmen in that direction, which, indeed, was the shortest line towards the town. That part of the rabble he was pursuing seemed to think of making a stand under the house; a volley fired by his followers from behind an aloe hedge made the rascals fly. In a gap chopped out for the rails of the harbour branch line Nostromo appeared, mounted on his silver-grey mare. He shouted, sent after them one shot from his revolver, and galloped up to the café window. He had an idea that old Giorgio would choose that part of the house for a refuge.

His voice had penetrated to them, sounding breathlessly hurried: 'Hola! Vecchio! O, Vecchio! Is it all well with you in there?'

'You see – ' murmured old Viola to his wife.

Signora Teresa was silent now. Outside Nostromo laughed.

'I can hear the padrona is not dead.'

'You have done your best to kill me with fear,' cried Signora Teresa. She wanted to say something more, but her voice failed her.

Linda raised her eyes to her face for a moment, but old Giorgio shouted apologetically; 'She is a little upset.'

Outside Nostromo shouted back with another laugh; 'She cannot upset me.'

Signora Teresa found her voice.

'It is what I say. You have no heart – and you have no conscience, Gian' Battista – '

They heard him wheel his horse away from the shutters. The party he led were babbling excitedly in Italian and Spanish, inciting each other to the pursuit. He put himself at their head, crying, 'Avanti!'

'He has not stopped very long with us. There is no praise from strangers to be got here,' Signora Teresa said, tragically. 'Avanti! Yes! That is all he cares for. To be first somewhere – somehow – to be first with these English. They will be showing him to everybody. "This is our Nostromo!" ' She laughed ominously. 'What a name! What is that? Nostromo? He would take a name that is properly no word from them.'

Meantime Giorgio, with tranquil movements, had been unfastening the door; the flood of light fell on Signora Teresa, with her two girls gathered to her side, a picturesque woman in a pose of maternal exaltation. Behind her the wall was dazzlingly white, and the crude colours of the Garibaldi lithograph paled in the sunshine.

Old Viola, at the door, moved his arm upwards as if referring all his quick, fleeting thoughts to the picture of his old chief on the wall. Even when he was cooking for the 'Signori Inglesi' – the engineers (he was a famous cook, though the kitchen was a dark place) – he was, as it were, under the eye of the great man who had led him in a glorious struggle where, under the walls of Gaeta, tyranny would have expired for ever had it not been for that accursed Piedmontese race of kings and ministers. When sometimes a frying-pan caught fire during a delicate operation with some shredded onions, and the old man was seen backing out of the doorway, swearing and coughing violently in an acrid cloud of smoke, the name of Cavour – the arch intriguer sold to kings and tyrants – could be heard involved in imprecations against the China girls, cooking in general, and the brute of a country where he was reduced to live for the love of liberty that traitor had strangled.

Then Signora Teresa, all in black, issuing from another door, advanced, portly and anxious, inclining her fine, black-browed head, opening her arms, and crying in a profound tone – 'Giorgio! thou passionate man! Misericordia Divina! In the sun like this! He will make himself ill.'

At her feet the hens made off in all directions, with immense strides; if there were any engineers from up the line staying in Sulaco, a young English face or two would appear at the billiard-room occupying one end of the house; but at the other end, in the café, Luis, the mulatto, took good care not to show himself. The Indian girls, with hair like flowing black manes, and dressed only in a shift and short petticoat, stared dully from under the square-cut fringes on their foreheads; the noisy frizzling of fat had stopped, the fumes floated upwards in sunshine, a strong smell of burnt onions hung in the drowsy heat, enveloping the house; and the eye lost itself in a vast flat expanse of grass to the west, as if the plain between the Sierra overtopping Sulaco and the coast range away there towards Esmeralda had been as big as half the world.

Signora Teresa, after an impressive pause, remonstrated: 'Eh, Giorgio! Leave Cavour alone and take care of yourself now we are lost in this country all alone with the two children, because you cannot live under a king.'

And while she looked at him she would sometimes put her hand hastily to her side with a short twitch of her fine lips and a knitting of her black, straight eyebrows like a flicker of angry pain or an angry thought on her handsome, regular features.

It was pain; she suppressed the twinge. It had come to her first a few years after they had left Italy to emigrate to America and settle at last in Sulaco after wandering from town to town, trying shopkeeping in a small way here and there; and once an organised enterprise of fishing – in Maldonado – for Giorgio, like the great Garibaldi, had been a sailor in his time.

Sometimes she had no patience with pain. For years its gnawing had been part of the landscape embracing the glitter of the harbour under the wooded spurs of the range; and the sunshine itself was heavy and dull – heavy with pain – not like the sunshine of her girlhood, in which middle-aged Giorgio had wooed her gravely and passionately on the shores of the gulf of Spezzia.

'You go in at once, Giorgio,' she directed. 'One would think you do not wish to have any pity on me – with four Signori Inglesi staying in the house.'

'Va bene, va bene,' Giorgio would mutter.

He obeyed. The Signori Inglesi would require their midday meal presently. He had been one of the immortal and invincible band of liberators who had made the mercenaries of tyranny fly like chaff before a hurricane, 'un uragano terribile'. But that was before he was married and had children; and before tyranny had reared its head again amongst the traitors who had imprisoned Garibaldi, his hero.

There were three doors in the front of the house, and each afternoon the Garibaldino could be seen at one or another of them with his big bush of white hair, his arms folded, his legs crossed, leaning back his leonine head against the lintel, and looking up the wooded slopes of the foothills at the snowy dome of Higuerota. The front of his house threw off a black long rectangle of shade, broadening slowly over the soft ox-cart track. Through the gaps, chopped out in the oleander hedges, the harbour branch railway, laid out temporarily on the level of the plain, curved away its shining parallel ribbons on a belt of scorched and withered grass within sixty yards of the end of the house. In the evening the empty material trains of flat cars circled round the dark green grove of Sulaco, and ran, undulating slightly with white jets of steam, over the plain towards the Casa Viola, on their way to the railway yards by the harbour. The Italian drivers saluted him from the footplate with raised hand, while the Negro brakesmen sat carelessly on the brakes, looking straight forward, with the rims of their big hats flapping in the wind. In return Giorgio would give a slight sideways jerk of the head, without unfolding his arms.

On this memorable day of the riot his arms were not folded on his chest. His hand grasped the barrel of the gun grounded on the threshold; he did not look up once at the white dome of Higuerota, whose cool purity seemed to hold itself aloof from a hot earth. His eyes examined the plain curiously. Tall trails of dust subsided here and there. In a speckless sky the sun hung clear and blinding. Knots of men ran headlong; others made a stand; and the irregular rattle of firearms came rippling to his ears in the fiery, still air. Single figures on foot raced desperately. Horsemen galloped towards each other, wheeled round together, separated at speed. Giorgio saw one fall, rider and horse disappearing as if they had galloped into a chasm, and the movements of the animated scene were like the passages of a violent game played upon the plain by dwarfs mounted and on foot, yelling with tiny throats, under the mountain that seemed a colossal embodiment of silence. Never before had Giorgio seen this bit of plain so full of active life; his gaze could not take in all its details at once; he shaded his eyes with his hand, till suddenly the thundering of many hoofs near by startled him.

A troop of horses had broken out of the fenced paddock of the Railway Company. They came on like a whirlwind, and dashed over the line snorting, kicking, squealing in a compact, piebald, tossing mob of bay, brown, grey backs, eyes staring, necks extended, nostrils red, long tails streaming. As soon as they had leaped upon the road the thick dust flew upwards from under their hoofs, and within six yards of Giorgio only a brown cloud with vague forms of necks and cruppers rolled by, making the soil tremble on its passage.

Viola coughed, turning his face away from the dust, and shaking his head slightly.

'There will be some horse-catching to be done before tonight,' he muttered.

In the square of sunlight falling through the door Signora Teresa, kneeling before the chair, had bowed her head, heavy with a twisted mass of ebony hair streaked with silver, into the palm of her hands. The black lace shawl she used to drape about her face had dropped to the ground by her side. The two girls got up, hand-in-hand, in short skirts, their loose hair falling in disorder. The younger had thrown her arm across her eyes, as if afraid to face the light.

Linda, with her hand on the other's shoulder, stared fearlessly. Viola looked at his children.

The sun brought out the deep lines on his face, and, energetic in expression, it had the immobility of a carving. It was impossible to discover what he thought. Bushy grey eyebrows shaded his dark glance.

'Well! And do you not pray like your mother?'

Linda pouted, advancing her red lips, which were almost too red; but she had admirable eyes, brown, with a sparkle of gold in the irises, full of intelligence and meaning, and so clear that they seemed to throw a glow upon her thin, colourless face. There were bronze glints in the sombre clusters of her hair, and the eyelashes, long and coal black, made her complexion appear still more pale.

'Mother is going to offer up a lot of candles in the church. She always does when Nostromo has been away fighting. I shall have some to carry up to the Chapel of the Madonna in the Cathedral.'

She said all this quickly, with great assurance, in an animated, penetrating voice. Then, giving her sister's shoulder a slight shake, she added; 'And she will be made to carry one, too!'

'Why made?' enquired Giorgio, gravely. 'Does she not want to?'

'She is timid,' said Linda, with a little burst of laughter. 'People notice her fair hair as she goes along with us. They call out after her, Look at the Rubiacita! "Look at the Rubia!" They call out in the streets. She is timid.'

'And you? You are not timid – eh?' the father pronounced, slowly.

She tossed back all her dark hair.

'Nobody calls out after me.'

Old Giorgio contemplated his children thoughtfully. There was two years difference between them. They had been born to him late, years after the boy had died. Had he lived he would have been nearly as old as Gian' Battista – he whom the English called Nostromo; but as to his daughters, the severity of his temper, his advancing age, his absorption in his memories, had prevented his taking much notice of them. He loved his children, but girls belong more to the mother, and much of his affection had been expended in the worship and service of liberty.

When quite a youth he had deserted from a ship trading to La Plata, to enlist in the navy of Montevideo, then under the command of Garibaldi. Afterwards, in the Italian legion of the Republic struggling against the encroaching tyranny of Rosas, he had taken part, on great plains, on the banks of immense rivers, in the fiercest fighting perhaps the world had ever known. He had lived amongst men who had declaimed about liberty, suffered for liberty, died for liberty, with a desperate exaltation, and with their eyes turned towards an oppressed Italy. His own enthusiasm had been fed on scenes of carnage, on the examples of lofty devotion, on the din of armed struggle, on the inflamed language of proclamations. He had never parted from the chief of his choice – the fiery apostle of independence – keeping by his side in America and in Italy till after the fatal day of Aspromonte, when the treachery of kings, emperors, and ministers had been revealed to the world in the wounding and imprisonment of his hero – a catastrophe that had instilled into him a gloomy doubt of ever being able to understand the ways of Divine justice.

He did not deny it, however. It required patience, he would say. Though he disliked priests, and would not put his foot inside a church for anything, he believed in God. Were not the proclamations against tyrants addressed to the peoples in the name of God and liberty? 'God for men – religions for women,' he muttered sometimes. In Sicily, an Englishman who had turned up in Palermo after its evacuation by the army of the king had given him a Bible in Italian – the publication of the British and Foreign Bible Society, bound in a dark leather cover. In periods of political adversity, in the pauses of silence when the revolutionists issued no proclamations, Giorgio earned his living with the first work that came to hand – as sailor, as dock labourer on the quays of Genoa, once as a hand on a farm in the hills above Spezzia – and in his spare time he studied the thick volume. He carried it with him into battles. Now it was his only reading, and in order not to be deprived of it (the print was small) he had consented to accept the present of a pair of silver-mounted spectacles from Señora Emilia Gould, the wife of the Englishman who managed the silver mine in the mountains three leagues from the town. She was the only Englishwoman in Sulaco.

Giorgio Viola had a great consideration for the English. This feeling, born on the battlefields of Uruguay, was forty years old at the very least. Several of them had poured their blood for the cause of freedom in America, and the first he had ever known he remembered by the name of Samuel; he commanded a Negro company under Garibaldi, during the famous siege of Montevideo, and died heroically with his Negroes at the fording of the Boyana. He, Giorgio, had reached the rank of ensign – *alferez* – and cooked for the general. Later, in Italy, he, with the rank of lieutenant, rode with the staff and still cooked for the general. He had cooked for him in Lombardy through the whole campaign; on the march to Rome he had lassoed his beef in the Campagna after the American manner; he had been wounded in the defence of the Roman Republic; he was one of the four fugitives who, with the general, carried out of the woods the inanimate body of the general's wife into the farmhouse where she died, exhausted by the hardships of that terrible retreat. He had survived that disastrous time to attend his general in Palermo when the Neapolitan shells from the castle crashed upon the town. He had cooked for him on the field of Volturno after fighting all day. And everywhere he had seen Englishmen in the front rank of the army of freedom. He respected their nation because they loved Garibaldi. Their very countesses and princesses had kissed the general's hands in London, it was said. He could well believe it; for the nation was noble, and the man was a saint. It was enough to look once at his face to see the divine force of faith in him and his great pity for all that was poor, suffering, and oppressed in this world.

The spirit of self-forgetfulness, the simple devotion to a vast humanitarian idea which inspired the thought and stress of that revolutionary time, had left its mark upon Giorgio in a sort of austere contempt for all personal advantage. This man, whom the lowest class in Sulaco suspected of having a buried hoard in his kitchen, had all his life despised money. The leaders of his youth had lived poor, had died poor. It had been a habit of his mind to disregard tomorrow. It was engendered partly by an existence of excitement, adventure, and wild warfare. But mostly it was a matter of principle. It did not resemble the carelessness of a condottiere, it was a puritanism of conduct, born of stern enthusiasm like the puritanism of religion.

This stern devotion to a cause had cast a gloom upon Giorgio's old age. It cast a gloom because the cause seemed lost. Too many kings and emperors flourished yet in the world which God had meant for the people.

He was sad because of his simplicity. Though always ready to help his countrymen, and greatly respected by the Italian emigrants wherever he lived (in his exile he called it), he could not conceal from himself that they cared nothing for the wrongs of downtrodden nations. They listened to his tales of war readily, but seemed to ask themselves what he had got out of it after all. There was nothing that they could see. 'We wanted nothing, we suffered for the love of all humanity!' he cried out furiously sometimes, and the powerful voice, the blazing eyes, the shaking of the white mane, the brown, sinewy hand pointing upwards as if to call heaven to witness, impressed his hearers. After the old man had broken off abruptly with a jerk of the head and a movement of the arm, meaning clearly, 'But what's the good of talking to you?' they nudged each other. There was in old Giorgio an energy of feeling, a personal quality of conviction, something they called 'terribilità' – 'an old lion', they used to say of him. Some slight incident, a chance word would set him off talking on the beach to the Italian fishermen of Maldonado, in the little shop he kept afterwards (in Valparaiso) to his countrymen customers; of an evening, suddenly, in the café at one end of the Casa Viola (the other was reserved for the English engineers) to the select clientele of engine-drivers and foremen of the railway shops.

With their handsome, bronzed, lean faces, shiny black ringlets, glistening eyes, broad-chested, bearded, sometimes a tiny gold ring in the lobe of the ear, the aristocracy of the railway works listened to him, turning away from their cards or dominoes. Here and there a fair-haired Basque studied his hand meantime, waiting without protest. No native of Costaguana intruded there. This was the Italian stronghold. Even the Sulaco policemen on a night patrol let their horses pace softly by, bending low in the saddle to glance through the window at the heads in a fog of smoke; and the drone of old Giorgio's declamatory narrative seemed to sink behind them into the plain. Only now and then the assistant of the chief of police, some broad-faced, brown little gentleman, with a great deal of Indian in him, would put in an appearance. Leaving his man outside with the horses he advanced with a confident, sly smile, and without a word up to the long trestle table. He pointed to one of the bottles on the shelf; Giorgio, thrusting his pipe into his mouth abruptly, served him in person. Nothing would be heard but the slight jingle of the spurs. His glass emptied, he would take a leisurely, scrutinising look all round the room, go out, and ride away slowly, circling towards the town.

Chapter 5

In this way only was the power of the local authorities vindicated amongst the great body of strong-limbed foreigners who dug the earth, blasted the rocks, drove the engines for the 'progressive and patriotic undertaking'. In these very words eighteen months before the Excellentísimo Señor Don Vincente Ribiera, the Dictator of Costaguana, had described the National Central Railway in his great speech at the turning of the first sod.

He had come on purpose to Sulaco, and there was a one-o'clock dinner-party, a *convité* offered by the OSN Company on board the *Juno* after the function on shore. Captain Mitchell had himself steered the cargo lighter, all draped with flags, which, in tow of the *Juno*'s steam launch, took the Excellentísimo from the jetty to the ship. Everybody of note in Sulaco had been invited – the one or two foreign merchants, all the representatives of the old Spanish families then in town, the great owners of estates on the plain, grave, courteous, simple men, caballeros of pure descent, with small hands and feet, conservative, hospitable, and kind. The Occidental Province was their stronghold; their Blanco party had triumphed now; it was their President-Dictator, a Blanco of the Blancos, who sat smiling urbanely between the representatives of two friendly foreign powers. They had come with him from Sta Marta to countenance by their presence the enterprise in which the capital of their countries was engaged.

The only lady of that company was Mrs Gould, the wife of Don Carlos, the administrator of the San Tomé silver mine. The ladies of Sulaco were not advanced enough to take part in the public life to that extent. They had come out strongly at the great ball at the Intendencia the evening before, but Mrs Gould alone had appeared, a bright spot in the group of black coats behind the President-Dictator, on the crimson cloth-covered stage erected under a shady tree on the shore of the harbour, where the ceremony of turning the first sod had taken place. She had come off in the cargo lighter, full of notabilities, sitting under the flutter of gay flags, in the place of honour by the side of Captain Mitchell, who steered, and her clear dress gave the only truly festive note to the sombre gathering in the long, gorgeous saloon of the *Juno*.

The head of the chairman of the railway board (from London), handsome and pale in a silvery mist of white hair and clipped beard, hovered near her shoulder attentive, smiling, and fatigued. The journey from London to Sta Marta in mail boats and the special carriages of the Sta Marta coastline (the only railway so far) had been tolerable – even pleasant – quite tolerable. But the trip over the mountains to Sulaco was another sort of experience, in an old diligencia over impassable roads skirting awful precipices.

'We have been upset twice in one day on the brink of very deep ravines,' he was telling Mrs Gould in an undertone. 'And when we arrived here at last I don't know what we should have done without your hospitality. What an out-of-the-way place Sulaco is! – and for a harbour, too! Astonishing!'

'Ah, but we are very proud of it. It used to be historically important. The highest ecclesiastical court, for two viceroyalties, sat here in the olden time,' she instructed him with animation.

'I am impressed. I didn't mean to be disparaging. You seem very patriotic.'

'The place is lovable, if only by its situation. Perhaps you don't know what an old resident I am.'

'How old, I wonder,' he murmured, looking at her with a slight smile. Mrs Gould's appearance was made youthful by the mobile intelligence of her face. 'We can't give you your ecclesiastical court back again; but you shall have more steamers, a railway, a telegraph-cable – a future in the great world which is worth infinitely more than any amount of ecclesiastical past. You shall be brought in touch with something greater than two viceroyalties. But I had no notion that a place on a seacoast could remain so isolated from the world. If it had been a thousand miles inland now – most remarkable! Has anything ever happened here for a hundred years before today?'

While he talked in a slow, humorous tone, she kept her little smile. Agreeing ironically, she assured him that certainly not – nothing ever happened in Sulaco. Even the revolutions, of which there had been two in her time, had respected the repose of the place. Their course ran in more populous southern parts of the Republic, and the great valley of Sta Marta, which was like one great battlefield of the parties, with the possession of the capital for a prize and an outlet to another ocean. They were more advanced over there. Here in Sulaco they heard only the echoes of these great questions, and, of course, their official world changed each time, coming to them over their rampart of mountains which he himself had traversed in an old diligencia, with such a risk to life and limb.

The chairman of the railway had been enjoying her hospitality for several days, and he was really grateful for it. It was only since he had left Sta Marta that he had utterly lost touch with the feeling of European life on the background of his exotic surroundings. In the capital he had been the guest of the Legation, and had been kept busy negotiating with the members of Don Vincente's Government – cultured men, men to whom the conditions of civilised business were not unknown.

What concerned him most at the time was the acquisition of land for the railway. In the Sta Marta Valley, where there was already one line in existence, the people were tractable, and it was only a matter of price. A commission had been nominated to fix the values, and the difficulty resolved itself into the judicious influencing of the Commissioners. But in Sulaco – the Occidental Province for whose very development the railway was intended – there had been trouble. It had been lying for ages ensconced behind its natural barriers, repelling modern enterprise by the precipices of its mountain range, by its shallow harbour opening into the everlasting calms of a gulf full of clouds, by the benighted state of mind of the owners of its fertile territory – all these aristocratic old Spanish families, all those Don Ambrosios this and Don Fernandos that, who seemed actually to dislike and distrust the coming of the railway over their lands. It had happened that some of the surveying parties scattered all over the province had been warned off with threats of violence. In other cases outrageous pretensions as to price had been raised. But the man of railways prided himself on being equal to every emergency. Since he was met by the inimical sentiment of blind conservatism in Sulaco he would meet it by sentiment, too, before taking his stand on his right alone. The Government was bound to carry out its part of the contract with the board of the new railway company, even if it had to use force for the purpose. But he desired nothing less than an armed disturbance in the smooth working of his plans. They were much too vast and far-reaching, and too promising to leave a stone unturned; and so he imagined to get the President-Dictator over there on a tour of ceremonies and speeches, culminating in a great function at the turning of the first sod by the harbour shore. After all he was their own creature – that Don Vincente. He was the embodied triumph of the best elements in the State. These were facts, and, unless facts meant nothing, Sir John argued to himself, such a man's influence must be real, and his personal action would produce the conciliatory effect he required. He had succeeded in arranging the trip with the help of a very clever advocate, who was known in Sta Marta as the agent of the Gould silver mine, the biggest thing in Sulaco, and even in the whole Republic. It was indeed a fabulously rich mine. Its so-called agent, evidently a man of culture and ability, seemed, without official position, to possess an extraordinary influence in the highest Government spheres. He was able to assure Sir John that the President-Dictator would make the journey. He regretted, however, in the course of the same conversation, that General Montero insisted upon going, too.

General Montero, whom the beginning of the struggle had found an obscure army captain employed on the wild eastern frontier of the State, had thrown in his lot with the Ribiera party at a moment when special circumstances had given that small adhesion a fortuitous importance. The fortunes of war served him marvellously, and the victory of Rio Seco (after a day of desperate fighting) put a seal to his success. At the end he emerged General, Minister of War, and the military head of the Blanco party, although there was nothing aristocratic in his descent. Indeed, it was said that he and his brother, orphans, had been brought up by the munificence of a famous European traveller, in whose service their father had lost his life. Another story was that their father had been nothing but a charcoal burner in the woods, and their mother a baptised Indian woman from the far interior.

However that might be, the Costaguana Press was in the habit of styling Montero's forest march from his commandancia to join the Blanco forces at the beginning of the troubles, the 'most heroic military exploit of modern times'. About the same time, too, his brother had turned up from Europe, where he had gone apparently as secretary to a consul. Having, however, collected a small band of outlaws, he showed some talent as guerrilla chief and had been rewarded at the pacification by the post of Military Commandant of the capital.

The Minister of War, then, accompanied the Dictator. The board of the OSN Company, working hand-in-hand with the railway people for the good of the Republic, had on this important occasion instructed Captain Mitchell to put the mail-boat *Juno* at the disposal of the distinguished party. Don Vincente, journeying south from Sta Marta, had embarked at Cayta, the principal port of Costaguana, and came to Sulaco by sea. But the chairman of the railway company had courageously crossed the mountains in a ramshackle diligencia, mainly for the purpose of meeting his engineer-in-chief engaged in the final survey of the road.

For all the indifference of a man of affairs to nature, whose hostility can always be overcome by the resources of finance, he could not help being impressed by his surroundings during his halt at the surveying camp established at the highest point his railway was to reach. He spent the night there, arriving just too late to see the last dying glow of sunlight upon the snowy flank of Higuerota. Pillared masses of black basalt framed like an open portal a portion of the white field lying aslant against the west. In the transparent air of the high altitudes everything seemed very near, steeped in a clear stillness as in an imponderable liquid; and with his ear ready to catch the first sound of the expected diligencia the engineer-in-chief, at the door of a hut of rough stones, had contemplated the changing hues on the enormous side of the mountain, thinking that in this sight, as in a piece of inspired music, there could be found together the utmost delicacy of shaded expression and a stupendous magnificence of effect.

Sir John arrived too late to hear the magnificent and inaudible strain sung by the sunset amongst the high peaks of the Sierra. It had sung itself out into the breathless pause of deep dusk before, climbing down the fore wheel of the diligencia with stiff limbs, he shook hands with the engineer.

They gave him his dinner in a stone hut like a cubical boulder, with no door or windows in its two openings; a bright fire of sticks (brought on muleback from the first valley below) burning outside, sent in a wavering glare; and two candles in tin candlesticks – lighted, it was explained to him, in his honour – stood on a sort of rough camp table, at which he sat on the right hand of the chief. He knew how to be amiable; and the young men of the engineering staff, for whom the surveying of the railway track had the glamour of the first steps on the path of life, sat there, too, listening modestly, with their smooth faces tanned by the weather, and very pleased to witness so much affability in so great a man.

Afterwards, late at night, pacing to and fro outside, he had a long talk with his chief engineer. He knew him well of old. This was not the first undertaking in which their gifts, as elementally different as fire and water, had worked in conjunction. From the contact of these two personalities, who had not the same vision of the world, there was generated a power for the world's service – a subtle force that could set in motion mighty machines, men's muscles, and awaken also in human breasts an unbounded devotion to the task. Of the young fellows at the table, to whom the survey of the track was like the tracing of the path of life, more than one would be called to meet death before the work was done. But the work would be done: the force would be almost as strong as a faith. Not quite, however. In the silence of the sleeping camp upon the moonlit plateau forming the top of the pass like the floor of a vast arena surrounded by the basalt walls of precipices, two strolling figures in thick ulsters stood still, and the voice of the engineer pronounced distinctly the words: 'We can't move mountains!'

Sir John, raising his head to follow the pointing gesture, felt the full force of the words. The white Higuerota soared out of the shadows of rock and earth like a frozen bubble under the moon. All was still, till near by, behind the wall of a corral for the camp animals, built roughly of loose stones in the circle, a pack mule stamped his forefoot heavily twice.

The engineer-in-chief had used the phrase in answer to the chairman's tentative suggestion that the tracing of the line could, perhaps, be altered in deference to the prejudices of the Sulaco landowners. The chief engineer believed that the obstinacy of men was the lesser obstacle. Moreover, to combat that they had the great influence of Charles Gould, whereas tunnelling under Higuerota would have been a colossal undertaking.

'Ah, yes! Gould. What sort of a man is he?'

Sir John had heard much of Charles Gould in Sta Marta, and wanted to know more. The engineer-in-chief assured him that the administrator of the San Tomé silver mine had an immense influence over all these Spanish Dons. He had also one of the best houses in Sulaco, and the Gould hospitality was beyond all praise.

'They received me as if they had known me for years,' he said. 'The little lady is kindness personified. I stayed with them for a month. He helped me to organise the surveying parties. His practical ownership of the San Tomé silver mine gives him a special position. He seems to have the ear of every provincial authority apparently, and, as I said, he can wind all the hidalgos of the province round his little finger. If you follow his advice the difficulties will fall away, because he wants the railway. Of course, you must be careful in what you say. He's English, and besides he must be immensely wealthy. The Holroyd house is in with him in that mine, so you may imagine – '

He interrupted himself as, from before one of the little fires burning outside the low wall of the corral, arose the figure of a man wrapped in a poncho up to the neck. The saddle which he had been using for a pillow made a dark patch on the ground against the red glow of embers.

'I shall see Holroyd himself on my way back through the States,' said Sir John. 'I've ascertained that he, too, wants the railway.'

The man who, perhaps disturbed by the proximity of the voices, had arisen from the ground, struck a match to light a cigarette. The flame showed a bronzed, black-whiskered face, a pair of eyes gazing straight; then, rearranging his wrappings, he sank full length and laid his head again on the saddle.

'That's our camp-master, whom I must send back to Sulaco now we are going to carry our survey into the Sta Marta Valley,' said the engineer. 'A most useful fellow, lent me by Captain Mitchell of the OSN Company. It was very good of Mitchell. Charles Gould told me I couldn't do better than take advantage of the offer. He seems to know how to rule all these muleteers and peóns. We had not the slightest trouble with our people. He shall escort your diligencia right into Sulaco with some of our railway peóns. The road at hand may save you an upset or two. He promised me to take care of your person all the way down as if you were his father.'

This camp-master was the Italian sailor whom all the Europeans in Sulaco, following Captain Mitchell's mispronunciation, were in the habit of calling Nostromo. And indeed, taciturn and ready, he did take excellent care of his charge at the bad parts of the road, as Sir John himself acknowledged to Mrs Gould afterwards.

Chapter 6

At this time Nostromo had been already long enough in the country to raise to the highest pitch Captain Mitchell's opinion of the extraordinary value of his discovery. Clearly he was one of those invaluable subordinates whom to possess is a legitimate cause of boasting. Captain Mitchell plumed himself upon his eye for men – but he was not selfish – and in the innocence of his pride was already developing that mania for 'lending you my Capataz de Cargadores' which was to bring Nostromo into personal contact, sooner or later, with every European in Sulaco, as a sort of universal factotum – a prodigy of efficiency in his own sphere of life.

'The fellow is devoted to me, body and soul!' Captain Mitchell was given to affirm; and though nobody, perhaps, could have explained why it should be so, it was impossible on a survey of their relation to throw doubt on that statement, unless, indeed, one were a bitter, eccentric character like Dr Monygham – for instance – whose short, hopeless laugh expressed somehow an immense mistrust of mankind. Not that Dr Monygham was a prodigal either of laughter or of words. He was bitterly taciturn when at his best. At his worst people feared the open scornfulness of his tongue. Only Mrs Gould could keep his unbelief in men's motives within due bounds; but even to her (on an occasion not connected with Nostromo, and in a tone which for him was gentle), even to her, he had said once, 'Really, it is most unreasonable to demand that a man should think of other people so much better than he is able to think of himself.'

And Mrs Gould had hastened to drop the subject. There were strange rumours of the English doctor. Years ago, in the time of Guzman Bento, he had been mixed up, it was whispered, in a conspiracy which was betrayed and, as people expressed it, drowned in blood. His hair had turned grey, his hairless, seamed face was of a brick-dust colour; the large check pattern of his flannel shirt and his old stained Panama hat were an established defiance to the conventionalities of Sulaco. Had it not been for the immaculate cleanliness of his apparel he might have been taken for one of those shiftless Europeans that are a moral eyesore to the respectability of a foreign colony in almost every exotic part of the world. The young ladies of Sulaco, adorning with clusters of pretty faces the balconies along the Street of the Constitution, when they saw him pass, with his limping gait and bowed head, a short linen jacket drawn on carelessly over the flannel check shirt, would remark to each other, 'Here is the Señor doctor going to call on Doña Emilia. He has got his little coat on.' The inference was true. Its deeper meaning was hidden from their simple intelligence. Moreover, they expended no store of thought on the doctor. He was old, ugly, learned – and a little 'loco' – mad, if not a bit of a sorcerer, as the common people suspected him of being. The little white jacket was in reality a concession to Mrs Gould's humanising influence. The doctor, with his habit of sceptical, bitter speech, had no other means of showing his profound respect for the character of the woman who was known in the country as the English Señora. He presented this tribute very seriously indeed; it was no trifle for a man of his habits. Mrs Gould felt that, too, perfectly. She would never have thought of imposing upon him this marked show of deference.

She kept her old Spanish house (one of the finest specimens in Sulaco) open for the dispensation of the small graces of existence. She dispensed them with simplicity and charm because she was guided by an alert perception of values. She was highly gifted in the art of human intercourse which consists in delicate shades of self-forgetfulness and in the suggestion of universal comprehension. Charles Gould (the Gould family, established in Costaguana for three generations, always went to England for their education and for their wives) imagined that he had fallen in love with a girl's sound common sense like any other man, but these were not exactly the reasons why, for instance, the whole surveying camp, from the youngest of the young men to their mature chief, should have found occasion to allude to Mrs Gould's house so frequently amongst the high peaks of the Sierra. She would have protested that she had done nothing for them, with a low laugh and a surprised widening of her grey eyes, had anybody told her how convincingly she was remembered on the edge of the snow-line above Sulaco. But directly, with a little capable air of setting her wits to work, she would have found an explanation. 'Of course, it was such a surprise for these boys to find any sort of welcome here. And I suppose they are homesick. I suppose everybody must be always just a little homesick.'

She was always sorry for homesick people.

Born in the country, as his father before him, spare and tall, with a flaming moustache, a neat chin, clear blue eyes, auburn hair, and a thin, fresh, red face, Charles Gould looked like a new arrival from over the sea. His grandfather had fought in the cause of independence under Bolívar, in that famous English legion which on the battlefield of Carabobo had been saluted by the great Liberator as Saviours of his country. One of Charles Gould's uncles had been the elected President of that very province of Sulaco (then called a State) in the days of Federation, and afterwards had been put up against the wall of a church and shot by the order of the barbarous Unionist general, Guzman Bento. It was the same Guzman Bento who, becoming later Perpetual President, famed for his ruthless and cruel tyranny, reached his apotheosis in the popular legend of a sanguinary land-haunting spectre whose body had been carried off by the devil in person from the brick mausoleum in the nave of the Church of Assumption in Sta Marta. Thus, at least, the priests explained its disappearance to the barefooted multitude that streamed in, awestruck, to gaze at the hole in the side of the ugly box of bricks before the great altar.

Guzman Bento of cruel memory had put to death great numbers of people besides Charles Gould's uncle; but with a relative martyred in the cause of aristocracy, the Sulaco Oligarchs (this was the phraseology of Guzman Bento's time; now they were called Blancos, and had given up the federal idea), which meant the families of pure Spanish descent, considered Charles as one of themselves. With such a family record, no one could be more of a Costaguanero than Don Carlos Gould; but his aspect was so characteristic that in the talk of common people he was just the Inglés – the Englishman of Sulaco. He looked more English than a casual tourist, a sort of heretic pilgrim, however, quite unknown in Sulaco. He looked more

English than the last arrived batch of young railway engineers, than anybody out of the hunting-field pictures in the numbers of *Punch* reaching his wife's drawing- room two months or so after date. It astonished you to hear him talk Spanish (Castillan, as the natives say) or the Indian dialect of the country-people so naturally. His accent had never been English; but there was something so indelible in all these ancestral Goulds – liberators, explorers, coffee planters, merchants, revolutionists – of Costaguana, that he, the only representative of the third generation in a continent possessing its own style of horsemanship, went on looking thoroughly English even on horseback. This is not said of him in the mocking spirit of the Llaneros – men of the great plains – who think that no one in the world knows how to sit a horse but themselves. Charles Gould, to use the suitably lofty phrase, rode like a centaur. Riding for him was not a special form of exercise; it was a natural faculty, as walking straight is to all men sound of mind and limb; but, all the same, when cantering beside the rutty ox-cart track to the mine he looked in his English clothes and with his imported saddlery as though he had come this moment to Costaguana at his easy swift *pasitrote*, straight out of some green meadow at the other side of the world.

His way would lie along the old Spanish road – the Camino Real of popular speech – the only remaining vestige of a fact and name left by that royalty old Giorgio Viola hated, and whose very shadow had departed from the land; for the big equestrian statue of Charles IV at the entrance of the Alameda, towering white against the trees, was only known to the folk from the country and to the beggars of the town that slept on the steps around the pedestal, as the Horse of Stone. The other Carlos, turning off to the left with a rapid clatter of hoofs on the disjointed pavement – Don Carlos Gould, in his English clothes, looked as incongruous, but much more at home than the kingly cavalier reining in his steed on the pedestal above the sleeping léperos, with his marble arm raised towards the marble rim of a plumed hat.

The weather-stained effigy of the mounted king, with its vague suggestion of a saluting gesture, seemed to present an inscrutable breast to the political changes which had robbed it of its very name; but neither did the other horseman, well known to the people, keen and alive on his well-shaped, slate-coloured beast with a white eye, wear his heart on the sleeve of his English coat. His mind preserved its steady poise as if sheltered in the passionless stability of private and public decencies at home in Europe. He accepted with a like calm the shocking manner in which the Sulaco ladies smothered their faces with pearl powder till they looked like white plaster casts with beautiful living eyes, the peculiar gossip of the town, and the continuous political changes, the constant 'saving of the country', which to his wife seemed a puerile and bloodthirsty game of murder and rapine played with terrible earnestness by depraved children. In the early days of her Costaguana life, the little lady used to clench her hands with exasperation at not being able to take the public affairs of the country as seriously as the incidental atrocity of methods deserved. She saw in them a comedy of naïve pretences, but hardly anything genuine except her own appalled indignation. Charles, very quiet and twisting his long moustaches, would decline to discuss them at all. Once, however, he observed to her gently: 'My dear, you seem to forget that I was born here.'

These few words made her pause as if they had been a sudden revelation. Perhaps the mere fact of being born in the country did make a difference. She had a great confidence in her husband; it had always been very great. He had struck her imagination from the first by his unsentimentalism, by that very quietude of mind which she had erected in her thought for a sign of perfect competency in the business of living. Don José Avellanos, their neighbour across the street, a statesman, a poet, a man of culture, who had represented his country at several European Courts (and had suffered untold indignities as a state prisoner in the time of the tyrant Guzman Bento), used to declare in Doña Emilia's drawing-room that Carlos had all the English qualities of character with a truly patriotic heart.

Mrs Gould, raising her eyes to her husband's thin, red and tan face, could not detect the slightest quiver of a feature at what he must have heard said of his patriotism. Perhaps he had just dismounted on his return from the mine; he was English enough to disregard the hottest hours of the day. Basilio, in a livery of white linen and a red sash, had squatted for a moment behind his heels to unstrap the heavy, blunt spurs in the patio; and then the Señor Administrator would go up the staircase into the gallery. Rows of plants in pots, ranged on the balustrade between the pilasters of the arches, screened the *corredor* with their leaves and flowers from the quadrangle below, whose paved space is the true hearthstone of a South American house, where the quiet hours of domestic life are marked by the shifting of light and shadow on the flagstones.

Señor Avellanos was in the habit of crossing the patio at five o'clock almost every day. Don José chose to come over at teatime because the English rite at Doña Emilia's house reminded him of the time he lived in London as Minister Plenipotentiary to the Court of St James. He did not like tea; and, usually, rocking his American chair, his neat little shiny boots crossed on the footrest, he would talk on and on with a sort of complacent virtuosity wonderful in a man of his age, while he held the cup in his hands for a long time. His close-cropped head was perfectly white; his eyes coal-black.

On seeing Charles Gould step into the sala he would nod provisionally and go on to the end of the oratorial period. Only then he would say: 'Carlos, my friend, you have ridden from San Tomé in the heat of the day. Always the true English activity. No? What?'

He drank up all the tea at once in one draught. This performance was invariably followed by a slight shudder and a low, involuntary 'br–r–r–r,' which was not covered by the hasty exclamation, 'Excellent!'

Then giving up the empty cup into his young friend's hand, extended with a smile, he continued to expatiate upon the patriotic nature of the San Tomé mine for the simple pleasure of talking fluently, it seemed, while his reclining body jerked backwards and forwards in a rocking-chair of the sort exported from the United States. The ceiling of the largest drawing-room of the Casa Gould extended its white level far above his head. The loftiness dwarfed the mixture of heavy, straight-backed Spanish chairs of brown wood with leathern seats, and European furniture, low, and cushioned all over, like squat little monsters gorged to bursting with steel springs and horsehair. There were knick-knacks on little tables, mirrors let into the wall above marble consoles, square spaces of carpet under the two groups of armchairs, each presided over by a deep sofa; smaller rugs scattered all over the floor of red tiles; three windows from ceiling down to the ground, opening on a balcony, and flanked by the perpendicular folds of the dark hangings. The stateliness of ancient days lingered between the four high, smooth walls, tinted a delicate primrose-colour; and Mrs Gould, with her little head and shining coils of hair, sitting in a cloud of muslin and lace before a slender mahogany table, resembled a fairy posed lightly before dainty philtres dispensed out of vessels of silver and porcelain.

Mrs Gould knew the history of the San Tomé mine. Worked in the early days mostly by means of lashes on the backs of slaves, its yield had been paid for in its own weight of human bones. Whole tribes of Indians had perished in the exploitation; and then the mine was abandoned, since with this primitive method it had ceased to make a profitable return, no matter how many corpses were thrown into its maw. Then it became forgotten. It was rediscovered after the War of Independence. An English company obtained the right to work it, and found so rich a vein that neither the exactions of successive governments, nor the periodical raids of recruiting officers upon the population of paid miners they had created, could discourage their perseverance. But in the end, during the long turmoil of pronunciamentos that followed the death of the famous Guzman Bento, the native miners, incited to revolt by the emissaries sent out from the capital, had risen upon their English chiefs and murdered them to a man. The decree of confiscation which appeared immediately afterwards in the *Diario Official*, published in Sta Marta, began with the words: 'Justly incensed at the grinding oppression of foreigners, actuated by sordid motives of gain rather than by love for a country where they come impoverished to seek their fortunes, the mining population of San Tomé, etc . . . ' and ended with the declaration: 'The chief of the State has resolved to exercise to the full his power of clemency. The mine, which by every law, international, human, and divine, reverts now to the Government as national property, shall remain closed till the sword drawn for the sacred defence of liberal principles has accomplished its mission of securing the happiness of our beloved country.'

And for many years this was the last of the San Tomé mine. What advantage that Government had expected from the spoliation, it is impossible to tell now. Costaguana was made with difficulty to pay a beggarly money compensation to the families of the victims, and then the matter dropped out of diplomatic despatches. But afterwards another Government bethought itself of that valuable asset. It was an ordinary Costaguana Government – the fourth in six years – but it judged of its opportunities sanely. It remembered the San Tomé mine with a secret conviction of its worthlessness in their own hands, but with an ingenious insight into the various uses a silver mine can be put to, apart from the sordid process of extracting the metal from under the ground. The father of Charles Gould, for a long time one of the most wealthy merchants of Costaguana, had already lost a considerable part of his fortune in forced loans to the successive Governments. He was a man of calm judgment, who never dreamed of pressing his claims; and when, suddenly, the perpetual concession of the San Tomé mine was offered to him in full settlement, his alarm became extreme. He was versed in the ways of Governments. Indeed, the intention of this affair, though no doubt deeply meditated in the closet, lay open on the surface of the document presented urgently for his signature. The third and most important clause stipulated that the concession-holder should pay at once to the Government five years' royalties on the estimated output of the mine.

Mr Gould, senior, defended himself from this fatal favour with many arguments and entreaties, but without success. He knew nothing of mining; he had no means to put his concession on the European market; the mine as a working concern did not exist. The buildings had been burnt down, the mining plant had been destroyed, the mining population had disappeared from the neighbourhood years and years ago; the very road had vanished under a flood of tropical vegetation as effectually as if swallowed by the sea; and the main gallery had fallen in within a hundred yards from the entrance. It was no longer an abandoned mine; it was a wild, inaccessible, and rocky gorge of the Sierra, where vestiges of charred timber, some heaps of smashed bricks, and a few shapeless pieces of rusty iron could have been found under the matted mass of thorny creepers covering the ground. Mr Gould, senior, did not desire the perpetual possession of that desolate locality; in fact, the mere vision of it arising before his mind in the still watches of the night had the power to exasperate him into hours of hot and agitated insomnia.

It so happened, however, that the Finance Minister of the time was a man to whom, in years gone by, Mr Gould had, unfortunately, declined to grant some small pecuniary assistance, basing his refusal on the ground that the applicant was a notorious gambler and cheat, besides being more than half suspected of a robbery with violence on a wealthy ranchero in a remote country district, where he was actually exercising the function of a judge. Now, after reaching his exalted position, that politician had proclaimed his intention to repay evil with good to Señor Gould – the poor man. He affirmed and reaffirmed this resolution in the drawing-rooms of Sta Marta,

in a soft and implacable voice, and with such malicious glances that Mr
Gould's best friends advised him earnestly to attempt no bribery to get the
matter dropped. It would have been useless. Indeed, it would not have been
a very safe proceeding. Such was also the opinion of a stout, loud-voiced
lady of French extraction, the daughter, she said, of an officer of high rank
(*officier supérieur de l'armée*), who was accommodated with lodgings within
the walls of a secularised convent next door to the Ministry of Finance. That
florid person, when approached on behalf of Mr Gould in a proper manner,
and with a suitable present, shook her head despondently. She was good-
natured, and her despondency was genuine. She imagined she could not take
money in consideration of something she could not accomplish. The friend
of Mr Gould, charged with the delicate mission, used to say afterwards that
she was the only honest person closely or remotely connected with the
Government he had ever met. 'No go,' she had said with a cavalier, husky
intonation which was natural to her, and using turns of expression more
suitable to a child of parents unknown than to the orphaned daughter of a
general officer. 'No; it's no go. Pas moyen, mon garçon. C'est dommage,
tout de même. Ah! zut! Je ne vole pas mon monde. Je ne suis pas ministre –
moi! Vous pouvez emporter votre petit sac.'

For a moment, biting her carmine lip, she deplored inwardly the tyranny
of the rigid principles governing the sale of her influence in high places.
Then, significantly, and with a touch of impatience, 'Allez,' she added, 'et
dites bien à votre bonhomme – entendez-vous? – qu'il faut avaler la pilule.'

After such a warning there was nothing for it but to sign and pay. Mr Gould
had swallowed the pill, and it was as though it had been compounded of some
subtle poison that acted directly on his brain. He became at once mine-ridden,
and as he was well read in light literature it took to his mind the form of the
Old Man of the Sea fastened upon his shoulders. He also began to dream of
vampires. Mr Gould exaggerated to himself the disadvantages of his new
position, because he viewed it emotionally. His position in Costaguana was no
worse than before. But man is a desperately conservative creature, and the
extravagant novelty of this outrage upon his purse distressed his sensibilities.
Everybody around him was being robbed by the grotesque and murderous
bands that played their game of governments and revolutions after the death of
Guzman Bento. His experience had taught him that, however short the
plunder might fall of their legitimate expectations, no gang in possession of
the Presidential Palace would be so incompetent as to suffer itself to be baffled
by the want of a pretext. The first casual colonel of the barefooted army of
scarecrows that came along was able to expose with force and precision to any
mere civilian his titles to a sum of 10,000 dollars; the while his hope would be
immutably fixed upon a gratuity, at any rate, of no less than a thousand. Mr
Gould knew that very well, and, armed with resignation, had waited for better
times. But to be robbed under the forms of legality and business was
intolerable to his imagination. Mr Gould, the father, had one fault in his

sagacious and honourable character: he attached too much importance to form. It is a failing common to mankind, whose views are tinged by prejudices. There was for him in that affair a malignancy of perverted justice which, by means of a moral shock, attacked his vigorous physique. 'It will end by killing me,' he used to affirm many times a day. And, in fact, since that time he began to suffer from fever, from liver pains, and mostly from a worrying inability to think of anything else. The Finance Minister could have formed no conception of the profound subtlety of his revenge. Even Mr Gould's letters to his fourteen-year-old boy Charles, then away in England for his education, came at last to talk of practically nothing but the mine. He groaned over the injustice, the persecution, the outrage of that mine; he occupied whole pages in the exposition of the fatal consequences attaching to the possession of that mine from every point of view, with every dismal inference, with words of horror at the apparently eternal character of that curse. For the Concession had been granted to him and his descendants for ever. He implored his son never to return to Costaguana, never to claim any part of his inheritance there, because it was tainted by the infamous Concession; never to touch it, never to approach it, to forget that America existed, and pursue a mercantile career in Europe. And each letter ended with bitter self-reproaches for having stayed too long in that cavern of thieves, intriguers, and brigands.

To be told repeatedly that one's future is blighted because of the possession of a silver mine is not, at the age of fourteen, a matter of prime importance as to its main statement; but in its form it is calculated to excite a certain amount of wonder and attention. In course of time the boy, at first only puzzled by the angry jeremiads, but rather sorry for his dad, began to turn the matter over in his mind in such moments as he could spare from play and study. In about a year he had evolved from the lecture of the letters a definite conviction that there was a silver mine in the Sulaco province of the Republic of Costaguana, where poor Uncle Harry had been shot by soldiers a great many years before. There was also connected closely with that mine a thing called the 'iniquitous Gould Concession', apparently written on a paper which his father desired ardently to 'tear and fling into the faces' of presidents, members of judicature, and ministers of State. And this desire persisted, though the names of these people, he noticed, seldom remained the same for a whole year together. This desire (since the thing was iniquitous) seemed quite natural to the boy, though why the affair was iniquitous he did not know. Afterwards, with advancing wisdom, he managed to clear the plain truth of the business from the fantastic intrusions of the Old Man of the Sea, vampires, and ghouls, which had lent to his father's correspondence the flavour of a gruesome Arabian Nights tale. In the end, the growing youth attained to as close an intimacy with the San Tomé mine as the old man who wrote these plaintive and enraged letters on the other side of the sea. He had been made several times already to pay heavy fines for neglecting to work the mine, he reported, besides other sums extracted from him on account of future royalties, on the ground that a man with such a valuable concession in his pocket could not refuse his financial assistance to the Government of the Republic. The last of his fortune was passing away from him against worthless receipts, he wrote, in a rage, whilst he was being pointed out as an individual who had known how to secure enormous advantages from the necessities of his country. And the young man in Europe grew more and more interested in that thing which could provoke such a tumult of words and passion.

He thought of it every day; but he thought of it without bitterness. It might have been an unfortunate affair for his poor dad, and the whole story threw a queer light upon the social and political life of Costaguana. The view he took of it was sympathetic to his father, yet calm and reflective. His personal feelings had not been outraged, and it is difficult to resent with proper and durable indignation the physical or mental anguish of another organism, even if that other organism is one's own father. By the time he was twenty Charles Gould had, in his turn, fallen under the spell of the San Tomé mine. But it was another form of enchantment, more suitable to his youth, into whose magic formula there entered hope, vigour, and self-confidence, instead of weary indignation and despair. Left after he was twenty to his own guidance (except for the severe injunction not to return to Costaguana), he had pursued his studies in Belgium and France with the idea of qualifying for a mining engineer. But this scientific aspect of his labours remained vague and imperfect in his mind. Mines had acquired for him a dramatic interest. He studied their peculiarities from a personal point of view, too, as one would study the varied characters of men. He visited them as one goes with curiosity to call upon remarkable persons. He visited mines in Germany, in Spain, in Cornwall. Abandoned workings had for him strong fascination. Their desolation appealed to him like the sight of human misery, whose causes are varied and profound. They might have been worthless, but also they might have been misunderstood. His future wife was the first, and perhaps the only person to detect this secret mood which governed the profoundly sensible, almost voiceless attitude of this man towards the world of material things. And at once her delight in him, lingering with half-open wings like those birds that cannot rise easily from a flat level, found a pinnacle from which to soar up into the skies.

They had become acquainted in Italy, where the future Mrs Gould was staying with an old and pale aunt who, years before, had married a middle-aged, impoverished Italian marquis. She now mourned that man, who had known how to give up his life to the independence and unity of his country, who had known how to be as enthusiastic in his generosity as the youngest of those who fell for that very cause of which old Giorgio Viola was a drifting relic, as a broken spar is suffered to float away disregarded after a naval victory. The Marchesa led a still, whispering existence, nunlike in her black robes and a white band over the forehead, in a corner of the first floor of an ancient and ruinous palace, whose big, empty halls downstairs sheltered under their painted ceilings the harvests, the fowls, and even the cattle, together with the whole family of the tenant farmer.

The two young people had met in Lucca. After that meeting Charles Gould visited no mines, though they went together in a carriage, once, to see some marble quarries, where the work resembled mining in so far that it also was the tearing of the raw material of treasure from the earth. Charles Gould did not open his heart to her in any set speeches. He simply went on acting and thinking in her sight. This is the true method of sincerity. One of his frequent remarks was, 'I think sometimes that poor father takes a wrong view of that San Tomé business.' And they discussed that opinion long and earnestly, as if they could influence a mind across half the globe; but in reality they discussed it because the sentiment of love can enter into any subject and live ardently in remote phrases. For this natural reason these discussions were precious to Mrs Gould in her engaged state. Charles feared that Mr Gould, senior, was wasting his strength and making himself ill by his efforts to get rid of the Concession. 'I fancy that this is not the kind of handling it requires,' he mused aloud, as if to himself.

And when she wondered frankly that a man of character should devote his energies to plotting and intrigues, Charles would remark, with a gentle concern that understood her wonder, 'You must not forget that he was born there.'

She would set her quick mind to work upon that, and then make the inconsequent retort, which he accepted as perfectly sagacious, because, in fact, it was so: 'Well, and you? You were born there, too.'

He knew his answer.

'That's different. I've been away ten years. Dad never had such a long spell; and it was more than thirty years ago.'

She was the first person to whom he opened his lips after receiving the news of his father's death.

'It has killed him!' he said.

He had walked straight out of town with the news, straight out before him in the noonday sun on the white road, and his feet had brought him face to face with her in the hall of the ruined palazzo, a room magnificent and naked, with here and there a long strip of damask, black with damp and age, hanging down on a bare panel of the wall. It was furnished with exactly one gilt armchair, with a broken back, and an octagon columnar stand bearing a heavy marble vase ornamented with sculptured masks and garlands of flowers, and cracked from top to bottom. Charles Gould was dusty with the white dust of the road lying on his boots, on his shoulders, on his cap with two peaks. Water dripped from under it all over his face, and he grasped a thick oaken cudgel in his bare right hand.

She went very pale under the roses of her big straw hat, gloved, swinging a clear sunshade, caught just as she was going out to meet him at the bottom of the hill, where three poplars stand near the wall of a vineyard.

'It has killed him!' he repeated. 'He ought to have had many years yet. We are a long-lived family.'

She was too startled to say anything; he was contemplating with a penetrating and motionless stare the cracked marble urn as though he had resolved to fix its shape for ever in his memory. It was only when, turning suddenly to her, he blurted out twice, 'I've come to you – I've come straight to you – ' without being able to finish his phrase, that the great pitifulness of that lonely and tormented death in Costaguana came to her with the full force of its misery. He caught hold of her hand, raised it to his lips, and at that she dropped her parasol to pat him on the cheek, murmured 'Poor boy,' and began to dry her eyes under the downward curve of her hat-brim, very small in her simple, white frock, almost like a lost child crying in the degraded grandeur of the noble hall, while he stood by her, again perfectly motionless in the contemplation of the marble urn.

Afterwards they went out for a long walk, which was silent till he exclaimed suddenly: 'Yes. But if he had only grappled with it in a proper way!'

And then they stopped. Everywhere there were long shadows lying on the hills, on the roads, on the enclosed fields of olive trees; the shadows of poplars, of wide chestnuts, of farm buildings, of stone walls; and in mid-air the sound of a bell, thin and alert, was like the throbbing pulse of the sunset glow. Her lips were slightly parted as though in surprise that he should not be looking at her with his usual expression. His usual expression was unconditionally approving and attentive. He was in his talks with her the most anxious and deferential of dictators, an attitude that pleased her immensely. It affirmed her power without detracting from his dignity. That slight girl, with her little feet, little hands, little face attractively overweighted by great coils of hair; with a rather large mouth, whose mere parting seemed to breathe upon you the fragrance of frankness and generosity, had the fastidious soul of an experienced woman. She was, before all things and all flatteries, careful of her pride in the object of her choice. But now he was actually not looking at her at all; and his expression was tense and irrational, as is natural in a man who elects to stare at nothing past a young girl's head.

'Well, yes. It was iniquitous. They corrupted him thoroughly, the poor old boy. Oh! why wouldn't he let me go back to him? But now I shall know how to grapple with this.'

After pronouncing these words with immense assurance, he glanced down at her, and at once fell a prey to distress, incertitude, and fear.

The only thing he wanted to know now, he said, was whether she did love him enough – whether she would have the courage to go with him so far away? He put these questions to her in a voice that trembled with anxiety – for he was a determined man.

She did. She would. And immediately the future hostess of all the Europeans in Sulaco had the physical experience of the earth falling away from under her. It vanished completely, even to the very sound of the bell. When her feet touched the ground again, the bell was still ringing in the valley; she put her hands up to her hair, breathing quickly, and glanced up and down the stony lane. It was reassuringly empty. Meantime, Charles, stepping with one foot into a dry and dusty ditch, picked up the open parasol, which had bounded away from them with a martial sound of drum taps. He handed it to her soberly, a little crestfallen.

They turned back, and after she had slipped her hand on his arm, the first words he pronounced were: 'It's lucky that we shall be able to settle in a coast town. You've heard its name. It is Sulaco. I am so glad poor father did get that house. He bought a big house there years ago, in order that there should always be a Casa Gould in the principal town of what used to be called the Occidental Province. I lived there once, as a small boy, with my dear mother, for a whole year, while poor father was away in the United States on business. You shall be the new mistress of the Casa Gould.'

And later, in the inhabited corner of the Palazzo above the vineyards, the marble hills, the pines and olives of Lucca, he also said: 'The name of Gould has been always highly respected in Sulaco. My uncle Harry was chief of the State for some time, and has left a great name amongst the first families. By this I mean the pure Creole families, who take no part in the miserable farce of governments. Uncle Harry was no adventurer. In Costaguana we Goulds are no adventurers. He was of the country, and he loved it, but he remained essentially an Englishman in his ideas. He made use of the political cry of his time. It was Federation. But he was no politician. He simply stood up for social order out of pure love for rational liberty and from his hate of oppression. There was no nonsense about him. He went to work in his own way because it seemed right, just as I feel I must lay hold of that mine.'

In such words he talked to her because his memory was very full of the country of his childhood, his heart of his life with that girl, and his mind of the San Tomé Concession. He added that he would have to leave her for a few days to find an American, a man from San Francisco, who was still somewhere in Europe. A few months before he had made his acquaintance in an old historic German town, situated in a mining district. The American had his womankind with him, but seemed lonely while they were sketching all day long the old doorways and the turreted corners of the mediaeval houses. Charles Gould had with him the inseparable companionship of the mine. The other man was interested in mining enterprises, knew something of Costaguana, and was no stranger to the name of Gould. They had talked together with some intimacy which was made possible by the difference of their ages. Charles wanted now to find that capitalist of shrewd mind and accessible character. His father's fortune in Costaguana, which he had supposed to be still considerable, seemed to have melted in the rascally crucible of revolutions. Apart from some ten thousand pounds deposited in England, there appeared to be nothing left except the house in Sulaco, a vague right of forest exploitation in a remote and savage district, and the San

Tomé Concession, which had attended his poor father to the very brink of the grave.

He explained those things. It was late when they parted. She had never before given him such a fascinating vision of herself. All the eagerness of youth for a strange life, for great distances, for a future in which there was an air of adventure, of combat – a subtle thought of redress and conquest, had filled her with an intense excitement, which she returned to the giver with a more open and exquisite display of tenderness.

He left her to walk down the hill, and directly he found himself alone he became sober. That irreparable change a death makes in the course of our daily thoughts can be felt in a vague and poignant discomfort of mind. It hurt Charles Gould to feel that never more, by no effort of will, would he be able to think of his father in the same way he used to think of him when the poor man was alive. His breathing image was no longer in his power. This consideration, closely affecting his own identity, filled his breast with a mournful and angry desire for action. In this his instinct was unerring. Action is consolatory. It is the enemy of thought and the friend of flattering illusions. Only in the conduct of our action can we find the sense of mastery over the Fates. For his action, the mine was obviously the only field. It was imperative sometimes to know how to disobey the solemn wishes of the dead. He resolved firmly to make his disobedience as thorough (by way of atonement) as it well could be. The mine had been the cause of an absurd moral disaster; its working must be made a serious and moral success. He owed it to the dead man's memory. Such were the – properly speaking – emotions of Charles Gould. His thoughts ran upon the means of raising a large amount of capital in San Francisco or elsewhere; and incidentally there occurred to him also the general reflection that the counsel of the departed must be an unsound guide. Not one of them could be aware beforehand what enormous changes the death of any given individual may produce in the very aspect of the world.

The latest phase in the history of the mine Mrs Gould knew from personal experience. It was in essence the history of her married life. The mantle of the Goulds' hereditary position in Sulaco had descended amply upon her little person; but she would not allow the peculiarities of the strange garment to weigh down the vivacity of her character, which was the sign of no mere mechanical sprightliness, but of an eager intelligence. It must not be supposed that Mrs Gould's mind was masculine. A woman with a masculine mind is not a being of superior efficiency; she is simply a phenomenon of imperfect differentiation – interestingly barren and without importance. Doña Emilia's intelligence being feminine led her to achieve the conquest of Sulaco, simply by lighting the way for her unselfishness and sympathy. She could converse charmingly, but she was not talkative. The wisdom of the heart having no concern with the erection or demolition of theories any more than with the defence of prejudices, has no random words at its command. The words it pronounces have the value of acts of integrity, tolerance, and compassion. A woman's true tenderness, like the true virility of man, is expressed in action of a conquering kind. The ladies of Sulaco adored Mrs Gould. 'They still look upon me as something of a monster,' Mrs Gould had said pleasantly to one of the three gentlemen from San Francisco she had to entertain in her new Sulaco house just about a year after her marriage.

They were her first visitors from abroad, and they had come to look at the San Tomé mine. She jested most agreeably, they thought; and Charles Gould, besides knowing thoroughly what he was about, had shown himself a real hustler. These facts caused them to be well disposed towards his wife. An unmistakable enthusiasm, pointed by a slight flavour of irony, made her talk of the mine absolutely fascinating to her visitors, and provoked them to grave and indulgent smiles in which there was a good deal of deference. Perhaps had they known how much she was inspired by an idealistic view of success they would have been amazed at the state of her mind as the Spanish-American ladies had been amazed at the tireless activity of her body. She would – in her own words – have been for them 'something of a monster'. However, the Goulds were in essentials a reticent couple, and their guests departed without the suspicion of any other purpose but simple profit in the working of a silver mine. Mrs Gould had out her own carriage, with two white mules, to drive them down to the harbour, whence the *Ceres* was to carry them off into the Olympus of plutocrats. Captain Mitchell had snatched at the occasion of leave-taking to remark to Mrs Gould, in a low, confidential mutter, 'This marks an epoch.'

Mrs Gould loved the patio of her Spanish house. A broad flight of stone steps was overlooked silently from a niche in the wall by a Madonna in blue robes with the crowned child sitting on her arm. Subdued voices ascended in the early mornings from the paved well of the quadrangle, with the stamping of horses and mules led out in pairs to drink at the cistern. A tangle of slender bamboo stems drooped its narrow, bladelike leaves over the square pool of water, and the fat coachman sat muffled up on the edge, holding lazily the ends of halters in his hand. Barefooted servants passed to and fro, issuing from dark, low doorways below; two laundry girls with baskets of washed linen; the baker with the tray of bread made for the day; Leonarda – her own camerista – bearing high up, swung from her hand raised above her raven black head, a bunch of starched underskirts dazzlingly white in the slant of sunshine. Then the old porter would hobble in, sweeping the flagstones, and the house was ready for the day. All the lofty rooms on three sides of the quadrangle opened into each other and into the *corredor*, with its wrought-iron railings and a border of flowers, whence, like the lady of the mediaeval castle, she could witness from above all the departures and arrivals of the Casa, to which the sonorous arched gateway lent an air of stately importance.

She had watched her carriage roll away with the three guests from the north. She smiled. Their three arms went up simultaneously to their three hats. Captain Mitchell, the fourth, in attendance, had already begun a pompous discourse. Then she lingered. She lingered, approaching her face to the clusters of flowers here and there as if to give time to her thoughts to catch up with her slow footsteps along the straight vista of the corridor.

A fringed Indian hammock from Aroa, gay with coloured featherwork, had been swung judiciously in a corner that caught the early sun; for the mornings are cool in Sulaco. The cluster of *flor de noche buena* blazed in great masses before the open glass doors of the reception rooms. A big green parrot, brilliant like an emerald in a cage that flashed like gold, screamed out ferociously, 'Vive Costaguana!' then called twice mellifluously, 'Leonarda! Leonarda!' in imitation of Mrs Gould's voice, and suddenly took refuge in immobility and silence. Mrs Gould reached the end of the gallery and put her head through the door of her husband's room.

Charles Gould, with one foot on a low wooden stool, was already strapping his spurs. He wanted to hurry back to the mine. Mrs Gould, without coming in, glanced about the room. One tall, broad bookcase, with glass doors, was full of books; but in the other, without shelves, and lined with red baize, were arranged firearms: Winchester carbines, revolvers, a couple of shotguns, and even two pairs of double-barrelled holster pistols. Between them, by itself, upon a strip of scarlet velvet, hung an old cavalry sabre, once the property of Don Enrique Gould, the hero of the Occidental Province, presented by Don José Avellanos, the hereditary friend of the family.

Otherwise, the plastered white walls were completely bare, except for a watercolour sketch of the San Tomé mountain – the work of Doña Emilia herself. In the middle of the red-tiled floor stood two long tables littered with plans and papers, a few chairs, and a glass showcase containing specimens of ore from the mine. Mrs Gould, looking at all these things in turn, wondered aloud why the talk of these wealthy and enterprising men discussing the prospects, the working, and the safety of the mine rendered her so impatient and uneasy, whereas she could talk of the mine by the hour with her husband with unwearied interest and satisfaction.

And dropping her eyelids expressively, she added: 'What do *you* feel about it, Charley?'

Then, surprised at her husband's silence, she raised her eyes, opened wide, as pretty as pale flowers. He had done with the spurs, and, twisting his moustache with both hands, horizontally, he contemplated her from the height of his long legs with a visible appreciation of her appearance. The consciousness of being thus contemplated pleased Mrs Gould.

'They are considerable men,' he said.

'I know. But have you listened to their conversation? They don't seem to have understood anything they have seen here.'

'They have seen the mine. They have understood that to some purpose,'

Charles Gould interjected, in defence of the visitors; and then his wife mentioned the name of the most considerable of the three. He was considerable in finance and in industry. His name was familiar to many millions of people. He was so considerable that he would never have travelled so far away from the centre of his activity if the doctors had not insisted, with veiled menaces, on his taking a long holiday.

'Mr Holroyd's sense of religion,' Mrs Gould pursued, 'was shocked and disgusted at the tawdriness of the dressed-up saints in the cathedral – the worship, he called it, of wood and tinsel. But it seemed to me that he looked upon his own God as a sort of influential partner, who gets his share of profits in the endowment of churches. That's a sort of idolatry. He told me he endowed churches every year, Charley.'

'No end of them,' said Mr Gould, marvelling inwardly at the mobility of her physiognomy. 'All over the country. He's famous for that sort of munificence.'

'Oh, he didn't boast,' Mrs Gould declared, scrupulously. 'I believe he's really a good man, but so stupid! A poor Cholo who offers a little silver arm or leg to thank his god for a cure is as rational and more touching.'

'He's at the head of immense silver and iron interests,' Charles Gould observed.

'Ah, yes! The religion of silver and iron. He's a very civil man, though he looked awfully solemn when he first saw the Madonna on the staircase, who's only wood and paint; but he said nothing to me. My dear Charley, I heard those men talk among themselves. Can it be that they really wish to become, for an immense consideration, drawers of water and hewers of wood to all the countries and nations of the earth?'

'A man must work to some end,' Charles Gould said, vaguely.

Mrs Gould, frowning, surveyed him from head to foot. With his riding breeches, leather leggings (an article of apparel never before seen in Costaguana), a Norfolk coat of grey flannel, and those great flaming moustaches, he suggested an officer of cavalry turned gentleman farmer. This combination was gratifying to Mrs Gould's tastes. 'How thin the poor boy is!' she thought. 'He overworks himself.' But there was no denying that his fine-drawn, keen red face, and his whole, long-limbed, lank person had an air of breeding and distinction. And Mrs Gould relented.

'I only wondered what you felt,' she murmured, gently.

During the last few days, as it happened, Charles Gould had been kept too busy thinking twice before he spoke to have paid much attention to the state of his feelings. But theirs was a successful match, and he had no difficulty in finding his answer.

'The best of my feelings are in your keeping, my dear,' he said, lightly; and there was so much truth in that obscure phrase that he experienced towards her at the moment a great increase of gratitude and tenderness.

Mrs Gould, however, did not seem to find this answer in the least obscure. She brightened up delicately; already he had changed his tone.

'But there are facts. The worth of the mine – as a mine – is beyond doubt. It shall make us very wealthy. The mere working of it is a matter of technical knowledge, which I have – which ten thousand other men in the world have. But its safety, its continued existence as an enterprise, giving a return to men – to strangers, comparative strangers – who invest money in it, is left altogether in my hands. I have inspired confidence in a man of wealth and position. You seem to think this perfectly natural – do you? Well, I don't know. I don't know why I have; but it is a fact. This fact makes everything possible, because without it I would never have thought of disregarding my father's wishes. I would never have disposed of the Concession as a speculator disposes of a valuable right to a company – for cash and shares, to grow rich eventually if possible, but at any rate to put some money at once in his pocket. No. Even if it had been feasible – which I doubt – I would not have done so. Poor father did not understand. He was afraid I would hang on to the ruinous thing, waiting for just some such chance, and waste my life miserably. That was the true sense of his prohibition, which we have deliberately set aside.'

They were walking up and down the corridor. Her head just reached to his shoulder. His arm, extended downwards, was about her waist. His spurs jingled slightly.

'He had not seen me for ten years. He did not know me. He parted from me for my sake, and he would never let me come back. He was always talking in his letters of leaving Costaguana, of abandoning everything and making his escape. But he was too valuable a prey. They would have thrown him into one of their prisons at the first suspicion.'

His spurred feet clinked slowly. He was bending over his wife as they walked. The big parrot, turning its head askew, followed their pacing figures with a round, unblinking eye.

'He was a lonely man. Ever since I was ten years old he used to talk to me as if I had been grown up. When I was in Europe he wrote to me every month. Ten, twelve pages every month of my life for ten years. And, after all, he did not know me! Just think of it – ten whole years away; the years I was growing up into a man. He could not know me. Do you think he could?'

Mrs Gould shook her head negatively; which was just what her husband had expected from the strength of the argument. But she shook her head negatively only because she thought that no one could know her Charles – really know him for what he was but herself. The thing was obvious. It could be felt. It required no argument. And poor Mr Gould, senior, who had died too soon to ever hear of their engagement, remained too shadowy a figure for her to be credited with knowledge of any sort whatever.

'No, he did not understand. In my view this mine could never have been a thing to sell. Never! After all his misery I simply could not have touched it for money alone,' Charles Gould pursued: and she pressed her head to his shoulder approvingly.

These two young people remembered the life which had ended wretchedly just when their own lives had come together in that splendour of hopeful love, which to the most sensible minds appears like a triumph of good over all the evils of the earth. A vague idea of rehabilitation had entered the plan of their life. That it was so vague as to elude the support of argument made it only the stronger. It had presented itself to them at the instant when the woman's instinct of devotion and the man's instinct of activity receive from the strongest of illusions their most powerful impulse. The very prohibition imposed the necessity of success. It was as if they had been morally bound to make good their vigorous view of life against the unnatural error of weariness and despair. If the idea of wealth was present to them it was only so far as it was bound with that other success. Mrs Gould, an orphan from early childhood and without fortune, brought up in an atmosphere of intellectual interests, had never considered the aspects of great wealth. They were too remote, and she had not learned that they were desirable. On the other hand, she had not known anything of absolute want. Even the very poverty of her aunt, the Marchesa, had nothing intolerable to a refined mind; it seemed in accord with a great grief: it had the austerity of a sacrifice offered to a noble ideal. Thus even the most legitimate touch of materialism was wanting in Mrs Gould's character. The dead man of whom she thought with tenderness (because he was Charley's father) and with some impatience (because he had been weak), must be put completely in the wrong. Nothing else would do to keep their prosperity without a stain on its only real, on its immaterial side!

Charles Gould, on his part, had been obliged to keep the idea of wealth well to the fore; but he brought it forward as a means, not as an end. Unless the mine was good business it could not be touched. He had to insist on that aspect of the enterprise. It was his lever to move men who had capital. And Charles Gould believed in the mine. He knew everything that could be known of it. His faith in the mine was contagious, though it was not served by a great eloquence; but business men are frequently as sanguine and imaginative as lovers. They are affected by a personality much oftener than people would suppose; and Charles Gould, in his unshaken assurance, was absolutely convincing. Besides, it was a matter of common knowledge to the men to whom he addressed himself that mining in Costaguana was a game that could be made considerably more than worth the candle. The men of affairs knew that very well. The real difficulty in touching it was elsewhere. Against that there was an implication of calm and implacable resolution in Charles Gould's very voice. Men of affairs venture sometimes on acts that the common judgment of the world would pronounce absurd; they make their decisions on apparently impulsive and human grounds. 'Very well,' had said the considerable personage to whom Charles Gould on his way out through San Francisco had lucidly exposed his point of view. 'Let us suppose that the mining affairs of Sulaco are taken in hand. There would then be in it: first, the house of Holroyd, which is all right; then, Mr Charles Gould, a citizen of Costaguana, who is also all right, and, lastly, the Government of the Republic. So far this resembles the first start of the Atacama nitrate fields, where there was a financing house, a gentleman of the name of Edwards, and – a Government; or, rather, two Governments – two South American Governments. And you know what came of it. War came of it; devastating and prolonged war came of it, Mr Gould. However, here we possess the advantage of having only one South American Government hanging around for plunder out of the deal. It is an advantage; but then there are degrees of badness, and that Government is the Costaguana Government.'

Thus spoke the considerable personage, the millionaire endower of churches on a scale befitting the greatness of his native land – the same to whom the doctors used the language of horrid and veiled menaces. He was a big-limbed, deliberate man, whose quiet burliness lent to an ample silk-faced frock-coat a superfine dignity. His hair was iron grey, his eyebrows were still black, and his massive profile was the profile of a Caesar's head on an old Roman coin. But his parentage was German and Scotch and English, with remote strains of Danish and French blood, giving him the temperament of a Puritan and an insatiable imagination of conquest. He was completely unbending to his visitor, because of the warm introduction the visitor had brought from Europe, and because of liking for earnestness and determination wherever met, to whatever end directed.

'The Costaguana Government shall play its hand for all it's worth – and don't you forget it, Mr Gould. Now; what is Costaguana? It is the bottomless pit of 10 per cent loans and other fool investments. European capital has been flung into it with both hands for years. Not ours, though. We in this country know just about enough to keep indoors when it rains. We can sit and watch. Of course, someday we shall step in. We are bound to. But there's no hurry. Time itself has got to wait on the greatest country in the whole of God's Universe. We shall be giving the word for everything: industry, trade, law, journalism, art, politics, and religion, from Cape Horn clear over to Smith's Sound, and beyond, too, if anything worth taking hold of turns up at the North Pole. And then we shall have the leisure to take in hand the outlying islands and continents of the earth. We shall run the world's business whether the world likes it or not. The world can't help it – and neither can we, I guess.'

By this he meant to express his faith in destiny in words suitable to his intelligence, which was unskilled in the presentation of general ideas. His intelligence was nourished on facts; and Charles Gould, whose imagination had been permanently affected by the one great fact of a silver mine, had no objection to this theory of the world's future. If it had seemed distasteful for a moment it was because the sudden statement of such vast eventualities dwarfed almost to nothingness the actual matter in hand. He and his plans and all the mineral wealth of the Occidental Province appeared suddenly robbed of every vestige of magnitude. The sensation was disagreeable; but Charles Gould was not dull. Already he felt that he was producing a favourable impression; the consciousness of that flattering fact helped him to a vague smile, which his big interlocutor took for a smile of discreet and admiring assent. He smiled quietly, too; and immediately Charles Gould, with that mental ability mankind will display in defence of a cherished hope, reflected that the very apparent insignificance of his aim would help him to success. His personality and his mine would be taken up because it was a matter of no great consequence, one way or another, to a man who referred his action to such a prodigious destiny. And Charles Gould was not humiliated by this consideration, because the thing remained as big as ever for him. Nobody else's vast conceptions of destiny could diminish the aspect of his desire for the redemption of the San Tomé mine. In comparison to the correctness of his aim, definite in space and absolutely attainable within a limited time, the other man appeared for an instant as a dreamy idealist of no importance.

The great man, massive and benignant, had been looking at him thoughtfully; when he broke the short silence it was to remark that concessions flew about thick in the air of Costaguana. Any simple soul that just yearned to be taken in could bring down a concession at the first shot.

'Our consuls get their mouths stopped with them,' he continued, with a twinkle of genial scorn in his eyes. But in a moment he became grave. 'A conscientious, upright man, that cares nothing for boodle, and keeps clear of their intrigues, conspiracies, and factions, soon gets his passports. See that, Mr Gould? *Persona non grata*. That's the reason our Government is never properly informed. On the other hand, Europe must be kept out of this continent, and for proper interference on our part the time is not yet ripe, I dare say. But we here – we are not this country's Government, neither are we simple souls. Your affair is all right. The main question for us is whether the second partner, and that's you, is the right sort to hold his own against the third and unwelcome partner, which is one or another of the high and mighty robber gangs that run the Costaguana Government. What do you think, Mr Gould, eh?'

He bent forward to look steadily into the unflinching eyes of Charles Gould, who, remembering the large box full of his father's letters, put the accumulated scorn and bitterness of many years into the tone of his answer: 'As far as the knowledge of these men and their methods and their politics is concerned, I can answer for myself. I have been fed on that sort of knowledge since I was a boy. I am not likely to fall into mistake from excess of optimism.'

'Not likely, eh? That's all right. Tact and a stiff upper lip is what you'll want; and you could bluff a little on the strength of your backing. Not too much, though. We will go with you as long as the thing runs straight. But we won't be drawn into any large trouble. This is the experiment which I am willing to make. There is some risk, and we will take it; but if you can't keep up your end, we will stand our loss, of course, and then – we'll let the thing go. This mine can wait; it has been shut up before, as you know. You must understand that under no circumstances will we consent to throw good money after bad.'

Thus the great personage had spoken then, in his own private office, in a great city where other men (very considerable in the eyes of a vain populace) waited with alacrity upon a wave of his hand. And rather more than a year later, during his unexpected appearance in Sulaco, he had emphasised his uncompromising attitude with a freedom of sincerity permitted to his wealth and influence. He did this with the less reserve, perhaps, because the inspection of what had been done, and more still the way in which successive steps had been taken, had impressed him with the conviction that Charles Gould was perfectly capable of keeping up his end.

'This young fellow,' he thought to himself, 'may yet become a power in the land.'

This thought flattered him, for hitherto the only account of this young man he could give to his intimates was: 'My brother-in-law met him in one of these one-horse old German towns, near some mines, and sent him on to me with a letter. He's one of the Costaguana Goulds, pure bred Englishmen, but all born in the country. His uncle went into politics, was the last Provincial President of Sulaco, and got shot after a battle. His father was a prominent business man in Sta Marta, tried to keep clear of their politics, and died ruined after a lot of revolutions. And that's your Costaguana in a nutshell.'

Of course, he was too great a man to be questioned as to his motives, even by his intimates. The outside world was at liberty to wonder respectfully at the hidden meaning of his actions. He was so great a man that his lavish patronage of the 'purer forms of Christianity' (which in its naive form of church-building amused Mrs Gould) was looked upon by his fellow-citizens as the manifestation of a pious and humble spirit. But in his own circles of the financial world the taking up of such a thing as the San Tomé mine was regarded with respect, indeed, but rather as a subject for discreet jocularity. It was a great man's caprice. In the great Holroyd building (an enormous pile of iron, glass, and blocks of stone at the corner of two streets, cobwebbed aloft by the radiation of telegraph wires) the heads of principal departments exchanged humorous glances, which meant that they were not let into the secrets of the San Tomé business. The Costaguana mail (it was never large – one fairly heavy envelope) was taken unopened straight into the great man's room, and no instructions dealing with it had ever been issued thence. The office whispered that he answered personally – and not by dictation either, but actually writing in his own hand, with pen and ink, and, it was to be supposed, taking a copy in his own private press copybook, inaccessible to profane eyes. Some scornful young men, insignificant pieces of minor machinery in that eleven-storey-high workshop of great affairs, expressed frankly their private opinion that the great chief had done at last something silly, and was ashamed of his folly; others, elderly and insignificant, but full of romantic reverence for the business that had devoured their best years, used to mutter darkly and knowingly that this was a portentous sign; that the Holroyd connection meant by and by to get hold of the whole Republic of Costaguana, lock, stock, and barrel. But, in fact, the hobby theory was the right one. It interested the great man to attend personally to the San Tomé mine; it interested him so much that he allowed this hobby to give a direction to the first complete holiday he had taken for quite a startling number of years. He was not running a great enterprise there; no mere railway board or industrial corporation. He was running a man! A success would have pleased him very much on refreshingly novel grounds; but, on the other side of the same feeling, it was incumbent upon him to cast it off utterly at the first sign of failure. A man may be thrown off. The papers had unfortunately trumpeted all over the land his journey to Costaguana. If he was pleased at the way Charles Gould was going on, he infused an added grimness into his assurances of support. Even at the very last interview, half an hour or so before he rolled out of the patio, hat in hand, behind Mrs Gould's white mules, he had said in Charles's room: 'You go ahead in your own way, and I shall know how to help you as long as you hold your own. But you may rest assured that in a given case we shall know how to drop you in time.'

To this Charles Gould's only answer had been: 'You may begin sending out the machinery as soon as you like.'

And the great man had liked this imperturbable assurance. The secret of it was that to Charles Gould's mind these uncompromising terms were agreeable. Like this the mine preserved its identity, with which he had endowed it as a boy; and it remained dependent on himself alone. It was a serious affair, and he, too, took it grimly.

'Of course,' he said to his wife, alluding to this last conversation with the departed guest, while they walked slowly up and down the corridor, followed by the irritated eye of the parrot – 'of course, a man of that sort can take up a thing or drop it when he likes. He will suffer from no sense of defeat. He may have to give in, or he may have to die tomorrow, but the great silver and iron interests shall survive, and someday shall get hold of Costaguana along with the rest of the world.'

They had stopped near the cage. The parrot, catching the sound of a word belonging to his vocabulary, was moved to interfere. Parrots are very human.

'Viva Costaguana!' he shrieked, with intense self-assertion, and, instantly ruffling up his feathers, assumed an air of puffed-up somnolence behind the glittering wires.

'And do you believe that, Charley?' Mrs Gould asked. 'This seems to me most awful materialism, and – '

'My dear, it's nothing to me,' interrupted her husband, in a reasonable tone. 'I make use of what I see. What's it to me whether his talk is the voice of destiny or simply a bit of claptrap eloquence? There's a good deal of eloquence of one sort or another produced in both Americas. The air of the

New World seems favourable to the art of declamation. Have you forgotten how dear Avellanos can hold forth for hours here – ?'

'Oh, but that's different,' protested Mrs Gould, almost shocked. The allusion was not to the point. Don José was a dear good man, who talked very well, and was enthusiastic about the greatness of the San Tomé mine. 'How can you compare them, Charles?' she exclaimed, reproachfully. 'He has suffered – and yet he hopes.'

The working competence of men – which she never questioned – was very surprising to Mrs Gould, because upon so many obvious issues they showed themselves strangely muddle-headed.

Charles Gould, with a careworn calmness which secured for him at once his wife's anxious sympathy, assured her that he was not comparing. He was an American himself, after all, and perhaps he could understand both kinds of eloquence – 'if it were worth while to try,' he added, grimly. But he had breathed the air of England longer than any of his people had done for three generations, and really he begged to be excused. His poor father could be eloquent, too. And he asked his wife whether she remembered a passage in one of his father's last letters where Mr Gould had expressed the conviction that 'God looked wrathfully at these countries, or else He would let some ray of hope fall through a rift in the appalling darkness of intrigue, bloodshed, and crime that hung over the Queen of Continents.'

Mrs Gould had not forgotten. 'You read it to me, Charley,' she murmured. 'It was a striking pronouncement. How deeply your father must have felt its terrible sadness!'

'He did not like to be robbed. It exasperated him,' said Charles Gould. 'But the image will serve well enough. What is wanted here is law, good faith, order, security. Anyone can declaim about these things, but I pin my faith to material interests. Only let the material interests once get a firm footing, and they are bound to impose the conditions on which alone they can continue to exist. That's how your money making is justified here in the face of lawlessness and disorder. It is justified because the security which it demands must be shared with an oppressed people. A better justice will come afterwards. That's your ray of hope.' His arm pressed her slight form closer to his side for a moment. 'And who knows whether in that sense even the San Tomé mine may not become that little rift in the darkness which poor father despaired of ever seeing?'

She glanced up at him with admiration. He was competent; he had given a vast shape to the vagueness of her unselfish ambitions.

'Charley,' she said, 'you are splendidly disobedient.'

He left her suddenly in the *corredor* to go and get his hat, a soft, grey sombrero, an article of national costume which combined unexpectedly well with his English get-up. He came back, a riding-whip under his arm, buttoning up a dogskin glove; his face reflected the resolute nature of his thoughts. His wife had waited for him at the head of the stairs, and before he gave her the parting kiss he finished the conversation: 'What should be perfectly clear to us,' he said, 'is the fact that there is no going back. Where could we begin life afresh? We are in now for all that there is in us.'

He bent over her upturned face very tenderly and a little remorsefully. Charles Gould was competent because he had no illusions. The Gould Concession had to fight for life with such weapons as could be found at once in the mire of corruption that was so universal as to almost lose its significance. He was prepared to stoop for his weapons. For a moment he felt as if the silver mine, which had killed his father, had decoyed him further than he meant to go; and with the roundabout logic of emotions, he felt that the worthiness of his life was bound up with success. There was no going back.

Chapter 7

Mrs Gould was too intelligently sympathetic not to share that feeling. It made life exciting, and she was too much of a woman not to like excitement. But it frightened her, too, a little; and when Don José Avellanos, rocking in the American chair, would go so far as to say, 'Even, my dear Carlos, if you had failed; even if some untoward event were yet to destroy your work – which God forbid! – you would have deserved well of your country,' Mrs Gould would look up from the tea-table profoundly at her unmoved husband stirring the spoon in the cup as though he had not heard a word.

Not that Don José anticipated anything of the sort. He could not praise enough dear Carlos's tact and courage. His English, rocklike quality of character was his best safeguard, Don José affirmed; and, turning to Mrs Gould, 'As to you, Emilia, my soul' – he would address her with the familiarity of his age and old friendship – 'you are as true a patriot as though you had been born in our midst.'

This might have been less or more than the truth. Mrs Gould, accompanying her husband all over the province in the search for labour, had seen the land with a deeper glance than a trueborn Costaguanera could have done. In her travel-worn riding habit, her face powdered white like a plaster cast, with a further protection of a small silk mask during the heat of the day, she rode on a well-shaped, light-footed pony in the centre of a little cavalcade. Two *mozos de campo*, picturesque in great hats, with spurred bare heels, in white embroidered calzoneras, leather jackets and striped ponchos, rode ahead with carbines across their shoulders, swaying in unison to the pace of the horses. A tropilla of pack mules brought up the rear in charge of a thin brown muleteer, sitting his long-eared beast very near the tail, legs thrust far forward, the wide brim of his hat set far back, making a sort of halo for his head. An old Costaguana officer, a retired senior major of humble origin, but patronised by the first families on account of his Blanco opinions, had been recommended by Don José for commissary and organiser of that expedition. The points of his grey moustache hung far below his chin, and, riding on Mrs Gould's left hand, he looked about with kindly eyes, pointing out the features of the country, telling the names of the little pueblos and of the estates, of the smooth-walled haciendas like long fortresses crowning the knolls above the level of the Sulaco Valley. It unrolled itself, with green young crops, plains, woodland, and gleams of water, park-like, from the blue vapour of the distant sierra to an immense quivering horizon of grass and sky, where big white clouds seemed to fall slowly into the darkness of their own shadows.

Men ploughed with wooden ploughs and yoked oxen, small on a boundless expanse, as if attacking immensity itself. The mounted figures of vaqueros galloped in the distance, and the great herds fed with all their horned heads one way, in one single wavering line as far as eye could reach across the broad *potreros*. A spreading cotton-wool tree shaded a thatched rancho by the road; the trudging files of burdened Indians taking off their hats, would lift sad, mute eyes to the cavalcade raising the dust of the crumbling *camino real* made by the hands of their enslaved forefathers. And Mrs Gould, with each day's journey, seemed to come nearer to the soul of the land in the tremendous disclosure of this interior unaffected by the slight European veneer of the coast towns, a great land of plain and mountain and people, suffering and mute, waiting for the future in a pathetic immobility of patience.

She knew its sights and its hospitality, dispensed with a sort of slumbrous dignity in those great houses presenting long, blind walls and heavy portals to the windswept pastures. She was given the head of the tables, where masters and dependants sat in a simple and patriarchal state. The ladies of the house would talk softly in the moonlight under the orange trees of the courtyards, impressing upon her the sweetness of their voices and the something mysterious in the quietude of their lives. In the morning the gentlemen, well mounted in braided sombreros and embroidered riding suits, with much silver on the trappings of their horses, would ride forth to escort the departing guests before committing them, with grave goodbyes, to the care of God at the boundary pillars of their estates. In all these households she could hear stories of political outrage; friends, relatives, ruined, imprisoned, killed in the battles of senseless civil wars, barbarously executed in ferocious proscriptions, as though the government of the country had been a struggle of lust between bands of absurd devils let loose upon the land with sabres and uniforms and grandiloquent phrases. And on all the lips she found a weary desire for peace, the dread of officialdom with its nightmarish parody of administration without law, without security, and without justice.

She bore a whole two months of wandering very well; she had that power of resistance to fatigue which one discovers here and there in some quite frail-looking women with surprise – like a state of possession by a remarkably stubborn spirit. Don Pépé – the old Costaguana major – after much display of solicitude for the delicate lady, had ended by conferring upon her the name of the 'Never-tired Señora.' Mrs Gould was indeed becoming a Costaguanera. Having acquired in Southern Europe a knowledge of true peasantry, she was able to appreciate the great worth of the people. She saw the man under the silent, sad-eyed beast of burden. She saw them on the road carrying loads, lonely figures upon the plain, toiling under great straw hats, with their white clothing flapping about their limbs in the wind; she remembered the villages by some group of Indian women at the fountain impressed upon her memory, by the face of some young Indian girl with a melancholy and sensual profile, raising an earthenware vessel of cool water at the door of a dark hut with a wooden porch cumbered with great brown jars. The solid wooden wheels of an ox-cart, halted with its shafts in the dust, showed the strokes of the axe; and a party of charcoal carriers, with each man's load resting above his head on the top of the low mud wall, slept stretched in a row within the strip of shade.

The heavy stonework of bridges and churches left by the conquerors proclaimed the disregard of human labour, the tribute-labour of vanished nations. The power of king and church was gone, but at the sight of some heavy ruinous pile overtopping from a knoll the low mud walls of a village, Don Pépé would interrupt the tale of his campaigns to exclaim: 'Poor Costaguana! Before, it was everything for the Padres, nothing for the people; and now it is everything for these great politicos in Sta Marta, for Negroes and thieves.'

Charles talked with the alcaldes, with the fiscales, with the principal people in towns, and with the caballeros on the estates. The commandantes of the districts offered him escorts – for he could show an authorisation from the Sulaco political chief of the day. How much the document had cost him in gold twenty-dollar pieces was a secret between himself, a great man in the United States (who condescended to answer the Sulaco mail with his own hand), and a great man of another sort, with a dark olive complexion and shifty eyes, inhabiting then the Palace of the Intendencia in Sulaco, and who piqued himself on his culture and Europeanism generally in a rather French style because he had lived in Europe for some years – in exile, he said. However, it was pretty well known that just before this exile he had incautiously gambled away all the cash in the Custom House of a small port where a friend in power had procured for him the post of sub-collector. That youthful indiscretion had, amongst other inconveniences, obliged him to earn his living for a time as a café waiter in Madrid; but his talents must have been great, after all, since they had enabled him to retrieve his political fortunes so splendidly. Charles Gould, exposing his business with an imperturbable steadiness, called him Excellency.

The provincial Excellency assumed a weary superiority, tilting his chair far back near an open window in the true Costaguana manner. The military band happened to be braying operatic selections on the plaza just then, and twice he raised his hand imperatively for silence in order to listen to a favourite passage.

'Exquisite, delicious!' he murmured; while Charles Gould waited, standing by with inscrutable patience. 'Lucia, Lucia di Lammermoor! I am passionate for music. It transports me. Ha! the divine – ha! – Mozart. Si! divine . . . What is it you were saying?'

Of course, rumours had reached him already of the newcomer's intentions. Besides, he had received official warning from Sta Marta. His manner was intended simply to conceal his curiosity and impress his visitor. But after he had locked up something valuable in the drawer of a large writing-desk in a distant part of the room, he became very affable, and walked back to his chair smartly.

'If you intend to build villages and assemble a population near the mine, you shall require a decree of the Minister of the Interior for that,' he suggested in a businesslike manner.

'I have already sent a memorial,' said Charles Gould, steadily, 'and I reckon now confidently upon your Excellency's favourable conclusions.'

The Excellency was a man of many moods. With the receipt of the money a great mellowness had descended upon his simple soul. Unexpectedly he fetched a deep sigh.

'Ah, Don Carlos! What we want is advanced men like you in the province. The lethargy – the lethargy of these aristocrats! The want of public spirit! The absence of all enterprise! I, with my profound studies in Europe, you understand – '

With one hand thrust into his swelling bosom, he rose and fell on his toes, and for ten minutes, almost without drawing breath, went on hurling himself intellectually to the assault of Charles Gould's polite silence; and when, stopping abruptly, he fell back into his chair, it was as though he had been beaten off from a fortress. To save his dignity he hastened to dismiss this silent man with a solemn inclination of the head and the words, pronounced with moody, fatigued condescension: 'You may depend upon my enlightened goodwill as long as your conduct as a good citizen deserves it.'

He took up a paper fan and began to cool himself with a consequential air, while Charles Gould bowed and withdrew. Then he dropped the fan at once, and stared with an appearance of wonder and perplexity at the closed door for quite a long time. At last he shrugged his shoulders as if to assure himself of his disdain. Cold, dull. No intellectuality. Red hair. A true Englishman. He despised him.

His face darkened. What meant this unimpressed and frigid behaviour? He was the first of the successive politicians sent out from the capital to rule the Occidental Province whom the manner of Charles Gould in official intercourse was to strike as offensively independent.

Charles Gould assumed that if the appearance of listening to deplorable balderdash must form part of the price he had to pay for being left unmolested, the obligation of uttering balderdash personally was by no means included in the bargain. He drew the line there. To these provincial autocrats, before whom the peaceable population of all classes had been accustomed to tremble, the reserve of that English-looking engineer caused an uneasiness which swung to and fro between cringing and truculence. Gradually all of them discovered that, no matter what party was in power, that man remained in most effective touch with the higher authorities in Sta Marta.

This was a fact, and it accounted perfectly for the Goulds being by no means so wealthy as the engineer-in-chief on the new railway could legitimately suppose. Following the advice of Don José Avellanos, who was a man of good counsel (though rendered timid by his horrible experiences of Guzman Bento's time), Charles Gould had kept clear of the capital; but in the current gossip of the foreign residents there he was known (with a good deal of seriousness underlying the irony) by the nickname of 'King of Sulaco'. An advocate of the Costaguana Bar, a man of reputed ability and good character, member of the distinguished Moraga family possessing extensive estates in the Sulaco Valley, was pointed out to strangers, with a shade of mystery and respect, as the agent of the San Tomé mine – 'political, you know.' He was tall, black-whiskered, and discreet. It was known that he had easy access to ministers, and that the numerous Costaguana generals were always anxious to dine at his house. Presidents granted him audience with facility. He corresponded actively with his maternal uncle, Don José Avellanos; but his letters – unless those expressing formally his dutiful affection – were seldom entrusted to the Costaguana Post Office. There the envelopes are opened, indiscriminately, with the frankness of a brazen and childish impudence characteristic of some Spanish-American Governments. But it must be noted that at about the time of the reopening of the San Tomé mine the muleteer who had been employed by Charles Gould in his preliminary travels on the Campo added his small train of animals to the thin stream of traffic carried over the mountain passes between the Sta Marta upland and the Valley of Sulaco. There are no travellers by that arduous and unsafe route unless under very exceptional circumstances, and the state of inland trade did not visibly require additional transport facilities; but the man seemed to find his account in it. A few packages were always found for him whenever he took the road. Very brown and wooden, in goatskin breeches with the hair outside, he sat near the tail of his own smart mule, his great hat turned against the sun, an expression of blissful vacancy on his long face, humming day after day a love-song in a plaintive key, or, without a change of expression, letting out a yell at his small tropilla in front. A round little guitar hung high up on his back; and there was a place scooped out artistically in the wood of one of his pack-saddles where a tightly rolled piece of paper could be slipped in, the wooden plug replaced, and the coarse canvas nailed on again. When in Sulaco it was his practice to smoke and doze all day long (as though he had no care in the world) on a stone bench outside the doorway of the Casa Gould and facing the windows of the Avellanos house. Years and years ago his mother had been chief laundrywoman in that family – very accomplished in the matter of clear-starching. He himself had been born on one of their haciendas. His name was Bonifacio, and Don José, crossing the street about five o'clock to call on Doña Emilia, always acknowledged his humble salute by some movement of hand or head. The porters of both houses conversed lazily with him in tones of grave intimacy. His evenings he devoted to gambling and to calls in a spirit of generous festivity upon the *peine de oro* girls in the more remote side-streets of the town. But he, too, was a discreet man.

Chapter 8

Those of us whom business or curiosity took to Sulaco in these years before the first advent of the railway can remember the steadying effect of the San Tomé mine upon the life of that remote province. The outward appearances had not changed then as they have changed since, as I am told, with cable cars running along the streets of the Constitution, and carriage roads far into the country, to Rincon and other villages, where the foreign merchants and the Ricos generally have their modern villas, and a vast railway goods yard by the harbour, which has a quayside, a long range of warehouses, and quite serious, organised labour troubles of its own.

Nobody had ever heard of labour troubles then. The Cargadores of the port formed, indeed, an unruly brotherhood of all sorts of scum, with a patron saint of their own. They went on strike regularly (every bullfight day), a form of trouble that even Nostromo at the height of his prestige could never cope with efficiently; but the morning after each fiesta, before the Indian market-women had opened their mat parasols on the plaza, when the snows of Higuerota gleamed pale over the town on a yet black sky, the appearance of a phantomlike horseman mounted on a silver-grey mare solved the problem of labour without fail. His steed paced the lanes of the slums and the weed-grown enclosures within the old ramparts, between the black, lightless cluster of huts, like cow-byres, like dog-kennels. The horseman hammered with the butt of a heavy revolver at the doors of low pulperías, of obscene lean-to sheds sloping against the tumbledown piece of a noble wall, at the wooden sides of dwellings so flimsy that the sound of snores and sleepy mùtters within could be heard in the pauses of the thundering clatter of his blows. He called out men's names menacingly from the saddle, once, twice.

The drowsy answers – grumpy, conciliating, savage, jocular, or deprecating – came out into the silent darkness in which the horseman sat still, and presently a dark figure would flit out coughing in the still air. Sometimes a low-toned woman cried through the window-hole softly, 'He's coming directly, señor,' and the horseman waited silent on a motionless horse. But if perchance he had to dismount, then, after a while, from the door of that hovel or of that pulpería, with a ferocious scuffle and stifled imprecations, a cargador would fly out head first and hands abroad, to sprawl under the forelegs of the silver-grey mare, who only pricked forward her sharp little ears. She was used to that work; and the man, picking himself up, would walk away hastily from Nostromo's revolver, reeling a little along the street and snarling low curses. At sunrise Captain Mitchell, coming out anxiously in his night attire on to the wooden balcony running the whole length of the OSN Company's lonely building by the shore, would see the lighters already under way, figures moving busily about the cargo cranes, perhaps hear the invaluable Nostromo, now dismounted and in the checked shirt and red sash of a Mediterranean sailor, bawling orders from the end of the jetty in a stentorian voice. A fellow in a thousand!

The material apparatus of perfected civilisation which obliterates the individuality of old towns under the stereotyped conveniences of modern life had not intruded as yet; but over the worn-out antiquity of Sulaco, so characteristic with its stuccoed houses and barred windows, with the great yellowy-white walls of abandoned convents behind the rows of sombre green cypresses, that fact – very modern in its spirit – the San Tomé mine had already thrown its subtle influence. It had altered, too, the outward character of the crowds on feast days on the plaza before the open portal of the cathedral, by the number of white ponchos with a green stripe affected as holiday wear by the San Tomé miners. They had also adopted white hats with green cord and braid – articles of good quality, which could be obtained in the storehouse of the administration for very little money. A peaceable Cholo wearing these colours (unusual in Costaguana) was somehow very seldom beaten to within an inch of his life on a charge of disrespect to the town police; neither ran he much risk of being suddenly lassoed on the road by a recruiting party of lanceros – a method of voluntary enlistment looked upon as almost legal in the Republic. Whole villages were known to have volunteered for the army in that way; but, as Don Pépé would say with a hopeless shrug to Mrs Gould, 'What would you! Poor people! Pobrecitos! Pobrecitos! But the State must have its soldiers.'

Thus professionally spoke Don Pépé, the fighter, with pendent moustaches, a nutbrown, lean face, and a clean run of a cast-iron jaw, suggesting the type of a cattle-herd horseman from the great Llanos of the South. 'If you will listen to an old officer of Paéz, señores,' was the exordium of all his speeches in the Aristocratic Club of Sulaco, where he was admitted on account of his past services to the extinct cause of Federation. The club, dating from the days of the proclamation of Costaguana's independence, boasted many names of liberators amongst its first founders. Suppressed arbitrarily innumerable times by various Governments, with memories of proscriptions and of at least one wholesale massacre of its members, sadly assembled for a banquet by the order of a zealous military commandante (their bodies were afterwards stripped naked and flung into the plaza out of the windows by the lowest scum of the populace), it was again flourishing, at that period, peacefully. It extended to strangers the large hospitality of the cool, big rooms of its historic quarters in the front part of a house, once the residence of a high official of the Holy Office. The two wings, shut up, crumbled behind the nailed doors, and what may be described as a grove of young orange trees grown in the unpaved patio concealed the utter ruin of the back part facing the gate. You turned in from the street, as if entering a secluded orchard, where you came upon the foot of a disjointed staircase, guarded by a moss-stained effigy of some saintly bishop, mitred and staffed, and bearing the indignity of a broken nose meekly, with his fine stone hands crossed on his breast. The chocolate-coloured faces of servants with mops of black hair peeped at you from above; the click of billiard balls came to your ears, and ascending the steps, you would perhaps see in the first sala, very stiff upon a straight-backed chair, in a good light, Don Pépé moving his long moustaches as he spelt his way, at arm's length, through an old Sta Marta newspaper. His horse – a stony-hearted but persevering black brute with a hammer head – you would have seen in the street dozing motionless under an immense saddle, with its nose almost touching the kerbstone of the sidewalk.

Don Pépé, when 'down from the mountain', as the phrase, often heard in Sulaco, went, could also be seen in the drawing-room of the Casa Gould. He sat with modest assurance at some distance from the tea-table. With his knees close together, and a kindly twinkle of drollery in his deep-set eyes, he would throw his small and ironic pleasantries into the current of conversation. There was in that man a sort of sane, humorous shrewdness, and a vein of genuine humanity so often found in simple old soldiers of proved courage who have seen much desperate service. Of course he knew nothing whatever of mining, but his employment was of a special kind. He was in charge of the whole population in the territory of the mine, which extended from the head of the gorge to where the cart track from the foot of the mountain enters the plain, crossing a stream over a little wooden bridge painted green – green, the colour of hope, being also the colour of the mine.

It was reported in Sulaco that up there 'at the mountain' Don Pépé walked about precipitous paths, girt with a great sword and in a shabby uniform with tarnished bullion epaulettes of a senior major. Most miners being Indians, with big wild eyes, addressed him as Taita (father), as these barefooted people of Costaguana will address anybody who wears shoes; but it was Basilio, Mr Gould's own mozo and the head servant of the Casa, who, in all good faith and from a sense of propriety, announced him once in the solemn words, 'El Señor Gobernador has arrived.'

Don José Avellanos, then in the drawing-room, was delighted beyond measure at the aptness of the title, with which he greeted the old major banteringly as soon as the latter's soldierly figure appeared in the doorway. Don Pépé only smiled in his long moustaches, as much as to say, 'You might have found a worse name for an old soldier.'

And El Señor Gobernador he had remained, with his small jokes upon his function and upon his domain, where he affirmed with humorous exaggeration to Mrs Gould: 'No two stones could come together anywhere without the Gobernador hearing the click, señora.'

And he would tap his ear with the tip of his forefinger knowingly. Even when the number of the miners alone rose to over six hundred he seemed to know each of them individually, all the innumerable Josés, Manuels, Ignacios, from the villages primero – segundo – or tercero (there were three mining villages) under his government. He could distinguish them not only by their flat, joyless faces, which to Mrs Gould looked all alike, as if run into the same ancestral mould of suffering and patience, but apparently also by the infinitely graduated shades of reddish-brown, of blackish-brown, of coppery-brown backs, as the two shifts, stripped to linen drawers and leather skullcaps, mingled together with a confusion of naked limbs, of shouldered picks, swinging lamps, in a great shuffle of sandalled feet on the open plateau before the entrance of the main tunnel. It was a time of pause. The Indian boys leaned idly against the long line of little cradle wagons standing empty; the screeners and ore-breakers squatted on their heels smoking long cigars; the great wooden shoots slanting over the edge of the tunnel plateau were silent; and only the ceaseless, violent rush of water in the open flumes could be heard, murmuring fiercely, with the splash and rumble of revolving turbine-wheels, and the thudding march of the stamps pounding to powder the treasure rock on the plateau below. The heads of gangs, distinguished by brass medals hanging on their bare breasts, marshalled their squads; and at last the mountain would swallow one-half of the silent crowd, while the other half would move off in long files down the zigzag paths leading to the bottom of the gorge. It was deep; and, far below, a thread of vegetation winding between the blazing rock faces resembled a slender green cord, in which three lumpy knots of banana patches, palm-leaf roots, and shady trees marked the Village One, Village Two, Village Three, housing the miners of the Gould Concession.

Whole families had been moving from the first towards the spot in the Higuerota range, whence the rumour of work and safety had spread over the pastoral Campo, forcing its way also, even as the waters of a high flood, into the nooks and crannies of the distant blue walls of the Sierras. Father first, in a pointed straw hat, then the mother with the bigger children, generally also a diminutive donkey, all under burdens, except the leader himself, or perhaps some grown girl, the pride of the family, stepping barefooted and straight as an arrow, with braids of raven hair, a thick, haughty profile, and no load to carry but the small guitar of the country and a pair of soft leather sandals tied together on her back. At the sight of such parties strung out on the cross trails between the pastures, or camped by the side of the royal road, travellers on horseback would remark to each other: 'More people going to the San Tomé mine. We shall see others tomorrow.'

And spurring on in the dusk they would discuss the great news of the province, the news of the San Tomé mine. A rich Englishman was going to work it – and perhaps not an Englishman, *Quién sabe!* A foreigner with much money. Oh, yes, it had begun. A party of men who had been to Sulaco with a herd of black bulls for the next corrida had reported that from the porch of the posada in Rincon, only a short league from the town, the lights on the mountain were visible, twinkling above the trees. And there was a woman seen riding a horse sideways, not in the chair seat, but upon a sort of saddle, and a man's hat on her head. She walked about, too, on foot up the mountain paths. A woman engineer, it seemed she was.

'What an absurdity! Impossible, señor!'

'Si! Si! Una Americana del Norte.'

'Ah, well! if your worship is informed. *Una Americana*; it need be something of that sort.'

And they would laugh a little with astonishment and scorn, keeping a wary eye on the shadows of the road, for one is liable to meet bad men when travelling late on the Campo.

And it was not only the men that Don Pépé knew so well, but he seemed able, with one attentive, thoughtful glance, to classify each woman, girl, or growing youth of his domain. It was only the small fry that puzzled him sometimes. He and the padre could be seen frequently side by side, meditative and gazing across the street of a village at a lot of sedate brown children, trying to sort them out, as it were, in low, consulting tones, or else they would together put searching questions as to the parentage of some small, staid urchin met wandering, naked and grave, along the road with a cigar in his baby mouth, and perhaps his mother's rosary, purloined for purposes of ornamentation, hanging in a loop of beads low down on his rotund little stomach. The spiritual and temporal pastors of the mine flock were very good friends. With Dr Monygham, the medical pastor, who had accepted the charge from Mrs Gould, and lived in the hospital building, they were on not so intimate terms. But no one could be on intimate terms with El Señor Doctor, who, with his twisted shoulders, drooping head, sardonic mouth, and sidelong bitter glance, was mysterious and uncanny. The other two authorities worked in harmony. Father Romàn, dried-up, small, alert, wrinkled, with big round eyes, a sharp chin, and a great snuff-taker, was an old campaigner, too; he had shriven many simple souls on the battlefields of the Republic, kneeling by the dying on hillsides, in the long grass, in the gloom of the forests, to hear the last confession with the smell of gunpowder smoke in his nostrils, the rattle of muskets, the hum and spatter of bullets in his ears. And where was the harm if, at the presbytery, they had a game with a pack of greasy cards in the early evening, before Don Pépé went his last rounds to see that all the watchmen of the mine – a body organised by himself – were at their posts? For that last duty before he slept Don Pépé did actually gird his old sword on the verandah of an unmistakable American white frame house, which Father Romàn called the presbytery. Near by, a long, low, dark building, steeple-roofed, like a vast barn with a wooden cross over the gable, was the miners' chapel. There Father Romàn said Mass every day before a sombre altarpiece representing the Resurrection, the grey slab of the tombstone balanced on one corner, a figure soaring upwards, long-limbed and livid, in an oval of pallid light, and a helmeted brown legionary smitten down, right across the bituminous foreground. 'This picture, my children, *muy linda e maravillosa*,' Father Romàn would say to some of his flock, 'which you behold here through the munificence of the wife of our Señor Administrador, has been painted in Europe, a country of saints and miracles, and much greater than our Costaguana.' And he would take a pinch of snuff with unction. But when once an inquisitive spirit desired to know in what direction this Europe was situated, whether up or down the coast, Father Romàn, to conceal his perplexity, became very reserved and severe. 'No doubt it is extremely far away. But ignorant sinners like you of the San Tomé mine should think earnestly of everlasting punishment instead of enquiring into the magnitude of the earth, with its countries and populations altogether beyond your understanding.'

With a 'Good-night, Padre;' 'Good-night, Don Pépé,' the Gobernador would go off, holding up his sabre against his side, his body bent forward, with a long, plodding stride in the dark. The jocularity proper to an innocent card game for a few cigars or a bundle of yerba was replaced at once by the stern duty mood of an officer setting out to visit the outposts of an encamped army. One loud blast of the whistle that hung from his neck provoked instantly a great shrilling of responding whistles, mingled with the barking of dogs, that would calm down slowly at last, away up at the head of the gorge; and in the stillness two serenos, on guard by the bridge, would appear walking noiselessly towards him. On one side of the road a long frame building – the store – would be closed and barricaded from end to end; facing it another white frame house, still longer, and with a verandah – the hospital – would have lights in the two windows of Dr Monygham's quarters. Even the delicate foliage of a clump of pepper trees did not stir, so breathless would be the darkness warmed by the radiation of the overheated rocks. Don Pépé would stand still for a moment with the two motionless serenos before him, and, abruptly, high up on the sheer face of the mountain, dotted with single torches, like drops of fire fallen from the two great blazing clusters of lights above, the ore shoots would begin to rattle. The great clattering, shuffling noise, gathering speed and weight, would be caught up by the walls of the gorge, and sent upon the plain in a growl of thunder. The posadero in Rincon swore that on calm nights, by listening intently, he could catch the sound in his doorway as of a storm in the mountains.

To Charles Gould's fancy it seemed that the sound must reach the uttermost limits of the province. Riding at night towards the mine, it would meet him at the edge of a little wood just beyond Rincon. There was no mistaking the growling mutter of the mountain pouring its stream of treasure under the stamps; and it came to his heart with the peculiar force of a proclamation thundered forth over the land and the marvellousness of an accomplished fact fulfilling an audacious desire. He had heard this desire. He had heard this very sound in his imagination on that far-off evening when his wife and himself, after a tortuous ride through a strip of forest, had reined in their horses near the stream, and had gazed for the first time upon the jungle-grown solitude of the gorge. The head of a palm rose here and there. In a high ravine round the corner of the San Tomé mountain (which is square like a blockhouse) the thread of a slender waterfall flashed bright and glassy through the dark green of the heavy fronds of tree-ferns. Don Pépé, in attendance, rode up, and, stretching his arm up the gorge, had declared with mock solemnity, 'Behold the very paradise of snakes, señora.'

And then they had wheeled their horses and ridden back to sleep that night at Rincon. The alcalde – an old, skinny Moreno, a sergeant of Guzman Bento's time – had cleared respectfully out of his house with his three pretty daughters, to make room for the foreign señora and their worships the Caballeros. All he asked Charles Gould (whom he took for a mysterious and official person) to do for him was to remind the supreme Government – El Gobierno supremo – of a pension (amounting to about a dollar a month) to which he believed himself entitled. It had been promised to him, he affirmed, straightening his bent back martially, 'many years ago, for my valour in the wars with the wild Indios when a young man, señor.'

The waterfall existed no longer. The tree-ferns that had luxuriated in its spray had dried around the dried-up pool, and the high ravine was only a big trench half filled up with the refuse of excavations and tailings. The torrent, dammed up above, sent its water rushing along the open flumes of scooped tree trunks striding on trestle-legs to the turbines working the stamps on the lower plateau – the *mesa grande* of the San Tomé mountain. Only the memory of the waterfall, with its amazing fernery, like a hanging garden above the rocks of the gorge, was preserved in Mrs Gould's watercolour sketch; she had made it hastily one day from a cleared patch in the bushes, sitting in the shade of a roof of straw erected for her on three rough poles under Don Pépé's direction.

Mrs Gould had seen it all from the beginning: the clearing of the wilderness, the making of the road, the cutting of new paths up the cliff face of San Tomé. For weeks together she had lived on the spot with her husband; and she was so little in Sulaco during that year that the appearance of the Gould carriage on the Alameda would cause a social excitement. From the heavy family coaches full of stately señoras and black-eyed señoritas rolling solemnly in the shaded alley white hands were waved towards her with animation in a flutter of greetings. Doña Emilia was 'down from the mountain'.

But not for long. Doña Emilia would be gone 'up to the mountain' in a day or two, and her sleek carriage mules would have an easy time of it for another long spell. She had watched the erection of the first frame-house put up on the lower mesa for an office and Don Pépé's quarters; she heard with a thrill of thankful emotion the first wagon load of ore rattle down the then only shoot; she had stood by her husband's side perfectly silent, and gone cold all over with excitement at the instant when the first battery of only fifteen stamps was put in motion for the first time. On the occasion when the fires under the first set of retorts in their shed had glowed far into the night she did not retire to rest on the rough catre set up for her in the as yet bare frame-house till she had seen the first spungy lump of silver yielded to the hazards of the world by the dark depths of the Gould Concession; she had laid her unmercenary hands, with an eagerness that made them tremble, upon the first silver ingot turned out still warm from the mould; and by her imaginative estimate of its power she endowed that lump of metal with a justificative conception, as though it were not a mere fact, but something far-reaching and impalpable, like the true expression of an emotion or the emergence of a principle.

Don Pépé, extremely interested, too, looked over her shoulder with a smile that, making longitudinal folds on his face, caused it to resemble a leathern mask with a benignantly diabolic expression.

'Would not the muchachos of Hernandez like to get hold of this insignificant object, that looks, por Dios, very much like a piece of tin?' he remarked, jocularly.

Hernandez, the robber, had been an inoffensive, small ranchero, kidnapped with circumstances of peculiar atrocity from his home during one of the civil wars, and forced to serve in the army. There his conduct as soldier was exemplary, till, watching his chance, he killed his colonel, and managed to get clear away. With a band of deserters, who chose him for their chief, he had taken refuge beyond the wild and waterless Bolson de Tonoro. The haciendas paid him blackmail in cattle and horses; extraordinary stories were told of his powers and of his wonderful escapes from capture. He used to ride, single-handed, into the villages and the little towns on the Campo, driving a pack mule before him, with two revolvers in his belt, go straight to the shop or store, select what he wanted, and ride away unopposed because of the terror his exploits and his audacity inspired. Poor country people he usually left alone; the upper class were often stopped on the roads and robbed; but any unlucky official that fell into his hands was sure to get a severe flogging. The army officers did not like his name to be mentioned in their presence. His followers, mounted on stolen horses, laughed at the pursuit of the regular cavalry sent to hunt them down, and whom they took pleasure to ambush most scientifically in the broken ground of their own fastness. Expeditions had been fitted out; a price had been put upon his head; even attempts had been made, treacherously of course, to open negotiations with him, without in the slightest way affecting the even tenor of his career. At last, in true Costaguana fashion, the Fiscal of Tonoro, who was ambitious of the glory of having reduced the famous Hernandez, offered him a sum of money and a safe conduct out of the country for the betrayal of his band. But Hernandez evidently was not of the stuff of which the distinguished military politicians and conspirators of Costaguana are made. This clever but common device (which frequently works like a charm in putting down revolutions) failed with the chief of vulgar salteadores. It promised well for the Fiscal at first, but ended very badly for the squadron of lanceros posted (by the Fiscal's directions) in a fold of the ground into which Hernandez had promised to lead his unsuspecting followers. They came, indeed, at the appointed time, but creeping on their hands and knees through the bush, and only let their presence be known by a general discharge of firearms, which emptied many saddles. The troopers who escaped came riding very hard into Tonoro. It is said that their commanding officer (who, being better mounted, rode far ahead of the rest) afterwards got into a state of despairing intoxication and beat the ambitious Fiscal severely with the flat of his sabre in the presence of his wife and daughters, for bringing this disgrace upon the National Army. The highest civil official of Tonoro, falling to the ground in a swoon, was further kicked all over the body and rowelled with sharp spurs about the neck and face because of the great sensitiveness of his military colleague. This gossip of the inland Campo, so characteristic of the rulers of the country with its story of oppression, inefficiency, fatuous methods, treachery, and savage brutality, was perfectly known to Mrs Gould. That it should be accepted with no indignant comment by people of intelligence, refinement, and character as something inherent in the nature of things was one of the symptoms of degradation that had the power to exasperate her almost to the verge of despair. Still looking at the ingot of silver, she shook her head at Don Pépé's remark: 'If it had not been for the lawless tyranny of your Government, Don Pépé, many an outlaw now with Hernandez would be living peaceably and happy by the honest work of his hands.'

'Señora,' cried Don Pépé, with enthusiasm, 'it is true! It is as if God had given you the power to look into the very breasts of people. You have seen them working round you, Doña Emilia – meek as lambs, patient like their own burros, brave like lions. I have led them to the very muzzles of guns – I, who stand here before you, señora – in the time of Paez, who was full of generosity, and in courage only approached by the uncle of Don Carlos here, as far as I know. No wonder there are bandits in the Campo when there are none but thieves, swindlers, and sanguinary macaques to rule us in

Sta Marta. However, all the same, a bandit is a bandit, and we shall have a dozen good straight Winchesters to ride with the silver down to Sulaco.'

Mrs Gould's ride with the first silver escort to Sulaco was the closing episode of what she called 'my camp life' before she had settled in her town-house permanently, as was proper and even necessary for the wife of the administrator of such an important institution as the San Tomé mine. For the San Tomé mine was to become an institution, a rallying point for everything in the province that needed order and stability to live. Security seemed to flow upon this land from the mountain-gorge. The authorities of Sulaco had learned that the San Tomé mine could make it worth their while to leave things and people alone. This was the nearest approach to the rule of common-sense and justice Charles Gould felt it possible to secure at first. In fact, the mine, with its organisation, its population growing fiercely attached to their position of privileged safety, with its armoury, with its Don Pépé, with its armed body of serenos (where, it was said, many an outlaw and deserter – and even some members of Hernandez's band – had found a place), the mine was a power in the land. As a certain prominent man in Sta Marta had exclaimed with a hollow laugh, once, when discussing the line of action taken by the Sulaco authorities at a time of political crisis: 'You call these men Government officials? They? Never! They are officials of the mine – officials of the Concession – I tell you.'

The prominent man (who was then a person in power, with a lemon-coloured face and a very short and curly, not to say woolly, head of hair) went so far in his temporary discontent as to shake his yellow fist under the nose of his interlocutor, and shriek: 'Yes! All! Silence! All! I tell you! The political Jefe, the chief of the police, the chief of the customs, the general, all, all, are the officials of that Gould.'

Thereupon an intrepid but low and argumentative murmur would flow on for a space in the ministerial cabinet, and the prominent man's passion would end in a cynical shrug of the shoulders. After all, he seemed to say, what did it matter as long as the minister himself was not forgotten during his brief day of authority? But all the same, the unofficial agent of the San Tomé mine, working for a good cause, had his moments of anxiety, which were reflected in his letters to Don José Avellanos, his maternal uncle.

'No sanguinary macaque from Sta Marta shall set foot on that part of Costaguana which lies beyond the San Tomé bridge,' Don Pépé used to assure Mrs Gould. 'Except, of course, as an honoured guest – for our Señor Administrador is a deep politico.' But to Charles Gould, in his own room, the old Major would remark with a grim and soldierly cheeriness, 'We are all playing our heads at this game.'

Don José Avellanos would mutter 'Imperium in imperio, Emilia, my soul,' with an air of profound self-satisfaction which, somehow, in a curious way, seemed to contain a queer admixture of bodily discomfort. But that, perhaps, could only be visible to the initiated.

And for the initiated it was a wonderful place, this drawing-room of the Casa Gould, with its momentary glimpses of the master – El Señor Administrador – older, harder, mysteriously silent, with the lines deepened on his English, ruddy, out-of-doors complexion; flitting on his thin cavalryman's legs across the doorways, either just 'back from the mountain' or with jingling spurs and riding-whip under his arm, on the point of starting 'for the mountain'. Then Don Pépé, modestly martial in his chair, the llanero who seemed somehow to have found his martial jocularity, his knowledge of the world, and his manner perfect for his station, in the midst of savage armed contests with his kind; Avellanos, polished and familiar, the diplomatist with his loquacity covering much caution and wisdom in delicate advice, with his manuscript of a historical work on Costaguana, entitled *Fifty Years of Misrule*, which, at present, he thought it was not prudent (even if it were possible) 'to give to the world'; these three, and also Doña Emilia amongst them, gracious, small, and fairylike, before the glittering tea-set, with one common master-thought in their heads, with one common feeling of a tense situation, with one ever-present aim to preserve the inviolable character of the mine at every cost. And there was also to be seen Captain Mitchell, a little apart, near one of the long windows, with an air of old-fashioned neat old bachelorhood about him, slightly pompous, in a white waistcoat, a little disregarded and unconscious of it; utterly in the dark, and imagining himself to be in the thick of things. The good man, having spent a clear thirty years of his life on the high seas before getting what he called a 'shore billet,' was astonished at the importance of transactions (other than relating to shipping) which take place on dry land. Almost every event out of the usual daily course 'marked an epoch' for him or else was 'history'; unless with his pomposity struggling with a discomfited droop of his rubicund, rather handsome face, set off by snow-white close hair and short whiskers, he would mutter: 'Ah, that! That, sir, was a mistake.'

The reception of the first consignment of San Tomé silver for shipment to San Francisco in one of OSN Co.'s mail-boats had, of course, 'marked an epoch' for Captain Mitchell. The ingots, packed in boxes of stiff oxhide with plaited handles, small enough to be carried easily by two men, were brought down by the serenos of the mine walking in careful couples down the half-mile or so of steep, zigzag paths to the foot of the mountain. There they would be loaded into a string of two-wheeled carts, resembling roomy coffers with a door at the back, and harnessed tandem with two mules each, waiting under the guard of armed and mounted serenos. Don Pépé padlocked each door in succession, and at the signal of his whistle the string of carts would move off, closely surrounded by the clank of spur and carbine, with jolts and cracking of whips, with a sudden deep rumble over the boundary bridge ('into the land of thieves and sanguinary macaques,' Don Pépé defined that crossing); hats bobbing in the first light of the dawn, on the heads of cloaked figures; Winchesters on hip; bridle hands protruding lean and brown from under the falling folds of the ponchos. The convoy skirting a little wood, along the mine trail, between the mud huts and low walls of Rincon, increased its pace on the *camino real*, mules urged to speed, escort galloping, Don Carlos riding alone ahead of a dust storm affording a vague vision of long ears of mules, of fluttering little green and white flags stuck upon each cart; of raised arms in a mob of sombreros with the white gleam of ranging eyes; and Don Pépé, hardly visible in the rear of that rattling dust trail, with a stiff seat and impassive face, rising and falling rhythmically on an ewe-necked silver-bitted black brute with a hammer head.

The sleepy people in the little clusters of huts, in the small ranchos near the road, recognised by the headlong sound the charge of the San Tomé silver escort towards the crumbling wall of the city on the Campo side. They came to the doors to see it dash by over ruts and stones, with a clatter and clank and cracking of whips, with the reckless rush and precise driving of a field battery hurrying into action, and the solitary English figure of the Señor Administrador riding far ahead in the lead.

In the fenced roadside paddocks loose horses galloped wildly for a while; the heavy cattle stood up breast deep in the grass, lowing mutteringly at the flying noise; a meek Indian villager would glance back once and hasten to shove his loaded little donkey bodily against a wall, out of the way of the San Tomé silver escort going to the sea; a small knot of chilly léperos under the Stone Horse of the Alameda would mutter: 'Caramba!' on seeing it take a wide curve at a gallop and dart into the empty street of the Constitution; for it was considered the correct thing, the only proper style by the mule-drivers of the San Tomé mine to go through the waking town from end to end without a check in the speed as if chased by a devil.

The early sunshine glowed on the delicate primrose, pale pink, pale blue fronts of the big houses with all their gates shut yet, and no face behind the iron bars of the windows. In the whole sunlit range of empty balconies along the street only one white figure would be visible high up above the clear pavement – the wife of the Señor Administrador – leaning over to see the escort go by to the harbour, a mass of heavy, fair hair twisted up negligently on her little head, and a lot of lace about the neck of her muslin wrapper. With a smile to her husband's single, quick, upward glance, she would watch the whole thing stream past below her feet with an orderly uproar, till she answered by a friendly sign the salute of the galloping Don Pépé, the stiff, deferential inclination with a sweep of the hat below the knee.

The string of padlocked carts lengthened, the size of the escort grew bigger as the years went on. Every three months an increasing stream of treasure swept through the streets of Sulaco on its way to the strong room in the OSN Co.'s building by the harbour, there to await shipment for the North. Increasing in volume, and of immense value also; for, as Charles Gould told his wife once with some exultation, there had never been seen anything in the world to approach the vein of the Gould Concession. For them both, each passing of the escort under the balconies of the Casa Gould was like another victory gained in the conquest of peace for Sulaco.

No doubt the initial action of Charles Gould had been helped at the beginning by a period of comparative peace which occurred just about that time; and also by the general softening of manners as compared with the epoch of civil wars whence had emerged the iron tyranny of Guzman Bento of fearful memory. In the contests that broke out at the end of his rule (which had kept peace in the country for a whole fifteen years) there was more fatuous imbecility, plenty of cruelty and suffering still, but much less of the old-time fierce and blindly ferocious political fanaticism. It was all more vile, more base, more contemptible, and infinitely more manageable in the very outspoken cynicism of motives. It was more clearly a brazen-faced scramble for a constantly diminishing quantity of booty; since all enterprise had been stupidly killed in the land. Thus it came to pass that the province of Sulaco, once the field of cruel party vengeances, had become in a way one of the considerable prizes of political career. The great of the earth (in Sta Marta) reserved the posts in the old Occidental State to those nearest and dearest to them: nephews, brothers, husbands of favourite sisters, bosom friends, trusty supporters – or prominent supporters of whom perhaps they were afraid. It was the blessed province of great opportunities and of largest salaries, for the San Tomé mine had its own unofficial pay list, whose items and amounts, fixed in consultation by Charles Gould and Señor Avellanos, were known to a prominent business man in the United States, who for twenty minutes or so in every month gave his undivided attention to Sulaco affairs. At the same time the material interests of all sorts, backed up by the influence of the San Tomé mine, were quietly gathering substance in that part of the Republic. If, for instance the Sulaco Collectorship was generally understood, in the political world of the capital, to open the way to the Ministry of Finance, and so on for every official post, then, on the other hand, the despondent business circles of the Republic had come to consider the Occidental Province as the promised land of safety, especially if a man managed to get on good terms with the administration of the mine. 'Charles Gould; excellent fellow! Absolutely necessary to make sure of him before taking a single step. Get an introduction to him from Moraga if you can – the agent of the King of Sulaco, don't you know.'

No wonder, then, that Sir John, coming from Europe to smooth the path for his railway, had been meeting the name (and even the nickname) of Charles Gould at every turn in Costaguana. The agent of the San Tomé Administration in Sta Marta (a polished, well-informed gentleman, Sir John thought him) had certainly helped so greatly in bringing about the presidential tour that he began to think that there was something in the faint whispers hinting at the immense occult influence of the Gould Concession. What was currently whispered was this – that the San Tomé Administration had, in part, at least, financed the last revolution, which had brought into a five-year dictatorship Don Vincente Ribiera, a man of culture and of unblemished character, invested with a mandate of reform by the best elements of the State. Serious, well-informed men seemed to believe the fact, to hope for better things, for the establishment of legality, of good faith and order in public life. So much the better, then, thought Sir John. He worked always on a great scale; there was a loan to the State, and a project for systematic colonisation of the Occidental Province, involved in one vast scheme with the construction of the National Central Railway. Good faith, order, honesty, peace, were badly wanted for this great development of material interests. Anybody on the side of these things, and especially if able to help, had an importance in Sir John's eyes. He had not been disappointed in the 'King of Sulaco'. The local difficulties had fallen away, as the engineer-in-chief had foretold they would, before Charles Gould's mediation. Sir John had been extremely fêted in Sulaco, next to the President-Dictator, a fact which might have accounted for the evident ill-humour General Montero displayed at a lunch given on board the *Juno* just before she was to sail, taking away from Sulaco the President-Dictator and the distinguished foreign guests in his train.

The Excellentísimo ('the hope of honest men', as Don José had addressed him in a public speech delivered in the name of the Provincial Assembly of Sulaco) sat at the head of the long table; Captain Mitchell, positively stony-eyed and purple in the face with the solemnity of this 'historical event', occupied the foot as the representative of the OSN Company in Sulaco, the hosts of that informal function, with the captain of the ship and some minor officials from the shore around him. Those cheery, swarthy little gentlemen cast jovial side-glances at the bottles of champagne beginning to pop behind the guests' backs in the hands of the ship's stewards. The amber wine creamed up to the rims of the glasses.

Charles Gould had his place next to a foreign envoy, who, in a listless undertone, had been talking to him fitfully of hunting and shooting. The well-nourished, pale face, with an eyeglass and drooping yellow moustache, made the Señor Administrador appear by contrast twice as sunbaked, more flaming red, a hundred times more intensely and silently alive. Don José Avellanos touched elbows with the other foreign diplomat, a dark man with a quiet, watchful, self-confident demeanour, and a touch of reserve. All etiquette being laid aside on the occasion, General Montero was the only one there in full uniform, so stiff with embroideries in front that his broad chest seemed protected by a cuirass of gold. Sir John at the beginning had got away from high places for the sake of sitting near Mrs Gould.

The great financier was trying to express to her his grateful sense of her hospitality and of his obligation to her husband's 'enormous influence in this part of the country', when she interrupted him by a low 'Hush!' The President was going to make an informal pronouncement.

The Excellentísimo was on his legs. He said only a few words, evidently deeply felt, and meant perhaps mostly for Avellanos – his old friend – as to the necessity of unremitting effort to secure the lasting welfare of the country emerging after this last struggle, he hoped, into a period of peace and material prosperity.

Mrs Gould, listening to the mellow, slightly mournful voice, looking at this rotund, dark, spectacled face, at the short body, obese to the point of infirmity, thought that this man of delicate and melancholy mind, physically almost a cripple, coming out of his retirement into a dangerous strife at the call of his fellows, had the right to speak with the authority of his self-sacrifice. And yet she was made uneasy. He was more pathetic than promising, this first civilian Chief of the State Costaguana had ever known, pronouncing, glass in hand, his simple watchwords of honesty, peace, respect for law, political good faith abroad and at home – the safeguards of national honour.

He sat down. During the respectful, appreciative buzz of voices that followed the speech, General Montero raised a pair of heavy, drooping eyelids and rolled his eyes with a sort of uneasy dullness from face to face. The military backwoods hero of the party, though secretly impressed by the sudden novelties and splendours of his position (he had never been on board a ship before, and had hardly ever seen the sea except from a distance), understood by a sort of instinct the advantage his surly, unpolished attitude of a savage fighter gave him amongst all these refined Blanco aristocrats. But why was it that nobody was looking at him? he wondered to himself angrily. He was able to spell out the print of newspapers, and knew that he had performed the 'greatest military exploit of modern times'.

'My husband wanted the railway,' Mrs Gould said to Sir John in the general murmur of resumed conversations. 'All this brings nearer the sort of future we desire for the country, which has waited for it in sorrow long enough, God knows. But I will confess that the other day, during my afternoon drive when I suddenly saw an Indian boy ride out of a wood with the red flag of a surveying party in his hand, I felt something of a shock. The future means change – an utter change. And yet even here there are simple and picturesque things that one would like to preserve.'

Sir John listened, smiling. But it was his turn now to hush Mrs Gould.

'General Montero is going to speak,' he whispered, and almost immediately added, in comic alarm, 'Heavens! he's going to propose my own health, I believe.'

General Montero had risen with a jingle of steel scabbard and a ripple of glitter on his gold-embroidered breast; a heavy sword-hilt appeared at his side above the edge of the table. In this gorgeous uniform, with his bull neck, his hooked nose flattened on the tip upon a blue-black, dyed moustache, he looked like a disguised and sinister vaquero. The drone of his voice had a strangely rasping, soulless ring. He floundered, lowering, through a few vague sentences; then suddenly raising his big head and his voice together, burst out harshly: 'The honour of the country is in the hands of the army. I assure you I shall be faithful to it.' He hesitated till his roaming eyes met Sir

John's face upon which he fixed a lurid, sleepy glance; and the figure of the lately negotiated loan came into his mind. He lifted his glass. 'I drink to the health of the man who brings us a million and a half of pounds.'

He tossed off his champagne, and sat down heavily with a half-surprised, half-bullying look all round the faces in the profound, as if appalled, silence which succeeded the felicitous toast. Sir John did not move.

'I don't think I am called upon to rise,' he murmured to Mrs Gould. 'That sort of thing speaks for itself.' But Don José Avellanos came to the rescue with a short oration, in which he alluded pointedly to England's goodwill towards Costaguana – 'a goodwill,' he continued, significantly, 'of which I, having been in my time accredited to the Court of St James, am able to speak with some knowledge.'

Only then Sir John thought fit to respond, which he did gracefully in bad French, punctuated by bursts of applause and the 'Hear! Hears!' of Captain Mitchell, who was able to understand a word now and then. Directly he had done, the financier of railways turned to Mrs Gould: 'You were good enough to say that you intended to ask me for something,' he reminded her, gallantly. 'What is it? Be assured that any request from you would be considered in the light of a favour to myself.'

She thanked him by a gracious smile. Everybody was rising from the table.

'Let us go on deck,' she proposed, 'where I'll be able to point out to you the very object of my request.'

An enormous national flag of Costaguana, diagonal red and yellow, with two green palm trees in the middle, floated lazily at the mainmast head of the *Juno*. A multitude of fireworks being let off in their thousands at the water's edge in honour of the President kept up a mysterious crepitating noise half round the harbour. Now and then a lot of rockets, swishing upwards invisibly, detonated overhead with only a puff of smoke in the bright sky. Crowds of people could be seen between the town gate and the harbour, under the bunches of multicoloured flags fluttering on tall poles.

Faint bursts of military music would be heard suddenly, and the remote sound of shouting. A knot of ragged Negroes at the end of the wharf kept on loading and firing a small iron cannon time after time. A greyish haze of dust hung thin and motionless against the sun.

Don Vincente Ribiera made a few steps under the deck-awning, leaning on the arm of Señor Avellanos; a wide circle was formed round him, where the mirthless smile of his dark lips and the sightless glitter of his spectacles could be seen turning amiably from side to side. The informal function arranged on purpose on board the *Juno* to give the President-Dictator an opportunity to meet intimately some of his most notable adherents in Sulaco was drawing to an end. On one side, General Montero, his bald head covered now by a plumed cocked hat, remained motionless on a skylight seat, a pair of big gauntleted hands folded on the hilt of the sabre standing upright between his legs. The white plume, the coppery tint of his broad face, the blue-black of the moustaches under the curved beak, the mass of gold on sleeves and breast, the high shining boots with enormous spurs, the working nostrils, the imbecile and domineering stare of the glorious victor of Rio Seco had in them something ominous and incredible; the exaggeration of a cruel caricature, the fatuity of solemn masquerading, the atrocious grotesqueness of some military idol of Aztec conception and European bedecking, awaiting the homage of worshippers. Don José approached diplomatically this weird and inscrutable portent, and Mrs Gould turned her fascinated eyes away at last.

Charles, coming up to take leave of Sir John, heard him say, as he bent over his wife's hand, 'Certainly. Of course, my dear Mrs Gould, for a protégé of yours! Not the slightest difficulty. Consider it done.'

Going ashore in the same boat with the Goulds, Don José Avellanos was very silent. Even in the Gould carriage he did not open his lips for a long time. The mules trotted slowly away from the wharf between the extended hands of the beggars, who for that day seemed to have abandoned in a body the portals of churches. Charles Gould sat on the back seat and looked away upon the plain. A multitude of booths made of green boughs, of rushes, of odd pieces of plank eked out with bits of canvas had been erected all over it for the sale of cana, of dulces, of fruit, of cigars. Over little heaps of glowing charcoal Indian women, squatting on mats, cooked food in black earthen pots, and boiled the water for the maté gourds, which they offered in soft, caressing voices to the country people. A racecourse had been staked out for the vaqueros; and away to the left, from where the crowd was massed thickly about a huge temporary erection, like a circus tent of wood with a conical grass roof, came the resonant twanging of harp strings, the sharp ping of guitars, with the grave drumming throb of an Indian gombo pulsating steadily through the shrill choruses of the dancers.

Charles Gould said presently: 'All this piece of land belongs now to the Railway Company. There will be no more popular feasts held here.'

Mrs Gould was rather sorry to think so. She took this opportunity to mention how she had just obtained from Sir John the promise that the house occupied by Giorgio Viola should not be interfered with. She declared she could never understand why the survey engineers ever talked of demolishing that old building. It was not in the way of the projected harbour branch of the line in the least.

She stopped the carriage before the door to reassure at once the old Genoese, who came out bareheaded and stood by the carriage step. She talked to him in Italian, of course, and he thanked her with calm dignity. An old Garibaldino was grateful to her from the bottom of his heart for keeping the roof over the heads of his wife and children. He was too old to wander any more.

'And is it for ever, signora?' he asked.

'For as long as you like.'

'Bene. Then the place must be named. It was not worth while before.'

He smiled ruggedly, with a running together of wrinkles at the corners of his eyes. 'I shall set about the painting of the name tomorrow.'

'And what is it going to be, Giorgio?'

'Albergo d'Italia Una,' said the old Garibaldino, looking away for a moment. 'More in memory of those who have died,' he added, 'than for the country stolen from us soldiers of liberty by the craft of that accursed Piedmontese race of kings and ministers.'

Mrs Gould smiled slightly, and, bending over a little, began to enquire about his wife and children. He had sent them into town on that day. The padrona was better in health; many thanks to the signora for enquiring.

People were passing in twos and threes, in whole parties of men and women attended by trotting children. A horseman mounted on a silver-grey mare drew rein quietly in the shade of the house after taking off his hat to the party in the carriage, who returned smiles and familiar nods. Old Viola, evidently very pleased with the news he had just heard, interrupted himself for a moment to tell him rapidly that the house was secured, by the kindness of the English signora, for as long as he liked to keep it. The other listened attentively, but made no response.

When the carriage moved on he took off his hat again, a grey sombrero with a silver cord and tassels. The bright colours of a Mexican serape twisted on the cantle, the enormous silver buttons on the embroidered leather jacket, the row of tiny silver buttons down the seam of the trousers, the snowy linen, a silk sash with embroidered ends, the silver plates on headstall and saddle, proclaimed the unapproachable style of the famous Capataz de Cargadores – a Mediterranean sailor – got up with more finished splendour than any well-to-do young ranchero of the Campo had ever displayed on a high holiday.

'It is a great thing for me,' murmured old Giorgio, still thinking of the house, for now he had grown weary of change. 'The signora just said a word to the Englishman.'

'The old Englishman who has enough money to pay for a railway? He is going off in an hour,' remarked Nostromo, carelessly. 'Buon viaggio, then. I've guarded his bones all the way from the Entrada pass down to the plain and into Sulaco, as though he had been my own father.'

Old Giorgio only moved his head sideways absently. Nostromo pointed after the Goulds' carriage, nearing the grass-grown gate in the old town wall that was like a wall of matted jungle.

'And I have sat alone at night with my revolver in the Company's warehouse time and again by the side of that other Englishman's heap of silver, guarding it as though it had been my own.'

Viola seemed lost in thought. 'It is a great thing for me,' he repeated again, as if to himself.

'It is,' agreed the magnificent Capataz de Cargadores, calmly. 'Listen, Vecchio – go in and bring me out a cigar, but don't look for it in my room. There's nothing there.'

Viola stepped into the café and came out directly, still absorbed in his idea, and tendered him a cigar, mumbling thoughtfully in his moustache, 'Children growing up – and girls, too! Girls!' He sighed and fell silent.

'What, only one?' remarked Nostromo, looking down with a sort of comic inquisitiveness at the unconscious old man. 'No matter,' he added, with lofty negligence; 'one is enough till another is wanted.'

He lit it and let the match drop from his passive fingers. Giorgio Viola looked up, and said abruptly: 'My son would have been just such a fine young man as you, Gian' Battista, if he had lived.'

'What? Your son? But you are right, padrone. If he had been like me he would have been a man.'

He turned his horse slowly, and paced on between the booths, checking the mare almost to a standstill now and then for children, for the groups of people from the distant Campo, who stared after him with admiration. The Company's lightermen saluted him from afar; and the greatly envied Capataz de Cargadores advanced, amongst murmurs of recognition and obsequious greetings, towards the huge circus-like erection. The throng thickened; the guitars tinkled louder; other horsemen sat motionless, smoking calmly above the heads of the crowd; it eddied and pushed before the doors of the high-roofed building, whence issued a shuffle and thumping of feet in time to the dance music vibrating and shrieking with a racking rhythm, overhung by the tremendous, sustained, hollow roar of the gombo. The barbarous and imposing noise of the big drum, that can madden a crowd, and that even Europeans cannot hear without a strange emotion, seemed to draw Nostromo on to its source, while a man, wrapped up in a faded, torn poncho, walked by his stirrup, and, buffeted right and left, begged 'his worship' insistently for employment on the wharf. He whined, offering the Señor Capataz half his daily pay for the privilege of being admitted to the swaggering fraternity of Cargadores; the other half would be enough for him, he protested. But Captain Mitchell's right-hand man – 'invaluable for our work – a perfectly incorruptible fellow' – after looking down critically at the ragged mozo, shook his head without a word in the uproar going on around.

The man fell back; and a little further on Nostromo had to pull up. From the doors of the dance hall men and women emerged tottering, streaming with sweat, trembling in every limb, to lean, panting, with staring eyes and parted lips, against the wall of the structure, where the harps and guitars played on with mad speed in an incessant roll of thunder. Hundreds of hands clapped in there; voices shrieked, and then all at once would sink low, chanting in unison the refrain of a love song, with a dying fall. A red flower, flung with a good aim from somewhere in the crowd, struck the resplendent Capataz on the cheek.

He caught it as it fell, neatly, but for some time did not turn his head. When at last he condescended to look round, the throng near him had parted to make way for a pretty Morenita, her hair held up by a small golden comb, who was walking towards him in the open space.

Her arms and neck emerged plump and bare from a snowy chemisette; the blue woollen skirt, with all the fullness gathered in front, scanty on the hips and tight across the back, disclosed the provoking action of her walk. She came straight on and laid her hand on the mare's neck with a timid, coquettish look upwards out of the corner of her eyes.

'Querido,' she murmured, caressingly, 'why do you pretend not to see me when I pass?'

'Because I don't love thee any more,' said Nostromo, deliberately, after a moment of reflective silence.

The hand on the mare's neck trembled suddenly. She dropped her head before all the eyes in the wide circle formed round the generous, the terrible, the inconstant Capataz de Cargadores, and his Morenita.

Nostromo, looking down, saw tears beginning to fall down her face.

'Has it come, then, ever beloved of my heart?' she whispered. 'Is it true?'

'No,' said Nostromo, looking away carelessly. 'It was a lie. I love thee as much as ever.'

'Is that true?' she cooed, joyously, her cheeks still wet with tears.

'It is true.'

'True on the life?'

'As true as that; but thou must not ask me to swear it on the Madonna that stands in thy room.' And the Capataz laughed a little in response to the grins of the crowd.

She pouted – very pretty – a little uneasy.

'No, I will not ask for that. I can see love in your eyes.' She laid her hand on his knee. 'Why are you trembling like this? From love?' she continued, while the cavernous thundering of the gombo went on without a pause. 'But if you love her as much as that, you must give your Paquita a gold-mounted rosary of beads for the neck of her Madonna.'

'No,' said Nostromo, looking into her uplifted, begging eyes, which suddenly turned stony with surprise.

'No? Then what else will your worship give me on the day of the fiesta?' she asked, angrily; 'so as not to shame me before all these people.'

'There is no shame for thee in getting nothing from thy lover for once.'

'True! The shame is your worship's – my poor lover's,' she flared up, sarcastically.

Laughs were heard at her anger, at her retort. What an audacious spitfire she was! The people aware of this scene were calling out urgently to others in the crowd. The circle round the silver-grey mare narrowed slowly.

The girl went off a pace or two, confronting the mocking curiosity of the eyes, then flung back to the stirrup, tiptoeing, her enraged face turned up to Nostromo with a pair of blazing eyes. He bent low to her in the saddle.

'Juan,' she hissed, 'I could stab thee to the heart!'

The dreaded Capataz de Cargadores, magnificent and carelessly public in his amours, flung his arm round her neck and kissed her spluttering lips. A murmur went round.

'A knife!' he demanded at large, holding her firmly by the shoulder.

Twenty blades flashed out together in the circle. A young man in holiday attire, bounding in, thrust one in Nostromo's hand and bounded back into the ranks, very proud of himself. Nostromo had not even looked at him.

'Stand on my foot,' he commanded the girl, who, suddenly subdued, rose lightly, and when he had her up, encircling her waist, her face near to his, he pressed the knife into her little hand.

'No, Morenita! You shall not put me to shame,' he said. 'You shall have your present; and so that everyone should know who is your lover today, you may cut all the silver buttons off my coat.'

There were shouts of laughter and applause at this witty freak, while the girl passed the keen blade, and the impassive rider jingled in his palm the increasing hoard of silver buttons. He eased her to the ground with both her hands full. After whispering for a while with a very strenuous face, she walked away, haughtily, and vanished into the crowd.

The circle had broken up, and the lordly Capataz de Cargadores, the indispensable man, the tried and trusty Nostromo, the Mediterranean sailor come ashore casually to try his luck in Costaguana, rode slowly towards the harbour. The *Juno* was just then swinging round; and even as Nostromo reined up again to look on, a flag ran up on the improvised flagstaff erected in an ancient and dismantled little fort at the harbour entrance. Half a battery of field guns had been hurried over there from the Sulaco barracks for the purpose of firing the regulation salutes for the President-Dictator and the War Minister. As the mail-boat headed through the pass, the badly timed reports announced the end of Don Vincente Ribiera's first official visit to Sulaco, and for Captain Mitchell the end of another 'historic occasion'. Next time when the 'Hope of honest men' was to come that way, a year and a half later, it was unofficially, over the mountain tracks, fleeing after a defeat on a lame mule, to be only just saved by Nostromo from an ignominious death at the hands of a mob. It was a very different event, of which Captain Mitchell used to say: 'It was history – history, sir! and that fellow of mine, Nostromo, you know, was right in it. Absolutely making history, sir.'

But this event, creditable to Nostromo, was to lead immediately to another, which could not be classed either as 'history' or as 'a mistake' in Captain Mitchell's phraseology. He had another word for it.

'Sir,' he used to say afterwards, 'that was no mistake. It was a fatality. A misfortune, pure and simple, sir. And that poor fellow of mine was right in it – right in the middle of it! A fatality, if ever there was one – and to my mind he has never been the same man since.'

PART SECOND
The Isabels

Chapter 1

Through good and evil report in the varying fortune of that struggle which Don José had characterised in the phrase, 'the fate of national honesty trembles in the balance', the Gould Concession, 'Imperium in Imperio', had gone on working; the square mountain had gone on pouring its treasure down the wooden shoots to the unresting batteries of stamps; the lights of San Tomé had twinkled night after night upon the great, limitless shadow of the Campo; every three months the silver escort had gone down to the sea as if neither the war nor its consequences could ever affect the ancient Occidental State secluded beyond its high barrier of the Cordillera. All the fighting took place on the other side of that mighty wall of serrated peaks lorded over by the white dome of Higuerota and as yet unbreached by the railway, of which only the first part, the easy Campo part from Sulaco to the Ivie Valley at the foot of the pass, had been laid. Neither did the telegraph line cross the mountains yet; its poles, like slender beacons on the plain, penetrated into the forest fringe of the foothills cut by the deep avenue of the track; and its wire ended abruptly in the construction camp at a white deal table supporting a Morse apparatus, in a long hut of planks with a corrugated iron roof overshadowed by gigantic cedar trees – the quarters of the engineer in charge of the advance section.

The harbour was busy, too, with the traffic in railway material, and with the movements of troops along the coast. The OSN Company found much occupation for its fleet. Costaguana had no navy, and, apart from a few coastguard cutters, there were no national ships except a couple of old merchant steamers used as transports.

Captain Mitchell, feeling more and more in the thick of history, found time for an hour or so during an afternoon in the drawing-room of the Casa Gould, where, with a strange ignorance of the real forces at work around him, he professed himself delighted to get away from the strain of affairs. He did not know what he would have done without his invaluable Nostromo, he declared. Those confounded Costaguana politics gave him more work – he confided to Mrs Gould – than he had bargained for.

Don José Avellanos had displayed in the service of the endangered Ribiera Government an organising activity and an eloquence of which the echoes reached even Europe. For, after the new loan to the Ribiera Government, Europe had become interested in Costaguana. The Sala of the Provincial Assembly (in the Municipal Buildings of Sulaco), with its portraits of the

Liberators on the walls and an old flag of Cortez preserved in a glass case above the President's chair, had heard all these speeches – the early one containing the impassioned declaration 'Militarism is the enemy', the famous one of the 'trembling balance' delivered on the occasion of the vote for the raising of a second Sulaco regiment in the defence of the reforming Government; and when the provinces again displayed their old flags (proscribed in Guzman Bento's time) there was another of those great orations, when Don José greeted these old emblems of the war of Independence, brought out again in the name of new Ideals. The old idea of Federalism had disappeared. For his part he did not wish to revive old political doctrines. They were perishable. They died. But the doctrine of political rectitude was immortal. The second Sulaco regiment, to whom he was presenting this flag, was going to show its valour in a contest for order, peace, progress; for the establishment of national self-respect without which – he declared with energy – 'we are a reproach and a byword amongst the powers of the world.'

Don José Avellanos loved his country. He had served it lavishly with his fortune during his diplomatic career, and the later story of his captivity and barbarous ill-usage under Guzman Bento was well known to his listeners. It was a wonder that he had not been a victim of the ferocious and summary executions which marked the course of that tyranny; for Guzman had ruled the country with the sombre imbecility of political fanaticism. The power of Supreme Government had become in his dull mind an object of strange worship, as if it were some sort of cruel deity. It was incarnated in himself, and his adversaries, the Federalists, were the supreme sinners, objects of hate, abhorrence, and fear, as heretics would be to a convinced Inquisitor. For years he had carried about at the tail of the Army of Pacification, all over the country, a captive band of such atrocious criminals, who considered themselves most unfortunate at not having been summarily executed. It was a diminishing company of nearly naked skeletons, loaded with irons, covered with dirt, with vermin, with raw wounds, all men of position, of education, of wealth, who had learned to fight amongst themselves for scraps of rotten beef thrown to them by soldiers, or to beg a Negro cook for a drink of muddy water in pitiful accents. Don José Avellanos, clanking his chains amongst the others, seemed only to exist in order to prove how much hunger, pain, degradation, and cruel torture a human body can stand without parting with the last spark of life. Sometimes interrogatories, backed by some primitive method of torture, were administered to them by a commission of officers hastily assembled in a hut of sticks and branches, and made pitiless by the fear for their own lives. A lucky one or two of that spectral company of prisoners would perhaps be led tottering behind a bush to be shot by a file of soldiers. Always an army chaplain – some unshaven, dirty man, girt with a sword and with a tiny cross embroidered in white cotton on the left breast of a lieutenant's uniform – would follow, cigarette in the corner of the mouth, wooden stool in hand, to hear the confession and give absolution; for the

Citizen Saviour of the Country (Guzman Bento was called thus officially in petitions) was not averse from the exercise of rational clemency. The irregular report of the firing squad would be heard, followed sometimes by a single finishing shot; a little bluish cloud of smoke would float up above the green bushes, and the Army of Pacification would move on over the savannas, through the forests, crossing rivers, invading rural pueblos, devastating the haciendas of the horrid aristocrats, occupying the inland towns in the fulfilment of its patriotic mission, and leaving behind a united land wherein the evil taint of Federalism could no longer be detected in the smoke of burning houses and the smell of spilt blood.

Don José Avellanos had survived that time.

Perhaps, when contemptuously signifying to him his release, the Citizen Saviour of the Country might have thought this benighted aristocrat too broken in health and spirit and fortune to be any longer dangerous. Or, perhaps, it may have been a simple caprice. Guzman Bento, usually full of fanciful fears and brooding suspicions, had sudden accesses of unreasonable self-confidence when he perceived himself elevated on a pinnacle of power and safety beyond the reach of mere mortal plotters. At such times he would impulsively command the celebration of a solemn Mass of thanksgiving, which would be sung in great pomp in the cathedral of Sta Marta by the trembling, subservient Archbishop of his creation. He heard it sitting in a gilt armchair placed before the high altar, surrounded by the civil and military heads of his Government. The unofficial world of Sta Marta would crowd into the cathedral, for it was not quite safe for anybody of mark to stay away from these manifestations of presidential piety. Having thus acknowledged the only power he was at all disposed to recognise as above himself, he would scatter acts of political grace in a sardonic wantonness of clemency. There was no other way left now to enjoy his power but by seeing his crushed adversaries crawl impotently into the light of day out of the dark, noisome cells of the colegio. Their harmlessness fed his insatiable vanity, and they could always be got hold of again. It was the rule for all the women of their families to present thanks afterwards in a special audience. The incarnation of that strange god: El Gobierno Supremo, received them standing, cocked hat on head, and exhorted them in a menacing mutter to show their gratitude by bringing up their children in fidelity to the democratic form of government, 'which I have established for the happiness of our country.' His front teeth having been knocked out in some accident of his former herdsman's life, his utterance was spluttering and indistinct. He had been working for Costaguana alone in the midst of treachery and opposition. Let it cease now lest he should become weary of forgiving!

Don José Avellanos had known this forgiveness.

He was broken in health and fortune deplorably enough to present a truly gratifying spectacle to the supreme chief of democratic institutions. He retired to Sulaco. His wife had an estate in that province, and she nursed him back to life out of the house of death and captivity. When she died, their daughter, an only child, was old enough to devote herself to 'poor papa'.

Miss Avellanos, born in Europe and educated partly in England, was a tall, grave girl, with a self-possessed manner, a wide, white forehead, a wealth of rich brown hair, and blue eyes.

The other young ladies of Sulaco stood in awe of her character and accomplishments. She was reputed to be terribly learned and serious. As to pride, it was well known that all the Corbelàns were proud, and her mother was a Corbelàn. Don José Avellanos depended very much upon the devotion of his beloved Antonia. He accepted it in the benighted way of men, who, though made in God's image, are like stone idols without sense before the smoke of certain burnt offerings. He was ruined in every way, but a man possessed of passion is not a bankrupt in life. Don José Avellanos desired passionately for his country: peace, prosperity, and (as the end of the preface to *Fifty Years of Misrule* has it) 'an honourable place in the comity of civilised nations'. In this last phrase the Minister Plenipotentiary, cruelly humiliated by the bad faith of his Government towards the foreign bondholders, stands disclosed in the patriot.

The fatuous turmoil of greedy factions succeeding the tyranny of Guzman Bento seemed to bring his desire to the very door of opportunity. He was too old to descend personally into the centre of the arena at Sta Marta. But the men who acted there sought his advice at every step. He himself thought that he could be most useful at a distance, in Sulaco. His name, his connections, his former position, his experience commanded the respect of his class. The discovery that this man, living in dignified poverty in the Corbelàn town residence (opposite the Casa Gould), could dispose of material means towards the support of the cause increased his influence. It was his open letter of appeal that decided the candidature of Don Vincente Ribiera for the Presidency. Another of these informal State papers drawn up by Don José (this time in the shape of an address from the Province) induced that scrupulous constitutionalist to accept the extraordinary powers conferred upon him for five years by an overwhelming vote of congress in Sta Marta. It was a specific mandate to establish the prosperity of the people on the basis of firm peace at home, and to redeem the national credit by the satisfaction of all just claims abroad.

In the afternoon the news of that vote had reached Sulaco by the usual roundabout postal way through Cayta, and up the coast by steamer. Don José, who had been waiting for the mail in the Goulds' drawing-room, got out of the rocking-chair, letting his hat fall off his knees. He rubbed his silvery, short hair with both hands, speechless with the excess of joy.

'Emilia, my soul,' he had burst out, 'let me embrace you! Let me – '

Captain Mitchell, had he been there, would no doubt have made an apt remark about the dawn of a new era; but if Don José thought something of the kind, his eloquence failed him on this occasion. The inspirer of that revival of the Blanco party tottered where he stood. Mrs Gould moved forward quickly and, as she offered her cheek with a smile to her old friend, managed very cleverly to give him the support of her arm he really needed.

Don José had recovered himself at once, but for a time he could do no more than murmur, 'Oh, you two patriots! Oh, you two patriots!' – looking from one to the other. Vague plans of another historical work, wherein all the devotions to the regeneration of the country he loved would be enshrined for the reverent worship of posterity, flitted through his mind. The historian who had enough elevation of soul to write of Guzman Bento: 'Yet this monster, imbrued in the blood of his countrymen, must not be held unreservedly to the execration of future years. It appears to be true that he, too, loved his country. He had given it twelve years of peace; and, absolute master of lives and fortunes as he was, he died poor. His worst fault, perhaps, was not his ferocity, but his ignorance;' the man who could write thus of a cruel persecutor (the passage occurs in his 'History of Misrule') felt at the foreshadowing of success an almost boundless affection for his two helpers, for these two young people from over the sea.

Just as years ago, calmly, from the conviction of practical necessity, stronger than any abstract political doctrine, Henry Gould had drawn the sword, so now, the times being changed, Charles Gould had flung the silver of the San Tomé into the fray. The Inglés of Sulaco, the 'Costaguana Englishman' of the third generation, was as far from being a political intriguer as his uncle from a revolutionary swashbuckler. Springing from the instinctive uprightness of their natures their action was reasoned. They saw an opportunity and used the weapon to hand.

Charles Gould's position – a commanding position in the background of that attempt to retrieve the peace and the credit of the Republic – was very clear. At the beginning he had had to accommodate himself to existing circumstances of corruption so naively brazen as to disarm the hatred of a man courageous enough not to be afraid of its irresponsible potency to ruin everything it touched. It seemed to him too contemptible for hot anger even. He made use of it with a cold, fearless scorn, manifested rather than concealed by the forms of stony courtesy which did away with much of the ignominy of the situation. At bottom, perhaps, he suffered from it, for he was not a man of cowardly illusions, but he refused to discuss the ethical view with his wife. He trusted that, though a little disenchanted, she would be intelligent enough to understand that his character safeguarded the enterprise of their lives as much or more than his policy. The extraordinary development of the mine had put a great power into his hands. To feel that prosperity always at the mercy of unintelligent greed had grown irksome to him. To Mrs Gould it was humiliating. At any rate, it was dangerous. In the confidential communications passing between Charles Gould, the King of Sulaco, and the head of the silver and steel interests far away in California, the conviction was growing that any attempt made by men of education and integrity ought to be discreetly supported. 'You may tell your friend Avellanos that I think so,' Mr Holroyd had written at the proper moment from his inviolable sanctuary within the eleven-storey-high factory of great affairs. And shortly afterwards, with a credit opened by the Third Southern Bank (located next door but one to the Holroyd Building), the Ribierist party in Costaguana took a practical shape under the eye of the administrator of the San Tomé mine. And Don José, the hereditary friend of the Gould family, could say: 'Perhaps, my dear Carlos, I shall not have believed in vain.'

Chapter 2

After another armed struggle, decided by Montero's victory of Rio Seco, had been added to the tale of civil wars, the 'honest men', as Don José called them, could breathe freely for the first time in half a century. The Five-Year-Mandate law became the basis of that regeneration, the passionate desire and hope for which had been like the elixir of everlasting youth for Don José Avellanos.

And when it was suddenly – and not quite unexpectedly – endangered by that 'brute Montero', it was a passionate indignation that gave him a new lease of life, as it were. Already, at the time of the President-Dictator's visit to Sulaco, Moraga had sounded a note of warning from Sta Marta about the War Minister. Montero and his brother made the subject of an earnest talk between the Dictator-President and the Nestor inspirer of the party. But Don Vincente, a doctor of philosophy from the Cordova University, seemed to have an exaggerated respect for military ability, whose mysteriousness – since it appeared to be altogether independent of intellect – imposed upon his imagination. The victor of Rio Seco was a popular hero. His services were so recent that the President-Dictator quailed before the obvious charge of political ingratitude. Great regenerating transactions were being initiated – the fresh loan, a new railway line, a vast colonisation scheme. Anything that could unsettle the public opinion in the capital was to be avoided. Don José bowed to these arguments and tried to dismiss from his mind the gold-laced portent in boots, and with a sabre, made meaningless now at last, he hoped, in the new order of things.

Less than six months after the President-Dictator's visit, Sulaco learned with stupefaction of the military revolt in the name of national honour. The Minister of War, in a barrack-square allocution to the officers of the artillery regiment he had been inspecting, had declared the national honour sold to foreigners. The Dictator, by his weak compliance with the demands of the

European powers – for the settlement of long outstanding money claims – had showed himself unfit to rule. A letter from Moraga explained afterwards that the initiative, and even the very text, of the incendiary allocution came, in reality, from the other Montero, the ex-guerrillero, the Commandante de Plaza. The energetic treatment of Dr Monygham, sent for in haste 'to the mountain', who came galloping three leagues in the dark, saved Don José from a dangerous attack of jaundice.

After getting over the shock, Don José refused to let himself be prostrated. Indeed, better news succeeded at first. The revolt in the capital had been suppressed after a night of fighting in the streets. Unfortunately, both the Monteros had been able to make their escape south, to their native province of Entre-Montes. The hero of the forest march, the victor of Rio Seco, had been received with frenzied acclamations in Nicoya, the provincial capital. The troops in garrison there had gone to him in a body. The brothers were organising an army, gathering malcontents, sending emissaries primed with patriotic lies to the people, and with promises of plunder to the wild llaneros. Even a Monterist press had come into existence, speaking oracularly of the secret promises of support given by 'our great sister Republic of the North' against the sinister land-grabbing designs of European powers, cursing in every issue the 'miserable Ribiera', who had plotted to deliver his country, bound hand and foot, for a prey to foreign speculators.

Sulaco, pastoral and sleepy, with its opulent Campo and the rich silver mine, heard the din of arms fitfully in its fortunate isolation. It was nevertheless in the very forefront of the defence with men and money; but the very rumours reached it circuitously – from abroad even, so much was it cut off from the rest of the Republic, not only by natural obstacles, but also by the vicissitudes of the war. The Monteristos were besieging Cayta, an important postal link. The overland couriers ceased to come across the mountains, and no muleteer would consent to risk the journey at last; even Bonifacio on one occasion failed to return from Sta Marta, either not daring to start, or perhaps captured by the parties of the enemy raiding the country between the Cordillera and the capital. Monterist publications, however, found their way into the province, mysteriously enough; and also Monterist emissaries preaching death to aristocrats in the villages and towns of the Campo. Very early, at the beginning of the trouble, Hernandez, the bandit, had proposed (through the agency of an old priest of a village in the wilds) to deliver two of them to the Ribierist authorities in Tonoro. They had come to offer him a free pardon and the rank of colonel from General Montero in consideration of joining the rebel army with his mounted band. No notice was taken at the time of the proposal. It was joined, as an evidence of good faith, to a petition praying the Sulaco Assembly for permission to enlist, with all his followers, in the forces being then raised in Sulaco for the defence of the Five-Year-Mandate of regeneration. The petition, like everything else, had found its way into Don José's hands. He had showed to Mrs Gould these pages of

dirty-greyish rough paper (perhaps looted in some village store), covered
with the crabbed, illiterate handwriting of the old padre, carried off from his
hut by the side of a mud-walled church to be the secretary of the dreaded
Salteador. They had both bent in the lamplight of the Gould drawing-room
over the document containing the fierce and yet humble appeal of the man
against the blind and stupid barbarity turning an honest ranchero into a
bandit. A postscript of the priest stated that, but for being deprived of his
liberty for ten days, he had been treated with humanity and the respect due
to his sacred calling. He had been, it appears, confessing and absolving the
chief and most of the band, and he guaranteed the sincerity of their good
disposition. He had distributed heavy penances, no doubt in the way of
litanies and fasts; but he argued shrewdly that it would be difficult for them
to make their peace with God durably till they had made peace with men.

Never before, perhaps, had Hernandez's head been in less jeopardy than
when he petitioned humbly for permission to buy a pardon for himself and his
gang of deserters by armed service. He could range afar from the waste lands
protecting his fastness, unchecked, because there were no troops left in the
whole province. The usual garrison of Sulaco had gone south to the war, with
its brass band playing the Bolívar march on the bridge of one of the OSN
Company's steamers. The great family coaches drawn up along the shore of
the harbour were made to rock on the high leathern springs by the enthusiasm
of the señoras and the señoritas standing up to wave their lace handkerchiefs,
as lighter after lighter packed full of troops left the end of the jetty.

Nostromo directed the embarkation, under the superintendence of Captain
Mitchell, red-faced in the sun, conspicuous in a white waistcoat, representing
the allied and anxious goodwill of all the material interests of civilisation.
General Barrios, who commanded the troops, assured Don José on parting
that in three weeks he would have Montero in a wooden cage drawn by three
pair of oxen ready for a tour through all the towns of the Republic.

'And then, señora,' he continued, baring his curly iron-grey head to Mrs
Gould in her landau – 'and then, señora, we shall convert our swords into
ploughshares and grow rich. Even I, myself, as soon as this little business is
settled, shall open a fundacíon on some land I have on the llanos and try to
make a little money in peace and quietness. Señora, you know, all Costaguana
knows – what do I say? – this whole South American continent knows, that
Pablo Barrios has had his fill of military glory.'

Charles Gould was not present at the anxious and patriotic send-off. It
was not his part to see the soldiers embark. It was neither his part, nor his
inclination, nor his policy. His part, his inclination, and his policy were
united in one endeavour to keep unchecked the flow of treasure he had
started single-handed from the re-opened scar in the flank of the mountain.
As the mine developed he had trained for himself some native help. There
were foremen, artificers and clerks, with Don Pépé for the gobernador of
the mining population. For the rest his shoulders alone sustained the whole

weight of the 'Imperium in Imperio', the great Gould Concession whose mere shadow had been enough to crush the life out of his father.

Mrs Gould had no silver mine to look after. In the general life of the Gould Concession she was represented by her two lieutenants, the doctor and the priest, but she fed her woman's love for excitement on events whose significance was purified to her by the fire of her imaginative purpose. On that day she had brought the Avellanos, father and daughter, down to the harbour with her.

Amongst his other activities of that stirring time, Don José had become the chairman of a Patriotic Committee which had armed a great proportion of troops in the Sulaco command with an improved model of a military rifle. It had been just discarded for something still more deadly by one of the great European powers. How much of the market-price for second-hand weapons was covered by the voluntary contributions of the principal families, and how much came from those funds Don José was understood to command abroad, remained a secret which he alone could have disclosed; but the Ricos, as the populace called them, had contributed under the pressure of their Nestor's eloquence. Some of the more enthusiastic ladies had been moved to bring offerings of jewels into the hands of the man who was the life and soul of the party.

There were moments when both his life and his soul seemed overtaxed by so many years of undiscouraged belief in regeneration. He appeared almost inanimate, sitting rigidly by the side of Mrs Gould in the landau, with his fine, old, clean-shaven face of a uniform tint as if modelled in yellow wax, shaded by a soft felt hat, the dark eyes looking out fixedly. Antonia, the beautiful Antonia, as Miss Avellanos was called in Sulaco, leaned back, facing them; and her full figure, the grave oval of her face with full red lips, made her look more mature than Mrs Gould, with her mobile expression and small, erect person under a slightly swaying sunshade.

Whenever possible Antonia attended her father; her recognised devotion weakened the shocking effect of her scorn for the rigid conventions regulating the life of Spanish-American girlhood. And, in truth, she was no longer girlish. It was said that she often wrote State papers from her father's dictation, and was allowed to read all the books in his library. At the receptions – where the situation was saved by the presence of a very decrepit old lady (a relation of the Corbelàns), quite deaf and motionless in an armchair – Antonia could hold her own in a discussion with two or three men at a time. Obviously she was not the girl to be content with peeping through a barred window at a cloaked figure of a lover ensconced in a doorway opposite – which is the correct form of Costaguana courtship. It was generally believed that with her foreign upbringing and foreign ideas the learned and proud Antonia would never marry – unless, indeed, she married a foreigner from Europe or North America, now that Sulaco seemed on the point of being invaded by all the world.

Chapter 3

When General Barrios stopped to address Mrs Gould, Antonia raised negligently her hand holding an open fan, as if to shade from the sun her head, wrapped in a light lace shawl. The clear gleam of her blue eyes gliding behind the black fringe of eyelashes paused for a moment upon her father, then travelled further to the figure of a young man of thirty at most, of medium height, rather thickset, wearing a light overcoat. Bearing down with the open palm of his hand upon the knob of a flexible cane, he had been looking on from a distance; but directly he saw himself noticed, he approached quietly and put his elbow over the door of the landau.

The shirt collar cut low in the neck, the big bow of his cravat, the style of his clothing, from the round hat to the varnished shoes, suggested an idea of French elegance; but otherwise he was the very type of a fair Spanish creole. The fluffy moustache and the short, curly, golden beard did not conceal his lips, rosy, fresh, almost pouting in expression. His full, round face was of that warm, healthy creole white which is never tanned by its native sunshine. Martin Decoud was seldom exposed to the Costaguana sun under which he was born. His people had been long settled in Paris, where he had studied law, had dabbled in literature, had hoped now and then in moments of exaltation to become a poet like that other foreigner of Spanish blood, José Maria Heredia. In other moments he had, to pass the time, condescended to write articles on European affairs for the *Semanario*, the principal newspaper in Sta Marta, which printed them under the heading 'From our special correspondent', though the authorship was an open secret. Everybody in Costaguana, where the tale of compatriots in Europe is jealously kept, knew that it was 'the son Decoud', a talented young man, supposed to be moving in the higher spheres of Society. As a matter of fact, he was an idle boulevardier, in touch with some smart journalists, made free of a few newspaper offices, and welcomed in the pleasure haunts of pressmen. This life, whose dreary superficiality is covered by the glitter of universal blague, like the stupid clowning of a harlequin by the spangles of a motley costume, induced in him a Frenchified – but most un-French – cosmopolitanism, in reality a mere barren indifferentism posing as intellectual superiority. Of his own country he used to say to his French associates: imagine an atmosphere of opéra-bouffe in which all the comic business of stage statesmen, brigands, etc., etc., all their farcical stealing, intriguing, and stabbing is done in dead earnest. It is screamingly funny, the blood flows all the time, and the actors believe themselves to be influencing the fate of the universe. Of course, government in general, any government anywhere, is a thing of exquisite comicality to a discerning mind; but really we Spanish-Americans do overstep the bounds. No man of ordinary intelligence can take part in the intrigues of *une farce macabre*. However, these Ribierists, of whom we hear so much just now, are really trying in their own comical way to make the country habitable, and even to pay some of its debts. My friends, you had better write up Señor Ribiera all you can in kindness to your own bondholders. Really, if what I am told in my letters is true, there is some chance for them at last.'

And he would explain with railing verve what Don Vincente Ribiera stood for – a mournful little man oppressed by his own good intentions, the significance of battles won, who Montero was *(un grotesque vaniteux et féroce)*, and the manner of the new loan connected with railway development, and the colonisation of vast tracts of land in one great financial scheme.

And his French friends would remark that evidently this little fellow Decoud *connaissait la question à fond*. An important Parisian review asked him for an article on the situation. It was composed in a serious tone and in a spirit of levity. Afterwards he asked one of his intimates: 'Have you read my thing about the regeneration of Costaguana – *une bonne blague, hein?*'

He imagined himself Parisian to the tips of his fingers. But far from being that he was in danger of remaining a sort of nondescript dilettante all his life. He had pushed the habit of universal raillery to a point where it blinded him to the genuine impulses of his own nature. To be suddenly selected for the executive member of the patriotic small-arms committee of Sulaco seemed to him the height of the unexpected, one of those fantastic moves of which only his 'dear countrymen' were capable.

'It's like a tile falling on my head. I – I – executive member! It's the first I hear of it! What do I know of military rifles? *C'est funambulesque!*' he had exclaimed to his favourite sister; for the Decoud family – except the old father and mother – used the French language amongst themselves. 'And you should see the explanatory and confidential letter! Eight pages of it – no less!'

This letter, in Antonia's handwriting, was signed by Don José, who appealed to the 'young and gifted Costaguanero' on public grounds, and privately opened his heart to his talented godson, a man of wealth and leisure, with wide relations, and by his parentage and bringing-up worthy of all confidence.

'Which means,' Martin commented, cynically, to his sister, 'that I am not likely to misappropriate the funds, or go blabbing to our Chargé d'Affaires here.'

The whole thing was being carried out behind the back of the War Minister, Montero, a member of the Ribiera Government, but difficult to get rid of at once. He was not to know anything of it till the troops under Barrios's command had the new rifle in their hands. The President-Dictator, whose position was very difficult, was alone in the secret.

'How funny!' commented Martin's sister and confidant; to which the brother, with an air of best Parisian blague, had retorted: 'It's immense! The idea of that Chief of the State engaged, with the help of private citizens, in digging a mine under his own indispensable War Minister. No! We are unapproachable!' And he laughed immoderately.

Afterwards his sister was surprised at the earnestness and ability he displayed in carrying out his mission, which circumstances made delicate, and his want of special knowledge rendered difficult. She had never seen Martin take so much trouble about anything in his whole life.

'It amuses me,' he had explained, briefly. 'I am beset by a lot of swindlers trying to sell all sorts of gas-pipe weapons. They are charming; they invite me to expensive luncheons; I keep up their hopes; it's extremely entertaining. Meanwhile, the real affair is being carried through in quite another quarter.'

When the business was concluded he declared suddenly his intention of seeing the precious consignment delivered safely in Sulaco. The whole burlesque business, he thought, was worth following up to the end. He mumbled his excuses, tugging at his golden beard, before the acute young lady who (after the first wide stare of astonishment) looked at him with narrowed eyes, and pronounced slowly: 'I believe you want to see Antonia.'

'What Antonia?' asked the Costaguana boulevardier, in a vexed and disdainful tone. He shrugged his shoulders, and spun round on his heel. His sister called out after him joyously: 'The Antonia you used to know when she wore her hair in two plaits down her back.'

He had known her some eight years since, shortly before the Avellanos had left Europe for good, as a tall girl of sixteen, youthfully austere, and of a character already so formed that she ventured to treat slightingly his pose of disabused wisdom. On one occasion, as though she had lost all patience, she flew out at him about the aimlessness of his life and the levity of his opinions. He was twenty then, an only son, spoiled by his adoring family. This attack disconcerted him so greatly that he had faltered in his affectation of amused superiority before that insignificant chit of a schoolgirl. But the impression left was so strong that ever since all the girl friends of his sisters recalled to him Antonia Avellanos by some faint resemblance, or by the great force of contrast. It was, he told himself, like a ridiculous fatality. And, of course, in the news the Decouds received regularly from Costaguana, the name of their friends, the Avellanos, cropped up frequently – the arrest and the abominable treatment of the ex-Minister, the dangers and hardships endured by the family, its withdrawal in poverty to Sulaco, the death of the mother.

The Monterist pronunciamento had taken place before Martin Decoud reached Costaguana. He came out in a roundabout way, through Magellan's Straits by the main line and the West Coast Service of the OSN Company. His precious consignment arrived just in time to convert the first feelings of consternation into a mood of hope and resolution. Publicly he was made much of by the *familias principales*. Privately Don José, still shaken and weak, embraced him with tears in his eyes.

'You have come out yourself! No less could be expected from a Decoud. Alas! our worst fears have been realised,' he moaned, affectionately. And again he hugged his godson. This was indeed the time for men of intellect and conscience to rally round the endangered cause.

It was then that Martin Decoud, the adopted child of Western Europe, felt the absolute change of atmosphere. He submitted to being embraced and talked to without a word. He was moved in spite of himself by that note of passion and sorrow unknown on the more refined stage of European politics. But when the tall Antonia, advancing with her light step in the dimness of the big bare sala of the Avellanos house, offered him her hand (in her emancipated way), and murmured, 'I am glad to see you here, Don Martin,' he felt how impossible it would be to tell these two people that he had intended to go away by the next month's packet. Don José, meantime, continued his praises. Every accession added to public confidence, and, besides, what an example to the young men at home from the brilliant defender of the country's regeneration, the worthy expounder of the party's political faith before the world!

Everybody had read the magnificent article in the famous Parisian Review. The world was now informed: and the author's appearance at this moment was like a public act of faith. Young Decoud felt overcome by a feeling of impatient confusion. His plan had been to return by way of the United States through California, visit Yellowstone Park, see Chicago, Niagara, have a look at Canada, perhaps make a short stay in New York, a longer one in Newport, use his letters of introduction. The pressure of Antonia's hand was so frank, the tone of her voice was so unexpectedly unchanged in its approving warmth, that all he found to say after his low bow was: 'I am inexpressibly grateful for your welcome; but why need a man be thanked for returning to his native country? I am sure Doña Antonia does not think so.'

'Certainly not, señor,' she said, with that perfectly calm openness of manner which characterised all her utterances. 'But when he returns, as you return, one may be glad – for the sake of both.'

Martin Decoud said nothing of his plans. He not only never breathed a word of them to anyone, but only a fortnight later asked the mistress of the Casa Gould (where he had of course obtained admission at once), leaning forward in his chair with an air of well-bred familiarity, whether she could not detect in him that day a marked change – an air, he explained, of more excellent gravity. At this Mrs Gould turned her face full towards him with the silent enquiry of slightly widened eyes and the merest ghost of a smile, an habitual movement with her, which was very fascinating to men by something subtly devoted, finely self-forgetful in its lively readiness of attention. Because, Decoud continued imperturbably, he felt no longer an idle cumberer of the earth. She was, he assured her, actually beholding at that moment the Journalist of Sulaco. At once Mrs Gould glanced towards Antonia, posed upright in the corner of a high, straight-backed Spanish sofa, a large black fan waving slowly against the curves of her fine figure, the tips of crossed feet peeping from under the hem of the black skirt. Decoud's eyes also remained fixed there, while in an undertone he added that Miss Avellanos was quite aware of his new and unexpected vocation, which in Costaguana was generally the speciality of half-educated Negroes and wholly penniless lawyers. Then, confronting with a sort of urbane effrontery Mrs Gould's gaze, now turned sympathetically upon himself, he breathed out the words, 'Pro Patria!'

What had happened was that he had all at once yielded to Don José's pressing entreaties to take the direction of a newspaper that would 'voice the aspirations of the province'. It had been Don José's old and cherished idea. The necessary plant (on a modest scale) and a large consignment of paper had been received from America some time before; the right man alone was wanted. Even Señor Moraga in Sta Marta had not been able to find one, and the matter was now becoming pressing; some organ was absolutely needed to counteract the effect of the lies disseminated by the Monterist press: the atrocious calumnies, the appeals of the people calling upon them to rise with their knives in their hands and put an end once for all to the Blancos, to these Gothic remnants, to these sinister mummies, these impotent paraliticos, who plotted with foreigners for the surrender of the lands and the slavery of the people.

The clamour of this 'Negro Liberalism' frightened Señor Avellanos. A newspaper was the only remedy. And now that the right man had been found in Decoud, great black letters appeared painted between the windows above the arcaded ground floor of a house on the Plaza. It was next to Anzani's great emporium of boots, silks, ironware, muslins, wooden toys, tiny silver arms, legs, heads, hearts (for ex-voto offerings), rosaries, champagne, women's hats, patent medicines, even a few dusty books in paper covers and mostly in the French language. The big black letters formed the words, 'Offices of the Porvenir'. From these offices a single folded sheet of Martin's journalism issued three times a week; and the sleek yellow Anzani prowling in a suit of ample black and carpet slippers, before the many doors of his establishment, greeted by a deep, sidelong inclination of his body the Journalist of Sulaco going to and fro on the business of his august calling.

Chapter 4

Perhaps it was in the exercise of his calling that he had come to see the troops depart. The *Porvenir* of the day after next would no doubt relate the event, but its editor, leaning his side against the landau, seemed to look at nothing. The front rank of the company of infantry drawn up three deep across the shore end of the jetty when pressed too close would bring their bayonets to the charge ferociously, with an awful rattle; and then the crowd of spectators swayed back bodily, even under the noses of the big white mules. Notwithstanding the great multitude there was only a low, muttering noise; the dust hung in a brown haze, in which the horsemen, wedged in the throng here and there, towered from the hips upwards, gazing all one way over the heads. Almost every one of them had mounted a friend, who steadied himself with both hands grasping his shoulders from behind; and the rims of their hats touching, made like one disc sustaining the cones of two pointed crowns with a double face underneath. A hoarse mozo would bawl out something to an acquaintance in the ranks, or a woman would shriek suddenly the word *Adios*! followed by the Christian name of a man.

General Barrios, in a shabby blue tunic and white peg-top trousers falling upon strange red boots, kept his head uncovered and stooped slightly, propping himself up with a thick stick. No! He had earned enough military glory to satiate any man, he insisted to Mrs Gould, trying at the same time to put an air of gallantry into his attitude. A few jetty hairs hung sparsely from his upper lip, he had a salient nose, a thin, long jaw, a black silk patch over one eye. His other eye, small and deep-set, twinkled erratically in all directions, aimlessly affable. The few European spectators, all men, who had naturally drifted into the neighbourhood of the Gould carriage, betrayed by the solemnity of their faces their impression that the general must have had too much punch (Swedish punch, imported in bottles by Anzani) at the Amarilla Club before he had started with his Staff on a furious ride to the harbour. But Mrs Gould bent forward, self-possessed, and declared her conviction that still more glory awaited the general in the near future.

'Señora!' he remonstrated, with great feeling, 'in the name of God, reflect! How can there be any glory for a man like me in overcoming that bald-headed *embustero* with the dyed moustaches?'

Pablo Ignacio Barrios, son of a village alcalde, general of division, commanding in chief the Occidental Military district, did not frequent the higher society of the town. He preferred the unceremonious gatherings of men where he could tell jaguar-hunt stories, boast of his powers with the lasso, with which he could perform extremely difficult feats of the sort 'no married man should attempt', as the saying goes amongst the llaneros; relate tales of extraordinary night rides, encounters with wild bulls, struggles with crocodile, adventures in the great forests, crossings of swollen rivers. And it was not mere boastfulness that prompted the general's reminiscences, but a genuine love of that wild life which he had led in his young days before he turned his back for ever on the thatched roof of the parental tolderia in the woods. Wandering away as far as Mexico he had fought against the French by the side (as he said) of Juarez, and was the only military man of Costaguana who had ever encountered European troops in the field. That fact shed a great lustre upon his name till it became eclipsed by the rising star of Montero. All his life he had been an inveterate gambler. He alluded himself quite openly to the current story how once, during some campaign (when in command of a brigade), he had gambled away his horses, pistols, and accoutrements, to the very epaulettes, playing *monte* with his colonels the night before the battle. Finally, he had sent under escort his sword (a presentation sword, with a gold hilt) to the town in the rear of his position to be immediately pledged for five hundred pesetas with a sleepy and frightened shopkeeper. By daybreak he had lost the last of that money, too, when his only remark, as he rose calmly, was, 'Now let us go and fight to the death.' From that time he had become aware that a general could lead his troops into battle very well with a simple stick in his hand. 'It has been my custom ever since,' he would say.

He was always overwhelmed with debts; even during the periods of splendour in his varied fortunes of a Costaguana general, when he held high military commands, his gold-laced uniforms were almost always in pawn with some tradesman. And at last, to avoid the incessant difficulties of costume caused by the anxious lenders, he had assumed a disdain of military trappings, an eccentric fashion of shabby old tunics, which had become like a second nature. But the faction Barrios joined needed to fear no political betrayal. He was too much of a real soldier for the ignoble traffic of buying and selling victories. A member of the foreign diplomatic body in Sta Marta had once passed a judgment upon him: 'Barrios is a man of perfect honesty and even of some talent for war, *mais il manque de tenue.*' After the triumph of the Ribierists he obtained the reputedly lucrative Occidental command, mainly through the exertions of his creditors (the Sta Marta shopkeepers, all great politicians), who moved heaven and earth in his interest publicly, and privately besieged Señor Moraga, the influential agent of the San Tomé mine, with the exaggerated lamentations that if the general were passed over, 'We shall all be ruined.' An incidental but favourable mention of his name in Mr Gould senior's long correspondence with his son had something to do with his appointment, too; but most of all undoubtedly his established political honesty. No one questioned the personal bravery of the Tiger-killer, as the populace called him. He was, however, said to be unlucky in the field – but this was to be the beginning of an era of peace. The soldiers liked him for his humane temper, which was like a strange and precious flower unexpectedly blooming on the hotbed of corrupt revolutions; and when he rode slowly through the streets during some military display, the contemptuous good humour of his solitary eye roaming over the crowds extorted the acclamations of the populace. The women of that class especially seemed positively fascinated by the long dropping nose, the peaked chin, the heavy lower lip, the black silk eye-patch and band slanting rakishly over the forehead. His high rank always procured an audience of Caballeros for his sporting stories, which he detailed very well with a simple, grave enjoyment. As to the society of ladies, it was irksome by the restraints it imposed without any equivalent, as far as he could see. He had not, perhaps, spoken three times on the whole to Mrs Gould since he had taken up his high command; but he had observed her frequently riding with the Señor Administrador, and had pronounced that there was more sense in her little bridle-hand than in all the female heads in Sulaco. His impulse had been to be very civil on parting to a woman who did not wobble in the saddle, and happened to be the wife of a personality very important to a man always short of money. He even pushed his attentions so far as to desire the aide-de-camp at his side (a thickset, short captain with a Tartar physiognomy) to bring along a corporal with a file of men in front of the carriage, lest the crowd in its backward surges should 'incommode the mules of the señora'.

Then, turning to the small knot of silent Europeans looking on within earshot, he raised his voice protectingly: 'Señores, have no apprehension. Go on quietly making your Ferrocarril – your railways, your telegraphs. Your – There's enough wealth in Costaguana to pay for everything – or else you would not be here. Ha! ha! Don't mind this little picardía of my friend Montero. In a little while you shall behold his dyed moustaches through the bars of a strong wooden cage. Si, señores! Fear nothing, develop the country, work, work!'

The little group of engineers received this exhortation without a word, and after waving his hand at them loftily, he addressed himself again to Mrs Gould: 'That is what Don José says we must do. Be enterprising! Work! Grow rich! To put Montero in a cage is my work; and when that insignificant piece of business is done, then, as Don José wishes us, we shall grow rich, one and all, like so many Englishmen, because it is money that saves a country, and – '

But a young officer in a very new uniform, hurrying up from the direction of the jetty, interrupted his interpretation of Señor Avellanos's ideals. The general made a movement of impatience; the other went on talking to him insistently, with an air of respect. The horses of the Staff had been embarked, the steamer's gig was awaiting the general at the boat steps; and Barrios, after a fierce stare of his one eye, began to take leave. Don José roused himself for an appropriate phrase pronounced mechanically. The terrible strain of hope and fear was telling on him, and he seemed to husband the last sparks of his fire for those oratorical efforts of which even the distant Europe was to hear. Antonia, her red lips firmly closed, averted her head behind the raised fan; and young Decoud, though he felt the girl's eyes upon him, gazed away persistently, hooked on his elbow, with a scornful and complete detachment. Mrs Gould heroically concealed her dismay at the appearance of men and events so remote from her racial conventions, dismay too deep to be uttered in words even to her husband. She understood his voiceless reserve better now. Their confidential intercourse fell, not in moments of privacy, but precisely in public, when the quick meeting of their glances would comment upon some fresh turn of events. She had gone to his school of uncompromising silence, the only one possible, since so much that seemed shocking, weird, and grotesque in the working out of their purposes had to be accepted as normal in this country. Decidedly, the stately Antonia looked more mature and infinitely calm; but she would never have known how to reconcile the sudden sinkings of her heart with an amiable mobility of expression.

Mrs Gould smiled a goodbye at Barrios, nodded round to the Europeans (who raised their hats simultaneously) with an engaging invitation, 'I hope to see you all presently, at home'; then said nervously to Decoud, 'Get in, Don Martin,' and heard him mutter to himself in French, as he opened the carriage door, '*Le sort en est jeté.*' She heard him with a sort of exasperation. Nobody ought to have known better than himself that the first cast of dice had been already thrown long ago in a most desperate game. Distant acclamations, words of command yelled out, and a roll of drums on the jetty greeted the departing general. Something like a slight faintness came over her, and she looked blankly at Antonia's still face, wondering what would happen to Charley if that absurd man failed. '*A la casa, Ignacio,*' she cried at the motionless broad back of the coachman, who gathered the reins without haste, mumbling to himself under his breadth, '*Si, la casa. Si, si niña.*'

The carriage rolled noiselessly on the soft track, the shadows fell long on the dusty little plain interspersed with dark bushes, mounds of turned-up earth, low wooden buildings with iron roofs of the Railway Company; the sparse row of telegraph poles strode obliquely clear of the town, bearing a single, almost invisible wire far into the great campo like a slender, vibrating feeler of that progress waiting outside for a moment of peace to enter and twine itself about the weary heart of the land.

The café window of the Albergo d'Italia Una was full of sunburnt, whiskered faces of railway men. But at the other end of the house, the end of the Signori Inglesi, old Giorgio, at the door with one of his girls on each side, bared his bushy head, as white as the snows of Higuerota. Mrs Gould stopped the carriage. She seldom failed to speak to her protégé; moreover, the excitement, the heat, and the dust had made her thirsty. She asked for a glass of water. Giorgio sent the children indoors for it, and approached with pleasure expressed in his whole rugged countenance. It was not often that he had occasion to see his benefactress, who was also an Englishwoman – another title to his regard. He offered some excuses for his wife. It was a bad day with her; her oppressions – he tapped his own broad chest. She could not move from her chair that day.

Decoud, ensconced in the corner of his seat, observed gloomily Mrs Gould's old revolutionist, then, offhand: 'Well, and what do you think of it all, Garibaldino?'

Old Giorgio, looking at him with some curiosity, said civilly that the troops had marched very well. One-eyed Barrios and his officers had done wonders with the recruits in a short time. Those Indios, only caught the other day, had gone swinging past in double quick time, like bersaglieri; they looked well fed, too, and had whole uniforms. 'Uniforms!' he repeated with a half-smile of pity. A look of grim retrospect stole over his piercing, steady eyes. It had been otherwise in his time when men fought against tyranny, in the forests of Brazil, or on the plains of Uruguay, starving on half-raw beef without salt, half naked, with often only a knife tied to a stick for a weapon. 'And yet we used to prevail against the oppressor,' he concluded, proudly.

His animation fell; the slight gesture of his hand expressed discouragement; but he added that he had asked one of the sergeants to show him the new rifle. There was no such weapon in his fighting days; and if Barrios could not: 'Yes, yes,' broke in Don José, almost trembling with eagerness. 'We are safe. The good Señor Viola is a man of experience. Extremely deadly – is it not so? You have accomplished your mission admirably, my dear Martin.'

Decoud, lolling back moodily, contemplated old Viola.

'Ah! Yes. A man of experience. But who are you for, really, in your heart?'

Mrs Gould leaned over to the children. Linda had brought out a glass of water on a tray, with extreme care; Giselle presented her with a bunch of flowers gathered hastily.

'For the people,' declared old Viola, sternly.

'We are all for the people – in the end.'

'Yes,' muttered old Viola, savagely. 'And meantime they fight for you. Blind. Esclavos!'

At that moment young Scarfe of the railway staff emerged from the door of the part reserved for the Signori Inglesi. He had come down to head-quarters from somewhere up the line on a light engine, and had had just time to get a bath and change his clothes. He was a nice boy, and Mrs Gould welcomed him.

'It's a delightful surprise to see you, Mrs Gould. I've just come down. Usual luck. Missed everything, of course. This show is just over, and I hear there has been a great dance at Don Juste Lopez's last night. Is it true?'

'The young patricians,' Decoud began suddenly in his precise English, 'have indeed been dancing before they started off to the war with the Great Pompey.'

Young Scarfe stared, astounded. 'You haven't met before,' Mrs Gould intervened. 'Mr Decoud – Mr Scarfe.'

'Ah! But we are not going to Pharsalia,' protested Don José, with nervous haste, also in English. 'You should not jest like this, Martin.'

Antonia's breast rose and fell with a deeper breath. The young engineer was utterly in the dark. 'Great what?' he muttered, vaguely.

'Luckily, Montero is not a Caesar,' Decoud continued. 'Not the two Monteros put together would make a decent parody of a Caesar.' He crossed his arms on his breast, looking at Señor Avellanos, who had returned to his immobility. 'It is only you, Don José, who are a genuine old Roman – vir Romanus – eloquent and inflexible.'

Since he had heard the name of Montero pronounced, young Scarfe had been eager to express his simple feelings. In a loud and youthful tone he hoped that this Montero was going to be licked once for all and done with. There was no saying what would happen to the railway if the revolution got the upper hand. Perhaps it would have to be abandoned. It would not be the first railway gone to pot in Costaguana. 'You know, it's one of their so-called national things,' he ran on, wrinkling up his nose as if the word had a suspicious flavour to his profound experience of South American affairs. And, of course, he chatted with animation, it had been such an immense piece of luck for him at his age to get appointed on the staff 'of a big thing like that – don't you know.' It would give him the pull over a lot of chaps all through life, he asserted. 'Therefore – down with Montero! Mrs Gould.' His artless grin disappeared slowly before the unanimous gravity of the faces turned upon him from the carriage; only that 'old chap,' Don José, presenting a motionless, waxy profile, stared straight on as if deaf. Scarfe did not know the Avellanos very well. They did not give balls, and Antonia never appeared at a ground-floor window, as some other young ladies used to do attended by elder women, to chat with the caballeros on horseback in the calle. The stares of these creoles did not matter much; but what on earth had come to Mrs Gould? She said, 'Go on, Ignacio,' and gave him a slow inclination of the head. He heard a short laugh from that round-faced, Frenchified fellow. He coloured up to the eyes, and stared at Giorgio Viola, who had fallen back with the children, hat in hand.

'I shall want a horse presently,' he said with some asperity to the old man.

'Si, señor. There are plenty of horses,' murmured the Garibaldino, smoothing absently, with his brown hands, the two heads, one dark with bronze glints, the other fair with a coppery ripple, of the two girls by his side. The returning stream of sightseers raised a great dust on the road. Horsemen noticed the group. 'Go to your mother,' he said. 'They are growing up as I am growing older, and there is nobody – '

He looked at the young engineer and stopped, as if awakened from a dream; then, folding his arms on his breast, took up his usual position, leaning back in the doorway with an upward glance fastened on the white shoulder of Higuerota far away.

In the carriage Martin Decoud, shifting his position as though he could not make himself comfortable, muttered as he swayed towards Antonia, 'I suppose you hate me.' Then in a loud voice he began to congratulate Don José upon all the engineers being convinced Ribierists. The interests of all those foreigners was gratifying. 'You have heard this one. He is an enlightened well-wisher. It is pleasant to think that the prosperity of Costaguana is of some use to the world.'

'He is very young,' Mrs Gould remarked, quietly.

'And so very wise for his age,' retorted Decoud. 'But here we have the naked truth from the mouth of that child. You are right, Don José. The natural treasures of Costaguana are of importance to the progressive Europe represented by this youth, just as three hundred years ago the wealth of our Spanish fathers was a serious object to the rest of Europe – as represented by the bold buccaneers. There is a curse of futility upon our character: Don Quixote and Sancho Panza, chivalry and materialism, high-sounding sentiments and a supine morality, violent efforts for an idea and a sullen acquiescence in every form of corruption. We convulsed a continent for our independence only to become the passive prey of a democratic parody, the helpless victims of scoundrels and cutthroats, our institutions a mockery, our laws a farce – a Guzman Bento our master! And we have sunk so low that when a man like you has awakened our conscience, a stupid barbarian of a Montero – Great Heavens! a Montero! – becomes a deadly danger, and an ignorant, boastful Indio, like Barrios, is our defender.'

But Don José, disregarding the general indictment as though he had not heard a word of it, took up the defence of Barrios. The man was competent enough for his special task in the plan of campaign. It consisted in an offensive movement, with Cayta as base, upon the flank of the Revolutionist forces advancing from the south against Sta Marta, which was covered by another army with the President-Dictator in its midst. Don José became quite animated with a great flow of speech, bending forward anxiously under the steady eyes of his daughter. Decoud, as if silenced by so much ardour, did not make a sound. The bells of the city were striking the hour of Oración when the carriage rolled under the old gateway facing the harbour like a shapeless monument of leaves and stones. The rumble of wheels under the sonorous arch was traversed by a strange, piercing shriek, and Decoud, from his back seat, had a view of the people behind the carriage trudging along the road outside, all turning their heads, in sombreros and rebozos, to look at a locomotive which rolled quickly out of sight behind Giorgio Viola's house, under a white trail of steam that seemed to vanish in the breathless, hysterically prolonged scream of warlike triumph. And it was all like a fleeting vision, the shrieking ghost of a railway engine fleeing across the frame of the archway, behind the startled movement of the people streaming back from a military spectacle with silent footsteps on the dust of the road. It was a material train returning from the Campo to the palisaded yards. The empty cars rolled lightly on the single track; there was no rumble of wheels, no tremor on the ground. The engine-driver, running past the Casa Viola with the salute of an uplifted arm, checked his speed smartly before entering the yard; and when the ear-splitting screech of the steam-whistle for the brakes had stopped, a series of hard, battering shocks, mingled with the clanking of chain-couplings, made a tumult of blows and shaken fetters under the vault of the gate.

Chapter 5

The Gould carriage was the first to return from the harbour to the empty town. On the ancient pavement, laid out in patterns, sunk into ruts and holes, the portly Ignacio, mindful of the springs of the Parisian-built landau, had pulled up to a walk, and Decoud in his corner contemplated moodily the inner aspect of the gate. The squat turreted sides held up between them a mass of masonry with bunches of grass growing at the top, and a grey, heavily scrolled, armorial shield of stone above the apex of the arch with the arms of Spain nearly smoothed out as if in readiness for some new device typical of the impending progress.

The explosive noise of the railway trucks seemed to augment Decoud's irritation. He muttered something to himself, then began to talk aloud in curt, angry phrases thrown at the silence of the two women. They did not look at him at all; while Don José, with his semi-translucent, waxy complexion, overshadowed by the soft grey hat, swayed a little to the jolts of the carriage by the side of Mrs Gould.

'This sound puts a new edge on a very old truth.'

Decoud spoke in French, perhaps because of Ignacio on the box above him; the old coachman, with his broad back filling a short, silver-braided jacket, had a big pair of ears, whose thick rims stood well away from his cropped head.

'Yes, the noise outside the city wall is new, but the principle is old.'

He ruminated his discontent for a while, then began afresh with a sidelong glance at Antonia: 'No, but just imagine our forefathers in morions and corselets drawn up outside this gate, and a band of adventurers just landed from their ships in the harbour there. Thieves, of course. Speculators, too. Their expeditions, each one, were the speculations of grave and reverend persons in England. That is history, as that absurd sailor Mitchell is always saying.'

'Mitchell's arrangements for the embarkation of the troops were excellent!' exclaimed Don José.

'That! – that! oh, that's really the work of that Genoese seaman! But to return to my noises; there used to be in the old days the sound of trumpets outside that gate. War trumpets! I'm sure they were trumpets. I have read somewhere that Drake, who was the greatest of these men, used to dine alone in his cabin on board ship to the sound of trumpets. In those days this town was full of wealth. Those men came to take it. Now the whole land is like a treasure-house, and all these people are breaking into it, whilst we are cutting each other's throats. The only thing that keeps them out is mutual jealousy. But they'll come to an agreement someday – and by the time we've settled our quarrels and become decent and honourable, there'll be nothing left for us. It has always been the same. We are a wonderful people, but it has always been our fate to be' – he did not say 'robbed,' but added, after a pause – 'exploited!'

Mrs Gould said, 'Oh, this is unjust!' And Antonia interjected, 'Don't answer him, Emilia. He is attacking me.'

'You surely do not think I was attacking Don Carlos!' Decoud answered.

And then the carriage stopped before the door of the Casa Gould. The young man offered his hand to the ladies. They went in first together; Don José walked by the side of Decoud, and the gouty old porter tottered after them with some light wraps on his arm.

Don José slipped his hand under the arm of the journalist of Sulaco.

'The *Porvenir* must have a long and confident article upon Barrios and the irresistibleness of his army of Cayta! The moral effect should be kept up in the country. We must cable encouraging extracts to Europe and the United States to maintain a favourable impression abroad.'

Decoud muttered, 'Oh, yes, we must comfort our friends, the speculators.'

The long open gallery was in shadow, with its screen of plants in vases along the balustrade, holding out motionless blossoms, and all the glass doors of the reception-rooms thrown open. A jingle of spurs died out at the further end.

Basilio, standing aside against the wall, said in a soft tone to the passing ladies, 'The Señor Administrador is just back from the mountain.'

In the great sala, with its groups of ancient Spanish and modern European furniture making as if different centres under the high white spread of the ceiling, the silver and porcelain of the tea-service gleamed among a cluster of dwarf chairs, like a bit of a lady's boudoir, putting in a note of feminine and intimate delicacy.

Don José in his rocking-chair placed his hat on his lap, and Decoud walked up and down the whole length of the room, passing between tables loaded with knick-knacks and almost disappearing behind the high backs of leathern sofas. He was thinking of the angry face of Antonia; he was confident that he would make his peace with her. He had not stayed in Sulaco to quarrel with Antonia.

Martin Decoud was angry with himself. All he saw and heard going on around him exasperated the preconceived views of his European civilisation. To contemplate revolutions from the distance of the Parisian Boulevards was quite another matter. Here on the spot it was not possible to dismiss their tragic comedy with the expression, '*Quelle farce!*'

The reality of the political action, such as it was, seemed closer, and acquired poignancy by Antonia's belief in the cause. Its crudeness hurt his feelings. He was surprised at his own sensitiveness.

'I suppose I am more of a Costaguanero than I would have believed possible,' he thought to himself.

His disdain grew like a reaction of his scepticism against the action into which he was forced by his infatuation for Antonia. He soothed himself by saying he was not a patriot, but a lover.

The ladies came in bareheaded, and Mrs Gould sank low before the little tea-table. Antonia took up her usual place at the reception hour – the corner of a leathern couch, with a rigid grace in her pose and a fan in her hand. Decoud, swerving from the straight line of his march, came to lean over the high back of her seat.

For a long time he talked into her ear from behind, softly, with a half smile and an air of apologetic familiarity. Her fan lay half grasped on her knees. She never looked at him. His rapid utterance grew more and more insistent and caressing. At last he ventured a slight laugh.

'No, really. You must forgive me. One must be serious sometimes.' He paused. She turned her head a little; her blue eyes glided slowly towards him, slightly upwards, mollified and questioning.

'You can't think I am serious when I call Montero a *gran bestia* every second day in the *Porvenir*? That is not a serious occupation. No occupation is serious, not even when a bullet through the heart is the penalty of failure!'

Her hand closed firmly on her fan.

'Some reason, you understand, I mean some sense, may creep into thinking; some glimpse of truth. I mean some effective truth, for which there is no room in politics or journalism. I happen to have said what I thought. And you are angry! If you do me the kindness to think a little you will see that I spoke like a patriot.'

She opened her red lips for the first time, not unkindly.

'Yes, but you never see the aim. Men must be used as they are. I suppose nobody is really disinterested, unless, perhaps, you, Don Martin.'

'God forbid! It's the last thing I should like you to believe of me.' He spoke lightly, and paused.

She began to fan herself without raising her hand. After a time he whispered passionately: 'Antonia!'

She smiled, and extended her hand after the English manner towards Charles Gould, who was bowing before her; while Decoud, with his elbows spread on the back of the sofa, dropped his eyes and murmured, '*Bonjour.*'

The Señor Administrador of the San Tomé mine bent over his wife for a moment. They exchanged a few words, of which only the phrase, 'The greatest enthusiasm', pronounced by Mrs Gould, could be heard.

'Yes,' Decoud began in a murmur. 'Even he!'

'This is sheer calumny,' said Antonia, not very severely.

'You just ask him to throw his mine into the melting-pot for the great cause,' Decoud whispered.

Don José had raised his voice. He rubbed his hands cheerily. The excellent aspect of the troops and the great quantity of new deadly rifles on the shoulders of those brave men seemed to fill him with an ecstatic confidence.

Charles Gould, very tall and thin before his chair, listened, but nothing could be discovered in his face except a kind and deferential attention.

Meantime, Antonia had risen, and, crossing the room, stood looking out of one of the three long windows giving on the street. Decoud followed her. The window was thrown open, and he leaned against the thickness of the wall. The long folds of the damask curtain, falling straight from the broad brass cornice, hid him partly from the room. He folded his arms on his breast, and looked steadily at Antonia's profile.

The people returning from the harbour filled the pavements; the shuffle of sandals and a low murmur of voices ascended to the window. Now and then a coach rolled slowly along the disjointed roadway of the Calle de la Constitucion. There were not many private carriages in Sulaco; at the most crowded hour on the Alameda they could be counted with one glance of the eye. The great family arks swayed on high leathern springs, full of pretty powdered faces in which the eyes looked intensely alive and black. And first Don Juste Lopez, the President of the Provincial Assembly, passed with his three lovely daughters, solemn in a black frock-coat and stiff white tie, as when directing a debate from a high tribune. Though they all raised their eyes, Antonia did not make the usual greeting gesture of a fluttered hand, and they affected not to see the two young people, Costaguaneros with European manners, whose eccentricities were discussed behind the barred windows of the first families in Sulaco. And then the widowed Señora Gavilaso de Valdes rolled by, handsome and dignified, in a great machine in which she used to travel to and from her country house, surrounded by an armed retinue in leather suits and big sombreros, with carbines at the bows of their saddles. She was a woman of most distinguished family, proud, rich, and kind-hearted. Her second son, Jaime, had just gone off on the Staff of Barrios. The eldest, a worthless fellow of a moody disposition, filled Sulaco with the noise of his dissipations, and gambled heavily at the club. The two youngest boys, with yellow Ribierist cockades in their caps, sat on the front seat. She, too, affected not to see the Señor Decoud talking publicly with Antonia in defiance of every convention. And he not even her *novio* as far as the world knew! Though, even in that case, it would have been scandal enough. But the dignified old lady, respected and admired by the first families, would have been still more shocked if she could have heard the words they were exchanging.

'Did you say I lost sight of the aim? I have only one aim in the world.'

She made an almost imperceptible negative movement of her head, still staring across the street at the Avellanos's house, grey, marked with decay, and with iron bars like a prison.

'And it would be so easy of attainment,' he continued, 'this aim which, whether knowingly or not, I have always had in my heart – ever since the day when you snubbed me so horribly once in Paris, you remember.'

A slight smile seemed to move the corner of the lip that was on his side.

'You know you were a very terrible person, a sort of Charlotte Corday in a schoolgirl's dress; a ferocious patriot. I suppose you would have stuck a knife into Guzman Bento?'

She interrupted him. 'You do me too much honour.'

'At any rate,' he said, changing suddenly to a tone of bitter levity, 'you would have sent me to stab him without compunction.'

'Ah, *par exemple!*' she murmured in a shocked tone.

'Well,' he argued, mockingly, 'you do keep me here writing deadly nonsense. Deadly to me! It has already killed my self-respect. And you may imagine,' he continued, his tone passing into light banter, 'that Montero, should he be successful, would get even with me in the only way such a brute can get even with a man of intelligence who condescends to call him a *gran bestia* three times a week. It's a sort of intellectual death; but there is the other one in the background for a journalist of my ability.'

'If he is successful!' said Antonia, thoughtfully.

'You seem satisfied to see my life hang on a thread,' Decoud replied, with a broad smile. 'And the other Montero, the "my trusted brother" of the proclamations, the guerrillero – haven't I written that he was taking the guests' overcoats and changing plates in Paris at our Legation in the intervals of spying on our refugees there, in the time of Rojas? He will wash out that sacred truth in blood. In my blood! Why do you look annoyed? This is simply a bit of the biography of one of our great men. What do you think he will do to me? There is a certain convent wall round the corner of the Plaza, opposite the door of the Bull Ring. You know? Opposite the door with the inscription, 'Entrada de la Sombra'. Appropriate, perhaps! That's where the uncle of our host gave up his Anglo-South-American soul. And, note, he might have run away. A man who has fought with weapons may run away. You might have let me go with Barrios if you had cared for me. I would have carried one of those rifles, in which Don José believes, with the greatest satisfaction, in the ranks of poor peóns and Indios, that know nothing either of reason or politics. The most forlorn hope in the most forlorn army on earth would have been safer than that for which you made me stay here. When you make war you may retreat, but not when you spend your time in inciting poor ignorant fools to kill and to die.'

His tone remained light, and as if unaware of his presence she stood motionless, her hands clasped lightly, the fan hanging down from her interlaced fingers. He waited for a while, and then: 'I shall go to the wall,' he said, with a sort of jocular desperation.

Even that declaration did not make her look at him. Her head remained still, her eyes fixed upon the house of the Avellanos, whose chipped pilasters, broken cornices, the whole degradation of dignity was hidden now by the gathering dusk of the street. In her whole figure her lips alone moved, forming the words: 'Martin, you will make me cry.'

He remained silent for a minute, startled, as if overwhelmed by a sort of awed happiness, with the lines of the mocking smile still stiffened about his mouth, and incredulous surprise in his eyes. The value of a sentence is in the personality which utters it, for nothing new can be said by man or woman; and those were the last words, it seemed to him, that could ever have been spoken by Antonia. He had never made it up with her so completely in all their intercourse of small encounters; but even before she had time to turn towards him, which she did slowly with a rigid grace, he had begun to plead: 'My sister is only waiting to embrace you. My father is transported with joy. I won't say anything of my mother! Our mothers were like sisters. There is the mail-boat for the south next week – let us go. That Moraga is a fool! A man like Montero is bribed. It's the practice of the country. It's tradition – it's politics. Read *Fifty Years of Misrule.*'

'Leave poor papa alone, Don Martin. He believes –'

'I have the greatest tenderness for your father,' he began, hurriedly. 'But I love you, Antonia! And Moraga has miserably mismanaged this business. Perhaps your father did, too; I don't know. Montero was bribeable. Why, I suppose he only wanted his share of this famous loan for national development. Why didn't the stupid Sta Marta people give him a mission to Europe, or something? He would have taken five years' salary in advance, and gone on loafing in Paris, this stupid, ferocious Indio!'

'The man,' she said, thoughtfully, and very calm before this outburst, 'was intoxicated with vanity. We had all the information, not from Moraga only; from others, too. There was his brother intriguing, too.'

'Oh, yes!' he said. 'Of course you know. You know everything. You read all the correspondence, you write all the papers – all those State papers that are inspired here, in this room, in blind deference to a theory of political purity. Hadn't you Charles Gould before your eyes? Rey de Sulaco! He and his mine are the practical demonstration of what could have been done. Do you think he succeeded by his fidelity to a theory of virtue? And all those railway people, with their honest work! Of course, their work is honest! But what if you cannot work honestly till the thieves are satisfied? Could he not, a gentleman, have told this Sir John what's-his-name that Montero had to be bought off – he and all his Negro Liberals hanging on to his gold-laced sleeve? He ought to have been bought off with his own stupid weight of gold – his weight of gold, I tell you, boots, sabre, spurs, cocked hat, and all.'

She shook her head slightly. 'It was impossible,' she murmured.

'He wanted the whole lot? What?'

She was facing him now in the deep recess of the window, very close and motionless. Her lips moved rapidly. Decoud, leaning his back against the wall, listened with crossed arms and lowered eyelids. He drank the tones of her even voice, and watched the agitated life of her throat, as if waves of emotion had run from her heart to pass out into the air in her reasonable words. He also had his aspirations, he aspired to carry her away out of these deadly futilities of pronunciamientos and reforms. All this was wrong – utterly wrong; but she fascinated him, and sometimes the sheer sagacity of a phrase would break the charm, replace the fascination by a sudden unwilling thrill of interest. Some women hovered, as it were, on the threshold of genius, he reflected. They did not want to know, or think, or understand. Passion stood for all that, and he was ready to believe that some startlingly profound remark, some appreciation of character, or a judgement upon an event, bordered on the miraculous. In the mature Antonia he could see with an extraordinary vividness the austere schoolgirl of the earlier days. She seduced his attention; sometimes he could not restrain a murmur of assent; now and then he advanced an objection quite seriously. Gradually they began to argue; the curtain half hid them from the people in the sala.

Outside it had grown dark. From the deep trench of shadow between the houses, lit up vaguely by the glimmer of street lamps, ascended the evening silence of Sulaco; the silence of a town with few carriages, of unshod horses, and a softly sandalled population. The windows of the Casa Gould flung their shining parallelograms upon the house of the Avellanos. Now and then a shuffle of feet passed below with the pulsating red glow of a cigarette at the foot of the walls; and the night air, as if cooled by the snows of Higuerota, refreshed their faces.

'We Occidentals,' said Martin Decoud, using the usual term the provincials of Sulaco applied to themselves, 'have been always distinct and separated. As long as we hold Cayta nothing can reach us. In all our troubles no army has marched over those mountains. A revolution in the central provinces isolates us at once. Look how complete it is now! The news of Barrios' movement will be cabled to the United States, and only in that way will it reach Sta Marta by the cable from the other seaboard. We have the greatest riches, the greatest fertility, the purest blood in our great families, the most laborious population. The Occidental Province should stand alone. The early Federalism was not bad for us. Then came this union which Don Henrique Gould resisted. It opened the road to tyranny; and, ever since, the rest of Costaguana hangs like a millstone round our necks. The Occidental territory is large enough to make any man's country. Look at the mountains! Nature itself seems to cry to us "Separate!" '

She made an energetic gesture of negation. A silence fell.

'Oh, yes, I know it's contrary to the doctrine laid down in the *History of Fifty Years' Misrule*. I am only trying to be sensible. But my sense seems always to give you cause for offence. Have I startled you very much with this perfectly reasonable aspiration?'

She shook her head. No, she was not startled, but the idea shocked her early convictions. Her patriotism was larger. She had never considered that possibility.

'It may yet be the means of saving some of your convictions,' he said, prophetically.

She did not answer. She seemed tired. They leaned side by side on the rail of the little balcony, very friendly, having exhausted politics, giving themselves up to the silent feeling of their nearness, in one of those profound pauses that fall upon the rhythm of passion. Towards the plaza end of the street the glowing coals in the brazeros of the market women cooking their evening meal gleamed red along the edge of the pavement. A man appeared without a sound in the light of a street lamp, showing the coloured inverted triangle of his bordered poncho, square on his shoulders, hanging to a point below his knees. From the harbour end of the Calle a horseman walked his soft-stepping mount, gleaming silver-grey abreast each lamp under the dark shape of the rider.

'Behold the illustrious Capataz de Cargadores,' said Decoud, gently, 'coming in all his splendour after his work is done. The next great man of Sulaco after Don Carlos Gould. But he is good-natured, and let me make friends with him.'

'Ah, indeed!' said Antonia. 'How did you make friends?'

'A journalist ought to have his finger on the popular pulse, and this man is one of the leaders of the populace. A journalist ought to know remarkable men – and this man is remarkable in his way.'

'Ah, yes!' said Antonia, thoughtfully. 'It is known that this Italian has a great influence.'

The horseman had passed below them, with a gleam of dim light on the shining broad quarters of the grey mare, on a bright heavy stirrup, on a long silver spur; but the short flick of yellowish flame in the dusk was powerless against the muffled-up mysteriousness of the dark figure with an invisible face concealed by a great sombrero.

Decoud and Antonia remained leaning over the balcony, side by side, touching elbows, with their heads overhanging the darkness of the street, and the brilliantly lighted sala at their backs. This was a tête-à-tête of extreme impropriety; something of which in the whole extent of the Republic only the extraordinary Antonia could be capable – the poor, motherless girl, never accompanied, with a careless father, who had thought only of making her learned. Even Decoud himself seemed to feel that this was as much as he could expect of having her to himself till – till the revolution was over and he could carry her off to Europe, away from the endlessness of civil strife, whose folly seemed even harder to bear than its ignominy. After one Montero there would be another, the lawlessness of a populace of all colours and races, barbarism, irremediable tyranny. As the great Liberator Bolívar had said in the bitterness of his spirit, 'America is ungovernable. Those who worked for her independence have ploughed the sea.' He did not care, he declared boldly; he seized every opportunity to tell her that though she had managed to make a Blanco journalist of him, he was no patriot. First of all, the word had no sense for cultured minds, to whom the narrowness of every belief is odious; and secondly, in connection with the everlasting troubles of this unhappy country it was hopelessly besmirched; it had been the cry of dark barbarism, the cloak of lawlessness, of crimes, of rapacity, of simple thieving.

He was surprised at the warmth of his own utterance. He had no need to drop his voice; it had been low all the time, a mere murmur in the silence of dark houses with their shutters closed early against the night air, as is the custom of Sulaco. Only the sala of the Casa Gould flung out defiantly the blaze of its four windows, the bright appeal of light in the whole dumb obscurity of the street. And the murmur on the little balcony went on after a short pause.

'But we are labouring to change all that,' Antonia protested. 'It is exactly what we desire. It is our object. It is the great cause. And the word you despise has stood also for sacrifice, for courage, for constancy, for suffering. Papa, who – '

'Ploughing the sea,' interrupted Decoud, looking down.

There was below the sound of hasty and ponderous footsteps.

'Your uncle, the grand-vicar of the cathedral, has just turned under the gate,' observed Decoud. 'He said Mass for the troops in the Plaza this morning. They had built for him an altar of drums, you know. And they brought outside all the painted blocks to take the air. All the wooden saints stood militarily in a row at the top of the great flight of steps. They looked like a gorgeous escort attending the Vicar-General. I saw the great function from the windows of the *Porvenir*. He is amazing, your uncle, the last of the Corbelàns. He glittered exceedingly in his vestments with a great crimson velvet cross down his back. And all the time our saviour Barrios sat in the Amarilla Club drinking punch at an open window. *Esprit fort* – our Barrios. I expected every moment your uncle to launch an excommunication there and then at the black eye-patch in the window across the Plaza. But not at all. Ultimately the troops marched off. Later Barrios came down with some of the officers, and stood with his uniform all unbuttoned, discoursing at the edge of the pavement. Suddenly your uncle appeared, no longer glittering, but all black, at the cathedral door with that threatening aspect he has – you know, like a sort of avenging spirit. He gives one look, strides over straight at the group of uniforms, and leads away the general by the elbow. He walked him for a quarter of an hour in the shade of a wall. Never let go his elbow for a moment, talking all the time with exaltation, and gesticulating with a long black arm. It was a curious scene. The officers seemed struck with astonishment. Remarkable man, your missionary uncle. He hates an infidel much less than a heretic, and prefers a heathen many times to an infidel. He condescends graciously to call me a heathen, sometimes, you know.'

Antonia listened with her hands over the balustrade, opening and shutting the fan gently; and Decoud talked a little nervously, as if afraid that she would leave him at the first pause. Their comparative isolation, the precious sense of intimacy, the slight contact of their arms, affected him softly; for now and then a tender inflection crept into the flow of his ironic murmurs.

'Any slight sign of favour from a relative of yours is welcome, Antonia. And perhaps he understands me, after all! But I know him, too, our Padre Corbelàn. The idea of political honour, justice, and honesty for him consists in the restitution of the confiscated Church property. Nothing else could have drawn that fierce converter of savage Indians out of the wilds to work for the Ribierist cause! Nothing else but that wild hope! He would make a pronunciamiento himself for such an object against any Government if he could only get followers! What does Don Carlos Gould think of that? But, of course, with his English impenetrability, nobody can tell what he thinks. Probably he thinks of nothing apart from his mine; of his 'Imperium in Imperio'. As to Mrs Gould, she thinks of her schools, of her hospitals, of the mothers with the young babies, of every sick old man in the three villages. If you were to turn your head now you would see her extracting a report from that sinister doctor in a check shirt – what's his name? Monygham – or else catechising Don Pépé or perhaps listening to Padre Romàn. They are all down here today – all her ministers of state. Well, she is a sensible woman, and perhaps Don Carlos is a sensible man. It's a part of solid English sense not to think too much; to see only what may be of practical use at the moment. These people are not like ourselves. We have no political reason; we have political passions – sometimes. What is a conviction? A particular view of our personal advantage either practical or emotional. No one is a patriot for nothing. The word serves us well. But I am clear-sighted, and I shall not use that word to you, Antonia! I have no patriotic illusions. I have only the supreme illusion of a lover.'

He paused, then muttered almost inaudibly, 'That can lead one very far, though.'

Behind their backs the political tide that once in every twenty-four hours set with a strong flood through the Gould drawing-room could be heard, rising higher in a hum of voices. Men had been dropping in singly, or in twos and threes: the higher officials of the province, engineers of the railway, sunburnt and in tweeds, with the frosted head of their chief smiling with slow, humorous indulgence amongst the young eager faces. Scarfe, the lover of fandangos, had already slipped out in search of some dance, no matter where, on the outskirts of the town. Don Juste Lopez, after taking his daughters home, had entered solemnly, in a black creased coat buttoned up under his spreading brown beard. The few members of the Provincial Assembly present clustered at once around their President to discuss the news of the war and the last proclamation of the rebel Montero, the miserable Montero, calling in the name of 'a justly incensed democracy' upon all the Provincial Assemblies of the Republic to suspend their sittings till his sword had made peace and the will of the people could be consulted. It was practically an invitation to dissolve: an unheard-of audacity of that evil madman.

The indignation ran high in the knot of deputies behind José Avellanos. Don José, lifting up his voice, cried out to them over the high back of his chair, 'Sulaco has answered by sending today an army upon his flank. If all the other provinces show only half as much patriotism as we, Occidentals – '

A great outburst of acclamations covered the vibrating treble of the life and soul of the party. Yes! Yes! This was true! A great truth! Sulaco was in the forefront, as ever! It was a boastful tumult, the hopefulness inspired by the event of the day breaking out amongst those caballeros of the Campo thinking of their herds, of their lands, of the safety of their families. Everything was at stake . . . No! It was impossible that Montero should succeed! This criminal, this shameless Indio! The clamour continued for some time, everybody else in the room looking towards the group where Don Juste had put on his air of impartial solemnity as if presiding at a sitting of the Provincial Assembly. Decoud had turned round at the noise, and, leaning his back on the balustrade, shouted into the room with all the strength of his lungs, '*Gran bestia!*'

This unexpected cry had the effect of stilling the noise. All the eyes were directed to the window with an approving expectation; but Decoud had already turned his back upon the room, and was again leaning out over the quiet street.

'This is the quintessence of my journalism; that is the supreme argument,' he said to Antonia. 'I have invented this definition, this last word on a great question. But I am no patriot. I am no more of a patriot than the Capataz of the Sulaco Cargadores, this Genoese who has done such great things for this harbour – this active usher-in of the material implements for our progress. You have heard Captain Mitchell confess over and over again that till he got this man he could never tell how long it would take to unload a ship. That is bad for progress. You have seen him pass by after his labours on his famous horse to dazzle the girls in some ballroom with an earthen floor. He is a fortunate fellow! His work is an exercise of personal powers; his leisure is spent in receiving the marks of extraordinary adulation. And he likes it, too. Can anybody be more fortunate? To be feared and admired is – '

'And are these your highest aspirations, Don Martin?' interrupted Antonia.

'I was speaking of a man of that sort,' said Decoud, curtly. 'The heroes of the world have been feared and admired. What more could he want?'

Decoud had often felt his familiar habit of ironic thought fall shattered against Antonia's gravity. She irritated him as if she, too, had suffered from that inexplicable feminine obtuseness which stands so often between a man and a woman of the more ordinary sort. But he overcame his vexation at once. He was very far from thinking Antonia ordinary, whatever verdict his

scepticism might have pronounced upon himself. With a touch of penetrating tenderness in his voice he assured her that his only aspiration was
to a felicity so high that it seemed almost unrealisable on this earth.

She coloured invisibly, with a warmth against which the breeze from the
sierra seemed to have lost its cooling power in the sudden melting of the
snows. His whisper could not have carried so far, though there was enough
ardour in his tone to melt a heart of ice. Antonia turned away abruptly, as if
to carry his whispered assurance into the room behind, full of light, noisy
with voices.

The tide of political speculation was beating high within the four walls of
the great sala, as if driven beyond the marks by a great gust of hope. Don
Juste's fan-shaped beard was still the centre of loud and animated discussions.
There was a self-confident ring in all the voices. Even the few Europeans
around Charles Gould – a Dane, a couple of Frenchmen, a discreet fat
German, smiling, with downcast eyes, the representatives of those material
interests that had got a footing in Sulaco under the protecting might of the
San Tomé mine – had infused a lot of good humour into their deference.
Charles Gould, to whom they were paying their court, was the visible sign of
the stability that could be achieved on the shifting ground of revolutions. They
felt hopeful about their various undertakings. One of the two Frenchmen,
small, black, with glittering eyes lost in an immense growth of bushy beard,
waved his tiny brown hands and delicate wrists.

He had been travelling in the interior of the province for a syndicate of
European capitalists. His forcible *'Monsieur l'Administrateur'* returning every
minute shrilled above the steady hum of conversations. He was relating his
discoveries. He was ecstatic. Charles Gould glanced down at him courteously.

At a given moment of these necessary receptions it was Mrs Gould's habit
to withdraw quietly into a little drawing-room, especially her own, next to
the great sala. She had risen, and, waiting for Antonia, listened with a slightly
worried graciousness to the engineer-in-chief of the railway, who stooped
over her, relating slowly, without the slightest gesture, something apparently
amusing, for his eyes had a humorous twinkle. Antonia, before she advanced
into the room to join Mrs Gould, turned her head over her shoulder towards
Decoud, only for a moment.

'Why should any one of us think his aspirations unrealisable?' she
said, rapidly.

'I am going to cling to mine to the end, Antonia,' he answered, through
clenched teeth, then bowed very low, a little distantly.

The engineer-in-chief had not finished telling his amusing story. The
humours of railway building in South America appealed to his keen appreciation of the absurd, and he told his instances of ignorant prejudice and as
ignorant cunning very well. Now, Mrs Gould gave him all her attention as he
walked by her side escorting the ladies out of the room. Finally all three
passed unnoticed through the glass doors in the gallery. Only a tall priest

stalking silently in the noise of the sala checked himself to look after them. Father Corbelàn, whom Decoud had seen from the balcony turning into the gateway of the Casa Gould, had addressed no one since coming in. The long, skimpy soutane accentuated the tallness of his stature; he carried his powerful torso thrown forward; and the straight, black bar of his joined eyebrows, the pugnacious outline of the bony face, the white spot of a scar on the bluish shaven cheeks (a testimonial to his apostolic zeal from a party of unconverted Indians), suggested something unlawful behind his priesthood, the idea of a chaplain of bandits.

He separated his bony, knotted hands clasped behind his back, to shake his finger at Martin.

Decoud had stepped into the room after Antonia. But he did not go far. He had remained just within, against the curtain, with an expression of not quite genuine gravity, like a grown-up person taking part in a game of children. He gazed quietly at the threatening finger.

'I have watched your reverence converting General Barrios by a special sermon on the Plaza,' he said, without making the slightest movement.

'What miserable nonsense!' Father Corbelàn's deep voice resounded all over the room, making all the heads turn on the shoulders. 'The man is a drunkard. Señores, the God of your General is a bottle!'

His contemptuous, arbitrary voice caused an uneasy suspension of every sound, as if the self-confidence of the gathering had been staggered by a blow. But nobody took up Father Corbelàn's declaration.

It was known that Father Corbelàn had come out of the wilds to advocate the sacred rights of the Church with the same fanatical fearlessness with which he had gone preaching to bloodthirsty savages, devoid of human compassion or worship of any kind. Rumours of legendary proportions told of his successes as a missionary beyond the eye of Christian men. He had baptised whole nations of Indians, living with them like a savage himself. It was related that the padre used to ride with his Indians for days, half naked, carrying a bullock-hide shield, and, no doubt, a long lance, too – who knows? That he had wandered clothed in skins, seeking for proselytes somewhere near the snow line of the Cordillera. Of these exploits Padre Corbelàn himself was never known to talk. But he made no secret of his opinion that the politicians of Sta Marta had harder hearts and more corrupt minds than the heathen to whom he had carried the word of God. His injudicious zeal for the temporal welfare of the Church was damaging the Ribierist cause. It was common knowledge that he had refused to be made titular bishop of the Occidental diocese till justice was done to a despoiled Church. The political Jefe of Sulaco (the same dignitary whom Captain Mitchell saved from the mob afterwards) hinted with naive cynicism that doubtless their Excellencies the Ministers sent the padre over the mountains to Sulaco in the worst season of the year in the hope that he would be frozen to death by the icy blasts of the high páramos. Every year a few hardy muleteers – men inured to exposure – were known to perish in that way. But what would you have? Their Excellencies possibly had not realised what a tough priest he was. Meantime, the ignorant were beginning to murmur that the Ribierist reforms meant simply the taking away of the land from the people. Some of it was to be given to foreigners who made the railway; the greater part was to go to the padres.

These were the results of the Grand Vicar's zeal. Even from the short allocution to the troops on the Plaza (which only the first ranks could have heard) he had not been able to keep out his fixed idea of an outraged Church waiting for reparation from a penitent country. The political Jefe had been exasperated. But he could not very well throw the brother-in-law of Don José into the prison of the Cabildo. The chief magistrate, an easy-going and popular official, visited the Casa Gould, walking over after sunset from the Intendencia, unattended, acknowledging with dignified courtesy the salutations of high and low alike. That evening he had walked up straight to Charles Gould and had hissed out to him that he would have liked to deport the Grand Vicar out of Sulaco, anywhere, to some desert island, to the Isabels, for instance. 'The one without water preferably – eh, Don Carlos?' he had added in a tone between jest and earnest. This uncontrollable priest, who had rejected his offer of the episcopal palace for a residence and preferred to hang his shabby hammock amongst the rubble and spiders of the sequestrated Dominican Convent, had taken into his head to advocate an unconditional pardon for Hernandez the Robber! And this was not enough; he seemed to have entered into communication with the most audacious criminal the country had known for years. The Sulaco police knew, of course, what was going on. Padre Corbelàn had got hold of that reckless Italian, the Capataz de Cargadores, the only man fit for such an errand, and had sent a message through him. Father Corbelàn had studied in Rome, and could speak Italian. The Capataz was known to visit the old Dominican Convent at night. An old woman who served the Grand Vicar had heard the name of Hernandez pronounced; and only last Saturday afternoon the Capataz had been observed galloping out of town. He did not return for two days. The police would have laid the Italian by the heels if it had not been for fear of the Cargadores, a turbulent body of men, quite apt to raise a tumult. Nowadays it was not so easy to govern Sulaco. Bad characters flocked into it, attracted by the money in the pockets of the railway workmen. The populace was made restless by Father Corbelàn's discourses. And the first magistrate explained to Charles Gould that now the province was stripped of troops any outbreak of lawlessness would find the authorities with their boots off, as it were.

Then he went away moodily to sit in an armchair, smoking a long, thin cigar, not very far from Don José, with whom, bending over sideways, he exchanged a few words from time to time. He ignored the entrance of the priest, and whenever Father Corbelàn's voice was raised behind him, he shrugged his shoulders impatiently.

Father Corbelàn had remained quite motionless for a time with that something vengeful in his immobility which seemed to characterise all his attitudes. A lurid glow of strong convictions gave its peculiar aspect to the black figure. But its fierceness became softened as the padre, fixing his eyes upon Decoud, raised his long, black arm slowly, impressively: 'And you – you are a perfect heathen,' he said, in a subdued, deep voice.

He made a step nearer, pointing a forefinger at the young man's breast. Decoud, very calm, felt the wall behind the curtain with the back of his head. Then, with his chin tilted well up, he smiled.

'Very well,' he agreed with the slightly weary nonchalance of a man well used to these passages. 'But is it perhaps that you have not discovered yet what is the God of my worship? It was an easier task with our Barrios.'

The priest suppressed a gesture of discouragement. 'You believe neither in stick nor stone,' he said.

'Nor bottle,' added Decoud without stirring. 'Neither does the other of your reverence's confidants. I mean the Capataz of the Cargadores. He does not drink. Your reading of my character does honour to your perspicacity. But why call me a heathen?'

'True,' retorted the priest. 'You are ten times worse. A miracle could not convert you.'

'I certainly do not believe in miracles,' said Decoud, quietly. Father Corbelàn shrugged his high, broad shoulders doubtfully.

'A sort of Frenchman – godless – a materialist,' he pronounced slowly, as if weighing the terms of a careful analysis. 'Neither the son of his own country nor of any other,' he continued, thoughtfully.

'Scarcely human, in fact,' Decoud commented under his breath, his head at rest against the wall, his eyes gazing up at the ceiling.

'The victim of this faithless age,' Father Corbelàn resumed in a deep but subdued voice.

'But of some use as a journalist.' Decoud changed his pose and spoke in a more animated tone. 'Has your worship neglected to read the last number of the *Porvenir?* I assure you it is just like the others. On the general policy it continues to call Montero a *gran bestia*, and stigmatise his brother, the guerrillero, for a combination of lackey and spy. What could be more effective? In local affairs it urges the Provincial Government to enlist bodily into the national army the band of Hernandez the Robber – who is apparently the protégé of the Church – or at least of the Great Vicar. Nothing could be more sound.'

The priest nodded and turned on the heels of his square-toed shoes with big steel buckles. Again, with his hands clasped behind his back, he paced to and fro, planting his feet firmly. When he swung about, the skirt of his soutane was inflated slightly by the brusqueness of his movements.

The great sala had been emptying itself slowly.

When the Jefe Politico rose to go, most of those remaining stood up suddenly in sign of respect, and José Avellanos stopped the rocking of his chair. But the good-natured First Official made a deprecatory gesture, waved his hand to Charles Gould, and went out discreetly.

In the comparative peace of the room the screaming '*Monsieur l'Administrateur*' of the frail, hairy Frenchman seemed to acquire a preternatural shrillness. The explorer of the Capitalist syndicate was still enthusiastic. 'Ten million dollars' worth of copper practically in sight, *Monsieur l'Administrateur*. Ten millions in sight! And a railway coming – a railway! They will never believe my report. *C'est trop beau*.' He fell a prey to a screaming ecstasy, in the midst of sagely nodding heads, before Charles Gould's imperturbable calm.

And only the priest continued his pacing, flinging round the skirt of his soutane at each end of his beat. Decoud murmured to him ironically: 'Those gentlemen talk about their gods.'

Father Corbelàn stopped short, looked at the journalist of Sulaco fixedly for a moment, shrugged his shoulders slightly, and resumed his plodding walk of an obstinate traveller.

And now the Europeans were dropping off from the group around Charles Gould till the Administrador of the Great Silver Mine could be seen in his whole lank length, from head to foot, left stranded by the ebbing tide of his guests on the great square of carpet, as it were a multicoloured shoal of flowers and arabesques under his brown boots. Father Corbelàn approached the rocking-chair of Don José Avellanos.

'Come, brother,' he said, with kindly brusqueness and a touch of relieved impatience a man may feel at the end of a perfectly useless ceremony. '*A la Casa! A la Casa!* This has been all talk. Let us now go and think and pray for guidance from Heaven.'

He rolled his black eyes upwards. By the side of the frail diplomatist – the life and soul of the party – he seemed gigantic, with a gleam of fanaticism in the glance. But the voice of the party, or, rather, its mouthpiece, the 'son Decoud' from Paris, turned journalist for the sake of Antonia's eyes, knew very well that it was not so, that he was only a strenuous priest with one idea, feared by the women and execrated by the men of the people. Martin Decoud, the dilettante in life, imagined himself to derive an artistic pleasure from watching the picturesque extreme of wrong-headedness into which an honest, almost sacred, conviction may drive a man. 'It is like madness. It must be because it's self-destructive,' Decoud had said to himself often. It seemed to him that every conviction, as soon as it became effective, turned into that form of dementia the gods send upon those they wish to destroy. But he enjoyed the bitter flavour of that example with the zest of a connoisseur in the art of his choice. Those two men got on well together, as if each had felt respectively that a masterful conviction, as well as utter scepticism, may lead a man very far on the by-paths of political action.

Don José obeyed the touch of the big hairy hand. Decoud followed out the brothers-in-law. And there remained only one visitor in the vast empty sala, bluishly hazy with tobacco smoke, a heavy-eyed, round-cheeked man, with a drooping moustache, a hide merchant from Esmeralda, who had come overland to Sulaco, riding with a few peóns across the coast range. He was very full of his journey, undertaken mostly for the purpose of seeing the Señor Administrador of San Tomé in relation to some assistance he required in his hide-exporting business. He hoped to enlarge it greatly now that the country was going to be settled. It was going to be settled, he repeated several times, degrading by a strange, anxious whine the sonority of the Spanish language, which he pattered rapidly, like some sort of cringing jargon. A plain man could carry on his little business now in the country, and even think of enlarging it – with safety. Was it not so? He seemed to beg Charles Gould for a confirmatory word, a grunt of assent, a simple nod even.

He could get nothing. His alarm increased, and in the pauses he would dart his eyes here and there; then, loth to give up, he would branch off into feeling allusion to the dangers of his journey. The audacious Hernandez, leaving his usual haunts, had crossed the Campo of Sulaco, and was known to be lurking in the ravines of the coast range. Yesterday, when distant only a few hours from Sulaco, the hide merchant and his servants had seen three men on the road arrested suspiciously, with their horses' heads together. Two of these rode off at once and disappeared in a shallow quebrada to the left. 'We stopped,' continued the man from Esmeralda, 'and I tried to hide behind a small bush. But none of my mozos would go forward to find out what it meant, and the third horseman seemed to be waiting for us to come up. It was no use. We had been seen. So we rode slowly on, trembling. He let us pass – a man on a grey horse with his hat down on his eyes – without a word of greeting; but by and by we heard him galloping after us. We faced about, but that did not seem to intimidate him. He rode up at speed, and touching my foot with the toe of his boot, asked me for a cigar, with a blood-curdling laugh. He did not seem armed, but when he put his hand back to reach for the matches I saw an enormous revolver strapped to his waist. I shuddered. He had very fierce whiskers, Don Carlos, and as he did not offer to go on we dared not move. At last, blowing the smoke of my cigar into the air through his nostrils, he said, 'Señor, it would be perhaps better for you if I rode behind your party. You are not very far from Sulaco now. Go you with God.' What would you? We went on. There was no resisting him. He might have been Hernandez himself; though my servant, who has been many times to Sulaco by sea, assured me that he had recognised him very well for the Capataz of the Steamship Company's Cargadores. Later, that same evening, I saw that very man at the corner of the Plaza talking to a girl, a Morenita, who stood by the stirrup with her hand on the grey horse's mane.'

'I assure you, Señor Hirsch,' murmured Charles Gould, 'that you ran no risk on this occasion.'

'That may be, señor, though I tremble yet. A most fierce man – to look at. And what does it mean? A person employed by the Steamship Company talking with salteadores – no less, señor; the other horsemen were salteadores – in a lonely place, and behaving like a robber himself! A cigar is nothing, but what was there to prevent him asking me for my purse?'

'No, no, Señor Hirsch,' Charles Gould murmured, letting his glance stray away a little vacantly from the round face, with its hooked beak upturned towards him in an almost childlike appeal. 'If it was the Capataz de Cargadores you met – and there is no doubt, is there? – you were perfectly safe.'

'Thank you. You are very good. A very fierce-looking man, Don Carlos. He asked me for a cigar in a most familiar manner. What would have happened if I had not had a cigar? I shudder yet. What business had he to be talking with robbers in a lonely place?'

But Charles Gould, openly preoccupied now, gave not a sign, made no sound. The impenetrability of the embodied Gould Concession had its surface shades. To be dumb is merely a fatal affliction; but the King of Sulaco had words enough to give him all the mysterious weight of a taciturn force. His silences, backed by the power of speech, had as many shades of significance as uttered words in the way of assent, of doubt, of negation – even of simple comment. Some seemed to say plainly, 'Think it over'; others meant clearly 'Go ahead', a simple, low 'I see', with an affirmative nod, at the end of a patient listening half-hour was the equivalent of a verbal contract, which men had learned to trust implicitly, since behind it all there was the great San Tomé mine, the head and front of the material interests, so strong that it depended on no man's goodwill in the whole length and breadth of the Occidental Province – that is, on no goodwill which it could not buy ten times over. But to the little hook-nosed man from Esmeralda, anxious about the export of hides, the silence of Charles Gould portended a failure. Evidently this was no time for extending a modest man's business. He enveloped in a swift mental malediction the whole country, with all its inhabitants, partisans of Ribiera and Montero alike; and there were incipient tears in his mute anger at the thought of the innumerable ox-hides going to waste upon the dreamy expanse of the Campo, with its single palms rising like ships at sea within the perfect circle of the horizon, its clumps of heavy timber motionless like solid islands of leaves above the running waves of grass. There were hides there, rotting, with no profit to anybody – rotting where they had been dropped by men called away to attend the urgent necessities of political revolutions. The practical, mercantile soul of Señor Hirsch rebelled against all that foolishess, while he was taking a respectful but disconcerted leave of the might and majesty of the San Tomé mine in the person of Charles Gould. He could not restrain a heartbroken murmur, wrung out of his very aching heart, as it were.

'It is a great, great foolishness, Don Carlos, all this. The price of hides in Hamburg is gone up – up. Of course the Ribierist Government will do away with all that – when it gets established firmly. Meantime –'

He sighed.

'Yes, meantime,' repeated Charles Gould inscrutably.

The other shrugged his shoulders. But he was not ready to go yet. There was a little matter he would like to mention very much if permitted. It appeared he had some good friends in Hamburg (he murmured the name of the firm) who were very anxious to do business, in dynamite, he explained. A contract for dynamite with the San Tomé mine, and then, perhaps, later on, other mines, which were sure to – The little man from Esmeralda was ready to enlarge, but Charles interrupted him. It seemed as though the patience of the Señor Administrador was giving way at last.

'Señor Hirsch,' he said, 'I have enough dynamite stored up at the mountain to send it down crashing into the valley' – his voice rose a little – 'to send half Sulaco into the air if I liked.'

Charles Gould smiled at the round, startled eyes of the dealer in hides, who was murmuring hastily, 'Just so. Just so.' And now he was going. It was impossible to do business in explosives with an Administrador so well provided and so discouraging. He had suffered agonies in the saddle and had exposed himself to the atrocities of the bandit Hernandez for nothing at all. Neither hides nor dynamite – and the very shoulders of the enterprising Israelite expressed dejection. At the door he bowed low to the engineer-in-chief. But at the bottom of the stairs in the patio he stopped short, with his podgy hand over his lips in an attitude of meditative astonishment.

'What does he want to keep so much dynamite for?' he muttered. 'And why does he talk like this to me?'

The engineer-in-chief, looking in at the door of the empty sala, whence the political tide had ebbed out to the last insignificant drop, nodded familiarly to the master of the house, standing motionless like a tall beacon amongst the deserted shoals of furniture.

'Good-night, I am going. Got my bike downstairs. The railway will know where to go for dynamite should we get short at any time. We have done cutting and chopping for a while now. We shall begin soon to blast our way through.'

'Don't come to me,' said Charles Gould, with perfect serenity. 'I shan't have an ounce to spare for anybody. Not an ounce. Not for my own brother, if I had a brother, and he were the engineer-in-chief of the most promising railway in the world.'

'What's that?' asked the engineer-in-chief, with equanimity. 'Unkindness?'

'No,' said Charles Gould, stolidly. 'Policy.'

'Radical, I should think,' the engineer-in-chief observed from the doorway.

'Is that the right name?' Charles Gould said, from the middle of the room.

'I mean, going to the roots, you know,' the engineer explained, with an air of enjoyment.

'Why, yes,' Charles pronounced, slowly. 'The Gould Concession has struck such deep roots in this country, in this province, in that gorge of the mountains, that nothing but dynamite shall be allowed to dislodge it from there. It's my choice. It's my last card to play.'

The engineer-in-chief whistled low. 'A pretty game,' he said, with a shade of discretion. 'And have you told Holroyd of that extraordinary trump card you hold in your hand?'

'Card only when it's played; when it falls at the end of the game. Till then you may call it a – a – '

'Weapon,' suggested the railway man.

'No. You may call it rather an argument,' corrected Charles Gould, gently. 'And that's how I've presented it to Mr Holroyd.'

'And what did he say to it?' asked the engineer, with undisguised interest.

'He' – Charles Gould spoke after a slight pause – 'he said something about holding on like grim death and putting our trust in God. I should imagine he must have been rather startled. But then' – pursued the Administrador of the San Tomé mine – 'but then, he is very far away, you know, and, as they say in this country, God is very high above.'

The engineer's appreciative laugh died away down the stairs, where the Madonna with the Child on her arm seemed to look after his shaking broad back from her shallow niche.

Chapter 6

A profound stillness reigned in the Casa Gould. The master of the house, walking along the corridor, opened the door of his room, and saw his wife sitting in a big armchair – his own smoking armchair – thoughtful, contemplating her little shoes. And she did not raise her eyes when he walked in.

'Tired?' asked Charles Gould.

'A little,' said Mrs Gould. Still without looking up, she added with feeling, 'There is an awful sense of unreality about all this.'

Charles Gould, before the long table strewn with papers, on which lay a hunting crop and a pair of spurs, stood looking at his wife: 'The heat and dust must have been awful this afternoon by the waterside,' he murmured, sympathetically. 'The glare on the water must have been simply terrible.'

'One could close one's eyes to the glare,' said Mrs Gould. 'But, my dear Charley, it is impossible for me to close my eyes to our position; to this awful . . . '

She raised her eyes and looked at her husband's face, from which all sign of sympathy or any other feeling had disappeared. 'Why don't you tell me something?' she almost wailed.

'I thought you had understood me perfectly from the first,' Charles Gould said, slowly. 'I thought we had said all there was to say a long time ago. There is nothing to say now. There were things to be done. We have done them; we have gone on doing them. There is no going back now. I don't suppose that, even from the first, there was really any possible way back. And, what's more, we can't even afford to stand still.'

'Ah, if one only knew how far you mean to go,' said his wife, inwardly trembling, but in an almost playful tone.

'Any distance, any length, of course,' was the answer, in a matter-of-fact tone, which caused Mrs Gould to make another effort to repress a shudder.

She stood up, smiling graciously, and her little figure seemed to be diminished still more by the heavy mass of her hair and the long train of her gown.

'But always to success,' she said, persuasively.

Charles Gould, enveloping her in the steely blue glance of his attentive eyes, answered without hesitation: 'Oh, there is no alternative.'

He put an immense assurance into his tone. As to the words, this was all that his conscience would allow him to say.

Mrs Gould's smile remained a shade too long upon her lips. She murmured: 'I will leave you; I've a slight headache. The heat, the dust, were indeed – I suppose you are going back to the mine before the morning?'

'At midnight,' said Charles Gould. 'We are bringing down the silver tomorrow. Then I shall take three whole days off in town with you.'

'Ah, you are going to meet the escort. I shall be on the balcony at five o'clock to see you pass. Till then, goodbye.'

Charles Gould walked rapidly round the table, and seizing her hands, bent down, pressing them both to his lips. Before he straightened himself up again to his full height she had disengaged one to smooth his cheek with a light touch, as if he were a little boy.

'Try to get some rest for a couple of hours,' she murmured, with a glance at a hammock stretched in a distant part of the room. Her long train swished softly after her on the red tiles. At the door she looked back.

Two big lamps with unpolished glass globes bathed in a soft and abundant light the four white walls of the room, with a glass case of arms, the brass hilt of Henry Gould's cavalry sabre on its square of velvet, and the watercolour sketch of the San Tomé gorge. And Mrs Gould, gazing at the last in its black wooden frame, sighed out: 'Ah, if we had left it alone, Charley!'

'No,' Charles Gould said, moodily; 'it was impossible to leave it alone.'

'Perhaps it was impossible,' Mrs Gould admitted, slowly. Her lips quivered a little, but she smiled with an air of dainty bravado. 'We have disturbed a good many snakes in that Paradise, Charley, haven't we?'

'Yes, I remember,' said Charles Gould, 'it was Don Pépé who called the gorge the Paradise of snakes. No doubt we have disturbed a great many. But remember, my dear, that it is not now as it was when you made that sketch.' He waved his hand towards the small watercolour hanging alone upon the great bare wall. 'It is no longer a Paradise of snakes. We have brought mankind into it, and we cannot turn our backs upon them to go and begin a new life elsewhere.'

He confronted his wife with a firm, concentrated gaze, which Mrs Gould returned with a brave assumption of fearlessness before she went out, closing the door gently after her.

In contrast with the white glaring room the dimly lit corridor had a restful mysteriousness of a forest glade, suggested by the stems and the leaves of the plants ranged along the balustrade of the open side. In the streaks of light falling through the open doors of the reception-rooms, the blossoms, white and red and pale lilac, came out vivid with the brilliance of flowers in a stream of sunshine; and Mrs Gould, passing on, had the vividness of a figure seen in the clear patches of sun that chequer the gloom of open glades in the woods. The stones in the rings upon her hand pressed to her forehead glittered in the lamplight abreast of the door of the sala.

'Who's there?' she asked, in a startled voice. 'Is that you, Basilio?' She looked in, and saw Martin Decoud walking about, with an air of having lost something, amongst the chairs and tables.

'Antonia has forgotten her fan in here,' said Decoud, with a strange air of distraction; 'so I entered to see.'

But, even as he said this, he had obviously given up his search, and walked straight towards Mrs Gould, who looked at him with doubtful surprise.

'Señora,' he began, in a low voice.

'What is it, Don Martin?' asked Mrs Gould. And then she added, with a slight laugh, 'I am so nervous today,' as if to explain the eagerness of the question.

'Nothing immediately dangerous,' said Decoud, who now could not conceal his agitation. 'Pray don't distress yourself. No, really, you must not distress yourself.'

Mrs Gould, with her candid eyes very wide open, her lips composed into a smile, was steadying herself in the doorway with a little bejewelled hand.

'Perhaps you don't know how alarming you are, appearing like this unexpectedly – '

'I! Alarming!' he protested, sincerely vexed and surprised. 'I assure you that I am not in the least alarmed myself. A fan is lost; well, it will be found again. But I don't think it is here. It is a fan I am looking for. I cannot understand how Antonia could – Well! Have you found it, amigo?'

'No, señor,' said behind Mrs Gould the soft voice of Basilio, the head servant of the Casa. 'I don't think the señorita could have left it in this house at all.'

'Go and look for it in the patio again. Go now, my friend; look for it on the steps, under the gate; examine every flagstone; search for it till I come down again. . . That fellow' – he addressed himself in English to Mrs Gould – 'is always stealing up behind one's back on his bare feet. I set him to look for that fan directly I came in to justify my reappearance, my sudden return.'

He paused and Mrs Gould said, amiably, 'You are always welcome.' She paused for a second, too. 'But I am waiting to learn the cause of your return.'

Decoud affected suddenly the utmost nonchalance.

'I can't bear to be spied upon. Oh, the cause? Yes, there is a cause; there is something else that is lost besides Antonia's favourite fan. As I was walking home after seeing Don José and Antonia to their house, the Capataz de Cargadores, riding down the street, spoke to me.'

'Has anything happened to the Violas?' enquired Mrs Gould.

'The Violas? You mean the old Garibaldino who keeps the hotel where the engineers live? Nothing happened there. The Capataz said nothing of them; he only told me that the telegraphist of the Cable Company was walking on the Plaza, bareheaded, looking out for me. There is news from the interior, Mrs Gould. I should rather say rumours of news.'

'Good news?' said Mrs Gould in a low voice.

'Worthless, I should think. But if I must define them, I would say bad. They are to the effect that a two days' battle had been fought near Sta Marta, and that the Ribierists are defeated. It must have happened a few days ago – perhaps a week. The rumour has just reached Cayta, and the man in charge of the cable station there has telegraphed the news to his colleague here. We might just as well have kept Barrios in Sulaco.'

'What's to be done now?' murmured Mrs Gould.

'Nothing. He's at sea with the troops. He will get to Cayta in a couple of days' time and learn the news there. What he will do then, who can say? Hold Cayta? Offer his submission to Montero? Disband his army – this last most likely, and go himself in one of the OSN Company's steamers, north or south – to Valparaiso or to San Francisco, no matter where. Our Barrios has a great practice in exiles and repatriations, which mark the points in the political game.'

Decoud, exchanging a steady stare with Mrs Gould, added, tentatively, as it were, 'And yet, if we had Barrios with his 2,000 improved rifles here, something could have been done.'

'Montero victorious, completely victorious!' Mrs Gould breathed out in a tone of unbelief.

'A canard, probably. That sort of bird is hatched in great numbers in such times as these. And even if it were true? Well, let us put things at their worst, let us say it is true.'

'Then everything is lost,' said Mrs Gould, with the calmness of despair.

Suddenly she seemed to divine, she seemed to see Decoud's tremendous excitement under its cloak of studied carelessness. It was, indeed, becoming visible in his audacious and watchful stare, in the curve, half-reckless, half-contemptuous, of his lips. And a French phrase came upon them as if, for this Costaguanero of the Boulevard, that had been the only forcible language: 'Non, Madame. Rien n'est perdu.'

It electrified Mrs Gould out of her benumbed attitude, and she said, vivaciously: 'What would you think of doing?'

But already there was something of mockery in Decoud's suppressed excitement.

'What would you expect a true Costaguanero to do? Another revolution, of course. On my word of honour, Mrs Gould, I believe I am a true *hijo del país*, a true son of the country, whatever Father Corbelàn may say. And I'm not so much of an unbeliever as not to have faith in my own ideas, in my desires.'

'Yes,' said Mrs Gould, doubtfully.

'You don't seem convinced,' Decoud went on again in French. 'Say, then, in my passions.'

Mrs Gould received this addition unflinchingly. To understand it thoroughly she did not require to hear his muttered assurance: 'There is nothing I would not do for the sake of Antonia. There is nothing I am not prepared to undertake. There is no risk I am not ready to run.'

Decoud seemed to find a fresh audacity in this voicing of his thoughts. 'You would not believe me if I were to say that it is the love of the country which – '

She made a sort of discouraged protest with her arm, as if to express that she had given up expecting that motive from anyone.

'A Sulaco revolution,' Decoud pursued in a forcible undertone. 'The Great Cause may be served here, on the very spot of its inception, in the place of its birth, Mrs Gould.'

Frowning, and biting her lower lip thoughtfully, she made a step away from the door.

'You are not going to speak to your husband?' Decoud arrested her anxiously.

'But you will need his help?'

'No doubt,' Decoud admitted without hesitation. 'Everything turns upon the San Tomé mine, but I would rather he didn't know anything as yet of my – my hopes.'

A puzzled look came upon Mrs Gould's face, and Decoud, approaching, explained confidentially: 'Don't you see, he's such an idealist.'

Mrs Gould flushed pink, and her eyes grew darker at the same time.

'Charley an idealist!' she said, as if to herself, wonderingly. 'What on earth do you mean?'

'Yes,' conceded Decoud, 'it's a wonderful thing to say with the sight of the San Tomé mine, the greatest fact in the whole of South America, perhaps, before our very eyes. But look even at that, he has idealised this fact to a point – ' He paused. 'Mrs Gould, are you aware to what point he has idealised the existence, the worth, the meaning of the San Tomé mine? Are you aware of it?'

He must have known what he was talking about.

The effect he expected was produced. Mrs Gould, ready to take fire, gave it up suddenly with a low little sound that resembled a moan.

'What do you know?' she asked in a feeble voice.

'Nothing,' answered Decoud, firmly. 'But, then don't you see, he's an Englishman?'

'Well, what of that?' asked Mrs Gould.

'Simply that he cannot act or exist without idealising every simple feeling, desire, or achievement. He could not believe his own motives if he did not make them first a part of some fairy tale. The earth is not quite good enough for him, I fear. Do you excuse my frankness? Besides, whether you excuse it or not, it is part of the truth of things which hurts the – what do you call them? – the Anglo-Saxon's susceptibilities, and at the present moment I don't feel as if I could treat seriously either his conception of things or – if you allow me to say so – or yet yours.'

Mrs Gould gave no sign of being offended. 'I suppose Antonia understands you thoroughly?'

'Understands? Well, yes. But I am not sure she approves. That, however, makes no difference. I am honest enough to tell you that, Mrs Gould.'

'Your idea, of course, is separation,' she said.

'Separation, of course,' declared Martin. 'Yes; separation of the whole Occidental Province from the rest of the unquiet body. But my true idea, the only one I care for, is not to be separated from Antonia.'

'And that is all?' asked Mrs Gould, without severity.

'Absolutely. I am not deceiving myself about my motives. She won't leave Sulaco for my sake, therefore Sulaco must leave the rest of the Republic to its fate. Nothing could be clearer than that. I like a clearly defined situation. I cannot part with Antonia, therefore the one and indivisible Republic of Costaguana must be made to part with its western province. Fortunately it happens to be also a sound policy. The richest, the most fertile part of this land may be saved from anarchy. Personally, I care little, very little; but it's a fact that the establishment of Montero in power would mean death to me. In all the proclamations of general pardon which I have seen, my name, with a few others, is specially excepted. The brothers hate me, as you know very well, Mrs Gould; and behold, here is the rumour of them having won a battle. You say that supposing it is true, I have plenty of time to run away.'

The slight, protesting murmur on the part of Mrs Gould made him pause for a moment, while he looked at her with a sombre and resolute glance.

'Ah, but I would, Mrs Gould. I would if it served that which at present is my only desire. I am courageous enough to say that, and to do it, too. But women, even our women, are idealists. It is Antonia that won't run away. A novel sort of vanity.'

'You call it vanity,' said Mrs Gould, in a shocked voice.

'Say pride, then, which, Father Corbelàn would tell you, is a mortal sin. But I am not proud. I am simply too much in love to run away. At the same time I want to live. There is no love for a dead man. Therefore it is necessary that Sulaco should not recognise the victorious Montero.'

'And you think my husband will give you his support?'

'I think he can be drawn into it, like all idealists, when he once sees a sentimental basis for his action. But I wouldn't talk to him. Mere clear facts won't appeal to his sentiment. It is much better for him to convince himself in his own way. And, frankly, I could not, perhaps, just now pay sufficient respect to either his motives or even, perhaps, to yours, Mrs Gould.'

It was evident that Mrs Gould was very determined not to be offended. She smiled vaguely, while she seemed to think the matter over. As far as she could judge from the girl's half-confidences, Antonia understood that young man. Obviously there was promise of safety in his plan, or rather in his idea. Moreover, right or wrong, the idea could do no harm. And it was quite possible, also, that the rumour was false.

'You have some sort of a plan,' she said.

'Simplicity itself. Barrios has started, let him go on then; he will hold Cayta, which is the door of the sea route to Sulaco. They cannot send a sufficient force over the mountains. No; not even to cope with the band of Hernandez. Meantime we shall organise our resistance here. And for that, this very Hernandez will be useful. He has defeated troops as a bandit; he will no doubt accomplish the same thing if he is made a colonel or even a general. You know the country well enough not to be shocked by what I say, Mrs Gould. I have heard you assert that this poor bandit was the living, breathing example of cruelty, injustice, stupidity, and oppression, that ruin men's souls as well as their fortunes in this country. Well, there would be some poetical retribution in that man arising to crush the evils which had driven an honest ranchero into a life of crime. A fine idea of retribution in that, isn't there?'

Decoud had dropped easily into English, which he spoke with precision, very correctly, but with too many z sounds.

'Think also of your hospitals, of your schools, of your ailing mothers and feeble old men, of all that population which you and your husband have brought into the rocky gorge of San Tomé. Are you not responsible to your conscience for all these people? Is it not worth while to make another effort; which is not at all so desperate as it looks, rather than – '

Decoud finished his thought with an upward toss of the arm, suggesting annihilation; and Mrs Gould turned away her head with a look of horror.

'Why don't you say all this to my husband?' she asked, without looking at Decoud, who stood watching the effect of his words.

'Ah! But Don Carlos is so English,' he began. Mrs Gould interrupted: 'Leave that alone, Don Martin. He's as much a Costaguanero – No! He's more of a Costaguanero than yourself.'

'Sentimentalist, sentimentalist,' Decoud almost cooed, in a tone of gentle and soothing deference. 'Sentimentalist, after the amazing manner of your people. I have been watching El Rey de Sulaco since I came here on a fool's errand, and perhaps impelled by some treason of fate lurking behind the unaccountable turns of a man's life. But I don't matter, I am not a sentimentalist, I cannot endow my personal desires with a shining robe of silk and jewels. Life is not for me a moral romance derived from the tradition of a pretty fairy tale. No, Mrs Gould; I am practical. I am not afraid of my motives. But, pardon me, I have been rather carried away. What I wish to say is that I have been observing. I won't tell you what I have discovered – '

'No. That is unnecessary,' whispered Mrs Gould, once more averting her head.

'It is. Except one little fact, that your husband does not like me. It's a small matter, which, in the circumstances, seems to acquire a perfectly ridiculous importance. Ridiculous and immense; for, clearly, money is required for my plan,' he reflected; then added, 'and we have two sentimentalists to deal with.'

'I don't know that I understand you, Don Martin,' said Mrs Gould, coldly, preserving the low key of their conversation. 'But, speaking as if I did, who is the other?'

'The great Holroyd in San Francisco, of course,' Decoud whispered, lightly. 'I think you understand me very well. Women are idealists; but then they are so perspicacious.'

But whatever was the reason of that remark, disparaging and complimentary at the same time, Mrs Gould seemed not to pay attention to it. The name of Holroyd had given a new tone to her anxiety.

'The silver escort is coming down to the harbour tomorrow; a whole six months' working, Don Martin!' she cried in dismay.

'Let it come down, then,' breathed out Decoud, earnestly, almost into her ear.

'But if the rumour should get about, and especially, if it turned out true, troubles might break out in the town,' objected Mrs Gould.

Decoud admitted that it was possible. He knew well the town children of the Sulaco Campo: sullen, thievish, vindictive, and bloodthirsty, whatever great qualities their brothers of the plain might have had. But then there was that other sentimentalist, who attached a strangely idealistic meaning to concrete facts. This stream of silver must be kept flowing north to return in the form of financial backing from the great house of Holroyd. Up at the mountain in the strong room of the mine the silver bars were worth less for his purpose than so much lead, from which at least bullets may be run. Let it come down to the harbour, ready for shipment.

The next north-going steamer would carry it off for the very salvation of the San Tomé mine, which has produced so much treasure. And, moreover, the rumour was probably false, he remarked, with much conviction in his hurried tone.

'Besides, señora,' concluded Decoud, 'we may suppress it for many days. I have been talking with the telegraphist in the middle of the Plaza Mayor; thus I am certain that we could not have been overheard. There was not even a bird in the air near us. And also let me tell you something more. I have been making friends with this man called Nostromo, the Capataz. We had a conversation this very evening, I walking by the side of his horse as he rode slowly out of the town just now. He promised me that if a riot took place for any reason – even for the most political of reasons, you understand – his Cargadores, an important part of the populace, you will admit, should be found on the side of the Europeans.'

'He has promised you that?' Mrs Gould enquired, with interest. 'What made him make that promise to you?'

'Upon my word, I don't know,' declared Decoud, in a slightly surprised tone. 'He certainly promised me that, but now you ask me why I certainly could not tell you his reasons. He talked with his usual carelessness, which, if he had been anything else but a common sailor, I would call a pose or an affectation.'

Decoud, interrupting himself, looked at Mrs Gould curiously.

'Upon the whole,' he continued, 'I suppose he expects something to his advantage from it. You mustn't forget that he does not exercise his extraordinary power over the lower classes without a certain amount of personal risk and without a great profusion in spending his money. One must pay in some way or other for such a solid thing as individual prestige. He told me after we made friends at a dance, in a Posada kept by a Mexican just outside the walls, that he had come here to make his fortune. I suppose he looks upon his prestige as a sort of investment.'

'Perhaps he prizes it for its own sake,' Mrs Gould said in a tone as if she were repelling an undeserved aspersion. 'Viola, the Garibaldino, with whom he has lived for some years, calls him the Incorruptible.'

'Ah! he belongs to the group of your protégés out there towards the harbour, Mrs Gould. *Muy bien.* And Captain Mitchell calls him wonderful. I have heard no end of tales of his strength, his audacity, his fidelity. No end of fine things. H'm! incorruptible! It is indeed a name of honour for the Capataz of the Cargadores of Sulaco. Incorruptible! Fine, but vague. However, I suppose he's sensible, too. And I talked to him upon that sane and practical assumption.'

'I prefer to think him disinterested, and therefore trustworthy,' Mrs Gould said, with the nearest approach to curtness it was in her nature to assume.

'Well, if so, then the silver will be still more safe. Let it come down, señora. Let it come down, so that it may go north and return to us in the shape of credit.'

Mrs Gould glanced along the corridor towards the door of her husband's room. Decoud, watching her as if she had his fate in her hands, detected an almost imperceptible nod of assent. He bowed with a smile, and, putting his hand into the breast pocket of his coat, pulled out a fan of light feathers set upon painted leaves of sandalwood. 'I had it in my pocket,' he murmured, triumphantly, 'for a plausible pretext.' He bowed again. 'Good-night, señora.'

Mrs Gould continued along the corridor away from her husband's room.

The fate of the San Tomé mine was lying heavy upon her heart. It was a long time now since she had begun to fear it. It had been an idea. She had watched it with misgivings turning into a fetish, and now the fetish had grown into a monstrous and crushing weight. It was as if the inspiration of their early years had left her heart to turn into a wall of silver-bricks, erected by the silent work of evil spirits, between her and her husband. He seemed to dwell alone within a circumvallation of precious metal, leaving her outside with her school, her hospital, the sick mothers and the feeble old men, mere insignificant vestiges of the initial inspiration. 'Those poor people!' she murmured to herself.

Below she heard the voice of Martin Decoud in the patio speaking loudly: 'I have found Doña Antonia's fan, Basilio. Look, here it is!'

Chapter 7

It was part of what Decoud would have called his sane materialism that he did not believe in the possibility of friendship between man and woman.

The one exception he allowed confirmed, he maintained, that absolute rule. Friendship was possible between brother and sister, meaning by friendship the frank unreserve, as before another human being, of thoughts and sensations; all the objectless and necessary sincerity of one's innermost life trying to react upon the profound sympathies of another existence.

His favourite sister, the handsome, slightly arbitrary and resolute angel, ruling the father and mother Decoud in the first-floor apartments of a very fine Parisian house, was the recipient of Martin Decoud's confidences as to his thoughts, actions, purposes, doubts, and even failures.

'Prepare our little circle in Paris for the birth of another South American Republic. One more or less, what does it matter? They may come into the world like evil flowers on a hotbed of rotten institutions; but the seed of this one has germinated in your brother's brain, and that will be enough for your devoted assent. I am writing this to you by the light of a single candle, in a sort of inn, near the harbour, kept by an Italian called Viola, a protégé of Mrs Gould. The whole building, which, for all I know, may have been contrived by a Conquistador farmer of the pearl fishery three hundred years ago, is perfectly silent. So is the plain between the town and the harbour; silent, but not so dark as the house, because the pickets of Italian workmen guarding the railway have lighted little fires all along the line. It was not so quiet around here yesterday. We had an awful riot – a sudden outbreak of the populace, which was not suppressed till late today. Its object, no doubt, was loot, and that was defeated, as you must have learned already from the cablegram sent via San Francisco and New York last night, when the cables were still open. You have read already there that the energetic action of the Europeans of the railway has saved the town from destruction, and you may believe that. I wrote out the cable myself. We have no Reuter's agency man here. I have also fired at the mob from the windows of the club, in company with some other young men of position. Our object was to keep the Calle de la Constitucion clear for the exodus of the ladies and children, who have taken refuge on board a couple of cargo ships now in the harbour here. That was yesterday. You should also have learned from the cable that the missing President, Ribiera, who had disappeared after the battle of Sta Marta, has turned up here in Sulaco by one of those strange coincidences that are almost incredible, riding on a lame mule into the very midst of the street fighting. It appears that he had fled, in company of a muleteer called Bonifacio, across the mountains from the threats of Montero into the arms of an enraged mob.

'The Capataz of Cargadores, that Italian sailor of whom I have written to you before, has saved him from an ignoble death. That man seems to have a particular talent for being on the spot whenever there is something picturesque to be done.

'He was with me at four o'clock in the morning at the offices of the *Porvenir*, where he had turned up so early in order to warn me of the coming trouble, and also to assure me that he would keep his Cargadores on the side of order. When the full daylight came we were looking together at the crowd on foot and on horseback, demonstrating on the Plaza and shying stones at the windows of the Intendencia. Nostromo (that is the name they call him by here) was pointing out to me his Cargadores interspersed in the mob.

'The sun shines late upon Sulaco, for it has first to climb above the mountains. In that clear morning light, brighter than twilight, Nostromo saw right across the vast Plaza, at the end of the street beyond the cathedral, a mounted man apparently in difficulties with a yelling knot of léperos. At once he said to me, "That's a stranger. What is it they are doing to him?" Then he took out the silver whistle he is in the habit of using on the wharf (this man seems to disdain the use of any metal less precious than silver) and blew into it twice, evidently a preconcerted signal for his Cargadores. He ran out immediately, and they rallied round him. I ran out, too, but was too late to follow them and help in the rescue of the stranger, whose animal had fallen. I was set upon at once as a hated aristocrat, and was only too glad to get into the club, where Don Jaime Berges (you may remember him visiting at our house in Paris some three years ago) thrust a sporting gun into my hands. They were already firing from the windows. There were little heaps of cartridges lying about on the open card-tables. I remember a couple of overturned chairs, some bottles rolling on the floor amongst the packs of cards scattered suddenly as the caballeros rose from their game to open fire upon the mob. Most of the young men had spent the night at the club in the expectation of some such disturbance. In two of the candelabra, on the consoles, the candles were burning down in their sockets. A large iron nut, probably stolen from the railway workshops, flew in from the street as I entered, and broke one of the large mirrors set in the wall. I noticed also one of the club servants tied up hand and foot with the cords of the curtain and flung in a corner. I have a vague recollection of Don Jaime assuring me hastily that the fellow had been detected putting poison into the dishes at supper. But I remember distinctly he was shrieking for mercy, without stopping at all, continuously, and so absolutely disregarded that nobody even took the trouble to gag him. The noise he made was so disagreeable that I had half a mind to do it myself. But there was no time to waste on such trifles. I took my place at one of the windows and began firing.

'I didn't learn till later in the afternoon whom it was that Nostromo, with his Cargadores and some Italian workmen as well, had managed to save from those drunken rascals. That man has a peculiar talent when anything striking to the imagination has to be done. I made that remark to him afterwards when we met after some sort of order had been restored in the town, and the answer he made rather surprised me. He said quite moodily, "And how much do I get for that, señor?" Then it dawned upon me that perhaps this man's vanity has been satiated by the adulation of the common people and the confidence of his superiors!'

Decoud paused to light a cigarette, then, with his head still over his writing, he blew a cloud of smoke, which seemed to rebound from the paper. He took up the pencil again.

'That was yesterday evening on the Plaza, while he sat on the steps of the cathedral, his hands between his knees, holding the bridle of his famous silver-grey mare. He had led his body of Cargadores splendidly all day long. He looked fatigued. I don't know how I looked. Very dirty, I suppose. But I suppose I also looked pleased. From the time the fugitive President had been got off to the S. S. *Minerva*, the tide had turned against the mob. They had been driven off the harbour, and out of the better streets of the town, into their own maze of ruins and tolderías. You must understand that this riot, whose primary object was undoubtedly the getting hold of the San Tomé silver stored in the lower rooms of the Custom House (besides the general looting of the Ricos), had acquired a political colouring from the fact of two Deputies to the Provincial Assembly, Señores Gamacho and Fuentes, both from Bolson, putting themselves at the head of it – late in the afternoon, it is true, when the mob, disappointed in their hopes of loot, made a stand in the narrow streets to the cries of "Viva la Libertad! Down with Feudalism!" (I wonder what they imagine feudalism to be?) "Down with the Goths and Paralytics." I suppose the Señores Gamacho and Fuentes knew what they were doing. They are prudent gentlemen. In the Assembly they called themselves Moderates, and opposed every energetic measure with philanthropic pensiveness. At the first rumours of Montero's victory, they began to show a subtle change of the pensive temper, and began to defy poor Don Juste Lopez in his Presidential tribune with an effrontery to which the poor man could only respond by a dazed smoothing of his beard and the ringing of the Presidential bell. Then, when the downfall of the Ribierist cause became confirmed beyond the shadow of a doubt, they have blossomed into convinced Liberals, acting together as if they were Siamese twins, and ultimately taking charge, as it were, of the riot in the name of Monterist principles.

'Their last move of eight o'clock last night was to organise themselves into a Monterist Committee which sits, as far as I know, in a posada kept by a retired Mexican bullfighter, a great politician, too, whose name I have forgotten. Thence they have issued a communication to us, the Goths and Paralytics of the Amarilla Club (who have our own committee), inviting us to come to some provisional understanding for a truce, in order, they have the impudence to say, that the noble cause of Liberty "should not be stained by the criminal excesses of Conservative selfishness"! As I came out to sit with Nostromo on the cathedral steps the club was busy considering a proper reply in the principal room, littered with exploded cartridges, with a lot of broken glass, blood smears, candlesticks, and all sorts of wreckage on the floor. But all this is nonsense. Nobody in the town has any real power except the railway engineers, whose men occupy the dismantled houses acquired by the Company for their town station on one side of the Plaza, and Nostromo, whose Cargadores were sleeping under the arcades along the front of Anzani's shops. A fire of broken furniture out of the Intendencia saloons, mostly gilt, was burning on the Plaza, in a high flame swaying right upon the statue of Charles IV. The dead body of a man was lying on the steps of the pedestal, his arms thrown wide open, and his sombrero covering his face – the attention of some friend, perhaps. The light of the flame touched the foliage of the first trees on the Alameda, and played on the end of a side street near by, blocked up by a jumble of ox-carts and dead bullocks. Sitting on one of the carcases, a lépero, muffled up, smoked a cigarette. It was a truce, you understand. The only other living being on the Plaza besides ourselves was a Cargador walking to and fro, with a long, bare knife in his hand, like a sentry before the Arcades, where his friends were sleeping. And the only other spot of light in the dark town were the lighted windows of the club, at the corner of the Calle.'

After having written so far, Don Martin Decoud, the exotic dandy of the Parisian boulevard, got up and walked across the sanded floor of the café at one end of the Albergo of United Italy, kept by Giorgio Viola, the old companion of Garibaldi. The highly coloured lithograph of the Faithful Hero seemed to look dimly, in the light of one candle, at the man with no faith in anything except the truth of his own sensations. Looking out of the window, Decoud was met by a darkness so impenetrable that he could see neither the mountains nor the town, nor yet the buildings near the harbour;

and there was not a sound, as if the tremendous obscurity of the Placid Gulf, spreading from the waters over the land, had made it dumb as well as blind. Presently Decoud felt a light tremor of the floor and a distant clank of iron. A bright white light appeared, deep in the darkness, growing bigger with a thundering noise. The rolling stock usually kept on the sidings in Rincon was being run back to the yards for safe keeping. Like a mysterious stirring of the darkness behind the headlight of the engine, the train passed in a gust of hollow uproar, by the end of the house, which seemed to vibrate all over in response. And nothing was clearly visible but, on the end of the last flat car, a Negro, in white trousers and naked to the waist, swinging a blazing torch basket incessantly with a circular movement of his bare arm. Decoud did not stir.

Behind him, on the back of the chair from which he had risen, hung his elegant Parisian overcoat, with a pearl-grey silk lining. But when he turned back to come to the table the candlelight fell upon a face that was grimy and scratched. His rosy lips were blackened with heat, the smoke of gunpowder. Dirt and rust tarnished the lustre of his short beard. His shirt collar and cuffs were crumpled; the blue silken tie hung down his breast like a rag; a greasy smudge crossed his white brow. He had not taken off his clothing nor used water, except to snatch a hasty drink greedily, for some forty hours. An awful restlessness had made him its own, had marked him with all the signs of desperate strife, and put a dry, sleepless stare into his eyes. He murmured to himself in a hoarse voice, 'I wonder if there's any bread here,' looked vaguely about him, then dropped into the chair and took the pencil up again. He became aware he had not eaten anything for many hours.

It occurred to him that no one could understand him so well as his sister. In the most sceptical heart there lurks at such moments, when the chances of existence are involved, a desire to leave a correct impression of the feelings, like a light by which the action may be seen when personality is gone, gone where no light of investigation can ever reach the truth which every death takes out of the world. Therefore, instead of looking for something to eat, or trying to snatch an hour or so of sleep, Decoud was filling the pages of a large pocketbook with a letter to his sister.

In the intimacy of that intercourse he could not keep out his weariness, his great fatigue, the close touch of his bodily sensations. He began again as if he were talking to her. With almost an illusion of her presence, he wrote the phrase, 'I am very hungry.'

'I have the feeling of a great solitude around me,' he continued. 'Is it, perhaps, because I am the only man with a definite idea in his head, in the complete collapse of every resolve, intention, and hope about me? But the solitude is also very real. All the engineers are out, and have been for two days, looking after the property of the National Central Railway, of that great Costaguana undertaking which is to put money into the pockets of Englishmen, Frenchmen, Americans, Germans, and God knows who else.

The silence about me is ominous. There is above the middle part of this house a sort of first floor, with narrow openings like loopholes for windows, probably used in old times for the better defence against the savages, when the persistent barbarism of our native continent did not wear the black coats of politicians, but went about yelling, half-naked, with bows and arrows in its hands. The woman of the house is dying up there, I believe, all alone with her old husband. There is a narrow staircase, the sort of staircase one man could easily defend against a mob, leading up there, and I have just heard, through the thickness of the wall, the old fellow going down into their kitchen for something or other. It was a sort of noise a mouse might make behind the plaster of a wall. All the servants they had ran away yesterday and have not returned yet, if ever they do. For the rest, there are only two children here, two girls. The father has sent them downstairs, and they have crept into this café, perhaps because I am here. They huddle together in a corner, in each other's arms; I just noticed them a few minutes ago, and I feel more lonely than ever.'

Decoud turned half round in his chair, and asked, 'Is there any bread here?'

Linda's dark head was shaken negatively in response, above the fair head of her sister nestling on her breast.

'You couldn't get me some bread?' insisted Decoud. The child did not move; he saw her large eyes stare at him very dark from the corner. 'You're not afraid of me?' he said.

'No,' said Linda, 'we are not afraid of you. You came here with Gian' Battista.'

'You mean Nostromo?' said Decoud.

'The English call him so, but that is no name either for man or beast,' said the girl, passing her hand gently over her sister's hair.

'But he lets people call him so,' remarked Decoud.

'Not in this house,' retorted the child.

'Ah! well, I shall call him the Capataz then.'

Decoud gave up the point, and after writing for a while turned round again. 'When do you expect him back?' he asked.

'After he brought you here he rode off to fetch the Señor Doctor from the town for mother. He will be back soon.'

'He stands a good chance of getting shot somewhere on the road,' Decoud murmured to himself audibly; and Linda declared in her high-pitched voice: 'Nobody would dare to fire a shot at Gian' Battista.'

'You believe that,' asked Decoud, 'do you?'

'I know it,' said the child, with conviction. 'There is no one in this place brave enough to attack Gian' Battista.'

'It doesn't require much bravery to pull a trigger behind a bush,' muttered Decoud to himself. 'Fortunately, the night is dark, or there would be but little chance of saving the silver of the mine.'

He turned again to his pocketbook, glanced back through the pages, and again started his pencil.

'That was the position yesterday, after the *Minerva* with the fugitive President had gone out of harbour, and the rioters had been driven back into the side lanes of the town. I sat on the steps of the cathedral with Nostromo, after sending out the cable message for the information of a more or less attentive world. Strangely enough, though the offices of the Cable Company are in the same building as the *Porvenir*, the mob, which has thrown my presses out of the window and scattered the type all over the Plaza, has been kept from interfering with the instruments on the other side of the court-yard. As I sat talking with Nostromo, Bernhardt, the telegraphist, came out from under the Arcades with a piece of paper in his hand. The little man had tied himself up to an enormous sword and was hung all over with revolvers. He is ridiculous, but the bravest German of his size that ever tapped the key of a Morse transmitter. He had received the message from Cayta reporting the transports with Barrios's army just entering the port, and ending with the words, "The greatest enthusiasm prevails." I walked off to drink some water at the fountain, and I was shot at from the Alameda by somebody hiding behind a tree. But I drank, and didn't care; with Barrios in Cayta and the great Cordillera between us and Montero's victorious army I seemed, notwithstanding Messrs. Gamacho and Fuentes, to hold my new State in the hollow of my hand. I was ready to sleep, but when I got as far as the Casa Gould I found the patio full of wounded laid out on straw. Lights were burning, and in that enclosed courtyard on that hot night a faint odour of chloroform and blood hung about. At one end Doctor Monygham, the doctor of the mine, was dressing the wounds; at the other, near the stairs, Father Corbelàn, kneeling, listened to the confession of a dying Cargador. Mrs Gould was walking about through these shambles with a large bottle in one hand and a lot of cotton wool in the other. She just looked at me and never even winked. Her camerista was following her, also holding a bottle, and sobbing gently to herself.

'I busied myself for some time in fetching water from the cistern for the wounded. Afterwards I wandered upstairs, meeting some of the first ladies of Sulaco, paler than I had ever seen them before, with bandages over their arms. Not all of them had fled to the ships. A good many had taken refuge for the day in the Casa Gould. On the landing a girl, with her hair half down, was kneeling against the wall under the niche where stands a Madonna in blue robes and a gilt crown on her head. I think it was the eldest Miss Lopez; I couldn't see her face, but I remember looking at the high French heel of her little shoe. She did not make a sound, she did not stir, she was not sobbing; she remained there, perfectly still, all black against the white wall, a silent figure of passionate piety. I am sure she was no more frightened than the other white-faced ladies I met carrying bandages. One was sitting on the top step tearing a piece of linen hastily into strips – the young wife of an elderly man of fortune here. She interrupted herself to wave her hand to my bow, as though she were in her carriage on the Alameda. The women of our country are worth looking at during a revolution. The rouge and pearl powder fall off, together with that passive attitude towards the outer world which education, tradition, custom impose upon them from the earliest infancy. I thought of your face, which from your infancy had the stamp of intelligence instead of that patient and resigned cast which appears when some political commotion tears down the veil of cosmetics and usage.

'In the great sala upstairs a sort of Junta of Notables was sitting, the remnant of the vanished Provincial Assembly. Don Juste Lopez had had half his beard singed off at the muzzle of a trabuco loaded with slugs, of which every one missed him, providentially. And as he turned his head from side to side it was exactly as if there had been two men inside his frock-coat, one nobly whiskered and solemn, the other scared.

'They raised a cry of "Decoud! Don Martin!" at my entrance. I asked them, "What are you upon, gentlemen?" There did not seem to be any president, though Don José Avellanos sat at the head of the table. They all answered together, "On the preservation of life and property." "Till the new officials arrive," Don Juste explained to me, with the solemn side of his face offered to my view. It was as if a stream of water had been poured upon my glowing idea of a new State. There was a hissing sound in my ears, and the room grew dim, as if suddenly filled with vapour.

'I walked up to the table blindly, as though I had been drunk. "You are deliberating upon surrender," I said. They all sat still, with their noses over the sheet of paper each had before him, God only knows why. Only Don José hid his face in his hands, muttering, 'Never, never!' But as I looked at him, it seemed to me that I could have blown him away with my breath, he looked so frail, so weak, so worn out. Whatever happens, he will not survive. The deception is too great for a man of his age; and hasn't he seen the sheets of *Fifty Years of Misrule*, which we have begun printing on the presses of the *Porvenir*, littering the Plaza, floating in the gutters, fired out as wads for trabucos loaded with handfuls of type, blown in the wind, trampled in the mud? I have seen pages floating upon the very waters of the harbour. It would be unreasonable to expect him to survive. It would be cruel.

' "Do you know," I cried, "what surrender means to you, to your women, to your children, to your property?" '

'I declaimed for five minutes without drawing breath, it seems to me, harping on our best chances, on the ferocity of Montero, whom I made out to be as great a beast as I have no doubt he would like to be if he had intelligence enough to conceive a systematic reign of terror. And then for another five minutes or more I poured out an impassioned appeal to their courage and manliness, with all the passion of my love for Antonia. For if ever man spoke well, it would be from a personal feeling, denouncing an enemy, defending himself, or pleading for what really may be dearer than life. My dear girl, I absolutely thundered at them. It seemed as if my voice would burst the walls asunder, and when I stopped I saw all their scared eyes looking at me dubiously. And that was all the effect I had produced! Only Don José's head had sunk lower and lower on his breast. I bent my ear to his withered lips, and made out his whisper, something like, "In God's name, then, Martin, my son!" I don't know exactly. There was the name of God in it, I am certain. It seems to me I have caught his last breath – the breath of his departing soul on his lips.

'He lives yet, it is true. I have seen him since; but it was only a senile body, lying on its back, covered to the chin, with open eyes, and so still that you might have said it was breathing no longer. I left him thus, with Antonia kneeling by the side of the bed, just before I came to this Italian's posada, where the ubiquitous death is also waiting. But I know that Don José has really died there, in the Casa Gould, with that whisper urging me to attempt what no doubt his soul, wrapped up in the sanctity of diplomatic treaties and solemn declarations, must have abhorred. I had exclaimed very loud, "There is never any God in a country where men will not help themselves."

'Meanwhile, Don Juste had begun a pondered oration whose solemn effect was spoiled by the ridiculous disaster to his beard. I did not wait to make it out. He seemed to argue that Montero's (he called him The General) intentions were probably not evil, though, he went on, "that distinguished man" (only a week ago we used to call him a *gran bestia)* "was perhaps mistaken as to the true means." As you may imagine, I didn't stay to hear the rest. I know the intentions of Montero's brother, Pedrito, the guerrillero, whom I exposed in Paris, some years ago, in a café frequented by South American students, where he tried to pass himself off for a Secretary of Legation. He used to come in and talk for hours, twisting his felt hat in his hairy paws, and his ambition seemed to be to become a sort of Duc de Morny to a sort of Napoleon. Already, then, he used to talk of his brother in inflated terms. He seemed fairly safe from being found out, because the students, all of the Blanco families, did not, as you may imagine, frequent the Legation. It was only Decoud, a man without faith and principles, as they used to say, that went in there sometimes for the sake of the fun, as it were to an assembly of trained monkeys. I know his intentions. I have seen him change the plates at table. Whoever is allowed to live on in terror, I must die the death.

'No, I didn't stay to the end to hear Don Juste Lopez trying to persuade himself in a grave oration of the clemency and justice, and honesty, and purity of the brothers Montero. I went out abruptly to seek Antonia. I saw her in the gallery. As I opened the door, she extended to me her clasped hands.

' "What are they doing in there?" she asked.

' "Talking," I said, with my eyes looking into hers.

' "Yes, yes, but – "

' "Empty speeches," I interrupted her. "Hiding their fears behind imbecile hopes. They are all great Parliamentarians there – on the English model, as you know." I was so furious that I could hardly speak. She made a gesture of despair.

'Through the door I held a little ajar behind me, we heard Don Juste's measured mouthing monotone go on from phrase to phrase, like a sort of awful and solemn madness.

' "After all, the Democratic aspirations have, perhaps, their legitimacy. The ways of human progress are inscrutable, and if the fate of the country is in the hand of Montero, we ought – "

'I crashed the door to on that; it was enough; it was too much. There was never a beautiful face expressing more horror and despair than the face of Antonia. I couldn't bear it; I seized her wrists.

' "Have they killed my father in there?" she asked.

'Her eyes blazed with indignation, but as I looked on, fascinated, the light in them went out.

' "It is a surrender," I said. And I remember I was shaking her wrists I held apart in my hands. "But it's more than talk. Your father told me to go on in God's name."

'My dear girl, there is that in Antonia which would make me believe in the feasibility of anything. One look at her face is enough to set my brain on fire. And yet I love her as any other man would – with the heart, and with that alone. She is more to me than his Church to Father Corbelàn (the Grand Vicar disappeared last night from the town; perhaps gone to join the band of Hernandez). She is more to me than his precious mine to that sentimental Englishman. I won't speak of his wife. She may have been sentimental once. The San Tomé mine stands now between those two people. "Your father himself, Antonia," I repeated; "your father, do you understand? has told me to go on."

'She averted her face, and in a pained voice: "He has?" she cried. "Then, indeed, I fear he will never speak again."

'She freed her wrists from my clutch and began to cry in her handkerchief. I disregarded her sorrow; I would rather see her miserable than not see her at all, never any more; for whether I escaped or stayed to die, there was for us no coming together, no future. And that being so, I had no pity to waste upon the passing moments of her sorrow. I sent her off in tears to fetch Doña Emilia and Don Carlos, too. Their sentiment was necessary to the very life of my plan; the sentimentalism of the people that will never do anything for the sake of their passionate desire, unless it comes to them clothed in the fair robes of an idea.

'Late at night we formed a small junta of four – the two women, Don Carlos, and myself – in Mrs Gould's blue-and-white boudoir.

'El Rey de Sulaco thinks himself, no doubt, a very honest man. And so he is, if one could look behind his taciturnity. Perhaps he thinks that this alone makes his honesty unstained. Those Englishmen live on illusions which somehow or other help them to get a firm hold of the substance.

When he speaks it is by a rare "yes" or "no" that seems as impersonal as the words of an oracle. But he could not impose on me by his dumb reserve. I knew what he had in his head; he has his mine in his head; and his wife had nothing in her head but his precious person, which he has bound up with the Gould Concession and tied up to that little woman's neck. No matter. The thing was to make him present the affair to Holroyd (the Steel and Silver King) in such a manner as to secure his financial support. At that time last night, just twenty-four hours ago, we thought the silver of the mine safe in the Custom House vaults till the northbound steamer came to take it away. And as long as the treasure flowed north, without a break, that utter sentimentalist, Holroyd, would not drop his idea of introducing, not only justice, industry, peace, to the benighted continents, but also that pet dream of his of a purer form of Christianity. Later on, the principal European really in Sulaco, the engineer-in-chief of the railway, came riding up the Calle, from the harbour, and was admitted to our conclave. Meantime, the Junta of the Notables in the great sala was still deliberating; only, one of them had run out in the corridor to ask the servant whether something to eat couldn't be sent in. The first words the engineer-in-chief said as he came into the boudoir were, "What is your house, dear Mrs Gould? A war hospital below, and apparently a restaurant above. I saw them carrying trays full of good things into the sala."

"And here, in this boudoir," I said, "you behold the inner cabinet of the Occidental Republic that is to be."

'He was so preoccupied that he didn't smile at that, he didn't even look surprised.

'He told us that he was attending to the general dispositions for the defence of the railway property at the railway yards when he was sent for to go into the railway telegraph office. The engineer of the railhead, at the foot of the mountains, wanted to talk to him from his end of the wire. There was nobody in the office but himself and the operator of the railway telegraph, who read off the clicks aloud as the tape coiled its length upon the floor. And the purport of that talk, clicked nervously from a wooden shed in the depths of the forests, had informed the chief that President Ribiera had been, or was being, pursued. This was news, indeed, to all of us in Sulaco. Ribiera himself, when rescued, revived, and soothed by us, had been inclined to think that he had not been pursued.

'Ribiera had yielded to the urgent solicitations of his friends, and had left the headquarters of his discomfited army alone, under the guidance of Bonifacio, the muleteer, who had been willing to take the responsibility with the risk. He had departed at daybreak of the third day. His remaining forces had melted away during the night. Bonifacio and he rode hard on horses towards the Cordillera; then they obtained mules, entered the passes, and crossed the Páramo of Ivie just before a freezing blast swept over that stony plateau, burying in a drift of snow the little shelter-hut of stones in which they had spent the night. Afterwards poor Ribiera had many adventures, got separated from his guide, lost his mount, struggled down to the Campo on foot, and if he had not thrown himself on the mercy of a ranchero would have perished a long way from Sulaco. That man, who, as a matter of fact, recognised him at once, let him have a fresh mule, which the fugitive, heavy and unskilful, had ridden to death. And it was true he had been pursued by a party commanded by no less a person than Pedro Montero, the brother of the general. The cold wind of the Páramo luckily caught the pursuers on the top of the pass. Some few men, and all the animals, perished in the icy blast. The stragglers died, but the main body kept on. They found poor Bonifacio lying half-dead at the foot of a snow slope, and bayoneted him promptly in the true Civil War style. They would have had Ribiera, too, if they had not, for some reason or other, turned off the track of the old Camino Real, only to lose their way in the forests at the foot of the lower slopes. And there they were at last, having stumbled in unexpectedly upon the construction camp. The engineer at the railhead told his chief by wire that he had Pedro Montero absolutely there, in the very office, listening to the clicks. He was going to take possession of Sulaco in the name of the Democracy. He was very overbearing. His men slaughtered some of the Railway Company's cattle without asking leave, and went to work broiling the meat on the embers. Pedrito made many pointed enquiries as to the silver mine, and what had become of the product of the last six months' working. He had said peremptorily, "Ask your chief up there by wire, he ought to know; tell him that Don Pedro Montero, Chief of the Campo and Minister of the Interior of the new Government, desires to be correctly informed."

'He had his feet wrapped up in bloodstained rags, a lean, haggard face, ragged beard and hair, and had walked in limping, with a crooked branch of a tree for a staff. His followers were perhaps in a worse plight, but apparently they had not thrown away their arms, and, at any rate, not all their ammunition. Their lean faces filled the door and the windows of the telegraph hut. As it was at the same time the bedroom of the engineer-in-charge there, Montero had thrown himself on his clean blankets and lay there shivering and dictating requisitions to be transmitted by wire to Sulaco. He demanded a train of cars to be sent down at once to transport his men up.

' "To this I answered from my end," the engineer-in-chief related to us, "that I dared not risk the rolling-stock in the interior, as there had been attempts to wreck trains all along the line several times. I did that for your sake, Gould," said the chief engineer. "The answer to this was, in the words of my subordinate, 'The filthy brute on my bed said, "Suppose I were to have you shot?" ' To which my subordinate, who, it appears, was himself operating, remarked that it would not bring the cars up. Upon that, the other, yawning, said, 'Never mind, there is no lack of horses on the Campo.' And, turning over, went to sleep on Harris's bed."

'This is why, my dear girl, I am a fugitive tonight. The last wire from railhead says that Pedro Montero and his men left at daybreak, after feeding on asado beef all night. They took all the horses; they will find more on the road; they'll be here in less than thirty hours, and thus Sulaco is no place either for me or the great store of silver belonging to the Gould Concession.

'But that is not the worst. The garrison of Esmeralda has gone over to the victorious party. We have heard this by means of the telegraphist of the Cable Company, who came to the Casa Gould in the early morning with the news. In fact, it was so early that the day had not yet quite broken over Sulaco. His colleague in Esmeralda had called him up to say that the garrison, after shooting some of their officers, had taken possession of a Government steamer laid up in the harbour. It is really a heavy blow for me. I thought I could depend on every man in this province. It was a mistake. It was a Monterist Revolution in Esmeralda, just such as was attempted in Sulaco, only that *that* one came off. The telegraphist was signalling to Bernhardt all the time, and his last transmitted words were, "They are bursting in the door, and taking possession of the cable office. You are cut off. Can do no more."

'But, as a matter of fact, he managed somehow to escape the vigilance of his captors, who had tried to stop the communication with the outer world. He did manage it. How it was done I don't know, but a few hours afterwards he called up Sulaco again, and what he said was, "The insurgent army has taken possession of the Government transport in the bay and are filling her with troops, with the intention of going round the coast to Sulaco. Therefore look out for yourselves. They will be ready to start in a few hours, and may be upon you before daybreak."

'This is all he could say. They drove him away from his instrument this time for good, because Bernhardt has been calling up Esmeralda ever since without getting an answer.'

After setting these words down in the pocketbook which he was filling up for the benefit of his sister, Decoud lifted his head to listen. But there were no sounds, neither in the room nor in the house, except the drip of the water from the filter into the vast earthenware jar under the wooden stand. And outside the house there was a great silence. Decoud lowered his head again over the pocketbook.

'I am not running away, you understand,' he wrote on. 'I am simply going away with that great treasure of silver which must be saved at all costs. Pedro Montero from the Campo and the revolted garrison of Esmeralda from the sea are converging upon it. That it is there lying ready for them is only an accident. The real objective is the San Tomé mine itself, as you may well imagine; otherwise the Occidental Province would have been, no doubt, left alone for many weeks, to be gathered at leisure into the arms of the victorious party. Don Carlos Gould will have enough to do to save his mine, with its organisation and its people; this "Imperium in Imperio", this wealth-producing thing, to which his sentimentalism attaches a strange idea of justice. He holds to it as some men hold to the idea of love or revenge. Unless I am much mistaken in the man, it must remain inviolate or perish by an act of his will alone. A passion has crept into his cold and idealistic life. A passion which I can only comprehend intellectually. A passion that is not like the passions we know, we men of another blood. But it is as dangerous as any of ours.

'His wife has understood it, too. That is why she is such a good ally of mine. She seizes upon all my suggestions with a sure instinct that in the end they make for the safety of the Gould Concession. And he defers to her because he trusts her perhaps, but I fancy more rather as if he wished to make up for some subtle wrong, for that sentimental unfaithfulness which surrenders her happiness, her life, to the seduction of an idea. The little woman has discovered that he lives for the mine rather than for her. But let them be. To each his fate, shaped by passion or sentiment. The principal thing is that she has backed up my advice to get the silver out of the town, out of the country, at once, at any cost, at any risk. Don Carlos' mission is to preserve unstained the fair fame of his mine; Mrs Gould's mission is to save him from the effects of that cold and overmastering passion, which she dreads more than if it were an infatuation for another woman. Nostromo's mission is to save the silver. The plan is to load it into the largest of the Company's lighters, and send it across the gulf to a small port out of Costaguana territory just on the other side of Azuera, where the first north bound steamer will get orders to pick it up. The waters here are calm. We shall slip away into the darkness of the gulf before the Esmeralda rebels arrive; and by the time the day breaks over the ocean we shall be out of sight, invisible, hidden by Azuera, which itself looks from the Sulaco shore like a faint blue cloud on the horizon.

'The incorruptible Capataz de Cargadores is the man for that work; and I, the man with a passion, but without a mission, I go with him to return – to play my part in the farce to the end, and, if successful, to receive my reward, which no one but Antonia can give me.

'I shall not see her again now before I depart. I left her, as I have said, by Don José's bedside. The street was dark, the houses shut up, and I walked out of the town in the night. Not a single street-lamp had been lit for two days, and the archway of the gate was only a mass of darkness in the vague form of a tower, in which I heard low, dismal groans, that seemed to answer the murmurs of a man's voice.

'I recognised something impassive and careless in its tone, characteristic of that Genoese sailor who, like me, has come casually here to be drawn into the events for which his scepticism as well as mine seems to entertain a sort of passive contempt. The only thing he seems to care for, as far as I have been able to discover, is to be well spoken of. An ambition fit for noble souls, but also a profitable one for an exceptionally intelligent scoundrel.

Yes. His very words, "To be well spoken of. Si, señor." He does not seem to make any difference between speaking and thinking. Is it sheer naiveness or the practical point of view, I wonder? Exceptional individualities always interest me, because they are true to the general formula expressing the moral state of humanity.

'He joined me on the harbour road after I had passed them under the dark archway without stopping. It was a woman in trouble he had been talking to. Through discretion I kept silent while he walked by my side. After a time he began to talk himself. It was not what I expected. It was only an old woman, an old lace-maker, in search of her son, one of the street-sweepers employed by the municipality. Friends had come the day before at daybreak to the door of their hovel calling him out. He had gone with them, and she had not seen him since; so she had left the food she had been preparing half-cooked on the extinct embers and had crawled out as far as the harbour, where she had heard that some town mozos had been killed on the morning of the riot. One of the Cargadores guarding the Custom House had brought out a lantern, and had helped her to look at the few dead left lying about there. Now she was creeping back, having failed in her search. So she sat down on the stone seat under the arch, moaning, because she was very tired. The Capataz had questioned her, and after hearing her broken and groaning tale had advised her to go and look amongst the wounded in the patio of the Casa Gould. He had also given her a quarter dollar, he mentioned carelessly.

' "Why did you do that?" I asked. "Do you know her?" '

' "No, señor. I don't suppose I have ever seen her before. How should I? She has not probably been out in the streets for years. She is one of those old women that you find in this country at the back of huts, crouching over fireplaces, with a stick on the ground by their side, and almost too feeble to drive away the stray dogs from their cooking-pots. Caramba! I could tell by her voice that death had forgotten her. But, old or young, they like money, and will speak well of the man who gives it to them." He laughed a little. "Señor, you should have felt the clutch of her paw as I put the piece in her palm." He paused. "My last, too," he added.

'I made no comment. He's known for his liberality and his bad luck at the game of monte, which keeps him as poor as when he first came here.

' "I suppose, Don Martin," he began, in a thoughtful, speculative tone, "that the Señor Administrador of San Tomé will reward me someday if I save his silver?"

'I said that it could not be otherwise, surely. He walked on, muttering to himself. "Si, si, without doubt, without doubt; and, look you, Señor Martin, what it is to be well spoken of! There is not another man that could have been even thought of for such a thing. I shall get something great for it someday. And let it come soon," he mumbled. "Time passes in this country as quick as anywhere else."

'This, *soeur chérie*, is my companion in the great escape for the sake of the great cause. He is more naive than shrewd, more masterful than crafty, more generous with his personality than the people who make use of him are with their money. At least, that is what he thinks himself with more pride than sentiment. I am glad I have made friends with him. As a companion he acquires more importance than he ever had as a sort of minor genius in his way – as an original Italian sailor whom I allowed to come in in the small hours and talk familiarly to the editor of the *Porvenir* while the paper was going through the press. And it is curious to have met a man for whom the value of life seems to consist in personal prestige.

'I am waiting for him here now. On arriving at the posada kept by Viola we found the children alone down below, and the old Genoese shouted to his countryman to go and fetch the doctor. Otherwise we would have gone on to the wharf, where it appears Captain Mitchell with some volunteer Europeans and a few picked Cargadores are loading the lighter with the silver that must be saved from Montero's clutches in order to be used for Montero's defeat. Nostromo galloped furiously back towards the town. He has been long gone already. This delay gives me time to talk to you. By the time this pocketbook reaches your hands much will have happened. But now it is a pause under the hovering wing of death in that silent house buried in the black night, with this dying woman, the two children crouching without a sound, and that old man whom I can hear through the thickness of the wall passing up and down with a light rubbing noise no louder than a mouse. And I, the only other with them, don't really know whether to count myself with the living or with the dead. "*Quien sabe?*" as the people here are prone to say in answer to every question. But no! feeling for you is certainly not dead, and the whole thing, the house, the dark night, the silent children in this dim room, my very presence here – all this is life, must be life, since it is so much like a dream.'

With the writing of the last line there came upon Decoud a moment of sudden and complete oblivion. He swayed over the table as if struck by a bullet. The next moment he sat up, confused, with the idea that he had heard his pencil roll on the floor. The low door of the café, wide open, was filled with the glare of a torch in which was visible half of a horse, switching its tail against the leg of a rider with a long iron spur strapped to the naked heel. The two girls were gone, and Nostromo, standing in the middle of the room, looked at him from under the round brim of the sombrero low down over his brow.

'I have brought that sour-faced English doctor in Señora Gould's carriage,' said Nostromo. 'I doubt if, with all his wisdom, he can save the Padrona this time. They have sent for the children. A bad sign that.'

He sat down on the end of a bench. 'She wants to give them her blessing, I suppose.'

Dazedly Decoud observed that he must have fallen sound asleep, and Nostromo said, with a vague smile, that he had looked in at the window and had seen him lying still across the table with his head on his arms. The English señora had also come in the carriage, and went upstairs at once with the doctor. She had told him not to wake up Don Martin yet; but when they sent for the children he had come into the café.

The half of the horse with its half of the rider swung round outside the door; the torch of tow and resin in the iron basket which was carried on a stick at the saddlebow flared right into the room for a moment, and Mrs Gould entered hastily with a very white, tired face. The hood of her dark, blue cloak had fallen back. Both men rose.

'Teresa wants to see you, Nostromo,' she said.

The Capataz did not move. Decoud, with his back to the table, began to button up his coat.

'The silver, Mrs Gould, the silver,' he murmured in English. 'Don't forget that the Esmeralda garrison have got a steamer. They may appear at any moment at the harbour entrance.'

'The doctor says there is no hope,' Mrs Gould spoke rapidly, also in English. 'I shall take you down to the wharf in my carriage and then come back to fetch away the girls.' She changed swiftly into Spanish to address Nostromo. 'Why are you wasting time? Old Giorgio's wife wishes to see you.'

'I am going to her, señora,' muttered the Capataz.

Dr Monygham now showed himself, bringing back the children. To Mrs Gould's enquiring glance he only shook his head and went outside at once, followed by Nostromo.

The horse of the torchbearer, motionless, hung his head low, and the rider had dropped the reins to light a cigarette. The glare of the torch played on the front of the house crossed by the big black letters of its inscription in which only the word italia was lighted fully. The patch of wavering glare reached as far as Mrs Gould's carriage waiting on the road, with the yellow-faced, portly Ignacio apparently dozing on the box. By his side Basilio, dark and skinny, held a Winchester carbine in front of him, with both hands, and peered fearfully into the darkness. Nostromo touched lightly the doctor's shoulder.

'Is she really dying, señor doctor?'

'Yes,' said the doctor, with a strange twitch of his scarred cheek. 'And why she wants to see you I cannot imagine.'

'She has been like that before,' suggested Nostromo, looking away.

'Well, Capataz, I can assure you she will never be like that again,' snarled Dr Monygham. 'You may go to her or stay away. There is very little to be got from talking to the dying. But she told Doña Emilia in my hearing that she has been like a mother to you ever since you first set foot ashore here.'

'Sí! And she never had a good word to say for me to anybody. It is more as if she could not forgive me for being alive, and such a man, too, as she would have liked her son to be.'

'Maybe!' exclaimed a mournful deep voice near them. 'Women have their own ways of tormenting themselves.' Giorgio Viola had come out of the house. He threw a heavy black shadow in the torchlight, and the glare fell on his big face, on the great bushy head of white hair. He motioned the Capataz indoors with his extended arm.

Dr Monygham, after busying himself with a little medicament box of polished wood on the seat of the landau, turned to old Giorgio and thrust into his big, trembling hand one of the glass-stoppered bottles out of the case.

'Give her a spoonful of this now and then, in water,' he said. 'It will make her easier.'

'And there is nothing more for her?' asked the old man, patiently.

'No. Not on earth,' said the doctor, with his back to him, clicking the lock of the medicine case.

Nostromo slowly crossed the large kitchen, all dark but for the glow of a heap of charcoal under the heavy mantel of the cooking-range, where water was boiling in an iron pot with a loud bubbling sound. Between the two walls of a narrow staircase a bright light streamed from the sickroom above; and the magnificent Capataz de Cargadores stepping noiselessly in soft leather sandals, bushy whiskered, his muscular neck and bronzed chest bare in the open check shirt, resembled a Mediterranean sailor just come ashore from some wine or fruit-laden felucca. At the top he paused, broad shouldered, narrow hipped and supple, looking at the large bed, like a white couch of state, with a profusion of snowy linen, amongst which the Padrona sat unpropped and bowed, her handsome, black-browed face bent over her chest. A mass of raven hair with only a few white threads in it covered her shoulders; one thick strand fallen forward half veiled her cheek. Perfectly motionless in that pose, expressing physical anxiety and unrest, she turned her eyes alone towards Nostromo.

The Capataz had a red sash wound many times round his waist, and a heavy silver ring on the forefinger of the hand he raised to give a twist to his moustache.

'Their revolutions, their revolutions,' gasped Señora Teresa. 'Look, Gian' Battista, it has killed me at last!'

Nostromo said nothing, and the sick woman with an upward glance insisted. 'Look, this one has killed me, while you were away fighting for what did not concern you, foolish man.'

'Why talk like this?' mumbled the Capataz between his teeth. 'Will you never believe in my good sense? It concerns me to keep on being what I am: every day alike.'

'You never change, indeed,' she said, bitterly. 'Always thinking of yourself and taking your pay out in fine words from those who care nothing for you.'

There was between them an intimacy of antagonism as close in its way as the intimacy of accord and affection. He had not walked along the way of

Teresa's expectations. It was she who had encouraged him to leave his ship, in the hope of securing a friend and defender for the girls. The wife of old Giorgio was aware of her precarious health, and was haunted by the fear of her aged husband's loneliness and the unprotected state of the children. She had wanted to annex that apparently quiet and steady young man, affectionate and pliable, an orphan from his tenderest age, as he had told her, with no ties in Italy except an uncle, owner and master of a felucca, from whose ill-usage he had run away before he was fourteen. He had seemed to her courageous, a hard worker, determined to make his way in the world. From gratitude and the ties of habit he would become like a son to herself and Giorgio; and then, who knows, when Linda had grown up . . .

Ten years' difference between husband and wife was not so much. Her own great man was nearly twenty years older than herself. Gian' Battista was an attractive young fellow, besides; attractive to men, women, and children, just by that profound quietness of personality which, like a serene twilight, rendered more seductive the promise of his vigorous form and the resolution of his conduct.

Old Giorgio, in profound ignorance of his wife's views and hopes, had a great regard for his young countryman. 'A man ought not to be tame,' he used to tell her, quoting the Spanish proverb in defence of the splendid Capataz. She was growing jealous of his success. He was escaping from her, she feared. She was practical, and he seemed to her to be an absurd spendthrift of these qualities which made him so valuable. He got too little for them. He scattered them with both hands amongst too many people, she thought. He laid no money by. She railed at his poverty, his exploits, his adventures, his loves and his reputation; but in her heart she had never given him up, as though, indeed, he had been her son.

Even now, ill as she was, ill enough to feel the chill, black breath of the approaching end, she had wished to see him. It was like putting out her benumbed hand to regain her hold. But she had presumed too much on her strength. She could not command her thoughts; they had become dim, like her vision. The words faltered on her lips, and only the paramount anxiety and desire of her life seemed to be too strong for death.

The Capataz said, 'I have heard these things many times. You are unjust, but it does not hurt me. Only now you do not seem to have much strength to talk, and I have but little time to listen. I am engaged in a work of very great moment.'

She made an effort to ask him whether it was true that he had found time to go and fetch a doctor for her. Nostromo nodded affirmatively.

She was pleased: it relieved her sufferings to know that the man had condescended to do so much for those who really wanted his help. It was a proof of his friendship. Her voice became stronger.

'I want a priest more than a doctor,' she said, pathetically. She did not move her head; only her eyes ran into the corners to watch the Capataz standing by the side of her bed. 'Would you go to fetch a priest for me now? Think! A dying woman asks you!'

Nostromo shook his head resolutely. He did not believe in priests in their sacerdotal character. A doctor was an efficacious person; but a priest, as priest, was nothing, incapable of doing either good or harm. Nostromo did not even dislike the sight of them as old Giorgio did. The utter uselessness of the errand was what struck him most.

'Padrona,' he said, 'you have been like this before, and got better after a few days. I have given you already the very last moments I can spare. Ask Señora Gould to send you one.'

He was feeling uneasy at the impiety of this refusal. The Padrona believed in priests, and confessed herself to them. But all women did that. It could not be of much consequence. And yet his heart felt oppressed for a moment – at the thought of what absolution would mean to her if she believed in it only ever so little. No matter. It was quite true that he had given her already the very last moment he could spare.

'You refuse to go?' she gasped. 'Ah! you are always yourself, indeed.'

'Listen to reason, Padrona,' he said. 'I am needed to save the silver of the mine. Do you hear? A greater treasure than the one which they say is guarded by ghosts and devils in Azuera. It is true. I am resolved to make this the most desperate affair I was ever engaged on in my whole life.'

She felt a despairing indignation. The supreme test had failed. Standing above her, Nostromo did not see the distorted features of her face, distorted by a paroxysm of pain and anger. Only she began to tremble all over. Her bowed head shook. The broad shoulders quivered.

'Then God, perhaps, will have mercy upon me! But do you look to it, man, that you get something for yourself out of it, besides the remorse that shall overtake you someday.'

She laughed feebly. 'Get riches at least for once, you indispensable, admired Gian' Battista, to whom the peace of a dying woman is less than the praise of people who have given you a silly name – and nothing besides – in exchange for your soul and body.'

The Capataz de Cargadores swore to himself under his breath.

'Leave my soul alone, Padrona, and I shall know how to take care of my body. Where is the harm of people having need of me? What are you envying me that I have robbed you and the children of? Those very people you are throwing in my teeth have done more for old Giorgio than they ever thought of doing for me.'

He struck his breast with his open palm; his voice had remained low though he had spoken in a forcible tone. He twisted his moustaches one after another, and his eyes wandered a little about the room.

'Is it my fault that I am the only man for their purposes? What angry nonsense are you talking, mother? Would you rather have me timid and foolish, selling watermelons on the marketplace or rowing a boat for passengers along the harbour, like a soft Neapolitan without courage or reputation? Would you have a young man live like a monk? I do not believe it. Would you want a monk for your eldest girl? Let her grow. What are you afraid of? You have been angry with me for everything I did for years; ever since you first spoke to me, in secret from old Giorgio, about your Linda. Husband to one and brother to the other, did you say? Well, why not! I like the little ones, and a man must marry sometime. But ever since that time you have been making little of me to everyone. Why? Did you think you could put a collar and chain on me as if I were one of the watchdogs they keep over there in the railway yards? Look here, Padrona, I am the same man who came ashore one evening and sat down in the thatched ranche you lived in at that time on the other side of the town and told you all about himself. You were not unjust to me then. What has happened since? I am no longer an insignificant youth. A good name, Giorgio says, is a treasure, Padrona.'

'They have turned your head with their praises,' gasped the sick woman. 'They have been paying you with words. Your folly shall betray you into poverty, misery, starvation. The very léperos shall laugh at you – the great Capataz.'

Nostromo stood for a time as if struck dumb. She never looked at him. A self-confident, mirthless smile passed quickly from his lips, and then he backed away. His disregarded figure sank down beyond the doorway. He descended the stairs backwards, with the usual sense of having been somehow baffled by this woman's disparagement of this reputation he had obtained and desired to keep.

Downstairs in the big kitchen a candle was burning, surrounded by the shadows of the walls, of the ceiling, but no ruddy glare filled the open square of the outer door. The carriage with Mrs Gould and Don Martin, preceded by the horseman bearing the torch, had gone on to the jetty. Dr Monygham, who had remained, sat on the corner of a hard wood table near the candlestick, his seamed, shaven face inclined sideways, his arms crossed on his breast, his lips pursed up, and his prominent eyes glaring stonily upon the floor of black earth. Near the overhanging mantel of the fireplace, where the pot of water was still boiling violently, old Giorgio held his chin in his hand, one foot advanced, as if arrested by a sudden thought.

'Adios, viejo,' said Nostromo, feeling the handle of his revolver in the belt and loosening his knife in its sheath. He picked up a blue poncho lined with red from the table, and put it over his head. 'Adios, look after the things in my sleeping-room, and if you hear from me no more, give up the box to Paquita. There is not much of value there, except my new serape from Mexico, and a few silver buttons on my best jacket. No matter! The things will look well enough on the next lover she gets, and the man need not be afraid I shall linger on earth after I am dead, like those Gringos that haunt the Azuera.'

Dr Monygham twisted his lips into a bitter smile. After old Giorgio, with an almost imperceptible nod and without a word, had gone up the narrow stairs, he said: 'Why, Capataz! I thought you could never fail in anything.'

Nostromo, glancing contemptuously at the doctor, lingered in the doorway rolling a cigarette, then struck a match, and, after lighting it, held the burning piece of wood above his head till the flame nearly touched his fingers.

'No wind!' he muttered to himself. 'Look here, señor – do you know the nature of my undertaking?'

Dr Monygham nodded sourly.

'It is as if I were taking up a curse upon me, señor doctor. A man with a treasure on this coast will have every knife raised against him in every place upon the shore. You see that, señor doctor? I shall float along with a spell upon my life till I meet somewhere the northbound steamer of the Company, and then indeed they will talk about the Capataz of the Sulaco Cargadores from one end of America to another.'

Dr Monygham laughed his short, throaty laugh. Nostromo turned round in the doorway.

'But if your worship can find any other man ready and fit for such business I will stand back. I am not exactly tired of my life, though I am so poor that I can carry all I have with myself on my horse's back.'

'You gamble too much, and never say "no" to a pretty face, Capataz,' said Dr Monygham, with sly simplicity. 'That's not the way to make a fortune. But nobody that I know ever suspected you of being poor. I hope you have made a good bargain in case you come back safe from this adventure.'

'What bargain would your worship have made?' asked Nostromo, blowing the smoke out of his lips through the doorway.

Dr Monygham listened up the staircase for a moment before he answered, with another of his short, abrupt laughs: 'Illustrious Capataz, for taking the curse of death upon my back, as you call it, nothing else but the whole treasure would do.'

Nostromo vanished out of the doorway with a grunt of discontent at this jeering answer. Dr Monygham heard him gallop away. Nostromo rode furiously in the dark. There were lights in the buildings of the OSN Company near the wharf, but before he got there he met the Gould carriage. The horseman preceded it with the torch, whose light showed the white mules trotting, the portly Ignacio driving, and Basilio with the carbine on the box. From the dark body of the landau Mrs Gould's voice cried, 'They are waiting for you, Capataz!' She was returning, chilly and excited, with Decoud's pocketbook still held in her hand. He had confided it to her to send to his sister. 'Perhaps my last words to her,' he had said, pressing Mrs Gould's hand.

The Capataz never checked his speed. At the head of the wharf vague figures with rifles leapt to the head of his horse; others closed upon him – cargadores of the company posted by Captain Mitchell on the watch. At a word from him they fell back with subservient murmurs, recognising his voice. At the other end of the jetty, near a cargo crane, in a dark group with glowing cigars, his name was pronounced in a tone of relief. Most of the Europeans in Sulaco were there, rallied round Charles Gould, as if the silver of the mine had been the emblem of a common cause, the symbol of the supreme importance of material interests. They had loaded it into the lighter with their own hands. Nostromo recognised Don Carlos Gould, a thin, tall shape standing a little apart and silent, to whom another tall shape, the engineer-in-chief, said aloud, 'If it must be lost, it is a million times better that it should go to the bottom of the sea.'

Martin Decoud called out from the lighter, 'Au revoir, messieurs, till we clasp hands again over the newborn Occidental Republic.' Only a subdued murmur responded to his clear, ringing tones, and then it seemed to him that the wharf was floating away into the night; but it was Nostromo, who was already pushing against a pile with one of the heavy sweeps. Decoud did not move; the effect was that of being launched into space. After a splash or two there was not a sound but the thud of Nostromo's feet leaping about the boat. He hoisted the big sail; a breath of wind fanned Decoud's cheek. Everything had vanished but the light of the lantern Captain Mitchell had hoisted upon the post at the end of the jetty to guide Nostromo out of the harbour.

The two men, unable to see each other, kept silent till the lighter, slipping before the fitful breeze, passed out between almost invisible headlands into the still deeper darkness of the gulf. For a time the lantern on the jetty shone after them. The wind failed, then fanned up again, but so faintly that the big, half-decked boat slipped along with no more noise than if she had been suspended in the air.

'We are out in the gulf now,' said the calm voice of Nostromo. A moment after he added, 'Señor Mitchell has lowered the light.'

'Yes,' said Decoud; 'nobody can find us now.'

A great recrudescence of obscurity embraced the boat. The sea in the gulf was as black as the clouds above. Nostromo, after striking a couple of matches to get a glimpse of the boat-compass he had with him in the lighter, steered by the feel of the wind on his cheek.

It was a new experience for Decoud, this mysteriousness of the great waters spread out strangely smooth, as if their restlessness had been crushed by the weight of that dense night. The Placido was sleeping profoundly under its black poncho.

The main thing now for success was to get away from the coast and gain the middle of the gulf before day broke. The Isabels were somewhere at hand. 'On your left as you look forward, señor,' said Nostromo, suddenly. When his voice ceased, the enormous stillness, without light or sound, seemed to affect Decoud's senses like a powerful drug. He didn't even know at times whether he were asleep or awake. Like a man lost in slumber, he heard nothing, he saw nothing. Even his hand held before his face did not exist for his eyes. The change from the agitation, the passions and the dangers, from the sights and sounds of the shore, was so complete that it would have resembled death had it not been for the survival of his thoughts. In this foretaste of eternal peace they floated vivid and light, like unearthly clear dreams of earthly things that may haunt the souls freed by death from the misty atmosphere of regrets and hopes. Decoud shook himself, shuddered a bit, though the air that drifted past him was warm. He had the strangest sensation of his soul having just returned into his body from the circumambient darkness in which land, sea, sky, the mountains, and the rocks were as if they had not been.

Nostromo's voice was speaking, though he, at the tiller, was also as if he were not. 'Have you been asleep, Don Martin? Caramba! If it were possible I would think that I, too, have dozed off. I have a strange notion somehow of having dreamt that there was a sound of blubbering, a sound a sorrowing man could make, somewhere near this boat. Something between a sigh and a sob.'

'Strange!' muttered Decoud, stretched upon the pile of treasure boxes covered by many tarpaulins. 'Could it be that there is another boat near us in the gulf? We could not see it, you know.'

Nostromo laughed a little at the absurdity of the idea. They dismissed it from their minds. The solitude could almost be felt. And when the breeze ceased, the blackness seemed to weigh upon Decoud like a stone.

'This is overpowering,' he muttered. 'Do we move at all, Capataz?'

'Not so fast as a crawling beetle tangled in the grass,' answered Nostromo, and his voice seemed deadened by the thick veil of obscurity that felt warm and hopeless all about them. There were long periods when he made no sound, invisible and inaudible as if he had mysteriously stepped out of the lighter.

In the featureless night Nostromo was not even certain which way the lighter headed after the wind had completely died out. He peered for the islands. There was not a hint of them to be seen, as if they had sunk to the bottom of the gulf. He threw himself down by the side of Decoud at last, and whispered into his ear that if daylight caught them near the Sulaco shore through want of wind, it would be possible to sweep the lighter behind the cliff at the high end of the Great Isabel, where she would lie concealed. Decoud was surprised at the grimness of his anxiety. To him the removal of the treasure was a political move. It was necessary for several reasons that it should not fall into the hands of Montero, but here was a man who took another view of this enterprise. The Caballeros over there did not seem to have the slightest idea of what they had given him to do. Nostromo, as if affected by the gloom around, seemed nervously resentful. Decoud was surprised. The Capataz, indifferent to those dangers that seemed obvious to his companion, allowed himself to become scornfully exasperated by the deadly nature of the trust put, as a matter of course, into his hands. It was more dangerous, Nostromo said, with a laugh and a curse, than sending a man to get the treasure that people said was guarded by devils and ghosts in the deep ravines of Azuera. 'Señor,' he said, 'we must catch the steamer at sea. We must keep out in the open looking for her till we have eaten and drunk all that has been put on board here. And if we miss her by some mischance, we must keep away from the land till we grow weak, and perhaps mad, and die, and drift dead, until one or another of the steamers of the Compania comes upon the boat with the two dead men who have saved the treasure. That, señor, is the only way to save it; for, don't you see? for us to come to the land anywhere in a hundred miles along this coast with this silver in our possession is to run the naked breast against the point of a knife. This thing has been given to me like a deadly disease. If men discover it I am dead, and you, too, señor, since you would come with me. There is enough silver to make a whole province rich, let alone a seaboard pueblo inhabited by thieves and vagabonds. Señor, they would think that heaven itself sent these riches into their hands, and would cut our throats without hesitation. I would trust no fair words from the best man around the shores of this wild gulf. Reflect that, even by giving up the treasure at the first demand, we would not be able to save our lives. Do you understand this, or must I explain?'

'No, you needn't explain,' said Decoud, a little listlessly. 'I can see it well enough myself, that the possession of this treasure is very much like a deadly disease for men situated as we are. But it had to be removed from Sulaco, and you were the man for the task.'

'I was; but I cannot believe,' said Nostromo, 'that its loss would have impoverished Don Carlos Gould very much. There is more wealth in the mountain. I have heard it rolling down the shoots on quiet nights when I used to ride to Rincon to see a certain girl, after my work at the harbour was done. For years the rich rocks have been pouring down with a noise like thunder, and the miners say that there is enough at the heart of the mountain to thunder on for years and years to come. And yet, the day before yesterday, we have been fighting to save it from the mob, and tonight I am sent out with it into this darkness, where there is no wind to get away with; as if it were the last lot of silver on earth to get bread for the hungry with. Ha! ha! Well, I am going to make it the most famous and desperate affair of my life – wind or no wind. It shall be talked about when the little children are grown up and the grown men are old. Aha! the Monterists must not get hold of it, I am told, whatever happens to Nostromo the Capataz; and they shall not have it, I tell you, since it has been tied for safety round Nostromo's neck.'

'I see it,' murmured Decoud. He saw, indeed, that his companion had his own peculiar view of this enterprise.

Nostromo interrupted his reflections upon the way men's qualities are made use of, without any fundamental knowledge of their nature, by the proposal they should slip the long oars out and sweep the lighter in the direction of the Isabels. It wouldn't do for daylight to reveal the treasure floating within a mile or so of the harbour entrance. The denser the darkness generally, the smarter were the puffs of wind on which he had reckoned to make his way; but tonight the gulf, under its poncho of clouds, remained breathless, as if dead rather than asleep.

Don Martin's soft hands suffered cruelly, tugging at the thick handle of the enormous oar. He stuck to it manfully, setting his teeth. He, too, was in the toils of an imaginative existence, and that strange work of pulling a lighter seemed to belong naturally to the inception of a new state, acquired an ideal meaning from his love for Antonia. For all their efforts, the heavily laden lighter hardly moved. Nostromo could be heard swearing to himself between the regular splashes of the sweeps. 'We are making a crooked path,' he muttered to himself. 'I wish I could see the islands.'

In his unskilfulness Don Martin over-exerted himself. Now and then a sort of muscular faintness would run from the tips of his aching fingers through every fibre of his body, and pass off in a flush of heat. He had fought, talked, suffered mentally and physically, exerting his mind and body for the last forty-eight hours without intermission. He had had no rest, very little food, no pause in the stress of his thoughts and his feelings. Even his love for Antonia, whence he drew his strength and his inspiration, had reached the point of tragic tension during their hurried interview by Don José's bedside. And now, suddenly, he was thrown out of all this into a dark gulf, whose very gloom, silence, and breathless peace added a torment to the necessity for physical exertion. He imagined the lighter sinking to the bottom with an extraordinary shudder of delight. 'I am on the verge of delirium,' he thought. He mastered the trembling of all his limbs, of his breast, the inward trembling of all his body exhausted of its nervous force.

'Shall we rest, Capataz?' he proposed in a careless tone. 'There are many hours of night yet before us.'

'True. It is but a mile or so, I suppose. Rest your arms, señor, if that is what you mean. You will find no other sort of rest, I can promise you, since you let yourself be bound to this treasure whose loss would make no poor man poorer. No, señor; there is no rest till we find a northbound steamer, or else some ship finds us drifting about stretched out dead upon the Englishman's silver. Or rather – no; *por Dios!* I shall cut down the gunwale with the axe right to the water's edge before thirst and hunger rob me of my strength. By all the saints and devils I shall let the sea have the treasure rather than give it up to any stranger. Since it was the good pleasure of the Caballeros to send me off on such an errand, they shall learn I am just the man they take me for.'

Decoud lay on the silver boxes panting. All his active sensations and feelings from as far back as he could remember seemed to him the maddest of dreams. Even his passionate devotion to Antonia into which he had worked himself up out of the depths of his scepticism had lost all appearance of reality. For a moment he was the prey of an extremely languid but not unpleasant indifference.

'I am sure they didn't mean you to take such a desperate view of this affair,' he said.

'What was it, then? A joke?' snarled the man, who on the pay-sheets of the OSN Company's establishment in Sulaco was described as 'Foreman of the wharf against the figure of his wages. 'Was it for a joke they woke me up from my sleep after two days of street fighting to make me stake my life upon a bad card? Everybody knows, too, that I am not a lucky gambler.'

'Yes, everybody knows of your good luck with women, Capataz,' Decoud propitiated his companion in a weary drawl.

'Look here, señor,' Nostromo went on. 'I never even remonstrated about this affair. Directly I heard what was wanted I saw what a desperate affair it must be, and I made up my mind to see it out. Every minute was of importance. I had to wait for you first. Then, when we arrived at the Italia Una, old Giorgio shouted to me to go for the English doctor. Later on, that poor dying woman wanted to see me, as you know. Señor, I was reluctant to go. I felt already this cursed silver growing heavy upon my back, and I was afraid that, knowing herself to be dying, she would ask me to ride off again for a priest. Father Corbelàn, who is fearless, would have come at a word; but Father Corbelàn is far away, safe with the band of Hernandez, and the populace, that would have liked to tear him to pieces, are much incensed against the priests. Not a single fat padre would have consented to put his head out of his hiding-place tonight to save a Christian soul, except, perhaps, under my protection. That was in her mind. I pretended I did not believe she was going to die. Señor, I refused to fetch a priest for a dying woman . . .'

Decoud was heard to stir.

'You did, Capataz!' he exclaimed. His tone changed. 'Well, you know – it was rather fine.'

'You do not believe in priests, Don Martin? Neither do I. What was the use of wasting time? But she – she believes in them. The thing sticks in my throat. She may be dead already, and here we are floating helpless with no wind at all. Curse on all superstition. She died thinking I deprived her of Paradise, I suppose. It shall be the most desperate affair of my life.'

Decoud remained lost in reflection. He tried to analyse the sensations awaked by what he had been told. The voice of the Capataz was heard again: 'Now, Don Martin, let us take up the sweeps and try to find the Isabels. It is either that or sinking the lighter if the day overtakes us. We must not forget that the steamer from Esmeralda with the soldiers may be coming along. We will pull straight on now. I have discovered a bit of a candle here, and we must take the risk of a small light to make a course by the boat compass. There is not enough wind to blow it out – may the curse of Heaven fall upon this blind gulf!'

A small flame appeared burning quite straight. It showed fragmentarily the stout ribs and planking in the hollow, empty part of the lighter. Decoud could see Nostromo standing up to pull. He saw him as high as the red sash on his waist, with a gleam of a white-handled revolver and the wooden haft of a long knife protruding on his left side. Decoud nerved himself for the effort of rowing. Certainly there was not enough wind to blow the candle out, but its flame swayed a little to the slow movement of the heavy boat. It was so big that with their utmost efforts they could not move it quicker than about a mile an hour. This was sufficient, however, to sweep them amongst the Isabels long before daylight came. There was a good six hours of darkness before them, and the distance from the harbour to the Great Isabel did not exceed two miles. Decoud put this heavy toil to the account of the Capataz's impatience. Sometimes they paused, and then strained their ears to hear the boat from Esmeralda. In this perfect quietness a steamer moving would have been heard from far off. As to seeing anything it was out of the question. They could not see each other. Even the lighter's sail, which remained set, was invisible. Very often they rested.

'Caramba!' said Nostromo, suddenly, during one of those intervals when they lolled idly against the heavy handles of the sweeps. 'What is it? Are you distressed, Don Martin?'

Decoud assured him that he was not distressed in the least. Nostromo for a time kept perfectly still, and then in a whisper invited Martin to come aft.

With lips touching Decoud's ear he declared his belief that there was somebody else besides themselves upon the lighter. Twice now he had heard the sound of stifled sobbing.

'Señor,' he whispered with awed wonder, 'I am certain that there is somebody weeping in this lighter.'

Decoud had heard nothing. He expressed his incredulity. However, it was easy to ascertain the truth of the matter.

'It is most amazing,' muttered Nostromo. 'Could anybody have concealed himself on board while the lighter was lying alongside the wharf?'

'And you say it was like sobbing?' asked Decoud, lowering his voice, too. 'If he is weeping, whoever he is he cannot be very dangerous.'

Clambering over the precious pile in the middle, they crouched low on the foreside of the mast and groped under the half-deck. Right forward, in the narrowest part, their hands came upon the limbs of a man, who remained as silent as death. Too startled themselves to make a sound, they dragged him aft by one arm and the collar of his coat. He was limp – lifeless.

The light of the bit of candle fell upon a round, hook-nosed face with black moustaches and little side-whiskers. He was extremely dirty. A greasy growth of beard was sprouting on the shaven parts of the cheeks. The thick lips were slightly parted, but the eyes remained closed. Decoud, to his immense astonishment, recognised Señor Hirsch, the hide merchant from Esmeralda. Nostromo, too, had recognised him. And they gazed at each other across the body, lying with its naked feet higher than its head, in an absurd pretence of sleep, faintness, or death.

For a moment, before this extraordinary find, they forgot their own concerns and sensations. Senor Hirsch's sensations as he lay there must have been those of extreme terror. For a long time he refused to give a sign of life, till at last Decoud's objurgations, and, perhaps more, Nostromo's impatient suggestion that he should be thrown overboard, as he seemed to be dead, induced him to raise one eyelid first, and then the other.

It appeared that he had never found a safe opportunity to leave Sulaco. He lodged with Anzani, the universal storekeeper, on the Plaza Mayor. But when the riot broke out he had made his escape from his host's house before daylight, and in such a hurry that he had forgotten to put on his shoes. He had run out impulsively in his socks, and with his hat in his hand, into the garden of Anzani's house. Fear gave him the necessary agility to climb over several low walls, and afterwards he blundered into the overgrown cloisters of the ruined Franciscan convent in one of the by-streets. He forced himself into the midst of matted bushes with the recklessness of desperation, and this accounted for his scratched body and his torn clothing. He lay hidden there all day, his tongue cleaving to the roof of his mouth with all the intensity of thirst engendered by heat and fear. Three times different bands of men invaded the place with shouts and imprecations, looking for Father Corbelàn; but towards the evening, still lying on his face in the bushes, he thought he would die from the fear of silence. He was not very clear as to what had induced him to leave the place, but evidently he had got out and slunk successfully out of town along the deserted back lanes. He wandered in the darkness near the railway, so maddened by apprehension that he dared not even approach the fires of the pickets of Italian workmen guarding the line. He had a vague idea evidently of finding refuge in the railway yards, but the dogs rushed upon him, barking; men began to shout; a shot was fired at random. He fled away from the gates. By the merest accident, as it happened, he took the direction of the OSN Company's offices. Twice he stumbled upon the bodies of men killed during the day. But everything living frightened him much more. He crouched, crept, crawled, made dashes, guided by a sort of animal instinct, keeping away from every light and from every sound of voices. His idea was to throw himself at the feet of Captain Mitchell and beg for shelter in the Company's offices. It was all dark there as he approached on his hands and knees, but suddenly someone on guard challenged loudly, '*Quien vive?*' There were more dead men lying about, and he flattened himself down at once by the side of a cold corpse. He heard a voice saying, 'There is one of those wounded rascals crawling about. Shall I go and finish him?' And another voice objected that it was not safe to go out without a lantern upon such an errand; perhaps it was only some Negro Liberal looking for a chance to stick a knife into the stomach of an honest man. Hirsch didn't stay to hear any more, but crawling away to the end of the wharf, hid himself amongst a lot of empty casks. After a while some people came along, talking, and with glowing cigarettes. He did not stop to ask himself whether they would be likely to do him any harm, but bolted incontinently along the jetty, saw a lighter lying moored at the end, and threw himself into it. In his desire to find cover he crept right forward under the half-deck, and he had remained there more dead than alive, suffering agonies of hunger and thirst, and almost fainting with terror, when he heard numerous footsteps and the voices of the Europeans who came in a body escorting the wagonload of treasure, pushed along the rails by a squad of Cargadores. He understood perfectly what was being done from the talk, but did not disclose his presence from the fear that he would not be allowed to remain. His only idea at the time, overpowering and masterful, was to get away from this terrible Sulaco. And now he regretted it very much. He had heard Nostromo talk to Decoud, and wished himself back on shore. He did not desire to be involved in any desperate affair – in a situation where one could not run away. The involuntary groans of his anguished spirit had betrayed him to the sharp ears of the Capataz.

They had propped him up in a sitting posture against the side of the lighter, and he went on with the moaning account of his adventures till his voice broke, his head fell forward. 'Water,' he whispered, with difficulty. Decoud held one of the cans to his lips. He revived after an extraordinarily short time, and scrambled up to his feet wildly. Nostromo, in an angry and threatening voice, ordered him forward. Hirsch was one of those men whom fear lashes like a whip, and he must have had an appalling idea of the Capataz's ferocity. He displayed an extraordinary agility in disappearing forward into the darkness. They heard him getting over the tarpaulin; then there was the sound of a heavy fall, followed by a weary sigh. Afterwards all was still in the forepart of the lighter, as though he had killed himself in his headlong tumble. Nostromo shouted in a menacing voice: 'Lie still there! Do not move a limb. If I hear as much as a loud breath from you I shall come over there and put a bullet through your head.'

The mere presence of a coward, however passive, brings an element of treachery into a dangerous situation. Nostromo's nervous impatience passed into gloomy thoughtfulness. Decoud, in an undertone, as if speaking to himself, remarked that, after all, this bizarre event made no great difference. He could not conceive what harm the man could do. At most he would be in the way, like an inanimate and useless object – like a block of wood, for instance.

'I would think twice before getting rid of a piece of wood,' said Nostromo, calmly. 'Something may happen unexpectedly where you could make use of it. But in an affair like ours a man like this ought to be thrown overboard. Even if he were as brave as a lion we would not want him here. We are not running away for our lives. Señor, there is no harm in a brave man trying to save himself with ingenuity and courage; but you have heard his tale, Don Martin. His being here is a miracle of fear – ' Nostromo paused. 'There is no room for fear in this lighter,' he added through his teeth.

Decoud had no answer to make. It was not a position for argument, for a display of scruples or feelings. There were a thousand ways in which a panic-stricken man could make himself dangerous. It was evident that Hirsch could not be spoken to, reasoned with, or persuaded into a rational line of conduct. The story of his own escape demonstrated that clearly enough. Decoud thought that it was a thousand pities the wretch had not died of fright. Nature, who had made him what he was, seemed to have calculated cruelly how much he could bear in the way of atrocious anguish without actually expiring. Some compassion was due to so much terror. Decoud, though imaginative enough for sympathy, resolved not to interfere with any action that Nostromo would take. But Nostromo did nothing. And the fate of Señor Hirsch remained suspended in the darkness of the gulf at the mercy of events which could not be foreseen.

The Capataz, extending his hand, put out the candle suddenly. It was to Decoud as if his companion had destroyed, by a single touch, the world of affairs, of loves, of revolution, where his complacent superiority analysed fearlessly all motives and all passions, including his own.

He gasped a little. Decoud was affected by the novelty of his position. Intellectually self-confident, he suffered from being deprived of the only weapon he could use with effect. No intelligence could penetrate the darkness of the Placid Gulf. There remained only one thing he was certain of, and that was the overweening vanity of his companion. It was direct, uncomplicated, naive, and effectual. Decoud, who had been making use of him, had tried to understand his man thoroughly. He had discovered a complete singleness of motive behind the varied manifestations of a consistent character. This was why the man remained so astonishingly simple in the jealous greatness of his conceit. And now there was a complication. It was evident that he resented having been given a task in which there were so many chances of failure. 'I wonder,' thought Decoud, 'how he would behave if I were not here.'

He heard Nostromo mutter again, 'No! there is no room for fear on this lighter. Courage itself does not seem good enough. I have a good eye and a steady hand; no man can say he ever saw me tired or uncertain what to do; but *por Dios*, Don Martin, I have been sent out into this black calm on a business where neither a good eye, nor a steady hand, nor judgment are any use . . .' He swore a string of oaths in Spanish and Italian under his breath. 'Nothing but sheer desperation will do for this affair.'

These words were in strange contrast to the prevailing peace – to this almost solid stillness of the gulf. A shower fell with an abrupt whispering sound all round the boat, and Decoud took off his hat, and, letting his head get wet, felt greatly refreshed. Presently a steady little draught of air caressed his cheek. The lighter began to move, but the shower distanced it. The drops ceased to fall upon his head and hands, the whispering died out in the distance. Nostromo emitted a grunt of satisfaction, and grasping the tiller, chirruped softly, as sailors do, to encourage the wind. Never for the last three days had Decoud felt less the need for what the Capataz would call desperation.

'I fancy I hear another shower on the water,' he observed in a tone of quiet content. 'I hope it will catch us up.'

Nostromo ceased chirruping at once. 'You hear another shower?' he said, doubtfully. A sort of thinning of the darkness seemed to have taken place, and Decoud could see now the outline of his companion's figure, and even the sail came out of the night like a square block of dense snow.

The sound which Decoud had detected came along the water harshly. Nostromo recognised that noise partaking of a hiss and a rustle which spreads out on all sides of a steamer making her way through a smooth water on a quiet night. It could be nothing else but the captured transport with troops from Esmeralda. She carried no lights. The noise of her steaming, growing louder every minute, would stop at times altogether, and then begin again abruptly, and sound startlingly nearer, as if that invisible vessel, whose position could not be precisely guessed, were making straight for the lighter. Meantime, that last kept on sailing slowly and noiselessly before a breeze so faint that it was only by leaning over the side and feeling the water slip through his fingers that Decoud convinced himself they were moving at all. His drowsy feeling had departed. He was glad to know that the lighter was moving. After so much stillness the noise of the steamer seemed uproarious and distracting. There was a weirdness in not being able to see her. Suddenly all was still. She had stopped, but so close to them that the steam, blowing off, sent its rumbling vibration right over their heads.

'They are trying to make out where they are,' said Decoud in a whisper. Again he leaned over and put his fingers into the water. 'We are moving quite smartly,' he informed Nostromo.

'We seem to be crossing her bows,' said the Capataz in a cautious tone. 'But this is a blind game with death. Moving on is of no use. We mustn't be seen or heard.'

His whisper was hoarse with excitement. Of all his face there was nothing visible but a gleam of white eyeballs. His fingers gripped Decoud's shoulder. 'That is the only way to save this treasure from this steamer full of soldiers. Any other would have carried lights. But you observe there is not a gleam to show us where she is.'

Decoud stood as if paralysed; only his thoughts were wildly active. In the space of a second he remembered the desolate glance of Antonia as he left her at the bedside of her father in the gloomy house of Avellanos, with shuttered windows, but all the doors standing open, and deserted by all the servants except an old Negro at the gate. He remembered the Casa Gould on his last visit, the arguments, the tones of his voice, the impenetrable attitude of Charles, Mrs Gould's face so blanched with anxiety and fatigue that her eyes seemed to have changed colour, appearing nearly black by contrast. Even whole sentences of the proclamation which he meant to make Barrios issue from his headquarters at Cayta as soon as he got there passed through his mind; the very germ of the new State, the Separationist proclamation which he had tried before he left to read hurriedly to Don José, stretched out on his bed under the fixed gaze of his daughter. God knows whether the old statesman had understood it; he was unable to speak, but he had certainly lifted his arm off the coverlet; his hand had moved as if to make the sign of the cross in the air, a gesture of blessing, of consent. Decoud had that very draft in his pocket, written in pencil on several loose sheets of paper, with the heavily-printed heading, 'Administration of the San Tomé Silver Mine. Sulaco. Republic of Costaguana'. He had written it furiously, snatching page after page on Charles Gould's table. Mrs Gould had looked several times over his shoulder as he wrote; but the Señor Administrador, standing straddle-legged, would not even glance at it when it was finished. He had waved it away firmly. It must have been scorn, and not caution, since he never made a remark about the use of the Administration's paper for such a compromising document. And that showed his disdain, the true English disdain of common prudence, as if everything outside the range of their own thoughts and feelings were unworthy of serious recognition. Decoud had the time in a second or two to become furiously angry with Charles Gould, and even resentful against Mrs Gould, in whose care, tacitly it is true, he had left the safety of Antonia. Better perish a thousand times than owe your preservation to such people, he exclaimed mentally. The grip of Nostromo's fingers never removed from his shoulder, tightening fiercely, recalled him to himself.

'The darkness is our friend,' the Capataz murmured into his ear. 'I am going to lower the sail, and trust our escape to this black gulf. No eyes could make us out lying silent with a naked mast. I will do it now, before this steamer closes still more upon us. The faint creak of a block would betray us and the San Tomé treasure into the hands of those thieves.'

He moved about as warily as a cat. Decoud heard no sound; and it was only by the disappearance of the square blotch of darkness that he knew the yard had come down, lowered as carefully as if it had been made of glass. Next moment he heard Nostromo's quiet breathing by his side.

'You had better not move at all from where you are, Don Martin,' advised the Capataz, earnestly. 'You might stumble or displace something which would make a noise. The sweeps and the punting poles are lying about. Move not for your life. *Por Dios*, Don Martin,' he went on in a keen but friendly whisper, 'I am so desperate that if I didn't know your worship to be a man of courage, capable of standing stock still whatever happens, I would drive my knife into your heart.'

A deathlike stillness surrounded the lighter. It was difficult to believe that there was near a steamer full of men with many pairs of eyes peering from her bridge for some hint of land in the night. Her steam had ceased blowing off, and she remained stopped too far off apparently for any other sound to reach the lighter.

'Perhaps you would, Capataz,' Decoud began in a whisper. 'However, you need not trouble. There are other things than the fear of your knife to keep my heart steady. It shall not betray you. Only, have you forgotten – '

'I spoke to you openly as to a man as desperate as myself,' explained the Capataz. 'The silver must be saved from the Monterists. I told Captain Mitchell three times that I preferred to go alone. I told Don Carlos Gould, too. It was in the Casa Gould. They had sent for me. The ladies were there; and when I tried to explain why I did not wish to have you with me, they promised me, both of them, great rewards for your safety. A strange way to talk to a man you are sending out to an almost certain death. Those gentlefolk do not seem to have sense enough to understand what they are giving one to do. I told them I could do nothing for you. You would have been safer with the bandit Hernandez. It would have been possible to ride out of the town with no greater risk than a chance shot sent after you in the dark. But it was as if they had been deaf. I had to promise I would wait for you under the harbour gate. I did wait. And now because you are a brave man you are as safe as the silver. Neither more nor less.'

At that moment, as if by way of comment upon Nostromo's words, the invisible steamer went ahead at half speed only, as could be judged by the leisurely beat of her propeller. The sound shifted its place markedly, but without coming nearer. It even grew a little more distant right abeam of the lighter, and then ceased again.

'They are trying for a sight of the Isabels,' muttered Nostromo, 'in order to make for the harbour in a straight line and seize the Custom House with the treasure in it. Have you ever seen the Commandant of Esmeralda, Sotillo? A handsome fellow, with a soft voice. When I first came here I used to see him in the Calle talking to the señoritas at the windows of the houses, and showing his white teeth all the time. But one of my Cargadores, who had been a soldier, told me that he had once ordered a man to be flayed alive in the remote Campo, where he was sent recruiting amongst the people of the Estancias. It has never entered his head that the Compania had a man capable of baffling his game.'

The murmuring loquacity of the Capataz disturbed Decoud like a hint of weakness. And yet, talkative resolution may be as genuine as grim silence.

'Sotillo is not baffled so far,' he said. 'Have you forgotten that crazy man forward?'

Nostromo had not forgotten Señor Hirsch. He reproached himself bitterly for not having visited the lighter carefully before leaving the wharf. He reproached himself for not having stabbed and flung Hirsch overboard at the very moment of discovery without even looking at his face. That would have been consistent with the desperate character of the affair. Whatever happened, Sotillo *was* already baffled. Even if that wretch, now as silent as death, did anything to betray the nearness of the lighter, Sotillo – if Sotillo it was in command of the troops on board – would be still baffled of his plunder.

'I have an axe in my hand,' Nostromo whispered, wrathfully, 'that in three strokes would cut through the side down to the water's edge. Moreover, each lighter has a plug in the stern, and I know exactly where it is. I feel it under the sole of my foot.'

Decoud recognised the ring of genuine determination in the nervous murmurs, the vindictive excitement of the famous Capataz. Before the steamer, guided by a shriek or two (for there could be no more than that, Nostromo said, gnashing his teeth audibly), could find the lighter there would be plenty of time to sink this treasure tied up round his neck.

The last words he hissed into Decoud's ear. Decoud said nothing. He was perfectly convinced. The usual characteristic quietness of the man was gone. It was not equal to the situation as he conceived it. Something deeper, something unsuspected by everyone, had come to the surface. Decoud, with careful movements, slipped off his overcoat and divested himself of his boots; he did not consider himself bound in honour to sink with the treasure. His object was to get down to Barrios, in Cayta, as the Capataz knew very well; and he, too, meant, in his own way, to put into that attempt all the desperation of which he was capable. Nostromo muttered, 'True, true! You are a politician, señor. Rejoin the army, and start another revolution.' He pointed out, however, that there was a little boat belonging to every lighter fit to carry two men, if not more. Theirs was towing behind.

Of that Decoud had not been aware. Of course, it was too dark to see, and it was only when Nostromo put his hand upon its painter fastened to a cleat in the stern that he experienced a full measure of relief. The prospect of finding himself in the water and swimming, overwhelmed by ignorance and darkness, probably in a circle, till he sank from exhaustion, was revolting. The barren and cruel futility of such an end intimidated his affectation of careless pessimism. In comparison to it, the chance of being left floating in a boat, exposed to thirst, hunger, discovery, imprisonment, execution, presented itself with an aspect of amenity worth securing even at the cost of some self-contempt. He did not accept Nostromo's proposal that he should get into the boat at once. 'Something sudden may overwhelm us, señor,' the Capataz remarked, promising faithfully, at the same time, to let go the painter at the moment when the necessity became manifest.

But Decoud assured him lightly that he did not mean to take to the boat till the very last moment, and that then he meant the Capataz to come along, too. The darkness of the gulf was no longer for him the end of all things. It was part of a living world since, pervading it, failure and death could be felt at your elbow. And at the same time it was a shelter. He exulted in its impenetrable obscurity. 'Like a wall, like a wall,' he muttered to himself.

The only thing which checked his confidence was the thought of Señor Hirsch. Not to have bound and gagged him seemed to Decoud now the height of improvident folly. As long as the miserable creature had the power to raise a yell he was a constant danger. His abject terror was mute now, but there was no saying from what cause it might suddenly find vent in shrieks.

This very madness of fear which both Decoud and Nostromo had seen in the wild and irrational glances, and in the continuous twitchings of his mouth, protected Señor Hirsch from the cruel necessities of this desperate affair. The moment of silencing him for ever had passed. As Nostromo remarked, in answer to Decoud's regrets, it was too late! It could not be done without noise, especially in the ignorance of the man's exact position. Wherever he had elected to crouch and tremble, it was too hazardous to go near him. He would begin probably to yell for mercy. It was much better to leave him quite alone since he was keeping so still. But to trust to his silence became every moment a greater strain upon Decoud's composure.

'I wish, Capataz, you had not let the right moment pass,' he murmured.

'What! To silence him for ever! I thought it good to hear first how he came to be here. It was too strange. Who could imagine that it was all an accident? Afterwards, señor, when I saw you giving him water to drink, I could not do it. Not after I had seen you holding up the can to his lips as though he were your brother. Señor, that sort of necessity must not be thought of too long. And yet it would have been no cruelty to take away from him his wretched life. It is nothing but fear. Your compassion saved him then, Don Martin, and now it is too late. It couldn't be done without noise.'

In the steamer they were keeping a perfect silence, and the stillness was so profound that Decoud felt as if the slightest sound conceivable must travel unchecked and audible to the end of the world. What if Hirsch coughed or sneezed? To feel himself at the mercy of such an idiotic contingency was too exasperating to be looked upon with irony. Nostromo, too, seemed to be getting restless. Was it possible, he asked himself, that the steamer, finding the night too dark altogether, intended to remain stopped where she was till daylight? He began to think that this, after all, was the real danger. He was afraid that the darkness, which was his protection, would, in the end, cause his undoing.

Sotillo, as Nostromo had surmised, was in command on board the transport. The events of the last forty-eight hours in Sulaco were not known to him; neither was he aware that the telegraphist in Esmeralda had managed to warn his colleague in Sulaco. Like a good many officers of the troops garrisoning the province, Sotillo had been influenced in his adoption of the Ribierist cause by the belief that it had the enormous wealth of the Gould

Concession on its side. He had been one of the frequenters of the Casa Gould, where he had aired his Blanco convictions and his ardour for reform before Don José Avellanos, casting frank glances towards Mrs Gould and Antonia the while. He was known to belong to a good family persecuted and impoverished during the tyranny of Guzman Bento. The opinions he expressed appeared eminently natural and proper in a man of his parentage and antecedents. And he was not a deceiver; it was perfectly natural for him to express elevated sentiments while his whole faculties were taken up with what seemed then a solid and practical notion – the notion that the husband of Antonia Avellanos would be, naturally, the intimate friend of the Gould Concession. He even pointed this out to Anzani once, when negotiating the sixth or seventh small loan in the gloomy, damp apartment with enormous iron bars, behind the principal shop in the whole row under the Arcades. He hinted to the universal shopkeeper at the excellent terms he was on with the emancipated señorita, who was like a sister to the Englishwoman. He would advance one leg and put his arms akimbo, posing for Anzani's inspection, and fixing him with a haughty stare.

'Look, miserable shopkeeper! How can a man like me fail with any woman, let alone an emancipated girl living in scandalous freedom?' he seemed to say.

His manner in the Casa Gould was, of course, very different – devoid of all truculence, and even slightly mournful. Like most of his countrymen, he was carried away by the sound of fine words, especially if uttered by himself. He had no convictions of any sort upon anything except as to the irresistible power of his personal advantages. But that was so firm that even Decoud's appearance in Sulaco, and his intimacy with the Goulds and the Avellanos, did not disquiet him. On the contrary, he tried to make friends with that rich Costaguanero from Europe in the hope of borrowing a large sum by and by. The only guiding motive of his life was to get money for the satisfaction of his expensive tastes, which he indulged recklessly, having no self-control. He imagined himself a master of intrigue, but his corruption was as simple as an animal instinct. At times, in solitude, he had his moments of ferocity, and also on such occasions as, for instance, when alone in a room with Anzani trying to get a loan.

He had talked himself into the command of the Esmeralda garrison. That small seaport had its importance as the station of the main submarine cable connecting the Occidental Provinces with the outer world, and the junction with it of the Sulaco branch. Don José Avellanos proposed him, and Barrios, with a rude and jeering guffaw, had said, 'Oh, let Sotillo go. He is a very good man to keep guard over the cable, and the ladies of Esmeralda ought to have their turn.' Barrios, an indubitably brave man, had no great opinion of Sotillo.

It was through the Esmeralda cable alone that the San Tomé mine could be kept in constant touch with the great financier, whose tacit approval made the strength of the Ribierist movement. This movement had its adversaries even there. Sotillo governed Esmeralda with repressive severity till the adverse course of events upon the distant theatre of civil war forced upon him the reflection that, after all, the great silver mine was fated to become the spoil of the victors. But caution was necessary. He began by assuming a dark and mysterious attitude towards the faithful Ribierist municipality of Esmeralda. Later on, the information that the commandant was holding assemblies of officers in the dead of night (which had leaked out somehow) caused those gentlemen to neglect their civil duties altogether, and remain shut up in their houses. Suddenly one day all the letters from Sulaco by the overland courier were carried off by a file of soldiers from the postoffice to the Comandancia, without disguise, concealment, or apology. Sotillo had heard through Cayta of the final defeat of Ribiera.

This was the first open sign of the change in his convictions. Presently notorious democrats, who had been living till then in constant fear of arrest, leg irons, and even floggings, could be observed going in and out at the great door of the Comandancia, where the horses of the orderlies doze under their heavy saddles, while the men, in ragged uniforms and pointed straw hats, lounge on a bench, with their naked feet stuck out beyond the strip of shade; and a sentry, in a red baize coat with holes at the elbows, stands at the top of the steps glaring haughtily at the common people, who uncover their heads to him as they pass.

Sotillo's ideas did not soar above the care for his personal safety and the chance of plundering the town in his charge, but he feared that such a late adhesion would earn but scant gratitude from the victors. He had believed just a little too long in the power of the San Tomé mine. The seized correspondence had confirmed his previous information of a large amount of silver ingots lying in the Sulaco Custom House. To gain possession of it would be a clear Monterist move; a sort of service that would have to be rewarded. With the silver in his hands he could make terms for himself and his soldiers. He was aware neither of the riots, nor of the President's escape to Sulaco and the close pursuit led by Montero's brother, the guerrillero. The game seemed in his own hands. The initial moves were the seizure of the cable telegraph office and the securing of the Government steamer lying in the narrow creek which is the harbour of Esmeralda. The last was effected without difficulty by a company of soldiers swarming with a rush over the gangways as she lay alongside the quay; but the lieutenant charged with the duty of arresting the telegraphist halted on the way before the only café in Esmeralda, where he distributed some brandy to his men, and refreshed himself at the expense of the owner, a known Ribierist. The whole party became intoxicated, and proceeded on their mission up the street yelling and firing random shots at the windows. This little festivity, which might have turned out dangerous to the telegraphist's life, enabled him in the end to send his warning to Sulaco. The lieutenant, staggering upstairs with a drawn sabre, was before long kissing him on both cheeks in one of those swift changes of mood peculiar to a state of drunkenness. He clasped the telegraphist close round the neck, assuring him that all the officers of the Esmeralda garrison were going to be made colonels, while tears of happiness streamed down his sodden face. Thus it came about that the town major, coming along later, found the whole party sleeping on the stairs and in passages, and the telegraphist (who scorned this chance of escape) very busy clicking the key of the transmitter. The major led him away bareheaded, with his hands tied behind his back, but concealed the truth from Sotillo, who remained in ignorance of the warning despatched to Sulaco.

The colonel was not the man to let any sort of darkness stand in the way of the planned surprise. It appeared to him a dead certainty; his heart was set upon his object with an ungovernable, childlike impatience. Ever since the steamer had rounded Punta Mala, to enter the deeper shadow of the gulf, he had remained on the bridge in a group of officers as excited as himself.

Distracted between the coaxings and menaces of Sotillo and his Staff, the miserable commander of the steamer kept her moving with as much prudence as they would let him exercise. Some of them had been drinking heavily, no doubt; but the prospect of laying hands on so much wealth made them absurdly foolhardy, and, at the same time, extremely anxious. The old major of the battalion, a stupid, suspicious man, who had never been afloat in his life, distinguished himself by putting out suddenly the binnacle light, the only one allowed on board for the necessities of navigation. He could not understand of what use it could be for finding the way. To the vehement protestations of the ship's captain, he stamped his foot and tapped the handle of his sword. 'Aha! I have unmasked you,' he cried, triumphantly. 'You are tearing your hair from despair at my acuteness. Am I a child to believe that a light in that brass box can show you where the harbour is? I am an old soldier, I am. I can smell a traitor a league off. You wanted that gleam to betray our approach to your friend the Englishman. A thing like that show you the way! What a miserable lie! *Que picardía!* You Sulaco people are all in the pay of those foreigners. You deserve to be run through the body with my sword.' Other officers, crowding round, tried to calm his indignation, repeating persuasively, 'No, no! This is an appliance of the mariners, major. This is no treachery.' The captain of the transport flung himself face downwards on the bridge, and refused to rise. 'Put an end to me at once,' he repeated in a stifled voice. Sotillo had to interfere.

The uproar and confusion on the bridge became so great that the helmsman fled from the wheel. He took refuge in the engine-room, and alarmed the engineers, who, disregarding the threats of the soldiers set on guard over them, stopped the engines, protesting that they would rather be shot than run the risk of being drowned down below.

This was the first time Nostromo and Decoud heard the steamer stop. After order had been restored, and the binnacle lamp relighted, she went ahead again, passing wide of the lighter in her search for the Isabels. The group could not be made out, and, at the pitiful entreaties of the captain,

Sotillo allowed the engines to be stopped again to wait for one of those periodical lightenings of darkness caused by the shifting of the cloud canopy spread above the waters of the gulf.

Sotillo, on the bridge, muttered from time to time angrily to the captain. The other, in an apologetic and cringing tone, begged *su merced* the colonel to take into consideration the limitations put upon human faculties by the darkness of the night. Sotillo swelled with rage and impatience. It was the chance of a lifetime.

'If your eyes are of no more use to you than this, I shall have them put out,' he burst out.

The captain of the steamer made no answer, for just then the mass of the Great Isabel loomed up darkly after a passing shower, then vanished, as if swept away by a wave of greater obscurity preceding another downpour. This was enough for him. In the voice of a man come back to life again, he informed Sotillo that in an hour he would be alongside the Sulaco wharf. The ship was put then full speed on the course, and a great bustle of preparation for landing arose among the soldiers on her deck.

It was heard distinctly by Decoud and Nostromo. The Capataz understood its meaning. They had made out the Isabels, and were going on now in a straight line for Sulaco. He judged that they would pass close; but believed that lying still like this, with the sail lowered, the lighter could not be seen. 'No, not even if they rubbed sides with us,' he muttered.

The rain began to fall again; first like a wet mist, then with a heavier touch, thickening into a smart, perpendicular downpour; and the hiss and thump of the approaching steamer was coming extremely near. Decoud, with his eyes full of water, and lowered head, asked himself how long it would be before she drew past, when unexpectedly he felt a lurch. An inrush of foam broke swishing over the stern, simultaneously with a crack of timbers and a staggering shock. He had the impression of an angry hand laying hold of the lighter and dragging it along to destruction. The shock, of course, had knocked him down, and he found himself rolling in a lot of water at the bottom of the lighter. A churning went on alongside; a strange and amazed voice cried out something above him in the night. He heard a piercing shriek for help from Señor Hirsch. He kept his teeth hard set all the time. It was a collision!

The steamer had struck the lighter obliquely, heeling her over till she was half swamped, starting some of her timbers, and swinging her head parallel to her own course with the force of the blow. The shock of it on board of her was hardly perceptible. All the violence of that collision was, as usual, felt only on board the smaller craft. Even Nostromo himself thought that this was perhaps the end of his desperate adventure. He, too, had been flung away from the long tiller, which took charge in the lurch. Next moment the steamer would have passed on, leaving the lighter to sink or swim after having shouldered her thus out of her way, and without even getting a glimpse of her form, had it not been that, being deeply laden with stores and the great number of people on board, her anchor was low enough to hook itself into one of the wire shrouds of the lighter's mast. For the space of two or three gasping breaths that new rope held against the sudden strain. It was this that gave Decoud the sensation of the snatching pull, dragging the lighter away to destruction. The cause of it, of course, was inexplicable to him. The whole thing was so sudden that he had no time to think. But all his sensations were perfectly clear; he had kept complete possession of himself; in fact, he was even pleasantly aware of that calmness at the very moment of being pitched head first over the transom, to struggle on his back in a lot of water. Señor Hirsch's shriek he had heard and recognised while he was regaining his feet, always with that mysterious sensation of being dragged headlong through the darkness. Not a word, not a cry escaped him; he had no time to see anything; and following upon the despairing screams for help, the dragging motion ceased so suddenly that he staggered forward with open arms and fell against the pile of the treasure boxes. He clung to them instinctively, in the vague apprehension of being flung about again; and immediately he heard another lot of shrieks for help, prolonged and despairing, not near him at all, but unaccountably in the distance, away from the lighter altogether, as if some spirit in the night were mocking at Señor Hirsch's terror and despair.

Then all was still – as still as when you wake up in your bed in a dark room from a bizarre and agitated dream. The lighter rocked slightly; the rain was still falling. Two groping hands took hold of his bruised sides from behind, and the Capataz's voice whispered, in his ear, 'Silence, for your life! Silence! The steamer has stopped.'

Decoud listened. The gulf was dumb. He felt the water nearly up to his knees. 'Are we sinking?' he asked in a faint breath.

'I don't know,' Nostromo breathed back to him. 'Señor, make not the slightest sound.'

Hirsch, when ordered forward by Nostromo, had not returned into his first hiding-place. He had fallen near the mast, and had no strength to rise; moreover, he feared to move. He had given himself up for dead, but not on any rational grounds. It was simply a cruel and terrifying feeling. Whenever he tried to think what would become of him his teeth would start chattering violently. He was too absorbed in the utter misery of his fear to take notice of anything.

Though he was stifling under the lighter's sail which Nostromo had unwittingly lowered on top of him, he did not even dare to put out his head till the very moment of the steamer striking. Then, indeed, he leaped right out, spurred on to new miracles of bodily vigour by this new shape of danger. The inrush of water when the lighter heeled over unsealed his lips. His shriek, 'Save me!' was the first distinct warning of the collision for the people on board the steamer. Next moment the wire shroud parted, and the released anchor swept over the lighter's forecastle. It came against the breast of Señor Hirsch, who simply seized hold of it, without in the least knowing what it was, but curling his arms and legs upon the part above the fluke with an invincible, unreasonable tenacity. The lighter yawed off wide, and the steamer, moving on, carried him away, clinging hard, and shouting for help. It was some time, however, after the steamer had stopped that his position was discovered. His sustained yelping for help seemed to come from somebody swimming in the water. At last a couple of men went over the bows and hauled him on board. He was carried straight off to Sotillo on the bridge. His examination confirmed the impression that some craft had been run over and sunk, but it was impracticable on such a dark night to look for the positive proof of floating wreckage. Sotillo was more anxious than ever now to enter the harbour without loss of time; the idea that he had destroyed the principal object of his expedition was too intolerable to be accepted. This feeling made the story he had heard appear the more incredible. Señor Hirsch, after being beaten a little for telling lies, was thrust into the chartroom. But he was beaten only a little. His tale had taken the heart out of Sotillo's Staff, though they all repeated round their chief, 'Impossible! impossible!' with the exception of the old major, who triumphed gloomily.

'I told you; I told you,' he mumbled. 'I could smell some treachery, some *diablura* a league off.'

Meantime, the steamer had kept on her way towards Sulaco, where only the truth of that matter could be ascertained. Decoud and Nostromo heard the loud churning of her propeller diminish and die out; and then, with no useless words, busied themselves in making for the Isabels. The last shower had brought with it a gentle but steady breeze. The danger was not over yet, and there was no time for talk. The lighter was leaking like a sieve. They splashed in the water at every step. The Capataz put into Decoud's hands the handle of the pump which was fitted at the side aft, and at once, without question or remark, Decoud began to pump in utter forgetfulness of every desire but that of keeping the treasure afloat. Nostromo hoisted the sail, flew back to the tiller, pulled at the sheet like mad. The short flare of a match (they had been kept dry in a tight tin box, though the man himself was completely wet), the vivid flare of a match, disclosed to the toiling Decoud the eagerness of his face, bent low over the box of the compass, and the attentive stare of his eyes. He knew now where he was, and he hoped to run the sinking lighter ashore in the shallow cove where the high, cliff-like end of the Great Isabel is divided in two equal parts by a deep and overgrown ravine.

Decoud pumped without intermission. Nostromo steered without relaxing for a second the intense, peering effort of his stare. Each of them was as if utterly alone with his task. It did not occur to them to speak. There was nothing in common between them but the knowledge that the damaged lighter must be slowly but surely sinking. In that knowledge, which was like the crucial test of their desires, they seemed to have become completely estranged, as if they had discovered in the very shock of the collision that the loss of the lighter would not mean the same thing to them both. This common danger brought their differences in aim, in view, in character, and in position, into absolute prominence in the private vision of each. There was no bond of conviction, of common idea; they were merely two adventurers pursuing each his own adventure, involved in the same imminence of deadly peril. Therefore they had nothing to say to each other. But this peril, this only incontrovertible truth in which they shared, seemed to act as an inspiration to their mental and bodily powers.

There was certainly something almost miraculous in the way the Capataz made the cove with nothing but the shadowy hint of the island's shape and the vague gleam of a small sandy strip for a guide. Where the ravine opens between the cliffs, and a slender, shallow rivulet meanders out of the bushes to lose itself in the sea, the lighter was run ashore; and the two men, with a taciturn, undaunted energy, began to discharge her precious freight, carrying each oxhide box up the bed of the rivulet beyond the bushes to a hollow place which the caving in of the soil had made below the roots of a large tree. Its big smooth trunk leaned like a falling column far over the trickle of water running amongst the loose stones.

A couple of years before Nostromo had spent a whole Sunday, all alone, exploring the island. He explained this to Decoud after their task was done, and they sat, weary in every limb, with their legs hanging down the low bank, and their backs against the tree, like a pair of blind men aware of each other and their surroundings by some indefinable sixth sense.

'Yes,' Nostromo repeated, 'I never forget a place I have carefully looked at once.' He spoke slowly, almost lazily, as if there had been a whole leisurely life before him, instead of the scanty two hours before daylight. The existence of the treasure, barely concealed in this improbable spot, laid a burden of secrecy upon every contemplated step, upon every intention and plan of future conduct. He felt the partial failure of this desperate affair entrusted to the great reputation he had known how to make for himself. However, it was also a partial success. His vanity was half appeased. His nervous irritation had subsided.

'You never know what may be of use,' he pursued with his usual quietness of tone and manner. 'I spent a whole miserable Sunday in exploring this crumb of land.'

'A misanthropic sort of occupation,' muttered Decoud, viciously. 'You had no money, I suppose, to gamble with, and to fling about amongst the girls in your usual haunts, Capataz.'

'È vero!' exclaimed the Capataz, surprised into the use of his native tongue by so much perspicacity. 'I had not! Therefore I did not want to go amongst those beggarly people accustomed to my generosity. It is looked for from the Capataz of the Cargadores, who are the rich men, and, as it were, the Caballeros amongst the common people. I don't care for cards but as a pastime; and as to those girls that boast of having opened their doors to my knock, you know I wouldn't look at any one of them twice except for what the people would say. They are queer, the good people of Sulaco, and I have got much useful information simply by listening patiently to the talk of the women that everybody believed I was in love with. Poor Teresa could never understand that. On that particular Sunday, señor, she scolded so that I went out of the house swearing that I would never darken their door again unless to fetch away my hammock and my chest of clothes. Señor, there is nothing more exasperating than to hear a woman you respect rail against your good reputation when you have not a single brass coin in your pocket. I untied one of the small boats and pulled myself out of the harbour with nothing but three cigars in my pocket to help me spend the day on this island. But the water of this rivulet you hear under your feet is cool and sweet and good, señor, both before and after a smoke.' He was silent for a while, then added reflectively, 'That was the first Sunday after I brought down the white-whiskered English *rico* all the way down the mountains from the Páramo on the top of the Entrada Pass – and in the coach, too! No coach had gone up or down that mountain road within the memory of man, señor, till I brought this one down in charge of fifty peóns working like one man with ropes, pickaxes, and poles under my direction. That was the rich Englishman, who, as people say, pays for the making of this railway. He was very pleased with me. But my wages were not due till the end of the month.'

He slid down the bank suddenly. Decoud heard the splash of his feet in the brook and followed his footsteps down the ravine. His form was lost among the bushes till he had reached the strip of sand under the cliff. As often happens in the gulf when the showers during the first part of the night had been frequent and heavy, the darkness had thinned considerably towards the morning though there were no signs of daylight as yet.

The cargo-lighter, relieved of its precious burden, rocked feebly, half-afloat, with her forefoot on the sand. A long rope stretched away like a black cotton thread across the strip of white beach to the grapnel Nostromo had carried ashore and hooked to the stem of a treelike shrub in the very opening of the ravine.

There was nothing for Decoud but to remain on the island. He received from Nostromo's hands whatever food the foresight of Captain Mitchell had put on board the lighter and deposited it temporarily in the little dinghy which on their arrival they had hauled up out of sight amongst the bushes. It was to be left with him. The island was to be a hiding-place, not a prison; he could pull out to a passing ship. The OSN Company's mail boats passed close to the islands when going into Sulaco from the north. But the *Minerva*, carrying off the ex-president, had taken the news up north of the disturbances in Sulaco. It was possible that the next steamer down would get instructions to miss the port altogether since the town, as far as the *Minerva*'s officers knew, was for the time being in the hands of the rabble. This would mean that there would be no steamer for a month, as far as the mail service went, but Decoud had to take his chance of that. The island was his only shelter from the proscription hanging over his head. The Capataz was, of course, going back. The unloaded lighter leaked much less, and he thought that she would keep afloat as far as the harbour.

He passed to Decoud, standing knee-deep alongside, one of the two spades which belonged to the equipment of each lighter for use when ballasting ships. By working with it carefully as soon as there was daylight enough to see, Decoud could loosen a mass of earth and stones overhanging the cavity in which they had deposited the treasure, so that it would look as if it had fallen naturally. It would cover up not only the cavity, but even all traces of their work, the footsteps, the displaced stones, and even the broken bushes.

'Besides, who would think of looking either for you or the treasure here?' Nostromo continued, as if he could not tear himself away from the spot. 'Nobody is ever likely to come here. What could any man want with this piece of earth as long as there is room for his feet on the mainland! The people in this country are not curious. There are even no fishermen here to intrude upon your worship. All the fishing that is done in the gulf goes on near Zapiga, over there. Señor, if you are forced to leave this island before anything can be arranged for you, do not try to make for Zapiga. It is a settlement of thieves and matreros, where they would cut your throat promptly for the sake of your gold watch and chain. And, señor, think twice before confiding in anyone whatever; even in the officers of the Company's steamers, if you ever get on board one. Honesty alone is not enough for security. You must look to discretion and prudence in a man. And always remember, señor, before you open your lips for a confidence, that this treasure may be left safely here for hundreds of years. Time is on its side, señor. And silver is an incorruptible metal that can be trusted to keep its value for ever . . . An incorruptible metal,' he repeated, as if the idea had given him a profound pleasure.

'As some men are said to be,' Decoud pronounced, inscrutably, while the Capataz, who busied himself in baling out the lighter with a wooden bucket, went on throwing the water over the side with a regular splash. Decoud, incorrigible in his scepticism, reflected, not cynically, but with general satisfaction, that this man was made incorruptible by his enormous vanity, that finest form of egoism which can take on the aspect of every virtue.

Nostromo ceased baling, and, as if struck with a sudden thought, dropped the bucket with a clatter into the lighter.

'Have you any message?' he asked in a lowered voice. 'Remember, I shall be asked questions.'

'You must find the hopeful words that ought to be spoken to the people in town. I trust for that your intelligence and your experience, Capataz. You understand?'

'Si, señor . . . For the ladies.'

'Yes, yes,' said Decoud, hastily. 'Your wonderful reputation will make them attach great value to your words; therefore be careful what you say. I am looking forward,' he continued, feeling the fatal touch of contempt for himself to which his complex nature was subject, 'I am looking forward to a glorious and successful ending to my mission. Do you hear, Capataz? Use the words glorious and successful when you speak to the señorita. Your own mission is accomplished gloriously and successfully. You have indubitably saved the silver of the mine. Not only this silver, but probably all the silver that shall ever come out of it.'

Nostromo detected the ironic tone. 'I dare say, Señor Don Martin,' he said, moodily. 'There are very few things that I am not equal to. Ask the foreign signori. I, a man of the people, who cannot always understand what you mean. But as to this lot which I must leave here, let me tell you that I would believe it in greater safety if you had not been with me at all.'

An exclamation escaped Decoud, and a short pause followed. 'Shall I go back with you to Sulaco?' he asked in an angry tone.

'Shall I strike you dead with my knife where you stand?' retorted Nostromo, contemptuously. 'It would be the same thing as taking you to Sulaco. Come, señor. Your reputation is in your politics, and mine is bound up with the fate of this silver. Do you wonder I wish there had been no other man to share my knowledge? I wanted no one with me, señor.'

'You could not have kept the lighter afloat without me,' Decoud almost shouted. 'You would have gone to the bottom with her.'

'Yes,' uttered Nostromo, slowly; 'alone.'

Here was a man, Decoud reflected, that seemed as though he would have preferred to die rather than deface the perfect form of his egoism. Such a man was safe. In silence he helped the Capataz to get the grapnel on board. Nostromo cleared the shelving shore with one push of the heavy oar, and Decoud found himself solitary on the beach like a man in a dream. A sudden desire to hear a human voice once more seized upon his heart. The lighter was hardly distinguishable from the black water upon which she floated.

'What do you think has become of Hirsch?' he shouted.

'Knocked overboard and drowned,' cried Nostromo's voice confidently out of the black wastes of sky and sea around the islet. 'Keep close in the ravine, señor. I shall try to come out to you in a night or two.'

A slight swishing rustle showed that Nostromo was setting the sail. It filled all at once with a sound as of a single loud drum-tap. Decoud went back to the ravine. Nostromo, at the tiller, looked back from time to time at the vanishing mass of the Great Isabel, which, little by little, merged into the uniform texture of the night. At last, when he turned his head again, he saw nothing but a smooth darkness, like a solid wall.

Then he, too, experienced that feeling of solitude which had weighed heavily on Decoud after the lighter had slipped off the shore. But while the man on the island was oppressed by a bizarre sense of unreality affecting the very ground upon which he walked, the mind of the Capataz of the Cargadores turned alertly to the problem of future conduct. Nostromo's faculties, working on parallel lines, enabled him to steer straight, to keep a lookout for Hermosa, near which he had to pass, and to try to imagine what would happen tomorrow in Sulaco. Tomorrow, or, as a matter of fact, today, since the dawn was not very far, Sotillo would find out in what way the treasure had gone. A gang of Cargadores had been employed in loading it into a railway truck from the Custom House storerooms, and running the truck on to the wharf. There would be arrests made, and certainly before noon Sotillo would know in what manner the silver had left Sulaco, and who it was that took it out.

Nostromo's intention had been to sail right into the harbour; but at this thought by a sudden touch of the tiller he threw the lighter into the wind and checked her rapid way. His reappearance with the very boat would raise suspicions, would cause surmises, would absolutely put Sotillo on the track. He himself would be arrested; and once in the Calabozo there was no saying what they would do to him to make him speak. He trusted himself, but he stood up to look round. Near by, Hermosa showed low its white surface as flat as a table, with the slight run of the sea raised by the breeze washing over its edges noisily. The lighter must be sunk at once.

He allowed her to drift with her sail aback. There was already a good deal of water in her. He allowed her to drift towards the harbour entrance, and, letting the tiller swing about, squatted down and busied himself in loosening the plug. With that out she would fill very quickly, and every lighter carried a little iron ballast – enough to make her go down when full of water. When he stood up again the noisy wash about the Hermosa sounded far away, almost inaudible; and already he could make out the shape of land about the harbour entrance. This was a desperate affair, and he was a good swimmer. A mile was nothing to him, and he knew of an easy place for landing just below the earthworks of the old abandoned fort. It occurred to him with a peculiar fascination that this fort was a good place in which to sleep the day through after so many sleepless nights.

With one blow of the tiller he unshipped for the purpose, he knocked the plug out, but did not take the trouble to lower the sail. He felt the water welling up heavily about his legs before he leaped on to the taffrail. There, upright and motionless, in his shirt and trousers only, he stood waiting. When he had felt her settle he sprang far away with a mighty splash.

At once he turned his head. The gloomy, clouded dawn from behind the mountains showed him on the smooth waters the upper corner of the sail, a dark wet triangle of canvas waving slightly to and fro. He saw it vanish, as if jerked under, and then struck out for the shore.

PART THIRD

The Lighthouse

Chapter 1

Directly the cargo boat had slipped away from the wharf and got lost in the darkness of the harbour the Europeans of Sulaco separated, to prepare for the coming of the Monterist régime, which was approaching Sulaco from the mountains, as well as from the sea.

This bit of manual work in loading the silver was their last concerted action. It ended the three days of danger, during which, according to the newspaper press of Europe, their energy had preserved the town from the calamities of popular disorder. At the shore end of the jetty, Captain Mitchell said good-night and turned back. His intention was to walk the planks of the wharf till the steamer from Esmeralda turned up. The engineers of the railway staff, collecting their Basque and Italian workmen, marched them away to the railway yards, leaving the Custom House, so well defended on the first day of the riot, standing open to the four winds of heaven. Their men had conducted themselves bravely and faithfully during the famous 'three days' of Sulaco. In a great part this faithfulness and that courage had been exercised in self-defence rather than in the cause of those material interests to which Charles Gould had pinned his faith. Amongst the cries of the mob not the least loud had been the cry of death to foreigners. It was, indeed, a lucky circumstance for Sulaco that the relations of those imported workmen with the people of the country had been uniformly bad from the first.

Doctor Monygham, going to the door of Viola's kitchen, observed this retreat marking the end of the foreign interference, this withdrawal of the army of material progress from the field of Costaguana revolutions.

Algarrobe torches carried on the outskirts of the moving body sent their penetrating aroma into his nostrils. Their light, sweeping along the front of the house, made the letters of the inscription, 'Albergo d'Italia Una', leap out black from end to end of the long wall. His eyes blinked in the clear blaze. Several young men, mostly fair and tall, shepherding this mob of dark bronzed heads, surmounted by the glint of slanting rifle barrels, nodded to him familiarly as they went by. The doctor was a well-known character. Some of them wondered what he was doing there. Then, on the flank of their workmen they tramped on, following the line of rails.

'Withdrawing your people from the harbour?' said the doctor, addressing himself to the chief engineer of the railway, who had accompanied Charles Gould so far in his way to the town, walking by the side of the horse, with his hand on the saddle-bow. They had stopped just outside the open door to let the workmen cross the road.

'As quick as I can. We are not a political faction,' answered the engineer, meaningly. 'And we are not going to give our new rulers a handle against the railway. You approve me, Gould?'

'Absolutely,' said Charles Gould's impassive voice, high up and outside the dim parallelogram of light falling on the road through the open door.

With Sotillo expected from one side, and Pedro Montero from the other, the engineer-in-chief's only anxiety now was to avoid a collision with either. Sulaco, for him, was a railway station, a terminus, workshops, a great accumulation of stores. As against the mob the railway defended its property, but politically the railway was neutral. He was a brave man; and in that spirit of neutrality he had carried proposals of truce to the self-appointed chiefs of the popular party, the deputies Fuentes and Gamacho. Bullets were still flying about when he had crossed the Plaza on that mission, waving above his head a white napkin belonging to the table linen of the Amarilla Club.

He was rather proud of this exploit; and reflecting that the doctor, busy all day with the wounded in the patio of the Casa Gould, had not had time to hear the news, he began a succinct narrative. He had communicated to them the intelligence from the Construction Camp as to Pedro Montero. The brother of the victorious general, he had assured them, could be expected at Sulaco at any time now. This news (as he anticipated), when shouted out of the window by Señor Gamacho, induced a rush of the mob along the Campo Road towards Rincon. The two deputies also, after shaking hands with him effusively, mounted and galloped off to meet the great man. 'I have misled them a little as to the time,' the chief engineer confessed. 'However hard he rides, he can scarcely get here before the morning. But my object is attained. I've secured several hours' peace for the losing party. But I did not tell them anything about Sotillo, for fear they would take it into their heads to try to get hold of the harbour again, either to oppose him or welcome him – there's no saying which. There was Gould's silver, on which rests the remnant of our hopes. Decoud's retreat had to be thought of, too. I think the railway has done pretty well by its friends without compromising itself hopelessly. Now the parties must be left to themselves.'

'Costaguana for the Costaguaneros,' interjected the doctor, sardonically. 'It is a fine country, and they have raised a fine crop of hates, vengeance, murder, and rapine – those sons of the country.'

'Well, I am one of them,' Charles Gould's voice sounded, calmly, 'and I must be going on to see to my own crop of trouble. My wife has driven straight on, doctor?'

'Yes. All was quiet on this side. Mrs Gould has taken the two girls with her.'

Charles Gould rode on, and the engineer-in-chief followed the doctor indoors.

'That man is calmness personified,' he said, appreciatively, dropping on a bench, and stretching his well-shaped legs in cycling stockings nearly across the doorway. 'He must be extremely sure of himself.'

'If that's all he is sure of, then he is sure of nothing,' said the doctor. He had perched himself again on the end of the table. He nursed his cheek in the palm of one hand, while the other sustained the elbow. 'It is the last thing a man ought to be sure of.' The candle, half-consumed and burning dimly with a long wick, lighted up from below his inclined face, whose expression, affected by the drawn-in cicatrices in the cheeks, had something vaguely unnatural, an exaggerated remorseful bitterness. As he sat there he had the air of meditating upon sinister things. The engineer-in-chief gazed at him for a time before he protested.

'I really don't see that. For me there seems to be nothing else. However – '

He was a wise man, but he could not quite conceal his contempt for that sort of paradox; in fact, Dr Monygham was not liked by the Europeans of Sulaco. His outward aspect of an outcast, which he preserved even in Mrs Gould's drawing-room, provoked unfavourable criticism. There could be no doubt of his intelligence; and as he had lived for over twenty years in the country, the pessimism of his outlook could not be altogether ignored. But instinctively, in self-defence of their activities and hopes, his hearers put it to the account of some hidden imperfection in the man's character. It was known that many years before, when quite young, he had been made by Guzman Bento chief medical officer of the army. Not one of the Europeans then in the service of Costaguana had been so much liked and trusted by the fierce old Dictator.

Afterwards his story was not so clear. It lost itself amongst the innumerable tales of conspiracies and plots against the tyrant as a stream is lost in an arid belt of sandy country before it emerges, diminished and troubled, perhaps, on the other side. The doctor made no secret of it that he had lived for years in the wildest parts of the Republic, wandering with almost unknown Indian tribes in the great forests of the far interior where the great rivers have their sources. But it was mere aimless wandering; he had written nothing, collected nothing, brought nothing for science out of the twilight of the forests, which seemed to cling to his battered personality limping about Sulaco, where it had drifted in casually, only to get stranded on the shores of the sea.

It was also known that he had lived in a state of destitution till the arrival of the Goulds from Europe. Don Carlos and Doña Emilia had taken up the mad English doctor, when it became apparent that for all his savage independence he could be tamed by kindness. Perhaps it was only hunger that had tamed him. In years gone by he had certainly been acquainted with Charles Gould's father in Sta Marta; and now, no matter what were the dark passages of his history, as the medical officer of the San Tomé mine he became a recognised personality. He was recognised, but not unreservedly accepted. So much defiant eccentricity and such an outspoken scorn for mankind seemed to point to mere recklessness of judgment, the bravado of guilt. Besides, since he had become again of some account, vague whispers had been heard that years ago, when fallen into disgrace and thrown into prison by Guzman Bento at the time of the so-called Great Conspiracy, he had betrayed some of his best friends amongst the conspirators. Nobody pretended to believe that whisper; the whole story of the Great Conspiracy was hopelessly involved and obscure; it is admitted in Costaguana that there never had been a conspiracy except in the diseased imagination of the Tyrant; and, therefore nothing and no one to betray; though the most distinguished Costaguaneros had been imprisoned and executed upon that accusation. The procedure dragged on for years, decimating the better class like a pestilence. The mere expression of sorrow for the fate of executed kinsmen had been punished with death. Don José Avellanos was perhaps the only one living who knew the whole story of those unspeakable cruelties. He had suffered from them himself, and he, with a shrug of the shoulders and a nervous, jerky gesture of the arm, was wont to put away from him, as it were, every allusion to it. But whatever the reason, Dr Monygham, a personage in the administration of the Gould Concession, treated with reverent awe by the miners, and indulged in his peculiarities by Mrs Gould, remained somehow outside the pale.

It was not from any liking for the doctor that the engineer-in-chief had lingered in the inn upon the plain. He liked old Viola much better. He had come to look upon the Albergo d'Italia Una as a dependence of the railway. Many of his subordinates had their quarters there. Mrs Gould's interest in the family conferred upon it a sort of distinction. The engineer-in-chief, with an army of workers under his orders, appreciated the moral influence of the old Garibaldino upon his countrymen. His austere, old-world Republicanism had a severe, soldier-like standard of faithfulness and duty, as if the world were a battlefield where men had to fight for the sake of universal love and brotherhood, instead of a more or less large share of booty.

'Poor old chap!' he said, after he had heard the doctor's account of Teresa. 'He'll never be able to keep the place going by himself. I shall be sorry.'

'He's quite alone up there,' grunted Dr Monygham, with a toss of his heavy head towards the narrow staircase. 'Every living soul has cleared out, and Mrs Gould took the girls away just now. It might not be over-safe for them out here before very long. Of course, as a doctor I can do nothing more here; but she has asked me to stay with old Viola, and as I have no horse to get back to the mine, where I ought to be, I made no difficulty to stay. They can do without me in the town.'

'I have a good mind to remain with you, doctor, till we see whether anything happens tonight at the harbour,' declared the engineer-in-chief. 'He must not be molested by Sotillo's soldiery, who may push on as far as this at once. Sotillo used to be very cordial to me at the Goulds' and at the club. How that man'll ever dare to look any of his friends here in the face I can't imagine.'

'He'll no doubt begin by shooting some of them to get over the first awkwardness,' said the doctor. 'Nothing in this country serves better your military man who has changed sides than a few summary executions.' He spoke with a gloomy positiveness that left no room for protest. The engineer-in-chief did not attempt any. He simply nodded several times regretfully, then said: 'I think we shall be able to mount you in the morning, doctor. Our peóns have recovered some of our stampeded horses. By riding hard and taking a wide circuit by Los Hatos and along the edge of the forest, clear of Rincon altogether, you may hope to reach the San Tomé bridge without being interfered with. The mine is just now, to my mind, the safest place for anybody at all compromised. I only wish the railway was as difficult to touch.'

'Am I compromised?' Dr Monygham brought out slowly after a short silence.

'The whole Gould Concession is compromised. I could not have remained for ever outside the political life of the country – if those convulsions may be called life. The thing is – can it be touched? The moment was bound to come when neutrality would become impossible, and Charles Gould understood this well. I believe he is prepared for every extremity. A man of his sort has never contemplated remaining indefinitely at the mercy of ignorance and corruption. It was like being a prisoner in a cavern of banditti with the price of your ransom in your pocket, and buying your life from day to day. Your mere safety, not your liberty, mind, doctor. I know what I am talking about. The image at which you shrug your shoulders is perfectly correct, especially if you conceive such a prisoner endowed with the power of replenishing his pocket by means as remote from the faculties of his captors as if they were magic. You must have understood that as well as I do, doctor. He was in the position of the goose with the golden eggs. I broached this matter to him as far back as Sir John's visit here. The prisoner of stupid and greedy banditti is always at the mercy of the first imbecile ruffian, who may blow out his brains in a fit of temper or for some prospect of an immediate big haul. The tale of killing the goose with the golden eggs has not been evolved for nothing out of the wisdom of mankind. It is a story that will never grow old. That is why Charles Gould in his deep, dumb way has countenanced the Ribierist Mandate, the first public act that promised him safety on other than venal grounds. Ribierism has failed, as everything merely rational fails in this country. But Gould remains logical in wishing to save this big lot of silver. Decoud's plan of a counter-revolution may be practicable or not, it may have a chance, or it may not have a chance. With all my experience of this revolutionary continent, I can hardly yet look at their methods seriously. Decoud has been reading to us his draft of a proclamation, and talking very well for two hours about his plan of action. He had arguments which should have appeared solid enough if we, members of old, stable political and national organisations, were not startled by the mere idea of a new State evolved like this out of the head of a scoffing young man fleeing for his life, with a proclamation in his pocket, to a rough, jeering, half-bred swashbuckler, who in this part of the world is called a general. It sounds like a comic fairy tale – and behold, it may come off; because it is true to the very spirit of the country.'

'Is the silver gone off then?' asked the doctor, moodily.

The chief engineer pulled out his watch. 'By Captain Mitchell's reckoning – and he ought to know – it has been gone long enough now to be some three or four miles outside the harbour; and, as Mitchell says, Nostromo is the sort of seaman to make the best of his opportunities.' Here the doctor grunted so heavily that the other changed his tone.

'You have a poor opinion of that move, doctor? But why? Charles Gould has got to play his game out, though he is not the man to formulate his conduct even to himself, perhaps, let alone to others. It may be that the game has been partly suggested to him by Holroyd; but it accords with his character, too; and that is why it has been so successful. Haven't they come to calling him 'El Rey de Sulaco' in Sta Marta? A nickname may be the best record of a success. That's what I call putting the face of a joke upon the body of a truth. My dear sir, when I first arrived in Sta Marta I was struck by the way all those journalists, demagogues, members of Congress, and all those generals and judges cringed before a sleepy-eyed advocate without practice simply because he was the plenipotentiary of the Gould Concession. Sir John when he came out was impressed, too.'

'A new State, with that plump dandy, Decoud, for the first President,' mused Dr Monygham, nursing his cheek and swinging his legs all the time.

'Upon my word, and why not?' the chief engineer retorted in an un-expectedly earnest and confidential voice. It was as if something subtle in the air of Costaguana had inoculated him with the local faith in 'pronunciamientos'. All at once he began to talk, like an expert revolutionist, of the instrument ready to hand in the intact army at Cayta, which could be brought back in a few days to Sulaco if only Decoud managed to make his way at once down the coast. For the military chief there was Barrios, who had nothing but a bullet to expect from Montero, his former professional rival and bitter enemy. Barrios's concurrence was assured. As to his army, it had nothing to expect from Montero either; not even a month's pay. From that point of view the existence of the treasure was of enormous importance. The mere knowledge that it had been saved from the Monterists would be a strong inducement for the Cayta troops to embrace the cause of the new State.

The doctor turned round and contemplated his companion for some time.

'This Decoud, I see, is a persuasive young beggar,' he remarked at last. 'And pray is it for this, then, that Charles Gould has let the whole lot of ingots go out to sea in charge of that Nostromo?'

'Charles Gould,' said the engineer-in-chief, 'has said no more about his motive than usual. You know, he doesn't talk. But we all here know his motive, and he has only one – the safety of the San Tomé mine with the preservation of the Gould Concession in the spirit of his compact with Holroyd. Holroyd is another uncommon man. They understand each other's imaginative side. One is thirty, the other nearly sixty, and they have been made for each other. To be a millionaire, and such a millionaire as Holroyd, is like being eternally young. The audacity of youth reckons upon what it fancies an unlimited time at its disposal; but a millionaire has unlimited means in his hand – which is better. One's time on earth is an uncertain quantity, but about the long reach of millions there is no doubt. The introduction of a pure form of Christianity into this continent is a dream for a youthful enthusiast, and I have been trying to explain to you why Holroyd at fifty-eight is like a man on the threshold of life, and better, too. He's not a missionary, but the San Tomé mine holds just that for him. I assure you, in sober truth, that he could not manage to keep this out of a strictly business conference upon the finances of Costaguana he had with Sir John a couple of years ago. Sir John mentioned it with amazement in a letter he wrote to me here, from San Francisco, when on his way home. Upon my word, doctor, things seem to be worth nothing by what they are in themselves. I begin to believe that the only solid thing about them is the spiritual value which everyone discovers in his own form of activity – '

'Bah!' interrupted the doctor, without stopping for an instant the idle swinging movement of his legs. 'Self-flattery. Food for that vanity which makes the world go round. Meantime, what do you think is going to happen to the treasure floating about the gulf with the great Capataz and the great politician?'

'Why are you uneasy about it, doctor?'

'I uneasy! And what the devil is it to me? I put no spiritual value into my desires, or my opinions, or my actions. They have not enough vastness to give me room for self-flattery. Look, for instance, I should certainly have liked to ease the last moments of that poor woman. And I can't. It's impossible. Have you met the impossible face to face – or have you, the Napoleon of railways, no such word in your dictionary?'

'Is she bound to have a very bad time of it?' asked the chief engineer, with humane concern.

Slow, heavy footsteps moved across the planks above the heavy hard wood beams of the kitchen. Then down the narrow opening of the staircase made in the thickness of the wall, and narrow enough to be defended by one man against twenty enemies, came the murmur of two voices, one faint and broken, the other deep and gentle answering it, and in its graver tone covering the weaker sound.

The two men remained still and silent till the murmurs ceased, then the doctor shrugged his shoulders and muttered: 'Yes, she's bound to. And I could do nothing if I went up now.'

A long period of silence above and below ensued.

'I fancy,' began the engineer, in a subdued voice, 'that you mistrust Captain Mitchell's Capataz.'

'Mistrust him!' muttered the doctor through his teeth. 'I believe him capable of anything – even of the most absurd fidelity. I am the last person he spoke to before he left the wharf, you know. The poor woman up there wanted to see him, and I let him go up to her. The dying must not be contradicted, you know. She seemed then fairly calm and resigned, but the scoundrel in those ten minutes or so has done or said something which seems to have driven her into despair. You know,' went on the doctor, hesitatingly, 'women are so very unaccountable in every position, and at all times of life, that I thought sometimes she was in a way, don't you see? in love with him – the Capataz. The rascal has his own charm indubitably, or he would not have made the conquest of all the populace of the town. No, no, I am not absurd. I may have given a wrong name to some strong sentiment for him on her part, to an unreasonable and simple attitude a woman is apt to take up emotionally towards a man. She used to abuse him to me frequently, which, of course, is not inconsistent with my idea. Not at all. It looked to me as if she were always thinking of him. He was something important in her life. You know, I have seen a lot of those people. Whenever I came down from the mine Mrs Gould used to ask me to keep my eye on them. She likes Italians; she has lived a long time in Italy, I believe, and she took a special fancy to that old Garibaldino. A remarkable chap enough. A rugged and dreamy character, living in the republicanism of his young days as if in a cloud. He has encouraged much of the Capataz's confounded nonsense – the high-strung, exalted old beggar!'

'What sort of nonsense?' wondered the chief engineer. 'I found the Capataz always a very shrewd and sensible fellow, absolutely fearless, and remarkably useful. A perfect handy man. Sir John was greatly impressed by his resourcefulness and attention when he made that overland journey from Sta Marta. Later on, as you might have heard, he rendered us a service by disclosing to the then chief of police the presence in the town of some professional thieves, who came from a distance to wreck and rob our monthly pay train. He has certainly organised the lighterage service of the harbour for the OSN Company with great ability. He knows how to make himself obeyed, foreigner though he is. It is true that the Cargadores are strangers here, too, for the most part – immigrants, Isleños.'

'His prestige is his fortune,' muttered the doctor, sourly.

'The man has proved his trustworthiness up to the hilt on innumerable occasions and in all sorts of ways,' argued the engineer. 'When this question of the silver arose, Captain Mitchell naturally was very warmly of the opinion that his Capataz was the only man fit for the trust. As a sailor, of course, I suppose so. But as a man, don't you know, Gould, Decoud, and myself judged that it didn't matter in the least who went. Any boatman would have done just as well. Pray, what could a thief do with such a lot of ingots? If he ran off with them he would have in the end to land somewhere, and how could he conceal his cargo from the knowledge of the people ashore? We dismissed that consideration from our minds. Moreover, Decoud was going.

There have been occasions when the Capataz has been more implicitly trusted.'

'He took a slightly different view,' the doctor said. 'I heard him declare in this very room that it would be the most desperate affair of his life. He made a sort of verbal will here in my hearing, appointing old Viola his executor; and, by Jove! do you know, he – he's not grown rich by his fidelity to you good people of the railway and the harbour. I suppose he obtains some – how do you say that? – some spiritual value for his labours, or else I don't know why the devil he should be faithful to you, Gould, Mitchell, or anybody else. He knows this country well. He knows, for instance, that Gamacho, the Deputy from Javira, has been nothing else but a 'tramposo' of the commonest sort, a petty pedlar of the Campo, till he managed to get enough goods on credit from Anzani to open a little store in the wilds, and got himself elected by the drunken mozos that hang about the Estancias and the poorest sort of rancheros who were in his debt. And Gamacho, who tomorrow will be probably one of our high officials, is a stranger, too – an Isleño. He might have been a Cargador on the OSN wharf had he not (the posadero of Rincon is ready to swear it) murdered a pedlar in the woods and stolen his pack to begin life on. And do you think that Gamacho, then, would have ever become a hero with the democracy of this place, like our Capataz? Of course not. He isn't half the man. No; decidedly, I think that Nostromo is a fool.'

The doctor's talk was distasteful to the builder of railways. 'It is impossible to argue that point,' he said, philosophically. 'Each man has his gifts. You should have heard Gamacho haranguing his friends in the street. He has a howling voice, and he shouted like mad, lifting his clenched fist right above his head, and throwing his body half out of the window. At every pause the rabble below yelled, "Down with the Oligarchs! *Viva la Libertad!*" Fuentes inside looked extremely miserable. You know, he is the brother of Jorge Fuentes, who has been Minister of the Interior for six months or so, some few years back. Of course, he has no conscience; but he is a man of birth and education – at one time the director of the Customs of Cayta. That idiot-brute Gamacho fastened himself upon him with his following of the lowest rabble. His sickly fear of that ruffian was the most rejoicing sight imaginable.'

He got up and went to the door to look out towards the harbour. 'All quiet,' he said; 'I wonder if Sotillo really means to turn up here?'

Chapter 2

Captain Mitchell, pacing the wharf, was asking himself the same question. There was always the doubt whether the warning of the Esmeralda telegraphist – a fragmentary and interrupted message – had been properly understood. However, the good man had made up his mind not to go to bed till daylight, if even then. He imagined himself to have rendered an enormous service to Charles Gould. When he thought of the saved silver he rubbed his hands together with satisfaction. In his simple way he was proud at being a party to this extremely clever expedient. It was he who had given it a practical shape by suggesting the possibility of intercepting at sea the northbound steamer. And it was advantageous to his Company, too, which would have lost a valuable freight if the treasure had been left ashore to be confiscated. The pleasure of disappointing the Monterists was also very great. Authoritative by temperament and the long habit of command, Captain Mitchell was no democrat. He even went so far as to profess a contempt for parliamentarism itself. 'His Excellency Don Vincente Ribiera,' he used to say, 'whom I and that fellow of mine, Nostromo, had the honour, sir, and the pleasure of saving from a cruel death, deferred too much to his Congress. It was a mistake – a distinct mistake, sir.'

The guileless old seaman superintending the OSN service imagined that the last three days had exhausted every startling surprise the political life of Costaguana could offer. He used to confess afterwards that the events which followed surpassed his imagination. To begin with, Sulaco (because of the seizure of the cables and the disorganisation of the steam service) remained for a whole fortnight cut off from the rest of the world like a besieged city.

'One would not have believed it possible; but so it was, sir. A full fortnight.'

The account of the extraordinary things that happened during that time, and the powerful emotions he experienced, acquired a comic impressiveness from the pompous manner of his personal narrative. He opened it always by assuring his hearer that he was 'in the thick of things from first to last'. Then he would begin by describing the getting away of the silver, and his natural anxiety lest 'his fellow' in charge of the lighter should make some mistake. Apart from the loss of so much precious metal, the life of Señor Martin Decoud, an agreeable, wealthy, and well-informed young gentleman, would have been jeopardised through his falling into the hands of his political enemies. Captain Mitchell also admitted that in his solitary vigil on the wharf he had felt a certain measure of concern for the future of the whole country.

'A feeling, sir,' he explained, 'perfectly comprehensible in a man properly grateful for the many kindnesses received from the best families of merchants and other native gentlemen of independent means, who, barely saved by us from the excesses of the mob, seemed, to my mind's eye, destined to become the prey in person and fortune of the native soldiery, which, as is well known, behave with regrettable barbarity to the inhabitants during their civil commotions. And then, sir, there were the Goulds, for both of whom, man and wife, I could not but entertain the warmest feelings deserved by their hospitality and kindness. I felt, too, the dangers of the gentlemen of the Amarilla Club, who had made me honorary member, and had treated me with uniform regard and civility, both in my capacity of Consular Agent and as Superintendent of an important Steam Service. Miss Antonia Avellanos, the most beautiful and accomplished young lady whom it had ever been my privilege to speak to, was not a little in my mind, I confess. How the interests of my Company would be affected by the impending change of officials claimed a large share of my attention, too. In short, sir, I was extremely anxious and very tired, as you may suppose, by the exciting and memorable events in which I had taken my little part. The Company's building containing my residence was within five minutes' walk, with the attraction of some supper and of my hammock (I always take my nightly rest in a hammock, as the most suitable to the climate); but somehow, sir, though evidently I could do nothing for anyone by remaining about, I could not tear myself away from that wharf, where the fatigue made me stumble painfully at times. The night was excessively dark – the darkest I remember in my life; so that I began to think that the arrival of the transport from Esmeralda could not possibly take place before daylight, owing to the difficulty of navigating the gulf. The mosquitoes bit like fury. We have been infested here with mosquitoes before the late improvements; a peculiar harbour brand, sir, renowned for its ferocity. They were like a cloud about my head, and I shouldn't wonder that but for their attacks I would have dozed off as I walked up and down, and got a heavy fall. I kept on smoking cigar after cigar, more to protect myself from being eaten up alive than from any real relish for the weed. Then, sir, when perhaps for the twentieth time I was approaching my watch to the lighted end in order to see the time, and observing with surprise that it wanted yet ten minutes to midnight, I heard the splash of a ship's propeller – an unmistakable sound to a sailor's ear on such a calm night. It was faint indeed, because they were advancing with precaution and dead slow, both on account of the darkness and from their desire of not revealing too soon their presence: a very unnecessary care, because, I verily believe, in all the enormous extent of this harbour I was the only living soul about. Even the usual staff of watchmen and others had been absent from their posts for several nights owing to the disturbances. I stood stock still, after dropping and stamping out my cigar – a circumstance highly agreeable, I should think, to the mosquitoes, if I may judge from the state of my face next morning. But that was a trifling inconvenience in comparison with the brutal proceedings I became victim of on the part of Sotillo. Something utterly inconceivable, sir; more like the proceedings of a maniac than the action of a sane man, however lost to all sense of honour and decency. But Sotillo was furious at the failure of his thievish scheme.'

In this Captain Mitchell was right. Sotillo was indeed infuriated. Captain Mitchell, however, had not been arrested at once; a vivid curiosity induced him to remain on the wharf (which is nearly four hundred feet long) to see, or rather hear, the whole process of disembarkation. Concealed by the railway truck used for the silver, which had been run back afterwards to the shore end of the jetty, Captain Mitchell saw the small detachment thrown forward, pass by, taking different directions upon the plain. Meantime, the troops were being landed and formed into a column, whose head crept up gradually so close to him that he made it out, barring nearly the whole width of the wharf, only a very few yards from him. Then the low, shuffling, murmuring, clinking sounds ceased, and the whole mass remained for about an hour motionless and silent, awaiting the return of the scouts. On land nothing was to be heard except the deep baying of the mastiffs at the railway yards, answered by the faint barking of the curs infesting the outer limits of the town. A detached knot of dark shapes stood in front of the head of the column.

Presently the picket at the end of the wharf began to challenge in under-tones single figures approaching from the plain. Those messengers sent back from the scouting parties flung to their comrades brief sentences and passed on rapidly, becoming lost in the great motionless mass, to make their report to the Staff. It occurred to Captain Mitchell that his position could become disagreeable and perhaps dangerous, when suddenly, at the head of the jetty, there was a shout of command, a bugle call, followed by a stir and a rattling of arms, and a murmuring noise that ran right up the column. Near by a loud voice directed hurriedly, 'Push that railway car out of the way!' At the rush of bare feet to execute the order Captain Mitchell skipped back a pace or two; the car, suddenly impelled by many hands, flew away from him along the rails, and before he knew what had happened he found himself surrounded and seized by his arms and the collar of his coat.

'We have caught a man hiding here, *mi teniente*!' cried one of his captors.

'Hold him ·on one side till the rearguard comes along,' answered the voice. The whole column streamed past Captain Mitchell at a run, the thundering noise of their feet dying away suddenly on the shore. His captors held him tightly, disregarding his declaration that he was an Englishman and his loud demands to be taken at once before their commanding officer. Finally he lapsed into dignified silence. With a hollow rumble of wheels on the planks a couple of field guns, dragged by hand, rolled by. Then, after a small body of men had marched past escorting four or five figures which walked in advance, with a jingle of steel scabbards, he felt a tug at his arms, and was ordered to come along. During the passage from the wharf to the

Custom House it is to be feared that Captain Mitchell was subjected to certain indignities at the hands of the soldiers – such as jerks, thumps on the neck, forcible application of the butt of a rifle to the small of his back. Their ideas of speed were not in accord with his notion of his dignity. He became flustered, flushed, and helpless. It was as if the world were coming to an end.

The long building was surrounded by troops, which were already piling arms by companies and preparing to pass the night lying on the ground in their ponchos with their sacks under their heads. Corporals moved with swinging lanterns posting sentries all round the walls wherever there was a door or an opening. Sotillo was taking his measures to protect his conquest as if it had indeed contained the treasure. His desire to make his fortune at one audacious stroke of genius had overmastered his reasoning faculties. He would not believe in the possibility of failure; the mere hint of such a thing made his brain reel with rage. Every circumstance pointing to it appeared incredible. The statement of Hirsch, which was so absolutely fatal to his hopes, could by no means be admitted. It is true, too, that Hirsch's story had been told so incoherently, with such excessive signs of distraction, that it really looked improbable. It was extremely difficult, as the saying is, to make head or tail of it. On the bridge of the steamer, directly after his rescue, Sotillo and his officers, in their impatience and excitement, would not give the wretched man time to collect such few wits as remained to him. He ought to have been quieted, soothed, and reassured, whereas he had been roughly handled, cuffed, shaken, and addressed in menacing tones. His struggles, his wriggles, his attempts to get down on his knees, followed by the most violent efforts to break away, as if he meant incontinently to jump overboard, his shrieks and shrinkings and cowering wild glances had filled them first with amazement, then with a doubt of his genuineness, as men are wont to suspect the sincerity of every great passion. His Spanish, too, became so mixed up with German that the better half of his statements remained incomprehensible. He tried to propitiate them by calling them *hochwohlgeborene Herren*, which in itself sounded suspicious. When admonished sternly not to trifle he repeated his entreaties and protestations of loyalty and innocence again in German, obstinately, because he was not aware in what language he was speaking. His identity, of course, was perfectly known as an inhabitant of Esmeralda, but this made the matter no clearer. As he kept on forgetting Decoud's name, mixing him up with several other people he had seen in the Casa Gould, it looked as if they all had been in the lighter together; and for a moment Sotillo thought that he had drowned every prominent Ribierist of Sulaco. The improbability of such a thing threw a doubt upon the whole statement. Hirsch was either mad or playing a part – pretending fear and distraction on the spur of the moment to cover the truth. Sotillo's rapacity, excited to the highest pitch by the prospect of an immense booty, could believe in nothing adverse. This Jew might have been very much frightened by the accident, but he knew where the silver was concealed, and had invented this story, with his Jewish cunning, to put him entirely off the track as to what had been done.

Sotillo had taken up his quarters on the upper floor in a vast apartment with heavy black beams. But there was no ceiling, and the eye lost itself in the darkness under the high pitch of the roof. The thick shutters stood open. On a long table could be seen a large inkstand, some stumpy, inky quill pens, and two square wooden boxes, each holding half a hundredweight of sand. Sheets of grey coarse official paper bestrewed the floor. It must have been a room occupied by some higher official of the Customs, because a large leathern armchair stood behind the table, with other high-backed chairs scattered about. A net hammock was swung under one of the beams – for the official's afternoon siesta, no doubt. A couple of candles stuck into tall iron candlesticks gave a dim reddish light. The colonel's hat, sword, and revolver lay between them, and a couple of his more trusty officers lounged gloomily against the table. The colonel threw himself into the armchair, and a big Negro with a sergeant's stripes on his ragged sleeve, kneeling down, pulled off his boots. Sotillo's ebony moustache contrasted violently with the livid colouring of his cheeks. His eyes were sombre and as if sunk very far into his head. He seemed exhausted by his perplexities, languid with disappointment; but when the sentry on the landing thrust his head in to announce the arrival of a prisoner, he revived at once.

'Let him be brought in,' he shouted, fiercely.

The door flew open, and Captain Mitchell, bareheaded, his waistcoat open, the bow of his tie under his ear, was hustled into the room.

Sotillo recognised him at once. He could not have hoped for a more precious capture; here was a man who could tell him, if he chose, everything he wished to know – and directly the problem of how best to make him talk to the point presented itself to his mind. The resentment of a foreign nation had no terrors for Sotillo. The might of the whole armed Europe would not have protected Captain Mitchell from insults and ill-usage, so well as the quick reflection of Sotillo that this was an Englishman who would most likely turn obstinate under bad treatment, and become quite unmanageable. At all events, the colonel smoothed the scowl on his brow.

'What! The excellent Señor Mitchell!' he cried, in affected dismay. The pretended anger of his swift advance and of his shout, 'Release the caballero at once,' was so effective that the astounded soldiers positively sprang away from their prisoner. Thus suddenly deprived of forcible support, Captain Mitchell reeled as though about to fall. Sotillo took him familiarly under the arm, led him to a chair, waved his hand at the room. 'Go out, all of you,' he commanded.

When they had been left alone he stood looking down, irresolute and silent, watching till Captain Mitchell had recovered his power of speech.

Here in his very grasp was one of the men concerned in the removal of the silver. Sotillo's temperament was of that sort that he experienced an ardent desire to beat him; just as formerly when negotiating with difficulty a loan from the cautious Anzani, his fingers always itched to take the shopkeeper by the throat. As to Captain Mitchell, the suddenness, unexpectedness, and general inconceivableness of this experience had confused his thoughts. Moreover, he was physically out of breath.

'I've been knocked down three times between this and the wharf,' he gasped out at last. 'Somebody shall be made to pay for this.' He had certainly stumbled more than once, and had been dragged along for some distance before he could regain his stride. With his recovered breath his indignation seemed to madden him. He jumped up, crimson, all his white hair bristling, his eyes glaring vengefully, and shook violently the flaps of his ruined waistcoat before the disconcerted Sotillo. 'Look! Those uniformed thieves of yours downstairs have robbed me of my watch.'

The old sailor's aspect was very threatening. Sotillo saw himself cut off from the table on which his sabre and revolver were lying.

'I demand restitution and apologies,' Mitchell thundered at him, quite beside himself. 'From you! Yes, from you!'

For the space of a second or so the colonel stood with a perfectly stony expression of face; then, as Captain Mitchell flung out an arm towards the table as if to snatch up the revolver, Sotillo, with a yell of alarm, bounded to the door and was gone in a flash, slamming it after him. Surprise calmed Captain Mitchell's fury. Behind the closed door Sotillo shouted and there was a great tumult of feet on the wooden staircase.

'Disarm him! Bind him!' the colonel could be heard vociferating.

Captain Mitchell had just the time to glance once at the windows, with three perpendicular bars of iron each and some twenty feet from the ground, as he well knew, before the door flew open and the rush upon him took place. In an incredibly short time he found himself bound with many turns of a hide rope to a high-backed chair, so that his head alone remained free. Not till then did Sotillo, who had been leaning in the doorway trembling visibly, venture again within. The soldiers, picking up from the floor the rifles they had dropped to grapple with the prisoner, filed out of the room. The officers remained leaning on their swords and looking on.

'The watch! the watch!' raved the colonel, pacing to and fro like a tiger in a cage. 'Give me that man's watch.'

It was true, that when searched for arms in the hall downstairs, before being taken into Sotillo's presence, Captain Mitchell had been relieved of his watch and chain; but at the colonel's clamour it was produced quickly enough, a corporal bringing it up, carried carefully in the palms of his joined hands. Sotillo snatched it, and pushed the clenched fist from which it dangled close to Captain Mitchell's face.

'Now then! You arrogant Englishman! You dare to call the soldiers of the army thieves! Behold your watch.'

He flourished his fist as if aiming blows at the prisoner's nose. Captain

Mitchell, helpless as a swathed infant, looked anxiously at the sixty-guinea gold half-chronometer, presented to him years ago by a Committee of Underwriters for saving a ship from total loss by fire. Sotillo, too, seemed to perceive its valuable appearance. He became silent suddenly, stepped aside to the table, and began a careful examination in the light of the candles. He had never seen anything so fine. His officers closed in and craned their necks behind his back.

He became so interested that for an instant he forgot his precious prisoner. There is always something childish in the rapacity of the passionate, clear-minded, Southern races, wanting in the misty idealism of the Northerners, who at the smallest encouragement dream of nothing less than the conquest of the earth. Sotillo was fond of jewels, gold trinkets, of personal adornment. After a moment he turned about, and with a commanding gesture made all his officers fall back. He laid down the watch on the table, then, negligently, pushed his hat over it.

'Ha!' he began, going up very close to the chair. 'You dare call my valiant soldiers of the Esmeralda regiment, thieves. You dare! What impudence! You foreigners come here to rob our country of its wealth. You never have enough! Your audacity knows no bounds.'

He looked towards the officers, amongst whom there was an approving murmur. The older major was moved to declare: 'Si, mi colonel. They are all traitors.'

'I shall say nothing,' continued Sotillo, fixing the motionless and powerless Mitchell with an uneasy stare. 'I shall say nothing of your treacherous attempt to get possession of my revolver to shoot me while I was trying to treat you with consideration you did not deserve. You have forfeited your life. Your only hope is in my clemency.'

He watched for the effect of his words, but there was no obvious sign of fear on Captain Mitchell's face. His white hair was full of dust, which covered also the rest of his helpless person. As if he had heard nothing, he twitched an eyebrow to get rid of a bit of straw which hung amongst the hairs.

Sotillo advanced one leg and put his arms akimbo. 'It is you, Mitchell,' he said, emphatically, 'who are the thief, not my soldiers!' He pointed at his prisoner a forefinger with a long, almond-shaped nail. 'Where is the silver of the San Tomé mine? I ask you, Mitchell, where is the silver that was deposited in this Custom House? Answer me that! You stole it. You were a party to stealing it. It was stolen from the Government. Aha! you think I do not know what I say; but I am up to your foreign tricks. It is gone, the silver! No? Gone in one of your lanchas, you miserable man! How dared you?'

This time he produced his effect. 'How on earth could Sotillo know that?' thought Mitchell. His head, the only part of his body that could move, betrayed his surprise by a sudden jerk.

'Ha! you tremble,' Sotillo shouted, suddenly. 'It is a conspiracy. It is a crime against the State. Did you not know that the silver belongs to the

Republic till the Government claims are satisfied? Where is it? Where have you hidden it, you miserable thief?'

At this question Captain Mitchell's sinking spirits revived. In whatever incomprehensible manner Sotillo had already got his information about the lighter, he had not captured it. That was clear. In his outraged heart, Captain Mitchell had resolved that nothing would induce him to say a word while he remained so disgracefully bound, but his desire to help the escape of the silver made him depart from this resolution. His wits were very much at work. He detected in Sotillo a certain air of doubt, of irresolution.

'That man,' he said to himself, 'is not certain of what he advances.' For all his pomposity in social intercourse, Captain Mitchell could meet the realities of life in a resolute and ready spirit. Now he had got over the first shock of the abominable treatment he was cool and collected enough. The immense contempt he felt for Sotillo steadied him, and he said oracularly, 'No doubt it is well concealed by this time.'

Sotillo, too, had time to cool down. '*Muy bien*, Mitchell,' he said in a cold and threatening manner. 'But can you produce the Government receipt for the royalty and the Custom House permit of embarkation, hey? Can you? No. Then the silver has been removed illegally, and the guilty shall be made to suffer, unless it is produced within five days from this.' He gave orders for the prisoner to be unbound and locked up in one of the smaller rooms downstairs. He walked about the room, moody and silent, till Captain Mitchell, with each of his arms held by a couple of men, stood up, shook himself, and stamped his feet.

'How did you like to be tied up, Mitchell?' he asked, derisively.

'It is the most incredible, abominable use of power!' Captain Mitchell declared in a loud voice. 'And whatever your purpose, you shall gain nothing from it, I can promise you.'

The tall colonel, livid, with his coal-black ringlets and moustache, crouched, as it were, to look into the eyes of the short, thickset, red-faced prisoner with rumpled white hair.

'That we shall see. You shall know my power a little better when I tie you up to a *potalón* outside in the sun for a whole day.' He drew himself up haughtily, and made a sign for Captain Mitchell to be led away.

'What about my watch?' cried Captain Mitchell, hanging back from the efforts of the men pulling him towards the door.

Sotillo turned to his officers. 'No! But only listen to this picaro, caballeros,' he pronounced with affected scorn, and was answered by a chorus of derisive laughter. 'He demands his watch!' . . . He ran up again to Captain Mitchell, for the desire to relieve his feelings by inflicting blows and pain upon this Englishman was very strong within him. 'Your watch! You are a prisoner in war time, Mitchell! In war time! You have no rights and no property! Caramba! The very breath in your body belongs to me. Remember that.'

'Bosh!' said Captain Mitchell, concealing a disagreeable impression.

Down below, in a great hall, with the earthen floor and with a tall mound thrown up by white ants in a corner, the soldiers had kindled a small fire with broken chairs and tables near the arched gateway, through which the faint murmur of the harbour waters on the beach could be heard. While Captain Mitchell was being led down the staircase, an officer passed him, running up to report to Sotillo the capture of more prisoners. A lot of smoke hung about in the vast gloomy place, the fire crackled, and, as if through a haze, Captain Mitchell made out, surrounded by short soldiers with fixed bayonets, the heads of three tall prisoners – the doctor, the engineer-in-chief, and the white leonine mane of old Viola, who stood half-turned away from the others with his chin on his breast and his arms crossed. Mitchell's astonishment knew no bounds. He cried out; the other two exclaimed also. But he hurried on, diagonally, across the big cavern-like hall. Lots of thoughts, surmises, hints of caution, and so on, crowded his head to distraction.

'Is he actually keeping you?' shouted the chief engineer, whose single eyeglass glittered in the firelight.

An officer from the top of the stairs was shouting urgently, 'Bring them all up – all three.'

In the clamour of voices and the rattle of arms, Captain Mitchell made himself heard imperfectly: 'By heavens! the fellow has stolen my watch.'

The engineer-in-chief on the staircase resisted the pressure long enough to shout, 'What? What did you say?'

'My chronometer!' Captain Mitchell yelled violently at the very moment of being thrust head foremost through a small door into a sort of cell, perfectly black, and so narrow that he fetched up against the opposite wall. The door had been instantly slammed. He knew where they had put him. This was the strong room of the Custom House, whence the silver had been removed only a few hours earlier. It was almost as narrow as a corridor, with a small square aperture, barred by a heavy grating, at the distant end. Captain Mitchell staggered for a few steps, then sat down on the earthen floor with his back to the wall. Nothing, not even a gleam of light from anywhere, interfered with Captain Mitchell's meditation. He did some hard but not very extensive thinking. It was not of a gloomy cast. The old sailor, with all his small weaknesses and absurdities, was constitutionally incapable of entertaining for any length of time a fear of his personal safety. It was not so much firmness of soul as the lack of a certain kind of imagination – the kind whose undue development caused intense suffering to Señor Hirsch; that sort of imagination which adds the blind terror of bodily suffering and of death, envisaged as an accident to the body alone, strictly – to all the other apprehensions on which the sense of one's existence is based. Unfortunately, Captain Mitchell had not much penetration of any kind; characteristic, illuminating trifles of expression, action, or movement, escaped him completely. He was too pompously and innocently aware of his own existence to observe that of others. For instance, he could not believe that Sotillo had been really afraid of him, and this simply because it would never have entered into his head to shoot anyone except in the most pressing case of self-defence. Anybody could see he was not a murdering kind of man, he reflected quite gravely. Then why this preposterous and insulting charge? he asked himself. But thoughts mainly clung around the astounding and unanswerable question: how the devil had the fellow got to know that the silver had gone off in the lighter? It was obvious that he had not captured it. And, obviously, he could not have captured it! In this last conclusion Captain Mitchell was misled by the assumption drawn from his observation of the weather during his long vigil on the wharf. He thought that there had been much more wind than usual that night in the gulf; whereas, as a matter of fact, the reverse was the case.

'How in the name of all that's marvellous did that confounded fellow get wind of the affair?' was the first question he asked directly after the bang, clatter, and flash of the open door (which was closed again almost before he could lift his dropped head) informed him that he had a companion of captivity. Dr Monygham's voice stopped muttering curses in English and Spanish.

'Is that you, Mitchell?' he made answer, surlily. 'I struck my forehead against this confounded wall with enough force to fell an ox. Where are you?'

Captain Mitchell, accustomed to the darkness, could make out the doctor stretching out his hands blindly.

'I am sitting here on the floor. Don't fall over my legs,' Captain Mitchell's voice announced with great dignity of tone. The doctor, entreated not to walk about in the dark, sank down to the ground, too. The two prisoners of Sotillo, with their heads nearly touching, began to exchange confidences.

'Yes,' the doctor related in a low tone to Captain Mitchell's vehement curiosity, 'we have been nabbed in old Viola's place. It seems that one of their pickets, commanded by an officer, pushed as far as the town gate. They had orders not to enter, but to bring along every soul they could find on the plain. We had been talking in there with the door open, and no doubt they saw the glimmer of our light. They must have been making their approaches for some time. The engineer laid himself on a bench in a recess by the fireplace, and I went upstairs to have a look. I hadn't heard any sound from there for a long time. Old Viola, as soon as he saw me come up, lifted his arm for silence. I stole in on tiptoe. By Jove, his wife was lying down and had gone to sleep. The woman had actually dropped off to sleep! "Señor Doctor," Viola whispers to me, "it looks as if her oppression was going to get better." "Yes," I said, very much surprised; "your wife is a wonderful woman, Giorgio." Just then a shot was fired in the kitchen, which made us jump and cower as if at a thunderclap. It seems that the party of soldiers had stolen quite close up, and one of them had crept up to the door. He looked in, thought there was no one there, and, holding his rifle ready, entered quietly. The chief told me that he had just closed his eyes for a moment.

When he opened them, he saw the man already in the middle of the room peering into the dark corners. The chief was so startled that, without thinking, he made one leap from the recess right out in front of the fireplace. The soldier, no less startled, up with his rifle and pulls the trigger, deafening and singeing the engineer, but in his flurry missing him completely. But, look what happens! At the noise of the report the sleeping woman sat up, as if moved by a spring, with a shriek, "The children, Gian' Battista! Save the children!" I have it in my ears now. It was the truest cry of distress I ever heard. I stood as if paralysed, but the old husband ran across to the bedside, stretching out his hands. She clung to them! I could see her eyes go glazed; the old fellow lowered her down on the pillows and then looked round at me. She was dead!

'All this took less than five minutes, and then I ran down to see what was the matter. It was no use thinking of any resistance. Nothing we two could say availed with the officer, so I volunteered to go up with a couple of soldiers and fetch down old Viola. He was sitting at the foot of the bed, looking at his wife's face, and did not seem to hear what I said; but after I had pulled the sheet over her head, he got up and followed us downstairs quietly, in a sort of thoughtful way. They marched us off along the road, leaving the door open and the candle burning. The chief engineer strode on without a word, but I looked back once or twice at the feeble gleam. After we had gone some considerable distance, the Garibaldino, who was walking by my side, suddenly said, "I have buried many men on battlefields on this continent. The priests talk of consecrated ground! Bah! All the earth made by God is holy; but the sea, which knows nothing of kings and priests and tyrants, is the holiest of all. Doctor! I should like to bury her in the sea. No mummeries, candles, incense, no holy water mumbled over by priests. The spirit of liberty is upon the waters." . . . Amazing old man. He was saying all this in an undertone as if talking to himself.'

'Yes, yes,' interrupted Captain Mitchell, impatiently. 'Poor old chap! But have you any idea how that ruffian Sotillo obtained his information? He did not get hold of any of our Cargadores who helped with the truck, did he? But no, it is impossible! These were picked men we've had in our boats for these five years, and I paid them myself specially for the job, with instructions to keep out of the way for twenty-four hours at least. I saw them with my own eyes march on with the Italians to the railway yards. The chief promised to give them rations as long as they wanted to remain there.'

'Well,' said the doctor, slowly, 'I can tell you that you may say goodbye for ever to your best lighter, and to the Capataz of Cargadores.'

At this, Captain Mitchell scrambled up to his feet in the excess of his excitement. The doctor, without giving him time to exclaim, stated briefly the part played by Hirsch during the night.

Captain Mitchell was overcome. 'Drowned!' he muttered, in a bewildered and appalled whisper. 'Drowned!' Afterwards he kept still, apparently listening, but too absorbed in the news of the catastrophe to follow the doctor's narrative with attention.

The doctor had taken up an attitude of perfect ignorance, till at last Sotillo was induced to have Hirsch brought in to repeat the whole story, which was got out of him again with the greatest difficulty, because every moment he would break out into lamentations. At last, Hirsch was led away, looking more dead than alive, and shut up in one of the upstairs rooms to be close at hand. Then the doctor, keeping up his character of a man not admitted to the inner councils of the San Tomé Administration, remarked that the story sounded incredible. Of course, he said, he couldn't tell what had been the action of the Europeans, as he had been exclusively occupied with his own work in looking after the wounded, and also in attending Don José Avellanos. He had succeeded in assuming so well a tone of impartial indifference, that Sotillo seemed to be completely deceived. Till then a show of regular enquiry had been kept up; one of the officers sitting at the table wrote down the questions and the answers, the others, lounging about the room, listened attentively, puffing at their long cigars and keeping their eyes on the doctor. But at that point Sotillo ordered everybody out.

Chapter 3

Directly they were alone, the colonel's severe official manner changed. He rose and approached the doctor. His eyes shone with rapacity and hope; he became confidential. 'The silver might have been indeed put on board the lighter, but it was not conceivable that it should have been taken out to sea.' The doctor, watching every word, nodded slightly, smoking with apparent relish the cigar which Sotillo had offered him as a sign of his friendly intentions. The doctor's manner of cold detachment from the rest of the Europeans led Sotillo on, till, from conjecture to conjecture, he arrived at hinting that in his opinion this was a put-up job on the part of Charles Gould, in order to get hold of that immense treasure all to himself. The doctor, observant and self-possessed, muttered, 'He is very capable of that.'

Here Captain Mitchell exclaimed with amazement, amusement, and indignation, 'You said that of Charles Gould!' Disgust, and even some suspicion, crept into his tone, for to him, too, as to other Europeans, there appeared to be something dubious about the doctor's personality.

'What on earth made you say that to this watch-stealing scoundrel?' he asked. 'What's the object of an infernal lie of that sort? That confounded pickpocket was quite capable of believing you.'

He snorted. For a time the doctor remained silent in the dark.

'Yes, that is exactly what I did say,' he uttered at last, in a tone which would have made it clear enough to a third party that the pause was not of a reluctant but of a reflective character. Captain Mitchell thought that he had never heard anything so brazenly impudent in his life.

'Well, well!' he muttered to himself, but he had not the heart to voice his thoughts. They were swept away by others full of astonishment and regret. A heavy sense of discomfiture crushed him: the loss of the silver, the death of Nostromo, which was really quite a blow to his sensibilities, because he had become attached to his Capataz as people get attached to their inferiors from love of ease and almost unconscious gratitude. And when he thought of Decoud being drowned, too, his sensibility was almost overcome by this miserable end. What a heavy blow for that poor young woman! Captain Mitchell did not belong to the species of crabbed old bachelors; on the contrary, he liked to see young men paying attentions to young women. It seemed to him a natural and proper thing. Proper especially. As to sailors, it was different; it was not their place to marry, he maintained, but it was on moral grounds as a matter of self-denial, for, he explained, life on board ship is not fit for a woman even at best, and if you leave her on shore, first of all it is not fair, and next she either suffers from it or doesn't care a bit, which, in both cases, is bad. He couldn't have told what upset him most – Charles Gould's immense material loss, the death of Nostromo, which was a heavy loss to himself, or the idea of that beautiful and accomplished young woman being plunged into mourning.

'Yes,' the doctor, who had been apparently reflecting some more, began again, 'he believed me right enough. I thought he would have hugged me. "Si, si," he said, "he will write to that partner of his, the rich Americano in San Francisco, that it is all lost. Why not? There is enough to share with many people." '

'But this is perfectly imbecile!' cried Captain Mitchell.

The doctor remarked that Sotillo *was* imbecile, and that his imbecility was ingenious enough to lead him completely astray. He had helped him only but a little way.

'I mentioned,' the doctor said, 'in a sort of casual way, that treasure is generally buried in the earth rather than being set afloat upon the sea. At this my Sotillo slapped his forehead. "*Por Dios*, yes," he said; "they must have buried it on the shores of this harbour somewhere before they sailed out." '

'Heavens and earth!' muttered Captain Mitchell, 'I should not have believed that anybody could be ass enough – ' He paused, then went on mournfully: 'But what's the good of all this? It would have been a clever enough lie if the lighter had been still afloat. It would have kept that inconceivable idiot perhaps from sending out the steamer to cruise in the gulf. That was the danger that worried me no end.' Captain Mitchell sighed profoundly.

'I had an object,' the doctor pronounced, slowly.

'Had you?' muttered Captain Mitchell. 'Well, that's lucky, or else I would have thought that you went on fooling him for the fun of the thing. And perhaps that was your object. Well, I must say I personally wouldn't condescend to that sort of thing. It is not to my taste. No, no. Blackening a friend's character is not my idea of fun, if it were to fool the greatest blackguard on earth.'

Had it not been for Captain Mitchell's depression, caused by the fatal news, his disgust of Dr Monygham would have taken a more outspoken shape; but he thought to himself that now it really did not matter what that man, whom he had never liked, would say and do.

'I wonder,' he grumbled, 'why they have shut us up together, or why Sotillo should have shut you up at all, since it seems to me you have been fairly chummy up there?'

'Yes, I wonder?' said the doctor, grimly.

Captain Mitchell's heart was so heavy that he would have preferred for the time being a complete solitude to the best of company. But any company would have been preferable to the doctor's, at whom he had always looked askance as a sort of beachcomber of superior intelligence partly reclaimed from his abased state. That feeling led him to ask: 'What has that ruffian done with the other two?'

'The chief engineer he would have let go in any case,' said the doctor. 'He wouldn't like to have a quarrel with the railway upon his hands. Not just yet, at any rate. I don't think, Captain Mitchell, that you understand exactly what Sotillo's position is – '

'I don't see why I should bother my head about it,' snarled Captain Mitchell.

'No,' assented the doctor, with the same grim composure. 'I don't see why you should. It wouldn't help a single human being in the world if you thought ever so hard upon any subject whatever.'

'No,' said Captain Mitchell, simply, and with evident depression. 'A man locked up in a confounded dark hole is not much use to anybody.'

'As to old Viola,' the doctor continued, as though he had not heard, 'Sotillo released him for the same reason he is presently going to release you.'

'Eh? What?' exclaimed Captain Mitchell, staring like an owl in the darkness. 'What is there in common between me and old Viola? More likely because the old chap has no watch and chain for the pickpocket to steal. And I tell you what, Dr Monygham,' he went on with rising choler, 'he will find it more difficult than he thinks to get rid of me. He will burn his fingers over that job yet, I can tell you. To begin with, I won't go without my watch, and as to the rest – we shall see. I dare say it is no great matter for you to be locked up. But Joe Mitchell is a different kind of man, sir. I don't mean to submit tamely to insult and robbery. I am a public character, sir.'

And then Captain Mitchell became aware that the bars of the opening had become visible, a black grating upon a square of grey. The coming of the day silenced Captain Mitchell as if by the reflection that now in all the future days he would be deprived of the invaluable services of his Capataz. He leaned against the wall with his arms folded on his breast, and the doctor walked up and down the whole length of the place with his peculiar hobbling gait, as if slinking about on damaged feet. At the end furthest from the grating he would be lost altogether in the darkness. Only the slight limping shuffle could be heard. There was an air of moody detachment in that painful prowl kept up without a pause. When the door of the prison was suddenly flung open and his name shouted out he showed no surprise. He swerved sharply in his walk, and passed out at once, as though much depended upon his speed; but Captain Mitchell remained for some time with his shoulders against the wall, quite undecided in the bitterness of his spirit whether it wouldn't be better to refuse to stir a limb in the way of protest. He had half a mind to get himself carried out, but after the officer at the door had shouted three or four times in tones of remonstrance and surprise he condescended to walk out.

Sotillo's manner had changed. The colonel's offhand civility was slightly irresolute, as though he were in doubt if civility were the proper course in this case. He observed Captain Mitchell attentively before he spoke from the big armchair behind the table in a condescending voice: 'I have concluded not to detain you, Señor Mitchell. I am of a forgiving disposition. I make allowances. Let this be a lesson to you, however.'

The peculiar dawn of Sulaco, which seems to break far away to the westward and creep back into the shade of the mountains, mingled with the reddish light of the candles. Captain Mitchell, in sign of contempt and indifference, let his eyes roam all over the room, and he gave a hard stare to the doctor, perched already on the casement of one of the windows, with his eyelids lowered, careless and thoughtful – or perhaps ashamed.

Sotillo, ensconced in the vast armchair, remarked, 'I should have thought that the feelings of a caballero would have dictated to you an appropriate reply.'

He waited for it, but Captain Mitchell remaining mute, more from extreme resentment than from reasoned intention, Sotillo hesitated, glanced towards the doctor, who looked up and nodded, then went on with a slight effort: 'Here, Señor Mitchell, is your watch. Learn how hasty and unjust has been your judgment of my patriotic soldiers.'

Lying back in his seat, he extended his arm over the table and pushed the watch away slightly. Captain Mitchell walked up with undisguised eagerness, put it to his ear, then slipped it into his pocket coolly.

Sotillo seemed to overcome an immense reluctance. Again he looked aside at the doctor, who stared at him unwinkingly.

But as Captain Mitchell was turning away, without as much as a nod or a glance, he hastened to say: 'You may go and wait downstairs for the señor doctor, whom I am going to liberate, too. You foreigners are insignificant, to my mind.'

He forced a slight, discordant laugh out of himself, while Captain Mitchell, for the first time, looked at him with some interest.

'The law shall take note later on of your transgressions,' Sotillo hurried on. 'But as for me, you can live free, unguarded, unobserved. Do you hear, Señor Mitchell? You may depart to your affairs. You are beneath my notice. My attention is claimed by matters of the very highest importance.'

Captain Mitchell was very nearly provoked to an answer. It displeased him to be liberated insultingly; but want of sleep, prolonged anxieties, a profound disappointment with the fatal ending of the silver-saving business weighed upon his spirits. It was as much as he could do to conceal his uneasiness, not about himself perhaps, but about things in general. It occurred to him distinctly that something underhand was going on. As he went out he ignored the doctor pointedly.

'A brute!' said Sotillo, as the door shut.

Dr Monygham slipped off the window-sill, thrusting his hands into the pockets of the long, grey dust coat he was wearing, and made a few steps into the room.

Sotillo got up, too, and, putting himself in the way, examined him from head to foot.

'So your countrymen do not confide in you much, señor doctor. They do not love you, eh? Why is that, I wonder?'

The doctor, lifting his head, answered by a long, lifeless stare and the words, 'Perhaps because I have lived too long in Costaguana.'

Sotillo had a gleam of white teeth under the black moustache.

'Aha! But you love yourself,' he said, encouragingly.

'If you leave them alone,' the doctor said, looking with the same lifeless stare at Sotillo's handsome face, 'they will betray themselves very soon. Meantime, I may try to make Don Carlos speak?'

'Ah! señor doctor,' said Sotillo, wagging his head, 'you are a man of quick intelligence. We were made to understand each other.' He turned away. He could bear no longer that expressionless and motionless stare, which seemed to have a sort of impenetrable emptiness like the black depth of an abyss.

Even in a man utterly devoid of moral sense there remains an appreciation of rascality which, being conventional, is perfectly clear. Sotillo thought that Dr Monygham, so different from all Europeans, was ready to sell his countrymen and Charles Gould, his employer, for some share of the San Tomé silver. Sotillo did not despise him for that. The colonel's want of moral sense was of a profound and innocent character. It bordered upon stupidity, moral stupidity. Nothing that served his ends could appear to him really reprehensible. Nevertheless, he despised Dr Monygham. He had for him an immense and satisfactory contempt. He despised him with all his heart because he did not mean to let the doctor have any reward at all. He despised him, not as a man without faith and honour, but as a fool. Dr Monygham's insight into his character had deceived Sotillo completely. Therefore he thought the doctor a fool.

Since his arrival in Sulaco the colonel's ideas had undergone some modification.

He no longer wished for a political career in Montero's administration. He had always doubted the safety of that course. Since he had learned from the chief engineer that at daylight most likely he would be confronted by Pedro Montero his misgivings on that point had considerably increased. The guerrillero brother of the general – the Pedrito of popular speech – had a reputation of his own. He wasn't safe to deal with. Sotillo had vaguely planned seizing not only the treasure but the town itself, and then negotiating at leisure. But in the face of facts learned from the chief engineer (who had frankly disclosed to him the whole situation) his audacity, never of a very dashing kind, had been replaced by a most cautious hesitation.

'An army – an army crossed the mountains under Pedrito already,' he had repeated, unable to hide his consternation. 'If it had not been that I am given the news by a man of your position I would never have believed it. Astonishing!'

'An armed force,' corrected the engineer, suavely.

His aim was attained. It was to keep Sulaco clear of any armed occupation for a few hours longer, to let those whom fear impelled leave the town. In the general dismay there were families hopeful enough to fly upon the road towards Los Hatos, which was left open by the withdrawal of the armed rabble under Señores Fuentes and Gamacho, to Rincon, with their enthusiastic welcome for Pedro Montero. It was a hasty and risky exodus, and it was said that Hernandez, occupying with his band the woods about Los Hatos, was receiving the fugitives. That a good many people he knew were contemplating such a flight had been well known to the chief engineer.

Father Corbelàn's efforts in the cause of that most pious robber had not been altogether fruitless. The political chief of Sulaco had yielded at the last moment to the urgent entreaties of the priest, had signed a provisional nomination appointing Hernandez a general, and calling upon him officially in this new capacity to preserve order in the town. The fact is that the political chief, seeing the situation desperate, did not care what he signed. It was the last official document he signed before he left the palace of the Intendencia for the refuge of the OSN Company's office. But even had he meant his act to be effective it was already too late. The riot which he feared and expected broke out in less than an hour after Father Corbelàn had left him. Indeed, Father Corbelàn, who had appointed a meeting with Nostromo in the Dominican Convent, where he had his residence in one of the cells, never managed to reach the place. From the Intendencia he had gone straight on to the Avellanos's house to tell his brother-in-law, and though he stayed there no more than half an hour he had found himself cut off from his ascetic abode. Nostromo, after waiting there for some time, watching uneasily the increasing uproar in the street, had made his way to the offices of the *Porvenir*, and stayed there till daylight, as Decoud had mentioned in the letter to his sister. Thus the Capataz, instead of riding towards the Los Hatos woods as bearer of Hernandez's nomination, had remained in town to save the life of the President Dictator, to assist in repressing the outbreak of the mob, and at last to sail out with the silver of the mine.

But Father Corbelàn, escaping to Hernandez, had the document in his pocket, a piece of official writing turning a bandit into a general in a memorable last official act of the Ribierist party, whose watchwords were honesty, peace, and progress. Probably neither the priest nor the bandit saw the irony of it. Father Corbelàn must have found messengers to send into the town, for early on the second day of the disturbances there were rumours of Hernandez being on the road to Los Hatos ready to receive those who would put themselves under his protection. A strange-looking horseman, elderly and audacious, had appeared in the town, riding slowly while his eyes examined the fronts of the houses, as though he had never seen such high buildings before. Before the cathedral he had dismounted, and, kneeling in the middle of the Plaza, his bridle over his arm and his hat lying in front of him on the ground, had bowed his head, crossing himself and beating his breast for some little time. Remounting his horse, with a fearless but not unfriendly look round the little gathering formed about his public devotions, he had asked for the Casa Avellanos. A score of hands were extended in answer, with fingers pointing up the Calle de la Constitucion.

The horseman had gone on with only a glance of casual curiosity upwards to the windows of the Amarilla Club at the corner. His stentorian voice shouted periodically in the empty street, 'Which is the Casa Avellanos?' till an answer came from the scared porter, and he disappeared under the gate. The letter he was bringing, written by Father Corbelàn with a pencil by the campfire of Hernandez, was addressed to Don José, of whose critical state the priest was not aware. Antonia read it, and, after consulting Charles Gould, sent it on for the information of the gentlemen garrisoning the Amarilla Club. For herself, her mind was made up; she would rejoin her uncle; she would entrust the last day – the last hours perhaps – of her father's life to the keeping of the bandit, whose existence was a protest against the irresponsible tyranny of all parties alike, against the moral darkness of the land. The gloom of Los Hatos woods was preferable; a life of hardships in the train of a robber band less debasing. Antonia embraced with all her soul her uncle's obstinate defiance of misfortune. It was grounded in the belief in the man whom she loved.

In his message the Vicar-General answered upon his head for Hernandez's fidelity. As to his power, he pointed out that he had remained unsubdued for so many years. In that letter Decoud's idea of the new Occidental State (whose flourishing and stable condition is a matter of common knowledge now) was for the first time made public and used as an argument. Hernandez, ex-bandit and the last general of Ribierist creation, was confident of being able to hold the tract of country between the woods of Los Hatos and the coast range till that devoted patriot, Don Martin Decoud, could bring General Barrios back to Sulaco for the reconquest of the town.

'Heaven itself wills it. Providence is on our side,' wrote Father Corbelàn; there was no time to reflect upon or to controvert his statement; and if the discussion started upon the reading of that letter in the Amarilla Club was violent, it was also shortlived. In the general bewilderment of the collapse some jumped at the idea with joyful astonishment as upon the amazing discovery of a new hope. Others became fascinated by the prospect of immediate personal safety for their women and children. The majority caught at it as a drowning man catches at a straw. Father Corbelàn was unexpectedly offering them a refuge from Pedrito Montero with his llaneros allied to Señores Fuentes and Gamacho with their armed rabble.

All the latter part of the afternoon an animated discussion went on in the big rooms of the Amarilla Club. Even those members posted at the windows with rifles and carbines to guard the end of the street in case of an offensive return of the populace shouted their opinions and arguments over their shoulders. As dusk fell Don Juste Lopez, inviting those caballeros who were of his way of thinking to follow him, withdrew into the corridor, where at a little table in the light of two candles he busied himself in composing an address, or rather a solemn declaration to be presented to Pedrito Montero by a deputation of such members of Assembly as had elected to remain in town. His idea was to propitiate him in order to save the form at least of parliamentary institutions. Seated before a blank sheet of paper, a goose-quill pen in his hand and surged upon from all sides, he turned to the right and to the left, repeating with solemn insistence: 'Caballeros, a moment of silence! A moment of silence! We ought to make it clear that we bow in all good faith to the accomplished facts.'

The utterance of that phrase seemed to give him a melancholy satisfaction. The hubbub of voices round him was growing strained and hoarse. In the sudden pauses the excited grimacing of the faces would sink all at once into the stillness of profound dejection.

Meantime, the exodus had begun. Carretas full of ladies and children rolled swaying across the Plaza, with men walking or riding by their side; mounted parties followed on mules and horses; the poorest were setting out on foot, men and women carrying bundles, clasping babies in their arms, leading old people, dragging along the bigger children. When Charles Gould, after leaving the doctor and the engineer at the Casa Viola, entered the town by the harbour gate, all those that had meant to go were gone, and the others had barricaded themselves in their houses. In the whole dark street there was only one spot of flickering lights and moving figures, where the Señor Administrador recognised his wife's carriage waiting at the door of the Avellanos's house. He rode up, almost unnoticed, and looked on without a word while some of his own servants came out of the gate carrying Don José Avellanos, who, with closed eyes and motionless features, appeared perfectly lifeless. His wife and Antonia walked on each side of the improvised stretcher, which was put at once into the carriage. The two women embraced; while from the other side of the landau Father Corbelàn's emissary, with his ragged beard all streaked with grey, and high, bronzed cheek-bones, stared, sitting upright in the saddle. Then Antonia, dry-eyed, got in by the side of the stretcher, and, after making the sign of the cross rapidly, lowered a thick veil upon her face. The servants and the three or four neighbours who had come to assist, stood back, uncovering their heads. On the box, Ignacio, resigned now to driving all night (and to having perhaps his throat cut before daylight) looked back surlily over his shoulder.

'Drive carefully,' cried Mrs Gould in a tremulous voice.

'Sí, carefully, sí niña,' he mumbled, chewing his lips, his round leathery cheeks quivering. And the landau rolled slowly out of the light.

'I will see them as far as the ford,' said Charles Gould to his wife. She stood on the edge of the sidewalk with her hands clasped lightly, and nodded to him as he followed after the carriage. And now the windows of the Amarilla Club were dark. The last spark of resistance had died out. Turning his head at the corner, Charles Gould saw his wife crossing over to their own gate in the lighted patch of the street. One of their neighbours, a well-known merchant and landowner of the province, followed at her elbow, talking with great gestures. As she passed in all the lights went out in the street, which remained dark and empty from end to end.

The houses of the vast Plaza were lost in the night. High up, like a star, there was a small gleam in one of the towers of the cathedral; and the equestrian statue gleamed pale against the black trees of the Alameda, like a ghost of royalty haunting the scenes of revolution. The rare prowlers they met ranged themselves against the wall. Beyond the last houses the carriage rolled noiselessly on the soft cushion of dust, and with a greater obscurity a feeling of freshness seemed to fall from the foliage of the trees bordering the country road. The emissary from Hernandez's camp pushed his horse close to Charles Gould.

'Caballero,' he said in an interested voice, 'you are he whom they call the King of Sulaco, the master of the mine? Is it not so?'

'Yes, I am the master of the mine,' answered Charles Gould.

The man cantered for a time in silence, then said, 'I have a brother, a sereno in your service in the San Tomé valley. You have proved yourself a just man. There had been no wrong done to anyone since you called upon the people to work in the mountains. My brother says that no official of the Government, no oppressor of the Campo, had been seen on your side of the stream. Your own officials do not oppress the people in the gorge. Doubtless they are afraid of your severity. You are a just man and a powerful one,' he added.

He spoke in an abrupt, independent tone, but evidently he was communicative with a purpose. He told Charles Gould that he had been a ranchero in one of the lower valleys, far south, a neighbour of Hernandez in the old days, and godfather to his eldest boy; one of those who joined him in his resistance to the recruiting raid which was the beginning of all their misfortunes. It was he that, when his compadre had been carried off, had buried his wife and children, murdered by the soldiers.

'Si, señor,' he muttered, hoarsely, 'I and two or three others, the lucky ones left at liberty, buried them all in one grave near the ashes of their ranch, under the tree that had shaded its roof.'

It was to him, too, that Hernandez came after he had deserted, three years afterwards. He had still his uniform on with the sergeant's stripes on the sleeve, and the blood of his colonel upon his hands and breast. Three troopers followed him, of those who had started in pursuit but had ridden on for liberty. And he told Charles Gould how he and a few friends, seeing those soldiers, lay in ambush behind some rocks ready to pull the trigger on them, when he recognised his compadre and jumped up from cover, shouting his name, because he knew that Hernandez could not have been coming back on an errand of injustice and oppression. Those three soldiers, together with the party who lay behind the rocks, had formed the nucleus of the famous band; and he, the narrator, had been the favourite lieutenant of Hernandez for many, many years. He mentioned proudly that the officials had put a price upon his head, too; but it did not prevent it getting sprinkled with grey upon his shoulders. And now he had lived long enough to see his compadre made a general.

He had a burst of muffled laughter. 'And now from robbers we have become soldiers. But look, Caballero, at those who made us soldiers and him a general! Look at these people!'

Ignacio shouted. The light of the carriage lamps, running along the nopal hedges that crowned the bank on each side, flashed upon the scared faces of people standing aside in the road, sunk deep, like an English country lane, into the soft soil of the Campo. They cowered; their eyes glistened very big for a second; and then the light, running on, fell upon the half-denuded roots of a big tree, on another stretch of nopal hedge, caught up another bunch of faces glaring back apprehensively. Three women – of whom one was carrying a child – and a couple of men in civilian dress – one armed with a sabre and another with a gun – were grouped about a donkey carrying two bundles tied up in blankets. Further on Ignacio shouted again to pass a carreta, a long wooden box on two high wheels, with the door at the back swinging open. Some ladies in it must have recognised the white mules, because they screamed out, 'Is it you, Doña Emilia?'

At the turn of the road the glare of a big fire filled the short stretch vaulted over by the branches meeting overhead. Near the ford of a shallow stream a roadside rancho of woven rushes and a roof of grass had been set on fire by accident, and the flames, roaring viciously, lit up an open space blocked with horses, mules, and a distracted, shouting crowd of people. When Ignacio pulled up, several ladies on foot assailed the carriage, begging Antonia for a seat. To their clamour she answered by pointing silently to her father.

'I must leave you here,' said Charles Gould, in the uproar. The flames leaped up sky-high, and in the recoil from the scorching heat across the road the stream of fugitives pressed against the carriage. A middle-aged lady dressed in black silk, but with a coarse manta over her head and a rough branch for a stick in her hand, staggered against the front wheel. Two young girls, frightened and silent, were clinging to her arms. Charles Gould knew her very well.

'*Misericordia!* We are getting terribly bruised in this crowd!' she exclaimed, smiling up courageously to him. 'We have started on foot. All our servants ran away yesterday to join the democrats. We are going to put ourselves under the protection of Father Corbelàn, of your sainted uncle, Antonia. He has wrought a miracle in the heart of a most merciless robber. A miracle!'

She raised her voice gradually up to a scream as she was borne along by the pressure of people getting out of the way of some carts coming up out of the ford at a gallop, with loud yells and cracking of whips. Great masses of sparks mingled with black smoke flew over the road; the bamboos of the walls detonated in the fire with the sound of an irregular fusillade. And then the bright blaze sank suddenly, leaving only a red dusk crowded with aimless dark shadows drifting in contrary directions; the noise of voices seemed to die away with the flame; and the tumult of heads, arms, quarrelling, and imprecations passed on fleeing into the darkness.

'I must leave you now,' repeated Charles Gould to Antonia. She turned her head slowly and uncovered her face. The emissary and compadre of Hernandez spurred his horse close up.

'Has not the master of the mine any message to send to Hernandez, the master of the Campo?'

The truth of the comparison struck Charles Gould heavily. In his determined purpose he held the mine, and the indomitable bandit held the Campo by the same precarious tenure. They were equals before the lawlessness of the land. It was impossible to disentangle one's activity from its debasing contacts. A close-meshed net of crime and corruption lay upon the whole country. An immense and weary discouragement sealed his lips for a time.

'You are a just man,' urged the emissary of Hernandez. 'Look at those people who made my compadre a general and have turned us all into soldiers. Look at those oligarchs fleeing for life, with only the clothes on their backs. My compadre does not think of that, but our followers may be wondering greatly, and I would speak for them to you. Listen, señor! For many months now the Campo has been our own. We need ask no man for anything; but soldiers must have their pay to live honestly when the wars are over. It is believed that your soul is so just that a prayer from you would cure the sickness of every beast, like the orison of the upright judge. Let me have some words from your lips that would act like a charm upon the doubts of our *partido*, where all are men.'

'Do you hear what he says?' Charles Gould said in English to Antonia.

'Forgive us our misery!' she exclaimed, hurriedly. 'It is your character that is the inexhaustible treasure which may save us all yet; your character, Carlos, not your wealth. I entreat you to give this man your word that you will accept any arrangement my uncle may make with their chief. One word. He will want no more.'

On the site of the roadside hut there remained nothing but an enormous heap of embers, throwing afar a darkening red glow, in which Antonia's face appeared deeply flushed with excitement. Charles Gould, with only a short hesitation, pronounced the required pledge. He was like a man who had ventured on a precipitous path with no room to turn, where the only chance of safety is to press forward. At that moment he understood it thoroughly as he looked down at Don José stretched out, hardly breathing, by the side of the erect Antonia, vanquished in a lifelong struggle with the powers of moral darkness, whose stagnant depths breed monstrous crimes and monstrous illusions. In a few words the emissary from Hernandez expressed his complete satisfaction. Stoically Antonia lowered her veil, resisting the longing to enquire about Decoud's escape. But Ignacio leered morosely over his shoulder.

'Take a good look at the mules, *mi amo*,' he grumbled. 'You shall never see them again!'

Chapter 4

Charles Gould turned towards the town. Before him jagged peaks of the Sierra came out all black in the clear dawn. Here and there a muffled lépero whisked round the corner of a grass-grown street before the ringing hoofs of his horse. Dogs barked behind the walls of the gardens; and with the colourless light the chill of the snows seemed to fall from the mountains upon the disjointed pavements and the shuttered houses with broken cornices and the plaster peeling in patches between the flat pilasters of the fronts. The daybreak struggled with the gloom under the arcades on the Plaza, with no signs of country people disposing their goods for the day's market, piles of fruit, bundles of vegetables ornamented with flowers, on low benches under enormous mat umbrellas; with no cheery early morning bustle of villagers, women, children, and loaded donkeys. Only a few scattered knots of revolutionists stood in the vast space, looking all one way from under their slouched hats for some sign of news from Rincon. The largest of those groups turned about like one man as Charles Gould passed, and shouted, *'Viva la libertad!'* after him in a menacing tone.

Charles Gould rode on, and turned into the archway of his house. In the patio littered with straw, a practicante, one of Dr Monygham's native assistants, sat on the ground with his back against the rim of the fountain, fingering a guitar discreetly, while two girls of the lower class, standing up before him, shuffled their feet a little and waved their arms, humming a popular dance tune. Most of the wounded during the two days of rioting had been taken away already by their friends and relations, but several figures could be seen sitting up balancing their bandaged heads in time to the music. Charles Gould dismounted. A sleepy mozo coming out of the bakery door took hold of the horse's bridle; the practicante endeavoured to conceal his guitar hastily; the girls, unabashed, stepped back smiling; and Charles Gould, on his way to the staircase, glanced into a dark corner of the patio at another group, a mortally wounded Cargador with a woman kneeling by his side; she mumbled prayers rapidly, trying at the same time to force a piece of orange between the stiffening lips of the dying man.

The cruel futility of things stood unveiled in the levity and sufferings of that incorrigible people; the cruel futility of lives and of deaths thrown away in the vain endeavour to attain an enduring solution of the problem. Unlike Decoud, Charles Gould could not play lightly a part in a tragic farce. It was tragic enough for him in all conscience, but he could see no farcical element. He suffered too much under a conviction of irremediable folly. He was too severely practical and too idealistic to look upon its terrible humours with amusement, as Martin Decoud, the imaginative materialist, was able to do in the dry light of his scepticism. To him, as to all of us, the compromises with his conscience appeared uglier than ever in the light of failure. His taciturnity, assumed with a purpose, had prevented him from tampering openly with his thoughts; but the Gould Concession had insidiously corrupted his judgment. He might have known, he said to himself, leaning over the balustrade of the corridor, that Ribierism could never come to anything. The mine had corrupted his judgment by making him sick of bribing and intriguing merely to have his work left alone from day to day. Like his father, he did not like to be robbed. It exasperated him. He had persuaded himself that, apart from higher considerations, the backing up of Don José's hopes of reform was good business. He had gone forth into the senseless fray as his poor uncle, whose sword hung on the wall of his study, had gone forth – in the defence of the commonest decencies of organised society. Only his weapon was the wealth of the mine, more far-reaching and subtle than an honest blade of steel fitted into a simple brass guard.

More dangerous to the wielder, too, this weapon of wealth, double-edged with the cupidity and misery of mankind, steeped in all the voices of self-indulgence in a concoction of poisonous roots, tainting the very cause for which it is drawn, always ready to turn awkwardly in the hand. There was nothing for it now but to go on using it. But he promised himself to see it shattered into small bits before he let it be wrenched from his grasp.

After all, with his English parentage and English upbringing, he perceived that he was an adventurer in Costaguana, the descendant of adventurers enlisted in a foreign legion, of men who had sought fortune in a revolutionary war, who had planned revolutions, who had believed in revolutions. For all the uprightness of his character, he had something of an adventurer's easy morality which takes count of personal risk in the ethical appraising of his action. He was prepared, if need be, to blow up the whole San Tomé mountain sky high out of the territory of the Republic. This resolution expressed the tenacity of his character, the remorse of that subtle conjugal infidelity through which his wife was no longer the sole mistress of his thoughts, something of his father's imaginative weakness, and something, too, of the spirit of a buccaneer throwing a lighted match into the magazine rather than surrender his ship.

Down below in the patio the wounded Cargador had breathed his last. The woman cried out once, and her cry, unexpected and shrill, made all the wounded sit up. The practicante scrambled up to his feet, and guitar in hand, gazed steadily in her direction with elevated eyebrows. The two girls – sitting now one on each side of their wounded relative, with their knees drawn up and long cigars between their lips – nodded at each other significantly.

Charles Gould, looking down over the balustrade, saw three men dressed ceremoniously in black frock-coats with white shirts, and wearing European round hats, enter the patio from the street. One of them, head and shoulders taller than the two others, advanced with marked gravity, leading the way. This was Don Juste Lopez, accompanied by two of his friends, members of Assembly, coming to call upon the Administrador of the San Tomé mine at this early hour. They saw him, too, waved their hands to him urgently, walking up the stairs as if in procession.

Don Juste, astonishingly changed by having shaved off altogether his damaged beard, had lost with it nine-tenths of his outward dignity. Even at that time of serious preoccupation Charles Gould could not help noting the revealed ineptitude in the aspect of the man. His companions looked crestfallen and sleepy. One kept on passing the tip of his tongue over his parched lips; the other's eyes strayed dully over the tiled floor of the corridor, while Don Juste, standing a little in advance, harangued the Señor Administrador of the San Tomé mine. It was his firm opinion that forms had to be observed. A new governor is always visited by deputations from the Cabildo, which is the Municipal Council, from the Consulado, the commercial Board, and it was proper that the Provincial Assembly should send a deputation, too, if only to assert the existence of parliamentary institutions. Don Juste proposed that Don Carlos Gould, as the most prominent citizen of the province, should join the Assembly's deputation. His position was exceptional, his personality known through the length and breadth of the whole Republic. Official courtesies must not be neglected, if they are gone through with a bleeding heart. The acceptance of accomplished facts may save yet the precious vestiges of parliamentary institutions. Don Juste's eyes glowed dully; he believed in parliamentary institutions – and the convinced drone of his voice lost itself in the stillness of the house like the deep buzzing of some ponderous insect.

Charles Gould had turned round to listen patiently, leaning his elbow on the balustrade. He shook his head a little, refusing, almost touched by the anxious gaze of the President of the Provincial Assembly. It was not Charles Gould's policy to make the San Tomé mine a party to any formal proceedings.

'My advice, señores, is that you should wait for your fate in your houses. There is no necessity for you to give yourselves up formally into Montero's hands. Submission to the inevitable, as Don Juste calls it, is all very well, but when the inevitable is called Pedrito Montero there is no need to exhibit pointedly the whole extent of your surrender. The fault of this country is the want of measure in political life. Flat acquiescence in illegality, followed by sanguinary reaction – that, señores, is not the way to a stable and prosperous future.'

Charles Gould stopped before the sad bewilderment of the faces, the wondering, anxious glances of the eyes. The feeling of pity for those men, putting all their trust into words of some sort, while murder and rapine stalked over the land, had betrayed him into what seemed empty loquacity. Don Juste murmured: 'You are abandoning us, Don Carlos . . . And yet, parliamentary institutions – '

He could not finish from grief. For a moment he put his hand over his eyes. Charles Gould, in his fear of empty loquacity, made no answer to the charge. He returned in silence their ceremonious bows. His taciturnity was his refuge. He understood that what they sought was to get the influence of the San Tomé mine on their side. They wanted to go on a conciliating errand to the victor under the wing of the Gould Concession. Other public bodies – the Cabildo, the Consulado – would be coming, too, presently, seeking the support of the most stable, the most effective force they had ever known to exist in their province.

The doctor, arriving with his sharp, jerky walk, found that the master had retired into his own room with orders not to be disturbed on any account. But Dr Monygham was not anxious to see Charles Gould at once. He spent some time in a rapid examination of his wounded. He gazed down upon each in turn, rubbing his chin between his thumb and forefinger; his steady stare met without expression their silently inquisitive look. All these cases were doing well; but when he came to the dead Cargador he stopped a little longer, surveying not the man who had ceased to suffer, but the woman kneeling in silent contemplation of the rigid face, with its pinched nostrils and a white gleam in the imperfectly closed eyes. She lifted her head slowly, and said in a dull voice: 'It is not long since he had become a Cargador – only a few weeks. His worship the Capataz had accepted him after many entreaties.'

'I am not responsible for the great Capataz,' muttered the doctor, moving off.

Directing his course upstairs towards the door of Charles Gould's room, the doctor at the last moment hesitated; then, turning away from the handle with a shrug of his uneven shoulders, slunk off hastily along the corridor in search of Mrs Gould's camerista.

Leonarda told him that the señora had not risen yet. The señora had given into her charge the girls belonging to that Italian posadero. She, Leonarda, had put them to bed in her own room. The fair girl had cried herself to sleep, but the dark one – the bigger – had not closed her eyes yet. She sat up in bed clutching the sheets right up under her chin and staring before her like a little witch. Leonarda did not approve of the Viola children being admitted to the house. She made this feeling clear by the indifferent tone in which she enquired whether their mother was dead yet. As to the señora, she must be asleep. Ever since she had gone into her room after seeing the departure of Doña Antonia with her dying father, there had been no sound behind her door.

The doctor, rousing himself out of profound reflection, told her abruptly to call her mistress at once. He hobbled off to wait for Mrs Gould in the sala. He was very tired, but too excited to sit down. In this great drawing-room, now empty, in which his withered soul had been refreshed after many arid years and his outcast spirit had accepted silently the toleration of many side-glances, he wandered haphazard amongst the chairs and tables till Mrs Gould, enveloped in a morning wrapper, came in rapidly.

'You know that I never approved of the silver being sent away,' the doctor began at once, as a preliminary to the narrative of his night's adventures in association with Captain Mitchell, the engineer-in-chief, and old Viola, at Sotillo's headquarters. To the doctor, with his special conception of this political crisis, the removal of the silver had seemed an irrational and ill-omened measure. It was as if a general were sending the best part of his troops away on the eve of battle upon some recondite pretext. The whole lot of ingots might have been concealed somewhere where they could have been got at for the purpose of staving off the dangers which were menacing the security of the Gould Concession. The Administrador had acted as if the immense and powerful prosperity of the mine had been founded on methods of probity, on the sense of usefulness. And it was nothing of the kind. The method followed had been the only one possible. The Gould Concession had ransomed its way through all those years. It was a nauseous process. He quite understood that Charles Gould had got sick of it and had left the old path to back up that hopeless attempt at reform. The doctor did not believe in the reform of Costaguana. And now the mine was back again in its old path, with the disadvantage that henceforth it had to deal not only with the greed provoked by its wealth, but with the resentment awakened by the attempt to free itself from its bondage to moral corruption. That was the penalty of failure. What made him uneasy was that Charles Gould seemed to him to have weakened at the decisive moment when a frank return to the old methods was the only chance. Listening to Decoud's wild scheme had been a weakness.

The doctor flung up his arms, exclaiming, 'Decoud! Decoud!' He hobbled about the room with slight, angry laughs. Many years ago both his ankles had been seriously damaged in the course of a certain investigation conducted in the castle of Sta Marta by a commission composed of military men. Their nomination had been signified to them unexpectedly at the dead of night, with scowling brow, flashing eyes, and in a tempestuous voice, by Guzman Bento. The old tyrant, maddened by one of his sudden accesses of suspicion, mingled spluttering appeals to their fidelity with imprecations and horrible menaces. The cells and casements of the castle on the hill had been already filled with prisoners. The commission was charged now with the task of discovering the iniquitous conspiracy against the Citizen-Saviour of his country.

The dread of the raving tyrant translated itself into a hasty ferocity of procedure. The Citizen-Saviour was not accustomed to wait. A conspiracy had to be discovered. The courtyards of the castle resounded with the clanking of leg-irons, sounds of blows, yells of pain; and the commission of high officers laboured feverishly, concealing their distress and apprehensions from each other, and especially from their secretary, Father Beron, an army chaplain, at that time very much in the confidence of the Citizen-Saviour. That priest was a big round-shouldered man, with an unclean-looking, overgrown tonsure on the top of his flat head, of a dingy, yellow complexion, softly fat, with greasy stains all down the front of his lieutenant's uniform, and a small cross embroidered in white cotton on his left breast. He had a heavy nose and a pendant lip. Dr Monygham remembered him still. He remembered him against all the force of his will striving its utmost to forget. Father Beron had been adjoined to the commission by Guzman Bento expressly for the purpose that his enlightened zeal should assist them in their labours. Dr Monygham could by no manner of means forget the zeal of Father Beron, or his face, or the pitiless, monotonous voice in which he pronounced the words, 'Will you confess now?'

The memory did not make him shudder, but it had made of him what he was in the eyes of respectable people, a man careless of common decencies, something between a clever vagabond and a disreputable doctor. But not all respectable people would have had the necessary delicacy of sentiment to understand with what trouble of mind and accuracy of vision Dr Monygham, medical officer of the San Tomé mine, remembered Father Beron, army chaplain, and once a secretary of a military commission. After all these years Dr Monygham, in his rooms at the end of the hospital building in the San Tomé gorge, remembered Beron as distinctly as ever. He remembered that priest at night, sometimes, in his sleep. On such nights the doctor waited for daylight with a candle lighted, and walking the whole length of his rooms to and fro, staring down at his bare feet, his arms hugging his sides tightly. He would dream of Father Beron sitting at the end of a long black table, behind which, in a row, appeared the heads, shoulders, and epaulettes of the military members, nibbling the feather of a quill pen, and listening with weary and impatient scorn to the protestations of some prisoner calling heaven to witness of his innocence, till he burst out, 'What's the use of wasting time over that miserable nonsense! Let me take him outside for a while.' And Father Beron would go outside after the clanking prisoner, led away between two soldiers. Such interludes happened on many days, many times, with many prisoners. When the prisoner returned he was ready to make a full confession, Father Beron would declare, leaning forward with that dull, surfeited look which can be seen in the eyes of gluttonous persons after a heavy meal.

The priest's inquisitorial instincts suffered but little from the want of classical apparatus of the Inquisition.

At no time of the world's history have men been at a loss how to inflict mental and bodily anguish upon their fellow-creatures. This aptitude came to them in the growing complexity of their passions and the early refinement of their ingenuity. But it may safely be said that primeval man did not go to the trouble of inventing tortures. He was indolent and pure of heart. He brained his neighbour ferociously with a stone axe from necessity and without malice. The stupidest mind may invent a rankling phrase or brand the innocent with a cruel aspersion. A piece of string and a ramrod; a few muskets in combination with a length of hide rope; or even a simple mallet of heavy, hard wood applied with a swing to human fingers or to the joints of a human body is enough for the infliction of the most exquisite torture. The doctor had been a very stubborn prisoner, and, as a natural consequence of that 'bad disposition' (so Father Beron called it), his subjugation had been very crushing and very complete. That is why the limp in his walk, the twist of his shoulders, the scars on his cheeks were so pronounced. His confessions, when they came at last, were very complete, too. Sometimes on the nights when he walked the floor, he wondered, grinding his teeth with shame and rage, at the fertility of his imagination when stimulated by a sort of pain which makes truth, honour, self-respect, and life itself matters of little moment.

And he could not forget Father Beron with his monotonous phrase, 'Will you confess now?' reaching him in an awful iteration and lucidity of meaning through the delirious incoherence of unbearable pain. He could not forget. But that was not the worst. Had he met Father Beron in the street after all these years Dr Monygham was sure he would have quailed before him. This contingency was not to be feared now. Father Beron was dead; but the sickening certitude prevented Dr Monygham from looking anybody in the face.

Dr Monygham had become, in a manner, the slave of a ghost. It was obviously impossible to take his knowledge of Father Beron home to Europe. When making his extorted confessions to the Military Board, Dr Monygham was not seeking to avoid death. He longed for it. Sitting half-naked for hours on the wet earth of his prison, and so motionless that the spiders, his companions, attached their webs to his matted hair, he consoled the misery of his soul with acute reasonings that he had confessed to crimes enough for a sentence of death – that they had gone too far with him to let him live to tell the tale.

But, as if by a refinement of cruelty, Dr Monygham was left for months to decay slowly in the darkness of his grave-like prison. It was no doubt hoped that it would finish him off without the trouble of an execution; but Dr Monygham had an iron constitution. It was Guzman Bento who died, not by the knife thrust of a conspirator, but from a stroke of apoplexy, and Dr Monygham was liberated hastily. His fetters were struck off by the light of a candle, which, after months of gloom, hurt his eyes so much that he had to cover his face with his hands. He was raised up. His heart was beating violently with the fear of this liberty. When he tried to walk the extraordinary lightness of his feet made him giddy, and he fell down. Two sticks were thrust into his hands, and he was pushed out of the passage. It was dusk; candles glimmered already in the windows of the officers' quarters round the courtyard; but the twilight sky dazed him by its enormous and overwhelming brilliance. A thin poncho hung over his naked, bony shoulders; the rags of his trousers came down no lower than his knees; an eighteen months' growth of hair fell in dirty grey locks on each side of his sharp cheek-bones. As he dragged himself past the guardroom door, one of the soldiers, lolling outside, moved by some obscure impulse, leaped forward with a strange laugh and rammed a broken old straw hat on his head. And Dr Monygham, after having tottered, continued on his way. He advanced one stick, then one maimed foot, then the other stick; the other foot followed only a very short distance along the ground, toilfully, as though it were almost too heavy to be moved at all; and yet his legs under the hanging angles of the poncho appeared no thicker than the two sticks in his hands. A ceaseless trembling agitated his bent body, all his wasted limbs, his bony head, the conical, ragged crown of the sombrero, whose ample flat rim rested on his shoulders.

In such conditions of manner and attire did Dr Monygham go forth to take possession of his liberty. And these conditions seemed to bind him indissolubly to the land of Costaguana like an awful procedure of naturalisation, involving him deep in the national life, far deeper than any amount of success and honour could have done. They did away with his Europeanism; for Dr Monygham had made himself an ideal conception of his disgrace. It was a conception eminently fit and proper for an officer and a gentleman. Dr Monygham, before he went out to Costaguana, had been surgeon in one of Her Majesty's regiments of foot. It was a conception which took no account of physiological facts or reasonable arguments; but it was not stupid for all that. It was simple. A rule of conduct resting mainly on severe rejections is necessarily simple. Dr Monygham's view of what it behoved him to do was severe; it was an ideal view, in so much that it was the imaginative exaggeration of a correct feeling. It was also, in its force, influence, and persistency, the view of an eminently loyal nature.

There was a great fund of loyalty in Dr Monygham's nature. He had settled it all on Mrs Gould's head. He believed her worthy of every devotion. At the bottom of his heart he felt an angry uneasiness before the prosperity of the San Tomé mine, because its growth was robbing her of all peace of mind. Costaguana was no place for a woman of that kind. What could Charles Gould have been thinking of when he brought her out there! It was outrageous! And the doctor had watched the course of events with a grim and distant reserve which, he imagined, his lamentable history imposed upon him.

Loyalty to Mrs Gould could not, however, leave out of account the safety of her husband. The doctor had contrived to be in town at the critical time because he mistrusted Charles Gould. He considered him hopelessly infected with the madness of revolutions. That is why he hobbled in distress in the drawing-room of the Casa Gould on that morning, exclaiming, 'Decoud, Decoud!' in a tone of mournful irritation.

Mrs Gould, her colour heightened, and with glistening eyes, looked straight before her at the sudden enormity of that disaster. The fingertips on one hand rested lightly on a low little table by her side, and the arm trembled right up to the shoulder. The sun, which looks late upon Sulaco, issuing in all the fullness of its power high up on the sky from behind the dazzling snow-edge of Higuerota, had precipitated the delicate, smooth, pearly greyness of light, in which the town lies steeped during the early hours, into sharp-cut masses of black shade and spaces of hot, blinding glare. Three long rectangles of sunshine fell through the windows of the sala; while just across the street the front of the Avellanos's house appeared very sombre in its own shadow seen through the flood of light.

A voice said at the door, 'What of Decoud?'

It was Charles Gould. They had not heard him coming along the corridor. His glance just glided over his wife and struck full at the doctor.

'You have brought some news, doctor?'

Dr Monygham blurted it all at once, in the rough. For some time after he had done, the Administrador of the San Tomé mine remained looking at him without a word. Mrs Gould sank into a low chair with her hands lying on her lap. A silence reigned between those three motionless persons. Then Charles Gould spoke: 'You must want some breakfast.'

He stood aside to let his wife pass first. She caught up her husband's hand and pressed it as she went out, raising the handkerchief to her eyes. The sight of her husband had brought Antonia's position to her mind, and she could not contain her tears at the thought of the poor girl. When she rejoined the two men in the dining-room after having bathed her face, Charles Gould was saying to the doctor across the table: 'No, there does not seem any room for doubt.'

And the doctor assented.

'No, I don't see myself how we could question that wretched Hirsch's tale. It's only too true, I fear.'

She sat down desolately at the head of the table and looked from one to the other. The two men, without absolutely turning their heads away, tried to avoid her glance. The doctor even made a show of being hungry; he seized his knife and fork, and began to eat with emphasis, as if on the stage. Charles Gould made no pretence of the sort; with his elbows raised squarely, he twisted both ends of his flaming moustaches – they were so long that his hands were quite away from his face.

'I am not surprised,' he muttered, abandoning his moustaches and throwing one arm over the back of his chair. His face was calm with that immobility of expression which betrays the intensity of a mental struggle. He felt that this accident had brought to a point all the consequences involved in his line of conduct, with its conscious and subconscious intentions. There must be an end now of this silent reserve, of that air of impenetrability behind which he had been safeguarding his dignity. It was the least ignoble form of dissembling forced upon him by that parody of civilised institutions which offended his intelligence, his uprightness, and his sense of right. He was like his father. He had no ironic eye. He was not amused at the absurdities that prevail in this world. They hurt him in his innate gravity. He felt that the miserable death of that poor Decoud took from him his inaccessible position of a force in the background. It committed him openly unless he wished to throw up the game – and that was impossible. The material interests required from him the sacrifice of his aloofness – perhaps his own safety too. And he reflected that Decoud's separationist plan had not gone to the bottom with the lost silver.

The only thing that was not changed was his position towards Mr Holroyd. The head of silver and steel interests had entered into Costaguana affairs with a sort of passion. Costaguana had become necessary to his existence; in the San Tomé mine he had found the imaginative satisfaction which other minds would get from drama, from art, or from sport. It was a special form of the great man's extravagance, sanctioned by a moral intention, big enough to flatter his vanity. Even in this aberration of his genius he served the progress of the world. Charles Gould felt sure of being understood with precision and judged with the indulgence of their common passion. Nothing now could surprise or startle this great man. And Charles Gould imagined himself writing a letter to San Francisco in some such words: '. . . The men at the head of the movement are dead or have fled; the civil organisation of the province is at an end for the present; the Blanco party in Sulaco has collapsed inexcusably, but in the characteristic manner of this country. But Barrios, untouched in Cayta, remains still available. I am forced to take up openly the plan of a provincial revolution as the only way of placing the enormous material interests involved in the prosperity and peace of Sulaco in a position of permanent safety . . .' That was clear. He saw these words as if written in letters of fire upon the wall at which he was gazing abstractedly.

Mrs Gould watched his abstraction with dread. It was a domestic and frightful phenomenon that darkened and chilled the house for her like a thundercloud passing over the sun. Charles Gould's fits of abstraction depicted the energetic concentration of a will haunted by a fixed idea. A man haunted by a fixed idea is insane. He is dangerous even if that idea is an idea of justice; for may he not bring the heaven down pitilessly upon a loved head? The eyes of Mrs Gould, watching her husband's profile, filled with tears again. And again she seemed to see the despair of the unfortunate Antonia.

'What would I have done if Charley had been drowned while we were engaged?' she exclaimed, mentally, with horror. Her heart turned to ice, while her cheeks flamed up as if scorched by the blaze of a funeral pyre consuming all her earthly affections. The tears burst out of her eyes.

'Antonia will kill herself!' she cried out.

This cry fell into the silence of the room with strangely little effect. Only the doctor, crumbling up a piece of bread, with his head inclined on one side, raised his face, and the few long hairs sticking out of his shaggy eyebrows stirred in a slight frown. Dr Monygham thought quite sincerely that Decoud was a singularly unworthy object for any woman's affection. Then he lowered his head again, with a curl of his lip, and his heart full of tender admiration for Mrs Gould.

'She thinks of that girl,' he said to himself; 'she thinks of the Viola children; she thinks of me; of the wounded; of the miners; she always thinks of everybody who is poor and miserable! But what will she do if Charles gets the worst of it in this infernal scrimmage those confounded Avellanos have drawn him into? No one seems to be thinking of her.'

Charles Gould, staring at the wall, pursued his reflections subtly.

'I shall write to Holroyd that the San Tomé mine is big enough to take in hand the making of a new State. It'll please him. It'll reconcile him to the risk.'

But was Barrios really available? Perhaps. But he was inaccessible. To send off a boat to Cayta was no longer possible, since Sotillo was master of the harbour, and had a steamer at his disposal. And now, with all the democrats in the province up, and every Campo township in a state of disturbance, where could he find a man who would make his way successfully overland to Cayta with a message, a ten days' ride at least; a man of courage and resolution, who would avoid arrest or murder, and if arrested would faithfully eat the paper? The Capataz de Cargadores would have been just such a man. But the Capataz of the Cargadores was no more.

And Charles Gould, withdrawing his eyes from the wall, said gently, 'That Hirsch! What an extraordinary thing! Saved himself by clinging to the anchor, did he? I had no idea that he was still in Sulaco. I thought he had gone back overland to Esmeralda more than a week ago. He came here once to talk to me about his hide business and some other things. I made it clear to him that nothing could be done.'

'He was afraid to start back on account of Hernandez being about,' remarked the doctor.

'And but for him we might not have known anything of what has happened,' marvelled Charles Gould.

Mrs Gould cried out: 'Antonia must not know! She must not be told. Not now.'

'Nobody's likely to carry the news,' remarked the doctor. 'It's no one's interest. Moreover, the people here are afraid of Hernandez as if he were the devil.' He turned to Charles Gould. 'It's even awkward, because if you wanted to communicate with the refugees you could find no messenger. When Hernandez was ranging hundreds of miles away from here the Sulaco populace used to shudder at the tales of him roasting his prisoners alive.'

'Yes,' murmured Charles Gould; 'Captain Mitchell's Capataz was the only man in the town who had seen Hernandez eye to eye. Father Corbelàn employed him. He opened the communications first. It is a pity that – '

His voice was covered by the booming of the great bell of the cathedral. Three single strokes, one after another, burst out explosively, dying away in deep and mellow vibrations. And then all the bells in the tower of every church, convent, or chapel in town, even those that had remained shut up for years, pealed out together with a crash. In this furious flood of metallic uproar there was a power of suggesting images of strife and violence which blanched Mrs Gould's cheek. Basilio, who had been waiting at table, shrinking within himself, clung to the sideboard with chattering teeth. It was impossible to hear yourself speak.

'Shut these windows!' Charles Gould yelled at him, angrily. All the other servants, terrified at what they took for the signal of a general massacre, had rushed upstairs, tumbling over each other, men and women, the obscure and generally invisible population of the ground floor on the four sides of the patio. The women, screaming *'Misericordia!'* ran right into the room, and, falling on their knees against the walls, began to cross themselves convulsively. The staring heads of men blocked the doorway in an instant – mozos from the stable, gardeners, nondescript helpers living on the crumbs of the munificent house – and Charles Gould beheld all the extent of his domestic establishment, even to the gatekeeper. This was a half-paralysed old man, whose long white locks fell down to his shoulders: an heirloom taken up by Charles Gould's familial piety. He could remember Henry Gould, an Englishman and a Costaguanero of the second generation, chief of the Sulaco province; he had been his personal mozo years and years ago in peace and war; had been allowed to attend his master in prison; had, on the fatal morning, followed the firing squad; and, peeping from behind one of the cypresses growing along the wall of the Franciscan Convent, had seen, with his eyes starting out of his head, Don Enrique throw up his hands and fall with his face in the dust. Charles Gould noted particularly the big patriarchal head of that witness in the rear of the other servants. But he was surprised to see a shrivelled old hag or two, of whose existence within the walls of his house he had not been aware. They must have been the mothers, or even the grandmothers of some of his people. There were a few children, too, more or less naked, crying and clinging to the legs of their elders. He had never before noticed any sign of a child in his patio. Even Leonarda, the camerista, came in a fright, pushing through, with her spoiled, pouting face of a favourite maid, leading the Viola girls by the hand. The crockery rattled on table and sideboard, and the whole house seemed to sway in the deafening wave of sound.

Chapter 5

During the night the expectant populace had taken possession of all the belfries in the town in order to welcome Pedrito Montero, who was making his entry after having slept the night in Rincon. And first came straggling in through the land gate the armed mob of all colours, complexions, types, and states of raggedness, calling themselves the Sulaco National Guard, and commanded by Señor Gamacho. Through the middle of the street streamed, like a torrent of rubbish, a mass of straw hats, ponchos, gun-barrels, with an enormous green and yellow flag flapping in their midst, in a cloud of dust, to the furious beating of drums. The spectators recoiled against the walls of the houses shouting their Vivas! Behind the rabble could be seen the lances of the cavalry, the 'army' of Pedro Montero. He advanced between Señores Fuentes and Gamacho at the head of his llaneros, who had accomplished the feat of crossing the Páramos of the Higuerota in a snowstorm. They rode four abreast, mounted on confiscated Campo horses, clad in the hetero-geneous stock of roadside stores they had looted hurriedly in their rapid ride through the northern part of the province; for Pedro Montero had been in a great hurry to occupy Sulaco. The handkerchiefs knotted loosely around their bare throats were glaringly new, and all the right sleeves of their cotton shirts had been cut off close to the shoulder for greater freedom in throwing the lazo. Emaciated greybeards rode by the side of lean dark youths, marked by all the hardships of campaigning, with strips of raw beef twined round the crowns of their hats, and huge iron spurs fastened to their naked heels. Those that in the passes of the mountain had lost their lances had provided themselves with the goads used by the Campo cattlemen: slender shafts of palm fully ten feet long, with a lot of loose rings jingling under the ironshod point. They were armed with knives and revolvers. A haggard fearlessness characterised the expression of all these sun-blacked countenances; they glared down haughtily with their scorched eyes at the crowd, or, blinking upwards insolently, pointed out to each other some particular head amongst the women at the windows. When they had ridden into the Plaza and caught sight of the equestrian statue of the King dazzlingly white in the sunshine, towering enormous and motionless above the surges of the crowd, with its eternal gesture of saluting, a murmur of surprise ran through their ranks. 'What is that saint in the big hat?' they asked each other.

They were a good sample of the cavalry of the plains with which Pedro Montero had helped so much the victorious career of his brother the general. The influence which that man, brought up in coast towns, acquired in a short time over the plainsmen of the Republic can be ascribed only to a genius for treachery of so effective a kind that it must have appeared to those violent men but little removed from a state of utter savagery, as the perfection of sagacity and virtue. The popular lore of all nations testifies that duplicity and cunning, together with bodily strength, were looked upon, even more than courage, as heroic virtues by primitive mankind. To overcome your adversary was the great affair of life. Courage was taken for granted. But the use of intelligence awakened wonder and respect. Stratagems, providing they did not fail, were honourable; the easy massacre of an unsuspecting enemy evoked no feelings but those of gladness, pride, and admiration. Not perhaps that primitive men were more faithless than their descendants of today, but that they went straighter to their aim, and were more artless in their recognition of success as the only standard of morality.

We have changed since. The use of intelligence awakens little wonder and less respect. But the ignorant and barbarous plainsmen engaging in civil strife followed willingly a leader who often managed to deliver their enemies bound, as it were, into their hands. Pedro Montero had a talent for lulling his adversaries into a sense of security. And as men learn wisdom with extreme slowness, and are always ready to believe promises that flatter their secret hopes, Pedro Montero was successful time after time. Whether only a servant or some inferior official in the Costaguana Legation in Paris, he had rushed back to his country directly he heard that his brother had emerged from the obscurity of his frontier comandancia. He had managed to deceive by his gift of plausibility the chiefs of the Ribierist movement in the capital, and even the acute agent of the San Tomé mine had failed to understand him thoroughly.

At once he had obtained an enormous influence over his brother. They were very much alike in appearance, both bald, with bunches of crisp hair above their ears, arguing the presence of some Negro blood. Only Pedro was smaller than the general, more delicate altogether, with an apelike faculty for imitating all the outward signs of refinement and distinction, and with a parrotlike talent for languages. Both brothers had received some elementary instruction by the munificence of a great European traveller, to whom their father had been a body-servant during his journeys in the interior of the country. In General Montero's case it enabled him to rise from the ranks. Pedrito, the younger, incorrigibly lazy and slovenly, had drifted aimlessly from one coast town to another, hanging about counting-houses, attaching himself to strangers as a sort of *valet-de-place*, picking up an easy and disreputable living. His ability to read did nothing for him but fill his head with absurd visions. His actions were usually determined by motives so improbable in themselves as to escape the penetration of a rational person.

Thus at first sight the agent of the Gould Concession in Sta Marta had credited him with the possession of sane views, and even with a restraining power over the general's everlastingly discontented vanity. It could never have entered his head that Pedrito Montero, lackey or inferior scribe, lodged in the garrets of the various Parisian hotels where the Costaguana Legation used to shelter its diplomatic dignity, had been devouring the lighter sort of historical works in the French language, such, for instance as the books of Imbert de Saint Amand upon the Second Empire. But Pedrito had been struck by the splendour of a brilliant court, and had conceived the idea of an existence for himself where, like the Duc de Morny, he would associate the command of every pleasure with the conduct of political affairs and enjoy power supremely in every way. Nobody could have guessed that. And yet this was one of the immediate causes of the Monterist Revolution. This will appear less incredible by the reflection that the fundamental causes were the same as ever, rooted in the political immaturity of the people, in the indolence of the upper classes and the lower.

Pedrito Montero saw in the elevation of his brother the road wide open to his wildest imaginings. This was what made the Monterist pronunciamiento so unpreventable. The general himself probably could have been bought off, pacified with flatteries, despatched on a diplomatic mission to Europe. It was his brother who had egged him on from first to last. He wanted to become the most brilliant statesman of South America. He did not desire supreme power. He would have been afraid of its labour and risk, in fact. Before all, Pedrito Montero, taught by his European experience, meant to acquire a serious fortune for himself. With this object in view he obtained from his brother, on the very morrow of the successful battle, the permission to push on over the mountains and take possession of Sulaco. Sulaco was the land of future prosperity, the chosen land of material progress, the only province in the Republic of interest to European capitalists. Pedrito Montero, following the example of the Duc de Morny, meant to have his share of this prosperity. This is what he meant literally. Now his brother was master of the country, whether as president, dictator, or even as Emperor – why not as an Emperor? – he meant to demand a share in every enterprise – in railways, in mines, in sugar estates, in cotton mills, in land companies, in each and every under-taking – as the price of his protection. The desire to be on the spot early was the real cause of the celebrated ride over the mountains with some two hundred llaneros, an enterprise of which the dangers had not appeared at first clearly to his impatience. Coming from a series of victories, it seemed to him that a Montero had only to appear to be master of the situation. This illusion had betrayed him into a rashness of which he was becoming aware. As he rode at the head of his llaneros he regretted that there were so few of them. The enthusiasm of the populace reassured him. They yelled '*Viva* Montero! *Viva* Pedrito!' In order to make them still more enthusiastic, and from the natural pleasure he had in dissembling, he dropped the reins on his horse's neck, and with a tremendous effect of familiarity and confidence slipped his hands under the arms of Señores Fuentes and Gamacho. In that posture, with a ragged town mozo holding his horse by the bridle, he rode triumphantly across the Plaza to the door of the Intendencia. Its old gloomy walls seemed to shake in the acclamations that rent the air and covered the crashing peals of the cathedral bells.

Pedro Montero, the brother of the general, dismounted into a shouting and perspiring throng of enthusiasts whom the ragged Nationals were pushing back fiercely. Ascending a few steps he surveyed the large crowd gaping at him and the bullet-speckled walls of the houses opposite lightly veiled by a sunny haze of dust. The word 'porvenir' in immense black capitals, alternating with broken windows, stared at him across the vast space; and he thought with delight of the hour of vengeance, because he was very sure of laying his hands upon Decoud. On his left hand, Gamacho, big and hot, wiping his hairy wet face, uncovered a set of yellow fangs in a grin of stupid hilarity. On his right, Señor Fuentes, small and lean, looked on with compressed lips. The crowd stared literally open-mouthed, lost in eager stillness, as though they had expected the great guerrillero, the famous Pedrito, to begin scattering at once some sort of visible largesse. What he began was a speech. He began it with the shouted word 'Citizens!' which reached even those in the middle of the Plaza. Afterwards the greater part of the citizens remained fascinated by the orator's action alone, his tiptoeing, the arms flung above his head with the fists clenched, a hand laid flat upon the heart, the silver gleam of rolling eyes, the sweeping, pointing, embracing gestures, a hand laid familiarly on Gamacho's shoulder; a hand waved formally towards the little black-coated person of Señor Fuentes, advocate and politician and a true friend of the people. The vivas of those nearest to the orator bursting out suddenly propagated them-selves irregularly to the confines of the crowd, like flames running over dry grass, and expired in the opening of the streets. In the intervals, over the swarming Plaza brooded a heavy silence, in which the mouth of the orator went on opening and shutting, and detached phrases – 'The happiness of the people', 'Sons of the country', 'The entire world, *el mundo entiero*' – reached even the packed steps of the cathedral with a feeble clear ring, thin as the buzzing of a mosquito. But the orator struck his breast; he seemed to prance between his two supporters. It was the supreme effort of his peroration. Then the two smaller figures disappeared from the public gaze and the enormous Gamacho, left alone, advanced, raising his hat high above his head. Then he covered himself proudly and yelled out, 'Ciudadanos!' A dull roar greeted Señor Gamacho, ex-pedlar of the Campo, Commandante of the National Guards.

Upstairs Pedrito Montero walked about rapidly from one wrecked room of the Intendencia to another, snarling incessantly: 'What stupidity! What destruction!'

Señor Fuentes, following, would relax his taciturn disposition to murmur: 'It is all the work of Gamacho and his Nationals;' and then, inclining his head on his left shoulder, would press together his lips so firmly that a little hollow would appear at each corner. He had his nomination for Political Chief of the town in his pocket, and was all impatience to enter upon his functions.

In the long audience room, with its tall mirrors all starred by stones, the hangings torn down and the canopy over the platform at the upper end pulled to pieces, the vast, deep muttering of the crowd and the howling voice of Gamacho speaking just below reached them through the shutters as they stood idly in dimness and desolation.

'The brute!' observed his Excellency Don Pedro Montero through clenched teeth. 'We must contrive as quickly as possible to send him and his Nationals out there to fight Hernandez.'

The new Jefe Politico only jerked his head sideways, and took a puff at his cigarette in sign of his agreement with his method for ridding the town of Gamacho and his inconvenient rabble.

Pedrito Montero looked with disgust at the absolutely bare floor, and at the belt of heavy gilt picture-frames running round the room, out of which the remnants of torn and slashed canvases fluttered like dingy rags.

'We are not barbarians,' he said.

This was what said his Excellency, the popular Pedrito, the guerrillero skilled in the art of laying ambushes, charged by his brother at his own demand with the organisation of Sulaco on democratic principles. The night before, during the consultation with his partisans, who had come out to meet him in Rincon, he had opened his intentions to Señor Fuentes: 'We shall organise a popular vote, by yes or no, confiding the destinies of our beloved country to the wisdom and valiance of my heroic brother, the invincible general. A plebiscite. Do you understand?'

And Señor Fuentes, puffing out his leathery cheeks, had inclined his head slightly to the left, letting a thin, bluish jet of smoke escape through his pursed lips. He had understood.

His Excellency was exasperated at the devastation. Not a single chair, table, sofa, *étagère* or console had been left in the state rooms of the Intendencia. His Excellency, though twitching all over with rage, was restrained from bursting into violence by a sense of his remoteness and isolation. His heroic brother was very far away. Meantime, how was he going to take his siesta? He had expected to find comfort and luxury in the Intendencia after a year of hard camp life, ending with the hardships and privations of the daring dash upon Sulaco – upon the province which was worth more in wealth and influence than all the rest of the Republic's territory. He would get even with Gamacho by and by. And Señor Gamacho's oration, delectable to popular ears, went on in the heat and glare of the Plaza like the uncouth howlings of an inferior sort of devil cast into a white-hot furnace. Every moment he had to wipe his streaming face with his bare forearm; he had flung off his coat, and had turned up the sleeves of his shirt high above the elbows; but he kept on his head the large cocked hat with white plumes. His ingenuousness cherished this sign of his rank as Commandante of the National Guards. Approving and grave murmurs greeted his periods. His opinion was that war should be declared at once against France, England, Germany, and the United States, who, by introducing railways, mining enterprises, colonisation, and under such other shallow pretences, aimed at robbing poor people of their lands, and with the help of these Goths and paralytics, the aristocrats would convert them into toiling and miserable slaves. And the léperos, flinging about the corners of their dirty white mantas, yelled their approbation. General Montero, Gamacho howled with conviction, was the only man equal to the patriotic task. They assented to that, too.

The morning was wearing on; there were already signs of disruption, currents and eddies in the crowd. Some were seeking the shade of the walls and under the trees of the Alameda. Horsemen spurred through, shouting; groups of sombreros set level on heads against the vertical sun were drifting away into the streets, where the open doors of pulperías revealed an enticing gloom resounding with the gentle tinkling of guitars. The National Guards were thinking of siesta, and the eloquence of Gamacho, their chief, was exhausted. Later on, when, in the cooler hours of the afternoon, they tried to assemble again for further consideration of public affairs, detachments of Montero's cavalry camped on the Alameda charged them without parley, at speed, with long lances levelled at their flying backs as far as the ends of the streets. The National Guards of Sulaco were surprised by this proceeding. But they were not indignant. No Costaguanero had ever learned to question the eccentricities of a military force. They were part of the natural order of things. This must be, they concluded, some kind of administrative measure, no doubt. But the motive of it escaped their unaided intelligence, and their chief and orator, Gamacho, Commandante of the National Guard, was lying drunk and asleep in the bosom of his family. His bare feet were upturned in the shadows repulsively, in the manner of a corpse. His eloquent mouth had dropped open. His youngest daughter, scratching her head with one hand, with the other waved a green bough over his scorched and peeling face.

Chapter 6

The declining sun had shifted the shadows from west to east amongst the houses of the town. It had shifted them upon the whole extent of the immense Campo, with the white walls of its haciendas on the knolls dominating the green distances; with its grass-thatched ranchos crouching in the folds of ground by the banks of streams; with the dark islands of clustered trees on a clear sea of grass, and the precipitous range of the Cordillera, immense and motionless, emerging from the billows of the lower forests like the barren coast of a land of giants. The sunset rays striking the snow-slope of Higuerota from afar gave it an air of rosy youth, while the serrated mass of distant peaks remained black, as if calcined in the fiery radiance. The undulating surface of the forests seemed powdered with pale gold dust; and away there, beyond Rincon, hidden from the town by two wooded spurs, the rocks of the San Tomé gorge, with the flat wall of the mountain itself crowned by gigantic ferns, took on warm tones of brown and yellow, with red rusty streaks, and the dark green clumps of bushes rooted in crevices. From the plain the stamp sheds and the houses of the mine appeared dark and small, high up, like the nests of birds clustered on the ledges of a cliff. The zigzag paths resembled faint tracings scratched on the wall of a cyclopean blockhouse. To the two serenos of the mine on patrol duty, strolling, carbine in hand, and watchful eyes, in the shade of the trees lining the stream near the bridge, Don Pépé, descending the path from the upper plateau, appeared no bigger than a large beetle.

With his air of aimless, insect-like going to and fro upon the face of the rock, Don Pépé's figure kept on descending steadily, and, when near the bottom, sank at last behind the roofs of storehouses, forges, and workshops. For a time the pair of serenos strolled back and forth before the bridge, on which they had stopped a horseman holding a large white envelope in his hand. Then Don Pépé, emerging in the village street from amongst the houses, not a stone's throw from the frontier bridge, approached, striding in wide dark trousers tucked into boots, a white linen jacket, sabre at his side, and revolver at his belt. In this disturbed time nothing could find the Señor Gobernador with his boots off, as the saying is.

At a slight nod from one of the serenos, the man, a messenger from the town, dismounted, and crossed the bridge, leading his horse by the bridle.

Don Pépé received the letter from his other hand, slapped his left side and his hips in succession, feeling for his spectacle case. After settling the heavy silver-mounted affair astride his nose, and adjusting it carefully behind his ears, he opened the envelope, holding it up at about a foot in front of his eyes. The paper he pulled out contained some three lines of writing. He looked at them for a long time. His grey moustache moved slightly up and down, and the wrinkles, radiating at the corners of his eyes, ran together. He nodded serenely. '*Bueno,*' he said. 'There is no answer.'

Then, in his quiet, kindly way, he engaged in a cautious conversation with the man, who was willing to talk cheerily, as if something lucky had happened to him recently. He had seen from a distance Sotillo's infantry camped along the shore of the harbour on each side of the Custom House. They had done no damage to the buildings. The foreigners of the railway remained shut up within the yards. They were no longer anxious to shoot poor people. He cursed the foreigners; then he reported Montero's entry and the rumours of the town. The poor were going to be made rich now. That was very good. More he did not know, and, breaking into propitiatory smiles, he intimated that he was hungry and thirsty. The old major directed him to go to the alcalde of the first village. The man rode off, and Don Pépé, striding slowly in the direction of a little wooden belfry, looked over a hedge into a little garden, and saw Father Romàn sitting in a white hammock slung between two orange trees in front of the presbytery.

An enormous tamarind shaded with its dark foliage the whole white framehouse. A young Indian girl with long hair, big eyes, and small hands and feet, carried out a wooden chair, while a thin old woman, crabbed and vigilant, watched her all the time from the verandah.

Don Pépé sat down in the chair and lighted a cigar; the priest drew in an immense quantity of snuff out of the hollow of his palm. On his reddish-brown face, worn, hollowed as if crumbled, the eyes, fresh and candid, sparkled like two black diamonds.

Don Pépé, in a mild and humorous voice, informed Father Romàn that Pedrito Montero, by the hand of Señor Fuentes, had asked him on what terms he would surrender the mine in proper working order to a legally constituted commission of patriotic citizens, escorted by a small military force. The priest cast his eyes up to heaven. However, Don Pépé continued, the mozo who brought the letter said that Don Carlos Gould was alive, and so far unmolested.

Father Romàn expressed in a few words his thankfulness at hearing of the Señor Administrador's safety.

The hour of oration had gone by in the silvery ringing of a bell in the little belfry. The belt of forest closing the entrance of the valley stood like a screen between the low sun and the street of the village. At the other end of the rocky gorge, between the walls of basalt and granite, a forest-clad mountain, hiding all the range from the San Tomé dwellers, rose steeply, lighted up and leafy to the very top. Three small rosy clouds hung motionless overhead in the great depth of blue. Knots of people sat in the street between the wattled huts. Before the casa of the alcalde, the foremen of the night-shift, already assembled to lead their men, squatted on the ground in a circle of leather skullcap, and, bowing their bronze backs, were passing round the gourd of maté. The mozo from the town, having fastened his horse to a wooden post before the door, was telling them the news of Sulaco as the blackened gourd of the decoction passed from hand to hand. The grave alcalde himself, in a white waistcloth and a flowered chintz gown with sleeves, open wide upon his naked stout person with an effect of a gaudy bathing robe, stood by, wearing a rough beaver hat at the back of his head, and grasping a tall staff with a silver knob in his hand. These insignia of his dignity had been conferred upon him by the Administration of the mine, the fountain of honour, of prosperity, and peace. He had been one of the first immigrants into this valley; his sons and sons-in-law worked within the mountain which seemed with its treasures to pour down the thundering ore shoots of the upper mesa, the gifts of well-being, security, and justice upon the toilers. He listened to the news from the town with curiosity and indifference, as if concerning another world than his own. And it was true that they appeared to him so. In a very few years the sense of belonging to a powerful organisation had been developed in these harassed, half-wild Indians. They were proud of, and attached to, the mine. It had secured their confidence and belief. They invested it with a protecting and invincible virtue as though it were a fetish made by their own hands, for they were ignorant, and in other respects did not differ appreciably from the rest of mankind which puts infinite trust in its own creations. It never entered the alcalde's head that the mine could fail in its protection and force. Politics were good enough for the people of the town and the Campo. His yellow, round face, with wide nostrils, and motionless in expression, resembled a fierce full moon. He listened to the excited vapourings of the mozo without misgivings, without surprise, without any active sentiment whatever.

Padre Romàn sat dejectedly balancing himself, his feet just touching the ground, his hands gripping the edge of the hammock. With less confidence, but as ignorant as his flock, he asked the major what did he think was going to happen now.

Don Pépé, bolt upright in the chair, folded his hands peacefully on the hilt of his sword, standing perpendicular between his thighs, and answered that he did not know. The mine could be defended against any force likely to be sent to take possession. On the other hand, from the arid character of the valley, when the regular supplies from the Campo had been cut off, the population of the three villages could be starved into submission. Don Pépé exposed these contingencies with serenity to Father Romàn, who, as an old campaigner, was able to understand the reasoning of a military man. They talked with simplicity and directness. Father Romàn was saddened at the idea of his flock being scattered or else enslaved. He had no illusions as to their fate, not from penetration, but from experience of political atrocities, which seemed to him fatal and unavoidable in the life of a State. The working of the usual public institutions presented itself to him most distinctly as a series of calamities overtaking private individuals and flowing logically from each other through hate, revenge, folly, and rapacity, as though they had been part of a divine dispensation. Father Romàn's clear-sightedness was served by an uninformed intelligence; but his heart, preserving its tenderness amongst scenes of carnage, spoliation, and violence, abhorred these calamities the more as his association with the victims was closer. He entertained towards the Indians of the valley feelings of paternal scorn. He had been marrying, baptising, confessing, absolving, and burying the workers of the San Tomé mine with dignity and unction for five years or more; and he believed in the sacredness of these ministrations, which made them his own in a spiritual sense. They were dear to his sacerdotal supremacy. Mrs Gould's earnest interest in the concerns of these people enhanced their importance in the priest's eyes, because it really augmented his own. When talking over with her the innumerable Marias and Brigidas of the villages, he felt his own humanity expand. Padre Romàn was incapable of fanaticism to an almost reprehensible degree. The English señora was evidently a heretic; but at the same time she seemed to him wonderful and angelic. Whenever that confused state of his feelings occurred to him, while strolling, for instance, his breviary under his arm, in the wide shade of the tamarind, he would stop short to inhale with a strong snuffling noise a large quantity of snuff, and shake his head profoundly. At the thought of what might befall the illustrious señora presently, he became gradually overcome with dismay.

He voiced it in an agitated murmur. Even Don Pépé lost his serenity for a moment. He leaned forward stiffly.

'Listen, Padre. The very fact that those thieving macaques in Sulaco are trying to find out the price of my honour proves that Señor Don Carlos and all in the Casa Gould are safe. As to my honour, that also is safe, as every man, woman, and child knows. But the Negro Liberals who have snatched the town by surprise do not know that. Bueno. Let them sit and wait. While they wait they can do no harm.'

And he regained his composure. He regained it easily, because whatever happened his honour of an old officer of Paez was safe. He had promised Charles Gould that at the approach of an armed force he would defend the gorge just long enough to give himself time to destroy scientifically the whole plant, buildings, and workshops of the mine with heavy charges of dynamite; block with ruins the main tunnel, break down the pathways, blow up the dam of the water-power, shatter the famous Gould Concession into fragments, flying sky high out of a horrified world. The mine had got hold of Charles Gould with a grip as deadly as ever it had laid upon his father. But this extreme resolution had seemed to Don Pépé the most natural thing in the world. His measures had been taken with judgment. Everything was prepared with a careful completeness. And Don Pépé folded his hands pacifically on his sword hilt, and nodded at the priest. In his excitement, Father Romàn had flung snuff in handfuls at his face, and, all besmeared with tobacco, round-eyed, and beside himself, had got out of the hammock to walk about, uttering exclamations.

Don Pépé stroked his grey and pendant moustache, whose fine ends hung far below the clean-cut line of his jaw, and spoke with a conscious pride in his reputation.

'So, Padre, I don't know what will happen. But I know that as long as I am here Don Carlos can speak to that macaque, Pedrito Montero, and threaten the destruction of the mine with perfect assurance that will be taken seriously. For people know me.'

He began to turn the cigar in his lips a little nervously, and went on: 'But that is talk – good for the politicos. I am a military man. I do not know what may happen. But I know what ought to be done – the mine should march upon the town with guns, axes, knives tied up to sticks – *por Dios*. That is what should be done. Only – '

His folded hands twitched on the hilt. The cigar turned faster in the corner of his lips.

'And who should lead but I? Unfortunately – observe – I have given my word of honour to Don Carlos not to let the mine fall into the hands of these thieves. In war – you know this, Padre – the fate of battles is uncertain, and whom could I leave here to act for me in case of defeat? The explosives are ready. But it would require a man of high honour, of intelligence, of judgment, of courage, to carry out the prepared destruction. Somebody I can trust with my honour as I can trust myself. Another old officer of Paez, for instance. Or – or – perhaps one of Paez's old chaplains would do.'

He got up, long, lank, upright, hard, with his martial moustache and the bony structure of his face, from which the glance of the sunken eyes seemed to transfix the priest, who stood still, an empty wooden snuffbox held upside down in his hand, and glared back, speechless, at the governor of the mine.

Chapter 7

At about that time, in the Intendencia of Sulaco, Charles Gould was assuring
Pedrito Montero, who had sent a request for his presence there, that he
would never let the mine pass out of his hands for the profit of a Government
who had robbed him of it. The Gould Concession could not be resumed.
His father had not desired it. The son would never surrender it. He would
never surrender it alive. And once dead, where was the power capable of
resuscitating such an enterprise in all its vigour and wealth out of the ashes
and ruin of destruction? There was no such power in the country. And
where was the skill and capital abroad that would condescend to touch such
an ill-omened corpse? Charles Gould talked in the impassive tone which had
for many years served to conceal his anger and contempt. He suffered. He
was disgusted with what he had to say. It was too much like heroics. In him
the strictly practical instinct was in profound discord with the almost mystic
view he took of his right. The Gould Concession was symbolic of abstract
justice. Let the heavens fall. But since the San Tomé mine had developed
into worldwide fame his threat had enough force and effectiveness to reach
the rudimentary intelligence of Pedro Montero, wrapped up as it was in the
futilities of historical anecdotes. The Gould Concession was a serious asset
in the country's finance, and, what was more, in the private budgets of
many officials as well. It was traditional. It was known. It was said. It was
credible. Every Minister of Interior drew a salary from the San Tomé mine.
It was natural. And Pedrito intended to be Minister of the Interior and
President of the Council in his brother's Government. The Duc de Morny
had occupied those high posts during the Second French Empire with
conspicuous advantage to himself.

A table, a chair, a wooden bedstead had been procured for His Excellency,
who, after a short siesta, rendered absolutely necessary by the labours and the
pomps of his entry into Sulaco, had been getting hold of the administrative
machine by making appointments, giving orders, and signing proclamations.
Alone with Charles Gould in the audience room, His Excellency managed
with his well-known skill to conceal his annoyance and consternation. He
had begun at first to talk loftily of confiscation, but the want of all proper
feeling and mobility in the Señor Administrador's features ended by affecting
adversely his power of masterful expression. Charles Gould had repeated:
'The Government can certainly bring about the destruction of the San Tomé
mine if it likes; but without me it can do nothing else.' It was an alarming

pronouncement, and well calculated to hurt the sensibilities of a politician whose mind is bent upon the spoils of victory. And Charles Gould said also that the destruction of the San Tomé mine would cause the ruin of other undertakings, the withdrawal of European capital, the withholding, most probably, of the last instalment of the foreign loan. That stony fiend of a man said all these things (which were accessible to His Excellency's intelligence) in a cold-blooded manner which made one shudder.

A long course of reading historical works, light and gossipy in tone, carried out in garrets of Parisian hotels, sprawling on an untidy bed, to the neglect of his duties, menial or otherwise, had affected the manners of Pedro Montero. Had he seen around him the splendour of the old Intendencia, the magnificent hangings, the gilt furniture ranged along the walls; had he stood upon a dais on a noble square of red carpet, he would have probably been very dangerous from a sense of success and elevation. But in this sacked and devastated residence, with the three pieces of common furniture huddled up in the middle of the vast apartment, Pedrito's imagination was subdued by a feeling of insecurity and impermanence. That feeling and the firm attitude of Charles Gould who had not once, so far, pronounced the word 'Excellency', diminished him in his own eyes. He assumed the tone of an enlightened man of the world, and begged Charles Gould to dismiss from his mind every cause for alarm. He was now conversing, he reminded him, with the brother of the master of the country, charged with a reorganising mission. The trusted brother of the master of the country, he repeated. Nothing was further from the thoughts of that wise and patriotic hero than ideas of destruction. 'I entreat you, Don Carlos, not to give way to your anti-democratic prejudices,' he cried, in a burst of condescending effusion.

Pedrito Montero surprised one at first sight by the vast development of his bald forehead, a shiny yellow expanse between the crinkly coal-black tufts of hair without any lustre, the engaging form of his mouth, and an unexpectedly cultivated voice. But his eyes, very glistening as if freshly painted on each side of his hooked nose, had a round, hopeless, birdlike stare when opened fully. Now, however, he narrowed them agreeably, throwing his square chin up and speaking with closed teeth slightly through the nose, with what he imagined to be the manner of a grand seigneur.

In that attitude, he declared suddenly that the highest expression of democracy was Caesarism: the imperial rule based upon the direct popular vote. Caesarism was conservative. It was strong. It recognised the legitimate needs of democracy which requires orders, titles, and distinctions. They would be showered upon deserving men. Caesarism was peace. It was progressive. It secured the prosperity of a country. Pedrito Montero was carried away. Look at what the Second Empire had done for France. It was a régime which delighted to honour men of Don Carlos's stamp. The Second Empire fell, but that was because its chief was devoid of that military genius which had raised General Montero to the pinnacle of fame and glory. Pedrito elevated his hand jerkily to help the idea of pinnacle, of fame. 'We shall have many talks yet. We shall understand each other thoroughly, Don Carlos!' he cried in a tone of fellowship. Republicanism had done its work. Imperial democracy was the power of the future. Pedrito, the guerrillero, showing his hand, lowered his voice forcibly. A man singled out by his fellow-citizens for the honourable nickname of El Rey de Sulaco could not but receive a full recognition from an imperial democracy as a great captain of industry and a person of weighty counsel, whose popular designation would be soon replaced by a more solid title. 'Eh, Don Carlos? No! What do you say? Conde de Sulaco – Eh? – or marquis . . .'

He ceased. The air was cool on the Plaza, where a patrol of cavalry rode round and round without penetrating into the streets, which resounded with shouts and the strumming of guitars issuing from the open doors of pulperías. The orders were not to interfere with the enjoyments of the people. And above the roofs, next to the perpendicular lines of the cathedral towers the snowy curve of Higuerota blocked a large space of darkening blue sky before the windows of the Intendencia. After a time Pedrito Montero, thrusting his hand in the bosom of his coat, bowed his head with slow dignity. The audience was over.

Charles Gould on going out passed his hand over his forehead as if to disperse the mists of an oppressive dream, whose grotesque extravagance leaves behind a subtle sense of bodily danger and intellectual decay. In the passages and on the staircases of the old palace Montero's troopers lounged about insolently, smoking and making way for no one; the clanking of sabres and spurs resounded all over the building. Three silent groups of civilians in severe black waited in the main gallery, formal and helpless, a little huddled up, each keeping apart from the others, as if in the exercise of a public duty they had been overcome by a desire to shun the notice of every eye. These were the deputations waiting for their audience. The one from the Provincial Assembly, more restless and uneasy in its corporate expression, was overtopped by the big face of Don Juste Lopez, soft and white, with prominent eyelids and wreathed in impenetrable solemnity as if in a dense cloud. The President of the Provincial Assembly, coming bravely to save the last shred of parliamentary institutions (on the English model), averted his eyes from the Administrador of the San Tomé mine as a dignified rebuke of his little faith in that only saving principle.

The mournful severity of that reproof did not affect Charles Gould, but he was sensible to the glances of the others directed upon him without reproach, as if only to read their own fate upon his face. All of them had talked, shouted, and declaimed in the great sala of the Casa Gould. The feeling of compassion for those men, struck with a strange impotence in the toils of moral degradation, did not induce him to make a sign. He suffered from his fellowship in evil with them too much. He crossed the Plaza unmolested. The Amarilla Club was full of festive ragamuffins. Their frowsy heads protruded from every window, and from within came drunken shouts, the thumping of feet, and the twanging of harps. Broken bottles strewed the pavement below. Charles Gould found the doctor still in his house.

Dr Monygham came away from the crack in the shutter through which he had been watching the street.

'Ah! You are back at last!' he said in a tone of relief. 'I have been telling Mrs Gould that you were perfectly safe, but I was not by any means certain that the fellow would have let you go.'

'Neither was I,' confessed Charles Gould, laying his hat on the table.

'You will have to take action.'

The silence of Charles Gould seemed to admit that this was the only course. This was as far as Charles Gould was accustomed to go towards intentions.

'I hope you did not warn Montero of what you mean to do,' the doctor said, anxiously.

'I tried to make him see that the existence of the mine was bound up with my personal safety,' continued Charles Gould, looking away from the doctor, and fixing his eyes upon the watercolour sketch upon the wall.

'He believed you?' the doctor asked, eagerly.

'God knows!' said Charles Gould. 'I owed it to my wife to say that much. He is well enough informed. He knows that I have Don Pépé there. Fuentes must have told him. They know that the old major is perfectly capable of blowing up the San Tomé mine without hesitation or compunction. Had it not been for that I don't think I'd have left the Intendencia a free man. He would blow everything up from loyalty and from hate – from hate of these Liberals, as they call themselves. Liberals! The words one knows so well have a nightmarish meaning in this country. Liberty, democracy, patriotism, government – all of them have a flavour of folly and murder. Haven't they, doctor? . . . I alone can restrain Don Pépé. If they were to – to do away with me, nothing could prevent him.'

'They will try to tamper with him,' the doctor suggested, thoughtfully.

'It is very possible,' Charles Gould said very low, as if speaking to himself, and still gazing at the sketch of the San Tomé gorge upon the wall. 'Yes, I expect they will try that.' Charles Gould looked for the first time at the doctor. 'It would give me time,' he added.

'Exactly,' said Dr Monygham, suppressing his excitement. 'Especially if Don Pépé behaves diplomatically. Why shouldn't he give them some hope of success? Eh? Otherwise you wouldn't gain so much time. Couldn't he be instructed to –'

Charles Gould, looking at the doctor steadily, shook his head, but the doctor continued with a certain amount of fire: 'Yes, to enter into negotiations for the surrender of the mine. It is a good notion. You would mature your plan. Of course, I don't ask what it is. I don't want to know. I would refuse to listen to you if you tried to tell me. I am not fit for confidences.'

'What nonsense!' muttered Charles Gould, with displeasure.

He disapproved of the doctor's sensitiveness about that far-off episode of his life. So much memory shocked Charles Gould. It was like morbidness. And again he shook his head. He refused to tamper with the open rectitude of Don Pépé's conduct, both from taste and from policy. Instructions would have to be either verbal or in writing. In either case they ran the risk of being intercepted. It was by no means certain that a messenger could reach the mine; and, besides, there was no one to send. It was on the tip of Charles's tongue to say that only the late Capataz de Cargadores could have been employed with some chance of success and the certitude of discretion. But he did not say that. He pointed out to the doctor that it would have been bad policy. Directly Don Pépé let it be supposed that he could be bought over, the Administrador's personal safety and the safety of his friends would become endangered. For there would be then no reason for moderation. The incorruptibility of Don Pépé was the essential and restraining fact. The doctor hung his head and admitted that in a way it was so.

He couldn't deny to himself that the reasoning was sound enough. Don Pépé's usefulness consisted in his unstained character. As to his own useful-ness, he reflected bitterly it was also his own character. He declared to Charles Gould that he had the means of keeping Sotillo from joining his forces with Montero at least for the present.

'If you had had all this silver here,' the doctor said, 'or even if it had been known to be at the mine, you could have bribed Sotillo to throw off his recent Monterism. You could have induced him either to go away in his steamer or even to join you.'

'Certainly not that last,' Charles Gould declared, firmly. 'What could one do with a man like that, afterwards – tell me, doctor? The silver is gone, and I am glad of it. It would have been an immediate and strong temptation. The scramble for that visible plunder would have precipitated a disastrous ending. I would have had to defend it, too. I am glad we've removed it – even if it is lost. It would have been a danger and a curse.'

'Perhaps he is right,' the doctor, an hour later, said hurriedly to Mrs Gould, whom he met in the corridor. 'The thing is done, and the shadow of the treasure may do just as well as the substance. Let me try to serve you to the whole extent of my evil reputation. I am off now to play my game of betrayal with Sotillo, and keep him off the town.'

She put out both her hands impulsively. 'Dr Monygham, you are running a terrible risk,' she whispered, averting from his face her eyes, full of tears, for a short glance at the door of her husband's room. She pressed both his hands, and the doctor stood as if rooted to the spot, looking down at her, and trying to twist his lips into a smile.

'Oh, I know you will defend my memory,' he uttered at last, and ran tottering down the stairs across the patio, and out of the house. In the street he kept up a great pace with his smart hobbling walk, a case of instruments under his arm. He was known for being *loco*. Nobody interfered with him. From under the seaward gate, across the dusty, arid plain, interspersed with low bushes, he saw, more than a mile away, the ugly enormity of the Custom House, and the two or three other buildings which at that time constituted the seaport of Sulaco. Far away to the south groves of palm trees edged the curve of the harbour shore. The distant peaks of the Cordillera had lost their identity of clear-cut shapes in the steadily deepening blue of the eastern sky. The doctor walked briskly. A darkling shadow seemed to fall upon him from the zenith. The sun had set. For a time the snows of Higuerota continued to glow with the reflected glory of the west. The doctor, holding a straight course for the Custom House, appeared lonely, hopping amongst the dark bushes like a tall bird with a broken wing.

Tints of purple, gold, and crimson were mirrored in the clear water of the harbour. A long tongue of land, straight as a wall, with the grass-grown ruins of the fort making a sort of rounded green mound, plainly visible from the inner shore, closed its circuit; while beyond the Placid Gulf repeated those splendours of colouring on a greater scale and with a more sombre magnificence. The great mass of cloud filling the head of the gulf had long red smears amongst its convoluted folds of grey and black, as of a floating mantle stained with blood. The three Isabels, overshadowed and clear cut in a great smoothness confounding the sea and sky, appeared suspended, purple-black, in the air. The little wavelets seemed to be tossing tiny red sparks upon the sandy beaches. The glassy bands along the horizon gave out a fiery red glow, as if fire and water had been mingled together in the vast bed of the ocean.

At last the conflagration of sea and sky, lying embraced and still in a flaming contact upon the edge of the world, went out. The red sparks in the water vanished together with the stains of blood in the black mantle draping the sombre head of the Placid Gulf; a sudden breeze sprang up and died out after rustling heavily the growth of bushes on the ruined earthwork of the fort. Nostromo woke up from a fourteen hours' sleep, and arose full length from his lair in the long grass. He stood knee deep amongst the whispering undulations of the green blades with the lost air of a man just born into the world. Handsome, robust, and supple, he threw back his head, flung his arms open, and stretched himself with a slow twist of the waist and a leisurely growling yawn of white teeth, as natural and free from evil in the moment of waking as a magnificent and unconscious wild beast. Then, in the suddenly steadied glance fixed upon nothing from under a thoughtful frown, appeared the man.

Chapter 8

After landing from his swim Nostromo had scrambled up, all dripping, into the main quadrangle of the old fort; and there, amongst ruined bits of walls and rotting remnants of roofs and sheds, he had slept the day through. He had slept in the shadow of the mountains, in the white blaze of noon, in the stillness and solitude of that overgrown piece of land between the oval of the harbour and the spacious semicircle of the gulf. He lay as if dead. A reyzamuro, appearing like a tiny black speck in the blue, stooped, circling prudently with a stealthiness of flight startling in a bird of that great size. The shadow of his pearly-white body, of his black-tipped wings, fell on the grass no more silently than he alighted himself on a hillock of rubbish within three yards of that man, lying as still as a corpse. The bird stretched his bare neck, craned his bald head, loathsome in the brilliance of varied colouring, with an air of voracious anxiety towards the promising stillness of that prostrate body. Then, sinking his head deeply into his soft plumage, he settled himself to wait. The first thing upon which Nostromo's eyes fell on waking was this patient watcher for the signs of death and corruption. When the man got up the vulture hopped away in great, sidelong, fluttering jumps. He lingered for a while, morose and reluctant, before he rose, circling noiselessly with a sinister droop of beak and claws.

Long after he had vanished, Nostromo, lifting his eyes up to the sky, muttered, 'I am not dead yet.'

The Capataz of the Sulaco Cargadores had lived in splendour and publicity up to the very moment, as it were, when he took charge of the lighter containing the treasure of silver ingots.

The last act he had performed in Sulaco was in complete harmony with his vanity, and as such perfectly genuine. He had given his last dollar to an old woman moaning with the grief and fatigue of a dismal search under the arch of the ancient gate. Performed in obscurity and without witnesses, it had still the characteristics of splendour and publicity, and was in strict keeping with his reputation. But this awakening in solitude, except for the watchful vulture, amongst the ruins of the fort, had no such characteristics. His first confused feeling was exactly this – that it was not in keeping. It was more like the end of things. The necessity of living concealed somehow, for God knows how long, which assailed him on his return to consciousness, made everything that had gone before for years appear vain and foolish, like a flattering dream come suddenly to an end.

He climbed the crumbling slope of the rampart, and, putting aside the bushes, looked upon the harbour. He saw a couple of ships at anchor upon the sheet of water reflecting the last gleams of light, and Sotillo's steamer moored to the jetty. And behind the pale long front of the Custom House, there appeared the extent of the town like a grove of thick timber on the plain with a gateway in front, and the cupolas, towers, and miradors rising above the trees, all dark, as if surrendered already to the night. The thought that it was no longer open to him to ride through the streets, recognised by everyone, great and little, as he used to do every evening on his way to play monte in the posada of the Mexican Domingo; or to sit in the place of honour, listening to songs and looking at dances, made it appear to him a town that had no existence.

For a long time he gazed on, then let the parted bushes spring back, and, crossing over to the other side of the fort, surveyed the vaster emptiness of the great gulf. The Isabels stood out heavily upon the narrowing long band of red in the west, which gleamed low between their black shapes, and the Capataz thought of Decoud alone there with the treasure. That man was the only one who cared whether he fell into the hands of the Monterists or not, the Capataz reflected bitterly. And that merely would be an anxiety for his own sake. As to the rest, they neither knew nor cared. What he had heard Giorgio Viola say once was very true. Kings, ministers, aristocrats, the rich in general, kept the people in poverty and subjection; they kept them as they kept dogs, to fight and hunt for their service.

The darkness of the sky had descended to the line of the horizon, enveloping the whole gulf, the islets, and the lover of Antonia alone with the treasure on the Great Isabel. The Capataz, turning his back on these things invisible and existing, sat down and took his face between his fists. He felt the pinch of poverty for the first time in his life. To find himself without money after a run of bad luck at monte in the low, smoky room of Domingo's posada, where the fraternity of Cargadores gambled, sang, and danced of an evening; to remain with empty pockets after a burst of public generosity to some *peine de oro* girl or other (for whom he did not care), had none of the humiliation of destitution. He remained rich in glory and reputation. But since it was no longer possible for him to parade the streets of the town, and be hailed with respect in the usual haunts of his leisure, this sailor felt himself destitute indeed.

His mouth was dry. It was dry with heavy sleep and extremely anxious thinking, as it had never been dry before. It may be said that Nostromo tasted the dust and ashes of the fruit of life into which he had bitten deeply in his hunger for praise. Without removing his head from between his fists, he tried to spit before him – 'Tfui' – and muttered a curse upon the selfishness of all the rich people.

Since everything seemed lost in Sulaco (and that was the feeling of his waking), the idea of leaving the country altogether had presented itself to

Nostromo. At that thought he had seen, like the beginning of another dream, a vision of steep and tideless shores, with dark pines on the heights and white houses low down near a very blue sea. He saw the quays of a big port, where the coasting feluccas, with their lateen sails outspread like motionless wings, enter gliding silently between the end of long moles of squared blocks that project angularly towards each other, hugging a cluster of shipping to the superb bosom of a hill covered with palaces. He remembered these sights not without some filial emotion, though he had been habitually and severely beaten as a boy on one of these feluccas by a short-necked, shaven Genoese, with a deliberate and distrustful manner, who (he firmly believed) had cheated him out of his orphan's inheritance. But it is mercifully decreed that the evils of the past should appear but faintly in retrospect. Under the sense of loneliness, abandonment, and failure, the idea of return to these things appeared tolerable. But, what? Return? With bare feet and head, with one check shirt and a pair of cotton calzoneras for all worldly possessions?

The renowned Capataz, his elbows on his knees and a fist dug into each cheek, laughed with self-derision, as he had spat with disgust, straight out before him into the night. The confused and intimate impressions of universal dissolution which beset a subjective nature at any strong check to its ruling passion had a bitterness approaching that of death itself. He was simple. He was as ready to become the prey of any belief, superstition, or desire as a child.

The facts of his situation he could appreciate like a man with a distinct experience of the country. He saw them clearly. He was as if sobered after a long bout of intoxication. His fidelity had been taken advantage of. He had persuaded the body of Cargadores to side with the Blancos against the rest of the people; he had had interviews with Don José; he had been made use of by Father Corbelàn for negotiating with Hernandez; it was known that Don Martin Decoud had admitted him to a sort of intimacy, so that he had been free of the offices of the *Porvenir*. All these things had flattered him in the usual way. What did he care about their politics? Nothing at all. And at the end of it all – Nostromo here and Nostromo there – where is Nostromo? Nostromo can do this and that – work all day and ride all night – behold! he found himself a marked Ribierist for any sort of vengeance Gamacho, for instance, would choose to take, now the Montero party had, after all, mastered the town. The Europeans had given up; the Caballeros had given up. Don Martin had indeed explained it was only temporary – that he was going to bring Barrios to the rescue. Where was that now – with Don Martin (whose ironic manner of talk had always made the Capataz feel vaguely uneasy) stranded on the Great Isabel? Everybody had given up. Even Don Carlos had given up. The hurried removal of the treasure out to sea meant nothing else than that. The Capataz de Cargadores, on a revulsion of subjectiveness, exasperated almost to insanity, beheld all his world without faith and courage. He had been betrayed!

With the boundless shadows of the sea behind him, out of his silence and immobility, facing the lofty shapes of the lower peaks crowded around the white, misty sheen of Higuerota, Nostromo laughed aloud again, sprang abruptly to his feet, and stood still. He must go. But where?

'There is no mistake. They keep us and encourage us as if we were dogs born to fight and hunt for them. The vecchio is right,' he said, slowly and scathingly. He remembered old Giorgio taking his pipe out of his mouth to throw these words over his shoulder at the café, full of engine-drivers and fitters from the railway workshops. This image fixed his wavering purpose. He would try to find old Giorgio if he could. God knows what might have happened to him! He made a few steps, then stopped again and shook his head. To the left and right, in front and behind him, the scrubby bush rustled mysteriously in the darkness.

'Teresa was right, too,' he added in a low tone touched with awe. He wondered whether she was dead in her anger with him or still alive. As if in answer to this thought, half of remorse and half of hope, with a soft flutter and oblique flight, a big owl, whose appalling cry: 'Ya-acabo! Ya-acabo! – it is finished; it is finished' – announces calamity and death in the popular belief, drifted vaguely like a large dark ball across his path. In the downfall of all the realities that made his force, he was affected by the superstition, and shuddered slightly. Signora Teresa must have died, then. It could mean nothing else. The cry of the ill-omened bird, the first sound he was to hear on his return, was a fitting welcome for his betrayed individuality. The unseen powers which he had offended by refusing to bring a priest to a dying woman were lifting up their voice against him. She was dead. With admirable and human consistency he referred everything to himself. She had been a woman of good counsel always. And the bereaved old Giorgio remained stunned by his loss just as he was likely to require the advice of his sagacity. The blow would render the dreamy old man quite stupid for a time.

As to Captain Mitchell, Nostromo, after the manner of trusted subordinates, considered him as a person fitted by education perhaps to sign papers in an office and to give orders, but otherwise of no use whatever, and something of a fool. The necessity of winding round his little finger, almost daily, the pompous and testy self-importance of the old seaman had grown irksome with use to Nostromo. At first it had given him an inward satisfaction. But the necessity of overcoming small obstacles becomes wearisome to a self-confident personality as much by the certitude of success as by the monotony of effort. He mistrusted his superior's proneness to fussy action. That old Englishman had no judgment, he said to himself. It was useless to suppose that, acquainted with the true state of the case, he would keep it to himself. He would talk of doing impracticable things. Nostromo feared him as one would fear saddling one's self with some persistent worry. He had no discretion. He would betray the treasure. And Nostromo had made up his mind that the treasure should not be betrayed.

The word had fixed itself tenaciously in his intelligence. His imagination had seized upon the clear and simple notion of betrayal to account for the dazed feeling of enlightenment as to being done for, of having inadvertently gone out of his existence on an issue in which his personality had not been taken into account. A man betrayed is a man destroyed. Signora Teresa (may God have her soul!) had been right. He had never been taken into account. Destroyed! Her white form sitting up bowed in bed, the falling black hair, the wide-browed suffering face raised to him, the anger of her denunciations appeared to him now majestic with the awfulness of inspiration and of death. For it was not for nothing that the evil bird had uttered its lamentable shriek over his head. She was dead – may God have her soul!

Sharing in the anti-priestly freethought of the masses, his mind used the pious formula from the superficial force of habit, but with a deep-seated sincerity. The popular mind is incapable of scepticism; and that incapacity delivers their helpless strength to the wiles of swindlers and to the pitiless enthusiasms of leaders inspired by visions of a high destiny. She was dead. But would God consent to receive her soul? She had died without confession or absolution, because he had not been willing to spare her another moment of his time. His scorn of priests as priests remained; but after all, it was impossible to know whether what they affirmed was not true. Power, punishment, pardon, are simple and credible notions. The magnificent Capataz de Cargadores, deprived of certain simple realities, such as the admiration of women, the adulation of men, the admired publicity of his life, was ready to feel the burden of sacrilegious guilt descend upon his shoulders.

Bareheaded, in a thin shirt and drawers, he felt the lingering warmth of the fine sand under the soles of his feet. The narrow strand gleamed far ahead in a long curve, defining the outline of this wild side of the harbour. He flitted along the shore like a pursued shadow between the sombre palm-groves and the sheet of water lying as still as death on his right hand. He strode with headlong haste in the silence and solitude as though he had forgotten all prudence and caution. But he knew that on this side of the water he ran no risk of discovery. The only inhabitant was a lonely, silent, apathetic Indian in charge of the palmeras, who brought sometimes a load of cocoanuts to the town for sale. He lived without a woman in an open shed, with a perpetual fire of dry sticks smouldering near an old canoe lying bottom up on the beach. He could be easily avoided.

The barking of the dogs about that man's rancho was the first thing that checked his speed. He had forgotten the dogs. He swerved sharply, and plunged into the palm-grove, as into a wilderness of columns in an immense hall, whose dense obscurity seemed to whisper and rustle faintly high above his head. He traversed it, entered a ravine, climbed to the top of a steep ridge free of trees and bushes.

From there, open and vague in the starlight, he saw the plain between the town and the harbour. In the woods above some night-bird made a strange drumming noise. Below beyond the palmera on the beach, the Indian's dogs continued to bark uproariously. He wondered what had upset them so much, and, peering down from his elevation, was surprised to detect unaccountable movements of the ground below, as if several oblong pieces of the plain had been in motion. Those dark, shifting patches, alternately catching and eluding the eye, altered their place always away from the harbour, with a suggestion of consecutive order and purpose. A light dawned upon him. It was a column of infantry on a night march towards the higher broken country at the foot of the hills. But he was too much in the dark about everything for wonder and speculation.

The plain had resumed its shadowy immobility. He descended the ridge and found himself in the open solitude, between the harbour and the town. Its spaciousness, extended indefinitely by an effect of obscurity, rendered more sensible his profound isolation. His pace became slower. No one waited for him; no one thought of him; no one expected or wished his return. 'Betrayed! Betrayed!' he muttered to himself. No one cared. He might have been drowned by this time. No one would have cared – unless, perhaps, the children, he thought to himself. But they were with the English signora, and not thinking of him at all.

He wavered in his purpose of making straight for the Casa Viola. To what end? What could he expect there? His life seemed to fail him in all its details, even to the scornful reproaches of Teresa. He was aware painfully of his reluctance. Was it that remorse she had prophesied with what he saw now, was her last breath?

Meantime, he had deviated from the straight course, inclining by a sort of instinct to the right, towards the jetty and the harbour, the scene of his daily labours. The great length of the Custom House loomed up all at once like the wall of a factory. Not a soul challenged his approach, and his curiosity became excited as he passed cautiously towards the front by the unexpected sight of two lighted windows.

They had the fascination of a lonely vigil kept by some mysterious watcher up there, those two windows shining dimly upon the harbour in the whole vast extent of the abandoned building. The solitude could almost be felt. A strong smell of wood smoke hung about in a thin haze, which was faintly perceptible to his raised eyes against the glitter of the stars. As he advanced in the profound silence, the shrilling of innumerable cicalas in the dry grass seemed positively deafening to his strained ears. Slowly, step by step, he found himself in the great hall, sombre and full of acrid smoke.

A fire built against the staircase had burnt down impotently to a low heap of embers. The hard wood had failed to catch; only a few steps at the bottom smouldered, with a creeping glow of sparks defining their charred edges. At the top he saw a streak of light from an open door. It fell upon the vast landing, all foggy with a slow drift of smoke. That was the room. He climbed the stairs, then checked himself, because he had seen within the shadow of a man cast upon one of the walls. It was a shapeless, high shouldered shadow of somebody standing still, with lowered head, out of his line of sight. The Capataz, remembering that he was totally unarmed, stepped aside, and, effacing himself upright in a dark corner, waited with his eyes fixed on the door.

The whole enormous ruined barrack of a place, unfinished, without ceilings under its lofty roof, was pervaded by the smoke swaying to and fro in the faint cross draughts playing in the obscurity of many lofty rooms and barnlike passages. Once one of the swinging shutters came against the wall with a single sharp crack, as if pushed by an impatient hand. A piece of paper scurried out from somewhere, rustling along the landing. The man, whoever he was, did not darken the lighted doorway. Twice the Capataz, advancing a couple of steps out of his corner, craned his neck in the hope of catching sight of what he could be at, so quietly, in there. But every time he saw only the distorted shadow of broad shoulders and bowed head.

He was doing apparently nothing, and stirred not from the spot, as though he were meditating – or, perhaps, reading a paper. And not a sound issued from the room.

Once more the Capataz stepped back. He wondered who it was – some Monterist? But he dreaded to show himself. To discover his presence on shore, unless after many days, would, he believed, endanger the treasure. With his own knowledge possessing his whole soul, it seemed impossible that anybody in Sulaco should fail to jump at the right surmise. After a couple of weeks or so it would be different. Who could tell he had not returned overland from some port beyond the limits of the Republic? The existence of the treasure confused his thoughts with a peculiar sort of anxiety, as though his life had become bound up with it. It rendered him timorous for a moment before that enigmatic, lighted door. Devil take the fellow! He did not want to see him. There would be nothing to learn from his face, known or unknown. He was a fool to waste his time there in waiting.

Less than five minutes after entering the place the Capataz began his retreat. He got away down the stairs with perfect success, gave one upward look over his shoulder at the light on the landing, and ran stealthily across the hall. But at the very moment he was turning out of the great door, with his mind fixed upon escaping the notice of the man upstairs, somebody he had not heard coming briskly along the front ran full into him. Both muttered a stifled exclamation of surprise, and leaped back and stood still, each indistinct to the other. Nostromo was silent. The other man spoke first, in an amazed and deadened tone.

'Who are you?'

Already Nostromo had seemed to recognise Dr Monygham. He had no doubt now. He hesitated the space of a second. The idea of bolting without a word presented itself to his mind. No use! An inexplicable repugnance to pronounce the name by which he was known kept him silent a little longer. At last he said in a low voice: 'A Cargador.'

He walked up to the other. Dr Monygham had received a shock. He flung his arms up and cried out his wonder aloud, forgetting himself before the marvel of this meeting. Nostromo angrily warned him to moderate his voice. The Custom House was not so deserted as it looked. There was somebody in the lighted room above.

There is no more evanescent quality in an accomplished fact than its wonderfulness. Solicited incessantly by the considerations affecting its fears and desires, the human mind turns naturally away from the marvellous side of events. And it was in the most natural way possible that the doctor asked this man whom only two minutes before he believed to have been drowned in the gulf –

'You have seen somebody up there? Have you?'

'No, I have not seen him.' .

'Then how do you know?'

'I was running away from his shadow when we met.'

'His shadow?'

'Yes. His shadow in the lighted room,' said Nostromo, in a contemptuous tone. Leaning back with folded arms at the foot of the immense building, he dropped his head, biting his lips slightly, and not looking at the doctor. 'Now,' he thought to himself, 'he will begin asking me about the treasure.'

But the doctor's thoughts were concerned with an event not as marvellous as Nostromo's appearance, but in itself much less clear. Why had Sotillo taken himself off with his whole command with this suddenness and secrecy? What did this move portend? However, it dawned upon the doctor that the man upstairs was one of the officers left behind by the disappointed colonel to communicate with him.

'I believe he is waiting for me,' he said.

'It is possible.'

'I must see. Do not go away yet, Capataz.'

'Go away where?' muttered Nostromo.

Already the doctor had left him. He remained leaning against the wall, staring at the dark water of the harbour; the shrilling of cicalas filled his ears. An invincible vagueness coming over his thoughts took from them all power to determine his will.

'Capataz! Capataz!' the doctor's voice called urgently from above.

The sense of betrayal and ruin floated upon his sombre indifference as upon a sluggish sea of pitch. But he stepped out from under the wall, and, looking up, saw Dr Monygham leaning out of a lighted window.

'Come up and see what Sotillo has done. You need not fear the man up here.'

He answered by a slight, bitter laugh. Fear a man! The Capataz of the Sulaco Cargadores fear a man! It angered him that anybody should suggest such a thing. It angered him to be disarmed and skulking and in danger because of the accursed treasure, which was of so little account to the people who had tied it round his neck. He could not shake off the worry of it. To

Nostromo the doctor represented all these people . . . And he had never even asked after it. Not a word of enquiry about the most desperate undertaking of his life.

Thinking these thoughts, Nostromo passed again through the cavernous hall, where the smoke was considerably thinned, and went up the stairs, not so warm to his feet now, towards the streak of light at the top. The doctor appeared in it for a moment, agitated and impatient.

'Come up! Come up!'

At the moment of crossing the doorway the Capataz experienced a shock of surprise. The man had not moved. He saw his shadow in the same place. He started, then stepped in with a feeling of being about to solve a mystery.

It was very simple. For an infinitesimal fraction of a second, against the light of two flaring and guttering candles, through a blue, pungent, thin haze which made his eyes smart, he saw the man standing, as he had imagined him, with his back to the door, casting an enormous and distorted shadow upon the wall. Swifter than a flash of lightning followed the impression of his constrained, toppling attitude – the shoulders projecting forward, the head sunk low upon the breast. Then he distinguished the arms behind his back, and wrenched so terribly that the two clenched fists, lashed together, had been forced up higher than the shoulder-blades. From there his eyes traced in one instantaneous glance the hide rope going upwards from the tied wrists over a heavy beam and down to a staple in the wall. He did not want to look at the rigid legs, at the feet hanging down nervelessly, with their bare toes some six inches above the floor, to know that the man had been given the estrapade till he had swooned. His first impulse was to dash forward and sever the rope at one blow. He felt for his knife. He had no knife – not even a knife. He stood quivering, and the doctor, perched on the edge of the table, facing thoughtfully the cruel and lamentable sight, his chin in his hand, uttered, without stirring: 'Tortured – and shot dead through the breast – getting cold.'

This information calmed the Capataz. One of the candles flickering in the socket went out. 'Who did this?' he asked.

'Sotillo, I tell you. Who else? Tortured – of course. But why shot?' The doctor looked fixedly at Nostromo, who shrugged his shoulders slightly. 'And mark, shot suddenly, on impulse. It is evident. I wish I had his secret.'

Nostromo had advanced, and stooped slightly to look. 'I seem to have seen that face somewhere,' he muttered. 'Who is he?'

The doctor turned his eyes upon him again. 'I may yet come to envying his fate. What do you think of that, Capataz, eh?'

But Nostromo did not even hear these words. Seizing the remaining light, he thrust it under the drooping head. The doctor sat oblivious, with a lost gaze. Then the heavy iron candlestick, as if struck out of Nostromo's hand, clattered on the floor.

'Hullo!' exclaimed the doctor, looking up with a start. He could hear the

Capataz stagger against the table and gasp. In the sudden extinction of the light within, the dead blackness sealing the window-frames became alive with stars to his sight.

'Of course, of course,' the doctor muttered to himself in English. 'Enough to make him jump out of his skin.'

Nostromo's heart seemed to force itself into his throat. His head swam. Hirsch! The man was Hirsch! He held on tight to the edge of the table.

'But he was hiding in the lighter,' he almost shouted. His voice fell. 'In the lighter, and – and – '

'And Sotillo brought him in,' said the doctor. 'He is no more startling to you than you were to me. What I want to know is how he induced some compassionate soul to shoot him.'

'So Sotillo knows – ' began Nostromo, in a more equable voice.

'Everything!' interrupted the doctor.

The Capataz was heard striking the table with his fist. 'Everything? What are you saying, there? Everything? Know everything? It is impossible! Everything?'

'Of course. What do you mean by impossible? I tell you I have heard this Hirsch questioned last night, here, in this very room. He knew your name, Decoud's name, and all about the loading of the silver . . . The lighter was cut in two. He was grovelling in abject terror before Sotillo, but he remembered that much. What do you want more? He knew least about himself. They found him clinging to their anchor. He must have caught at it just as the lighter went to the bottom.'

'Went to the bottom?' repeated Nostromo, slowly. 'Sotillo believes that? *Bueno!*'

The doctor, a little impatiently, was unable to imagine what else could anybody believe. Yes, Sotillo believed that the lighter was sunk, and the Capataz de Cargadores, together with Martin Decoud and perhaps one or two other political fugitives, had been drowned.

'I told you well, señor doctor,' remarked Nostromo at that point, 'that Sotillo did not know everything.'

'Eh? What do you mean?'

'He did not know I was not dead.'

'Neither did we.'

'And you did not care – none of you caballeros on the wharf – once you got off a man of flesh and blood like yourselves on a fool's business that could not end well.'

'You forget, Capataz, I was not on the wharf. And I did not think well of the business. So you need not taunt me. I tell you what, man, we had but little leisure to think of the dead. Death stands near behind us all. You were gone.'

'I went, indeed!' broke in Nostromo. 'And for the sake of what – tell me?'

'Ah! that is your own affair,' the doctor said, roughly. 'Do not ask me.'

Their flowing murmurs paused in the dark. Perched on the edge of the table with slightly averted faces, they felt their shoulders touch, and their eyes remained directed towards an upright shape nearly lost in the obscurity of the inner part of the room, that with projecting head and shoulders, in ghastly immobility, seemed intent on catching every word.

'*Muy bien!*' Nostromo muttered at last. 'So be it. Teresa was right. It is my own affair.'

'Teresa is dead,' remarked the doctor, absently, while his mind followed a new line of thought suggested by what might have been called Nostromo's return to life. 'She died, the poor woman.'

'Without a priest?' the Capataz asked, anxiously.

'What a question! Who could have got a priest for her last night?'

'May God keep her soul!' ejaculated Nostromo, with a gloomy and hopeless fervour which had no time to surprise Dr Monygham, before, reverting to their previous conversation, he continued in a sinister tone, 'Si, señor doctor. As you were saying, it is my own affair. A very desperate affair.'

'There are no two men in this part of the world that could have saved themselves by swimming as you have done,' the doctor said, admiringly.

And again there was silence between those two men. They were both reflecting, and the diversity of their natures made their thoughts born from their meeting swing afar from each other. The doctor, impelled to risky action by his loyalty to the Goulds, wondered with thankfulness at the chain of accident which had brought that man back where he would be of the greatest use in the work of saving the San Tomé mine. The doctor was loyal to the mine. It presented itself to his fifty-years' old eyes in the shape of a little woman in a soft dress with a long train, with a head attractively overweighted by a great mass of fair hair and the delicate preciousness of her inner worth, partaking of a gem and a flower, revealed in every attitude of her person. As the dangers thickened round the San Tomé mine this illusion acquired force, permanency, and authority. It claimed him at last! This claim, exalted by a spiritual detachment from the usual sanctions of hope and reward, made Dr Monygham's thinking, acting, individuality extremely dangerous to himself and to others, all his scruples vanishing in the proud feeling that his devotion was the only thing that stood between an admirable woman and a frightful disaster.

It was a sort of intoxication which made him utterly indifferent to Decoud's fate, but left his wits perfectly clear for the appreciation of Decoud's political idea. It was a good idea – and Barrios was the only instrument of its realisation. The doctor's soul, withered and shrunk by the shame of a moral disgrace, became implacable in the expansion of its tenderness. Nostromo's return was providential. He did not think of him humanely, as of a fellow-creature just escaped from the jaws of death. The Capataz for him was the only possible messenger to Cayta. The very man. The doctor's misanthropic mistrust of mankind (the bitterer because based on personal failure) did not lift him sufficiently above common weaknesses. He was under the spell of an established reputation. Trumpeted by Captain Mitchell, grown in repetition, and fixed in general assent, Nostromo's faithfulness had never been questioned by Dr Monygham as a fact. It was not likely to be questioned now he stood in desperate need of it himself. Dr Monygham was human; he accepted the popular conception of the Capataz's incorruptibility simply because no word or fact had ever contradicted a mere affirmation. It seemed to be a part of the man, like his whiskers or his teeth. It was impossible to conceive him otherwise. The question was whether he would consent to go on such a dangerous and desperate errand. The doctor was observant enough to have become aware from the first of something peculiar in the man's temper. He was no doubt sore about the loss of the silver.

'It will be necessary to take him into my fullest confidence,' he said to himself, with a certain acuteness of insight into the nature he had to deal with.

On Nostromo's side the silence had been full of black irresolution, anger, and mistrust. He was the first to break it, however.

'The swimming was no great matter,' he said. 'It is what went before – and what comes after that – '

He did not quite finish what he meant to say, breaking off short, as though his thought had butted against a solid obstacle. The doctor's mind pursued its own schemes with Machiavellian subtlety. He said as sympathetically as he was able: 'It is unfortunate, Capataz. But no one would think of blaming you. Very unfortunate. To begin with, the treasure ought never to have left the mountain. But it was Decoud who – however, he is dead. There is no need to talk of him.'

'No,' assented Nostromo, as the doctor paused, 'there is no need to talk of dead men. But I am not dead yet.'

'You are all right. Only a man of your intrepidity could have saved himself.'

In this Dr Monygham was sincere. He esteemed highly the intrepidity of that man, whom he valued but little, being disillusioned as to mankind in general, because of the particular instance in which his own manhood had failed. Having had to encounter single-handed during his period of eclipse many physical dangers, he was well aware of the most dangerous element common to them all: of the crushing, paralysing sense of human littleness, which is what really defeats a man struggling with natural forces, alone, far from the eyes of his fellows. He was eminently fit to appreciate the mental image he made for himself of the Capataz, after hours of tension and anxiety, precipitated suddenly into an abyss of waters and darkness, without earth or sky, and confronting it not only with an undismayed mind, but with sensible success. Of course, the man was an incomparable swimmer, that was known, but the doctor judged that this instance testified to a still greater intrepidity of spirit. It was pleasing to him; he augured well from it for the success of the arduous mission with which he meant to entrust the Capataz so marvellously restored to usefulness. And in a tone vaguely gratified, he observed: 'It must have been terribly dark!'

'It was the worst darkness of the Golfo,' the Capataz assented, briefly. He was mollified by what seemed a sign of some faint interest in such things as had befallen him, and dropped a few descriptive phrases with an affected and curt nonchalance. At that moment he felt communicative. He expected the continuance of that interest which, whether accepted or rejected, would have restored to him his personality – the only thing lost in that desperate affair. But the doctor, engrossed by a desperate adventure of his own, was terrible in the pursuit of his idea. He let an exclamation of regret escape him.

'I could almost wish you had shouted and shown a light.'

This unexpected utterance astounded the Capataz by its character of cold-blooded atrocity. It was as much as to say, 'I wish you had shown yourself a coward; I wish you had had your throat cut for your pains.' Naturally he referred it to himself, whereas it related only to the silver, being uttered simply and with many mental reservations. Surprise and rage rendered him speechless, and the doctor pursued, practically unheard by Nostromo, whose stirred blood was beating violently in his ears.

'For I am convinced Sotillo in possession of the silver would have turned short round and made for some small port abroad. Economically it would have been wasteful, but still less wasteful than having it sunk. It was the next best thing to having it at hand in some safe place, and using part of it to buy up Sotillo. But I doubt whether Don Carlos would have ever made up his mind to it. He is not fit for Costaguana, and that is a fact, Capataz.'

The Capataz had mastered the fury that was like a tempest in his ears in time to hear the name of Don Carlos. He seemed to have come out of it a changed man – a man who spoke thoughtfully in a soft and even voice.

'And would Don Carlos have been content if I had surrendered this treasure?'

'I should not wonder if they were all of that way of thinking now,' the doctor said, grimly. 'I was never consulted. Decoud had it his own way. Their eyes are opened by this time, I should think. I for one know that if that silver turned up this moment miraculously ashore I would give it to Sotillo. And, as things stand, I would be approved.'

'Turned up miraculously,' repeated the Capataz very low; then raised his voice. 'That, señor, would be a greater miracle than any saint could perform.'

'I believe you, Capataz,' said the doctor, drily.

He went on to develop his view of Sotillo's dangerous influence upon the situation. And the Capataz, listening as if in a dream, felt himself of as little account as the indistinct, motionless shape of the dead man whom he saw upright under the beam, with his air of listening also, disregarded, forgotten, like a terrible example of neglect.

'Is it for an unconsidered and foolish whim that they came to me, then?' he interrupted, suddenly. 'Had I not done enough for them to be of some account, por Dios? Is it that the hombres finos – the gentlemen – need not think as long as there is a man of the people ready to risk his body and soul? Or perhaps, we have no souls – like dogs?'

'There was Decoud, too, with his plan,' the doctor reminded him again.

'Si! And the rich man in San Francisco who had something to do with that treasure, too – what do I know? No! I have heard too many things. It seems to me that everything is permitted to the rich.'

'I understand, Capataz,' the doctor began.

'What Capataz?' broke in Nostromo, in a forcible but even voice. 'The Capataz is undone, destroyed. There is no Capataz. Oh, no! You will find the Capataz no more.'

'Come, this is childish!' remonstrated the doctor; and the other calmed down suddenly.

'I have been indeed like a little child,' he muttered.

And as his eyes met again the shape of the murdered man suspended in his awful immobility, which seemed the uncomplaining immobility of attention, he asked, wondering gently: 'Why did Sotillo give the estrapade to this pitiful wretch? Do you know? No torture could have been worse than his fear. Killing I can understand. His anguish was intolerable to behold. But why should he torment him like this? He could tell no more.'

'No; he could tell nothing more. Any sane man would have seen that. He had told him everything. But I tell you what it is, Capataz. Sotillo would not believe what he was told. Not everything.'

'What is it he would not believe? I cannot understand.'

'I can, because I have seen the man. He refuses to believe that the treasure is lost.'

'What?' the Capataz cried out in a discomposed tone.

'That startles you – eh?'

'Am I to understand, señor,' Nostromo went on in a deliberate and, as it were, watchful tone, 'that Sotillo thinks the treasure has been saved by some means?'

'No! no! That would be impossible,' said the doctor, with conviction; and Nostromo emitted a grunt in the dark. 'That would be impossible. He thinks that the silver was no longer in the lighter when she was sunk. He has convinced himself that the whole show of getting it away to sea is a mere sham got up to deceive Gamacho and his Nationals, Pedrito Montero, Señor Fuentes, our new Jefe Politico, and himself, too. Only, he says, he is no such fool.'

'But he is devoid of sense. He is the greatest imbecile that ever called himself a colonel in this country of evil,' growled Nostromo.

'He is no more unreasonable than many sensible men,' said the doctor. 'He has convinced himself that the treasure can be found because he desires passionately to possess himself of it. And he is also afraid of his officers turning upon him and going over to Pedrito, whom he has not the courage either to fight or trust. Do you see that, Capataz? He need fear no desertion as long as some hope remains of that enormous plunder turning up. I have made it my business to keep this very hope up.'

'You have!' the Capataz de Cargadores repeated cautiously. 'Well, that is wonderful. And how long do you think you are going to keep it up?'

'As long as I can.'

'What does that mean?'

'I can tell you exactly. As long as I live,' the doctor retorted in a stubborn voice. Then, in a few words, he described the story of his arrest and the circumstances of his release. 'I was going back to that silly scoundrel when we met,' he concluded.

Nostromo had listened with profound attention. 'You have made up your mind, then, to a speedy death,' he muttered through his clenched teeth.

'Perhaps, my illustrious Capataz,' the doctor said, testily. 'You are not the only one here who can look an ugly death in the face.'

'No doubt,' mumbled Nostromo, loud enough to be overheard. 'There may be even more than two fools in this place. Who knows?'

'And that is my affair,' said the doctor, curtly.

'As taking out the accursed silver to sea was my affair,' retorted Nostromo. 'I see. *Bueno*. Each of us has his reasons. But you were the last man I conversed with before I started, and you talked to me as if I were a fool.'

Nostromo had a great distaste for the doctor's sardonic treatment of his great reputation. Decoud's faintly ironic recognition used to make him uneasy; but the familiarity of a man like Don Martin was flattering, whereas the doctor was a nobody. He could remember him a penniless outcast, slinking about the streets of Sulaco, without a single friend or acquaintance, till Don Carlos Gould took him into the service of the mine.

'You may be very wise,' he went on, thoughtfully, staring into the obscurity of the room, pervaded by the gruesome enigma of the tortured and murdered Hirsch. 'But I am not such a fool as when I started. I have learned one thing since, and that is that you are a dangerous man.'

Dr Monygham was too startled to do more than exclaim: 'What is it you say?'

'If he could speak he would say the same thing,' pursued Nostromo, with a nod of his shadowy head silhouetted against the starlit window.

'I do not understand you,' said Dr Monygham, faintly.

'No? Perhaps, if you had not confirmed Sotillo in his madness, he would have been in no haste to give the estrapade to that miserable Hirsch.'

The doctor started at the suggestion. But his devotion, absorbing all his sensibilities, had left his heart steeled against remorse and pity. Still, for complete relief, he felt the necessity of repelling it loudly and contemptuously.

'Bah! You dare to tell me that, with a man like Sotillo. I confess I did not give a thought to Hirsch. If I had it would have been useless. Anybody can see that the luckless wretch was doomed from the moment he caught hold of the anchor. He was doomed, I tell you! Just as I myself am doomed – most probably.'

This is what Dr Monygham said in answer to Nostromo's remark, which was plausible enough to prick his conscience. He was not a callous man. But the necessity, the magnitude, the importance of the task he had taken upon himself dwarfed all merely humane considerations. He had undertaken it in a fanatical spirit. He did not like it. To lie, to deceive, to circumvent even the basest of mankind was odious to him. It was odious to him by training, instinct, and tradition. To do these things in the character of a traitor was abhorrent to his nature and terrible to his feelings. He had made that sacrifice in a spirit of abasement. He had said to himself bitterly, 'I am the only one fit for that dirty work.' And he believed this. He was not subtle. His simplicity was such that, though he had no sort of heroic idea of seeking death, the risk, deadly enough, to which he exposed himself, had a sustaining and comforting effect. To that spiritual state the fate of Hirsch presented itself as part of the general atrocity of things. He considered that episode practically. What did it mean? Was it a sign of some dangerous change in Sotillo's delusion? That the man should have been killed like this was what the doctor could not understand.

'Yes. But why shot?' he murmured to himself.

Nostromo kept very still.

Chapter 9

Distracted between doubts and hopes, dismayed by the sound of bells pealing out the arrival of Pedrito Montero, Sotillo had spent the morning in battling with his thoughts; a contest to which he was unequal, from the vacuity of his mind and the violence of his passions. Disappointment, greed, anger, and fear made a tumult in the colonel's breast louder than the din of bells in the town. Nothing he had planned had come to pass. Neither Sulaco nor the silver of the mine had fallen into his hands. He had performed no military exploit to secure his position, and had obtained no enormous booty to make off with. Pedrito Montero, either as friend or foe, filled him with dread. The sound of bells maddened him.

Imagining at first that he might be attacked at once, he had made his battalion stand to arms on the shore. He walked to and fro all the length of the room, stopping sometimes to gnaw the fingertips of his right hand with a lurid sideways glare fixed on the floor; then, with a sullen, repelling glance all round, he would resume his tramping in savage aloofness. His hat, horsewhip, sword, and revolver were lying on the table. His officers, crowding the window giving the view of the town gate, disputed amongst themselves the use of his field-glass bought last year on long credit from Anzani. It passed from hand to hand, and the possessor for the time being was besieged by anxious enquiries.

'There is nothing; there is nothing to see!' he would repeat, impatiently.

There was nothing. And when the picket in the bushes near the Casa Viola had been ordered to fall back upon the main body, no stir of life appeared on the stretch of dusty and arid land between the town and the waters of the port. But late in the afternoon a horseman issuing from the gate was made out riding up fearlessly. It was an emissary from Señor Fuentes. Being all alone he was allowed to come on. Dismounting at the great door he greeted the silent bystanders with cheery impudence, and begged to be taken up at once to the 'muy valiente' colonel.

Señor Fuentes, on entering upon his functions of Jefe Politico, had turned his diplomatic abilities to getting hold of the harbour as well as of the mine. The man he pitched upon to negotiate with Sotillo was a Notary Public, whom the revolution had found languishing in the common jail on a charge of forging documents. Liberated by the mob along with the other 'victims of Blanco tyranny', he had hastened to offer his services to the new Government.

He set out determined to display much eloquence in trying to induce Sotillo to come into town alone for a conference with Pedrito Montero. Nothing was further from the colonel's intentions. The mere fleeting idea of trusting himself into the famous Pedrito's hands had made him feel unwell several times. It was out of the question – it was madness. And to put himself in open hostility was madness, too. It would render impossible a systematic search for that treasure, for that wealth of silver which he seemed to feel somewhere about, to scent somewhere near.

But where? Where? Heavens! Where? Oh! why had he allowed that doctor to go! Imbecile that he was. But no! It was the only right course, he reflected distractedly, while the messenger waited downstairs chatting agreeably to the officers. It was in that scoundrelly doctor's true interest to return with positive information. But what if anything stopped him? A general prohibition to leave the town, for instance! There would be patrols!

The colonel, seizing his head in his hands, turned in his tracks as if struck with vertigo. A flash of craven inspiration suggested to him an expedient – not unknown to European statesmen when they wish to delay a difficult negotiation. Booted and spurred, he scrambled into the hammock with undignified haste. His handsome face had turned yellow with the strain of weighty cares. The ridge of his shapely nose had grown sharp; the audacious nostrils appeared mean and pinched. The velvety, caressing glance of his fine eyes seemed dead, and even decomposed; for these almond-shaped, languishing orbs had become inappropriately bloodshot with much sinister sleeplessness. He addressed the surprised envoy of Señor Fuentes in a deadened, exhausted voice. It came pathetically feeble from under a pile of ponchos, which buried his elegant person right up to the black moustaches, uncurled, pendant, in sign of bodily prostration and mental incapacity. Fever, fever – a heavy fever had overtaken the 'muy valliente' colonel. A wavering wildness of expression, caused by the passing spasms of a slight colic which had declared itself suddenly, and the rattling teeth of repressed panic, had a genuineness which impressed the envoy. It was a cold fit. The colonel explained that he was unable to think, to listen, to speak. With an appearance of superhuman effort the colonel gasped out that he was not in a state to return a suitable reply or to execute any of his Excellency's orders. But tomorrow! Tomorrow! Ah! tomorrow! Let his Excellency Don Pedro be without uneasiness. The brave Esmeralda Regiment held the harbour, held – And closing his eyes, he rolled his aching head like a half-delirious invalid under the inquisitive stare of the envoy, who was obliged to bend down over the hammock in order to catch the painful and broken accents. Meantime, Colonel Sotillo trusted that his Excellency's humanity would permit the doctor, the English doctor, to come out of town with his case of foreign remedies to attend upon him. He begged anxiously his worship the caballero now present for the grace of looking in as he passed the Casa Gould, and informing the English doctor, who was probably there, that his services were immediately required by Colonel Sotillo, lying ill of fever in the Custom House. Immediately. Most urgently required. Awaited with extreme impatience. A thousand thanks. He closed his eyes wearily and would not open them again, lying perfectly still, deaf, dumb, insensible, overcome, vanquished, crushed, annihilated by the fell disease.

But as soon as the other had shut after him the door of the landing, the colonel leaped out with a fling of both feet in an avalanche of woollen coverings. His spurs having become entangled in a perfect welter of ponchos he nearly pitched on his head, and did not recover his balance till the middle of the room. Concealed behind the half-closed jalousies he listened to what went on below.

The envoy had already mounted, and turning to morose officers occupying the great doorway, took off his hat formally.

'Caballeros,' he said, in a very loud tone, 'allow me to recommend you to take great care of your colonel. It has done me much honour and gratification to have seen you all, a fine body of men exercising the soldierly virtue of patience in this exposed situation, where there is much sun, and no water to speak of, while a town full of wine and feminine charms is ready to embrace you for the brave men you are. Caballeros, I have the honour to salute you. There will be much dancing tonight in Sulaco. Goodbye!'

But he reined in his horse and inclined his head sideways on seeing the old major step out, very tall and meagre, in a straight narrow coat coming down to his ankles as it were the casing of the regimental colours rolled round their staff.

The intelligent old warrior, after enunciating in a dogmatic tone the general proposition that the 'world was full of traitors', went on pronouncing deliberately a panegyric upon Sotillo. He ascribed to him with leisurely emphasis every virtue under heaven, summing it all up in an absurd colloquialism current amongst the lower class of Occidentals (especially about Esmeralda). 'And,' he concluded, with a sudden rise in the voice, 'a man of many teeth – "*hombre de muchos dientes*". *Si, señor*. As to us,' he pursued, portentous and impressive, 'your worship is beholding the finest body of officers in the Republic, men unequalled for valour and sagacity, '*y hombres de muchos dientes*." '

'What? All of them?' enquired the disreputable envoy of Señor Fuentes, with a faint, derisive smile.

'*Todos. Si, señor*,' the major affirmed, gravely, with conviction. 'Men of many teeth.'

The other wheeled his horse to face the portal resembling the high gate of a dismal barn. He raised himself in his stirrups, extended one arm. He was a facetious scoundrel, entertaining for these stupid Occidentals a feeling of great scorn natural in a native from the central provinces. The folly of Esmeraldians especially aroused his amused contempt. He began an oration upon Pedro Montero, keeping a solemn countenance. He flourished his hand as if introducing him to their notice. And when he saw every face set, all the eyes fixed upon his lips, he began to shout a sort of catalogue of perfections: 'Generous, valorous, affable, profound' – (he snatched off his hat enthusiastically) – 'a statesman, an invincible chief of partisans – ' He dropped his voice startlingly to a deep, hollow note – 'and a dentist.'

He was off instantly at a smart walk; the rigid straddle of his legs, the turned-out feet, the stiff back, the rakish slant of the sombrero above the square, motionless set of the shoulders expressing an infinite, awe-inspiring impudence.

Upstairs, behind the jalousies, Sotillo did not move for a long time. The audacity of the fellow appalled him. What were his officers saying below? They were saying nothing. Complete silence. He quaked. It was not thus that he had imagined himself at that stage of the expedition. He had seen himself triumphant, unquestioned, appeased, the idol of the soldiers, weighing in secret complacency the agreeable alternatives of power and wealth open to his choice. Alas! How different! Distracted, restless, supine, burning with fury, or frozen with terror, he felt a dread as fathomless as the sea creep upon him from every side. That rogue of a doctor had to come out with his information. That was clear. It would be of no use to him – alone. He could do nothing with it. Malediction! The doctor would never come out. He was probably under arrest already, shut up together with Don Carlos. He laughed aloud insanely. Ha! ha! ha! ha! It was Pedrito Montero who would get the information. Ha! ha! ha! ha! – and the silver. Ha!

All at once, in the midst of the laugh, he became motionless and silent as if turned into stone. He, too, had a prisoner. A prisoner who must, must know the real truth. He would have to be made to speak. And Sotillo, who all that time had not quite forgotten Hirsch, felt an inexplicable reluctance at the notion of proceeding to extremities.

He felt a reluctance – part of that unfathomable dread that crept on all sides upon him. He remembered reluctantly, too, the dilated eyes of the hide merchant, his contortions, his loud sobs and protestations. It was not compassion or even mere nervous sensibility. The fact was that though Sotillo did never for a moment believe his story – he could not believe it; nobody could believe such nonsense – yet those accents of despairing truth impressed him disagreeably. They made him feel sick. And he suspected also that the man might have gone mad with fear. A lunatic is a hopeless subject. Bah! A pretence. Nothing but a pretence. He would know how to deal with that.

He was working himself up to the right pitch of ferocity. His fine eyes squinted slightly; he clapped his hands; a barefooted orderly appeared noiselessly; a corporal, with his bayonet hanging on his thigh and a stick in his hand.

The colonel gave his orders, and presently the miserable Hirsch, pushed in by several soldiers, found him frowning awfully in a broad armchair, hat on head, knees wide apart, arms akimbo, masterful, imposing, irresistible, haughty, sublime, terrible.

Hirsch, with his arms tied behind his back, had been bundled violently into one of the smaller rooms. For many hours he remained apparently forgotten, stretched lifelessly on the floor. From that solitude, full of despair and terror, he was torn out brutally, with kicks and blows, passive, sunk in hebetude. He listened to threats and admonitions, and afterwards made his usual answers to questions, with his chin sunk on his breast, his hands tied behind his back, swaying a little in front of Sotillo, and never looking up. When he was forced to hold up his head, by means of a bayonet-point prodding him under the chin, his eyes had a vacant, trancelike stare, and drops of perspiration as big as peas were seen hailing down the dirt, bruises, and scratches of his white face. Then they stopped suddenly.

Sotillo looked at him in silence. 'Will you depart from your obstinacy, you rogue?' he asked. Already a rope, whose one end was fastened to Señor Hirsch's wrists, had been thrown over a beam, and three soldiers held the other end, waiting. He made no answer. His heavy lower lip hung stupidly. Sotillo made a sign. Hirsch was jerked up off his feet, and a yell of despair and agony burst out in the room, filled the passage of the great buildings, rent the air outside, caused every soldier of the camp along the shore to look up at the windows, started some of the officers in the hall babbling excitedly, with shining eyes; others, setting their lips, looked gloomily at the floor.

Sotillo, followed by the soldiers, had left the room. The sentry on the landing presented arms. Hirsch went on screaming all alone behind the half-closed jalousies while the sunshine, reflected from the water of the harbour, made an ever-running ripple of light high up on the wall. He screamed with uplifted eyebrows and a wide-open mouth – incredibly wide, black, enormous, full of teeth – comical.

In the still burning air of the windless afternoon he made the waves of his agony travel as far as the OSN Company's offices. Captain Mitchell on the balcony, trying to make out what went on generally, had heard him faintly but distinctly, and the feeble and appalling sound lingered in his ears after he had retreated indoors with blanched cheeks. He had been driven off the balcony several times during that afternoon.

Sotillo, irritable, moody, walked restlessly about, held consultations with his officers, gave contradictory orders in this shrill clamour pervading the whole empty edifice. Sometimes there would be long and awful silences. Several times he had entered the torture-chamber where his sword, horse-whip, revolver, and field-glass were lying on the table, to ask with forced calmness 'Will you speak the truth now? No? I can wait.' But he could not afford to wait much longer. That was just it. Every time he went in and came out with a slam of the door, the sentry on the landing presented arms, and got in return a black, venomous, unsteady glance, which, in reality, saw nothing at all, being merely the reflection of the soul within – a soul of gloomy hatred, irresolution, avarice, and fury.

The sun had set when he went in once more. A soldier carried in two lighted candles and slunk out, shutting the door without noise.

'Speak, thou Jewish child of the devil! The silver. The silver, I say! Where is it? Where have you foreign rogues hidden it? Confess or – '

A slight quiver passed up the taut rope from the racked limbs, but the body of Señor Hirsch, enterprising business man from Esmeralda, hung under the heavy beam perpendicular and silent, facing the colonel awfully. The inflow of the night air, cooled by the snows of the Sierra, spread gradually a delicious freshness through the close heat of the room.

'Speak – thief – scoundrel – picaro – or – '

Sotillo had seized the riding-whip, and stood with his arm lifted up. For a word, for one little word, he felt he would have knelt, cringed, grovelled on the floor before the drowsy, conscious stare of those fixed eyeballs starting out of the grimy, dishevelled head that drooped very still with its mouth closed askew. The colonel ground his teeth with rage and struck. The rope vibrated leisurely to the blow, like the long string of a pendulum starting from a rest. But no swinging motion was imparted to the body of Señor Hirsch, the well-known hide merchant on the coast. With a convulsive effort of the twisted arms it leaped up a few inches, curling upon itself like a fish on the end of a line. Señor Hirsch's head was flung back on his straining throat; his chin trembled. For a moment the rattle of his chattering teeth pervaded the vast, shadowy room, where the candles made a patch of light round the two flames burning side by side. And as Sotillo, staying his raised hand, waited for him to speak, with the sudden flash of a grin and a straining forward of the wrenched shoulders, he spat violently into his face.

The uplifted whip fell, and the colonel sprang back with a low cry of dismay, as if aspersed by a jet of deadly venom. Quick as thought he snatched up his revolver, and fired twice. The report and the concussion of the shots seemed to throw him at once from ungovernable rage into idiotic stupor. He stood with drooping jaw and stony eyes. What had he done, *Sangre de Dios!* What had he done? He was basely appalled at his impulsive act, sealing for ever these lips from which so much was to be extorted. What could he say? How could he explain? Ideas of headlong flight somewhere, anywhere, passed through his mind; even the craven and absurd notion of hiding under the table occurred to his cowardice. It was too late; his officers had rushed in tumultuously, in a great clatter of scabbards, clamouring, with astonishment and wonder. But since they did not immediately proceed to plunge their swords into his breast, the brazen side of his character asserted itself. Passing the sleeve of his uniform over his face he pulled himself together. His truculent glance turned slowly here and there, checked the noise where it fell; and the stiff body of the late Señor Hirsch, merchant, after swaying imperceptibly, made a half turn, and came to a rest in the midst of awed murmurs and uneasy shuffling.

A voice remarked loudly, 'Behold a man who will never speak again.' And another, from the back row of faces, timid and pressing, cried out: 'Why did you kill him, *mi colonel*?'

'Because he has confessed everything,' answered Sotillo, with the hardihood of desperation. He felt himself cornered. He brazened it out on the strength of his reputation with very fair success. His hearers thought him very capable of such an act. They were disposed to believe his flattering tale. There is no credulity so eager and blind as the credulity of covetousness, which, in its universal extent, measures the moral misery and the intellectual destitution of mankind. Ah! he had confessed everything, this fractious Jew, this *bribón*. Good! Then he was no longer wanted. A sudden dense guffaw was heard from the senior captain – a big-headed man, with little round eyes and monstrously fat cheeks which never moved. The old major, tall and fantastically ragged like a scarecrow, walked round the body of the late Señor Hirsch, muttering to himself with ineffable complacency that like this there was no need to guard against any future treacheries of that scoundrel. The others stared, shifting from foot to foot, and whispering short remarks to each other.

Sotillo buckled on his sword and gave curt, peremptory orders to hasten the retirement decided upon in the afternoon. Sinister, impressive, his sombrero pulled right down upon his eyebrows, he marched first through the door in such disorder of mind that he forgot utterly to provide for Dr Monygham's possible return. As the officers trooped out after him, one or two looked back hastily at the late Señor Hirsch, merchant from Esmeralda, left swinging rigidly at rest, alone with the two burning candles. In the emptiness of the room the burly shadow of head and shoulders on the wall had an air of life.

Below, the troops fell in silently and moved off by companies without drum or trumpet. The old scarecrow major commanded the rearguard; but the party he left behind with orders to fire the Custom House (and 'burn the carcass of the treacherous Jew where it hung') failed somehow in their haste to set the staircase properly alight. The body of the late Señor Hirsch dwelt alone for a time in the dismal solitude of the unfinished building, resounding weirdly with sudden slams and clicks of doors and latches, with rustling scurries of torn papers, and the tremulous sighs that at each gust of wind passed under the high roof. The light of the two candles burning before the perpendicular and breathless immobility of the late Señor Hirsch threw a gleam afar over land and water, like a signal in the night. He remained to startle Nostromo by his presence, and to puzzle Dr Monygham by the mystery of his atrocious end.

'But why shot?' the doctor again asked himself, audibly. This time he was answered by a dry laugh from Nostromo.

'You seem much concerned at a very natural thing, señor doctor. I wonder why? It is very likely that before long we shall all get shot one after another, if not by Sotillo, then by Pedrito, or Fuentes, or Gamacho. And we may even get the estrapade, too, or worse – *quien sabe?* – with your pretty tale of the silver you put into Sotillo's head.'

'It was in his head already,' the doctor protested. 'I only – '

'Yes. And you only nailed it there so that the devil himself – '

'That is precisely what I meant to do,' caught up the doctor.

'That is what you meant to do. *Bueno.* It is as I say. You are a dangerous man.'

Their voices, which without rising had been growing quarrelsome, ceased suddenly. The late Señor Hirsch, erect and shadowy against the stars, seemed to be waiting attentive, in impartial silence.

But Dr Monygham had no mind to quarrel with Nostromo. At this supremely critical point of Sulaco's fortunes it was borne upon him at last that this man was really indispensable, more indispensable than ever the infatuation of Captain Mitchell, his proud discoverer, could conceive; far beyond what Decoud's best dry raillery about 'my illustrious friend, the unique Capataz de Cargadores', had ever intended. The fellow was unique. He was not 'one in a thousand'. He was absolutely the only one. The doctor surrendered. There was something in the genius of that Genoese seaman which dominated in the destinies of great enterprises and of many people, the fortunes of Charles Gould, the fate of an admirable woman. At this last thought the doctor had to clear his throat before he could speak.

In a completely changed tone he pointed out to the Capataz that, to begin with, he personally ran no great risk. As far as everybody knew he was dead. It was an enormous advantage. He had only to keep out of sight in the Casa Viola, where the old Garibaldino was known to be alone – with his dead wife. The servants had all run away. No one would think of searching for him there, or anywhere else on earth, for that matter.

'That would be very true,' Nostromo spoke up, bitterly, 'if I had not met you.'

For a time the doctor kept silent. 'Do you mean to say that you think I may give you away?' he asked in an unsteady voice. 'Why? Why should I do that?'

'What do I know? Why not? To gain a day perhaps. It would take Sotillo a day to give me the estrapade, and try some other things perhaps, before he puts a bullet through my heart – as he did to that poor wretch here. Why not?'

The doctor swallowed with difficulty. His throat had gone dry in a moment. It was not from indignation. The doctor, pathetically enough, believed that he had forfeited the right to be indignant with anyone – for anything. It was simple dread. Had the fellow heard his story by some chance? If so, there was an end of his usefulness in that direction. The indispensable man escaped his influence, because of that indelible blot which made him fit for dirty work. A feeling as of sickness came upon the doctor. He would have given anything to know, but he dared not clear up the point. The fanaticism of his devotion, fed on the sense of his abasement, hardened his heart in sadness and scorn.

'Why not, indeed?' he re-echoed, sardonically. 'Then the safe thing for you is to kill me on the spot. I would defend myself. But you may just as well know I am going about unarmed.'

'*Por Dios!*' said the Capataz, passionately. 'You fine people are all alike. All dangerous. All betrayers of the poor who are your dogs.'

'You do not understand,' began the doctor, slowly.

'I understand you all!' cried the other with a violent movement, as shadowy to the doctor's eyes as the persistent immobility of the late Señor Hirsch. 'A poor man amongst you has got to look after himself. I say that you do not care for those that serve you. Look at me! After all these years, suddenly, here I find myself like one of these curs that bark outside the walls – without a kennel or a dry bone for my teeth. Caramba!' But he relented with a contemptuous fairness. 'Of course,' he went on, quietly, 'I do not suppose that you would hasten to give me up to Sotillo, for example. It is not that. It is that I am nothing! Suddenly – ' He swung his arm downwards. 'Nothing to anyone,' he repeated.

The doctor breathed freely. 'Listen, Capataz,' he said, stretching out his arm almost affectionately towards Nostromo's shoulder. 'I am going to tell you a very simple thing. You are safe because you are needed. I would not give you away for any conceivable reason, because I want you.'

In the dark Nostromo bit his lip. He had heard enough of that. He knew what that meant. No more of that for him. But he had to look after himself now, he thought. And he thought, too, that it would not be prudent to part in anger from his companion. The doctor, admitted to be a great healer, had, amongst the populace of Sulaco, the reputation of being an evil sort of man. It was based solidly on his personal appearance, which was strange, and on his rough ironic manner – proofs visible, sensible, and incontrovertible of the doctor's malevolent disposition. And Nostromo was of the people. So he only grunted incredulously.

'You, to speak plainly, are the only man,' the doctor pursued. 'It is in your power to save this town and . . . everybody from the destructive rapacity of men who – '

'No, señor,' said Nostromo, sullenly. 'It is not in my power to get the treasure back for you to give up to Sotillo, or Pedrito, or Gamacho. What do I know?'

'Nobody expects the impossible,' was the answer.

'You have said it yourself – nobody,' muttered Nostromo, in a gloomy, threatening tone.

But Dr Monygham, full of hope, disregarded the enigmatic words and the threatening tone. To their eyes, accustomed to obscurity, the late Señor Hirsch, growing more distinct, seemed to have come nearer. And the doctor lowered his voice in exposing his scheme as though afraid of being overheard.

He was taking the indispensable man into his fullest confidence. Its implied flattery and suggestion of great risks came with a familiar sound to the Capataz. His mind, floating in irresolution and discontent, recognised it with bitterness. He understood well that the doctor was anxious to save the San Tomé mine from annihilation. He would be nothing without it. It was his interest. Just as it had been the interest of Señor Decoud, of the Blancos, and of the Europeans to get his Cargadores on their side. His thought became arrested upon Decoud. What would happen to him?

Nostromo's prolonged silence made the doctor uneasy. He pointed out, quite unnecessarily, that though for the present he was safe, he could not live concealed for ever. The choice was between accepting the mission to Barrios, with all its dangers and difficulties, and leaving Sulaco by stealth, ingloriously, in poverty.

'None of your friends could reward you and protect you just now, Capataz. Not even Don Carlos himself.'

'I would have none of your protection and none of your rewards. I only wish I could trust your courage and your sense. When I return in triumph, as you say, with Barrios, I may find you all destroyed. You have the knife at your throat now.'

It was the doctor's turn to remain silent in the contemplation of horrible contingencies.

'Well, we would trust your courage and your sense. And you, too, have a knife at your throat.'

'Ah! And whom am I to thank for that? What are your politics and your mines to me – your silver and your constitutions – your Don Carlos this, and Don José that – '

'I don't know,' burst out the exasperated doctor. 'There are innocent people in danger whose little finger is worth more than you or I and all the Ribierists together. I don't know. You should have asked yourself before you allowed Decoud to lead you into all this. It was your place to think like a man; but if you did not think then, try to act like a man now. Did you imagine Decoud cared very much for what would happen to you?'

'No more than you care for what will happen to me,' muttered the other.

'No; I care for what will happen to you as little as I care for what will happen to myself.'

'And all this because you are such a devoted Ribierist?' Nostromo said in an incredulous tone.

'All this because I am such a devoted Ribierist,' repeated Dr Monygham, grimly.

Again Nostromo, gazing abstractedly at the body of the late Señor Hirsch, remained silent, thinking that the doctor was a dangerous person in more than one sense. It was impossible to trust him.

'Do you speak in the name of Don Carlos?' he asked at last.

'Yes. I do,' the doctor said, loudly, without hesitation. 'He must come forward now. He must,' he added in a mutter, which Nostromo did not catch.

'What did you say, señor?'

The doctor started. 'I say that you must be true to yourself, Capataz. It would be worse than folly to fail now.'

'True to myself,' repeated Nostromo. 'How do you know that I would not be true to myself if I told you to go to the devil with your propositions?'

'I do not know. Maybe you would,' the doctor said, with a roughness of tone intended to hide the sinking of his heart and the faltering of his voice. 'All I know is, that you had better get away from here. Some of Sotillo's men may turn up here looking for me.'

He slipped off the table, listened intently. The Capataz, too, stood up.

'Suppose I went to Cayta, what would you do meantime?' he asked.

'I would go to Sotillo directly you had left – in the way I am thinking of.'

'A very good way – if only that engineer-in-chief consents. Remind him, señor, that I looked after the old rich Englishman who pays for the railway, and that I saved the lives of some of his people that time when a gang of thieves came from the south to wreck one of his pay-trains. It was I who discovered it all at the risk of my life, by pretending to enter into their plans. Just as you are doing with Sotillo.'

'Yes. Yes, of course. But I can offer him better arguments,' the doctor said, hastily. 'Leave it to me.'

'Ah, yes! True. I am nothing.'

'Not at all. You are everything.'

They moved a few paces towards the door. Behind them the late Señor Hirsch preserved the immobility of a disregarded man.

'That will be all right. I know what to say to the engineer,' pursued the doctor, in a low tone. 'My difficulty will be with Sotillo.'

And Dr Monygham stopped short in the doorway as if intimidated by the difficulty. He had made the sacrifice of his life. He considered this a fitting opportunity. But he did not want to throw his life away too soon. In his quality of betrayer of Don Carlos' confidence, he would have ultimately to indicate the hiding-place of the treasure. That would be the end of his deception, and the end of himself as well, at the hands of the infuriated colonel. He wanted to delay him to the very last moment; and he had been racking his brains to invent some place of concealment at once plausible and difficult of access.

He imparted his trouble to Nostromo, and concluded: 'Do you know what, Capataz? I think that when the time comes and some information must be given, I shall indicate the Great Isabel. That is the best place I can think of. What is the matter?'

A low exclamation had escaped Nostromo. The doctor waited, surprised, and after a moment of profound silence, heard a thick voice stammer out, 'Utter folly,' and stop with a gasp.

'Why folly?'

'Ah! You do not see it,' began Nostromo, scathingly, gathering scorn as he went on. 'Three men in half an hour would see that no ground had been disturbed anywhere on that island. Do you think that such a treasure can be buried without leaving traces of the work – eh! señor doctor? Why! you would not gain half a day more before having your throat cut by Sotillo. The Isabel! What stupidity! What miserable invention! Ah! you are all alike, you fine men of intelligence. All you are fit for is to betray men of the people into undertaking deadly risks for objects that you are not even sure about. If it comes off you get the benefit. If not, then it does not matter. He is only a dog. Ah! *Madre de Dios*, I would – ' He shook his fists above his head.

The doctor was overwhelmed at first by this fierce, hissing vehemence.

'Well! It seems to me on your own showing that the men of the people are no mean fools, too,' he said sullenly. 'No, but come. You are so clever. Have you a better place?'

Nostromo had calmed down as quickly as he had flared up.

'I am clever enough for that,' he said quietly, almost with indifference. 'You want to tell him of a hiding-place big enough to take days in ransacking – a place where a treasure of silver ingots can be buried without leaving a sign on the surface.'

'And close at hand,' the doctor put in.

'Just so, señor. Tell him it is sunk.'

'This has the merit of being the truth,' the doctor said, contemptuously. 'He will not believe it.'

'You tell him that it is sunk where he may hope to lay his hands on it, and he will believe you quick enough. Tell him it has been sunk in the harbour in order to be recovered afterwards by divers. Tell him you found out that I had orders from Don Carlos Gould to lower the cases quietly overboard somewhere in a line between the end of the jetty and the entrance. The depth is not too great there. He has no divers, but he has a ship, boats, ropes, chains, sailors – of a sort. Let him fish for the silver. Let him set his fools to drag backwards and forwards and crossways while he sits and watches till his eyes drop out of his head.'

'Really, this is an admirable idea,' muttered the doctor.

'Si. You tell him that, and see whether he will not believe you ! He will spend days in rage and torment – and still he will believe. He will have no thought for anything else. He will not give up till he is driven off – why, he may even forget to kill you. He will neither eat nor sleep. He – '

'The very thing! The very thing!' the doctor repeated in an excited whisper. 'Capataz, I begin to believe that you are a great genius in your way.'

Nostromo had paused; then began again in a changed tone, sombre, speaking to himself as though he had forgotten the doctor's existence.

'There is something in a treasure that fastens upon a man's mind. He will pray and blaspheme and still persevere, and will curse the day he ever heard of it, and will let his last hour come upon him unawares, still believing that he missed it only by a foot. He will see it every time he closes his eyes. He will never forget it till he is dead – and even then – Doctor, did you ever hear of the miserable gringos on Azuera, that cannot die? Ha! ha! Sailors like myself. There is no getting away from a treasure that once fastens upon your mind.'

'You are a devil of a man, Capataz. It is the most plausible thing.'

Nostromo pressed his arm.

'It will be worse for him than thirst at sea or hunger in a town full of people. Do you know what that is? He shall suffer greater torments than he inflicted upon that terrified wretch who had no invention. None! none! Not like me. I could have told Sotillo a deadly tale for very little pain.'

He laughed wildly and turned in the doorway towards the body of the late Señor Hirsch, an opaque long blotch in the semi-transparent obscurity of the room between the two tall parallelograms of the windows full of stars.

'You man of fear!' he cried. 'You shall be avenged by me – Nostromo. Out of my way, doctor! Stand aside – or, by the suffering soul of a woman dead without confession, I will strangle you with my two hands.'

He bounded downwards into the black, smoky hall. With a grunt of astonishment, Dr Monygham threw himself recklessly into the pursuit. At the bottom of the charred stairs he had a fall, pitching forward on his face with a force that would have stunned a spirit less intent upon a task of love and devotion. He was up in a moment, jarred, shaken, with a queer impression of the terrestrial globe having been flung at his head in the dark. But it wanted more than that to stop Dr Monygham's body, possessed by the exaltation of self-sacrifice; a reasonable exaltation, determined not to lose whatever advantage chance put into its way. He ran with headlong, tottering swiftness, his arms going like a windmill in his effort to keep his balance on his crippled feet. He lost his hat; the tails of his open gaberdine flew behind him. He had no mind to lose sight of the indispensable man. But it was a long time, and a long way from the Custom House, before he managed to seize his arm from behind, roughly, out of breath.

'Stop! Are you mad?'

Already Nostromo was walking slowly, his head dropping, as if checked in his pace by the weariness of irresolution.

'What is that to you? Ah! I forgot you want me for something. Always. Siempre Nostromo.'

'What do you mean by talking of strangling me?' panted the doctor.

'What do I mean? I mean that the king of the devils himself has sent you out of this town of cowards and talkers to meet me tonight of all the nights of my life.'

Under the starry sky the Albergo d'Italia Una emerged, black and low, breaking the dark level of the plain. Nostromo stopped altogether.

'The priests say he is a tempter, do they not?' he added, through his clenched teeth.

'My good man, you drivel. The devil has nothing to do with this. Neither has the town, which you may call by what name you please. But Don Carlos Gould is neither a coward nor an empty talker. You will admit that?' He waited. 'Well?'

'Could I see Don Carlos?'

'Great heavens! No! Why? What for?' exclaimed the doctor in agitation. 'I tell you it is madness. I will not let you go into the town for anything.'

'I must.'

'You must not!' hissed the doctor, fiercely, almost beside himself with the fear of the man doing away with his usefulness for an imbecile whim of some sort. 'I tell you you shall not. I would rather – '

He stopped at loss for words, feeling fagged out, powerless, holding on to Nostromo's sleeve, absolutely for support after his run.

'I am betrayed!' muttered the Capataz to himself; and the doctor, who overheard the last word, made an effort to speak calmly.

'That is exactly what would happen to you. You would be betrayed.'

He thought with a sickening dread that the man was so well known that he could not escape recognition. The house of the Señor Administrador was beset by spies, no doubt. And even the very servants of the casa were not to be trusted. 'Reflect, Capataz,' he said, impressively . . . 'What are you laughing at?'

'I am laughing to think that if somebody that did not approve of my presence in town, for instance – you understand, señor doctor – if somebody were to give me up to Pedrito, it would not be beyond my power to make friends even with him. It is true. What do you think of that?'

'You are a man of infinite resource, Capataz,' said Dr Monygham, dismally. 'I recognise that. But the town is full of talk about you; and those few Cargadores that are not in hiding with the railway people have been shouting "Viva Montero" on the Plaza all day.'

'My poor Cargadores!' muttered Nostromo. 'Betrayed! Betrayed!'

'I understand that on the wharf you were pretty free in laying about you with a stick amongst your poor Cargadores,' the doctor said in a grim tone, which showed that he was recovering from his exertions. 'Make no mistake. Pedrito is furious at Señor Ribiera's rescue, and at having lost the pleasure of shooting Decoud. Already there are rumours in the town of the treasure having been spirited away. To have missed that does not please Pedrito either; but let me tell you that if you had all that silver in your hand for your ransom it would not save you.'

Turning swiftly, and catching the doctor by the shoulders, Nostromo thrust his face close to his.

'Maledetto! You follow me speaking of the treasure. You have sworn my ruin. You were the last man who looked upon me before I went out with it. And Sidoni the engine-driver says you have an evil eye.'

'He ought to know. I saved his broken leg for him last year,' the doctor said, stoically. He felt on his shoulders the weight of these hands famed amongst the populace for snapping thick ropes and bending horseshoes. 'And to you I offer the best means of saving yourself – let me go – and of retrieving your great reputation. You boasted of making the Capataz de Cargadores famous from one end of America to the other about this wretched silver. But I bring you a better opportunity – let me go, hombre!'

Nostromo released him abruptly, and the doctor feared that the indispensable man would run off again. But he did not. He walked on slowly. The doctor hobbled by his side till, within a stone's throw from the Casa Viola, Nostromo stopped again.

Silent in inhospitable darkness, the Casa Viola seemed to have changed its nature; his home appeared to repel him with an air of hopeless and inimical mystery. The doctor said: 'You will be safe there. Go in, Capataz.'

'How can I go in?' Nostromo seemed to ask himself in a low, inward tone. 'She cannot unsay what she said, and I cannot undo what I have done.'

'I tell you it is all right. Viola is all alone in there. I looked in as I came out of the town. You will be perfectly safe in that house till you leave it to make your name famous on the Campo. I am going now to arrange for your departure with the engineer-in-chief, and I shall bring you news here long before daybreak.'

Dr Monygham, disregarding, or perhaps fearing to penetrate the meaning of Nostromo's silence, clapped him lightly on the shoulder, and starting off with his smart, lame walk, vanished utterly at the third or fourth hop in the direction of the railway track. Arrested between the two wooden posts for people to fasten their horses to Nostromo did not move, as if he, too, had been planted solidly in the ground. At the end of half an hour he lifted his head to the deep baying of the dogs at the railway yards, which had burst out suddenly, tumultuous and deadened as if coming from under the plain. That lame doctor with the evil eye had got there pretty fast.

Step by step Nostromo approached the Albergo d'Italia Una, which he had never known so lightless, so silent, before. The door, all black in the pale wall, stood open as he had left it twenty-four hours before, when he had nothing to hide from the world. He remained before it, irresolute, like a fugitive, like a man betrayed. Poverty, misery, starvation! Where had he heard these words? The anger of a dying woman had prophesied that fate for his folly. It looked as if it would come true very quickly. And the léperos would laugh – she had said. Yes, they would laugh if they knew that the Capataz de Cargadores was at the mercy of the mad doctor whom they could remember, only a few years ago, buying cooked food from a stall on the Plaza for a copper coin – like one of themselves.

At that moment the notion of seeking Captain Mitchell passed through his mind. He glanced in the direction of the jetty and saw a small gleam of light in the OSN Company's building. The thought of lighted windows was not attractive. Two lighted windows had decoyed him into the empty Custom House, only to fall into the clutches of that doctor. No! He would not go near lighted windows again on that night. Captain Mitchell was there. And what could he be told? That doctor would worm it all out of him as if he were a child.

On the threshold he called out 'Giorgio!' in an undertone. Nobody answered. He stepped in. '*Olà! viejo!* Are you there? . . . ' In the impenetrable darkness his head swam with the illusion that the obscurity of the kitchen was as vast as the Placid Gulf, and that the floor dipped forward like a sinking lighter. '*Olà! viejo!*' he repeated, falteringly, swaying where he stood. His hand, extended to steady himself, fell upon the table. Moving a step forward, he shifted it, and felt a box of matches under his fingers. He fancied he had heard a quiet sigh. He listened for a moment, holding his breath; then, with trembling hands, tried to strike a light.

The tiny piece of wood flamed up quite blindingly at the end of his fingers, raised above his blinking eyes. A concentrated glare fell upon the leonine white head of old Giorgio against the black fireplace – showed him leaning forward in a chair in staring immobility, surrounded, overhung, by great masses of shadow, his legs crossed, his cheek in his hand, an empty pipe in the corner of his mouth. It seemed hours before he attempted to turn his face; at the very moment the match went out, and he disappeared, overwhelmed by the shadows, as if the walls and roof of the desolate house had collapsed upon his white head in ghostly silence.

Nostromo heard him stir and utter dispassionately the words: 'It may have been a vision.'

'No,' he said, softly. 'It is no vision, old man.'

A strong chest voice asked in the dark: 'Is that you I hear, Giovann' Battista?'

'*Si, viejo.* Steady. Not so loud.'

After his release by Sotillo, Giorgio Viola, attended to the very door by the good-natured engineer-in-chief, had re-entered his house, which he had been made to leave almost at the very moment of his wife's death. All was still. The lamp above was burning. He nearly called out to her by name; and the thought that no call from him would ever again evoke the answer of her voice, made him drop heavily into the chair with a loud groan, wrung out by the pain as of a keen blade piercing his breast.

The rest of the night he made no sound. The darkness turned to grey, and on the colourless, clear, glassy dawn the jagged sierra stood out flat and opaque, as if cut out of paper.

The enthusiastic and severe soul of Giorgio Viola, sailor, champion of oppressed humanity, enemy of kings, and, by the grace of Mrs Gould, hotel-keeper of the Sulaco harbour, had descended into the open abyss of desolation amongst the shattered vestiges of his past. He remembered his wooing between two campaigns a single short week in the season of gathering olives. Nothing approached the grave passion of that time but the deep, passionate sense of his bereavement. He discovered all the extent of his dependence upon the silenced voice of that woman. It was her voice that he missed. Abstracted, busy, lost in inward contemplation, he seldom looked at his wife in those later years. The thought of his girls was a matter of concern, not of consolation. It was her voice that he would miss. And he remembered the other child – the little boy who died at sea. Ah! a man would have been something to lean upon. And, alas! even Gian' Battista – he of whom, and of Linda, his wife had spoken to him so anxiously before she dropped off into her last sleep on earth, he on whom she had called aloud to save the children, just before she died – even he was dead!

And the old man, bent forward, his head in his hand, sat through the day in immobility and solitude. He never heard the brazen roar of the bells in town. When it ceased the earthenware filter in the corner of the kitchen kept on its swift musical drip, drip into the great porous jar below.

Towards sunset he got up, and with slow movements disappeared up the narrow staircase. His bulk filled it; and the rubbing of his shoulders made a small noise as of a mouse running behind the plaster of a wall. While he remained up there the house was as dumb as a grave. Then, with the same faint rubbing noise, he descended. He had to catch at the chairs and tables to regain his seat. He seized his pipe off the high mantel of the fireplace – but made no attempt to reach the tobacco – thrust it empty into the corner of his mouth, and sat down again in the same staring pose. The sun of Pedrito's entry into Sulaco, the last sun of Señor Hirsch's life, the first of Decoud's solitude on the Great Isabel, passed over the Albergo d'Italia Una on its way to the west. The tinkling drip, drip of the filter had ceased, the lamp upstairs had burnt itself out, and the night beset Giorgio Viola and his dead wife with its obscurity and silence that seemed invincible till the Capataz de Cargadores, returning from the dead, put them to flight with the splutter and flare of a match.

'*Si, viejo*. It is me. Wait.'

Nostromo, after barricading the door and closing the shutters carefully, groped upon a shelf for a candle, and lit it.

Old Viola had risen. He followed with his eyes in the dark the sounds made by Nostromo. The light disclosed him standing without support, as if the mere presence of that man who was loyal, brave, incorruptible, who was all his son would have been, were enough for the support of his decaying strength.

He extended his hand grasping the briar-wood pipe, whose bowl was charred on the edge, and knitted his bushy eyebrows heavily at the light.

'You have returned,' he said, with shaky dignity. 'Ah! Very well! I – '

He broke off. Nostromo, leaning back against the table, his arms folded on his breast, nodded at him slightly.

'You thought I was drowned! No! The best dog of the rich, of the aristocrats, of these fine men who can only talk and betray the people, is not dead yet.'

The Garibaldino, motionless, seemed to drink in the sound of the well-known voice. His head moved slightly once as if in sign of approval; but Nostromo saw clearly that the old man understood nothing of the words. There was no one to understand; no one he could take into the confidence of Decoud's fate, of his own, into the secret of the silver. That doctor was an enemy of the people – a tempter . . .

Old Giorgio's heavy frame shook from head to foot with the effort to overcome his emotion at the sight of that man, who had shared the intimacies of his domestic life as though he had been a grown-up son.

'She believed you would return,' he said, solemnly.

Nostromo raised his head.

'She was a wise woman. How could I fail to come back?'

He finished the thought mentally: 'Since she has prophesied for me an end of poverty, misery, and starvation.' These words of Teresa's anger, from the circumstances in which they had been uttered, like the cry of a soul prevented from making its peace with God, stirred the obscure superstition of personal fortune from which even the greatest genius amongst men of adventure and action is seldom free. They reigned over Nostromo's mind with the force of a potent malediction. And what a curse it was that which her words had laid upon him! He had been orphaned so young that he could remember no other woman whom he called mother. Henceforth there would be no enterprise in which he would not fail. The spell was working already. Death itself would elude him now . . . He said violently-

'Come, viejo! Get me something to eat. I am hungry! *Sangre de Dios!* The emptiness of my belly makes me lightheaded.'

With his chin dropped again upon his bare breast above his folded arms, barefooted, watching from under a gloomy brow the movements of old Viola foraging amongst the cupboards, he seemed as if indeed fallen under a curse – a ruined and sinister Capataz.

Old Viola walked out of a dark corner, and, without a word, emptied upon the table out of his hollowed palms a few dry crusts of bread and half a raw onion.

While the Capataz began to devour his beggar's fare, taking up with stony-eyed voracity piece after piece lying by his side, the Garibaldino went off, and squatting down in another corner filled an earthenware mug with red wine out of a wicker-covered demijohn. With a familiar gesture, as when serving customers in the café, he had thrust his pipe between his teeth to have his hands free.

The Capataz drank greedily. A slight flush deepened the bronze of his cheek. Before him, Viola, with a turn of his white and massive head towards the staircase, took his empty pipe out of his mouth, and pronounced slowly: 'After the shot was fired down here, which killed her as surely as if the bullet had struck her oppressed heart, she called upon you to save the children. Upon you, Gian' Battista.'

The Capataz looked up.

'Did she do that, Padrone? To save the children! They are with the English señora, their rich benefactress. Hey! old man of the people. Thy benefactress . . .'

'I am old,' muttered Giorgio Viola. 'An Englishwoman was allowed to give a bed to Garibaldi lying wounded in prison. The greatest man that ever lived. A man of the people, too – a sailor. I may let another keep a roof over my head. È . . . I am old. I may let her. Life lasts too long sometimes.'

'And she herself may not have a roof over her head before many days are out, unless I . . . What do you say? Am I to keep a roof over her head? Am I to try – and save all the Blancos together with her?'

'You shall do it,' said old Viola in a strong voice. 'You shall do it as my son would have . . .'

'Thy son, viejo! . . . There never has been a man like thy son. Ha, I must try . . . But what if it were only a part of the curse to lure me on? . . . And so she called upon me to save – and then – ?'

'She spoke no more.' The heroic follower of Garibaldi, at the thought of the eternal stillness and silence fallen upon the shrouded form stretched out on the bed upstairs, averted his face and raised his hand to his furrowed brow. 'She was dead before I could seize her hands,' he stammered out, pitifully.

Before the wide eyes of the Capataz, staring at the doorway of the dark staircase, floated the shape of the Great Isabel, like a strange ship in distress, freighted with enormous wealth and the solitary life of a man. It was impossible for him to do anything. He could only hold his tongue, since there was no one to trust. The treasure would be lost, probably – unless Decoud . . . And his thought came abruptly to an end. He perceived that he could not imagine in the least what Decoud was likely to do.

Old Viola had not stirred. And the motionless Capataz dropped his long, soft eyelashes, which gave to the upper part of his fierce, black-whiskered face a touch of feminine ingenuousness. The silence had lasted for a long time.

'God rest her soul!' he murmured, gloomily.

Chapter 10

The next day was quiet in the morning, except for the faint sound of firing to the northward, in the direction of Los Hatos. Captain Mitchell had listened to it from his balcony anxiously. The phrase, 'In my delicate position as the only consular agent then in the port, everything, sir, everything was a just cause for anxiety,' had its place in the more or less stereotyped relation of the 'historical events' which for the next few years was at the service of distinguished strangers visiting Sulaco. The mention of the dignity and neutrality of the flag, so difficult to preserve in his position, 'right in the thick of these events between the lawlessness of that piratical villain Sotillo and the more regularly established but scarcely less atrocious tyranny of his Excellency Don Pedro Montero,' came next in order. Captain Mitchell was not the man to enlarge upon mere dangers much. But he insisted that it was a memorable day. On that day, towards dusk, he had seen 'that poor fellow of mine – Nostromo. The sailor whom I discovered, and, I may say, made, sir. The man of the famous ride to Cayta, sir. An historical event, sir!'

Regarded by the OSN Company as an old and faithful servant, Captain Mitchell was allowed to attain the term of his usefulness in ease and dignity at the head of the enormously extended service. The augmentation of the establishment, with its crowds of clerks, an office in town, the old office in the harbour, the division into departments – passenger, cargo, lighterage, and so on – secured a greater leisure for his last years in the regenerated Sulaco, the capital of the Occidental Republic. Liked by the natives for his good nature and the formality of his manner, self-important and simple, known for years as a 'friend of our country', he felt himself a personality of mark in the town. Getting up early for a turn in the marketplace while the gigantic shadow of Higuerota was still lying upon the fruit and flower stalls piled up with masses of gorgeous colouring, attending easily to current affairs, welcomed in houses, greeted by ladies on the Alameda, with his entry into all the clubs and a footing in the Casa Gould, he led his privileged old bachelor, man-about-town existence with great comfort and solemnity. But on mail-boat days he was down at the Harbour Office at an early hour, with his own gig, manned by a smart crew in white and blue, ready to dash off and board the ship directly she showed her bows between the harbour heads.

It would be into the Harbour Office that he would lead some privileged passenger he had brought off in his own boat, and invite him to take a seat for a moment while he signed a few papers. And Captain Mitchell, seating himself at his desk, would keep on talking hospitably: 'There isn't much time if you are to see everything in a day. We shall be off in a moment. We'll have lunch at the Amarilla Club – though I belong also to the Anglo-American – mining engineers and business men, don't you know – and to the Mirliflores as well, a new club – English, French, Italians, all sorts – lively young fellows mostly, who wanted to pay a compliment to an old resident, sir. But we'll lunch at the Amarilla. Interest you, I fancy. Real thing of the country. Men of the first families. The President of the Occidental Republic himself belongs to it, sir. Fine old bishop with a broken nose in the patio. Remarkable piece of statuary, I believe. Cavaliere Parrochetti – you know Parrochetti, the famous Italian sculptor – was working here for two years – thought very highly of our old bishop . . . There! I am very much at your service now.'

Proud of his experience, penetrated by the sense of historical importance of men, events, and buildings, he talked pompously in jerky periods, with slight sweeps of his short, thick arm, letting nothing 'escape the attention' of his privileged captive.

'Lot of building going on, as you observe. Before the Separation it was a plain of burnt grass smothered in clouds of dust, with an ox-cart track to our Jetty. Nothing more. This is the Harbour Gate. Picturesque, is it not? Formerly the town stopped short there. We enter now the Calle de la Constitucion. Observe the old Spanish houses. Great dignity. Eh? I suppose it's just as it was in the time of the Viceroys, except for the pavement. Wood blocks now. Sulaco National Bank there, with the sentry boxes each side of the gate. Casa Avellanos this side, with all the ground-floor windows shuttered. A wonderful woman lives there – Miss Avellanos – the beautiful Antonia. A character, sir! A historical woman! Opposite – Casa Gould. Noble gateway. Yes, *the* Goulds of the original Gould Concession, that all the world knows of now. I hold seventeen of the thousand-dollar shares in the Consolidated San Tomé mines. All the poor savings of my lifetime, sir, and it will be enough to keep me in comfort to the end of my days at home when I retire. I got in on the ground-floor, you see. Don Carlos, great friend of mine. Seventeen shares – quite a little fortune to leave behind one, too. I have a niece – married a parson – most worthy man, incumbent of a small parish in Sussex; no end of children. I was never married myself. A sailor should exercise self-denial. Standing under that very gateway, sir, with some young engineer-fellows, ready to defend that house where we had received so much kindness and hospitality, I saw the first and last charge of Pedrito's horsemen upon Barrios's troops, who had just taken the Harbour Gate. They could not stand the new rifles brought out by that poor Decoud. It was a murderous fire. In a moment the street became blocked with a mass of dead men and horses. They never came on again.'

And all day Captain Mitchell would talk like this to his more or less willing victim: 'The Plaza. I call it magnificent. Twice the area of Trafalgar Square.'

From the very centre, in the blazing sunshine, he pointed out the buildings: 'The Intendencia, now President's Palace – Cabildo, where the Lower Chamber of Parliament sits. You notice the new houses on that side of the Plaza? Compañia Anzani, a great general store, like those co-operative things at home. Old Anzani was murdered by the National Guards in front of his safe. It was even for that specific crime that the deputy Gamacho, commanding the Nationals, a bloodthirsty and savage brute, was executed publicly by garrotte upon the sentence of a court-martial ordered by Barrios. Anzani's nephews converted the business into a company. All that side of the Plaza had been burnt; used to be colonnaded before. A terrible fire, by the light of which I saw the last of the fighting, the llaneros flying, the Nationals throwing their arms down, and the miners of San Tomé, all Indians from the Sierra, rolling by like a torrent to the sound of pipes and cymbals, green flags flying, a wild mass of men in white ponchos and green hats, on foot, on mules, on donkeys. Such a sight, sir, will never be seen again. The miners, sir, had marched upon the town, Don Pépé leading on his black horse, and their very wives in the rear on burros, screaming encouragement, sir, and beating tambourines. I remember one of these women had a green parrot seated on her shoulder, as calm as a bird of stone. They had just saved their Señor Administrador; for Barrios, though he ordered the assault at once, at night, too, would have been too late. Pedrito Montero had Don Carlos led out to be shot – like his uncle many years ago – and then, as Barrios said afterwards, 'Sulaco would not have been worth fighting for.' Sulaco without the Concession was nothing; and there were tons and tons of dynamite distributed all over the mountain with detonators arranged, and an old priest, Father Romàn, standing by to annihilate the San Tomé mine at the first news of failure. Don Carlos had made up his mind not to leave it behind, and he had the right men to see to it, too.'

Thus Captain Mitchell would talk in the middle of the Plaza, holding over his head a white umbrella with a green lining; but inside the cathedral, in the dim light, with a faint scent of incense floating in the cool atmosphere, and here and there a kneeling female figure, black or all white, with a veiled head, his lowered voice became solemn and impressive.

'Here,' he would say, pointing to a niche in the wall of the dusky aisle, 'you see the bust of Don José Avellanos, "Patriot and Statesman", as the inscription says, "Minister to Courts of England and Spain, etc., etc., died in the woods of Los Hatos worn out with his lifelong struggle for Right and Justice at the dawn of the New Era." A fair likeness. Parrochetti's work from some old photographs and a pencil sketch by Mrs Gould. I was well acquainted with that distinguished Spanish-American of the old school, a true Hidalgo, beloved by everybody who knew him. The marble medallion in the wall, in the antique style, representing a veiled woman seated with her hands clasped loosely over her knees, commemorates that unfortunate young gentleman who sailed out with Nostromo on that fatal night, sir. See, "To the memory of Martin Decoud, his betrothed Antonia Avellanos." Frank, simple, noble. There you have that lady, sir, as she is. An exceptional woman. Those who thought she would give way to despair were mistaken, sir. She has been blamed in many quarters for not having taken the veil. It was expected of her. But Doña Antonia is not the stuff they make nuns of. Bishop Corbelàn, her uncle, lives with her in the Corbelàn town house. He is a fierce sort of priest, everlastingly worrying the Government about the old Church lands and convents. I believe they think a lot of him in Rome. Now let us go to the Amarilla Club, just across the Plaza, to get some lunch.'

Directly outside the cathedral on the very top of the noble flight of steps, his voice rose pompously, his arm found again its sweeping gesture.

'*Porvenir*, over there on that first floor, above those French plate-glass shop-fronts; our biggest daily. Conservative, or, rather, I should say, Parliamentary. We have the Parliamentary party here of which the actual Chief of the State, Don Juste Lopez, is the head; a very sagacious man, I think. A first-rate intellect, sir. The Democratic party in opposition rests mostly, I am sorry to say, on these socialistic Italians, sir, with their secret societies, camorras, and suchlike. There are lots of Italians settled here on the railway lands, dismissed navvies, mechanics, and so on, all along the trunk line. There are whole villages of Italians on the Campo. And the natives, too, are being drawn into these ways . . . American bar? Yes. And over there you can see another. New Yorkers mostly frequent that one – Here we are at the Amarilla. Observe the bishop at the foot of the stairs to the right as we go in.'

And the lunch would begin and terminate its lavish and leisurely course at a little table in the gallery, Captain Mitchell nodding, bowing, getting up to speak for a moment to different officials in black clothes, merchants in jackets, officers in uniform, middle-aged caballeros from the Campo – sallow, little, nervous men, and fat, placid, swarthy men, and Europeans or North Americans of superior standing, whose faces looked very white amongst the majority of dark complexions and black, glistening eyes.

Captain Mitchell would lie back in the chair, casting around looks of satisfaction, and tender over the table a case full of thick cigars.

'Try a weed with your coffee. Local tobacco. The black coffee you get at the Amarilla, sir, you don't meet anywhere in the world. We get the bean from a famous cafeteria in the foothills, whose owner sends three sacks every year as a present to his fellow members in remembrance of the fight against Gamacho's Nationals, carried on from these very windows by the caballeros. He was in town at the time, and took part, sir, to the bitter end. It arrives on three mules – not in the common way, by rail; no fear! – right into the patio, escorted by mounted peóns, in charge of the Mayoral of his estate, who walks upstairs, booted and spurred, and delivers it to our committee formally with the words, "For the sake of those fallen the third of May." We call it Très de Mayo coffee. Taste it.'

Captain Mitchell, with an expression as though making ready to hear a sermon in a church, would lift the tiny cup to his lips. And the nectar would be sipped to the bottom during a restful silence in a cloud of cigar smoke.

'Look at this man in black just going out,' he would begin, leaning forward hastily. 'This is the famous Hernandez, Minister of War. *The Times* special correspondent, who wrote that striking series of letters calling the Occidental Republic the "Treasure House of the World", gave a whole article to him and the force he has organised – the renowned Carabineers of the Campo.'

Captain Mitchell's guest, staring curiously, would see a figure in a long-tailed black coat walking gravely, with downcast eyelids in a long, composed face, a brow furrowed horizontally, a pointed head, whose grey hair, thin at the top, combed down carefully on all sides and rolled at the ends, fell low on the neck and shoulders. This, then, was the famous bandit of whom Europe had heard with interest. He put on a high-crowned sombrero with a wide flat brim; a rosary of wooden beads was twisted about his right wrist. And Captain Mitchell would proceed: 'The protector of the Sulaco refugees from the rage of Pedrito. As general of cavalry with Barrios he distinguished himself at the storming of Tonoro, where Señor Fuentes was killed with the last remnant of the Monterists. He is the friend and humble servant of Bishop Corbelàn. Hears three Masses every day. I bet you he will step into the cathedral to say a prayer or two on his way home to his siesta.'

He took several puffs at his cigar in silence; then, in his best important manner, pronounced: 'The Spanish race, sir, is prolific of remarkable characters in every rank of life ... I propose we go now into the billiard-room, which is cool, for a quiet chat. There's never anybody there till after five. I could tell you episodes of the Separationist revolution that would astonish you. When the great heat's over, we'll take a turn on the Alameda.'

The programme went on relentless, like a law of Nature. The turn on the Alameda was taken with slow steps and stately remarks.

'All the great world of Sulaco here, sir.' Captain Mitchell bowed right and left with no end of formality; then with animation, 'Doña Emilia, Mrs Gould's carriage. Look. Always white mules. The kindest, most gracious woman the sun ever shone upon. A great position, sir. A great position. First lady in Sulaco – far before the President's wife. And worthy of it.' He took off his hat; then, with a studied change of tone, added, negligently, that the man in black by her side, with a high white collar and a scarred, snarly face, was Dr Monygham, Inspector of State Hospitals, chief medical officer of the Consolidated San Tomé mines. 'A familiar of the house. Everlastingly there. No wonder. The Goulds made him. Very clever man and all that, but I never liked him. Nobody does. I can recollect him limping about the streets in a check shirt and native sandals with a watermelon under his arm – all he would get to eat for the day. A bigwig now, sir, and as nasty as ever. However . . . There's no doubt he played his part fairly well at the time. He saved us all from the deadly incubus of Sotillo, where a more particular man might have failed – '

His arm went up.

'The equestrian statue that used to stand on the pedestal over there has been removed. It was an anachronism,' Captain Mitchell commented, obscurely. 'There is some talk of replacing it by a marble shaft commemorative of Separation, with angels of peace at the four corners, and bronze Justice holding an even balance, all gilt, on the top. Cavaliere Parrochetti was asked to make a design, which you can see framed under glass in the Municipal Sala. Names are to be engraved all round the base. Well! They could do no better than begin with the name of Nostromo. He has done for Separation as much as anybody else, and,' added Captain Mitchell, 'has got less than many others by it – when it comes to that.' He dropped on to a stone seat under a tree, and tapped invitingly at the place by his side. 'He carried to Barrios the letters from Sulaco which decided the General to abandon Cayta for a time, and come back to our help here by sea. The transports were still in harbour fortunately. Sir, I did not even know that my Capataz de Cargadores was alive. I had no idea. It was Dr Monygham who came upon him, by chance, in the Custom House, evacuated an hour or two before by the wretched Sotillo. I was never told; never given a hint, nothing – as if I were unworthy of confidence. Monygham arranged it all. He went to the railway yards, and got admission to the engineer-in-chief, who, for the sake of the Goulds as much as for anything else, consented to let an engine make a dash down the line, one hundred and eighty miles, with Nostromo aboard. It was the only way to get him off. In the Construction Camp at the railhead, he obtained a horse, arms, some clothing, and started alone on that marvellous ride – four hundred miles in six days, through a disturbed country, ending by the feat of passing through the Monterist lines outside Cayta. The history of that ride, sir, would make a most exciting book. He carried all our lives in his pocket. Devotion, courage, fidelity, intelligence were not enough. Of course, he was perfectly fearless and incorruptible. But a man was wanted that would know how to succeed. He was that man, sir. On the fifth of May, being practically a prisoner in the Harbour Office of my Company, I suddenly heard the whistle of an engine in the railway yards, a quarter of a mile away. I could not believe my ears. I made one jump on to the balcony, and beheld a locomotive under a great head of steam run out of the yard gates, screeching like mad, enveloped in a white cloud, and then, just abreast of old Viola's inn, check almost to a standstill. I made out, sir, a man – I couldn't tell who – dash out of the Albergo d'Italia Una, climb into the cab, and then, sir, that engine seemed positively to leap clear of the house, and was gone in the twinkling of an eye. As you blow a candle out, sir! There was a first-rate driver on the footplate, sir, I can tell you. They were fired heavily upon by the National Guards in Rincon and one other place. Fortunately the line had not been torn up. In four hours they reached the Construction Camp. Nostromo had his start . . . The rest you know. You've got only to look round you. There are people on this Alameda that ride in their carriages, or even are alive at all today, because years ago I engaged a runaway Italian sailor for a foreman of our wharf simply on the strength of his looks. And that's a fact. You can't get over it, sir. On the seventeenth of May, just twelve days after I saw the man from the Casa Viola get on the engine, and wondered what it meant, Barrios's transports were entering this harbour, and the "Treasure House of the World", as *The Times* man calls Sulaco in his book, was saved intact for civilisation – for a great future, sir. Pedrito, with Hernandez on the west, and the San Tomé miners pressing on the land gate, was not able to oppose the landing. He had been sending messages to Sotillo for a week to join him. Had Sotillo done so, there would have been massacres and proscription that would have left no man or woman of position alive. But that's where Dr Monygham comes in. Sotillo, blind and deaf to everything, stuck on board his steamer watching the dragging for silver, which he believed to be sunk at the bottom of the harbour. They say that for the last three days he was out of his mind raving and foaming with disappointment at getting nothing, flying about the deck, and yelling curses at the boats with the drags, ordering them in, and then suddenly stamping his foot and crying out, "And yet it is there! I see it! I feel it!"

'He was preparing to hang Dr Monygham (whom he had on board) at the end of the after-derrick, when the first of Barrios's transports, one of our own ships at that, steamed right in, and ranging close alongside opened a small-arm fire without as much preliminaries as a hail. It was the completest surprise in the world, sir. They were too astounded at first to bolt below. Men were falling right and left like ninepins. It's a miracle that Monygham, standing on the after-hatch with the rope already round his neck, escaped being riddled through and through like a sieve. He told me since that he had given himself up for lost, and kept on yelling with all the strength of his lungs: "Hoist a white flag! Hoist a white flag!" Suddenly an old major of the Esmeralda regiment, standing by, unsheathed his sword with a shriek: "Die, perjured traitor!" and ran Sotillo clean through the body, just before he fell himself shot through the head.'

Captain Mitchell stopped for a while.

'Begad, sir! I could spin you a yarn for hours. But it's time we started off to Rincon. It would not do for you to pass through Sulaco and not see the lights of the San Tomé mine, a whole mountain ablaze like a lighted palace above the dark Campo. It's a fashionable drive . . . But let me tell you one little anecdote, sir; just to show you. A fortnight or more later, when Barrios, declared Generalísimo, was gone in pursuit of Pedrito away south, when the

Provisional Junta, with Don Juste Lopez at its head, had promulgated the new Constitution, and our Don Carlos Gould was packing up his trunks bound on a mission to San Francisco and Washington (the United States, sir, were the first great power to recognise the Occidental Republic) – a fortnight later, I say, when we were beginning to feel that our heads were safe on our shoulders, if I may express myself so, a prominent man, a large shipper by our line, came to see me on business, and, says he, the first thing: "I say, Captain Mitchell, is that fellow" (meaning Nostromo) "still the Capataz of your Cargadores or not?" "What's the matter?" says I. "Because, if he is, then I don't mind; I send and receive a good lot of cargo by your ships; but I have observed him several days loafing about the wharf, and just now he stopped me as cool as you please, with a request for a cigar. Now, you know, my cigars are rather special, and I can't get them so easily as all that." "I hope you stretched a point," I said, very gently. "Why, yes. But it's a confounded nuisance. The fellow's everlastingly cadging for smokes." Sir, I turned my eyes away, and then asked, "Weren't you one of the prisoners in the Cabildo?" "You know very well I was, and in chains, too," says he. "And under a fine of fifteen thousand dollars?" He coloured, sir, because it got about that he fainted from fright when they came to arrest him, and then behaved before Fuentes in a manner to make the very *policias*, who had dragged him there by the hair of his head, smile at his cringing. "Yes," he says, in a sort of shy way. "Why?" "Oh, nothing. You stood to lose a tidy bit," says I, "even if you saved your life . . . But what can I do for you?" He never even saw the point. Not he. And that's how the world wags, sir.'

He rose a little stiffly, and the drive to Rincon would be taken with only one philosophical remark, uttered by the merciless cicerone, with his eyes fixed upon the lights of San Tomé, that seemed suspended in the dark night between earth and heaven.

'A great power, this, for good and evil, sir. A great power.'

And the dinner of the Mirliflores would be eaten, excellent as to cooking, and leaving upon the traveller's mind an impression that there were in Sulaco many pleasant, able young men with salaries apparently too large for their discretion, and amongst them a few, mostly Anglo-Saxon, skilled in the art of, as the saying is, 'taking a rise' out of his kind host.

With a rapid, jingling drive to the harbour in a two-wheeled machine (which Captain Mitchell called a curricle) behind a fleet and scraggy mule beaten all the time by an obviously Neapolitan driver, the cycle would be nearly closed before the lighted-up offices of the OSN Company, remaining open so late because of the steamer. Nearly – but not quite.

'Ten o'clock. Your ship won't be ready to leave till half-past twelve, if by then. Come in for a brandy-and-soda and one more cigar.'

And in the superintendent's private room the privileged passenger by the *Ceres*, or *Juno*, or *Pallas*, stunned and as it were annihilated mentally by a sudden surfeit of sights, sounds, names, facts, and complicated information imperfectly apprehended, would listen like a tired child to a fairy tale; would hear a voice, familiar and surprising in its pompousness, tell him, as if from another world, how there was 'in this very harbour' an international naval demonstration, which put an end to the Costaguana-Sulaco War. How the United States cruiser, *Powhattan*, was the first to salute the Occidental flag – white, with a wreath of green laurel in the middle encircling a yellow amarilla flower. Would hear how General Montero, in less than a month after proclaiming himself Emperor of Costaguana, was shot dead (during a solemn and public distribution of orders and crosses) by a young artillery officer, the brother of his then mistress.

'The abominable Pedrito, sir, fled the country,' the voice would say. And it would continue: 'A captain of one of our ships told me lately that he recognised Pedrito the Guerrillero, arrayed in purple slippers and a velvet smoking-cap with a gold tassel, keeping a disorderly house in one of the southern ports.'

'Abominable Pedrito! Who the devil was he?' would wonder the distinguished bird of passage hovering on the confines of waking and sleep with resolutely open eyes and a faint but amiable curl upon his lips, from between which stuck out the eighteenth or twentieth cigar of that memorable day.

'He appeared to me in this very room like a haunting ghost, sir,' – Captain Mitchell was talking of his Nostromo with true warmth of feeling and a touch of wistful pride. 'You may imagine, sir, what an effect it produced on me. He had come round by sea with Barrios, of course. And the first thing he told me after I became fit to hear him was that he had picked up the lighter's boat floating in the gulf! He seemed quite overcome by the circumstance. And a remarkable enough circumstance it was, when you remember that it was then sixteen days since the sinking of the silver. At once I could see he was another man. He stared at the wall, sir, as if there had been a spider or something running about there. The loss of the silver preyed on his mind. The first thing he asked me about was whether Doña Antonia had heard yet of Decoud's death. His voice trembled. I had to tell him that Doña Antonia, as a matter of fact, was not then back in town yet. Poor girl! And just as I was making ready to ask him a thousand questions, with a sudden, "Pardon me, señor," he cleared out of the office altogether. I did not see him again for three days. I was terribly busy, you know. It seems that he wandered about in and out of the town, and on two nights turned up to sleep in the baracoons of the railway people. He seemed absolutely indifferent to what went on. I asked him on the wharf, "When are you going to take hold again, Nostromo? There will be plenty of work for the Cargadores presently."

' "Señor," says he, looking at me in a slow, inquisitive manner, 'would it surprise you to hear that I am too tired to work just yet? And what work could I do now? How can I look my Cargadores in the face after losing a lighter?"

'I begged him not to think any more about the silver, and he smiled. A smile that went to my heart, sir. "It was no mistake," I told him. "It was a fatality. A thing that could not be helped." "*Si, si!*" he said, and turned away. I thought it best to leave him alone for a bit to get over it. Sir, it took him years really, to get over it. I was present at his interview with Don Carlos. I must say that Gould is rather a cold man. He had to keep a tight hand on his feelings, dealing with thieves and rascals, in constant danger of ruin for himself and wife for so many years, that it had become a second nature. They looked at each other for a long time. Don Carlos asked what he could do for him, in his quiet, reserved way.

' "My name is known from one end of Sulaco to the other," he said, as quiet as the other. "What more can you do for me?" That was all that passed on that occasion. Later, however, there was a very fine coasting schooner for sale, and Mrs Gould and I put our heads together to get her bought and presented to him. It was done, but he paid all the price back within the next three years. Business was booming all along this seaboard, sir. Moreover, that man always succeeded in everything except in saving the silver. Poor Doña Antonia, fresh from her terrible experiences in the woods of Los Hatos, had an interview with him, too. Wanted to hear about Decoud: what they said, what they did, what they thought up to the last on that fatal night. Mrs Gould told me his manner was perfect for quietness and sympathy. Miss Avellanos burst into tears only when he told her how Decoud had happened to say that his plan would be a glorious success. And there's no doubt, sir, that it is. It is a success.'

The cycle was about to close at last. And while the privileged passenger, shivering with the pleasant anticipations of his berth, forgot to ask himself what on earth Decoud's plan could be? Captain Mitchell was saying, 'Sorry we must part so soon. Your intelligent interest made this a pleasant day to me. I shall see you now on board. You had a glimpse of the "Treasure House of the World". A very good name that.' And the coxswain's voice at the door, announcing that the gig was ready, closed the cycle.

Nostromo had, indeed, found the lighter's boat, which he had left on the Great Isabel with Decoud, floating empty far out in the gulf. He was then on the bridge of the first of Barrios's transports, and within an hour's steaming from Sulaco. Barrios, always delighted with a feat of daring and a good judge of courage, had taken a great liking to the Capataz. During the passage round the coast the General kept Nostromo near his person, addressing him frequently in that abrupt and boisterous manner which was the sign of his high favour.

Nostromo's eyes were the first to catch, broad on the bow, the tiny, elusive dark speck, which, alone with the forms of the Three Isabels right ahead, appeared on the flat, shimmering emptiness of the gulf. There are times when no fact should be neglected as insignificant; a small boat so far from the land might have had some meaning worth finding out. At a nod of consent from Barrios the transport swept out of her course, passing near enough to ascertain that no one manned the little cockleshell. It was merely a common small boat gone adrift with her oars in her. But Nostromo, to whose mind Decoud had been insistently present for days, had long before recognised with excitement the dinghy of the lighter.

There could be no question of stopping to pick up that thing. Every minute of time was momentous with the lives and futures of a whole town. The head of the leading ship, with the General on board, fell off to her course. Behind her, the fleet of transports, scattered haphazard over a mile or so in the offing, like the finish of an ocean race, pressed on, all black and smoking on the western sky.

'Mi General,' Nostromo's voice rang out loud, but quiet, from behind a group of officers, 'I should like to save that little boat. *Por Dios*, I know her. She belongs to my Company.'

'And, *por Dios*,' guffawed Barrios, in a noisy, good-humoured voice, 'you belong to me. I am going to make you a captain of cavalry directly we get within sight of a horse again.'

'I can swim far better than I can ride, mi General,' cried Nostromo, pushing through to the rail with a set stare in his eyes. 'Let me – '

'Let you? What a conceited fellow that is,' bantered the General, jovially, without even looking at him. 'Let him go! Ha! ha! ha! He wants me to admit that we cannot take Sulaco without him! Ha! ha! ha! Would you like to swim off to her, my son?'

A tremendous shout from one end of the ship to the other stopped his guffaw. Nostromo had leaped overboard; and his black head bobbed up far away already from the ship. The General muttered an appalled '*Cielo!* Sinner that I am!' in a thunderstruck tone. One anxious glance was enough to show him that Nostromo was swimming with perfect ease; and then he thundered terribly, 'No! no! We shall not stop to pick up this impertinent fellow. Let him drown – that mad Capataz.'

Nothing short of main force would have kept Nostromo from leaping overboard. That empty boat, coming out to meet him mysteriously, as if rowed by an invisible spectre, exercised the fascination of some sign, of some warning, seemed to answer in a startling and enigmatic way the persistent thought of a treasure and of a man's fate. He would have leaped if there had been death in that half-mile of water. It was as smooth as a pond, and for some reason sharks are unknown in the Placid Gulf, though on the other side of the Punta Mala the coastline swarms with them.

The Capataz seized hold of the stern and blew with force. A queer, faint feeling had come over him while he swam. He had got rid of his boots and coat in the water. He hung on for a time, regaining his breath. In the distance the transports, more in a bunch now, held on straight for Sulaco, with their air of friendly contest, of nautical sport, of a regatta; and the united smoke of their funnels drove like a thin, sulphurous fogbank right over his head. It was his daring, his courage, his act that had set these ships in motion upon the sea, hurrying on to save the lives and fortunes of the Blancos, the taskmasters of the people; to save the San Tomé mine; to save the children.

With a vigorous and skilful effort he clambered over the stern. The very boat! No doubt of it; no doubt whatever. It was the dinghy of the lighter No. 3 – the dinghy left with Martin Decoud on the Great Isabel so that he should have some means to help himself if nothing could be done for him from the shore. And here she had come out to meet him empty and inexplicable. What had become of Decoud? The Capataz made a minute examination. He looked for some scratch, for some mark, for some sign. All he discovered was a brown stain on the gunwale abreast of the thwart. He bent his face over it and rubbed hard with his finger. Then he sat down in the stern sheets, passive, with his knees close together and legs aslant.

Streaming from head to foot, with his hair and whiskers hanging lank and dripping and a lustreless stare fixed upon the bottom boards, the Capataz of the Sulaco Cargadores resembled a drowned corpse come up from the bottom to idle away the sunset hour in a small boat. The excitement of his adventurous ride, the excitement of the return in time, of achievement, of success, all these excitements centred round the associated ideas of the great treasure and of the only other man who knew of its existence, had departed from him. To the very last moment he had been cudgelling his brains as to how he could manage to visit the Great Isabel without loss of time and undetected. For the idea of secrecy had come to be connected with the treasure so closely that even to Barrios himself he had refrained from mentioning the existence of Decoud and of the silver on the island.

The letters he carried to the General, however, made brief mention of the loss of the lighter, as having its bearing upon the situation in Sulaco. In the circumstances, the one-eyed tiger-slayer, scenting battle from afar, had not wasted his time in making enquiries from the messenger. In fact, Barrios, talking with Nostromo, assumed that both Don Martin Decoud and the ingots of San Tomé were lost together, and Nostromo, not questioned directly, had kept silent, under the influence of some indefinable form of resentment and distrust. Let Don Martin speak of everything with his own lips – was what he told himself mentally.

And now, with the means of gaining the Great Isabel thrown thus in his way at the earliest possible moment his excitement had departed, as when the soul takes flight leaving the body inert upon an earth it knows no more. Nostromo did not seem to know the gulf. For a long time even his eyelids did not flutter once upon the glazed emptiness of his stare. Then slowly, without a limb having stirred, without a twitch of muscle or quiver of an eyelash, an expression, a living expression came upon the still features, deep thought crept into the empty stare – as if an outcast soul, a quiet, brooding soul, finding that untenanted body in its way, had come in stealthily to take possession.

The Capataz frowned: and in the immense stillness of sea, islands, and coast, of cloud forms on the sky and trails of light upon the water, the knitting of that brow had the emphasis of a powerful gesture. Nothing else budged for a long time; then the Capataz shook his head and again surrendered himself to the universal repose of all visible things. Suddenly he seized the oars, and with one movement made the dinghy spin round, head-on to the Great Isabel. But before he began to pull he bent once more over the brown stain on the gunwale.

'I know that thing,' he muttered to himself, with a sagacious jerk of the head. 'That's blood.'

His stroke was long, vigorous, and steady. Now and then he looked over his shoulder at the Great Isabel, presenting its low cliff to his anxious gaze like an impenetrable face. At last the stem touched the strand. He flung rather than dragged the boat up the little beach. At once, turning his back upon the sunset, he plunged with long strides into the ravine, making the water of the stream spurt and fly upwards at every step, as if spurning its shallow, clear, murmuring spirit with his feet. He wanted to save every moment of daylight.

A mass of earth, grass, and smashed bushes had fallen down very naturally from above upon the cavity under the leaning tree. Decoud had attended to the concealment of the silver as instructed, using the spade with some intelligence. But Nostromo's half-smile of approval changed into a scornful curl of the lip by the sight of the spade itself flung there in full view, as if in utter carelessness or sudden panic, giving away the whole thing. Ah! They were all alike in their folly, these *hombres finos* that invented laws and governments and barren tasks for the people.

The Capataz picked up the spade, and with the feel of the handle in his palm the desire to have a look at the horse-hide boxes of treasure came upon him suddenly. In a very few strokes he uncovered the edges and corners of several; then, clearing away more earth, became aware that one of them had been slashed with a knife.

He exclaimed at that discovery in a stifled voice, and dropped on his knees with a look of irrational apprehension over one shoulder, then over the other. The stiff hide had closed, and he hesitated before he pushed his hand through the long slit and felt the ingots inside. There they were. One, two, three. Yes, four gone. Taken away. Four ingots. But who? Decoud? Nobody else. And why? For what purpose? For what cursed fancy? Let him explain. Four ingots carried off in a boat, and – blood!

In the face of the open gulf, the sun, clear, unclouded, unaltered, plunged into the waters in a grave and untroubled mystery of self-immolation consummated far from all mortal eyes, with an infinite majesty of silence and peace. Four ingots short! – and blood!

The Capataz got up slowly.

'He might simply have cut his hand,' he muttered. 'But, then –'

He sat down on the soft earth, unresisting, as if he had been chained to the treasure, his drawn-up legs clasped in his hands with an air of hopeless submission, like a slave set on guard. Once only he lifted his head smartly: the rattle of hot musketry fire had reached his ears, like pouring from on high a stream of dry peas upon a drum. After listening for a while, he said, half aloud: 'He will never come back to explain.'

And he lowered his head again.

'Impossible!' he muttered, gloomily.

The sounds of firing died out. The loom of a great conflagration in Sulaco flashed up red above the coast, played on the clouds at the head of the gulf, seemed to touch with a ruddy and sinister reflection the forms of the Three Isabels. He never saw it, though he raised his head.

'But, then, I cannot know,' he pronounced, distinctly, and remained silent and staring for hours.

He could not know. Nobody was to know. As might have been supposed, the end of Don Martin Decoud never became a subject of speculation for anyone except Nostromo. Had the truth of the facts been known, there would always have remained the question, Why? Whereas the version of his death at the sinking of the lighter had no uncertainty of motive. The young apostle of Separation had died striving for his idea by an ever-lamented accident. But the truth was that he died from solitude, the enemy known but to few on this earth, and whom only the simplest of us are fit to withstand. The brilliant Costaguanero of the boulevards had died from solitude and want of faith in himself and others.

For some good and valid reasons beyond mere human comprehension, the sea-birds of the gulf shun the Isabels. The rocky head of Azuera is their haunt, whose stony levels and chasms resound with their wild and tumultuous clamour as if they were for ever quarrelling over the legendary treasure.

At the end of his first day on the Great Isabel, Decoud, turning in his lair of coarse grass, under the shade of a tree, said to himself: 'I have not seen as much as one single bird all day.'

And he had not heard a sound, either, all day but that one now of his own muttering voice. It had been a day of absolute silence – the first he had known in his life. And he had not slept a wink. Not for all these wakeful nights and the days of fighting, planning, talking; not for all that last night of danger and hard physical toil upon the gulf, had he been able to close his eyes for a moment. And yet from sunrise to sunset he had been lying prone on the ground, either on his back or on his face.

He stretched himself, and with slow steps descended into the gully to spend the night by the side of the silver. If Nostromo returned – as he might have done at any moment – it was there that he would look first; and night would, of course, be the proper time for an attempt to communicate. He remembered with indifference that he had not eaten anything yet since he had been left alone on the island.

He spent the night open-eyed, and when the day broke he ate something with the same indifference. The brilliant 'Son Decoud,' the spoiled darling of the family, the lover of Antonia and journalist of Sulaco, was not fit to grapple with himself single-handed. Solitude from mere outward condition of existence becomes very swiftly a state of soul in which the affectations of irony and scepticism have no place. It takes possession of the mind, and drives forth the thought into the exile of utter unbelief. After three days of waiting for the sight of some human face, Decoud caught himself entertaining a doubt of his own individuality. It had merged into the world of cloud and water, of natural forces and forms of nature. In our activity alone do we find the sustaining illusion of an independent existence as against the whole scheme of things of which we form a helpless part. Decoud lost all belief in the reality of his action past and to come. On the fifth day an immense melancholy descended upon him palpably. He resolved not to give himself up to these people in Sulaco, who had beset him, unreal and terrible, like jibbering and obscene spectres. He saw himself struggling feebly in their midst, and Antonia, gigantic and lovely like an allegorical statue, looking on with scornful eyes at his weakness.

Not a living being, not a speck of distant sail, appeared within the range of his vision; and, as if to escape from this solitude, he absorbed himself in his melancholy. The vague consciousness of a misdirected life given up to impulses whose memory left a bitter taste in his mouth was the first moral sentiment of his manhood. But at the same time he felt no remorse. What should he regret? He had recognised no other virtue than intelligence, and had erected passions into duties. Both his intelligence and his passion were swallowed up easily in this great unbroken solitude of waiting without faith. Sleeplessness had robbed his will of all energy, for he had not slept seven hours in the seven days. His sadness was the sadness of a sceptical mind. He beheld the universe as a succession of incomprehensible images. Nostromo was dead. Everything had failed ignominiously. He no longer dared to think of Antonia. She had not survived. But if she survived he could not face her. And all exertion seemed senseless.

On the tenth day, after a night spent without even dozing off once (it had occurred to him that Antonia could not possibly have ever loved a being so impalpable as himself), the solitude appeared like a great void, and the silence of the gulf like a tense, thin cord to which he hung suspended by both hands, without fear, without surprise, without any sort of emotion whatever. Only towards the evening, in the comparative relief of coolness, he began to wish that this cord would snap. He imagined it snapping with a report as of a pistol – a sharp, full crack. And that would be the end of him. He contemplated that eventuality with pleasure, because he dreaded the sleepless nights in which the silence, remaining unbroken in the shape of a cord to which he hung with both hands, vibrated with senseless phrases, always the same but utterly incomprehensible, about Nostromo, Antonia,

Barrios, and proclamations mingled into an ironical and senseless buzzing. In the daytime he could look at the silence like a still cord stretched to breaking-point, with his life, his vain life, suspended to it like a weight.

'I wonder whether I would hear it snap before I fell,' he asked himself.

The sun was two hours above the horizon when he got up, gaunt, dirty, white-faced, and looked at it with his red-rimmed eyes. His limbs obeyed him slowly, as if full of lead, yet without tremor; and the effect of that physical condition gave to his movements an unhesitating, deliberate dignity. He acted as if accomplishing some sort of rite. He descended into the gully; for the fascination of all that silver, with its potential power, survived alone outside of himself. He picked up the belt with the revolver, that was lying there, and buckled it round his waist. The cord of silence could never snap on the island. It must let him fall and sink into the sea, he thought. And sink! He was looking at the loose earth covering the treasure. In the sea! His aspect was that of a somnambulist. He lowered himself down on his knees slowly and went on grubbing with his fingers with industrious patience till he uncovered one of the boxes. Without a pause, as if doing some work done many times before, he slit it open and took four ingots, which he put in his pockets. He covered up the exposed box again and step by step came out of the gully. The bushes closed after him with a swish.

It was on the third day of his solitude that he dragged the dinghy near the water with an idea of rowing away somewhere, but had desisted partly at the whisper of lingering hope that Nostromo would return, partly from conviction of utter uselessness of all effort. Now she wanted only a slight shove to be set afloat. He had eaten a little every day after the first, and had some muscular strength left yet. Taking up the oars slowly, he pulled away from the cliff of the Great Isabel, that stood behind him warm with sunshine, as if with the heat of life, bathed in a rich light from head to foot as if in a radiance of hope and joy. He pulled straight towards the setting sun. When the gulf had grown dark, he ceased rowing and flung the sculls in. The hollow clatter they made in falling was the loudest noise he had ever heard in his life. It was a revelation. It seemed to recall him from far away. Actually the thought, 'Perhaps I may sleep tonight,' passed through his mind. But he did not believe it. He believed in nothing; and he remained sitting on the thwart.

The dawn from behind the mountains put a gleam into his unwinking eyes. After a clear daybreak the sun appeared splendidly above the peaks of the range. The great gulf burst into a glitter all around the boat; and in this glory of merciless solitude the silence appeared again before him, stretched taut like a dark, thin string.

His eyes looked at it while, without haste, he shifted his seat from the thwart to the gunwale. They looked at it fixedly, while his hand, feeling about his waist, unbuttoned the flap of the leather case, drew the revolver, cocked it, brought it forward pointing at his breast, pulled the trigger, and, with convulsive force, sent the still-smoking weapon hurtling through the air. His eyes looked at it while he fell forward and hung with his breast on the gunwale and the fingers of his right hand hooked under the thwart. They looked: 'It is done,' he stammered out, in a sudden flow of blood. His last thought was: 'I wonder how that Capataz died.' The stiffness of the fingers relaxed, and the lover of Antonia Avellanos rolled overboard without having heard the cord of silence snap in the solitude of the Placid Gulf, whose glittering surface remained untroubled by the fall of his body.

A victim of the disillusioned weariness which is the retribution meted out to intellectual audacity, the brilliant Don Martin Decoud, weighted by the bars of San Tomé silver, disappeared without a trace, swallowed up in the immense indifference of things. His sleepless, crouching figure was gone from the side of the San Tomé silver; and for a time the spirits of good and evil that hover near every concealed treasure of the earth might have thought that this one had been forgotten by all mankind. Then, after a few days, another form appeared striding away from the setting sun to sit motionless and awake in the narrow black gully all through the night, in nearly the same pose, in the same place in which had sat that other sleepless man who had gone away for ever so quietly in a small boat, about the time of sunset. And the spirits of good and evil that hover about a forbidden treasure understood well that the silver of San Tomé was provided now with a faithful and lifelong slave.

The magnificent Capataz de Cargadores, victim of the disenchanted vanity which is the reward of audacious action, sat in the weary pose of a hunted outcast through a night of sleeplessness as tormenting as any known to Decoud, his companion in the most desperate affair of his life. And he wondered how Decoud had died. But he knew the part he had played himself. First a woman, then a man, abandoned each in their last extremity, for the sake of this accursed treasure. It was paid for by a soul lost and by a vanished life. The blank stillness of awe was succeeded by a gust of immense pride. There was no one in the world but Gian' Battista Fidanza, Capataz de Cargadores, the incorruptible and faithful Nostromo, to pay such a price.

He had made up his mind that nothing should be allowed now to rob him of his bargain. Nothing. Decoud had died. But how? That he was dead he had not a shadow of a doubt. But four ingots . . . What for? Did he mean to come for more – some other time?

The treasure was putting forth its latent power. It troubled the clear mind of the man who had paid the price. He was sure that Decoud was dead. The island seemed full of that whisper. Dead? Gone! And he caught himself listening for the swish of bushes and the splash of the footfalls in the bed of the brook. Dead! The talker, the novio of Doña Antonia!

'Ha!' he murmured, with his head on his knees, under the livid clouded dawn breaking over the liberated Sulaco and upon the gulf as grey as ashes. 'It is to her that he will fly. To her that he will fly!'

And four ingots! Did he take them in revenge, to cast a spell, like the angry woman who had prophesied remorse and failure, and yet had laid upon him the task of saving the children? Well, he had saved the children. He had defeated starvation. He had done it all alone – or perhaps helped by the devil. Who cared? He had done it, betrayed as he was, and saving by the same stroke the San Tomé mine, which appeared to him hateful and immense, lording it by its vast wealth over the valour, the toil, the fidelity of the poor, over war and peace, over the labours of the town, the sea, and the Campo.

The sun lit up the sky behind the peaks of the Cordillera. The Capataz looked down for a time upon the fall of loose earth, stones, and smashed bushes, concealing the hiding-place of the silver.

'I must grow rich very slowly,' he meditated, aloud.

Chapter 11

Sulaco outstripped Nostromo's prudence, growing rich swiftly on the hidden treasures of the earth, hovered over by the anxious spirits of good and evil, torn out by the labouring hands of the people. It was like a second youth, like a new life, full of promise, of unrest, of toil, scattering lavishly its wealth to the four corners of an excited world. Material changes swept along in the train of material interests. And other changes more subtle, outwardly unmarked, affected the minds and hearts of the workers. Captain Mitchell had gone home to live on his savings invested in the San Tomé mine; and Dr Monygham had grown older, with his head steel-grey and the unchanged expression of his face, living on the inexhaustible treasure of his devotion drawn upon in the secret of his heart like a store of unlawful wealth.

The Inspector-General of State Hospitals (whose maintenance is a charge upon the Gould Concession), Official Adviser on Sanitation to the Municipality, Chief Medical Officer of the San Tomé Consolidated Mines (whose territory, containing gold, silver, copper, lead, cobalt, extends for miles along the foothills of the Cordillera), had felt poverty-stricken, miserable, and starved during the prolonged, second visit the Goulds paid to Europe and the United States of America. Intimate of the casa, proved friend, a bachelor without ties and without establishment (except of the professional sort), he had been asked to take up his quarters in the Gould house. In the eleven months of their absence the familiar rooms, recalling at every glance the woman to whom he had given all his loyalty, had grown intolerable. As the day approached for the arrival of the mail boat *Hermes* (the latest addition to the OSN Co.'s splendid fleet), the doctor hobbled about more vivaciously, snapped more sardonically at simple and gentle out of sheer nervousness.

He packed up his modest trunk with speed, with fury, with enthusiasm, and saw it carried out past the old porter at the gate of the Casa Gould with delight, with intoxication; then, as the hour approached, sitting alone in the great landau behind the white mules, a little sideways, his drawn-in face positively venomous with the effort of self-control, and holding a pair of new gloves in his left hand, he drove to the harbour.

His heart dilated within him so, when he saw the Goulds on the deck of the *Hermes*, that his greetings were reduced to a casual mutter. Driving back to town, all three were silent. And in the patio the doctor, in a more natural manner, said: 'I'll leave you now to yourselves. I'll call tomorrow if I may?'

'Come to lunch, dear Dr Monygham, and come early,' said Mrs Gould, in her travelling dress and her veil down, turning to look at him at the foot of the stairs; while at the top of the flight the Madonna, in blue robes and the Child on her arm, seemed to welcome her with an aspect of pitying tenderness.

'Don't expect to find me at home,' Charles Gould warned him. 'I'll be off early to the mine.'

After lunch, Doña Emilia and the señor doctor came slowly through the inner gateway of the patio. The large gardens of the Casa Gould, surrounded by high walls, and the red-tile slopes of neighbouring roofs, lay open before them, with masses of shade under the trees and level surfaces of sunlight upon the lawns. A triple row of old orange trees surrounded the whole. Barefooted, brown gardeners, in snowy white shirts and wide calzoneras, dotted the grounds, squatting over flower-beds, passing between the trees, dragging slender india-rubber tubes across the gravel of the paths; and the fine jets of water crossed each other in graceful curves, sparkling in the sunshine with a slight pattering noise upon the bushes, and an effect of showered diamonds upon the grass.

Doña Emilia, holding up the train of a clear dress, walked by the side of Dr Monygham, in a longish black coat and severe black bow on an immaculate shirt-front. Under a shady clump of trees, where stood scattered little tables and wicker easy-chairs, Mrs Gould sat down in a low and ample seat.

'Don't go yet,' she said to Dr Monygham, who was unable to tear himself away from the spot. His chin nestling within the points of his collar, he devoured her stealthily with his eyes, which, luckily, were round and hard like clouded marbles, and incapable of disclosing his sentiments. His pitying emotion at the marks of time upon the face of that woman, the air of frailty and weary fatigue that had settled upon the eyes and temples of the 'Never-tired Señora' (as Don Pépé years ago used to call her with admiration), touched him almost to tears. 'Don't go yet. Today is all my own,' Mrs Gould urged, gently. 'We are not back yet officially. No one will come. It's only tomorrow that the windows of the Casa Gould are to be lit up for a reception.'

The doctor dropped into a chair.

'Giving a tertulía?' he said, with a detached air.

'A simple greeting for all the kind friends who care to come.'

'And only tomorrow?'

'Yes. Charles would be tired out after a day at the mine, and so I – It would be good to have him to myself for one evening on our return to this house I love. It has seen all my life.'

'Ah, yes!' snarled the doctor, suddenly. 'Women count time from the marriage feast. Didn't you live a little before?'

'Yes; but what is there to remember? There were no cares.'

Mrs Gould sighed. And as two friends, after a long separation, will revert to the most agitated period of their lives, they began to talk of the Sulaco Revolution. It seemed strange to Mrs Gould that people who had taken part in it seemed to forget its memory and its lesson.

'And yet,' struck in the doctor, 'we who played our part in it had our reward. Don Pépé, though superannuated, still can sit a horse. Barrios is drinking himself to death in jovial company away somewhere on his *fundacíon* beyond the Bolsón de Tonoro. And the heroic Father Romàn – I imagine the old padre blowing up systematically the San Tomé mine, uttering a pious exclamation at every bang, and taking handfuls of snuff between the explosions – the heroic Padre Romàn says that he is not afraid of the harm Holroyd's missionaries can do to his flock, as long as *he* is alive.'

Mrs Gould shuddered a little at the allusion to the destruction that had come so near to the San Tomé mine.

'Ah, but you, dear friend?'

'I did the work I was fit for.'

'You faced the most cruel dangers of all. Something more than death.'

'No, Mrs Gould! Only death – by hanging. And I am rewarded beyond my deserts.'

Noticing Mrs Gould's gaze fixed upon him, he dropped his eyes.

'I've made my career – as you see,' said the Inspector-General of State Hospitals, taking up lightly the lapels of his superfine black coat. The doctor's self-respect marked inwardly by the almost complete disappearance from his dreams of Father Beron, appeared visibly in what, by contrast with former carelessness, seemed an immoderate cult of personal appearance. Carried out within severe limits of form and colour, and in perpetual freshness, this change of apparel gave to Dr Monygham an air at the same time professional and festive; while his gait and the unchanged crabbed character of his face acquired from it a startling force of incongruity.

'Yes,' he went on. 'We all had our rewards – the engineer-in-chief, Captain Mitchell – '

'We saw him,' interrupted Mrs Gould, in her charming voice. 'The poor dear man came up from the country on purpose to call on us in our hotel in London. He comported himself with great dignity, but I fancy he regrets Sulaco. He rambled feebly about "historical events" till I felt I could have a cry.'

'H'm,' grunted the doctor; 'getting old, I suppose. Even Nostromo is getting older – though he is not changed. And, speaking of that fellow, I wanted to tell you something – '

For some time the house had been full of murmurs, of agitation. Suddenly the two gardeners, busy with rose trees at the side of the garden arch, fell upon their knees with bowed heads on the passage of Antonia Avellanos, who appeared walking beside her uncle.

Invested with the red hat after a short visit to Rome, where he had been invited by the Propaganda, Father Corbelàn, missionary to the wild Indians, conspirator, friend and patron of Hernandez the robber, advanced with big, slow strides, gaunt and leaning forward, with his powerful hands clasped behind his back. The first Cardinal-Archbishop of Sulaco had preserved his fanatical and morose air; the aspect of a chaplain of bandits. It was believed that his unexpected elevation to the purple was a countermove to the Protestant invasion of Sulaco organised by the Holroyd Missionary Fund. Antonia, the beauty of her face as if a little blurred, her figure slightly fuller, advanced with her light walk and her high serenity, smiling from a distance at Mrs Gould. She had brought her uncle over to see dear Emilia, without ceremony, just for a moment before the siesta.

When all were seated again, Dr Monygham, who had come to dislike heartily everybody who approached Mrs Gould with any intimacy, kept aside, pretending to be lost in profound meditation. A louder phrase of Antonia made him lift his head.

'How can we abandon, groaning under oppression, those who have been our countrymen only a few years ago, who are our countrymen now?' Miss Avellanos was saying. 'How can we remain blind, and deaf without pity to the cruel wrongs suffered by our brothers? There is a remedy.'

'Annex the rest of Costaguana to the order and prosperity of Sulaco,' snapped the doctor. 'There is no other remedy.'

'I am convinced, señor doctor,' Antonia said, with the earnest calm of invincible resolution, 'that this was from the first poor Martin's intention.'

'Yes, but the material interests will not let you jeopardise their development for a mere idea of pity and justice,' the doctor muttered, grumpily. 'And it is just as well perhaps.'

The Cardinal-Archbishop straightened up his gaunt, bony frame.

'We have worked for them; we have made them, these material interests of the foreigners,' the last of the Corbelàns uttered in a deep, denunciatory tone.

'And without them you are nothing,' cried the doctor from the distance. 'They will not let you.'

'Let them beware, then, lest the people, prevented from their aspirations, should rise and claim their share of the wealth and their share of the power,' the popular Cardinal-Archbishop of Sulaco declared, significantly, menacingly.

A silence ensued, during which his Eminence stared frowning at the ground, and Antonia, graceful and rigid in her chair, breathed calmly in the strength of her convictions. Then the conversation took a social turn, touching on the visit of the Goulds to Europe. The Cardinal-Archbishop, when in Rome, had suffered from neuralgia in the head all the time. It was the climate – the bad air.

When uncle and niece had gone away, with the servants again falling on their knees, and the old porter, who had known Henry Gould, almost totally blind and impotent now, creeping up to kiss his Eminence's extended hand, Dr Monygham, looking after them, pronounced the one word: 'Incorrigible!'

Mrs Gould, with a look upwards, dropped wearily on her lap her white hands flashing with the gold and stones of many rings.

'Conspiring. Yes!' said the doctor. 'The last of the Avellanos and the last of the Corbelàns are conspiring with the refugees from Sta Marta that flock here after every revolution. The Café Lambroso at the corner of the Plaza is full of them; you can hear their chatter across the street like the noise of a parrot-house. They are conspiring for the invasion of Costaguana. And do you know where they go for strength, for the necessary force? To the secret societies amongst immigrants and natives, where Nostromo – I should say Captain Fidanza – is the great man. What gives him that position? Who can say? Genius? He has genius. He is greater with the populace than ever he was before. It was as if he had some secret power; some mysterious means to keep up his influence. He holds conferences with the Archbishop, as in those old days which you and I remember. Barrios is useless. But for a military head they have the pious Hernandez. And they may raise the country with the new cry of the wealth for the people.'

'Will there be never any peace? Will there be no rest?' Mrs Gould whispered. 'I thought that we – '

'No!' interrupted the doctor. 'There is no peace and no rest in the development of material interests. They have their law, and their justice. But it is founded on expediency, and is inhuman; it is without rectitude, without the continuity and the force that can be found only in a moral principle. Mrs Gould, the time approaches when all that the Gould Concession stands for shall weigh as heavily upon the people as the barbarism, cruelty, and misrule of a few years back.'

'How can you say that, Dr Monygham?' she cried out, as if hurt in the most sensitive place of her soul.

'I can say what is true,' the doctor insisted, obstinately. 'It'll weigh as heavily, and provoke resentment, bloodshed, and vengeance, because the men have grown different. Do you think that now the mine would march upon the town to save their Señor Administrador? Do you think that?'

She pressed the backs of her entwined hands on her eyes and murmured hopelessly: 'Is it this we have worked for, then?'

The doctor lowered his head. He could follow her silent thought. Was it for this that her life had been robbed of all the intimate felicities of daily affection which her tenderness needed as the human body needs air to breathe? And the doctor, indignant with Charles Gould's blindness, hastened to change the conversation.

'It is about Nostromo that I wanted to talk to you. Ah! that fellow has some continuity and force. Nothing will put an end to him. But never mind that. There's something inexplicable going on – or perhaps only too easy to explain. You know, Linda is practically the lighthouse keeper of the Great Isabel light. The Garibaldino is too old now. His part is to clean the lamps and to cook in the house; but he can't get up the stairs any longer. The black-eyed Linda sleeps all day and watches the light all night. Not all day, though. She is up towards five in the afternoon, when our Nostromo, whenever he is in harbour with his schooner, comes out on his courting visit, pulling in a small boat.'

'Aren't they married yet?' Mrs Gould asked. 'The mother wished it, as far as I can understand, while Linda was yet quite a child. When I had the girls with me for a year or so during the War of Separation, that extraordinary Linda used to declare quite simply that she was going to be Gian' Battista's wife.'

'They are not married yet,' said the doctor, curtly. 'I have looked after them a little.'

'Thank you, dear Dr Monygham,' said Mrs Gould; and under the shade of the big trees her little, even teeth gleamed in a youthful smile of gentle malice. 'People don't know how really good you are. You will not let them know, as if on purpose to annoy me, who have put my faith in your good heart long ago.'

The doctor, with a lifting up of his upper lip, as though he were longing to bite, bowed stiffly in his chair. With the utter absorption of a man to whom love comes late, not as the most splendid of illusions, but like an enlightening and priceless misfortune, the sight of that woman (of whom he had been deprived for nearly a year) suggested ideas of adoration, of kissing the hem of her robe. And this excess of feeling translated itself naturally into an augmented grimness of speech.

'I am afraid of being overwhelmed by too much gratitude. However, these people interest me. I went out several times to the Great Isabel light to look after old Giorgio.'

He did not tell Mrs Gould that it was because he found there, in her absence, the relief of an atmosphere of congenial sentiment in old Giorgio's austere admiration for the 'English signora – the benefactress', in black-eyed Linda's voluble, torrential, passionate affection for 'our Doña Emilia – that angel'; in the white-throated, fair Giselle's adoring upward turn of the eyes, which then glided towards him with a sidelong, half-arch, half-candid glance, which made the doctor exclaim to himself mentally, 'If I weren't what I am, old and ugly, I would think the minx is making eyes at me. And perhaps she

is. I dare say she would make eyes at anybody.' Dr Monygham said nothing of
this to Mrs Gould, the providence of the Viola family, but reverted to what
he called 'our great Nostromo'.

'What I wanted to tell you is this: our great Nostromo did not take much
notice of the old man and the children for some years. It's true, too, that he
was away on his coasting voyages certainly ten months out of the twelve. He
was making his fortune, as he told Captain Mitchell once. He seems to have
done uncommonly well. It was only to be expected. He's a man full of
resource, full of confidence in himself, ready to take chances and risks of
every sort. I remember being in Mitchell's office one day, when he came in
with that calm, grave air he always carries everywhere. He had been away
trading in the Gulf of California, he said, looking straight past us at the wall,
as his manner is, and was glad to see on his return that a lighthouse was
being built on the cliff of the Great Isabel. Very glad, he repeated. Mitchell
explained that it was the OSN Co. who was building it, for the convenience
of the mail service, on his own advice. Captain Fidanza was good enough to
say that it was excellent advice. I remember him twisting up his moustaches
and looking all round the cornice of the room before he proposed that old
Giorgio should be made the keeper of that light.'

'I heard of this. I was consulted at the time,' Mrs Gould said. 'I doubted
whether it would be good for these girls to be shut up on that island as if in a
prison.'

'The proposal fell in with the old Garibaldino's humour. As to Linda, any
place was lovely and delightful enough for her as long as it was Nostromo's
suggestion. She could wait for her Gian' Battista's good pleasure there as
well as anywhere else. My opinion is that she was always in love with that
incorruptible Capataz. Moreover, both father and sister were anxious to get
Giselle away from the attentions of a certain Ramirez.'

'Ah!' said Mrs Gould, interested. 'Ramirez? What sort of man is that?'

'Just a mozo of the town. His father was a Cargador. As a lanky boy he ran
about the wharf in rags, till Nostromo took him up and made a man of him.
When he got a little older, he put him into a lighter and very soon gave him
charge of the No. 3 boat – the boat which took the silver away, Mrs Gould.
Nostromo selected that lighter for the work because she was the best sailing
and the strongest boat of all the Company's fleet. Young Ramirez was one of
the five Cargadores entrusted with the removal of the treasure from the
Custom House on that famous night. As the boat he had charge of was sunk,
Nostromo, on leaving the Company's service, recommended him to Captain
Mitchell for his successor. He had trained him in the routine of work
perfectly, and thus Mr Ramirez, from a starving waif, becomes a man and
the Capataz of the Sulaco Cargadores.'

'Thanks to Nostromo,' said Mrs Gould, with warm approval.

'Thanks to Nostromo,' repeated Dr Monygham. 'Upon my word, the
fellow's power frightens me when I think of it. That our poor old Mitchell

was only too glad to appoint somebody trained to the work, who saved him trouble, is not surprising. What is wonderful is the fact that the Sulaco Cargadores accepted Ramirez for their chief, simply because such was Nostromo's good pleasure. Of course, he is not a second Nostromo, as he fondly imagined he would be; but still, the position was brilliant enough. It emboldened him to make up to Giselle Viola, who, you know, is the recognised beauty of the town. The old Garibaldino, however, took a violent dislike to him. I don't know why. Perhaps because he was not a model of perfection like his Gian' Battista, the incarnation of the courage, the fidelity, the honour of "the people". Signor Viola does not think much of Sulaco natives. Both of them, the old Spartan and that white-faced Linda, with her red mouth and coal-black eyes, were looking rather fiercely after the fair one. Ramirez was warned off. Father Viola, I am told, threatened him with his gun once.'

'But what of Giselle herself?' asked Mrs Gould.

'She's a bit of a flirt, I believe,' said the doctor. 'I don't think she cared much one way or another. Of course she likes men's attentions. Ramirez was not the only one, let me tell you, Mrs Gould. There was one engineer, at least, on the railway staff who got warned off with a gun, too. Old Viola does not allow any trifling with his honour. He has grown uneasy and suspicious since his wife died. He was very pleased to remove his youngest girl away from the town. But look what happens, Mrs Gould. Ramirez, the honest, lovelorn swain, is forbidden the island. Very well. He respects the prohibition, but naturally turns his eyes frequently towards the Great Isabel. It seems as though he had been in the habit of gazing late at night upon the light. And during these sentimental vigils he discovers that Nostromo, Captain Fidanza that is, returns very late from his visits to the Violas. As late as midnight at times.'

The doctor paused and stared meaningly at Mrs Gould.

'Yes. But I don't understand,' she began, looking puzzled.

'Now comes the strange part,' went on Dr Monygham. 'Viola, who is king on his island, will allow no visitor on it after dark. Even Captain Fidanza has got to leave after sunset, when Linda has gone up to tend the light. And Nostromo goes away obediently. But what happens afterwards? What does he do in the gulf between half-past six and midnight? He has been seen more than once at that late hour pulling quietly into the harbour. Ramirez is devoured by jealousy. He dared not approach old Viola; but he plucked up courage to rail Linda about it on Sunday morning as she came on the mainland to hear Mass and visit her mother's grave. There was a scene on the wharf, which, as a matter of fact, I witnessed. It was early morning. He must have been waiting for her on purpose. I was there by the merest chance, having been called to an urgent consultation by the doctor of the German gunboat in the harbour. She poured wrath, scorn, and flame upon Ramirez, who seemed out of his mind. It was a strange sight, Mrs Gould: the long jetty, with this raving Cargador in his crimson sash and the girl all in black, at the end; the early Sunday morning quiet of the harbour in the shade of the mountains; nothing but a canoe or two moving between the ships at anchor, and the German gunboat's gig coming to take me off. Linda passed me within a foot. I noticed her wild eyes. I called out to her. She never heard me. She never saw me. But I looked at her face. It was awful in its anger and wretchedness.'

Mrs Gould sat up, opening her eyes very wide.

'What do you mean, Dr Monygham? Do you mean to say that you suspect the younger sister?'

'*Quien sabe!* Who can tell?' said the doctor, shrugging his shoulders like a born Costaguanero. 'Ramirez came up to me on the wharf. He reeled – he looked insane. He took his head into his hands. He had to talk to someone – simply had to. Of course for all his mad state he recognised me. People know me well here. I have lived too long amongst them to be anything else but the evil-eyed doctor, who can cure all the ills of the flesh, and bring bad luck by a glance. He came up to me. He tried to be calm. He tried to make it out that he wanted merely to warn me against Nostromo. It seems that Captain Fidanza at some secret meeting or other had mentioned me as the worst despiser of all the poor – of the people. It's very possible. He honours me with his undying dislike. And a word from the great Fidanza may be quite enough to send some fool's knife into my back. The Sanitary Commission I preside over is not in favour with the populace. "Beware of him, señor doctor. Destroy him, señor doctor," Ramirez hissed right into my face. And then he broke out. "That man," he spluttered, "has cast a spell upon both these girls." As to himself, he had said too much. He must run away now – run away and hide somewhere. He moaned tenderly about Giselle, and then called her names that cannot be repeated. If he thought she could be made to love him by any means, he would carry her off from the island. Off into the woods. But it was no good . . . He strode away, flourishing his arms above his head. Then I noticed an old Negro, who had been sitting behind a pile of cases, fishing from the wharf. He wound up his lines and slunk away at once. But he must have heard something, and must have talked, too, because some of the old Garibaldino's railway friends, I suppose, warned him against Ramirez. At any rate, the father had been warned. But Ramirez has disappeared from the town.'

'I feel I have a duty towards these girls,' said Mrs Gould, uneasily. 'Is Nostromo in Sulaco now?'

'He is, since last Sunday.'

'He ought to be spoken to – at once.'

'Who will dare speak to him? Even the love-mad Ramirez runs away from the mere shadow of Captain Fidanza.'

'I can. I will,' Mrs Gould declared. 'A word will be enough for a man like Nostromo.'

The doctor smiled sourly.

'He must end this situation which lends itself to – I can't believe it of that child,' pursued Mrs Gould.

'He's very attractive,' muttered the doctor, gloomily.

'He'll see it, I am sure. He must put an end to all this by marrying Linda at once,' pronounced the first lady of Sulaco with immense decision.

Through the garden gate emerged Basilio, grown fat and sleek, with an elderly hairless face, wrinkles at the corners of his eyes, and his jet-black, coarse hair plastered down smoothly. Stooping carefully behind an ornamental clump of bushes, he put down with precaution a small child he had been carrying on his shoulder – his own and Leonarda's last born. The pouting, spoiled Camerista and the head mozo of the Casa Gould had been married for some years now.

He remained squatting on his heels for a time, gazing fondly at his offspring, which returned his stare with imperturbable gravity, then, solemn and respectable, walked down the path.

'What is it, Basilio?' asked Mrs Gould.

'A telephone came through from the office of the mine. The master remains to sleep at the mountain tonight.'

Dr Monygham had got up and stood looking away. A profound silence reigned for a time under the shade of the biggest trees in the lovely gardens of the Casa Gould.

'Very well, Basilio,' said Mrs Gould. She watched him walk away along the path, step aside behind the flowering bush, and reappear with the child seated on his shoulder. He passed through the gateway between the garden and the patio with measured steps, careful of his light burden.

The doctor, with his back to Mrs Gould, contemplated a flower-bed away in the sunshine. People believed him scornful and soured. The truth of his nature consisted in his capacity for passion and in the sensitiveness of his temperament. What he lacked was the polished callousness of men of the world, the callousness from which springs an easy tolerance for oneself and others; the tolerance wide as poles asunder from true sympathy and human compassion. This want of callousness accounted for his sardonic turn of mind and his biting speeches.

In profound silence, and glaring viciously at the brilliant flower-bed, Dr Monygham poured mental imprecations on Charles Gould's head. Behind him the immobility of Mrs Gould added to the grace of her seated figure the charm of art, of an attitude caught and interpreted for ever. Turning abruptly, the doctor took his leave.

Mrs Gould leaned back in the shade of the big trees planted in a circle. She leaned back with her eyes closed and her white hands lying idle on the arms of her seat. The half-light under the thick mass of leaves brought out the youthful prettiness of her face; made the clear, light fabrics and white lace of her dress appear luminous. Small and dainty, as if radiating a light of her own in the deep shade of the interlaced boughs, she resembled a good fairy, weary with a long career of well-doing, touched by the withering suspicion of the uselessness of her labours, the powerlessness of her magic.

Had anybody asked her of what she was thinking, alone in the garden of the Casa, with her husband at the mine and the house closed to the street like an empty dwelling, her frankness would have had to evade the question. It had come into her mind that for life to be large and full, it must contain the care of the past and of the future in every passing moment of the present. Our daily work must be done to the glory of the dead, and for the good of those who come after. She thought that, and sighed without opening her eyes – without moving at all. Mrs Gould's face became set and rigid for a second, as if to receive, without flinching, a great wave of loneliness that swept over her head. And it came into her mind, too, that no one would ever ask her with solicitude what she was thinking of. No one. No one, but perhaps the man who had just gone away. No; no one who could be answered with careless sincerity in the ideal perfection of confidence.

The word 'incorrigible' – a word lately pronounced by Dr Monygham – floated into her still and sad immobility. Incorrigible in his devotion to the great silver mine was the Señor Administrador! Incorrigible in his hard, determined service of the material interests to which he had pinned his faith in the triumph of order and justice. Poor boy! She had a clear vision of the grey hairs on his temples. He was perfect – perfect. What more could she have expected? It was a colossal and lasting success; and love was only a short moment of forgetfulness, a short intoxication, whose delight one remembered with a sense of sadness, as if it had been a deep grief lived through. There was something inherent in the necessities of successful action which carried with it the moral degradation of the idea. She saw the San Tomé mountain hanging over the Campo, over the whole land, feared, hated, wealthy; more soulless than any tyrant, more pitiless and autocratic than the worst Government; ready to crush innumerable lives in the expansion of its greatness. He did not see it. He could not see it. It was not his fault. He was perfect, perfect; but she would never have him to herself. Never; not altogether to herself in this old Spanish house she loved so well! Incorrigible, the last of the Corbelàns, the last of the Avellanos, the doctor had said; but she saw clearly the San Tomé mine possessing, consuming, burning up the life of the last of the Costaguana Goulds; mastering the energetic spirit of the son as it had mastered the lamentable weakness of the father. A terrible success for the last of the Goulds. The last! She had hoped for a long, long time, that perhaps – But no! There were to be no more. An immense desolation, the dread of her own continued life, descended upon the first lady of Sulaco. With a prophetic vision she saw herself surviving alone the degradation of her young ideal of life, of love, of work – all alone in the Treasure House of the World. The profound, blind, suffering expression of a painful dream settled on her face with its closed eyes. In the indistinct voice of an unlucky sleeper, lying passive in the grip of a merciless nightmare, she stammered out aimlessly the words: 'Material interest.'

Chapter 12

Nostromo had been growing rich very slowly. It was an effect of his prudence. He could command himself even when thrown off his balance. And to become the slave of a treasure with full self-knowledge is an occurrence rare and mentally disturbing. But it was also in a great part because of the difficulty of converting it into a form in which it could become available. The mere act of getting it away from the island piecemeal, little by little, was surrounded by difficulties, by the dangers of imminent detection. He had to visit the Great Isabel in secret, between his voyages along the coast, which were the ostensible source of his fortune. The crew of his own schooner were to be feared as if they had been spies upon their dreaded captain. He did not dare stay too long in port. When his coaster was unloaded, he hurried away on another trip, for he feared arousing suspicion even by a day's delay. Sometimes during a week's stay, or more, he could only manage one visit to the treasure. And that was all. A couple of ingots. He suffered through his fears as much as through his prudence. To do things by stealth humiliated him. And he suffered most from the concentration of his thought upon the treasure.

A transgression, a crime entering a man's existence, eats it up like a malignant growth, consumes it like a fever. Nostromo had lost his peace; the genuineness of all his qualities was destroyed. He felt it himself, and often cursed the silver of San Tomé. His courage, his magnificence, his leisure, his work, everything was as before, only everything was a sham. But the treasure was real. He clung to it with a more tenacious, mental grip. But he hated the feel of the ingots. Sometimes, after putting away a couple of them in his cabin – the fruit of a secret night expedition to the Great Isabel – he would look fixedly at his fingers, as if surprised they had left no stain on his skin.

He had found means of disposing of the silver bars in distant ports. The necessity to go far afield made his coasting voyages long, and caused his visits to the Viola household to be rare and far between. He was fated to have his wife from there. He had said so once to Giorgio himself. But the Garibaldino had put the subject aside with a majestic wave of his hand, clutching a smouldering black briar-root pipe. There was plenty of time; he was not the man to force his girls upon anybody.

As time went on, Nostromo discovered his preference for the younger of the two. They had some profound similarities of nature, which must exist for complete confidence and understanding, no matter what outward differences of temperament there may be to exercise their own fascination of contrast. His wife would have to know his secret or else life would be impossible. He was attracted by Giselle, with her candid gaze and white throat, pliable, silent, fond of excitement under her quiet indolence; whereas Linda, with her intense, passionately pale face, energetic, all fire and words, touched with gloom and scorn, a chip of the old block, true daughter of the austere republican, but with Teresa's voice, inspired him with a deep-seated mistrust. Moreover, the poor girl could not conceal her love for Gian' Battista. He could see it would be violent, exacting, suspicious, uncompromising – like her soul. Giselle, by her fair but warm beauty, by the surface placidity of her nature holding a promise of submissiveness, by the charm of her girlish mysteriousness, excited his passion and allayed his fears as to the future.

His absences from Sulaco were long. On returning from the longest of them, he made out lighters loaded with blocks of stone lying under the cliff of the Great Isabel; cranes and scaffolding above; workmen's figures moving about, and a small lighthouse already rising from its foundations on the edge of the cliff.

At this unexpected, undreamt-of, startling sight, he thought himself lost irretrievably. What could save him from detection now? Nothing! He was struck with amazed dread at this turn of chance, that would kindle a far-reaching light upon the only secret spot of his life; that life whose very essence, value, reality, consisted in its reflection from the admiring eyes of men. All of it but that thing which was beyond common comprehension; which stood between him and the power that hears and gives effect to the evil intention of curses. It was dark. Not every man had such a darkness. And they were going to put a light there. A light! He saw it shining upon disgrace, poverty, contempt. Somebody was sure to . . . Perhaps somebody had already . . .

The incomparable Nostromo, the Capataz, the respected and feared Captain Fidanza, the unquestioned patron of secret societies, a republican like old Giorgio, and a revolutionist at heart (but in another manner), was on the point of jumping overboard from the deck of his own schooner. That man, subjective almost to insanity, looked suicide deliberately in the face. But he never lost his head. He was checked by the thought that this was no escape. He imagined himself dead, and the disgrace, the shame going on. Or, rather, properly speaking, he could not imagine himself dead. He was possessed too strongly by the sense of his own existence, a thing of infinite duration in its changes, to grasp the notion of finality. The earth goes on for ever.

And he was courageous. It was a corrupt courage, but it was as good for his purposes as the other kind. He sailed close to the cliff of the Great Isabel, throwing a penetrating glance from the deck at the mouth of the ravine, tangled in an undisturbed growth of bushes. He sailed close enough to exchange hails with the workmen, shading their eyes on the edge of the sheer drop of the cliff overhung by the jib-head of a powerful crane. He perceived that none of them had any occasion even to approach the ravine where the silver lay hidden; let alone to enter it. In the harbour he learned that no one slept on the island. The labouring gangs returned to port every evening, singing chorus songs in the empty lighters towed by a harbour tug. For the moment he had nothing to fear.

But afterwards? he asked himself. Later, when a keeper came to live in the cottage that was being built some hundred and fifty yards back from the low light-tower, and four hundred or so from the dark, shaded, jungly ravine, containing the secret of his safety, of his influence, of his magnificence, of his power over the future, of his defiance of ill-luck, of every possible betrayal from rich and poor alike – what then? He could never shake off the treasure. His audacity, greater than that of other men, had welded that vein of silver into his life. And the feeling of fearful and ardent subjection, the feeling of his slavery – so irremediable and profound that often, in his thoughts, he compared himself to the legendary Gringos, neither dead nor alive, bound down to their conquest of unlawful wealth on Azuera – weighed heavily on the independent Captain Fidanza, owner and master of a coasting schooner, whose smart appearance (and fabulous good-luck in trading) were so well known along the western seaboard of a vast continent.

Fiercely whiskered and grave, a shade less supple in his walk, the vigour and symmetry of his powerful limbs lost in the vulgarity of a brown tweed suit, made by Jews in the slums of London, and sold by the clothing department of the Compañia Anzani, Captain Fidanza was seen in the streets of Sulaco attending to his business, as usual, that trip. And, as usual, he allowed it to get about that he had made a great profit on his cargo. It was a cargo of salt fish, and Lent was approaching. He was seen in tramcars going to and fro between the town and the harbour; he talked with people in a café or two in his measured, steady voice. Captain Fidanza was *seen*. The generation that would know nothing of the famous ride to Cayta was not born yet.

Nostromo, the miscalled Capataz de Cargadores, had made for himself, under his rightful name, another public existence, but modified by the new conditions, less picturesque, more difficult to keep up in the increased size and varied population of Sulaco, the progressive capital of the Occidental Republic.

Captain Fidanza, unpicturesque, but always a little mysterious, was recognised quite sufficiently under the lofty glass and iron roof of the Sulaco railway station. He took a local train, and got out in Rincon, where he visited the widow of the Cargador who had died of his wounds (at the dawn of the New Era, like Avellanos) in the patio of the Casa Gould. He consented to sit down and drink a glass of cool lemonade in the hut, while the woman, standing up, poured a perfect torrent of words to which he did not listen. He left some money with her, as usual. The orphaned children, growing up and well schooled, calling him uncle, clamoured for his blessing. He gave that, too; and in the doorway paused for a moment to look at the flat face of the San Tomé mountain with a faint frown. This slight contraction of his bronzed brow casting a marked tinge of severity upon his usual unbending expression, was observed at the Lodge which he attended – but went away before the banquet. He wore it at the meeting of some good comrades, Italians and Occidentals, assembled in his honour under the presidency of an indigent, sickly, somewhat hunchbacked little photographer, with a white face and a magnanimous soul dyed crimson by a bloodthirsty hate of all capitalists, oppressors of the two hemispheres. The heroic Giorgio Viola, old revolutionist, would have understood nothing of his opening speech; and Captain Fidanza, lavishly generous as usual to some poor comrades, made no speech at all. He had listened, frowning with his mind far away, and walked off unapproachable, silent, like a man full of cares.

His frown deepened as, in the early morning, he watched the stonemasons go off to the Great Isabel, in lighters loaded with squared blocks of stone, enough to add another course to the squat light-tower. That was the rate of the work. One course per day.

And Captain Fidanza meditated. The presence of strangers on the island would cut him completely off the treasure. It had been difficult and dangerous enough before. He was afraid, and he was angry. He thought with the resolution of a master and the cunning of a cowed slave. Then he went ashore.

He was a man of resource and ingenuity; and, as usual, the expedient he found at a critical moment was effective enough to alter the situation radically. He had the gift of evolving safety out of the very danger, this incomparable Nostromo, this 'fellow in a thousand'. With Giorgio established on the Great Isabel, there would be no need for concealment. He would be able to go openly, in daylight, to see his daughters – one of his daughters – and stay late talking to the old Garibaldino. Then in the dark . . . Night after night . . . He would dare to grow rich quicker now. He yearned to clasp, embrace, absorb, subjugate in unquestioned possession this treasure, whose tyranny had weighed upon his mind, his actions, his very sleep.

He went to see his friend Captain Mitchell – and the thing was done as Dr Monygham had related to Mrs Gould. When the project was mooted to the Garibaldino, something like the faint reflection, the dim ghost of a very ancient smile, stole under the white and enormous moustaches of the old hater of kings and ministers. His daughters were the object of his anxious care. The younger, especially. Linda, with her mother's voice, had taken more her mother's place. Her deep, vibrating 'Eh, Padre?' seemed, but for the change of the word, the very echo of the impassioned, remonstrating 'Eh, Giorgio?' of poor Signora Teresa. It was his fixed opinion that the town was no proper place for his girls. The infatuated but guileless Ramirez was the object of his profound aversion, as resuming the sins of the country whose people were blind, vile *esclavos*.

On his return from his next voyage, Captain Fidanza found the Violas settled in the light-keeper's cottage. His knowledge of Giorgio's idiosyncrasies had not played him false. The Garibaldino had refused to entertain the idea of any companion whatever, except his girls. And Captain Mitchell, anxious to please his poor Nostromo, with that felicity of inspiration which only true affection can give, had formally appointed Linda Viola as under-keeper of the Isabel's Light.

'The light is private property,' he used to explain. 'It belongs to my Company. I've the power to nominate whom I like, and Viola it shall be. It's about the only thing Nostromo – a man worth his weight in gold, mind you – has ever asked me to do for him.'

Directly his schooner was anchored opposite the New Custom House, with its sham air of a Greek temple, flat-roofed, with a colonnade, Captain Fidanza went pulling his small boat out of the harbour, bound for the Great Isabel, openly in the light of a declining day, before all men's eyes, with a sense of having mastered the fates. He must establish a regular position. He would ask him for his daughter now. He thought of Giselle as he pulled. Linda loved him, perhaps, but the old man would be glad to keep the eldest, who had his wife's voice.

He did not pull for the narrow strand where he had landed with Decoud, and afterwards alone on his first visit to the treasure. He made for the beach at the other end, and walked up the regular and gentle slope of the wedge-shaped island. Giorgio Viola, whom he saw from afar, sitting on a bench under the front wall of the cottage, lifted his arm slightly to his loud hail. He walked up. Neither of the girls appeared.

'It is good here,' said the old man, in his austere, faraway manner.

Nostromo nodded; then, after a short silence: 'You saw my schooner pass in not two hours ago? Do you know why I am here before, so to speak, my anchor has fairly bitten into the ground of this port of Sulaco?'

'You are welcome like a son,' the old man declared, quietly, staring away upon the sea.

'Ah! thy son. I know. I am what thy son would have been. It is well, viejo. It is a very good welcome. Listen, I have come to ask you for – '

A sudden dread came upon the fearless and incorruptible Nostromo. He dared not utter the name in his mind. The slight pause only imparted a marked weight and solemnity to the changed end of the phrase.

'For my wife!' . . . His heart was beating fast. 'It is time you – '

The Garibaldino arrested him with an extended arm. 'That was left for you to judge.'

He got up slowly. His beard, unclipped since Teresa's death, thick, snow-white, covered his powerful chest. He turned his head to the door, and called out in his strong voice: 'Linda.'

Her answer came sharp and faint from within; and the appalled Nostromo stood up, too, but remained mute, gazing at the door. He was afraid. He was not afraid of being refused the girl he loved – no mere refusal could stand between him and a woman he desired – but the shining spectre of the treasure rose before him, claiming his allegiance in a silence that could not be gainsaid. He was afraid, because, neither dead nor alive, like the Gringos on Azuera, he belonged body and soul to the unlawfulness of his audacity. He was afraid of being forbidden the island. He was afraid, and said nothing.

Seeing the two men standing up side by side to await her, Linda stopped in the doorway. Nothing could alter the passionate dead whiteness of her face; but her black eyes seemed to catch and concentrate all the light of the low sun in a flaming spark within the black depths, covered at once by the slow descent of heavy eyelids.

'Behold thy husband, master, and benefactor.' Old Viola's voice resounded with a force that seemed to fill the whole gulf.

She stepped forward with her eyes nearly closed, like a sleepwalker in a beatific dream.

Nostromo made a superhuman effort. 'It is time, Linda, we two were betrothed,' he said, steadily, in his level, careless, unbending tone.

She put her hand into his offered palm, lowering her head, dark with bronze glints, upon which her father's hand rested for a moment.

'And so the soul of the dead is satisfied.'

This came from Giorgio Viola, who went on talking for a while of his dead wife; while the two, sitting side by side, never looked at each other. Then the old man ceased; and Linda, motionless, began to speak.

'Ever since I felt I lived in the world, I have lived for you alone, Gian' Battista. And that you knew! You knew it . . . Battistino.'

She pronounced the name exactly with her mother's intonation. A gloom as of the grave covered Nostromo's heart.

'Yes. I knew,' he said.

The heroic Garibaldino sat on the same bench bowing his hoary head, his old soul dwelling alone with its memories, tender and violent, terrible and dreary – solitary on the earth full of men.

And Linda, his best-loved daughter, was saying, 'I was yours ever since I can remember. I had only to think of you for the earth to become empty to my eyes. When you were there, I could see no one else. I was yours. Nothing is changed. The world belongs to you, and you let me live in it,' . . . She dropped her low, vibrating voice to a still lower note, and found other things to say – torturing for the man at her side. Her murmur ran on ardent and voluble. She did not seem to see her sister, who came out with an altar-cloth she was embroidering in her hands, and passed in front of them, silent, fresh, fair, with a quick faint smile, to sit a little away on the other side of Nostromo.

The evening was still. The sun sank almost to the edge of a purple ocean; and the white lighthouse, livid against the background of clouds filling the head of the gulf, bore the lantern red and glowing, like a live ember kindled by the fire of the sky. Giselle, indolent and demure, raised the altar-cloth from time to time to hide nervous yawns, as of a young panther.

Suddenly Linda rushed at her sister, and seizing her head, covered her face with kisses. Nostromo's brain reeled. When she left her, as if stunned by the violent caresses, with her hands lying in her lap, the slave of the treasure felt as if he could shoot that woman. Old Giorgio lifted his leonine head.

'Where are you going, Linda?'

'To the light, padre mio.'

'Si, si – to your duty.'

He got up, too, looked after his eldest daughter; then, in a tone whose festive note seemed the echo of a mood lost in the night of ages: 'I am going in to cook something. Aha! Son! The old man knows where to find a bottle of wine, too.'

He turned to Giselle, with a change to austere tenderness.

'And you, little one, pray not to the God of priests and slaves, but to the God of orphans, of the oppressed, of the poor, of little children, to give thee a man like this one for a husband.'

His hand rested heavily for a moment on Nostromo's shoulder; then he went in. The hopeless slave of the San Tomé silver felt at these words the venomous fangs of jealousy biting deep into his heart. He was appalled by the novelty of the experience, by its force, by its physical intimacy. A husband! A husband for her! And yet it was natural that Giselle should have a husband at sometime or other. He had never realised that before. In discovering that her beauty could belong to another he felt as though he could kill this one of old Giorgio's daughters also. He muttered moodily: 'They say you love Ramirez.'

She shook her head without looking at him. Coppery glints rippled to and fro on the wealth of her gold hair. Her smooth forehead had the soft, pure sheen of a priceless pearl in the splendour of the sunset, mingling the gloom of starry spaces, the purple of the sea, and the crimson of the sky in a magnificent stillness.

'No,' she said, slowly. 'I never loved him. I think I never . . . He loves me – perhaps.'

The seduction of her slow voice died out of the air, and her raised eyes remained fixed on nothing, as if indifferent and without thought.

'Ramirez told you he loved you?' asked Nostromo, restraining himself.

'Ah! once – one evening . . .'

'The miserable . . . Ha!'

He had jumped up as if stung by a gadfly, and stood before her mute with anger.

'*Misericordia Divina!* You, too, Gian' Battista! Poor wretch that I am!' she lamented in ingenuous tones. 'I told Linda, and she scolded – she scolded. Am I to live blind, dumb, and deaf in this world? And she told father, who took down his gun and cleaned it. Poor Ramirez! Then you came, and she told you.'

He looked at her. He fastened his eyes upon the hollow of her white throat, which had the invincible charm of things young, palpitating, delicate, and alive. Was this the child he had known? Was it possible? It dawned upon him that in these last years he had really seen very little – nothing – of her. Nothing. She had come into the world like a thing unknown. She had come upon him unawares. She was a danger. A frightful danger. The instinctive mood of fierce determination that had never failed him before the perils of this life added its steady force to the violence of his passion. She, in a voice that recalled to him the song of running water, the tinkling of a silver bell, continued: 'And between you three you have brought me here into this captivity to the sky and water. Nothing else. Sky and water. Oh, *Santissima Madre*. My hair shall turn grey on this tedious island. I could hate you, Gian' Battista!'

He laughed loudly. Her voice enveloped him like a caress. She bemoaned her fate, spreading unconsciously, like a flower its perfume in the coolness of the evening, the indefinable seduction of her person. Was it her fault that nobody ever had admired Linda? Even when they were little, going out with their mother to Mass, she remembered that people took no notice of Linda, who was fearless, and chose instead to frighten her, who was timid, with their attention. It was her hair like gold, she supposed.

He broke out: 'Your hair like gold, and your eyes like violets, and your lips like the rose; your round arms, your white throat . . .'

Imperturbable in the indolence of her pose, she blushed deeply all over to the roots of her hair. She was not conceited. She was no more self-conscious than a flower. But she was pleased. And perhaps even a flower loves to hear itself praised. He glanced down, and added, impetuously: 'Your little feet!'

Leaning back against the rough cottage, she seemed to bask languidly in the warmth of the rosy flush. Only her lowered eyes glanced at her little feet.

'And so you are going at last to marry our Linda. She is terrible. Ah! now she will understand better since you have told her you love her. She will not be so fierce.'

'*Chica!*' said Nostromo, 'I have not told her anything.'

'Then make haste. Come tomorrow. Come and tell her, so that I may have some peace from her scolding and – perhaps – who knows . . .'

'Be allowed to listen to your Ramirez, eh? Is that it? You . . .'

'Mercy of God! How violent you are, Giovanni,' she said, unmoved. 'Who is Ramirez . . . Ramirez . . . Who is he?' she repeated, dreamily, in the dusk and gloom of the clouded gulf, with a low red streak in the west like a hot bar of glowing iron laid across the entrance of a world sombre as a cavern, where the magnificent Capataz de Cargadores had hidden his conquests of love and wealth.

'Listen, Giselle,' he said, in measured tones; 'I will tell no word of love to your sister. Do you want to know why?'

'Alas! I could not understand perhaps, Giovanni. Father says you are not

like other men; that no one had ever understood you properly; that the rich
will be surprised yet . . . Oh! saints in heaven! I am weary.'

She raised her embroidery to conceal the lower part of her face, then let
it fall on her lap. The lantern was shaded on the land side, but slanting away
from the dark column of the lighthouse they could see the long shaft of
light, kindled by Linda, go out to strike the expiring glow in a horizon of
purple and red.

Giselle Viola, with her head resting against the wall of the house, her
eyes half closed, and her little feet, in white stockings and black slippers,
crossed over each other, seemed to surrender herself, tranquil and fatal, to
the gathering dusk. The charm of her body, the promising mysteriousness
of her indolence, went out into the night of the Placid Gulf like a fresh and
intoxicating fragrance spreading out in the shadows, impregnating the air.
The incorruptible Nostromo breathed her ambient seduction in the tumultuous heaving of his breast. Before leaving the harbour he had thrown off
the store clothing of Captain Fidanza, for greater ease in the long pull out
to the islands. He stood before her in the red sash and check shirt as he used
to appear on the Company's wharf – a Mediterranean sailor come ashore to
try his luck in Costaguana. The dusk of purple and red enveloped him, too
– close, soft, profound, as no more than fifty yards from that spot it had
gathered evening after evening about the self-destructive passion of Don
Martin Decoud's utter scepticism, flaming up to death in solitude.

'You have got to hear,' he began at last, with perfect self-control. 'I shall
say no word of love to your sister, to whom I am betrothed from this
evening, because it is you that I love. It is you!'

The dusk let him see yet the tender and voluptuous smile that came
instinctively upon her lips shaped for love and kisses, freeze hard in the
drawn, haggard lines of terror. He could not restrain himself any longer.

While she shrank from his approach, her arms went out to him, abandoned
and regal in the dignity of her languid surrender. He held her head in his two
hands, and showered rapid kisses upon the upturned face that gleamed in the
purple dusk. Masterful and tender, he was entering slowly upon the fullness of
his possession. And he perceived that she was crying. Then the incomparable
Capataz, the man of careless loves, became gentle and caressing, like a woman
to the grief of a child. He murmured to her fondly. He sat down by her and
nursed her fair head on his breast. He called her his star and his little flower.

It had grown dark. From the living-room of the light-keeper's cottage,
where Giorgio, one of the Immortal Thousand, was bending his leonine and
heroic head over a charcoal fire, there came the sound of sizzling and the
aroma of an artistic *frittura*.

In the obscure disarray of that thing, happening like a cataclysm, it was in
her feminine head that some gleam of reason survived. He was lost to the
world in their embraced stillness. But she said, whispering into his ear: 'God
of mercy! What will become of me – here – now – between sky and this water

I hate? Linda, Linda – I see her!' . . . She tried to get out of his arms, suddenly relaxed at the sound of that name. But there was no one approaching their black shapes, enlaced and struggling on the white background of the wall. 'Linda! Poor Linda! I tremble! I shall die of fear before my poor sister Linda, betrothed today to Giovanni – my lover! Giovanni, you must have been mad! I cannot understand you! You are not like other men! I will not give you up – never – only to God himself! But why have you done this blind, mad, cruel, frightful thing?'

Released, she hung her head, let fall her hands. The altar-cloth, as if tossed by a great wind, lay far away from them, gleaming white on the black ground.

'From fear of losing my hope of you,' said Nostromo.

'You knew that you had my soul! You know everything! It was made for you! But what could stand between you and me? What? Tell me!' she repeated, without impatience, in superb assurance.

'Your dead mother,' he said, very low.

'Ah! . . . Poor mother! She has always . . . She is a saint in heaven now, and I cannot give you up to her. No, Giovanni. Only to God alone. You were mad – but it is done. Oh! what have you done? Giovanni, my beloved, my life, my master, do not leave me here in this grave of clouds. You cannot leave me now. You must take me away – at once – this instant – in the little boat. Giovanni, carry me off tonight, from my fear of Linda's eyes, before I have to look at her again.'

She nestled close to him. The slave of the San Tomé silver felt the weight as of chains upon his limbs, a pressure as of a cold hand upon his lips. He struggled against the spell.

'I cannot,' he said. 'Not yet. There is something that stands between us two and the world.'

She pressed her form closer to his side with a subtle and naive instinct of seduction.

'You rave, Giovanni – my lover!' she whispered engagingly. 'What can there be? Carry me off – in thy very hands – to Doña Emilia – away from here. I am not very heavy.'

It seemed as though she expected him to lift her up at once in his two palms. She had lost the notion of all impossibility. Anything could happen on this night of wonder. As he made no movement, she almost cried aloud: 'I tell you I am afraid of Linda!' And still he did not move. She became quiet and wily. 'What can there be?' she asked, coaxingly.

He felt her warm, breathing, alive, quivering in the hollow of his arm. In the exulting consciousness of his strength, and the triumphant excitement of his mind, he struck out for his freedom.

'A treasure,' he said. All was still. She did not understand. 'A treasure. A treasure of silver to buy a gold crown for thy brow.'

'A treasure?' she repeated in a faint voice, as if from the depths of a dream. 'What is it you say?'

She disengaged herself gently. He got up and looked down at her, aware of her face, of her hair, her lips, the dimples on her cheeks – seeing the fascination of her person in the night of the gulf as if in the blaze of noonday. Her nonchalant and seductive voice trembled with the excitement of admiring awe and ungovernable curiosity.

'A treasure of silver!' she stammered out. Then pressed on faster: 'What? Where? How did you get it, Giovanni?'

He wrestled with the spell of captivity. It was as if striking a heroic blow that he burst out: 'Like a thief!'

The densest blackness of the Placid Gulf seemed to fall upon his head. He could not see her now. She had vanished into a long, obscure abysmal silence, whence her voice came back to him after a time with a faint glimmer, which was her face.

'I love you! I love you!'

These words gave him an unwonted sense of freedom, they cast a spell stronger than the accursed spell of the treasure; they changed his weary subjection to that dead thing into an exulting conviction of his power. He would cherish her, he said, in a splendour as great as Doña Emilia's. The rich lived on wealth stolen from the people, but he had taken from the rich nothing – nothing that was not lost to them already by their folly and their betrayal. For he had been betrayed – he said – deceived, tempted. She believed him . . . He had kept the treasure for purposes of revenge; but now he cared nothing for it. He cared only for her. He would put her beauty in a palace on a hill crowned with olive trees – a white palace above a blue sea. He would keep her there like a jewel in a casket. He would get land for her – her own land fertile with vines and corn – to set her little feet upon. He kissed them . . .

He had already paid for it all with the soul of a woman and the life of a man . . . The Capataz de Cargadores tasted the supreme intoxication of his generosity. He flung the mastered treasure superbly at her feet in the impenetrable darkness of the gulf, in the darkness defying – as men said – the knowledge of God and the wit of the devil. But she must let him grow rich first – he warned her.

She listened as if in a trance. Her fingers stirred in his hair. He got up from his knees reeling, weak, empty, as though he had flung his soul away.

'Make haste, then,' she said. 'Make haste, Giovanni, my lover, my master, for I will give thee up to no one but God. And I am afraid of Linda.'

He guessed at her shudder, and swore to do his best. He trusted the courage of her love. She promised to be brave in order to be loved always far away in a white palace upon a hill above a blue sea. Then with a timid, tentative eagerness she murmured: 'Where is it? Where? Tell me that, Giovanni.'

He opened his mouth and remained silent – thunderstruck.

'Not that! Not that!' he gasped out, appalled at the spell of secrecy that had kept him dumb before so many people falling upon his lips again with unimpaired force. Not even to her. Not even to her. It was too dangerous. 'I forbid thee to ask,' he cried at her, deadening cautiously the anger of his voice.

He had not regained his freedom. The spectre of the unlawful treasure arose, standing by her side like a figure of silver, pitiless and secret, with a finger on its pale lips. His soul died within him at the vision of himself creeping in presently along the ravine, with the smell of earth, of damp foliage in his nostrils – creeping in, determined in a purpose that numbed his breast, and creeping out again loaded with silver, with his ears alert to every sound. It must be done on this very night – that work of a craven slave!

He stooped low, pressed the hem of her skirt to his lips, with a muttered command: 'Tell him I would not stay,' and was gone suddenly from her, silent, without as much as a footfall in the dark night.

She sat still, her head resting indolently against the wall, and her little feet in white stockings and black slippers crossed over each other.

Old Giorgio, coming out, did not seem to be surprised at the intelligence as much as she had vaguely feared. For she was full of inexplicable fear now – fear of everything and everybody except of her Giovanni and his treasure. But that was incredible.

The heroic Garibaldino accepted Nostromo's abrupt departure with a sagacious indulgence. He remembered his own feelings, and exhibited a masculine penetration of the true state of the case.

'*Va bene.* Let him go. Ha! ha! No matter how fair the woman, it galls a little. Liberty, liberty. There's more than one kind! He has said the great word, and son Gian' Battista is not tame.' He seemed to be instructing the motionless and scared Giselle . . . 'A man should not be tame,' he added, dogmatically out of the doorway. Her stillness and silence seemed to displease him. 'Do not give way to the enviousness of your sister's lot,' he admonished her, very grave, in his deep voice.

Presently he had to come to the door again to call in his younger daughter. It was late. He shouted her name three times before she even moved her head. Left alone, she had become the helpless prey of astonishment. She walked into the bedroom she shared with Linda like a person profoundly asleep. That aspect was so marked that even old Giorgio, spectacled, raising his eyes from the Bible, shook his head as she shut the door behind her.

She walked right across the room without looking at anything, and sat down at once by the open window. Linda, stealing down from the tower in the exuberance of her happiness, found her with a lighted candle at her back, facing the black night full of sighing gusts of wind and the sound of distant showers – a true night of the gulf, too dense for the eye of God and the wiles of the devil. She did not turn her head at the opening of the door.

There was something in that immobility which reached Linda in the depths of her paradise. The elder sister guessed angrily: the child is thinking of that wretched Ramirez. Linda longed to talk. She said in her arbitrary voice, 'Giselle!' and was not answered by the slightest movement.

The girl that was going to live in a palace and walk on ground of her own was ready to die with terror. Not for anything in the world would she have turned her head to face her sister. Her heart was beating madly. She said with subdued haste: 'Do not speak to me. I am praying.'

Linda, disappointed, went out quietly; and Giselle sat on unbelieving, lost, dazed, patient, as if waiting for the confirmation of the incredible. The hopeless blackness of the clouds seemed part of a dream, too. She waited.

She did not wait in vain. The man whose soul was dead within him, creeping out of the ravine, weighted with silver, had seen the gleam of the lighted window, and could not help retracing his steps from the beach.

On that impenetrable background, obliterating the lofty mountains by the seaboard, she saw the slave of the San Tomé silver, as if by an extraordinary power of a miracle. She accepted his return as if henceforth the world could hold no surprise for all eternity.

She rose, compelled and rigid, and began to speak long before the light from within fell upon the face of the approaching man.

'You have come back to carry me off. It is well! Open thy arms, Giovanni, my lover. I am coming.'

His prudent footsteps stopped, and with his eyes glistening wildly, he spoke in a harsh voice: 'Not yet. I must grow rich slowly.' . . . A threatening note came into his tone. 'Do not forget that you have a thief for your lover.'

'Yes! Yes!' she whispered, hastily. 'Come nearer! Listen! Do not give me up, Giovanni! Never, never! . . . I will be patient! . . .' Her form drooped consolingly over the low casement towards the slave of the unlawful treasure. The light in the room went out, and weighted with silver, the magnificent Capataz clasped her round her white neck in the darkness of the gulf as a drowning man clutches at a straw.

Chapter 13

On the day Mrs Gould was going, in Dr Monygham's words, to 'give a tertulia', Captain Fidanza went down the side of his schooner lying in Sulaco harbour, calm, unbending, deliberate in the way he sat down in his dinghy and took up his sculls. He was later than usual. The afternoon was well advanced before he landed on the beach of the Great Isabel, and with a steady pace climbed the slope of the island.

From a distance he made out Giselle sitting in a chair tilted back against the end of the house, under the window of the girls' room. She had her embroidery in her hands, and held it well up to her eyes. The tranquillity of that girlish figure exasperated the feeling of perpetual struggle and strife he carried in his breast. He became angry. It seemed to him that she ought to hear the clanking of his fetters – his silver fetters, from afar. And while ashore that day, he had met the doctor with the evil eye, who had looked at him very hard.

The raising of her eyes mollified him. They smiled in their flower-like freshness straight upon his heart. Then she frowned. It was a warning to be cautious. He stopped some distance away, and in a loud, indifferent tone, said: 'Good-day, Giselle. Is Linda up yet?'

'Yes. She is in the big room with father.'

He approached then, and, looking through the window into the bedroom for fear of being detected by Linda returning there for some reason, he said, moving only his lips: 'You love me?'

'More than my life.' She went on with her contemplating gaze and continued to speak, looking at her work, 'Or I could not live. I could not, Giovanni. For this life is like death. Oh, Giovanni, I shall perish if you do not take me away.'

He smiled carelessly. 'I will come to the window when it's dark,' he said.

'No, don't, Giovanni. Not tonight. Linda and father have been talking together for a long time today.'

'What about?'

'Ramirez, I fancy I heard. I do not know. I am afraid. I am always afraid. It is like dying a thousand times a day. Your love is to me like your treasure to you. It is there, but I can never get enough of it.'

He looked at her very still. She was beautiful. His desire had grown within him. He had two masters now. But she was incapable of sustained emotion. She was sincere in what she said, but she slept placidly at night. When she saw him she flamed up always. Then only an increased taciturnity marked the change in her. She was afraid of betraying herself. She was afraid of pain, of bodily harm, of sharp words, of facing anger, and witnessing violence. For her soul was light and tender with a pagan sincerity in its impulses. She murmured: 'Give up the palazzo, Giovanni, and the vineyard on the hills, for which we are starving our love.'

She ceased, seeing Linda standing silent at the corner of the house.

Nostromo turned to his affianced wife with a greeting, and was amazed at her sunken eyes, at her hollow cheeks, at the air of illness and anguish in her face.

'Have you been ill?' he asked, trying to put some concern into this question. Her black eyes blazed at him. 'Am I thinner?' she asked.

'Yes – perhaps – a little.'

'And older?'

'Every day counts – for all of us.'

'I shall go grey, I fear, before the ring is on my finger,' she said, slowly, keeping her gaze fastened upon him.

She waited for what he would say, rolling down her turned-up sleeves.

'No fear of that,' he said, absently.

She turned away as if it had been something final, and busied herself with household cares while Nostromo talked with her father. Conversation with the old Garibaldino was not easy. Age had left his faculties unimpaired, only they seemed to have withdrawn somewhere deep within him. His answers were slow in coming, with an effect of august gravity. But that day he was more animated, quicker; there seemed to be more life in the old lion. He was uneasy for the integrity of his honour. He believed Sidoni's warning as to Ramirez's designs upon his younger daughter. And he did not trust her. She was flighty. He said nothing of his cares to 'Son Gian' Battista.' It was a touch of senile vanity. He wanted to show that he was equal yet to the task of guarding alone the honour of his house.

Nostromo went away early. As soon as he had disappeared, walking towards the beach, Linda stepped over the threshold and with a haggard smile, sat down by the side of her father.

Ever since that Sunday, when the infatuated and desperate Ramirez had waited for her on the wharf, she had no doubts whatever. The jealous ravings of that man were no revelation. They had only fixed with precision, as with a nail driven into her heart, that sense of unreality and deception which, instead of bliss and security, she had found in her intercourse with her promised husband. She had passed on, pouring indignation and scorn upon Ramirez; but, that Sunday, she nearly died of wretchedness and shame, lying on the carved and lettered stone of Teresa's grave, subscribed for by the engine-drivers and the fitters of the railway workshops, in sign of their respect for the hero of Italian Unity. Old Viola had not been able to carry out his desire of burying his wife in the sea; and Linda wept upon the stone.

The gratuitous outrage appalled her. If he wished to break her heart – well and good. Everything was permitted to Gian' Battista. But why trample upon the pieces; why seek to humiliate her spirit? Aha! He could not break that. She dried her tears. And Giselle! Giselle! The little one that, ever since she could toddle, had always clung to her skirt for protection. What duplicity! But she could not help it probably. When there was a man in the case the poor featherheaded wretch could not help herself.

Linda had a good share of the Viola stoicism. She resolved to say nothing. But woman-like she put passion into her stoicism. Giselle's short answers, prompted by fearful caution, drove her beside herself by their curtness that resembled disdain. One day she flung herself upon the chair in which her indolent sister was lying and impressed the mark of her teeth at the base of the whitest neck in Sulaco. Giselle cried out. But she had her share of the Viola heroism. Ready to faint with terror, she only said, in a lazy voice, '*Madre de Dios!* Are you going to eat me alive, Linda?' And this outburst passed off leaving no trace upon the situation. 'She knows nothing. She cannot know anything,' reflected Giselle. 'Perhaps it is not true. It cannot be true,' Linda tried to persuade herself.

But when she saw Captain Fidanza for the first time after her meeting with the distracted Ramirez, the certitude of her misfortune returned. She watched him from the doorway go away to his boat, asking herself stoically, 'Will they meet tonight?' She made up her mind not to leave the tower for a second. When he had disappeared she came out and sat down by her father.

The venerable Garibaldino felt, in his own words, 'a young man yet'. In one way or another a good deal of talk about Ramirez had reached him of late; and his contempt and dislike of that man who obviously was not what his son would have been, had made him restless. He slept very little now; but for several nights past instead of reading – or only sitting, with Mrs Gould's silver spectacles on his nose, before the open Bible, he had been prowling actively all about the island with his old gun, on watch over his honour.

Linda, laying her thin brown hand on his knee, tried to soothe his excitement. Ramirez was not in Sulaco. Nobody knew where he was. He was gone. His talk of what he would do meant nothing.

'No,' the old man interrupted. 'But son Gian' Battista told me – quite of himself – that the cowardly *esclavo* was drinking and gambling with the rascals of the north side of the gulf. He may get some of the worst scoundrels of that scoundrelly town of Negroes to help him in his attempt upon the little one . . . But I am not so old. No!'

She argued earnestly against the probability of any attempt being made; and at last the old man fell silent, chewing his white moustache. Women had their obstinate notions which must be humoured – his poor wife was like that, and Linda resembled her mother. It was not seemly for a man to argue. 'May be. May be,' he mumbled.

She was by no means easy in her mind. She loved Nostromo. She turned her eyes upon Giselle, sitting at a distance, with something of maternal tenderness, and the jealous anguish of a rival outraged in her defeat. Then she rose and walked over to her.

'Listen – you,' she said, roughly.

The invincible candour of the gaze, raised up all violet and dew, excited her rage and admiration. She had beautiful eyes – the *Chica* – this vile thing of white flesh and black deception. She did not know whether she wanted to tear them out with shouts of vengeance or cover up their mysterious and shameless innocence with kisses of pity and love. And suddenly they became empty, gazing blankly at her, except for a little fear not quite buried deep enough with all the other emotions in Giselle's heart.

Linda said, 'Ramirez is boasting in town that he will carry you off from the island.'

'What folly!' answered the other, and in a perversity born of long restraint, she added: 'He is not the man,' in a jesting tone with a trembling audacity.

'No?' said Linda, through her clenched teeth. 'Is he not? Well, then, look to it; because father has been walking about with a loaded gun at night.'

'It is not good for him. You must tell him not to, Linda. He will not listen to me.'

'I shall say nothing – never any more – to anybody,' cried Linda, passionately.

This could not last, thought Giselle. Giovanni must take her away soon – the very next time he came. She would not suffer these terrors for ever so much silver. To speak with her sister made her ill. But she was not uneasy at her father's watchfulness. She had begged Nostromo not to come to the window that night. He had promised to keep away for this once. And she did not know, could not guess or imagine, that he had another reason for coming on the island.

Linda had gone straight to the tower. It was time to light up. She unlocked the little door, and went heavily up the spiral staircase, carrying her love for the magnificent Capataz de Cargadores like an ever-increasing load of shameful fetters. No; she could not throw it off. No; let Heaven dispose of these two. And moving about the lantern, filled with twilight and the sheen of the moon, with careful movements she lighted the lamp. Then her arms fell along her body.

'And with our mother looking on,' she murmured. 'My own sister – the Chica!'

The whole refracting apparatus, with its brass fittings and rings of prisms, glittered and sparkled like a dome-shaped shrine of diamonds, containing not a lamp, but some sacred flame, dominating the sea. And Linda, the keeper, in black, with a pale face, drooped low in a wooden chair, alone with her jealousy, far above the shames and passions of the earth. A strange, dragging pain as if somebody were pulling her about brutally by her dark hair with bronze glints, made her put her hands up to her temples. They would meet. They would meet. And she knew where, too. At the window. The sweat of torture fell in drops on her cheeks, while the moonlight in the offing closed as if with a colossal bar of silver the entrance of the Placid Gulf – the sombre cavern of clouds and stillness in the surf-fretted seaboard.

Linda Viola stood up suddenly with a finger on her lip. He loved neither her nor her sister. The whole thing seemed so objectless as to frighten her, and also give her some hope. Why did he not carry her off? What prevented him? He was incomprehensible. What were they waiting for? For what end were these two lying and deceiving? Not for the ends of their love. There was no such thing. The hope of regaining him for herself made her break her vow of not leaving the tower that night. She must talk at once to her father, who was wise, and would understand. She ran down the spiral stairs. At the moment of opening the door at the bottom she heard the sound of the first shot ever fired on the Great Isabel.

She felt a shock, as though the bullet had struck her breast. She ran on without pausing. The cottage was dark. She cried at the door, 'Giselle!

Giselle!' then dashed round the corner and screamed her sister's name at the open window, without getting an answer; but as she was rushing, distracted, round the house, Giselle came out of the door, and darted past her, silently, her hair loose, and her eyes staring ahead. She seemed to skim along the grass as if on tiptoe, and vanished.

Linda walked on slowly, with her arms stretched out before her. All was still on the island; she did not know where she was going. The tree under which Martin Decoud spent his last days, beholding life like a succession of senseless images, threw a large blotch of black shade upon the grass. Suddenly she saw her father, standing quietly all alone in the moonlight.

The Garibaldino – big, erect, with his snow-white hair and beard – had a monumental repose in his immobility, leaning upon a rifle. She put her hand upon his arm lightly. He never stirred.

'What have you done?' she asked, in her ordinary voice.

'I have shot Ramirez – *infame!*' he answered, with his eyes directed to where the shade was blackest. 'Like a thief he came, and like a thief he fell. The child had to be protected.'

He did not offer to move an inch, to advance a single step. He stood there, rugged and unstirring, like a statue of an old man guarding the honour of his house. Linda removed her trembling hand from his arm, firm and steady like an arm of stone, and, without a word, entered the blackness of the shade. She saw a stir of formless shapes on the ground, and stopped short. A murmur of despair and tears grew louder to her strained hearing.

'I entreated you not to come tonight. Oh, my Giovanni! And you promised. Oh! Why – why did you come, Giovanni?'

It was her sister's voice. It broke on a heartrending sob. And the voice of the resourceful Capataz de Cargadores, master and slave of the San Tomé treasure, who had been caught unawares by old Giorgio while stealing across the open towards the ravine to get some more silver, answered careless and cool, but sounding startlingly weak from the ground.

'It seemed as though I could not live through the night without seeing thee once more – my star, my little flower.'

The brilliant tertulía was just over, the last guests had departed, and the Señor Administrador had gone to his room already, when Dr Monygham, who had been expected in the evening but had not turned up, arrived driving along the wood-block pavement under the electric-lamps of the deserted Calle de la Constitucion, and found the great gateway of the Casa still open.

He limped in, stumped up the stairs, and found the fat and sleek Basilio on the point of turning off the lights in the sala. The prosperous majordomo remained open-mouthed at this late invasion.

'Don't put out the lights,' commanded the doctor. 'I want to see the señora.'

'The señora is in the Señor Adminstrador's cancillería,' said Basilio, in an unctuous voice. 'The Señor Administrador starts for the mountain in an hour. There is some trouble with the workmen to be feared, it appears. A shameless people without reason and decency. And idle, señor. Idle.'

'You are shamelessly lazy and imbecile yourself,' said the doctor, with that faculty for exasperation which made him so generally beloved. 'Don't put the lights out.'

Basilio retired with dignity. Dr Monygham, waiting in the brilliantly lighted sala, heard presently a door close at the further end of the house. A jingle of spurs died out. The Señor Administrador was off to the mountain.

With a measured swish of her long train, flashing with jewels and the shimmer of silk, her delicate head bowed as if under the weight of a mass of fair hair, in which the silver threads were lost, the 'first lady of Sulaco', as Captain Mitchell used to describe her, moved along the lighted corridor, wealthy beyond great dreams of wealth, considered, loved, respected, honoured, and as solitary as any human being had ever been, perhaps, on this earth.

The doctor's 'Mrs Gould! One minute!' stopped her with a start at the door of the lighted and empty sala. From the similarity of mood and circumstance, the sight of the doctor, standing there all alone amongst the groups of furniture, recalled to her emotional memory her unexpected meeting with Martin Decoud; she seemed to hear in the silence the voice of that man, dead miserably so many years ago, pronounce the words, 'Antonia left her fan here.' But it was the doctor's voice that spoke, a little altered by his excitement. She remarked his shining eyes.

'Mrs Gould, you are wanted. Do you know what has happened? You remember what I told you yesterday about Nostromo. Well, it seems that a lancha, a decked boat, coming from Zapiga, with four Negroes in her, passing close to the Great Isabel, was hailed from the cliff by a woman's voice – Linda's, as a matter of fact – commanding them (it's a moonlight night) to go round to the beach and take up a wounded man to the town. The *patron* (from whom I've heard all this), of course, did so at once. He told me that when they got round to the low side of the Great Isabel, they found Linda Viola waiting for them. They followed her: she led them under a tree not far from the cottage. There they found Nostromo lying on the ground with his head in the younger girl's lap, and father Viola standing some distance off leaning on his gun. Under Linda's direction they got a table out of the cottage for a stretcher, after breaking off the legs. They are here, Mrs Gould. I mean Nostromo and – and Giselle. The Negroes brought him in to the first-aid hospital near the harbour. He made the attendant send for me. But it is not me he wanted to see – it was you, Mrs Gould! It was you.'

'Me?' whispered Mrs Gould, shrinking a little.

'Yes, you!' the doctor burst out. 'He begged me – his enemy, as he thinks – to bring you to him at once. It seems he has something to say to you alone.'

'Impossible!' murmured Mrs Gould.

'He said to me, "Remind her that I have done something to keep a roof over her head." . . . Mrs Gould,' the doctor pursued, in the greatest excitement. 'Do you remember the silver? The silver in the lighter – that was lost !'

Mrs Gould remembered. But she did not say she hated the mere mention of that silver. Frankness personified, she remembered with an exaggerated horror that for the first and last time of her life she had concealed the truth from her husband about that very silver. She had been corrupted by her fears at that time, and she had never forgiven herself. Moreover, that silver, which would never have come down if her husband had been made acquainted with the news brought by Decoud, had been in a roundabout way nearly the cause of Dr Monygham's death. And these things appeared to her very dreadful.

'Was it lost, though?' the doctor exclaimed. 'I've always felt that there was a mystery about our Nostromo ever since. I do believe he wants now, at the point of death – '

'The point of death,' repeated Mrs Gould.

'Yes. Yes . . . He wants perhaps to tell you something concerning that silver which – '

'Oh, no! No!' exclaimed Mrs Gould, in a low voice. 'Isn't it lost and done with? Isn't there enough treasure without it to make everybody in the world miserable?'

The doctor remained still, in a submissive, disappointed silence. At last he ventured, very low: 'And there is that Viola girl, Giselle. What are we to do? It looks as though father and sister had – '

Mrs Gould admitted that she felt in duty bound to do her best for these girls.

'I have a volante here,' the doctor said. 'If you don't mind getting into that – '

He waited, all impatience, till Mrs Gould reappeared, having thrown over her dress a grey cloak with a deep hood.

It was thus that, cloaked and monastically hooded over her evening costume, this woman, full of endurance and compassion, stood by the side of the bed on which the splendid Capataz de Cargadores lay stretched out motionless on his back. The whiteness of sheets and pillows gave a sombre and energetic relief to his bronzed face, to the dark, nervous hands, so good on a tiller, upon a bridle and on a trigger, lying open and idle upon a white coverlet.

'She is innocent,' the Capataz was saying in a deep and level voice, as though afraid that a louder word would break the slender hold his spirit still kept upon his body. 'She is innocent. It is I alone. But no matter. For these things I would answer to no man or woman alive.'

He paused. Mrs Gould's face, very white within the shadow of the hood, bent over him with an invincible and dreary sadness. And the low sobs of Giselle Viola, kneeling at the end of the bed, her gold hair with coppery gleams loose and scattered over the Capataz's feet, hardly troubled the silence of the room.

'Ha! Old Giorgio – the guardian of thine honour! Fancy the Vecchio coming upon me so light of foot, so steady of aim. I myself could have done no better. But the price of a charge of powder might have been saved. The honour was safe . . . Señora, she would have followed to the end of the world Nostromo the thief . . . I have said the word. The spell is broken!'

A low moan from the girl made him cast his eyes down.

'I cannot see her . . . No matter,' he went on, with the shadow of the old magnificent carelessness in his voice. 'One kiss is enough, if there is no time for more. An airy soul, señora! Bright and warm, like sunshine – soon clouded, and soon serene. They would crush it there between them. Señora, cast on her the eye of your compassion, as famed from one end of the land to the other as the courage and daring of the man who speaks to you. She will console herself in time. And even Ramirez is not a bad fellow. I am not angry. No! It is not Ramirez who overcame the Capataz of the Sulaco Cargadores.' He paused, made an effort, and in louder voice, a little wildly, declared: 'I die betrayed – betrayed by – '

But he did not say by whom or by what he was dying betrayed.

'She would not have betrayed me,' he began again, opening his eyes very wide. 'She was faithful. We were going very far – very soon. I could have torn myself away from that accursed treasure for her. For that child I would have left boxes and boxes of it – full. And Decoud took four. Four ingots. Why? *Picardía!* To betray me? How could I give back the treasure with four ingots missing? They would have said I had purloined them. The doctor would have said that. Alas! it holds me yet!'

Mrs Gould bent low, fascinated – cold with apprehension.

'What became of Don Martin on that night, Nostromo?'

'Who knows! I wondered what would become of me. Now I know. Death was to come upon me unawares. He went away! He betrayed me! And you think I have killed him! You are all alike, you fine people. The silver has killed me. It has held me. It holds me yet. Nobody knows where it is. But you are the wife of Don Carlos, who put it into my hands and said, "Save it on your life." And when I returned, and you all thought it was lost, what do I hear? It was nothing of importance. Let it go. Up, Nostromo, the faithful, and ride away to save us, for dear life!'

'Nostromo!' Mrs Gould whispered, bending low. 'I, too, have hated the idea of that silver from the bottom of my heart.'

'Marvellous! – that one of you should hate the wealth that you know so well how to take from the hands of the poor. The world rests upon the poor, as old Giorgio says. You have been always good to the poor. But there is something accursed in wealth. Señora, shall I tell you where the treasure is? To you alone . . . Shining! Incorruptible!'

A pained, involuntary reluctance lingered in his tone, in his eyes, plain to the woman with the genius of sympathetic intuition. She averted her glance from the miserable subjection of the dying man, appalled, wishing to hear no more of the silver.

'No, Capataz,' she said. 'No one misses it now. Let it be lost for ever.'

After hearing these words, Nostromo closed his eyes, uttered no word, made no movement. Outside the door of the sickroom Dr Monygham, excited to the highest pitch, his eyes shining with eagerness, came up to the two women.

'Now, Mrs Gould,' he said, almost brutally in his impatience, 'tell me, was I right? There is a mystery. You have got the word of it, have you not? He told you – '

'He told me nothing,' said Mrs Gould, steadily.

The light of his temperamental enmity to Nostromo went out of Dr Monygham's eyes. He stepped back submissively. He did not believe Mrs Gould. But her word was law. He accepted her denial like an inexplicable fatality affirming the victory of Nostromo's genius over his own. Even before that woman, whom he loved with secret devotion, he had been defeated by the magnificent Capataz de Cargadores, the man who had lived his own life on the assumption of unbroken fidelity, rectitude, and courage!

'Pray send at once somebody for my carriage,' spoke Mrs Gould from within her hood. Then, turning to Giselle Viola, 'Come nearer me, child; come closer. We will wait here.'

Giselle Viola, heartbroken and childlike, her face veiled in her falling hair, crept up to her side. Mrs Gould slipped her hand through the arm of the unworthy daughter of old Viola, the immaculate republican, the hero without a stain. Slowly, gradually, as a withered flower droops, the head of the girl, who would have followed a thief to the end of the world, rested on the shoulder of Doña Emilia, the first lady of Sulaco, the wife of the Señor Administrador of the San Tomé mine. And Mrs Gould, feeling her suppressed sobbing, nervous and excited, had the first and only moment of bitterness in her life. It was worthy of Dr Monygham himself.

'Console yourself, child. Very soon he would have forgotten you for his treasure.'

'Señora, he loved me. He loved me,' Giselle whispered, despairingly. 'He loved me as no one had ever been loved before.'

'I have been loved, too,' Mrs Gould said in a severe tone.

Giselle clung to her convulsively. 'Oh, señora, but you shall live adored to the end of your life,' she sobbed out.

Mrs Gould kept an unbroken silence till the carriage arrived. She helped in the half-fainting girl. After the doctor had shut the door of the landau, she leaned over to him.

'You can do nothing?' she whispered.

'No, Mrs Gould. Moreover, he won't let us touch him. It does not matter. I just had one look . . . Useless.'

But he promised to see old Viola and the other girl that very night. He could get the police-boat to take him off to the island. He remained in the street, looking after the landau rolling away slowly behind the white mules.

The rumour of some accident – an accident to Captain Fidanza – had been spreading along the new quays with their rows of lamps and the dark shapes of towering cranes. A knot of night prowlers – the poorest of the poor – hung about the door of the first-aid hospital, whispering in the moonlight of the empty street.

There was no one with the wounded man but the pale photographer, small, frail, bloodthirsty, the hater of capitalists, perched on a high stool near the head of the bed with his knees up and his chin in his hands. He had been fetched by a comrade who, working late on the wharf, had heard from a Negro belonging to a lancha, that Captain Fidanza had been fatally wounded.

'Have you any dispositions to make, comrade?' he asked, anxiously. 'Do not forget that we want money for our work. The rich must be fought with their own weapons.'

Nostromo made no answer. The other did not insist, remaining huddled up on the stool, shockheaded, wildly hairy, like a hunchbacked monkey. Then, after a long silence: 'Comrade Fidanza,' he began, solemnly, 'you have refused all aid from that doctor. Is he really a dangerous enemy of the people?'

In the dimly lit room Nostromo rolled his head slowly on the pillow and opened his eyes, directing at the weird figure perched by his bedside a glance of enigmatic and profound enquiry. Then his head rolled back, his eyelids fell, and the Capataz de Cargadores died without a word or moan after an hour of immobility, broken by short shudders testifying to the most atrocious sufferings.

Dr Monygham, going out in the police-galley to the islands, beheld the glitter of the moon upon the gulf and the high black shape of the Great Isabel sending a shaft of light afar, from under the canopy of clouds.

'Pull easy,' he said, wondering what he would find there. He tried to imagine Linda and her father, and discovered a strange reluctance within himself. 'Pull easy,' he repeated.

From the moment he fired at the thief of his honour, Giorgio Viola had not stirred from the spot. He stood, his old gun grounded, his hand grasping the barrel near the muzzle. After the lancha carrying off Nostromo for ever from her had left the shore, Linda, coming up, stopped before him. He did not seem to be aware of her presence, but when, losing her forced calmness, she cried out: 'Do you know whom you have killed?' he answered: 'Ramirez the vagabond.'

White, and staring insanely at her father, Linda laughed in his face. After a time he joined her faintly in a deep-toned and distant echo of her peals. Then she stopped, and the old man spoke as if startled: 'He cried out in son Gian' Battista's voice.'

The gun fell from his opened hand, but the arm remained extended for a moment as if still supported. Linda seized it roughly.

'You are too old to understand. Come into the house.'

He let her lead him. On the threshold he stumbled heavily, nearly coming to the ground together with his daughter. His excitement, his activity of the last few days, had been like the flare of a dying lamp. He caught at the back of his chair.

'In son Gian' Battista's voice,' he repeated in a severe tone. 'I heard him – Ramirez – the miserable – '

Linda helped him into the chair, and, bending low, hissed into his ear: 'You have killed Gian' Battista.'

The old man smiled under his thick moustache. Women had strange fancies.

'Where is the child?' he asked, surprised at the penetrating chilliness of the air and the unwonted dimness of the lamp by which he used to sit up half the night with the open Bible before him.

Linda hesitated a moment, then averted her eyes.

'She is asleep,' she said. 'We shall talk of her tomorrow.'

She could not bear to look at him. He filled her with terror and with an almost unbearable feeling of pity. She had observed the change that came over him. He would never understand what he had done; and even to her the whole thing remained incomprehensible. He said with difficulty: 'Give me the book.'

Linda laid on the table the closed volume in its worn leather cover, the Bible given him ages ago by an Englishman in Palermo.

'The child had to be protected,' he said, in a strange, mournful voice.

Behind his chair Linda wrung her hands, crying without noise. Suddenly she started for the door. He heard her move.

'Where are you going?' he asked.

'To the light,' she answered, turning round to look at him balefully.

'The light! Si – duty.'

Very upright, white-haired, leonine, heroic in his absorbed quietness, he felt in the pocket of his red shirt for the spectacles given him by Doña Emilia. He put them on. After a long period of immobility he opened the book, and from on high looked through the glasses at the small print in double columns. A rigid, stern expression settled upon his features with a slight frown, as if in response to some gloomy thought or unpleasant sensation. But he never detached his eyes from the book while he swayed forward, gently, gradually, till his snow-white head rested upon the open pages. A wooden clock ticked methodically on the whitewashed wall, and growing slowly cold the Garibaldino lay alone, rugged, undecayed, like an old oak uprooted by a treacherous gust of wind.

The light of the Great Isabel burned unfailing above the lost treasure of the San Tomé mine. Into the bluish sheen of a night without stars the lantern sent out a yellow beam towards the far horizon. Like a black speck upon the shining panes, Linda, crouching in the outer gallery, rested her head on the rail. The moon, drooping in the western board, looked at her radiantly.

Below, at the foot of the cliff, the regular splash of oars from a passing boat ceased, and Dr Monygham stood up in the stern sheets.

'Linda!' he shouted, throwing back his head. 'Linda!'

Linda stood up. She had recognised the voice.

'Is he dead?' she cried, bending over.

'Yes, my poor girl. I am coming round,' the doctor answered from below. 'Pull to the beach,' he said to the rowers.

Linda's black figure detached itself upright on the light of the lantern with her arms raised above her head as though she were going to throw herself over.

'It is I who loved you,' she whispered, with a face as set and white as marble in the moonlight. 'I! Only I! She will forget thee, killed miserably for her pretty face. I cannot understand. I cannot understand. But I shall never forget thee. Never!'

She stood silent and still, collecting her strength to throw all her fidelity, her pain, bewilderment, and despair into one great cry.

'Never! Gian' Battista!'

Dr Monygham, pulling round in the police-galley, heard the name pass over his head. It was another of Nostromo's triumphs, the greatest, the most enviable, the most sinister of all. In that true cry of undying passion that seemed to ring aloud from Punta Mala to Azuera and away to the bright line of the horizon, overhung by a big white cloud shining like a mass of solid silver, the genius of the magnificent Capataz de Cargadores dominated the dark gulf containing his conquests of treasure and love.

THE SECRET AGENT

A Simple Tale

The Secret Agent

A Simple Tale

A novel by

JOSEPH CONRAD

first published in 1907

Author's Note

The origin of *The Secret Agent* – subject, treatment, artistic purpose and every other motive that may induce an author to take up his pen can, I believe, be traced to a period of mental and emotional reaction.

The actual facts are that I began this book impulsively and wrote it continuously. When in due course it was bound and delivered to the public gaze I found myself reproved for having produced it at all. Some of the admonitions were severe, others had a sorrowful note. I have not got them textually before me but I remember perfectly the general argument, which was very simple; and also my surprise at its nature. All this sounds a very old story now! And yet it is not such a long time ago. I must conclude that I had still preserved much of my pristine innocence in the year 1907. It seems to me now that even an artless person might have foreseen that some criticisms would be based on the ground of sordid surroundings and the moral squalor of the tale.

That of course is a serious objection. It was not universal. In fact it seems ungracious to remember so little reproof amongst so much intelligent and sympathetic appreciation; and I trust that the readers of this preface will not hasten to put it down to wounded vanity or a natural disposition to ingratitude. I suggest that a charitable heart could very well ascribe my choice to natural modesty. Yet it isn't exactly modesty that makes me select reproof for the illustration of my case. No, it isn't exactly modesty. I am not at all certain that I am modest; but those who have read so far through my work will credit me with enough decency, tact, *savoir-faire*, what you will, to prevent me from making a song for my own glory out of the words of other people. No! The true motive of any selection lies in quite a different trait. I have always had a propensity to justify my action. Not to defend. To justify. Not to insist that I was right but simply to explain that there was no perverse intention, no secret scorn for the natural sensibilities of mankind at the bottom of my impulses.

That kind of weakness is dangerous only so far that it exposes one to the risk of becoming a bore; for the world generally is not interested in the motives of any overt act but in its consequences. Man may smile and smile but he is not an investigating animal. He loves the obvious. He shrinks from explanations. Yet I will go on with mine. It's obvious that I need not have written that book. I was under no necessity to deal with that subject; using the word subject both in the sense of the tale itself and in the larger one of a special manifestation in the life of mankind. This I fully admit. But the thought of elaborating mere ugliness in order to shock, or even simply to surprise my readers by a change of front, has never entered my head. In making this statement I expect to be believed, not only on the evidence of my general character but also for the reason, which anybody can see, that the whole treatment of the tale, its inspiring indignation and underlying pity and contempt, prove my detachment from the squalor and sordidness which lie simply in the outward circumstances of the setting.

The inception of *The Secret Agent* followed immediately on a two years' period of intense absorption in the task of writing that remote novel, *Nostromo*, with its far off Latin-American atmosphere; and the profoundly personal *Mirror of the Sea*. The first an intense creative effort on what I suppose will always remain my largest canvas, the second an unreserved attempt to unveil for a moment the profounder intimacies of the sea and the formative influences of nearly half my lifetime. It was a period, too, in which my sense of the truth of things was attended by a very intense imaginative and emotional readiness which, all genuine and faithful to facts as it was, yet made me feel (the task once done) as if I were left behind, aimless amongst mere husks of sensations and lost in a world of other, of inferior, values.

I don't know whether I really felt that I wanted a change, change in my imagination, in my vision and in my mental attitude. I rather think that a change in the fundamental mood had already stolen over me unawares. I don't remember anything definite happening. With *The Mirror of the Sea* finished in the full consciousness that I had dealt honestly with myself and my readers in every line of that book, I gave myself up to a not unhappy pause. Then, while I was yet standing still, as it were, and certainly not thinking of going out of my way to look for anything ugly, the subject of *The Secret Agent* – I mean the tale – came to me in the shape of a few words uttered by a friend in a casual conversation about anarchists or rather anarchist activities; how brought about I don't remember now.

I remember, however, remarking on the criminal futility of the whole thing, doctrine, action, mentality; and on the contemptible aspect of the half-crazy pose as of a brazen cheat exploiting the poignant miseries and passionate credulities of a mankind always so tragically eager for self-destruction. That was what made for me its philosophical pretences so unpardonable. Presently, passing to particular instances, we recalled the already old story of the attempt to blow up the Greenwich Observatory; a blood-stained inanity of so fatuous a kind that it was impossible to fathom its origin by any reasonable or even unreasonable process of thought. For perverse unreason has its own logical processes. But that outrage could not be laid hold of mentally in any sort of way, so that one remained faced by the fact of a man blown to bits for nothing even most remotely resembling an idea, anarchistic or other. As to the outer wall of the Observatory it did not show as much as the faintest crack.

I pointed all this out to my friend who remained silent for a while and
then remarked in his characteristically casual and omniscient manner: 'Oh,
that fellow was half an idiot. His sister committed suicide afterwards.' These
were absolutely the only words that passed between us; for extreme surprise
at this unexpected piece of information kept me dumb for a moment and he
began at once to talk of something else. It never occurred to me later to ask
how he arrived at his knowledge. I am sure that if he had seen once in his life
the back of an anarchist that must have been the whole extent of his
connection with the underworld. He was, however, a man who liked to talk
with all sorts of people, and he may have gathered those illuminating facts at
second or third hand, from a crossing-sweeper, from a retired police officer,
from some vague man in his club, or even, perhaps, from a Minister of State
met at some public or private reception.

Of the illuminating quality there could be no doubt whatever. One felt like
walking out of a forest on to a plain – there was not much to see but one had
plenty of light. No, there was not much to see and, frankly, for a considerable
time I didn't even attempt to perceive anything. It was only the illuminating
impression that remained. It remained satisfactory but in a passive way. Then,
about a week later, I came upon a book which as far as I know had never
attained any prominence, the rather summary recollections of an Assistant
Commissioner of Police, an obviously able man with a strong religious strain
in his character who was appointed to his post at the time of the dynamite
outrages in London, away back in the eighties. The book was fairly interesting,
very discreet of course; and I have by now forgotten the bulk of its contents. It
contained no revelations, it ran over the surface agreeably, and that was all. I
won't even try to explain why I should have been arrested by a little passage of
about seven lines, in which the author (I believe his name was Anderson)
reproduced a short dialogue held in the Lobby of the House of Commons
after some unexpected anarchist outrage, with the Home Secretary. I think it
was Sir William Harcourt then. He was very much irritated and the official
was very apologetic. The phrase, amongst the three which passed between
them, that struck me most was Sir W. Harcourt's angry sally: 'All that's
very well. But your idea of secrecy over there seems to consist of keeping
the Home Secretary in the dark.' Characteristic enough of Sir W. Harcourt's
temper but not much in itself. There must have been, however, some sort
of atmosphere in the whole incident because all of a sudden I felt myself
stimulated. And then ensued in my mind what a student of chemistry would
best understand from the analogy of the addition of the tiniest little drop of
the right kind, precipitating the process of crystallisation in a test tube
containing some colourless solution.

It was at first for me a mental change, disturbing a quieted-down imagination, in which strange forms, sharp in outline but imperfectly apprehended,
appeared and claimed attention as crystals will do by their bizarre and
unexpected shapes. One fell to musing before the phenomenon – even of the

past: of South America, a continent of crude sunshine and brutal revolutions, of the sea, the vast expanse of salt waters, the mirror of heaven's frowns and smiles, the reflector of the world's light. Then the vision of an enormous town presented itself, of a monstrous town more populous than some continents and in its man-made might as if indifferent to heaven's frowns and smiles; a cruel devourer of the world's light. There was room enough there to place any story, depth enough there for any passion, variety enough there for any setting, darkness enough to bury five millions of lives. Irresistibly the town became the background for the ensuing period of deep and tentative meditations. Endless vistas opened before me in various directions. It would take years to find the right way! It seemed to take years! . . . Slowly the dawning conviction of Mrs Verloc's maternal passion grew up to a flame between me and that background, tingeing it with its secret ardour and receiving from it in exchange some of its own sombre colouring. At last the story of Winnie Verloc stood out complete from the days of her childhood to the end, unproportioned as yet, with everything still on the first plan, as it were; but ready now to be dealt with. It was a matter of about three days.

This book is *that* story, reduced to manageable proportions, its whole course suggested and centred round the absurd cruelty of the Greenwich Park explosion. I had there a task I will not say arduous but of the most absorbing difficulty. But it had to be done. It was a necessity. The figures grouped about Mrs Verloc and related directly or indirectly to her tragic suspicion that 'life doesn't stand much looking into,' are the outcome of that very necessity. Personally I have never had any doubt of the reality of Mrs Verloc's story; but it had to be disengaged from its obscurity in that immense town, it had to be made credible, I don't mean so much as to her soul but as to her surroundings, not so much as to her psychology but as to her humanity. For the surroundings hints were not lacking. I had to fight hard to keep at arm's-length the memories of my solitary and nocturnal walks all over London in my early days, lest they should rush in and overwhelm each page of the story as these emerged one after another from a mood as serious in feeling and thought as any in which I ever wrote a line. In that respect I really think that *The Secret Agent* is a perfectly genuine piece of work. Even the purely artistic purpose, that of applying an ironic method to a subject of that kind, was formulated with deliberation and in the earnest belief that ironic treatment alone would enable me to say all I felt I would have to say in scorn as well as in pity. It is one of the minor satisfactions of my writing life that having taken that resolve I did manage, it seems to me, to carry it right through to the end. As to the personages whom the absolute necessity of the case – Mrs Verloc's case – brings out in front of the London background, from them, too, I obtained those little satisfactions which really count for so much against the mass of oppressive doubts that haunt so persistently every attempt at creative work. For instance, of Mr Vladimir himself (who was fair game for a caricatural presentation) I was gratified to hear that an experienced man of the world had said 'that Conrad must have been in touch with that sphere or else has an excellent intuition of things', because Mr Vladimir was 'not only possible in detail but quite right in essentials'. Then a visitor from America informed me that all sorts of revolutionary refugees in New York would have it that the book was written by somebody who knew a lot about them. This seemed to me a very high compliment, considering that, as a matter of hard fact, I had seen even less of their kind than the omniscient friend who gave me the first suggestion for the novel. I have no doubt, however, that there had been moments during the writing of the book when I was an extreme revolutionist, I won't say more convinced than they but certainly cherishing a more concentrated purpose than any of them had ever done in the whole course of his life. I don't say this to boast. I was simply attending to my business. In the matter of all my books I have always attended to my business. I have attended to it with complete self surrender. And this statement, too, is not a boast. I could not have done otherwise. It would have bored me too much to make-believe.

The suggestions for certain personages of the tale, both law-abiding and lawless, came from various sources which, perhaps, here and there, some reader may have recognised. They are not very recondite. But I am not concerned here to legitimise any of those people, and even as to my general view of the moral reactions as between the criminal and the police all I will venture to say is that it seems to me to be at least arguable.

The twelve years that have elapsed since the publication of the book have not changed my attitude. I do not regret having written it. Lately, circumstances which have nothing to do with the general tenor of this preface, have compelled me to strip this tale of the literary robe of indignant scorn it cost me so much to fit on it, decently, years ago. I have been forced, so to speak, to look upon its bare bones. I confess that it makes a grisly skeleton. But still I will submit that in telling Winnie Verloc's story to its anarchistic end of utter desolation, madness and despair, and telling it as I have told it here, I have not intended to commit a gratuitous outrage on the feelings of mankind.

JOSEPH CONRAD
1920

Chapter 1

Mr Verloc, going out in the morning, left his shop nominally in charge of his brother-in-law. It could be done, because there was very little business at any time, and practically none at all before the evening. Mr Verloc cared but little about his ostensible business. And, moreover, his wife was in charge of his brother-in-law.

The shop was small, and so was the house. It was one of those grimy brick houses which existed in large quantities before the era of reconstruction dawned upon London. The shop was a square box of a place, with the front glazed in small panes. In the daytime the door remained closed; in the evening it stood discreetly but suspiciously ajar.

The window contained photographs of more or less undressed dancing girls; nondescript packages in wrappers like patent medicines; closed yellow paper envelopes, very flimsy, and marked two-and-six in heavy black figures; a few numbers of ancient French comic publications hung across a string as if to dry; a dingy blue china bowl, a casket of black wood, bottles of marking ink, and rubber stamps; a few books, with titles hinting at impropriety; a few apparently old copies of obscure newspapers, badly printed, with titles like *The Torch, The Gong* – rousing titles. And the two gas-jets inside the pane were always turned low, either for economy's sake or for the sake of the customers.

These customers were either very young men, who hung about the window for a time before slipping in suddenly; or men of a more mature age, but looking generally as if they were not in funds. Some of that last kind had the collars of their overcoats turned right up to their moustaches, and traces of mud on the bottom of their nether garments, which had the appearance of being much worn and not very valuable. And the legs inside them did not, as a general rule, seem of much account either. With their hands plunged deep in the side pockets of their coats, they dodged in sideways, one shoulder first, as if afraid to start the bell going.

The bell, hung on the door by means of a curved ribbon of steel, was difficult to circumvent. It was hopelessly cracked; but of an evening, at the slightest provocation, it clattered behind the customer with impudent virulence.

It clattered; and at that signal, through the dusty glass door behind the painted deal counter, Mr Verloc would issue hastily from the parlour at the back. His eyes were naturally heavy; he had an air of having wallowed, fully dressed, all day on an unmade bed. Another man would have felt such an appearance a distinct disadvantage. In a commercial transaction of the retail order much depends on the seller's engaging and amiable aspect. But Mr Verloc knew his business, and remained undisturbed by any sort of aesthetic doubt about his appearance. With a firm, steady-eyed impudence, which seemed to hold back the threat of some abominable menace, he would proceed to sell over the counter some object looking obviously and scandalously not worth the money which passed in the transaction: a small cardboard box with apparently nothing inside, for instance, or one of those carefully closed yellow flimsy envelopes, or a soiled volume in paper covers with a promising title. Now and then it happened that one of the faded, yellow dancing girls would get sold to an amateur, as though she had been alive and young.

Sometimes it was Mrs Verloc who would appear at the call of the cracked bell. Winnie Verloc was a young woman with a full bust, in a tight bodice, and with broad hips. Her hair was very tidy. Steady-eyed like her husband, she preserved an air of unfathomable indifference behind the rampart of the counter. Then the customer of comparatively tender years would get suddenly disconcerted at having to deal with a woman, and with rage in his heart would proffer a request for a bottle of marking ink, retail value sixpence (price in Verloc's shop one-and-sixpence), which, once outside, he would drop stealthily into the gutter.

The evening visitors – the men with collars turned up and soft hats rammed down – nodded familiarly to Mrs Verloc, and with a muttered greeting, lifted up the flap at the end of the counter in order to pass into the back parlour, which gave access to a passage and to a steep flight of stairs. The door of the shop was the only means of entrance to the house in which Mr Verloc carried on his business of a seller of shady wares, exercised his vocation of a protector of society, and cultivated his domestic virtues. These last were pronounced. He was thoroughly domesticated. Neither his spiritual, nor his mental, nor his physical needs were of the kind to take him much abroad. He found at home the ease of his body and the peace of his conscience, together with Mrs Verloc's wifely attentions and Mrs Verloc's mother's deferential regard.

Winnie's mother was a stout, wheezy woman, with a large brown face. She wore a black wig under a white cap. Her swollen legs rendered her inactive. She considered herself to be of French descent, which might have been true; and after a good many years of married life with a licensed victualler of the more common sort, she provided for the years of widowhood by letting furnished apartments for gentlemen near Vauxhall Bridge Road in a square once of some splendour and still included in the district of Belgravia. This topographical fact was of some advantage in advertising her rooms; but the patrons of the worthy widow were not exactly of the fashionable kind. Such as they were, her daughter Winnie, helped to look after them. Traces of the French descent which the widow boasted of were apparent in Winnie, too. They were apparent in the extremely neat and artistic arrangement of her glossy dark hair. Winnie had also other charms: her youth; her full, rounded form; her clear complexion; the provocation of her unfathomable reserve, which never went so far as to prevent conversation, carried on on the lodger's part with animation, and on hers with an equable amiability. It must be that Mr Verloc was susceptible to these fascinations. Mr Verloc was an intermittent patron. He came and went without any very apparent reason. He generally arrived in London (like the influenza) from the Continent, only he arrived unheralded by the Press; and his visitations set in with great severity. He breakfasted in bed and remained wallowing there with an air of quiet enjoyment till noon every day – and sometimes even to a later hour. But when he went out he seemed to experience a great difficulty in finding his way back to his temporary home in the Belgravian square. He left it late, and returned to it early – as early as three or four in the morning; and on waking up at ten addressed Winnie, bringing in the breakfast tray, with jocular, exhausted civility, in the hoarse, failing tones of a man who had been talking vehemently for many hours together. His prominent, heavy-lidded eyes rolled sideways amorously and languidly, the bedclothes were pulled up to his chin, and his dark smooth moustache covered his thick lips capable of much honeyed banter.

In Winnie's mother's opinion Mr Verloc was a very nice gentleman. From her life's experience gathered in various 'business houses' the good woman had taken into her retirement an ideal of gentlemanliness as exhibited by the patrons of private-saloon bars. Mr Verloc approached that ideal; he attained it, in fact.

'Of course, we'll take over your furniture, mother,' Winnie had remarked.

The lodging-house was to be given up. It seems it would not answer to carry it on. It would have been too much trouble for Mr Verloc. It would not have been convenient for his other business. What his business was he did not say; but after his engagement to Winnie he took the trouble to get up before noon, and descending the basement stairs, make himself pleasant to Winnie's mother in the breakfast-room downstairs where she had her motionless being. He stroked the cat, poked the fire, had his lunch served to him there. He left its slightly stuffy cosiness with evident reluctance, but, all the same, remained out till the night was far advanced. He never offered to take Winnie to theatres, as such a nice gentleman ought to have done. His evenings were occupied. His work was in a way political, he told Winnie once. She would have, he warned her, to be very nice to his political friends. And with her straight, unfathomable glance she answered that she would be so, of course.

How much more he told her as to his occupation it was impossible for Winnie's mother to discover. The married couple took her over with the furniture. The mean aspect of the shop surprised her. The change from the Belgravian square to the narrow street in Soho affected her legs adversely. They became of an enormous size. On the other hand, she experienced a complete relief from material cares. Her son-in-law's heavy good nature inspired her with a sense of absolute safety. Her daughter's future was obviously assured, and even as to her son Stevie she need have no anxiety. She had not been able to conceal from herself that he was a terrible encumbrance, that poor Stevie. But in view of Winnie's fondness for her delicate brother, and of Mr Verloc's kind and generous disposition, she felt that the poor boy was pretty safe in this rough world. And in her heart of hearts she was not perhaps displeased that the Verlocs had no children. As that circumstance seemed perfectly indifferent to Mr Verloc, and as Winnie found an object of quasi-maternal affection in her brother, perhaps this was just as well for poor Stevie.

For he was difficult to dispose of, that boy. He was delicate and, in a frail way, good-looking, too, except for the vacant droop of his lower lip. Under our excellent system of compulsory education he had learned to read and write, notwithstanding the unfavourable aspect of the lower lip. But as errand-boy he did not turn out a great success. He forgot his messages; he was easily diverted from the straight path of duty by the attractions of stray cats and dogs, which he followed down narrow alleys into unsavoury courts; by the comedies of the streets, which he contemplated open-mouthed, to the detriment of his employer's interests; or by the dramas of fallen horses, whose pathos and violence induced him sometimes to shriek piercingly in a crowd, which disliked to be disturbed by sounds of distress in its quiet enjoyment of the national spectacle. When led away by a grave and protecting policeman, it would often become apparent that poor Stevie had forgotten his address – at least for a time. A brusque question caused him to stutter to the point of suffocation. When startled by anything perplexing he used to squint horribly. However, he never had any fits (which was encouraging); and before the natural outbursts of impatience on the part of his father he could always, in his childhood's days, run for protection behind the short skirts of his sister Winnie. On the other hand, he might have been suspected of hiding a fund of reckless naughtiness. When he had reached the age of fourteen a friend of his late father, an agent for a foreign preserved milk firm, having given him an opening as office-boy, he was discovered one foggy afternoon, in his chief's absence, busy letting off fireworks on the staircase. He touched off in quick succession a set of fierce rockets, angry Catherine wheels, loudly exploding squibs – and the matter might have turned out very serious. An awful panic spread through the whole building. Wild-eyed, choking clerks stampeded through the passages full of smoke, silk hats and elderly business men could be seen rolling independently down the stairs. Stevie did not seem to derive any personal gratification from what he had done. His motives for this stroke of originality were difficult to discover. It was only later on that Winnie obtained from him a misty and confused confession. It seems that two other office-boys in the building had worked upon his feelings by tales of injustice and oppression till they had wrought his compassion to the pitch of that frenzy.

But his father's friend, of course, dismissed him summarily as likely to ruin his business. After that altruistic exploit Stevie was put to help wash the dishes in the basement kitchen, and to black the boots of the gentlemen patronising the Belgravian mansion. There was obviously no future in such work. The gentlemen tipped him a shilling now and then. Mr Verloc showed himself the most generous of lodgers. But altogether all that did not amount to much either in the way of gain or prospects; so that when Winnie announced her engagement to Mr Verloc her mother could not help wondering, with a sigh and a glance towards the scullery, what would become of poor Stephen now.

It appeared that Mr Verloc was ready to take him over together with his wife's mother and with the furniture, which was the whole visible fortune of the family. Mr Verloc gathered everything as it came to his broad, good-natured breast. The furniture was disposed to the best advantage all over the house, but Mrs Verloc's mother was confined to two back rooms on the first floor. The luckless Stevie slept in one of them. By this time a growth of thin fluffy hair had come to blur, like a golden mist, the sharp line of his small lower jaw. He helped his sister with blind love and docility in her household duties. Mr Verloc thought that some occupation would be good for him. His spare time he occupied by drawing circles with compass and pencil on a piece of paper. He applied himself to that pastime with great industry, with his elbows spread out and bowed low over the kitchen table. Through the open door of the parlour at the back of the shop Winnie, his sister, glanced at him from time to time with maternal vigilance.

Chapter 2

Such was the house, the household, and the business Mr Verloc left behind him on his way westward at the hour of half-past ten in the morning. It was unusually early for him; his whole person exhaled the charm of almost dewy freshness; he wore his blue cloth overcoat unbuttoned; his boots were shiny; his cheeks, freshly shaven, had a sort of gloss; and even his heavy-lidded eyes, refreshed by a night of peaceful slumber, sent out glances of comparative alertness. Through the park railings these glances beheld men and women riding in the Row, couples cantering past harmoniously, others advancing sedately at a walk, loitering groups of three or four, solitary horsemen looking unsociable, and solitary women followed at a long distance by a groom with a cockade to his hat and a leather belt over his tight-fitting coat. Carriages went bowling by, mostly two horse broughams, with here and there a victoria with the skin of some wild beast inside and a woman's face and hat emerging above the folded hood. And a peculiarly London sun – against which nothing could be said except that it looked bloodshot – glorified all this by its stare. It hung at a moderate elevation above Hyde Park Corner with an air of punctual and benign vigilance. The very pavement under Mr Verloc's feet had an old-gold tinge in that diffused light, in which neither wall, nor tree, nor beast, nor man cast a shadow. Mr Verloc was going westward through a town without shadows in an atmosphere of powdered old gold. There were red, coppery gleams on the roofs of houses, on the corners of walls, on the panels of carriages, on the very coats of the horses, and on the broad back of Mr Verloc's overcoat, where they produced a dull effect of rustiness. But Mr Verloc was not in the least conscious of having got rusty. He surveyed through the park railings the evidences of the town's opulence and luxury with an approving eye. All these people had to be protected. Protection is the first necessity of opulence and luxury. They had to be protected; and their horses, carriages, houses, servants had to be protected; and the source of their wealth had to be protected in the heart of the city and the heart of the country; the whole social order favourable to their hygienic idleness had to be protected against the shallow enviousness of unhygienic labour. It had to – and Mr Verloc would have rubbed his hands with satisfaction had he not been constitutionally averse from every superfluous exertion. His idleness was not hygienic, but it suited him very well. He was in a manner devoted to it with a sort of inert fanaticism, or perhaps rather with a fanatical inertness. Born of industrious parents for a life of toil, he had embraced indolence from an impulse as profound as inexplicable and as imperious as the impulse which directs a man's preference for one particular woman in a given thousand. He was too lazy even for a mere demagogue, for a workman orator, for a leader of labour. It was too much trouble. He required a more perfect form of ease; or it might have been that he was the victim of a philosophical unbelief in the effectiveness of every human effort. Such a form of indolence requires, implies, a certain amount of intelligence. Mr Verloc was not devoid of intelligence – and at the notion of a menaced social order he would perhaps have winked to himself if there had not been an effort to make in that sign of scepticism. His big, prominent eyes were not well adapted to winking. They were rather of the sort that closes solemnly in slumber with majestic effect.

Undemonstrative and burly in a fat-pig style, Mr Verloc, without either rubbing his hands with satisfaction or winking sceptically at his thoughts, proceeded on his way. He trod the pavement heavily with his shiny boots, and his general get-up was that of a well-to-do mechanic in business for himself. He might have been anything from a picture-frame maker to a locksmith; an employer of labour in a small way. But there was also about him an indescribable air which no mechanic could have acquired in the practice of his handicraft however dishonestly exercised: the air common to men who live on the vices, the follies, or the baser fears of mankind; the air of moral nihilism common to keepers of gambling halls and disorderly houses; to private detectives and inquiry agents; to drink sellers and, I should say, to the sellers of invigorating electric belts and to the inventors of patent medicines. But of that last I am not sure, not having carried my investigations so far into the depths. For all I know, the expression of these last may be perfectly diabolic. I shouldn't be surprised. What I want to affirm is that Mr Verloc's expression was by no means diabolic.

Before reaching Knightsbridge, Mr Verloc took a turn to the left out of the busy main thoroughfare, uproarious with the traffic of swaying omnibuses and trotting vans, in the almost silent, swift flow of hansoms. Under his hat, worn with a slight backward tilt, his hair had been carefully brushed into respectful sleekness; for his business was with an Embassy. And Mr Verloc, steady like a rock – a soft kind of rock – marched now along a street which could with every propriety be described as private. In its breadth, emptiness, and extent it had the majesty of inorganic nature, of matter that never dies. The only reminder of mortality was a doctor's brougham arrested in august solitude close to the kerbstone. The polished knockers of the doors gleamed as far as the eye could reach, the clean windows shone with a dark opaque lustre. And all was still. But a milk cart rattled noisily across the distant perspective; a butcher boy, driving with the noble recklessness of a charioteer at Olympic Games, dashed round the corner sitting high above a pair of red wheels. A guilty-looking cat issuing from under the stones ran for a while in front of Mr Verloc, then dived into another basement; and a thick police constable, looking a stranger to every emotion, as if he, too, were part of inorganic nature, surging apparently out of a lamp-post, took not the slightest notice of Mr Verloc. With a turn to the left Mr Verloc pursued his way along a narrow street by the side of a yellow wall which, for some inscrutable reason, had No. 1 Chesham Square written on it in black letters. Chesham Square was at least sixty yards away, and Mr Verloc, cosmopolitan enough not to be deceived by London's topographical mysteries, held on steadily, without a sign of surprise or indignation. At last, with businesslike persistency, he reached the Square, and made diagonally for the number 10. This belonged to an imposing carriage gate in a high, clean wall between two houses, of which one rationally enough bore the number 9 and the other was numbered 37; but the fact that this last belonged to Porthill Street, a street well known in the neighbourhood, was proclaimed by an inscription placed above the ground-floor windows by whatever highly efficient authority is charged with the duty of keeping track of London's strayed houses. Why powers are not asked of Parliament (a short act would do) for compelling those edifices to return where they belong is one of the mysteries of municipal administration. Mr Verloc did not trouble his head about it, his mission in life being the protection of the social mechanism, not its perfectionment or even its criticism.

It was so early that the porter of the Embassy issued hurriedly out of his lodge still struggling with the left sleeve of his livery coat. His waistcoat was red, and he wore knee-breeches, but his aspect was flustered. Mr Verloc, aware of the rush on his flank, drove it off by simply holding out an envelope stamped with the arms of the Embassy, and passed on. He produced the same talisman also to the footman who opened the door, and stood back to let him enter the hall.

A clear fire burned in a tall fireplace, and an elderly man standing with his back to it, in evening dress and with a chain round his neck, glanced up from the newspaper he was holding spread out in both hands before his calm and severe face. He didn't move; but another lackey, in brown trousers and claw-hammer coat edged with thin yellow cord, approaching Mr Verloc listened to the murmur of his name, and turning round on his heel in silence, began to walk, without looking back once. Mr Verloc, thus led along a ground-floor passage to the left of the great carpeted staircase, was suddenly motioned to enter a quite small room furnished with a heavy writing-table and a few chairs. The servant shut the door, and Mr Verloc remained alone. He did not take a seat. With his hat and stick held in one hand he glanced about, passing his other podgy hand over his uncovered sleek head.

Another door opened noiselessly, and Mr Verloc immobilising his glance in that direction saw at first only black clothes, the bald top of a head, and a drooping dark grey whisker on each side of a pair of wrinkled hands. The person who had entered was holding a batch of papers before his eyes and walked up to the table with a rather mincing step, turning the papers over the while. Privy Councillor Wurmt, *Chancelier d'Ambassade*, was rather short-sighted. This meritorious official, laying the papers on the table, disclosed a face of pasty complexion and of melancholy ugliness surrounded by a lot of fine, long dark grey hairs, barred heavily by thick and bushy eyebrows. He put on a black-framed pince-nez upon a blunt and shapeless nose, and seemed struck by Mr Verloc's appearance. Under the enormous eyebrows his weak eyes blinked pathetically through the glasses.

He made no sign of greeting; neither did Mr Verloc, who certainly knew his place; but a subtle change about the general outlines of his shoulders and back suggested a slight bending of Mr Verloc's spine under the vast surface of his overcoat. The effect was of unobtrusive deference.

'I have here some of your reports,' said the bureaucrat in an unexpectedly soft and weary voice, and pressing the tip of his forefinger on the papers with force. He paused; and Mr Verloc, who had recognised his own hand-writing very well, waited in an almost breathless silence. 'We are not very satisfied with the attitude of the police here,' the other continued, with every appearance of mental fatigue.

The shoulders of Mr Verloc, without actually moving, suggested a shrug. And for the first time since he left his home that morning his lips opened.

'Every country has its police,' he said, philosophically. But as the official of the Embassy went on blinking at him steadily he felt constrained to add: 'Allow me to observe that I have no means of action upon the police here.'

'What is desired,' said the man of papers, 'is the occurrence of something definite which should stimulate their vigilance. That is within your province is it not so?'

Mr Verloc made no answer except by a sigh, which escaped him involuntarily, for instantly he tried to give his face a cheerful expression. The official blinked doubtfully, as if affected by the dim light of the room. He repeated vaguely: 'The vigilance of the police – and the severity of the magistrates. The general leniency of the judicial procedure here, and the utter absence of all repressive measures, are a scandal to Europe. What is wished for just now is the accentuation of the unrest of the fermentation which undoubtedly exists . . .'

'Undoubtedly, undoubtedly,' broke in Mr Verloc in a deep, deferential bass of an oratorical quality, so utterly different from the tone in which he had spoken before that his interlocutor remained profoundly surprised. 'It exists to a dangerous degree. My reports for the last twelve months make it sufficiently clear.'

'Your reports for the last twelve months,' State Councillor Wurmt began in his gentle and dispassionate tone, 'have been read by me. I failed to discover why you wrote them at all.'

A sad silence reigned for a time. Mr Verloc seemed to have swallowed his tongue, and the other gazed at the papers on the table fixedly. At last he gave them a slight push.

'The state of affairs you expose there is assumed to exist as the first condition of your employment. What is required at present is not writing, but the bringing to light of a distinct, significant fact – I would almost say of an alarming fact.'

'I need not say that all my endeavours shall be directed to that end,' Mr Verloc said, with convinced modulations in his conversational husky tone. But the sense of being blinked at watchfully behind the blind glitter of these eyeglasses on the other side of the table disconcerted him. He stopped short with a gesture of absolute devotion. The useful, hard-working, if obscure member of the Embassy had an air of being impressed by some newly-born thought.

'You are very corpulent,' he said.

This observation, really of a psychological nature and advanced with the modest hesitation of an office-man more familiar with ink and paper than with the requirements of active life, stung Mr Verloc in the manner of a rude personal remark. He stepped back a pace.

'Eh? What were you pleased to say?' he exclaimed, with husky resentment.

The *Chancelier d'Ambassade*, entrusted with the conduct of this interview, seemed to find it too much for him.

'I think,' he said, 'that you had better see Mr Vladimir. Yes, decidedly I think you ought to see Mr Vladimir. Be good enough to wait here,' he added, and went out with mincing steps.

At once Mr Verloc passed his hand over his hair. A slight perspiration had broken out on his forehead. He let the air escape from his pursed-up lips like a man blowing at a spoonful of hot soup. But when the servant in brown appeared at the door silently, Mr Verloc had not moved an inch from the place he had occupied throughout the interview. He had remained motionless, as if feeling himself surrounded by pitfalls.

He walked along a passage lighted by a lonely gas-jet, then up a flight of winding stairs, and through a glazed and cheerful corridor on the first floor. The footman threw open a door, and stood aside. The feet of Mr Verloc felt a thick carpet. The room was large, with three windows; and a young man with a shaven, big face, sitting in a roomy armchair before a vast mahogany writing-table, said in French to the *Chancelier d'Ambassade*, who was going out with the papers in his hand: 'You are quite right, *mon cher*. He's fat – the animal.'

Mr Vladimir, First Secretary, had a drawing-room reputation as an agreeable and entertaining man. He was something of a favourite in society. His wit consisted in discovering droll connections between incongruous ideas; and when talking in that strain he sat well forward on his seat, with his left hand raised, as if exhibiting his funny demonstrations between the thumb and forefinger, while his round and clean-shaven face wore an expression of merry perplexity.

But there was no trace of merriment or perplexity in the way he looked at Mr Verloc. Lying far back in the deep armchair, with squarely spread elbows, and throwing one leg over a thick knee, he had with his smooth and rosy countenance the air of a preternaturally thriving baby that will not stand nonsense from anybody.

'You understand French, I suppose?' he said.

Mr Verloc stated huskily that he did. His whole vast bulk had a forward inclination. He stood on the carpet in the middle of the room, clutching his hat and stick in one hand; the other hung lifelessly by his side. He muttered unobtrusively somewhere deep down in his throat something about having done his military service in the French artillery. At once, with contemptuous perversity, Mr Vladimir changed the language, and began to speak idiomatic English without the slightest trace of a foreign accent.

'Ah! Yes. Of course. Let's see. How much did you get for obtaining the design of the improved breech-block of their new field-gun?'

'Five years rigorous confinement in a fortress,' Mr Verloc answered, unexpectedly, but without any sign of feeling.

'You got off easily,' was Mr Vladimir's comment. 'And, anyhow, it served you right for letting yourself get caught. What made you go in for that sort of thing – eh?'

Mr Verloc's husky conversational voice was heard speaking of youth, of a fatal infatuation for an unworthy . . .

'Aha! *Cherchez la femme*,' Mr Vladimir deigned to interrupt, unbending, but without affability; there was, on the contrary, a touch of grimness in his condescension. How long have you been employed by the Embassy here?' he asked.

'Ever since the time of the late Baron Stott Wartenheim,' Mr Verloc answered in subdued tones, and protruding his lips sadly, in sign of sorrow for the deceased diplomat. The First Secretary observed this play of physiognomy steadily.

'Ah! ever since . . . Well! What have you got to say for yourself?' he asked, sharply.

Mr Verloc answered with some surprise that he was not aware of having anything special to say. He had been summoned by a letter. And he plunged his hand busily into the side pocket of his overcoat, but before the mocking, cynical watchfulness of Mr Vladimir, concluded to leave it there.

'Bah,' said the latter. 'What do you mean by getting out of condition like this? You haven't got even the physique of your profession. You – a member of a starving proletariat – never! You – a desperate socialist or anarchist – which is it?'

'Anarchist,' stated Mr Verloc in a deadened tone.

'Bosh!' went on Mr Vladimir, without raising his voice. 'You startled old Wurmt himself. You wouldn't deceive an idiot. They all are that by the by, but you seem to me simply impossible. So you began your connection with us by stealing the French gun designs. And you got yourself caught. That must have been very disagreeable to our Government. You don't seem to be very smart.'

Mr Verloc tried to exculpate himself huskily.

'As I've had occasion to observe before, a fatal infatuation for an un-worthy . . .'

Mr Vladimir raised a large, white, plump hand.

'Ah, yes. The unlucky attachment – of your youth. She got hold of the money, and then sold you to the police eh?'

The doleful change in Mr Verloc's physiognomy, the momentary drooping of his whole person, confessed that such was the regrettable case. Mr Vladimir's hand clasped the ankle reposing on his knee. The sock was of dark blue silk.

'You see, that was not very clever of you. Perhaps you are too susceptible.'

Mr Verloc intimated in a throaty, veiled murmur that he was no longer young.

'Oh! That's a failing which age does not cure,' Mr Vladimir remarked, with sinister familiarity. But no! You are too fat for that. You could not have come to look like this if you had been at all susceptible. I'll tell you what I think is the matter: you are a lazy fellow. How long have you been drawing pay from this Embassy?'

'Eleven years,' was the answer, after a moment of sulky hesitation. 'I've been charged with several missions to London while His Excellency Baron

Stott-Wartenheim was still Ambassador in Paris. Then by his Excellency's instructions I settled down in London. I am English.'

'You are! Are you? Eh?'

'A natural-born British subject,' Mr Verloc said, stolidly. 'But my father was French, and so . . . '

'Never mind explaining,' interrupted the other. 'I dare say you could have been legally a Marshal of France and a Member of Parliament in England – and then, indeed, you would have been of some use to our Embassy.'

This flight of fancy provoked something like a faint smile on Mr Verloc's face. Mr Vladimir retained an imperturbable gravity.

'But, as I've said, you are a lazy fellow; you don't use your opportunities. In the time of Baron Stott-Wartenheim we had a lot of soft-headed people running this Embassy. They caused fellows of your sort to form a false conception of the nature of a secret service fund. It is my business to correct this misapprehension by telling you what the secret service is not. It is not a philanthropic institution. I've had you called here on purpose to tell you this.'

Mr Vladimir observed the forced expression of bewilderment on Verloc's face, and smiled sarcastically.

'I see that you understand me perfectly. I dare say you are intelligent enough for your work. What we want now is activity – activity.'

On repeating this last word Mr Vladimir laid a long white forefinger on the edge of the desk. Every trace of huskiness disappeared from Verloc's voice. The nape of his gross neck became crimson above the velvet collar of his overcoat. His lips quivered before they came widely open.

'If you'll only be good enough to look up my record,' he boomed out in his great, clear, oratorical bass, 'you'll see I gave a warning only three months ago on the occasion of the Grand Duke Romuald's visit to Paris, which was telegraphed from here to the French police, and . . . '

'Tut, tut!' broke out Mr Vladimir, with a frowning grimace. 'The French police had no use for your warning. Don't roar like this. What the devil do you mean?'

With a note of proud humility Mr Verloc apologised for forgetting himself. His voice, famous for years at open-air meetings and at workmen's assemblies in large halls, had contributed, he said, to his reputation of a good and trustworthy comrade. It was, therefore, a part of his usefulness. It had inspired confidence in his principles. 'I was always put up to speak by the leaders at a critical moment,' Mr Verloc declared, with obvious satisfaction. There was no uproar above which he could not make himself heard, he added; and suddenly he made a demonstration.

'Allow me,' he said. With lowered forehead, without looking up, swiftly and ponderously, he crossed the room to one of the French windows. As if giving way to an uncontrollable impulse, he opened it a little. Mr Vladimir, jumping up amazed from the depths of the armchair, looked over his shoulder; and below, across the courtyard of the Embassy, well beyond the open gate, could be seen the broad back of a policeman watching idly the gorgeous perambulator of a wealthy baby being wheeled in state across the Square.

'Constable!' said Mr Verloc, with no more effort than if he were whispering; and Mr Vladimir burst into a laugh on seeing the policeman spin round as if prodded by a sharp instrument. Mr Verloc shut the window quietly, and returned to the middle of the room.

'With a voice like that,' he said, putting on the husky conversational pedal, 'I was naturally trusted. And I knew what to say, too.'

Mr Vladimir, arranging his cravat, observed him in the glass over the mantelpiece.

'I dare say you have the social revolutionary jargon by heart well enough,' he said, contemptuously. '*Vox et . . .* You haven't ever studied Latin – have you?'

'No,' growled Mr Verloc. 'You did not expect me to know it. I belong to the million. Who knows Latin? Only a few hundred imbeciles who aren't fit to take care of themselves.'

For some thirty seconds longer Mr Vladimir studied in the mirror the fleshy profile, the gross bulk, of the man behind him. And at the same time he had the advantage of seeing his own face, clean-shaved and round, rosy about the gills, and with the thin, sensitive lips formed exactly for the utterance of those delicate witticisms which had made him such a favourite in the very highest society. Then he turned, and advanced into the room with such determination that the very ends of his quaintly old-fashioned bow necktie seemed to bristle with unspeakable menaces. The movement was so swift and fierce that Mr Verloc, casting an oblique glance, quailed inwardly.

'Aha! You dare be impudent,' Mr Vladimir began, with an amazingly guttural intonation not only utterly un-English, but absolutely un-European, and startling even to Mr Verloc's experience of cosmopolitan slums. 'You dare! Well, I am going to speak plain English to you. Voice won't do. We have no use for your voice. We don't want a voice. We want facts – startling facts – damn you,' he added, with a sort of ferocious discretion, right into Mr Verloc's face.

'Don't you try to come over me with your Hyperborean manners,' Mr Verloc defended himself, huskily, looking at the carpet. At this his interlocutor, smiling mockingly above the bristling bow of his necktie, switched the conversation into French.

'You give yourself for an "agent provocateur". The proper business of an "agent provocateur" is to provoke. As far as I can judge from your record kept here, you have done nothing to earn your money for the last three years.'

'Nothing!' exclaimed Verloc, stirring not a limb, and not raising his eyes, but with the note of sincere feeling in his tone. 'I have several times prevented what might have been . . .'

'There is a proverb in this country which says prevention is better than cure,' interrupted Mr Vladimir, throwing himself into the armchair. 'It is stupid in a general way. There is no end to prevention. But it is characteristic. They dislike finality in this country. Don't you be too English. And in this particular instance, don't be absurd. The evil is already here. We don't want prevention – we want cure.'

He paused, turned to the desk, and turning over some papers lying there, spoke in a changed, businesslike tone, without looking at Mr Verloc.

'You know, of course, of the International Conference assembled in Milan?'

Mr Verloc intimated hoarsely that he was in the habit of reading the daily papers. To a further question his answer was that, of course, he understood what he read. At this Mr Vladimir, smiling faintly at the documents he was still scanning one after another, murmured, 'As long as it is not written in Latin, I suppose.'

'Or Chinese,' added Mr Verloc, stolidly.

'H'm. Some of your revolutionary friends' effusions are written in a *charabia* every bit as incomprehensible as Chinese – ' Mr Vladimir let fall disdainfully a grey sheet of printed matter. 'What are all these leaflets headed F. P., with a hammer, pen, and torch crossed? What does it mean, this F. P.?' Mr Verloc approached the imposing writing-table.

'The Future of the Proletariat. It's a society,' he explained, standing ponderously by the side of the armchair, 'not anarchist in principle, but open to all shades of revolutionary opinion.'

'Are you in it?'

'One of the Vice-Presidents,' Mr Verloc breathed out heavily; and the First Secretary of the Embassy raised his head to look at him.

'Then you ought to be ashamed of yourself,' he said, incisively. 'Isn't your society capable of anything else but printing this prophetic bosh in blunt type on this filthy paper – eh? Why don't you do something? Look here. I've this matter in hand now, and I tell you plainly that you will have to earn your money. The good old Stott-Wartenheim times are over. No work, no pay.'

Mr Verloc felt a queer sensation of faintness in his stout legs. He stepped back one pace, and blew his nose loudly.

He was, in truth, startled and alarmed. The rusty London sunshine struggling clear of the London mist shed a lukewarm brightness into the First Secretary's private room: and in the silence Mr Verloc heard against a window-pane the faint buzzing of a fly – his first fly of the year – heralding better than any number of swallows the approach of spring. The useless fussing of that tiny, energetic organism affected unpleasantly this big man threatened in his indolence.

In the pause Mr Vladimir formulated in his mind a series of disparaging remarks concerning Mr Verloc's face and figure. The fellow was unexpectedly vulgar, heavy, and impudently unintelligent. He looked uncommonly like a master plumber come to present his bill. The First Secretary of the Embassy, from his occasional excursions into the field of American humour, had formed a special notion of that class of mechanic as the embodiment of fraudulent laziness and incompetency.

This was then the famous and trusty secret agent, so secret that he was never designated otherwise but by the symbol Δ in the late Baron Stott-Wartenheim's official, semi-official and confidential correspondence; the celebrated agent Δ, whose warnings had the power to change the schemes and the dates of royal, imperial, grand-ducal journeys, and sometimes cause them to be put off altogether! This fellow! And Mr Vladimir indulged mentally in an enormous and derisive fit of merriment, partly at his own astonishment, which he judged naïve, but mostly at the expense of the universally regretted Baron Stott-Wartenheim. His late Excellency, whom the august favour of his Imperial master had imposed as Ambassador upon several reluctant Ministers of Foreign Affairs, had enjoyed in his lifetime a fame for an owlish, pessimistic gullibility. His Excellency had the social revolution on the brain. He imagined himself to be a diplomatist set apart by a special dispensation to watch the end of diplomacy, and pretty nearly the end of the world, in a horrid, democratic upheaval. His prophetic and doleful despatches had been for years the joke of Foreign Offices. He was said to have exclaimed on his deathbed (visited by his Imperial friend and master): 'Unhappy Europe! Thou shalt perish by the moral insanity of thy children!' He was fated to be the victim of the first humbugging rascal that came along, thought Mr Vladimir, smiling vaguely at Mr Verloc.

'You ought to venerate the memory of Baron Stott-Wartenheim,' he exclaimed, suddenly.

The lowered physiognomy of Mr Verloc expressed a sombre and weary annoyance.

'Permit me to observe to you,' he said, 'that I came here because I was summoned by a peremptory letter. I have been here only twice before in the last eleven years, and certainly never at eleven in the morning. It isn't very wise to call me up like this. There is just a chance of being seen. And that would be no joke for me.'

Mr Vladimir shrugged his shoulders.

'It would destroy my usefulness,' continued the other hotly.

'That's your affair,' murmured Mr Vladimir, with soft brutality. 'When you cease to be useful you shall cease to be employed. Yes. Right off. Cut short. You shall . . . ' Mr Vladimir, frowning, paused, at a loss for a sufficiently idiomatic expression, and instantly brightened up, with a grin of beautifully white teeth. 'You shall be chucked,' he brought out, ferociously.

Once more Mr Verloc had to react with all the force of his will against that sensation of faintness running down one's legs which once upon a time had inspired some poor devil with the felicitous expression: 'My heart went down into my boots.' Mr Verloc, aware of the sensation, raised his head bravely.

Mr Vladimir bore the look of heavy enquiry with perfect serenity.

'What we want is to administer a tonic to the Conference in Milan,' he said, airily. 'Its deliberations upon international action for the suppression of political crime don't seem to get anywhere. England lags. This country is absurd with its sentimental regard for individual liberty. It's intolerable to think that all your friends have got only to come over to . . . '

'In that way I have them all under my eye,' Mr Verloc interrupted, huskily.

'It would be much more to the point to have them all under lock and key. England must be brought into line. The imbecile bourgeoisie of this country make themselves the accomplices of the very people whose aim is to drive them out of their houses to starve in ditches. And they have the political power still, if they only had the sense to use it for their preservation. I suppose you agree that the middle classes are stupid?'

Mr Verloc agreed hoarsely.

'They are.'

'They have no imagination. They are blinded by an idiotic vanity. What they want just now is a jolly good scare. This is the psychological moment to set your friends to work. I have had you called here to develop to you my idea.'

And Mr Vladimir developed his idea from on high, with scorn and condescension, displaying at the same time an amount of ignorance as to the real aims thoughts, and methods of the revolutionary world which filled the silent Mr Verloc with inward consternation. He confounded causes with effects more than was excusable; the most distinguished propagandists with impulsive bomb throwers; assumed organisation where in the nature of things it could not exist; spoke of the social revolutionary party one moment as of a perfectly disciplined army, where the word of chiefs was supreme, and at another as if it had been the loosest association of desperate brigands that ever camped in a mountain gorge. Once Mr Verloc had opened his mouth for a protest, but the raising of a shapely, large white hand arrested him. Very soon he became too appalled to even try to protest. He listened in a stillness of dread which resembled the immobility of profound attention.

'A series of outrages,' Mr Vladimir continued, calmly, 'executed here in this country; not only *planned* here – that would not do – they would not mind. Your friends could set half the Continent on fire without influencing the public opinion here in favour of a universal repressive legislation. They will not look outside their backyard here.'

Mr Verloc cleared his throat, but his heart failed him, and he said nothing.

'These outrages need not be especially sanguinary,' Mr Vladimir went on, as if delivering a scientific lecture, 'but they must be sufficiently startling – effective. Let them be directed against buildings, for instance. What is the fetish of the hour that all the bourgeoisie recognise – eh, Mr Verloc?'

Mr Verloc opened his hands and shrugged his shoulders slightly.

'You are too lazy to think,' was Mr Vladimir's comment upon that gesture. 'Pay attention to what I say. The fetish of today is neither royalty nor religion. Therefore the palace and the church should be left alone. You understand what I mean, Mr Verloc?'

The dismay and the scorn of Mr Verloc found vent in an attempt at levity.

'Perfectly. But what of the Embassies? A series of attacks on the various Embassies,' he began; but he could not withstand the cold, watchful stare of the First Secretary.

'You can be facetious, I see,' the latter observed, carelessly. 'That's all right. It may enliven your oratory at socialistic congresses. But this room is no place for it. It would be infinitely safer for you to follow carefully what I am saying. As you are being called upon to furnish facts instead of cock-and-bull stories, you had better try to make your profit off what I am taking the trouble to explain to you. The sacrosanct fetish of today is science. Why don't you get some of your friends to go for that wooden-faced panjandrum – eh? Is it not part of these institutions which must be swept away before the F. P. comes along?'

Mr Verloc said nothing. He was afraid to open his lips lest a groan should escape him.

'This is what you should try for. An attempt upon a crowned head or on a president is sensational enough in a way, but not so much as it used to be. It has entered into the general conception of the existence of all chiefs of state. It's almost conventional – especially since so many presidents have been assassinated. Now let us take an outrage upon – say a church. Horrible enough at first sight, no doubt, and yet not so effective as a person of an ordinary mind might think. No matter how revolutionary and anarchist in inception, there would be fools enough to give such an outrage the character of a religious manifestation. And that would detract from the especial alarming significance we wish to give to the act. A murderous attempt on a restaurant or a theatre would suffer in the same way from the suggestion of non-political passion; the exasperation of a hungry man, an act of social revenge. All this is used up; it is no longer instructive as an object lesson in revolutionary anarchism. Every newspaper has ready-made phrases to explain such manifestations away. I am about to give you the philosophy of bomb throwing from my point of view; from the point of view you pretend to have been serving for the last eleven years. I will try not to talk above your head. The sensibilities of the class you are attacking are soon blunted. Property seems to them an indestructible thing. You can't count upon their emotions either of pity or fear for very long. A bomb outrage to have any influence on public opinion now must go beyond the intention of vengeance or terrorism. It must be purely destructive. It must be that, and only that, beyond the faintest suspicion of any other object. You anarchists should make it clear that you are perfectly determined to make a clean sweep of the whole social creation. But how to get that appallingly absurd notion into the heads of the middle classes so that there should be no mistake? That's the question. By directing your blows at something outside the ordinary passions of humanity is the answer. Of course, there is art. A bomb in the National Gallery would make some noise. But it would not be serious enough. Art has never been their fetish. It's like breaking a few back windows in a man's house; whereas, if you want to make him really sit up, you must try at least to raise the roof. There would be some screaming of course, but from whom? Artists – art critics and suchlike people of no account. Nobody minds what they say. But there is learning – science. Any imbecile that has got an income believes in that. He does not know why, but he believes it matters somehow. It is the sacrosanct fetish. All the damned professors are radicals at heart. Let them know that their great panjandrum has got to go, too, to make room for the Future of the Proletariat. A howl from all these intellectual idiots is bound to help forward the labours of the Milan Conference. They will be writing to the papers. Their indignation would be above suspicion, no material interests being openly at stake, and it will alarm every selfishness of the class which should be impressed. They believe that in some mysterious way science is at the source of their material prosperity. They do. And the absurd ferocity of such a demonstration will affect them more profoundly than the mangling of a whole street – or theatre – full of their own kind. To that last they can always say: "Oh! it's mere class hate." But what is one to say to an act of destructive ferocity so absurd as to be incomprehensible, inexplicable, almost unthinkable; in fact, mad? Madness alone is truly terrifying, inasmuch as you cannot placate it either by threats, persuasion, or bribes. Moreover, I am a civilised man. I would never dream of directing you to organise a mere butchery, even if I expected the best results from it. But I wouldn't expect from a butchery the result I want. Murder is always with us. It is almost an institution. The demonstration must be against learning – science. But not every science will do. The attack must have all the shocking senselessness of gratuitous blasphemy. Since bombs are your means of expression, it would be really telling if one could throw a bomb into pure mathematics. But that is impossible. I have been trying to educate you; I have expounded to you the higher philosophy of your usefulness, and suggested to you some serviceable arguments. The practical application of my teaching interests *you* mostly. But from the moment I have undertaken to interview you I have also given some attention to the practical aspect of the question. What do you think of having a go at astronomy?'

For sometime already Mr Verloc's immobility by the side of the armchair resembled a state of collapsed coma – a sort of passive insensibility interrupted by slight convulsive starts, such as may be observed in the domestic dog having a nightmare on the hearthrug. And it was in an uneasy, doglike growl that he repeated the word: 'Astronomy.'

He had not recovered thoroughly as yet from the state of bewilderment brought about by the effort to follow Mr Vladimir's rapid, incisive utterance. It had overcome his power of assimilation. It had made him angry. This anger was complicated by incredulity. And suddenly it dawned upon him that all this was an elaborate joke. Mr Vladimir exhibited his white teeth in a smile, with dimples on his round, full face posed with a complacent inclination above the bristling bow of his necktie. The favourite of intelligent society women had assumed his drawing-room attitude accompanying the delivery of delicate witticisms. Sitting well forward, his white hand upraised, he seemed to hold delicately between his thumb and forefinger the subtlety of his suggestion.

'There could be nothing better. Such an outrage combines the greatest possible regard for humanity with the most alarming display of ferocious imbecility. I defy the ingenuity of journalists to persuade their public that any given member of the proletariat can have a personal grievance against astronomy. Starvation itself could hardly be dragged in there – eh? And there are other advantages. The whole civilised world has heard of Greenwich. The very boot-blacks in the basement of Charing Cross Station know something of it. See?'

The features of Mr Vladimir, so well known in the best society by their humorous urbanity, beamed with cynical self-satisfaction, which would have astonished the intelligent women his wit entertained so exquisitely. 'Yes,' he continued, with a contemptuous smile, 'the blowing up of the first meridian is bound to raise a howl of execration.'

'A difficult business,' Mr Verloc mumbled, feeling that this was the only safe thing to say.

'What is the matter? Haven't you the whole gang under your hand? The very pick of the basket? That old terrorist Yundt is here. I see him walking about Piccadilly in his green Havelock almost every day. And Michaelis, the ticket-of-leave apostle – you don't mean to say you don't know where he is? Because if you don't, I can tell you,' Mr Vladimir went on menacingly. 'If you imagine that you are the only one on the secret fund list, you are mistaken.'

This perfectly gratuitous suggestion caused Mr Verloc to shuffle his feet slightly.

'And the whole Lausanne lot – eh? Haven't they been flocking over here at the first hint of the Milan Conference? This is an absurd country.'

'It will cost money,' Mr Verloc said, by a sort of instinct.

'That cock won't fight,' Mr Vladimir retorted, with an amazingly genuine English accent. 'You'll get your screw every month, and no more till something happens. And if nothing happens very soon you won't get even that. What's your ostensible occupation? What are you supposed to live by?'

'I keep a shop,' answered Mr Verloc.

'A shop! What sort of shop?'

'Stationery, newspapers. My wife . . . '

'Your what?' interrupted Mr Vladimir in his guttural Central Asian tones.

'My wife.' Mr Verloc raised his husky voice slightly. 'I am married.'

'That be damned for a yarn,' exclaimed the other in unfeigned astonishment. 'Married! And you a professed anarchist, too! What is this confounded nonsense? But I suppose it's merely a manner of speaking. Anarchists don't marry. It's well known. They can't. It would be apostasy.'

'My wife isn't one,' Mr Verloc mumbled, sulkily. 'Moreover, it's no concern of yours.'

'Oh, yes, it is,' snapped Mr Vladimir. 'I am beginning to be convinced that you are not at all the man for the work you've been employed on. Why you must have discredited yourself completely in your own world by your marriage. Couldn't you have managed without? This is your virtuous attachment – eh? What with one sort of attachment and another you are doing away with your usefulness.'

Mr Verloc, puffing out his cheeks, let the air escape violently, and that was all. He had armed himself with patience. It was not to be tried much longer. The First Secretary became suddenly very curt, detached, final.

'You may go now,' he said. 'A dynamite outrage must be provoked. I give you a month. The sittings of the Conference are suspended. Before it reassembles again something must have happened here, or your connection with us ceases.'

He changed the note once more with an unprincipled versatility.

'Think over my philosophy, Mr – Mr – Verloc,' he said, with a sort of chaffing condescension, waving his hand towards the door. 'Go for the first meridian. You don't know the middle classes as well as I do. Their sensibilities are jaded. The first meridian. Nothing better, and nothing easier, I should think.'

He had got up, and with his thin sensitive lips twitching humorously, watched in the glass over the mantelpiece Mr Verloc backing out of the room heavily, hat and stick in hand. The door closed.

The footman in trousers, appearing suddenly in the corridor, let Mr Verloc another way out and through a small door in the corner of the courtyard. The porter standing at the gate ignored his exit completely; and Mr Verloc retraced the path of his morning's pilgrimage as if in a dream – an angry dream. This detachment from the material world was so complete that, though the mortal envelope of Mr Verloc had not hastened unduly along the streets, that part of him to which it would be unwarrantably rude to refuse immortality, found itself at the shop door all at once, as borne from west to east on the wings of a great wind. He walked straight behind the counter, and sat down on a wooden chair that stood there. No one appeared to disturb his solitude. Stevie, put into a green baize apron, was now sweeping and dusting upstairs, intent and conscientious, as though he were playing at it; and Mrs Verloc, warned in the kitchen by the clatter of the cracked bell, had merely come to the glazed door of the parlour, and putting the curtain aside a little, had peered into the dim shop. Seeing her husband sitting there shadowy and bulky, with his hat tilted far back on his head, she had at once returned to her stove. An hour or more later she took the green baize apron off her brother Stevie, and instructed him to wash his hands and face in the peremptory tone she had used in that connection for fifteen years or so ever since she had, in fact, ceased to attend to the boy's hands and face herself. She spared presently a glance away from her dishing-up for the inspection of that face and those hands which Stevie, approaching the kitchen table, offered for her approval with an air of self-assurance hiding a perpetual residue of anxiety. Formerly the anger of the father was the supremely effective sanction of these rites, but Mr Verloc's placidity in domestic life would have made all mention of anger incredible – even to poor Stevie's nervousness. The theory was that Mr Verloc would have been inexpressibly pained and shocked by any deficiency of cleanliness at meal times. Winnie after the death of her father found considerable consolation in the feeling that she need no longer tremble for poor Stevie. She could not bear to see the boy hurt. It maddened her. As a little girl she had often faced with blazing eyes the irascible licensed victualler in defence of her brother. Nothing now in Mrs Verloc's appearance could lead one to suppose that she was capable of a passionate demonstration.

She finished her dishing-up. The table was laid in the parlour. Going to the foot of the stairs she screamed out 'Mother!' Then opening the glazed door leading to the shop, she said quietly 'Adolf!' Mr Verloc had not changed his position; he had not apparently stirred a limb for an hour and a half. He got up heavily, and came to his dinner in his overcoat and with his hat on, without uttering a word. His silence in itself had nothing startlingly unusual in this household, hidden in the shades of the sordid street seldom touched by the sun, behind the dim shop with its wares of disreputable rubbish. Only that day Mr Verloc's taciturnity was so obviously thoughtful that the two women were impressed by it. They sat silent themselves, keeping a watchful eye on poor Stevie, lest he should break out into one of his fits of loquacity. He faced Mr Verloc across the table, and remained very good and quiet, staring vacantly. The endeavour to keep him from making himself objectionable in any way to the master of the house put no inconsiderable anxiety into these two women's lives. 'That boy', as they alluded to him softly between themselves, had been a source of that sort of anxiety almost from the very day of his birth. The late licensed victualler's humiliation at having such a very peculiar boy for a son manifested itself by a propensity to brutal treatment; for he was a person of fine sensibilities, and his sufferings as a man and a father were perfectly genuine. Afterwards Stevie had to be kept from making himself a nuisance to the single gentlemen lodgers, who are themselves a queer lot, and are easily aggrieved. And there was always the anxiety of his mere existence to face. Visions of a workhouse infirmary for her child had haunted the old woman in the basement breakfast-room of the decayed Belgravian house. 'If you had not found such a good husband, my dear,' she used to say to her daughter, 'I don't know what would have become of that poor boy.'

Mr Verloc extended as much recognition to Stevie as a man not particularly fond of animals may give to his wife's beloved cat; and this recognition, benevolent and perfunctory, was essentially of the same quality. Both women admitted to themselves that not much more could be reasonably expected. It was enough to earn for Mr Verloc the old woman's reverential gratitude. In the early days, made sceptical by the trials of friendless life, she used sometimes to ask anxiously: 'You don't think, my dear, that Mr Verloc is getting tired of seeing Stevie about?' To this Winnie replied habitually by a slight toss of her head. Once, however, she retorted, with a rather grim pertness: 'He'll have to get tired of me first.' A long silence ensued. The mother, with her feet propped up on a stool, seemed to be trying to get to the bottom of that answer, whose feminine profundity had struck her all of a heap. She had never really understood why Winnie had married Mr Verloc. It was very sensible of her, and evidently had turned out for the best, but her girl might have naturally hoped to find somebody of a more suitable age. There had been a steady young fellow, only son of a butcher in the next street, helping his father in business, with whom Winnie had been walking out with obvious gusto. He was dependent on his father, it is true; but the business was good, and his prospects excellent. He took her girl to the theatre on several evenings. Then just as she began to dread to hear of their engagement (for what could she have done with that big house alone, with Stevie on her hands), that romance came to an abrupt end, and Winnie went about looking very dull. But Mr Verloc, turning up providentially to occupy the first-floor front bedroom, there had been no more question of the young butcher. It was clearly providential.

Chapter 3

' . . . All idealisation makes life poorer. To beautify it is to take away its character of complexity – it is to destroy it. Leave that to the moralists, me boy. History is made by men, but they do not make it in their heads. The ideas that are born in their consciousness play an insignificant part in the march of events. History is dominated and determined by the tool and the production – by the force of economic conditions. Capitalism has made socialism, and the laws made by the capitalism for the protection of property are responsible for anarchism. No one can tell what form the social organisation may take in the future. Then why indulge in prophetic fantasies? At best they can only interpret the mind of the prophet, and can have no objective value. Leave that pastime to the moralists, my boy.'

Michaelis, the ticket-of-leave apostle, was speaking in an even voice, a voice that wheezed as if deadened and oppressed by the layer of fat on his chest. He had come out of a highly hygienic prison round like a tub, with an enormous stomach and distended cheeks of a pale, semi-transparent complexion, as though for fifteen years the servants of an outraged society had made a point of stuffing him with fattening foods in a damp and lightless cellar. And ever since he had never managed to get his weight down as much as an ounce.

It was said that for three seasons running a very wealthy old lady had sent him for a cure to Marienbad – where he was about to share the public curiosity once with a crowned head – but the police on that occasion ordered him to leave within twelve hours. His martyrdom was continued by forbidding him all access to the healing waters. But he was resigned now.

With his elbow presenting no appearance of a joint, but more like a bend in a dummy's limb, thrown over the back of a chair, he leaned forward slightly over his short and enormous thighs to spit into the grate.

'Yes! I had the time to think things out a little,' he added without emphasis. 'Society has given me plenty of time for meditation.'

On the other side of the fireplace, in the horsehair armchair where Mrs Verloc's mother was generally privileged to sit, Karl Yundt giggled grimly, with a faint black grimace of a toothless mouth. The terrorist, as he called himself, was old and bald, with a narrow, snow-white wisp of a goatee hanging limply from his chin. An extraordinary expression of underhand malevolence survived in his extinguished eyes. When he rose painfully the thrusting forward of a skinny groping hand deformed by gouty swellings suggested the effort of a moribund murderer summoning all his remaining strength for a last stab. He leaned on a thick stick, which trembled under his other hand.

'I have always dreamed,' he mouthed, fiercely, 'of a band of men absolute in their resolve to discard all scruples in the choice of means, strong enough to give themselves frankly the name of destroyers, and free from the taint of that resigned pessimism which rots the world. No pity for anything on earth, including themselves, and death enlisted for good and all in the service of humanity – that's what I would have liked to see.'

His little bald head quivered, imparting a comical vibration to the wisp of white goatee. His enunciation would have been almost totally unintelligible to a stranger. His worn-out passion, resembling in its impotent fierceness the excitement of a senile sensualist, was badly served by a dried throat and toothless gums which seemed to catch the tip of his tongue. Mr Verloc, established in the corner of the sofa at the other end of the room, emitted two hearty grunts of assent.

The old terrorist turned slowly his head on his skinny neck from side to side.

'And I could never get as many as three such men together. So much for your rotten pessimism,' he snarled at Michaelis, who uncrossed his thick legs similar to bolsters, and slid his feet abruptly under his chair in sign of exasperation.

He a pessimist! Preposterous! He cried out that the charge was outrageous. He was so far from pessimism that he saw already the end of all private property coming along logically, unavoidably, by the mere development of its inherent viciousness. The possessors of property had not only to face the awakened proletariat, but they had also to fight amongst themselves. Yes. Struggle, warfare, was the condition of private ownership. It was fatal. Ah! he did not depend upon emotional excitement to keep up his belief, no declamations, no anger, no visions of blood-red flags waving, or metaphorical lurid suns of vengeance rising above the horizon of a doomed society. Not he! Cold reason, he boasted, was the basis of his optimism. Yes, optimism . . .

His laborious wheezing stopped, then, after a gasp or two, he added: 'Don't you think that, if I had not been the optimist I am, I could not have found in fifteen years some means to cut my throat? And, in the last instance, there were always the walls of my cell to dash my head against.'

The shortness of breath took all fire, all animation out of his voice; his great, pale cheeks hung like filled pouches, motionless, without a quiver; but in his blue eyes, narrowed as if peering, there was the same look of confident shrewdness, a little crazy in its fixity, they must have had while the indomitable optimist sat thinking at night in his cell. Before him, Karl Yundt remained standing, one wing of his faded greenish Havelock thrown back cavalierly over his shoulder. Seated in front of the fireplace, Comrade Ossipon, ex-medical student, the principal writer of the F. P. leaflets, stretched out his robust legs, keeping the soles of his boots turned up to the glow in the grate. A bush of crinkly yellow hair topped his red, freckled face, with a flattened nose and prominent mouth cast in the rough mould of the Negro type. His almond-shaped eyes leered languidly over the high cheek-bones. He wore a grey flannel shirt, the loose ends of a black silk tie hung down the buttoned breast of his serge coat; and his head resting on the back of his chair, his throat largely exposed, he raised to his lips a cigarette in a long wooden tube, puffing jets of smoke straight up at the ceiling.

Michaelis pursued his idea – *the* idea of his solitary reclusion – the thought vouchsafed to his captivity and growing like a faith revealed in visions. He talked to himself, indifferent to the sympathy or hostility of his hearers, indifferent indeed to their presence, from the habit he had acquired of thinking aloud hopefully in the solitude of the four whitewashed walls of his cell, in the sepulchral silence of the great blind pile of bricks near a river, sinister and ugly like a colossal mortuary for the socially drowned.

He was no good in discussion, not because any amount of argument could shake his faith, but because the mere fact of hearing another voice disconcerted him painfully, confusing his thoughts at once – these thoughts that for so many years, in a mental solitude more barren than a waterless desert, no living voice had ever combated, commented, or approved.

No one interrupted him now, and he made again the confession of his faith, mastering him irresistible and complete like an act of grace: the secret of fate discovered in the material side of life; the economic condition of the world responsible for the past and shaping the future; the source of all history, of all ideas, guiding the mental development of mankind and the very impulses of their passion ...

A harsh laugh from Comrade Ossipon cut the tirade dead short in a sudden faltering of the tongue and a bewildered unsteadiness of the apostle's mildly exalted eyes. He closed them slowly for a moment, as if to collect his routed thoughts. A silence fell; but what with the two gas-jets over the table and the glowing grate the little parlour behind Mr Verloc's shop had become frightfully hot. Mr Verloc, getting off the sofa with ponderous reluctance, opened the door leading into the kitchen to get more air, and thus disclosed the innocent Stevie, seated very good and quiet at a deal table, drawing circles, circles, circles; innumerable circles, concentric, eccentric; a coruscating whirl of circles that by their tangled multitude of repeated curves, uniformity of form, and confusion of intersecting lines suggested a rendering of cosmic chaos, the symbolism of a mad art attempting the inconceivable. The artist never turned his head; and in all his soul's application to the task his back quivered, his thin neck, sunk into a deep hollow at the base of the skull, seemed ready to snap.

Mr Verloc, after a grunt of disapproving surprise, returned to the sofa. Alexander Ossipon got up, tall in his threadbare blue serge suit under the low ceiling, shook off the stiffness of long immobility, and strolled away into the kitchen (down two steps) to look over Stevie's shoulder. He came back, pronouncing oracularly: 'Very good. Very characteristic, perfectly typical.'

'What's very good?' grunted, enquiringly, Mr Verloc, settled again in the corner of the sofa. The other explained his meaning negligently, with a shade of condescension and a toss of his head towards the kitchen: 'Typical of this form of degeneracy – these drawings, I mean.'

'You would call that lad a degenerate, would you?' mumbled Mr Verloc.

Comrade Alexander Ossipon – nicknamed the Doctor, ex-medical student without a degree; afterwards wandering lecturer to working-men's associations upon the socialistic aspects of hygiene; author of a popular quasi-medical study (in the form of a cheap pamphlet seized promptly by the police) entitled 'The Corroding Vices of the Middle Classes'; special delegate of the more or less mysterious Red Committee, together with Karl Yundt and Michaelis for the work of literary propaganda – turned upon the obscure familiar of at least two Embassies that glance of insufferable, hopelessly dense sufficiency which nothing but the frequentation of science can give to the dullness of common mortals.

'That's what he may be called scientifically. Very good type, too, altogether, of that sort of degenerate. It's enough to glance at the lobes of his ears. If you read Lombroso ...'

Mr Verloc, moody and spread largely on the sofa, continued to look down the row of his waistcoat buttons; but his cheeks became tinged by a faint blush. Of late even the merest derivative of the word science (a term in itself inoffensive and of indefinite meaning) had the curious power of evoking a definitely offensive mental vision of Mr Vladimir, in his body as he lived, with almost supernatural clearness. And this phenomenon, deserving justly to be classed amongst the marvels of science, induced in Mr Verloc an emotional state of dread and exasperation tending to express itself in violent swearing. But he said nothing. It was Karl Yundt who was heard, implacable to his last breath: 'Lombroso is an ass.'

Comrade Ossipon met the shock of this blasphemy by an awful, vacant stare. And the other, his extinguished eyes without gleams blackening the deep shadows under the great, bony forehead, mumbled, catching the tip of his tongue between his lips at every second word as though he were chewing it angrily: 'Did you ever see such an idiot? For him the criminal is the prisoner. Simple, is it not? What about those who shut him up there – forced him in there? Exactly. Forced him in there. And what is crime? Does he know that, this imbecile who has made his way in this world of gorged fools by looking at the ears and teeth of a lot of poor, luckless devils? Teeth and ears mark the criminal? Do they? And what about the law that marks him still better – the pretty branding instrument invented by the overfed to protect themselves against the hungry? Red-hot applications on their vile skins – hey? Can't you smell and hear from here the thick hide of the people burn and sizzle? That's how criminals are made for your Lombrosos to write their silly stuff about.'

The knob of his stick and his legs shook together with passion, whilst the trunk, draped in the wings of the Havelock, preserved his historic attitude of defiance. He seemed to sniff the tainted air of social cruelty, to strain his ear for its atrocious sounds. There was an extraordinary force of suggestion in this posturing. The all but moribund veteran of dynamite wars had been a great actor in his time – actor on platforms, in secret assemblies, in private interviews. The famous terrorist had never in his life raised personally as much as his little finger against the social edifice. He was no man of action; he was not even an orator of torrential eloquence, sweeping the masses along in the rushing noise and foam of a great enthusiasm. With a more subtle intention, he took the part of an insolent and venomous evoker of sinister impulses which lurk in the blind envy and exasperated vanity of ignorance, in the suffering and misery of poverty, in all the hopeful and noble illusions of righteous anger, pity, and revolt. The shadow of his evil gift clung to him yet like the smell of a deadly drug in an old vial of poison, emptied now, useless, ready to be thrown away upon the rubbish heap of things that had served their time.

Michaelis, the ticket-of-leave apostle, smiled vaguely with his glued lips; his pasty moon face drooped under the weight of melancholy assent. He had been a prisoner himself. His own skin had sizzled under the red-hot brand, he murmured softly. But Comrade Ossipon, nicknamed the Doctor, had got over the shock by that time.

'You don't understand,' he began, disdainfully, but stopped short, intimidated by the dead blackness of the cavernous eyes in the face turned slowly towards him with a blind stare, as if guided only by the sound. He gave the discussion up, with a slight shrug of the shoulders.

Stevie, accustomed to move about disregarded, had got up from the kitchen table, carrying off his drawing to bed with him. He had reached the parlour door in time to receive in full the shock of Karl Yundt's eloquent imagery. The sheet of paper covered with circles dropped out of his fingers, and he remained staring at the old terrorist, as if rooted suddenly to the spot by his morbid horror and dread of physical pain. Stevie knew very well that hot iron applied to one's skin hurt very much. His scared eyes blazed with indignation: it would hurt terribly. His mouth dropped open.

Michaelis by staring unwinkingly at the fire had regained that sentiment of isolation necessary for the continuity of his thought. His optimism had begun to flow from his lips. He saw Capitalism doomed in its cradle, born with the poison of the principle of competition in its system. The great capitalists devouring the little capitalists, concentrating the power and the tools of production in great masses, perfecting industrial processes, and in the madness of self-aggrandisement only preparing, organising, enriching, making ready the lawful inheritance of the suffering proletariat. Michaelis pronounced the great word 'Patience' – and his clear blue glance, raised to the low ceiling of Mr Verloc's parlour, had a character of seraphic trustfulness. In the doorway Stevie, calmed, seemed sunk in hebetude.

Comrade Ossipon's face twitched with exasperation.

'Then it's no use doing anything – no use whatever.'

'I don't say that,' protested Michaelis, gently. His vision of truth had grown so intense that the sound of a strange voice failed to rout it this time. He continued to look down at the red coals. Preparation for the future was necessary, and he was willing to admit that the great change would perhaps come in the upheaval of a revolution. But he argued that revolutionary propaganda was a delicate work of high conscience. It was the education of the masters of the world. It should be as careful as the education given to kings. He would have it advance its tenets cautiously, even timidly, in our ignorance of the effect that may be produced by any given economic change upon the happiness, the morals, the intellect, the history of mankind. For history is made with tools, not with ideas; and everything is changed by economic conditions – art, philosophy, love, virtue – truth itself!

The coals in the grate settled down with a slight crash; and Michaelis, the hermit of visions in the desert of a penitentiary, got up impetuously. Round like a distended balloon, he opened his short, thick arms, as if in a pathetically hopeless attempt to embrace and hug to his breast a self-regenerated universe. He gasped with ardour.

'The future is as certain as the past – slavery, feudalism, individualism, collectivism. This is the statement of a law, not an empty prophecy.'

The disdainful pout of Comrade Ossipon's thick lips accentuated the Negro type of his face.

'Nonsense,' he said, calmly enough. 'There is no law and no certainty. The teaching propaganda be hanged. What the people knows does not matter, were its knowledge ever so accurate. The only thing that matters to us is the emotional state of the masses. Without emotion there is no action.'

He paused, then added with modest firmness: 'I am speaking now to you scientifically – scientifically – Eh? What did you say, Verloc?'

'Nothing,' growled from the sofa Mr Verloc, who, provoked by the abhorrent sound, had merely muttered a 'Damn.'

The venomous spluttering of the old terrorist without teeth was heard.

'Do you know how I would call the nature of the present economic conditions? I would call it cannibalistic. That's what it is! They are nourishing their greed on the quivering flesh and the warm blood of the people – nothing else.'

Stevie swallowed the terrifying statement with an audible gulp, and at once, as though it had been swift poison, sank limply in a sitting posture on the steps of the kitchen door.

Michaelis gave no signs of having heard anything. His lips seemed glued together for good; not a quiver passed over his heavy cheeks. With troubled eyes he looked for his round, hard hat, and put it on his round head. His round and obese body seemed to float low between the chairs under the sharp elbow of Karl Yundt. The old terrorist, raising an uncertain and clawlike hand, gave a swaggering tilt to a black felt sombrero shading the hollows and ridges of his wasted face. He got in motion slowly, striking the floor with his stick at every step. It was rather an affair to get him out of the house because, now and then, he would stop, as if to think, and did not offer to move again till impelled forward by Michaelis. The gentle apostle grasped his arm with brotherly care; and behind them, his hands in his pockets, the robust Ossipon yawned vaguely. A blue cap with a patent leather peak set well at the back of his yellow bush of hair gave him the aspect of a Norwegian sailor bored with the world after a thundering spree. Mr Verloc saw his guests off the premises, attending them bareheaded, his heavy overcoat hanging open, his eyes on the ground.

He closed the door behind their backs with restrained violence, turned the key, shot the bolt. He was not satisfied with his friends. In the light of Mr Vladimir's philosophy of bomb throwing they appeared hopelessly futile. The part of Mr Verloc in revolutionary politics having been to observe, he could not all at once, either in his own home or in larger assemblies, take the initiative of action. He had to be cautious. Moved by the just indignation of a man well over forty, menaced in what is dearest to him – his repose and his security – he asked himself scornfully what else could have been expected from such a lot, this Karl Yundt, this Michaelis – this Ossipon.

Pausing in his intention to turn off the gas burning in the middle of the shop, Mr Verloc descended into the abyss of moral reflections. With the insight of a kindred temperament he pronounced his verdict. A lazy lot – this Karl Yundt, nursed by a blear-eyed old woman, a woman he had years ago enticed away from a friend, and afterwards had tried more than once to shake off into the gutter. Jolly lucky for Yundt that she had persisted in coming up time after time, or else there would have been no one now to help him out of the bus by the Green Park railings, where that spectre took its constitutional crawl every fine morning. When that indomitable snarling old witch died the swaggering spectre would have to vanish, too – there would be an end to fiery Karl Yundt. And Mr Verloc's morality was offended also by the optimism of Michaelis, annexed by his wealthy old lady, who had taken lately to sending him to a cottage she had in the country. The ex-prisoner could moon about the shady lanes for days together in a delicious and humanitarian idleness. As to Ossipon, that beggar was sure to want for nothing as long as there were silly girls with savings-bank books in the world. And Mr Verloc, temperamentally identical with his associates, drew fine distinctions in his mind on the strength of insignificant differences. He drew them with a certain complacency, because the instinct of conventional respectability was strong within him, being only overcome by his dislike of all kinds of recognised labour – a temperamental defect which he shared with a large proportion of revolutionary reformers of a given social state. For obviously one does not revolt against the advantages and opportunities of that state, but against the price which must be paid for the same in the coin of accepted morality, self-restraint, and toil. The majority of revolutionists are the enemies of discipline and fatigue mostly. There are natures, too, to whose sense of justice the price exacted looms up monstrously enormous, odious, oppressive, worrying, humiliating, extortionate, intolerable. Those are the fanatics. The remaining portion of social rebels is accounted for by vanity, the mother of all noble and vile illusions, the companion of poets, reformers, charlatans, prophets, and incendiaries.

Lost for a whole minute in the abyss of meditation, Mr Verloc did not reach the depth of these abstract considerations. Perhaps he was not able. In any case he had not the time. He was pulled up painfully by the sudden recollection of Mr Vladimir, another of his associates, whom in virtue of subtle moral affinities he was capable of judging correctly. He considered him as dangerous. A shade of envy crept into his thoughts. Loafing was all very well for these fellows who knew not Mr Vladimir, and had women to fall back upon; whereas he had a woman to provide for . . .

At this point, by a simple association of ideas, Mr Verloc was brought face to face with the necessity of going to bed sometime or other that evening. Then why not go now – at once? He sighed. The necessity was not so normally pleasurable as it ought to have been for a man of his age and temperament. He dreaded the demon of sleeplessness, which he felt had marked him for its own. He raised his arm, and turned off the flaring gas-jet above his head.

A bright band of light fell through the parlour door into the part of the shop behind the counter. It enabled Mr Verloc to ascertain at a glance the number of silver coins in the till. These were but few; and for the first time since he opened his shop he took a commercial survey of its value. This survey was unfavourable. He had gone into trade for no commercial reasons. He had been guided in the selection of this peculiar line of business by an instinctive leaning towards shady transactions, where money is picked up easily. Moreover, it did not take him out of his own sphere – the sphere which is watched by the police. On the contrary, it gave him a publicly confessed standing in that sphere, and as Mr Verloc had unconfessed relations which made him familiar with yet careless of the police, there was a distinct advantage in such a situation. But as a means of livelihood it was by itself insufficient.

He took the cash-box out of the drawer, and turning to leave the shop, became aware that Stevie was still downstairs.

What on earth is he doing there? Mr Verloc asked himself. What's the meaning of these antics? He looked dubiously at his brother-in-law, but he did not ask him for information. Mr Verloc's intercourse with Stevie was limited to the casual mutter of a morning, after breakfast, 'My boots', and even that was more a communication at large of a need than a direct order or request. Mr Verloc perceived with some surprise that he did not know really what to say to Stevie. He stood still in the middle of the parlour, and looked into the kitchen in silence. Nor yet did he know what would happen if he did say anything. And this appeared very queer to Mr Verloc in view of the fact, borne upon him suddenly, that he had to provide for this fellow, too. He had never given a moment's thought till then to that aspect of Stevie's existence.

Positively he did not know how to speak to the lad. He watched him gesticulating and murmuring in the kitchen. Stevie prowled round the table like an excited animal in a cage. A tentative 'Hadn't you better go to bed now?' produced no effect whatever; and Mr Verloc, abandoning the stony contemplation of his brother-in-law's behaviour, crossed the parlour wearily, cashbox in hand. The cause of the general lassitude he felt while climbing the stairs being purely mental, he became alarmed by its inexplicable character. He hoped he was not sickening for anything. He stopped on the dark landing to examine his sensations. But a slight and continuous sound of snoring pervading the obscurity interfered with their clearness. The sound came from his mother-in-law's room. Another one to provide for, he thought – and on this thought walked into the bedroom.

Mrs Verloc had fallen asleep with the lamp (no gas was laid upstairs) turned up full on the table by the side of the bed. The light thrown down by the shade fell dazzlingly on the white pillow sunk by the weight of her head reposing with closed eyes and dark hair done up in several plaits for the night. She woke up with the sound of her name in her ears, and saw her husband standing over her.

'Winnie! Winnie!'

At first she did not stir, lying very quiet and looking at the cash-box in Mr Verloc's hand. But when she understood that her brother was 'capering all over the place downstairs' she swung out in one sudden movement on to the edge of the bed. Her bare feet, as if poked through the bottom of an unadorned, sleeved calico sack buttoned tightly at neck and wrists, felt over the rug for the slippers while she looked upward into her husband's face.

'I don't know how to manage him,' Mr Verloc explained, peevishly. 'Won't do to leave him downstairs alone with the lights.'

She said nothing, glided across the room swiftly, and the door closed upon her white form.

Mr Verloc deposited the cash-box on the night table, and began the operation of undressing by flinging his overcoat on to a distant chair. His coat and waistcoat followed. He walked about the room in his stockinged feet, and his burly figure, with the hands worrying nervously at his throat, passed and repassed across the long strip of looking-glass in the door of his wife's wardrobe. Then after slipping his braces off his shoulders he pulled up violently the Venetian blind, and leaned his forehead against the cold window-pane – a fragile film of glass stretched between him and the enormity of cold, black, wet, muddy, inhospitable accumulation of bricks, slates, and stones, things in themselves unlovely and unfriendly to man.

Mr Verloc felt the latent unfriendliness of all out of doors with a force approaching to positive bodily anguish. There is no occupation that fails a man more completely than that of a secret agent of police. It's like your horse suddenly falling dead under you in the midst of an uninhabited and thirsty plain. The comparison occurred to Mr Verloc because he had sat astride various army horses in his time, and had now the sensation of an incipient fall. The prospect was as black as the window-pane against which he was leaning his forehead. And suddenly the face of Mr Vladimir, clean-shaved and witty, appeared enhaloed in the glow of its rosy complexion like a sort of pink seal impressed on the fatal darkness.

This luminous and mutilated vision was so ghastly physically that Mr Verloc started away from the window, letting down the venetian blind with a great rattle. Discomposed and speechless with the apprehension of more such visions, he beheld his wife re-enter the room and get into bed in a calm, businesslike manner which made him feel hopelessly lonely in the world. Mrs Verloc expressed her surprise at seeing him up yet.

'I don't feel very well,' he muttered, passing his hands over his moist brow.

'Giddiness?'

'Yes. Not at all well.'

Mrs Verloc, with all the placidity of an experienced wife, expressed a confident opinion as to the cause, and suggested the usual remedies; but her husband, rooted in the middle of the room, shook his lowered head sadly.

'You'll catch cold standing there,' she observed.

Mr Verloc made an effort, finished undressing, and got into bed. Down below in the quiet, narrow street measured footsteps approached the house, then died away, unhurried and firm, as if the passer-by had started to pace out all eternity, from gas-lamp to gas-lamp in a night without end; and the drowsy ticking of the old clock on the landing became distinctly audible in the bedroom.

Mrs Verloc, on her back, and staring at the ceiling, made a remark.

'Takings very small today.'

Mr Verloc, in the same position, cleared his throat as if for an important statement, but merely enquired: 'Did you turn off the gas downstairs?'

'Yes; I did,' answered Mrs Verloc, conscientiously. 'That poor boy is in a very excited state tonight,' she murmured, after a pause which lasted for three ticks of the clock.

Mr Verloc cared nothing for Stevie's excitement, but he felt horribly wakeful, and dreaded facing the darkness and silence that would follow the extinguishing of the lamp. This dread led him to make the remark that Stevie had disregarded his suggestion to go to bed. Mrs Verloc, falling into the trap, started to demonstrate at length to her husband that this was not 'impudence' of any sort, but simply 'excitement.' There was no young man of his age in London more willing and docile than Stephen, she affirmed; none more affectionate and ready to please, and even useful, as long as people did not upset his poor head. Mrs Verloc, turning towards her recumbent husband, raised herself on her elbow, and hung over him in her anxiety that he should believe Stevie to be a useful member of the family. That ardour of protecting compassion exalted morbidly in her childhood by the misery of another child tinged her sallow cheeks with a faint dusky blush, made her big eyes gleam under the dark lids. Mrs Verloc then looked younger; she looked as young as Winnie used to look, and much more animated than the Winnie of the Belgravian mansion days had ever allowed herself to appear to gentlemen lodgers. Mr Verloc's anxieties had prevented him from attaching any sense to what his wife was saying. It was as if her voice was talking on the other side of a very thick wall. It was her aspect that recalled him to himself.

He appreciated this woman, and the sentiment of this appreciation, stirred by a display of something resembling emotion, only added another pang to his mental anguish. When her voice ceased he moved uneasily, and said: 'I haven't been feeling well for the last few days.'

He might have meant this as an opening to a complete confidence; but Mrs Verloc laid her head on the pillow again, and staring upward, went on: 'That boy hears too much of what is talked about here. If I had known they were coming tonight I would have seen to it that he went to bed at the same time I did. He was out of his mind with something he overheard about eating people's flesh and drinking blood. What's the good of talking like that?'

There was a note of indignant scorn in her voice. Mr Verloc was fully responsive now.

'Ask Karl Yundt,' he growled, savagely.

Mrs Verloc, with great decision, pronounced Karl Yundt 'a disgusting old man.' She declared openly her affection for Michaelis. Of the robust Ossipon, in whose presence she always felt uneasy behind an attitude of stony reserve, she said nothing whatever. And continuing to talk of that brother, who had been for so many years an object of care and fears: 'He isn't fit to hear what's said here. He believes it's all true. He knows no better. He gets into his passions over it.'

Mr Verloc made no comment.

'He glared at me, as if he didn't know who I was, when I went downstairs. His heart was going like a hammer. He can't help being excitable. I woke mother up, and asked her to sit with him till he went to sleep. It isn't his fault. He's no trouble when he's left alone.'

Mr Verloc made no comment.

'I wish he had never been to school,' Mrs Verloc began again, brusquely. 'He's always taking away those newspapers from the window to read. He gets a red face poring over them. We don't get rid of a dozen numbers in a month. They only take up room in the front window. And Mr Ossipon brings every week a pile of these F. P. tracts to sell at a halfpenny each. I wouldn't give a halfpenny for the whole lot. It's silly reading – that's what it is. There's no sale for it. The other day Stevie got hold of one, and there was a story in it of a German soldier officer tearing half-off the ear of a recruit, and nothing was done to him for it. The brute! I couldn't do anything with Stevie that afternoon. The story was enough, too, to make one's blood boil. But what's the use of printing things like that? We aren't German slaves here, thank God. It's not our business – is it?'

Mr Verloc made no reply.

'I had to take the carving knife from the boy,' Mrs Verloc continued, a little sleepily now. 'He was shouting and stamping and sobbing. He can't stand the notion of any cruelty. He would have stuck that officer like a pig if he had seen him then. It's true, too! Some people don't deserve much mercy.' Mrs Verloc's voice ceased, and the expression of her motionless eyes became more and more contemplative and veiled during the long pause. 'Comfortable, dear?' she asked in a faint, far-away voice. 'Shall I put out the light now?'

The dreary conviction that there was no sleep for him held Mr Verloc mute and hopelessly inert in his fear of darkness. He made a great effort.

'Yes. Put it out,' he said at last in a hollow tone.

Chapter 4

Most of the thirty or so little tables covered by red cloths with a white design stood ranged at right angles to the deep brown wainscoting of the underground hall. Bronze chandeliers with many globes depended from the low, slightly vaulted ceiling, and the fresco paintings ran flat and dull all round the walls without windows, representing scenes of the chase and of outdoor revelry in medieval costumes. Varlets in green jerkins brandished hunting knives and raised on high tankards of foaming beer.

'Unless I am very much mistaken, you are the man who would know the inside of this confounded affair,' said the robust Ossipon, leaning over, his elbows far out on the table and his feet tucked back completely under his chair. His eyes stared with wild eagerness.

An upright semi-grand piano near the door, flanked by two palms in pots, executed suddenly all by itself a valse tune with aggressive virtuosity. The din it raised was deafening. When it ceased, as abruptly as it had started, the bespectacled, dingy little man who faced Ossipon behind a heavy glass mug full of beer emitted calmly what had the sound of a general proposition.

'In principle what one of us may or may not know as to any given fact can't be a matter for enquiry to the others.'

'Certainly not,' Comrade Ossipon agreed in a quiet undertone. 'In principle.'

With his big florid face held between his hands he continued to stare hard, while the dingy little man in spectacles coolly took a drink of beer and stood the glass mug back on the table. His flat, large ears departed widely from the sides of his skull, which looked frail enough for Ossipon to crush between thumb and forefinger; the dome of the forehead seemed to rest on the rim of the spectacles; the flat cheeks, of a greasy, unhealthy complexion, were merely smudged by the miserable poverty of a thin dark whisker. The lamentable inferiority of the whole physique was made ludicrous by the supremely self-confident bearing of the individual. His speech was curt, and he had a particularly impressive manner of keeping silent.

Ossipon spoke again from between his hands in a mutter.

'Have you been out much today?'

'No. I stayed in bed all the morning,' answered the other. 'Why?'

'Oh! Nothing,' said Ossipon, gazing earnestly and quivering inwardly with the desire to find out something, but obviously intimidated by the little man's overwhelming air of unconcern. When talking with this comrade – which happened but rarely – the big Ossipon suffered from a sense of moral and even physical insignificance. However, he ventured another question. 'Did you walk down here?'

'No; omnibus,' the little man answered, readily enough. He lived far away in Islington, in a small house down a shabby street, littered with straw and dirty paper, where out of school hours a troop of assorted children ran and squabbled with a shrill, joyless, rowdy clamour. His single back room, remarkable for having an extremely large cupboard, he rented furnished from two elderly spinsters, dressmakers in a humble way with a clientele of servant girls mostly. He had a heavy padlock put on the cupboard, but otherwise he was a model lodger, giving no trouble, and requiring practically no attendance. His oddities were that he insisted on being present when his room was being swept, and that when he went out he locked his door, and took the key away with him.

Ossipon had a vision of these round black-rimmed spectacles progressing along the streets on the top of an omnibus, their self-confident glitter falling here and there on the walls of houses or lowered upon the heads of the unconscious stream of people on the pavements. The ghost of a sickly smile altered the set of Ossipon's thick lips at the thought of the walls nodding, of people running for life at the sight of those spectacles. If they had only known! What a panic! He murmured interrogatively: 'Been sitting long here?'

'An hour or more,' answered the other, negligently, and took a pull at the dark beer. All his movements – he way he grasped the mug, the act of drinking, the way he set the heavy glass down and folded his arms – had a firmness, an assured precision which made the big and muscular Ossipon, leaning forward with staring eyes and protruding lips, look the picture of eager indecision.

'An hour,' he said. 'Then it may be you haven't heard yet the news I've heard just now – in the street. Have you?'

The little man shook his head negatively the least bit. But as he gave no indication of curiosity, Ossipon ventured to add that he had heard it just outside the place. A newspaper boy had yelled the thing under his very nose, and not being prepared for anything of that sort, he was very much startled and upset. He had to come in there with a dry mouth. 'I never thought of finding you here,' he added, murmuring steadily, with his elbows planted on the table.

'I come here sometimes,' said the other, preserving his provoking coolness of demeanour.

'It's wonderful that you of all people should have heard nothing of it,' the big Ossipon continued. His eyelids snapped nervously upon the shining eyes. 'You of all people,' he repeated, tentatively. This obvious restraint argued an incredible and inexplicable timidity of the big fellow before the calm little man, who again lifted the glass mug, drank, and put it down with brusque and assured movements. And that was all.

Ossipon, after waiting for something, word or sign, that did not come, made an effort to assume a sort of indifference.

'Do you,' he said, deadening his voice still more, 'give your stuff to anybody who's up to asking you for?

'My absolute rule is never to refuse anybody – as long as I have a pinch by me,' answered the little man with decision.

'That's a principle?' commented Ossipon.

'It's a principle.'

'And you think it's sound?'

The large round spectacles, which gave a look of staring self-confidence to the sallow face, confronted Ossipon like sleepless, unwinking orbs flashing a cold fire.

'Perfectly. Always. Under every circumstance. What could stop me? Why should I not? Why should I think twice about it?'

Ossipon gasped, as it were, discreetly.

'Do you mean to say you would hand it over to a 'tec if one came to ask you for your wares?'

The other smiled faintly.

'Let them come and try it on, and you will see,' he said. 'They know me, but I know also every one of them. They won't come near me, not they.'

His thin, livid lips snapped together firmly. Ossipon began to argue.

'But they could send someone – rig a plant on you. Don't you see? Get the stuff from you in that way, and then arrest you with the proof in their hands.'

'Proof of what? Dealing in explosives without a licence perhaps.' This was meant for a contemptuous jeer, though the expression of the thin, sickly face remained unchanged, and the utterance was negligent. 'I don't think there's one of them anxious to make that arrest. I don't think they could get one of them to apply for a warrant. I mean one of the best. Not one.'

'Why?' Ossipon asked.

'Because they know very well I take care never to part with the last handful of my wares. I've it always by me.' He touched the breast of his coat lightly. 'In a thick glass flask,' he added, 'So I have been told,' said Ossipon, with a shade of wonder in his voice. 'But I didn't know if . . . '

'They know,' interrupted the little man, crisply, leaning against the straight chair back, which rose higher than his fragile head. 'I shall never be arrested. The game isn't good enough for any policeman of them all. To deal with a man like me you require sheer, naked, inglorious heroism.'

Again his lips closed with a self-confident snap. Ossipon repressed a movement of impatience.

'Or recklessness – or simply ignorance,' he retorted. 'They've only to get somebody for the job who does not know you carry enough stuff in your pocket to blow yourself and everything within sixty yards of you to pieces.'

'I never affirmed I could not be eliminated,' rejoined the other. 'But that wouldn't be an arrest. Moreover, it's not so easy as it looks.'

'Bah!' Ossipon contradicted. 'Don't be too sure of that. What's to prevent half a dozen of them jumping upon you from behind in the street? With your arms pinned to your sides you could do nothing – could you?'

'Yes; I could. I am seldom out in the streets after dark,' said the little man, impassively, 'and never very late. I walk always with my right hand closed round the india-rubber ball which I have in my trouser pocket. The pressing of this ball actuates a detonator inside the flask I carry in my pocket. It's the principle of the pneumatic instantaneous shutter for a camera lens. The tube leads up . . .'

With a swift, disclosing gesture he gave Ossipon a glimpse of an india-rubber tube, resembling a slender brown worm, issuing from the armhole of his waistcoat and plunging into the inner breast pocket of his jacket. His clothes, of a nondescript brown mixture, were threadbare and marked with stains, dusty in the folds, with ragged buttonholes. 'The detonator is partly mechanical, partly chemical,' he explained, with casual condescension.

'It is instantaneous, of course?' murmured Ossipon, with a slight shudder.

'Far from it,' confessed the other, with a reluctance which seemed to twist his mouth dolorously. 'A full twenty seconds must elapse from the moment I press the ball till the explosion takes place.'

'Phew!' whistled Ossipon, completely appalled. 'Twenty seconds! Horrors! You mean to say that you could face that? I should go crazy . . .'

'Wouldn't matter if you did. Of course, it's the weak point of this special system, which is only for my own use. The worst is that the manner of exploding is always the weak point with us. I am trying to invent a detonator that would adjust itself to all conditions of action, and even to unexpected changes of conditions. A variable and yet perfectly precise mechanism. A really intelligent detonator.'

'Twenty seconds,' muttered Ossipon again. 'Ough! And then . . .'

With a slight turn of the head the glitter of the spectacles seemed to gauge the size of the beer saloon in the basement of the renowned Silenus Restaurant.

'Nobody in this room could hope to escape,' was the verdict of that survey. 'Nor yet this couple going up the stairs now.'

The piano at the foot of the staircase clanged through a mazurka with brazen impetuosity, as though a vulgar and impudent ghost were showing off. The keys sank and rose mysteriously. Then all became still. For a moment Ossipon imagined the overlighted place changed into a dreadful black hole belching horrible fumes choked with ghastly rubbish of smashed brickwork and mutilated corpses. He had such a distinct perception of ruin and death that he shuddered again. The other observed, with an air of calm sufficiency: 'In the last instance it is character alone that makes for one's safety. There are very few people in the world whose character is as well established as mine.'

'I wonder how you managed it,' growled Ossipon.

'Force of personality,' said the other, without raising his voice; and coming from the mouth of that obviously miserable organism the assertion caused the robust Ossipon to bite his lower lip. 'Force of personality,' he repeated, with ostentatious calm.

'I have the means to make myself deadly, but that by itself, you understand, is absolutely nothing in the way of protection. What is effective is the belief those people have in my will to use the means. That's their impression. It is absolute. Therefore I am deadly.'

'There are individuals of character amongst that lot, too,' muttered Ossipon ominously.

'Possibly. But it is a matter of degree obviously since, for instance, I am not impressed by them. Therefore they are inferior. They cannot be otherwise. Their character is built upon conventional morality. It leans on the social order. Mine stands free from everything artificial. They are bound in all sorts of conventions. They depend on life, which, in this connection, is a historical fact surrounded by all sorts of restraints and considerations, a complex, organised fact open to attack at every point; whereas I depend on death, which knows no restraint and cannot be attacked. My superiority is evident.'

'This is a transcendental way of putting it,' said Ossipon, watching the cold glitter of the round spectacles. 'I've heard Karl Yundt say much the same thing not very long ago.'

'Karl Yundt,' mumbled the other, contemptuously, 'the delegate of the International Red Committee, has been a posturing shadow all his life. There are three of you delegates, aren't there? I won't define the other two, as you are one of them. But what you say means nothing. You are the worthy delegates for revolutionary propaganda, but the trouble is not only that you are as unable to think independently as any respectable grocer or journalist of them all, but that you have no character whatever.'

Ossipon could not restrain a start of indignation.

'But what do you want from us?' he exclaimed in a deadened voice. 'What is it you are after yourself?'

'A perfect detonator,' was the peremptory answer. 'What are you making that face for? You see, you can't even bear the mention of something conclusive.'

'I am not making a face,' growled the annoyed Ossipon, bearishly.

'You revolutionists,' the other continued, with leisurely self-confidence, 'are the slaves of the social convention, which is afraid of you; slaves of it as much as the very police that stands up in the defence of that convention. Clearly you are, since you want to revolutionise it. It governs your thought, of course, and your action, too, and thus neither your thought nor your action can ever be conclusive.' He paused, tranquil, with that air of close, endless silence, then almost immediately went on: 'You are not a bit better than the forces arrayed against you – than the police, for instance. The other day I came suddenly upon Chief Inspector Heat at the corner of Tottenham Court Road. He looked at me very steadily. But I did not look at him. Why should I give

him more than a glance? He was thinking of many things – of his superiors, of
his reputation, of the law courts, of his salary, of newspapers – of a hundred
things. But I was thinking of my perfect detonator only. He meant nothing to
me. He was as insignificant as – I can't call to mind anything insignificant
enough to compare him with except Karl Yundt perhaps. Like to like. The
terrorist and the policeman both come from the same basket. Revolution,
legality – counter moves in the same game; forms of idleness at bottom
identical. He plays his little game; so do you propagandists. But I don't play:
I work fourteen hours a day and go hungry sometimes. My experiments cost
money now and again, and then I must do without food for a day or two.
You're looking at my beer. Yes. I have had two glasses already, and shall
have another presently. This is a little holiday, and I celebrate it alone. Why
not? I've the grit to work alone, quite alone, absolutely alone. I've worked
alone for years.'

Ossipon's face had turned dusky red.

'At the perfect detonator – eh?' he sneered, very low.

'Yes,' retorted the other. 'It is a good definition. You couldn't find anything
half so precise to define the nature of your activity with all your committees
and delegations. It is I who am the true propagandist.'

'We won't discuss that point,' said Ossipon, with an air of rising above
personal considerations. 'I am afraid I'll have to spoil your holiday for you,
though. There's a man blown up in Greenwich Park this morning.'

'How do you know?'

'They have been yelling the news in the streets since two o'clock. I bought
the paper, and just ran in here. Then I saw you sitting at this table. I've got it
in my pocket now.'

He pulled the newspaper out. It was a good-sized, rosy sheet, as if flushed
by the warmth of its own convictions, which were optimistic. He scanned
the pages rapidly.

'Ah! Here it is. Bomb in Greenwich Park. There isn't much so far. Half-
past eleven. Foggy morning. Effects of explosion felt as far as Romney Road
and Park Place. Enormous hole in the ground under a tree filled with smashed
roots and broken branches. All round fragments of a man's body blown to
pieces. That's all. The rest's mere newspaper gup. No doubt a wicked attempt
to blow up the Observatory, they say. H'm. That's hardly credible.'

He looked at the paper for a while longer in silence then passed it to
the other, who after gazing abstractedly at the print laid it down without
comment.

It was Ossipon who spoke first – still resentful.

'The fragments of only *one* man, you note. Ergo: blew *himself* up. That
spoils your day off for you – don't it? Were you expecting that sort of
move? I hadn't the slightest idea – not the ghost of a notion of anything of
the sort being planned to come off here – in this country. Under the present
circumstances it's nothing short of criminal.'

The little man lifted his thin black eyebrows with dispassionate scorn.

'Criminal! What is that? What is crime? What can be the meaning of such an assertion?'

'How am I to express myself? One must use the current words,' said Ossipon, impatiently. 'The meaning of this assertion is that this business may affect our position very adversely in this country. Isn't that crime enough for you? I am convinced you have been giving away some of your stuff lately.'

Ossipon stared hard. The other, without flinching, lowered and raised his head slowly.

'You have!' burst out the editor of the F. P. leaflets in an intense whisper. 'No! And are you really handing it over at large like this, for the asking, to the first fool that comes along?'

'Just so! The condemned social order has not been built up on paper and ink, and I don't fancy that a combination of paper and ink will ever put an end to it, whatever you may think. Yes, I would give the stuff with both hands to every man, woman, or fool that likes to come along. I know what you are thinking about. But I am not taking my cue from the Red Committee. I would see you all hounded out of here, or arrested – or beheaded for that matter – without turning a hair. What happens to us as individuals is not of the least consequence.'

He spoke carelessly, without heat, almost without feeling, and Ossipon, secretly much affected, tried to copy this detachment.

'If the police here knew their business they would shoot you full of holes with revolvers, or else try to sandbag you from behind in broad daylight.'

The little man seemed already to have considered that point of view in his dispassionate, self-confident manner.

'Yes,' he assented with the utmost readiness. 'But for that they would have to face their own institutions. Do you see? That requires uncommon grit. Grit of a special kind.'

Ossipon blinked.

'I fancy that's exactly what would happen to you if you were to set up your laboratory in the States. They don't stand on ceremony with their institutions there.'

'I am not likely to go and see. Otherwise your remark is just,' admitted the other. 'They have more character over there, and their character is essentially anarchistic. Fertile ground for us, the States – very good ground. The great Republic has the root of the destructive matter in her. The collective temperament is lawless. Excellent. They may shoot us down, but . . .'

'You are too transcendental for me,' growled Ossipon, with moody concern.

'Logical,' protested the other. 'There are several kinds of logic. This is the enlightened kind. America is all right. It is this country that is dangerous, with her idealistic conception of legality. The social spirit of this people is wrapped up in scrupulous prejudices, and that is fatal to our work. You talk of England being our only refuge! So much the worse. Capua! What do we want with refuges? Here you talk, print, plot, and do nothing. I dare say it's very convenient for such Karl Yundts.'

He shrugged his shoulders slightly, then added with the same leisurely assurance: 'To break up the superstition and worship of legality should be our aim. Nothing would please me more than to see Inspector Heat and his likes take to shooting us down in broad daylight with the approval of the public. Half our battle would be won then; the disintegration of the old morality would have set in in its very temple. That is what you ought to aim at. But you revolutionists will never understand that. You plan the future, you lose yourselves in reveries of economical systems derived from what is; whereas what's wanted is a clean sweep and a clear start for a new conception of life. That sort of future will take care of itself if you will only make room for it. Therefore I would shovel my stuff in heaps at the corners of the streets if I had enough for that; and as I haven't, I do my best by perfecting a really dependable detonator.'

Ossipon, who had been mentally swimming in deep waters, seized upon the last word as if it were a saving plank.

'Yes. Your detonators. I shouldn't wonder if it weren't one of your detonators that made a clean sweep of the man in the park.'

A shade of vexation darkened the determined, sallow face confronting Ossipon.

'My difficulty consists precisely in experimenting practically with the various kinds. They must be tried, after all. Besides . . . '

Ossipon interrupted.

'Who could that fellow be? I assure you that we in London had no knowledge . . . Couldn't you describe the person you gave the stuff to?'

The other turned his spectacles upon Ossipon like a pair of searchlights.

'Describe him,' he repeated, slowly. 'I don't think there can be the slightest objection now. I will describe him to you in one word – Verloc.'

Ossipon, whom curiosity had lifted a few inches off his seat, dropped back, as if hit in the face.

'Verloc! Impossible.'

The self-possessed little man nodded slightly once.

'Yes. He's the person. You can't say that in this case I was giving my stuff to the first fool that came along. He was a prominent member of the group as far as I understand.'

'Yes,' said Ossipon. 'Prominent. No, not exactly. He was the centre for general intelligence, and usually received comrades coming over here. More useful than important. Man of no ideas. Years ago he used to speak at meetings – in France, I believe. Not very well, though. He was trusted by such men as Latorre, Moser, and all that old lot. The only talent he showed really was his ability to elude the attentions of the police somehow. Here, for instance, he did not seem to be looked after very closely. He was regularly married, you know. I suppose it's with her money that he started that shop. Seemed to make it pay, too.'

Ossipon paused abruptly, muttered to himself, 'I wonder what that woman will do now?' and fell into thought.

The other waited with ostentatious indifference. His parentage was obscure, and he was generally known only by his nickname of Professor. His title to that designation consisted in his having been once assistant demonstrator in chemistry at some technical institute. He quarrelled with the authorities upon a question of unfair treatment. Afterwards he obtained a post in the laboratory of a manufactory of dyes. There, too, he had been treated with revolting injustice. His struggles, his privations, his hard work to raise himself in the social scale, had filled him with such an exalted conviction of his merits that it was extremely difficult for the world to treat him with justice – the standard of that notion depending so much upon the patience of the individual. The Professor had genius, but lacked the great social virtue of resignation.

'Intellectually a nonentity,' Ossipon pronounced aloud, abandoning suddenly the inward contemplation of Mrs Verloc's bereaved person and business. 'Quite an ordinary personality. You are wrong in not keeping more in touch with the comrades, Professor,' he added in a reproving tone. 'Did he say anything to you – give you some idea of his intentions? I hadn't seen him for a month. It seems impossible that he should be gone.'

'He told me it was going to be a demonstration against a building,' said the Professor. 'I had to know that much to prepare the missile. I pointed out to him that I had hardly a sufficient quantity for a completely destructive result, but he pressed me very earnestly to do my best. As he wanted something that could be carried openly in the hand, I proposed to make use of an old one-gallon copal varnish can I happened to have by me. He was pleased at the idea. It gave me some trouble, because I had to cut out the bottom first and solder it on again afterwards. When prepared for use, the can enclosed a wide-mouthed, well-corked jar of thick glass packed around with some wet clay and containing sixteen ounces of X_2 green powder. The detonator was connected with the screw top of the can. It was ingenious – a combination of time and shock. I explained the system to him. It was a thin tube of tin enclosing a . . .'

Ossipon's attention had wandered.

'What do you think has happened?' he interrupted.

'Can't tell. Screwed the top on tight, which would make the connection, and then forgot the time. It was set for twenty minutes. On the other hand, the time contact being made, a sharp shock would bring about the explosion at once. He either ran the time too close, or simply let the thing fall. The contact was made all right – that's clear to me at any rate. The system's worked perfectly. And yet you would think that a common fool in a hurry would be much more likely to forget to make the contact altogether. I was worrying myself about that sort of failure mostly. But there are more kinds of fools than one can guard against. You can't expect a detonator to be absolutely foolproof.'

He beckoned to a waiter. Ossipon sat rigid, with the abstracted gaze of mental travail. After the man had gone away with the money he roused himself, with an air of profound dissatisfaction.

'It's extremely unpleasant for me,' he mused. 'Karl has been in bed with bronchitis for a week, There's an even chance that he will never get up again. Michaelis is luxuriating in the country somewhere. A fashionable publisher has offered him five hundred pounds for a book. It will be a ghastly failure. He has lost the habit of consecutive thinking in prison, you know.'

The Professor on his feet, now buttoning his coat, looked about him with perfect indifference.

'What are you going to do?' asked Ossipon, wearily. He dreaded the blame of the Central Red Committee, a body which had no permanent place of abode, and of whose membership he was not exactly informed. If this affair eventuated in the stoppage of the modest subsidy allotted to the publication of the F. P. pamphlets, then indeed he would have to regret Verloc's inexplicable folly.

'Solidarity with the extremist form of action is one thing, and silly reckless-ness is another,' he said, with a sort of moody brutality. 'I don't know what came to Verloc. There's some mystery there. However, he's gone. You may take it as you like, but under the circumstances the only policy for the militant revolutionary group is to disclaim all connection with this damned freak of yours. How to make the disclaimer convincing enough is what bothers me.'

The little man on his feet, buttoned up and ready to go, was no taller than the seated Ossipon. He levelled his spectacles at the latter's face point-blank.

'You might ask the police for a testimonial of good conduct. They know where every one of you slept last night. Perhaps if you asked them they would consent to publish some sort of official statement.'

'No doubt they are aware well enough that we had nothing to do with this,' mumbled Ossipon, bitterly. 'What they will say is another thing.' He remained thoughtful, disregarding the short, owlish, shabby figure standing by his side. 'I must lay hands on Michaelis at once, and get him to speak from his heart at one of our gatherings. The public has a sort of sentimental regard for that fellow. His name is known. And I am in touch with a few reporters on the big dailies. What he would say would be utter bosh, but he has a turn of talk that makes it go down all the same.'

'Like treacle,' interjected the Professor, rather low, keeping an impassive expression.

The perplexed Ossipon went on communing with himself half audibly, after the manner of a man reflecting in perfect solitude.

'Confounded ass! To leave such an imbecile business on my hands. And I don't even know if . . .'

He sat with compressed lips. The idea of going for news straight to the shop lacked charm. His notion was that Verloc's shop might have been turned already into a police trap. They will be bound to make some arrests, he thought, with something resembling virtuous indignation, for the even tenor of his revolutionary life was menaced by no fault of his. And yet unless he went there he ran the risk of remaining in ignorance of what perhaps it would be very material for him to know. Then he reflected that, if the man in the park had been so very much blown to pieces as the evening papers said, he could not have been identified. And if so, the police could have no special reason for watching Verloc's shop more closely than any other place known to be frequented by marked anarchists – no more reason, in fact, than for watching the doors of the Silenus. There would be a lot of watching all round, no matter where he went. Still . . .'

'I wonder what I had better do now?' he muttered, taking counsel with himself.

A rasping voice at his elbow said, with sedate scorn: 'Fasten yourself upon the woman for all she's worth.'

After uttering these words the Professor walked away from the table. Ossipon, whom that piece of insight had taken unawares, gave one ineffectual start, and remained still, with a helpless gaze, as though nailed fast to the seat of his chair. The lonely piano, without as much as a music stool to help it, struck a few chords courageously, and beginning a selection of national airs, played him out at last to the tune of 'Blue Bells of Scotland.' The painfully detached notes grew faint behind his back while he went slowly upstairs, across the hall, and into the street.

In front of the great doorway a dismal row of newspaper sellers standing clear of the pavement dealt out their wares from the gutter. It was a raw, gloomy day of the early spring; and the grimy sky, the mud of the streets, the rags of the dirty men harmonised excellently with the eruption of the damp, rubbishy sheets of paper soiled with printers' ink. The posters, maculated with filth, garnished like tapestry the sweep of the kerbstone. The trade in afternoon paper was brisk, yet, in comparison with the swift, constant march of foot traffic, the effect was of indifference, of a disregarded distribution. Ossipon looked hurriedly both ways before stepping out into the cross-currents, but the Professor was already out of sight.

Chapter 5

The Professor had turned into a street to the left, and walked along, with his head carried rigidly erect, in a crowd whose every individual almost overtopped his stunted stature. It was vain to pretend to himself that he was not disappointed. But that was mere feeling; the stoicism of his thought could not be disturbed by this or any other failure. Next time, or the time after next, a telling stroke would be delivered – something really startling – a blow fit to open the first crack in the imposing front of the great edifice of legal conceptions sheltering the atrocious injustice of society. Of humble origin, and with an appearance really so mean as to stand in the way of his considerable natural abilities, his imagination had been fired early by the tales of men rising from the depths of poverty to positions of authority and affluence. The extreme, almost ascetic purity of his thought, combined with an astounding ignorance of worldly conditions, had set before him a goal of power and prestige to be attained without the medium of arts, graces, tact, wealth – by sheer weight of merit alone. On that view he considered himself entitled to undisputed success. His father, a delicate dark enthusiast with a sloping forehead, had been an itinerant and rousing preacher of some obscure but rigid Christian sect – a man supremely confident in the privileges of his righteousness. In the son, individualist by temperament, once the science of colleges had replaced thoroughly the faith of conventicles, this moral attitude translated itself into a frenzied puritanism of ambition. He nursed it as some-thing secularly holy. To see it thwarted opened his eyes to the true nature of the world, whose morality was artificial, corrupt, and blasphemous. The way of even the most justifiable revolutions is prepared by personal impulses disguised into creeds. The Professor's indignation found in itself a final cause that absolved him from the sin of turning to destruction as the agent of his ambition. To destroy public faith in legality was the imperfect formula of his pedantic fanaticism; but the subconscious conviction that the framework of an established social order cannot be effectually shattered except by some form of collective or individual violence was precise and correct. He was a moral agent – that was settled in his mind. By exercising his agency with ruthless defiance he procured for himself the appearances of power and personal prestige. That was undeniable to his vengeful bitterness. It pacified its unrest; and in their own way the most ardent of revolutionaries are perhaps doing no more but seeking for peace in common with the rest of mankind – the peace of soothed vanity, of satisfied appetites, or perhaps of appeased conscience.

Lost in the crowd, miserable and undersized, he meditated confidently on his power, keeping his hand in the left pocket of his trousers, grasping lightly the india-rubber ball, the supreme guarantee of his sinister freedom; but after a while he became disagreeably affected by the sight of the roadway thronged with vehicles and of the pavement crowded with men and women. He was in a long, straight street, peopled by a mere fraction of an immense multitude; but all round him, on and on, even to the limits of the horizon hidden by the enormous piles of bricks, he felt the mass of mankind mighty in its numbers. They swarmed numerous like locusts, industrious like ants, thoughtless like a natural force, pushing on blind and orderly and absorbed, impervious to sentiment, to logic, to terror, too, perhaps . . .

That was the form of doubt he feared most. Impervious to fear! Often while walking abroad, when he happened also to come out of himself, he had such moments of dreadful and sane mistrust of mankind. What if nothing could move them? Such moments come to all men whose ambition aims at a direct grasp upon humanity – to artists, politicians, thinkers, reformers, or saints. A despicable emotional state this, against which solitude fortifies a superior character; and with severe exultation the Professor thought of the refuge of his room, with its padlocked cupboard, lost in a wilderness of poor houses, the hermitage of the perfect anarchist. In order to reach sooner the point where he could take his omnibus, he turned brusquely out of the populous street into a narrow and dusky alley paved with flagstones. On one side the low brick houses had in their dusty windows the sightless, moribund look of incurable decay – empty shells awaiting demolition. From the other side life had not departed wholly as yet. Facing the only gas-lamp yawned the cavern of a second-hand furniture dealer, where, deep in the gloom of a sort of narrow avenue winding through a bizarre forest of wardrobes, with an undergrowth tangle of table legs, a tall pier-glass glimmered like a pool of water in a wood. An unhappy, homeless couch, accompanied by two unrelated chairs, stood in the open. The only human being making use of the alley besides the Professor, coming stalwart and erect from the opposite direction checked his swinging pace suddenly . . .

'Hallo!' he said, and stood a little on one side watchfully.

The Professor had already stopped, with a ready half turn which brought his shoulders very near the other wall. His right hand fell lightly on the back of the outcast couch, the left remained purposefully plunged deep in the trousers pocket, and the roundness of the heavy rimmed spectacles imparted an owlish character to his moody, unperturbed face.

It was like a meeting in a side corridor of a mansion full of life. The stalwart man was buttoned up in a dark overcoat, and carried an umbrella. His hat, tilted back, uncovered a good deal of forehead, which appeared very white in the dusk. In the dark patches of the orbits the eyeballs glimmered piercingly. Long, drooping moustaches, the colour of ripe corn, framed with their points the square block of his shaved chin.

'I am not looking for you,' he said, curtly.

The Professor did not stir an inch. The blended noises of the enormous town sank down to an inarticulate low murmur. Chief Inspector Heat of the Special Crime Department changed his tone.

'Not in a hurry to get home?' he asked, with mocking simplicity.

The unwholesome-looking little moral agent of destruction exulted silently in the possession of personal prestige, keeping in check this man armed with the defensive mandate of a menaced society. More fortunate than Caligula, who wished that the Roman senate had only one head for the better satisfaction of his cruel lust, he beheld in that one man all the forces he had set at defiance: the force of law, property, oppression, and injustice. He beheld all his enemies and fearlessly confronted them all in a supreme satisfaction of his vanity. They stood perplexed before him as if before a dreadful portent. He gloated inwardly over the chance of this meeting affirming his superiority over all the multitude of mankind.

It was in reality a chance meeting. Chief Inspector Heat had had a disagreeably busy day since his department received the first telegram from Greenwich a little before eleven in the morning. First of all, the fact of the outrage being attempted less than a week after he had assured a high official that no outbreak of anarchist activity was to be apprehended was sufficiently annoying. If he ever thought himself safe in making a statement, it was then. He had made that statement with infinite satisfaction to himself, because it was clear that the high official desired greatly to hear that very thing. He had affirmed that nothing of the sort could even be thought of without the department being aware of it within twenty-four hours; and he had spoken thus in his consciousness of being the great expert of his department. He had gone even so far as to utter words which true wisdom would have kept back. But Chief Inspector Heat was not very wise, at least not truly so. True wisdom, which is not certain of anything in this world of contradictions, would have prevented him from attaining his present position. It would have alarmed his superiors, and done away with his chances of promotion. His promotion had been very rapid.

'There isn't one of them, sir, that we couldn't lay our hands on at any time of night and day. We know what each of them is doing hour by hour,' he had declared. And the high official had deigned to smile. This was so obviously the right thing to say for an officer of Chief Inspector Heat's reputation that it was perfectly delightful. The high official believed the declaration, which chimed in with his idea of the fitness of things. His wisdom was of an official kind, or else he might have reflected upon a matter not of theory but of experience that in the close-woven stuff of relations between conspirator and police there occur unexpected solutions of continuity, sudden holes in space and time. A given anarchist may be watched inch by inch and minute by minute, but a moment always comes when somehow all sight and touch of him are lost for a few hours, during which something (generally an explosion) more or less deplorable does happen. But the high official, carried away by his sense of the fitness of things, had smiled, and now the recollection of that smile was very annoying to Chief Inspector Heat, principal expert in anarchist procedure.

This was not the only circumstance whose recollection depressed the usual serenity of the eminent specialist. There was another dating back only to that very morning. The thought that when called urgently to his Assistant Commissioner's private room he had been unable to conceal his astonishment was distinctly vexing. His instinct of a successful man had taught him long ago that, as a general rule, a reputation is built on manner as much as on achievement. And he felt that his manner when confronted with the telegram had not been impressive. He had opened his eyes widely, and had exclaimed 'Impossible! ' exposing himself thereby to the unanswerable retort of a fingertip laid forcibly on the telegram which the Assistant Commissioner, after reading it aloud, had flung on the desk. To be crushed, as it were, under the tip of a forefinger was an unpleasant experience. Very damaging, too! Furthermore, Chief Inspector Heat was conscious of not having mended matters by allowing himself to express a conviction.

'One thing I can tell you at once: none of our lot had anything to do with this.'

He was strong in his integrity of a good detective, but he saw now that an impenetrably attentive reserve towards this incident would have served his reputation better. On the other hand, he admitted to himself that it was difficult to preserve one's reputation if rank outsiders were going to take a hand in the business. Outsiders are the bane of the police as of other professions. The tone of the Assistant Commissioner's remarks had been sour enough to set one's teeth on edge.

And since breakfast Chief Inspector Heat had not managed to get anything to eat.

Starting immediately to begin his investigation on the spot, he had swallowed a good deal of raw, unwholesome fog in the park. Then he had walked over to the hospital; and when the investigation in Greenwich was concluded at last he had lost his inclination for food. Not accustomed, as the doctors are, to examine closely the mangled remains of human beings, he had been shocked by the sight disclosed to his view when a waterproof sheet had been lifted off a table in a certain apartment of the hospital.

Another waterproof sheet was spread over that table in the manner of a tablecloth, with the corners turned up over a sort of mound – a heap of rags, scorched and bloodstained, half concealing what might have been an accumulation of raw material for a cannibal feast. It required considerable firmness of mind not to recoil before that sight. Chief Inspector Heat, an efficient officer of his department, stood his ground, but for a whole minute he did not advance. A local constable in uniform cast a sidelong glance, and said with stolid simplicity: 'He's all there. Every bit of him. It was a job.'

He had been the first man on the spot after the explosion. He mentioned the fact again. He had seen something like a heavy flash of lightning in the fog. At that time he was standing at the door of the King William Street Lodge talking to the keeper. The concussion made him tingle all over. He ran between the trees towards the Observatory. 'As fast as my legs would carry me,' he repeated twice.

Chief Inspector Heat, bending forward over the table in a gingerly and horrified manner, let him run on. The hospital porter and another man turned down the corners of the cloth, and stepped aside. The Chief Inspector's eyes searched the gruesome detail of that heap of mixed things, which seemed to have been collected in shambles and rag shops.

'You used a shovel,' he remarked, observing a sprinkling of small gravel, tiny brown bits of bark, and particles of splintered wood as fine as needles.

'Had to in one place,' said the stolid constable. 'I sent a keeper to fetch a spade. When he heard me scraping the ground with it he leaned his forehead against a tree, and was as sick as a dog.'

The Chief Inspector, stooping guardedly over the table, fought down the unpleasant sensation in his throat. The shattering violence of destruction which had made of that body a heap of nameless fragments affected his feelings with a sense of ruthless cruelty, though his reason told him the effect must have been as swift as a flash of lightning. The man, whoever he was, had died instantaneously; and yet it seemed impossible to believe that a human body could have reached that state of disintegration without passing through the pangs of inconceivable agony. No physiologist, and still less of a metaphysician, Chief Inspector Heat rose by the force of sympathy, which is a form of fear, above the vulgar conception of time. Instantaneous! He remembered all he had ever read in popular publications of long and terrifying dreams dreamed in the instant of waking; of the whole past life lived with frightful intensity by a drowning man as his doomed head bobs up, streaming, for the last time. The inexplicable mysteries of conscious existence beset Chief Inspector Heat till he evolved a horrible notion that ages of atrocious pain and mental torture could be contained between two successive winks of an eye. And meantime the Chief Inspector went on peering at the table with a calm face and the slightly anxious attention of an indigent customer bending over what may be called the by-products of a butcher's shop with a view to an inexpensive Sunday dinner. All the time his trained faculties of an excellent investigator who scorns no chance of information, followed the self-satisfied, disjointed loquacity of the constable.

'A fair-haired fellow,' the last observed in a placid tone, and paused. 'The old woman who spoke to the sergeant noticed a fair-haired fellow coming out of Maze Hill Station.' He paused. 'And he was a fair-haired fellow. She noticed two men coming out of the station after the up-train had gone on,' he continued, slowly. 'She couldn't tell if they were together. She took no particular notice of the big one, but the other was a fair, slight chap, carrying a tin varnish can in one hand.' The constable ceased.

'Know the woman?' muttered the Chief Inspector, with his eyes fixed on the table, and a vague notion in his mind of an inquest to be held presently upon a person likely to remain for ever unknown.

'Yes. She's housekeeper to a retired publican, and attends the chapel in Park Place sometimes,' the constable uttered weightily, and paused, with another oblique glance at the table. Then suddenly: 'Well, here he is – all of him I could see. Fair. Slight – slight enough. Look at that foot there. I picked up the legs first, one after another. He was that scattered you didn't know where to begin.'

The constable paused; the least flicker of an innocent, self-laudatory smile invested his round face with an infantile expression.

'Stumbled,' he announced, positively. 'I stumbled once myself, and pitched on my head, too, while running up. Them roots do stick out all about the place. Stumbled against the root of a tree and fell, and that thing he was carrying must have gone off right under his chest, I expect.'

The echo of the words 'Person unknown' repeating itself in his inner consciousness bothered the Chief Inspector considerably. He would have liked to trace this affair back to its mysterious origin for his own information. He was professionally curious. Before the public he would have liked to vindicate the efficiency of his department by establishing the identity of that man. He was a loyal servant. That, however, appeared impossible. The first term of the problem was unreadable – lacked all suggestion but that of atrocious cruelty.

Overcoming his physical repugnance, Chief Inspector Heat stretched out his hand without conviction for the salving of his conscience, and took up the least soiled of the rags. It was a narrow strip of velvet with a larger triangular piece of dark blue cloth hanging from it. He held it up to his eyes; and the police constable spoke.

'Velvet collar. Funny the old woman should have noticed the velvet collar. Dark blue overcoat with a velvet collar, she has told us. He was the chap she saw, and no mistake. And here he is all complete, velvet collar and all. I don't think I missed a single piece as big as a postage stamp.'

At this point the trained faculties of the Chief Inspector ceased to hear the voice of the constable. He moved to one of the windows for better light. His face, averted from the room, expressed a startled, intense interest while he examined closely the triangular piece of broadcloth. By a sudden jerk he detached it, and only after stuffing it into his pocket turned round to the room, and flung the velvet collar back on the table.

'Cover up,' he directed the attendants, curtly, without another look, and, saluted by the constable, carried off his spoil hastily.

A convenient train whirled him up to town, alone and pondering deeply, in a third-class compartment. That singed piece of cloth was incredibly valuable, and he could not defend himself from astonishment at the casual manner it had come into his possession. It was as if Fate had thrust that clue into his hands. And after the manner of the average man, whose ambition is to command events, he began to mistrust such a gratuitous and accidental success – just because it seemed forced upon him. The practical value of success depends not a little on the way you look at it. But Fate looks at nothing. It has no discretion. He no longer considered it eminently desirable all round to establish publicly the identity of the man who had blown himself up that morning with such horrible completeness. But he was not certain of the view his department would take. A department is to those it employs a complex personality with ideas and even fads of its own. It depends on the loyal devotion of its servants and the devoted loyalty of trusted servants is associated with a certain amount of affectionate contempt, which keeps it sweet, as it were. By a benevolent provision of Nature no man is a hero to his valet, or else the heroes would have to brush their own clothes. Likewise no department appears perfectly wise to the intimacy of its workers. A department does not know so much as some of its servants. Being a dispassionate organism, it can never be perfectly informed. It would not be good for its efficiency to know too much. Chief Inspector Heat got out of the train in a state of thoughtfulness entirely untainted with disloyalty, but not quite free of that jealous mistrust which so often springs on the ground of perfect devotion, whether to women or to institutions.

It was in this mental disposition, physically very empty, but still nauseated by what he had seen, that he had come upon the Professor. Under these conditions which make for irascibility in a sound, normal man, this meeting was specially unwelcome to Chief Inspector Heat. He had not been thinking of the Professor; he had not been thinking of any individual anarchist at all. The complexion of that case had somehow forced upon him the general idea of the absurdity of things human, which in the abstract is sufficiently annoying to an unphilosophical temperament, and in concrete instances becomes exasperating beyond endurance. At the beginning of his career Chief Inspector Heat had been concerned with the more energetic forms of thieving. He had gained his spurs in that sphere, and naturally enough had kept for it, after his promotion to another department, a feeling not very far removed from affection. Thieving was not a sheer absurdity. It was a form of human industry, perverse indeed, but still an industry exercised in an industrious world; it was work undertaken for the same reason as the work in potteries, in coal mines, in fields, in tool-grinding shops. It was labour, whose practical difference from the other forms of labour consisted in the nature of its risk, which did not lie in ankylosis, or lead poisoning, or fire-damp, or gritty dust, but in what may be briefly defined in its own special phraseology as 'Seven years hard.' Chief Inspector Heat was, of course, not insensible to the gravity of moral differences. But neither were the thieves he had been looking after. They submitted to the severe sanctions of a morality familiar to Chief Inspector Heat with a certain resignation. They were his fellow-citizens gone wrong because of imperfect education, Chief Inspector Heat believed; but allowing for that difference, he could understand the mind of a burglar, because, as a matter of fact, the mind and the instincts of a burglar are of the same kind as the mind and the instincts of a police officer. Both recognise the same conventions, and have a working knowledge of each other's methods and of the routine of their respective trades. They understand each other, which is advantageous to both, and establishes a sort of amenity in their relations. Products of the same machine, one classed as useful and the other as noxious, they take the machine for granted in different ways, but with a seriousness essentially the same. The mind of Chief Inspector Heat was inaccessible to ideas of revolt. But his thieves were not rebels. His bodily vigour, his cool, inflexible manner, his courage, and his fairness, had secured for him much respect and some adulation in the sphere of his early successes. He had felt himself revered and admired. And Chief Inspector Heat, arrested within six paces of the anarchist nicknamed the Professor, gave a thought of regret to the world of thieves – sane, without morbid ideals, working by routine, respectful of constituted authorities, free from all taint of hate and despair.

After paying this tribute to what is normal in the constitution of society (for the idea of thieving appeared to his instinct as normal as the idea of property), Chief Inspector Heat felt very angry with himself for having stopped, for having spoken, for having taken that way at all on the ground of it being a short cut from the station to the headquarters. And he spoke again in his big, authoritative voice, which, being moderated, had a threatening character.

'You are not wanted, I tell you,' he repeated.

The anarchist did not stir. An inward laugh of derision uncovered not only his teeth but his gums as well, shook him all over, without the slightest sound. Chief Inspector Heat was led to add, against his better judgement: 'Not yet. When I want you I will know where to find you.'

Those were perfectly proper words, within the tradition and suitable to his character of a police officer addressing one of his special flock. But the reception they got departed from tradition and propriety. It was outrageous. The stunted, weakly figure before him spoke at last.

'I've no doubt the papers would give you an obituary notice then. You know best what that would be worth to you. I should think you can imagine easily the sort of stuff that would be printed. But you may be exposed to the unpleasantness of being buried together with me, though I suppose your friends would make an effort to sort us out as much as possible.'

With all his healthy contempt for the spirit dictating such speeches, the atrocious allusiveness of the words had its effect on Chief Inspector Heat. He had too much insight, and too much exact information as well, to dismiss them as rot. The dusk of this narrow lane took on a sinister tint from the dark, frail little figure, its back to the wall, and speaking with a weak, self-confident voice. To the vigorous, tenacious vitality of the Chief Inspector, the physical wretchedness of that being, so obviously not fit to live, was ominous; for it seemed to him that if he had the misfortune to be such a miserable object he would not have cared how soon he died. Life had such a strong hold upon him that a fresh wave of nausea broke out in slight perspiration upon his brow. The murmur of town life, the subdued rumble of wheels in the two invisible streets to the right and left, came through the curve of the sordid lane to his ears with a precious familiarity and an appealing sweetness. He was human. But Chief Inspector Heat was also a man, and he could not let such words pass.

'All this is good to frighten children with,' he said. 'I'll have you yet.'

It was very well said, without scorn, with an almost austere quietness.

'Doubtless,' was the answer; 'but there's no time like the present, believe me. For a man of real convictions this is a fine opportunity of self-sacrifice. You may not find another so favourable, so humane. There isn't even a cat near us, and these condemned old houses would make a good heap of bricks where you stand. You'll never get me at so little cost to life and property, which you are paid to protect.'

'You don't know who you're speaking to,' said Chief Inspector Heat, firmly. 'If I were to lay my hands on you now I would be no better than yourself.'

'Ah! The game!'

'You may be sure our side will win in the end. It may yet be necessary to make people believe that some of you ought to be shot at sight like mad dogs. Then that will be the game. But I'll be damned if I know what yours is. I don't believe you know yourselves. You'll never get anything by it.'

'Meantime, it's you who get something from it – so far. And you get it easily, too. I won't speak of your salary, but haven't you made your name simply by not understanding what we are after?'

'What are you after, then?' asked Chief Inspector Heat, with scornful haste, like a man in a hurry who perceives he is wasting his time.

The perfect anarchist answered by a smile which did not part his thin, colourless lips; and the celebrated Chief Inspector felt a sense of superiority which induced him to raise a warning finger.

'Give it up – whatever it is,' he said in an admonishing tone, but not so kindly as if he were condescending to give good advice to a cracksman of repute. 'Give it up. You'll find we are too many for you.'

The fixed smile on the Professor's lips wavered, as if the mocking spirit within had lost its assurance. Chief Inspector Heat went on: 'Don't you believe me – eh? Well, you've only got to look about you. We are. And anyway, you're not doing it well. You're always making a mess of it. Why, if the thieves didn't know their work better they would starve.'

The hint of an invincible multitude behind that man's back roused a sombre indignation in the breast of the Professor. He smiled no longer his enigmatic and mocking smile. The resisting power of numbers, the unattackable stolidity of a great multitude, was the haunting fear of his sinister loneliness. His lips trembled for some time before he managed to say in a strangled voice: 'I am doing my work better than you're doing yours.'

'That'll do now,' interrupted Chief Inspector Heat hurriedly; and the Professor laughed right out this time. While still laughing he moved on; but he did not laugh long. It was a sad-faced, miserable little man who emerged from the narrow passage into the bustle of the broad thoroughfare. He walked with the nerveless gait of a tramp going on, still going on, indifferent to rain or sun in a sinister detachment from the aspects of sky and earth. Chief Inspector Heat, on the other hand, after watching him for a while, stepped out with the purposeful briskness of a man disregarding indeed the inclemencies of the weather, but conscious of having an authorised mission on this earth and the moral support of his kind. All the inhabitants of the immense town, the population of the whole country, and even the teeming millions struggling upon the planet, were with him – down to the very thieves and mendicants. Yes, the thieves themselves were sure to be with him in his present work. The consciousness of universal support in his general activity heartened him to grapple with the particular problem.

The problem immediately before the Chief Inspector was that of managing the Assistant Commissioner of his department, his immediate superior. This is the perennial problem of trusty and loyal servants; anarchism gave it its particular complexion, but nothing more. Truth to say, Chief Inspector Heat thought but little of anarchism. He did not attach undue importance to it, and could never bring himself to consider it seriously. It had more the character of disorderly conduct; disorderly without the human excuse of drunkenness, which at any rate implies good feeling and an amiable leaning towards festivity. As criminals, anarchists were distinctly no class – no class at all. And recalling the Professor, Chief Inspector Heat, without checking his swinging pace, muttered through his teeth: 'Lunatic.'

Catching thieves was another matter altogether. It had that quality of seriousness belonging to every form of open sport where the best man wins under perfectly comprehensible rules. There were no rules for dealing with anarchists. And that was distasteful to the Chief Inspector. It was all foolishness, but that foolishness excited the public mind, affected persons in high places, and touched upon international relations. A hard, merciless contempt settled rigidly on the Chief Inspector's face as he walked on. His mind ran over all the anarchists of his flock. Not one of them had half the spunk of this or that burglar he had known. Not half – not one tenth.

At headquarters the Chief Inspector was admitted at once to the Assistant Commissioner's private room. He found him, pen in hand, bent over a great table bestrewn with papers, as if worshipping an enormous double inkstand of bronze and crystal. Speaking tubes resembling snakes were tied by the heads to the back of the Assistant Commissioner's wooden armchair, and their gaping mouths seemed ready to bite his elbows. And in this attitude he raised only his eyes, whose lids were darker than his face and very much creased. The reports had come in: every anarchist had been exactly accounted for.

After saying this he lowered his eyes, signed rapidly two single sheets of paper, and only then laid down his pen, and sat well back, directing an enquiring gaze at his renowned subordinate. The Chief Inspector stood it well, deferential but inscrutable.

'I dare say you were right,' said the Assistant Commissioner, 'in telling me at first that the London anarchists had nothing to do with this. I quite appreciate the excellent watch kept on them by your men. On the other hand, this, for the public, does not amount to more than a confession of ignorance.'

The Assistant Commissioner's delivery was leisurely, as it were cautious. His thought seemed to rest poised on a word before passing to another, as though words had been the stepping-stones for his intellect picking its way across the waters of error. 'Unless you have brought something useful from Greenwich,' he added.

The Chief Inspector began at once the account of his investigation in a clear, matter-of-fact manner. His superior turning his chair a little, and crossing his thin legs, leaned sideways on his elbow, with one hand shading his eyes. His listening attitude had a sort of angular and sorrowful grace. Gleams as of highly burnished silver played on the sides of his ebony black head when he inclined it slowly at the end.

Chief Inspector Heat waited with the appearance of turning over in his mind all he had just said, but, as a matter of fact, considering the advisability of saying something more. The Assistant Commissioner cut his hesitation short.

'You believe there were two men?' he asked, without uncovering his eyes.

The Chief Inspector thought it more than probable. In his opinion, the two men had parted from each other within a hundred yards from the Observatory walls. He explained also how the other man could have got out of the park speedily without being observed. The fog, though not very dense, was in his favour. He seemed to have escorted the other to the spot, and then to have left him there to do the job single-handed. Taking the time those two were seen coming out of Maze Hill Station by the old woman, and the time when the explosion was heard, the Chief Inspector thought that the other man might have been actually at the Greenwich Park Station, ready to catch the next train up, at the moment his comrade was destroying himself so thoroughly.

'Very thoroughly – eh?' murmured the Assistant Commissioner from under the shadow of his hand.

The Chief Inspector in a few vigorous words described the aspect of the remains. 'The coroner's jury will have a treat,' he added, grimly.

The Assistant Commissioner uncovered his eyes.

'We shall have nothing to tell them,' he remarked, languidly.

He looked up, and for a time watched the markedly non-committal attitude of his Chief Inspector. His nature was one that is not easily accessible to illusions. He knew that a department is at the mercy of its subordinate officers, who have their own conceptions of loyalty. His career had begun in a tropical colony. He had liked his work there. It was police work. He had been very successful in tracking and breaking up certain nefarious secret societies amongst the natives. Then he took his long leave, and got married rather impulsively. It was a good match from a worldly point of view, but his wife formed an unfavourable opinion of the colonial climate on hearsay evidence. On the other hand, she had influential connections. It was an excellent match. But he did not like the work he had to do now. He felt himself dependent on too many subordinates and too many masters. The near presence of that strange emotional phenomenon called public opinion weighed upon his spirits, and alarmed him by its irrational nature. No doubt that from ignorance he exaggerated to himself its power for good and evil – especially for evil; and the rough east winds of the English spring (which agreed with his wife) augmented his general mistrust of men's motives and of the efficiency of their organisation. The futility of police work especially appalled him on those days so trying to his sensitive liver.

He got up, unfolding himself to his full height, and with a heaviness of step remarkable in so slender a man, moved across the room to the window. The panes streamed with rain, and the short street he looked down into lay wet and empty, as if swept clear suddenly by a great flood. It was a very trying day, choked in raw fog to begin with, and now drowned in cold rain. The flickering, blurred flames of gas-lamps seemed to be dissolving in a watery atmosphere. And the lofty pretensions of a mankind oppressed by the miserable indignities of the weather appeared as a colossal and hopeless vanity deserving of scorn, wonder, and compassion.

'Horrible, horrible!' thought the Assistant Commissioner to himself, with his face near the window-pane. 'We have been having this sort of thing now for ten days; no, a fortnight – a fortnight.' He ceased to think completely for a time. That utter stillness of his brain lasted about three seconds. Then he said, perfunctorily: 'You have set enquiries on foot for tracing that other man up and down the line?'

He had no doubt that everything needful had been done. Chief Inspector Heat knew, of course, thoroughly the business of man-hunting. And these were the routine steps, too, that would be taken as a matter of course by the merest beginner. A few enquiries amongst the ticket collectors and the porters of the two small railway stations would give additional details as to the appearance of the two men; the inspection of the collected tickets would show at once where they came from that morning. It was elementary, and could not have been neglected. Accordingly, the Chief Inspector answered that all this had been done directly the old woman had come forward with her deposition. And he mentioned the name of a station. 'That's where they came from, sir,' he went on. 'The porter who took the tickets at Maze Hill remembers two chaps answering to the description passing the barrier. They seemed to him two respectable working-men of a superior sort – sign painters or house decorators. The big man got out of a third-class compartment backward, with a bright tin can in his hand. On the platform he gave it to carry to the fair young fellow who followed him. All this agrees exactly with what the old woman told the police sergeant in Greenwich.'

The Assistant Commissioner, still with his face turned to the window, expressed his doubt as to these two men having had anything to do with the outrage. All this theory rested upon the utterances of an old charwoman who had been nearly knocked down by a man in a hurry. Not a very substantial authority indeed, unless on the ground of sudden inspiration, which was hardly tenable.

'Frankly now, could she have been really inspired?' he queried, with grave irony, keeping his back to the room, as if entranced by the contemplation of the town's colossal forms half lost in the night. He did not even look round when he heard the mutter of the word 'Providential' from the principal subordinate of his department, whose name, printed sometimes in the papers, was familiar to the great public as that of one of its zealous and hard-working protectors. Chief Inspector Heat raised his voice a little.

'Strips and bits of bright tin were quite visible to me,' he said. 'That's a pretty good corroboration.'

'And these men came from that little country station,' the Assistant Commissioner mused aloud, wondering. He was told that such was the name on two tickets out of three given up out of that train at Maze Hill. The third person who got out was a hawker from Gravesend well known to the porters. The Chief Inspector imparted that information in a tone of finality with some ill humour, as loyal servants will do in the consciousness of their fidelity and with the sense of the value of their loyal exertions. And still the Assistant Commissioner did not turn away from the darkness outside, as vast as a sea.

'Two foreign anarchists coming from that place,' he said, apparently to the window-pane. 'It's rather unaccountable.'

'Yes, sir. But it would be still more unaccountable if that Michaelis weren't staying in a cottage in the neighbourhood.'

At the sound of that name, falling unexpectedly into this annoying affair, the Assistant Commissioner dismissed brusquely the vague remembrance of his daily whist party at his club. It was the most comforting habit of his life, in a mainly successful display of his skill without the assistance of any subordinate. He entered his club to play from five to seven, before going home to dinner, forgetting for those two hours whatever was distasteful in his life, as though the game were a beneficent drug for allaying the pangs of moral discontent. His partners were the gloomily humorous editor of a celebrated magazine; a silent, elderly barrister with malicious little eyes; and a highly martial, simple-minded old Colonel with nervous brown hands. They were his club acquaintances merely. He never met them elsewhere except at the card-table. But they all seemed to approach the game in the spirit of co-sufferers, as if it were indeed a drug against the secret ills of existence; and every day as the sun declined over the countless roofs of the town, a mellow, pleasurable impatience, resembling the impulse of a sure and profound friendship, lightened his professional labours. And now this pleasurable sensation went out of him with something resembling a physical shock, and was replaced by a special kind of interest in his work of social protection – an improper sort of interest, which may be defined best as a sudden and alert mistrust of the weapon in his hand.

Chapter 6

The lady patroness of Michaelis, the ticket-of-leave apostle of humanitarian hopes, was one of the most influential and distinguished connections of the Assistant Commissioner's wife, whom she called Annie, and treated still rather as a not very wise and utterly inexperienced young girl. But she had consented to accept him on a friendly footing, which was by no means the case with all of his wife's influential connections. Married young and splendidly at some remote epoch of the past, she had had for a time a close view of great affairs and even of some great men. She herself was a great lady. Old now in the number of her years, she had that sort of exceptional temperament which defies time with scornful disregard, as if it were a rather vulgar convention submitted to by the mass of inferior mankind. Many other conventions easier to set aside, alas! failed to obtain her recognition, also on temperamental grounds – either because they bored her, or else because they stood in the way of her scorns and sympathies. Admiration was a sentiment unknown to her (it was one of the secret griefs of her most noble husband against her) – first, as always more or less tainted with mediocrity, and next as being in a way an admission of inferiority. And both were frankly inconceivable to her nature. To be fearlessly outspoken in her opinions came easily to her, since she judged solely from the standpoint of her social position. She was equally untrammelled in her actions; and as her tactfulness proceeded from genuine humanity, her bodily vigour remained remarkable and her superiority was serene and cordial, three generations had admired her infinitely, and the last she was likely to see had pronounced her a wonderful woman. Meantime, intelligent, with a sort of lofty simplicity, and curious at heart, but not like many women merely of social gossip, she amused her age by attracting within her ken through the power of her great, almost historical, social prestige everything that rose above the dead level of mankind, lawfully or unlawfully, by position, wit, audacity, fortune or misfortune. Royal Highnesses, artists, men of science, young statesmen, and charlatans of all ages and conditions, who, unsubstantial and light, bobbing up like corks, show best the direction of the surface currents, had been welcomed in that house, listened to, penetrated, understood, appraised, for her own edification. In her own words, she liked to watch what the world was coming to. And as she had a practical mind her judgement of men and things, though based on special prejudices, was seldom totally wrong, and almost never wrong-headed. Her drawing-room was probably the only place in the wide world where an Assistant Commissioner of Police could meet a convict liberated on a ticket-of-leave on other than professional and official ground. Who had brought Michaelis there one afternoon the Assistant Commissioner did not remember very well. He had a notion it must have been a certain Member of Parliament of illustrious parentage and unconventional sympathies, which were the standing joke of the comic papers. The notabilities and even the simple notorieties of the day brought each other freely to that temple of an old woman's not ignoble curiosity. You never could guess whom you were likely to come upon being received in semi-privacy within the faded blue silk and gilt frame screen, making a cosy nook for a couch and a few armchairs in the great drawing-room, with its hum of voices and the groups of people seated or standing in the light of six tall windows.

Michaelis had been the object of a revulsion of popular sentiment, the same sentiment which years ago had applauded the ferocity of the life sentence passed upon him for complicity in a rather mad attempt to rescue some prisoners from a police van. The plan of the conspirators had been to shoot down the horses and overpower the escort. Unfortunately, one of the police constables got shot, too. He left a wife and three small children, and the death of that man aroused through the length and breadth of a realm for whose defence, welfare, and glory men die every day as matter of duty, an outburst of furious indignation, of a raging implacable pity for the victim. Three ring-leaders got hanged. Michaelis, young and slim, locksmith by trade, and great frequenter of evening schools, did not even know that anybody had been killed, his part with a few others being to force open the door at the back of the special conveyance. When arrested he had a bunch of skeleton keys in one pocket, a heavy chisel in another, and a short crowbar in his hand: neither more nor less than a burglar. But no burglar would have received such a heavy sentence. The death of the constable had made him miserable at heart, but the failure of the plot also. He did not conceal either of these sentiments from his empanelled countrymen, and that sort of compunction appeared shockingly imperfect to the crammed court. The judge on passing sentence commented feelingly upon the depravity and callousness of the young prisoner.

That made the groundless fame of his condemnation; the fame of his release was made for him on no better grounds by people who wished to exploit the sentimental aspect of his imprisonment either for purposes of their own or for no intelligible purpose. He let them do so in the innocence of his heart and the simplicity of his mind. Nothing that happened to him individually had any importance. He was like those saintly men whose personality is lost in the contemplation of their faith. His ideas were not in the nature of convictions. They were inaccessible to reasoning. They formed in all their contradictions and obscurities an invincible and humanitarian creed, which he confessed rather than preached, with an obstinate gentleness, a smile of pacific assurance on his lips, and his candid blue eyes cast down because the sight of faces troubled his inspiration developed in solitude. In that characteristic attitude, pathetic in his grotesque and incurable obesity which he had to drag like a galley slave's bullet to the end of his days, the Assistant Commissioner of Police beheld the ticket-of-leave apostle filling a privileged armchair within the screen. He sat there by the head of the old lady's couch, mild-voiced and quiet, with no more self-consciousness than a very small child, and with something of a child's charm – the appealing charm of trustfulness. Confident of the future, whose secret ways had been revealed to him within the four walls of a well-known penitentiary, he had no reason to look with suspicion upon anybody. If he could not give the great and curious lady a very definite idea as to what the world was coming to, he had managed without effort to impress her by his unembittered faith, by the sterling quality of his optimism.

A certain simplicity of thought is common to serene souls at both ends of the social scale. The great lady was simple in her own way. His views and beliefs had nothing in them to shock or startle her, since she judged them from the standpoint of her lofty position. Indeed, her sympathies were easily accessible to a man of that sort. She was not an exploiting capitalist herself; she was, as it were, above the play of economic conditions. And she had a great capacity of pity for the more obvious forms of common human miseries precisely because she was such a complete stranger to them that she had to translate her conception into terms of mental suffering before she could grasp the notion of their cruelty. The Assistant Commissioner remembered very well the conversation between these two. He had listened in silence. It was something as exciting in a way, and even touching in its foredoomed futility, as the efforts at moral intercourse between the inhabitants of remote planets. But this grotesque incarnation of humanitarian passion appealed, somehow to one's imagination. At last Michaelis rose, and taking the great lady's extended hand, shook it, retained it for a moment in his great cushioned palm with unembarrassed friendliness, and turned upon the semi-private nook of the drawing-room his back, vast and square, and as if distended under the short tweed jacket. Glancing about in serene benevolence, he waddled along to the distant door between the knots of other visitors. The murmur of conversations paused on his passage. He smiled innocently at a tall, brilliant girl, whose eyes met his accidentally, and went out unconscious of the glances following him across the room. Michaelis' first appearance in the world was a success – a success of esteem unmarred by a single murmur of derision. The interrupted conversations were resumed in their proper tone, grave or light. Only a well-set-up, long-limbed, active-looking man of forty talking with two ladies near a window remarked aloud, with an unexpected depth of feeling: 'Eighteen stone, I should say, and not five foot six. Poor fellow! It's terrible – terrible.'

The lady of the house, gazing absently at the Assistant Commissioner, left alone with her on the private side of the screen, seemed to be re-arranging her mental impressions behind her thoughtful immobility of a handsome old face. Men with grey moustaches and full, healthy, vaguely smiling countenances approached, circling round the screen; two mature women with a matronly air of gracious resolution; a clean-shaved individual with sunken cheeks, and dangling a gold mounted eyeglass on a broad black ribbon with an old-world, dandified effect. A silence deferential, but full of reserves, reigned for a moment, and then the great lady exclaimed, not with resentment, but with a sort of protesting indignation: 'And that officially is supposed to be a revolutionist! What nonsense.' She looked hard at the Assistant Commissioner, who murmured, apologetically: 'Not a dangerous one perhaps.'

'Not dangerous – I should think not indeed. He is a mere believer. It's the temperament of a saint,' declared the great lady in a firm tone. 'And they kept him shut up for twenty years. One shudders at the stupidity of it. And now they have let him out everybody belonging to him is gone away somewhere or dead. His parents are dead; the girl he was to marry has died while he was in prison; he has lost the skill necessary for his manual occupation. He told me all this himself with the sweetest patience; but then, he said, he had had plenty of time to think out things for himself. A pretty compensation! If that's the stuff revolutionists are made of some of us may well go on their knees to them,' she continued in a slightly bantering voice, while the banal society smiles hardened on the worldly faces turned towards her with conventional deference. 'The poor creature is obviously no longer in a position to take care of himself. Somebody will have to look after him a little.'

'He should be recommended to follow a treatment of some sort,' the soldierly voice of the active-looking man was heard advising earnestly from a distance. He was in the pink of condition for his age, and even the texture of his long frock coat had a character of elastic soundness, as if it were a living tissue. 'The man is virtually a cripple,' he added with unmistakable feeling.

Other voices, as if glad of the opening, murmured hasty compassion. 'Quite startling,' 'Monstrous,' 'Most painful to see.' The lank man, with the eyeglass on a broad ribbon, pronounced mincingly the word, 'Grotesque,' whose justness was appreciated by those standing near him. They smiled at each other.

The Assistant Commissioner had expressed no opinion either then or later, his position making it impossible for him to ventilate any independent view of a ticket-of-leave convict. But, in truth, he shared the view of his wife's friend and patron that Michaelis was a humanitarian sentimentalist, a little mad, but upon the whole incapable of hurting a fly intentionally. So when that name cropped up suddenly in this vexing bomb affair he realised all the danger of it for the ticket-of-leave apostle, and his mind reverted at once to the old lady's well-established infatuation. Her arbitrary kindness would not brook patiently any interference with Michaelis' freedom. It was a deep, calm, convinced infatuation. She had not only felt him to be inoffensive, but she had said so, which last by a confusion of her absolutist mind became a sort of incontrovertible demonstration. It was as if the monstrosity of the man, with his candid infant's eyes and a fat angelic smile, had fascinated her. She had come to believe almost his theory of the future, since it was not repugnant to her prejudices. She disliked the new element of plutocracy in the social compound, and industrialism as a method of human development appeared to her singularly repulsive in its mechanical and unfeeling character. The humanitarian hopes of the mild Michaelis tended not towards utter destruction, but merely towards the complete economic ruin of the system. And she did not really see where was the moral harm of it. It would do away with all the multitude of the 'parvenus,' whom she disliked and mistrusted, not because they had arrived anywhere (she denied that), but because of their profound unintelligence of the world, which was the primary cause of the crudity of their perceptions and the aridity of their hearts. With the annihilation of all capital they would vanish, too; but universal ruin (providing it was universal, as it was revealed to Michaelis) would leave the social values untouched. The disappearance of the last piece of money could not affect people of position. She could not conceive how it could affect her position, for instance. She had developed these discoveries to the Assistant Commissioner with all the serene fearlessness of an old woman who had escaped the blight of indifference. He had made for himself the rule to receive everything of that sort in a silence which he took care from policy and inclination not to make offensive. He had an affection for the aged disciple of Michaelis, a complex sentiment depending a little on her prestige, on her personality, but most of all on the instinct of flattered gratitude. He felt himself really liked in her house. She was kindness personified. And she was practically wise, too, after the manner of experienced women. She made his married life much easier than it would have been without her generously full recognition of his rights as Annie's husband. Her influence upon his wife, a woman devoured by all sorts of small selfishnesses, small envies, small jealousies, was excellent. Unfortunately, both her kindness and her wisdom were of unreasonable complexion, distinctly feminine, and difficult to deal with. She remained a perfect woman all along her full tale of years, and not as some of them do become, a sort of slippery, pestilential old man in petticoats. And it was as of a woman that he thought of her – the specially choice incarnation of the feminine, wherein is recruited the tender, ingenuous, and fierce bodyguard for all sorts of men who talk under the influence of an emotion, true or fraudulent; for preachers, seers, prophets, or reformers.

Appreciating the distinguished and good friend of his wife, and himself, in that way, the Assistant Commissioner became alarmed at the convict Michaelis' possible fate. Once arrested on suspicion of being in some way, however remote, a party to this outrage, the man could hardly escape being sent back to finish his sentence at least. And that would kill him; he would never come out alive. The Assistant Commissioner made a reflection extremely unbecoming his official position without being really creditable to his humanity.

'If the fellow is laid hold of again,' he thought, 'she will never forgive me.'

The frankness of such a secretly outspoken thought could not go without some derisive self-criticism. No man engaged in a work he does not like can preserve many saving illusions about himself. The distaste, the absence of glamour, extend from the occupation to the personality. It is only when our appointed activities seem by a lucky accident to obey the particular earnestness of our temperament that we can taste the comfort of complete self-deception. The Assistant Commissioner did not like his work at home. The police work he had been engaged on in a distant part of the globe had the saving character of an irregular sort of warfare or at least the risk and excitement of open-air sport. His real abilities, which were mainly of an administrative order, were combined with an adventurous disposition. Chained to a desk in the thick of four millions of men, he considered himself the victim of an ironic fate; the same, no doubt, which had brought about his marriage with a woman exceptionally sensitive in the matter of colonial climate, besides other limitations testifying to the delicacy of her nature – and her tastes. Though he judged his alarm sardonically he did not dismiss the improper thought from his mind. The instinct of self-preservation was strong within him. On the contrary, he repeated it mentally with profane emphasis and a fuller precision: 'Damn it! If that infernal Heat has his way the fellow'll die in prison smothered in his fat, and she'll never forgive me.'

His black, narrow figure, with the white band of the collar under the silvery gleams on the close-cropped hair at the back of the head, remained motionless. The silence had lasted such a long time that Chief Inspector Heat ventured to clear his throat. This noise produced its effect. The zealous and intelligent officer was asked by his superior, whose back remained turned to him immovably: 'You connect Michaelis with this affair?'

Chief Inspector Heat was very positive, but cautious.

'Well, sir,' he said, 'we have enough to go upon. A man like that has no business to be at large, anyhow.'

'You will want some conclusive evidence,' came the observation in a murmur.

Chief Inspector Heat raised his eyebrows at the black, narrow back, which remained obstinately presented to his intelligence and his zeal.

'There will be no difficulty in getting up sufficient evidence against *him*,' he said, with virtuous complacency. 'You may trust me for that, sir,' he added, quite unnecessarily, out of the fullness of his heart; for it seemed to him an excellent thing to have that man in hand to be thrown down to the public should it think fit to roar with any special indignation in this case. It was impossible to say yet whether it would roar or not. That in the last instance depended, of course, on the newspaper press. But in any case, Chief Inspector Heat, purveyor of prisons by trade, and a man of legal instincts, did logically believe that incarceration was the proper fate for every declared enemy of the law. In the strength of that conviction he committed a fault of tact. He allowed himself a little conceited laugh, and repeated: 'Trust me for that, sir.'

This was too much for the forced calmness under which the Assistant Commissioner had for upwards of eighteen months concealed his irritation with the system and the subordinates of his office. A square peg forced into a round hole, he had felt like a daily outrage that long-established smooth roundness into which a man of less sharply angular shape would have fitted himself, with voluptuous acquiescence, after a shrug or two. What he resented most was just the necessity of taking so much on trust. At the little laugh of Chief Inspector Heat's he spun swiftly on his heels, as if whirled away from the window-pane by an electric shock. He caught on the latter's face not only the complacency proper to the occasion lurking under the moustache, but the vestiges of experimental watchfulness in the round eyes, which had been, no doubt, fastened on his back, and now met his glance for a second before the intent character of their stare had the time to change to a merely startled appearance.

The Assistant Commissioner of Police had really some qualifications for his post. Suddenly his suspicion was awakened. It is but fair to say that his suspicions of the police methods (unless the police happened to be a semi-military body organised by himself) was not difficult to arouse. If it ever slumbered from sheer weariness, it was but lightly; and his appreciation of Chief Inspector Heat's zeal and ability, moderate in itself, excluded all notion of moral confidence. 'He's up to something,' he exclaimed, mentally, and at once became angry. Crossing over to his desk with headlong strides, he sat down violently. 'Here I am stuck in a litter of paper,' he reflected, with unreasonable resentment, 'supposed to hold all the threads in my hands, and yet I can but hold what is put in my hand, and nothing else. And they can fasten the other ends of the threads where they please.'

He raised his head, and turned towards his subordinate a long, meagre face with the accentuated features of an energetic Don Quixote.

'Now what is it you've got up your sleeve?'

The other stared. He stared without winking in a perfect immobility of his round eyes, as he was used to stare at the various members of the criminal class when, after being duly cautioned, they made their statements in the tones of injured innocence, or false simplicity, or sullen resignation. But behind that professional and stony fixity there was some surprise, too, for in such a tone, combining nicely the note of contempt and impatience, Chief Inspector Heat, the right-hand man of the department, was not used to be addressed. He began in a procrastinating manner, like a man taken unawares by a new and unexpected experience.

'What I've got against that man Michaelis you mean, sir?'

The Assistant Commissioner watched the bullet head; the points of that Norse rover's moustache, falling below the line of the heavy jaw; the whole full and pale physiognomy, whose determined character was marred by too much flesh; at the cunning wrinkles radiating from the outer corners of the eyes – and in that purposeful contemplation of the valuable and trusted officer he drew a conviction so sudden that it moved him like an inspiration.

'I have reason to think that when you came into this room,' he said in measured tones, 'it was not Michaelis who was in your mind; not principally – perhaps not at all.'

'You have reason to think, sir?' muttered Chief Inspector Heat, with every appearance of astonishment, which up to a certain point was genuine enough. He had discovered in this affair a delicate and perplexing side, forcing upon the discoverer a certain amount of insincerity – that sort of insincerity which, under the names of skill, prudence, discretion, turns up at one point or another in most human affairs. He felt at the moment like a tight-rope artist might feel if suddenly, in the middle of the performance, the manager of the Music Hall were to rush out of the proper managerial seclusion and begin to shake the rope. Indignation, the sense of moral insecurity engendered by such a treacherous proceeding joined to the immediate apprehension of a broken neck, would, in the colloquial phrase, put him in a state. And there would be also some scandalised concern for his art, too, since a man must identify himself with something more tangible than his own personality, and establish his pride somewhere, either in his social position, or in the quality of the work he is obliged to do, or simply in the superiority of the idleness he may be fortunate enough to enjoy.

'Yes,' said the Assistant Commissioner; 'I have. I do not mean to say that you have not thought of Michaelis at all. But you are giving the fact you've mentioned a prominence which strikes me as not quite candid, Inspector Heat. If that is really the track of discovery, why haven't you followed it up at once, either personally or by sending one of your men to that village? '

'Do you think, sir, I have failed in my duty there?' the Chief Inspector asked, in a tone which he sought to make simply reflective. Forced unexpectedly to concentrate his faculties upon the task of preserving his balance, he had seized upon that point, and exposed himself to a rebuke; for the Assistant Commissioner, frowning slightly, observed that this was a very improper remark to make.

'But since you've made it,' he continued, coldly, 'I'll tell you that this is not my meaning.'

He paused, with a straight glance of his sunken eyes which was a full equivalent of the unspoken termination 'and you know it.' The head of the so-called Special Crimes Department, debarred by his position from going out of doors personally in quest of secrets locked up in guilty breasts, had a propensity to exercise his considerable gifts for the detection of incriminating truth upon his own subordinates. That peculiar instinct could hardly be called a weakness. It was natural. He was a born detective. It had unconsciously governed his choice of a career, and if it ever failed him in life it was perhaps in the one exceptional circumstance of his marriage, which was also natural. It fed, since it could not roam abroad upon the human material which was brought to it in its official seclusion. We can never cease to be ourselves.

His elbow on the desk, his thin legs crossed and nursing his cheek in the palm of his meagre hand, the Assistant Commissioner in charge of the Special Crimes branch was getting hold of the case with growing interest. His Chief Inspector, if not an absolutely worthy foeman of his penetration, was at any rate the most worthy of all within his reach. A mistrust of established reputations was strictly in character with the Assistant Commissioner's ability as detector. His memory evoked a certain old fat and wealthy native chief in the distant colony whom it was a tradition for the successive Colonial Governors to trust and make much of as a firm friend and supporter of the order and legality established by white men; whereas, when examined sceptically, he was found out to be principally his own good friend, and nobody else's. Not precisely a traitor, but still a man of many dangerous reservations in his fidelity, caused by a due regard for his own advantage, comfort, and safety. A fellow of some innocence in his naïve duplicity, but none the less dangerous. He took some finding out. He was physically a big man, too, and (allowing for the difference of colour, of course) Chief Inspector Heat's appearance recalled him to the memory of his superior. It was not the eyes nor yet the lips exactly. It was bizarre. But does not Alfred Wallace relate in his famous book on the Malay Archipelago how, amongst the Aru Islanders, he discovered in an old and naked savage with a sooty skin a peculiar resemblance to a dear friend at home?

For the first time since he took up his appointment the Assistant Commissioner felt as if he were going to do some real work for his salary. And that was a pleasurable sensation. 'I'll turn him inside out like an old glove,' thought the Assistant Commissioner, with his eyes resting pensively upon Chief Inspector Heat.

'No, that was not my thought,' he began again. 'There is no doubt about you knowing your business no doubt at all; and that is precisely why I – ' He stopped short, and changing his tone: 'What could you bring up against

Michaelis of a definite nature? I mean apart from the fact that the two men under suspicion – you're certain there were two of them – came last from a railway station within three miles of the village where Michaelis is living now.'

'This by itself is enough for us to go upon, sir, with that sort of man,' said the Chief Inspector, with returning composure. The slight, approving movement of the Assistant Commissioner's head went far to pacify the resentful astonishment of the renowned officer. For Chief Inspector Heat was a kind man, an excellent husband, a devoted father; and the public and departmental confidence he enjoyed acting favourably upon an amiable nature, disposed him to feel friendly towards the successive Assistant Commissioners he had seen pass through that very room. There had been three in his time. The first one, a soldierly, abrupt, red-faced person, with white eyebrows and an explosive temper, could be managed with a silken thread. He left on reaching the age limit. The second, a perfect gentleman, knowing his own and everybody else's place to a nicety, on resigning to take up a higher appointment out of England got decorated for (really) Inspector Heat's services. To work with him had been a pride and a pleasure. The third, a bit of a dark horse from the first, was at the end of eighteen months something of a dark horse still to the department. Upon the whole Chief Inspector Heat believed him to be in the main harmless – odd-looking, but harmless. He was speaking now, and the Chief Inspector listened with outward deference (which means nothing, being a matter of duty) and inwardly with benevolent toleration.

'Michaelis reported himself before leaving London for the country?'

'Yes, sir. He did.'

'And what may he be doing there?' continued the Assistant Commissioner, who was perfectly informed on that point. Fitted with painful tightness into an old wooden armchair, before a worm-eaten oak table in an upstairs room of a four-roomed cottage with a roof of moss-grown tiles, Michaelis was writing night and day in a shaky, slanting hand that 'Autobiography of a Prisoner' which was to be like a book of Revelation in the history of mankind. The conditions of confined space, seclusion, and solitude in a small four-roomed cottage were favourable to his inspiration. It was like being in prison, except that one was never disturbed for the odious purpose of taking exercise according to the tyrannical regulations of his old home in the penitentiary. He could not tell whether the sun still shone on the earth or not. The perspiration of the literary labour dropped from his brow. A delightful enthusiasm urged him on. It was the liberation of his inner life, the letting out of his soul into the wide world. And the zeal of his guileless vanity (first awakened by the offer of five hundred pounds from a publisher) seemed something predestined and holy.

'It would be, of course, most desirable to be informed exactly,' insisted the Assistant Commissioner uncandidly.

Chief Inspector Heat, conscious of renewed irritation at this display of scrupulousness, said that the county police had been notified from the first of Michaelis' arrival, and that a full report could be obtained in a few hours. A wire to the superintendent . . .

Thus he spoke, rather slowly, while his mind seemed already to be weighing the consequences. A slight knitting of the brow was the outward sign of this. But he was interrupted by a question.

'You've sent that wire already?'

'No, sir,' he answered, as if surprised.

The Assistant Commissioner uncrossed his legs suddenly. The briskness of that movement contrasted with the casual way in which he threw out a suggestion.

'Would you think that Michaelis had anything to do with the preparation of that bomb, for instance?'

The Chief Inspector assumed a reflective manner.

'I wouldn't say so. There's no necessity to say anything at present. He associates with men who are classed as dangerous. He was made a delegate of the Red Committee less than a year after his release on licence. A sort of compliment, I suppose.'

And the Chief Inspector laughed a little angrily, a little scornfully. With a man of that sort scrupulousness was a misplaced and even an illegal sentiment. The celebrity bestowed upon Michaelis on his release two years ago by some emotional journalists in want of special copy had rankled ever since in his breast. It was perfectly legal to arrest that man on the barest suspicion. It was legal and expedient on the face of it. His two former chiefs would have seen the point at once; whereas this one, without saying either yes or no, sat there, as if lost in a dream. Moreover, besides being legal and expedient, the arrest of Michaelis solved a little personal difficulty which worried Chief Inspector Heat somewhat. This difficulty had its bearing upon his reputation, upon his comfort, and even upon the efficient performance of his duties. For, if Michaelis no doubt knew something about this outrage, the Chief Inspector was fairly certain that he did not know too much. This was just as well. He knew much less – the Chief Inspector was positive – than certain other individuals he had in his mind, but whose arrest seemed to him inexpedient, besides being a more complicated matter, on account of the rules of the game. The rules of the game did not protect so much Michaelis, who was an ex-convict. It would be stupid not to take advantage of legal facilities, and the journalists who had written him up with emotional gush would be ready to write him down with emotional indignation.

This prospect, viewed with confidence, had the attraction of a personal triumph for Chief Inspector Heat. And deep down in his blameless bosom of an average married citizen, almost unconscious but potent nevertheless, the dislike of being compelled by events to meddle with the desperate ferocity of the Professor had its say. This dislike had been strengthened by the chance meeting in the lane. The encounter did not leave behind with Chief Inspector

Heat that satisfactory sense of superiority the members of the police force get from the unofficial but intimate side of their intercourse with the criminal classes, by which the vanity of power is soothed, and the vulgar love of domination over our fellow-creatures is flattered as worthily as it deserves.

The perfect anarchist was not recognised as a fellow-creature by Chief Inspector Heat. He was impossible – a mad dog to be left alone. Not that the Chief Inspector was afraid of him; on the contrary, he meant to have him someday. But not yet: he meant to get hold of him in his own time, properly and effectively, according to the rules of the game. The present was not the right time for attempting that feat, not the right time for many reasons, personal and of public service. This being the strong feeling of Inspector Heat, it appeared to him just and proper that this affair should be shunted off its obscure and inconvenient track, leading goodness knows where, into a quiet (and lawful) siding called Michaelis. And he repeated, as if reconsidering the suggestion conscientiously: 'The bomb. No, I would not say that exactly. We may never find that out. But it's clear that he is connected with this in some way, which we can find out without much trouble.'

His countenance had that look of grave, overbearing indifference once well known and much dreaded by the better sort of thieves. Chief Inspector Heat, though what is called a man, was not a smiling animal. But his inward state was that of satisfaction at the passively receptive attitude of the Assistant Commissioner, who murmured gently: 'And you really think that the investigation should be made in that direction?'

'I do, sir.'

'Quite convinced?

'I am, sir. That's the true line for us to take.'

The Assistant Commissioner withdrew the support of his hand from his reclining head with a suddenness that, considering his languid attitude, seemed to menace his whole person with collapse. But, on the contrary, he sat up, extremely alert, behind the great writing-table on which his hand had fallen with the sound of a sharp blow.

'What I want to know is what put it out of your head till now.'

'Put it out of my head,' repeated the Chief Inspector very slowly.

'Yes. Till you were called into this room – you know.'

The Chief Inspector felt as if the air between his clothing and his skin had become unpleasantly hot. It was the sensation of an unprecedented and incredible experience.

'Of course,' he said, exaggerating the deliberation of his utterance to the utmost limits of possibility, 'if there is a reason, of which I know nothing, for not interfering with the convict Michaelis, perhaps it's just as well I didn't start the county police after him.'

This took such a long time to say that the unflagging attention of the Assistant Commissioner seemed a wonderful feat of endurance. His retort came without delay.

'No reason whatever that I know of. Come, Chief Inspector, this finessing with me is highly improper on your part – highly improper. And it's also unfair, you know. You shouldn't leave me to puzzle things out for myself like this. Really, I am surprised.'

He paused, then added smoothly: 'I need scarcely tell you that this conversation is altogether unofficial.'

These words were far from pacifying the Chief Inspector. The indignation of a betrayed tight-rope performer was strong within him. In his pride of a trusted servant he was affected by the assurance that the rope was not shaken for the purpose of breaking his neck, as by an exhibition of impudence. As if anybody were afraid! Assistant Commissioners come and go, but a valuable Chief Inspector is not an ephemeral office phenomenon. He was not afraid of getting a broken neck. To have his performance spoiled was more than enough to account for the glow of honest indignation. And as thought is no respecter of persons, the thought of Chief Inspector Heat took a threatening and prophetic shape. 'You, my boy,' he said to himself, keeping his round and habitually roving eyes fastened upon the Assistant Commissioner's face – 'you, my boy, you don't know your place, and your place won't know you very long either, I bet.'

As if in provoking answer to that thought, something like the ghost of an amiable smile passed on the lips of the Assistant Commissioner. His manner was easy and businesslike while he persisted in administering another shake to the tight rope.

'Let us come now to what you have discovered on the spot, Chief Inspector,' he said.

'A fool and his job are soon parted,' went on the train of prophetic thought in Chief Inspector Heat's head. But it was immediately followed by the reflection that a higher official, even when 'fired out' (this was the precise image), has still the time as he flies through the door to launch a nasty kick at the shinbones of a subordinate. Without softening very much the basilisk nature of his stare, he said, impassively: 'We are coming to that part of my investigation, sir,'

'That's right. Well, what have you brought away from it?'

The Chief Inspector, who had made up his mind to jump off the rope, came to the ground with gloomy frankness.

'I've brought away an address,' he said, pulling out of his pocket without haste a singed rag of dark blue cloth. 'This belongs to the overcoat the fellow who got himself blown to pieces was wearing. Of course, the overcoat may not have been his, and may even have been stolen. But that's not at all probable if you look at this.'

The Chief Inspector, stepping up to the table, smoothed out carefully the rag of blue cloth. He had picked it up from the repulsive heap in the mortuary, because a tailor's name is found sometimes under the collar. It is not often of much use, but still . . . He only half expected to find anything useful, but certainly he did not expect to find – not under the collar at all, but stitched carefully on the under side of the lapel – a square piece of calico with an address written on it in marking ink.

The Chief Inspector removed his smoothing hand.

'I carried it off with me without anybody taking notice,' he said. 'I thought it best. It can always be produced if required.'

The Assistant Commissioner, rising a little in his chair, pulled the cloth over to his side of the table. He sat looking at it in silence. Only the number 32 and the name of Brett Street were written in marking ink on a piece of calico slightly larger than an ordinary cigarette paper. He was genuinely surprised.

'Can't understand why he should have gone about labelled like this,' he said, looking up at Chief Inspector Heat. 'It's a most extraordinary thing.'

'I met once in the smoking-room of a hotel an old gentleman who went about with his name and address sewn on in all his coats in case of an accident or sudden illness,' said the Chief Inspector. 'He professed to be eighty-four years old, but he didn't look his age. He told me he was also afraid of losing his memory suddenly, like those people he had been reading of in the papers.'

A question from the Assistant Commissioner, who wanted to know what was No. 32 Brett Street, interrupted that reminiscence abruptly. The Chief Inspector, driven down to the ground by unfair artifices, had elected to walk the path of unreserved openness. If he believed firmly that to know too much was not good for the department, the judicious holding back of knowledge was as far as his loyalty dared to go for the good of the service. If the Assistant Commissioner wanted to mismanage this affair nothing, of course, could prevent him. But, on his own part, he now saw no reason for a display of alacrity. So he answered concisely: 'It's a shop, sir.'

The Assistant Commissioner, with his eyes lowered on the rag of blue cloth, waited for more information. As that did not come he proceeded to obtain it by a series of questions propounded with gentle patience. Thus he acquired an idea of the nature of Mr Verloc's commerce, of his personal appearance, and heard at last his name. In a pause the Assistant Commissioner raised his eyes, and discovered some animation on the Chief Inspector's face. They looked at each other in silence.

'Of course,' said the latter, 'the department has no record of that man.'

'Did any of my predecessors have any knowledge of what you have told me now?' asked the Assistant Commissioner, putting his elbows on the table and raising his joined hands before his face, as if about to offer prayer, only that his eyes had not a pious expression.

'No, sir; certainly not. What would have been the object? That sort of man could never be produced publicly to any good purpose. It was sufficient for me to know who he was, and to make use of him in a way that could be used publicly.'

'And do you think that sort of private knowledge consistent with the official position you occupy?'

'Perfectly, sir. I think it's quite proper. I will take the liberty to tell you, sir, that it makes me what I am – and I am looked upon as a man who knows his work. It's a private affair of my own. A personal friend of mine in the French police gave me the hint that the fellow was an Embassy spy. Private friendship, private information, private use of it – that's how I look upon it.'

The Assistant Commissioner, after remarking to himself that the mental state of the renowned Chief Inspector seemed to affect the outline of his lower jaw, as if the lively sense of his high professional distinction had been located in that part of his anatomy, dismissed the point for the moment with a calm 'I see.' Then leaning his cheek on his joined hands: 'Well, then – speaking privately if you like how long have you been in private touch with this Embassy spy?'

To this enquiry the private answer of the Chief Inspector, so private that it was never shaped into audible words, was: 'Long before you were even thought of for your place here.'

The so-to-speak public utterance was much more precise.

'I saw him for the first time in my life a little more than seven years ago, when two Imperial Highnesses and the Imperial Chancellor were on a visit here. I was put in charge of all the arrangements for looking after them. Baron Stott-Wartenheim was Ambassador then. He was a very nervous old gentleman. One evening, three days before the Guildhall Banquet, he sent word that he wanted to see me for a moment. I was downstairs, and the carriages were at the door to take the Imperial Highnesses and the Chancellor to the opera. I went up at once. I found the Baron walking up and down his bedroom in a pitiable state of distress, squeezing his hands together. He assured me he had the fullest confidence in our police and in my abilities, but he had there a man just come over from Paris whose information could be trusted implicitly. He wanted me to hear what that man had to say. He took me at once into a dressing-room next door, where I saw a big fellow in a heavy overcoat sitting all alone on a chair, and holding his hat and stick in one hand. The Baron said to him in French 'Speak, my friend.' The light in that room was not very good. I talked with him for some five minutes perhaps. He certainly gave me a piece of very startling news. Then the Baron took me aside nervously to praise him up to me, and when I turned round again I discovered that the fellow had vanished like a ghost. Got up and sneaked out down some back stairs, I suppose. There was no time to run after him, as I had to hurry off after the Ambassador down the great staircase, and see the party started safe for the opera. However, I acted upon the information that very night. Whether it was perfectly correct or not, it did look serious enough. Very likely it saved us from an ugly trouble on the day of the Imperial visit to the City.

'Sometime later, a month or so after my promotion to Chief Inspector, my attention was attracted to a big burly man, I thought I had seen somewhere before, coming out in a hurry from a jeweller's shop in the Strand. I went after him, as it was on my way towards Charing Cross, and there seeing one of our detectives across the road, I beckoned him over, and pointed out the fellow to him, with instructions to watch his movements for a couple of days, and then report to me. No later than next afternoon my man turned up to tell mc that the fellow had married his landlady's daughter at a registrar's office that very day at 11.30 a.m., and had gone off with her to Margate for a week. Our man had seen the luggage being put on the cab. There were some old Paris labels on one of the bags. Somehow I couldn't get the fellow out of my head, and the very next time I had to go to Paris on service I spoke about him to that friend of mine in the Paris police. My friend said: 'From what you tell me I think you must mean a rather well-known hanger-on and emissary of the Revolutionary Red Committee. He says he is an Englishman by birth. We have an idea that he has been for a good few years now a secret agent of one of the foreign Embassies in London.' This woke up my memory completely. He was the vanishing fellow I saw sitting on a chair in Baron Stott-Wartenheim's bathroom. I told my friend that he was quite right. The fellow was a secret agent to my certain knowledge. Afterwards my friend took the trouble to ferret out the complete record of that man for me. I thought I had better know all there was to know; but I don't suppose you want to hear his history now, sir?'

The Assistant Commissioner shook his supported head. 'The history of your relations with that useful personage is the only thing that matters just now,' he said, closing slowly his weary, deep-set eyes, and then opening them swiftly with a greatly refreshed glance.

'There's nothing official about them,' said the Chief Inspector, bitterly. 'I went into his shop one evening, told him who I was, and reminded him of our first meeting. He didn't as much as twitch an eyebrow. He said that he was married and settled now, and that all he wanted was not to be interfered in his little business. I took it upon myself to promise him that, as long as he didn't go in for anything obviously outrageous, he would be left alone by the police. That was worth something to him, because a word from us to the Custom-House people would have been enough to get some of these packages he gets from Paris and Brussels opened in Dover, with confiscation to follow for certain, and perhaps a prosecution as well at the end of it.'

'That's a very precarious trade,' murmured the Assistant Commissioner. 'Why did he go in for that?'

The Chief Inspector raised scornful eyebrows dispassionately.

'Most likely got a connection – friends on the Continent – amongst people who deal in such wares. They would be just the sort he would consort with. He's a lazy dog, too – like the rest of them.'

'What do you get from him in exchange for your protection?'

The Chief Inspector was not inclined to enlarge on the value of Mr Verloc's services.

'He would not be much good to anybody but myself. One has got to know a good deal beforehand to make use of a man like that. I can understand the sort of hint he can give. And when I want a hint he can generally furnish it to me.'

The Chief Inspector lost himself suddenly in a discreet reflective mood; and the Assistant Commissioner repressed a smile at the fleeting thought that the reputation of Chief Inspector Heat might possibly have been made in a great part by the Secret Agent Verloc.

'In a more general way of being of use, all our men of the Special Crimes section on duty at Charing Cross and Victoria have orders to take careful notice of anybody they may see with him. He meets the new arrivals frequently and afterwards keeps track of them. He seems to have been told off for that sort of duty. When I want an address in a hurry, I can always get it from him. Of course, I know how to manage our relations. I haven't seen him to speak to three times in the last two years. I drop him a line, unsigned, and he answers me in the same way at my private address.'

From time to time the Assistant Commissioner gave an almost imperceptible nod. The Chief Inspector added that he did not suppose Mr Verloc to be deep in the confidence of the prominent members of the Revolutionary International Council, but that he was generally trusted, of that there could be no doubt. 'Whenever I've had reason to think there was something in the wind,' he concluded, 'I've always found he could tell me something worth knowing.'

The Assistant Commissioner made a significant remark.

'He failed you this time.'

'Neither had I wind of anything in any other way,' retorted Chief Inspector Heat. 'I asked him nothing so he could tell me nothing. He isn't one of our men. It isn't as if he were in our pay.'

'No,' muttered the Assistant Commissioner. 'He's a spy in the pay of a foreign government. We could never confess to him.'

'I must do my work in my own way,' declared the Chief Inspector. 'When it comes to that I would deal with the devil himself, and take the consequences. There are things not fit for everybody to know.'

'Your idea of secrecy seems to consist in keeping the chief of your department in the dark. That's stretching it perhaps a little too far, isn't it? He lives over his shop?'

'Who – Verloc? Oh, yes. He lives over his shop. The wife's mother, I fancy, lives with them.'

'Is the house watched?'

'Oh, dear, no. It wouldn't do. Certain people who come there are watched. My opinion is that he knows nothing of this affair.'

'How do you account for this?' The Assistant Commissioner nodded at the cloth rag lying before him on the table.

'I don't account for it at all, sir. It's simply unaccountable. It can't be explained by what I know.' The Chief Inspector made those admissions with the frankness of a man whose reputation is established as if on a rock. 'At any rate not at this present moment. I think that the man who had most to do with it will turn out to be Michaelis.'

'You do?'

'Yes, sir; because I can answer for all the others.'

'What about that other man supposed to have escaped from the park?'

'I should think he's far away by this time,' opined the Chief Inspector.

The Assistant Commissioner looked hard at him, and rose suddenly, as though having made up his mind to some course of action. As a matter of fact, he had that very moment succumbed to a fascinating temptation. The Chief Inspector heard himself dismissed with instructions to meet his superior early next morning for further consultation upon the case. He listened with an impenetrable face, and walked out of the room with measured steps.

Whatever might have been the plans of the Assistant Commissioner they had nothing to do with that desk work, which was the bane of his existence because of its confined nature and apparent lack of reality. It could not have had, or else the general air of alacrity that came upon the Assistant Commissioner would have been inexplicable. As soon as he was left alone he looked for his hat impulsively, and put it on his head. Having done that, he sat down again to reconsider the whole matter. But as his mind was already made up, this did not take long. And before Chief Inspector Heat had gone very far on the way home, he also left the building.

Chapter 7

The Assistant Commissioner walked along a short and narrow street like a wet, muddy trench, then crossing a very broad thoroughfare entered a public edifice, and sought speech with a young private secretary (unpaid) of a great personage.

This fair, smooth-faced young man, whose symmetrically arranged hair gave him the air of a large and neat schoolboy, met the Assistant Commissioner's request with a doubtful look, and spoke with bated breath.

'Would he see you? I don't know about that. He has walked over from the House an hour ago to talk with the permanent Under-Secretary, and now he's ready to walk back again. He might have sent for him; but he does it for the sake of a little exercise, I suppose. It's all the exercise he can find time for while this session lasts. I don't complain; I rather enjoy these little strolls.

He leans on my arm, and doesn't open his lips. But, I say, he's very tired, and – well – not in the sweetest of tempers just now.'

'It's in connection with that Greenwich affair.'

'Oh! I say! He's very bitter against you people. But I will go and see, if you insist.'

'Do. That's a good fellow,' said the Assistant Commissioner.

The unpaid secretary admired this pluck. Composing for himself an innocent face, he opened a door, and went in with the assurance of a nice and privileged child. And presently he reappeared, with a nod to the Assistant Commissioner, who passing through the same door left open for him, found himself with the great personage in a large room.

Vast in bulk and stature, with a long white face, which, broadened at the base by a big double chin, appeared egg-shaped in the fringe of thin greyish whisker, the great personage seemed an expanding man. Unfortunate from a tailoring point of view, the crossfolds in the middle of a buttoned black coat added to the impression, as if the fastenings of the garment were tried to the utmost. From the head, set upward on a thick neck, the eyes, with puffy lower lids, stared with a haughty droop on each side of a hooked, aggressive nose, nobly salient in the vast pale circumference of the face. A shiny silk hat and a pair of worn gloves lying ready on the end of a long table looked expanded, too, enormous.

He stood on the hearthrug in big, roomy boots, and uttered no word of greeting.

'I would like to know if this is the beginning of another dynamite campaign,' he asked at once in a deep, very smooth voice. 'Don't go into details. I have no time for that.'

The Assistant Commissioner's figure before this big and rustic Presence had the frail slenderness of a reed addressing an oak. And indeed the unbroken record of that man's descent surpassed in the number of centuries the age of the oldest oak in the country.

'No. As far as one can be positive about anything I can assure you that it is not.'

'Yes. But your idea of assurances over there,' said the great man, with a contemptuous wave of his hand towards a window giving on the broad thoroughfare, 'seems to consist mainly in making the Secretary of State look a fool. I have been told positively in this very room less than a month ago that nothing of the sort was even possible.'

The Assistant Commissioner glanced in the direction of the window calmly.

'You will allow me to remark, Sir Ethelred, that so far I have had no opportunity to give you assurances of any kind.'

The haughty droop of the eyes was focused now upon the Assistant Commissioner.

'True,' confessed the deep, smooth voice. 'I sent for Heat. You are still rather a novice in your new berth. And how are you getting on over there?'

'I believe I am learning something every day.'

'Of course, of course. I hope you will get on.'

'Thank you, Sir Ethelred. I've learned something today, and even within the last hour or so. There is much in this affair of a kind that does not meet the eye in a usual anarchist outrage, even if one looked into it as deep as can be. That's why I am here.'

The great man put his arms akimbo, the backs of his big hands resting on his hips.

'Very well. Go on. Only no details, pray. Spare me the details.'

'You shall not be troubled with them, Sir Ethelred,' the Assistant Commissioner began, with a calm and untroubled assurance. While he was speaking the hands on the face of the clock behind the great man's back – a heavy, glistening affair of massive scrolls in the same dark marble as the mantelpiece, and with a ghostly, evanescent tick – had moved through the space of seven minutes. He spoke with a studious fidelity to a parenthetical manner, into which every little fact – that is, every detail – fitted with delightful ease. Not a murmur nor even a movement hinted at interruption. The great Personage might have been the statue of one of his own princely ancestors stripped of a crusader's war harness, and put into an ill-fitting frock coat. The Assistant Commissioner felt as though he were at liberty to talk for an hour. But he kept his head, and at the end of the time mentioned above he broke off with a sudden conclusion, which, reproducing the opening statement, pleasantly surprised Sir Ethelred by its apparent swiftness and force.

'The kind of thing which meets us under the surface of this affair, otherwise without gravity, is unusual – in this precise form at least – and requires special treatment.'

The tone of Sir Ethelred was deepened, full of conviction.

'I should think so – involving the Ambassador of a foreign power!'

'Oh! The Ambassador!' protested the other, erect and slender, allowing himself a mere half smile. 'It would be stupid of me to advance anything of the kind. And it is absolutely unnecessary, because if I am right in my surmises, whether ambassador or hall porter it's a mere detail.'

Sir Ethelred opened a wide mouth, like a cavern, into which the hooked nose seemed anxious to peer; there came from it a subdued rolling sound, as from a distant organ with the scornful indignation stop.

'No! These people are too impossible. What do they mean by importing their methods of Crim-Tartary here? A Turk would have more decency.'

'You forget, Sir Ethelred, that strictly speaking we know nothing positively – as yet.'

'No! But how would you define it? Shortly?'

'Barefaced audacity amounting to childishness of a peculiar sort.'

'We can't put up with the innocence of nasty little children,' said the great and expanded personage, expanding a little more, as it were. The haughty, drooping glance struck crushingly the carpet at the Assistant Commissioner's feet. 'They'll have to get a hard rap on the knuckles over this affair. We must be in a position to . . . What is your general idea, stated shortly? No need to go into details.'

'No, Sir Ethelred. In principle, I should lay it down that the existence of secret agents should not be tolerated, as tending to augment the positive dangers of the evil against which they are used. That the spy will fabricate his information is a mere commonplace. But in the sphere of political and revolutionary action, relying partly on violence, the professional spy has every facility to fabricate the very facts themselves, and will spread the double evil of emulation in one direction, and of panic, hasty legislation, unreflecting hate, on the other. However, this is an imperfect world . . . '

The deep-voiced Presence on the hearthrug, motionless, with big elbows stuck out, said hastily: 'Be lucid, please.'

'Yes, Sir Ethelred . . . An imperfect world. Therefore directly the character of this affair suggested itself to me, I thought it should be dealt with with special secrecy, and ventured to come over here.'

'That's right,' approved the great Personage, glancing down complacently over his double chin. 'I am glad there's somebody over at your shop who thinks that the Secretary of State may be trusted now and then.'

The Assistant Commissioner had an amused smile. 'I was really thinking that it might be better at this stage for Heat to be replaced by . . . '

'What! Heat? An ass – eh?' exclaimed the great man, with distinct animosity.

'Not at all. Pray, Sir Ethelred, don't put that unjust interpretation on my remarks.'

'Then what? Too clever by half?'

'Neither – at least not as a rule. All the grounds of my surmises I have from him. The only thing I've discovered by myself is that he has been making use of that man privately. Who could blame him? He's an old police hand. He told me virtually that he must have tools to work with. It occurred to me that this tool should be surrendered to the Special Crimes division as a whole, instead of remaining the private property of Chief Inspector Heat. I extended my conception of our departmental duties to the suppression of the secret agent. But Chief Inspector Heat is an old departmental hand. He would accuse me of perverting its morality and attacking its efficiency. He would define it bitterly as protection extended to the criminal class of revolutionists. It would mean just that to him.'

'Yes. But what do you mean?'

'I mean to say, first, that there's but poor comfort in being able to declare that any given act of violence damaging property or destroying life – is not the work of anarchism at all, but of something else altogether – some species of authorised scoundrelism. This, I fancy, is much more frequent than we suppose. Next, it's obvious that the existence of these people in the pay of foreign governments destroys in a measure the efficiency of our supervision. A spy of that sort can afford to be more reckless than the most reckless of conspirators. His occupation is free from all restraint. He's without as much faith as is necessary for complete negation, and without that much law as is implied in lawlessness. Thirdly, the existence of these spies amongst the revolutionary groups, which we are reproached for harbouring here, does away with all certitude. You have received a reassuring statement from Chief Inspector Heat some time ago. It was by no means groundless – and yet this episode happens. I call it an episode, because this affair, I make bold to say, is episodic; it is no part of any general scheme, however wild. The very peculiarities which surprise and perplex Chief Inspector Heat establish its character in my eyes. I am keeping clear of details, Sir Ethelred.'

The Personage on the hearthrug had been listening with profound attention.

'Just so. Be as concise as you can.'

The Assistant Commissioner intimated by an earnest, deferential gesture that he was anxious to be concise.

'There is a peculiar stupidity and feebleness in the conduct of this affair which gives me excellent hopes of getting behind it and finding there something else than an individual freak of fanaticism. For it is a planned thing, undoubtedly. The actual perpetrator seems to have been led by the hand to the spot, and then abandoned hurriedly to his own devices. The inference is that he was imported from abroad for the purpose of committing this outrage. At the same time one is forced to the conclusion that he did not know enough English to ask his way, unless one were to accept the fantastic theory that he was a deaf mute. I wonder now . . . But this is idle. He has destroyed himself by an accident, obviously. Not an extraordinary accident. But an extraordinary little fact remains: the address on his clothing discovered by the merest accident, too. It is an incredible little fact, so incredible that the explanation which will account for it is bound to touch the bottom of this affair. Instead of instructing Heat to go on with this case, my intention is to seek this explanation personally – by myself, I mean – where it may be picked up. That is in a certain shop in Brett Street, and on the lips of a certain secret agent once upon a time the confidential and trusted spy of the late Baron Stott-Wartenheim, Ambassador of a Great Power to the Court of St James.'

The Assistant Commissioner paused, then added: 'Those fellows are a perfect pest.' In order to raise his drooping glance to the speaker's face, the Personage on the hearthrug had gradually tilted his head farther back, which gave him an aspect of extraordinary haughtiness.

'Why not leave it to Heat?'

'Because he is an old departmental hand. They have their own morality. My line of enquiry would appear to him an awful perversion of duty. For him the plain duty is to fasten the guilt upon as many prominent anarchists as he can on some slight indications he had picked up in the course of his investigation on the spot; whereas I, he would say, am bent upon vindicating their innocence. I am trying to be as lucid as I can in presenting this obscure matter to you without details.'

'He would, would he?' muttered the proud head of Sir Ethelred from its lofty elevation.

'I am afraid so – with an indignation and disgust of which you or I can have no idea. He's an excellent servant. We must not put an undue strain on his loyalty. That's always a mistake. Besides, I want a free hand – a freer hand than it would be perhaps advisable to give Chief Inspector Heat. I haven't the slightest wish to spare this man Verloc. He will, I imagine, be extremely startled to find his connection with this affair, whatever it may be, brought home to him so quickly. Frightening him will not be very difficult. But our true objective lies behind him somewhere. I want your authority to give him such assurances of personal safety as I may think proper.'

'Certainly,' said the Personage on the hearthrug. 'Find out as much as you can; find it out in your own way.'

'I must set about it without loss of time, this very evening,' said the Assistant Commissioner.

Sir Ethelred shifted one hand under his coat tails, and tilting back his head, looked at him steadily.

'We'll have a late sitting tonight,' he said. 'Come to the House with your discoveries if we are not gone home. I'll warn Toodles to look out for you. He'll take you into my room.'

The numerous family and the wide connections of the youthful-looking Private Secretary cherished for him the hope of an austere and exalted destiny. Meantime, the social sphere he adorned in his hours of idleness chose to pet him under the above nickname. And Sir Ethelred, hearing it on the lips of his wife and girls every day (mostly at breakfast-time), had conferred upon it the dignity of unsmiling adoption.

The Assistant Commissioner was surprised and gratified extremely.

'I shall certainly bring my discoveries to the House on the chance of you having the time to . . . '

'I won't have the time,' interrupted the great Personage. 'But I will see you. I haven't the time now. And you are going yourself?'

'Yes, Sir Ethelred. I think it the best way.'

The Personage had tilted his head so far back that, in order to keep the Assistant Commissioner under his observation, he had to nearly close his eyes.

'H'm. Ha! And how do you propose . . . Will you assume a disguise?'

'Hardly a disguise! I'll change my clothes, of course.'

'Of course,' repeated the great man, with a sort of absent-minded loftiness. He turned his big head slowly, and over his shoulder gave a haughty, oblique stare to the ponderous marble timepiece with the sly, feeble tick. The gilt hands had taken the opportunity to steal through no less than five and twenty minutes behind his back.

The Assistant Commissioner, who could not see them, grew a little nervous in the interval. But the great man presented to him a calm and undismayed face.

'Very well,' he said, and paused, as if in deliberate contempt of the official clock. 'But what first put you in motion in this direction?'

'I have been always of opinion,' began the Assistant Commissioner.

'Ah. Yes! Opinion. That's of course. But the immediate motive?'

'What shall I say, Sir Ethelred? A new man's antagonism to old methods. A desire to know something at first hand. Some impatience. It's my old work, but the harness is different. It has been chafing me a little in one or two tender places.'

'I hope you'll get on over there,' said the great man, kindly, extending his hand, soft to the touch, but broad and powerful like the hand of a glorified farmer. The Assistant Commissioner shook it, and withdrew.

In the outer room Toodles, who had been waiting perched on the edge of a table, advanced to meet him, subduing his natural buoyancy.

'Well? Satisfactory?' he asked, with airy importance.

'Perfectly. You've earned my undying gratitude,' answered the Assistant Commissioner, whose long face looked wooden in contrast with the peculiar character of the other's gravity, which seemed perpetually ready to break into ripples and chuckles.

'That's all right. But, seriously, you can't imagine how irritated he is by the attacks on his Bill for the Nationalisation of Fisheries. They call it the beginning of social revolution. Of course, it is a revolutionary measure. But these fellows have no decency. The personal attacks.'

'I read the papers,' remarked the Assistant Commissioner.

'Odious? Eh? And you have no notion what a mass of work he has got to get through every day. He does it all himself. Seems unable to trust anyone with these Fisheries.'

'And yet he's given a whole half hour to the consideration of my very small sprat,' interjected the Assistant Commissioner.

'Small! Is it? I'm glad to hear that. But it's a pity you didn't keep away, then. This fight takes it out of him frightfully. The man's getting exhausted. I feel it by the way he leans on my arm as we walk over. And, I say, is he safe in the streets? Mullins has been marching his men up here this afternoon. There's a constable stuck by every lamp-post, and every second person we meet between this and Palace Yard is an obvious 'tec. It will get on his nerves presently. I say, these foreign scoundrels aren't likely to throw something at him – are they? It would be a national calamity. The country can't spare him.'

'Not to mention yourself. He leans on your arm,' suggested the Assistant Commissioner, soberly. 'You would both go.'

'It would be an easy way for a young man to go down into history? Not so many British Ministers have been assassinated as to make it a minor incident. But seriously now . . . '

'I am afraid that if you want to go down into history you'll have to do something for it. Seriously, there's no danger whatever for both of you but from overwork.'

The sympathetic Toodles welcomed this opening for a chuckle.

'The Fisheries won't kill me. I am used to late hours,' he declared, with ingenuous levity. But, feeling an instant compunction, he began to assume an air of statesmanlike moodiness, as one draws on a glove.

'His massive intellect will stand any amount of work. It's his nerves that I am afraid of. The reactionary gang, with that abusive brute Cheeseman at their head, insult him every night.'

'If he will insist on beginning a revolution!' murmured the Assistant Commissioner.

'The time has come, and he is the only man great enough for the work,' protested the revolutionary Toodles, flaring up under the calm, speculative gaze of the Assistant Commissioner. Somewhere in a corridor a distant bell tinkled urgently, and with devoted vigilance the young man pricked up his ears at the sound. 'He's ready to go now,' he exclaimed in a whisper, snatched up his hat, and vanished from the room.

The Assistant Commissioner went out by another door in a less elastic manner. Again he crossed the wide thoroughfare, walked along a narrow street, and re-entered hastily his own departmental buildings. He kept up this accelerated pace to the door of his private room. Before he had closed it fairly his eyes sought his desk. He stood still for a moment, then walked up, looked all round on the floor, sat down in his chair, rang a bell, and waited.

'Chief Inspector Heat gone yet?'

'Yes, sir. Went away half an hour ago.'

He nodded. 'That will do.' And sitting still, with his hat pushed off his forehead, he thought that it was just like Heat's confounded cheek to carry off quietly the only piece of material evidence. But he thought this without animosity. Old and valued servants will take liberties. The piece of overcoat with the address sewn on was certainly not a thing to leave about. Dismissing from his mind this manifestation of Chief Inspector Heat's mistrust, he wrote and despatched a note to his wife, charging her to make his apologies to Michaelis' great lady, with whom they were engaged to dine that evening.

The short jacket and the low, round hat he assumed in a sort of curtained alcove containing a washstand, a row of wooden pegs and a shelf, brought out wonderfully the length of his grave, brown face. He stepped back into the full light of the room, looking like the vision of a cool, reflective Don Quixote, with the sunken eyes of a dark enthusiast and a very deliberate manner. He left the scene of his daily labours quickly like an unobtrusive shadow. His descent into the street was like the descent into a slimy aquarium from which the water had been run off. A murky, gloomy dampness enveloped him. The walls of the houses were wet, the mud of the roadway glistened with an effect of phosphorescence, and when he emerged into the Strand out of a narrow street by the side of Charing Cross Station the genius of the locality assimilated him. He might have been but one more of the queer foreign fish that can be seen of an evening about there flitting round the dark corners.

He came to a stand on the very edge of the pavement, and waited. His exercised eyes had made out in the confused movements of lights and shadows thronging the roadway the crawling approach of a hansom. He gave no sign; but when the low step gliding along the kerbstone came to his feet he dodged in skilfully in front of the big turning wheel, and spoke up through the little trap door almost before the man gazing supinely ahead from his perch was aware of having been boarded by a fare.

It was not a long drive. It ended by signal abruptly, nowhere in particular, between two lamp-posts before a large drapery establishment – a long range of shops already lapped up in sheets of corrugated iron for the night. Tendering a coin through the trap door the fare slipped out and away, leaving an effect of uncanny eccentric ghostliness upon the driver's mind. But the size of the coin was satisfactory to his touch, and his education not being literary, he remained untroubled by the fear of finding it presently turned to a dead leaf in his pocket. Raised above the world of fares by the nature of his calling, he contemplated their action with a limited interest. The sharp pulling of his horse right round expressed his philosophy.

Meantime, the Assistant Commissioner was already giving his order to a waiter in a little Italian restaurant round the corner – one of those traps for the hungry, long and narrow, baited with a perspective of mirrors and white napery; without air, but with an atmosphere of their own – an atmosphere of fraudulent cookery mocking an abject mankind in the most pressing of its miserable necessities. In this immoral atmosphere the Assistant Commissioner, reflecting upon his enterprise, seemed to lose some more of his identity. He had a sense of loneliness, of evil freedom. It was rather pleasant. When, after paying for his short meal, he stood up and waited for his change, he saw himself in the sheet of glass, and was struck by his foreign appearance. He contemplated his own image with a melancholy and inquisitive gaze, then by sudden inspiration raised the collar of his jacket. This arrangement appeared to him commendable, and he completed it by giving an upward twist to the ends of his black moustache. He was satisfied by the subtle modification of his personal aspect caused by these small changes. 'That'll do very well,' he thought. 'I'll get a little wet, a little splashed . . . '

He became aware of the waiter at his elbow and of a small pile of silver coins on the edge of the table before him. The waiter kept one eye on it, while his other eye followed the long back of a tall, not very young girl, who passed up to a distant table looking perfectly sightless and altogether unapproachable. She seemed to be an habitual customer.

On going out the Assistant Commissioner made to himself the observation that the patrons of the place had lost in the frequentation of fraudulent cookery all their national and private characteristics. And this was strange, since the Italian restaurant is such a peculiarly British institution. But these people were as denationalised as the dishes set before them with every circumstance of unstamped respectability. Neither was their personality stamped in any way, professionally, socially, or racially. They seemed created for the Italian restaurant unless the Italian restaurant had been perchance created for them. But that last hypothesis was unthinkable, since one could not place them anywhere outside those special establishments. One never met these enigmatical persons elsewhere. It was impossible to form a precise idea what occupations they followed by day and where they went to bed at night. And he himself had become unplaced. It would have been impossible for anybody to guess his occupation. As to going to bed, there was a doubt even in his own mind. Not indeed in regard to his domicile itself, but very much so in respect of the time when he would be able to return there. A pleasurable feeling of independence possessed him when he heard the glass doors swing to behind his back with a sort of imperfect baffled thud. He advanced at once into an immensity of greasy slime and damp plaster interspersed with lamps, and enveloped, oppressed, penetrated, choked, and suffocated by the blackness of a wet London night, which is composed of soot and drops of water.

Brett Street was not very far away. It branched off, narrow, from the side of an open triangular space surrounded by dark and mysterious houses, temples of petty commerce emptied of traders for the night. Only a fruiterer's stall at the corner made a violent blaze of light and colour. Beyond all was black, and the few people passing in that direction vanished at one stride beyond the glowing heaps of oranges and lemons. No footsteps echoed. They would never be heard of again. The adventurous head of the Special Crimes Department watched these disappearances from a distance with an interested eye. He felt light-hearted, as though he had been ambushed all alone in a jungle many thousands of miles away from departmental desks and official inkstands. This joyousness and dispersion of thought before a task of some importance seems to prove that this world of ours is not such a very serious affair after all. For the Assistant Commissioner was not constitutionally inclined to levity.

The policeman on the beat projected his sombre and moving form against the luminous glory of oranges and lemons, and entered Brett Street without haste. The Assistant Commissioner, as though he were a member of the criminal classes, lingered out of sight, awaiting his return. But this constable seemed to be lost for ever to the force. He never returned: must have gone out at the other end of Brett Street.

The Assistant Commissioner, reaching this conclusion, entered the street in his turn, and came upon a large van arrested in front of the dimly lit windowpanes of a carter's eating-house. The man was refreshing himself inside, and the horses, their big heads lowered to the ground, fed out of nose-bags steadily. Farther on, on the opposite side of the street, another suspect patch of dim light issued from Mr Verloc's shop front, hung with papers, heaving with vague piles of cardboard boxes and the shapes of books. The Assistant Commissioner stood observing it across the roadway. There could be no mistake. By the side of the front window, encumbered by the shadows of nondescript things, the door, standing ajar, let escape on the pavement a narrow, clear streak of gaslight within.

Behind the Assistant Commissioner the van and horses, merged into one mass, seemed something alive – a square-backed black monster blocking half the street, with sudden iron-shod stampings, fierce jingles, and heavy, blowing sighs. The harshly festive, ill-omened glare of a large and prosperous public-house faced the other end of Brett Street across a wide road. This barrier of blazing lights, opposing the shadows gathered about the humble abode of Mr Verloc's domestic happiness, seemed to drive the obscurity of the street back upon itself, make it more sullen, brooding, and sinister.

Chapter 8

Having infused by persistent importunities some sort of heat into the chilly interest of several licensed victuallers (the acquaintances once upon a time of her late unlucky husband), Mrs Verloc's mother had at last secured her admission to certain almshouses founded by a wealthy innkeeper for the destitute widows of the trade.

This end, conceived in the astuteness of her uneasy heart, the old woman had pursued with secrecy and determination. That was the time when her daughter Winnie could not help passing a remark to Mr Verloc that 'mother has been spending half-crowns and five shillings almost every day this last week in cab fares.' But the remark was not made grudgingly. Winnie respected her mother's infirmities. She was only a little surprised at this sudden mania for locomotion. Mr Verloc, who was sufficiently magnificent in his way, had grunted the remark impatiently aside as interfering with his meditations. These were frequent, deep, and prolonged; they bore upon a matter more important than five shillings. Distinctly more important, and beyond all comparison more difficult to consider in all its aspects with philosophical serenity.

Her object attained in astute secrecy, the heroic old woman had made a clean breast of it to Mrs Verloc. Her soul was triumphant and her heart tremulous. Inwardly she quaked, because she dreaded and admired the calm, self-contained character of her daughter Winnie, whose displeasure was made redoubtable by a diversity of dreadful silences. But she did not allow her inward apprehensions to rob her of the advantage of venerable placidity conferred upon her outward person by her triple chin, the floating ampleness of her ancient form, and the impotent condition of her legs.

The shock of the information was so unexpected that Mrs Verloc, against her usual practice when addressed, interrupted the domestic occupation she was engaged upon. It was the dusting of the furniture in the parlour behind the shop. She turned her head towards her mother.

'Whatever did you want to do that for?' she exclaimed, in scandalised astonishment.

The shock must have been severe to make her depart from that distant and unenquiring acceptance of facts which was her force and her safeguard in life.

'Weren't you made comfortable enough here?'

She had lapsed into these enquiries, but next moment she saved the consistency of her conduct by resuming her dusting, while the old woman sat scared and dumb under her dingy white cap and lustreless dark wig.

Winnie finished the chair, and ran the duster along the mahogany at the back of the horsehair sofa on which Mr Verloc loved to take his ease in hat and overcoat. She was intent on her work, but presently she permitted herself another question.

'How in the world did you manage it, mother?'

As not affecting the inwardness of things, which it was Mrs Verloc's principle to ignore, this curiosity was excusable. It bore merely on the methods. The old woman welcomed it eagerly as bringing forward something that could be talked about with much sincerity.

She favoured her daughter by an exhaustive answer full of names and enriched by side comments upon the ravages of time as observed in the alteration of human countenances. The names were principally the names of licensed victuallers – 'poor daddy's friends, my dear'. She enlarged with special appreciation on the kindness and condescension of a large brewer, a Baronet and an MP, the Chairman of the Governors of the Charity. She expressed herself thus warmly because she had been allowed to interview by appointment his Private Secretary – 'A very polite gentleman, all in black, with a gentle, sad voice, but so very, very thin and quiet. He was like a shadow, my dear.'

Winnie, prolonging her dusting operations till the tale was told to the end, walked out of the parlour into the kitchen (down two steps) in her usual manner, without the slightest comment.

Shedding a few tears in sign of rejoicing at her daughter's mansuetude in this terrible affair, Mrs Verloc's mother gave play to her astuteness in the direction of her furniture, because it was her own; and sometimes she wished it hadn't been. Heroism is all very well, but there are circumstances when the disposal of a few tables and chairs, brass bedsteads, and so on, may be big with remote and disastrous consequences. She required a few pieces herself, the Foundation which, after many importunities, had gathered her to its charitable breast, giving nothing but bare planks and cheaply papered bricks to the objects of its solicitude. The delicacy guiding her choice to the least valuable and most dilapidated articles passed unacknowledged, because Winnie's philosophy consisted in not taking notice of the inside of facts; she assumed that mother took what suited her best. As to Mr Verloc, his intense meditation, like a sort of Chinese wall, isolated him completely from the phenomena of this world of vain effort and illusory appearances.

Her selection made, the disposal of the rest became a perplexing question in a particular way. She was leaving it in Brett Street, of course. But she had two children. Winnie was provided for by her sensible union with that excellent husband, Mr Verloc. Stevie was destitute and a little peculiar. His position had to be considered before the claims of legal justice and even the promptings of partiality. The possession of the furniture would not be in any sense a provision. He ought to have it – the poor boy. But to give it to him would be like tampering with his position of complete dependence. It was a sort of claim which she feared to weaken. Moreover, the susceptibilities of Mr Verloc would perhaps not brook being beholden to his brother-in-law for the chairs he sat on. In a long experience of gentlemen lodgers, Mrs Verloc's mother had acquired a dismal but resigned notion of the fantastic side of human nature. What if Mr Verloc suddenly took it into his head to tell Stevie to take his blessed sticks somewhere out of that? A division, on the other hand, however carefully made, might give some cause of offence to Winnie. No. Stevie must remain destitute and dependent. And at the moment of leaving Brett Street she had said to her daughter: 'No use waiting till I am dead, is there? Everything I leave here is altogether your own now, my dear.'

Winnie, with her hat on, silent behind her mother's back, went on arranging the collar of the old woman's cloak. She got her handbag, an umbrella, with an impassive face. The time had come for the expenditure of the sum of three-and-sixpence on what might well be supposed the last cab drive of Mrs Verloc's mother's life. They went out at the shop door.

The conveyance awaiting them would have illustrated the proverb that 'truth can be more cruel than caricature,' if such a proverb existed. Crawling behind an infirm horse, a metropolitan hackney carriage drew up on wobbly wheels and with a maimed driver on the box. This last peculiarity caused some embarrassment. Catching sight of a hooked iron contrivance protruding from the left sleeve of the man's coat, Mrs Verloc's mother lost suddenly the heroic courage of these days. She really couldn't trust herself. 'What do you think, Winnie?' She hung back. The passionate expostulations of the big-faced cabman seemed to be squeezed out of a blocked throat. Leaning over from his box, he whispered with mysterious indignation. What was the matter now? Was it possible to treat a man so? His enormous and unwashed countenance flamed red in the muddy stretch of the street. Was it likely they would have given him a licence, he enquired desperately, if . . .

The police constable of the locality quieted him by a friendly glance; then addressing himself to the two women without marked consideration, said: 'He's been driving a cab for twenty years. I never knew him to have an accident.'

'Accident!' shouted the driver in a scornful whisper.

The policeman's testimony settled it. The modest assemblage of seven people, mostly under age, dispersed. Winnie followed her mother into the cab. Stevie climbed on the box. His vacant mouth and distressed eyes depicted the state of his mind in regard to the transactions which were taking place. In the narrow streets the progress of the journey was made sensible to those within by the near fronts of the houses gliding past slowly and shakily, with a great rattle and jingling of glass, as if about to collapse behind the cab; and the infirm horse, with the harness hung over his sharp backbone flapping very loose about his thighs, appeared to be dancing mincingly on his toes with infinite patience. Later on, in the wider space of Whitehall, all visual evidences of motion became imperceptible. The rattle and jingle of glass went on indefinitely in front of the long Treasury building – and time itself seemed to stand still.

At last Winnie observed: 'This isn't a very good horse.'

Her eyes gleamed in the shadow of the cab straight ahead, immovable. On the box, Stevie shut his vacant mouth first, in order to ejaculate earnestly: 'Don't.'

The driver, holding high the reins twisted around the hook, took no notice. Perhaps he had not heard. Stevie's breast heaved.

'Don't whip.'

The man turned slowly his bloated and sodden face of many colours bristling with white hairs. His little red eyes glistened with moisture. His big lips had a violet tint. They remained closed. With the dirty back of his whip-hand he rubbed the stubble sprouting on his enormous chin.

'You mustn't,' stammered out Stevie, violently, 'it hurts.'

'Mustn't whip?' queried the other in a thoughtful whisper, and immediately whipped. He did this, not because his soul was cruel and his heart evil, but because he had to earn his fare. And for a time the walls of St Stephen's, with its towers and pinnacles, contemplated in immobility and silence a cab that jingled. It rolled, too, however. But on the bridge there was a commotion. Stevie suddenly proceeded to get down from the box. There were shouts on the pavement, people ran forward, the driver pulled up, whispering curses of indignation and astonishment. Winnie lowered the window, and put her head out, white as a ghost. In the depths of the cab her mother was exclaiming, in tones of anguish: 'Is that boy hurt? Is that boy hurt?'

Stevie was not hurt, he had not even fallen, but excitement as usual had robbed him of the power of connected speech. He could do no more than stammer at the window: 'Too heavy. Too heavy.' Winnie put out her hand on to his shoulder.

'Stevie! Get up on the box directly, and don't try to get down again.'

'No. No. Walk. Must walk.'

In trying to state the nature of that necessity he stammered himself into utter incoherence. No physical impossibility stood in the way of his whim. Stevie could have managed easily to keep pace with the infirm, dancing horse without getting out of breath. But his sister withheld her consent decisively. 'The idea! Who ever heard of such a thing! Run after a cab!' Her mother, frightened and helpless in the depths of the conveyance, entreated: 'Oh, don't let him, Winnie. He'll get lost. Don't let him.'

'Certainly not. What next! Mr Verloc will be sorry to hear of this nonsense, Stevie, I can tell you. He won't be happy at all.'

The idea of Mr Verloc's grief and unhappiness acting as usual powerfully upon Stevie's fundamentally docile disposition, he abandoned all resistance, and climbed up again on the box, with a face of despair.

The cabby turned at him his enormous and inflamed countenance truculently. 'Don't you go for trying this silly game again, young fellow.'

After delivering himself thus in a stern whisper, strained almost to extinction, he drove on, ruminating solemnly. To his mind the incident remained somewhat obscure. But his intellect, though it had lost its pristine vivacity in the benumbing years of sedentary exposure to the weather, lacked not independence or sanity. Gravely he dismissed the hypothesis of Stevie being a drunken young nipper.

Inside the cab the spell of silence, in which the two women had endured shoulder to shoulder the jolting, rattling, and jingling of the journey, had been broken by Stevie's outbreak. Winnie raised her voice.

'You've done what you wanted, mother. You'll have only yourself to thank for it if you aren't happy afterwards. And I don't think you'll be. That I don't. Weren't you comfortable enough in the house? Whatever people'll think of us – you throwing yourself like this on a Charity?'

'My dear,' screamed the old woman earnestly above the noise, 'you've been the best of daughters to me. As to Mr Verloc – there . . .'

Words failing her on the subject of Mr Verloc's excellence, she turned her old tearful eyes to the roof of the cab. Then she averted her head on the pretence of looking out of the window, as if to judge of their progress. It was insignificant, and went on close to the kerbstone. Night, the early dirty night, the sinister, noisy, hopeless, and rowdy night of South London, had overtaken her on her last cab drive. In the gaslight of the low-fronted shops her big cheeks glowed with an orange hue under a black and mauve bonnet.

Mrs Verloc's mother's complexion had become yellow by the effect of age and from a natural predisposition to biliousness, favoured by the trials of a difficult and worried existence first as wife, then as widow. It was a complexion that under the influence of a blush would take on an orange tint. And this woman, modest indeed but hardened in the fires of adversity, of an age, moreover, when blushes are not expected, had positively blushed before her daughter. In the privacy of a four-wheeler, on her way to a charity cottage (one of a row) which by the exiguity of its dimensions and the simplicity of its accommodation, might well have been devised in kindness as a place of training for the still more straitened circumstances of the grave, she was forced to hide from her own child a blush of remorse and shame.

Whatever people will think? She knew very well what they did think, the people Winnie had in her mind – the old friends of her husband, and others too, whose interest she had solicited with such flattering success. She had not known before what a good beggar she could be. But she guessed very well what inference was drawn from her application. On account of that shrinking delicacy, which exists side by side with aggressive brutality in masculine nature, the enquiries into her circumstances had not been pushed very far. She had checked them by a visible compression of the lips and some display of an emotion determined to be eloquently silent. And the men would become suddenly incurious, after the manner of their kind. She congratulated herself more than once on having nothing to do with women, who being naturally more callous and avid of details, would have been anxious to be exactly informed by what sort of unkind conduct her daughter and son-in-law had driven her to that sad extremity. It was only before the Secretary of the great brewer M. P. and Chairman of the Charity, who, acting for his principal, felt bound to be conscientiously inquisitive as to the real circumstances of the applicant, that she had burst into tears outright and aloud, as a cornered woman will weep. The thin and polite gentleman, after contemplating her with an air of being 'struck all of a heap', abandoned his position under the cover of soothing remarks. She must not distress herself. The deed of the Charity did not absolutely specify 'childless widows'. In fact, it did not by any means disqualify her. But the discretion of the Committee must be an informed discretion. One could understand very well her unwillingness to be a burden, etc., etc. Thereupon, to his profound disappointment, Mrs Verloc's mother wept some more with an augmented vehemence.

The tears of that large female in a dark, dusty wig, and ancient silk dress festooned with dingy white cotton lace, were the tears of genuine distress. She had wept because she was heroic and unscrupulous and full of love for both her children. Girls frequently get sacrificed to the welfare of the boys. In this case she was sacrificing Winnie. By the suppression of truth she was slandering her. Of course, Winnie was independent, and need not care for the opinion of people that she would never see and who would never see her; whereas poor Stevie had nothing in the world he could call his own except his mother's heroism and unscrupulousness.

The first sense of security following on Winnie's marriage wore off in time (for nothing lasts), and Mrs Verloc's mother, in the seclusion of the back bedroom, had recalled the teaching of that experience which the world impresses upon a widowed woman. But she had recalled it without vain bitterness; her store of resignation amounted almost to dignity. She reflected stoically that everything decays, wears out, in this world; that the way of kindness should be made easy to the well disposed; that her daughter Winnie was a most devoted sister, and a very self-confident wife indeed. As regards Winnie's sisterly devotion, her stoicism flinched. She excepted that sentiment from the rule of decay affecting all things human and some things divine. She could not help it; not to do so would have frightened her too much. But in considering the conditions of her daughter's married state, she rejected firmly all flattering illusions. She took the cold and reasonable view that the less strain put on Mr Verloc's kindness the longer its effects were likely to last. That excellent man loved his wife, of course, but he would, no doubt, prefer to keep as few of her relations as was consistent with the proper display of that sentiment. It would be better if its whole effect were concentrated on poor Stevie. And the heroic old woman resolved on going away from her children as an act of devotion and as a move of deep policy.

The 'virtue' of this policy consisted in this (Mrs Verloc's mother was subtle in her way), that Stevie's moral claim would be strengthened. The poor boy – a good, useful boy, if a little peculiar – had not a sufficient standing. He had been taken over with his mother, somewhat in the same way as the furniture of the Belgravian mansion had been taken over, as if on the ground of belonging to her exclusively. What will happen, she asked herself (for Mrs Verloc's mother was in a measure imaginative), when I die? And when she asked herself that question it was with dread. It was also terrible to think that she would not then have the means of knowing what happened to the poor boy. But by making him over to his sister, by going thus away, she gave him the advantage of a directly dependent position. This was the more subtle sanction of Mrs Verloc's mother's heroism and un-scrupulousness. Her act of abandonment was really an arrangement for settling her son permanently in life. Other people made material sacrifices for such an object, she in that way. It was the only way. Moreover, she would be able to see how it worked. Ill or well she would avoid the horrible incertitude on the deathbed. But it was hard, hard, cruelly hard.

The cab rattled, jingled, jolted; in fact, the last was quite extraordinary. By its disproportionate violence and magnitude it obliterated every sensation of onward movement; and the effect was of being shaken in a stationary apparatus like a medieval device for the punishment of crime, or some very new-fangled invention for the cure of a sluggish liver. It was extremely distressing; and the raising of Mrs Verloc's mother's voice sounded like a wail of pain.

'I know, my dear, you'll come to see me as often as you can spare the time. Won't you?'

'Of course,' answered Winnie, shortly, staring straight before her.

And the cab jolted in front of a steamy, greasy shop in a blaze of gas and in the smell of fried fish.

The old woman raised a wail again.

'And, my dear, I must see that poor boy every Sunday. He won't mind spending the day with his old mother.'

Winnie screamed out stolidly: 'Mind! I should think not. That poor boy will miss you something cruel. I wish you had thought a little of that, mother.'

Not think of it! The heroic woman swallowed a playful and inconvenient object like a billiard ball, which had tried to jump out of her throat. Winnie sat mute for a while, pouting at the front of the cab, then snapped out, which was an unusual tone with her: 'I expect I'll have a job with him at first, he'll be that restless . . .'

'Whatever you do, don't let him worry your husband, my dear.' Thus they discussed on familiar lines the bearings of a new situation. And the cab jolted. Mrs Verloc's mother expressed some misgivings. Could Stevie be trusted to come all that way alone? Winnie maintained that he was much less 'absent-minded' now. They agreed as to that. It could not be denied. Much less – hardly at all. They shouted at each other in the jingle with comparative cheerfulness. But suddenly the maternal anxiety broke out afresh. There were two omnibuses to take, and a short walk between. It was too difficult! The old woman gave way to grief and consternation.

Winnie stared forward.

'Don't you upset yourself like this, mother. You must see him, of course.'

'No, my dear. I'll try not to.'

She mopped her streaming eyes.

'But you can't spare the time to come with him, and if he should forget himself and lose his way and somebody spoke to him sharply, his name and address may slip his memory, and he'll remain lost for days and days.'

The vision of a workhouse infirmary for poor Stevie – if only during enquiries – wrung her heart. For she was a proud woman. Winnie's stare had grown hard, intent, inventive.

'I can't bring him to you myself every week,' she cried. 'But don't you worry, mother. I'll see to it that he don't get lost for long.'

They felt a peculiar bump; a vision of brick pillars lingered before the rattling windows of the cab; a sudden cessation of atrocious jolting and uproarious jingling dazed the two women. What had happened? They sat motionless and scared in the profound stillness, till the door came open, and a rough, strained whispering was heard: ' 'Ere you are!'

A range of gabled little houses, each with one dim yellow window, on the ground floor, surrounded the dark open space of a grass plot planted with shrubs and railed off from the patchwork of lights and shadows in the wide road, resounding with the dull rumble of traffic. Before the door of one of these tiny houses – one without a light in the little downstairs window – the cab had come to a standstill. Mrs Verloc's mother got out first, backwards, with a key in her hand. Winnie lingered on the flagstone path to pay the cabman. Stevie, after helping to carry inside a lot of small parcels, came out and stood under the light of a gas-lamp belonging to the Charity. The cabman looked at the pieces of silver, which, appearing very minute in his big, grimy palm, symbolised the insignificant results which reward the ambitious courage and toil of a mankind whose day is short on this earth of evil.

He had been paid decently – four one-shilling pieces – and he contemplated them in perfect stillness, as if they had been the surprising terms of a melancholy problem. The slow transfer of that treasure to an inner pocket demanded much laborious groping in the depths of decayed clothing. His form was squat and without flexibility. Stevie, slender, his shoulders a little up, and his hands thrust deep in the side pockets of his warm overcoat, stood at the edge of the path, pouting.

The cabman, pausing in his deliberate movements, seemed struck by some misty recollection.

'Oh! 'Ere you are, young fellow,' he whispered. 'You'll know him again – won't you?'

Stevie was staring at the horse, whose hind quarters appeared unduly elevated by the effect of emaciation. The little stiff tail seemed to have been fitted in for a heartless joke; and at the other end the thin, flat neck, like a plank covered with old horse-hide, drooped to the ground under the weight of an enormous bony head. The ears hung at different angles, negligently; and the macabre figure of that mute dweller on the earth steamed straight up from ribs and backbone in the muggy stillness of the air.

The cabman struck lightly Stevie's breast with the iron hook protruding from a ragged, greasy sleeve.

'Look 'ere, young feller. 'Ow'd *you* like to sit behind this 'oss up to two o'clock in the morning p'raps? '

Stevie looked vacantly into the fierce little eyes with red-edged lids.

'He ain't lame,' pursued the other, whispering with energy. 'He ain't got no sore places on 'im. 'Ere he is. 'Ow would *you* like?'

His strained, extinct voice invested his utterance with a character of vehement secrecy. Stevie's vacant gaze was changing slowly into dread.

'You may well look! Till three and four o'clock in the morning. Cold and 'ungry. Looking for fares. Drunks.'

His jovial purple cheeks bristled with white hairs; and like Virgil's Silenus, who, his face smeared with the juice of berries, discoursed of Olympian Gods to the innocent shepherds of Sicily, he talked to Stevie of domestic matters and the affairs of men whose sufferings are great and immortality by no means assured.

'I am a night cabby, I am,' he whispered, with a sort of boastful exasperation.

'I've got to take out what they will blooming well give me at the yard. I've got my missus and four kids at 'ome.'

The monstrous nature of that declaration of paternity seemed to strike the world dumb. A silence reigned, during which the flanks of the old horse, the steed of apocalyptic misery, smoked upwards in the light of the charitable gas-lamp.

The cabman grunted, then added in his mysterious whisper: 'This ain't an easy world.'

Stevie's face had been twitching for some time and at last his feelings burst out in their usual concise form.

'Bad! Bad!'

His gaze remained fixed on the ribs of the horse, self-conscious and sombre, as though he were afraid to look about him at the badness of the world. And his slenderness, his rosy lips and pale, clear complexion, gave him the aspect of a delicate boy, notwithstanding the fluffy growth of golden hair on his cheeks. He pouted in a scared way like a child. The cabman, short and broad, eyed him with his fierce little eyes that seemed to smart in a clear and corroding liquid.

' 'Ard on 'osses, but dam' sight 'arder on poor chaps like me,' he wheezed just audibly.

'Poor! Poor!' stammered out Stevie, pushing his hands deeper into his pocket with convulsive sympathy. He could say nothing; for the tenderness to all pain and all misery, the desire to make the horse happy and the cabman happy, had reached the point of a bizarre longing to take them to bed with him. And that, he knew, was impossible. For Stevie was not mad. It was, as it were, a symbolic longing; and at the same time it was very distinct, because springing from experience, the mother of wisdom. Thus when as a child he cowered in a dark corner scared, wretched, sore, and miserable with the black, black misery of the soul, his sister Winnie used to come along, and carry him off to bed with her, as into a heaven of consoling peace. Stevie, though apt to forget mere facts, such as his name and address for instance, had a faithful memory of sensations. To be taken into a bed of compassion was the supreme remedy, with the only one disadvantage of being difficult of application on a large scale. And looking at the cabman, Stevie perceived this clearly, because he was reasonable.

The cabman went on with his leisurely preparations as if Stevie had not existed. He made as if to hoist himself on the box, but at the last moment, from some obscure motive, perhaps merely from disgust with carriage exercise, desisted. He approached instead the motionless partner of his labours, and stooping to seize the bridle, lifted up the big, weary head to the height of his shoulder with one effort of his right arm, like a feat of strength.

'Come on,' he whispered, secretly.

Limping, he led the cab away. There was an air of austerity in this departure, the scrunched gravel of the drive crying out under the slowly turning wheels, the horse's lean thighs moving with ascetic deliberation away from the light into the obscurity of the open space bordered dimly by the pointed roofs and the feebly shining windows of the little almshouses. The plaint of the gravel travelled slowly all round the drive. Between the lamps of the charitable gateway the slow cortège reappeared, lighted up for a moment, the short, thick man limping busily, with the horse's head held aloft in his fist, the lank animal walking in stiff and forlorn dignity, the dark, low box on wheels rolling behind comically with an air of waddling. They turned to the left. There was a pub down the street, within fifty yards of the gate.

Stevie left alone beside the private lamp-post of the Charity, his hands thrust deep into his pockets, glared with vacant sulkiness. At the bottom of his pockets his incapable, weak hands were clinched hard into a pair of angry fists. In the face of anything which affected directly or indirectly his morbid dread of pain, Stevie ended by turning vicious. A magnanimous indignation swelled his frail chest to bursting, and caused his candid eyes to squint. Supremely wise in knowing his own powerlessness, Stevie was not wise enough to restrain his passions. The tenderness of his universal charity had two phases as indissolubly joined and connected as the reverse and obverse sides of a medal. The anguish of immoderate compassion was succeeded by the pain of an innocent but pitiless rage. Those two states expressing themselves outwardly by the same signs of futile bodily agitation, his sister Winnie soothed his excitement without ever fathoming its twofold character. Mrs Verloc wasted no portion of this transient life in seeking for fundamental information. This is a sort of economy having all the appearances and some of the advantages of prudence. Obviously it may be good for one not to know too much. And such a view accords very well with constitutional indolence.

On that evening on which it may be said that Mrs Verloc's mother having parted for good from her children had also departed this life, Winnie Verloc did not investigate her brother's psychology. The poor boy was excited, of course. After once more assuring the old woman on the threshold that she would know how to guard against the risk of Stevie losing himself for very long on his pilgrimages of filial piety, she took her brother's arm to walk away. Stevie did not even mutter to himself, but with the special sense of sisterly devotion developed in her earliest infancy, she felt that the boy was very much excited indeed. Holding tight to his arm, under the appearance of leaning on it, she thought of some words suitable to the occasion.

'Now, Stevie, you must look well after me at the crossings, and get first into the bus, like a good brother.'

This appeal to manly protection was received by Stevie with his usual docility. It flattered him. He raised his head and threw out his chest.

'Don't be nervous, Winnie. Mustn't be nervous! Bus all right,' he answered in a brusque, slurring stammer partaking of the timorousness of a child and the resolution of a man. He advanced fearlessly with the woman on his arm, but his lower lip dropped. Nevertheless, on the pavement of the squalid and wide thoroughfare, whose poverty in all the amenities of life stood foolishly exposed by a mad profusion of gaslights, their resemblance to each other was so pronounced as to strike the casual passers-by.

Before the doors of the public-house at the corner, where the profusion of gaslight reached the height of positive wickedness, a four-wheeled cab standing by the kerbstone, with no one on the box, seemed cast out into the gutter on account of irremediable decay. Mrs Verloc recognised the conveyance. Its aspect was so profoundly lamentable, with such a perfection of grotesque misery and weirdness of macabre detail, as if it were the Cab of Death itself, that Mrs Verloc, with that ready compassion of a woman for a horse (when she is not sitting behind him), exclaimed vaguely: 'Poor brute.'

Hanging back suddenly, Stevie inflicted an arresting jerk upon his sister.

'Poor! Poor!' he ejaculated, appreciatively. 'Cabman poor, too. He told me himself.'

The contemplation of the infirm and lonely steed overcame him. Jostled, but obstinate, he would remain there, trying to express the view newly opened to his sympathies of the human and equine misery in close association. But it was very difficult. 'Poor brute, poor people!' was all he could repeat. It did not seem forcible enough, and he came to a stop with an angry splutter: 'Shame!' Stevie was no master of phrases, and perhaps for that very reason his thoughts lacked clearness and precision. But he felt with greater completeness and some profundity. That the little word contained all his sense of indignation and horror at one sort of wretchedness having to feed upon the anguish of the other – at the poor cabman beating the poor horse in the name, as it were, of his poor kids at home. And Stevie knew what it was to be beaten. He knew it from experience. It was a bad world. Bad! Bad!

Mrs Verloc, his only sister, guardian, and protector, could not pretend to such depths of insight. Moreover, she had not experienced the magic of the cabman's eloquence. She was in the dark as to the inwardness of the word 'Shame.' And she said placidly: 'Come along, Stevie. You can't help that.'

The docile Stevie went along; but now he went along without pride, shamblingly, and muttering half words, and even words that would have been whole if they had not been made up of halves that did not belong to each other. It was as though he had been trying to fit all the words he could remember to his sentiments in order to get some sort of corresponding idea. And, as a matter of fact, he got it at last. He hung back to utter it at once.

'Bad world for poor people.'

Directly he had expressed that thought he became aware that it was familiar to him already in all its consequences. This circumstance strengthened his conviction immensely, but also augmented his indignation. Somebody, he felt, ought to be punished for it – punished with great severity. Being no sceptic, but a moral creature, he was in a manner at the mercy of his righteous passions.

'Beastly!' he added, concisely.

It was clear to Mrs Verloc that he was greatly excited.

'Nobody can help that,' she said. 'Do come along. Is that the way you're taking care of me?'

Stevie mended his pace obediently. He prided himself on being a good brother. His morality, which was very complete, demanded that from him. Yet he was pained at the information imparted by his sister Winnie – who was good. Nobody could help that! He came along gloomily, but presently he brightened up. Like the rest of mankind, perplexed by the mystery of the universe, he had his moments of consoling trust in the organised powers of the earth.

'Police,' he suggested, confidently.

'The police aren't for that,' observed Mrs Verloc cursorily, hurrying on her way.

Stevie's face lengthened considerably. He was thinking. The more intense his thinking, the slacker was the droop of his lower jaw. And it was with an aspect of hopeless vacancy that he gave up his intellectual enterprise.

'Not for that?' he mumbled, resigned but surprised. 'Not for that?' He had formed for himself an ideal conception of the metropolitan police as a sort of benevolent institution for the suppression of evil. The notion of benevolence especially was very closely associated with his sense of the power of the men in blue. He had liked all police constables tenderly, with a guileless trustfulness. And he was pained. He was irritated, too, by a suspicion of duplicity in the members of the force. For Stevie was frank and as open as the day himself. What did they mean by pretending then? Unlike his sister, who put her trust in face values, he wished to go to the bottom of the matter. He carried on his enquiry by means of an angry challenge.

'What are they for then, Winn? What are they for? Tell me.'

Winnie disliked controversy. But fearing most a fit of black depression consequent on Stevie missing his mother very much at first, she did not altogether decline the discussion. Guiltless of all irony, she answered yet in a form which was not perhaps unnatural in the wife of Mr Verloc, Delegate of the Central Red Committee, personal friend of certain anarchists, and a votary of social revolution.

'Don't you know what the police are for, Stevie? They are there so that them as have nothing shouldn't take anything away from them who have.'

She avoided using the verb 'to steal', because it always made her brother uncomfortable. For Stevie was delicately honest. Certain simple principles had been instilled into him so anxiously (on account of his 'queerness') that the mere names of certain transgressions filled him with horror. He had been always easily impressed by speeches. He was impressed and startled now, and his intelligence was very alert.

'That?' he asked at once, anxiously. 'Not even if they were hungry? Mustn't they?'

The two had paused in their walk.

'Not if they were ever so,' said Mrs Verloc, with the equanimity of a person untroubled by the problem of the distribution of wealth, and exploring the perspective of the roadway for an omnibus of the right colour. 'Certainly not. But what's the use of talking about all that? You aren't ever hungry.'

She cast a swift glance at the boy, like a young man, by her side. She saw him amiable, attractive, affectionate, and only a little, a very little peculiar. And she could not see him otherwise, for he was connected with what there was of the salt of passion in her tasteless life – the passion of indignation, of courage, of pity, and even of self-sacrifice. She did not add: 'And you aren't likely ever to be as long as I live.' But she might very well have done so, since she had taken effectual steps to that end. Mr Verloc was a very good husband. It was her honest impression that nobody could help liking the boy. She cried out suddenly: 'Quick, Stevie. Stop that green bus.'

And Stevie, tremulous and important with his sister Winnie on his arm, flung up the other high above his head at the approaching bus, with complete success.

An hour afterwards Mr Verloc raised his eyes from a newspaper he was reading, or at any rate looking at, behind the counter, and in the expiring clatter of the doorbell beheld Winnie, his wife, enter and cross the shop on her way upstairs, followed by Stevie, his brother-in-law. The sight of his wife was agreeable to Mr Verloc. It was his idiosyncrasy. The figure of his brother-in-law remained imperceptible to him because of the morose thoughtfulness that lately had fallen like a veil between Mr Verloc and the appearances of the world of senses. He looked after his wife fixedly, without a word, as though she had been a phantom. His voice for home use was husky and placid, but now it was heard not at all. It was not heard at supper, to which he was called by his wife in the usual brief manner: 'Adolf.' He sat down to consume it without conviction, wearing his hat pushed far back on his head. It was not devotion to an outdoor life, but the frequentation of foreign cafes which was responsible for that habit, investing with a character of unceremonious impermanency Mr Verloc's steady fidelity to his own fireside. Twice at the clatter of the cracked bell he arose without a word, disappeared into the shop, and came back silently. During these absences Mrs Verloc, becoming acutely aware of the vacant place at her right hand, missed her mother very much, and stared stonily; while Stevie, from the same reason, kept on shuffling his feet, as though the floor under the table were uncomfortably hot. When Mr Verloc returned to sit in his place, like the very embodiment of silence, the character of Mrs Verloc's stare underwent a subtle change, and Stevie ceased to fidget with his feet, because of his great and awed regard for his sister's husband. He directed at him glances of respectful compassion. Mr Verloc was sorry. His sister Winnie had impressed upon him (in the omnibus) that Mr Verloc would be found at home in a state of sorrow, and must not be worried. His father's anger, the irritability of gentlemen lodgers, and Mr Verloc's predisposition to immoderate grief, had been the main sanctions of Stevie's self-restraint. Of these sentiments, all easily provoked, but not always easy to understand, the last had the greatest moral efficiency – because Mr Verloc was *good*. His mother and his sister had established that ethical fact on an unshakable foundation. They had established, erected, consecrated it behind Mr Verloc's back, for reasons that had nothing to do with abstract morality. And Mr Verloc was not aware of it. It is but bare justice to him to say that he had no notion of appearing good to Stevie. Yet so it was. He was even the only man so qualified in Stevie's knowledge, because the gentlemen lodgers had been too transient and too remote to have anything very distinct about them but perhaps their boots; and as regards the disciplinary measures of his father, the desolation of his mother and sister shrank from setting up a theory of goodness before the victim. It would have been too cruel. And it was even possible that Stevie would not have believed them. As far as Mr Verloc was concerned, nothing could stand in the way of Stevie's belief. Mr Verloc was obviously yet mysteriously *good*. And the grief of a good man is august.

Stevie gave glances of reverential compassion to his brother-in-law. Mr Verloc was sorry. The brother of Winnie had never before felt himself in such close communion with the mystery of that man's goodness. It was an understandable sorrow. And Stevie himself was sorry. He was very sorry. The same sort of sorrow. And his attention being drawn to this unpleasant state, Stevie shuffled his feet. His feelings were habitually manifested by the agitation of his limbs.

'Keep your feet quiet, dear,' said Mrs Verloc, with authority and tenderness; then turning towards her husband in an indifferent voice, the masterly achievement of instinctive tact: 'Are you going out tonight?' she asked.

The mere suggestion seemed repugnant to Mr Verloc. He shook his head moodily, and then sat still with downcast eyes, looking at the piece of cheese on his plate for a whole minute. At the end of that time he got up, and went out – went right out in the clatter of the shop-door bell. He acted thus inconsistently, not from any desire to make himself unpleasant, but because of an unconquerable restlessness. It was no earthly good going out. He could not find anywhere in London what he wanted. But he went out. He led a cortege of dismal thoughts along dark streets, through lighted streets, in and out of two flash bars, as if in a half-hearted attempt to make a night of it, and finally back again to his menaced home, where he sat down fatigued behind the counter, and they crowded urgently round him, like a pack of hungry black hounds. After locking up the house and putting out the gas he took them upstairs with him – a dreadful escort for a man going to bed. His wife had preceded him some time before, and with her ample form defined vaguely under the counterpane, her head on the pillow, and a hand under the cheek, offered to his distraction the view of early drowsiness arguing the possession of an equable soul. Her big eyes stared wide open, inert and dark against the snowy whiteness of the linen. She did not move.

She had an equable soul. She felt profoundly that things do not stand much looking into. She made her force and her wisdom of that instinct. But the taciturnity of Mr Verloc had been lying heavily upon her for a good many days. It was, as a matter of fact, affecting her nerves. Recumbent and motionless, she said placidly: 'You'll catch cold walking about in your socks like this.'

This speech, becoming the solicitude of the wife and the prudence of the woman, took Mr Verloc unawares. He had left his boots downstairs, but he had forgotten to put on his slippers, and he had been turning about the bedroom on noiseless pads like a bear in a cage. At the sound of his wife's voice he stopped and stared at her with a somnambulistic, expressionless gaze so long that Mrs Verloc moved her limbs slightly under the bedclothes. But she did not move her black head sunk in the white pillow, one hand under her cheek and the big, dark, unwinking eyes.

Under her husband's expressionless stare, and remembering her mother's empty room across the landing, she felt an acute pang of loneliness. She had never been parted from her mother before. They had stood by each other. She felt that they had, and she said to herself that now mother was gone – gone for good. Mrs Verloc had no illusions. Stevie remained, however. And she said: 'Mother's done what she wanted to do. There's no sense in it that I can see. I'm sure she couldn't have thought you had enough of her. It's perfectly wicked, leaving us like that.'

Mr Verloc was not a well-read person, his range of allusive phrases was limited, but there was a peculiar aptness in circumstances which made him think of rats leaving a doomed ship. He very nearly said so. He had grown suspicious and embittered. Could it be that the old woman had such an excellent nose? But the unreasonableness of such a suspicion was patent, and Mr Verloc held his tongue. Not altogether, however. He muttered, heavily: 'Perhaps it's just as well.'

He began to undress. Mrs Verloc kept very still, perfectly still, with her eyes fixed in a dreamy, quiet stare. And her heart for the fraction of a second seemed to stand still, too. That night she was 'not quite herself', as the saying is, and it was borne upon her with some force that a simple sentence may hold several diverse meanings – mostly disagreeable. How was it just as well? And why? But she did not allow herself to fall into the idleness of barren speculation. She was rather confirmed in her belief that things did not stand being looked into. Practical and subtle in her way, she brought Stevie to the front without loss of time, because in her the singleness of purpose had the unerring nature and the force of an instinct.

'What I am going to do to cheer up that boy for the first few days I'm sure I don't know. He'll be worrying himself from morning till night before he gets used to mother being away. And he's such a good boy. I couldn't do without him.'

Mr Verloc went on divesting himself of his clothing with the unnoticing inward concentration of a man undressing in the solitude of a vast and hopeless desert. For thus inhospitably did this fair earth, our common inheritance, present itself to the mental vision of Mr Verloc. All was so still without and within that the lonely ticking of the clock on the landing stole into the room as if for the sake of company.

Mr Verloc, getting into bed on his own side, remained prone and mute behind Mrs Verloc's back. His thick arms rested abandoned on the outside of the counterpane like dropped weapons, like discarded tools. At that moment he was within a hair's breadth of making a clean breast of it all to his wife. The moment seemed propitious. Looking out of the corners of his eyes, he saw her ample shoulders draped in white, the back of her head, with the hair done for the night in three plaits tied up with black tapes at the ends. And he forbore. Mr Verloc loved his wife as a wife should be loved – that is, maritally, with the regard one has for one's chief possession. This head arranged for the night, those ample shoulders, had an aspect of familiar sacredness – the sacredness of domestic peace. She moved not, massive and shapeless like a recumbent statue in the rough; he remembered her wide-open eyes looking into the empty room. She was mysterious, with the mysteriousness of living beings. The far-famed secret agent Δ of the late Baron Stott-Wartenheim's alarmist despatches was not the man to break into such mysteries. He was easily intimidated. And he was also indolent, with the indolence which is so often the secret of good nature. He forbore touching that mystery out of love, timidity, and indolence. There would be always time enough. For several minutes he bore his sufferings silently in the drowsy silence of the room. And then he disturbed it by a resolute declaration.

'I am going on the Continent tomorrow.'

His wife might have fallen asleep already. He could not tell. As a matter of fact, Mrs Verloc had heard him. Her eyes remained very wide open, and she lay very still, confirmed in her instinctive conviction that things don't bear looking into very much. And yet it was nothing very unusual for Mr Verloc to take such a trip. He renewed his stock from Paris and Brussels. Often he went over to make his purchases personally. A little select connection of amateurs was forming around the shop in Brett Street, a secret connection eminently proper for any business undertaken by Mr Verloc, who, by a mystic accord of temperament and necessity, had been set apart to be a secret agent all his life.

He waited for a while, then added: 'I'll be away a week or perhaps a fortnight. Get Mrs Neale to come for the day.'

Mrs Neale was the charwoman of Brett Street. Victim of her marriage with a debauched joiner, she was oppressed by the needs of many infant children. Red-armed, and aproned in coarse sacking up to the armpits, she exhaled the anguish of the poor in a breath of soapsuds and rum, in the uproar of scrubbing, in the clatter of tin pails.

Mrs Verloc, full of deep purpose, spoke in the tone of the shallowest indifference.

'There is no need to have the woman here all day. I shall do very well with Stevie.'

She let the lonely clock on the landing count off fifteen ticks into the abyss of eternity, and asked: 'Shall I put the light out?'

Mr Verloc snapped at his wife huskily.

'Put it out.'

Chapter 9

Mr Verloc returning from the Continent at the end of ten days, brought back a mind evidently unrefreshed by the wonders of foreign travel and a countenance unlighted by the joys of home-coming. He entered in the clatter of the shop-bell with an air of sombre and vexed exhaustion. His bag in hand, his head lowered, he strode straight behind the counter, and let himself fall into the chair, as though he had tramped all the way from Dover. It was early morning. Stevie, dusting various objects displayed in the front windows, turned to gape at him with reverence and awe.

'Here!' said Mr Verloc, giving a slight kick to the Gladstone bag on the floor; and Stevie flung himself upon it, seized it, bore it off with triumphant devotion. He was so prompt that Mr Verloc was distinctly surprised.

Already at the clatter of the shop-bell Mrs Neale, black-leading the parlour grate, had looked through the door, and rising from her knees had gone, aproned, and grimy with everlasting toil, to tell Mrs Verloc in the kitchen that 'there was the master come back.'

Winnie came no farther than the inner shop door.

'You'll want some breakfast,' she said from a distance.

Mr Verloc moved his hands slightly, as if overcome by an impossible suggestion. But once enticed into the parlour he did not reject the food set before him. He ate as if in a public place, his hat pushed off his forehead, the skirts of his heavy overcoat hanging in a triangle on each side of the chair. And across the length of the table covered with brown oilcloth Winnie, his wife, talked evenly at him the wifely talk, as artfully adapted, no doubt, to the circumstances of this return as the talk of Penelope to the return of the wandering Odysseus. Mrs Verloc, however, had done no weaving during her husband's absence. But she had had all the upstairs room cleaned thoroughly, had sold some wares, had seen Mr Michaelis several times. He had told her the last time that he was going away to live in a cottage in the country, somewhere on the London, Chatham, and Dover line. Karl Yundt had come, too, once, led under the arm by that 'wicked old housekeeper of his'. He was 'a disgusting old man'. Of Comrade Ossipon, whom she had received curtly, entrenched behind the counter with a stony face and a faraway gaze, she said nothing, her mental reference to the robust anarchist being marked by a short pause, with the faintest possible blush. And bringing in her brother Stevie as soon as she could into the current of domestic events, she mentioned that the boy had moped a good deal.

'It's all along of mother leaving us like this.' Mr Verloc neither said 'Damn!' nor yet 'Stevie be hanged!' And Mrs Verloc, not let into the secret of his thoughts, failed to appreciate the generosity of this restraint.

'It isn't that he doesn't work as well as ever,' she continued. 'He's been making himself very useful. You'd think he couldn't do enough for us.'

Mr Verloc directed a casual and somnolent glance at Stevie, who sat on his right, delicate, pale-faced, his rosy mouth open vacantly. It was not a critical glance. It had no intention. And if Mr Verloc thought for a moment that his wife's brother looked uncommonly useless, it was only a dull and fleeting thought, devoid of that force and durability which enables sometimes a thought to move the world. Leaning back, Mr Verloc uncovered his head. Before his extended arm could put down the hat Stevie pounced upon it, and bore it off reverently into the kitchen. And again Mr Verloc was surprised.

'You could do anything with that boy, Adolf.' Mrs Verloc said, with her best air of inflexible calmness. 'He would go through fire for you. He . . .'

She paused attentive, her ear turned towards the door of the kitchen.

There Mrs Neale was scrubbing the floor. At Stevie's appearance she groaned lamentably, having observed that he could be induced easily to bestow for the benefit of her infant children the shilling his sister Winnie presented him with from time to time. On all fours amongst the puddles, wet and begrimed, like a sort of amphibious and domestic animal living in ashbins and dirty water, she uttered the usual exordium: 'It's all very well for you, kept doing nothing like a gentleman.' And she followed it with the everlasting plaint of the poor, pathetically mendacious, miserably authenticated by the horrible breath of cheap rum and soapsuds. She scrubbed hard, snuffling all the time, and talking volubly. And she was sincere. And on each side of her thin red nose her bleared, misty eyes swam in tears, because she felt really the want of some sort of stimulant in the morning.

In the parlour Mrs Verloc observed, with knowledge: 'There's Mrs Neale at it again with her harrowing tales about her little children. They can't be all so little as she makes them out. Some of them must be big enough by now to try to do something for themselves. It only makes Stevie angry.'

These words were confirmed by a thud as of a fist striking the kitchen table. In the normal evolution of his sympathy Stevie had become angry on discovering that he had no shilling in his pocket. In his inability to relieve at once Mrs Neale's 'little 'uns' ' privations, he felt that somebody should be made to suffer for it. Mrs Verloc rose, and went into the kitchen to 'stop that nonsense.' And she did it firmly but gently. She was well aware that directly Mrs Neale received her money she went round the corner to drink ardent spirits in a mean and musty public-house, the unavoidable station on the *via dolorosa* of her life. Mrs Verloc's comment upon this practice had an unexpected profundity, as coming from a person disinclined to look under the surface of things. 'Of course, what is she to do to keep up? If I were like Mrs Neale I expect I wouldn't act any different.'

In the afternoon of the same day, as Mr Verloc, coming with a start out of the last of a long series of dozes before the parlour fire, declared his intention of going out for a walk, Winnie said from the shop: 'I wish you would take that boy out with you, Adolf.'

For the third time that day Mr Verloc was surprised. He stared stupidly at his wife. She continued in her steady manner. The boy, whenever he was not doing anything, moped in the house. It made her uneasy; it made her nervous, she confessed. And that from the calm Winnie sounded like exaggeration. But, in truth, Stevie moped in the striking fashion of an unhappy domestic animal. He would go up on the dark landing, to sit on the floor at the foot of the tall clock, with his knees drawn up and his head in his hands. To come upon his pallid face, with its big eyes gleaming in the dusk, was discomposing; to think of him up there was uncomfortable.

Mr Verloc got used to the startling novelty of the idea. He was fond of his wife as a man should be – that is, generously. But a weighty objection presented itself to his mind, and he formulated it.

'He'll lose sight of me perhaps, and get lost in the street,' he said.

Mrs Verloc shook her head competently.

'He won't. You don't know him. That boy just worships you. But if you should miss him – '

Mrs Verloc paused for a moment, but only for a moment.

'You just go on, and have your walk out. Don't worry. He'll be all right. He's sure to turn up safe here before very long.'

This optimism procured for Mr Verloc his fourth surprise of the day.

'Is he?' he grunted, doubtfully. But perhaps his brother-in-law was not such an idiot as he looked. His wife would know best. He turned away his heavy eyes, saying huskily: 'Well, let him come along, then,' and relapsed into the clutches of black care, that perhaps prefers to sit behind a horseman, but knows also how to tread close on the heels of people not sufficiently well off to keep horses – like Mr Verloc, for instance.

Winnie, at the shop door, did not see this fatal attendant upon Mr Verloc's walks. She watched the two figures down the squalid street, one tall and burly, the other slight and short, with a thin neck, and the peaked shoulders raised slightly under the large semi-transparent ears. The material of their overcoats was the same, their hats were black and round in shape. Inspired by the similarity of wearing apparel, Mrs Verloc gave rein to her fancy.

'Might be father and son,' she said to herself. She thought also that Mr Verloc was as much of a father as poor Stevie ever had in his life. She was aware also that it was her work. And with peaceful pride she congratulated herself on a certain resolution she had taken a few years before. It had cost her some effort, and even a few tears.

She congratulated herself still more on observing in the course of days that Mr Verloc seemed to be taking kindly to Stevie's companionship. Now, when ready to go out for his walk, Mr Verloc called aloud to the boy, in the spirit, no doubt, in which a man invites the attendance of the household dog, though, of course, in a different manner. In the house Mr Verloc could be detected staring curiously at Stevie a good deal. His own demeanour had changed. Taciturn still, he was not so listless. Mrs Verloc thought that he was rather jumpy at times. It might have been regarded as an improvement. As to Stevie, he moped no longer at the foot of the clock, but muttered to himself in corners instead in a threatening tone. When asked, 'What is it you're saying, Stevie?' he merely opened his mouth, and squinted at his sister. At odd times he clenched his fists without apparent cause, and when discovered in solitude would be scowling at the wall, with the sheet of paper and the pencil given him for drawing circles lying blank and idle on the kitchen table. This was a change, but it was no improvement. Mrs Verloc, including all these vagaries under the general definition of excitement began to fear that Stevie was hearing more than was good for him of her husband's conversations with his friends. During his 'walks' Mr Verloc, of course, met and conversed with various persons. It could hardly be otherwise. His walks were an integral part of his outdoor activities, which his wife had never looked deeply into. Mrs Verloc felt that the position was delicate, but she faced it with the same impenetrable calmness which impressed and even astonished the customers of the shop and made the other visitors keep their distance a little wonderingly. No! She feared that there were things not good for Stevie to hear of, she told her husband. It only excited the poor boy, because he could not help them being so. Nobody could.

It was in the shop. Mr Verloc made no comment. He made no retort, and yet the retort was obvious. But he refrained from pointing out to his wife that the idea of making Stevie the companion of his walks was her own, and nobody else's. At that moment, to an impartial observer, Mr Verloc would have appeared more than human in his magnanimity. He took down a small cardboard box from a shelf, peeped in to see that the contents were all right, and put it down gently on the counter. Not till that was done did he break the silence, to the effect that most likely Stevie would profit greatly by being sent out of town for a while; only he supposed his wife could not get on without him.

'Could not get on without him!' repeated Mrs Verloc, slowly. 'I couldn't get on without him if it were for his good! The idea! Of course, I can get on without him. But there's nowhere for him to go.'

Mr Verloc got out some brown paper and a ball of string; and meanwhile he muttered that Michaelis was living in a little cottage in the country. Michaelis wouldn't mind giving Stevie a room to sleep in. There were no visitors and no talk there. Michaelis was writing a book.

Mrs Verloc declared her affection for Michaelis; mentioned her abhorrence of Karl Yundt, 'nasty old man'; and of Ossipon she said nothing. As to Stevie, he could be no other than very pleased. Mr Michaelis was always so nice and kind to him. He seemed to like the boy. Well, the boy was a good boy.

'You, too, seem to have grown quite fond of him of late,' she added, after a pause, with her inflexible assurance.

Mr Verloc, tying up the cardboard box into a parcel for the post, broke the string by an injudicious jerk, and muttered several swear words confidentially to himself. Then raising his tone to the usual husky mutter, he announced his willingness to take Stevie into the country himself, and leave him all safe with Michaelis.

He carried out this scheme on the very next day. Stevie offered no objection. He seemed rather eager, in a bewildered sort of way. He turned his candid gaze inquisitively to Mr Verloc's heavy countenance at frequent intervals, especially when his sister was not looking at him. His expression was proud, apprehensive, and concentrated, like that of a small child entrusted for the first time with a box of matches and the permission to strike a light. But Mrs Verloc, gratified by her brother's docility, recommended him not to dirty his clothes unduly in the country. At this Stevie gave his sister, guardian, and protector a look, which for the first time in his life seemed to lack the quality of perfect childlike trustfulness. It was haughtily gloomy. Mrs Verloc smiled.

'Goodness me! You needn't be offended. You know you do get yourself very untidy when you get a chance, Stevie.'

Mr Verloc was already gone some way down the street.

Thus in consequence of her mother's heroic proceedings, and of her brother's absence on this *villegiature*, Mrs Verloc found herself oftener than usual all alone not only in the shop, but in the house. For Mr Verloc had to take his walks. She was alone longer than usual on the day of the attempted bomb outrage in Greenwich Park, because Mr Verloc went out very early that morning and did not come back till nearly dusk. She did not mind being alone. She had no desire to go out. The weather was too bad, and the shop was cosier than the streets. Sitting behind the counter with some sewing, she did not raise her eyes from her work when Mr Verloc entered in the aggressive clatter of the bell. She had recognised his step on the pavement outside.

She did not raise her eyes, but as Mr Verloc, silent, and with his hat rammed down upon his forehead, made straight for the parlour door, she said, serenely: 'What a wretched day. You've been perhaps to see Stevie?'

'No! I haven't,' said Mr Verloc, softly, and slammed the glazed parlour door behind him with unexpected energy.

For some time Mrs Verloc remained quiescent, with her work dropped in her lap, before she put it away under the counter and got up to light the gas. This done, she went into the parlour on her way to the kitchen. Mr Verloc would want his tea presently. Confident of the power of her charms, Winnie did not expect from her husband in the daily intercourse of their married life a ceremonious amenity of address and courtliness of manner; vain and antiquated forms at best, probably never very exactly observed, discarded nowadays even in the highest spheres, and always foreign to the standard of her class. She did not look for courtesies from him. But he was a good husband, and she had a loyal respect for his rights.

Mrs Verloc would have gone through the parlour and on to her domestic duties in the kitchen with the perfect serenity of a woman sure of the power of her charms. But a slight, very slight, and rapid rattling sound grew upon her hearing. Bizarre and incomprehensible, it arrested Mrs Verloc's attention. Then as his character became plain to the ear she stopped short, amazed and concerned. Striking a match on the box she held in her hand, she turned on and lighted, above the parlour table, one of the two gas-burners, which, being defective, first whistled as if astonished, and then went on purring comfortably like a cat.

Mr Verloc, against his usual practice, had thrown off his overcoat. It was lying on the sofa. His hat, which he must also have thrown off, rested overturned under the edge of the sofa. He had dragged a chair in front of the fireplace, and his feet planted inside the fender, his head held between his hands, he was hanging low over the glowing grate. His teeth rattled with an ungovernable violence, causing his whole enormous back to tremble at the same rate. Mrs Verloc was startled.

'You've been getting wet,' she said.

'Not very,' Mr Verloc managed to falter out, in a profound shudder. By a great effort he suppressed the rattling of his teeth.

'I'll have you laid up on my hands,' she said, with genuine uneasiness.

'I don't think so,' remarked Mr Verloc, snuffling huskily.

He had certainly contrived somehow to catch an abominable cold between seven in the morning and five in the afternoon. Mrs Verloc looked at his bowed back.

'Where have you been today?' she asked.

'Nowhere,' answered Mr Verloc in a low, choked nasal tone. His attitude suggested aggrieved sulks or a severe headache. The insufficiency and un-candidness of his answer became painfully apparent in the dead silence of the room. He snuffled apologetically, and added: 'I've been to the bank.'

Mrs Verloc became attentive.

'You have!' she said, dispassionately. 'What for?'

Mr Verloc mumbled, with his nose over the grate, and with marked unwillingness: 'Draw the money out!'

'What do you mean? All of it?'

'Yes. All of it.'

Mrs Verloc spread out with care the scanty tablecloth, got two knives and two forks out of the table drawer, and suddenly stopped in her methodical proceedings.

'What did you do that for?'

'May want it soon,' snuffled vaguely Mr Verloc, who was coming to the end of his calculated indiscretions.

'I don't know what you mean,' remarked his wife in a tone perfectly casual, but standing stock still between the table and the cupboard.

'You know you can trust me,' Mr Verloc remarked to the grate, with hoarse feeling.

Mrs Verloc turned slowly towards the cupboard, saying with deliberation: 'Oh, yes. I can trust you.'

And she went on with her methodical proceedings. She laid two plates, got the bread, the butter, going to and fro quietly between the table and the cupboard in the peace and silence of her home. On the point of taking out the jam, she reflected practically: 'He will be feeling hungry, having been away all day,' and she returned to the cupboard once more to get the cold beef. She set it under the purring gas-jet, and with a passing glance at her motionless husband hugging the fire, she went (down two steps) into the kitchen. It was only when coming back, carving knife and fork in hand, that she spoke again.

'If I hadn't trusted you I wouldn't have married you.'

Bowed under the overmantel, Mr Verloc, holding his head in both hands, seemed to have gone to sleep. Winnie made the tea, and called out in an undertone: 'Adolf.'

Mr Verloc got up at once, and staggered a little before he sat down at the table. His wife, examining the sharp edge of the carving knife, placed it on the dish, and called his attention to the cold beef. He remained insensible to the suggestion, with his chin on his breast.

'You should feed your cold,' Mrs Verloc said, dogmatically.

He looked up, and shook his head. His eyes were bloodshot and his face red. His fingers had ruffled his hair into a dissipated untidiness. Altogether he had a disreputable aspect, expressive of the discomfort, the irritation, and the gloom following a heavy debauch. But Mr Verloc was not a debauched man. In his conduct he was respectable. His appearance might have been the effect of a feverish cold. He drank three cups of tea, but abstained from food entirely. He recoiled from it with sombre aversion when urged by Mrs Verloc, who said at last: 'Aren't your feet wet? You had better put on your slippers. You aren't going out any more this evening.'

Mr Verloc intimated by morose grunts and signs that his feet were not wet, and that anyhow he did not care. The proposal as to slippers was disregarded as beneath his notice. But the question of going out in the evening received an unexpected development. It was not of going out in the evening that Mr Verloc was thinking. His thoughts embraced a vaster scheme. From moody and incomplete phrases it became apparent that Mr Verloc had been considering the expediency of emigrating. It was not very clear whether he had in his mind France or California.

The utter unexpectedness, improbability, and inconceivableness of such an event robbed this vague declaration of all its effect. Mrs Verloc, as placidly as if her husband had been threatening her with the end of the world, said: 'The idea!'

Mr Verloc declared himself sick and tired of everything, and besides . . . She interrupted him.

'You've a bad cold.'

It was indeed obvious that Mr Verloc was not in his usual state, physically and even mentally. A sombre irresolution held him silent for a while. Then he murmured a few ominous generalities on the theme of necessity.

'Will have to,' repeated Winnie, sitting calmly back, with folded arms, opposite her husband. 'I should like to know who's to make you. You ain't a slave. No one need be a slave in this country – and don't you make yourself one.' She paused, and with invincible and steady candour: 'The business isn't so bad,' she went on. 'You've a comfortable home.'

She glanced all round the parlour, from the corner cupboard to the good fire in the grate. Ensconced cosily behind the shop of doubtful wares, with the mysteriously dim window, and its door suspiciously ajar in the obscure and narrow street, it was in all essentials of domestic propriety and domestic comfort a respectable home. Her devoted affection missed out of it her brother Stevie, now enjoying a damp *villegiature* in the Kentish lanes under the care of Mr Michaelis. She missed him poignantly, with all the force of her protecting passion. This was the boy's home, to the roof, the cupboard, the stoked grate. On this thought Mrs Verloc rose, and walking to the other end of the table, said in the fullness of her heart: 'And you are not tired of me.'

Mr Verloc made no sound. Winnie leaned on his shoulder from behind, and pressed her lips to his forehead. Thus she lingered. Not a whisper reached them from the outside world. The sound of footsteps on the pavement died out in the discreet dimness of the shop. Only the gas-jet above the table went on purring equably in the brooding silence of the parlour.

During the contact of that unexpected and lingering kiss Mr Verloc, gripping with both hands the edges of his chair, preserved a hieratic immobility. When the pressure was removed he let go the chair, rose, and went to stand before the fireplace. He turned no longer his back to the room. With his features swollen and an air of being drugged, he followed his wife's movements with his eyes.

Mrs Verloc went about serenely, clearing up the table. Her tranquil voice commented on the idea thrown out in a reasonable and domestic tone. It wouldn't stand examination. She condemned it from every point of view. But her only real concern was Stevie's welfare. He appeared to her thought in that connection as sufficiently 'peculiar' not to be taken rashly abroad. And that was all. But talking round that vital point, she approached absolute vehemence in her delivery. Meanwhile, with brusque movements, she arrayed herself in an apron for the washing up of cups. And as if excited by the sound of her uncontradicted voice, she went so far as to say in a tone almost tart: 'If you go abroad you'll have to go without me.'

'You know I wouldn't,' said Mr Verloc, huskily, and the unresonant voice of his private life trembled with an enigmatical emotion.

Already Mrs Verloc was regretting her words. They had sounded more unkind than she meant them to be. They had also the unwisdom of un-necessary things. In fact, she had not meant them at all. It was a sort of phrase that is suggested by the demon of perverse inspiration. But she knew a way to make it as if it had not been.

She turned her head over her shoulder and gave that man planted heavily in front of the fireplace a glance, half arch, half cruel, out of her large eyes – a glance of which the Winnie of the Belgravian mansion days would have been incapable, because of her respectability and her ignorance. But the man was her husband now, and she was no longer ignorant. She kept it on him for a whole second, with her grave face motionless like a mask, while she said playfully: 'You couldn't. You would miss me too much.'

Mr Verloc started forward.

'Exactly,' he said in a louder tone, throwing his arms out and making a step towards her. Something wild and doubtful in his expression made it appear uncertain whether he meant to strangle or to embrace his wife. But Mrs Verloc's attention was called away from that manifestation by the clatter of the shop-bell.

'Shop, Adolf. You go.'

He stopped, his arms came down slowly.

'You go,' repeated Mrs Verloc. 'I've got my apron on.'

Mr Verloc obeyed woodenly, stony-eyed, and like an automaton whose face had been painted red. And this resemblance to a mechanical figure went so far that he had an automaton's absurd air of being aware of the machinery inside of him.

He closed the parlour door, and Mrs Verloc, moving briskly, carried the tray into the kitchen. She washed the cups and some other things before she stopped in her work to listen. No sound reached her. The customer was a long time in the shop. It was a customer, because if he had not been Mr Verloc would have taken him inside. Undoing the strings of her apron with a jerk, she threw it on a chair, and walked back to the parlour slowly.

At that precise moment Mr Verloc entered from the shop.

He had gone in red. He came out a strange papery white. His face, losing its drugged, feverish stupor, had in that short time acquired a be-wildered and harassed expression. He walked straight to the sofa, and stood looking down at his overcoat lying there, as though he were afraid to touch it.

'What's the matter?' asked Mrs Verloc in a subdued voice. Through the door left ajar she could see that the customer was not gone yet.

'I find I'll have to go out this evening,' said Mr Verloc. He did not attempt to pick up his outer garment.

Without a word Winnie made for the shop, and shutting the door after her, walked in behind the counter. She did not look overtly at the customer till she had established herself comfortably on the chair. But by that time she had noted that he was tall and thin, and wore his moustaches twisted up. In fact, he gave the sharp points a twist just then. His long, bony face rose out of a turned-up collar. He was a little splashed, a little wet. A dark man, with the ridge of the cheek-bone well defined under the slightly hollow temple. A complete stranger. Not a customer, either.

Mrs Verloc looked at him placidly.

'You came over from the Continent?' she said after a time.

The long, thin stranger, without exactly looking at Mrs Verloc, answered only by a faint and peculiar smile.

Mrs Verloc's steady, incurious gaze rested on him.

'You understand English, don't you?'

'Oh, yes. I understand English.'

There was nothing foreign in his accent, except that he seemed in his slow enunciation to be taking pains with it. And Mrs Verloc, in her varied experience, had come to the conclusion that some foreigners could speak better English than the natives. She said, looking at the door of the parlour fixedly: 'You don't think perhaps of staying in England for good?'

The stranger gave her again a silent smile. He had a kindly mouth and probing eyes. And he shook his head a little sadly, it seemed.

'My husband will see you through all right. Meantime, for a few days you couldn't do better than take lodgings with Mr Guigliani. Continental Hotel it's called. Private. It's quiet. My husband will take you there.'

'A good idea,' said the thin, dark man, whose glance had hardened suddenly.

'You knew Mr Verloc before, didn't you? Perhaps in France?'

'I have heard of him,' admitted the visitor in his slow, painstaking tone, which yet had a certain curtness of intention.

There was a pause. Then he spoke again, in a far less elaborate manner.

'Your husband has not gone out to wait for me in the street by chance?'

'In the street!' repeated Mrs Verloc, surprised. 'He couldn't. There's no other door to the house.' For a moment she sat impassive, then left her seat to go and peep through the glazed door. Suddenly she opened it, and disappeared into the parlour.

Mr Verloc had done no more than put on his overcoat. But why he should remain afterwards leaning over the table propped up on his two arms as though he were feeling giddy or sick, she could not understand. 'Adolf,' she called out half aloud; and when he had raised himself: 'Do you know that man?' she asked, rapidly.

'I've heard of him,' whispered uneasily Mr Verloc, darting a wild glance at the door.

Mrs Verloc's fine, incurious eyes lighted up with a flash of abhorrence.

'One of Karl Yundt's friends – beastly old man.'

'No! No!' protested Mr Verloc, busy fishing for his hat. But when he got it from under the sofa he held it as if he did not know the use of a hat.

'Well – he's waiting for you,' said Mrs Verloc at last. 'I say, Adolf, he ain't one of them Embassy people you have been bothered with of late?'

'Bothered with Embassy people,' repeated Mr Verloc, with a heavy start of surprise and fear. 'Who's been talking to you of the Embassy people?'

'Yourself.'

'I! I! Talked of the Embassy to you!'

Mr Verloc seemed scared and bewildered beyond measure. His wife explained: 'You've been talking a little in your sleep of late, Adolf.'

'What – what did I say? What do you know?'

'Nothing much. It seemed mostly nonsense. Enough to let me guess that something worried you.'

Mr Verloc rammed his hat on his head. A crimson flood of anger ran over his face.

'Nonsense – eh? The Embassy people! I would cut their hearts out one after another. But let them look out. I've got a tongue in my head.'

He fumed, pacing up and down between the table and the sofa, his open overcoat catching against the angles. The red flood of anger ebbed out, and left his face all white, with quivering nostrils. Mrs Verloc, for the purposes of practical existence, put down these appearances to the cold.

'Well,' she said, 'get rid of the man whoever he is, as soon as you can, and come back home to me. You want looking after for a day or two.'

Mr Verloc calmed down, and, with resolution imprinted on his pale face, had already opened the door, when his wife called him back in a whisper: 'Adolf! Adolf!' He came back, startled. 'What about that money you drew out?' she asked. 'You've got it in your pocket? Hadn't you better . . . '

Mr Verloc gazed stupidly into the palm of his wife's extended hand for some time before he slapped his brow.

'Money! Yes! Yes! I didn't know what you meant.'

He drew out of his breast pocket a new pigskin pocket-book. Mrs Verloc received it without another word, and stood still till the bell, clattering after Mr Verloc and Mr Verloc's visitor, had quieted down. Only then she peeped in at the amount, drawing the notes out for the purpose. After this inspection she looked round thoughtfully, with an air of mistrust in the silence and solitude of the house. This abode of her married life appeared to her as lonely and unsafe as though it had been situated in the midst of a forest. No receptacle she could think of amongst the solid, heavy furniture seemed other but flimsy and particularly tempting to her conception of a house-breaker. It was an ideal conception, endowed with sublime faculties and a miraculous insight. The till was not to be thought of. It was the first spot a thief would make for. Mrs Verloc, unfastening hastily a couple of hooks, slipped the pocket-book under the bodice of her dress. Having thus disposed of her husband's capital, she was rather glad to hear the clatter of the doorbell, announcing an arrival. Assuming the fixed, unabashed stare and the stony expression reserved for the casual customer, she walked in behind the counter.

A man standing in the middle of the shop was inspecting it with a swift, cool, all-round glance. His eyes ran over the walls, took in the ceiling, noted the floor, all in a moment. The points of a long fair moustache fell below the line of the jaw. He smiled the smile of an old if distant acquaintance and Mrs Verloc remembered having seen him before. Not a customer. She softened her 'customer stare' to mere indifference, and faced him across the counter.

He approached, on his side, confidentially, but not too markedly so.

'Husband at home, Mrs Verloc?' he asked in an easy, full tone.

'No. He's gone out.'

'I am sorry for that. I've called to get from him a little private information.'

This was the exact truth. Chief Inspector Heat had been all the way home and had even gone so far as to think of getting into his slippers, since practically he was, he told himself, chucked out of that case. He indulged in some scornful and in a few angry thoughts, and found the occupation so unsatisfactory that he resolved to seek relief out of doors. Nothing prevented him paying a friendly call on Mr Verloc, casually as it were. It was in the character of a private citizen that walking out privately he made use of his customary conveyances. Their general direction was towards Mr Verloc's home. Chief Inspector Heat respected his own private character so con-sistently that he took especial pains to avoid all the police constables on point and patrol duty in the vicinity of Brett Street. This precaution was much more necessary for a man of his standing than for an obscure Assistant Commissioner. Private Citizen Heat entered the street, manoeuvring in a way which in a member of the criminal classes would have been stigmatised as slinking. The piece of cloth picked up in Greenwich was in his pocket. Not that he had the slightest intention of producing it in his private capacity. On the contrary, he wanted to know just what Mr Verloc would be disposed to say voluntarily. He hoped Mr Verloc's talk would be of a nature to incriminate Michaelis. It was a conscientiously professional hope in the main, but not without its moral value. For Chief Inspector Heat was a servant of justice. Finding Mr Verloc from home, he felt disappointed.

'I would wait for him a little if I were sure he wouldn't be long,' he said.

Mrs Verloc volunteered no assurance of any kind. 'The information I need is quite private,' he repeated. 'You understand what I mean? I wonder if you could give me a notion where he's gone to?'

Mrs Verloc shook her head.

'Can't say.'

She turned away to range some boxes on the shelves behind the counter. Chief Inspector Heat looked at her thoughtfully for a time.

'I suppose you know who I am?' he said.

Mrs Verloc glanced over her shoulder. Chief Inspector Heat was amazed at her coolness.

'Come! You know I am in the police,' he said, sharply.

'I don't trouble my head much about it,' Mrs Verloc remarked, returning to the ranging of her boxes.

'My name is Heat. Chief Inspector Heat of the Special Crimes section.'

Mrs Verloc adjusted nicely in its place a small cardboard box, and turning round, faced him again, heavy-eyed, with idle hands hanging down. A silence reigned for a time.

'So your husband went out a quarter of an hour ago! And he didn't say when he would be back?'

'He didn't go out alone,' Mrs Verloc let fall negligently.

'A friend?'

Mrs Verloc touched the back of her hair. It was in perfect order.

'A stranger who called.'

'I see. What sort of man was that stranger? Would you mind telling me?'

Mrs Verloc did not mind. And when Chief Inspector Heat heard of a man dark, thin, with a long face and turned-up moustaches, he gave signs of perturbation, and exclaimed: 'Dash me if I didn't think so! He hasn't lost any time.'

He was intensely disgusted in the secrecy of his heart at the unofficial conduct of his immediate chief. But he was not quixotic. He lost all desire to await Mr Verloc's return. What they had gone out for he did not know, but he imagined it possible that they would return together. The case is not followed properly, it's being tampered with, he thought, bitterly.

'I am afraid I haven't time to wait for your husband,' he said.

Mrs Verloc received this declaration listlessly. Her detachment had impressed Chief Inspector Heat all along. At this precise moment it whetted his curiosity. Chief Inspector Heat hung in the wind, swayed by his passions like the most private of citizens.

'I think,' he said, looking at her steadily, 'that you could give me a pretty good notion of what's going on if you liked.'

Forcing her fine, inert eyes to return his gaze, Mrs Verloc murmured: 'Going on! What is going on?'

'Why, the affair I came to talk about a little with your husband.'

That day Mrs Verloc had glanced at a morning paper as usual. But she had not stirred out of doors. The newsboys never invaded Brett Street. It was not a street for their business. And the echo of their cries drifting along the populous thoroughfares expired between the dirty brick walls without reaching the threshold of the shop. Her husband had not brought an evening paper home. At any rate she had not seen it. Mrs Verloc knew nothing whatever of any affair. And she said so, with a genuine note of wonder in her quiet voice.

Chief Inspector Heat did not believe for a moment in so much ignorance. Curtly, without amiability, he stated the bare fact.

Mrs Verloc turned away her eyes.

'I call it silly,' she pronounced, slowly. She paused. 'We ain't downtrodden slaves here.'

The Chief Inspector waited watchfully. Nothing more came.

'And your husband didn't mention anything to you when he came home?'

Mrs Verloc simply turned her face from right to left in sign of negation. A languid, baffling silence reigned in the shop. Chief Inspector Heat felt provoked beyond endurance.

'There was another small matter,' he began in a detached tone, 'which I wanted to speak to your husband about. There came into our hands a – a – what we believe is – a stolen overcoat.'

Mrs Verloc, with her mind specially aware of thieves that evening, touched lightly the bosom of her dress.

'We have lost no overcoat,' she said, calmly.

'That's funny,' continued Private Citizen Heat. 'I see you keep a lot of marking ink here.'

He took up a small bottle, and looked at it against the gas-jet in the middle of the shop.

'Purple – isn't it?' he remarked, setting it down again. 'As I said, it's strange. Because the overcoat has got a label sewn on the inside with your address written in marking ink.'

Mrs Verloc leaned over the counter with a low exclamation.

'That's my brother's, then.'

'Where's your brother? Can I see him?' asked the Chief Inspector, briskly. Mrs Verloc leaned a little more over the counter.

'No. He isn't here. I wrote that label myself.'

'Where's your brother now?'

'He's been away living with – a friend – in the country.'

'The overcoat comes from the country. And what's the name of the friend?'

'Michaelis,' confessed Mrs Verloc in an awed whisper.

The Chief Inspector let out a whistle. His eyes snapped.

'Just so. Capital. And your brother now, what's he like, a sturdy, darkish chap – eh?'

'Oh, no,' exclaimed Mrs Verloc, fervently. 'That must be the thief. Stevie's slight and fair.'

'Good,' said the Chief Inspector in an approving tone. And while Mrs Verloc, wavering between alarm and wonder, stared at him, he sought for information. Why have the address sewn like this inside the coat? And he heard that the mangled remains he had inspected that morning with extreme repugnance were those of a youth, nervous, absent-minded, peculiar, and also that the woman who was speaking to him had the charge of that boy since he was a baby.

'Easily excitable?' he suggested.

'Oh, yes. He is. But how did he come to lose his coat.'

Chief Inspector Heat suddenly pulled out a pink newspaper he had bought less than half an hour ago. He was interested in horses. Forced by his calling into an attitude of doubt and suspicion towards his fellow citizens, Chief Inspector Heat relieved the instinct of credulity implanted in the human breast by putting unbounded faith in the sporting prophets of that particular evening publication. Dropping the extra special on to the counter, he plunged his hand again into his pocket, and pulling out the piece of cloth fate had presented him with out of a heap of things that seemed to have been collected in shambles and rag shop, he offered it to Mrs Verloc for inspection.

'I suppose you recognise this?'

She took it mechanically in both her hands. Her eyes seemed to grow bigger as she looked.

'Yes,' she whispered, then raised her head, and staggered backward a little.

'Whatever for is it torn out like this?'

The Chief Inspector snatched across the counter the cloth out of her hands, and she sat heavily on the chair. He thought: identification's perfect. And in that moment he had a glimpse into the whole amazing truth. Verloc was the 'other man.'

'Mrs Verloc,' he said, 'it strikes me that you know more of this bomb affair than even you yourself are aware of.'

Mrs Verloc sat still, amazed, lost in boundless astonishment. What was the connection? And she became so rigid all over that she was not able to turn her head at the clatter of the bell, which caused the private investigator Heat to spin round on his heel. Mr Verloc had shut the door, and for a moment the two men looked at each other.

Mr Verloc, without looking at his wife, walked up to the Chief Inspector, who was relieved to see him return alone.

'You here!' muttered Mr Verloc, heavily. 'Who are you after?'

'No one,' said Chief Inspector Heat in a low tone. 'Look here, I would like a word or two with you.'

Mr Verloc, still pale, had brought an air of resolution with him. Still he didn't look at his wife. He said: 'Come in here, then.' And he led the way into the parlour.

The door was hardly shut when Mrs Verloc, jumping up from the chair, ran to it as if to fling it open, but instead of doing so fell on her knees, with her ear to the keyhole. The two men must have stopped directly they were through, because she heard plainly the Chief Inspector's voice, though she could not see his finger pressed against her husband's breast emphatically.

'You are the other man, Verloc. Two men were seen entering the park.'

And the voice of Mr Verloc said: 'Well, take me now. What's to prevent you? You have the right.'

'Oh, no! I know too well who you have been giving yourself away to. He'll have to manage this little affair all by himself. But don't you make a mistake, it's I who found you out.'

Then she heard only muttering. Inspector Heat must have been showing to Mr Verloc the piece of Stevie's overcoat, because Stevie's sister, guardian, and protector heard her husband a little louder.

'I never noticed that she had hit upon that dodge.'

Again for a time Mrs Verloc heard nothing but murmurs, whose mysteriousness was less nightmarish to her brain than the horrible suggestions of shaped words. Then Chief Inspector Heat, on the other side of the door, raised his voice: 'You must have been mad.'

And Mr Verloc's voice answered, with a sort of, gloomy fury: 'I have been mad for a month or more, but I am not mad now. It's all over. It shall all come out of my head, and hang the consequences.'

There was a silence, and then Private Citizen Heat murmured: 'What's coming out?'

'Everything,' exclaimed the voice of Mr Verloc, and then sank very low.

After a while it rose again.

'You have known me for several years now, and you've found me useful, too. You know I was a straight man. Yes, straight.'

This appeal to old acquaintance must have been extremely distasteful to the Chief Inspector.

His voice took on a warning note.

'Don't you trust so much to what you have been promised. If I were you I would clear out. I don't think we will run after you.'

Mr Verloc was heard to laugh a little.

'Oh, yes; you hope the others will get rid of me for you – don't you? No, no; you don't shake me off now. I have been a straight man to those people too long, and now everything must come out.'

'Let it come out, then,' the indifferent voice of Chief Inspector Heat assented. 'But tell me now how did you get away?'

'I was making for Chesterfield Walk,' Mrs Verloc heard her husband's voice, 'when I heard the bang. I started running then. Fog. I saw no one till I was past the end of George Street. Don't think I met anyone till then.'

'So easy as that!' marvelled the voice of Chief Inspector Heat. 'The bang startled you, eh?'

'Yes; it came too soon,' confessed the gloomy, husky voice of Mr Verloc.

Mrs Verloc pressed her ear to the keyhole; her lips were blue, her hands cold as ice, and her pale face, in which the two eyes seemed like two black holes, felt to her as if it were enveloped in flames.

On the other side of the door the voices sank very low. She caught words now and then, sometimes in her husband's voice, sometimes in the smooth tones of the Chief Inspector. She heard this last say, 'We believe he stumbled against the root of a tree?'

There was a husky, voluble murmur, which lasted for some time, and then the Chief Inspector, as if answering some enquiry, spoke emphatically: 'Of course. Blown to small bits: limbs, gravel, clothing, bones, splinters – all mixed up together. I tell you they had to fetch a shovel to gather him up with.'

Mrs Verloc sprang up suddenly from her crouching position, and stopping her ears, reeled to and fro between the counter and the shelves on the wall towards the chair. Her crazed eyes noted the sporting sheet left by the Chief Inspector, and as she knocked herself against the counter she snatched it up, fell into the chair, tore the optimistic, rosy sheet right across in trying to open it, then flung it on the floor. On the other side of the door, Chief Inspector Heat was saying to Mr Verloc, the secret agent: 'So your defence will be practically a full confession?'

'It will. I am going to tell the whole story.'

'You won't be believed as much as you fancy you will.'

And the Chief Inspector remained thoughtful. The turn this affair was taking meant the disclosure of many things – the laying waste of fields of knowledge, which, cultivated by a capable man, had a distinct value for the individual and for the society. It was sorry, sorry meddling. It would leave Michaelis unscathed; it would drag to light the Professor's home industry; disorganise the whole system of supervision; make no end of a row in the papers, which, from that point of view, appeared to him by a sudden illumination as invariably written by fools for the reading of imbeciles. Mentally he agreed with the words Mr Verloc let fall at last in answer to his last remark.

'Perhaps not. But it will upset many things. I have been a straight man, and I shall keep straight in this.'

'If they let you,' said the Chief Inspector, cynically. 'You will be preached to, no doubt, before they put you into the dock. And in the end you may yet get let in for a sentence that will surprise you. I wouldn't trust too much the gentleman who's been talking to you.'

Mr Verloc listened, frowning.

'My advice to you is to clear out while you may. I have no instructions. There are some of them,' continued Chief Inspector Heat, laying a peculiar stress on the word 'them,' 'who think you are already out of the world.'

'Indeed!' Mr Verloc was moved to say. Though since his return from Greenwich he had spent most of his time sitting in the tap-room of an obscure little public-house, he could hardly have hoped for such favourable news.

'That's the impression about you.' The Chief Inspector nodded at him. 'Vanish. Clear out.'

'Where to?' snarled Mr Verloc. He raised his head, and gazing at the closed door of the parlour, muttered feelingly: 'I only wish you would take me away tonight. I would go quietly.'

'I dare say,' assented sardonically the Chief Inspector, following the direction of his glance.

The brow of Mr Verloc broke into slight moisture. He lowered his husky voice confidentially before the unmoved Chief Inspector.

'The lad was half-witted, irresponsible. Any court would have seen that at once. Only fit for the asylum. And that was the worst that would've happened to him if . . . '

The Chief Inspector, his hand on the door handle, whispered into Mr Verloc's face: 'He may've been half-witted, but you must have been crazy. What drove you off your head like this?'

Mr Verloc, thinking of Mr Vladimir, did not hesitate in the choice of words.

'A Hyperborean swine,' he hissed, forcibly. 'A what you might call a – a gentleman.'

The Chief Inspector, steady-eyed, nodded briefly his comprehension, and opened the door. Mrs Verloc, behind the counter, might have heard but did not see his departure, pursued by the aggressive clatter of the bell. She sat at her post of duty behind the counter. She sat rigidly erect in the chair with two dirty pink pieces of paper lying spread out at her feet. The palms of her hands were pressed convulsively to her face, with the tips of the fingers contracted against the forehead, as though the skin had been a mask which she was ready to tear off violently. The perfect immobility of her pose expressed the agitation of rage and despair, all the potential violence of tragic passions, better than any shallow display of shrieks, with the beating of a distracted head against the walls, could have done. Chief Inspector Heat, crossing the shop at his busy, swinging pace, gave her only a cursory glance. And when the cracked bell ceased to tremble on its curved ribbon of steel nothing stirred near Mrs Verloc, as if her attitude had the locking power of a spell. Even the butterfly-shaped gas flames posed on the ends of the suspended T-bracket burned without a quiver. In that shop of shady wares fitted with deal shelves painted a dull brown, which seemed to devour the sheen of the light, the gold circlet of the wedding ring on Mrs Verloc's left hand glittered exceedingly with the untarnished glory of a piece from some splendid treasure of jewels, dropped in a dustbin.

Chapter 10

The Assistant Commissioner, driven rapidly in a hansom from the neighbour-hood of Soho in the direction of Westminster, got out at the very centre of the Empire on which the sun never sets. Some stalwart constables, who did not seem particularly impressed by the duty of watching the august spot, saluted him. Penetrating through a portal by no means lofty into the precincts of the House which is *the* House, *par excellence*, in the minds of many millions of men, he was met at last by the volatile and revolutionary Toodles.

That neat and nice young man concealed his astonishment at the early appearance of the Assistant Commissioner, whom he had been told to look out for sometime about midnight. His turning up so early he concluded to be the sign that things, whatever they were, had gone wrong. With an extremely ready sympathy, which in nice youngsters goes often with a joyous tempe-rament, he felt sorry for the great Presence he called 'The Chief,' and also for the Assistant Commissioner, whose face appeared to him more ominously wooden than ever before, and quite wonderfully long. 'What a queer, foreign-looking chap he is,' he thought to himself, smiling from a distance with friendly buoyancy. And directly they came together he began to talk with the kind intention of burying the awkwardness of failure under a heap of words. It looked as if the great assault threatened for that night were going to fizzle out. An inferior henchman of 'that brute Chessman' was up boring mercilessly a very thin House with some shamelessly cooked statistics. He, Toodles, hoped he would bore them into a count out every minute. But then he might be only marking time to let that guzzling Cheeseman dine at his leisure. Anyway, the Chief could not be persuaded to go home.

'He will see you at once, I think. He's sitting all alone in his room thinking of all the fishes of the sea,' concluded Toodles, airily. 'Come along.'

Notwithstanding the kindness of his disposition, the young private secre-tary (unpaid) was accessible to the common failings of humanity. He did not wish to harrow the feelings of the Assistant Commissioner, who looked to him uncommonly like a man who has made a mess of his job. But his curiosity was too strong to be restrained by mere compassion. He could not help, as they went along, to throw over his shoulder lightly: 'And your sprat?'

'Got him,' answered the Assistant Commissioner with a concision which did not mean to be repellent in the least.

'Good. You've no idea how these great men dislike to be disappointed in small things.'

After this profound observation the experienced Toodles seemed to reflect. At any rate he said nothing for quite two seconds. Then: 'I'm glad. But – I say – is it really such a very small thing as you make it out?'

'Do you know what may be done with a sprat?' the Assistant Commissioner asked in his turn.

'He's sometimes put into a sardine box,' chuckled Toodles, whose erudition on the subject of the fishing industry was fresh and, in comparison with his ignorance of all other industrial matters, immense. 'There are sardine canneries on the Spanish coast which . . .'

The Assistant Commissioner interrupted the apprentice statesman.

'Yes. Yes. But a sprat is also thrown away sometimes in order to catch a whale.'

'A whale. Phew!' exclaimed Toodles, with bated breath. 'You're after a whale, then?'

'Not exactly. What I am after is more like a dogfish. You don't know perhaps what a dogfish is like.'

'Yes; I do. We're buried in special books up to our necks – whole shelves full of them – with plates . . . It's a noxious, rascally-looking, altogether detestable beast, with a sort of smooth face and moustaches.'

'Described to a T,' commended the Assistant Commissioner. 'Only mine is clean-shaven altogether. You've seen him. It's a witty fish.'

'I have seen him!' said Toodles, incredulously. 'I can't conceive where I could have seen him.'

'At the Explorers, I should say,' dropped the Assistant Commissioner, calmly. At the name of that extremely exclusive club Toodles looked scared, and stopped short.

'Nonsense,' he protested, but in an awestruck tone. 'What do you mean? A member?'

'Honorary,' muttered the Assistant Commissioner through his teeth.

'Heavens!'

Toodles looked so thunderstruck that the Assistant Commissioner smiled faintly.

'That's between ourselves strictly,' he said.

'That's the beastliest thing I've ever heard in my life,' declared Toodles, feebly, as if astonishment had robbed him of all his buoyant strength in a second.

The Assistant Commissioner gave him an unsmiling glance. Till they came to the door of the great man's room, Toodles preserved a scandalised and solemn silence, as though he were offended with the Assistant Commissioner for exposing such an unsavoury and disturbing fact. It revolutionised his idea of the Explorers' Club's extreme selectness, of its social purity. Toodles was revolutionary only in politics; his social beliefs and personal feelings he wished to preserve unchanged through all the years allotted to him on this earth which, upon the whole, he believed to be a nice place to live on.

He stood aside.

'Go in without knocking,' he said.

Shades of green silk fitted low over all the lights imparted to the room something of a forest's deep gloom. The haughty eyes were physically the great man's weak point. This point was wrapped up in secrecy. When an opportunity offered, he rested them conscientiously. The Assistant Commissioner entering saw at first only a big pale hand supporting a big head, and concealing the upper part of a big pale face. An open despatch-box stood on the writing-table near a few oblong sheets of paper and a scattered handful of quill pens. There was absolutely nothing else on the large flat surface except a little bronze statuette draped in a toga, mysteriously watchful in its shadowy immobility. The Assistant Commissioner, invited to take a chair, sat down. In the dim light, the salient points of his personality, the long face, the black hair, his lankness, made him look more foreign than ever.

The great man manifested no surprise, no eagerness, no sentiment whatever. The attitude in which he rested his menaced eyes was profoundly meditative. He did not alter it the least bit. But his tone was not dreamy.

'Well! What is it that you've found out already? You came upon something unexpected on the first step.'

'Not exactly unexpected, Sir Ethelred. What I mainly came upon was a psychological state.'

The Great Presence made a slight movement.

'You must be lucid, please.'

'Yes, Sir Ethelred. You know no doubt that most criminals at sometime or other feel an irresistible need of confessing – of making a clean breast of it to somebody – to anybody. And they do it often to the police. In that Verloc whom Heat wished so much to screen I've found a man in that particular psychological state. The man, figuratively speaking, flung himself on my breast. It was enough on my part to whisper to him who I was and to add, 'I know that you are at the bottom of this affair.' It must have seemed miraculous to him that we should know already, but he took it all in the stride. The wonderfulness of it never checked him for a moment. There remained for me only to put to him the two questions: Who put you up to it? and, Who was the man who did it? He answered the first with remarkable emphasis. As to the second question, I gather that the fellow with the bomb was his brother - in - law – quite a lad – a weak-minded creature . . . It is rather a curious affair – too long perhaps to state fully just now.'

'What then have you learned?' asked the great man.

'First, I've learned that the ex-convict Michaelis had nothing to do with it, though indeed the lad had been living with him temporarily in the country up to eight o'clock this morning. It is more than likely that Michaelis knows nothing of it to this moment.'

'You are positive as to that?' asked the great man.

'Quite certain, Sir Ethelred. This fellow Verloc went there this morning, and took away the lad on the pretence of going out for a walk in the lanes. As it was not the first time that he did this, Michaelis could not have the slightest suspicion of anything unusual. For the rest, Sir Ethelred, the indignation of this man Verloc had left nothing in doubt – nothing whatever. He had been driven out of his mind almost by an extraordinary performance, which for you or me it would be difficult to take as seriously meant, but which produced a great impression obviously on him.'

The Assistant Commissioner then imparted briefly to the great man, who sat still, resting his eyes under the screen of his hand, Mr Verloc's appreciation of Mr Vladimir's proceedings and character. The Assistant Commissioner did not seem to refuse it a certain amount of competency. But the great personage remarked: 'All this seems very fantastic.'

'Doesn't it? One would think a ferocious joke. But our man took it seriously, it appears. He felt himself threatened. Formerly, you know, he was in direct communication with old Stott-Wartenheim himself, and had come to regard his services as indispensable. It was an extremely rude awakening. I imagine that he lost his head. He became angry and frightened. Upon my word, my impression is that he thought these Embassy people quite capable not only to throw him out, but to give him away, too, in some manner or other . . . '

'How long were you with him?' interrupted the Presence from behind his big hand.

'Some forty minutes, Sir Ethelred, in a house of bad repute called Continental Hotel, closeted in a room which by the by I took for the night. I found him under the influence of that reaction which follows the effort of crime. The man cannot be defined as a hardened criminal. It is obvious that he did not plan the death of that wretched lad – his brother-in-law. That was a shock to him – I could see that. Perhaps he is a man of strong sensibilities. Perhaps he was even fond of the lad – who knows? He might have hoped that the fellow would get clear away; in which case it would have been almost impossible to bring this thing home to anyone. At any rate, he risked consciously nothing more but arrest for him.'

The Assistant Commissioner paused in his speculations to reflect for a moment.

'Though how, in that last case, he could hope to have his own share in the business concealed is more than I can tell,' he continued, in his ignorance of poor Stevie's devotion to Mr Verloc (who was *good*), and of his truly peculiar dumbness, which in the old affair of fireworks on the stairs had for many years resisted entreaties, coaxing, anger, and other means of investigation used by his beloved sister. For Stevie was loyal . . . 'No, I can't imagine. It's possible that he never thought of that at all. It sounds an extravagant way of putting it, Sir Ethelred, but his state of dismay suggested to me an impulsive man who, after committing suicide with the notion that it would end all his troubles, had discovered that it did nothing of the kind.'

The Assistant Commissioner gave this definition in an apologetic voice. But in truth there is a sort of lucidity proper to extravagant language, and the great man was not offended. A slight jerky movement of the big body half lost in the gloom of the green silk shades, of the big head leaning on the big hand, accompanied an intermittent stifled but powerful sound. The great man had laughed.

'What have you done with him?'

The Assistant Commissioner answered very readily: 'As he seemed very anxious to get back to his wife in the shop I let him go, Sir Ethelred.'

'You did? But the fellow will disappear.'

'Pardon me. I don't think so. Where could he go to? Moreover, you must remember that he has got to think of the danger from his comrades, too. He's there at his post. How could he explain leaving it? But even if there were no obstacles to his freedom of action he would do nothing. At present he hasn't enough moral energy to take a resolution of any sort. Permit me also to point out that if I had detained him we would have been committed to a course of action on which I wished to know your precise intentions first.'

The great personage rose heavily, an imposing, shadowy form in the greenish gloom of the room.

'I'll see the Attorney-General tonight, and will send for you tomorrow morning. Is there anything more you'd wish to tell me now?'

The Assistant Commissioner had stood up also, slender and flexible.

'I think not, Sir Ethelred, unless I were to enter into details which . . .'

'No. No details, please.'

The great shadowy form seemed to shrink away as if in physical dread of details; then came forward, expanded, enormous, and weighty, offering a large hand. 'And you say that this man has got a wife?'

'Yes, Sir Ethelred,' said the Assistant Commissioner, pressing deferentially the extended hand. 'A genuine wife and a genuinely, respectably, marital relation. He told me that after his interview at the Embassy he would have thrown everything up, would have tried to sell his shop, and leave the country, only he felt certain that his wife would not even hear of going abroad. Nothing could be more characteristic of the respectable bond than that,' went on, with a touch of grimness, the Assistant Commissioner, whose own wife, too, had refused to hear of going abroad. 'Yes, a genuine wife. And the victim was a genuine brother-in-law. From a certain point of view we are here in the presence of a domestic drama.'

The Assistant Commissioner laughed a little; but the great man's thoughts seemed to have wandered far away, perhaps to the questions of his country's domestic policy, the battleground of his crusading valour against the paynim Cheeseman. The Assistant Commissioner withdrew quietly, unnoticed, as if already forgotten.

He had his own crusading instincts. This affair, which, in one way or another, disgusted Chief Inspector Heat, seemed to him a providentially given starting point for a crusade. He had it much at heart to begin. He walked slowly home, meditating that enterprise on the way, and thinking over Mr Verloc's psychology in a composite mood of repugnance and satisfaction. He walked all the way home. Finding the drawing-room dark, he went upstairs, and spent some time between the bedroom and the dressing-room, changing his clothes, going to and fro with the air of a thoughtful somnambulist. But he shook it off before going out again to join his wife at the house of the great lady patroness of Michaelis.

He knew he would be welcomed there. On entering the smaller of the two drawing-rooms he saw his wife in a small group near the piano. A youngish composer in pass of becoming famous was discoursing from a music stool to two thick men whose backs looked old, and three slender women whose backs looked young. Behind the screen the great lady had only two persons with her: a man and a woman, who sat side by side on armchairs at the foot of her couch. She extended her hand to the Assistant Commissioner.

'I never hoped to see you here tonight. Annie told me . . .'

'Yes. I had no idea myself that my work would be over so soon.'

The Assistant Commissioner added in a low tone: 'I am glad to tell you that Michaelis is altogether clear of this . . .'

The patroness of the ex-convict received this assurance indignantly.

'Why? Were your people stupid enough to connect him with . . .'

'Not stupid,' interrupted the Assistant Commissioner, contradicting deferentially. 'Clever enough – quite clever enough for that.'

A silence fell. The man at the foot of the couch had stopped speaking to the lady, and looked on with a faint smile.

'I don't know whether you ever met before,' said the great lady.

Mr Vladimir and the Assistant Commissioner, introduced, acknowledged each other's existence with punctilious and guarded courtesy.

'He's been frightening me,' declared suddenly the lady who sat by the side of Mr Vladimir, with an inclination of the head towards that gentleman. The Assistant Commissioner knew the lady.

'You do not look frightened,' he pronounced, after surveying her conscientiously with his tired and equable gaze. He was thinking meantime to himself that in this house one met everybody sooner or later. Mr Vladimir's rosy countenance was wreathed in smiles, because he was witty, but his eyes remained serious, like the eyes of convinced man.

'Well, he tried to at least,' amended the lady.

'Force of habit perhaps,' said the Assistant Commissioner, moved by an irresistible inspiration.

'He has been threatening society with all sorts of horrors,' continued the lady, whose enunciation was caressing and slow, 'apropos of this explosion in Greenwich Park. It appears we all ought to quake in our shoes at what's coming if those people are not suppressed all over the world. I had no idea this was such a grave affair.'

Mr Vladimir, affecting not to listen, leaned towards the couch, talking amiably in subdued tones, but he heard the Assistant Commissioner say: 'I've no doubt that Mr Vladimir has a very precise notion of the true importance of this affair.'

Mr Vladimir asked himself what that confounded and intrusive policeman was driving at. Descended from generations victimised by the instruments of an arbitrary power, he was racially, nationally, and individually afraid of the police. It was an inherited weakness, altogether independent of his judgement, of his reason, of his experience. He was born to it. But that sentiment, which resembled the irrational horror some people have of cats, did not stand in the way of his immense contempt for the English police. He finished the sentence addressed to the great lady, and turned slightly in his chair.

'You mean that we have a great experience of these people. Yes; indeed, we suffer greatly from their activity, while you' – Mr Vladimir hesitated for a moment, in smiling perplexity – 'While you suffer their presence gladly in your midst,' he finished, displaying a dimple in each clean-shaven cheek. Then he added more gravely: 'I may even say – because you do.'

When Mr Vladimir ceased speaking the Assistant Commissioner lowered his glance, and the conversation dropped. Almost immediately afterwards Mr Vladimir took leave. Directly his back was turned on the couch the Assistant Commissioner rose, too.

'I thought you were going to stay and take Annie home,' said the lady patroness of Michaelis.

'I find that I've yet a little work to do tonight.'

'In connection . . . ?'

'Well, yes – in a way.'

'Tell me, what is it really – this horror?'

'It's difficult to say what it is, but it may yet be a *cause célèbre*,' said the Assistant Commissioner.

He left the drawing-room hurriedly, and found Mr Vladimir still in the hall, wrapping up his throat carefully in a large silk handkerchief. Behind him a footman waited, holding his overcoat. Another stood ready to open the door. The Assistant Commissioner was duly helped into his coat, and let out at once. After descending the front steps he stopped, as if to consider the way he should take. On seeing this through the door held open, Mr Vladimir lingered in the hall to get out a cigar and asked for a light. It was furnished to him by an elderly man out of livery with an air of calm solicitude. But the match went out; the footman then closed the door, and Mr Vladimir lighted his large Havana with leisurely care. When at last he got out of the house, he saw with disgust the 'confounded policeman' still standing on the pavement.

'Can he be waiting for me,' thought Mr Vladimir, looking up and down for some signs of a hansom. He saw none. A couple of carriages waited by

the kerbstone, their lamps blazing steadily, the horses standing perfectly
still, as if carved in stone, the coachmen sitting motionless under the big fur
capes, without as much as a quiver stirring the white thongs of their big
whips. Mr Vladimir walked on, and the 'confounded policeman' fell into
step at his elbow. He said nothing. At the end of the fourth stride Mr
Vladimir felt infuriated and uneasy. This could not last.

'Rotten weather,' he growled, savagely.

'Mild,' said the Assistant Commissioner without passion. He remained
silent for a little while. 'We've got hold of a man called Verloc,' he announced,
casually.

Mr Vladimir did not stumble, did not stagger back, did not change his
stride. But he could not prevent himself from exclaiming: 'What?' The
Assistant Commissioner did not repeat his statement. 'You know him,' he
went on in the same tone.

Mr Vladimir stopped, and became guttural.

'What makes you say that?'

'I don't. It's Verloc who says that.'

'A lying dog of some sort,' said Mr Vladimir in somewhat Oriental
phraseology. But in his heart he was almost awed by the miraculous cleverness of the English police. The change of his opinion on the subject was so
violent that it made him for a moment feel slightly sick. He threw away his
cigar, and moved on.

'What pleased me most in this affair,' the Assistant went on, talking
slowly, 'is that it makes such an excellent starting-point for a piece of work
which I've felt must be taken in hand – that is, the clearing out of this
country of all the foreign political spies, police, and that sort of – of – dogs.
In my opinion they are a ghastly nuisance; also an element of danger. But we
can't very well seek them out individually. The only way is to make their
employment unpleasant to their employers. The thing's becoming indecent.
And dangerous, too, for us, here.'

Mr Vladimir stopped again for a moment.

'What do you mean?'

'The prosecution of this Verloc will demonstrate to the public both the
danger and the indecency.'

'Nobody will believe what a man of that sort says,' said Mr Vladimir,
contemptuously.

'The wealth and precision of detail will carry conviction to the great mass
of the public,' advanced the Assistant Commissioner gently.

'So that is seriously what you mean to do.'

'We've got the man; we have no choice.'

'You will be only feeding up the lying spirit of these revolutionary scoundrels,' Mr Vladimir protested. 'What do you want to make a scandal for? –
from morality – or what?'

Mr Vladimir's anxiety was obvious. The Assistant Commissioner, having ascertained in this way that there must be some truth in the summary statements of Mr Verloc, said indifferently: 'There's a practical side, too. We have really enough to do to look after the genuine article. You can't say we are not effective. But we don't intend to let ourselves be bothered by shams under any pretext whatever.'

Mr Vladimir's tone became lofty.

'For my part, I can't share your view. It is selfish. My sentiments for my own country cannot be doubted; but I've always felt that we ought to be good Europeans besides – I mean governments and men.'

'Yes,' said the Assistant Commissioner simply. 'Only you look at Europe from its other end. But,' he went on in a good-natured tone, 'the foreign governments cannot complain of the inefficiency of our police. Look at this outrage; a case specially difficult to trace inasmuch as it was a sham. In less than twelve hours we have established the identity of a man literally blown to shreds, have found the organiser of the attempt, and have had a glimpse of the inciter behind him. And we could have gone further; only we stopped at the limits of our territory.'

'So this instructive crime was planned abroad,' Mr Vladimir said, quickly. 'You admit it was planned abroad?'

'Theoretically. Theoretically only, on foreign territory; abroad only by a fiction,' said the Assistant Commissioner, alluding to the character of Embassies which are supposed to be part and parcel of the country to which they belong. 'But that's a detail. I talked to you of this business because it's your government that grumbles most at our police. You see that we are not so bad. I wanted particularly to tell you of our success.'

'I'm sure I'm very grateful,' muttered Mr Vladimir through his teeth.

'We can put our finger on every anarchist here,' went on the Assistant Commissioner, as though he were quoting Chief Inspector Heat. 'All that's wanted now is to do away with the agent provocateur to make everything safe.'

Mr Vladimir held up his hand to a passing hansom.

'You're not going in here,' remarked the Assistant Commissioner, looking at a building of noble proportions and hospitable aspect, with the light of a great hall falling through its glass doors on a broad flight of steps.

But Mr Vladimir, sitting, stony-eyed, inside the hansom, drove off without a word.

The Assistant Commissioner himself did not turn into the noble building. It was the Explorers' Club. The thought passed through his mind that Mr Vladimir, honorary member, would not be seen very often there in the future. He looked at his watch. It was only half-past ten. He had had a very full evening.

Chapter 11

After Chief Inspector Heat had left him Mr Verloc moved about the parlour. From time to time he eyed his wife through the open door. 'She knows all about it now,' he thought to himself with commiseration for her sorrow and with some satisfaction as regarded himself. Mr Verloc's soul, if lacking greatness perhaps, was capable of tender sentiments. The prospect of having to break the news to her had put him into a fever. Chief Inspector Heat had relieved him of the task. That was good as far as it went. It remained for him now to face her grief.

Mr Verloc had never expected to have to face it on account of death, whose catastrophic character cannot be argued away by sophisticated reasoning or persuasive eloquence. Mr Verloc never meant Stevie to perish with such abrupt violence. He did not mean him to perish at all. Stevie dead was a much greater nuisance than ever he had been when alive. Mr Verloc had augured a favourable issue to his enterprise, basing himself not on Stevie's intelligence, which sometimes plays queer tricks with a man, but on the blind docility and on the blind devotion of the boy. Though not much of a psychologist, Mr Verloc had gauged the depth of Stevie's fanaticism. He dared cherish the hope of Stevie walking away from the walls of the Observatory as he had been instructed to do, taking the way shown to him several times previously, and rejoining his brother-in-law, the wise and good Mr Verloc, outside the precincts of the park. Fifteen minutes ought to have been enough for the veriest fool to deposit the engine and walk away. And the Professor had guaranteed more than fifteen minutes. But Stevie had stumbled within five minutes of being left to himself. And Mr Verloc was shaken morally to pieces. He had foreseen everything but that. He had foreseen Stevie distracted and lost – sought for – found in some police station or provincial workhouse in the end. He had foreseen Stevie arrested, and was not afraid, because Mr Verloc had a great opinion of Stevie's loyalty, which had been carefully indoctrinated with the necessity of silence in the course of many walks. Like a peripatetic philosopher, Mr Verloc, strolling along the streets of London, had modified Stevie's view of the police by conversations full of subtle reasonings. Never had a sage a more attentive and admiring disciple. The submission and worship were so apparent that Mr Verloc had come to feel something like a liking for the boy. In any case, he had not foreseen the swift bringing home of his connection. That his wife should hit upon the precaution of sewing the boy's address inside his overcoat was the last thing Mr Verloc would have thought of. One can't think of everything. That was what she meant when she said that he need not worry if he lost Stevie during their walks. She had assured him that the boy would turn up all right. Well, he had turned up with a vengeance!

'Well, well,' muttered Mr Verloc in his wonder. What did she mean by it? Spare him the trouble of keeping an anxious eye on Stevie? Most likely she had meant well. Only she ought to have told him of the precaution she had taken.

Mr Verloc walked behind the counter of the shop. His intention was not to overwhelm his wife with bitter reproaches. Mr Verloc felt no bitterness. The unexpected march of events had converted him to the doctrine of fatalism. Nothing could be helped now. He said: 'I didn't mean any harm to come to the boy.'

Mrs Verloc shuddered at the sound of her husband's voice. She did not uncover her face. The trusted secret agent of the late Baron Stott-Wartenheim looked at her for a time with a heavy, persistent, undiscerning glance. The torn evening paper was lying at her feet. It could not have told her much. Mr Verloc felt the need of talking to his wife.

'It's that damned Heat - eh?' he said. 'He upset you. He's a brute, blurting it out like this to a woman. I made myself ill thinking how to break it to you. I sat for hours in the little parlour of Cheshire Cheese thinking over the best way. You understand I never meant any harm to come to that boy.'

Mr Verloc, the Secret Agent, was speaking the truth. It was his marital affection that had received the greatest shock from the premature explosion. He added: 'I didn't feel particularly gay sitting there and thinking of you.'

He observed another slight shudder of his wife, which affected his sensibility. As she persisted in hiding her face in her hands, he thought he had better leave her alone for a while. On this delicate impulse Mr Verloc withdrew into the parlour again, where the gas-jet purred like a contented cat. Mrs Verloc's wifely forethought had left the cold beef on the table with carving knife and fork and half a loaf of bread for Mr Verloc's supper. He noticed all these things now for the first time, and cutting himself a piece of bread and meat, he began to eat.

His appetite did not proceed from callousness. Mr Verloc had not eaten any breakfast that day. He had left his home fasting. Not being an energetic man, he found his resolution in nervous excitement, which seemed to hold him mainly by the throat. He could not have swallowed anything solid. Michaelis' cottage was as destitute of provisions as the cell of a prisoner. The ticket-of-leave apostle lived on a little milk and crusts of stale bread. Moreover, when Mr Verloc arrived he had already gone upstairs after his frugal meal. Absorbed in the toil and delight of literary composition, he had not even answered Mr Verloc's shout up the little staircase.

'I am taking this young fellow home for a day or two.'

And, in truth, Mr Verloc did not wait for an answer, but had marched out of the cottage at once, followed by the obedient Stevie.

Now that all action was over and his fate taken out of his hands with unexpected swiftness, Mr Verloc felt terribly empty physically. He carved the meat, cut the bread, and devoured his supper standing by the table, and now and then casting a glance towards his wife. Her prolonged immobility disturbed the comfort of his reflection. He walked again into the shop, and came up very close to her. This sorrow with a veiled face made Mr Verloc uneasy. He expected, of course, his wife to be very much upset, but he wanted her to pull herself together. He needed all her assistance and all her loyalty in these new conjunctures his fatalism had already accepted.

'Can't be helped,' he said in a tone of gloomy sympathy. 'Come, Winnie, we've got to think of tomorrow. You'll want all your wits about you after I am taken away.'

He paused. Mrs Verloc's breast heaved convulsively. This was not re-assuring to Mr Verloc, in whose view the newly created situation required from the two people most concerned in it calmness, decision, and other qualities incompatible with the mental disorder of passionate sorrow. Mr Verloc was a humane man; he had come home prepared to allow every latitude to his wife's affection for her brother. Only he did not understand either the nature or the whole extent of that sentiment. And in this he was excusable, since it was impossible for him to understand it without ceasing to be himself. He was startled and disappointed, and his speech conveyed it by a certain roughness of tone.

'You might look at a fellow,' he observed after waiting a while.

As if forced through the hands covering Mrs Verloc's face the answer came, deadened, almost pitiful.

'I don't want to look at you as long as I live.'

'Eh? What!' Mr Verloc was merely startled by the superficial and literal meaning of this declaration. It was obviously unreasonable, the mere cry of exaggerated grief. He threw over it the mantle of his marital indulgence. The mind of Mr Verloc lacked profundity. Under the mistaken impression that the value of individuals consists in what they are in themselves, he could not possibly comprehend the value of Stevie in the eyes of Mrs Verloc. She was taking it confoundedly hard, he thought to himself. It was all the fault of that damned Heat. What did he want to upset the woman for? But she mustn't be allowed, for her own good, to carry on so till she got quite beside herself.

'Look here! You can't sit like this in the shop,' he said with affected severity, in which there was some real annoyance; for urgent practical matters must be talked over if they had to sit up all night. 'Somebody might come in at any minute,' he added, and waited again. No effect was produced, and the idea of the finality of death occurred to Mr Verloc during the pause. He changed his tone. 'Come. This won't bring him back,' he said, gently, feeling ready to take her in his arms and press her to his breast, where impatience and compassion dwelt side by side. But except for a short shudder Mrs Verloc remained apparently unaffected by the force of that terrible truism. It was Mr

Verloc himself who was moved. He was moved in his simplicity to urge moderation by asserting the claims of his own personality.

'Do be reasonable, Winnie. What would it have been if you had lost me?'

He had vaguely expected to hear her cry out. But she did not budge. She leaned back a little, quieted down to a complete, unreadable stillness. Mr Verloc's heart began to beat faster with exasperation and something resembling alarm. He laid his hand on her shoulder, saying: 'Don't be a fool, Winnie.'

She gave no sign. It was impossible to talk to any purpose with a woman whose face one cannot see. Mr Verloc caught hold of his wife's wrists. But her hands seemed glued fast. She swayed forward bodily to his tug, and nearly went off the chair. Startled to feel her so helplessly limp, he was trying to put her back on the chair when she stiffened suddenly all over, tore herself out of his hands, ran out of the shop, across the parlour, and into the kitchen. This was very swift. He had just a glimpse of her face and that much of her eyes that he knew she had not looked at him.

It all had the appearance of a struggle for the possession of a chair, because Mr Verloc instantly took his wife's place in it. Mr Verloc did not cover his face with his hands, but a sombre thoughtfulness veiled his features. A term of imprisonment could not be avoided. He did not wish now to avoid it. A prison was a place as safe from certain unlawful vengeance as the grave, with this advantage, that in a prison there is room for hope. What he saw before him was a term of imprisonment, an early release, and then life abroad somewhere, such as he had contemplated already, in case of failure. Well, it was a failure, if not exactly the sort of failure he had feared. It had been so near success that he could have positively terrified Mr Vladimir out of his ferocious scoffing with this proof of occult efficiency. So at least it seemed now to Mr Verloc. His prestige with the Embassy would have been immense if – if his wife had not had the unlucky notion of sewing on the address inside Stevie's overcoat. Mr Verloc, who was no fool, had soon perceived the extraordinary character of the influence he had over Stevie, though he did not understand exactly its origin – the doctrine of his supreme wisdom and goodness inculcated by two anxious women. In all the eventualities he had foreseen Mr Verloc had calculated with correct insight on Stevie's instinctive loyalty and blind discretion. The eventuality he had not foreseen had appalled him as a humane man and a fond husband. From every other point of view it was rather advantageous. Nothing can equal the everlasting discretion of death. Mr Verloc, sitting perplexed and frightened in the small parlour of the Cheshire Cheese, could not help acknowledging that to himself, because his sensibility did not stand in the way of his judgement. Stevie's violent disintegration, however disturbing to think about, only assured the success; for, of course, the knocking down of a wall was not the aim of Mr Vladimir's menaces, but the production of a moral effect. With much trouble and distress on Mr Verloc's part the effect might be said to have been produced. When, however, most unexpectedly, it came home to roost in Brett Street, Mr Verloc, who had been struggling like a man in a nightmare for the preservation of his position, accepted the blow in the spirit of a convinced fatalist. The position was gone through no one's fault really. A small, tiny fact had done it. It was like slipping on a bit of orange peel in the dark and breaking your leg.

Mr Verloc drew a weary breath. He nourished no resentment against his wife. He thought: She will have to look after the shop while they keep me locked up. And thinking also how cruelly she would miss Stevie at first, he felt greatly concerned about her health and spirits. How would she stand her solitude absolutely alone in that house? It would not do for her to break down while he was locked up. What would become of the shop then? The shop was an asset. Though Mr Verloc's fatalism accepted his undoing as a secret agent, he had no mind to be utterly ruined; mostly, it must be owned, from regard for his wife.

Silent, and out of his line of sight in the kitchen, she frightened him. If only she had her mother with her. But that silly old woman . . . An angry dismay possessed Mr Verloc. He must talk with his wife. He could tell her certainly that a man does get desperate under certain circumstances. But he did not go incontinently to impart to her that information. First of all, it was clear to him that this evening was no time for business. He got up to close the street door and put the gas out in the shop.

Having thus assured a solitude around his hearthstone Mr Verloc walked into the parlour, and glanced down into the kitchen. Mrs Verloc was sitting in the place where poor Stevie usually established himself of an evening with paper and pencil for the pastime of drawing these coruscations of innumerable circles suggesting chaos and eternity. Her arms were folded on the table, and her head was lying on her arms. Mr Verloc contemplated her back and the arrangement of her hair for a time, then walked away from the kitchen door. Mrs Verloc's philosophical, almost disdainful incuriosity, the foundation of their accord in domestic life, made it extremely difficult to get into contact with her, now this tragic necessity had arisen. Mr Verloc felt this difficulty acutely. He turned around the table in the parlour with his usual air of a large animal in a cage.

Curiosity being one of the forms of self-revelation, a systematically incurious person remains always partly mysterious. Every time he passed near the door Mr Verloc glanced at his wife uneasily. It was not that he was afraid of her. Mr Verloc imagined himself loved by that woman. But she had not accustomed him to make confidences. And the confidence he had to make was of a profound psychological order. How with his want of practice could he tell her what he himself felt but vaguely: that there are conspiracies of fatal destiny, that a notion grows in a mind sometimes till it acquires an outward existence, an independent power of its own, and even a suggestive voice? He could not inform her that a man may be haunted by a fat, witty, clean-shaved face till the wildest expedient to get rid of it appears a child of wisdom.

On this mental reference to a First Secretary of a great Embassy, Mr Verloc stopped in the doorway, and looking down into the kitchen with an angry face and clenched fists, addressed his wife.

'You don't know what a brute I had to deal with.'

He started off to make another perambulation of the table; then when he had come to the door again he stopped, glaring in from the height of two steps.

'A silly, jeering, dangerous brute, with no more sense than . . . After all these years! A man like me! And I have been playing my head at that game. You didn't know. Quite right, too. What was the good of telling you that I stood the risk of having a knife stuck into me any time these seven years we've been married? I am not a chap to worry a woman that's fond of me. You had no business to know.'

Mr Verloc took another turn round the parlour, fuming.

'A venomous beast,' he began again from the doorway. 'Drive me out into a ditch to starve for a joke. I could see he thought it was a damned good joke. A man like me! Look here! Some of the highest in the world have got to thank me for walking on their two legs to this day. That's the man you've got married to, my girl!'

He perceived that his wife had sat up. Mrs Verloc's arms remained lying stretched on the table. Mr Verloc watched her back as if he could read there the effect of his words.

'There isn't a murdering plot for the last eleven years that I hadn't my finger in at the risk of my life. There's scores of these revolutionists I've sent off, with their bombs in their blamed pockets, to get themselves caught on the frontier. The old Baron knew what I was worth to his country. And here suddenly a swine comes along – an ignorant, overbearing swine.'

Mr Verloc, stepping slowly down two steps, entered the kitchen, took a tumbler off the dresser, and holding it in his hand, approached the sink, without looking at his wife.

'It wasn't the old Baron who would have had the wicked folly of getting me to call on him at eleven in the morning. There are two or three in this town that, if they had seen me going in, would have made no bones about knocking me on the head sooner or later. It was a silly, murderous trick to expose for nothing a man – like me.'

Mr Verloc, turning on the tap above the sink, poured three glasses of water, one after another, down his throat to quench the fires of his indignation. Mr Vladimir's conduct was like a hot brand which set his internal economy in a blaze. He could not get over the disloyalty of it. This man, who would not work at the usual hard tasks which society sets to its humbler members, had exercised his secret industry with an indefatigable devotion. There was in Mr Verloc a fund of loyalty. He had been loyal to his employers, to the cause of social stability – and to his affections, too – as became apparent when, after standing the tumbler in the sink, he turned about, saying: 'If I hadn't thought of you I would have taken the bullying brute by the throat and rammed his head into the fireplace. I'd have been more than a match for that pink-faced, smooth-shaved . . . '

Mr Verloc neglected to finish the sentence, as if there could be no doubt of the terminal word. For the first time in his life he was taking that incurious woman into his confidence. The singularity of the event, the force and importance of the personal feelings aroused in the course of this confession, drove Stevie's fate clean out of Mr Verloc's mind. The boy's stuttering existence of fears and indignations, together with the violence of his end, had passed out of Mr Verloc's mental sight for a time. For that reason, when he looked up he was startled by the inappropriate character of his wife's stare. It was not a wild stare, and it was not inattentive, but its attention was peculiar and not satisfactory, inasmuch that it seemed concentrated upon some point beyond Mr Verloc's person. The impression was so strong that Mr Verloc glanced over his shoulder. There was nothing behind him: there was just the whitewashed wall. The excellent husband of Winnie Verloc saw no writing on the wall. He turned to his wife again, repeating, with some emphasis: 'I would have taken him by the throat. As true as I stand here, if I hadn't thought of you then I would have half choked the life out of the brute before I let him get up. And don't you think he would have been anxious to call the police – either. He wouldn't have dared. You understand why – don't you?'

He blinked at his wife knowingly.

'No,' said Mrs Verloc in an unresonant voice, and without looking at him at all. 'What are you talking about?'

A great discouragement, the result of fatigue, came upon Mr Verloc. He had had a very full day, and his nerves had been tried to the utmost. After a month of maddening worry, ending in an unexpected catastrophe, the storm-tossed spirit of Mr Verloc longed for repose. His career as a secret agent had come to an end in a way no one could have foreseen; only, now, perhaps he could manage to get a night's sleep at last. But looking at his wife, he doubted it. She was taking it very hard – not at all like herself, he thought. He made an effort to speak.

'You'll have to pull yourself together, my girl,' he said, sympathetically. 'What's done can't be undone.'

Mrs Verloc gave a slight start, though not a muscle of her white face moved in the least. Mr Verloc, who was not looking at her, continued ponderously: 'You go to bed now. What you want is a good cry.'

This opinion had nothing to recommend it but the general consent of mankind. It is universally understood that, as if it were nothing more substantial than vapour floating in the sky, every emotion of a woman is bound to end in a shower. And it is very probable that had Stevie died in his bed under her despairing gaze, in her protecting arms, Mrs Verloc's grief would have found relief in a flood of bitter and pure tears. Mrs Verloc, in common with other human beings, was provided with a fund of unconscious resignation sufficient to meet the normal manifestation of human destiny. Without 'troubling her head about it,' she was aware that it 'did not stand looking into very much.' But the lamentable circumstances of Stevie's end, which to Mr Verloc's mind had only an episodic character, as part of a greater disaster, dried her tears at their very source. It was the effect of a white-hot iron drawn across her eyes; at the same time her heart, hardened and chilled into a lump of ice, kept her body in an inward shudder, set her features into a frozen, contemplative immobility addressed to a whitewashed wall with no writing on it. The exigencies of Mrs Verloc's temperament, which, when stripped of its philosophical reserve, was maternal and violent, forced her to roll a series of thoughts in her motionless head. These thoughts were rather imagined than expressed. Mrs Verloc was a woman of singularly few words, either for public or private use. With the rage and dismay of a betrayed woman, she reviewed the tenor of her life in visions concerned mostly with Stevie's difficult existence from its earliest days. It was a life of single purpose and of a noble unity of inspiration, like those rare lives that have left their mark on the thoughts and feelings of mankind. But the visions of Mrs Verloc lacked nobility and magnificence. She saw herself putting the boy to bed by the light of a single candle on the deserted top floor of a 'business house,' dark under the roof and scintillating exceedingly with lights and cut glass at the level of the street like a fairy palace. That meretricious splendour was the only one to be met in Mrs Verloc's visions. She remembered brushing the boy's hair and tying his pinafores – herself in a pinafore still; the consolations administered to a small and badly scared creature by another creature nearly as small but not quite so badly scared; she had the vision of the blows intercepted (often with her own head), of a door held desperately shut against a man's rage (not for very long); of a poker flung once (not very far), which stilled that particular storm into the dumb and awful silence which follows a thunderclap. And all these scenes of violence came and went accompanied by the unrefined noise of deep vociferations proceeding from a man wounded in his paternal pride, declaring himself obviously accursed since one of his kids was a 'slobbering idjut and the other a wicked she-devil.' It was of her that this had been said many years ago.

Mrs Verloc heard the words again in a ghostly fashion, and then the dreary shadow of the Belgravian mansion descended upon her shoulders. It was a crushing memory, an exhausting vision of countless breakfast trays carried up and down innumerable stairs, of endless haggling over pence, of the endless drudgery of sweeping, dusting, cleaning, from basement to attics; while the impotent mother, staggering on swollen legs, cooked in a grimy kitchen, and poor Stevie, the unconscious presiding genius of all their toil, blacked the gentlemen's boots in the scullery. But this vision had a breath of a hot London summer in it, and for a central figure a young man wearing his Sunday best, with a straw hat on his dark head and a wooden pipe in his mouth. Affectionate and jolly, he was a fascinating companion for a voyage down the sparkling stream of life; only his boat was very small. There was room in it for a girl-partner at the oar, but no accommodation for passengers. He was allowed to drift away from the threshold of the Belgravian mansion while Winnie averted her tearful eyes. He was not a lodger. The lodger was Mr Verloc, indolent and keeping late hours, sleepily jocular of a morning from under his bedclothes, but with gleams of infatuation in his heavy-lidded eyes, and always with some money in his pockets. There was no sparkle of any kind on the lazy stream of his life. It flowed through secret places. But his barque seemed a roomy craft, and his taciturn magnanimity accepted as a matter of course the presence of passengers.

Mrs Verloc pursued the visions of seven years' security for Stevie loyally paid for on her part; of security growing into confidence, into a domestic feeling, stagnant and deep like a placid pool, whose guarded surface hardly shuddered on the occasional passage of Comrade Ossipon, the robust anarchist with shamelessly inviting eyes, whose glance had a corrupt clearness sufficient to enlighten any woman not absolutely imbecile.

A few seconds only had elapsed since the last word had been uttered aloud in the kitchen, and Mrs Verloc was staring already at the vision of an episode not more than a fortnight old. With eyes whose pupils were extremely dilated she stared at the vision of her husband and poor Stevie walking up Brett Street side by side away from the shop. It was the last scene of an existence created by Mrs Verloc's genius; an existence foreign to all grace and charm, without beauty and almost without decency, but admirable in the continuity of feeling and tenacity of purpose. And this last vision had such plastic relief, such nearness of form, such a fidelity of suggestive detail, that it wrung from Mrs Verloc an anguished and faint murmur, reproducing the supreme illusion of her life, an appalled murmur that died out on her blanched lips.

'Might have been father and son.'

Mr Verloc stopped, and raised a careworn face. 'Eh? What did you say?' he asked. Receiving no reply, he resumed his sinister tramping. Then with a menacing flourish of a thick, fleshy fist, he burst out: 'Yes. The Embassy people. A pretty lot, ain't they! Before a week's out I'll make some of them wish themselves twenty feet under ground. Eh? What?'

He glanced sideways, with his head down. Mrs Verloc gazed at the whitewashed wall. A blank wall – perfectly blank. A blankness to run at and dash your head against. Mrs Verloc remained immovably seated. She kept still as the population of half the globe would keep still in astonishment and despair, were the sun suddenly put out in the summer sky by the perfidy of a trusted providence.

'The Embassy,' Mr Verloc began again, after a preliminary grimace which bared his teeth wolfishly. 'I wish I could get loose in there with a cudgel for half an hour. I would keep on hitting till there wasn't a single unbroken bone left amongst the whole lot. But never mind, I'll teach them yet what it means trying to throw out a man like me to rot in the streets. I've a tongue in my head. All the world shall know what I've done for them. I am not afraid. I don't care. Everything'll come out. Every damned thing. Let them look out!'

In these terms did Mr Verloc declare his thirst for revenge. It was a very appropriate revenge. It was in harmony with the promptings of Mr Verloc's genius. It had also the advantage of being within the range of his powers and of adjusting itself easily to the practice of his life, which had consisted precisely in betraying the secret and unlawful proceedings of his fellow-men. Anarchists or diplomats were all one to him. Mr Verloc was temperamentally no respecter of persons. His scorn was equally distributed over the whole field of his operations. But as a member of a revolutionary proletariat – which he undoubtedly was – he nourished a rather inimical sentiment against social distinction.

'Nothing on earth can stop me now,' he added, and paused, looking fixedly at his wife, who was looking fixedly at a blank wall.

The silence in the kitchen was prolonged, and Mr Verloc felt disappointed. He had expected his wife to say something. But Mrs Verloc's lips, composed in their usual form, preserved a statuesque immobility like the rest of her face. And Mr Verloc was disappointed. Yet the occasion did not, he recognised, demand speech from her. She was a woman of very few words. For reasons involved in the very foundation of his psychology, Mr Verloc was inclined to put his trust in any woman who had given herself to him. Therefore he trusted his wife. Their accord was perfect, but it was not precise. It was a tacit accord, congenial to Mrs Verloc's incuriosity and to Mr Verloc's habits of mind, which were indolent and secret. They refrained from going to the bottom of facts and motives.

This reserve, expressing, in a way, their profound confidence in each other, introduced at the same time a certain element of vagueness into their intimacy. No system of conjugal relations is perfect. Mr Verloc presumed that his wife had understood him but he would have been glad to hear her say what she thought at the moment. It would have been a comfort.

There were several reasons why this comfort was denied him. There was a physical obstacle: Mrs Verloc had not sufficient command over her voice. She did not see any alternative between screaming and silence, and instinctively she chose the silence. Winnie Verloc was temperamentally a silent person. And there was the paralysing atrocity of the thought which occupied her. Her cheeks were blanched, her lips ashy, her immobility amazing. And she thought without looking at Mr Verloc: 'This man took the boy away to murder him. He took the boy away from his home to murder him. He took the boy away from me to murder him!'

Mrs Verloc's whole being was racked by that inconclusive and maddening thought. It was in her veins, in her bones, in the roots of her hair. Mentally she assumed the biblical attitude of mourning – the covered face, the rent garments; the sound of wailing and lamentation filled her head. But her teeth were violently clenched, and her tearless eyes were hot with rage, because she was not a submissive creature. The protection she had extended over her brother had been in its origin of a fierce and indignant complexion. She had to love him with a militant love. She had battled for him – even against herself. His loss had the bitterness of defeat, with the anguish of a baffled passion. It was not an ordinary stroke of death. Moreover, it was not death that took Stevie from her. It was Mr Verloc who took him away. She had seen him. She had watched him, without raising a hand, take the boy away. And she had let him go, like – like a fool – a blind fool. Then after he had murdered the boy he came home to her. Just came home like any other man would come home to his wife . . .

Through her set teeth Mrs Verloc muttered at the wall: 'And I thought he had caught a cold.'

Mr Verloc heard these words and appropriated them.

'It was nothing,' he said, moodily. 'I was upset. I was upset on your account.'

Mrs Verloc, turning her head slowly, transferred her stare from the wall to her husband's person. Mr Verloc, with the tips of his fingers between his lips, was looking on the ground.

'Can't be helped,' he mumbled, letting his hand fall. 'You must pull yourself together. You'll want all your wits about you. It is you who brought the police about our ears. Never mind, I won't say anything more about it,' continued Mr Verloc, magnanimously. 'You couldn't know.'

'I couldn't,' breathed out Mrs Verloc. It was as if a corpse had spoken. Mr Verloc took up the thread of his discourse.

'I don't blame you. I'll make them sit up. Once under lock and key it will be safe enough for me to talk – you understand. You must reckon on me being two years away from you,' he continued, in a tone of sincere concern. 'It will be easier for you than for me. You'll have something to do, while I – Look here, Winnie, what you must do is to keep this business going for two years. You know enough for that. You've a good head on you. I'll send you word when it's time to go about trying to sell. You'll have to be extra careful. The comrades will be keeping an eye on you all the time. You'll have to be as artful as you know how, and as close as the grave. No one must know what you are going to do. I have no mind to get a knock on the head or a stab in the back directly I am let out.'

Thus spoke Mr Verloc, applying his mind with ingenuity and forethought to the problems of the future. His voice was sombre, because he had a correct sentiment of the situation. Everything which he did not wish to pass had come to pass. The future had become precarious. His judgement, perhaps, had been momentarily obscured by his dread of Mr Vladimir's truculent folly. A man somewhat over forty may be excusably thrown into considerable disorder by the prospect of losing his employment, especially if the man is a secret agent of political police, dwelling secure in the consciousness of his high value and in the esteem of high personages. He was excusable.

Now the thing had ended in a crash. Mr Verloc was cool; but he was not cheerful. A secret agent who throws his secrecy to the winds from desire of vengeance, and flaunts his achievements before the public eye, becomes the mark for desperate and bloodthirsty indignations. Without unduly exaggerating the danger, Mr Verloc tried to bring it clearly before his wife's mind. He repeated that he had no intention of letting the revolutionists do away with him.

He looked straight into his wife's eyes. The enlarged pupils of the woman received his stare into their unfathomable depths.

'I am too fond of you for that,' he said, with a little nervous laugh.

A faint flush coloured Mrs Verloc's ghastly and motionless face. Having done with the visions of the past, she had not only heard, but had also understood the words uttered by her husband. By their extreme disaccord with her mental condition these words produced on her a slightly suffocating effect. Mrs Verloc's mental condition had the merit of simplicity; but it was not sound. It was governed too much by a fixed idea. Every nook and cranny of her brain was filled with the thought that this man, with whom she had lived without distaste for seven years, had taken the 'poor boy' away from her in order to kill him – the man to whom she had grown accustomed in body and mind; the man whom she had trusted, took the boy away to kill him! In its form, in its substance, in its effect, which was universal, altering even the aspect of inanimate things, it was a thought to sit still and marvel at for ever and ever. Mrs Verloc sat still. And across that thought (not across the kitchen) the form of Mr Verloc went to and fro, familiarly in hat and overcoat, stamping with his boots upon her brain. He was probably talking, too; but Mrs Verloc's thought for the most part covered the voice.

Now and then, however, the voice would make itself heard. Several connected words emerged at times. Their purport was generally hopeful. On each of these occasions Mrs Verloc's dilated pupils, losing their far-off fixity, followed her husband's movements with the effect of black care and impenetrable attention. Well informed upon all matters relating to his secret calling, Mr Verloc augured well for the success of his plans and combinations. He really believed that it would be upon the whole easy for him to escape the knife of infuriated revolutionists. He had exaggerated the strength of their fury and the length of their arm (for professional purposes) too often to have many illusions one way or the other. For to exaggerate with judgement one must begin by measuring with nicety. He knew also how much virtue and how much infamy is forgotten in two years – two long years. His first really confidential discourse to his wife was optimistic from conviction. He also thought it good policy to display all the assurance he could muster. It would put heart into the poor woman. On his liberation, which, harmonising with the whole tenor of his life, would be secret, of course, they would vanish together without loss of time. As to covering up the tracks, he begged his wife to trust him for that. He knew how it was to be done so that the devil himself . . . '

He waved his hand. He seemed to boast. He wished only to put heart into her. It was a benevolent intention, but Mr Verloc had the misfortune not to be in accord with his audience.

The self-confident tone grew upon Mrs Verloc's ear, which let most of the words go by; for what were words to her now? What could words do to her for good or evil in the face of her fixed idea? Her black glance followed that man who was asserting his impunity – the man who had taken poor Stevie from home to kill him somewhere. Mrs Verloc could not remember exactly where, but her heart began to beat very perceptibly.

Mr Verloc, in a soft and conjugal tone, was now expressing his firm belief that there were yet a good few years of quiet life before them both. He did not go into the question of means. A quiet life it must be and, as it were, nestling in the shade, concealed among men whose flesh is grass; modest, like the life of violets. The words used by Mr Verloc were: 'Lie low for a bit.' And far from England, of course. It was not clear whether Mr Verloc had in his mind Spain or South America; but at any rate somewhere abroad.

This last word, falling into Mrs Verloc's ear, produced a definite impression. This man was talking of going abroad. The impression was completely disconnected; and such is the force of mental habit that Mrs Verloc at once and automatically asked herself: 'And what of Stevie?'

It was a sort of forgetfulness; but instantly she became aware that there was no longer any occasion for anxiety on that score. There would never be any occasion any more. The poor boy had been taken out and killed. The poor boy was dead.

This shaking piece of forgetfulness stimulated Mrs Verloc's intelligence. She began to perceive certain consequences which would have surprised Mr Verloc. There was no need for her now to stay there, in that kitchen, in that house, with that man – since the boy was gone for ever. No need whatever. And on that Mrs Verloc rose as if raised by a spring. But neither could she see what there was to keep her in the world at all. And this inability arrested her. Mr Verloc watched her with marital solicitude.

'You're looking more like yourself,' he said, uneasily. Something peculiar in the blackness of his wife's eyes disturbed his optimism. At that precise moment Mrs Verloc began to look upon herself as released from all earthly ties. She had her freedom. Her contract with existence, as represented by that man standing over there, was at an end. She was a free woman. Had this view become in some way perceptible to Mr Verloc he would have been extremely shocked. In his affairs of the heart Mr Verloc had been always carelessly generous, yet always with no other idea than that of being loved for himself. Upon this matter, his ethical notions being in agreement with his vanity, he was completely incorrigible. That this should be so in the case of his virtuous and legal connection he was perfectly certain. He had grown older, fatter, heavier, in the belief that he lacked no fascination for being loved for his own sake. When he saw Mrs Verloc starting to walk out of the kitchen without a word he was disappointed.

'Where are you going to?' he called out rather sharply. 'Upstairs?'

Mrs Verloc in the doorway turned at the voice. An instinct of prudence born of fear, the excessive fear of being approached and touched by that man, induced her to nod at him slightly (from the height of two steps), with a stir of the lips which the conjugal optimism of Mr Verloc took for a wan and uncertain smile.

'That's right,' he encouraged her gruffly. 'Rest and quiet's what you want. Go on. It won't be long before I am with you.'

Mrs Verloc, the free woman who had had really no idea where she was going to, obeyed the suggestion with rigid steadiness.

Mr Verloc watched her. She disappeared up the stairs. He was disappointed. There was that within him which would have been more satisfied if she had been moved to throw herself upon his breast. But he was generous and indulgent. Winnie was always undemonstrative and silent. Neither was Mr Verloc himself prodigal of endearments and words as a rule. But this was not an ordinary evening. It was an occasion when a man wants to be fortified and strengthened by open proofs of sympathy and affection. Mr Verloc sighed, and put out the gas in the kitchen. Mr Verloc's sympathy with his wife was genuine and intense. It almost brought tears into his eyes as he stood in the parlour reflecting on the loneliness hanging over her head. In this mood Mr Verloc missed Stevie very much out of a difficult world. He thought mournfully of his end. If only that lad had not stupidly destroyed himself!

The sensation of unappeasable hunger, not unknown after the strain of a hazardous enterprise to adventurers of tougher fibre than Mr Verloc, overcame him again. The piece of roast beef, laid out in the likeness of funereal baked meats for Stevie's obsequies, offered itself largely to his notice. And Mr Verloc again partook. He partook ravenously, without restraint and decency, cutting thick slices with the sharp carving knife, and swallowing them without bread. In the course of that refection it occurred to Mr Verloc that he was not hearing his wife move about the bedroom as he should have done. The thought of finding her perhaps sitting on the bed in the dark not only cut Mr Verloc's appetite, but also took from him the inclination to follow her upstairs just yet. Laying down the carving knife, Mr Verloc listened with careworn attention.

He was comforted by hearing her move at last. She walked suddenly across the room, and threw the window up. After a period of stillness up there, during which he figured her to himself with her head out, he heard the sash being lowered slowly. Then she made a few steps, and sat down. Every resonance of his house was familiar to Mr Verloc, who was thoroughly domesticated. When next he heard his wife's footsteps overheard he knew, as well as if he had seen her doing it, that she had been putting on her walking shoes. Mr Verloc wriggled his shoulders slightly at this ominous symptom, and moving away from the table, stood with his back to the fireplace, his head on one side, and gnawing perplexedly at the tips of his fingers. He kept track of her movements by the sound. She walked here and there violently, with abrupt stoppages, now before the chest of drawers, then in front of the wardrobe. An immense load of weariness, the harvest of a day of shocks and surprises, weighed Mr Verloc's energies to the ground.

He did not raise his eyes till he heard his wife descending the stairs. It was as he had guessed, she was dressed for going out.

Mrs Verloc was a free woman. She had thrown open the window of the bedroom either with the intention of screaming Murder! Help! or of throwing herself out. For she did not exactly know what use to make of her freedom. Her personality seemed to have been torn into two pieces, whose mental operations did not adjust themselves very well to each other. The street, silent and deserted from end to end, repelled her by taking sides with that man who was so certain of his impunity. She was afraid to shout lest no one should come. Obviously no one would come. Her instinct of self-preservation recoiled from the depth of the fall into that sort of slimy, deep trench. Mrs Verloc closed the window, and dressed herself to go out into the street by another way. She was a free woman. She had dressed herself thoroughly, down to the tying of a black veil over her face. As she appeared before him in the light of the parlour, Mr Verloc observed that she had even her little handbag hanging from her left wrist . . . Flying off to her mother, of course.

The thought that women were wearisome creatures after all presented itself to his fatigued brain. But he was too generous to harbour it for more than an instant. This man, hurt cruelly in his vanity, remained magnanimous in his conduct, allowing himself no satisfaction of a bitter smile or of a contemptuous gesture. With true greatness of soul, he only glanced at the wooden clock on the wall, and said in a perfectly calm but forcible manner: 'Five and twenty minutes past eight, Winnie. There's no sense in going over there so late. You will never manage to get back tonight.'

Before his extended hand Mrs Verloc had stopped short. He added, heavily: 'Your mother will be gone to bed before you get there. This is the sort of news that can wait.'

Nothing was further from Mrs Verloc's thoughts than going to her mother. She recoiled at the mere idea, and feeling a chair behind her, she obeyed the suggestion of the touch, and sat down. Her intention had been simply to get outside the door for ever. And if this feeling was correct, its mental form took an unrefined shape corresponding to her origin and station. 'I would rather walk the streets all the days of my life,' she thought. But this creature, whose moral nature had been subjected to a shock of which, in the physical order, the most violent earthquake of history could only be a faint and languid rendering, was at the mercy of mere trifles, of casual contacts. She sat down. With her hat and veil she had the air of a visitor, of having looked in on Mr Verloc for a moment. Her instant docility encouraged him, whilst her aspect of only temporary and silent acquiescence provoked him a little.

'Let me tell you, Winnie,' he said with authority, 'that your place is here this evening. Hang it all! you brought the damned police high and low about my ears. I don't blame you – but it's your doing all the same. You'd better take this confounded hat off. I can't let you go out, old girl,' he added in a softened voice.

Mrs Verloc's mind got hold of that declaration with morbid tenacity. The man who had taken Stevie out from under her very eyes to murder him in a locality whose name was at the moment not present to her memory would not allow her to go out. Of course he wouldn't. Now he had murdered Stevie he would never let her go. He would want to keep her for nothing. And on this characteristic reasoning, having all the force of insane logic, Mrs Verloc's disconnected wits went to work practically. She could slip by him, open the door, run out. But he would dash out after her, seize her round the body, drag her back into the shop. She could scratch, kick, and bite and stab, too; but for stabbing she wanted a knife. Mrs Verloc sat still under her black veil, in her own house, like a masked and mysterious visitor of impenetrable intentions.

Mr Verloc's magnanimity was not more than human. She had exasperated him at last.

'Can't you say something? You have your own dodges for vexing a man. Oh, yes! I know your deaf-and-dumb trick. I've seen you at it before today. But just now it won't do. And to begin with, take this damned thing off. One can't tell whether one is talking to a dummy or to a live woman.'

He advanced, and stretching out his hand, dragged the veil off, unmasking a still unreadable face, against which his nervous exasperation was shattered like a glass bubble flung against a rock. 'That's better,' he said, to cover his momentary uneasiness, and retreated back to his old station by the mantelpiece. It never entered his head that his wife could give him up. He felt a little ashamed of himself, for he was fond and generous. What could he do? Everything had been said already. He protested vehemently.

'By heavens! You know that I hunted high and low. I ran the risk of giving myself away to find somebody for that accursed job. And I tell you again I couldn't find anyone crazy enough or hungry enough. What do you take me for – a murderer, or what? The boy is gone. Do you think I wanted him to blow himself up? He's gone. His troubles are over. Ours are just going to begin, I tell you, precisely because he did blow himself up. I don't blame you. But just try to understand that it was a pure accident; as much an accident as if he had been run over by a bus while crossing the street.'

His generosity was not infinite, because he was a human being – and not a monster, as Mrs Verloc believed him to be. He paused, and a snarl lifting his moustaches above a gleam of white teeth gave him the expression of a reflective beast, not very dangerous – a slow beast with a sleek head, gloomier than a seal, and with a husky voice.

'And when it comes to that, it's as much your doing as mine. That's so. You may glare as much as you like. I know what you can do in that way. Strike me dead if I ever would have thought of the lad for that purpose. It was you who kept on shoving him in my way when I was half distracted with the worry of keeping the lot of us out of trouble. What the devil made you? One would think you were doing it on purpose. And I am damned if I know that you didn't. There's no saying how much of what's going on you have got hold of on the sly with your infernal don't-care-a-damn way of looking nowhere in particular, and saying nothing at all . . . '

His husky, domestic voice ceased for a while. Mrs Verloc made no reply. Before that silence he felt ashamed of what he had said. But as often happens to peaceful men in domestic tiffs, being ashamed he pushed another point.

'You have a devilish way of holding your tongue sometimes,' he began again, without raising his voice. 'Enough to make some men go mad. It's lucky for you that I am not so easily put out as some of them would be by your deaf-and-dumb sulks. I am fond of you. But don't you go too far. This isn't the time for it. We ought to be thinking of what we've got to do. And I can't let you go out tonight, galloping off to your mother with some crazy tale or other about me. I won't have it. Don't you make any mistake about it: if you will have it that I killed the boy, then you've killed him as much as I.'

In sincerity of feeling and openness of statement, these words went far beyond anything that had ever been said in this home, kept up on the wages of a secret industry eked out by the sale of more or less secret wares: the poor expedients devised by a mediocre mankind for preserving an imperfect society from the dangers of moral and physical corruption, both secret, too, of their kind. They were spoken because Mr Verloc had felt himself really outraged; but the reticent decencies of this home life, nestling in a shady street behind a shop where the sun never shone, remained apparently undisturbed. Mrs Verloc heard him out with perfect propriety, and then rose from her chair in her hat and jacket like a visitor at the end of a call. She advanced towards her husband, one palm extended as if for a silent leave-taking. Her net veil dangling down by one end on the left side of her face gave an air of disorderly formality to her restrained movements. But when she arrived as far as the hearthrug, Mr Verloc was no longer standing there. He had moved off in the direction of the sofa, without raising his eyes to watch the effect of his tirade. He was tired, resigned in a truly marital spirit. But he felt hurt in the tender spot of his secret weakness. If she would go on sulking in that dreadful overcharged silence – why then she must. She was a master in that domestic art. Mr Verloc flung himself heavily upon the sofa, disregarding as usual the fate of his hat, which, as if accustomed to take care of itself, made for a safe shelter under the table.

He was tired. The last particle of his nervous force had been expended in the wonders and agonies of this day full of surprising failures coming at the end of a harassing month of scheming and insomnia. He was tired. A man isn't made of stone. Hang everything! Mr Verloc reposed characteristically, clad in his outdoor garments. One side of his open overcoat was lying partly on the ground. Mr Verloc wallowed on his back. But he longed for a more perfect rest – for sleep – for a few hours of delicious forgetfulness. That would come later. Provisionally he rested. And he thought: 'I wish she would give over this damned nonsense. It's exasperating.'

There must have been something imperfect in Mrs Verloc's sentiment of regained freedom. Instead of taking the way of the door she leaned back, with her shoulders against the tablet of the mantelpiece, as a wayfarer rests against a fence. A tinge of wildness in her aspect was derived from the black veil hanging like a rag against her cheek, and from the fixity of her black gaze where the light of the room was absorbed and lost without the trace of a single gleam. This woman, capable of a bargain the mere suspicion of which would have been infinitely shocking to Mr Verloc's idea of love, remained irresolute, as if scrupulously aware of something wanting on her part for the formal closing of the transaction.

On the sofa Mr Verloc wriggled his shoulders into perfect comfort, and from the fullness of his heart emitted a wish which was certainly as pious as anything likely to come from such a source.

'I wish to goodness,' he growled, huskily, 'I had never seen Greenwich Park or anything belonging to it.'

The veiled sound filled the small room with its moderate volume, well adapted to the modest nature of the wish. The waves of air of the proper length, propagated in accordance with correct mathematical formulas, flowed around all the inanimate things in the room, lapped against Mrs Verloc's head as if it had been a head of stone. And incredible as it may appear, the eyes of Mrs Verloc seemed to grow still larger. The audible wish of Mr Verloc's overflowing heart flowed into an empty place in his wife's memory. Greenwich Park. A park! That's where the boy was killed. A park – smashed branches, torn leaves, gravel, bits of brotherly flesh and bone, all spouting up together in the manner of a firework. She remembered now what she had heard, and she remembered it pictorially. They had to gather him up with the shovel. Trembling all over with irrepressible shudders, she saw before her the very implement with its ghastly load scraped up from the ground. Mrs Verloc closed her eyes desperately, throwing upon that vision the night of her eyelids, where after a rainlike fall of mangled limbs the decapitated head of Stevie lingered suspended alone, and fading out slowly like the last star of a pyrotechnic display. Mrs Verloc opened her eyes.

Her face was no longer stony. Anybody could have noted the subtle change on her features, in the stare of her eyes, giving her a new and startling expression; an expression seldom observed by competent persons under the conditions of leisure and security demanded for thorough analysis, but whose meaning could not he mistaken at a glance. Mrs Verloc's doubts as to the end of the bargain no longer existed; her wits, no longer disconnected, were working under the control of her will. But Mr Verloc observed nothing. He was reposing in that pathetic condition of optimism induced by excess of fatigue. He did not want any more trouble – with his wife, too – of all people in the world. He had been unanswerable in his vindication. He was loved for himself. The present phase of her silence he interpreted favourably. This was the time to make it up with her. The silence had lasted long enough. He broke it by calling to her in an undertone.

'Winnie.'

'Yes,' answered obediently Mrs Verloc the free woman. She commanded her wits now, her vocal organs; she felt herself to be in an almost preter-naturally perfect control of every fibre of her body. It was all her own, because the bargain was at an end. She was clear sighted. She had become cunning. She chose to answer him so readily for a purpose. She did not wish that man to change his position on the sofa which was very suitable to the circumstances. She succeeded. The man did not stir. But after answering him she remained leaning negligently against the mantelpiece in the attitude of a resting wayfarer. She was unhurried. Her brow was smooth. The head and shoulders of Mr Verloc were hidden from her by the high side of the sofa. She kept her eyes fixed on his feet.

She remained thus mysteriously still and suddenly collected till Mr Verloc was heard with an accent of marital authority, and moving slightly to make room for her to sit on the edge of the sofa.

'Come here,' he said in a peculiar tone, which might have been the tone of brutality, but was intimately known to Mrs Verloc as the note of wooing. She started forward at once, as if she were still a loyal woman bound to that man by an unbroken contract. Her right hand skimmed slightly the end of the table, and when she had passed on towards the sofa the carving knife had vanished without the slightest sound from the side of the dish. Mr Verloc heard the creaky plank in the floor, and was content. He waited. Mrs Verloc was coming. As if the homeless soul of Stevie had flown for shelter straight to the breast of his sister, guardian, and protector, the resemblance of her face with that of her brother grew at every step, even to the droop of the lower lip, even to the slight divergence of the eyes. But Mr Verloc did not see that. He was lying on his back and staring upwards. He saw partly on the ceiling and partly on the wall the moving shadow of an arm with a clenched hand holding a carving knife. It flickered up and down. Its movements were leisurely. They were leisurely enough for Mr Verloc to recognise the limb and the weapon.

They were leisurely enough for him to take in the full meaning of the portent, and to taste the flavour of death rising in his gorge. His wife had gone raving mad – murdering mad. They were leisurely enough for the first para-lysing effect of this discovery to pass away before a resolute determination to come out victorious from the ghastly struggle with that armed lunatic. They were leisurely enough for Mr Verloc to elaborate a plan of defence involving a dash behind the table, and the felling of the woman to the ground with a heavy wooden chair. But they were not leisurely enough to allow Mr Verloc the time to move either hand or foot. The knife was already planted in his breast. It met no resistance on its way. Hazard has such accuracies. Into that plunging blow, delivered over the side of the couch, Mrs Verloc had put all the inheritance of her immemorial and obscure descent, the simple ferocity of the age of caverns, and the unbalanced nervous fury of the age of bar-rooms. Mr Verloc, the Secret Agent, turning slightly on his side with the force of the blow, expired without stirring a limb, in the muttered sound of the word 'Don't' by way of protest.

Mrs Verloc had let go the knife, and her extraordinary resemblance to her late brother had faded, had become very ordinary now. She drew a deep breath, the first easy breath since Chief Inspector Heat had exhibited to her the labelled piece of Stevie's overcoat. She leaned forward on her folded arms over the side of the sofa. She adopted that easy attitude not in order to watch or gloat over the body of Mr Verloc, but because of the undulatory and swinging movements of the parlour, which for some time behaved as though it were at sea in a tempest. She was giddy but calm. She had become a free woman with a perfection of freedom which left her nothing to desire and absolutely nothing to do, since Stevie's urgent claim on her devotion no longer existed. Mrs Verloc, who thought in images, was not troubled now by visions, because she did not think at all. And she did not move. She was a woman enjoying her complete irresponsibility and endless leisure, almost in the manner of a corpse. She did not move, she did not think. Neither did the mortal envelope of the late Mr Verloc reposing on the sofa. Except for the fact that Mrs Verloc breathed these two would have been perfectly in accord: that accord of prudent reserve without superfluous words, and sparing of signs, which had been the foundation of their respectable home life. For it had been respectable, covering by a decent reticence the problems that may arise in the practice of a secret profession and the commerce of shady wares. To the last its decorum had remained undisturbed by unseemly shrieks and other misplaced sincerities of conduct. And after the striking of the blow, this respectability was continued in immobility and silence.

Nothing moved in the parlour till Mrs Verloc raised her head slowly and looked at the clock with enquiring mistrust. She had become aware of a ticking sound in the room. It grew upon her ear, while she remembered clearly that the clock on the wall was silent, had no audible tick. What did it mean by beginning to tick so loudly all of a sudden? Its face indicated ten minutes to nine. Mrs Verloc cared nothing for time, and the ticking went on. She concluded it could not be the clock, and her sullen gaze moved along the walls, wavered, and became vague, while she strained her hearing to locate the sound. Tic, tic, tic.

After listening for some time Mrs Verloc lowered her gaze deliberately on her husband's body. Its attitude of repose was so homelike and familiar that she could do so without feeling embarrassed by any pronounced novelty in the phenomena of her home life. Mr Verloc was taking his habitual ease. He looked comfortable.

By the position of the body the face of Mr Verloc was not visible to Mrs Verloc, his widow. Her fine, sleepy eyes, travelling downward on the track of the sound, became contemplative on meeting a flat object of bone which protruded a little beyond the edge of the sofa. It was the handle of the domestic carving knife with nothing strange about it but its position at right angles to Mr Verloc's waistcoat and the fact that something dripped from it. Dark drops fell on the floor-cloth one after another, with a sound of ticking growing fast and furious like the pulse of an insane clock. At its highest speed this ticking changed into a continuous sound of trickling. Mrs Verloc watched that transformation with shadows of anxiety coming and going on her face. It was a trickle, dark, swift, thin . . . Blood!

At this unforeseen circumstance Mrs Verloc abandoned her pose of idleness and irresponsibility.

With a sudden snatch at her skirts and a faint shriek she ran to the door, as if the trickle had been the first sign of a destroying flood. Finding the table in her way she gave it a push with both hands as though it had been alive, with such force that it went for some distance on its four legs, making a loud, scraping racket, whilst the big dish with the joint crashed heavily on the floor.

Then all became still. Mrs Verloc on reaching the door had stopped. A round hat disclosed in the middle of the floor by the moving of the table rocked slightly on its crown in the wind of her flight.

Chapter 12

Winnie Verloc, the widow of Mr Verloc, the sister of the late faithful Stevie (blown to fragments in a state of innocence and in the conviction of being engaged in a humanitarian enterprise), did not run beyond the door of the parlour. She had indeed run away so far from a mere trickle of blood, but that was a movement of instinctive repulsion. And there she had paused, with staring eyes and lowered head. As though she had run through long years in her flight across the small parlour, Mrs Verloc by the door was quite a different person from the woman who had been leaning over the sofa, a little swimmy in her head, but otherwise free to enjoy the profound calm of idleness and irresponsibility. Mrs Verloc was no longer giddy. Her head was steady. On the other hand, she was no longer calm. She was afraid.

If she avoided looking in the direction of her reposing husband it was not because she was afraid of him. Mr Verloc was not frightful to behold. He looked comfortable. Moreover, he was dead. Mrs Verloc entertained no vain delusions on the subject of the dead. Nothing brings them back, neither love nor hate. They can do nothing to you. They are as nothing. Her mental state was tinged by a sort of austere contempt for that man who had let himself be killed so easily. He had been the master of a house, the husband of a woman, and the murderer of her Stevie. And now he was of no account in every respect. He was of less practical account than the clothing on his body, than his overcoat, than his boots – than that hat lying on the floor. He was nothing. He was not worth looking at. He was even no longer the murderer of poor Stevie. The only murderer that would be found in the room when people came to look for Mr Verloc would be – herself!

Her hands shook so that she failed twice in the task of refastening her veil. Mrs Verloc was no longer a person of leisure and irresponsibility. She was afraid. The stabbing of Mr Verloc had been only a blow. It had relieved the pent-up agony of shrieks strangled in her throat, of tears dried up in her hot eyes, of the maddening and indignant rage at the atrocious part played by that man, who was less than nothing now, in robbing her of the boy. It had been an obscurely prompted blow. The blood trickling on the floor off the handle of the knife had turned it into an extremely plain case of murder. Mrs Verloc, who always refrained from looking deep into things, was compelled to look into the very bottom of this thing. She saw there no haunting face, no reproachful shade, no vision of remorse, no sort of ideal conception. She saw there an object. That object was the gallows. Mrs Verloc was afraid of the gallows.

She was terrified of them ideally. Having never set eyes on that last argument of men's justice except in illustrative woodcuts to a certain type of tales, she first saw them erect against a black and stormy background, festooned with chains and human bones, circled about by birds that peck at dead men's eyes. This was frightful enough, but Mrs Verloc, though not a well-informed woman, had a sufficient knowledge of the institutions of her country to know that gallows are no longer erected romantically on the banks of dismal rivers or on wind-swept headlands, but in the yards of jails. There within four high walls, as if into a pit, at dawn of day, the murderer was brought out to be executed, with a horrible quietness and, as the reports in the newspapers always said, 'in the presence of the authorities.' With her eyes staring on the floor, her nostrils quivering with anguish and shame, she imagined herself all alone amongst a lot of strange gentlemen in silk hats who were calmly proceeding about the business of hanging her by the neck. That – never! Never! And how was it done? The impossibility of imagining the details of such quiet execution added something maddening to her abstract terror. The newspapers never gave any details except one, but that one with some affectation was always there at the end of a meagre report. Mrs Verloc remembered its nature. It came with a cruel burning pain into her head, as if the words 'The drop given was fourteen feet' had been scratched on her brain with a hot needle. 'The drop given was fourteen feet.'

These words affected her physically, too. Her throat became convulsed in waves to resist strangulation; and the apprehension of the jerk was so vivid that she seized her head in both hands as if to save it from being torn off her shoulders. 'The drop given was fourteen feet.' No! that must never be. She could not stand *that*. The thought of it even was not bearable. She could not stand thinking of it. Therefore Mrs Verloc formed the resolution to go at once and throw herself into the river off one of the bridges.

This time she managed to refasten her veil. With her face as if masked, all black from head to foot except for some flowers in her hat, she looked up mechanically at the clock. She thought it must have stopped. She could not believe that only two minutes had passed since she had looked at it last. Of course not. It had been stopped all the time. As a matter of fact, only three minutes had elapsed from the moment she had drawn the first deep, easy breath after the blow, to this moment when Mrs Verloc formed the resolution to drown herself in the Thames. But Mrs Verloc could not believe that. She seemed to have heard or read that clocks and watches always stopped at the moment of murder for the undoing of the murderer. She did not care. 'To the bridge – and over I go.' . . . But her movements were slow.

She dragged herself painfully across the shop, and had to hold on to the handle of the door before she found the necessary fortitude to open it. The street frightened her, since it led either to the gallows or to the river. She floundered over the doorstep head forward, arms thrown out, like a person falling over the parapet of a bridge. This entrance into the open air had a foretaste of drowning; a slimy dampness enveloped her, entered her nostrils, clung to her hair. It was not actually raining, but each gas lamp had a rusty little halo of mist. The van and horses were gone, and in the black street the curtained window of the carters' eating-house made a square patch of soiled blood-red light glowing faintly very near the level of the pavement. Mrs Verloc, dragging herself slowly towards it, thought that she was a very friendless woman. It was true. It was so true that, in a sudden longing to see some friendly face, she could think of no one else but of Mrs Neale, the charwoman. She had no acquaintances of her own. Nobody would miss her in a social way. It must not be imagined that the Widow Verloc had forgotten her mother. This was not so. Winnie had been a good daughter because she had been a devoted sister. Her mother had always leaned on her for support. No consolation or advice could be expected there. Now that Stevie was dead the bond seemed to be broken. She could not face the old woman with the horrible tale. Moreover, it was too far. The river was her present destination. Mrs Verloc tried to forget her mother.

Each step cost her an effort of will which seemed the last possible. Mrs Verloc had dragged herself past the red glow of the eating-house window. 'To the bridge – and over I go,' she repeated to herself with fierce obstinacy. She put out her hand just in time to steady herself against a lamp-post. 'I'll never get there before morning,' she thought. The fear of death paralysed her efforts to escape the gallows. It seemed to her she had been staggering in that street for hours. 'I'll never get there,' she thought. 'They'll find me knocking about the streets. It's too far.' She held on, panting under her black veil.

'The drop given was fourteen feet.'

She pushed the lamp-post away from her violently, and found herself walking. But another wave of faintness overtook her like a great sea, washing away her heart clean out of her breast. 'I will never get there,' she muttered, suddenly arrested, swaying lightly where she stood. 'Never.'

And perceiving the utter impossibility of walking as far as the nearest bridge, Mrs Verloc thought of a flight abroad.

It came to her suddenly. Murderers escaped. They escaped abroad. Spain or California. Mere names. The vast world created for the glory of man was only a vast blank to Mrs Verloc. She did not know which way to turn. Murderers had friends, relations, helpers – they had knowledge. She had nothing. She was the most lonely of murderers that ever struck a mortal blow. She was alone in London: and the whole town of marvels and mud, with its maze of streets and its mass of lights, was sunk in a hopeless night, rested at the bottom of a black abyss from which no unaided woman could hope to scramble out.

She swayed forward, and made a fresh start blindly, with an awful dread of falling down; but at the end of a few steps, unexpectedly, she found a sensation of support, of security. Raising her head, she saw a man's face peering closely at her veil. Comrade Ossipon was not afraid of strange women, and no feeling of false delicacy could prevent him from striking an acquaintance with a woman apparently very much intoxicated. Comrade Ossipon was interested in women. He held up this one between his two large palms, peering at her in a businesslike way till he heard her say faintly 'Mr Ossipon!' and then he very nearly let her drop to the ground.

'Mrs Verloc!' he exclaimed. 'You here!'

It seemed impossible to him that she should have been drinking. But one never knows. He did not go into that question, but attentive not to discourage kind fate surrendering to him the widow of Comrade Verloc, he tried to draw her to his breast. To his astonishment she came quite easily, and even rested on his arm for a moment before she attempted to disengage herself. Comrade Ossipon would not be brusque with kind fate. He withdrew his arm in a natural way.

'You recognised me,' she faltered out, standing before him, fairly steady on her legs.

'Of course I did,' said Ossipon with perfect readiness. 'I was afraid you were going to fall. I've thought of you too often lately not to recognise you anywhere, at any time. I've always thought of you – ever since I first set eyes on you.'

Mrs Verloc seemed not to hear. 'You were coming to the shop?' she said, nervously.

'Yes; at once,' answered Ossipon. 'Directly I read the paper.'

In fact, Comrade Ossipon had been skulking for a good two hours in the neighbourhood of Brett Street, unable to make up his mind for a bold move. The robust anarchist was not exactly a bold conqueror. He remembered that Mrs Verloc had never responded to his glances by the slightest sign of encouragement. Besides, he thought the shop might be watched by the police, and Comrade Ossipon did not wish the police to form an exaggerated notion of his revolutionary sympathies. Even now he did not know precisely what to do. In comparison with his usual amatory speculations this was a big and serious undertaking. He ignored how much there was in it and how far he would have to go in order to get hold of what there was to get – supposing there was a chance at all. These perplexities checking his elation imparted to his tone a soberness well in keeping with the circumstances.

'May I ask you where you were going?' he enquired in a subdued voice.

'Don't ask me!' cried Mrs Verloc with a shuddering, repressed violence. All her strong vitality recoiled from the idea of death. 'Never mind where I was going . . .'

Ossipon concluded that she was very much excited but perfectly sober. She remained silent by his side for a moment, then all at once she did something which he did not expect. She slipped her hand under his arm. He was startled by the act itself certainly, and quite as much, too, by the palpably resolute character of this movement. But this being a delicate affair, Comrade Ossipon behaved with delicacy. He contented himself by pressing the hand slightly against his robust ribs. At the same time he felt himself being impelled forward, and yielded to the impulse. At the end of Brett Street he became aware of being directed to the left. He submitted.

The fruiterer at the corner had put out the blazing glory of his oranges and lemons, and Brett Place was all darkness, interspersed with the misty halos of the few lamps defining its triangular shape, with a cluster of three lights on one stand in the middle. The dark forms of the man and woman glided slowly arm in arm along the walls with a loverlike and homeless aspect in the miserable night.

'What would you say if I were to tell you that I was going to find you?' Mrs Verloc asked, gripping his arm with force.

'I would say that you couldn't find anyone more ready to help you in your trouble,' answered Ossipon, with a notion of making tremendous headway. In fact, the progress of this delicate affair was almost taking his breath away.

'In my trouble!' Mrs Verloc repeated, slowly.

'Yes.'

'And do you know what my trouble is?' she whispered with strange intensity.

'Ten minutes after seeing the evening paper,' explained Ossipon with ardour, 'I met a fellow whom you may have seen once or twice at the shop perhaps, and I had a talk with him which left no doubt whatever in my mind. Then I started for here, wondering whether you – I've been fond of you beyond words ever since I set eyes on your face,' he cried, as if unable to command his feelings.

Comrade Ossipon assumed correctly that no woman was capable of wholly disbelieving such a statement. But he did not know that Mrs Verloc accepted it with all the fierceness the instinct of self-preservation imparts to the grip of a drowning person. To the widow of Mr Verloc the robust anarchist was like a radiant messenger of life.

They walked slowly, in step. 'I thought so,' Mrs Verloc murmured, faintly.

'You've read it in my eyes,' suggested Ossipon with great assurance.

'Yes,' she breathed out into his inclined ear.

'A love like mine could not be concealed from a woman like you,' he went on, trying to detach his mind from material considerations such as the business value of the shop, and the amount of money Mr Verloc might have left in the bank. He applied himself to the sentimental side of the affair. In his heart of hearts he was a little shocked at his success. Verloc had been a good fellow, and certainly a very decent husband as far as one could see. However, Comrade Ossipon was not going to quarrel with his luck for the sake of a dead man. Resolutely he suppressed his sympathy for the ghost of Comrade Verloc, and went on: 'I could not conceal it. I was too full of you. I dare say you could not help seeing it in my eyes. But I could not guess it. You were always so distant . . .'

'What else did you expect?' burst out Mrs Verloc. 'I was a respectable woman . . .'

She paused, then added, as if speaking to herself, in sinister resentment: 'Till he made me what I am.'

Ossipon let that pass, and took up his running.

'He never did seem to me to be quite worthy of you,' he began, throwing loyalty to the winds. 'You were worthy of a better fate.'

Mrs Verloc interrupted bitterly: 'Better fate! He cheated me out of seven years of life.'

'You seemed to live so happily with him.' Ossipon tried to exculpate the lukewarmness of his past conduct. 'It's that what's made me timid. You seemed to love him. I was surprised – and jealous,' he added.

'Love him!' Mrs Verloc cried out in a whisper full of scorn and rage. 'Love him! I was a good wife to him. I am a respectable woman. You thought I loved him! You did! Look here, Tom . . .'

The sound of this name thrilled Comrade Ossipon with pride. For his name was Alexander, and he was called Tom by arrangement with the most familiar of his intimates. It was a name of friendship – of moments of expansion. He had no idea that she had ever heard it used by anybody. It was apparent that she had not only caught it, but had treasured it in her memory – perhaps in her heart.

'Look here, Tom! I was a young girl. I was done up. I was tired. I had two people depending on what I could do, and it did seem as if I couldn't do any more. Two people – mother and the boy. He was much more mine than mother's. I sat up nights and nights with him on my lap, all alone upstairs, when I wasn't more than eight years old myself. And then . . . He was mine, I tell you . . . You can't understand that. No man can understand it. What was I to do? There was a young fellow . . . '

The memory of the early romance with the young butcher survived, tenacious, like the image of a glimpsed ideal in that heart quailing before the fear of the gallows and full of revolt against death.

'That was the man I loved then,' went on the widow of Mr Verloc. 'I suppose he could see it in my eyes, too. Five and twenty shillings a week, and his father threatened to kick him out of the business if he made such a fool of himself as to marry a girl with a crippled mother and a crazy idiot of a boy on her hands. But he would hang about me, till one evening I found the courage to slam the door in his face. I had to do it. I loved him dearly. Five and twenty shillings a week! There was that other man – a good lodger. What is a girl to do? Could I've gone on the streets? He seemed kind. He wanted me, anyhow. What was I to do with mother and that poor boy? Eh? I said yes. He seemed good-natured, he was freehanded, he had money, he never said anything. Seven years – seven years a good wife to him, the kind, the good, the generous, the . . . And he loved me. Oh, yes. He loved me till I sometimes wished myself . . . Seven years. Seven years a wife to him. And do you know what he was, that dear friend of yours? Do you know what he was? . . . He was a devil!'

The superhuman vehemence of that whispered statement completely stunned Comrade Ossipon. Winnie Verloc turning about held him by both arms, facing him under the falling mist in the darkness and solitude of Brett Place, in which all sounds of life seemed lost as if in a triangular well of asphalt and bricks, of blind houses and unfeeling stones.

'No; I didn't know,' he declared, with a sort of flabby stupidity, whose comical aspect was lost upon a woman haunted by the fear of the gallows, 'but I do now. I – I understand,' he floundered on, his mind speculating as to what sort of atrocities Verloc could have practised under the sleepy, placid appearances of his married estate. It was positively awful. 'I understand,' he repeated, and then by a sudden inspiration uttered an 'Unhappy woman!' of lofty commiseration instead of the more familiar 'Poor darling!' of his usual practice. This was no usual case. He felt conscious of something abnormal going on, while he never lost sight of the greatness of the stake. 'Unhappy, brave woman!'

He was glad to have discovered that variation; but he could discover nothing else. 'Ah, but he is dead now,' was the best he could do. And he put a remarkable amount of animosity into his guarded exclamation. Mrs Verloc caught at his arm with a sort of frenzy. 'You guessed then he was dead,' she murmured, as if beside herself. 'You! You guessed what I had to do. Had to!'

There were suggestions of triumph, relief, gratitude in the indefinable tone of these words. It engrossed the whole attention of Ossipon to the detriment of mere literal sense. He wondered what was up with her, why she had worked herself into this state of wild excitement. He even began to wonder whether the hidden causes of that Greenwich Park affair did not lie deep in the unhappy circumstances of the Verloc's' married life. He went so far as to suspect Mr Verloc of having selected that extraordinary manner of committing suicide. By Jove! that would account for the utter inanity and wrong-headedness of the thing. No anarchist manifestation was required by the circumstances. Quite the contrary; and Verloc was as well aware of that as any other revolutionist of his standing. What an immense joke if Verloc had simply made fools of the whole of Europe, of the revolutionary world, of the police, of the press, and of the cocksure Professor as well. Indeed, thought Ossipon, in astonishment, it seemed almost certain that he did! Poor beggar! It struck him as very possible that of that household of two it wasn't precisely the man who was the devil.

Alexander Ossipon, nicknamed the Doctor, was naturally inclined to think indulgently of his men friends. He eyed Mrs Verloc hanging on his arm. Of his women friends he thought in a specially practical way. Why Mrs Verloc should exclaim at his knowledge of Mr Verloc's death, which was no guess at all, did not disturb him beyond measure. Women often talked like lunatics. But he was curious to know how she had been informed. The papers could tell her nothing beyond the mere fact: the man blown to pieces in Greenwich Park not having been identified. It was inconceivable on any theory that Verloc should have given her an inkling of his intention – whatever it was. This problem interested Comrade Ossipon immensely. He stopped short. They had gone then along the three sides of Brett Place, and were near the end of Brett Street again.

'How did you first come to hear of it?' he asked in a tone he tried to render appropriate to the character of the revelations which had been made to him by the woman at his side.

She shook violently for a while before she answered in a listless voice: 'From the police. A chief inspector came. Chief Inspector Heat he said he was. He showed me . . . '

Mrs Verloc choked. 'Oh, Tom, they had to gather him up with a shovel.' Her breast heaved with dry sobs. In a moment Ossipon found his tongue.

'The police! Do you mean to say the police came already? That Chief Inspector Heat himself actually came to tell you.'

'Yes,' she confirmed in the same listless tone. 'He came. Just like this.

He came. I didn't know. He showed me a piece of overcoat, and . . . Just like that. Do you know this? he says.'

'Heat! Heat! And what did he do?'

Mrs Verloc's head dropped. 'Nothing. He did nothing. He went away. The police were on that man's side,' she murmured, tragically. 'Another one came, too.'

'Another – another inspector, do you mean?' asked Ossipon, in great excitement, and very much in the tone of a scared child.

'I don't know. He came. He looked like a foreigner. He may have been one of them Embassy people.'

Comrade Ossipon nearly collapsed under this new shock.

'Embassy! Are you aware what you are saying? What Embassy? What on earth do you mean by Embassy?'

'It's that place in Chesham Square. The people he cursed so. I don't know. What does it matter!'

'And that fellow, what did he do or say to you?'

'I don't remember . . . Nothing . . . I don't care. Don't ask me,' she pleaded in a weary voice.

'All right. I won't,' assented Ossipon, tenderly. And he meant it, too, not because he was touched by the pathos of the pleading voice, but because he felt himself losing his footing in the depths of this tenebrous affair. Police! Embassy! Phew! For fear of adventuring his intelligence into ways where its natural lights might fail to guide it safely he dismissed resolutely all suppositions, surmises, and theories out of his mind. He had the woman there, absolutely flinging herself at him, and that was the principal consideration. But after what he had heard nothing could astonish him any more. And when Mrs Verloc, as if startled suddenly out of a dream of safety, began to urge upon him wildly the necessity of an immediate flight on the Continent, he did not exclaim in the least. He simply said with unaffected regret that there was no train till the morning, and stood looking thoughtfully at her face, veiled in black net, in the light of a gas-lamp veiled in a gauze of mist.

Near him, her black form merged in the night, like a figure half chiselled out of a block of black stone. It was impossible to say what she knew, how deep she was involved with policemen and Embassies. But if she wanted to get away, it was not for him to object. He was anxious to be off himself. He felt that the business, the shop so strangely familiar to chief inspectors and members of foreign Embassies, was not the place for him. That must be dropped. But there was the rest. These savings. The money!

'You must hide me till the morning somewhere,' she said in a dismayed voice.

'Fact is, my dear, I can't take you where I live. I share the room with a friend.'

He was somewhat dismayed himself. In the morning the blessed 'tecs will be out in all the stations, no doubt. And if they once got hold of her, for one reason or another she would be lost to him indeed.

'But you must. Don't you care for me at all – at all? What are you thinking of?'

She said this violently, but she let her clasped hands fall in discouragement. There was a silence, while the mist fell, and darkness reigned undisturbed over Brett Place. Not a soul, not even the vagabond, lawless, and amorous soul of a cat, came near the man and the woman facing each other.

'It would be possible perhaps to find a safe lodging somewhere,' Ossipon spoke at last. 'But the truth is, my dear, I have not enough money to go and try with – only a few pence. We revolutionists are not rich.'

He had fifteen shillings in his pocket. He added: 'And there's the journey before us, too – first thing in the morning at that.'

She did not move, made no sound, and Comrade Ossipon's heart sank a little. Apparently she had no suggestion to offer. Suddenly she clutched at her breast, as if she had felt a sharp pain there.

'But I have,' she gasped. 'I have the money. I have enough money. Tom! Let us go from here.'

'How much have you got?' he enquired, without stirring to her tug; for he was a cautious man.

'I have the money, I tell you. All the money.'

'What do you mean by it? All the money there was in the bank, or what?' he asked, incredulously, but ready not to be surprised at anything in the way of luck.

'Yes, yes!' she said, nervously. 'All there was. I've it all.'

'How on earth did you manage to get hold of it already?' he marvelled.

'He gave it to me,' she murmured, suddenly subdued and trembling. Comrade Ossipon put down his rising surprise with a firm hand.

'Why, then – we are saved,' he uttered, slowly.

She leaned forward, and sank against his breast. He welcomed her there. She had all the money. Her hat was in the way of very marked effusion; her veil, too. He was adequate in his manifestations, but no more. She received them without resistance and without abandonment, passively, as if only half-sensible. She freed herself from his lax embrace without difficulty.

'You will save me, Tom,' she broke out, recoiling, but still keeping her hold on him by the two lapels of his damp coat. 'Save me. Hide me. Don't let them have me. You must kill me first. I couldn't do it myself – I couldn't, I couldn't – not even for what I am afraid of.'

She was confoundedly bizarre, he thought. She was beginning to inspire him with an indefinite uneasiness. He said surlily, for he was busy with important thoughts: 'What the devil *are* you afraid of?'

'Haven't you guessed what I was driven to do?' cried the woman. Distracted by the vividness of her dreadful apprehensions, her head ringing with forceful words, that kept the horror of her position before her mind, she had imagined her incoherence to be clearness itself. She had no conscience of how little she had audibly said in the disjointed phrases completed only in her thought. She had felt the relief of a full confession, and she gave a special meaning to every sentence spoken by Comrade Ossipon, whose knowledge did not in the least resemble her own. 'Haven't you guessed what I was driven to do?' Her voice fell. 'You needn't be long in guessing then what I am afraid of,' she continued, in a bitter and sombre murmur. 'I won't have it. I won't. I won't. I won't. You must promise to kill me first!' She shook the lapels of his coat. 'It must never be!'

He assured her curtly that no promises on his part were necessary, but he took good care not to contradict her in set terms, because he had had much to do with excited women, and he was inclined in general to let his experience guide his conduct in preference to applying his sagacity to each special case. His sagacity in this case was busy in other directions. Women's words fell into water, but the shortcomings of time-tables remained. The insular nature of Great Britain obtruded itself upon his notice in an odious form. 'Might just as well be put under lock and key every night,' he thought irritably, as nonplussed as though he had a wall to scale with the woman on his back. Suddenly he slapped his forehead. He had by dint of cudgelling his brains just thought of the Southampton – St Malo service. The boat left about midnight. There was a train at 10:30. He became cheery and ready to act.

'From Waterloo. Plenty of time. We are all right after all . . . What's the matter now? This isn't the way,' he protested.

Mrs Verloc, having hooked her arm into his, was trying to drag him into Brett Street again.

'I've forgotten to shut the shop door as I went out,' she whispered, terribly agitated.

The shop and all that was in it had ceased to interest Comrade Ossipon. He knew how to limit his desires. He was on the point of saying 'What of that? Let it be,' but he refrained. He disliked argument about trifles. He even mended his pace considerably on the thought that she might have left the money in the drawer. But his willingness lagged behind her feverish impatience. The shop seemed to be quite dark at first. The door stood ajar. Mrs Verloc, leaning against the front, gasped out: 'Nobody has been in. Look! The light – the light in the parlour.'

Ossipon, stretching his head forward, saw a faint gleam in the darkness of the shop.

'There is,' he said.

'I forgot it.' Mrs Verloc's voice came from behind her veil faintly. And as he stood waiting for her to enter first, she said louder: 'Go in and put it out – or I'll go mad.'

He made no immediate objection to this proposal, so strangely motived. 'Where's all that money?' he asked.

'On me! Go, Tom. Quick! Put it out . . . Go in!' she cried, seizing him by both shoulders from behind.

Not prepared for a display of physical force, Comrade Ossipon stumbled far into the shop before her push. He was astonished at the strength of the woman and scandalised by her proceedings. But he did not retrace his steps in order to remonstrate with her severely in the street. He was beginning to be disagreeably impressed by her fantastic behaviour. Moreover, this or never was the time to humour the woman. Comrade Ossipon avoided easily the end of the counter, and approached calmly the glazed door of the parlour. The curtain over the panes being drawn back a little he, by a very natural impulse, looked in, just as he made ready to turn the handle. He looked in without a thought, without intention, without curiosity of any sort. He looked in because he could not help looking in. He looked in, and discovered Mr Verloc reposing quietly on the sofa.

A yell coming from the innermost depths of his chest died out unheard and transformed into a sort of greasy, sickly taste on his lips. At the same time the mental personality of Comrade Ossipon executed a frantic leap backwards. But his body, left thus without intellectual guidance, held on to the door handle with the unthinking force of an instinct. The robust anarchist did not even totter. And he stared, his face close to the glass, his eyes protruding out of his head. He would have given anything to get away, but his returning reason informed him that it would not do to let go the door handle. What was it – madness, a nightmare, or a trap into which he had been decoyed with fiendish artfulness? Why – what for? He did not know. Without any sense of guilt in his breast, in the full peace of his conscience as far as these people were concerned, the idea that he would be murdered for mysterious reasons by the couple Verloc passed not so much across his mind as across the pit of his stomach, and went out, leaving behind a trail of sickly faintness – an indisposition. Comrade Ossipon did not feel very well in a very special way for a moment – a long moment. And he stared. Mr Verloc lay very still meanwhile, simulating sleep for reasons of his own, while that savage woman of his was guarding the door – invisible and silent in the dark and deserted street. Was all this some sort of terrifying arrangement invented by the police for his especial benefit? His modesty shrank from that explanation.

But the true sense of the scene he was beholding came to Ossipon through the contemplation of the hat. It seemed an extraordinary thing, an ominous object, a sign. Black, and rim upward, it lay on the floor before the couch as if prepared to receive the contributions of pence from people who would come presently to behold Mr Verloc in the fullness of his domestic ease reposing on a sofa. From the hat the eyes of the robust anarchist wandered to the displaced table, gazed at the broken dish for a time, received a kind of optical shock from observing a white gleam under the imperfectly closed eyelids of the man on the couch. Mr Verloc did not seem so much asleep now as lying down with a bent head and looking insistently at his left breast. And when

Comrade Ossipon had made out the handle of the knife he turned away from the glazed door, and retched violently.

The crash of the street door flung to made his very soul leap in a panic. This house with its harmless tenant could still be made a trap of – a trap of a terrible kind. Comrade Ossipon had no settled conception now of what was happening to him. Catching his thigh against the end of the counter, he spun round, staggered with a cry of pain, felt in the distracting clatter of the bell his arms pinned to his side by a convulsive hug, while the cold lips of a woman moved creepily on his very ear to form the words: 'Policeman! He has seen me!'

He ceased to struggle; she never let him go. Her hands had locked themselves with an inseparable twist of fingers on his robust back. While the footsteps approached, they breathed quickly, breast to breast with hard, laboured breaths, as if theirs had been the attitude of a deadly struggle, while, in fact, it was the attitude of deadly fear. And the time was long.

The constable on the beat had in truth seen something of Mrs Verloc; only coming from the lighted thoroughfare at the other end of Brett Street, she had been no more to him than a flutter in the darkness. And he was not even quite sure that there had been a flutter. He had no reason to hurry up. On coming abreast of the shop he observed that it had been closed early. There was nothing very unusual in that. The men on duty had special instructions about that shop: what went on about there was not to be meddled with unless absolutely disorderly, but any observations made were to be reported. There were no observations to make; but from a sense of duty and for the peace of his conscience, owing also to that doubtful flutter of the darkness, the constable crossed the road, and tried the door. The spring latch, whose key was reposing for ever off duty in the late Mr Verloc's waistcoat pocket, held as well as usual. While the conscientious officer was shaking the handle, Ossipon felt the cold lips of the woman stirring again creepily against his very ear: 'If he comes in kill me – kill me, Tom.'

The constable moved away, flashing as he passed the light of his dark lantern, merely for form's sake, at the shop window. For a moment longer the man and the woman inside stood motionless, panting, breast to breast; then her fingers came unlocked, her arms fell by her side slowly. Ossipon leaned against the counter. The robust anarchist wanted support badly. This was awful. He was almost too disgusted for speech. Yet he managed to utter a plaintive thought, showing at least that he realised his position.

'Only a couple of minutes later and you'd have made me blunder against the fellow poking about here with his damned dark lantern.'

The widow of Mr Verloc, motionless in the middle of the shop, said insistently: 'Go in and put that light out, Tom. It will drive me crazy.'

She saw vaguely his vehement gesture of refusal. Nothing in the world would have induced Ossipon to go into the parlour. He was not superstitious, but there was too much blood on the floor; a beastly pool of it all round the hat. He judged he had been already too near that corpse for his peace of mind – for the safety of his neck, perhaps!

'At the meter then! There. Look. In that corner.'

The robust form of Comrade Ossipon, striding brusque and shadowy across the shop, squatted in a corner obediently; but this obedience was without grace. He fumbled nervously – and suddenly in the sound of a muttered curse the light behind the glazed door flicked out to a gasping, hysterical sigh of a woman. Night, the inevitable reward of men's faithful labours on this earth, night had fallen on Mr Verloc, the tried revolutionist – 'one of the old lot' – the humble guardian of society; the invaluable Secret Agent Δ of Baron Stott-Wartenheim's despatches; a servant of law and order, faithful, trusted, accurate, admirable, with perhaps one single amiable weakness: the idealistic belief in being loved for himself.

Ossipon groped his way back through the stuffy atmosphere, as black as ink now, to the counter. The voice of Mrs Verloc, standing in the middle of the shop, vibrated after him in that blackness with a desperate protest.

'I will not be hanged, Tom. I will not . . .'

She broke off. Ossipon from the counter issued a warning: 'Don't shout like this,' then seemed to reflect profoundly. 'You did this thing quite by yourself?' he enquired in a hollow voice, but with an appearance of masterful calmness which filled Mrs Verloc's heart with grateful confidence in his protecting strength.

'Yes,' she whispered, invisible.

'I wouldn't have believed it possible,' he muttered. 'Nobody would.' She heard him move about and the snapping of a lock in the parlour door. Comrade Ossipon had turned the key on Mr Verloc's repose; and this he did not from reverence for its eternal nature or any other obscurely sentimental consideration, but for the precise reason that he was not at all sure that there was not someone else hiding somewhere in the house. He did not believe the woman, or rather he was incapable by now of judging what could be true, possible, or even probable on this astounding universe. He was terrified out of all capacity for belief or disbelief in regard to this extraordinary affair, which began with police inspectors and Embassies and would end goodness knows where – on the scaffold for someone. He was terrified at the thought that he could not prove the use he made of his time ever since seven o'clock, for he had been skulking about Brett Street. He was terrified at this savage woman who had brought him in there, and would probably saddle him with complicity, at least if he were not careful. He was terrified at the rapidity with which he had been involved in such danger – decoyed into it. It was some twenty minutes since he had met her – not more.

The voice of Mrs Verloc rose subdued, pleading piteously: 'Don't let them hang me, Tom! Take me out of the country. I'll work for you. I'll slave for you. I'll love you. I've no one in the world . . . Who would look at me if you don't!' She ceased for a moment; then in the depths of the loneliness made round her by an insignificant thread of blood trickling off the handle of a knife, she found a dreadful inspiration to her – who had been the respectable girl of the Belgravian mansion, the loyal, respectable wife of Mr Verloc. 'I won't ask you to marry me,' she breathed out in shamefaced accents.

She moved a step forward in the darkness. He was terrified at her. He would not have been surprised if she had suddenly produced another knife destined for his breast. He certainly would have made no resistance. He had really not enough fortitude in him just then to tell her to keep back. But he enquired in a cavernous, strange tone, 'Was he asleep?'

'No,' she cried, and went on rapidly: 'He wasn't. Not he. He had been telling me that nothing could touch him. After taking the boy away from under my very eyes to kill him – the loving, innocent, harmless lad. My own, I tell you. He was lying on the couch quite easy – after killing the boy – my boy. I would have gone on the streets to get out of his sight. And he says to me like this: "Come here," after telling me I had helped to kill the boy. You hear, Tom? He says like this: "Come here," after taking my very heart out of me along with the boy to smash in the dirt.'

She ceased, then dreamily repeated twice: 'Blood and dirt. Blood and dirt.' A great light broke upon Comrade Ossipon. It was that half-witted lad then who had perished in the park. And the fooling of everybody all round appeared more complete than ever – colossal. He exclaimed scientifically, in the extremity of his astonishment: 'The degenerate by heavens!'

'Come here.' The voice of Mrs Verloc rose again. 'What did he think I was made of? Tell me, Tom. Come here! Me! Like this! I had been looking at the knife, and I thought I would come then if he wanted me so much. Oh, yes! I came – for the last time . . . With the knife.'

He was excessively terrified at her – the sister of the degenerate a degenerate herself of a murdering type . . . or else of the lying type. Comrade Ossipon might have been said to be terrified scientifically in addition to all other kinds of fear. It was an immeasurable and composite funk, which from its very excess gave him in the dark a false appearance of calm and thoughtful deliberation. For he moved and spoke with difficulty, being as if half frozen in his will and mind – and no one could see his ghastly face. He felt half dead.

He leaped a foot high. Unexpectedly Mrs Verloc had desecrated the unbroken, reserved decency of her home by a shrill and terrible shriek.

'Help, Tom! Save me. I won't be hanged!'

He rushed forward, groping for her mouth with a silencing hand, and the shriek died out. But in his rush he had knocked her over. He felt her now clinging round his legs, and his terror reached its culminating point, became a sort of intoxication, entertained delusions, acquired the characteristics of delirium tremens. He positively saw snakes now. He saw the woman twined round him like a snake, not to be shaken off. She was not deadly. She was death itself – the companion of life.

Mrs Verloc, as if relieved by the outburst, was very far from behaving noisily now. She was pitiful.

'Tom, you can't throw me off now,' she murmured from the floor. 'Not unless you crush my head under your heel. I won't leave you.'

'Get up,' said Ossipon.

His face was so pale as to be quite visible in the profound black darkness of the shop; while Mrs Verloc, veiled, had no face, almost no discernible form. The trembling of something small and white, a flower in her hat, marked her place, her movements.

It rose in the blackness. She had got up from the floor, and Ossipon regretted not having run out at once into the street. But he perceived easily that it would not do. It would not do. She would run after him. She would pursue him shrieking till she sent every policeman within hearing in chase. And then goodness only knew what she would say of him. He was so frightened that for a moment the insane notion of strangling her in the dark passed through his mind. And he became more frightened than ever! She had him! He saw himself living in abject terror in some obscure hamlet in Spain or Italy; till some fine morning they found him dead, too, with a knife in his breast – like Mr Verloc. He sighed deeply. He dared not move. And Mrs Verloc waited in silence the good pleasure of her saviour, deriving comfort from his reflective silence.

Suddenly he spoke up in an almost natural voice. His reflections had come to an end.

'Let's get out, or we will lose the train.'

'Where are we going to, Tom?' she asked, timidly. Mrs Verloc was no longer a free woman.

'Let's get to Paris first, the best way we can . . . Go out first, and see if the way's clear.'

She obeyed. Her voice came subdued through the cautiously opened door.

'It's all right.'

Ossipon came out. Notwithstanding his endeavours to be gentle, the cracked bell clattered behind the closed door in the empty shop, as if trying in vain to warn the reposing Mr Verloc of the final departure of his wife accompanied by his friend.

In the hansom they presently picked up, the robust anarchist became explanatory. He was still awfully pale, with eyes that seemed to have sunk a whole half-inch into his tense face. But he seemed to have thought of everything with extraordinary method.

'When we arrive,' he discoursed in a queer, monotonous tone, 'you must go into the station ahead of me, as if we did not know each other. I will take the tickets, and slip yours into your hand as I pass you. Then you will go into the first-class ladies' waiting-room, and sit there till ten minutes before the train starts. Then you come out. I will be outside. You go in first on the platform, as if you did not know me. There may be eyes watching there that know what's what. Alone you are only a woman going off by train. I am known. With me, you may be guessed at as Mrs Verloc running away. Do you understand, my dear?' he added, with an effort.

'Yes,' said Mrs Verloc, sitting there against him in the hansom all rigid with the dread of the gallows and the fear of death. 'Yes, Tom.' And she added to herself, like an awful refrain: 'The drop given was fourteen feet.'

Ossipon, not looking at her, and with a face like a fresh plaster cast of himself after a wasting illness, said: 'By the by, I ought to have the money for the tickets now.'

Mrs Verloc, undoing some hooks of her bodice, while she went on staring ahead beyond the splashboard, handed over to him the new pigskin pocketbook. He received it without a word, and seemed to plunge it deep somewhere into his very breast. Then he slapped his coat on the outside.

All this was done without the exchange of a single glance; they were like two people looking out for the first sight of a desired goal. It was not till the hansom swung round a corner and towards the bridge that Ossipon opened his lips again.

'Do you know how much money there is in that thing?' he asked, as if addressing slowly some hobgoblin sitting between the ears of the horse.

'No,' said Mrs Verloc. 'He gave it to me. I didn't count. I thought nothing of it at the time. Afterwards . . . '

She moved her right hand a little. It was so expressive that little movement of that right hand which had struck the deadly blow into a man's heart less than an hour before that Ossipon could not repress a shudder. He exaggerated it then purposely, and muttered: 'I am cold. I got chilled through.'

Mrs Verloc looked straight ahead at the perspective of her escape. Now and then, like a sable streamer blown across a road, the words 'The drop given was fourteen feet' got in the way of her tense stare. Through her black veil the whites of her big eyes gleamed lustrously like the eyes of a masked woman.

Ossipon's rigidity had something businesslike, a queer official expression. He was heard again all of a sudden, as though he had released a catch in order to speak.

'Look here! Do you know whether your – whether he kept his account at the bank in his own name or in some other name.'

Mrs Verloc turned upon him her masked face and the big white gleam of her eyes.

'Other name?' she said, thoughtfully.

'Be exact in what you say,' Ossipon lectured in the swift motion of the hansom. 'It's extremely important. I will explain to you. The bank has the numbers of these notes. If they were paid to him in his own name, then when his – his death becomes known, the notes may serve to track us since we have no other money. You have no other money on you?'

She shook her head negatively.

'None whatever?' he insisted.

'A few coppers.'

'It would be dangerous in that case. The money would have then to be dealt specially with. Very specially. We'd have perhaps to lose more than half the amount in order to get these notes changed in a certain safe place I know of in Paris. In the other case I mean if he had his account and got paid out under some other name say Smith, for instance – the money is perfectly safe to use. You understand? The bank has no means of knowing that Mr Verloc and, say, Smith are one and the same person. Do you see how important it is that you should make no mistake in answering me? Can you answer that query at all? Perhaps not. Eh?'

She said composedly: 'I remember now! He didn't bank in his own name. He told me once that it was on deposit in the name of Prozor.'

'You are sure?'

'Certain.'

'You don't think the bank had any knowledge of his real name? Or anybody in the bank or . . . '

She shrugged her shoulders.

'How can I know? Is it likely, Tom?'

'No. I suppose it's not likely. It would have been more comfortable to know . . . Here we are. Get out first, and walk straight in. Move smartly.'

He remained behind, and paid the cabman out of his own loose silver. The programme traced by his minute foresight was carried out. When Mrs Verloc, with her ticket for St Malo in her hand, entered the ladies' waiting-room, Comrade Ossipon walked into the bar, and in seven minutes absorbed three goes of hot brandy and water.

'Trying to drive out a cold,' he explained to the barmaid, with a friendly nod and a grimacing smile. Then he came out, bringing out from that festive interlude the face of a man who had drunk at the very Fountain of Sorrow. He raised his eyes to the clock. It was time. He waited.

Punctual, Mrs Verloc came out, with her veil down, and all black – black as commonplace death itself, crowned with a few cheap and pale flowers. She passed close to a little group of men who were laughing, but whose laughter could have been struck dead by a single word. Her walk was indolent, but her back was straight, and Comrade Ossipon looked after it in terror before making a start himself.

The train was drawn up, with hardly anybody about its row of open doors. Owing to the time of the year and to the abominable weather there were but few passengers. Mrs Verloc walked slowly along the line of empty compartments till Ossipon touched her elbow from behind.

'In here.'

She got in, and he remained on the platform looking about. She bent forward, and in a whisper: 'What is it, Tom? Is there any danger?'

'Wait a moment. There's the guard.'

She saw him accost the man in uniform. They talked for a while. She heard the guard say 'Very well, sir,' and saw him touch his cap. Then Ossipon came back, saying: 'I told him not to let anybody get into our compartment.'

She was leaning forward on her seat. 'You think of everything . . . You'll get me off, Tom?' she asked in a gust of anguish, lifting her veil brusquely to look at her saviour.

She had uncovered a face like adamant. And out of this face the eyes looked on, big, dry, enlarged, lightless, burnt out like two black holes in the white, shining globes.

'There is no danger,' he said, gazing into them with an earnestness almost rapt, which to Mrs Verloc, flying from the gallows, seemed to be full of force and tenderness. This devotion deeply moved her – and the adamantine face lost the stern rigidity of its terror. Comrade Ossipon gazed at it as no lover ever gazed at his mistress's face. Alexander Ossipon, anarchist, nicknamed the Doctor, author of a medical (and improper) pamphlet, late lecturer on the social aspects of hygiene to working men's clubs, was free from the trammels of conventional morality – but he submitted to the rule of science. He was scientific, and he gazed scientifically at that woman, the sister of a degenerate, a degenerate herself – of a murdering type. He gazed at her, and invoked Lombroso, as an Italian peasant recommends himself to his favourite saint. He gazed scientifically. He gazed at her cheeks, at her nose, at her eyes, at her ears . . . Bad! . . . Fatal! Mrs Verloc's pale lips parting, slightly relaxed under his passionately attentive gaze, he gazed also at her teeth . . . Not a doubt remained . . . a murdering type. If Comrade Ossipon did not recommend his terrified soul to Lombroso, it was only because on scientific grounds he could not believe that he carried about him such a thing as a soul. But he had in him the scientific spirit, which moved him to testify on the platform of a railway station in nervous, jerky phrases.

'He was an extraordinary lad, that brother of yours. Most interesting to study. A perfect type in a way. Perfect!'

He spoke scientifically in his secret fear. And Mrs Verloc, hearing these words of commendation vouchsafed to her beloved dead, swayed forward with a flicker of light in her sombre eyes, like a ray of sunshine heralding a tempest of rain.

'He was that indeed,' she whispered, softly, with quivering lips. 'You took a lot of notice of him, Tom. I loved you for it.'

'It's almost incredible the resemblance there was between you two,' pursued Ossipon, giving a voice to his abiding dread, and trying to conceal his nervous, sickening impatience for the train to start. 'Yes, he resembled you.'

These words were not especially touching or sympathetic. But the fact of that resemblance insisted upon was enough in itself to act upon her emotions powerfully. With a little faint cry, and throwing her arms out, Mrs Verloc burst into tears at last.

Ossipon entered the carriage, hastily closed the door and looked out to see the time by the station clock. Eight minutes more. For the first three of these Mrs Verloc wept violently and helplessly without pause or interruption. Then she recovered somewhat, and sobbed gently in an abundant fall of tears. She tried to talk to her saviour, to the man who was the messenger of life.

'Oh, Tom! How could I fear to die after he was taken away from me so cruelly! How could I! How could I be such a coward!'

She lamented aloud her love of life, that life without grace or charm, and almost without decency, but of an exalted faithfulness of purpose, even unto murder. And, as often happens in the lament of poor humanity rich in suffering but indigent in words, the truth – the very cry of truth – was found in a worn and artificial shape picked up somewhere among the phrases of sham sentiment.

'How could I be so afraid of death! Tom, I tried. But I am afraid. I tried to do away with myself. And I couldn't. Am I hard? I suppose the cup of horrors was not full enough for such as me. Then when you came . . . '

She paused. Then in a gust of confidence and gratitude, 'I will live all my days for you, Tom!' she sobbed out.

'Go over into the other corner of the carriage, away from the platform,' said Ossipon, solicitously. She let her saviour settle her comfortably, and he watched the coming on of another crisis of weeping, still more violent than the first. He watched the symptoms with a sort of medical air, as if counting seconds. He heard the guard's whistle at last. An involuntary contraction of the upper lip bared his teeth with all the aspect of savage resolution as he felt the train beginning to move. Mrs Verloc heard and felt nothing, and Ossipon, her saviour, stood still. He felt the train roll quicker, rumbling heavily to the sound of the woman's loud sobs, and then crossing the carriage in two long strides he opened the door deliberately, and leaped out.

He had leaped out at the very end of the platform; and such was his determination in sticking to his desperate plan that he managed by a sort of miracle, performed almost in the air, to slam to the door of the carriage. Only then did he find himself rolling head over heels like a shot rabbit. He was bruised, shaken, pale as death, and out of breath when he got up. But he was calm, and perfectly able to meet the excited crowd of railway men who had gathered round him in a moment. He explained, in gentle and convincing tones, that his wife had started at a moment's notice for Brittany to her dying mother; that, of course, she was greatly upset, and he considerably concerned at her state; that he was trying to cheer her up, and had absolutely failed to notice at first that the train was moving out. To the general exclamation 'Why didn't you go on to Southampton, then, sir?' he objected the inexperience of a young sister-in-law left alone in the house with three small children, and her alarm at his absence, the telegraph offices being closed. He had acted on impulse. 'But I don't think I'll ever try that again,' he concluded; smiled all round; distributed some small change, and marched without a limp out of the station.

Outside, Comrade Ossipon, flush of safe banknotes as never before in his life, refused the offer of a cab.

'I can walk,' he said, with a little friendly laugh to the civil driver.

He could walk. He walked. He crossed the bridge. Later on the towers of the Abbey saw in their massive immobility the yellow bush of his hair passing under the lamps. The lights of Victoria saw him, too, and Sloane Square, and the railings of the park. And Comrade Ossipon once more found himself on a bridge. The river, a sinister marvel of still shadows and flowing gleams mingling below in a black silence, arrested his attention. He stood looking over the parapet for a long time. The clock tower boomed a brazen blast above his drooping head. He looked up at the dial . . . Half-past twelve of a wild night in the Channel.

And again Comrade Ossipon walked. His robust form was seen that night in distant parts of the enormous town slumbering monstrously on a carpet of mud under a veil of raw mist. It was seen crossing the streets without life and sound, or diminishing in the interminable straight perspectives of shadowy houses bordering empty roadways lined by strings of gas-lamps. He walked through Squares, Places, Ovals, Commons, through monotonous streets with unknown names where the dust of humanity settles inert and hopeless out of the stream of life. He walked. And suddenly turning into a strip of a front garden with a mangy grass plot, he let himself into a small grimy house with a latchkey he took out of his pocket.

He threw himself down on his bed all dressed, and lay still for a whole quarter of an hour. Then he sat up suddenly, drawing up his knees, and clasping his legs. The first dawn found him open-eyed, in that same posture. This man who could walk so long, so far, so aimlessly, without showing a sign of fatigue, could also remain sitting still for hours without stirring a limb or an eyelid. But when the late sun sent its rays into the room he unclasped his hands, and fell back on the pillow. His eyes stared at the ceiling. And suddenly they closed. Comrade Ossipon slept in the sunlight.

Chapter 13

The enormous iron padlock on the doors of the wall cupboard was the only object in the room on which the eye could rest without becoming afflicted by the miserable unloveliness of forms and the poverty of material. Unsaleable in the ordinary course of business on account of its noble proportions, it had been ceded to the Professor for a few pence by a marine dealer in the east of London. The room was large, clean, respectable, and poor with that poverty suggesting the starvation of every human need except mere bread. There was nothing on the walls but the paper, an expanse of arsenical green, soiled with indelible smudges here and there, and with stains resembling faded maps of uninhabited continents.

At a deal table near a window sat Comrade Ossipon, holding his head between his fists. The Professor, dressed in his only suit of shoddy tweeds, but flapping to and fro on the bare boards a pair of incredibly dilapidated slippers, had thrust his hands deep into the overstrained pockets of his jacket. He was relating to his robust guest a visit he had lately been paying to the Apostle Michaelis. The Perfect Anarchist had even been unbending a little.

'The fellow didn't know anything of Verloc's death. Of course! He never looks at the newspapers. They make him too sad, he says. But never mind. I walked into his cottage. Not a soul anywhere. I had to shout half a dozen times before he answered me. I thought he was fast asleep yet, in bed. But not at all. He had been writing his book for four hours already. He sat in that tiny cage in a litter of manuscript. There was a half-eaten raw carrot on the table near him. His breakfast. He lives on a diet of raw carrots and a little milk now.'

'How does he look on it?' asked Comrade Ossipon, listlessly.

'Angelic . . . I picked up a handful of his pages from the floor. The poverty of reasoning is astonishing. He has no logic. He can't think consecutively. But that's nothing. He has divided his biography into three parts, entitled – "Faith, Hope, Charity." He is elaborating now the idea of a world planned out like an immense and nice hospital, with gardens and flowers, in which the strong are to devote themselves to the nursing of the weak.'

The Professor paused.

'Conceive you this folly, Ossipon? The weak! The source of all evil on this earth!' he continued with his grim assurance. 'I told him that I dreamt of a world like shambles, where the weak would be taken in hand for utter extermination.

'Do you understand, Ossipon? The source of all evil! They are our sinister masters – the weak, the flabby, the silly, the cowardly, the faint of heart, and the slavish of mind. They have power. They are the multitude. Theirs is the kingdom of the earth. Exterminate, exterminate! That is the only way of progress. It is! Follow me, Ossipon. First the great multitude of the weak must go, then the only relatively strong. You see? First the blind, then the deaf and the dumb, then the halt and the lame and so on. Every taint, every vice, every prejudice, every convention must meet its doom.'

'And what remains?' asked Ossipon in a stifled voice.

'I remain – if I am strong enough,' asserted the sallow little Professor, whose large ears, thin like membranes, and standing far out from the sides of his frail skull, took on suddenly a deep red tint. .

'Haven't I suffered enough from this oppression of the weak?' he continued, forcibly. Then tapping the breast-pocket of his jacket: 'And yet I *am* the force,' he went on. 'But the time! The time! Give me time! Ah! that multitude, too stupid to feel either pity or fear. Sometimes I think they have everything on their side. Everything – even death – my own weapon.'

'Come and drink some beer with me at the Silenus,' said the robust Ossipon after an interval of silence pervaded by the rapid flap, flap of the slippers on the feet of the Perfect Anarchist. This last accepted. He was jovial that day in his own peculiar way. He slapped Ossipon's shoulder.

'Beer! So be it! Let us drink and be merry, for we are strong, and tomorrow we die.'

He busied himself with putting on his boots, and talked meanwhile in his curt, resolute tones.

'What's the matter with you, Ossipon? You look glum and seek even my company. I hear that you are seen constantly in places where men utter foolish things over glasses of liquor. Why? Have you abandoned your collection of women? They are the weak who feed the strong – eh?'

He stamped one foot, and picked up his other laced boot, heavy, thick-soled, unblacked, mended many times. He smiled to himself grimly.

'Tell me, Ossipon, terrible man, has ever one of your victims killed herself for you – or are your triumphs so far incomplete – for blood alone puts a seal on greatness? Blood. Death. Look at history.'

'You be damned,' said Ossipon, without turning his head.

'Why? Let that be the hope of the weak, whose theology has invented hell for the strong. Ossipon, my feeling for you is amicable contempt. You couldn't kill a fly.'

But rolling to the feast on the top of the omnibus the Professor lost his high spirits. The contemplation of the multitudes thronging the pavements extinguished his assurance under a load of doubt and uneasiness which he could shake off after a period of seclusion in the room with the large cupboard closed by an enormous padlock.

'And so,' said over his shoulder Comrade Ossipon, who sat on the seat behind. 'And so Michaelis dreams of a world like a beautiful and cheery hospital.'

'Just so. An immense charity for the healing of the weak,' assented the Professor, sardonically.

'That's silly,' admitted Ossipon. 'You can't heal weakness. But after all Michaelis may not be so far wrong. In two hundred years doctors will rule the world. Science reigns already. It reigns in the shade maybe – but it reigns. And all science must culminate at last in the science of healing – not the weak, but the strong. Mankind wants to live – to live.'

'Mankind,' asserted the Professor with a self-confident glitter of his iron-rimmed spectacles, 'does not know what it wants.'

'But you do,' growled Ossipon. 'Just now you've been crying for time –

time. Well, the doctors will serve you out your time if you are good. You profess yourself to be one of the strong because you carry in your pocket enough stuff to send yourself and, say, twenty other people into eternity. But eternity is a damned hole. It's time that you need. You – if you met a man who could give you for certain ten years of time, you would call him your master.'

'My device is: No God! No master,' said the Professor, sententiously, as he rose to get off the bus.

Ossipon followed. 'Wait till you are lying flat on your back at the end of your time,' he retorted, jumping off the footboard after the other. 'Your scurvy, shabby, mangy little bit of time,' he continued across the street, and hopping on to the kerbstone.

'Ossipon, I think that you are a humbug,' the Professor said, opening masterfully the doors of the renowned Silenus. And when they had established themselves at a little table he developed further this gracious thought. 'You are not even a doctor. But you are funny. Your notion of a humanity universally putting out the tongue and taking the pill from pole to pole at the bidding of a few solemn jokers is worthy of the prophet. Prophecy! What's the good of thinking of what will be!' He raised his glass. 'To the destruction of what is,' he said, calmly.

He drank and relapsed into his peculiarly close manner of silence. The thought of a mankind as numerous as the sands of the seashore, as indestructible, as difficult to handle, oppressed him. The sound of exploding bombs was lost in their immensity of passive grains without an echo. For instance, this Verloc affair. Who thought of it now?

Ossipon, as if suddenly compelled by some mysterious force, pulled a much-folded newspaper out of his pocket. The Professor raised his head at the rustle.

'What's that paper? Anything in it?' he asked.

Ossipon started like a scared somnambulist.

'Nothing. Nothing whatever. The thing's ten days old. I forgot it in my pocket, I suppose.'

But he did not throw the old thing away. Before returning it to his pocket he stole a glance at the last lines of a paragraph. They ran thus: '*An impenetrable mystery seems destined to hang for ever over this act of madness or despair.*'

Such were the end words of an item of news headed: 'Suicide of Lady Passenger from a cross-Channel Boat.' Comrade Ossipon was familiar with the beauties of its journalistic style. '*An impenetrable mystery seems destined to hang for ever . . .* ' He knew every word by heart. '*An impenetrable mystery . . .* ' And the robust anarchist, hanging his head on his breast, fell into a long reverie.

He was menaced by this thing in the very sources of his existence. He could not issue forth to meet his various conquests, those that he courted on benches in Kensington Gardens, and those he met near area railings, without the dread of beginning to talk to them of an impenetrable mystery destined . . . He was becoming scientifically afraid of insanity lying in wait for him amongst these lines. '*To hang for ever over.*' It was an obsession, a torture. He had lately failed to keep several of these appointments, whose note used to be an unbounded trustfulness in the language of sentiment and manly tenderness. The confiding disposition of various classes of women satisfied the needs of his self-love, and put some material means into his hand. He needed it to live. It was there. But if he could no longer make use of it, he ran the risk of starving his ideals and his body . . . '*This act of madness or despair.*'

'An impenetrable mystery' was sure 'to hang for ever' as far as all mankind was concerned. But what of that if he alone of all men could never get rid of the cursed knowledge? And Comrade Ossipon's knowledge was as precise as the newspaper man could make it – up to the very threshold of the '*mystery destined to hang for ever . . .* '

Comrade Ossipon was well informed. He knew what the gangway man of the steamer had seen: 'A lady in a black dress and a black veil, wandering at midnight alongside, on the quay. "Are you going by the boat, ma'am," he had asked her, encouragingly. "This way." She seemed not to know what to do. He helped her on board. She seemed weak.'

And Ossipon knew also what the stewardess had seen: A lady in black with a white face standing in the middle of the empty ladies' cabin. The stewardess induced her to lie down there. The lady seemed quite unwilling to speak, and as if she were in some awful trouble. The next the stewardess knew she was gone from the ladies' cabin. The stewardess then went on deck to look for her, and Comrade Ossipon was informed that the good woman found the unhappy lady lying down in one of the hooded seats. Her eyes were open, but she would not answer anything that was said to her. She seemed very ill. The stewardess fetched the chief steward, and those two people stood by the side of the hooded seat consulting over their extraordinary and tragic passenger. They talked in audible whispers (for she seemed past hearing) of St Malo and the Consul there, of communicating with her people in England. Then they went away to arrange for her removal down below, for indeed by what they could see of her face she seemed to them to be dying. But Comrade Ossipon knew that behind that white mask of despair there was struggling against terror and despair a vigour of vitality, a love of life that could resist the furious anguish which drives to murder and the fear, the blind, mad fear of the gallows. He knew. But the stewardess and the chief steward knew nothing, except that when they came back for her in less than five minutes the lady in black was no longer in the hooded seat. She was nowhere. She was gone. It was then five o'clock in the morning, and it was no accident either. An hour afterwards one of the steamer's hands found a wedding ring left lying on the seat. It had stuck to the wood in a bit of wet, and its glitter caught the man's eye. There was a date, 24th June, 1879, engraved inside. '*An impenetrable mystery is destined to hang for ever . . .*'

And Comrade Ossipon raised his bowed head, beloved of various humble women of these isles, Apollo-like in the sunniness of its bush of hair.

The Professor had grown restless meantime. He rose.

'Stay,' said Ossipon, hurriedly. 'Here, what do you know of madness and despair?'

The Professor passed the tip of his tongue on his dry, thin lips, and said doctorally: 'There are no such things. All passion is lost now. The world is mediocre, limp, without force. And madness and despair are a force. And force is a crime in the eyes of the fools, the weak and the silly who rule the roost. You are mediocre. Verloc, whose affair the police has managed to smother so nicely, was mediocre. And the police murdered him. He was mediocre. Everybody is mediocre, madness and despair! Give me that for a lever, and I'll move the world. Ossipon, you have my cordial scorn. You are incapable of conceiving even what the fat-fed citizen would call a crime. You have no force.' He paused, smiling sardonically under the fierce glitter of his thick glasses.

'And let me tell you that this little legacy they say you've come into has not improved your intelligence. You sit at your beer like a dummy. Goodbye.'

'Will you have it?' said Ossipon, looking up with an idiotic grin.

'Have what?'

'The legacy. All of it.'

The incorruptible Professor only smiled. His clothes were all but falling off him, his boots, shapeless with repairs, heavy like lead, let water in at every step. He said: 'I will send you by and by a small bill for certain chemicals which I shall order tomorrow. I need them badly. Understood eh?'

Ossipon lowered his head slowly. He was alone. '*An impenetrable mystery . . .*' It seemed to him that suspended in the air before him he saw his own brain pulsating to the rhythm of an impenetrable mystery. It was diseased clearly. '*This act of madness or despair . . .*'

The mechanical piano near the door played through a valse cheekily, then fell silent all at once, as if gone grumpy. Comrade Ossipon, nicknamed the Doctor, went out of the Silenus beer-hall. At the door he hesitated, blinking at a not too splendid sunlight – and the paper with the report of the suicide of a lady was in his pocket. His heart was beating against it. The suicide of a lady – *this act of madness or despair.*

He walked along the street without looking where he put his feet; and he walked in a direction which would not bring him to the place of appointment with another lady (an elderly nursery governess putting her trust in an Apollo-like ambrosial head). He was walking away from it. He could face no woman. It was ruin. He could neither think, work, sleep, nor eat. But he was beginning to drink with pleasure, with anticipation, with hope. It was ruin. His revolutionary career, sustained by the sentiment and trustfulness of many women, was menaced by an impenetrable mystery – the mystery of a human brain pulsating wrongfully to the rhythm of journalistic phrases. ' . . . *Will hang for ever over this act . . .* ' It was inclining towards the gutter . . . '*of madness or despair . . .* '

'I am seriously ill,' he muttered to himself with scientific insight. Already his robust form, with an Embassy's secret-service money (inherited from Mr Verloc) in his pockets, was marching in the gutter as if in training for the task of an inevitable future. Already he bowed his broad shoulders, his head of ambrosial locks, as if ready to receive the leather yoke of the sandwich board. As on that night, more than a week ago, Comrade Ossipon walked without looking where he put his feet, feeling no fatigue, feeling nothing, seeing nothing, hearing not a sound. '*An impenetrable mystery . . .* ' He walked disregarded . . . '*This act of madness or despair.*'

And the incorruptible Professor walked, too, averting his eyes from the odious multitude of mankind. He had no future. He disdained it. He was a force. His thoughts caressed the images of ruin and destruction. He walked frail, insignificant, shabby, miserable – and terrible in the simplicity of his idea calling madness and despair to the regeneration of the world. Nobody looked at him. He passed on unsuspected and deadly, like a pest in the street full of men.

SHORT STORIES

Short Stories

by

JOSEPH CONRAD

CONTENTS

The Lagoon   769

An Outpost of Progress   781

Karain: A Memory   801

Youth: A Narrative   833

Amy Foster   859

Typhoon   883

Falk   947

Heart of Darkness   1003

The End of the Tether   1071

An Anarchist   1171

The Informer   1189

Il Conde   1209

The Secret Sharer   1223

Prince Roman   1257

The Shadow-Line   1275

The Tale   1357

THE LAGOON

The white man, leaning with both arms over the roof of the little house in the stern of the boat, said to the steersman – 'We will pass the night in Arsat's clearing. It is late.'

The Malay only grunted, and went on looking fixedly at the river. The white man rested his chin on his crossed arms and gazed at the wake of the boat. At the end of the straight avenue of forests cut by the intense glitter of the river, the sun appeared unclouded and dazzling, poised low over the water that shone smoothly like a band of metal. The forests, sombre and dull, stood motionless and silent on each side of the broad stream. At the foot of big, towering trees, trunkless nipa palms rose from the mud of the bank, in bunches of leaves enormous and heavy, that hung unstirring over the brown swirl of eddies. In the stillness of the air every tree, every leaf, every bough, every tendril of creeper and every petal of minute blossoms seemed to have been bewitched into an immobility perfect and final. Nothing moved on the river but the eight paddles that rose flashing regularly, dipped together with a single splash; while the steersman swept right and left with a periodic and sudden flourish of his blade describing a glinting semicircle above his head. The churned-up water frothed alongside with a confused murmur. And the white man's canoe, advancing upstream in the short-lived disturbance of its own making, seemed to enter the portals of a land from which the very memory of motion had for ever departed.

The white man, turning his back upon the setting sun, looked along the empty and broad expanse of the sea-reach. For the last three miles of its course the wandering, hesitating river, as if enticed irresistibly by the freedom of an open horizon, flows straight into the sea, flows straight to the east – to the east that harbours both light and darkness. Astern of the boat the repeated call of some bird, a cry discordant and feeble, skipped along over the smooth water and lost itself, before it could reach the other shore, in the breathless silence of the world.

The steersman dug his paddle into the stream, and held hard with stiffened arms, his body thrown forward. The water gurgled aloud; and suddenly the long straight reach seemed to pivot on its centre, the forests swung in a semicircle, and the slanting beams of sunset touched the broadside of the canoe with a fiery glow, throwing the slender and distorted shadows of its crew upon the streaked glitter of the river. The white man turned to look ahead. The course of the boat had been altered at right-angles to the stream, and the carved dragon-head of its prow was pointing now at a gap in the fringing bushes of the bank. It glided through, brushing the overhanging twigs, and disappeared from the river like some slim and amphibious creature leaving the water for its lair in the forests.

The narrow creek was like a ditch: tortuous, fabulously deep; filled with gloom under the thin strip of pure and shining blue of the heaven. Immense trees soared up, invisible behind the festooned draperies of creepers. Here and there, near the glistening blackness of the water, a twisted root of some tall tree showed amongst the tracery of small ferns, black and dull, writhing and motionless, like an arrested snake. The short words of the paddlers reverberated loudly between the thick and sombre walls of vegetation. Darkness oozed out from between the trees, through the tangled maze of the creepers, from behind the great fantastic and unstirring leaves; the darkness, mysterious and invincible; the darkness scented and poisonous of impenetrable forests.

The men poled in the shoaling water. The creek broadened, opening out into a wide sweep of a stagnant lagoon. The forests receded from the marshy bank, leaving a level strip of bright green, reedy grass to frame the reflected blueness of the sky. A fleecy pink cloud drifted high above, trailing the delicate colouring of its image under the floating leaves and the silvery blossoms of the lotus. A little house, perched on high piles, appeared black in the distance. Near it, two tall nibong palms, that seemed to have come out of the forests in the background, leaned slightly over the ragged roof, with a suggestion of sad tenderness and care in the droop of their leafy and soaring heads.

The steersman, pointing with his paddle, said, 'Arsat is there. I see his canoe fast between the piles.'

The polers ran along the sides of the boat glancing over their shoulders at the end of the day's journey. They would have preferred to spend the night somewhere else than on this lagoon of weird aspect and ghostly reputation. Moreover, they disliked Arsat, first as a stranger, and also because he who repairs a ruined house, and dwells in it, proclaims that he is not afraid to live amongst the spirits that haunt the places abandoned by mankind. Such a man can disturb the course of fate by glances or words; while his familiar ghosts are not easy to propitiate by casual wayfarers upon whom they long to wreak the malice of their human master. White men care not for such things, being unbelievers and in league with the Father of Evil, who leads them unharmed through the invisible dangers of this world. To the warnings of the righteous they oppose an offensive pretence of disbelief. What is there to be done?

So they thought, throwing their weight on the end of their long poles. The big canoe glided on swiftly, noiselessly, and smoothly, towards Arsat's clearing, till, in a great rattling of poles thrown down, and the loud murmurs of 'Allah be praised!' it came with a gentle knock against the crooked piles below the house.

The boatmen with uplifted faces shouted discordantly, 'Arsat! O Arsat!' Nobody came. The white man began to climb the rude ladder giving access to the bamboo platform before the house. The juragan of the boat said sulkily, 'We will cook in the sampan, and sleep on the water.'

'Pass my blankets and the basket,' said the white man curtly.

He knelt on the edge of the platform to receive the bundle. Then the boat shoved off, and the white man, standing up, confronted Arsat, who had come out through the low door of his hut. He was a man young, powerful, with a broad chest and muscular arms. He had nothing on but his sarong. His head was bare. His big, soft eyes stared eagerly at the white man, but his voice and demeanour were composed as he asked, without any words of greeting – 'Have you medicine, Tuan?'

'No,' said the visitor in a startled tone. 'No. Why? Is there sickness in the house?'

'Enter and see,' replied Arsat, in the same calm manner, and turning short round, passed again through the small doorway. The white man, dropping his bundles, followed.

In the dim light of the dwelling he made out on a couch of bamboos a woman stretched on her back under a broad sheet of red cotton cloth. She lay still, as if dead; but her big eyes, wide open, glittered in the gloom, staring upwards at the slender rafters, motionless and unseeing. She was in a high fever, and evidently unconscious. Her cheeks were sunk slightly, her lips were partly open, and on the young face there was the ominous and fixed expression – the absorbed, contemplating expression of the unconscious who are going to die. The two men stood looking down at her in silence.

'Has she been long ill?' asked the traveller.

'I have not slept for five nights,' answered the Malay, in a deliberate tone. 'At first she heard voices calling her from the water and struggled against me who held her. But since the sun of today rose she hears nothing – she hears not me. She sees nothing. She sees not me – me!'

He remained silent for a minute, then asked softly – 'Tuan, will she die?'

'I fear so,' said the white man sorrowfully. He had known Arsat years ago, in a far country in times of trouble and danger, when no friendship is to be despised. And since his Malay friend had come unexpectedly to dwell in the hut on the lagoon with a strange woman, he had slept many times there, in his journeys up and down the river. He liked the man who knew how to keep faith in council and how to fight without fear by the side of his white friend. He liked him – not so much perhaps as a man likes his favourite dog – but still he liked him well enough to help and ask no questions, to think sometimes vaguely and hazily in the midst of his own pursuits, about the lonely man and the long-haired woman with audacious face and triumphant eyes, who lived together hidden by the forests – alone and feared.

The white man came out of the hut in time to see the enormous conflagration of sunset put out by the swift and stealthy shadows that, rising like a black and impalpable vapour above the tree-tops, spread over the heaven, extinguishing the crimson glow of floating clouds and the red brilliance of departing daylight. In a few moments all the stars came out above the intense blackness of the earth, and the great lagoon gleaming suddenly with reflected lights resembled an oval patch of night sky flung down into the hopeless and abysmal night of the wilderness. The white man had some supper out of the basket, then collecting a few sticks that lay about the platform, made up a small fire, not for warmth, but for the sake of the smoke, which would keep off the mosquitos. He wrapped himself in his blankets and sat with his back against the reed wall of the house, smoking thoughtfully.

Arsat came through the doorway with noiseless steps and squatted down by the fire. The white man moved his outstretched legs a little.

'She breathes,' said Arsat in a low voice, anticipating the expected question. 'She breathes and burns as if with a great fire. She speaks not; she hears not – and burns!'

He paused for a moment, then asked in a quiet, incurious tone – 'Tuan . . . will she die?'

The white man moved his shoulders uneasily, and muttered in a hesitating manner – 'If such is her fate.'

'No, Tuan,' said Arsat calmly. 'If such is my fate. I hear, I see, I wait. I remember . . . Tuan, do you remember the old days? Do you remember my brother?'

'Yes,' said the white man. The Malay rose suddenly and went in. The other, sitting still outside, could hear the voice in the hut. Arsat said: 'Hear me! Speak!' His words were succeeded by a complete silence. 'O Diamelen!' he cried suddenly. After that cry there was a deep sigh. Arsat came out and sank down again in his old place.

They sat in silence before the fire. There was no sound within the house, there was no sound near them; but far away on the lagoon they could hear the voices of the boatmen ringing fitful and distinct on the calm water. The fire in the bows of the sampan shone faintly in the distance with a hazy red glow. Then it died out. The voices ceased. The land and the water slept invisible, unstirring and mute. It was as though there had been nothing left in the world but the glitter of stars streaming, ceaseless and vain, through the black stillness of the night.

The white man gazed straight before him into the darkness with wide-open eyes. The fear and fascination, the inspiration and the wonder of death – of death near, unavoidable, and unseen, soothed the unrest of his race and stirred the most indistinct, the most intimate of his thoughts. The ever-ready suspicion of evil, the gnawing suspicion that lurks in our hearts, flowed out into the stillness round him – into the stillness profound and dumb, and made it appear untrustworthy and infamous like the placid and impenetrable mask of an unjustifiable violence. In that fleeting and powerful disturbance of his being the earth enfolded in the starlight peace became a shadowy country of inhuman strife, a battlefield of phantoms terrible and charming, august or ignoble, struggling ardently for the possession of our helpless hearts. An unquiet and mysterious country of inextinguishable desires and fears.

A plaintive murmur rose in the night; a murmur saddening and startling, as if the great solitudes of surrounding woods had tried to whisper into his ear the wisdom of their immense and lofty indifference. Sounds hesitating and vague floated in the air round him, shaped themselves slowly into words; and at last flowed on gently in a murmuring stream of soft and monotonous sentences. He stirred like a man waking up and changed his position slightly. Arsat, motionless and shadowy, sitting with bowed head under the stars, was speaking in a low and dreamy tone – ' . . . for where can we lay down the heaviness of our trouble but in a friend's heart? A man must speak of war and of love. You, Tuan, know what war is, and you have seen me in time of danger seek death as other men seek life! A writing may be lost; a lie may be written; but what the eye has seen is truth and remains in the mind!'

'I remember,' said the white man quietly. Arsat went on with mournful composure – 'Therefore I shall speak to you of love. Speak in the night. Speak before both night and love are gone – and the eye of day looks upon my sorrow and my shame; upon my blackened face; upon my burnt-up heart.'

A sigh, short and faint, marked an almost imperceptible pause, and then his words flowed on, without a stir, without a gesture.

'After the time of trouble and war was over and you went away from my country in the pursuit of your desires, which we, men of the islands, cannot understand, I and my brother became again, as we had been before, the sword-bearers of the Ruler. You know we were men of family, belonging to a ruling race, and more fit than any to carry on our right shoulder the emblem of power. And in the time of prosperity Si Dendring showed us favour, as we, in time of sorrow, had showed to him the faithfulness of our courage. It was a time of peace. A time of deer-hunts and cock-fights; of idle talks and foolish squabbles between men whose bellies are full and weapons are rusty. But the sower watched the young rice-shoots grow up without fear, and the traders came and went, departed lean and returned fat into the river of peace. They brought news too. Brought lies and truth mixed together, so that no man knew when to rejoice and when to be sorry. We heard from them about you also. They had seen you here and had seen you there. And I was glad to hear, for I remembered the stirring times, and I always remembered you, Tuan, till the time came when my eyes could see nothing in the past, because they had looked upon the one who is dying there – in the house.'

He stopped to exclaim in an intense whisper, 'O Mara bahia! O Calamity!' then went on speaking a little louder.

'There's no worse enemy and no better friend than a brother, Tuan, for one brother knows another, and in perfect knowledge is strength for good or evil. I loved my brother. I went to him and told him that I could see nothing but one face, hear nothing but one voice. He told me: "Open your heart so that she can see what is in it – and wait. Patience is wisdom. Inchi Midah may die or our Ruler may throw off his fear of a woman!" . . . I waited! . . . You remember the lady with the veiled face, Tuan, and the fear of our Ruler before her cunning and temper. And if she wanted her servant, what could I do? But I fed the hunger of my heart on short glances and stealthy words. I loitered on the path to the bath-houses in the daytime, and when the sun had fallen behind the forest I crept along the jasmine hedges of the women's courtyard. Unseeing, we spoke to one another through the scent of flowers, through the veil of leaves, through the blades of long grass that stood still before our lips; so great was our prudence, so faint was the murmur of our great longing. The time passed swiftly. . . and there were whispers amongst women – and our enemies watched – my brother was gloomy, and I began to think of killing and of a fierce death . . . We are of a people who take what they want – like you whites. There is a time when a man should forget loyalty and respect. Might and authority are given to rulers, but to all men is given love and strength and courage. My brother said, "You shall take her from their midst. We are two who are like one." And I answered, "Let it be soon, for I find no warmth in sunlight that does not shine upon her." Our time came when the Ruler and all the great people went to the mouth of the river to fish by torchlight. There were hundreds of boats, and on the white sand, between the water and the forests, dwellings of leaves were built for the households of the Rajahs. The smoke of cooking-fires was like a blue mist of the evening, and many voices rang in it joyfully. While they were making the boats ready to beat up the fish, my brother came to me and said, "Tonight!" I looked to my weapons, and when the time came our canoe took its place in the circle of boats carrying the torches. The lights blazed on the water, but behind the boats there was darkness. When the shouting began and the excitement made them like mad we dropped out. The water swallowed our fire, and we floated back to the shore that was dark with only here and there the glimmer of embers. We could hear the talk of slave-girls amongst the sheds. Then we found a place deserted and silent. We waited there. She came. She came running along the shore, rapid and leaving no trace, like a leaf driven by the wind into the sea. My brother said gloomily, "Go and take her; carry her into our boat." I lifted her in my arms. She panted. Her heart was beating against my breast. I said, "I take you from those people. You came to the cry of my heart, but my arms take you into my boat against the will of the great!" "It is right," said my brother. "We are men who take what we want and can hold it against many. We should have taken her in daylight." I said, "Let us be off;" for since she was in my boat I began to think of our ruler's many men. "Yes. Let us be off," said my brother. "We are cast out and this boat is our country now – and the sea is our refuge." He lingered with his foot on the shore, and I entreated him to hasten, for I remembered the strokes of her heart against my breast and thought that two men cannot withstand a hundred. We left, paddling downstream close to the bank; and as we passed by the creek where they were fishing, the great shouting had ceased, but the murmur of voices was loud like the humming of insects flying at noonday. The boats floated, clustered together, in the red light of torches, under a black roof of smoke; and men talked of their sport. Men that boasted, and praised, and jeered – men that would have been our friends in the morning, but on that night were already our enemies. We paddled swiftly past. We had no more friends in the country of our birth. She sat in the middle of the canoe with covered face; silent as she is now; unseeing as she is now – and I had no regret at what I was leaving because I could hear her breathing close to me – as I can hear her now.'

He paused, listened with his ear turned to the doorway, then shook his head and went on.

'My brother wanted to shout the cry of challenge – one cry only – to let the people know we were freeborn robbers who trusted our arms and the great sea. And again I begged him in the name of our love to be silent. Could I not hear her breathing close to me? I knew the pursuit would come quick enough. My brother loved me. He dipped his paddle without a splash. He only said, "There is half a man in you now – the other half is in that woman. I can wait. When you are a whole man again, you will come back with me here to shout defiance. We are sons of the same mother." I made no answer. All my strength and all my spirit were in my hands that held the paddle – for I longed to be with her in a safe place beyond the reach of men's anger and of women's spite. My love was so great, that I thought it could guide me to a country where death was unknown, if I could only escape from Inchi Midah's fury and from our Ruler's sword. We paddled with haste, breathing through our teeth. The blades bit deep into the smooth water. We passed out of the river; we flew in clear channels amongst the shallows. We skirted the black coast; we skirted the sand beaches where the sea speaks in whispers to the land; and the gleam of white sand flashed back past our boat, so swiftly she ran upon the water. We spoke not. Only once I said, "Sleep, Diamelen, for soon you may want all your strength." I heard the sweetness of her voice, but I never turned my head. The sun rose and still we went on. Water fell from my face like rain from a cloud. We flew in the light and heat. I never looked back; but I knew that my brother's eyes, behind me, were looking steadily ahead, for the boat went as straight as a bushman's dart, when it leaves the end of the sumpitan. There was no better paddler, no better steersman than my brother. Many times, together, we had won races in that canoe. But we never had put out our strength as we did then – then, when for the last time we paddled together! There was no braver or stronger man in our country than my brother. I could not spare the strength to turn my head and look at him, but every moment I heard the hiss of his breath getting louder behind me. Still he did not speak. The sun was high. The heat clung to my back like a flame of fire. My ribs were ready to burst, but I could no longer get enough air into my chest. And then I felt I must cry out with my last breath, "Let us rest!" . . . "Good!" he answered; and his voice was firm. He was strong. He was brave. He knew not fear and no fatigue . . . My brother!'

A murmur powerful and gentle, a murmur vast and faint; the murmur of trembling leaves, of stirring boughs, ran through the tangled depths of the forests, ran over the starry smoothness of the lagoon, and the water between the piles lapped the slimy timber once with a sudden splash. A breath of warm air touched the two men's faces and passed on with a mournful sound – a breath loud and short like an uneasy sigh of the dreaming earth.

Arsat went on in an even, low voice.

'We ran our canoe on the white beach of a little bay close to a long tongue of land that seemed to bar our road; a long wooded cape going far into the sea. My brother knew that place. Beyond the cape a river has its entrance, and . through the jungle of that land there is a narrow path. We made a fire and cooked rice. Then we lay down to sleep on the soft sand in the shade of our canoe, while she watched. No sooner had I closed my eyes than I heard her cry of alarm. We leaped up. The sun was halfway down the sky already, and coming in sight in the opening of the bay we saw a prau manned by many paddlers. We knew it at once; it was one of our Rajah's praus. They were watching the shore, and saw us. They beat the gong, and turned the head of the prau into the bay. I felt my heart become weak within my breast. Diamelen sat on the sand and covered her face. There was no escape by sea. My brother laughed. He had the gun you had given him, Tuan, before you went away, but there was only a handful of powder. He spoke to me quickly: "Run with her along the path. I shall keep them back, for they have no firearms, and landing in the face of a man with a gun is certain death for some. Run with her. On the other side of that wood there is a fisherman's house – and a canoe. When I have fired all the shots I will follow. I am a great runner, and before they can come up we shall be gone. I will hold out as long as I can, for she is but a woman – that can neither run nor fight, but she has your heart in her weak hands." He dropped behind the canoe. The prau was coming. She and I ran, and as we rushed along the path I heard shots. My brother fired – once – twice – and the booming of the gong ceased. There was silence behind us. That neck of land is narrow. Before I heard my brother fire the third shot I saw the shelving shore, and I saw the water again: the mouth of a broad river. We crossed a grassy glade. We ran down to the water. I saw a low hut above the black mud, and a small canoe hauled up. I heard another shot behind me. I thought, "That is his last charge." We rushed down to the canoe; a man came running from the hut, but I leaped on him, and we rolled together in the mud. Then I got up, and he lay still at my feet. I don't know whether I had killed him or not. I and Diamelen pushed the canoe afloat. I heard yells behind me, and I saw my brother run across the glade. Many men were bounding after him, I took her in my arms and threw her into the boat, then leaped in myself. When I looked back I saw that my brother had fallen. He fell and was up again, but the men were closing round him. He shouted, "I am coming!" The men were close to him. I looked. Many men. Then I looked at her. Tuan, I pushed the canoe! I pushed it into deep water. She was kneeling forward looking at me, and I said, "Take your paddle," while I struck the water with mine. Tuan, I heard him cry. I heard him cry my name twice; and I heard voices shouting, "Kill! Strike!" I never turned back. I heard him calling my name again with a great shriek, as when life is going out together with the voice – and I never turned my head. My own name! . . . My brother! Three times he called – but I was not afraid of life. Was she not there in that canoe? And could I not with her find a country where death is forgotten – where death is unknown!'

The white man sat up. Arsat rose and stood, an indistinct and silent figure above the dying embers of the fire. Over the lagoon a mist drifting and low had crept, erasing slowly the glittering images of the stars. And now a great expanse of white vapour covered the land: it flowed cold and grey in the darkness, eddied in noiseless whirls round the tree-trunks and about the platform of the house, which seemed to float upon a restless and impalpable illusion of a sea. Only far away the tops of the trees stood outlined on the twinkle of heaven, like a sombre and forbidding shore – a coast deceptive, pitiless and black.

Arsat's voice vibrated loudly in the profound peace.

'I had her there! I had her! To get her I would have faced all mankind. But I had her – and –'

His words went out ringing into the empty distances. He paused, and seemed to listen to them dying away very far – beyond help and beyond recall. Then he said quietly – 'Tuan, I loved my brother.'

A breath of wind made him shiver. High above his head, high above the silent sea of mist the drooping leaves of the palms rattled together with a mournful and expiring sound. The white man stretched his legs. His chin rested on his chest, and he murmured sadly without lifting his head – 'We all love our brothers.'

Arsat burst out with an intense whispering violence – 'What did I care who died? I wanted peace in my own heart.'

He seemed to hear a stir in the house – listened – then stepped in noiselessly. The white man stood up. A breeze was coming in fitful puffs. The stars shone paler as if they had retreated into the frozen depths of immense space. After a chill gust of wind there were a few seconds of perfect calm and absolute silence. Then from behind the black and wavy line of the forests a column of golden light shot up into the heavens and spread over the semicircle of the eastern horizon. The sun had risen. The mist lifted, broke into drifting patches, vanished into thin flying wreaths; and the unveiled lagoon lay, polished and black, in the heavy shadows at the foot of the wall of trees. A white eagle rose over it with a slanting and ponderous flight, reached the clear sunshine and appeared dazzlingly brilliant for a moment, then soaring higher, became a dark and motionless speck before it vanished into the blue as if it had left the earth for ever. The white man, standing gazing upwards before the doorway, heard in the hut a confused and broken murmur of distracted words ending with a loud groan. Suddenly Arsat stumbled out with outstretched hands, shivered, and stood still for some time with fixed eyes. Then he said – 'She burns no more.'

Before his face the sun showed its edge above the tree-tops, rising steadily. The breeze freshened; a great brilliance burst upon the lagoon, sparkled on the rippling water. The forests came out of the clear shadows of the morning, became distinct, as if they had rushed nearer – to stop short in a great stir of leaves, of nodding boughs, of swaying branches. In the merciless sunshine the whisper of unconscious life grew louder, speaking in an incomprehensible voice round the dumb darkness of that human sorrow. Arsat's eyes wandered slowly, then stared at the rising sun.

'I can see nothing,' he said half aloud to himself.

'There is nothing,' said the white man, moving to the edge of the platform and waving his hand to his boat. A shout came faintly over the lagoon and the sampan began to glide towards the abode of the friend of ghosts.

'If you want to come with me, I will wait all the morning,' said the white man, looking away upon the water.

'No, Tuan,' said Arsat softly. 'I shall not eat or sleep in this house, but I must first see my road. Now I can see nothing – see nothing! There is no light and no peace in the world; but there is death – death for many. We were sons of the same mother – and I left him in the midst of enemies; but I am going back now.'

He drew a long breath and went on in a dreamy tone.

'In a little while I shall see clear enough to strike – to strike. But she has died, and . . . now . . . darkness.'

He flung his arms wide open, let them fall along his body, then stood still with unmoved face and stony eyes, staring at the sun. The white man got down into his canoe. The polers ran smartly along the sides of the boat, looking over their shoulders at the beginning of a weary journey. High in the stern, his head muffled up in white rags, the juragan sat moody, letting his paddle trail in the water. The white man, leaning with both arms over the grass roof of the little cabin, looked back at the shining ripple of the boat's wake. Before the sampan passed out of the lagoon into the creek he lifted his eyes. Arsat had not moved. He stood lonely in the searching sunshine; and he looked beyond the great light of a cloudless day into the darkness of a world of illusions.

1896

AN OUTPOST OF PROGRESS

There were two white men in charge of the trading station. Kayerts, the chief, was short and fat; Carlier, the assistant, was tall, with a large head and a very broad trunk perched upon a long pair of thin legs. The third man on the staff was a Sierra Leone nigger, who maintained that his name was Henry Price. However, for some reason or other, the natives down the river had given him the name of Makola, and it stuck to him through all his wanderings about the country. He spoke English and French with a warbling accent, wrote a beautiful hand, understood bookkeeping, and cherished in his innermost heart the worship of evil spirits. His wife was a Negress from Loanda, very large and very noisy. Three children rolled about in sunshine before the door of his low, shed-like dwelling. Makola, taciturn and impenetrable, despised the two white men. He had charge of a small clay storehouse with a dried-grass roof, and pretended to keep a correct account of beads, cotton cloth, red kerchiefs, brass wire, and other trade goods it contained. Besides the storehouse and Makola's hut, there was only one large building in the cleared ground of the station. It was built neatly of reeds, with a verandah on all the four sides. There were three rooms in it. The one in the middle was the living-room, and had two rough tables and a few stools in it. The other two were the bedrooms for the white men. Each had a bedstead and a mosquito net for all furniture. The plank floor was littered with the belongings of the white men: open half-empty boxes, torn wearing apparel, old boots; all the things dirty, and all the things broken, that accumulate mysteriously round untidy men. There was also another dwelling-place some distance away from the buildings. In it, under a tall cross much out of the perpendicular, slept the man who had seen the beginning of all this; who had planned and had watched the construction of this outpost of progress. He had been, at home, an unsuccessful painter who, weary of pursuing fame on an empty stomach, had gone out there through high protections. He had been the first chief of that station. Makola had watched the energetic artist die of fever in the just finished house with his usual kind of 'I told you so' indifference. Then, for a time, he dwelt alone with his family, his account books, and the Evil Spirit that rules the lands under the equator. He got on very well with his god. Perhaps he had propitiated him by a promise of more white men to play with, by and by. At any rate the director of the Great Trading Company, coming up in a steamer that resembled an enormous sardine box with a flat-roofed shed erected on it, found the station in good order, and Makola as usual quietly diligent. The director had the cross put up over the first agent's grave, and appointed Kayerts to the post. Carlier was told off as second in charge. The director was a man ruthless and efficient, who at times, but very imperceptibly, indulged in grim humour. He made a speech to Kayerts and Carlier, pointing out to them the promising aspect of their station. The nearest trading-post was about three hundred miles away. It was an exceptional opportunity for them to distinguish themselves and to earn percentages on the trade. This appointment was a favour done to beginners. Kayerts was moved almost to tears by his director's kindness. He would, he said, by doing his best, try to justify the flattering confidence, etc., etc. Kayerts had been in the Administration of the Telegraphs, and knew how to express himself correctly. Carlier, an ex-non-commissioned officer of cavalry in an army guaranteed from harm by several European Powers, was less impressed. If there were commissions to get, so much the better; and, trailing a sulky glance over the river, the forests, the impenetrable bush that seemed to cut off the station from the rest of the world, he muttered between his teeth, 'We shall see, very soon.'

Next day, some bales of cotton goods and a few cases of provisions having been thrown on shore, the sardine-box steamer went off, not to return for another six months. On the deck the director touched his cap to the two agents, who stood on the bank waving their hats, and turning to an old servant of the company on his passage to headquarters, said, 'Look at those two imbeciles. They must be mad at home to send me such specimens. I told those fellows to plant a vegetable garden, build new storehouses and fences, and construct a landing-stage. I bet nothing will be done! They won't know how to begin. I always thought the station on this river useless, and they just fit the station!'

'They will form themselves there,' said the old stager with a quiet smile.

'At any rate, I am rid of them for six months,' retorted the director.

The two men watched the steamer round the bend, then, ascending arm in arm the slope of the bank, returned to the station. They had been in this vast and dark country only a very short time, and as yet always in the midst of other white men, under the eye and guidance of their superiors. And now, dull as they were to the subtle influences of surroundings, they felt themselves very much alone when suddenly left unassisted to face the wilderness: a wilderness rendered more strange, more incomprehensible by the mysterious glimpses of the vigorous life it contained. They were two perfectly insignificant and incapable individuals, whose existence is only rendered possible through the high organisation of civilised crowds. Few men realise that their life, the very essence of their character, their capabilities and their audacities, are only the expression of their belief in the safety of their surroundings. The courage, the composure, the confidence; the emotions and principles; every great and every insignificant thought belongs not to the individual but to the crowd: to the crowd that believes blindly in the irresistible force of its institutions and of its morals, in the power of its police and of its opinion. But the contact with pure unmitigated savagery, with primitive nature and primitive man, brings sudden and profound trouble into the heart. To the sentiment of being alone of one's kind, to the clear perception of the loneliness of one's thoughts, of one's sensations – to the negation of the habitual, which is safe, there is added the affirmation of the unusual, which is dangerous; a suggestion of things vague, uncontrollable, and repulsive, whose discomposing intrusion excites the imagination and tries the civilised nerves of the foolish and the wise alike.

Kayerts and Carlier walked arm in arm drawing close to one another as children do in the dark; and they had the same, not altogether unpleasant, sense of danger which one half suspects to be imaginary. They chatted persistently in familiar tones. 'Our station is prettily situated,' said one. The other assented with enthusiasm, enlarging volubly on the beauties of the situation. Then they passed near the grave. 'Poor devil!' said Kayerts. 'He died of fever, didn't he?' muttered Carlier, stopping short. 'Why,' retorted Kayerts, with indignation, 'I've been told that the fellow exposed himself recklessly to the sun. The climate here, everybody says, is not at all worse than at home, as long as you keep out of the sun. Do you hear that, Carlier? I am chief here, and my orders are that you should not expose yourself to the sun!' He assumed his superiority jocularly, but his meaning was serious. The idea that he would, perhaps, have to bury Carlier and remain alone, gave him an inward shiver. He felt suddenly that this Carlier was more precious to him here, in the centre of Africa, than a brother could be anywhere else. Carlier, entering into the spirit of the thing, made a military salute and answered in a brisk tone, 'Your orders shall be attended to, chief!' Then he burst out laughing, slapped Kayerts on the back, and shouted, 'We shall let life run easily here! Just sit still and gather in the ivory those savages will bring. This country has its good points, after all!' They both laughed loudly while Carlier thought: That poor Kayerts; he is so fat and unhealthy. It would be awful if I had to bury him here. He is a man I respect . . . Before they reached the verandah of their house they called one another 'my dear fellow'.

The first day they were very active, pottering about with hammers and nails and red calico, to put up curtains, make their house habitable and pretty; resolved to settle down comfortably to their new life. For them an impossible task. To grapple effectually with even purely material problems requires more serenity of mind and more lofty courage than people generally imagine. No two beings could have been more unfitted for such a struggle. Society, not from any tenderness, but because of its strange needs, had taken care of those two men, forbidding them all independent thought, all initiative, all departure from routine; and forbidding it under pain of death. They could only live on condition of being machines. And now, released from the fostering care of men with pens behind the ears, or of men with gold lace on the sleeves, they were like those lifelong prisoners who, liberated after many years, do not know what use to make of their freedom. They did not know what use to make of their faculties, being both, through want of practice, incapable of independent thought.

At the end of two months Kayerts often would say, 'If it was not for my Melie, you wouldn't catch me here.' Melie was his daughter. He had thrown up his post in the Administration of the Telegraphs, though he had been for seventeen years perfectly happy there, to earn a dowry for his girl. His wife was dead, and the child was being brought up by his sisters. He regretted the streets, the pavements, the cafés, his friends of many years; all the things he used to see, day after day; all the thoughts suggested by familiar things – the thoughts effortless, monotonous, and soothing of a government clerk; he regretted all the gossip, the small enmities, the mild venom, and the little jokes of government offices. 'If I had had a decent brother-in-law,' Carlier would remark, 'a fellow with a heart, I would not be here.' He had left the army and had made himself so obnoxious to his family by his laziness and impudence, that an exasperated brother-in-law had made superhuman efforts to procure him an appointment in the Company as a second-class agent. Having not a penny in the world, he was compelled to accept this means of livelihood as soon as it became quite clear to him that there was nothing more to squeeze out of his relations. He, like Kayerts, regretted his old life. He regretted the clink of sabre and spurs on a fine afternoon, the barrack-room witticisms, the girls of garrison towns; but, besides, he had also a sense of grievance. He was evidently a much ill-used man. This made him moody, at times. But the two men got on well together in the fellowship of their stupidity and laziness. Together they did nothing, absolutely nothing, and enjoyed the sense of the idleness for which they were paid. And in time they came to feel something resembling affection for one another.

They lived like blind men in a large room, aware only of what came in contact with them (and of that only imperfectly), but unable to see the general aspect of things. The river, the forest, all the great land throbbing with life, were like a great emptiness. Even the brilliant sunshine disclosed nothing intelligible. Things appeared and disappeared before their eyes in an un-connected and aimless kind of way. The river seemed to come from nowhere and flow nowhither. It flowed through a void. Out of that void, at times, came canoes, and men with spears in their hands would suddenly crowd the yard of the station. They were naked, glossy black, ornamented with snowy shells and glistening brass wire, perfect of limb. They made an uncouth babbling noise when they spoke, moved in a stately manner, and sent quick, wild glances out of their startled, never-resting eyes. Those warriors would squat in long rows, four or more deep, before the verandah, while their chiefs bargained for hours with Makola over an elephant tusk. Kayerts sat on his chair and looked down on the proceedings, understanding nothing. He stared at them with his round blue eyes, called out to Carlier, 'Here, look! look at that fellow there – and that other one, to the left. Did you ever see such a face? Oh, the funny brute!'

Carlier, smoking native tobacco in a short wooden pipe, would swagger up twirling his moustaches, and, surveying the warriors with haughty indulgence, would say – 'Fine animals. Brought any bone? Yes? It's not any too soon. Look at the muscles of that fellow – third from the end. I wouldn't care to get a punch on the nose from him. Fine arms, but legs no good below the knee. Couldn't make cavalry men of them.' And after glancing down complacently at his own shanks, he always concluded: 'Pah! Don't they stink! You, Makola! Take that herd over to the fetish' (the storehouse was in every station called the fetish, perhaps because of the spirit of civilisation it contained) 'and give them up some of the rubbish you keep there. I'd rather see it full of bone than full of rags.'

Kayerts approved.

'Yes, yes! Go and finish that palaver over there, Mr Makola. I will come round when you are ready, to weigh the tusk. We must be careful.' Then, turning to his companion: 'This is the tribe that lives down the river; they are rather aromatic. I remember, they have been once before here. D'ye hear that row? What a fellow has got to put up with in this dog of a country! My head is split.'

Such profitable visits were rare. For days the two pioneers of trade and progress would look on their empty courtyard in the vibrating brilliance of vertical sunshine. Below the high bank, the silent river flowed on, glittering and steady. On the sands in the middle of the stream, hippos and alligators sunned themselves side by side. And stretching away in all directions, surrounding the insignificant cleared spot of the trading post, immense forests, hiding fateful complications of fantastic life, lay in the eloquent silence of mute greatness. The two men understood nothing, cared for nothing but for the passage of days that separated them from the steamer's return. Their predecessor had left some torn books. They took up these wrecks of novels, and, as they had never read anything of the kind before, they were surprised and amused. Then during long days there were interminable and silly discussions about plots and personages. In the centre of Africa they made the acquaintance of Richelieu and of d'Artagnan, of Hawk's Eye and of Father Goriot, and of many other people. All these imaginary personages became subjects for gossip as if they had been living friends. They discounted their virtues, suspected their motives, decried their successes; were scandalised at their duplicity or were doubtful about their courage. The accounts of crimes filled them with indignation, while tender or pathetic passages moved them deeply. Carlier cleared his throat and said in a soldierly voice, 'What nonsense!' Kayerts, his round eyes suffused with tears, his fat cheeks quivering, rubbed his bald head, and declared, 'This is a splendid book. I had no idea there were such clever fellows in the world.' They also found some old copies of a home paper. That print discussed what it was pleased to call 'Our Colonial Expansion' in high-flown language. It spoke much of the rights and duties of civilisation, of the sacredness of the civilising work, and extolled the merits of those who went about bringing light, and faith, and commerce to the dark places of the earth. Carlier and Kayerts read, wondered, and began to think better of themselves. Carlier said one evening, waving his hand about, 'In a hundred years, there will be perhaps a town here. Quays, and warehouses, and barracks, and – and – billiard-rooms. Civilisation, my boy, and virtue – and all. And then, chaps will read that two good fellows, Kayerts and Carlier, were the first civilised men to live in this very spot!' Kayerts nodded, 'Yes, it is a consolation to think of that.' They seemed to forget their dead predecessor; but, early one day, Carlier went out and replanted the cross firmly. 'It used to make me squint whenever I walked that way,' he explained to Kayerts over the morning coffee. 'It made me squint, leaning over so much. So I just planted it upright. And solid, I promise you! I suspended myself with both hands to the cross-piece. Not a move. Oh, I did that properly.'

At times Gobila came to see them. Gobila was the chief of the neighbouring villages. He was a grey-headed savage, thin and black, with a white cloth round his loins and a mangy panther skin hanging over his back. He came up with long strides of his skeleton legs, swinging a staff as tall as himself, and, entering the common room of the station, would squat on his heels to the left of the door. There he sat, watching Kayerts, and now and then making a speech which the other did not understand. Kayerts, without interrupting his occupation, would from time to time say in a friendly manner: 'How goes it, you old image?' and they would smile at one another. The two whites had a liking for that old and incomprehensible creature, and called him Father Gobila. Gobila's manner was paternal, and he seemed really to love all white men. They all appeared to him very young, indistinguishably alike (except for stature), and he knew that they were all brothers, and also immortal. The death of the artist, who was the first white man whom he knew intimately, did not disturb this belief, because he was firmly convinced that the white stranger had pretended to die and got himself buried for some mysterious purpose of his own, into which it was useless to enquire. Perhaps it was his way of going home to his own country? At any rate, these were his brothers, and he transferred his absurd affection to them. They returned it in a way. Carlier slapped him on the back, and recklessly struck off matches for his amusement. Kayerts was always ready to let him have a sniff at the ammonia bottle. In short, they behaved just like that other white creature that had hidden itself in a hole in the ground. Gobila considered them attentively. Perhaps they were the same being with the other – or one of them was. He couldn't decide – clear up that mystery; but he remained always very friendly. In consequence of that friendship the women of Gobila's village walked in single file through the reedy grass, bringing every morning to the station, fowls, and sweet potatoes, and palm wine, and sometimes a goat. The Company never provisioned the stations fully, and the agents required those local supplies to live. They had them through the goodwill of Gobila, and lived well. Now and then one of them had a bout of fever, and the other nursed him with gentle devotion. They did not think much of it. It left them weaker, and their appearance changed for the worse. Carlier was hollow-eyed and irritable. Kayerts showed a drawn, flabby face above the rotundity of his stomach, which gave him a weird aspect. But being constantly together, they did not notice the change that took place gradually in their appearance, and also in their dispositions.

Five months passed in that way.

Then, one morning, as Kayerts and Carlier, lounging in their chairs under the verandah, talked about the approaching visit of the steamer, a knot of armed men came out of the forest and advanced towards the station. They were strangers to that part of the country. They were tall, slight, draped classically from neck to heel in blue fringed cloths, and carried percussion muskets over their bare right shoulders. Makola showed signs of excitement, and ran out of the storehouse (where he spent all his days) to meet these visitors. They came into the courtyard and looked about them with steady, scornful glances. Their leader, a powerful and determined-looking Negro with bloodshot eyes, stood in front of the verandah and made a long speech. He gesticulated much, and ceased very suddenly.

There was something in his intonation, in the sounds of the long sentences he used, that startled the two whites. It was like a reminiscence of something not exactly familiar, and yet resembling the speech of civilised men. It sounded like one of those impossible languages which sometimes we hear in our dreams.

'What lingo is that?' said the amazed Carlier. 'In the first moment I fancied the fellow was going to speak French. Anyway, it is a different kind of gibberish to what we ever heard.'

'Yes,' replied Kayerts. 'Hey, Makola, what does he say? Where do they come from? Who are they?'

But Makola, who seemed to be standing on hot bricks, answered hurriedly, 'I don't know. They come from very far. Perhaps Mrs Price will understand. They are perhaps bad men.'

The leader, after waiting for a while, said something sharply to Makola, who shook his head. Then the man, after looking round, noticed Makola's hut and walked over there. The next moment Mrs Makola was heard speaking with great volubility. The other strangers – they were six in all – strolled about with an air of ease, put their heads through the door of the store-room, congregated round the grave, pointed understandingly at the cross, and generally made themselves at home.

'I don't like those chaps – and, I say, Kayerts, they must be from the coast; they've got firearms,' observed the sagacious Carlier.

Kayerts also did not like those chaps. They both, for the first time, became aware that they lived in conditions where the unusual may be dangerous, and that there was no power on earth outside of themselves to stand between them and the unusual. They became uneasy, went in and loaded their revolvers. Kayerts said, 'We must order Makola to tell them to go away before dark.'

The strangers left in the afternoon, after eating a meal prepared for them by Mrs Makola. The immense woman was excited, and talked much with the visitors. She rattled away shrilly, pointing here and pointing there at the forests and at the river. Makola sat apart and watched. At times he got up and whispered to his wife. He accompanied the strangers across the ravine at the back of the station-ground, and returned slowly looking very thoughtful. When questioned by the white men he was very strange, seemed not to understand, seemed to have forgotten French – seemed to have forgotten how to speak altogether. Kayerts and Carlier agreed that the nigger had had too much palm wine.

There was some talk about keeping a watch in turn, but in the evening everything seemed so quiet and peaceful that they retired as usual. All night they were disturbed by a lot of drumming in the villages. A deep, rapid roll near by would be followed by another far off – then all ceased. Soon short appeals would rattle out here and there, then all mingle together, increase, become vigorous and sustained, would spread out over the forest, roll through the night, unbroken and ceaseless, near and far, as if the whole land had been one immense drum booming out steadily an appeal to heaven. And through the deep and tremendous noise sudden yells that resembled snatches of songs from a madhouse darted shrill and high in discordant jets of sound which seemed to rush far above the earth and drive all peace from under the stars.

Carlier and Kayerts slept badly. They both thought they had heard shots fired during the night – but they could not agree as to the direction. In the morning Makola was gone somewhere. He returned about noon with one of yesterday's strangers, and eluded all Kayerts' attempts to close with him: had become deaf apparently. Kayerts wondered. Carlier, who had been fishing off the bank, came back and remarked while he showed his catch, 'The niggers seem to be in a deuce of a stir; I wonder what's up. I saw about fifteen canoes cross the river during the two hours I was there fishing.' Kayerts, worried, said, 'Isn't this Makola very queer today?' Carlier advised, 'Keep all our men together in case of some trouble.'

2

There were ten station men who had been left by the director. Those fellows, having engaged themselves to the Company for six months (without having any idea of a month in particular and only a very faint notion of time in general), had been serving the cause of progress for upwards of two years. Belonging to a tribe from a very distant part of this land of darkness and sorrow, they did not run away, naturally supposing that as wandering strangers they would be killed by the inhabitants of the country; in which they were right. They lived in straw huts on the slope of a ravine overgrown with reedy grass, just behind the station buildings. They were not happy, regretting the festive incantations, the sorceries, the human sacrifices of their own land; where they also had parents, brothers, sisters, admired chiefs, respected magicians, loved friends, and other ties supposed generally to be human. Besides, the rice rations served out by the Company did not agree with them, being a food unknown to their land, and to which they could not get used. Consequently they were unhealthy and miserable. Had they been of any other tribe they would have made up their minds to die – for nothing is easier to certain savages than suicide – and so have escaped from the puzzling difficulties of existence. But belonging, as they did, to a warlike tribe with filed teeth, they had more grit, and went on stupidly living through disease and sorrow. They did very little work, and had lost their splendid physique. Carlier and Kayerts doctored them assiduously without being able to bring them back into condition again. They were mustered every morning and told off to different tasks – grass-cutting, fence-building, tree-felling, etc., etc., which no power on earth could induce them to execute efficiently. The two whites had practically very little control over them.

In the afternoon Makola came over to the big house and found Kayerts watching three heavy columns of smoke rising above the forests. 'What is that?' asked Kayerts. 'Some villages burn,' answered Makola, who seemed to have regained his wits. Then he said abruptly: 'We have got very little ivory; bad six months' trading. Do you like get a little more ivory?'

'Yes,' said Kayerts eagerly. He thought of percentages which were low.

'Those men who came yesterday are traders from Loanda who have got more ivory than they can carry home. Shall I buy? I know their camp.'

'Certainly,' said Kayerts. 'What are those traders?'

'Bad fellows,' said Makola indifferently. 'They fight with people, and catch women and children. They are bad men, and got guns. There is a great disturbance in the country. Do you want ivory?'

'Yes,' said Kayerts. Makola said nothing for a while. Then: 'Those workmen of ours are no good at all,' he muttered, looking round. 'Station in very bad order, sir. Director will growl. Better get a fine lot of ivory, then he say nothing.'

'I can't help it; the men won't work,' said Kayerts. 'When will you get that ivory?'

'Very soon,' said Makola. 'Perhaps tonight. You leave it to me, and keep indoors, sir. I think you had better give some palm wine to our men to make a dance this evening. Enjoy themselves. Work better tomorrow. There's plenty palm wine – gone a little sour.'

Kayerts said yes, and Makola, with his own hands, carried the big calabashes to the door of his hut. They stood there till the evening, and Mrs

Makola looked into every one. The men got them at sunset. When Kayerts and Carlier retired, a big bonfire was flaring before the men's huts. They could hear their shouts and drumming. Some men from Gobila's village had joined the station hands, and the entertainment was a great success.

In the middle of the night, Carlier, waking suddenly, heard a man shout loudly; then a shot was fired. Only one. Carlier ran out and met Kayerts on the verandah. They were both startled. As they went across the yard to call Makola, they saw shadows moving in the night. One of them cried, 'Don't shoot! It's me, Price.' Then Makola appeared close to them. 'Go back, go back, please,' he urged, 'you spoil all.' 'There are strange men about,' said Carlier. 'Never mind; I know,' said Makola. Then he whispered, 'All right. Bring ivory. Say nothing! I know my business.' The two white men reluctantly went back to the house, but did not sleep. They heard footsteps, whispers, some groans. It seemed as if a lot of men came in, dumped heavy things on the ground, squabbled a long time, then went away. They lay on their hard beds and thought: 'This Makola is invaluable.' In the morning Carlier came out, very sleepy, and pulled at the cord of the big bell. The station hands mustered every morning to the sound of the bell. That morning nobody came. Kayerts turned out also, yawning. Across the yard they saw Makola come out of his hut, a tin basin of soapy water in his hand. Makola, a civilised nigger, was very neat in his person. He threw the soapsuds skilfully over a wretched little yellow cur he had, then turning his face to the agent's house, he shouted from the distance, 'All the men gone last night!'

They heard him plainly, but in their surprise they both yelled out together: 'What!' Then they stared at one another. 'We are in a proper fix now,' growled Carlier. 'It's incredible!' muttered Kayerts. 'I will go to the huts and see,' said Carlier, striding off. Makola coming up found Kayerts standing alone.

'I can hardly believe it,' said Kayerts tearfully. 'We took care of them as if they had been our children.'

'They went with the coast people,' said Makola after a moment of hesitation.

'What do I care with whom they went – the ungrateful brutes!' exclaimed the other. Then with sudden suspicion, and looking hard at Makola, he added: 'What do you know about it?'

Makola moved his shoulders, looking down on the ground. 'What do I know? I think only. Will you come and look at the ivory I've got there? It is a fine lot. You never saw such.'

He moved towards the store. Kayerts followed him mechanically, thinking about the incredible desertion of the men. On the ground before the door of the fetish lay six splendid tusks.

'What did you give for it?' asked Kayerts, after surveying the lot with satisfaction.

'No regular trade,' said Makola. 'They brought the ivory and gave it to me. I told them to take what they most wanted in the station. It is a beautiful lot. No station can show such tusks. Those traders wanted carriers badly, and our men were no good here. No trade, no entry in books; all correct.'

Kayerts nearly burst with indignation. 'Why!' he shouted, 'I believe you have sold our men for these tusks!' Makola stood impassive and silent. 'I – I – will – I,' stuttered Kayerts. 'You fiend!' he yelled out.

'I did the best for you and the Company,' said Makola imperturbably. 'Why you shout so much? Look at this tusk.'

'I dismiss you! I will report you – I won't look at the tusk. I forbid you to touch them. I order you to throw them into the river. You – you!'

'You very red, Mr Kayerts. If you are so irritable in the sun, you will get fever and die – like the first chief!' pronounced Makola impressively.

They stood still, contemplating one another with intense eyes, as if they had been looking with effort across immense distances. Kayerts shivered. Makola had meant no more than he said, but his words seemed to Kayerts full of ominous menace! He turned sharply and went away to the house. Makola retired into the bosom of his family; and the tusks, left lying before the store, looked very large and valuable in the sunshine.

Carlier came back on the verandah. 'They're all gone, hey?' asked Kayerts from the far end of the common room in a muffled voice. 'You did not find anybody?'

'Oh, yes,' said Carlier, 'I found one of Gobila's people lying dead before the huts – shot through the body. We heard that shot last night.'

Kayerts came out quickly. He found his companion staring grimly over the yard at the tusks, away by the store. They both sat in silence for a while. Then Kayerts related his conversation with Makola. Carlier said nothing. At the midday meal they ate very little. They hardly exchanged a word that day. A great silence seemed to lie heavily over the station and press on their lips. Makola did not open the store; he spent the day playing with his children. He lay full-length on a mat outside his door, and the youngsters sat on his chest and clambered all over him. It was a touching picture. Mrs Makola was busy cooking all day as usual. The white men made a somewhat better meal in the evening. Afterwards, Carlier smoking his pipe strolled over to the store; he stood for a long time over the tusks, touched one or two with his foot, even tried to lift the largest one by its small end. He came back to his chief, who had not stirred from the verandah, threw himself in the chair and said – 'I can see it! They were pounced upon while they slept heavily after drinking all that palm wine you'd allowed Makola to give them. A put-up job! See? The worst is, some of Gobila's people were there, and got carried off too, no doubt. The least drunk woke up, and got shot for his sobriety. This is a funny country. What will you do now?'

'We can't touch it, of course,' said Kayerts.

'Of course not,' assented Carlier.

'Slavery is an awful thing,' stammered out Kayerts in an unsteady voice.

'Frightful – the sufferings,' grunted Carlier, with conviction.

They believed their words. Everybody shows a respectful deference to certain sounds that he and his fellows can make. But about feelings people really know nothing. We talk with indignation or enthusiasm; we talk about oppression, cruelty, crime, devotion, self-sacrifice, virtue, and we know nothing real beyond the words. Nobody knows what suffering or sacrifice mean – except, perhaps, the victims of the mysterious purpose of these illusions.

Next morning they saw Makola very busy setting up in the yard the big scales used for weighing ivory. By and by Carlier said: 'What's that filthy scoundrel up to?' and lounged out into the yard. Kayerts followed. They stood by watching. Makola took no notice. When the balance was swung true, he tried to lift a tusk into the scale. It was too heavy. He looked up helplessly without a word, and for a minute they stood round that balance as mute and still as three statues. Suddenly Carlier said: 'Catch hold of the other end, Makola – you beast!' and together they swung the tusk up. Kayerts trembled in every limb. He muttered, 'I say! Oh! I say!' and putting his hand in his pocket found there a dirty bit of paper and the stump of a pencil. He turned his back on the others, as if about to do something tricky, and noted stealthily the weights which Carlier shouted out to him with unnecessary loudness. When all was over, Makola whispered to himself: 'The sun's very strong here for the tusks.' Carlier said to Kayerts in a careless tone: 'I say, chief, I might just as well give him a lift with this lot into the store.'

As they were going back to the house Kayerts observed with a sigh: 'It had to be done.' And Carlier said: 'It's deplorable, but, the men being Company's men, the ivory is Company's ivory. We must look after it.'

'I will report to the director, of course,' said Kayerts. 'Of course; let him decide,' approved Carlier.

At midday they made a hearty meal. Kayerts sighed from time to time. Whenever they mentioned Makola's name they always added to it an opprobrious epithet. It eased their conscience. Makola gave himself a half-holiday, and bathed his children in the river. No one from Gobila's villages came near the station that day. No one came the next day, and the next, nor for a whole week. Gobila's people might have all been dead and buried for any sign of life they gave. But they were only mourning for those they had lost by the witchcraft of white men, who had brought wicked people into their country. The wicked people were gone, but fear remained. Fear always remains. A man may destroy everything within himself, love and hate and belief, and even doubt; but as long as he clings to life he cannot destroy fear: the fear, subtle, indestructible, and terrible, that pervades his being; that tinges his thoughts; that lurks in his heart; that watches on his lips the struggle of his last breath. In his fear, the mild old Gobila offered extra human sacrifices to all the evil spirits that had taken possession of his white friends. His heart was heavy. Some warriors spoke about burning and killing, but the cautious old savage dissuaded them. Who could foresee the woe those mysterious creatures, if irritated, might bring? They should be left alone. Perhaps in time they would disappear into the earth as the first one had disappeared. His people must keep away from them, and hope for the best.

Kayerts and Carlier did not disappear, but remained above on this earth, that, somehow, they fancied had become bigger and very empty. It was not the absolute and dumb solitude of the post that impressed them so much as an inarticulate feeling that something from within them was gone, something that worked for their safety, and had kept the wilderness from interfering with their hearts. The images of home; the memory of people like them, of men that thought and felt as they used to think and feel, receded into distances made indistinct by the glare of unclouded sunshine. And out of the great silence of the surrounding wilderness, its very hopelessness and savagery seemed to approach them nearer, to draw them gently, to look upon them, to envelop them with a solicitude irresistible, familiar, and disgusting.

Days lengthened into weeks, then into months. Gobila's people drummed and yelled to every new moon, as of yore, but kept away from the station. Makola and Carlier tried once in a canoe to open communications, but were received with a shower of arrows, and had to fly back to the station for dear life. That attempt set the country up and down the river into an uproar that could be very distinctly heard for days. The steamer was late. At first they spoke of delay jauntily, then anxiously, then gloomily. The matter was becoming serious. Stores were running short. Carlier cast his lines off the bank, but the river was low, and the fish kept out in the stream. They dared not stroll far away from the station to shoot. Moreover, there was no game in the impenetrable forest. Once Carlier shot a hippo in the river. They had no boat to secure it, and it sank. When it floated up it drifted away, and Gobila's people secured the carcase. It was the occasion for a national holiday, but Carlier had a fit of rage over it, and talked about the necessity of exterminating all the niggers before the country could be made habitable. Kayerts mooned about silently; spent hours looking at the portrait of his Melie. It represented a little girl with long bleached tresses and a rather sour face. His legs were much swollen, and he could hardly walk. Carlier, undermined by fever, could not swagger any more, but kept tottering about, still with a devil-may-care air, as became a man who remembered his crack regiment. He had become hoarse, sarcastic, and inclined to say unpleasant things. He called it 'being frank with you'. They had long ago reckoned their percentages on trade, including in them that last deal of 'this infamous Makola'. They had also concluded not to say anything about it. Kayerts hesitated at first – was afraid of the director.

'He has seen worse things done on the quiet,' maintained Carlier, with a hoarse laugh. 'Trust him! He won't thank you if you blab. He is no better than you or me. Who will talk if we hold our tongues? There is nobody here.'

That was the root of the trouble! There was nobody there; and being left there alone with their weakness, they became daily more like a pair of accomplices than like a couple of devoted friends. They had heard nothing from home for eight months. Every evening they said, 'Tomorrow we shall see the steamer.' But one of the Company's steamers had been wrecked, and the director was busy with the other, relieving very distant and important stations on the main river. He thought that the useless station, and the useless men, could wait. Meantime Kayerts and Carlier lived on rice boiled without salt, and cursed the Company, all Africa, and the day they were born. One must have lived on such diet to discover what ghastly trouble the necessity of swallowing one's food may become. There was literally nothing else in the station but rice and coffee; they drank the coffee without sugar. The last fifteen lumps Kayerts had solemnly locked away in his box, together with a half-bottle of Cognac, 'in case of sickness', he explained. Carlier approved. 'When one is sick,' he said, 'any little extra like that is cheering.'

They waited. Rank grass began to sprout over the courtyard. The bell never rang now. Days passed, silent, exasperating, and slow. When the two men spoke, they snarled; and their silences were bitter, as if tinged by the bitterness of their thoughts.

One day after a lunch of boiled rice, Carlier put down his cup untasted, and said: 'Hang it all! Let's have a decent cup of coffee for once. Bring out that sugar, Kayerts!'

'For the sick,' muttered Kayerts, without looking up.

'For the sick,' mocked Carlier. 'Bosh! . . . Well! I am sick.'

'You are no more sick than I am, and I go without,' said Kayerts in a peaceful tone.

'Come! out with that sugar, you stingy old slave-dealer.'

Kayerts looked up quickly. Carlier was smiling with marked insolence. And suddenly it seemed to Kayerts that he had never seen that man before. Who was he? He knew nothing about him. What was he capable of? There was a surprising flash of violent emotion within him, as if in the presence of something undreamt of, dangerous, and final. But he managed to pronounce with composure – 'That joke is in very bad taste. Don't repeat it.'

'Joke!' said Carlier, hitching himself forward on his seat. 'I am hungry – I am sick – I don't joke! I hate hypocrites. You are a hypocrite. You are a slave-dealer. I am a slave-dealer. There's nothing but slave-dealers in this cursed country. I mean to have sugar in my coffee today, anyhow!'

'I forbid you to speak to me in that way,' said Kayerts with a fair show of resolution.

'You! – What?' shouted Carlier, jumping up.

Kayerts stood up also. 'I am your chief,' he began, trying to master the shakiness of his voice.

'What?' yelled the other. 'Who's chief? There's no chief here. There's nothing here: there's nothing but you and I. Fetch the sugar – you pot-bellied ass.'

'Hold your tongue. Go out of this room,' screamed Kayerts. 'I dismiss you – you scoundrel!'

Carlier swung a stool. All at once he looked dangerously in earnest. 'You flabby, good-for-nothing civilian – take that!' he howled.

Kayerts dropped under the table, and the stool struck the grass inner wall of the room. Then, as Carlier was trying to upset the table, Kayerts in desperation made a blind rush, head low, like a cornered pig would do, and overturning his friend, bolted along the verandah and into his room. He locked the door, snatched his revolver, and stood panting. In less than a minute Carlier was kicking at the door furiously, howling, 'If you don't bring out that sugar, I will shoot you at sight, like a dog. Now then – one – two – three. You won't? I will show you who's the master.'

Kayerts thought the door would fall in, and scrambled through the square hole that served for a window in his room. There was then the whole breadth of the house between them. But the other was apparently not strong enough to break in the door, and Kayerts heard him running round. Then he also began to run laboriously on his swollen legs. He ran as quickly as he could, grasping the revolver, and unable yet to understand what was happening to him. He saw in succession Makola's house, the store, the river, the ravine, and the low bushes; and he saw all those things again as he ran for the second time round the house. Then again they flashed past him. That morning he could not have walked a yard without a groan.

And now he ran. He ran fast enough to keep out of sight of the other man.

Then as, weak and desperate, he thought, 'Before I finish the next round I shall die,' he heard the other man stumble heavily, then stop. He stopped also. He had the back and Carlier the front of the house, as before. He heard him drop into a chair cursing, and suddenly his own legs gave way, and he slid down into a sitting posture with his back to the wall. His mouth was as dry as a cinder, and his face was wet with perspiration – and tears. What was it all about? He thought it must be a horrible illusion; he thought he was dreaming; he thought he was going mad! After a while he collected his senses. What did they quarrel about? That sugar! How absurd! He would give it to him – didn't want it himself. And he began scrambling to his feet with a sudden feeling of security. But before he had fairly stood upright, a common-sense reflection occurred to him and drove him back into despair. He thought: If I give way now to that brute of a soldier, he will begin this horror again tomorrow – and the day after – every day – raise other pretensions, trample on me, torture me, make me his slave – and I will be lost! Lost! The steamer may not come for days – may never come. He shook so that he had to sit down on the floor again. He shivered forlornly. He felt he could not, would not move any more. He was completely distracted by the sudden perception that the position was without issue – that death and life had in a moment become equally difficult and terrible.

All at once he heard the other push his chair back; and he leaped to his feet with extreme facility. He listened and got confused. Must run again! Right or left? He heard footsteps. He darted to the left, grasping his revolver, and at the very same instant, as it seemed to him, they came into violent collision. Both shouted with surprise. A loud explosion took place between them; a roar of red fire, thick smoke; and Kayerts, deafened and blinded, rushed back thinking: I am hit – it's all over. He expected the other to come round – to gloat over his agony. He caught hold of an upright of the roof – 'All over!' Then he heard a crashing fall on the other side of the house, as if somebody had tumbled headlong over a chair – then silence. Nothing more happened. He did not die. Only his shoulder felt as if it had been badly wrenched, and he had lost his revolver. He was disarmed and helpless! He waited for his fate. The other man made no sound. It was stratagem. He was stalking him now! Along what side? Perhaps he was taking aim this very minute!

After a few moments of an agony frightful and absurd, he decided to go and meet his doom. He was prepared for every surrender. He turned the corner, steadying himself with one hand on the wall, made a few paces, and nearly swooned. He had seen on the floor, protruding past the other corner, a pair of turned-up feet. A pair of white naked feet in red slippers. He felt deadly sick, and stood for a time in profound darkness. Then Makola appeared before him, saying quietly: 'Come along, Mr Kayerts. He is dead.' He burst into tears of gratitude; a loud, sobbing fit of crying. After a time he found himself sitting in a chair and looking at Carlier, who lay stretched on his back. Makola was kneeling over the body.

'Is this your revolver?' asked Makola, getting up.

'Yes,' said Kayerts; then he added very quickly, 'He ran after me to shoot me – you saw!'

'Yes, I saw,' said Makola. 'There is only one revolver; where's his?'

'Don't know,' whispered Kayerts in a voice that had become suddenly very faint.

'I will go and look for it,' said the other gently. He made the round along the verandah, while Kayerts sat still and looked at the corpse. Makola came back empty-handed, stood in deep thought, then stepped quietly into the dead man's room, and came out directly with a revolver, which he held up before Kayerts. Kayerts shut his eyes. Everything was going round. He found life more terrible and difficult than death. He had shot an unarmed man.

After meditating for a while, Makola said softly, pointing at the dead man who lay there with his right eye blown out – 'He died of fever.' Kayerts looked at him with a stony stare. 'Yes,' repeated Makola thoughtfully, stepping over the corpse, 'I think he died of fever. Bury him tomorrow.'

And he went away slowly to his expectant wife, leaving the two white men alone on the verandah.

Night came, and Kayerts sat unmoving on his chair. He sat quiet as if he had taken a dose of opium. The violence of the emotions he had passed through produced a feeling of exhausted serenity. He had plumbed in one short afternoon the depths of horror and despair, and now found repose in the conviction that life had no more secrets for him: neither had death! He sat by the corpse thinking; thinking very actively, thinking very new thoughts. He seemed to have broken loose from himself altogether. His old thoughts, convictions, likes and dislikes, things he respected and things he abhorred, appeared in their true light at last! Appeared contemptible and childish, false and ridiculous. He revelled in his new wisdom while he sat by the man he had killed. He argued with himself about all things under heaven with that kind of wrong-headed lucidity which may be observed in some lunatics. Incidentally he reflected that the fellow dead there had been a noxious beast anyway; that men died every day in thousands; perhaps in hundreds of thousands – who could tell? – and that, in the number, that one death could not possibly make any difference; couldn't have any importance, at least to a thinking creature. He, Kayerts, was a thinking creature. He had been all his life, till that moment, a believer in a lot of nonsense like the rest of mankind – who are fools; but now he thought! He knew! He was at peace; he was familiar with the highest wisdom! Then he tried to imagine himself dead, and Carlier sitting in his chair watching him; and his attempt met with such unexpected success, that in a very few moments he became not at all sure who was dead and who was alive. This extraordinary achievement of his fancy startled him, however, and by a clever and timely effort of mind he saved himself just in time from becoming Carlier. His heart thumped, and he felt hot all over at the thought of that danger. Carlier! What a beastly thing! To compose his now disturbed nerves – and no wonder! – he tried to whistle a little. Then, suddenly, he fell asleep, or thought he had slept; but at any rate there was a fog, and somebody had whistled in the fog.

He stood up. The day had come, and a heavy mist had descended upon the land: the mist penetrating, enveloping, and silent; the morning mist of tropical lands; the mist that clings and kills; the mist white and deadly, immaculate and poisonous. He stood up, saw the body, and threw his arms above his head with a cry like that of a man who, waking from a trance, finds himself immured for ever in a tomb. 'Help! . . . My God!'

A shriek, inhuman, vibrating and sudden, pierced like a sharp dart the white shroud of that land of sorrow. Three short, impatient screeches followed, and then, for a time, the fog-wreaths rolled on, undisturbed, through a formidable silence. Then many more shrieks, rapid and piercing, like the yells of some exasperated and ruthless creature, rent the air. Progress was calling to Kayerts from the river. Progress and civilisation and all the virtues. Society was calling to its accomplished child to come, to be taken care of, to be instructed, to be judged, to be condemned; it called him to return to that rubbish heap from which he had wandered away, so that justice could be done.

Kayerts heard and understood. He stumbled out of the verandah, leaving the other man quite alone for the first time since they had been thrown there together. He groped his way through the fog, calling in his ignorance upon the invisible heaven to undo its work. Makola flitted by in the mist, shouting as he ran – 'Steamer! Steamer! They can't see. They whistle for the station. I go ring the bell. Go down to the landing, sir. I ring.'

He disappeared. Kayerts stood still. He looked upwards; the fog rolled low over his head. He looked round like a man who has lost his way; and he saw a dark smudge, a cross-shaped stain, upon the shifting purity of the mist. As he began to stumble towards it, the station bell rang in a tumultuous peal its answer to the impatient clamour of the steamer.

The managing director of the Great Civilising Company (since we know that civilisation follows trade) landed first, and incontinently lost sight of the steamer. The fog down by the river was exceedingly dense; above, at the station, the bell rang unceasing and brazen.

The director shouted loudly to the steamer: 'There is nobody down to meet us; there may be something wrong, though they are ringing. You had better come, too!'

And he began to toil up the steep bank. The captain and the engine-driver of the boat followed behind. As they scrambled up the fog thinned, and they could see their director a good way ahead. Suddenly they saw him start forward, calling to them over his shoulder: 'Run! Run to the house! I've found one of them. Run, look for the other!'

He had found one of them! And even he, the man of varied and startling experience, was somewhat discomposed by the manner of this finding. He stood and fumbled in his pockets (for a knife) while he faced Kayerts, who was hanging by a leather strap from the cross. He had evidently climbed the grave, which was high and narrow, and after tying the end of the strap to the arm, had swung himself off. His toes were only a couple of inches above the ground; his arms hung stiffly down; he seemed to be standing rigidly at attention, but with one purple cheek playfully posed on the shoulder. And, irreverently, he was putting out a swollen tongue at his managing director.

1896

KARAIN: A MEMORY

We knew him in those unprotected days when we were content to hold in our hands our lives and our property. None of us, I believe, has any property now, and I hear that many, negligently, have lost their lives; but I am sure that the few who survive are not yet so dim-eyed as to miss in the befogged respectability of their newspapers the intelligence of various native risings in the Eastern Archipelago. Sunshine gleams between the lines of those short paragraphs – sunshine and the glitter of the sea. A strange name wakes up memories; the printed words scent the smoky atmosphere of today faintly, with the subtle and penetrating perfume as of land breezes breathing through the starlight of bygone nights; a signal fire gleams like a jewel on the high brow of a sombre cliff; great trees, the advanced sentries of immense forests, stand watchful and still over sleeping stretches of open water; a line of white surf thunders on an empty beach, the shallow water foams on the reefs; and green islets scattered through the calm of noonday lie upon the level of a polished sea, like a handful of emeralds on a buckler of steel.

There are faces too – faces dark, truculent, and smiling; the frank audacious faces of men barefooted, well armed and noiseless. They thronged the narrow length of our schooner's decks with their ornamented and barbarous crowd, with the variegated colours of checkered sarongs, red turbans, white jackets, embroideries; with the gleam of scabbards, gold rings, charms, armlets, lance blades, and jewelled handles of their weapons. They had an independent bearing, resolute eyes, a restrained manner; and we seem yet to hear their soft voices speaking of battles, travels, and escapes; boasting with composure, joking quietly; sometimes in well-bred murmurs extolling their own valour, our generosity; or celebrating with loyal enthusiasm the virtues of their ruler. We remember the faces, the eyes, the voices, we see again the gleam of silk and metal; the murmuring stir of that crowd, brilliant, festive, and martial; and we seem to feel the touch of friendly brown hands that, after one short grasp, return to rest on a chased hilt. They were Karain's people – a devoted following. Their movements hung on his lips; they read their thoughts in his eyes; he murmured to them nonchalantly of life and death, and they accepted his words humbly, like gifts of fate. They were all free men, and when speaking to him said, 'Your slave.' On his passage voices died out as though he had walked guarded by silence; awed whispers followed him. They called him their war-chief. He was the ruler of three villages on a narrow plain; the master of an insignificant foothold on the earth – of a conquered foothold that, shaped like a young moon, lay ignored between the hills and the sea.

From the deck of our schooner, anchored in the middle of the bay, he indicated by a theatrical sweep of his arm along the jagged outline of the hills the whole of his domain; and the ample movement seemed to drive back its limits, augmenting it suddenly into something so immense and vague that for a moment it appeared to be bounded only by the sky. And really, looking at that place, landlocked from the sea and shut off from the land by the precipitous slopes of mountains, it was difficult to believe in the existence of any neighbourhood. It was still, complete, unknown, and full of a life that went on stealthily with a troubling effect of solitude; of a life that seemed unaccountably empty of anything that would stir the thought, touch the heart, give a hint of the ominous sequence of days. It appeared to us a land without memories, regrets, and hopes; a land where nothing could survive the coming of the night, and where each sunrise, like a dazzling act of special creation, was disconnected from the eve and the morrow.

Karain swept his hand over it. 'All mine!' He struck the deck with his long staff; the gold head flashed like a falling star; very close behind him a silent old fellow in a richly embroidered black jacket alone of all the Malays around did not follow the masterful gesture with a look. He did not even lift his eyelids. He bowed his head behind his master, and without stirring held hilt up over his right shoulder a long blade in a silver scabbard. He was there on duty, but without curiosity, and seemed weary, not with age, but with the possession of a burdensome secret of existence. Karain, heavy and proud, had a lofty pose and breathed calmly. It was our first visit, and we looked about curiously.

The bay was like a bottomless pit of intense light. The circular sheet of water reflected a luminous sky, and the shores enclosing it made an opaque ring of earth floating in an emptiness of transparent blue. The hills, purple and arid, stood out heavily on the sky: their summits seemed to fade into a coloured tremble as of ascending vapour; their steep sides were streaked with the green of narrow ravines; at their foot lay rice-fields, plantain-patches, yellow sands. A torrent wound about like a dropped thread. Clumps of fruit-trees marked the villages; slim palms put their nodding heads together above the low houses; dried-palm-leaf roofs shone afar, like roofs of gold, behind the dark colonnades of tree-trunks; figures passed vivid and vanishing; the smoke of fires stood upright above the masses of flowering bushes; bamboo fences glittered, running away in broken lines between the fields. A sudden cry on the shore sounded plaintive in the distance, and ceased abruptly, as if stifled in the downpour of sunshine; a puff of breeze made a flash of darkness on the smooth water, touched our faces, and became forgotten. Nothing moved. The sun blazed down into a shadowless hollow of colours and stillness.

It was the stage where, dressed splendidly for his part, he strutted, incomparably dignified, made important by the power he had to awaken an absurd expectation of something heroic going to take place – a burst of action or song – upon the vibrating tone of a wonderful sunshine. He was ornate and disturbing, for one could not imagine what depth of horrible void such an elaborate front could be worthy to hide. He was not masked – there was too much life in him, and a mask is only a lifeless thing; but he presented himself essentially as an actor, as a human being aggressively disguised. His smallest acts were prepared and unexpected, his speeches grave, his sentences ominous like hints and complicated like arabesques. He was treated with a solemn respect accorded in the irreverent West only to the monarchs of the stage, and he accepted the profound homage with a sustained dignity seen nowhere else but behind the footlights and in the condensed falseness of some grossly tragic situation. It was almost impossible to remember who he was – only a petty chief of a conveniently isolated corner of Mindanao, where we could in comparative safety break the law against the traffic in firearms and ammunition with the natives. What would happen should one of the moribund Spanish gunboats be suddenly galvanised into a flicker of active life did not trouble us, once we were inside the bay – so completely did it appear out of the reach of a meddling world; and besides, in those days we were imaginative enough to look with a kind of joyous equanimity on any chance there was of being quietly hanged somewhere out of the way of diplomatic remonstrance. As to Karain, nothing could happen to him unless what happens to all – failure and death; but his quality was to appear clothed in the illusion of unavoidable success. He seemed too effective, too necessary there, too much of an essential condition for the existence of his land and his people, to be destroyed by anything short of an earthquake. He summed up his race, his country, the elemental force of ardent life, of tropical nature. He had its luxuriant strength, its fascination; and, like it, he carried the seed of peril within.

In many successive visits we came to know his stage well – the purple semicircle of hills, the slim trees leaning over houses, the yellow sands, the streaming green of ravines. All that had the crude and blended colouring, the appropriateness almost excessive, the suspicious immobility of a painted scene; and it enclosed so perfectly the accomplished acting of his amazing pretences that the rest of the world seemed shut out for ever from the gorgeous spectacle. There could be nothing outside. It was as if the earth had gone on spinning, and had left that crumb of its surface alone in space. He appeared utterly cut off from everything but the sunshine, and that even seemed to be made for him alone. Once when asked what was on the other side of the hills, he said, with a meaning smile, 'Friends and enemies – many enemies; else why should I buy your rifles and powder?' He was always like this – word-perfect in his part, playing up faithfully to the mysteries and certitudes of his surroundings. 'Friends and enemies –' nothing else. It was impalpable and vast. The earth had indeed rolled away from under his land, and he, with his handful of people, stood surrounded by a silent tumult as of contending shades. Certainly no sound came from outside. 'Friends and enemies!' He might have added, 'and memories', at least as far as he himself was concerned; but he neglected to make that point then. It made itself later on, though; but it was after the daily performance – in the wings, so to speak, and with the lights out. Meantime he filled the stage with barbarous dignity. Some ten years ago he had led his people – a scratch lot of wandering Bugis – to the conquest of the bay, and now in his august care they had forgotten all the past, and had lost all concern for the future. He gave them wisdom, advice, reward, punishment, life or death, with the same serenity of attitude and voice. He understood irrigation and the art of war – the qualities of weapons and the craft of boat-building. He could conceal his heart; had more endurance; he could swim longer, and steer a canoe better than any of his people; he could shoot straighter, and negotiate more tortuously than any man of his race I knew. He was an adventurer of the sea, an outcast, a ruler – and my very good friend. I wish him a quick death in a stand-up fight, a death in sunshine; for he had known remorse and power, and no man can demand more from life. Day after day he appeared before us, incomparably faithful to the illusions of the stage, and at sunset the night descended upon him quickly, like a falling curtain. The seamed hills became black shadows towering high upon a clear sky; above them the glittering confusion of stars resembled a mad turmoil stilled by a gesture; sounds ceased, men slept, forms vanished – and the reality of the universe alone remained – a marvellous thing of darkness and glimmers.

2

But it was at night that he talked openly, forgetting the exactions of his stage. In the daytime there were affairs to be discussed in state. There were at first between him and me his own splendour, my shabby suspicions, and the scenic landscape that intruded upon the reality of our lives by its motionless fantasy of outline and colour. His followers thronged round him; above his head the broad blades of their spears made a spiked halo of iron points, and they hedged him from humanity by the shimmer of silks, the gleam of weapons, the excited and respectful hum of eager voices. Before sunset he would take leave with ceremony, and go off sitting under a red umbrella, and escorted by a score of boats. All the paddles flashed and struck together with a mighty splash that reverberated loudly in the monumental amphitheatre of hills. A broad stream of dazzling foam trailed behind the flotilla. The canoes appeared very black on the white hiss of water; turbaned heads swayed back and forth; a multitude of arms in crimson and yellow rose and fell with one movement; the spearmen upright in the bows of canoes had variegated sarongs and gleaming shoulders like bronze statues; the muttered strophes of the paddlers' song ended periodically in a plaintive shout. They diminished in the distance; the song ceased; they swarmed on the beach in the long shadows of the western hills. The sunlight lingered on the purple crests, and we could see him leading the way to his stockade, a burly bareheaded figure walking far in advance of a straggling *cortège*, and swinging regularly an ebony staff taller than himself. The darkness deepened fast; torches gleamed fitfully, passing behind bushes; a long hail or two trailed in the silence of the evening; and at last the night stretched its smooth veil over the shore, the lights, and the voices.

Then, just as we were thinking of repose, the watchmen of the schooner would hail a splash of paddles away in the starlit gloom of the bay; a voice would respond in cautious tones, and our serang, putting his head down the open skylight, would inform us without surprise, 'That Rajah, he coming. He here now.' Karain appeared noiselessly in the doorway of the little cabin. He was simplicity itself then; all in white; muffled about his head; for arms only a kriss with a plain buffalo-horn handle, which he would politely conceal within a fold of his sarong before stepping over the threshold. The old sword-bearer's face, the worn-out and mournful face so covered with wrinkles that it seemed to look out through the meshes of a fine dark net, could be seen close above his shoulder. Karain never moved without that attendant, who stood or squatted close at his back. He had a dislike of an open space behind him. It was more than a dislike – it resembled fear, a nervous preoccupation of what went on where he could not see. This, in view of the evident and fierce loyalty that surrounded him, was inexplicable. He was there alone in the midst of devoted men; he was safe from neighbourly ambushes, from fraternal ambitions; and yet more than one of our visitors had assured us that their ruler could not bear to be alone. They said, 'Even when he eats and sleeps there is always one on the watch near him who has strength and weapons.' There was indeed always one near him, though our informants had no conception of that watcher's strength and weapons, which were both shadowy and terrible. We knew, but only later on, when we had heard the story. Meantime we noticed that, even during the most important interviews, Karain would often give a start, and interrupting his discourse, would sweep his arm back with a sudden movement, to feel whether the old fellow was there. The old fellow, impenetrable and weary, was always there. He shared his food, his repose, and his thoughts; he knew his plans, guarded his secrets; and, impassive behind his master's agitation, without stirring the least bit, murmured above his head in a soothing tone some words difficult to catch.

It was only on board the schooner, when surrounded by white faces, by unfamiliar sights and sounds, that Karain seemed to forget the strange obsession that wound like a black thread through the gorgeous pomp of his public life. At night we treated him in a free and easy manner, which just stopped short of slapping him on the back, for there are liberties one must not take with a Malay. He said himself that on such occasions he was only a private gentleman coming to see other gentlemen whom he supposed as well born as himself. I fancy that to the last he believed us to be emissaries of Government, darkly official persons furthering by our illegal traffic some dark scheme of high statecraft. Our denials and protestations were unavailing. He only smiled with discreet politeness and enquired about the Queen. Every visit began with that enquiry; he was insatiable of details; he was fascinated by the holder of a sceptre the shadow of which, stretching from the westward over the earth and over the seas, passed far beyond his own hand's-breadth of conquered land. He multiplied questions; he could never know enough of the monarch of whom he spoke with wonder and chivalrous respect – with a kind of affectionate awe! Afterwards, when we had learned that he was the son of a woman who had many years ago ruled a small Bugis state, we came to suspect that the memory of his mother (of whom he spoke with enthusiasm) mingled somehow in his mind with the image he tried to form for himself of the far-off Queen whom he called great, invincible, pious, and fortunate. We had to invent details at last to satisfy his craving curiosity; and our loyalty must be pardoned, for we tried to make them fit for his august and resplendent ideal. We talked. The night slipped over us, over the still schooner, over the sleeping land, and over the sleepless sea that thundered amongst the reefs outside the bay. His paddlers, two trustworthy men, slept in the canoe at the foot of our side-ladder. The old confidant, relieved from duty, dozed on his heels, with his back against the companion-doorway; and Karain sat squarely in the ship's wooden armchair, under the slight sway of the cabin lamp, a cheroot between his dark fingers, and a glass of lemonade before him. He was amused by the fizz of the thing, but after a sip or two would let it get flat, and with a courteous wave of his hand ask for a fresh bottle. He decimated our slender stock; but we did not begrudge it to him, for, when he began, he talked well. He must have been a great Bugis dandy in his time, for even then (and when we knew him he was no longer young) his splendour was spotlessly neat, and he dyed his hair a light shade of brown. The quiet dignity of his bearing transformed the dim-lit cuddy of the schooner into an audience-hall. He talked of inter-island politics with an ironic and melancholy shrewdness. He had travelled much, suffered not a little, intrigued, fought. He knew native courts, European settlements, the forests, the sea, and, as he said himself, had spoken in his time to many great men. He liked to talk with me because I had known some of these men: he seemed to think that I could understand him, and, with a fine confidence, assumed that I, at least, could appreciate how much greater he was himself. But he preferred to talk of his native country – a small Bugis state on the island of Celebes. I had visited it some time before, and he asked eagerly for news. As men's names came up in conversation he would say, 'We swam against one another when we were boys;' or, 'We hunted the deer together – he could use the noose and the spear as well as I.' Now and then his big dreamy eyes would roll restlessly; he frowned or smiled, or he would become pensive, and, staring in silence, would nod slightly for a time at some regretted vision of the past.

His mother had been the ruler of a small semi-independent state on the sea-coast at the head of the Gulf of Boni. He spoke of her with pride. She had been a woman resolute in affairs of state and of her own heart. After the death of her first husband, undismayed by the turbulent opposition of the chiefs, she married a rich trader, a Korinchi man of no family. Karain was her son by that second marriage, but his unfortunate descent had apparently nothing to do with his exile. He said nothing as to its cause, though once he let slip with a sigh, 'Ha! my land will not feel any more the weight of my body.' But he related winningly the story of his wanderings, and told us all about the conquest of the bay. Alluding to the people beyond the hills, he would murmur gently, with a careless wave of the hand, 'They came over the hills once to fight us, but those who got away never came again.' He thought for a while, smiling to himself. 'Very few got away,' he added, with proud serenity. He cherished the recollections of his successes; he had an exulting eagerness for endeavour; when he talked, his aspect was warlike, chivalrous, and uplifting. No wonder his people admired him. We saw him once walking in daylight amongst the houses of the settlement. At the doors of huts groups of women turned to look after him, warbling softly, and with gleaming eyes; armed men stood out of the way, submissive and erect; others approached from the side, bending their backs to address him humbly; an old woman stretched out a draped lean arm – 'Blessings on thy head!' she cried from a dark doorway; a fiery-eyed man showed above the low fence of a plantain-patch a streaming face, a bare breast scarred in two places, and bellowed out pantingly after him, 'God give victory to our master!' Karain walked fast, and with firm long strides; he answered greetings right and left by quick piercing glances. Children ran forward between the houses, peeped fearfully round corners; young boys kept up with him, gliding between bushes: their eyes gleamed through the dark leaves. The old sword-bearer, shouldering the silver scabbard, shuffled hastily at his heels with bowed head, and his eyes on the ground. And in the midst of a great stir they passed swift and absorbed, like two men hurrying through a great solitude.

In his council hall he was surrounded by the gravity of armed chiefs, while two long rows of old headmen dressed in cotton stuffs squatted on their heels, with idle arms hanging over their knees. Under the thatch roof supported by smooth columns, of which each one had cost the life of a straight-stemmed young palm, the scent of flowering hedges drifted in warm waves. The sun was sinking. In the open courtyard suppliants walked through the gate, raising, when yet far off, their joined hands above bowed heads, and bending low in the bright stream of sunlight. Young girls, with flowers in their laps, sat under the wide-spreading boughs of a big tree. The blue smoke of wood fires spread in a thin mist above the high-pitched roofs of houses that had glistening walls of woven reeds, and all round them rough wooden pillars under the sloping eaves. He dispensed justice in the shade; from a high seat he gave orders, advice, reproof. Now and then the hum of approbation rose louder, and idle spearmen that lounged listlessly against the posts, looking at the girls, would turn their heads slowly. To no man had been given the shelter of so much respect, confidence, and awe. Yet at times he would lean forward and appear to listen as for a far-off note of discord as if expecting to hear some faint voice, the sound of light footsteps; or he would start half up in his seat, as though he had been familiarly touched on the shoulder. He glanced back with apprehension; his aged follower whispered inaudibly at his ear; the chiefs turned their eyes away in silence, for the old wizard, the man who could command ghosts and send evil spirits against enemies, was speaking low to their ruler. Around the short stillness of the open place the trees rustled faintly, the soft laughter of girls playing with the flowers rose in clear bursts of joyous sound. At the end of upright spear-shafts the long tufts of dyed horsehair waved crimson and filmy in the gust of wind; and beyond the blaze of hedges the brook of limpid quick water ran invisible and loud under the drooping grass of the bank, with a great murmur, passionate and gentle.

After sunset, far across the fields and over the bay, clusters of torches could be seen burning under the high roofs of the council shed. Smoky red flames swayed on high poles, and the fiery blaze flickered over faces, clung to the smooth trunks of palm-trees, kindled bright sparks on the rims of metal dishes standing on fine floor-mats. That obscure adventurer feasted like a king. Small groups of men crouched in tight circles round the wooden platters; brown hands hovered over snowy heaps of rice. Sitting upon a rough couch apart from the others, he leaned on his elbow with inclined head; and near him a youth improvised in a high tone a song that celebrated his valour and wisdom. The singer rocked himself to and fro, rolling frenzied eyes; old women hobbled about with dishes, and men, squatting low, lifted their heads to listen gravely without ceasing to eat. The song of triumph vibrated in the night, and the stanzas rolled out mournfully and fiery like the thoughts of a hermit. He silenced it with a sign, 'Enough!' An owl hooted far away, exulting in the delight of deep gloom in dense foliage; overhead lizards ran in the attap thatch, calling softly; the dry leaves of the roof rustled; the rumour of mingled voices grew louder suddenly. After a circular and startled glance, as of a man waking up abruptly to the sense of danger, he would throw himself back, and under the downward gaze of the old sorcerer take up, wide-eyed, the slender thread of his dream. They watched his moods; the swelling rumour of animated talk subsided like a wave on a sloping beach. The chief is pensive. And above the spreading whisper of lowered voices only a light rattle of weapons would be heard, a single louder word distinct and alone, or the grave ring of a big brass tray.

For two years at short intervals we visited him. We came to like him, to trust him, almost to admire him. He was plotting and preparing a war with patience, with foresight – with a fidelity to his purpose and with a steadfastness of which I would have thought him racially incapable. He seemed fearless of the future, and in his plans displayed a sagacity that was only limited by his profound ignorance of the rest of the world. We tried to enlighten him, but our attempts to make clear the irresistible nature of the forces which he desired to arrest failed to discourage his eagerness to strike a blow for his own primitive ideas. He did not understand us, and replied by arguments that almost drove one to desperation by their childish shrewdness. He was absurd and unanswerable. Sometimes we caught glimpses of a sombre, glowing fury within him – a brooding and vague sense of wrong, and a concentrated lust of violence which is dangerous in a native. He raved like one inspired. On one occasion, after we had been talking to him late in his campong, he jumped up. A great, clear fire blazed in the grove; lights and shadows danced together between the trees; in the still night bats flitted in and out of the boughs like fluttering flakes of denser darkness. He snatched the sword from the old man, whizzed it out of the scabbard, and thrust the point into the earth. Upon the thin, upright blade the silver hilt, released, swayed before him like something alive. He stepped back a pace, and in a deadened tone spoke fiercely to the vibrating steel: 'If there is virtue in the fire, in the iron, in the hand that forged thee, in the words spoken over thee, in the desire of my heart, and in the wisdom of thy makers – then we shall be victorious together!' He drew it out, looked along the edge. 'Take,' he said over his shoulder to the old sword-bearer. The other, unmoved on his hams, wiped the point with a corner of his sarong, and returning the weapon to its scabbard, sat nursing it on his knees without a single look upwards. Karain, suddenly very calm, reseated himself with dignity. We gave up remonstrating after this, and let him go his way to an honourable disaster. All we could do for him was to see to it that the powder was good for the money and the rifles serviceable, if old.

But the game was becoming at last too dangerous; and if we, who had faced it pretty often, thought little of the danger, it was decided for us by some very respectable people sitting safely in counting-houses that the risks were too great, and that only one more trip could be made. After giving in the usual way many misleading hints as to our destination, we slipped away quietly, and after a very quick passage entered the bay. It was early morning, and even before the anchor went to the bottom the schooner was surrounded by boats.

The first thing we heard was that Karain's mysterious sword-bearer had died a few days ago. We did not attach much importance to the news. It was certainly difficult to imagine Karain without his inseparable follower; but the fellow was old, he had never spoken to one of us, we hardly ever had heard the sound of his voice; and we had come to look upon him as something inanimate, as part of our friend's trappings of state – like that sword he had carried, or the fringed red umbrella displayed during an official progress. Karain did not visit us in the afternoon as usual. A message of greeting and a present of fruit and vegetables came off for us before sunset. Our friend paid us like a banker, but treated us like a prince. We sat up for him till midnight. Under the stern awning bearded Jackson jingled an old guitar and sang, with an execrable accent, Spanish love-songs; while young Hollis and I, sprawling on the deck, had a game of chess by the light of a cargo lantern. Karain did not appear. Next day we were busy unloading, and heard that the Rajah was unwell. The expected invitation to visit him ashore did not come. We sent friendly messages, but, fearing to intrude upon some secret council, remained on board. Early on the third day we had landed all the powder and rifles, and also a six-pounder brass gun with its carriage, which we had subscribed together for a present to our friend. The afternoon was sultry. Ragged edges of black clouds peeped over the hills, and invisible thunderstorms circled outside, growling like wild beasts. We got the schooner ready for sea, intending to leave next morning at daylight. All day a merciless sun blazed down into the bay, fierce and pale, as if at white heat. Nothing moved on the land. The beach was empty, the villages seemed deserted; the trees far off stood in unstirring clumps, as if painted; the white smoke of some invisible bush-fire spread itself low over the shores of the bay like a settling fog. Late in the day three of Karain's chief men, dressed in their best and armed to the teeth, came off in a canoe, bringing a case of dollars. They were gloomy and languid, and told us they had not seen their Rajah for five days. No one had seen him! We settled all accounts, and after shaking hands in turn and in profound silence, they descended one after another into their boat, and were paddled to the shore, sitting close together, clad in vivid colours, with hanging heads: the gold embroideries of their jackets flashed dazzlingly as they went away gliding on the smooth water, and not one of them looked back once. Before sunset the growling clouds carried with a rush the ridge of hills, and came tumbling down the inner slopes. Everything disappeared; black whirling vapours filled the bay, and in the midst of them the schooner swung here and there in the shifting gusts of wind. A single clap of thunder detonated in the hollow with a violence that seemed capable of bursting into small pieces the ring of high land, and a warm deluge descended. The wind died out. We panted in the close cabin; our faces streamed; the bay outside hissed as if boiling; the water fell in perpendicular shafts as heavy as lead; it swished about the deck, poured off the spars, gurgled, sobbed, splashed, murmured in the blind night. Our lamp burned low. Hollis, stripped to the waist, lay stretched out on the lockers, with closed eyes and motionless like a despoiled corpse; at his head Jackson twanged the guitar, and gasped out in sighs a mournful dirge about hopeless love and eyes like stars. Then we heard startled voices on deck crying in the rain, hurried footsteps overhead, and suddenly Karain appeared in the doorway of the cabin. His bare breast and his face glistened in the light; his sarong, soaked, clung about his legs; he had his sheathed kriss in his left hand; and wisps of wet hair, escaping from under his red kerchief, stuck over his eyes and down his cheeks. He stepped in with a headlong stride and looking over his shoulder like a man pursued. Hollis turned on his side quickly and opened his eyes. Jackson clapped his big hand over the strings and the jingling vibration died suddenly. I stood up.

'We did not hear your boat's hail!' I exclaimed.

'Boat! The man's swum off,' drawled out Hollis from the locker. 'Look at him!'

He breathed heavily, wild-eyed, while we looked at him in silence. Water dripped from him, made a dark pool, and ran crookedly across the cabin floor. We could hear Jackson, who had gone out to drive away our Malay seamen from the doorway of the companion; he swore menacingly in the patter of a heavy shower, and there was a great commotion on deck. The watchmen, scared out of their wits by the glimpse of a shadowy figure leaping over the rail, straight out of the night as it were, had alarmed all hands.

Then Jackson, with glittering drops of water on his hair and beard, came back looking angry, and Hollis, who, being the youngest of us, assumed an indolent superiority, said without stirring, 'Give him a dry sarong – give him mine; it's hanging up in the bathroom.' Karain laid the kriss on the table, hilt inwards, and murmured a few words in a strangled voice.

'What's that?' asked Hollis, who had not heard.

'He apologises for coming in with a weapon in his hands,' I said, dazedly.

'Ceremonious beggar. Tell him we forgive a friend . . . on such a night,' drawled out Hollis. 'What's wrong?'

Karain slipped the dry sarong over his head, dropped the wet one at his feet, and stepped out of it. I pointed to the wooden armchair – his armchair. He sat down very straight, said 'Ha!' in a strong voice; a short shiver shook his broad frame. He looked over his shoulder uneasily, turned as if to speak to us, but only stared in a curious blind manner, and again looked back. Jackson bellowed out, 'Watch well on deck there!' heard a faint answer from above, and reaching out with his foot slammed-to the cabin door.

'All right now,' he said.

Karain's lips moved slightly. A vivid flash of lightning made the two round sternports facing him glimmer like a pair of cruel and phosphorescent eyes. The flame of the lamp seemed to wither into brown dust for an instant, and the looking-glass over the little sideboard leaped out behind his back in a smooth sheet of livid light. The roll of thunder came near, crashed over us; the schooner trembled, and the great voice went on, threatening terribly, into the distance. For less than a minute a furious shower rattled on the decks. Karain looked slowly from face to face, and then the silence became so profound that we all could hear distinctly the two chronometers in my cabin ticking along with unflagging speed against one another.

And we three, strangely moved, could not take our eyes from him. He had become enigmatical and touching, in virtue of that mysterious cause that had driven him through the night and through the thunderstorm to the shelter of the schooner's cuddy. Not one of us doubted that we were looking at a fugitive, incredible as it appeared to us. He was haggard, as though he had not slept for weeks; he had become lean, as though he had not eaten for days. His cheeks were hollow, his eyes sunk, the muscles of his chest and arms twitched slightly as if after an exhausting contest. Of course, it had been a long swim off to the schooner; but his face showed another kind of fatigue, the tormented weariness, the anger and the fear of a struggle against a thought, an idea – against something that cannot be grappled, that never rests – a shadow, a nothing, unconquerable and immortal, that preys upon life. We knew it as though he had shouted it at us. His chest expanded time after time, as if it could not contain the beating of his heart. For a moment he had the power of the possessed – the power to awaken in the beholders wonder, pain, pity, and a fearful near sense of things invisible, of things dark and mute, that surround the loneliness of mankind. His eyes roamed about aimlessly for a moment, then became still. He said with effort – 'I came here . . . I leaped out of my stockade as after a defeat. I ran in the night. The water was black. I left him calling on the edge of black water . . . I left him standing alone on the beach. I swam . . . he called out after me . . . I swam . . .'

He trembled from head to foot, sitting very upright and gazing straight before him. Left whom? Who called? We did not know. We could not understand. I said at all hazards – 'Be firm.'

The sound of my voice seemed to steady him into a sudden rigidity, but otherwise he took no notice. He seemed to listen, to expect something for a moment, then went on – 'He cannot come here – therefore I sought you. You men with white faces who despise the invisible voices. He cannot abide your unbelief and your strength.'

He was silent for a while, then exclaimed softly – 'Oh! the strength of unbelievers!'

'There's no one here but you – and we three,' said Hollis, quietly. He reclined with his head supported on his elbow and did not budge.

'I know,' said Karain. 'He has never followed me here. Was not the wise man ever by my side? But since the old wise man, who knew of my trouble, has died, I have heard the voice every night. I shut myself up – for many days – in the dark. I can hear the sorrowful murmurs of women, the whisper of the wind, of the running waters; the clash of weapons in the hands of faithful men, their footsteps – and his voice! . . . Near . . . So! In my ear! I felt him near . . . His breath passed over my neck. I leaped out without a cry. All about me men slept quietly. I ran to the sea. He ran by my side without footsteps, whispering, whispering old words – whispering into my ear in his old voice. I ran into the sea; I swam off to you, with my kriss between my teeth. I, armed, I fled before a breath – to you. Take me away to your land. The wise old man has died, and with him is gone the power of his words and charms. And I can tell no one. No one. There is no one here faithful enough and wise enough to know. It is only near you, unbelievers, that my trouble fades like a mist under the eye of day.'

He turned to me.

'With you I go!' he cried in a contained voice. 'With you, who know so many of us. I want to leave this land – my people . . . and him – there!'

He pointed a shaking finger at random over his shoulder. It was hard for us to bear the intensity of that undisclosed distress. Hollis stared at him hard. I asked gently – 'Where is the danger?'

'Everywhere outside this place,' he answered, mournfully. 'In every place where I am. He waits for me on the paths, under the trees, in the place where I sleep – everywhere but here.'

He looked round the little cabin, at the painted beams, at the tarnished varnish of bulkheads; he looked round as if appealing to all its shabby strangeness, to the disorderly jumble of unfamiliar things that belong to an inconceivable life of stress, of power, of endeavour, of unbelief – to the strong life of white men, which rolls on irresistible and hard on the edge of outer darkness. He stretched out his arms as if to embrace it and us. We waited. The wind and rain had ceased, and the stillness of the night round the schooner was as dumb and complete as if a dead world had been laid to rest in a grave of clouds. We expected him to speak. The necessity within him tore at his lips. There are those who say that a native will not speak to a white man. Error. No man will speak to his master; but to a wanderer and a friend, to him who does not come to teach or to rule, to him who asks for nothing and accepts all things, words are spoken by the camp-fires, in the shared solitude of the sea, in riverside villages, in resting-places surrounded by forests – words are spoken that take no account of race or colour. One heart speaks – another one listens; and the earth, the sea, the sky, the passing wind and the stirring leaf, hear also the futile tale of the burden of life.

He spoke at last. It is impossible to convey the effect of his story. It is undying, it is but a memory, and its vividness cannot be made clear to another mind any more than the vivid emotions of a dream. One must have seen his infinite splendour, one must have known him before – looked at him then. The wavering gloom of the little cabin; the breathless stillness outside, through which only the lapping of water against the schooner's sides could be heard; Hollis's pale face, with steady dark eyes; the energetic head of

Jackson held up between two big palms, and with the long yellow hair of his beard flowing over the strings of the guitar lying on the table; Karain's upright and motionless pose, his tone – all this made an impression that cannot be forgotten. He faced us across the table. His dark head and bronze torso appeared above the tarnished slab of wood, gleaming and still as if cast in metal. Only his lips moved, and his eyes glowed, went out, blazed again, or stared mournfully. His expressions came straight from his tormented heart. His words sounded low, in a sad murmur as of running water; at times they rang loud like the clash of a war-gong – or trailed slowly like weary travellers – or rushed forward with the speed of fear.

4

This is, imperfectly, what he said – 'It was after the great trouble that broke the alliance of the four states of Wajo. We fought amongst ourselves, and the Dutch watched from afar till we were weary. Then the smoke of their fire-ships was seen at the mouth of our rivers, and their great men came in boats full of soldiers to talk to us of protection and peace. We answered with caution and wisdom, for our villages were burnt, our stockades weak, the people weary, and the weapons blunt. They came and went; there had been much talk, but after they went away everything seemed to be as before, only their ships remained in sight from our coast, and very soon their traders came amongst us under a promise of safety. My brother was a Ruler, and one of those who had given the promise. I was young then, and had fought in the war, and Pata Matara had fought by my side. We had shared hunger, danger, fatigue, and victory. His eyes saw my danger quickly, and twice my arm had preserved his life. It was his destiny. He was my friend. And he was great amongst us – one of those who were near my brother, the ruler. He spoke in council, his courage was great, he was the chief of many villages round the great lake that is in the middle of our country as the heart is in the middle of a man's body. When his sword was carried into a campong in advance of his coming, the maidens whispered wonderingly under the fruit-trees, the rich men consulted together in the shade, and a feast was made ready with rejoicing and songs. He had the favour of the Ruler and the affection of the poor. He loved war, deer hunts, and the charms of women. He was the possessor of jewels, of lucky weapons, and of men's devotion. He was a fierce man; and I had no other friend.

'I was the chief of a stockade at the mouth of the river, and collected tolls for my brother from the passing boats. One day I saw a Dutch trader go up the river. He went up with three boats, and no toll was demanded from him, because the smoke of Dutch warships stood out from the open sea, and we were too weak to forget treaties. He went up under the promise of safety, and my brother gave him protection. He said he came to trade. He listened to our voices, for we are men who speak openly and without fear; he counted the number of our spears, he examined the trees, the running waters, the grasses of the bank, the slopes of our hills. He went up to Matara's country and obtained permission to build a house. He traded and planted. He despised our joys, our thoughts, and our sorrows. His face was red, his hair like flame, and his eyes pale, like a river mist; he moved heavily, and spoke with a deep voice; he laughed aloud like a fool, and knew no courtesy in his speech. He was a big, scornful man, who looked into women's faces and put his hand on the shoulders of free men as though he had been a noble-born chief. We bore with him. Time passed.

'Then Pata Matara's sister fled from the campong and went to live in the Dutchman's house. She was a great and wilful lady: I had seen her once carried high on slaves' shoulders amongst the people, with uncovered face, and I had heard all men say that her beauty was extreme, silencing the reason and ravishing the heart of the beholders. The people were dismayed; Matara's face was blackened with that disgrace, for she knew she had been promised to another man. Matara went to the Dutchman's house, and said, "Give her up to die – she is the daughter of chiefs." The white man refused, and shut himself up, while his servants kept guard night and day with loaded guns. Matara raged. My brother called a council. But the Dutch ships were near, and watched our coast greedily. My brother said, "If he dies now our land will pay for his blood. Leave him alone till we grow stronger and the ships are gone." Matara was wise; he waited and watched. But the white man feared for her life and went away.

'He left his house, his plantations, and his goods! He departed, armed and menacing, and left all – for her! She had ravished his heart! From my stockade I saw him put out to sea in a big boat. Matara and I watched him from the fighting platform behind the pointed stakes. He sat cross-legged, with his gun in his hands, on the roof at the stern of his prau. The barrel of his rifle glinted aslant before his big, red face. The broad river was stretched under him – level, smooth, shining, like a plain of silver; and his prau, looking very short and black from the shore, glided along the silver plain and over into the blue of the sea.

'Thrice Matara, standing by my side, called aloud her name with grief and imprecations. He stirred my heart. It leaped three times; and three times with the eye of my mind I saw in the gloom within the enclosed space of the prau a woman with streaming hair going away from her land and her people. I was angry – and sorry. Why? And then I also cried out insults and threats. Matara said, "Now they have left our land their lives are mine. I shall follow and strike – and, alone, pay the price of blood." A great wind was sweeping

towards the setting sun over the empty river. I cried, "By your side I will go!"
He lowered his head in sign of assent. It was his destiny. The sun had set, and
the trees swayed their boughs with a great noise above our heads.

'On the third night we two left our land together in a trading prau.

'The sea met us – the sea, wide, pathless, and without voice. A sailing prau
leaves no track. We went south. The moon was full; and, looking up, we said
to one another, "When the next moon shines as this one, we shall return
and they will be dead." It was fifteen years ago. Many moons have grown
full and withered, and I have not seen my land since. We sailed south; we
overtook many praus; we examined the creeks and the bays; we saw the end of
our coast, of our island – a steep cape over a disturbed strait, where drift the
shadows of shipwrecked praus and drowned men clamour in the night. The
wide sea was all round us now. We saw a great mountain burning in the midst
of water; we saw thousands of islets scattered like bits of iron fired from a big
gun; we saw a long coast of mountain and lowlands stretching away in
sunshine from west to east. It was Java. We said, "They are there; their time
is near, and we shall return or die cleansed from dishonour."

'We landed. Is there anything good in that country? The paths run
straight and hard and dusty. Stone campongs, full of white faces, are
surrounded by fertile fields, but every man you meet is a slave. The rulers live
under the edge of a foreign sword. We ascended mountains, we traversed
valleys; at sunset we entered villages. We asked everyone, 'Have you seen
such a white man?' Some stared; others laughed; women gave us food,
sometimes, with fear and respect, as though we had been distracted by the
visitation of God; but some did not understand our language, and some
cursed us, or, yawning, asked with contempt the reason of our quest. Once, as
we were going away, an old man called after us, "Desist!"

'We went on. Concealing our weapons, we stood humbly aside before the
horsemen on the road; we bowed low in the courtyards of chiefs who were no
better than slaves. We lost ourselves in the fields, in the jungle; and one
night, in a tangled forest, we came upon a place where crumbling old walls
had fallen amongst the trees, and where strange stone idols – carved images
of devils with many arms and legs, with snakes twined round their bodies,
with twenty heads and holding a hundred swords – seemed to live and
threaten in the light of our camp-fire. Nothing dismayed us. And on the
road, by every fire, in resting-places, we always talked of her and of him.
Their time was near. We spoke of nothing else. No! not of hunger, thirst,
weariness, and faltering hearts. No! we spoke of him and her! Of her! And
we thought of them – of her! Matara brooded by the fire. I sat and thought
and thought, till suddenly I could see again the image of a woman, beautiful,
and young, and great, and proud, and tender, going away from her land and
her people. Matara said, "When we find them we shall kill her first to cleanse
the dishonour – then the man must die." I would say, "It shall be so; it is your
vengeance." He stared long at me with his big sunken eyes.

'We came back to the coast. Our feet were bleeding, our bodies thin. We slept in rags under the shadow of stone enclosures; we prowled, soiled and lean, about the gateways of white men's courtyards. Their hairy dogs barked at us, and their servants shouted from afar, "Begone!" Low-born wretches, that keep watch over the streets of stone campongs, asked us who we were. We lied, we cringed, we smiled with hate in our hearts, and we kept looking here, looking there, for them – for the white man with hair like flame, and for her, for the woman who had broken faith, and therefore must die. We looked. At last in every woman's face I thought I could see hers. We ran swiftly. No! Sometimes Matara would whisper, "Here is the man," and we waited, crouching. He came near. It was not the man – those Dutchmen are all alike. We suffered the anguish of deception. In my sleep I saw her face, and was both joyful and sorry . . . Why? . . . I seemed to hear a whisper near me. I turned swiftly. She was not there! And as we trudged wearily from stone city to stone city I seemed to hear a light footstep near me. A time came when I heard it always, and I was glad. I thought, walking dizzy and weary in sunshine on the hard paths of white men – I thought, She is there – with us! . . . Matara was sombre. We were often hungry.

'We sold the carved sheaths of our krisses – the ivory sheaths with golden ferules. We sold the jewelled hilts. But we kept the blades – for them. The blades that never touch but kill – we kept the blades for her . . . Why? She was always by our side . . . We starved. We begged. We left Java at last.

'We went West, we went East. We saw many lances, crowds of strange faces, men that live in trees and men who eat their old people. We cut rattans in the forest for a handful of rice, and for a living swept the decks of big ships and heard curses heaped upon our heads. We toiled in villages; we wandered upon the seas with the Bajow people, who have no country. We fought for pay; we hired ourselves to work for Goram men, and were cheated; and under the orders of rough white-faces we dived for pearls in barren bays, dotted with black rocks, upon a coast of sand and desolation. And everywhere we watched, we listened, we asked. We asked traders, robbers, white men. We heard jeers, mockery, threats – words of wonder and words of contempt. We never knew rest; we never thought of home, for our work was not done. A year passed, then another. I ceased to count the number of nights, of moons, of years. I watched over Matara. He had my last handful of rice; if there was water enough for one he drank it; I covered him up when he shivered with cold; and when the hot sickness came upon him I sat sleepless through many nights and fanned his face. He was a fierce man, and my friend. He spoke of her with fury in the daytime, with sorrow in the dark; he remembered her in health, in sickness. I said nothing; but I saw her every day always! At first I saw only her head, as of a woman walking in the low mist on a river bank. Then she sat by our fire. I saw her! I looked at her! She had tender eyes and a ravishing face. I murmured to her in the night. Matara said sleepily sometimes, "To whom are you talking? Who is there?" I answered quickly, "No one" . . . It was a lie! She never left me. She shared the warmth of our fire, she sat on my couch of leaves, she swam on the sea to follow me . . . I saw her! . . . I tell you I saw her long black hair spread behind her upon the moonlit water as she struck out with bare arms by the side of a swift prau. She was beautiful, she was faithful, and in the silence of foreign countries she spoke to me very low in the language of my people. No one saw her; no one heard her; she was mine only! In daylight she moved with a swaying walk before me upon the weary paths; her figure was straight and flexible like the stem of a slender tree; the heels of her feet were round and polished like shells of eggs; with her round arm she made signs. At night she looked into my face. And she was sad! Her eyes were tender and frightened; her voice soft and pleading. Once I murmured to her, "You shall not die," and she smiled . . . ever after she smiled! . . . She gave me courage to bear weariness and hardships. Those were times of pain, and she soothed me. We wandered patient in our search. We knew deception, false hopes; we knew captivity, sickness, thirst, misery, despair . . . Enough! We found them! . . . '

He cried out the last words and paused. His face was impassive, and he kept still like a man in a trance. Hollis sat up quickly, and spread his elbows on the table. Jackson made a brusque movement, and accidentally touched the guitar. A plaintive resonance filled the cabin with confused vibrations and died out slowly. Then Karain began to speak again. The restrained fierceness of his tone seemed to rise like a voice from outside, like a thing unspoken but heard; it filled the cabin and enveloped in its intense and deadened murmur the motionless figure in the chair.

'We were on our way to Atjeh, where there was war; but the vessel ran on a sandbank, and we had to land in Delli. We had earned a little money, and had bought a gun from some Selangore traders; only one gun, which was fired by the spark of a stone: Matara carried it. We landed. Many white men lived there, planting tobacco on conquered plains, and Matara . . . But no matter. He saw him! . . . The Dutchman! . . . At last! . . . We crept and watched. Two nights and a day we watched. He had a house – a big house in a clearing in the midst of his fields; flowers and bushes grew around; there were narrow paths of yellow earth between the cut grass, and thick hedges to keep people out. The third night we came armed, and lay behind a hedge.

'A heavy dew seemed to soak through our flesh and made our very entrails cold. The grass, the twigs, the leaves, covered with drops of water, were grey in the moonlight. Matara, curled up in the grass, shivered in his sleep. My teeth rattled in my head so loud that I was afraid the noise would wake up all the land. Afar, the watchmen of white men's houses struck wooden clappers and hooted in the darkness. And, as every night, I saw her by my side. She smiled no more! . . . The fire of anguish burned in my breast, and she whispered to me with compassion, with pity, softly – as women will; she soothed the pain of my mind; she bent her face over me – the face of a woman who ravishes the hearts and silences the reason of men. She was all mine, and no one could see her – no one of living mankind! Stars shone through her bosom, through her floating hair. I was overcome with regret, with tenderness, with sorrow. Matara slept . . . Had I slept? Matara was shaking me by the shoulder, and the fire of the sun was drying the grass, the bushes, the leaves. It was day. Shreds of white mist hung between the branches of trees.

'Was it night or day? I saw nothing again till I heard Matara breathe quickly where he lay, and then outside the house I saw her. I saw them both. They had come out. She sat on a bench under the wall, and twigs laden with flowers crept high above her head, hung over her hair. She had a box on her lap, and gazed into it, counting the increase of her pearls. The Dutchman stood by looking on; he smiled down at her; his white teeth flashed; the hair on his lip was like two twisted flames. He was big and fat, and joyous, and without fear. Matara tipped fresh priming from the hollow of his palm, scraped the flint with his thumb-nail, and gave the gun to me. To me! I took it . . . O fate!

'He whispered into my ear, lying on his stomach, "I shall creep close and then amok . . . let her die by my hand. You take aim at the fat swine there. Let him see me strike my shame off the face of the earth – and then . . . you are my friend – kill with a sure shot." I said nothing; there was no air in my chest – there was no air in the world. Matara had gone suddenly from my side. The grass nodded. Then a bush rustled. She lifted her head.

'I saw her! The consoler of sleepless nights, of weary days; the companion of troubled years! I saw her! She looked straight at the place where I crouched. She was there as I had seen her for years – a faithful wanderer by my side. She looked with sad eyes and had smiling lips; she looked at me . . . Smiling lips! Had I not promised that she should not die!

'She was far off and I felt her near. Her touch caressed me, and her voice murmured, whispered above me, around me, "Who shall be thy companion, who shall console thee if I die?" I saw a flowering thicket to the left of her stir a little . . . Matara was ready . . . I cried aloud – "Return!"

'She leaped up; the box fell; the pearls streamed at her feet. The big Dutchman by her side rolled menacing eyes through the still sunshine. The gun went up to my shoulder. I was kneeling and I was firm – firmer than the trees, the rocks, the mountains. But in front of the steady long barrel the fields, the house, the earth, the sky swayed to and fro like shadows in a forest on a windy day. Matara burst out of the thicket; before him the petals of torn flowers whirled high as if driven by a tempest. I heard her cry; I saw her spring with open arms in front of the white man. She was a woman of my country and of noble blood. They are so! I heard her shriek of anguish and fear – and all stood still! The fields, the house, the earth, the sky stood still – while Matara leaped at her with uplifted arm. I pulled the trigger, saw a spark, heard nothing; the smoke drove back into my face, and then I could see Matara roll over head first and lie with stretched arms at her feet. Ha! A sure shot! The sunshine fell on my back colder than the running water. A sure shot! I flung the gun after the shot. Those two stood over the dead man as though they had been bewitched by a charm. I shouted at her, "Live and remember!" Then for a time I stumbled about in a cold darkness.

'Behind me there were great shouts, the running of many feet; strange men surrounded me, cried meaningless words into my face, pushed me, dragged me, supported me . . . I stood before the big Dutchman: he stared as if bereft of his reason. He wanted to know, he talked fast, he spoke of gratitude, he offered me food, shelter, gold – he asked many questions. I laughed in his face. I said, "I am a Korinchi traveller from Perak over there, and know nothing of that dead man. I was passing along the path when I heard a shot, and your senseless people rushed out and dragged me here." He lifted his arms, he wondered, he could not believe, he could not understand, he clamoured in his own tongue! She had her arms clasped round his neck, and over her shoulder stared back at me with wide eyes. I smiled and looked at her; I smiled and waited to hear the sound of her voice. The white man asked her suddenly, "Do you know him?" I listened – my life was in my ears! She looked at me long, she looked at me with unflinching eyes, and said aloud, "No! I never saw him before." . . . What! Never before? Had she forgotten already? Was it possible? Forgotten already – after so many years – so many years of wandering, of companionship, of trouble, of tender words! Forgotten already! . . . I tore myself out from the hands that held me and went away without a word . . . They let me go.

'I was weary. Did I sleep? I do not know. I remember walking upon a broad path under a clear starlight; and that strange country seemed so big, the rice-fields so vast, that, as I looked around, my head swam with the fear of space. Then I saw a forest. The joyous starlight was heavy upon me. I turned off the path and entered the forest, which was very sombre and very sad.'

5

Karain's tone had been getting lower and lower, as though he had been going away from us, till the last words sounded faint but clear, as if shouted on a calm day from a very great distance. He moved not. He stared fixedly past the motionless head of Hollis, who faced him, as still as himself. Jackson had turned sideways, and with elbow on the table shaded his eyes with the palm of his hand. And I looked on, surprised and moved; I looked at that man, loyal to a vision, betrayed by his dream, spurned by his illusion, and coming to us unbelievers for help – against a thought. The silence was profound; but it seemed full of noiseless phantoms, of things sorrowful, shadowy, and mute, in whose invisible presence the firm, pulsating beat of the two ship's chronometers ticking off steadily the seconds of Greenwich Time seemed to me a protection and a relief. Karain stared stonily; and looking at his rigid figure, I thought of his wanderings, of that obscure odyssey of revenge, of all the men that wander amongst illusions; of the illusions as restless as men; of the illusions faithful, faithless; of the illusions that give joy, that give sorrow, that give pain, that give peace; of the invincible illusions that can make life and death appear serene, inspiring, tormented, or ignoble.

A murmur was heard; that voice from outside seemed to flow out of a dreaming world into the lamplight of the cabin. Karain was speaking.

'I lived in the forest.

'She came no more. Never! Never once! I lived alone. She had forgotten. It was well. I did not want her; I wanted no one. I found an abandoned house in an old clearing. Nobody came near. Sometimes I heard in the distance the voices of people going along a path. I slept; I rested; there was wild rice, water from a running stream and peace! Every night I sat alone by my small fire before the hut. Many nights passed over my head.

'Then, one evening, as I sat by my fire after having eaten, I looked down on the ground and began to remember my wanderings. I lifted my head. I had heard no sound, no rustle, no footsteps – but I lifted my head. A man was coming towards me across the small clearing. I waited. He came up without a greeting and squatted down into the firelight. Then he turned his face to me. It was Matara. He stared at me fiercely with his big sunken eyes. The night was cold; the heat died suddenly out of the fire, and he stared at me. I rose and went away from there, leaving him by the fire that had no heat.

'I walked all that night, all next day, and in the evening made up a big blaze and sat down to wait for him. He did not come into the light. I heard him in the bushes here and there, whispering, whispering. I understood at last – I had heard the words before, "You are my friend – kill with a sure shot."

'I bore it as long as I could then leaped away, as on this very night I leaped from my stockade and swam to you. I ran – I ran crying like a child left alone and far from the houses. He ran by my side, without footsteps, whispering, whispering – invisible and heard. I sought people – I wanted men around me! Men who had not died! And again we two wandered. I sought danger, violence and death. I fought in the Atjeh war, and a brave people wondered at the valiance of a stranger. But we were two; he warded off the blows . . . Why? I wanted peace, not life. And no one could see him; no one knew – I dared tell no one. At times he would leave me, but not for long; then he would return and whisper or stare. My heart was torn with a strange fear, but could not die. Then I met an old man.

'You all knew him. People here called him my sorcerer, my servant and sword-bearer; but to me he was father, mother, protection, refuge, and peace. When I met him he was returning from a pilgrimage, and I heard him intoning the prayer of sunset. He had gone to the holy place with his son, his son's wife, and a little child; and on their return, by the favour of the Most High, they all died: the strong man, the young mother, the little child – they died; and the old man reached his country alone. He was a pilgrim serene and pious, very wise and very lonely. I told him all. For a time we lived together. He said over me words of compassion, of wisdom, of prayer. He warded from me the shade of the dead. I begged him for a charm that would make me safe. For a long time he refused; but at last, with a sigh and a smile, he gave me one. Doubtless he could command a spirit stronger than the unrest of my dead friend, and again I had peace; but I had become restless, and a lover of turmoil and danger. The old man never left me. We travelled together. We were welcomed by the great; his wisdom and my courage are remembered where your strength, O white men, is forgotten! We served the Sultan of Sula. We fought the Spaniards. There were victories, hopes, defeats, sorrow, blood, women's tears . . . What for? . . . We fled. We collected wanderers of a warlike race and came here to fight again. The rest you know. I am the ruler of a conquered land, a lover of war and danger, a fighter and a plotter. But the old man has died, and I am again the slave of the dead. He is not here now to drive away the reproachful shade – to silence the lifeless voice! The power of his charm has died with him. And I know fear; and I hear the whisper, "Kill! kill! kill!" . . . Have I not killed enough? . . . '

For the first time that night a sudden convulsion of madness and rage passed over his face. His wavering glances darted here and there like scared birds in a thunderstorm. He jumped up, shouting – 'By the spirits that drink blood: by the spirits that cry in the night: by all the spirits of fury, misfortune, and death, I swear some day I will strike into every heart I meet – I . . . '

He looked so dangerous that we all three leaped to our feet, and Hollis, with the back of his hand, sent the kriss flying off the table. I believe we shouted together. It was a short scare, and the next moment he was again composed in his chair, with three white men standing over him in rather foolish attitudes. We felt a little ashamed of ourselves. Jackson picked up the kriss, and, after an enquiring glance at me, gave it to him. He received it with a stately inclination of the head and stuck it in the twist of his sarong, with punctilious care to give his weapon a pacific position. Then he looked up at us with an austere smile. We were abashed and reproved. Hollis sat sideways on the table and, holding his chin in his hand, scrutinised him in pensive silence. I said – 'You must abide with your people. They need you. And there is forgetfulness in life. Even the dead cease to speak in time.'

'Am I a woman, to forget long years before an eyelid has had the time to beat twice?' he exclaimed, with bitter resentment. He startled me. It was amazing. To him his life – that cruel mirage of love and peace – seemed as real, as undeniable, as theirs would be to any saint, philosopher, or fool of us all. Hollis muttered – 'You won't soothe him with your platitudes.'

Karain spoke to me.

'You know us. You have lived with us. Why? – we cannot know; but you understand our sorrows and thoughts. You have lived with my people, and you understand our desires and our fears. With you I will go. To your land – to your people. To your people, who live in unbelief; to whom day is day and night is night – nothing more, because you understand all things seen, and despise all else! To your land of unbelief, where the dead do not speak, where every man is wise, and alone – and at peace!'

'Capital description,' murmured Hollis, with the flicker of a smile.

Karain hung his head.

'I can toil, and fight – and be faithful,' he whispered, in a weary tone, 'but I cannot go back to him who waits for me on the shore. No! Take me with you . . . Or else give me some of your strength – of your unbelief . . . A charm! . . .'

He seemed utterly exhausted.

'Yes, take him home,' said Hollis, very low, as if debating with himself. 'That would be one way. The ghosts there are in society, and talk affably to ladies and gentlemen, but would scorn a naked human being – like our princely friend . . . Naked . . . Flayed! I should say. I am sorry for him. Impossible – of course. The end of all this shall be,' he went on, looking up at us – 'the end of this shall be, that some day he will run amok amongst his faithful subjects and send *ad patres* ever so many of them before they make up their minds to the disloyalty of knocking him on the head.'

I nodded. I thought it more than probable that such would be the end of Karain. It was evident that he had been hunted by his thought along the very limit of human endurance, and very little more pressing was needed to make him swerve over into the form of madness peculiar to his race. The respite he had had during the old man's life made the return of the torment unbearable. That much was clear.

He lifted his head suddenly; we had imagined for a moment that he had been dozing.

'Give me your protection – or your strength!' he cried. 'A charm . . . a weapon!'

Again his chin fell on his breast. We looked at him, then looked at one another with suspicious awe in our eyes, like men who come unexpectedly upon the scene of some mysterious disaster. He had given himself up to us; he had thrust into our hands his errors and his torment, his life and his peace; and we did not know what to do with that problem from the outer darkness. We three white men, looking at that Malay, could not find one word to the purpose amongst us – if indeed there existed a word that could solve that problem. We pondered, and our hearts sank. We felt as though we three had been called to the very gate of Infernal Regions to judge, to decide the fate of a wanderer coming suddenly from a world of sunshine and illusions.

'By Jove, he seems to have a great idea of our power,' whispered Hollis, hopelessly. And then again there was a silence, the feeble plash of water, the steady tick of chronometers. Jackson, with bare arms crossed, leaned his shoulders against the bulkhead of the cabin. He was bending his head under the deck beam, his fair beard spread out magnificently over his chest; he looked colossal, ineffectual, and mild. There was something lugubrious in the aspect of the cabin; the air in it seemed to become slowly charged with the cruel chill of helplessness, with the pitiless anger of egoism against the incomprehensible form of an intruding pain. We had no idea what to do; we began to resent bitterly the hard necessity to get rid of him.

Hollis mused, muttered suddenly with a short laugh, 'Strength . . . Protection. . . Charm.' He slipped off the table and left the cuddy without a look at us. It seemed a base desertion. Jackson and I exchanged indignant glances. We could hear him rummaging in his pigeon-hole of a cabin. Was the fellow actually going to bed? Karain sighed. It was intolerable!

Then Hollis reappeared, holding in both hands a small leather box. He put it down gently on the table and looked at us with a queer gasp, we thought, as though he had from some cause become speechless for a moment, or were ethically uncertain about producing that box. But in an instant the insolent and unerring wisdom of his youth gave him the needed courage. He said, as he unlocked the box with a very small key, 'Look as solemn as you can, you fellows.'

Probably we looked only surprised and stupid, for he glanced over his shoulder, and said angrily – 'This is no play; I am going to do something for him. Look serious. Confound it! . . . Can't you lie a little . . . for a friend!'

Karain seemed to take no notice of us, but when Hollis threw open the lid of the box his eyes flew to it – and so did ours. The quilted crimson satin of the inside put a violent patch of colour into the sombre atmosphere; it was something positive to look at – it was fascinating.

6

Hollis looked smiling into the box. He had lately made a dash home through the Canal. He had been away six months, and only joined us again just in time for this last trip. We had never seen the box before. His hands hovered above it; and he talked to us ironically, but his face became as grave as though he were pronouncing a powerful incantation over the things inside.

'Every one of us,' he said, with pauses that somehow were more offensive than his words – 'every one of us, you'll admit, has been haunted by some woman . . . And . . . as to friends . . . dropped by the way . . . Well! . . . ask yourselves . . .'

He paused. Karain stared. A deep rumble was heard high up under the deck. Jackson spoke seriously – 'Don't be so beastly cynical.'

'Ah! You are without guile,' said Hollis, sadly. 'You will learn . . . Meantime this Malay has been our friend . . .'

He repeated several times thoughtfully, 'Friend . . . Malay. Friend, Malay,' as though weighing the words against one another, then went on more briskly – 'A good fellow – a gentleman in his way. We can't, so to speak, turn our backs on his confidence and belief in us. Those Malays are easily impressed – all nerves, you know – therefore . . .

He turned to me sharply.

'You know him best,' he said, in a practical tone. 'Do you think he is fanatical – I mean very strict in his faith?'

I stammered in profound amazement that 'I did not think so.'

'It's on account of its being a likeness – an engraved image,' muttered Hollis, enigmatically, turning to the box. He plunged his fingers into it. Karain's lips were parted and his eyes shone. We looked into the box.

There were there a couple of reels of cotton, a packet of needles, a bit of silk ribbon, dark blue; a cabinet photograph, at which Hollis stole a glance before laying it on the table face downwards. A girl's portrait, I could see. There were, amongst a lot of various small objects, a bunch of flowers, a narrow white glove with many buttons, a slim packet of letters carefully tied up. Amulets of white men! Charms and talismans! Charms that keep them straight, that drive them crooked, that have the power to make a young man sigh, an old man smile. Potent things that procure dreams of joy, thoughts of regret; that soften hard hearts, and can temper a soft one to the hardness of steel. Gifts of heaven – things of earth.

Hollis rummaged in the box.

And it seemed to me, during that moment of waiting, that the cabin of the schooner was becoming filled with a stir invisible and living as of subtle breaths. All the ghosts driven out of the unbelieving West by men who pretend to be wise and alone and at peace – all the homeless ghosts of an unbelieving world – appeared suddenly round the figure of Hollis bending over the box; all the exiled and charming shades of loved women; all the beautiful and tender ghosts of ideals, remembered, forgotten, cherished, execrated; all the cast-out and reproachful ghosts of friends admired, trusted, traduced, betrayed, left dead by the way – they all seemed to come from the inhospitable regions of the earth to crowd into the gloomy cabin, as though it had been a refuge and, in all the unbelieving world, the only place of avenging belief . . . It lasted a second – all disappeared. Hollis was facing us alone with something small that glittered between his fingers. It looked like a coin.

'Ah! here it is,' he said.

He held it up. It was a sixpence – a Jubilee sixpence. It was gilt; it had a hole punched near the rim. Hollis looked towards Karain.

'A charm for our friend,' he said to us. 'The thing itself is of great power – money, you know – and his imagination is struck. A loyal vagabond; if only his puritanism doesn't shy at a likeness . . .'

We said nothing. We did not know whether to be scandalised, amused, or relieved. Hollis advanced towards Karain, who stood up as if startled, and then, holding the coin up, spoke in Malay.

'This is the image of the Great Queen, and the most powerful thing the white men know,' he said, solemnly.

Karain covered the handle of his kriss in sign of respect, and stared at the crowned head.

'The Invincible, the Pious,' he muttered.

'She is more powerful than Suleiman the Wise, who commanded the genii, as you know,' said Hollis, gravely. 'I shall give this to you.'

He held the sixpence in the palm of his hand, and looking at it thoughtfully, spoke to us in English.

'She commands a spirit, too – the spirit of her nation; a masterful, conscientious, unscrupulous, unconquerable devil . . . that does a lot of good – incidentally . . . a lot of good . . . at times – and wouldn't stand any fuss from the best ghost out for such a little thing as our friend's shot. Don't look thunderstruck, you fellows. Help me to make him believe – everything's in that.'

'His people will be shocked,' I murmured.

Hollis looked fixedly at Karain, who was the incarnation of the very essence of still excitement. He stood rigid, with head thrown back; his eyes rolled wildly, flashing; the dilated nostrils quivered.

'Hang it all!' said Hollis at last, 'he is a good fellow. I'll give him something that I shall really miss.'

He took the ribbon out of the box, smiled at it scornfully, then with a pair of scissors cut out a piece from the palm of the glove.

'I shall make him a thing like those Italian peasants wear, you know.'

He sewed the coin in the delicate leather, sewed the leather to the ribbon, tied the ends together. He worked with haste. Karain watched his fingers all the time.

'Now then,' he said – then stepped up to Karain. They looked close into one another's eyes. Those of Karain stared in a lost glance, but Hollis's seemed to grow darker and looked out masterful and compelling. They were in violent contrast together – one motionless and the colour of bronze, the other dazzling white and lifting his arms, where the powerful muscles rolled slightly under a skin that gleamed like satin. Jackson moved near with the air of a man closing up to a chum in a tight place. I said impressively, pointing to Hollis – 'He is young, but he is wise. Believe him!'

Karain bent his head: Hollis threw lightly over it the dark-blue ribbon and stepped back.

'Forget, and be at peace!' I cried.

Karain seemed to wake up from a dream. He said, 'Ha!' shook himself as if throwing off a burden. He looked round with assurance. Someone on deck dragged off the skylight cover, and a flood of light fell into the cabin. It was morning already.

'Time to go on deck,' said Jackson.

Hollis put on a coat, and we went up, Karain leading.

The sun had risen beyond the hills, and their long shadows stretched far over the bay in the pearly light. The air was clear, stainless, and cool. I pointed at the curved line of yellow sands.

'He is not there,' I said, emphatically, to Karain. 'He waits no more. He has departed for ever.'

A shaft of bright hot rays darted into the bay between the summits of two hills, and the water all round broke out as if by magic into a dazzling sparkle.

'No! He is not there waiting,' said Karain, after a long look over the beach. 'I do not hear him,' he went on, slowly. 'No!'

He turned to us.

'He has departed again – for ever!' he cried.

We assented vigorously, repeatedly, and without compunction. The great thing was to impress him powerfully; to suggest absolute safety – the end of all trouble. We did our best; and I hope we affirmed our faith in the power of Hollis's charm efficiently enough to put the matter beyond the shadow of a doubt. Our voices rang around him joyously in the still air, and above his head the sky, pellucid, pure, stainless, arched its tender blue from shore to shore and over the bay, as if to envelop the water, the earth, and the man in the caress of its light.

The anchor was up, the sails hung still, and half a dozen big boats were seen sweeping over the bay to give us a tow out. The paddlers in the first one that came alongside lifted their heads and saw their ruler standing amongst us. A low murmur of surprise arose then a shout of greeting.

He left us, and seemed straightway to step into the glorious splendour of his stage, to wrap himself in the illusion of unavoidable success. For a moment he stood erect, one foot over the gangway, one hand on the hilt of his kriss, in a martial pose; and, relieved from the fear of outer darkness, he held his head high, he swept a serene look over his conquered foothold on the earth. The boats far off took up the cry of greeting; a great clamour rolled on the water; the hills echoed it, and seemed to toss back at him the words invoking life and victories.

He descended into a canoe, and as soon as he was clear of the side we gave him three cheers. They sounded faint and orderly after the wild tumult of his loyal subjects, but it was the best we could do. He stood up in the boat, lifted up both his arms, then pointed to the infallible charm. We cheered again; and the Malays in the boats stared – very much puzzled and impressed. I wonder what they thought; what he thought . . . what the reader thinks?

We towed out slowly. We saw him land and watch us from the beach.

A figure approached him humbly but openly – not at all like a ghost with a grievance. We could see other men running towards him. Perhaps he had been missed? At any rate there was a great stir. A group formed itself rapidly near him, and he walked along the sands, followed by a growing *cortège*, and kept nearly abreast of the schooner. With our glasses we could see the blue ribbon on his neck and a patch of white on his brown chest. The bay was waking up. The smoke of morning fires stood in faint spirals higher than the heads of palms; people moved between the houses; a herd of buffaloes galloped clumsily across a green slope; the slender figures of boys brandishing sticks appeared black and leaping in the long grass; a coloured line of women, with water bamboos on their heads, moved swaying through a thin grove of fruit-trees. Karain stopped in the midst of his men and waved his hand; then, detaching himself from the splendid group, walked alone to the water's edge and waved his hand again. The schooner passed out to sea between the steep headlands that shut in the bay, and at the same instant Karain passed out of our life for ever.

But the memory remains. Some years afterwards I met Jackson, in the Strand. He was magnificent as ever. His head was high above the crowd. His beard was gold, his face red, his eyes blue; he had a wide-brimmed grey hat and no collar or waistcoat; he was inspiring; he had just come home – had landed that very day! Our meeting caused an eddy in the current of humanity. Hurried people would run against us, then walk round us, and turn back to look at that giant. We tried to compress seven years of life into seven exclamations; then, suddenly appeased, walked sedately along, giving one another the news of yesterday. Jackson gazed about him, like a man who looks for landmarks, then stopped before Bland's window. He always had a passion for firearms; so he stopped short and contemplated the row of weapons, perfect and severe, drawn up in a line behind the black-framed panes. I stood by his side. Suddenly he said – 'Do you remember Karain?'

I nodded.

'The sight of all this made me think of him,' he went on, with his face near the glass . . . and I could see another man, powerful and bearded, peering at him intently from amongst the dark and polished tubes that can cure so many illusions. 'Yes; it made me think of him,' he continued, slowly. 'I saw a paper this morning; they are fighting over there again. He's sure to be in it. He will make it hot for the caballeros. Well, good luck to him, poor devil! He was perfectly stunning.'

We walked on.

'I wonder whether the charm worked – you remember Hollis's charm, of course. If it did . . . never was a sixpence wasted to better advantage! Poor devil! I wonder whether he got rid of that friend of his. Hope so . . . Do you know, I sometimes think that –'

I stood still and looked at him.

'Yes . . . I mean, whether the thing was so, you know . . . whether it really happened to him . . . What do you think?'

'My dear chap,' I cried, 'you have been too long away from home. What a question to ask! Only look at all this.'

A watery gleam of sunshine flashed from the west and went out between two long lines of walls; and then the broken confusion of roofs, the chimney-stacks, the gold letters sprawling over the fronts of houses, the sombre polish of windows, stood resigned and sullen under the falling gloom. The whole length of the street, deep as a well and narrow like a corridor, was full of a sombre and ceaseless stir. Our ears were filled by a headlong shuffle and beat of rapid footsteps and an underlying rumour – a rumour vast, faint, pulsating, as of panting breaths, of beating hearts, of gasping voices. Innumerable eyes stared straight in front, feet moved hurriedly, blank faces flowed, arms swung. Over all, a narrow ragged strip of smoky sky wound about between the high roofs, extended and motionless, like a soiled streamer flying above the rout of a mob.

'Ye–e–e–s,' said Jackson, meditatively.

The big wheels of hansoms turned slowly along the edge of side-walks; a pale-faced youth strolled, overcome by weariness, by the side of his stick and with the tails of his overcoat flapping gently near his heels; horses stepped gingerly on the greasy pavement, tossing their heads; two young girls passed by, talking vivaciously and with shining eyes; a fine old fellow strutted, red-faced, stroking a white moustache; and a line of yellow boards with blue letters on them approached us slowly, tossing on high behind one another like some queer wreckage adrift upon a river of hats.

'Ye–e–es,' repeated Jackson. His clear blue eyes looked about, con-temptuous, amused and hard, like the eyes of a boy. A clumsy string of red, yellow, and green omnibuses rolled swaying, monstrous and gaudy; two shabby children ran across the road; a knot of dirty men with red neckerchiefs round their bare throats lurched along, discussing filthily; a ragged old man with a face of despair yelled horribly in the mud the name of a paper; while far off, amongst the tossing heads of horses, the dull flash of harnesses, the jumble of lustrous panels and roofs of carriages, we could see a policeman, helmeted and dark, stretching out a rigid arm at the crossing of the streets.

'Yes; I see it,' said Jackson, slowly. 'It is there; it pants, it runs, it rolls; it is strong and alive; it would smash you if you didn't look out; but I'll be hanged if it is yet as real to me as . . . as the other thing . . . say, Karain's story.'

I think that, decidedly, he had been too long away from home.

1897

YOUTH: A NARRATIVE

This could have occurred nowhere but in England, where men and sea interpenetrate, so to speak – the sea entering into the life of most men, and the men knowing something or everything about the sea, in the way of amusement, of travel, or of bread-winning.

We were sitting round a mahogany table that reflected the bottle, the claret-glasses, and our faces as we leaned on our elbows. There was a director of companies, an accountant, a lawyer, Marlow, and myself. The director had been a *Conway* boy, the accountant had served four years at sea, the lawyer – a fine crusted Tory, High Churchman, the best of old fellows, the soul of honour – had been chief officer in the P. & O. service in the good old days when mail-boats were square-rigged at least on two masts, and used to come down the China Sea before a fair monsoon with stun'-sails set alow and aloft. We all began life in the merchant service. Between the five of us there was the strong bond of the sea, and also the fellowship of the craft, which no amount of enthusiasm for yachting, cruising, and so on can give, since one is only the amusement of life and the other is life itself.

Marlow (at least I think that is how he spelt his name) told the story, or rather the chronicle, of a voyage: 'Yes, I have seen a little of the Eastern seas; but what I remember best is my first voyage there. You fellows know there are those voyages that seem ordered for the illustration of life, that might stand for a symbol of existence. You fight, work, sweat, nearly kill yourself, sometimes do kill yourself, trying to accomplish something – and you can't. Not from any fault of yours. You simply can do nothing, neither great nor little – not a thing in the world – not even marry an old maid, or get a wretched 600-ton cargo of coal to its port of destination.

'It was altogether a memorable affair. It was my first voyage to the East, and my first voyage as second mate; it was also my skipper's first command. You'll admit it was time. He was sixty if a day; a little man, with a broad, not very straight back, with bowed shoulders and one leg more bandy than the other, he had that queer twisted-about appearance you see so often in men who work in the fields. He had a nut-cracker face – chin and nose trying to come together over a sunken mouth – and it was framed in iron-grey fluffy hair, that looked like a chin-strap of cotton-wool sprinkled with coal-dust. And he had blue eyes in that old face of his, which were amazingly like a boy's, with that candid expression some quite common men preserve to the end of their days by a rare internal gift of simplicity of heart and rectitude of soul.

What induced him to accept me was a wonder. I had come out of a crack Australian clipper, where I had been third officer, and he seemed to have a prejudice against crack clippers as aristocratic and high-toned. He said to me, "You know, in this ship you will have to work." I said I had to work in every ship I had ever been in. "Ah, but this is different, and you gentlemen out of them big ships; . . . but there! I dare say you will do. Join tomorrow."

'I joined tomorrow. It was twenty-two years ago; and I was just twenty. How time passes! It was one of the happiest days of my life. Fancy! Second mate for the first time – a really responsible officer! I wouldn't have thrown up my new billet for a fortune. The mate looked me over carefully. He was also an old chap, but of another stamp. He had a Roman nose, a snow-white, long beard, and his name was Mahon, but he insisted that it should be pronounced Mann. He was well connected; yet there was something wrong with his luck, and he had never got on.

'As to the captain, he had been for years in coasters, then in the Mediterranean, and last in the West Indian trade. He had never been round the Capes. He could just write a kind of sketchy hand, and didn't care for writing at all. Both were thorough good seamen of course, and between those two old chaps I felt like a small boy between two grandfathers.

'The ship also was old. Her name was the *Judea*. Queer name, isn't it? She belonged to a man Wilmer, Wilcox – some name like that; but he has been bankrupt and dead these twenty years or more, and his name don't matter. She had been laid up in Shadwell basin for ever so long. You may imagine her state. She was all rust, dust, grime – soot aloft, dirt on deck. To me it was like coming out of a palace into a ruined cottage. She was about 400 tons, had a primitive windlass, wooden latches to the doors, not a bit of brass about her, and a big square stern. There was on it, below her name in big letters, a lot of scrollwork, with the gilt off, and some sort of a coat of arms, with the motto "Do or Die" underneath. I remember it took my fancy immensely. There was a touch of romance in it, something that made me love the old thing – something that appealed to my youth!

'We left London in ballast – sand ballast – to load a cargo of coal in a northern port for Bangkok. Bangkok! I thrilled. I had been six years at sea, but had only seen Melbourne and Sydney, very good places, charming places in their way – but Bangkok!

'We worked out of the Thames under canvas, with a North Sea pilot on board. His name was Jermyn, and he dodged all day long about the galley drying his handkerchief before the stove. Apparently he never slept. He was a dismal man, with a perpetual tear sparkling at the end of his nose, who either had been in trouble, or was in trouble, or expected to be in trouble – couldn't be happy unless something went wrong. He mistrusted my youth, my common-sense, and my seamanship, and made a point of showing it in a hundred little ways. I dare say he was right. It seems to me I knew very little then, and I know not much more now; but I cherish a hate for that Jermyn to this day.

'We were a week working up as far as Yarmouth Roads, and then we got into a gale – the famous October gale of twenty-two years ago. It was wind, lightning, sleet, snow, and a terrific sea. We were flying light, and you may imagine how bad it was when I tell you we had smashed bulwarks and a flooded deck. On the second night she shifted her ballast into the lee bow, and by that time we had been blown off somewhere on the Dogger Bank. There was nothing for it but go below with shovels and try to right her, and there we were in that vast hold, gloomy like a cavern, the tallow dips stuck and flickering on the beams, the gale howling above, the ship tossing about like mad on her side; there we all were, Jermyn, the captain, everyone, hardly able to keep our feet, engaged on that gravedigger's work, and trying to toss shovelfuls of wet sand up to windward. At every tumble of the ship you could see vaguely in the dim light men falling down with a great flourish of shovels. One of the ship's boys (we had two), impressed by the weirdness of the scene, wept as if his heart would break. We could hear him blubbering somewhere in the shadows.

'On the third day the gale died out, and by and by a north-country tug picked us up. We took sixteen days in all to get from London to the Tyne! When we got into dock we had lost our turn for loading, and they hauled us off to a tier where we remained for a month. Mrs Beard (the captain's name was Beard) came from Colchester to see the old man. She lived on board. The crew of runners had left, and there remained only the officers, one boy, and the steward, a mulatto who answered to the name of Abraham. Mrs Beard was an old woman with a face all wrinkled and ruddy like a winter apple, and the figure of a young girl. She caught sight of me once, sewing on a button, and insisted on having my shirts to repair. This was something different from the captains' wives I had known on board crack clippers. When I brought her the shirts, she said: "And the socks? They want mending, I am sure, and John's – Captain Beard's – things are all in order now. I would be glad of something to do." Bless the old woman. She overhauled my outfit for me, and meantime I read for the first time *Sartor Resartus* and Burnaby's *Ride to Khiva*. I didn't understand much of the first then; but I remember I preferred the soldier to the philosopher at the time; a preference which life has only confirmed. One was a man, and the other was either more – or less. However, they are both dead, and Mrs Beard is dead, and youth, strength, genius, thoughts, achievements, simple hearts – all dies . . . No matter.

'They loaded us at last. We shipped a crew. Eight able seamen and two boys. We hauled off one evening to the buoys at the dock-gates, ready to go out, and with a fair prospect of beginning the voyage next day. Mrs Beard was to start for home by a late train. When the ship was fast we went to tea. We sat rather silent through the meal – Mahon, the old couple, and I. I finished first, and slipped away for a smoke, my cabin being in a deck-house just against the poop. It was high water, blowing fresh with a drizzle; the double dock-gates were opened, and the steam-colliers were going in and out in the darkness with their lights burning bright, a great plashing of propellers, rattling of winches, and a lot of hailing on the pier-heads. I watched the procession of headlights gliding high and of green lights gliding low in the night, when suddenly a red gleam flashed at me, vanished, came into view again, and remained. The fore-end of a steamer loomed up close. I shouted down the cabin, "Come up, quick!" and then heard a startled voice saying afar in the dark, "Stop her, sir." A bell jingled. Another voice cried warningly, "We are going right into that barque, sir." The answer to this was a gruff "All right," and the next thing was a heavy crash as the steamer struck a glancing blow with the bluff of her bow about our fore-rigging. There was a moment of confusion, yelling, and running about. Steam roared. Then somebody was heard saying, "All clear, sir." . . . "Are you all right?" asked the gruff voice. I had jumped forward to see the damage, and hailed back, "I think so." "Easy astern," said the gruff voice. A bell jingled. "What steamer is that?" screamed Mahon. By that time she was no more to us than a bulky shadow manoeuvring a little way off. They shouted at us some name – a woman's name, Miranda or Melissa – or some such thing. "This means another month in this beastly hole," said Mahon to me, as we peered with lamps about the splintered bulwarks and broken braces. "But where's the captain?"

'We had not heard or seen anything of him all that time. We went aft to look. A doleful voice arose hailing somewhere in the middle of the dock, "*Judea* ahoy!" . . . How the devil did he get there? . . . "Hallo!" we shouted. "I am adrift in our boat without oars," he cried. A belated waterman offered his services, and Mahon struck a bargain with him for half a crown to tow our skipper alongside; but it was Mrs Beard that came up the ladder first. They had been floating about the dock in that mizzly cold rain for nearly an hour. I was never so surprised in my life.

'It appears that when he heard my shout "Come up" he understood at once what was the matter, caught up his wife, ran on deck, and across, and down into our boat, which was fast to the ladder. Not bad for a sixty-year-old. Just imagine that old fellow saving heroically in his arms that old woman – the woman of his life. He set her down on a thwart, and was ready to climb back on board when the painter came adrift somehow, and away they went together. Of course in the confusion we did not hear him shouting. He looked abashed. She said cheerfully, "I suppose it does not matter my losing the train now?" "No, Jenny – you go below and get warm," he growled. Then to us: "A sailor has no business with a wife – I say. There I was, out of the ship. Well, no harm done this time. Let's go and look at what that fool of a steamer smashed."

'It wasn't much, but it delayed us three weeks. At the end of that time, the captain being engaged with his agents, I carried Mrs Beard's bag to the railway-station and put her all comfy into a third-class carriage. She lowered the window to say, "You are a good young man. If you see John – Captain Beard – without his muffler at night, just remind him from me to keep his throat well wrapped up." "Certainly, Mrs Beard," I said. "You are a good young man; I noticed how attentive you are to John – to Captain – " The train pulled out suddenly; I took my cap off to the old woman: I never saw her again . . . Pass the bottle.

'We went to sea next day. When we made that start for Bangkok we had been already three months out of London. We had expected to be a fortnight or so – at the outside.

'It was January, and the weather was beautiful – the beautiful sunny winter weather that has more charm than in the summer-time, because it is unexpected, and crisp, and you know it won't, it can't, last long. It's like a windfall, like a godsend, like an unexpected piece of luck.

'It lasted all down the North Sea, all down Channel; and it lasted till we were three hundred miles or so to the westward of the Lizards: then the wind went round to the sou'west and began to pipe up. In two days it blew a gale. The *Judea*, hove to, wallowed on the Atlantic like an old candlebox. It blew day after day: it blew with spite, without interval, without mercy, without rest. The world was nothing but an immensity of great foaming waves rushing at us, under a sky low enough to touch with the hand and dirty like a smoked ceiling. In the stormy space surrounding us there was as much flying spray as air. Day after day and night after night there was nothing round the ship but the howl of the wind, the tumult of the sea, the noise of water pouring over her deck. There was no rest for her and no rest for us. She tossed, she pitched, she stood on her head, she sat on her tail, she rolled, she groaned, and we had to hold on while on deck and cling to our bunks when below, in a constant effort of body and worry of mind.

'One night Mahon spoke through the small window of my berth. It opened right into my very bed, and I was lying there sleepless, in my boots, feeling as though I had not slept for years, and could not if I tried. He said excitedly – "You got the sounding-rod in here, Marlow? I can't get the pumps to suck. By God! it's no child's play."

'I gave him the sounding-rod and lay down again, trying to think of various things – but I thought only of the pumps. When I came on deck they were still at it, and my watch relieved at the pumps. By the light of the lantern brought on deck to examine the sounding-rod I caught a glimpse of their weary, serious faces. We pumped all the four hours. We pumped all night, all day, all the week – watch and watch. She was working herself loose, and leaked badly – not enough to drown us at once, but enough to kill us with the work at the pumps. And while we pumped the ship was going from us piecemeal: the bulwarks went, the stanchions were torn out, the ventilators smashed, the cabin-door burst in. There was not a dry spot in the ship. She was being gutted bit by bit. The long-boat changed, as if by magic, into matchwood where she stood in her gripes. I had lashed her myself, and was rather proud of my handiwork, which had withstood so long the malice of the sea. And we pumped. And there was no break in the weather. The sea was white like a sheet of foam, like a caldron of boiling milk; there was not a break in the clouds, no – not the size of a man's hand – no, not for so much as ten seconds. There was for us no sky, there were for us no stars, no sun, no universe – nothing but angry clouds and an infuriated sea. We pumped watch and watch, for dear life; and it seemed to last for months, for years, for all eternity, as though we had been dead and gone to a hell for sailors. We forgot the day of the week, the name of the month, what year it was, and whether we had ever been ashore. The sails blew away, she lay broadside on under a weather-cloth, the ocean poured over her, and we did not care. We turned those handles, and had the eyes of idiots. As soon as we had crawled on deck I used to take a round turn with a rope about the men, the pumps, and the mainmast, and we turned, we turned incessantly, with the water to our waists, to our necks, over our heads. It was all one. We had forgotten how it felt to be dry.

'And there was somewhere in me the thought: By Jove! this is the deuce of an adventure – something you read about; and it is my first voyage as second mate – and I am only twenty – and here I am lasting it out as well as any of these men, and keeping my chaps up to the mark. I was pleased. I would not have given up the experience for worlds. I had moments of exultation. Whenever the old dismantled craft pitched heavily with her counter high in the air, she seemed to me to throw up, like an appeal, like a defiance, like a cry to the clouds without mercy, the words written on her stern: "*Judea*, London. Do or Die."

'O youth! The strength of it, the faith of it, the imagination of it! To me she was not an old rattle-trap carting about the world a lot of coal for a freight – to me she was the endeavour, the test, the trial of life. I think of her with pleasure, with affection, with regret – as you would think of someone dead you have loved. I shall never forget her . . . Pass the bottle.

'One night when tied to the mast, as I explained, we were pumping on, deafened with the wind, and without spirit enough in us to wish ourselves dead, a heavy sea crashed aboard and swept clean over us. As soon as I got my breath I shouted, as in duty bound, "Keep on, boys!" when suddenly I felt something hard floating on deck strike the calf of my leg. I made a grab at it and missed. It was so dark we could not see each other's faces within a foot – you understand.

'After that thump the ship kept quiet for a while, and the thing, whatever it was, struck my leg again. This time I caught it – and it was a saucepan. At first, being stupid with fatigue and thinking of nothing but the pumps, I did not understand what I had in my hand. Suddenly it dawned upon me, and I shouted, "Boys, the house on deck is gone. Leave this, and let's look for the cook."

'There was a deck-house forward, which contained the galley, the cook's berth, and the quarters of the crew. As we had expected for days to see it swept away, the hands had been ordered to sleep in the cabin – the only safe place in the ship. The steward, Abraham, however, persisted in clinging to his berth, stupidly, like a mule – from sheer fright I believe, like an animal that won't leave a stable falling in an earthquake. So we went to look for him. It was chancing death, since once out of our lashings we were as exposed as if on a raft. But we went. The house was shattered as if a shell had exploded inside. Most of it had gone overboard – stove, men's quarters, and their property, all was gone; but two posts, holding a portion of the bulkhead to which Abraham's bunk was attached, remained as if by a miracle. We groped in the ruins and came upon this, and there he was, sitting in his bunk, surrounded by foam and wreckage, jabbering cheerfully to himself. He was out of his mind; completely and for ever mad, with this sudden shock coming upon the fag-end of his endurance. We snatched him up, lugged him aft, and pitched him head-first down the cabin companion. You understand there was no time to carry him down with infinite precautions and wait to see how he got on. Those below would pick him up at the bottom of the stairs all right. We were in a hurry to go back to the pumps. That business could not wait. A bad leak is an inhuman thing.

'One would think that the sole purpose of that fiendish gale had been to make a lunatic of that poor devil of a mulatto. It eased before morning, and next day the sky cleared, and as the sea went down the leak took up. When it came to bending a fresh set of sails the crew demanded to put back – and really there was nothing else to do. Boats gone, decks swept clean, cabin gutted, men without a stitch but what they stood in, stores spoiled, ship strained. We put her head for home, and – would you believe it? The wind came east right in our teeth. It blew fresh, it blew continuously. We had to beat up every inch of the way, but she did not leak so badly, the water keeping comparatively smooth. Two hours' pumping in every four is no joke – but it kept her afloat as far as Falmouth.

'The good people there live on casualties of the sea, and no doubt were glad to see us. A hungry crowd of shipwrights sharpened their chisels at the sight of that carcass of a ship. And, by Jove! they had pretty pickings off us before they were done. I fancy the owner was already in a tight place. There were delays. Then it was decided to take part of the cargo out and caulk her topsides. This was done, the repairs finished, cargo reshipped; a new crew came on board, and we went out – for Bankok. At the end of a week we were back again. The crew said they weren't going to Bankok – a hundred and fifty days' passage – in a something hooker that wanted pumping eight hours out of the twenty-four; and the nautical papers inserted again the little paragraph: "*Judea*. Barque. Tyne to Bankok; coals; put back to Falmouth leaky and with crew refusing duty."

'There were more delays – more tinkering. The owner came down for a day, and said she was as right as a little fiddle. Poor old Captain Beard looked like the ghost of a Geordie skipper – through the worry and humiliation of it. Remember he was sixty, and it was his first command. Mahon said it was a foolish business, and would end badly. I loved the ship more than ever, and wanted awfully to get to Bankok. To Bankok! Magic name, blessed name. Mesopotamia wasn't a patch on it. Remember I was twenty, and it was my first second mate's billet, and the East was waiting for me.

'We went out and anchored in the outer roads with a fresh crew – the third. She leaked worse than ever. It was as if those confounded shipwrights had actually made a hole in her. This time we did not even go outside. The crew simply refused to man the windlass."

'They towed us back to the inner harbour, and we became a fixture, a feature, an institution of the place. People pointed us out to visitors as "That 'ere barque that's going to Bankok – has been here six months – put back three times." On holidays the small boys pulling about in boats would hail, "*Judea*, ahoy!" and if a head showed above the rail shouted, "Where you bound to? – Bankok?" and jeered. We were only three on board. The poor old skipper mooned in the cabin. Mahon undertook the cooking, and unexpectedly developed all a Frenchman's genius for preparing nice little messes. I looked languidly after the rigging. We became citizens of Falmouth. Every shopkeeper knew us. At the barber's or tobacconist's they asked familiarly, "Do you think you will ever get to Bankok?" Meantime the owner, the underwriters, and the charterers squabbled amongst themselves in London, and our pay went on . . . Pass the bottle.

'It was horrid. Morally it was worse than pumping for life. It seemed as though we had been forgotten by the world, belonged to nobody, would get nowhere; it seemed that; as if bewitched, we would have to live for ever and ever in that inner harbour, a derision and a byword to generations of long-shore loafers and dishonest boatmen. I obtained three months' pay and a five days' leave, and made a rush for London. It took me a day to get there and pretty well another to come back – but three months' pay went all the same. I don't know what I did with it. I went to a music-hall, I believe, lunched, dined, and supped in a swell place in Regent Street, and was back to time, with nothing but a complete set of Byron's works and a new railway rug to show for three months' work. The boatman who pulled me off to the ship said: "Hallo! I thought you had left the old thing. *She* will never get to Bankok." "That's all *you* know about it," I said, scornfully – but I didn't like that prophecy at all.

'Suddenly a man, some kind of agent to somebody, appeared with full powers. He had grog-blossoms all over his face, an indomitable energy, and was a jolly soul. We leaped into life again. A hulk came alongside, took our cargo, and then we went into dry dock to get our copper stripped. No wonder she leaked. The poor thing, strained beyond endurance by the gale, had, as if in disgust, spat out all the oakum of her lower seams. She was recaulked, new coppered, and made as tight as a bottle. We went back to the hulk and reshipped our cargo.

'Then, on a fine moonlight night, all the rats left the ship.

'We had been infested with them. They had destroyed our sails, consumed more stores than the crew, affably shared our beds and our dangers, and now, when the ship was made seaworthy, concluded to clear out. I called Mahon to enjoy the spectacle. Rat after rat appeared on our rail, took a last look over his shoulder, and leaped with a hollow thud into the empty hulk. We tried to count them, but soon lost the tale. Mahon said: "Well, well! don't talk to me about the intelligence of rats. They ought to have left before, when we had that narrow squeak from foundering. There you have the proof how silly is the superstition about them. They leave a good ship for an old rotten hulk, where there is nothing to eat, too, the fools! . . . I don't believe they know what is safe or what is good for them, any more than you or I."

'And after some more talk we agreed that the wisdom of rats had been grossly overrated, being in fact no greater than that of men.

'The story of the ship was known, by this, all up the Channel from Land's End to the Forelands, and we could get no crew on the south coast. They sent us one all complete from Liverpool, and we left once more – for Bankok.

'We had fair breezes, smooth water right into the tropics, and the old *Judea* lumbered along in the sunshine. When she went eight knots everything cracked aloft, and we tied our caps to our heads; but mostly she strolled on at the rate of three miles an hour. What could you expect? She was tired – that old ship. Her youth was where mine is – where yours is – you fellows who listen to this yarn; and what friend would throw your years and your weariness in your face? We didn't grumble at her. To us aft, at least, it seemed as though we had been born in her, reared in her, had lived in her for ages, had never known any other ship. I would just as soon have abused the old village church at home for not being a cathedral.

'And for me there was also my youth to make me patient. There was all the East before me, and all life, and the thought that I had been tried in that ship and had come out pretty well. And I thought of men of old who, centuries ago, went that road in ships that sailed no better, to the land of palms, and spices, and yellow sands, and of brown nations ruled by kings more cruel than Nero the Roman and more splendid than Solomon the Jew. The old bark lumbered on, heavy with her age and the burden of her cargo, while I lived the life of youth in ignorance and hope. She lumbered on through an interminable procession of days; and the fresh gilding flashed back at the setting sun, seemed to cry out over the darkening sea the words painted on her stern, "*Judea*, London. Do or Die."

'Then we entered the Indian Ocean and steered northerly for Java Head. The winds were light. Weeks slipped by. She crawled on, do or die, and people at home began to think of posting us as overdue.

'One Saturday evening, I being off duty, the men asked me to give them an extra bucket of water or so – for washing clothes. As I did not wish to screw on the freshwater pump so late, I went forward whistling, and with a key in my hand to unlock the forepeak scuttle, intending to serve the water out of a spare tank we kept there.

'The smell down below was as unexpected as it was frightful. One would have thought hundreds of paraffin-lamps had been flaring and smoking in that hole for days. I was glad to get out. The man with me coughed and said, "Funny smell, sir." I answered negligently, "It's good for the health they say," and walked aft.

'The first thing I did was to put my head down the square of the midship ventilator. As I lifted the lid a visible breath, something like a thin fog, a puff of faint haze, rose from the opening. The ascending air was hot, and had a heavy, sooty, paraffiny smell. I gave one sniff, and put down the lid gently. It was no use choking myself. The cargo was on fire.

'Next day she began to smoke in earnest. You see it was to be expected, for though the coal was of a safe kind, that cargo had been so handled, so broken up with handling, that it looked more like smithy coal than anything else. Then it had been wetted – more than once. It rained all the time we were taking it back from the hulk, and now with this long passage it got heated, and there was another case of spontaneous combustion.

'The captain called us into the cabin. He had a chart spread on the table, and looked unhappy. He said, "The coast of West Australia is near, but I mean to proceed to our destination. It is the hurricane month too; but we will just keep her head for Bankok, and fight the fire. No more putting back anywhere, if we all get roasted. We will try first to stifle this 'ere damned combustion by want of air."

'We tried. We battened down everything, and still she smoked. The smoke kept coming out through imperceptible crevices; it forced itself through bulkheads and covers; it oozed here and there and everywhere in slender threads, in an invisible film, in an incomprehensible manner. It made its way into the cabin, into the forecastle; it poisoned the sheltered places on the deck, it could be sniffed as high as the mainyard. It was clear that if the smoke came out the air came in. This was disheartening. This combustion refused to be stifled.

'We resolved to try water, and took the hatches off. Enormous volumes of smoke, whitish, yellowish, thick, greasy, misty, choking, ascended as high as the trucks. All hands cleared out aft. Then the poisonous cloud blew away, and we went back to work in a smoke that was no thicker now than that of an ordinary factory chimney.

'We rigged the force-pump, got the hose along, and by and by it burst. Well, it was as old as the ship – a prehistoric hose, and past repair. Then we pumped with the feeble head-pump, drew water with buckets, and in this way managed in time to pour lots of Indian Ocean into the main hatch. The bright stream flashed in sunshine, fell into a layer of white crawling smoke, and vanished on the black surface of coal. Steam ascended mingling with the smoke. We poured salt water as into a barrel without a bottom. It was our fate to pump in that ship, to pump out of her, to pump into her; and after keeping water out of her to save ourselves from being drowned, we frantically poured water into her to save ourselves from being burnt.

'And she crawled on, do or die, in the serene weather. The sky was a miracle of purity, a miracle of azure. The sea was polished, was blue, was pellucid, was sparkling like a precious stone, extending on all sides, all round to the horizon – as if the whole terrestrial globe had been one jewel, one colossal sapphire, a single gem fashioned into a planet. And on the lustre of the great calm waters the *Judea* glided imperceptibly, enveloped in languid and unclean vapours, in a lazy cloud that drifted to leeward, light and slow: a pestiferous cloud defiling the splendour of sea and sky.

'All this time of course we saw no fire. The cargo smouldered at the bottom somewhere. Once Mahon, as we were working side by side, said to me with a queer smile: "Now, if she only would spring a tidy leak – like that time when we first left the Channel – it would put a stopper on this fire. Wouldn't it?" I remarked irrelevantly, "Do you remember the rats?"

'We fought the fire and sailed the ship too as carefully as though nothing had been the matter. The steward cooked and attended on us. Of the other twelve men, eight worked while four rested. Everyone took his turn, captain included. There was equality, and if not exactly fraternity, then a deal of good feeling. Sometimes a man, as he dashed a bucketful of water down the hatchway, would yell out, "Hurrah for Bankok!" and the rest laughed. But generally we were taciturn and serious – and thirsty. Oh! how thirsty! And we had to be careful with the water. Strict allowance. The ship smoked, the sun blazed . . . Pass the bottle.

'We tried everything. We even made an attempt to dig down to the fire. No good, of course. No man could remain more than a minute below. Mahon, who went first, fainted there, and the man who went to fetch him out did likewise. We lugged them out on deck. Then I leaped down to show how easily it could be done. They had learned wisdom by that time, and contented themselves by fishing for me with a chain-hook tied to a broom-handle, I believe. I did not offer to go and fetch up my shovel, which was left down below.

'Things began to look bad. We put the long-boat into the water. The second boat was ready to swing out. We had also another, a fourteen-foot thing, on davits aft, where it was quite safe.

"Then, behold, the smoke suddenly decreased. We redoubled our efforts to flood the bottom of the ship. In two days there was no smoke at all. Everybody was on the broad grin. This was on a Friday. On Saturday no work, but sailing the ship of course, was done. The men washed their clothes and their faces for the first time in a fortnight, and had a special dinner given them. They spoke of spontaneous combustion with contempt, and implied *they* were the boys to put out combustions. Somehow we all felt as though we each had inherited a large fortune. But a beastly smell of burning hung about the ship. Captain Beard had hollow eyes and sunken cheeks. I had never noticed so much before how twisted and bowed he was. He and Mahon prowled soberly about hatches and ventilators, sniffing. It struck me suddenly poor Mahon was a very, very old chap. As to me, I was as pleased and proud as though I had helped to win a great naval battle. O! Youth!

'The night was fine. In the morning a homeward-bound ship passed us hull down – the first we had seen for months; but we were nearing the land at last, Java Head being about a hundred and ninety miles off, and nearly due north.

'Next day it was my watch on deck from eight to twelve. At breakfast the captain observed, "It's wonderful how that smell hangs about the cabin." About ten, the mate being on the poop, I stepped down on the main-deck for a moment. The carpenter's bench stood abaft the mainmast: I leaned against it sucking at my pipe, and the carpenter, a young chap, came to talk to me. He remarked, "I think we have done very well, haven't we?" and then I perceived with annoyance the fool was trying to tilt the bench. I said curtly, "Don't, Chips," and immediately became aware of a queer sensation, of an absurd delusion – I seemed somehow to be in the air. I heard all round me like a pent-up breath released – as if a thousand giants simultaneously had said Phoo! – and felt a dull concussion which made my ribs ache suddenly. No doubt about it – I was in the air, and my body was describing a short parabola. But short as it was, I had the time to think several thoughts in, as far as I can remember, the following order: "This can't be the carpenter – What is it? – Some accident – Submarine volcano? – Coals, gas! – By Jove! we are being blown up – Everybody's dead – I am falling into the after-hatch – I see fire in it."

'The coal-dust suspended in the air of the hold had glowed dull-red at the moment of the explosion. In the twinkling of an eye, in an infinitesimal fraction of a second since the first tilt of the bench, I was sprawling full length on the cargo. I picked myself up and scrambled out. It was quick like a rebound. The deck was a wilderness of smashed timber, lying crosswise like trees in a wood after a hurricane; an immense curtain of soiled rags waved gently before me – it was the mainsail blown to strips. I thought, the masts will be toppling over directly; and to get out of the way bolted on all-fours towards the poop-ladder. The first person I saw was Mahon, with eyes like saucers, his mouth open, and the long white hair standing straight on end round his head like a silver halo. He was just about to go down when the sight of the main-deck stirring, heaving up, and changing into splinters before his eyes, petrified him on the top step. I stared at him in unbelief, and he stared at me with a queer kind of shocked curiosity. I did not know that I had no hair, no eyebrows, no eyelashes, that my young moustache was burnt off, that my face was black, one cheek laid open, my nose cut, and my chin bleeding. I had lost my cap, one of my slippers, and my shirt was torn to rags. Of all this I was not aware. I was amazed to see the ship still afloat, the poop-deck whole – and, most of all, to see anybody alive. Also the peace of the sky and the serenity of the sea were distinctly surprising. I suppose I expected to see them convulsed with horror . . . Pass the bottle.

'There was a voice hailing the ship from somewhere – in the air, in the sky – I couldn't tell. Presently I saw the captain – and he was mad. He asked me eagerly, "Where's the cabin-table?" and to hear such a question was a frightful shock. I had just been blown up, you understand, and vibrated with that experience – I wasn't quite sure whether I was alive. Mahon began to stamp with both feet and yelled at him, "Good God! don't you see the deck's blown out of her?" I found my voice, and stammered out as if conscious of some gross neglect of duty, "I don't know where the cabin-table is." It was like an absurd dream.

'Do you know what he wanted next? Well, he wanted to trim the yards. Very placidly, and as if lost in thought, he insisted on having the foreyard squared. "I don't know if there's anybody alive," said Mahon, almost tearfully. "Surely," he said, gently, "there will be enough left to square the foreyard."

'The old chap, it seems, was in his own berth, winding up the chronometers, when the shock sent him spinning. Immediately it occurred to him – as he said afterwards – that the ship had struck something, and he ran out into the cabin. There, he saw, the cabin-table had vanished somewhere. The deck being blown up, it had fallen down into the lazarette of course. Where we had our breakfast that morning he saw only a great hole in the floor. This appeared to him so awfully mysterious, and impressed him so immensely, that what he saw and heard after he got on deck were mere trifles in comparison. And, mark, he noticed directly the wheel deserted and his barque off her course – and his only thought was to get that miserable, stripped, undecked, smouldering shell of a ship back again with her head pointing at her port of destination. Bankok! That's what he was after. I tell you this quiet, bowed, bandy-legged, almost deformed little man was immense in the singleness of his idea and in his placid ignorance of our agitation. He motioned us forward with a commanding gesture, and went to take the wheel himself.

'Yes; that was the first thing we did – trim the yards of that wreck! No one was killed, or even disabled, but everyone was more or less hurt. You should have seen them! Some were in rags, with black faces, like coalheavers, like sweeps, and had bullet heads that seemed closely cropped, but were in fact singed to the skin. Others, of the watch below, awakened by being shot out from their collapsing bunks, shivered incessantly, and kept on groaning even as we went about our work. But they all worked. That crew of Liverpool hard cases had in them the right stuff. It's my experience they always have. It is the sea that gives it – the vastness, the loneliness surrounding their dark stolid souls. Ah! Well! we stumbled, we crept, we fell, we barked our shins on the wreckage, we hauled. The masts stood, but we did not know how much they might be charred down below. It was nearly calm, but a long swell ran from the west and made her roll. They might go at any moment. We looked at them with apprehension. One could not foresee which way they would fall.

'Then we retreated aft and looked about us. The deck was a tangle of planks on edge, of planks on end, of splinters, of ruined woodwork. The masts rose from that chaos like big trees above a matted undergrowth. The interstices of that mass of wreckage were full of something whitish, sluggish, stirring – of something that was like a greasy fog. The smoke of the invisible fire was coming up again, was trailing, like a poisonous thick mist in some valley choked with dead wood. Already lazy wisps were beginning to curl upwards amongst the mass of splinters. Here and there a piece of timber, stuck upright, resembled a post. Half of a fife-rail had been shot through the foresail, and the sky made a patch of glorious blue in the ignobly soiled canvas. A portion of several boards holding together had fallen across the rail, and one end protruded overboard, like a gangway leading upon nothing, like a gangway leading over the deep sea, leading to death – as if inviting us to walk the plank at once and be done with our ridiculous troubles. And still the air, the sky – a ghost, something invisible was hailing the ship.

'Someone had the sense to look over, and there was the helmsman, who had impulsively jumped overboard, anxious to come back. He yelled and swam lustily like a merman, keeping up with the ship. We threw him a rope, and presently he stood amongst us streaming with water and very crestfallen. The captain had surrendered the wheel, and apart, elbow on rail and chin in hand, gazed at the sea wistfully. We asked ourselves, What next? I thought, Now, this is something like. This is great. I wonder what will happen. O youth!

'Suddenly Mahon sighted a steamer far astern. Captain Beard said, "We may do something with her yet." We hoisted two flags, which said in the international language of the sea, "On fire. Want immediate assistance." The steamer grew bigger rapidly, and by and by spoke with two flags on her foremast, "I am coming to your assistance."

'In half an hour she was abreast, to windward, within hail, and rolling slightly, with her engines stopped. We lost our composure, and yelled all together with excitement, "We've been blown up." A man in a white helmet, on the bridge, cried, "Yes! All right! all right!" and he nodded his head, and smiled, and made soothing motions with his hand as though at a lot of frightened children. One of the boats dropped in the water, and walked towards us upon the sea with her long oars. Four Calashes pulled a swinging stroke. This was my first sight of Malay seamen. I've known them since, but what struck me then was their unconcern: they came alongside, and even the bowman standing up and holding to our main-chains with the boat-hook did not deign to lift his head for a glance. I thought people who had been blown up deserved more attention.

'A little man, dry like a chip and agile like a monkey, clambered up. It was the mate of the steamer. He gave one look, and cried, ' O boys – you had better quit.'

'We were silent. He talked apart with the captain for a time – seemed to argue with him. Then they went away together to the steamer.

'When our skipper came back we learned that the steamer was the *Sommerville*, Captain Nash, from West Australia to Singapore *via* Batavia with mails, and that the agreement was she should tow us to Anjer or Batavia, if possible, where we could extinguish the fire by scuttling, and then proceed on our voyage to Bankok! The old man seemed excited. 'We will do it yet,' he said to Mahon, fiercely. He shook his fist at the sky. Nobody else said a word.

'At noon the steamer began to tow. She went ahead slim and high, and what was left of the *Judea* followed at the end of seventy fathom of tow-rope – followed her swiftly like a cloud of smoke with mastheads protruding above. We went aloft to furl the sails. We coughed on the yards, and were careful about the bunts. Do you see the lot of us there, putting a neat furl on the sails of that ship doomed to arrive nowhere? There was not a man who didn't think that at any moment the masts would topple over. From aloft we could not see the ship for smoke, and they worked carefully, passing the gaskets with even turns. "Harbour furl – aloft there!" cried Mahon from below.

'You understand this? I don't think one of those chaps expected to get down in the usual way. When we did I heard them saying to each other, "I thought we would come down overboard, in a lump – sticks and all – blame me if I didn't." "That's what I was thinking to myself," would answer wearily another battered and bandaged scarecrow. And, mind, these were men without the drilled-in habit of obedience. To an onlooker they would be a lot of profane scallywags without a redeeming point. What made them do it – what made them obey me when I, thinking consciously how fine it was, made them drop the bunt of the foresail twice to try and do it better? What? They had no professional reputation – no examples, no praise. It wasn't a sense of duty; they all knew well enough how to shirk, and laze, and dodge – when they had a mind to it – and mostly they had. Was it the two pounds ten a-month that sent them there? They didn't think their pay half good enough. No; it was something in them, something inborn and subtle and everlasting. I don't say positively that the crew of a French or German merchantman wouldn't have done it, but I doubt whether it would have been done in the same way. There was a completeness in it, something solid like a principle, and masterful like an instinct – a disclosure of something secret – of that hidden something, that gift of good or evil that makes racial difference, that shapes the fate of nations.

'It was that night at ten that, for the first time since we had been fighting it, we saw the fire. The speed of the towing had fanned the smouldering destruction. A blue gleam appeared forward, shining below the wreck of the deck. It wavered in patches, it seemed to stir and creep like the light of a glowworm. I saw it first, and told Mahon. "Then the game's up," he said. "We had better stop this towing, or she will burst out suddenly fore and aft before we can clear out." We set up a yell; rang bells to attract their attention; they towed on. At last Mahon and I had to crawl forward and cut the rope with an axe. There was no time to cast off the lashings. Red tongues could be seen licking the wilderness of splinters under our feet as we made our way back to the poop.

'Of course they very soon found out in the steamer that the rope was gone. She gave a loud blast of her whistle, her lights were seen sweeping in a wide circle, she came up ranging close alongside, and stopped. We were all in a tight group on the poop looking at her. Every man had saved a little bundle or a bag. Suddenly a conical flame with a twisted top shot up forward and threw upon the black sea a circle of light, with the two vessels side by side and heaving gently in its centre. Captain Beard had been sitting on the gratings still and mute for hours, but now he rose slowly and advanced in front of us, to the mizzen-shrouds. Captain Nash hailed: "Come along! Look sharp. I have mailbags on board. I will take you and your boats to Singapore."

' "Thank you! No!" said our skipper. "We must see the last of the ship."

' "I can't stand by any longer," shouted the other. "Mails – you know."

' "Ay! ay! We are all right."

' "Very well! I'll report you in Singapore. . . Goodbye!"

'He waved his hand. Our men dropped their bundles quietly. The steamer moved ahead, and passing out of the circle of light, vanished at once from our sight, dazzled by the fire which burned fiercely. And then I knew that I would see the East first as commander of a small boat. I thought it fine; and the fidelity to the old ship was fine. We should see the last of her. Oh, the glamour of youth! Oh, the fire of it, more dazzling than the flames of the burning ship, throwing a magic light on the wide earth, leaping audaciously to the sky, presently to be quenched by time, more cruel, more pitiless, more bitter than the sea – and like the flames of the burning ship surrounded by an impenetrable night.'

*   *   *

'The old man warned us in his gentle and inflexible way that it was part of our duty to save for the underwriters as much as we could of the ship's gear. Accordingly we went to work aft, while she blazed forward to give us plenty of light. We lugged out a lot of rubbish. What didn't we save? An old barometer fixed with an absurd quantity of screws nearly cost me my life: a sudden rush of smoke came upon me, and I just got away in time. There were various stores, bolts of canvas, coils of rope; the poop looked like a marine bazaar, and the boats were lumbered to the gunwales. One would have thought the old man wanted to take as much as he could of his first command with him. He was very, very quiet, but off his balance evidently. Would you believe it? He wanted to take a length of old stream-cable and a kedge-anchor with him in the long-boat. We said, "Ay, ay, sir," deferentially, and on the quiet let the things slip overboard. The heavy medicine-chest went that way, two bags of green coffee, tins of paint – fancy, paint! – a whole lot of things. Then I was ordered with two hands into the boats to make a stowage and get them ready against the time it would be proper for us to leave the ship.

'We put everything straight, stepped the long-boat's mast for our skipper, who was to take charge of her, and I was not sorry to sit down for a moment. My face felt raw, every limb ached as if broken, I was aware of all my ribs, and would have sworn to a twist in the backbone. The boats, fast astern, lay in a deep shadow, and all around I could see the circle of the sea lighted by the fire. A gigantic flame arose forward straight and clear. It flared fierce, with noises like the whirr of wings, with rumbles as of thunder. There were cracks, detonations, and from the cone of flame the sparks flew upwards, as man is born to trouble, to leaky ships, and to ships that burn.

'What bothered me was that the ship, lying broadside to the swell and to such wind as there was – a mere breath – the boats would not keep astern where they were safe, but persisted, in a pig-headed way boats have, in getting under the counter and then swinging alongside. They were knocking about dangerously and coming near the flame, while the ship rolled on them, and, of course, there was always the danger of the masts going over the side at any moment. I and my two boat-keepers kept them off as best we could, with oars and boat-hooks; but to be constantly at it became exasperating, since there was no reason why we should not leave at once. We could not see those on board, nor could we imagine what caused the delay. The boat-keepers were swearing feebly, and I had not only my share of the work but also had to keep at it two men who showed a constant inclination to lay themselves down and let things slide.

'At last I hailed, "On deck there," and someone looked over. "We're ready here," I said. The head disappeared, and very soon popped up again. "The captain says, All right, sir, and to keep the boats well clear of the ship."

'Half an hour passed. Suddenly there was a frightful racket, rattle, clanking of chain, hiss of water, and millions of sparks flew up into the shivering column of smoke that stood leaning slightly above the ship. The cat-heads had burned away, and the two red-hot anchors had gone to the bottom, tearing out after them two hundred fathom of red-hot chain. The ship trembled, the mass of flame swayed as if ready to collapse, and the fore top-gallant-mast fell. It darted down like an arrow of fire, shot under, and instantly leaping up within an oar's-length of the boats, floated quietly, very black on the luminous sea. I hailed the deck again. After some time a man in an unexpectedly cheerful but also muffled tone, as though he had been trying to speak with his mouth shut, informed me, "Coming directly, sir," and vanished. For a long time I heard nothing but the whirr and roar of the fire. There were also whistling sounds. The boats jumped, tugged at the painters, ran at each other playfully, knocked their sides together, or, do what we would, swung in a bunch against the ship's side. I couldn't stand it any longer, and swarming up a rope, clambered aboard over the stern.

'It was as bright as day. Coming up like this, the sheet of fire facing me was a terrifying sight, and the heat seemed hardly bearable at first. On a settee cushion dragged out of the cabin Captain Beard, his legs drawn up and one arm under his head, slept with the light playing on him. Do you know what the rest were busy about? They were sitting on deck right aft, round an open case, eating bread and cheese and drinking bottled stout.

'On the background of flames twisting in fierce tongues above their heads they seemed at home like salamanders, and looked like a band of desperate pirates. The fire sparkled in the whites of their eyes, gleamed on patches of white skin seen through the torn shirts. Each had the marks as of a battle about him – bandaged heads, tied-up arms, a strip of dirty rag round a knee – and each man had a bottle between his legs and a chunk of cheese in his hand. Mahon got up. With his handsome and disreputable head, his hooked profile, his long white beard, and with an uncorked bottle in his hand, he resembled one of those reckless sea-robbers of old making merry amidst violence and disaster. "The last meal on board," he explained solemnly. "We had nothing to eat all day, and it was no use leaving all this." He flourished the bottle and indicated the sleeping skipper. "He said he couldn't swallow anything, so I got him to lie down," he went on; and as I stared, "I don't know whether you are aware, young fellow, the man had no sleep to speak of for days – and there will be dam' little sleep in the boats." "There will be no boats by and by if you fool about much longer," I said, indignantly. I walked up to the skipper and shook him by the shoulder. At last he opened his eyes, but did not move. "Time to leave her, sir," I said, quietly.

'He got up painfully, looked at the flames, at the sea sparkling round the ship, and black, black as ink farther away; he looked at the stars shining dim through a thin veil of smoke in a sky black, black as Erebus.

' "Youngest first," he said.

'And the ordinary seaman, wiping his mouth with the back of his hand, got up, clambered over the taffrail, and vanished. Others followed. One, on the point of going over, stopped short to drain his bottle, and with a great swing of his arm flung it at the fire. "Take this!" he cried.

'The skipper lingered disconsolately, and we left him to commune alone for a while with his first command. Then I went up again and brought him away at last. It was time. The ironwork on the poop was hot to the touch.

'Then the painter of the long-boat was cut, and the three boats, tied together, drifted clear of the ship. It was just sixteen hours after the explosion when we abandoned her. Mahon had charge of the second boat, and I had the smallest – the fourteen-foot thing. The long-boat would have taken the lot of us; but the skipper said we must save as much property as we could – for the underwriters – and so I got my first command. I had two men with me, a bag of biscuits, a few tins of meat, and a breaker of water. I was ordered to keep close to the long-boat, that in case of bad weather we might be taken into her.

'And do you know what I thought? I thought I would part company as soon as I could. I wanted to have my first command all to myself. I wasn't going to sail in a squadron if there were a chance for independent cruising. I would make land by myself. I would beat the other boats. Youth! All youth! The silly, charming, beautiful youth.

'But we did not make a start at once. We must see the last of the ship. And so the boats drifted about that night, heaving and setting on the swell. The men dozed, waked, sighed, groaned. I looked at the burning ship.

'Between the darkness of earth and heaven she was burning fiercely upon a disc of purple sea shot by the blood-red play of gleams; upon a disc of water glittering and sinister. A high, clear flame, an immense and lonely flame, ascended from the ocean, and from its summit the black smoke poured continuously at the sky. She burned furiously, mournful and imposing like a funeral pile kindled in the night, surrounded by the sea, watched over by the stars. A magnificent death had come like a grace, like a gift, like a reward to that old ship at the end of her laborious days. The surrender of her weary ghost to the keeping of stars and sea was stirring like the sight of a glorious triumph. The masts fell just before daybreak, and for a moment there was a burst and turmoil of sparks that seemed to fill with flying fire the night patient and watchful, the vast night lying silent upon the sea. At daylight she was only a charred shell, floating still under a cloud of smoke and bearing a glowing mass of coal within.

'Then the oars were got out, and the boats forming in a line moved round her remains as if in procession – the long-boat leading. As we pulled across her stern a slim dart of fire shot out viciously at us, and suddenly she went down, head first, in a great hiss of steam. The unconsumed stern was the last to sink; but the paint had gone, had cracked, had peeled off, and there were no letters, there was no word, no stubborn device that was like her soul, to flash at the rising sun her creed and her name.

'We made our way north. A breeze sprang up, and about noon all the boats came together for the last time. I had no mast or sail in mine, but I made a mast out of a spare oar and hoisted a boat-awning for a sail, with a boat-hook for a yard. She was certainly over-masted, but I had the satisfaction of knowing that with the wind aft I could beat the other two. I had to wait for them. Then we all had a look at the captain's chart, and, after a sociable meal of hard bread and water, got our last instructions. These were simple: steer north, and keep together as much as possible. "Be careful with that jury-rig, Marlow," said the captain; and Mahon, as I sailed proudly past his boat, wrinkled his curved nose and hailed, "You will sail that ship of yours under water, if you don't look out, young fellow." He was a malicious old man – and may the deep sea where he sleeps now rock him gently, rock him tenderly to the end of time!

'Before sunset a thick rain-squall passed over the two boats, which were far astern, and that was the last I saw of them for a time. Next day I sat steering my cockle-shell – my first command – with nothing but water and sky around me. I did sight in the afternoon the upper sails of a ship far away, but said nothing, and my men did not notice her. You see I was afraid she might be homeward bound, and I had no mind to turn back from the portals of the East. I was steering for Java – another blessed name – like Bankok, you know. I steered many days.

'I need not tell you what it is to be knocking about in an open boat. I remember nights and days of calm, when we pulled, we pulled, and the boat seemed to stand still, as if bewitched within the circle of the sea horizon. I remember the heat, the deluge of rain-squalls that kept us baling for dear life (but filled our water-cask), and I remember sixteen hours on end with a mouth dry as a cinder and a steering-oar over the stern to keep my first command head on to a breaking sea. I did not know how good a man I was till then. I remember the drawn faces, the dejected figures of my two men, and I remember my youth and the feeling that will never come back any more – the feeling that I could last for ever, outlast the sea, the earth, and all men; the deceitful feeling that lures us on to joys, to perils, to love, to vain effort – to death; the triumphant conviction of strength, the heat of life in the handful of dust, the glow in the heart that with every year grows dim, grows cold, grows small, and expires – and expires, too soon, too soon – before life itself.

'And this is how I see the East. I have seen its secret places and have looked into its very soul; but now I see it always from a small boat, a high outline of mountains, blue and afar in the morning; like faint mist at noon; a jagged wall of purple at sunset. I have the feel of the oar in my hand, the vision of a scorching blue sea in my eyes. And I see a bay, a wide bay, smooth as glass and polished like ice, shimmering in the dark. A red light burns far off upon the gloom of the land, and the night is soft and warm. We drag at the oars with aching arms, and suddenly a puff of wind, a puff faint and tepid and laden with strange odours of blossoms, of aromatic wood, comes out of the still night – the first sigh of the East on my face. That I can never forget. It was impalpable and enslaving, like a charm, like a whispered promise of mysterious delight.

'We had been pulling this finishing spell for eleven hours. Two pulled, and he whose turn it was to rest sat at the tiller. We had made out the red light in that bay and steered for it, guessing it must mark some small coasting port. We passed two vessels, outlandish and high-sterned, sleeping at anchor, and, approaching the light, now very dim, ran the boat's nose against the end of a jutting wharf. We were blind with fatigue. My men dropped the oars and fell off the thwarts as if dead. I made fast to a pile. A current rippled softly. The scented obscurity of the shore was grouped into vast masses, a density of colossal clumps of vegetation, probably – mute and fantastic shapes. And at their foot the semicircle of a beach gleamed faintly, like an illusion. There was not a light, not a stir, not a sound. The mysterious East faced me, perfumed like a flower, silent like death, dark like a grave.

'And I sat weary beyond expression, exulting like a conqueror, sleepless and entranced as if before a profound, a fateful enigma.

'A splashing of oars, a measured dip reverberating on the level of water, intensified by the silence of the shore into loud claps, made me jump up. A boat, a European boat, was coming in. I invoked the name of the dead; I hailed: *Judea* ahoy! A thin shout answered.

'It was the captain, I had beaten the flagship by three hours, and I was glad to hear the old man's voice again, tremulous and tired. "Is it you, Marlow?" "Mind the end of that jetty, sir," I cried.

'He approached cautiously, and brought up with the deep-sea lead-line which we had saved – for the underwriters. I eased my painter and fell alongside. He sat, a broken figure at the stern, wet with dew, his hands clasped in his lap. His men were asleep already. "I had a terrible time of it," he murmured. "Mahon is behind – not very far." We conversed in whispers, in low whispers, as if afraid to wake up the land. Guns, thunder, earthquakes would not have awakened the men just then.

'Looking round as we talked, I saw away at sea a bright light travelling in the night. "There's a steamer passing the bay," I said. She was not passing, she was entering, and she even came close and anchored. "I wish," said the old man, "you would find out whether she is English. Perhaps they could give us a passage somewhere." He seemed nervously anxious. So by dint of punching and kicking I started one of my men into a state of somnambulism, and giving him an oar, took another and pulled towards the lights of the steamer.

'There was a murmur of voices in her, metallic hollow clangs of the engine-room, footsteps on the deck. Her ports shone, round like dilated eyes. Shapes moved about, and there was a shadowy man high up on the bridge. He heard my oars.

'And then, before I could open my lips, the East spoke to me, but it was in a Western voice. A torrent of words was poured into the enigmatical, the fateful silence; outlandish, angry words, mixed with words and even whole sentences of good English, less strange but even more surprising. The voice swore and cursed violently; it riddled the solemn peace of the bay by a volley of abuse. It began by calling me Pig, and from that went crescendo into unmentionable adjectives – in English. The man up there raged aloud in two languages, and with a sincerity in his fury that almost convinced me I had, in some way, sinned against the harmony of the universe. I could hardly see him, but began to think he would work himself into a fit.

'Suddenly he ceased, and I could hear him snorting and blowing like a porpoise. I said – ' "What steamer is this, pray?"

' "Eh? What's this? And who are you?"

' "Castaway crew of an English barque burnt at sea. We came here tonight. I am the second mate. The captain is in the long-boat, and wishes to know if you would give us a passage somewhere."

' "Oh, my goodness! I say . . . This is the *Celestial* from Singapore on her return trip. I'll arrange with your captain in the morning, . . . and, . . . I say, . . . did you hear me just now?"

' "I should think the whole bay heard you."

' "I thought you were a shore-boat. Now, look here – this infernal lazy scoundrel of a caretaker has gone to sleep again – curse him. The light is out, and I nearly ran foul of the end of this damned jetty. This is the third time he plays me this trick. Now, I ask you, can anybody stand this kind of thing? It's enough to drive a man out of his mind. I'll report him . . . I'll get the Assistant Resident to give him the sack, by . . . ! See – there's no light. It's out, isn't it? I take you to witness the light's out. There should be a light, you know. A red light on the – "

' "There was a light," I said, mildly.

' "But it's out, man! What's the use of talking like this? You can see for yourself it's out – don't you? If you had to take a valuable steamer along this God-forsaken coast you would want a light too. I'll kick him from end to end of his miserable wharf. You'll see if I don't. I will – "

' "So I may tell my captain you'll take us?" I broke in.

' "Yes, I'll take you. Good-night," he said, brusquely.

'I pulled back, made fast again to the jetty, and then went to sleep at last. I had faced the silence of the East. I had heard some of its language. But when I opened my eyes again the silence was as complete as though it had never been broken. I was lying in a flood of light, and the sky had never looked so far, so high, before. I opened my eyes and lay without moving.

'And then I saw the men of the East – they were looking at me. The whole length of the jetty was full of people. I saw brown, bronze, yellow faces, the black eyes, the glitter, the colour of an Eastern crowd. And all these beings stared without a murmur, without a sigh, without a movement. They stared down at the boats, at the sleeping men who at night had come to them from the sea. Nothing moved. The fronds of palms stood still against the sky. Not a branch stirred along the shore, and the brown roofs of hidden houses peeped through the green foliage, through the big leaves that hung shining and still like leaves forged of heavy metal. This was the East of the ancient navigators, so old, so mysterious, resplendent and sombre, living and unchanged, full of danger and promise. And these were the men. I sat up suddenly. A wave of movement passed through the crowd from end to end, passed along the heads, swayed the bodies, ran along the jetty like a ripple on the water, like a breath of wind on a field – and all was still again. I see it now – the wide sweep of the bay, the glittering sands, the wealth of green infinite and varied, the sea blue like the sea of a dream, the crowd of attentive faces, the blaze of vivid colour – the water reflecting it all, the curve of the shore, the jetty, the high-sterned outlandish craft floating still, and the three boats with the tired men from the West sleeping, unconscious of the land and the people and of the violence of sunshine. They slept thrown across the thwarts, curled on bottom-boards, in the careless attitudes of death. The head of the old skipper, leaning back in the stern of the long-boat, had fallen on his breast, and he looked as though he would never wake. Farther out old Mahon's face was upturned to the sky, with the long white beard spread out on his breast, as though he had been shot where he sat at the tiller; and a man, all in a heap in the bows of the boat, slept with both arms embracing the stem-head and with his cheek laid on the gunwale. The East looked at them without a sound.

'I have known its fascination since; I have seen the mysterious shores, the still water, the lands of brown nations, where a stealthy Nemesis lies in wait, pursues, overtakes so many of the conquering race, who are proud of their wisdom, of their knowledge, of their strength. But for me all the East is contained in that vision of my youth. It is all in that moment when I opened my young eyes on it. I came upon it from a tussle with the sea – and I was young – and I saw it looking at me. And this is all that is left of it! Only a moment; a moment of strength, of romance, of glamour – of youth! . . . A flick of sunshine upon a strange shore, the time to remember, the time for a sigh, and – goodbye! – Night – Goodbye . . . !'

He drank.

'Ah! The good old time – the good old time. Youth and the sea. Glamour and the sea! The good, strong sea, the salt, bitter sea, that could whisper to you and roar at you and knock your breath out of you.'

He drank again.

'By all that's wonderful it is the sea, I believe, the sea itself – or is it youth alone? Who can tell? But you here – you all had something out of life: money, love – whatever one gets on shore – and, tell me, wasn't that the best time, that time when we were young at sea; young and had nothing, on the sea that gives nothing, except hard knocks – and sometimes a chance to feel your strength – that only – what you all regret?'

And we all nodded at him: the man of finance, the man of accounts, the man of law, we all nodded at him over the polished table that like a still sheet of brown water reflected our faces, lined, wrinkled; our faces marked by toil, by deceptions, by success, by love; our weary eyes looking still, looking always, looking anxiously for something out of life, that while it is expected is already gone – has passed unseen, in a sigh, in a flash – together with the youth, with the strength, with the romance of illusions.

1898

AMY FOSTER

Kennedy is a country doctor, and lives in Colebrook, on the shores of Eastbay. The high ground rising abruptly behind the red roofs of the little town crowds the quaint High Street against the wall which defends it from the sea. Beyond the sea-wall there curves for miles in a vast and regular sweep the barren beach of shingle, with the village of Brenzett standing out darkly across the water, a spire in a clump of trees; and still further out the perpendicular column of a lighthouse, looking in the distance no bigger than a lead-pencil, marks the vanishing-point of the land. The country at the back of Brenzett is low and flat; but the bay is fairly well sheltered from the seas, and occasionally a big ship, windbound or through stress of weather, makes use of the anchoring ground a mile and a half due north from you as you stand at the back door of the Ship Inn in Brenzett. A dilapidated windmill near by lifting its shattered arms from a mound no loftier than a rubbish-heap, and a Martello tower squatting at the water's edge half a mile to the south of the coastguard cottages, are familiar to the skippers of small craft. These are the official sea marks for the patch of trustworthy bottom represented on the Admiralty charts by an irregular oval of dots enclosing several figures six, with a tiny anchor engraved among them, and the legend 'mud and shells' over all.

The brow of the upland overtops the square tower of the Colebrook Church. The slope is green and looped by a white road. Ascending along this road, you open a valley broad and shallow, a wide green trough of pastures and hedges merging inland into a vista of purple tints and flowing lines closing the view.

In this valley down to Brenzett and Colebrook and up to Darnford, the market town fourteen miles away, lies the practice of my friend Kennedy. He had begun life as a surgeon in the Navy, and afterwards had been the companion of a famous traveller, in the days when there were continents with unexplored interiors. His papers on the fauna and flora made him known to scientific societies. And now he had come to a country practice – from choice. The penetrating power of his mind, acting like a corrosive fluid, had destroyed his ambition, I fancy. His intelligence is of a scientific order, of an investigating habit, and of that unappeasable curiosity which believes that there is a particle of a general truth in every mystery.

A good many years ago now, on my return from abroad, he invited me to stay with him. I came readily enough, and as he could not neglect his patients to keep me company, he took me on his rounds – thirty miles or so of an afternoon, sometimes. I waited for him on the roads; the horse reached after the leafy twigs, and, sitting high in the dogcart, I could hear Kennedy's laugh through the half-open door of some cottage. He had a big, hearty laugh that would have fitted a man twice his size, a brisk manner, a bronzed face, and a pair of grey, profoundly attentive eyes. He had the talent of making people talk to him freely, and an inexhaustible patience in listening to their tales.

One day, as we trotted out of a large village into a shady bit of road, I saw on our left hand a low, black cottage, with diamond panes in the windows, a creeper on the end wall, a roof of shingle, and some roses climbing on the rickety trellis-work of the tiny porch. Kennedy pulled up to a walk. A woman, in full sunlight, was throwing a dripping blanket over a line stretched between two old apple-trees. And as the bobtailed, long-necked chestnut, trying to get his head, jerked the left hand, covered by a thick dogskin glove, the doctor raised his voice over the hedge: 'How's your child, Amy?'

I had the time to see her dull face, red, not with a mantling blush, but as if her flat cheeks had been vigorously slapped, and to take in the squat figure, the scanty, dusty brown hair drawn into a tight knot at the back of the head. She looked quite young. With a distinct catch in her breath, her voice sounded low and timid.

'He's well, thank you.'

We trotted again. 'A young patient of yours,' I said; and the doctor, flicking the chestnut absently, muttered, 'Her husband used to be.'

'She seems a dull creature,' I remarked listlessly.

'Precisely,' said Kennedy. 'She is very passive. It's enough to look at the red hands hanging at the end of those short arms, at those slow, prominent brown eyes, to know the inertness of her mind – an inertness that one would think made it everlastingly safe from all the surprises of imagination. And yet which of us is safe? At any rate, such as you see her, she had enough imagination to fall in love. She's the daughter of one Isaac Foster, who from a small farmer has sunk into a shepherd; the beginning of his misfortunes dating from his runaway marriage with the cook of his widowed father – a well-to-do, apoplectic grazier, who passionately struck his name off his will, and had been heard to utter threats against his life. But this old affair, scandalous enough to serve as a motive for a Greek tragedy, arose from the similarity of their characters. There are other tragedies, less scandalous and of a subtler poignancy, arising from irreconcilable differences and from that fear of the Incomprehensible that hangs over all our heads – over all our heads . . . '

The tired chestnut dropped into a walk; and the rim of the sun, all red in a speckless sky, touched familiarly the smooth top of a ploughed rise near the road as I had seen it times innumerable touch the distant horizon of the sea. The uniform brownness of the harrowed field glowed with a rosy tinge, as though the powdered clods had sweated out in minute pearls of blood the toil of uncounted ploughmen. From the edge of a copse a waggon with two horses was rolling gently along the ridge. Raised above our heads upon the skyline, it loomed up against the red sun, triumphantly big, enormous, like a chariot of giants drawn by two slow-stepping steeds of legendary proportions. And the clumsy figure of the man plodding at the head of the leading horse projected itself on the background of the Infinite with a heroic uncouthness. The end of his carter's whip quivered high up in the blue. Kennedy discoursed – 'She's the eldest of a large family. At the age of fifteen they put her out to service at the New Barns Farm. I attended Mrs Smith, the tenant's wife, and saw that girl there for the first time. Mrs Smith, a genteel person with a sharp nose, made her put on a black dress every afternoon. I don't know what induced me to notice her at all. There are faces that call your attention by a curious want of definiteness in their whole aspect, as, walking in a mist, you peer attentively at a vague shape which, after all, may be nothing more curious or strange than a signpost. The only peculiarity I perceived in her was a slight hesitation in her utterance, a sort of preliminary stammer which passes away with the first word. When sharply spoken to, she was apt to lose her head at once; but her heart was of the kindest. She had never been heard to express a dislike for a single human being, and she was tender to every living creature. She was devoted to Mrs Smith, to Mr Smith, to their dogs, cats, canaries; and as to Mrs Smith's grey parrot, its peculiarities exercised upon her a positive fascination. Nevertheless, when that outlandish bird, attacked by the cat, shrieked for help in human accents, she ran out into the yard stopping her ears, and did not prevent the crime. For Mrs Smith this was another evidence of her stupidity; on the other hand, her want of charm, in view of Smith's well-known frivolousness, was a great recommendation. Her short-sighted eyes would swim with pity for a poor mouse in a trap, and she had been seen once by some boys on her knees in the wet grass helping a toad in difficulties. If it's true, as some German fellow has said, that without phosphorus there is no thought, it is still more true that there is no kindness of heart without a certain amount of imagination. She had some. She had even more than is necessary to understand suffering and to be moved by pity. She fell in love under circumstances that leave no room for doubt in the matter; for you need imagination to form a notion of beauty at all, and still more to discover your ideal in an unfamiliar shape.

'How this aptitude came to her, what it did feed upon, is an inscrutable mystery. She was born in the village, and had never been further away from it than Colebrook or perhaps Darnford. She lived for four years with the Smiths. New Barns is an isolated farmhouse a mile away from the road, and she was content to look day after day at the same fields, hollows, rises; at the trees and the hedgerows; at the faces of the four men about the farm, always the same – day after day, month after month, year after year. She never showed a desire for conversation, and, as it seemed to me, she did not know how to smile. Sometimes of a fine Sunday afternoon she would put on her best dress, a pair of stout boots, a large grey hat trimmed with a black feather (I've seen her in that finery), seize an absurdly slender parasol, climb over two stiles, tramp over three fields and along two hundred yards of road – never further. There stood Foster's cottage. She would help her mother to give their tea to the younger children, wash up the crockery, kiss the little ones, and go back to the farm. That was all. All the rest, all the change, all the relaxation. She never seemed to wish for anything more. And then she fell in love. She fell in love silently, obstinately – perhaps helplessly. It came slowly, but when it came it worked like a powerful spell; it was love as the Ancients understood it: an irresistible and fateful impulse – a possession! Yes, it was in her to become haunted and possessed by a face, by a presence, fatally, as though she had been a pagan worshipper of form under a joyous sky – and to be awakened at last from that mysterious forgetfulness of self, from that enchantment, from that transport, by a fear resembling the unaccountable terror of a brute . . . '

With the sun hanging low on its western limit, the expanse of the grasslands framed in the counterscarps of the rising ground took on a gorgeous and sombre aspect. A sense of penetrating sadness, like that inspired by a grave strain of music, disengaged itself from the silence of the fields. The men we met walked past, slow, unsmiling, with downcast eyes, as if the melancholy of an overburdened earth had weighted their feet, bowed their shoulders, borne down their glances.

'Yes,' said the doctor to my remark, 'one would think the earth is under a curse, since of all her children these that cling to her the closest are uncouth in body and as leaden of gait as if their very hearts were loaded with chains. But here on this same road you might have seen amongst these heavy men a being lithe, supple and long-limbed, straight like a pine, with something striving upwards in his appearance as though the heart within him had been buoyant. Perhaps it was only the force of the contrast, but when he was passing one of these villagers here, the soles of his feet did not seem to me to touch the dust of the road. He vaulted over the stiles, paced these slopes with a long elastic stride that made him noticeable at a great distance, and had lustrous black eyes. He was so different from the mankind around that, with his freedom of movement, his soft – a little startled, glance, his olive complexion and graceful bearing, his humanity suggested to me the nature of a woodland creature. He came from there.'

The doctor pointed with his whip, and from the summit of the descent seen over the rolling tops of the trees in a park by the side of the road, appeared the level sea far below us, like the floor of an immense edifice inlaid with bands of dark ripple, with still trails of glitter, ending in a belt of glassy water at the foot of the sky. The light blur of smoke, from an invisible steamer, faded on the great clearness of the horizon like the mist of a breath on a mirror; and, inshore, the white sails of a coaster, with the appearance of disentangling themselves slowly from under the branches, floated clear of the foliage of the trees.

'Shipwrecked in the bay?' I said.

'Yes; he was a castaway. A poor emigrant from central Europe bound to America and washed ashore here in a storm. And for him, who knew nothing of the earth, England was an undiscovered country. It was some time before he learned its name; and for all I know he might have expected to find wild beasts or wild men here, when, crawling in the dark over the sea-wall, he rolled down the other side into a dyke, where it was another miracle he didn't get drowned. But he struggled instinctively like an animal under a net, and this blind struggle threw him out into a field. He must have been, indeed, of a tougher fibre than he looked to withstand without expiring such buffetings, the violence of his exertions, and so much fear. Later on, in his broken English that resembled curiously the speech of a young child, he told me himself that he put his trust in God, believing he was no longer in this world. And truly – he would add – how was he to know? He fought his way against the rain and the gale on all fours, and crawled at last among some sheep huddled close under the lee of a hedge. They ran off in all directions, bleating in the darkness, and he welcomed the first familiar sound he heard on these shores. It must have been two in the morning then. And this is all we know of the manner of his landing, though he did not arrive unattended by any means. Only his grisly company did not begin to come ashore till much later in the day . . . '

The doctor gathered the reins, clicked his tongue; we trotted down the hill. Then turning, almost directly, a sharp corner into the High Street, we rattled over the stones and were home.

Late in the evening Kennedy, breaking a spell of moodiness that had come over him, returned to the story. Smoking his pipe, he paced the long room from end to end. A reading-lamp concentrated all its light upon the papers on his desk; and, sitting by the open window, I saw, after the windless, scorching day, the frigid splendour of a hazy sea lying motionless under the moon. Not a whisper, not a splash, not a stir of the shingle, not a footstep, not a sigh came up from the earth below – never a sign of life but the scent of climbing jasmine; and Kennedy's voice, speaking behind me, passed through the wide casement, to vanish outside in a chill and sumptuous stillness.

' . . . The relations of shipwrecks in the olden time tell us of much suffering. Often the castaways were only saved from drowning to die miserably from starvation on a barren coast; others suffered violent death or else slavery, passing through years of precarious existence with people to whom their strangeness was an object of suspicion, dislike or fear. We read about these things, and they are very pitiful. It is indeed hard upon a man to find himself a lost stranger, helpless, incomprehensible, and of a mysterious origin, in some obscure corner of the earth. Yet amongst all the adventurers shipwrecked in all the wild parts of the world, there is not one, it seems to me, that ever had to suffer a fate so simply tragic as the man I am speaking of, the most innocent of adventurers cast out by the sea in the bight of this bay, almost within sight from this very window.

'He did not know the name of his ship. Indeed, in the course of time we discovered he did not even know that ships had names – 'like Christian people'; and when, one day, from the top of the Talfourd Hill, he beheld the sea lying open to his view, his eyes roamed afar, lost in an air of wild surprise, as though he had never seen such a sight before. And probably he had not. As far as I could make out, he had been hustled together with many others on board an emigrant ship lying at the mouth of the Elbe, too bewildered to take note of his surroundings, too weary to see anything, too anxious to care. They were driven below into the 'tween-deck and battened down from the very start. It was a low timber dwelling – he would say – with wooden beams overhead, like the houses in his country, but you went into it down a ladder. It was very large, very cold, damp and sombre, with places in the manner of wooden boxes where people had to sleep one above another, and it kept on rocking all ways at once all the time. He crept into one of these boxes and lay down there in the clothes in which he had left his home many days before, keeping his bundle and his stick by his side. People groaned, children cried, water dripped, the lights went out, the walls of the place creaked, and everything was being shaken so that in one's little box one dared not lift one's head. He had lost touch with his only companion (a young man from the same valley, he said), and all the time a great noise of wind went on outside and heavy blows fell – boom! boom! An awful sickness overcame him, even to the point of making him neglect his prayers. Besides, one could not tell whether it was morning or evening. It seemed always to be night in that place.

'Before that he had been travelling a long, long time on the iron track. He looked out of the window, which had a wonderfully clear glass in it, and the trees, the houses, the fields, and the long roads seemed to fly round and round about him till his head swam. He gave me to understand that he had on his passage beheld uncounted multitudes of people – whole nations – all dressed in such clothes as the rich wear. Once he was made to get out of the carriage, and slept through a night on a bench in a house of bricks with his bundle under his head; and once for many hours he had to sit on a floor of flat stones dozing, with his knees up and with his bundle between his feet. There was a roof over him, which seemed made of glass, and was so high that the tallest mountain-pine he had ever seen would have had room to grow under it. Steam-machines rolled in at one end and out at the other. People swarmed more than you can see on a feast-day round the miraculous Holy Image in the yard of the Carmelite Convent down in the plains where, before he left his home, he drove his mother in a wooden cart – a pious old woman who wanted to offer prayers and make a vow for his safety. He could not give me an idea of how large and lofty and full of noise and smoke and gloom, and clang of iron, the place was, but someone had told him it was called Berlin. Then they rang a bell, and another steam-machine came in, and again he was taken on and on through a land that wearied his eyes by its flatness without a single bit of a hill to be seen anywhere. One more night he spent shut up in a building like a good stable with a litter of straw on the floor, guarding his bundle amongst a lot of men, of whom not one could understand a single word he said. In the morning they were all led down to the stony shores of an extremely broad muddy river, flowing not between hills but between houses that seemed immense. There was a steam-machine that went on the water, and they all stood upon it packed tight, only now there were with them many women and children who made much noise. A cold rain fell, the wind blew in his face; he was wet through, and his teeth chattered. He and the young man from the same valley took each other by the hand.

'They thought they were being taken to America straight away, but suddenly the steam-machine bumped against the side of a thing like a great house on the water. The walls were smooth and black, and there uprose, growing from the roof as it were, bare trees in the shape of crosses, extremely high. That's how it appeared to him then, for he had never seen a ship before. This was the ship that was going to swim all the way to America. Voices shouted, everything swayed; there was a ladder dipping up and down. He went up on his hands and knees in mortal fear of falling into the water below, which made a great splashing. He got separated from his companion, and when he descended into the bottom of that ship his heart seemed to melt suddenly within him.

'It was then also, as he told me, that he lost contact for good and all with one of those three men who the summer before had been going about through all the little towns in the foothills of his country. They would arrive on market-days driving in a peasant's cart, and would set up an office in an inn or some other Jew's house. There were three of them, of whom one with a long beard looked venerable; and they had red cloth collars round their necks and gold lace on their sleeves like Government officials. They sat proudly behind a long table; and in the next room, so that the common people shouldn't hear, they kept a cunning telegraph machine, through which they could talk to the Emperor of America. The fathers hung about the door, but the young men of the mountains would crowd up to the table asking many questions, for there was work to be got all the year round at three dollars a day in America, and no military service to do.

'But the American Kaiser would not take everybody. Oh no! He himself had great difficulty in getting accepted, and the venerable man in uniform had to go out of the room several times to work the telegraph on his behalf. The American Kaiser engaged him at last at three dollars, he being young and strong. However, many able young men backed out, afraid of the great distance; besides, those only who had some money could be taken. There were some who had sold their huts and their land because it cost a lot of money to get to America; but then, once there, you had three dollars a day, and if you were clever you could find places where true gold could be picked up on the ground. His father's house was getting over full. Two of his brothers were married and had children. He promised to send money home from America by post twice a year. His father sold an old cow, a pair of piebald mountain ponies of his own raising, and a cleared plot of fair pasture land on the sunny slope of a pine-clad pass to a Jew innkeeper, in order to pay the people of the ship that took men to America to get rich in a short time.

'He must have been a real adventurer at heart, for how many of the greatest enterprises in the conquest of the earth had for their beginning just such a bargaining away of the paternal cow for the mirage of true gold far away! I have been telling you more or less in my own words what I learned fragmentarily in the course of two or three years, during which I seldom missed an opportunity of a friendly chat with him. He told me this story of his adventure with many flashes of white teeth and lively glances of black eyes, at first in a sort of anxious baby-talk, then, as he acquired the language, with great fluency, but always with that singing, soft, and at the same time vibrating intonation that instilled a strangely penetrating power into the sound of the most familiar English words, as if they had been the words of an unearthly language. And he always would come to an end, with many emphatic shakes of his head, upon that awful sensation of his heart melting within him directly he set foot on board that ship. Afterwards there seemed to come for him a period of blank ignorance, at any rate as to facts. No doubt he must have been abominably seasick and abominably unhappy – this soft and passionate adventurer, taken thus out of his knowledge, and feeling bitterly as he lay in his emigrant bunk his utter loneliness; for his was a highly sensitive nature. The next thing we know of him for certain is that he had been hiding in Hammond's pig-pound by the side of the road to Norton, six miles, as the crow flies, from the sea. Of these experiences he was unwilling to speak: they seemed to have seared into his soul a sombre sort of wonder and indignation. Through the rumours of the countryside, which lasted for a good many days after his arrival, we know that the fishermen of West Colebrook had been disturbed and startled by heavy knocks against the walls of weatherboard cottages, and by a voice crying piercingly strange words in the night. Several of them turned out even, but, no doubt, he had fled in sudden alarm at their rough angry tones hailing each other in the darkness. A sort of frenzy must have helped him up the steep Norton Hill. It was he, no doubt, who early the following morning had been seen lying (in a swoon, I should say) on the roadside grass by the Brenzett carrier, who actually got down to have a nearer look, but drew back, intimidated by the perfect immobility, and by something queer in the aspect of that tramp, sleeping so still under the showers. As the day advanced, some children came dashing into school at Norton in such a fright that the schoolmistress went out and spoke indignantly to a "horrid-looking man" on the road. He edged away, hanging his head, for a few steps, and then suddenly ran off with extraordinary fleetness. The driver of Mr Bradley's milk-cart made no secret of it that he had lashed with his whip at a hairy sort of gypsy fellow who, jumping up at a turn of the road by the Vents, made a snatch at the pony's bridle. And he caught him a good one too, right over the face, he said, that made him drop down in the mud a jolly sight quicker than he had jumped up; but it was a good half a mile before he could stop the pony. Maybe that in his desperate endeavours to get help, and in his need to get in touch with someone, the poor devil had tried to stop the cart. Also three boys confessed afterwards to throwing stones at a funny tramp, knocking about all wet and muddy, and, it seemed, very drunk, in the narrow deep lane by the limekilns. All this was the talk of three villages for days; but we have Mrs Finn's (the wife of Smith's waggoner) unimpeachable testimony that she saw him get over the low wall of Hammond's pig-pound and lurch straight at her, babbling aloud in a voice that was enough to make one die of fright. Having the baby with her in a perambulator, Mrs Finn called out to him to go away, and as he persisted in coming nearer, she hit him courageously with her umbrella over the head, and, without once looking back, ran like the wind with the perambulator as far as the first house in the village. She stopped then, out of breath, and spoke to old Lewis, hammering there at a heap of stones; and the old chap, taking off his immense black wire goggles, got up on his shaky legs to look where she pointed. Together they followed with their eyes the figure of the man running over a field; they saw him fall down, pick himself up, and run on again, staggering and waving his long arms above his head, in the direction of the New Barns Farm. From that moment he is plainly in the toils of his obscure and touching destiny. There is no doubt after this of what happened to him. All is certain now: Mrs Smith's intense terror; Amy Foster's stolid conviction held against the other's nervous attack, that the man "meant no harm"; Smith's exasperation (on his return from Darnford Market) at finding the dog barking himself into a fit, the back-door locked, his wife in hysterics; and all for an unfortunate dirty tramp, supposed to be even then lurking in his stackyard. Was he? He would teach him to frighten women.

'Smith is notoriously hot-tempered, but the sight of some nondescript and miry creature sitting cross-legged amongst a lot of loose straw, and swinging itself to and fro like a bear in a cage, made him pause. Then this tramp stood up silently before him, one mass of mud and filth from head to foot. Smith, alone amongst his stacks with this apparition, in the stormy twilight ringing with the infuriated barking of the dog, felt the dread of an inexplicable strangeness. But when that being, parting with his black hands the long matted locks that hung before his face, as you part the two halves of a curtain, looked out at him with glistening, wild, black-and-white eyes, the weirdness of this silent encounter fairly staggered him. He has admitted since (for the story has been a legitimate subject of conversation about here for years) that he made more than one step backwards. Then a sudden burst of rapid, senseless speech persuaded him at once that he had to do with an escaped lunatic. In fact, that impression never wore off completely. Smith has not in his heart given up his secret conviction of the man's essential insanity to this very day.

'As the creature approached him, jabbering in a most discomposing manner, Smith (unaware that he was being addressed as "gracious lord", and adjured in God's name to afford food and shelter) kept on speaking firmly but gently to it, and retreating all the time into the other yard. At last, watching his chance, by a sudden charge he bundled him headlong into the wood-lodge, and instantly shot the bolt. Thereupon he wiped his brow, though the day was cold. He had done his duty to the community by shutting up a wandering and probably dangerous maniac. Smith isn't a hard man at all, but he had room in his brain only for that one idea of lunacy. He was not imaginative enough to ask himself whether the man might not be perishing with cold and hunger. Meantime, at first, the maniac made a great deal of noise in the lodge. Mrs Smith was screaming upstairs, where she had locked herself in her bedroom; but Amy Foster sobbed piteously at the kitchen-door, wringing her hands and muttering, "Don't! don't!" I dare say Smith had a rough time of it that evening with one noise and another, and this insane, disturbing voice crying obstinately through the door only added to his irritation. He couldn't possibly have connected this troublesome lunatic with the sinking of a ship in Eastbay, of which there had been a rumour in the Darnford market-place. And I dare say the man inside had been very near to insanity on that night. Before his excitement collapsed and he became unconscious he was throwing himself violently about in the dark, rolling on some dirty sacks, and biting his fists with rage, cold, hunger, amazement, and despair.

'He was a mountaineer of the eastern range of the Carpathians, and the vessel sunk the night before in Eastbay was the Hamburg emigrant ship *Herzogin Sophia-Dorothea*, of appalling memory.

'A few months later we could read in the papers the accounts of the bogus "Emigration Agencies" among the Sclavonian peasantry in the more remote provinces of Austria. The object of these scoundrels was to get hold of the poor ignorant people's homesteads, and they were in league with the local usurers. They exported their victims through Hamburg mostly. As to the ship, I had watched her out of this very window, reaching close-hauled under short canvas into the bay on a dark, threatening afternoon. She came to an anchor, correctly by the chart, off the Brenzett coastguard station. I remember before the night fell looking out again at the outlines of her spars and rigging that stood out dark and pointed on a background of ragged, slaty clouds like another and a slighter spire to the left of the Brenzett church-tower. In the evening the wind rose. At midnight I could hear in my bed the terrific gusts and the sounds of a driving deluge.

'About that time the coastguardmen thought they saw the lights of a steamer over the anchoring-ground. In a moment they vanished; but it is clear that another vessel of some sort had tried for shelter in the bay on that awful, blind night, had rammed the German ship amidships (a breach – as one of the divers told me afterwards – 'that you could sail a Thames barge through'), and then had gone out either scathless or damaged, who shall say; but had gone out, unknown, unseen, and fatal, to perish mysteriously at sea. Of her nothing ever came to light, and yet the hue and cry that was raised all over the world would have found her out if she had been in existence anywhere on the face of the waters.

'A completeness without a clue, and a stealthy silence as of a neatly executed crime, characterise this murderous disaster, which, as you may remember, had its gruesome celebrity. The wind would have prevented the loudest outcries from reaching the shore; there had been evidently no time for signals of distress. It was death without any sort of fuss. The Hamburg ship, filling all at once, capsized as she sank, and at daylight there was not even the end of a spar to be seen above water. She was missed, of course, and at first the coastguardmen surmised that she had either dragged her anchor or parted her cable some time during the night, and had been blown out to sea. Then, after the tide turned, the wreck must have shifted a little and released some of the bodies, because a child – a little fair-haired child in a red frock – came ashore abreast of the Martello tower. By the afternoon you could see along three miles of beach dark figures with bare legs dashing in and out of the tumbling foam, and rough-looking men, women with hard faces, children, mostly fair-haired, were being carried, stiff and dripping, on stretchers, on wattles, on ladders, in a long procession past the door of the Ship Inn, to be laid out in a row under the north wall of the Brenzett Church.

'Officially, the body of the little girl in the red frock is the first thing that came ashore from that ship. But I have patients amongst the seafaring population of West Colebrook, and, unofficially, I am informed that very early that morning two brothers, who went down to look after their cobble hauled up on the beach, found, a good way from Brenzett, an ordinary ship's hencoop lying high and dry on the shore, with eleven drowned ducks inside. Their families ate the birds, and the hencoop was split into firewood with a hatchet. It is possible that a man (supposing he happened to be on deck at the time of the accident) might have floated ashore on that hencoop. He might. I admit it is improbable, but there was the man – and for days, nay, for weeks – it didn't enter our heads that we had amongst us the only living soul that had escaped from that disaster. The man himself, even when he learned to speak intelligibly, could tell us very little. He remembered he had felt better (after the ship had anchored, I suppose), and that the darkness, the wind, and the rain took his breath away. This looks as if he had been on deck some time during that night. But we mustn't forget he had been taken out of his knowledge, that he had been seasick and battened down below for four days, that he had no general notion of a ship or of the sea, and therefore could have no definite idea of what was happening to him. The rain, the wind, the darkness he knew; he understood the bleating of the sheep, and he remembered the pain of his wretchedness and misery, his heartbroken astonishment that it was neither seen nor understood, his dismay at finding all the men angry and all the women fierce. He had approached them as a beggar, it is true, he said; but in his country, even if they gave nothing, they spoke gently to beggars. The children in his country were not taught to throw stones at those who asked for compassion. Smith's strategy overcame him completely. The wood-lodge presented the horrible aspect of a dungeon. What would be done to him next? . . . No wonder that Amy Foster appeared to his eyes with the aureole of an angel of light. The girl had not been able to sleep for thinking of the poor man, and in the morning, before the Smiths were up, she slipped out across the back yard. Holding the door of the wood-lodge ajar, she looked in and extended to him half a loaf of white bread – "such bread as the rich eat in my country," he used to say.

'At this he got up slowly from amongst all sorts of rubbish, stiff, hungry, trembling, miserable, and doubtful. "Can you eat this?" she asked in her soft and timid voice. He must have taken her for a "gracious lady". He devoured ferociously, and tears were falling on the crust. Suddenly he dropped the bread, seized her wrist, and imprinted a kiss on her hand. She was not frightened. Through his forlorn condition she had observed that he was good-looking. She shut the door and walked back slowly to the kitchen. Much later on, she told Mrs Smith, who shuddered at the bare idea of being touched by that creature.

'Through this act of impulsive pity he was brought back again within the pale of human relations with his new surroundings. He never forgot it – never.

'That very same morning old Mr Swaffer (Smith's nearest neighbour) came over to give his advice, and ended by carrying him off. He stood, unsteady on his legs, meek, and caked over in half-dried mud, while the two men talked around him in an incomprehensible tongue. Mrs Smith had refused to come downstairs till the madman was off the premises; Amy Foster, from far within the dark kitchen, watched through the open back door; and he obeyed the signs that were made to him to the best of his ability. But Smith was full of mistrust. "Mind, sir! It may be all his cunning," he cried repeatedly in a tone of warning. When Mr Swaffer started the mare, the deplorable being sitting humbly by his side, through weakness, nearly fell out over the back of the high two-wheeled cart. Swaffer took him straight home. And it is then that I come upon the scene.

'I was called in by the simple process of the old man beckoning to me with his forefinger over the gate of his house as I happened to be driving past. I got down, of course.

"I've got something here,' he mumbled, leading the way to an outhouse at a little distance from his other farm-buildings.

'It was there that I saw him first, in a long low room taken upon the space of that sort of coach-house. It was bare and whitewashed, with a small square aperture glazed with one cracked, dusty pane at its further end. He was lying on his back upon a straw pallet; they had given him a couple of horse-blankets, and he seemed to have spent the remainder of his strength in the exertion of cleaning himself. He was almost speechless; his quick breathing under the blankets pulled up to his chin, his glittering, restless black eyes reminded me of a wild bird caught in a snare. While I was examining him, old Swaffer stood silently by the door, passing the tips of his fingers along his shaven upper lip. I gave some directions, promised to send a bottle of medicine, and naturally made some enquiries.

'Smith caught him in the stackyard at New Barns,' said the old chap in his deliberate, unmoved manner, and as if the other had been indeed a sort of wild animal, 'That's how I came by him. Quite a curiosity, isn't he? Now tell me, doctor – you've been all over the world – don't you think that's a bit of a Hindu we've got hold of here?'

'I was greatly surprised. His long black hair scattered over the straw bolster contrasted with the olive pallor of his face. It occurred to me he might be a Basque. It didn't necessarily follow that he should understand Spanish; but I tried him with the few words I know, and also with some French. The whispered sounds I caught by bending my ear to his lips puzzled me utterly. That afternoon the young ladies from the rectory (one of them read Goethe with a dictionary, and the other had struggled with Dante for years), coming to see Miss Swaffer, tried their German and Italian on him from the doorway. They retreated, just the least bit scared by the flood of passionate speech which, turning on his pallet, he let out at them. They admitted that the sound was pleasant, soft, musical – but, in conjunction with his looks perhaps, it was startling – so excitable, so utterly unlike anything one had ever heard. The village boys climbed up the bank to have a peep through the little square aperture. Everybody was wondering what Mr Swaffer would do with him.

'He simply kept him.

'Swaffer would be called eccentric were he not so much respected. They will tell you that Mr Swaffer sits up as late as ten o'clock at night to read books, and they will tell you also that he can write a cheque for two hundred pounds without thinking twice about it. He himself would tell you that the Swaffers have owned land between this and Darnford for these three hundred years. He must be eighty-five today, but he does not look a bit older than when I first came here. He is a great breeder of sheep, and deals extensively in cattle. He attends market days for miles around in every sort of weather, and drives sitting bowed low over the reins, his lank grey hair curling over the collar of his warm coat, and with a green plaid rug round his legs. The calmness of advanced age gives a solemnity to his manner. He is clean-shaved; his lips are thin and sensitive; something rigid and monachal in the set of his features lends a certain elevation to the character of his face. He has been known to drive miles in the rain to see a new kind of rose in somebody's garden, or a monstrous cabbage grown by a cottager. He loves to hear tell of or to be shown something what he calls "outlandish". Perhaps it was just that outlandishness of the man which influenced old Swaffer. Perhaps it was only an inexplicable caprice. All I know is that at the end of three weeks I caught sight of Smith's lunatic digging in Swaffer's kitchen garden. They had found out he could use a spade. He dug barefooted.

'His black hair flowed over his shoulders. I suppose it was Swaffer who had given him the striped old cotton shirt; but he wore still the national brown cloth trousers (in which he had been washed ashore) fitting to the leg almost like tights; was belted with a broad leathern belt studded with little brass discs; and had never yet ventured into the village. The land he looked upon seemed to him kept neatly, like the grounds round a landowner's house; the size of the cart-horses struck him with astonishment; the roads resembled garden walks, and the aspect of the people, especially on Sundays, spoke of opulence. He wondered what made them so hardhearted and their children so bold. He got his food at the back door, carried it in both hands, carefully, to his outhouse, and, sitting alone on his pallet, would make the sign of the cross before he began. Beside the same pallet, kneeling in the early darkness of the short days, he recited aloud the Lord's Prayer before he slept. Whenever he saw old Swaffer he would bow with veneration from the waist, and stand erect while the old man, with his fingers over his upper lip, surveyed him silently. He bowed also to Miss Swaffer, who kept house frugally for her father – a broad-shouldered, big-boned woman of forty-five, with the pocket of her dress full of keys, and a grey, steady eye. She was Church – as people said (while her father was one of the trustees of the Baptist Chapel) – and wore a little steel cross at her waist. She dressed severely in black, in memory of one of the innumerable Bradleys of the neighbourhood, to whom she had been engaged some twenty-five years ago – a young farmer who broke his neck out hunting on the eve of the wedding-day. She had the unmoved countenance of the deaf, spoke very seldom, and her lips, thin like her father's, astonished one sometimes by a mysteriously ironic curl.

'These were the people to whom he owed allegiance, and an overwhelming loneliness seemed to fall from the leaden sky of that winter without sunshine. All the faces were sad. He could talk to no one, and had no hope of ever understanding anybody. It was as if these had been the faces of people from the other world – dead people – he used to tell me years afterwards. Upon my word, I wonder he did not go mad. He didn't know where he was. Somewhere very far from his mountains – somewhere over the water. Was this America, he wondered?

'If it hadn't been for the steel cross at Miss Swaffer's belt he would not, he confessed, have known whether he was in a Christian country at all. He used to cast stealthy glances at it, and feel comforted. There was nothing here the same as in his country! The earth and the water were different; there were no images of the Redeemer by the roadside. The very grass was different, and the trees. All the trees but the three old Norway pines on the bit of lawn before Swaffer's house, and these reminded him of his country. He had been detected once, after dusk, with his forehead against the trunk of one of them, sobbing, and talking to himself. They had been like brothers to him at that time, he affirmed. Everything else was strange. Conceive you the kind of an existence overshadowed, oppressed, by the everyday material appearances, as if by the visions of a nightmare. At night, when he could not sleep, he kept on thinking of the girl who gave him the first piece of bread he had eaten in this foreign land. She had been neither fierce nor angry, nor frightened. Her face he remembered as the only comprehensible face amongst all these faces that were as closed, as mysterious, and as mute as the faces of the dead who are possessed of a knowledge beyond the comprehension of the living. I wonder whether the memory of her compassion prevented him from cutting his throat. But there! I suppose I am an old sentimentalist, and forget the instinctive love of life which it takes all the strength of an uncommon despair to overcome.

'He did the work which was given him with an intelligence which surprised old Swaffer. By and by it was discovered that he could help at the ploughing, could milk the cows, feed the bullocks in the cattle-yard, and was of some use with the sheep. He began to pick up words, too, very fast; and suddenly, one fine morning in spring, he rescued from an untimely death a grandchild of old Swaffer.

'Swaffer's younger daughter is married to Willcox, a solicitor and the Town Clerk of Colebrook. Regularly twice a year they come to stay with the old man for a few days. Their only child, a little girl not three years old at the time, ran out of the house alone in her little white pinafore, and, toddling across the grass of a terraced garden, pitched herself over a low wall head first into the horsepond in the yard below.

'Our man was out with the waggoner and the plough in the field nearest to the house, and as he was leading the team round to begin a fresh furrow, he saw, through the gap of a gate, what for anybody else would have been a mere flutter of something white. But he had straight-glancing, quick, far-reaching eyes, that only seemed to flinch and lose their amazing power before the immensity of the sea. He was barefooted, and looking as outlandish as the heart of Swaffer could desire. Leaving the horses on the turn, to the inexpressible disgust of the waggoner he bounded off, going over the ploughed ground in long leaps, and suddenly appeared before the mother, thrust the child into her arms, and strode away.

'The pond was not very deep; but still, if he had not had such good eyes, the child would have perished – miserably suffocated in the foot or so of sticky mud at the bottom. Old Swaffer walked out slowly into the field, waited till the plough came over to his side, had a good look at him, and without saying a word went back to the house. But from that time they laid out his meals on the kitchen table; and at first, Miss Swaffer, all in black and with an inscrutable face, would come and stand in the doorway of the living-room to see him make a big sign of the cross before he fell to. I believe that from that day, too, Swaffer began to pay him regular wages.

'I can't follow step by step his development. He cut his hair short, was seen in the village and along the road going to and fro his work like any other man.

Children ceased to shout after him. He became aware of social differences, but remained for a long time surprised at the bare poverty of the churches among so much wealth. He couldn't understand either why they were kept shut up on weekdays. There was nothing to steal in them. Was it to keep people from praying too often? The rectory took much notice of him about that time, and I believe the young ladies attempted to prepare the ground for his conversion. They could not, however, break him of his habit of crossing himself, but he went so far as to take off the string with a couple of brass medals the size of a sixpence, a tiny metal cross, and a square sort of scapulary which he wore round his neck. He hung them on the wall by the side of his bed, and he was still to be heard every evening reciting the Lord's Prayer, in incomprehensible words and in a slow, fervent tone, as he had heard his old father do at the head of all the kneeling family, big and little, on every evening of his life. And though he wore corduroys at work, and a slop-made pepper-and-salt suit on Sundays, strangers would turn round to look after him on the road. His foreignness had a peculiar and indelible stamp. At last people became used to see him. But they never became used to him. His rapid, skimming walk; his swarthy complexion; his hat cocked on the left ear; his habit, on warm evenings, of wearing his coat over one shoulder, like a hussar's dolman; his manner of leaping over the stiles, not as a feat of agility, but in the ordinary course of progression – all these peculiarities were, as one may say, so many causes of scorn and offence to the inhabitants of the village. *They* wouldn't in their dinner hour lie flat on their backs on the grass to stare at the sky. Neither did they go about the fields screaming dismal tunes. Many times have I heard his high-pitched voice from behind the ridge of some sloping sheep-walk, a voice light and soaring, like a lark's, but with a melancholy human note, over our fields that hear only the song of birds. And I would be startled myself. Ah! He was different: innocent of heart, and full of good will, which nobody wanted, this castaway, that, like a man transplanted into another planet, was separated by an immense space from his past and by an immense ignorance from his future. His quick, fervent utterance positively shocked everybody. "An excitable devil", they called him. One evening, in the taproom of the Coach and Horses (having drunk some whisky), he upset them all by singing a love-song of his country. They hooted him down, and he was pained; but Preble, the lame wheelwright, and Vincent, the fat blacksmith, and the other notables too, wanted to drink their evening beer in peace. On another occasion he tried to show them how to dance. The dust rose in clouds from the sanded floor; he leaped straight up amongst the deal tables, struck his heels together, squatted on one heel in front of old Preble, shooting out the other leg, uttered wild and exulting cries, jumped up to whirl on one foot, snapping his fingers above his head – and a strange carter who was having a drink in there began to swear, and cleared out with his half-pint in his hand into the bar. But when suddenly he sprang upon a table and continued to dance among the glasses, the landlord interfered. He didn't want any "acrobat tricks in the taproom". They laid their hands on him. Having had a glass or two, Mr Swaffer's foreigner tried to expostulate: was ejected forcibly: got a black eye.

'I believe he felt the hostility of his human surroundings. But he was tough – tough in spirit, too, as well as in body. Only the memory of the sea frightened him, with that vague terror that is left by a bad dream. His home was far away; and he did not want now to go to America. I had often explained to him that there is no place on earth where true gold can be found lying ready and to be got for the trouble of the picking up. How then, he asked, could he ever return home with empty hands when there had been sold a cow, two ponies, and a bit of land to pay for his going? His eyes would fill with tears, and, averting them from the immense shimmer of the sea, he would throw himself face down on the grass. But sometimes, cocking his hat with a little conquering air, he would defy my wisdom. He had found his bit of true gold. That was Amy Foster's heart; which was "a golden heart, and soft to people's misery", he would say in the accents of overwhelming conviction.

'He was called Yanko. He had explained that this meant Little John; but as he would also repeat very often that he was a mountaineer (some word sounding in the dialect of his country like Goorall) he got it for his surname. And this is the only trace of him that the succeeding ages may find in the marriage register of the parish. There it stands – Yanko Goorall – in the rector's handwriting. The crooked cross made by the castaway, a cross whose tracing no doubt seemed to him the most solemn part of the whole ceremony, is all that remains now to perpetuate the memory of his name.

'His courtship had lasted some time – ever since he got his precarious footing in the community. It began by his buying for Amy Foster a green satin ribbon in Darnford. This was what you did in his country. You bought a ribbon at a Jew's stall on a fair-day. I don't suppose the girl knew what to do with it, but he seemed to think that his honourable intentions could not be mistaken.

'It was only when he declared his purpose to get married that I fully understood how, for a hundred futile and inappreciable reasons, how – shall I say odious? – he was to all the countryside. Every old woman in the village was up in arms. Smith, coming upon him near the farm, promised to break his head for him if he found him about again. But he twisted his little black moustache with such a bellicose air and rolled such big, black fierce eyes at Smith that this promise came to nothing. Smith, however, told the girl that she must be mad to take up with a man who was surely wrong in his head. All the same, when she heard him in the gloaming whistle from beyond the orchard a couple of bars of a weird and mournful tune, she would drop whatever she had in her hand – she would leave Mrs Smith in the middle of a sentence – and she would run out to his call. Mrs Smith called her a shameless hussy. She answered nothing. She said nothing at all to anybody, and went on her way as if she had been deaf. She and I alone in all the land, I fancy, could see his very real beauty. He was very good-looking, and most graceful in his bearing, with that something wild as of a woodland creature in his aspect. Her mother moaned over her dismally whenever the girl came to see her on her day out. The father was surly, but pretended not to know; and Mrs Finn once told her plainly that "this man, my dear, will do you some harm someday yet". And so it went on. They could be seen on the roads, she tramping stolidly in her finery – grey dress, black feather, stout boots, prominent white cotton gloves that caught your eye a hundred yards away; and he, his coat slung picturesquely over one shoulder, pacing by her side, gallant of bearing and casting tender glances upon the girl with the golden heart. I wonder whether he saw how plain she was. Perhaps, among types so different from what he had ever seen, he had not the power to judge; or perhaps he was seduced by the divine quality of her pity.

'Yanko was in great trouble meantime. In his country you get an old man for an ambassador in marriage affairs. He did not know how to proceed. However, one day in the midst of sheep in a field (he was now Swaffer's under-shepherd with Foster) he took off his hat to the father and declared himself humbly. "I dare say she's fool enough to marry you," was all Foster said. "And then," he used to relate, "he puts his hat on his head, looks black at me as if he wanted to cut my throat, whistles the dog, and off he goes, leaving me to do the work." The Fosters, of course, didn't like to lose the wages the girl earned: Amy used to give all her money to her mother. But there was in Foster a very genuine aversion to that match. He contended that the fellow was very good with sheep, but was not fit for any girl to marry. For one thing, he used to go along the hedges muttering to himself like a dam' fool; and then, these foreigners behave very queerly to women sometimes. And perhaps he would want to carry her off somewhere – or run off himself. It was not safe. He preached it to his daughter that the fellow might ill-use her in some way. She made no answer. It was, they said in the village, as if the man had done something to her. People discussed the matter. It was quite an excitement, and the two went on "walking out" together in the face of opposition. Then something unexpected happened.

'I don't know whether old Swaffer ever understood how much he was regarded in the light of a father by his foreign retainer. Anyway the relation was curiously feudal. So when Yanko asked formally for an interview – "and the Miss too" (he called the severe, deaf Miss Swaffer simply *Miss*) – it was to obtain their permission to marry. Swaffer heard him unmoved, dismissed him by a nod, and then shouted the intelligence into Miss Swaffer's best ear. She showed no surprise, and only remarked grimly, in a veiled blank voice, "He certainly won't get any other girl to marry him."

'It is Miss Swaffer who has all the credit of the munificence: but in a very few days it came out that Mr Swaffer had presented Yanko with a cottage (the cottage you've seen this morning) and something like an acre of ground – had made it over to him in absolute property. Willcox expedited the deed, and I remember him telling me he had a great pleasure in making it ready. It recited: "In consideration of saving the life of my beloved grandchild, Bertha Willcox."

'Of course, after that no power on earth could prevent them from getting married.

'Her infatuation endured. People saw her going out to meet him in the evening. She stared with unblinking, fascinated eyes up the road where he was expected to appear, walking freely, with a swing from the hip, and humming one of the love-tunes of his country. When the boy was born, he got elevated at the Coach and Horses, essayed again a song and a dance, and was again ejected. People expressed their commiseration for a woman married to that Jack-in-the-box. He didn't care. There was a man now (he told me boastfully) to whom he could sing and talk in the language of his country, and show how to dance by and by.

'But I don't know. To me he appeared to have grown less springy of step, heavier in body, less keen of eye. Imagination, no doubt; but it seems to me now as if the net of fate had been drawn closer round him already.

'One day I met him on the footpath over the Talfourd Hill. He told me that "women were funny". I had heard already of domestic differences. People were saying that Amy Foster was beginning to find out what sort of man she had married. He looked upon the sea with indifferent, unseeing eyes. His wife had snatched the child out of his arms one day as he sat on the doorstep crooning to it a song such as the mothers sing to babies in his mountains. She seemed to think he was doing it some harm. Women are funny. And she had objected to him praying aloud in the evening. Why? He expected the boy to repeat the prayer aloud after him by and by, as he used to do after his old father when he was a child – in his own country. And I discovered he longed for their boy to grow up so that he could have a man to talk with in that language that to our ears sounded so disturbing, so passionate, and so bizarre. Why his wife should dislike the idea he couldn't tell. But that would pass, he said. And tilting his head knowingly, he tapped his breastbone to indicate that she had a good heart: not hard, not fierce, open to compassion, charitable to the poor!

'I walked away thoughtfully; I wondered whether his difference, his strangeness, were not penetrating with repulsion that dull nature they had begun by irresistibly attracting. I wondered . . . '

The doctor came to the window and looked out at the frigid splendour of the sea, immense in the haze, as if enclosing all the earth with all the hearts lost among the passions of love and fear.

'Physiologically, now,' he said, turning away abruptly, 'it was possible. It was possible.'

He remained silent. Then went on – 'At all events, the next time I saw him he was ill – lung trouble. He was tough, but I dare say he was not acclimatised as well as I had supposed. It was a bad winter; and, of course, these mountaineers do get fits of home sickness; and a state of depression would make him vulnerable. He was lying half dressed on a couch downstairs.

'A table covered with a dark oilcloth took up all the middle of the little room. There was a wicker cradle on the floor, a kettle spouting steam on the hob, and some child's linen lay drying on the fender. The room was warm, but the door opens right into the garden, as you noticed perhaps.

'He was very feverish, and kept on muttering to himself. She sat on a chair and looked at him fixedly across the table with her brown, blurred eyes. "Why don't you have him upstairs?" I asked. With a start and a confused stammer she said, "Oh! ah! I couldn't sit with him upstairs, sir."

'I gave her certain directions; and going outside, I said again that he ought to be in bed upstairs. She wrung her hands. "I couldn't. I couldn't. He keeps on saying something – I don't know what." With the memory of all the talk against the man that had been dinned into her ears, I looked at her narrowly. I looked into her short-sighted eyes, at her dumb eyes that once in her life had seen an enticing shape, but seemed, staring at me, to see nothing at all now. But I saw she was uneasy.

'"What's the matter with him?" she asked in a sort of vacant trepidation. "He doesn't look very ill. I never did see anybody look like this before . . . "

'"Do you think," I asked indignantly, "he is shamming?"

'"I can't help it, sir," she said stolidly. And suddenly she clapped her hands and looked right and left. "And there's the baby. I am so frightened. He wanted me just now to give him the baby. I can't understand what he says to it."

'"Can't you ask a neighbour to come in tonight?" I asked.

'"Please, sir, nobody seems to care to come," she muttered, dully resigned all at once.

'I impressed upon her the necessity of the greatest care, and then had to go. There was a good deal of sickness that winter. "Oh, I hope he won't talk!" she exclaimed softly just as I was going away.

'I don't know how it is I did not see – but I didn't. And yet, turning in my trap, I saw her lingering before the door, very still, and as if meditating a flight up the miry road.

'Towards the night his fever increased.

'He tossed, moaned, and now and then muttered a complaint. And she sat with the table between her and the couch, watching every movement and every sound, with the terror, the unreasonable terror, of that man she could not understand creeping over her. She had drawn the wicker cradle close to her feet. There was nothing in her now but the maternal instinct and that unaccountable fear.

'Suddenly coming to himself, parched, he demanded a drink of water. She did not move. She had not understood, though he may have thought he was speaking in English. He waited, looking at her, burning with fever, amazed at her silence and immobility, and then he shouted impatiently, "Water! Give me water!"

'She jumped to her feet, snatched up the child, and stood still. He spoke to her, and his passionate remonstrances only increased her fear of that strange man. I believe he spoke to her for a long time, entreating, wondering, pleading, ordering, I suppose. She says she bore it as long as she could. And then a gust of rage came over him.

'He sat up and called out terribly one word – some word. Then he got up as though he hadn't been ill at all, she says. And as in fevered dismay, indignation, and wonder he tried to get to her round the table, she simply opened the door and ran out with the child in her arms. She heard him call twice after her down the road in a terrible voice – and fled. . . . Ah! but you should have seen stirring behind the dull, blurred glance of those eyes the spectre of the fear which had hunted her on that night three miles and a half to the door of Foster's cottage! I did the next day.

'And it was I who found him lying face down and his body in a puddle, just outside the little wicket-gate.

'I had been called out that night to an urgent case in the village, and on my way home at daybreak passed by the cottage. The door stood open. My man helped me to carry him in. We laid him on the couch. The lamp smoked, the fire was out, the chill of the stormy night oozed from the cheerless yellow paper on the wall. "Amy!" I called aloud, and my voice seemed to lose itself in the emptiness of this tiny house as if I had cried in a desert. He opened his eyes. "Gone!" he said distinctly. "I had only asked for water – only for a little water . . . "

'He was muddy. I covered him up and stood waiting in silence, catching a painfully gasped word now and then. They were no longer in his own language. The fever had left him, taking with it the heat of life. And with his panting breast and lustrous eyes he reminded me again of a wild creature under the net; of a bird caught in a snare. She had left him. She had left him – sick – helpless – thirsty. The spear of the hunter had entered his very soul. "Why?" he cried in the penetrating and indignant voice of a man calling to a responsible Maker. A gust of wind and a swish of rain answered.

'And as I turned away to shut the door he pronounced the word "Merciful!" and expired.

'Eventually I certified heart-failure as the immediate cause of death. His heart must have indeed failed him, or else he might have stood this night of storm and exposure, too. I closed his eyes and drove away. Not very far from the cottage I met Foster walking sturdily between the dripping hedges with his collie at his heels.

'"Do you know where your daughter is?" I asked.

'"Don't I!" he cried. "I am going to talk to him a bit. Frightening a poor woman like this."

'"He won't frighten her any more," I said. "He is dead."

'He struck with his stick at the mud.

'"And there's the child."

'Then, after thinking deeply for a while – "'I don't know that it isn't for the best."

'That's what he said. And she says nothing at all now. Not a word of him. Never. Is his image as utterly gone from her mind as his lithe and striding figure, his carolling voice are gone from our fields? He is no longer before her eyes to excite her imagination into a passion of love or fear; and his memory seems to have vanished from her dull brain as a shadow passes away upon a white screen. She lives in the cottage and works for Miss Swaffer. She is Amy Foster for everybody, and the child is "Amy Foster's boy". She calls him Johnny – which means Little John.

'It is impossible to say whether this name recalls anything to her. Does she ever think of the past? I have seen her hanging over the boy's cot in a very passion of maternal tenderness. The little fellow was lying on his back, a little frightened at me, but very still, with his big black eyes, with his fluttered air of a bird in a snare. And looking at him I seemed to see again the other one – the father, cast out mysteriously by the sea to perish in the supreme disaster of loneliness and despair.'

1901

TYPHOON

Far as the mariner on highest mast
Can see all around upon the calmed vast,
So wide was Neptune's hall . . .

KEATS

To
R. B. CUNNINGHAME GRAHAM

Author's Note
(to volume containing 'Typhoon' and 'Falk', 1919)

The main characteristic of this volume consists in this, that all the stories composing it belong not only to the same period but have been written one after another in the order in which they appear in the book.

The period is that which follows on my connection with *Blackwood's Magazine*. I had just finished writing 'The End of the Tether' and was casting about for some subject which could be developed in a shorter form than the tales in the volume of 'Youth' when the instance of a steamship full of returning coolies from Singapore to some port in northern China occurred to my recollection. Years before I had heard it being talked about in the East as a recent occurrence. It was for us merely one subject of conversation amongst many others of the kind. Men earning their bread in any very specialised occupation will talk shop, not only because it is the most vital interest of their lives but also because they have not much knowledge of other subjects. They have never had the time to get acquainted with them. Life, for most of us, is not so much a hard as an exacting taskmaster.

I never met anybody personally concerned in this affair, the interest of which for us was, of course, not the bad weather but the extraordinary complication brought into the ship's life at a moment of exceptional stress by the human element below her deck. Neither was the story itself ever enlarged upon in my hearing. In that company each of us could imagine easily what the whole thing was like. The financial difficulty of it, presenting also a human problem, was solved by a mind much too simple to be perplexed by anything in the world except men's idle talk for which it was not adapted.

From the first the mere anecdote, the mere statement I might say, that such a thing had happened on the high seas, appeared to me a sufficient subject for meditation. Yet it was but a bit of a sea yarn after all. I felt that to bring out its deeper significance, which was quite apparent to me, something other, something more was required; a leading motive that would harmonise all these violent noises, and a point of view that would put all that elemental fury into its proper place.

What was needed of course was Captain MacWhirr. Directly I perceived him I could see that he was the man for the situation. I don't mean to say that I ever saw Captain MacWhirr in the flesh, or had ever come in contact with his literal mind and his dauntless temperament. MacWhirr is not an acquaintance of a few hours, or a few weeks, or a few months. He is the product of twenty years of life. My own life. Conscious invention had little to do with him. If it is true that Captain MacWhirr never walked and breathed on this earth (which I find for my part extremely difficult to believe) I can also assure my readers that he is perfectly authentic. I may venture to assert the same of every aspect of the story, while I confess that the particular typhoon of the tale was not a typhoon of my actual experience.

At its first appearance 'Typhoon', the story, was classed by some critics as a deliberately intended storm-piece. Others picked out MacWhirr, in whom they perceived a definite symbolic intention. Neither was exclusively my intention. Both the typhoon and Captain MacWhirr presented themselves to me as the necessities of the deep conviction with which I approached the subject of the story. It was their opportunity. It was also my opportunity; and it would be vain to discourse about what I made of it in a handful of pages, since the pages themselves are here, between the covers of this volume, to speak for themselves.

This is a belated reflection. If it had occurred to me before it would have perhaps done away with the existence of this Author's Note; for, indeed, the same remark applies to every story in this volume. None of them are stories of experience in the absolute sense of the word. Experience in them is but the canvas of the attempted picture. Each of them has its more than one intention. With each the question is what the writer has done with his opportunity; and each answers the question for itself in words which, if I may say so without undue solemnity, were written with a conscientious regard for the truth of my own sensations. And each of those stories, to mean something, must justify itself in its own way to the conscience of each successive reader.

'Falk' – the second story in the volume – offended the delicacy of one critic at least by certain peculiarities of its subject. But what is the subject of 'Falk'? I personally do not feel so very certain about it. He who reads must find out for himself. My intention in writing 'Falk' was not to shock anybody. As in most of my writings I insist not on the events but on their effect upon the persons in the tale. But in everything I have written there is always one invariable intention, and that is to capture the reader's attention, by securing his interest and enlisting his sympathies for the matter in hand, whatever it may be, within the limits of the visible world and within the boundaries of human emotions.

I may safely say that Falk is absolutely true to my experience of certain straightforward characters combining a perfectly natural ruthlessness with a certain amount of moral delicacy. Falk obeys the laws of self-preservation without the slightest misgivings as to his right, but at a crucial turn of that ruthlessly preserved life he will not condescend to dodge the truth. As he is presented as sensitive enough to be affected permanently by a certain unusual experience, that experience had to be set by me before the reader vividly; but it is not the subject of the tale. If we go by mere facts then the subject is Falk's attempt to get married; in which the narrator of the tale finds himself unexpectedly involved both on its ruthless and its delicate side.

'Falk' shares with one other of my stories ('The Return' in the 'Tales of Unrest' volume) the distinction of never having been serialised. I think the copy was shown to the editor of some magazine who rejected it indignantly on the sole ground that 'the girl never says anything'. This is perfectly true. From first to last Hermann's niece utters no word in the tale – and it is not because she is dumb, but for the simple reason that whenever she happens to come under the observation of the narrator she has either no occasion or is too profoundly moved to speak. The editor, who obviously had read the story, might have perceived that for himself. Apparently he did not, and I refrained from pointing out the impossibility to him because, since he did not venture to say that 'the girl' did not live, I felt no concern at his indignation . . .

Joseph Conrad

1919

Chapter 1

Captain MacWhirr, of the steamer *Nan-Shan*, had a physiognomy that, in the order of material appearances, was the exact counterpart of his mind: it presented no marked characteristics of firmness or stupidity; it had no pronounced characteristics whatever; it was simply ordinary, irresponsive, and unruffled.

The only thing his aspect might have been said to suggest, at times, was bashfulness; because he would sit, in business offices ashore, sunburnt and smiling faintly, with downcast eyes. When he raised them, they were perceived to be direct in their glance and of blue colour. His hair was fair and extremely fine, clasping from temple to temple the bald dome of his skull in a clamp as of fluffy silk. The hair of his face, on the contrary, carroty and flaming, resembled a growth of copper wire clipped short to the line of the lip; while, no matter how close he shaved, fiery metallic gleams passed, when he moved his head, over the surface of his cheeks. He was rather below the medium height, a bit round-shouldered, and so sturdy of limb that his clothes always looked a shade too tight for his arms and legs. As if unable to grasp what is due to the difference of latitudes, he wore a brown bowler hat, a complete suit of a brownish hue, and clumsy black boots. These harbour togs gave to his thick figure an air of stiff and uncouth smartness. A thin silver watch-chain looped his waistcoat, and he never left his ship for the shore without clutching in his powerful, hairy fist an elegant umbrella of the very best quality, but generally unrolled. Young Jukes, the chief mate, attending his commander to the gangway, would sometimes venture to say, with the greatest gentleness, 'Allow me, sir' – and possessing himself of the umbrella deferentially, would elevate the ferule, shake the folds, twirl a neat furl in a jiffy, and hand it back; going through the performance with a face of such portentous gravity, that Mr Solomon Rout, the chief engineer, smoking his morning cigar over the skylight, would turn away his head in order to hide a smile. 'Oh! aye! The blessed gamp . . . Thank 'ee, Jukes, thank 'ee,' would mutter Captain MacWhirr heartily, without looking up.

Having just enough imagination to carry him through each successive day, and no more, he was tranquilly sure of himself; and from the very same cause he was not in the least conceited. It is your imaginative superior who is touchy, overbearing, and difficult to please; but every ship Captain MacWhirr commanded was the floating abode of harmony and peace. It was, in truth, as impossible for him to take a flight of fancy as it would be for a watchmaker to put together a chronometer with nothing except a two-pound hammer and a whip-saw in the way of tools. Yet the uninteresting lives of men so entirely given to the actuality of the bare existence have their mysterious side. It was impossible in Captain MacWhirr's case, for instance, to understand what under heaven could have induced that perfectly satisfactory son of a petty grocer in Belfast to run away to sea. And yet he had done that very thing at the age of fifteen. It was enough, when you thought it over, to give you the idea of an immense, potent, and invisible hand thrust into the ant-heap of the earth, laying hold of shoulders, knocking heads together, and setting the unconscious faces of the multitude towards inconceivable goals and in undreamt-of directions.

His father never really forgave him for this undutiful stupidity. 'We could have got on without him,' he used to say later on, 'but there's the business. And he an only son too!' His mother wept very much after his disappearance. As it had never occurred to him to leave word behind, he was mourned over for dead till, after eight months, his first letter arrived from Talcahuano. It was short, and contained the statement: 'We had very fine weather on our passage out.' But evidently, in the writer's mind, the only important intelligence was to the effect that his captain had, on the very day of writing, entered him regularly on the ship's articles as Ordinary Seaman. 'Because I can do the work,' he explained. The mother again wept copiously, while the remark, 'Tom's an ass,' expressed the emotions of the father. He was a corpulent man, with a gift for sly chaffing, which to the end of his life he exercised in his intercourse with his son, a little pityingly, as if upon a half-witted person.

MacWhirr's visits to his home were necessarily rare, and in the course of years he despatched other letters to his parents, informing them of his successive promotions and of his movements upon the vast earth. In these missives could be found sentences like this: 'The heat here is very great.' Or: 'On Christmas day at 4 p.m. we fell in with some icebergs.' The old people ultimately became acquainted with a good many names of ships, and with the names of the skippers who commanded them – with the names of Scots and English shipowners – with the names of seas, oceans, straits, promontories – with outlandish names of lumber-ports, of rice-ports, of cotton-ports – with the names of islands – with the name of their son's young woman. She was called Lucy. It did not suggest itself to him to mention whether he thought the name pretty. And then they died.

The great day of MacWhirr's marriage came in due course, following shortly upon the great day when he got his first command.

All these events had taken place many years before the morning when, in the chart-room of the steamer *Nan-Shan*, he stood confronted by the fall of a barometer he had no reason to distrust. The fall – taking into account the excellence of the instrument, the time of the year, and the ship's position on the terrestrial globe – was of a nature ominously prophetic; but the red face of the man betrayed no sort of inward disturbance. Omens were as nothing to him, and he was unable to discover the message of a prophecy till the fulfilment had brought it home to his very door. 'That's a fall, and no mistake,' he thought. 'There must be some uncommonly dirty weather knocking about.'

The *Nan-Shan* was on her way from the southward to the treaty port of Fu-chau, with some cargo in her lower holds, and two hundred Chinese coolies returning to their village homes in the province of Fo-kien, after a few years of work in various tropical colonies. The morning was fine, the oily sea heaved without a sparkle, and there was a queer white misty patch in the sky like a halo of the sun. The fore-deck, packed with Chinamen, was full of sombre clothing, yellow faces, and pigtails, sprinkled over with a good many naked shoulders, for there was no wind, and the heat was close. The coolies lounged, talked, smoked, or stared over the rail; some, drawing water over the side, sluiced each other; a few slept on hatches, while several small parties of six sat on their heels surrounding iron trays with plates of rice and tiny teacups; and every single Celestial of them was carrying with him all he had in the world – a wooden chest with a ringing lock and brass on the corners, containing the savings of his labours: some clothes of ceremony, sticks of incense, a little opium maybe, bits of nameless rubbish of conventional value, and a small hoard of silver dollars, toiled for in coal lighters, won in gambling-houses or in petty trading, grubbed out of earth, sweated out in mines, on railway lines, in deadly jungle, under heavy burdens – amassed patiently, guarded with care, cherished fiercely.

A cross swell had set in from the direction of Formosa Channel about ten o'clock, without disturbing these passengers much, because the *Nan-Shan*, with her flat bottom, rolling chocks on bilges, and great breadth of beam, had the reputation of an exceptionally steady ship in a sea-way. Mr Jukes, in moments of expansion on shore, would proclaim loudly that the 'old girl was as good as she was pretty'. It would never have occurred to Captain MacWhirr to express his favourable opinion so loud or in terms so fanciful.

She was a good ship, undoubtedly, and not old either. She had been built in Dumbarton less than three years before, to the order of a firm of merchants in Siam – Messrs Sigg and Son. When she lay afloat, finished in every detail and ready to take up the work of her life, the builders contemplated her with pride.

'Sigg has asked us for a reliable skipper to take her out,' remarked one of the partners; and the other, after reflecting for a while, said: 'I think MacWhirr is ashore just at present.' 'Is he? Then wire him at once. He's the very man,' declared the senior, without a moment's hesitation.

Next morning MacWhirr stood before them unperturbed, having travelled from London by the midnight express after a sudden but undemonstrative parting with his wife. She was the daughter of a superior couple who had seen better days.

'We had better be going together over the ship, Captain,' said the senior partner; and the three men started to view the perfections of the *Nan-Shan* from stem to stern, and from her keelson to the trucks of her two stumpy pole-masts.

Captain MacWhirr had begun by taking off his coat, which he hung on the end of a steam windlass embodying all the latest improvements.

'My uncle wrote of you favourably by yesterday's mail to our good friends – Messrs Sigg, you know – and doubtless they'll continue you out there in command,' said the junior partner. 'You'll be able to boast of being in charge of the handiest boat of her size on the coast of China, Captain,' he added.

'Have you? Thank 'ee,' mumbled vaguely MacWhirr, to whom the view of a distant eventuality could appeal no more than the beauty of a wide landscape to a purblind tourist; and his eyes happening at the moment to be at rest upon the lock of the cabin door, he walked up to it, full of purpose, and began to rattle the handle vigorously, while he observed, in his low, earnest voice, 'You can't trust the workmen nowadays. A brand-new lock, and it won't act at all. Stuck fast. See? See?'

As soon as they found themselves alone in their office across the yard: 'You praised that fellow up to Sigg. What is it you see in him?' asked the nephew, with faint contempt.

'I admit he has nothing of your fancy skipper about him, if that's what you mean,' said the elder man curtly. 'Is the foreman of the joiners on the *Nan-Shan* outside? . . . Come in, Bates. How is it that you let Tait's people put us off with a defective lock on the cabin door? The Captain could see directly he set eye on it. Have it replaced at once. The little straws, Bates . . . the little straws . . . '

The lock was replaced accordingly, and a few days afterwards the *Nan-Shan* steamed out to the East, without MacWhirr having offered any further remark as to her fittings, or having been heard to utter a single word hinting at pride in his ship, gratitude for his appointment, or satisfaction at his prospects.

With a temperament neither loquacious nor taciturn, he found very little occasion to talk. There were matters of duty, of course – directions, orders, and so on; but the past being to his mind done with, and the future not there yet, the more general actualities of the day required no comment – because facts can speak for themselves with overwhelming precision.

Old Mr Sigg liked a man of few words, and one that 'you could be sure would not try to improve upon his instructions'. MacWhirr, satisfying these requirements, was continued in command of the *Nan-Shan*, and applied himself to the careful navigation of his ship in the China seas. She had come out on a British register, but after some time Messrs Sigg judged it expedient to transfer her to the Siamese flag.

At the news of the contemplated transfer Jukes grew restless, as if under a sense of personal affront. He went about grumbling to himself, and uttering short scornful laughs. 'Fancy having a ridiculous Noah's Ark elephant in the ensign of one's ship,' he said once at the engine-room door. 'Dash me if I can stand it: I'll throw up the billet. Don't it make *you* sick, Mr Rout?' The chief engineer only cleared his throat with the air of a man who knows the value of a good billet.

The first morning the new flag floated over the stern of the *Nan-Shan* Jukes stood looking at it bitterly from the bridge. He struggled with his feelings for a while, and then remarked, 'Queer flag for a man to sail under, sir.'

'What's the matter with the flag?' enquired Captain MacWhirr. 'Seems all right to me.' And he walked across to the end of the bridge to have a good look.

'Well, it looks queer to me,' burst out Jukes, greatly exasperated, and flung off the bridge.

Captain MacWhirr was amazed at these manners. After a while he stepped quietly into the chart-room, and opened his International Signal Code-book at the plate where the flags of all the nations are correctly figured in gaudy rows. He ran his finger over them, and when he came to Siam he contemplated with great attention the red field and the white elephant. Nothing could be more simple; but to make sure he brought the book out on the bridge for the purpose of comparing the coloured drawing with the real thing at the flagstaff astern. When next Jukes, who was carrying on the duty that day with a sort of suppressed fierceness, happened on the bridge, his commander observed: 'There's nothing amiss with that flag.'

'Isn't there?' mumbled Jukes, falling on his knees before a deck-locker and jerking therefrom viciously a spare lead-line.

'No. I looked up the book. Length twice the breadth and the elephant exactly in the middle. I thought the people ashore would know how to make the local flag. Stands to reason. You were wrong, Jukes . . . '

'Well, sir,' began Jukes, getting up excitedly, 'all I can say – ' He fumbled for the end of the coil of line with trembling hands.

'That's all right.' Captain MacWhirr soothed him, sitting heavily on a little canvas folding-stool he greatly affected. 'All you have to do is to take care they don't hoist the elephant upside-down before they get quite used to it.'

Jukes flung the new lead-line over on the fore-deck with a loud 'Here you are, bo'ss'en – don't forget to wet it thoroughly,' and turned with immense resolution towards his commander; but Captain MacWhirr spread his elbows on the bridge-rail comfortably.

'Because it would be, I suppose, understood as a signal of distress,' he went on. 'What do you think? That elephant there, I take it, stands for something in the nature of the Union Jack in the flag . . . '

'Does it!' yelled Jukes, so that every head on the *Nan-Shan*'s decks looked towards the bridge. Then he sighed, and with sudden resignation: 'It would certainly be a dam' distressful sight,' he said meekly.

Later in the day he accosted the chief engineer with a confidential, 'Here, let me tell you the old man's latest.'

Mr Solomon Rout (frequently alluded to as Long Sol, Old Sol, or Father Rout), from finding himself almost invariably the tallest man on board every ship he joined, had acquired the habit of a stooping, leisurely condescension. His hair was scant and sandy, his flat cheeks were pale, his bony wrists and long scholarly hands were pale too, as though he had lived all his life in the shade.

He smiled from on high at Jukes, and went on smoking and glancing about quietly, in the manner of a kind uncle lending an ear to the tale of an excited schoolboy. Then, greatly amused but impassive, he asked: 'And did you throw up the billet?'

'No,' cried Jukes, raising a weary, discouraged voice above the harsh buzz of the *Nan-Shan*'s friction winches. All of them were hard at work, snatching slings of cargo, high up, to the end of long derricks, only, as it seemed, to let them rip down recklessly by the run. The cargo chains groaned in the gins, clinked on coamings, rattled over the side; and the whole ship quivered, with her long grey flanks smoking in wreaths of steam. 'No,' cried Jukes, 'I didn't. What's the good? I might just as well fling my resignation at this bulkhead. I don't believe you can make a man like that understand anything. He simply knocks me over.'

At that moment Captain MacWhirr, back from the shore, crossed the deck, umbrella in hand, escorted by a mournful, self-possessed Chinaman, walking behind in paper-soled silk shoes, and who also carried an umbrella.

The master of the *Nan-Shan*, speaking just audibly and gazing at his boots as his manner was, remarked that it would be necessary to call at Fu-chau this trip, and desired Mr Rout to have steam up tomorrow afternoon at one o'clock sharp. He pushed back his hat to wipe his forehead, observing at the same time that he hated going ashore anyhow; while overtopping him Mr Rout, without deigning a word, smoked austerely, nursing his right elbow in the palm of his left hand. Then Jukes was directed in the same subdued voice to keep the forward 'tween-deck clear of cargo. Two hundred coolies were going to be put down there. The Bun Hin Company were sending that lot home. Twenty-five bags of rice would be coming off in a sampan directly, for stores. All seven-years'-men they were, said Captain MacWhirr, with a camphor-wood chest to every man. The carpenter should be set to work nailing three-inch battens along the deck below, fore and aft, to keep these boxes from shifting in a sea-way. Jukes had better look to it at once. 'D'ye hear, Jukes?' This Chinaman here was coming with the ship as far as Fu-chau — a sort of interpreter he would be. Bun Hin's clerk he was, and wanted to have a look at the space. Jukes had better take him forward. 'D'ye hear, Jukes?'

Jukes took care to punctuate these instructions in proper places with the obligatory 'Yes, sir,' ejaculated without enthusiasm. His brusque 'Come along, John; make look see' set the Chinaman in motion at his heels.

'Wanchee look see, all same look see can do,' said Jukes, who having no talent for foreign languages mangled the very pidgin-English cruelly. He pointed at the open hatch. 'Catchee number one piecie place to sleep in. Eh?'

He was gruff, as became his racial superiority, but not unfriendly. The Chinaman, gazing sad and speechless into the darkness of the hatchway, seemed to stand at the head of a yawning grave.

'No catchee rain down there – savee?' pointed out Jukes. 'Suppose all'ee same fine weather, one piecie coolie-man come topside,' he pursued, warming up imaginatively. 'Make so – Phooooo!' He expanded his chest and blew out his cheeks. 'Savee, John? Breathe – fresh air. Good. Eh? Washee him piecie pants, chow-chow top-side – see, John?'

With his mouth and hands he made exuberant motions of eating rice and washing clothes; and the Chinaman, who concealed his distrust of this pantomime under a collected demeanour tinged by a gentle and refined melancholy, glanced out of his almond eyes from Jukes to the hatch and back again. 'Velly good,' he murmured, in a disconsolate undertone, and hastened smoothly along the decks, dodging obstacles in his course. He disappeared, ducking low under a sling of ten dirty gunny-bags full of some costly merchandise and exhaling a repulsive smell.

Captain MacWhirr meantime had gone on the bridge, and into the chart-room, where a letter, commenced two days before, awaited termination. These long letters began with the words, 'My darling wife', and the steward, between the scrubbing of the floors and the dusting of chronometer-boxes, snatched at every opportunity to read them. They interested him much more than they possibly could the woman for whose eye they were intended; and this for the reason that they related in minute detail each successive trip of the *Nan-Shan*.

Her master, faithful to facts, which alone his consciousness reflected, would set them down with painstaking care upon many pages. The house in a northern suburb to which these pages were addressed had a bit of garden before the bow-windows, a deep porch of good appearance, coloured glass with imitation lead frame in the front door. He paid five-and-forty pounds a year for it, and did not think the rent too high, because Mrs MacWhirr (a pretentious person with a scraggy neck and a disdainful manner) was admittedly ladylike, and in the neighbourhood considered as 'quite superior'. The only secret of her life was her abject terror of the time when her husband would come home to stay for good. Under the same roof there dwelt also a daughter called Lydia and a son, Tom. These two were but slightly acquainted with their father. Mainly, they knew him as a rare but privileged visitor, who of an evening smoked his pipe in the dining-room and slept in the house. The lanky girl, upon the whole, was rather ashamed of him; the boy was frankly and utterly indifferent in a straightforward, delightful, unaffected way manly boys have.

And Captain MacWhirr wrote home from the coast of China twelve times every year, desiring quaintly to be 'remembered to the children', and subscribing himself 'your loving husband', as calmly as if the words so long used by so many men were not, apart from their shape, worn-out things, and of a faded meaning.

The China seas north and south are narrow seas. They are seas full of everyday, eloquent facts, such as islands, sandbanks, reefs, swift and changeable currents – tangled facts that nevertheless speak to a seaman in clear and definite language. Their speech appealed to Captain MacWhirr's sense of realities so forcibly that he had given up his stateroom below and practically lived all his days on the bridge of his ship, often having his meals sent up, and sleeping at night in the chart-room. And he indited there his home letters. Each of them, without exception, contained the phrase, 'The weather has been very fine this trip,' or some other form of a statement to that effect. And this statement, too, in its wonderful persistence, was of the same perfect accuracy as all the others they contained.

Mr Rout likewise wrote letters; only no one on board knew how chatty he could be pen in hand, because the chief engineer had enough imagination to keep his desk locked. His wife relished his style greatly. They were a childless couple, and Mrs Rout, a big, high-bosomed, jolly woman of forty, shared with Mr Rout's toothless and venerable mother a little cottage near Teddington. She would run over her correspondence, at breakfast, with lively eyes, and scream out interesting passages in a joyous voice at the deaf old lady, prefacing each extract by the warning shout, 'Solomon says!' She had the trick of firing off Solomon's utterances also upon strangers, astonishing them easily by the unfamiliar text and the unexpectedly jocular vein of these quotations. On the day the new curate called for the first time at the cottage, she found occasion to remark, 'As Solomon says: "the engineers that go down to the sea in ships behold the wonders of sailor nature";' when a change in the visitor's countenance made her stop and stare.

'Solomon . . . Oh! . . . Mrs Rout,' stuttered the young man, very red in the face, 'I must say . . . I don't . . . '

'He's my husband,' she announced in a great shout, throwing herself back in the chair. Perceiving the joke, she laughed immoderately with a handkerchief to her eyes, while he sat wearing a forced smile, and, from his inexperience of jolly women, fully persuaded that she must be deplorably insane. They were excellent friends afterwards; for, absolving her from irreverent intention, he came to think she was a very worthy person indeed; and he learned in time to receive without flinching other scraps of Solomon's wisdom.

'For my part,' Solomon was reported by his wife to have said once, 'give me the dullest ass for a skipper before a rogue. There is a way to take a fool; but a rogue is smart and slippery.' This was an airy generalisation drawn from the particular case of Captain MacWhirr's honesty, which, in itself, had the heavy obviousness of a lump of clay. On the other hand, Mr Jukes, unable to generalise, unmarried, and unengaged, was in the habit of opening his heart after another fashion to an old chum and former shipmate, actually serving as second officer on board an Atlantic liner.

First of all he would insist upon the advantages of the Eastern trade, hinting at its superiority to the Western ocean service. He extolled the sky, the seas, the ships, and the easy life of the Far East. The *Nan-Shan*, he affirmed, was second to none as a sea-boat.

'We have no brass-bound uniforms, but then we are like brothers here,' he wrote. 'We all mess together and live like fighting-cocks . . . All the chaps of the black-squad are as decent as they make that kind, and old Sol, the Chief, is a dry stick. We are good friends. As to our old man, you could not find a quieter skipper. Sometimes you would think he hadn't sense enough to see anything wrong. And yet it isn't that. Can't be. He has been in command for a good few years now. He doesn't do anything actually foolish, and gets his ship along all right without worrying anybody. I believe he hasn't brains enough to enjoy kicking up a row. I don't take advantage of him. I would scorn it. Outside the routine of duty he doesn't seem to understand more than half of what you tell him. We get a laugh out of this at times; but it is dull, too, to be with a man like this – in the long-run. Old Sol says he hasn't much conversation. Conversation! O Lord! He never talks. The other day I had been yarning under the bridge with one of the engineers, and he must have heard us. When I came up to take my watch, he steps out of the chart-room and has a good look all round, peeps over at the sidelights, glances at the compass, squints upwards at the stars. That's his regular performance. By and by he says: "Was that you talking just now in the port alleyway?" "Yes, sir." "With the third engineer?" "Yes, sir." He walks off to starboard, and sits under the dodger on a little campstool of his, and for half an hour perhaps he makes no sound, except that I heard him sneeze once. Then after a while I hear him getting up over there, and he strolls across to port, where I was. "I can't understand what you can find to talk about," says he. "Two solid hours. I am not blaming you. I see people ashore at it all day long, and then in the evening they sit down and keep at it over the drinks. Must be saying the same things over and over again. I can't understand."

'Did you ever hear anything like that? And he was so patient about it. It made me quite sorry for him. But he is exasperating too sometimes. Of course one would not do anything to vex him even if it were worth while. But it isn't. He's so jolly innocent that if you were to put your thumb to your nose and wave your fingers at him he would only wonder gravely to himself what had got into you. He told me once quite simply that he found it very difficult to make out what made people always act so queerly. He's too dense to trouble about, and that's the truth.'

Thus wrote Mr Jukes to his chum in the Western ocean trade, out of the fullness of his heart and the liveliness of his fancy.

He had expressed his honest opinion. It was not worth while trying to impress a man of that sort. If the world had been full of such men, life would have probably appeared to Jukes an unentertaining and unprofitable business. He was not alone in his opinion. The sea itself, as if sharing Mr Jukes' good-natured forbearance, had never put itself out to startle the silent man, who seldom looked up, and wandered innocently over the waters with the only visible purpose of getting food, raiment, and house-room for three people ashore. Dirty weather he had known, of course. He had been made wet, uncomfortable, tired in the usual way, felt at the time and presently forgotten. So that upon the whole he had been justified in reporting fine weather at home. But he had never been given a glimpse of immeasurable strength and of immoderate wrath, the wrath that passes exhausted but never appeased – the wrath and fury of the passionate sea. He knew it existed, as we know that crime and abominations exist; he had heard of it as a peaceable citizen in a town hears of battles, famines, and floods, and yet knows nothing of what these things mean – though, indeed, he may have been mixed up in a street row, have gone without his dinner once, or been soaked to the skin in a shower. Captain MacWhirr had sailed over the surface of the oceans as some men go skimming over the years of existence to sink gently into a placid grave, ignorant of life to the last, without ever having been made to see all it may contain of perfidy, of violence, and of terror. There are on sea and land such men thus fortunate – or thus disdained by destiny or by the sea.

Chapter 2

Observing the steady fall of the barometer, Captain MacWhirr thought, 'There's some dirty weather knocking about.' This is precisely what he thought. He had had an experience of moderately dirty weather – the term dirty as applied to the weather implying only moderate discomfort to the seaman. Had he been informed by an indisputable authority that the end of the world was to be finally accomplished by a catastrophic disturbance of the atmosphere, he would have assimilated the information under the simple idea of dirty weather, and no other, because he had no experience of cataclysms, and belief does not necessarily imply comprehension. The wisdom of his country had pronounced by means of an Act of Parliament that before he could be considered as fit to take charge of a ship he should be able to answer certain simple questions on the subject of circular storms such as hurricanes, cyclones, typhoons; and apparently he had answered them, since he was now in command of the *Nan-Shan* in the China seas during the season of typhoons. But if he had answered he remembered nothing of it. He was, however, conscious of being made uncomfortable by the clammy heat. He came out on the bridge, and found no relief to this oppression. The air seemed thick. He gasped like a fish, and began to believe himself greatly out of sorts.

The *Nan-Shan* was ploughing a vanishing furrow upon the circle of the sea that had the surface and the shimmer of an undulating piece of grey silk. The sun, pale and without rays, poured down leaden heat in a strangely indecisive light, and the Chinamen were lying prostrate about the decks. Their bloodless, pinched, yellow faces were like the faces of bilious invalids. Captain MacWhirr noticed two of them especially, stretched out on their backs below the bridge. As soon as they had closed their eyes they seemed dead. Three others, however, were quarrelling barbarously away forward; and one big fellow, half naked, with herculean shoulders, was hanging limply over a winch; another, sitting on the deck, his knees up and his head drooping sideways in a girlish attitude, was plaiting his pigtail with infinite languor depicted in his whole person and in the very movement of his fingers. The smoke struggled with difficulty out of the funnel, and instead of streaming away spread itself out like an infernal sort of cloud, smelling of sulphur and raining soot all over the decks.

'What the devil are you doing there, Mr Jukes?' asked Captain MacWhirr.

This unusual form of address, though mumbled rather than spoken, caused the body of Mr Jukes to start as though it had been prodded under the fifth rib. He had had a low bench brought on the bridge, and sitting on it, with a length of rope curled about his feet and a piece of canvas stretched over his knees, was pushing a sail-needle vigorously. He looked up, and his surprise gave to his eyes an expression of innocence and candour.

'I am only roping some of that new set of bags we made last trip for whipping up coals,' he remonstrated gently. 'We shall want them for the next coaling, sir.'

'What became of the others?'

'Why, worn out of course, sir.'

Captain MacWhirr, after glaring down irresolutely at his chief mate, disclosed the gloomy and cynical conviction that more than half of them had been lost overboard, 'if only the truth was known', and retired to the other end of the bridge. Jukes, exasperated by this unprovoked attack, broke the needle at the second stitch, and dropping his work got up and cursed the heat in a violent undertone.

The propeller thumped, the three Chinamen forward had given up squabbling very suddenly, and the one who had been plaiting his tail clasped his legs and stared dejectedly over his knees. The lurid sunshine cast faint and sickly shadows. The swell ran higher and swifter every moment, and the ship lurched heavily in the smooth, deep hollows of the sea.

'I wonder where that beastly swell comes from,' said Jukes aloud, recovering himself after a stagger.

'North-east,' grunted the literal MacWhirr, from his side of the bridge. 'There's some dirty weather knocking about. Go and look at the glass.'

When Jukes came out of the chart-room, the cast of his countenance had changed to thoughtfulness and concern. He caught hold of the bridge-rail and stared ahead.

The temperature in the engine-room had gone up to a hundred and seventeen degrees. Irritated voices were ascending through the skylight and through the fiddle of the stokehold in a harsh and resonant uproar, mingled with angry clangs and scrapes of metal, as if men with limbs of iron and throats of bronze had been quarrelling down there. The second engineer was falling foul of the stokers for letting the steam go down. He was a man with arms like a blacksmith, and generally feared; but that afternoon the stokers were answering him back recklessly, and slammed the furnace doors with the fury of despair. Then the noise ceased suddenly, and the second engineer appeared, emerging out of the stokehold streaked with grime and soaking wet like a chimney-sweep coming out of a well. As soon as his head was clear of the fiddle he began to scold Jukes for not trimming properly the stokehold ventilators; and in answer Jukes made with his hands deprecatory soothing signs meaning: No wind – can't be helped – you can see for yourself. But the other wouldn't hear reason. His teeth flashed angrily in his dirty face. He didn't mind, he said, the trouble of punching their blanked heads down there, blank his soul, but did the condemned sailors think you could keep steam up in the God-forsaken boilers simply by knocking the blanked stokers about? No, by George! You had to get some draught too – may he be everlastingly blanked for a swab-headed deck-hand if you didn't! And the chief, too, rampaging before the steam-gauge and carrying on like a lunatic up and down the engine-room ever since noon. What did Jukes think he was stuck up there for, if he couldn't get one of his decayed, good-for-nothing deck-cripples to turn the ventilators to the wind?

The relations of the 'engine-room' and the 'deck' of the *Nan-Shan* were, as is known, of a brotherly nature; therefore Jukes leaned over and begged the other in a restrained tone not to make a disgusting ass of himself; the skipper was on the other side of the bridge. But the second declared mutinously that he didn't care a rap who was on the other side of the bridge, and Jukes, passing in a flash from lofty disapproval into a state of exaltation, invited him in unflattering terms to come up and twist the beastly things to please himself, and catch such wind as a donkey of his sort could find. The second rushed up to the fray. He flung himself at the port ventilator as though he meant to tear it out bodily and toss it overboard. All he did was to move the cowl round a few inches, with an enormous expenditure of force, and seemed spent in the effort. He leaned against the back of the wheelhouse, and Jukes walked up to him.

'Oh, Heavens!' ejaculated the engineer in a feeble voice. He lifted his eyes to the sky, and then let his glassy stare descend to meet the horizon that, tilting up to an angle of forty degrees, seemed to hang on a slant for a while and settled down slowly. 'Heavens! Phew! What's up, anyhow?'

Jukes, straddling his long legs like a pair of compasses, put on an air of superiority. 'We're going to catch it this time,' he said. 'The barometer is tumbling down like anything, Harry. And you trying to kick up that silly row . . .'

The word 'barometer' seemed to revive the second engineer's mad animosity. Collecting afresh all his energies, he directed Jukes in a low and brutal tone to shove the unmentionable instrument down his gory throat. Who cared for his crimson barometer? It was the steam – the steam – that was going down; and what between the firemen going faint and the chief going silly, it was worse than a dog's life for him; he didn't care a tinker's curse how soon the whole show was blown out of the water. He seemed on the point of having a cry, but after regaining his breath he muttered darkly, 'I'll faint them,' and dashed off. He stopped upon the fiddle long enough to shake his fist at the unnatural daylight, and dropped into the dark hole with a whoop.

When Jukes turned, his eyes fell upon the rounded back and the big red ears of Captain MacWhirr, who had come across. He did not look at his chief officer, but said at once, 'That's a very violent man, that second engineer.'

'Jolly good second, anyhow,' grunted Jukes. 'They can't keep up steam,' he added rapidly, and made a grab at the rail against the coming lurch.

Captain MacWhirr, unprepared, took a run and brought himself up with a jerk by an awning stanchion.

'A profane man,' he said obstinately. 'If this goes on, I'll have to get rid of him the first chance.'

'It's the heat,' said Jukes. 'The weather's awful. It would make a saint swear. Even up here I feel exactly as if I had my head tied up in a woollen blanket.'

Captain MacWhirr looked up. 'D'ye mean to say, Mr Jukes, you ever had your head tied up in a blanket? What was that for?'

'It's a manner of speaking, sir,' said Jukes stolidly.

'Some of you fellows do go on! What's that about saints swearing? I wish you wouldn't talk so wild. What sort of saint would that be that would swear? No more saint than yourself, I expect. And what's a blanket got to do with it – or the weather either . . . The heat does not make me swear – does it? It's filthy bad temper. That's what it is. And what's the good of your talking like this?'

Thus Captain MacWhirr expostulated against the use of images in speech, and at the end electrified Jukes by a contemptuous snort, followed by words of passion and resentment: 'Damme! I'll fire him out of the ship if he don't look out.'

And Jukes, incorrigible, thought: 'Goodness me! Somebody's put a new inside to my old man. Here's temper, if you like. Of course it's the weather; what else? It would make an angel quarrelsome – let alone a saint.'

All the Chinamen on deck appeared at their last gasp.

At its setting the sun had a diminished diameter and an expiring brown, rayless glow, as if millions of centuries elapsing since the morning had brought it near its end. A dense bank of cloud became visible to the northward; it had a sinister dark olive tint, and lay low and motionless upon the sea, resembling a solid obstacle in the path of the ship. She went floundering towards it like an exhausted creature driven to its death. The coppery twilight retired slowly, and the darkness brought out overhead a swarm of unsteady, big stars, that, as if blown upon, flickered exceedingly and seemed to hang very near the earth. At eight o'clock Jukes went into the chart-room to write up the ship's log.

He copied neatly out of the rough-book the number of miles, the course of the ship, and in the column for 'wind' scrawled the word 'calm' from top to bottom of the eight hours since noon. He was exasperated by the continuous, monotonous rolling of the ship. The heavy inkstand would slide away in a manner that suggested perverse intelligence in dodging the pen. Having written in the large space under the head of 'Remarks' 'Heat very oppressive', he stuck the end of the penholder in his teeth, pipe fashion, and mopped his face carefully.

'Ship rolling heavily in a high cross swell,' he began again, and commented to himself, 'Heavily is no word for it.' Then he wrote: 'Sunset threatening, with a low bank of clouds to N. and E. Sky clear overhead.'

Sprawling over the table with arrested pen, he glanced out of the door, and in that frame of his vision he saw all the stars flying upwards between the teakwood jambs on a black sky. The whole lot took flight together and disappeared, leaving only a blackness flecked with white flashes, for the sea was as black as the sky and speckled with foam afar. The stars that had flown to the roll came back on the return swing of the ship, rushing downwards in their glittering multitude, not of fiery points, but enlarged to tiny discs brilliant with a clear wet sheen.

Jukes watched the flying big stars for a moment, and then wrote: '8 p.m. Swell increasing. Ship labouring and taking water on her decks. Battened down the coolies for the night. Barometer still falling.' He paused, and thought to himself, 'Perhaps nothing whatever'll come of it.' And then he closed resolutely his entries: 'Every appearance of a typhoon coming on.'

On going out he had to stand aside, and Captain MacWhirr strode over the doorstep without saying a word or making a sign.

'Shut the door, Mr Jukes, will you?' he cried from within.

Jukes turned back to do so, muttering ironically: 'Afraid to catch cold, I suppose.' It was his watch below, but he yearned for communion with his kind; and he remarked cheerily to the second mate: 'Doesn't look so bad, after all – does it?'

The second mate was marching to and fro on the bridge, tripping down with small steps one moment, and the next climbing with difficulty the shifting slope of the deck. At the sound of Jukes's voice he stood still, facing forward, but made no reply.

'Hallo! That's a heavy one,' said Jukes, swaying to meet the long roll till his lowered hand touched the planks. This time the second mate made in his throat a noise of an unfriendly nature.

He was an oldish, shabby little fellow, with bad teeth and no hair on his face. He had been shipped in a hurry in Shanghai, that trip when the second officer brought from home had delayed the ship three hours in port by contriving (in some manner Captain MacWhirr could never understand) to fall overboard into an empty coal-lighter lying alongside, and had to be sent ashore to the hospital with concussion of the brain and a broken limb or two.

Jukes was not discouraged by the unsympathetic sound. 'The Chinamen must be having a lovely time of it down there,' he said. 'It's lucky for them the old girl has the easiest roll of any ship I've ever been in. There now! This one wasn't so bad.'

'You wait,' snarled the second mate.

With his sharp nose, red at the tip, and his thin pinched lips, he always looked as though he were raging inwardly; and he was concise in his speech to the point of rudeness. All his time off duty he spent in his cabin with the door shut, keeping so still in there that he was supposed to fall asleep as soon as he had disappeared; but the man who came in to wake him for his watch on deck would invariably find him with his eyes wide open, flat on his back in the bunk, and glaring irritably from a soiled pillow. He never wrote any letters, did not seem to hope for news from anywhere; and though he had been heard once to mention West Hartlepool, it was with extreme bitterness, and only in connection with the extortionate charges of a boarding-house. He was one of those men who are picked up at need in the ports of the world. They are competent enough, appear hopelessly hard up, show no evidence of any sort of vice, and carry about them all the signs of manifest failure. They come aboard on an emergency, care for no ship afloat, live in their own atmosphere of casual connection amongst their shipmates who know nothing of them, and make up their minds to leave at inconvenient times. They clear out with no words of leave-taking in some God-forsaken port other men would fear to be stranded in, and go ashore in company of a shabby sea-chest, corded like a treasure-box, and with an air of shaking the ship's dust off their feet.

'You wait,' he repeated, balanced in great swings with his back to Jukes, motionless and implacable.

'Do you mean to say we are going to catch it hot?' asked Jukes with boyish interest.

'Say? . . . I say nothing. You don't catch me,' snapped the little second mate, with a mixture of pride, scorn, and cunning, as if Jukes' question had been a trap cleverly detected. 'Oh no! None of you here shall make a fool of me if I know it,' he mumbled to himself.

Jukes reflected rapidly that this second mate was a mean little beast, and in his heart he wished poor Jack Allen had never smashed himself up in the coal-lighter. The far-off blackness ahead of the ship was like another night seen through the starry night of the earth – the starless night of the immensities beyond the created universe, revealed in its appalling stillness through a low fissure in the glittering sphere of which the earth is the kernel.

'Whatever there might be about,' said Jukes, 'we are steaming straight into it.'

'*You've* said it,' caught up the second mate, always with his back to Jukes. 'You've said it, mind – not I.'

'Oh, go to Jericho!' said Jukes frankly; and the other emitted a triumphant little chuckle.

'You've said it,' he repeated.

'And what of that?'

'I've known some real good men get into trouble with their skippers for saying a dam' sight less,' answered the second mate feverishly. 'Oh no! You don't catch me.'

'You seem deucedly anxious not to give yourself away,' said Jukes, completely soured by such absurdity. 'I wouldn't be afraid to say what I think.'

'Aye, to me! That's no great trick. I am nobody, and well I know it.'

The ship, after a pause of comparative steadiness, started upon a series of rolls, one worse than the other, and for a time Jukes, preserving his equilibrium, was too busy to open his mouth. As soon as the violent swinging had quieted down somewhat, he said: 'This is a bit too much of a good thing. Whether anything is coming or not I think she ought to be put head on to that swell. The old man is just gone in to lie down. Hang me if I don't speak to him.'

But when he opened the door of the chart-room he saw his captain reading a book. Captain MacWhirr was not lying down: he was standing up with one hand grasping the edge of the bookshelf and the other holding open before his face a thick volume. The lamp wriggled in the gimbals, the loosened books toppled from side to side on the shelf, the long barometer swung in jerky circles, the table altered its slant every moment. In the midst of all this stir and movement Captain MacWhirr, holding on, showed his eyes above the upper edge, and asked, 'What's the matter?'

'Swell getting worse, sir.'

'Noticed that in here,' muttered Captain MacWhirr. 'Anything wrong?'

Jukes, inwardly disconcerted by the seriousness of the eyes looking at him over the top of the book, produced an embarrassed grin.

'Rolling like old boots,' he said sheepishly.

'Aye! Very heavy – very heavy. What do you want?'

At this Jukes lost his footing and began to flounder.

'I was thinking of our passengers,' he said, in the manner of a man clutching at a straw.

'Passengers?' wondered the Captain gravely. 'What passengers?'

'Why, the Chinamen, sir,' explained Jukes, very sick of this conversation.

'The Chinamen! Why don't you speak plainly? Couldn't tell what you meant. Never heard a lot of coolies spoken of as passengers before. Passengers, indeed! What's come to you?'

Captain MacWhirr, closing the book on his forefinger, lowered his arm and looked completely mystified. 'Why are you thinking of the Chinamen, Mr Jukes?' he enquired.

Jukes took a plunge, like a man driven to it. 'She's rolling her decks full of water, sir. Thought you might put her head on perhaps – for a while. Till this goes down a bit – very soon, I dare say. Head to the eastward. I never knew a ship roll like this.'

He held on in the doorway, and Captain MacWhirr, feeling his grip on the shelf inadequate, made up his mind to let go in a hurry, and fell heavily on the couch.

'Head to the eastward?' he said, struggling to sit up. 'That's more than four points off her course.'

'Yes, sir. Fifty degrees . . . Would just bring her head far enough round to meet this . . .'

Captain MacWhirr was now sitting up. He had not dropped the book, and he had not lost his place.

'To the eastward?' he repeated, with dawning astonishment. 'To the . . . Where do you think we are bound to? You want me to haul a full-powered steamship four points off her course to make the Chinamen comfortable! Now, I've heard more than enough of mad things done in the world – but this . . . If I didn't know you, Jukes, I would think you were in liquor. Steer four points off . . . And what afterwards? Steer four points over the other way, I suppose, to make the course good. What put it into your head that I would start to tack a steamer as if she were a sailing-ship?'

'Jolly good thing she isn't,' threw in Jukes, with bitter readiness. 'She would have rolled every blessed stick out of her this afternoon.'

'Aye! And you just would have had to stand and see them go,' said Captain MacWhirr, showing a certain animation. 'It's a dead calm, isn't it?'

'It is, sir. But there's something out of the common coming, for sure.'

'Maybe. I suppose you have a notion I should be getting out of the way of that dirt,' said Captain MacWhirr, speaking with the utmost simplicity of manner and tone, and fixing the oilcloth on the floor with a heavy stare. Thus he noticed neither Jukes' discomfiture nor the mixture of vexation and astonished respect on his face.

'Now, here's this book,' he continued with deliberation, slapping his thigh with the closed volume. 'I've been reading the chapter on the storms there.'

This was true. He had been reading the chapter on the storms. When he had entered the chart-room, it was with no intention of taking the book down. Some influence in the air – the same influence, probably, that caused the steward to bring without orders the Captain's sea-boots and oilskin coat up to the chart-room – had as it were guided his hand to the shelf; and without taking the time to sit down he had waded with a conscious effort into the terminology of the subject. He lost himself amongst advancing semicircles, left- and right-hand quadrants, the curves of the tracks, the probable bearing of the centre, the shifts of wind and the readings of barometer. He tried to bring all these things into a definite relation to himself, and ended by becoming contemptuously angry with such a lot of words and with so much advice, all head-work and supposition, without a glimmer of certitude.

'It's the damnedest thing, Jukes,' he said. 'If a fellow was to believe all that's in there, he would be running most of his time all over the sea trying to get behind the weather.'

Again he slapped his leg with the book; and Jukes opened his mouth, but said nothing.

'Running to get behind the weather! Do you understand that, Mr Jukes? It's the maddest thing!' ejaculated Captain MacWhirr, with pauses, gazing at the floor profoundly. 'You would think an old woman had been writing this. It passes me. If that thing means anything useful, then it means that I should at once alter the course away, away to the devil somewhere, and come booming down on Fu-chau from the northward at the tail of this dirty weather that's supposed to be knocking about in our way. From the north! Do you understand, Mr Jukes? Three hundred extra miles to the distance, and a pretty coal bill to show. I couldn't bring myself to do that if every word in there was gospel truth, Mr Jukes. Don't you expect me . . . '

And Jukes, silent, marvelled at this display of feeling and loquacity.

'But the truth is that you don't know if the fellow is right anyhow. How can you tell what a gale is made of till you get it? He isn't aboard here, is he? Very well. Here he says that the centre of them things bears eight points off the wind; but we haven't got any wind, for all the barometer falling. Where's his centre now?'

'We will get the wind presently,' mumbled Jukes.

'Let it come, then,' said Captain MacWhirr, with dignified indignation. 'It's only to let you see, Mr Jukes, that you don't find everything in books. All these rules for dodging breezes and circumventing the winds of heaven, Mr Jukes, seem to me the maddest thing, when you come to look at it sensibly.'

He raised his eyes, saw Jukes gazing at him dubiously, and tried to illustrate his meaning.

'About as queer as your extraordinary notion of dodging the ship head to sea, for I don't know how long, to make the Chinamen comfortable; whereas all we've got to do is to take them to Fu-chau, being timed to get there before noon on Friday. If the weather delays me – very well. There's your log-book to talk straight about the weather. But suppose I went swinging off my course and came in two days late, and they asked me: "Where have you been all that time, Captain?" What could I say to that? "Went around to dodge the bad weather," I would say. "It must've been dam' bad," they would say. "Don't know," I would have to say; "I've dodged clear of it." See that, Jukes? I have been thinking it all out this afternoon.'

He looked up again in his unseeing, unimaginative way. No one had ever heard him say so much at one time. Jukes, with his arms open in the doorway, was like a man invited to behold a miracle. Unbounded wonder was the intellectual meaning of his eye, while incredulity was seated in his whole countenance.

'A gale is a gale, Mr Jukes,' resumed the Captain, 'and a full-powered steamship has got to face it. There's just so much dirty weather knocking about the world, and the proper thing is to go through it with none of what old Captain Wilson of the *Melita* calls "storm strategy". The other day ashore I heard him hold forth about it to a lot of shipmasters who came in and sat at a table next to mine. It seemed to me the greatest nonsense. He was telling them how he – outmanoeuvred, I think he said, a terrific gale, so that it never came nearer than fifty miles to him. A neat piece of head-work he called it. How he knew there was a terrific gale fifty miles off beats me altogether. It was like listening to a crazy man. I would have thought Captain Wilson was old enough to know better.'

Captain MacWhirr ceased for a moment, then said, 'It's your watch below, Mr Jukes?'

Jukes came to himself with a start. 'Yes, sir.'

'Leave orders to call me at the slightest change,' said the Captain. He reached up to put the book away, and tucked his legs up on the couch. 'Shut the door so that it don't fly open, will you? I can't stand a door banging. They've put a lot of rubbishy locks into this ship, I must say.'

Captain MacWhirr closed his eyes.

He did so to rest himself. He was tired, and he experienced that state of mental vacuity which comes at the end of an exhaustive discussion that has liberated some belief matured in the course of meditative years. He had indeed been making his confession of faith, had he only known it; and its effect was to make Jukes, on the other side of the door, stand scratching his head for a good while.

Captain MacWhirr opened his eyes.

He thought he must have been asleep. What was that loud noise? Wind? Why had he not been called? The lamp wriggled in its gimbals, the barometer swung in circles, the table altered its slant every moment; a pair of limp seaboots with collapsed tops went sliding past the couch. He put out his hand instantly, and captured one.

Jukes' face appeared in a crack of the door: only his face, very red, with staring eyes. The flame of the lamp leaped, a piece of paper flew up, a rush of air enveloped Captain MacWhirr. Beginning to draw on the boot, he directed an expectant gaze at Jukes' swollen, excited features.

'Came on like this,' shouted Jukes, 'five minutes ago . . . all of a sudden.'

The head disappeared with a bang, and a heavy splash and patter of drops swept past the closed door as if a pailful of melted lead had been flung against the house. A whistling could be heard now upon the deep vibrating noise outside. The stuffy chart-room seemed as full of draughts as a shed. Captain MacWhirr collared the other sea-boot on its violent passage along the floor. He was not flustered, but he could not find at once the opening for inserting his foot. The shoes he had flung off were scurrying from end to end of the cabin, gambolling playfully over each other like puppies. As soon as he stood up he kicked at them viciously, but without effect.

He threw himself into the attitude of a lunging fencer, to reach after his oilskin coat; and afterwards he staggered all over the confined space while he jerked himself into it. Very grave, straddling his legs far apart, and stretching his neck, he started to tie deliberately the strings of his sou'-wester under his chin, with thick fingers that trembled slightly. He went through all the movements of a woman putting on her bonnet before a glass, with a strained, listening attention, as though he expected every moment to hear the shout of his name in the confused clamour that had suddenly beset his ship. Its increase filled his ears while he was getting ready to go out and confront whatever it might mean. It was tumultuous and very loud – made up of the rush of the wind, the crashes of the sea, with that prolonged deep vibration of the air, like the roll of an immense and remote drum beating the charge of the gale.

He stood for a moment in the light of the lamp, thick, clumsy, shapeless in his panoply of combat, vigilant and red-faced.

'There's a lot of weight in this,' he muttered.

As soon as he attempted to open the door the wind caught it. Clinging to the handle, he was dragged out over the doorstep, and at once found himself engaged with the wind in a sort of personal scuffle whose object was the shutting of that door. At the last moment a tongue of air scurried in and licked out the flame of the lamp.

Ahead of the ship he perceived a great darkness lying upon a multitude of white flashes; on the starboard beam a few amazing stars drooped, dim and fitful, above an immense waste of broken seas, as if seen through a mad drift of smoke.

On the bridge a knot of men, indistinct and toiling, were making great efforts in the light of the wheelhouse windows that shone mistily on their heads and backs. Suddenly darkness closed upon one pane, then on another. The voices of the lost group reached him after the manner of men's voices in a gale, in shreds and fragments of forlorn shouting snatched past the ear. All at once Jukes appeared at his side, yelling, with his head down.

'Watch – put in – wheelhouse shutters – glass – afraid – blow in.'

Jukes heard his commander upbraiding.

'This – come – anything – warning – call me.'

He tried to explain, with the uproar pressing on his lips.

'Light air – remained – bridge – sudden – north-east – could turn – thought – you – sure – hear.'

They had gained the shelter of the weather-cloth, and could converse with raised voices, as people quarrel.

'I got the hands along to cover up all the ventilators. Good job I had remained on deck. I didn't think you would be asleep, and so . . . What did you say, sir? What?'

'Nothing,' cried Captain MacWhirr. 'I said – all right.'

'By all the powers! We've got it this time,' observed Jukes in a howl.

'You haven't altered her course?' enquired Captain MacWhirr, straining his voice.

'No, sir. Certainly not. Wind came out right ahead. And here comes the head sea.'

A plunge of the ship ended in a shock as if she had landed her forefoot upon something solid. After a moment of stillness a lofty flight of sprays drove hard with the wind upon their faces.

'Keep her at it as long as we can,' shouted Captain MacWhirr.

Before Jukes had squeezed the salt water out of his eyes all the stars had disappeared.

Chapter 3

Jukes was as ready a man as any half-dozen young mates that may be caught by casting a net upon the waters; and though he had been somewhat taken aback by the startling viciousness of the first squall, he had pulled himself together on the instant, had called out the hands and had rushed them along to secure such openings about the deck as had not been already battened down earlier in the evening. Shouting in his fresh, stentorian voice, 'Jump, boys, and bear a hand!' he led in the work, telling himself the while that he had 'just expected this'.

But at the same time he was growing aware that this was rather more than he had expected. From the first stir of the air felt on his cheek the gale seemed to take upon itself the accumulated impetus of an avalanche. Heavy sprays enveloped the *Nan-Shan* from stem to stern, and instantly in the midst of her regular rolling she began to jerk and plunge as though she had gone mad with fright.

Jukes thought, 'This is no joke.' While he was exchanging explanatory yells with his captain, a sudden lowering of the darkness came upon the night, falling before their vision like something palpable. It was as if the masked lights of the world had been turned down. Jukes was uncritically glad to have his captain at hand. It relieved him as though that man had, by simply coming on deck, taken most of the gale's weight upon his shoulders. Such is the prestige, the privilege, and the burden of command.

Captain MacWhirr could expect no relief of that sort from anyone on earth. Such is the loneliness of command. He was trying to see, with that watchful manner of a seaman who stares into the wind's eye as if into the eye of an adversary, to penetrate the hidden intention and guess the aim and force of the thrust. The strong wind swept at him out of a vast obscurity; he felt under his feet the uneasiness of his ship, and he could not even discern the shadow of her shape. He wished it were not so; and very still he waited, feeling stricken by a blind man's helplessness.

To be silent was natural to him, dark or shine. Jukes, at his elbow, made himself heard yelling cheerily in the gusts, 'We must have got the worst of it at once, sir.' A faint burst of lightning quivered all round, as if flashed into a cavern – into a black and secret chamber of the sea, with a floor of foaming crests.

It unveiled for a sinister, fluttering moment a ragged mass of clouds hanging low, the lurch of the long outlines of the ship, the black figures of men caught on the bridge heads forward, as if petrified in the act of butting. The darkness palpitated down upon all this, and then the real thing came at last.

It was something formidable and swift, like the sudden smashing of a vial of wrath. It seemed to explode all round the ship with an overpowering concussion and a rush of great waters, as if an immense dam had been blown up to windward. In an instant the men lost touch of each other. This is the disintegrating power of a great wind: it isolates one from one's kind. An earthquake, a landslip, an avalanche, overtake a man incidentally, as it were – without passion. A furious gale attacks him like a personal enemy, tries to grasp his limbs, fastens upon his mind, seeks to rout his very spirit out of him.

Jukes was driven away from his commander. He fancied himself whirled a great distance through the air. Everything disappeared – even, for a moment, his power of thinking; but his hand had found one of the rail-stanchions. His distress was by no means alleviated by an inclination to disbelieve the reality of this experience. Though young, he had seen some bad weather, and had never doubted his ability to imagine the worst; but this was so much beyond his powers of fancy that it appeared incompatible with the existence of any ship whatever. He would have been incredulous about himself in the same way, perhaps, had he not been so harassed by the necessity of exerting a wrestling effort against a force trying to tear him away from his hold. Moreover, the conviction of not being utterly destroyed returned to him through the sensations of being half-drowned, bestially shaken, and partly choked.

It seemed to him he remained there precariously alone with the stanchion for a long, long time. The rain poured on him, flowed, drove in sheets. He breathed in gasps; and sometimes the water he swallowed was fresh and sometimes it was salt. For the most part he kept his eyes shut tight, as if suspecting his sight might be destroyed in the immense flurry of the elements. When he ventured to blink hastily, he derived some moral support from the green gleam of the starboard light shining feebly upon the flight of rain and sprays. He was actually looking at it when its ray fell upon the uprearing sea which put it out. He saw the head of the wave topple over, adding the mite of its crash to the tremendous uproar raging around him, and almost at the same instant the stanchion was wrenched away from his embracing arms. After a crushing thump on his back he found himself suddenly afloat and borne upwards. His first irresistible notion was that the whole China Sea had climbed on the bridge. Then, more sanely, he concluded himself gone overboard. All the time he was being tossed, flung, and rolled in great volumes of water, he kept on repeating mentally, with the utmost precipitation, the words: 'My God! My God! My God! My God!'

All at once, in a revolt of misery and despair, he formed the crazy resolution to get out of that. And he began to thresh about with his arms and legs. But as soon as he commenced his wretched struggles he discovered that he had become somehow mixed up with a face, an oilskin coat, somebody's boots. He clawed ferociously all these things in turn, lost them, found them again, lost them once more, and finally was himself caught in the firm clasp of a pair of stout arms. He returned the embrace closely round a thick solid body. He had found his captain.

They tumbled over and over, tightening their hug. Suddenly the water let them down with a brutal bang; and, stranded against the side of the wheelhouse, out of breath and bruised, they were left to stagger up in the wind and hold on where they could.

Jukes came out of it rather horrified, as though he had escaped some unparalleled outrage directed at his feelings. It weakened his faith in himself. He started shouting aimlessly to the man he could feel near him in that fiendish blackness, 'Is it you, sir? Is it you, sir?' till his temples seemed ready to burst. And he heard in answer a voice, as if crying far away, as if screaming to him fretfully from a very great distance, the one word 'Yes!' Other seas swept again over the bridge. He received them defencelessly right over his bare head, with both his hands engaged in holding.

The motion of the ship was extravagant. Her lurches had an appalling helplessness: she pitched as if taking a header into a void, and seemed to find a wall to hit every time. When she rolled she fell on her side headlong, and she would be righted back by such a demolishing blow that Jukes felt her reeling as a clubbed man reels before he collapses. The gale howled and scuffled about gigantically in the darkness as though the entire world were one black gully. At certain moments the air streamed against the ship as if sucked through a tunnel with a concentrated solid force of impact that seemed to lift her clean out of the water and keep her up for an instant with only a quiver running through her from end to end. And then she would begin her tumbling again as if dropped back into a boiling cauldron. Jukes tried hard to compose his mind and judge things coolly.

The sea, flattened down in the heavier gusts, would uprise and overwhelm both ends of the *Nan-Shan* in snowy rushes of foam, expanding wide, beyond both rails, into the night. And on this dazzling sheet, spread under the blackness of the clouds and emitting a bluish glow, Captain MacWhirr could catch a desolate glimpse of a few tiny specks black as ebony, the tops of the hatches, the battened companions, the heads of the covered winches, the foot of a mast. This was all he could see of his ship. Her middle structure, covered by the bridge which bore him, his mate, the closed wheelhouse where a man was steering shut up with the fear of being swept overboard together with the whole thing in one great crash – her middle structure was like a half-tide rock awash upon a coast. It was like an outlying rock with the water boiling up, streaming over, pouring off, beating round – like a rock in the surf to which shipwrecked people cling before they let go – only it rose, it sank, it rolled continuously, without respite and rest, like a rock that should have miraculously struck adrift from a coast and gone wallowing upon the sea.

The *Nan-Shan* was being looted by the storm with a senseless, destructive fury: trysails torn out of the extra gaskets, double-lashed awnings blown away, bridge swept clean, weather-cloths burst, rails twisted, light-screens smashed – and two of the boats had gone already. They had gone unheard and unseen, melting, as it were, in the shock and smother of the wave. It was only later, when upon the white flash of another high sea hurling itself amidships, Jukes had a vision of two pairs of davits leaping black and empty out of the solid blackness, with one overhauled fall flying and an iron-bound block capering in the air, that he became aware of what had happened within about three yards of his back.

He poked his head forward, groping for the ear of his commander. His lips touched it – big, fleshy, very wet. He cried in an agitated tone, 'Our boats are going now, sir.'

And again he heard that voice, forced and ringing feebly, but with a penetrating effect of quietness in the enormous discord of noises, as if sent out from some remote spot of peace beyond the black wastes of the gale; again he heard a man's voice – the frail and indomitable sound that can be made to carry an infinity of thought, resolution and purpose, that shall be pronouncing confident words on the last day, when heavens fall, and justice is done – again he heard it, and it was crying to him, as if from very, very far – 'All right.'

He thought he had not managed to make himself understood. 'Our boats – I say boats – the boats, sir! Two gone!'

The same voice, within a foot of him and yet so remote, yelled sensibly, 'Can't be helped.'

Captain MacWhirr had never turned his face, but Jukes caught some more words on the wind.

'What can – expect – when hammering through – such – Bound to leave – something behind – stands to reason.'

Watchfully Jukes listened for more. No more came. This was all Captain MacWhirr had to say; and Jukes could picture to himself rather than see the broad squat back before him. An impenetrable obscurity pressed down upon the ghostly glimmers of the sea. A dull conviction seized upon Jukes that there was nothing to be done.

If the steering-gear did not give way, if the immense volumes of water did not burst the deck in or smash one of the hatches, if the engines did not give up, if way could be kept on the ship against this terrific wind, and she did not bury herself in one of these awful seas, of whose white crests alone, topping high above her bows, he could now and then get a sickening glimpse – then there was a chance of her coming out of it. Something within him seemed to turn over, bringing uppermost the feeling that the *Nan-Shan* was lost.

'She's done for,' he said to himself, with a surprising mental agitation, as though he had discovered an unexpected meaning in this thought. One of these things was bound to happen. Nothing could be prevented now, and nothing could be remedied. The men on board did not count, and the ship could not last. This weather was too impossible.

Jukes felt an arm thrown heavily over his shoulders; and to this overture he responded with great intelligence by catching hold of his captain round the waist.

They stood clasped thus in the blind night, bracing each other against the wind, cheek to cheek and lip to ear, in the manner of two hulks lashed stem to stern together.

And Jukes heard the voice of his commander hardly any louder than before, but nearer, as though, starting to march athwart the prodigious rush of the hurricane, it had approached him, bearing that strange effect of quietness like the serene glow of a halo.

'D'ye know where the hands got to?' it asked, vigorous and evanescent at the same time, overcoming the strength of the wind, and swept away from Jukes instantly.

Jukes didn't know. They were all on the bridge when the real force of the hurricane struck the ship. He had no idea where they had crawled to. Under the circumstances they were nowhere, for all the use that could be made of them. Somehow the Captain's wish to know distressed Jukes.

'Want the hands, sir?' he cried apprehensively.

'Ought to know,' asserted Captain MacWhirr. 'Hold hard.'

They held hard. An outburst of unchained fury, a vicious rush of the wind absolutely steadied the ship; she rocked only, quick and light like a child's cradle, for a terrific moment of suspense, while the whole atmosphere, as it seemed, streamed furiously past her, roaring away from the tenebrous earth.

It suffocated them, and with eyes shut they tightened their grasp. What from the magnitude of the shock might have been a column of water running upright in the dark, butted against the ship, broke short, and fell on her bridge, crushingly, from on high, with a dead burying weight.

A flying fragment of that collapse, a mere splash, enveloped them in one swirl from their feet over their heads, filling violently their ears, mouths and nostrils with salt water. It knocked out their legs, wrenched in haste at their arms, seethed away swiftly under their chins; and opening their eyes, they saw the piled-up masses of foam dashing to and fro amongst what looked like the fragments of a ship. She had given way as if driven straight in. Their panting hearts yielded too before the tremendous blow; and all at once she sprang up again to her desperate plunging, as if trying to scramble out from under the ruins.

The seas in the dark seemed to rush from all sides to keep her back where she might perish. There was hate in the way she was handled, and a ferocity in the blows that fell. She was like a living creature thrown to the rage of a mob: hustled terribly, struck at, borne up, flung down, leaped upon. Captain MacWhirr and Jukes kept hold of each other, deafened by the noise, gagged by the wind; and the great physical tumult beating about their bodies, brought, like an unbridled display of passion, a profound trouble to their souls. One of these wild and appalling shrieks that are heard at times passing mysteriously overhead in the steady roar of a hurricane, swooped, as if borne on wings, upon the ship, and Jukes tried to outscream it.

'Will she live through this?'

The cry was wrenched out of his breast. It was as unintentional as the birth of a thought in the head, and he heard nothing of it himself. It all became extinct at once – thought, intention, effort – and of his cry the inaudible vibration added to the tempest waves of the air.

He expected nothing from it. Nothing at all. For indeed what answer could be made? But after a while he heard with amazement the frail and resisting voice in his ear, the dwarf sound, unconquered in the giant tumult.

'She may!'

It was a dull yell, more difficult to seize than a whisper. And presently the voice returned again, half submerged in the vast crashes, like a ship battling against the waves of an ocean.

'Let's hope so!' it cried – small, lonely and unmoved, a stranger to the visions of hope or fear; and it flickered into disconnected words: 'Ship . . . This . . . Never – Anyhow . . . for the best.' Jukes gave it up.

Then, as if it had come suddenly upon the one thing fit to withstand the power of a storm, it seemed to gain force and firmness for the last broken shouts: 'Keep on hammering . . . builders . . . good men . . . And chance it . . . engines . . . Rout . . . good man.'

Captain MacWhirr removed his arm from Jukes' shoulders, and thereby ceased to exist for his mate, so dark it was; Jukes, after a tense stiffening of every muscle, would let himself go limp all over. The gnawing of profound discomfort existed side by side with an incredible disposition to somnolence, as though he had been buffeted and worried into drowsiness. The wind would get hold of his head and try to shake it off his shoulders; his clothes, full of water, were as heavy as lead, cold and dripping like an armour of melting ice: he shivered – it lasted a long time; and with his hands closed hard on his hold, he was letting himself sink slowly into the depths of bodily misery. His mind became concentrated upon himself in an aimless, idle way, and when something pushed lightly at the back of his knees he nearly, as the saying is, jumped out of his skin.

In the start forward he bumped the back of Captain MacWhirr, who didn't move; and then a hand gripped his thigh. A lull had come, a menacing lull of the wind, the holding of a stormy breath – and he felt himself pawed all over. It was the boatswain. Jukes recognised these hands, so thick and enormous that they seemed to belong to some new species of man.

The boatswain had arrived on the bridge, crawling on all fours against the wind, and had found the chief mate's legs with the top of his head. Immediately he crouched and began to explore Jukes' person upwards, with prudent, apologetic touches, as became an inferior.

He was an ill-favoured, undersized, gruff sailor of fifty, coarsely hairy, short-legged, long-armed, resembling an elderly ape. His strength was immense; and in his great lumpy paws, bulging like brown boxing-gloves on the end of furry forearms, the heaviest objects were handled like playthings. Apart from the grizzled pelt on his chest, the menacing demeanour and the hoarse voice, he had none of the classical attributes of his rating. His good nature almost amounted to imbecility: the men did what they liked with him, and he had not an ounce of initiative in his character, which was easy-going and talkative. For these reasons Jukes disliked him; but Captain MacWhirr, to Jukes' scornful disgust, seemed to regard him as a first-rate petty officer.

He pulled himself up by Jukes' coat, taking that liberty with the greatest moderation, and only so far as it was forced upon him by the hurricane.

'What is it, boss'n, what is it?' yelled Jukes, impatiently. What could that fraud of a boss'n want on the bridge? The typhoon had got on Jukes' nerves. The husky bellowings of the other, though unintelligible, seemed to suggest a state of lively satisfaction. There could be no mistake. The old fool was pleased with something.

The boatswain's other hand had found some other body, for in a changed tone he began to enquire: 'Is it you, sir? Is it you, sir?' The wind strangled his howls.

'Yes!' cried Captain MacWhirr.

Chapter 4

All that the boatswain, out of a superabundance of yells, could make clear to Captain MacWhirr was the bizarre intelligence that 'All them Chinamen in the fore 'tween deck have fetched away, sir.'

Jukes to leeward could hear these two shouting within six inches of his face, as you may hear on a still night half a mile away two men conversing across a field. He heard Captain MacWhirr's exasperated, 'What? What?'

and the strained pitch of the other's hoarseness. 'In a lump . . . seen them myself . . . Awful sight, sir . . . thought . . . tell you.'

Jukes remained indifferent, as if rendered irresponsible by the force of the hurricane, which made the very thought of action utterly vain. Besides, being very young, he had found the occupation of keeping his heart completely steeled against the worst so engrossing that he had come to feel an over-powering dislike towards any other form of activity whatever. He was not scared; he knew this because, firmly believing he would never see another sunrise, he remained calm in that belief.

These are the moments of do-nothing heroics to which even good men surrender at times. Many officers of ships can no doubt recall a case in their experience when just such a trance of confounded stoicism would come all at once over a whole ship's company. Jukes, however, had no wide experience of men or storms. He conceived himself to be calm – inexorably calm; but as a matter of fact he was daunted; not abjectly, but only so far as a decent man may, without becoming loathsome to himself.

It was rather like a forced-on numbness of spirit. The long, long stress of a gale does it; the suspense of the interminably culminating catastrophe; and there is a bodily fatigue in the mere holding on to existence within the excessive tumult; a searching and insidious fatigue that penetrates deep into a man's breast to cast down and sadden his heart, which is incorrigible, and of all the gifts of the earth – even before life itself – aspires to peace.

Jukes was benumbed much more than he supposed. He held on – very wet, very cold, stiff in every limb; and in a momentary hallucination of swift visions (it is said that a drowning man thus reviews all his life) he beheld all sorts of memories altogether unconnected with his present situation. He remembered his father, for instance: a worthy businessman, who at an unfortunate crisis in his affairs went quietly to bed and died forthwith in a state of resignation. Jukes did not recall these circumstances, of course, but remaining otherwise unconcerned he seemed to see distinctly the poor man's face; a certain game of nap played when quite a boy in Table Bay on board a ship, since lost with all hands; the thick eyebrows of his first skipper; and without any emotion, as he might years ago have walked listlessly into her room and found her sitting there with a book, he remembered his mother – dead, too, now – the resolute woman, left badly off, who had been very firm in his bringing up.

It could not have lasted more than a second, perhaps not so much. A heavy arm had fallen about his shoulders; Captain MacWhirr's voice was speaking his name into his ear.

'Jukes! Jukes!'

He detected the tone of deep concern. The wind had thrown its weight on the ship, trying to pin her down amongst the seas. They made a clean breach over her, as over a deep-swimming log; and the gathered weight of crashes menaced monstrously from afar. The breakers flung out of the night with a ghostly light on their crests – the light of sea-foam that in a ferocious, boiling-up pale flash showed upon the slender body of the ship the toppling rush, the downfall, and the seething mad scurry of each wave. Never for a moment could she shake herself clear of the water; Jukes, rigid, perceived in her motion the ominous sign of haphazard floundering. She was no longer struggling intelligently. It was the beginning of the end; and the note of busy concern in Captain MacWhirr's voice sickened him like an exhibition of blind and pernicious folly.

The spell of the storm had fallen upon Jukes. He was penetrated by it, absorbed by it; he was rooted in it with a rigour of dumb attention. Captain MacWhirr persisted in his cries, but the wind got between them like a solid wedge. He hung round Jukes' neck as heavy as a millstone, and suddenly the sides of their heads knocked together.

'Jukes! Mr Jukes, I say!'

He had to answer that voice that would not be silenced. He answered in the customary manner: ' . . . Yes, sir.'

And directly, his heart, corrupted by the storm that breeds a craving for peace, rebelled against the tyranny of training and command.

Captain MacWhirr had his mate's head fixed firm in the crook of his elbow, and pressed it to his yelling lips mysteriously. Sometimes Jukes would break in, admonishing hastily: 'Look out, sir!' or Captain MacWhirr would bawl an earnest exhortation to 'Hold hard, there!' and the whole black universe seemed to reel together with the ship. They paused. She floated yet. And Captain MacWhirr would resume his shouts. ' . . . Says . . . whole lot . . . fetched away . . . Ought to see . . . what's the matter.'

Directly the full force of the hurricane had struck the ship, every part of her deck became untenable; and the sailors, dazed and dismayed, took shelter in the port alleyway under the bridge. It had a door aft, which they shut; it was very black, cold, and dismal. At each heavy fling of the ship they would groan all together in the dark, and tons of water could be heard scuttling about as if trying to get at them from above. The boatswain had been keeping up a gruff talk, but a more unreasonable lot of men, he said afterwards, he had never been with. They were snug enough there, out of harm's way, and not wanted to do anything, either; and yet they did nothing but grumble and complain peevishly like so many sick kids. Finally, one of them said that if there had been at least some light to see each other's noses by, it wouldn't be so bad. It was making him crazy, he declared, to lie there in the dark waiting for the blamed hooker to sink.

'Why don't you step outside, then, and be done with it at once?' the boatswain turned on him.

This called up a shout of execration. The boatswain found himself overwhelmed with reproaches of all sorts. They seemed to take it ill that a lamp was not instantly created for them out of nothing. They would whine after a light to get drowned by – anyhow! And though the unreason of their revilings was patent – since no one could hope to reach the lamp-room, which was forward – he became greatly distressed. He did not think it was decent of them to be nagging at him like this. He told them so, and was met by general contumely. He sought refuge, therefore, in an embittered silence. At the same time their grumbling and sighing and muttering worried him greatly, but by and by it occurred to him that there were six globe lamps hung in the 'tween-deck, and that there could be no harm in depriving the coolies of one of them.

The *Nan-Shan* had an athwartship coal-bunker, which, being at times used as cargo space, communicated by an iron door with the fore 'tween-deck. It was empty then, and its manhole was the foremost one in the alleyway. The boatswain could get in, therefore, without coming out on deck at all; but to his great surprise he found he could induce no one to help him in taking off the manhole cover. He groped for it all the same, but one of the crew lying in his way refused to budge.

'Why, I only want to get you that blamed light you are crying for,' he expostulated, almost pitifully.

Somebody told him to go and put his head in a bag. He regretted he could not recognise the voice, and that it was too dark to see, otherwise, as he said, he would have put a head on *that* son of a sea-cook, anyway, sink or swim. Nevertheless, he had made up his mind to show them he could get a light, if he were to die for it.

Through the violence of the ship's rolling, every movement was dangerous. To be lying down seemed labour enough. He nearly broke his neck dropping into the bunker. He fell on his back, and was sent shooting helplessly from side to side in the dangerous company of a heavy iron bar – a coal-trimmer's slice probably – left down there by somebody. This thing made him as nervous as though it had been a wild beast. He could not see it, the inside of the bunker coated with coal-dust being perfectly and impenetrably black; but he heard it sliding and clattering, and striking here and there, always in the neighbour-hood of his head. It seemed to make an extraordinary noise, too – to give heavy thumps as though it had been as big as a bridge girder. This was remarkable enough for him to notice while he was flung from port to starboard and back again, and clawing desperately the smooth sides of the bunker in the endeavour to stop himself. The door into the 'tween-deck not fitting quite true, he saw a thread of dim light at the bottom.

Being a sailor, and a still active man, he did not want much of a chance to regain his feet; and as luck would have it, in scrambling up he put his hand on the iron slice, picking it up as he rose. Otherwise he would have been afraid of the thing breaking his legs, or at least knocking him down again. At first he stood still. He felt unsafe in this darkness that seemed to make the ship's motion unfamiliar, unforeseen, and difficult to counteract. He felt so much shaken for a moment that he dared not move for fear of 'taking charge again'. He had no mind to get battered to pieces in that bunker.

He had struck his head twice; he was dazed a little. He seemed to hear yet so plainly the clatter and bangs of the iron slice flying about his ears that he tightened his grip to prove to himself he had it there safely in his hand. He was vaguely amazed at the plainness with which down there he could hear the gale raging. Its howls and shrieks seemed to take on, in the emptiness of the bunker, something of the human character, of human rage and pain – being not vast but infinitely poignant. And there were, with every roll, thumps too – profound, ponderous thumps, as if a bulky object of five-ton weight or so had got play in the hold. But there was no such thing in the cargo. Something on deck? Impossible. Or alongside? Couldn't be.

He thought all this quickly, clearly, competently, like a seaman, and in the end remained puzzled. This noise, though, came deadened from outside, together with the washing and pouring of water on deck above his head. Was it the wind? Must be. It made down there a row like the shouting of a big lot of crazed men. And he discovered in himself a desire for a light too – if only to get drowned by – and a nervous anxiety to get out of that bunker as quickly as possible.

He pulled back the bolt: the heavy iron plate turned on its hinges; and it was as though he had opened the door to the sounds of the tempest. A gust of hoarse yelling met him: the air was still; and the rushing of water overhead was covered by a tumult of strangled, throaty shrieks that produced an effect of desperate confusion. He straddled his legs the whole width of the doorway and stretched his neck. And at first he perceived only what he had come to seek: six small yellow flames swinging violently on the great body of the dusk.

It was stayed like the gallery of a mine, with a row of stanchions in the middle, and cross-beams overhead, penetrating into the gloom ahead – indefinitely. And to port there loomed, like the caving in of one of the sides, a bulky mass with a slanting outline. The whole place, with the shadows and the shapes, moved all the time. The boatswain glared: the ship lurched to starboard, and a great howl came from that mass that had the slant of fallen earth.

Pieces of wood whizzed past. Planks, he thought, inexpressibly startled, and flinging back his head. At his feet a man went sliding over, open-eyed, on his back, straining with uplifted arms for nothing: and another came bounding like a detached stone with his head between his legs and his hands clenched. His pigtail whipped in the air; he made a grab at the boatswain's legs, and from his opened hand a bright white disc rolled against the boatswain's foot. He recognised a silver dollar, and yelled at it with astonishment. With a precipitated sound of trampling and shuffling of bare feet, and with guttural cries, the mound of writhing bodies piled up to port detached itself from the ship's side and shifted to starboard, sliding, inert and struggling, to a dull, brutal thump. The cries ceased. The boatswain heard a long moan through the roar and whistling of the wind; he saw an inextricable confusion of heads and shoulders, naked soles kicking upwards, fists raised, tumbling backs, legs, pigtails, faces.

'Good Lord!' he cried, horrified, and banged-to the iron door upon this vision.

This was what he had come on the bridge to tell. He could not keep it to himself; and on board ship there is only one man to whom it is worth while to unburden yourself. On his passage back the hands in the alleyway swore at him for a fool. Why didn't he bring that lamp? What the devil did the coolies matter to anybody? And when he came out, the extremity of the ship made what went on inside of her appear of little moment.

At first he thought he had left the alleyway in the very moment of her sinking. The bridge ladders had been washed away, but an enormous sea filling the after-deck floated him up. After that he had to lie on his stomach for some time, holding to a ring-bolt, getting his breath now and then, and swallowing salt water. He struggled farther on his hands and knees, too frightened and distracted to turn back. In this way he reached the after-part of the wheelhouse. In that comparatively sheltered spot he found the second mate. The boatswain was pleasantly surprised – his impression being that everybody on deck must have been washed away a long time ago. He asked eagerly where the captain was.

The second mate was lying low, like a malignant little animal under a hedge.

'Captain? Gone overboard, after getting us into this mess.' The mate, too, for all he knew or cared. Another fool. Didn't matter. Everybody was going by and by.

The boatswain crawled out again into the strength of the wind; not because he much expected to find anybody, he said, but just to get away from 'that man'. He crawled out as outcasts go to face an inclement world. Hence his great joy at finding Jukes and the Captain. But what was going on in the 'tween-deck was to him a minor matter by that time. Besides, it was difficult to make yourself heard. But he managed to convey the idea that the Chinamen had broken adrift together with their boxes, and that he had come up on purpose to report this. As to the hands, they were all right. Then, appeased, he subsided on the deck in a sitting posture, hugging with his arms and legs the stand of the engine-room telegraph – an iron casting as thick as a post. When that went, why, he expected he would go too. He gave no more thought to the coolies.

Captain MacWhirr had made Jukes understand that he wanted him to go down below – to see.

'What am I to do then, sir?' And the trembling of his whole wet body caused Jukes' voice to sound like bleating.

'See first . . . Boss'n . . . says . . . adrift.'

'That boss'n is a confounded fool,' howled Jukes shakily.

The absurdity of the demand made upon him revolted Jukes. He was as unwilling to go as if the moment he had left the deck the ship were sure to sink.

'I must know . . . can't leave . . .'

'They'll settle, sir.'

'Fight . . . boss'n says they fight . . . Why? Can't have . . . fighting . . . board ship . . . Much rather keep you here . . . case . . . I should . . . washed overboard myself . . . Stop it . . . some way. You see and tell me . . . through engine-room tube. Don't want you . . . come up here . . . too often. Dangerous . . . moving about . . . deck.'

Jukes, held with his head in chancery, had to listen to what seemed horrible suggestions.

'Don't want . . . you get lost . . . so long . . . ship isn't . . . Rout . . . Good man . . . Ship . . . may . . . through this . . . all right yet.'

All at once Jukes understood he would have to go.

'Do you think she may?' he screamed.

But the wind devoured the reply, out of which Jukes heard only the one word, pronounced with great energy ' . . . Always . . . '

Captain MacWhirr released Jukes, and bending over the boatswain, yelled, 'Get back with the mate.' Jukes only knew that the arm was gone off his shoulders. He was dismissed with his orders – to do what? He was exasperated into letting go his hold carelessly, and on the instant was blown away. It seemed to him that nothing could stop him from being blown right over the stern. He flung himself down hastily, and the boatswain, who was following, fell on him.

'Don't you get up yet, sir,' cried the boatswain. 'No hurry!'

A sea swept over. Jukes understood the boatswain to splutter that the bridge ladders were gone. 'I'll lower you down, sir, by your hands,' he screamed. He shouted also something about the smoke-stack being as likely to go overboard as not. Jukes thought it very possible, and imagined the fires out, the ship helpless . . . The boatswain by his side kept on yelling. 'What? What is it?' Jukes cried distressfully; and the other repeated, 'What would my old woman say if she saw me now?'

In the alleyway, where a lot of water had got in and splashed in the dark, the men were still as death, till Jukes stumbled against one of them and cursed him savagely for being in the way. Two or three voices then asked, eager and weak, 'Any chance for us, sir?'

'What's the matter with you fools?' he said brutally. He felt as though he could throw himself down amongst them and never move any more. But they seemed cheered; and in the midst of obsequious warnings, 'Look out! Mind that manhole lid, sir,' they lowered him into the bunker. The boatswain tumbled down after him, and as soon as he had picked himself up he remarked, 'She would say, "Serve you right, you old fool, for going to sea."'

The boatswain had some means, and made a point of alluding to them frequently. His wife – a fat woman – and two grown-up daughters kept a greengrocer's shop in the East End of London.

In the dark, Jukes, unsteady on his legs, listened to a faint thunderous patter. A deadened screaming went on steadily at his elbow, as it were; and from above the louder tumult of the storm descended upon these near sounds. His head swam. To him, too, in that bunker, the motion of the ship seemed novel and menacing, sapping his resolution as though he had never been afloat before.

He had half a mind to scramble out again; but the remembrance of Captain MacWhirr's voice made this impossible. His orders were to go and see. What was the good of it, he wanted to know. Enraged, he told himself he would see – of course. But the boatswain, staggering clumsily, warned him to be careful how he opened that door; there was a blamed fight going on. And Jukes, as if in great bodily pain, desired irritably to know what the devil they were fighting for.

'Dollars! Dollars, sir. All their rotten chests got burst open. Blamed money skipping all over the place, and they are tumbling after it head over heels – tearing and biting like anything. A regular little hell in there.'

Jukes convulsively opened the door. The short boatswain peered under his arm.

One of the lamps had gone out, broken perhaps. Rancorous, guttural cries burst out loudly on their ears, and a strange panting sound, the working of all these straining breasts. A hard blow hit the side of the ship: water fell above with a stunning shock, and in the forefront of the gloom, where the air was reddish and thick, Jukes saw a head bang the deck violently, two thick calves waving on high, muscular arms twined round a naked body, a yellow-face, open-mouthed and with a set wild stare, look up and slide away. An empty chest clattered turning over; a man fell head first with a jump, as if lifted by a kick; and farther off, indistinct, others streamed like a mass of rolling stones down a bank, thumping the deck with their feet and flourishing their arms wildly. The hatchway ladder was loaded with coolies swarming on it like bees on a branch. They hung on the steps in a crawling, stirring cluster, beating madly with their fists the underside of the battened hatch, and the headlong rush of the water above was heard in the intervals of their yelling. The ship heeled over more, and they began to drop off: first one, then two, then all the rest went away together, falling straight off with a great cry.

Jukes was confounded. The boatswain, with gruff anxiety, begged him, 'Don't you go in there, sir.'

The whole place seemed to twist upon itself, jumping incessantly the while; and when the ship rose to a sea Jukes fancied that all these men would be shot upon him in a body. He backed out, swung the door to, and with trembling hands pushed at the bolt . . .

As soon as his mate had gone Captain MacWhirr, left alone on the bridge, sidled and staggered as far as the wheelhouse. Its door being hinged forward, he had to fight the gale for admittance, and when at last he managed to enter, it was with an instantaneous clatter and a bang, as though he had been fired through the wood. He stood within, holding on to the handle.

The steering-gear leaked steam, and in the confined space the glass of the binnacle made a shiny oval of light in a thin white fog. The wind howled, hummed, whistled, with sudden booming gusts that rattled the doors and shutters in the vicious patter of sprays. Two coils of lead-line and a small canvas bag hung on a long lanyard, swung wide off, and came back clinging to the bulkheads. The gratings underfoot were nearly afloat; with every sweeping blow of a sea, water squirted violently through the cracks all round the door, and the man at the helm had flung down his cap, his coat, and stood propped against the gear-casing in a striped cotton shirt open on his breast. The little brass wheel in his hands had the appearance of a bright and fragile toy. The cords of his neck stood hard and lean, a dark patch lay in the hollow of his throat, and his face was still and sunken as in death.

Captain MacWhirr wiped his eyes. The sea that had nearly taken him overboard had, to his great annoyance, washed his sou'-wester hat off his bald head. The fluffy, fair hair, soaked and darkened, resembled a mean skein of cotton threads festooned round his bare skull. His face, glistening with sea-water, had been made crimson with the wind, with the sting of sprays. He looked as though he had come off sweating from before a furnace.

'You here?' he muttered heavily.

The second mate had found his way into the wheelhouse some time before. He had fixed himself in a corner with his knees up, a fist pressed against each temple; and this attitude suggested rage, sorrow, resignation, surrender, with a sort of concentrated unforgiveness. He said mournfully and defiantly, 'Well, it's my watch below now: ain't it?'

The steam gear clattered, stopped, clattered again; and the helmsman's eyeballs seemed to project out of a hungry face as if the compass card behind the binnacle glass had been meat. God knows how long he had been left there to steer, as if forgotten by all his shipmates. The bells had not been struck; there had been no reliefs; the ship's routine had gone down wind; but he was trying to keep her head north-north-east. The rudder might have been gone for all he knew, the fires out, the engines broken down, the ship ready to roll over like a corpse. He was anxious not to get muddled and lose control of her head, because the compass-card swung far both ways, wriggling on the pivot, and sometimes seemed to whirl right round. He suffered from mental stress. He was horribly afraid, also, of the wheelhouse going. Mountains of water kept on tumbling against it. When the ship took one of her desperate dives the corners of his lips twitched.

Captain MacWhirr looked up at the wheelhouse clock. Screwed to the bulkhead, it had a white face on which the black hands appeared to stand quite still. It was half-past one in the morning.

'Another day,' he muttered to himself.

The second mate heard him, and lifting his head as one grieving amongst ruins, 'You won't see it break,' he exclaimed. His wrists and his knees could be seen to shake violently. 'No, by God! You won't . . .'

He took his face again between his fists.

The body of the helmsman had moved slightly, but his head didn't budge on his neck – like a stone head fixed to look one way from a column. During a roll that all but took his booted legs from under him, and in the very stagger to save himself, Captain MacWhirr said austerely, 'Don't you pay any attention to what that man says.' And then, with an indefinable change of tone, very grave, he added, 'He isn't on duty.'

The sailor said nothing.

The hurricane boomed, shaking the little place, which seemed airtight; and the light of the binnacle flickered all the time.

'You haven't been relieved,' Captain MacWhirr went on, looking down. 'I want you to stick to the helm, though, as long as you can. You've got the hang of her. Another man coming here might make a mess of it. Wouldn't do. No child's play. And the hands are probably busy with a job down below . . . Think you can?'

The steering gear leaped into an abrupt short clatter, stopped smouldering like an ember; and the still man, with a motionless gaze, burst out, as if all the passion in him had gone into his lips: 'By Heavens, sir! I can steer for ever if nobody talks to me.'

'Oh! aye! All right . . . ' The Captain lifted his eyes for the first time to the man, ' . . . Hackett.'

And he seemed to dismiss this matter from his mind. He stooped to the engine-room speaking-tube, blew in, and bent his head. Mr Rout below answered, and at once Captain MacWhirr put his lips to the mouthpiece.

With the uproar of the gale around him he applied alternately his lips and his ear, and the engineer's voice mounted to him, harsh and as if out of the heat of an engagement. One of the stokers was disabled, the others had given in, the second engineer and the donkeyman were firing-up. The third engineer was standing by the steam-valve. The engines were being tended by hand. How was it above?

'Bad enough. It mostly rests with you,' said Captain MacWhirr. Was the mate down there yet? No? Well, he would be presently. Would Mr Rout let him talk through the speaking-tube? – through the deck speaking-tube, because he – the Captain – was going out again on the bridge directly. There was some trouble amongst the Chinamen. They were fighting, it seemed. Couldn't allow fighting anyhow . . .

Mr Rout had gone away, and Captain MacWhirr could feel against his ear the pulsation of the engines, like the beat of the ship's heart. Mr Rout's voice down there shouted something distantly. The ship pitched headlong, the pulsation leaped with a hissing tumult, and stopped dead. Captain MacWhirr's face was impassive, and his eyes were fixed aimlessly on the crouching shape of the second mate. Again Mr Rout's voice cried out in the depths, and the pulsating beats recommenced, with slow strokes – growing swifter.

Mr Rout had returned to the tube. 'It don't matter much what they do,' he said hastily; and then, with irritation, 'She takes these dives as if she never meant to come up again.'

'Awful sea,' said the Captain's voice from above.

'Don't let me drive her under,' barked Solomon Rout up the pipe.

'Dark and rain. Can't see what's coming,' uttered the voice. 'Must – keep – her – moving – enough to steer – and chance it,' it went on to state distinctly.

'I am doing as much as I dare.'

'We are – getting – smashed up – a good deal up here,' proceeded the voice mildly. 'Doing – fairly well – though. Of course, if the wheelhouse should go . . .'

Mr Rout, bending an attentive ear, muttered peevishly something under his breath.

But the deliberate voice up there became animated to ask: 'Jukes turned up yet?' Then, after a short wait, 'I wish he would bear a hand. I want him to be done and come up here in case of anything. To look after the ship. I am all alone. The second mate's lost . . .'

'What?' shouted Mr Rout into the engine-room, taking his head away. Then up the tube he cried, 'Gone overboard?' and clapped his ear to.

'Lost his nerve,' the voice from above continued in a matter-of-fact tone. 'Damned awkward circumstance.'

Mr Rout, listening with bowed neck, opened his eyes wide at this. However, he heard something like the sounds of a scuffle and broken exclamations coming down to him. He strained his hearing; and all the time Beale, the third engineer, with his arms uplifted, held between the palms of his hands the rim of a little black wheel projecting at the side of a big copper pipe. He seemed to be poising it above his head, as though it were a correct attitude in some sort of game.

To steady himself, he pressed his shoulder against the white bulkhead, one knee bent, and a sweat-rag tucked in his belt hanging on his hip. His smooth cheek was begrimed and flushed, and the coal dust on his eyelids, like the black pencilling of a make-up, enhanced the liquid brilliance of the whites, giving to his youthful face something of a feminine, exotic and fascinating aspect. When the ship pitched he would with hasty movements of his hands screw hard at the little wheel.

'Gone crazy,' began the Captain's voice suddenly in the tube. 'Rushed at me . . . Just now. Had to knock him down . . . This minute. You heard, Mr Rout?'

'The devil!' muttered Mr Rout. 'Look out, Beale!'

His shout rang out like the blast of a warning trumpet, between the iron walls of the engine-room. Painted white, they rose high into the dusk of the skylight, sloping like a roof; and the whole lofty space resembled the interior of a monument, divided by floors of iron grating, with lights flickering at different levels, and a mass of gloom lingering in the middle, within the columnar stir of machinery under the motionless swelling of the cylinders. A loud and wild resonance, made up of all the noises of the hurricane, dwelt in the still warmth of the air. There was in it the smell of hot metal, of oil, and a slight mist of steam. The blows of the sea seemed to traverse it in an unringing, stunning shock, from side to side.

Gleams, like pale long flames, trembled upon the polish of metal; from the flooring below the enormous crank-heads emerged in their turns with a flash of brass and steel – going over; while the connecting-rods, big-jointed, like skeleton limbs, seemed to thrust them down and pull them up again with an irresistible precision. And deep in the half-light other rods dodged deliberately to and fro, crossheads nodded, discs of metal rubbed smoothly against each other, slow and gentle, in a commingling of shadows and gleams.

Sometimes all those powerful and unerring movements would slow down simultaneously, as if they had been the functions of a living organism, stricken suddenly by the blight of languor; and Mr Rout's eyes would blaze darker in his long sallow face. He was fighting this fight in a pair of carpet slippers. A short shiny jacket barely covered his loins, and his white wrists protruded far out of the tight sleeves, as though the emergency had added to his stature, had lengthened his limbs, augmented his pallor, hollowed his eyes.

He moved, climbing high up, disappearing low down, with a restless, purposeful industry, and when he stood still, holding the guard-rail in front of the starting-gear, he would keep glancing to the right at the steam-gauge, at the water-gauge, fixed upon the white wall in the light of a swaying lamp. The mouths of two speaking-tubes gaped stupidly at his elbow, and the dial of the engine-room telegraph resembled a clock of large diameter, bearing on its face curt words instead of figures. The grouped letters stood out heavily black, around the pivot-head of the indicator, emphatically symbolic of loud exclamations: Ahead, Astern, Slow, Half, Stand by; and the fat black hand pointed downwards to the word Full, which, thus singled out, captured the eye as a sharp cry secures attention.

The wood-encased bulk of the low-pressure cylinder, frowning portly from above, emitted a faint wheeze at every thrust, and except for that low hiss the engines worked their steel limbs headlong or slow with a silent, determined smoothness. And all this, the white walls, the moving steel, the floor plates under Solomon Rout's feet, the floors of iron grating above his head, the dusk and the gleams, uprose and sank continuously, with one accord, upon the harsh wash of the waves against the ship's side. The whole loftiness of the place, booming hollow to the great voice of the wind, swayed at the top like a tree, would go over bodily, as if borne down this way and that by the tremendous blasts.

'You've got to hurry up,' shouted Mr Rout, as soon as he saw Jukes appear in the stokehold doorway.

Jukes' glance was wandering and tipsy; his red face was puffy, as though he had overslept himself. He had had an arduous road, and had travelled over it with immense vivacity, the agitation of his mind corresponding to the exertions of his body. He had rushed up out of the bunker, stumbling in the dark alleyway amongst a lot of bewildered men who, trod upon, asked 'What's up, sir?' in awed mutters all round him; down the stokehold ladder, missing many iron rungs in his hurry, down into a place deep as a well, black as Tophet, tipping over back and forth like a see-saw. The water in the bilges thundered at each roll, and lumps of coal skipped to and fro, from end to end, rattling like an avalanche of pebbles on a slope of iron.

Somebody in there moaned with pain, and somebody else could be seen crouching over what seemed the prone body of a dead man; a lusty voice blasphemed; and the glow under each fire-door was like a pool of flaming blood radiating quietly in a velvety blackness.

A gust of wind struck upon the nape of Jukes' neck, and next moment he felt it streaming about his wet ankles. The stokehold ventilators hummed: in front of the six fire-doors two wild figures, stripped to the waist, staggered and stooped, wrestling with two shovels.

'Hallo! Plenty of draught now,' yelled the second engineer at once, as though he had been all the time looking out for Jukes. The donkeyman, a dapper little chap with a dazzling fair skin and a tiny, gingery moustache, worked in a sort of mute transport. They were keeping a full head of steam, and a profound rumbling, as of an empty furniture van trotting over a bridge, made a sustained bass to all the other noises of the place.

'Blowing off all the time,' went on yelling the second. With a sound as of a hundred scoured saucepans, the orifice of a ventilator spat upon his shoulder a sudden gush of salt water, and he volleyed a stream of curses upon all things on earth including his own soul, ripping and raving, and all the time attending to his business. With a sharp clash of metal the ardent pale glare of the fire opened upon his bullet head showing his spluttering lips, his insolent face, and with another clang closed like the white-hot wink of an iron eye.

'Where's the blooming ship? Can you tell me? blast my eyes! Under water – or what? It's coming down here in tons. Are the condemned cowls gone to Hades? Hey? Don't you know anything – you jolly sailor-man you . . . ?'

Jukes, after a bewildered moment, had been helped by a roll to dart through; and as soon as his eyes took in the comparative vastness, peace and brilliance of the engine-room, the ship, setting her stern heavily in the water, sent him charging head down upon Mr Rout.

The chief's arm, long like a tentacle, and straightening as if worked by a spring, went out to meet him, and deflected his rush into a spin towards the speaking-tubes. At the same time Mr Rout repeated earnestly: 'You've got to hurry up, whatever it is.'

Jukes yelled, 'Are you there, sir?' and listened. Nothing. Suddenly the roar of the wind fell straight into his ear, but presently a small voice shoved aside the shouting hurricane quietly.

'You, Jukes? – Well?'

Jukes was ready to talk: it was only time that seemed to be wanting. It was easy enough to account for everything. He could perfectly imagine the coolies battened down in the reeking 'tween-deck, lying sick and scared between the rows of chests. Then one of these chests – or perhaps several at once – breaking loose in a roll, knocking out others, sides splitting, lids flying open, and all these clumsy Chinamen rising up in a body to save their property. Afterwards every fling of the ship would hurl that tramping, yelling mob here and there, from side to side, in a whirl of smashed wood, torn clothing, rolling dollars. A struggle once started, they would be unable to stop themselves. Nothing could stop them now except main force. It was a disaster. He had seen it, and that was all he could say. Some of them must be dead, he believed. The rest would go on fighting . . .

He sent up his words, tripping over each other, crowding the narrow tube. They mounted as if into a silence of an enlightened comprehension dwelling alone up there with a storm. And Jukes wanted to be dismissed from the face of that odious trouble intruding on the great need of the ship.

Chapter 5

He waited. Before his eyes the engines turned with slow labour, that in the moment of going off into a mad fling would stop dead at Mr Rout's shout, 'Look out, Beale!' They paused in an intelligent immobility, stilled in mid-stroke, a heavy crank arrested on the cant, as if conscious of danger and the passage of time. Then, with a 'Now, then!' from the chief, and the sound of a breath expelled through clenched teeth, they would accomplish the interrupted revolution and begin another.

There was the prudent sagacity of wisdom and the deliberation of enormous strength in their movements. This was their work – this patient coaxing of a distracted ship over the fury of the waves and into the very eye of the wind. At times Mr Rout's chin would sink on his breast, and he watched them with knitted eyebrows as if lost in thought.

The voice that kept the hurricane out of Jukes' ear began: 'Take the hands with you . . . ' and left off unexpectedly.

'What could I do with them, sir?'

A harsh, abrupt, imperious clang exploded suddenly. The three pairs of eyes flew up to the telegraph dial to see the hand jump from Full to Stop, as if snatched by a devil. And then these three men in the engine-room had the intimate sensation of a check upon the ship, of a strange shrinking, as if she had gathered herself for a desperate leap.

'Stop her!' bellowed Mr Rout.

Nobody – not even Captain MacWhirr, who alone on deck had caught sight of a white line of foam coming on at such a height that he couldn't believe his eyes – nobody was to know the steepness of that sea and the awful depth of the hollow the hurricane had scooped out behind the running wall of water.

It raced to meet the ship, and, with a pause, as of girding the loins, the *Nan-Shan* lifted her bows and leaped. The flames in all the lamps sank, darkening the engine-room. One went out. With a tearing crash and a swirling, raving tumult, tons of water fell upon the deck, as though the ship had darted under the foot of a cataract.

Down there they looked at each other, stunned.

'Swept from end to end, by God!' bawled Jukes.

She dipped into the hollow straight down, as if going over the edge of the world. The engine-room toppled forward menacingly, like the inside of a tower nodding in an earthquake. An awful racket, of iron things falling, came from the stokehold. She hung on this appalling slant long enough for Beale to drop on his hands and knees and begin to crawl as if he meant to fly on all fours out of the engine-room, and for Mr Rout to turn his head slowly, rigid, cavernous, with the lower jaw dropping. Jukes had shut his eyes, and his face in a moment became hopelessly blank and gentle, like the face of a blind man.

At last she rose slowly, staggering, as if she had to lift a mountain with her bows.

Mr Rout shut his mouth; Jukes blinked; and little Beale stood up hastily.

'Another one like this, and that's the last of her,' cried the chief.

He and Jukes looked at each other, and the same thought came into their heads. The Captain! Everything must have been swept away. Steering gear gone – ship like a log. All over directly.

'Rush!' ejaculated Mr Rout thickly, glaring with enlarged, doubtful eyes at Jukes, who answered him by an irresolute glance.

The clang of the telegraph gong soothed them instantly. The black hand dropped in a flash from Stop to Full.

'Now then, Beale!' cried Mr Rout.

The steam hissed low. The piston-rods slid in and out. Jukes put his ear to the tube. The voice was ready for him. It said: 'Pick up all the money. Bear a hand now. I'll want you up here.' And that was all.

'Sir?' called up Jukes. There was no answer.

He staggered away like a defeated man from the field of battle. He had got, in some way or other, a cut above his left eyebrow – a cut to the bone. He was not aware of it in the least: quantities of the China Sea, large enough to break his neck for him, had gone over his head, had cleaned, washed, and salted that wound. It did not bleed, but only gaped red; and this gash over the eye, his dishevelled hair, the disorder of his clothes, gave him the aspect of a man worsted in a fight with fists.

'Got to pick up the dollars.' He appealed to Mr Rout, smiling pitifully at random.

'What's that?' asked Mr Rout wildly. 'Pick up . . . ? I don't care . . .' Then, quivering in every muscle, but with an exaggeration of paternal tone, 'Go away now, for God's sake. You deck people'll drive me silly. There's that second mate been going for the old man. Don't you know? You fellows are going wrong for want of something to do . . .'

At these words Jukes discovered in himself the beginnings of anger. Want of something to do – indeed . . . Full of hot scorn against the chief, he turned to go the way he had come. In the stokehold the plump donkeyman toiled with his shovel mutely, as if his tongue had been cut out; but the second was carrying on like a noisy, undaunted maniac, who had preserved his skill in the art of stoking under a marine boiler.

'Hallo, you wandering officer! Hey! Can't you get some of your slush-slingers to wind up a few of them ashes? I am getting choked with them here. Curse it! Hallo! Hey! Remember the articles: *Sailors and firemen to assist each other*. Hey! D'ye hear?'

Jukes was climbing out frantically, and the other, lifting up his face after him, howled, 'Can't you speak? What are you poking about here for? What's your game, anyhow?'

A frenzy possessed Jukes. By the time he was back amongst the men in the darkness of the alleyway, he felt ready to wring all their necks at the slightest sign of hanging back. The very thought of it exasperated him. *He* couldn't hang back. They shouldn't.

The impetuosity with which he came amongst them carried them along. They had already been excited and startled at all his comings and goings – by the fierceness and rapidity of his movements; and more felt than seen in his rushes, he appeared formidable – busied with matters of life and death that brooked no delay. At his first word he heard them drop into the bunker one after another obediently, with heavy thumps.

They were not clear as to what would have to be done. 'What is it? What is it?' they were asking each other. The boatswain tried to explain; the sounds of a great scuffle surprised them: and the mighty shocks, reverberating awfully in the black bunker, kept them in mind of their danger. When the boatswain threw open the door it seemed that an eddy of the hurricane, stealing through the iron sides of the ship, had set all these bodies whirling like dust: there came to them a confused uproar, a tempestuous tumult, a fierce mutter, gusts of screams dying away, and the tramping of feet mingling with the blows of the sea.

For a moment they glared amazed, blocking the doorway. Jukes pushed through them brutally. He said nothing, and simply darted in. Another lot of coolies on the ladder, struggling suicidally to break through the battened hatch to a swamped deck, fell off as before, and he disappeared under them like a man overtaken by a landslide.

The boatswain yelled excitedly: 'Come along. Get the mate out. He'll be trampled to death. Come on.'

They charged in, stamping on breasts, on fingers, on faces, catching their feet in heaps of clothing, kicking broken wood; but before they could get hold of him Jukes emerged waist deep in a multitude of clawing hands. In the instant he had been lost to view, all the buttons of his jacket had gone, its back had got split up to the collar, his waistcoat had been torn open. The central struggling mass of Chinamen went over to the roll, dark, indistinct, helpless, with a wild gleam of many eyes in the dim light of the lamps.

'Leave me alone – damn you. I am all right,' screeched Jukes. 'Drive them forward. Watch your chance when she pitches. Forward with 'em. Drive them against the bulkhead. Jam 'em up.'

The rush of the sailors into the seething 'tween-deck was like a splash of cold water into a boiling cauldron. The commotion sank for a moment.

The bulk of Chinamen were locked in such a compact scrimmage that, linking their arms and aided by an appalling dive of the ship, the seamen sent it forward in one great shove, like a solid block. Behind their backs small clusters and loose bodies tumbled from side to side.

The boatswain performed prodigious feats of strength. With his long arms open, and each great paw clutching at a stanchion, he stopped the rush of seven entwined Chinamen rolling like a boulder. His joints cracked; he said, 'Ha!' and they flew apart. But the carpenter showed the greater intelligence. Without saying a word to anybody he went back into the alleyway, to fetch several coils of cargo gear he had seen there – chain and rope. With these lifelines were rigged.

There was really no resistance. The struggle, however it began, had turned into a scramble of blind panic. If the coolies had started up after their scattered dollars they were by that time fighting only for their footing. They took each other by the throat merely to save themselves from being hurled about. Whoever got a hold anywhere would kick at the others who caught at his legs and hung on, till a roll sent them flying together across the deck.

The coming of the white devils was a terror. Had they come to kill? The individuals torn out of the ruck became very limp in the seamen's hands: some, dragged aside by the heels, were passive, like dead bodies, with open, fixed eyes. Here and there a coolie would fall on his knees as if begging for mercy; several, whom the excess of fear made unruly, were hit with hard fists between the eyes, and cowered; while those who were hurt submitted to rough handling, blinking rapidly without a plaint. Faces streamed with blood; there were raw places on the shaven heads, scratches, bruises, torn wounds, gashes. The broken porcelain out of the chests was mostly responsible for the latter. Here and there a Chinaman, wild-eyed, with his tail unplaited, nursed a bleeding sole.

They had been ranged closely, after having been shaken into submission, cuffed a little to allay excitement, addressed in gruff words of encouragement that sounded like promises of evil. They sat on the deck in ghastly, drooping rows, and at the end the carpenter, with two hands to help him, moved busily from place to place, setting taut and hitching the lifelines. The boatswain, with one leg and one arm embracing a stanchion, struggled with a lamp pressed to his breast, trying to get a light, and growling all the time like an industrious gorilla. The figures of seamen stooped repeatedly, with the movements of gleaners, and everything was being flung into the bunker: clothing, smashed wood, broken china, and the dollars too, gathered up in men's jackets. Now and then a sailor would stagger towards the doorway with his arms full of rubbish; and dolorous, slanting eyes followed his movements.

With every roll of the ship the long rows of sitting Celestials would sway forward brokenly, and her headlong dives knocked together the line of shaven polls from end to end. When the wash of water rolling on the deck died away for a moment, it seemed to Jukes, yet quivering from his exertions, that in his mad struggle down there he had overcome the wind somehow: that a silence had fallen upon the ship, a silence in which the sea struck thunderously at her sides.

Everything had been cleared out of the 'tween-deck – all the wreckage, as the men said. They stood erect and tottering above the level of heads and drooping shoulders. Here and there a coolie sobbed for his breath. Where the high light fell, Jukes could see the salient ribs of one, the yellow, wistful face of another; bowed necks; or would meet a dull stare directed at his face. He was amazed that there had been no corpses; but the lot of them seemed at their last gasp, and they appeared to him more pitiful than if they had been all dead.

Suddenly one of the coolies began to speak. The light came and went on his lean, straining face; he threw his head up like a baying hound. From the bunker came the sounds of knocking and the tinkle of some dollars rolling loose; he stretched out his arm, his mouth yawned black, and the incomprehensible guttural hooting sounds, that did not seem to belong to a human language, penetrated Jukes with a strange emotion as if a brute had tried to be eloquent.

Two more started mouthing what seemed to Jukes fierce denunciations; the others stirred with grunts and growls. Jukes ordered the hands out of the 'tween-decks hurriedly. He left last himself, backing through the door, while the grunts rose to a loud murmur and hands were extended after him as after a malefactor. The boatswain shot the bolt, and remarked uneasily, 'Seems as if the wind had dropped, sir.'

The seamen were glad to get back into the alleyway. Secretly each of them thought that at the last moment he could rush out on deck – and that was a comfort. There is something horribly repugnant in the idea of being drowned under a deck. Now they had done with the Chinamen, they again became conscious of the ship's position.

Jukes on coming out of the alleyway found himself up to the neck in the noisy water. He gained the bridge, and discovered he could detect obscure shapes as if his sight had become preternaturally acute. He saw faint outlines. They recalled not the familiar aspect of the *Nan-Shan*, but something remembered – an old dismantled steamer he had seen years ago rotting on a mudbank. She recalled that wreck.

There was no wind, not a breath, except the faint currents created by the lurches of the ship. The smoke tossed out of the funnel was settling down upon her deck. He breathed it as he passed forward. He felt the deliberate throb of the engines, and heard small sounds that seemed to have survived the great uproar: the knocking of broken fittings, the rapid tumbling of some piece of wreckage on the bridge. He perceived dimly the squat shape of his captain holding on to a twisted bridge-rail, motionless and swaying as if rooted to the planks. The unexpected stillness of the air oppressed Jukes.

'We have done it, sir,' he gasped.

'Thought you would,' said Captain MacWhirr.

'Did you?' murmured Jukes to himself.

'Wind fell all at once,' went on the Captain.

Jukes burst out: 'If you think it was an easy job – '

But his captain, clinging to the rail, paid no attention. 'According to the books the worst is not over yet.'

'If most of them hadn't been half dead with seasickness and fright, not one of us would have come out of that 'tween-deck alive,' said Jukes.

'Had to do what's fair by them,' mumbled MacWhirr stolidly. 'You don't find everything in books.'

'Why, I believe they would have risen on us if I hadn't ordered the hands out of that pretty quick,' continued Jukes with warmth.

After the whisper of their shouts, their ordinary tones, so distinct, rang out very loud to their ears in the amazing stillness of the air. It seemed to them they were talking in a dark and echoing vault.

Through a jagged aperture in the dome of clouds the light of a few stars fell upon the black sea, rising and falling confusedly. Sometimes the head of a watery cone would topple on board and mingle with the rolling flurry of foam on the swamped deck; and the *Nan-Shan* wallowed heavily at the bottom of a circular cistern of clouds. This ring of dense vapours, gyrating madly round the calm of the centre, encompassed the ship like a motionless and unbroken wall of an aspect inconceivably sinister. Within, the sea, as if agitated by an internal commotion, leaped in peaked mounds that jostled each other, slapping heavily against her sides; and a low moaning sound, the infinite plaint of the storm's fury, came from beyond the limits of the menacing calm. Captain MacWhirr remained silent, and Jukes' ready ear caught suddenly the faint, long-drawn roar of some immense wave rushing unseen under that thick blackness, which made the appalling boundary of his vision.

'Of course,' he started resentfully, 'they thought we had caught at the chance to plunder them. Of course! You said – pick up the money. Easier said than done. They couldn't tell what was in our heads. We came in, smash – right into the middle of them. Had to do it by a rush.'

'As long as it's done . . . ' mumbled the Captain, without attempting to look at Jukes. 'Had to do what's fair.'

'We shall find yet there's the devil to pay when this is over,' said Jukes, feeling very sore. 'Let them only recover a bit, and you'll see. They will fly at our throats, sir. Don't forget, sir, she isn't a British ship now. These brutes know it well, too. The damn'd Siamese flag.'

'We are on board, all the same,' remarked Captain MacWhirr.

'The trouble's not over yet,' insisted Jukes prophetically, reeling and catching on. 'She's a wreck,' he added faintly.

'The trouble's not over yet,' assented Captain MacWhirr, half aloud . . . 'Look out for her a minute.'

'Are you going off the deck, sir?' asked Jukes hurriedly, as if the storm were sure to pounce upon him as soon as he had been left alone with the ship.

He watched her, battered and solitary, labouring heavily in a wild scene of mountainous black waters lit by the gleams of distant worlds. She moved slowly, breathing into the still core of the hurricane the excess of her strength in a white cloud of steam – and the deep-toned vibration of the escape was like the defiant trumpeting of a living creature of the sea impatient for the renewal of the contest. It ceased suddenly. The still air moaned. Above Jukes' head a few stars shone into the pit of black vapours. The inky edge of the cloud-disc frowned upon the ship under the patch of glittering sky. The stars too seemed to look at her intently, as if for the last time, and the cluster of their splendour sat like a diadem on a lowering brow.

Captain MacWhirr had gone into the chart-room. There was no light there; but he could feel the disorder of that place where he used to live tidily. His armchair was upset. The books had tumbled out on the floor: he scrunched a piece of glass under his boot. He groped for the matches, and found a box on a shelf with a deep ledge. He struck one, and puckering the corners of his eyes, held out the little flame towards the barometer whose glittering top of glass and metals nodded at him continuously.

It stood very low – incredibly low, so low that Captain MacWhirr grunted. The match went out, and hurriedly he extracted another, with thick, stiff fingers.

Again a little flame flared up before the nodding glass and metal of the top. His eyes looked at it, narrowed with attention, as if expecting an imperceptible sign. With his grave face he resembled a booted and misshapen pagan burning incense before the oracle of a Joss. There was no mistake. It was the lowest reading he had ever seen in his life.

Captain MacWhirr emitted a low whistle. He forgot himself till the flame diminished to a blue spark, burnt his fingers and vanished. Perhaps something had gone wrong with the thing!

There was an aneroid glass screwed above the couch. He turned that way, struck another match, and discovered the white face of the other instrument looking at him from the bulkhead, meaningly, not to be gainsaid, as though the wisdom of men were made unerring by the indifference of matter. There was no room for doubt now. Captain MacWhirr pshawed at it, and threw the match down.

The worst was to come, then – and if the books were right this worst would be very bad. The experience of the last six hours had enlarged his conception of what heavy weather could be like. 'It'll be terrific,' he pronounced mentally. He had not consciously looked at anything by the light of the matches except at the barometer; and yet somehow he had seen that his water-bottle and the two tumblers had been flung out of their stand. It seemed to give him a more intimate knowledge of the tossing the ship had gone through. 'I wouldn't have believed it,' he thought. And his table had been cleared too; his rulers, his pencils, the inkstand – all the things that had their safe appointed places – they were gone, as if a mischievous hand had plucked them out one by one and flung them on the wet floor. The hurricane had broken in upon the orderly arrangements of his privacy. This had never happened before, and the feeling of dismay reached the very seat of his composure. And the worst was to come yet! He was glad the trouble in the 'tween-deck had been discovered in time. If the ship had to go after all, then, at least, she wouldn't be going to the bottom with a lot of people in her fighting teeth and claw. That would have been odious. And in that feeling there was a humane intention and a vague sense of the fitness of things.

These instantaneous thoughts were yet in their essence heavy and slow, partaking of the nature of the man. He extended his hand to put back the matchbox in its corner of the shelf. There were always matches there – by his order. The steward had his instructions impressed upon him long before. 'A box . . . just there, see? Not so very full . . . where I can put my hand on it, steward. Might want a light in a hurry. Can't tell on board ship *what* you might want in a hurry. Mind, now.'

And of course on his side he would be careful to put it back in its place scrupulously. He did so now, but before he removed his hand it occurred to him that perhaps he would never have occasion to use that box any more. The vividness of the thought checked him, and for an infinitesimal fraction of a second his fingers closed again on the small object as though it had been the symbol of all these little habits that chain us to the weary round of life. He released it at last, and letting himself fall on the settee, listened for the first sounds of returning wind.

Not yet. He heard only the wash of water, the heavy splashes, the dull shocks of the confused seas boarding his ship from all sides. She would never have a chance to clear her decks.

But the quietude of the air was startlingly tense and unsafe, like a slender hair holding a sword suspended over his head. By this awful pause the storm penetrated the defences of the man and unsealed his lips. He spoke out in the solitude and the pitch darkness of the cabin, as if addressing another being awakened within his breast.

'I shouldn't like to lose her,' he said half aloud.

He sat unseen, apart from the sea, from his ship, isolated, as if withdrawn from the very current of his own existence, where such freaks as talking to himself surely had no place. His palms reposed on his knees, he bowed his short neck and puffed heavily, surrendering to a strange sensation of weariness he was not enlightened enough to recognise for the fatigue of mental stress.

From where he sat he could reach the door of a washstand locker. There should have been a towel there. There was. Good . . . He took it out, wiped his face, and afterwards went on rubbing his wet head. He towelled himself with energy in the dark, and then remained motionless with the towel on his knees. A moment passed, of a stillness so profound that no one could have guessed there was a man sitting in that cabin. Then a murmur arose.

'She may come out of it yet.'

When Captain MacWhirr came out on deck, which he did brusquely, as though he had suddenly become conscious of having stayed away too long, the calm had lasted already more than fifteen minutes – long enough to make itself intolerable even to his imagination. Jukes, motionless on the forepart of the bridge, began to speak at once. His voice, blank and forced as though he were talking through hard-set teeth, seemed to flow away on all sides into the darkness, deepening again upon the sea.

'I had the wheel relieved. Hackett began to sing out that he was done. He's lying in there alongside the steering gear with a face like death. At first I couldn't get anybody to crawl out and relieve the poor devil. That boss'en's worse than no good, I always said. Thought I would have had to go myself and haul out one of them by the neck.'

'Ah, well,' muttered the Captain. He stood watchful by Jukes' side.

'The second mate's in there too, holding his head. Is he hurt, sir?'

'No – crazy,' said Captain MacWhirr, curtly.

'Looks as if he had a tumble, though.'

'I had to give him a push,' explained the Captain.

Jukes gave an impatient sigh.

'It will come very sudden,' said Captain MacWhirr, 'and from over there, I fancy. God only knows, though. These books are only good to muddle your head and make you jumpy. It will be bad, and there's an end. If we only can steam her round in time to meet it . . . '

A minute passed. Some of the stars winked rapidly and vanished.

'You left them pretty safe?' began the Captain abruptly, as though the silence were unbearable.

'Are you thinking of the coolies, sir? I rigged lifelines all ways across that 'tween-deck.'

'Did you? Good idea, Mr Jukes.'

'I didn't . . . think you cared to . . . know,' said Jukes – the lurching of the ship cut his speech as though somebody had been jerking him around while he talked – 'how I got on with . . . that infernal job. We did it. And it may not matter in the end.'

'Had to do what's fair, for all – they are only Chinamen. Give them the same chance with ourselves – hang it all. She isn't lost yet. Bad enough to be shut up below in a gale – '

'That's what I thought when you gave me the job, sir,' interjected Jukes moodily.

' – without being battered to pieces,' pursued Captain MacWhirr with rising vehemence. 'Couldn't let that go on in my ship, if I knew she hadn't five minutes to live. Couldn't bear it, Mr Jukes.'

A hollow echoing noise, like that of a shout rolling in a rocky chasm, approached the ship and went away again. The last star, blurred, enlarged, as if returning to the fiery mist of its beginning, struggled with the colossal depth of blackness hanging over the ship – and went out.

'Now for it!' muttered Captain MacWhirr. 'Mr Jukes.'

'Here, sir.'

The two men were growing indistinct to each other.

'We must trust her to go through it and come out on the other side. That's plain and straight. There's no room for Captain Wilson's storm-strategy here.'

'No, sir.'

'She will be smothered and swept again for hours,' mumbled the Captain. 'There's not much left by this time above deck for the sea to take away – unless you or me.'

'Both, sir,' whispered Jukes breathlessly.

'You are always meeting trouble half-way, Jukes,' Captain MacWhirr remonstrated quaintly. 'Though it's a fact that the second mate is no good. D'ye hear, Mr Jukes? You would be left alone if . . . '

Captain MacWhirr interrupted himself, and Jukes, glancing on all sides, remained silent.

'Don't you be put out by anything,' the Captain continued, mumbling rather fast. 'Keep her facing it. They may say what they like, but the heaviest seas run with the wind. Facing it – always facing it – that's the way to get through. You are a young sailor. Face it. That's enough for any man. Keep a cool head.'

'Yes, sir,' said Jukes, with a flutter of the heart.

In the next few seconds the Captain spoke to the engine-room and got an answer.

For some reason Jukes experienced an access of confidence, a sensation that came from outside like a warm breath, and made him feel equal to every demand. The distant muttering of the darkness stole into his ears. He noted it unmoved, out of that sudden belief in himself, as a man safe in a shirt of mail would watch a point.

The ship laboured without intermission amongst the black hills of water, paying with this hard tumbling the price of her life. She rumbled in her depths, shaking a white plummet of steam into the night, and Jukes' thought skimmed like a bird through the engine-room, where Mr Rout – good man – was ready. When the rumbling ceased it seemed to him that there was a pause of every sound, a dead pause in which Captain MacWhirr's voice rang out startlingly.

'What's that? A puff of wind?' – it spoke much louder than Jukes had ever heard it before – 'On the bow. That's right. She may come out of it yet.'

The mutter of the winds drew near apace. In the forefront could be distinguished a drowsy waking plaint passing on, and far off the growth of a multiple clamour, marching and expanding. There was the throb as of many drums in it, a vicious rushing note, and like the chant of a tramping multitude.

Jukes could no longer see his captain distinctly. The darkness was absolutely piling itself upon the ship. At most he made out movements, a hint of elbows spread out, of a head thrown up.

Captain MacWhirr was trying to do up the top button of his oilskin coat with unwonted haste. The hurricane, with its power to madden the seas, to sink ships, to uproot trees, to overturn strong walls and dash the very birds of the air to the ground, had found this taciturn man in its path, and, doing its utmost, had managed to wring out a few words. Before the renewed wrath of winds swooped on his ship, Captain MacWhirr was moved to declare, in a tone of vexation, as it were: 'I wouldn't like to lose her.'

He was spared that annoyance.

Chapter 6

On a bright sunshiny day, with the breeze chasing her smoke far ahead, the *Nan-Shan* came into Fu-chau. Her arrival was at once noticed on shore, and the seamen in harbour said: 'Look! Look at that steamer. What's that? Siamese – isn't she? Just look at her!'

She seemed, indeed, to have been used as a running target for the secondary batteries of a cruiser. A hail of minor shells could not have given her upper works a more broken, torn, and devastated aspect: and she had about her the worn, weary air of ships coming from the far ends of the world – and indeed with truth, for in her short passage she had been very far; sighting, verily, even the coast of the Great Beyond, whence no ship ever returns to give up her crew to the dust of the earth. She was encrusted and grey with salt to the trucks of her masts and to the top of her funnel; as though (as some facetious seaman said) 'the crowd on board had fished her out somewhere from the bottom of the sea and brought her in here for salvage'. And further, excited by the felicity of his own wit, he offered to give five pounds for her – 'as she stands'.

Before she had been quite an hour at rest, a meagre little man, with a red-tipped nose and a face cast in an angry mould, landed from a sampan on the quay of the Foreign Concession, and incontinently turned to shake his fist at her.

A tall individual, with legs much too thin for a rotund stomach, and with watery eyes, strolled up and remarked, 'Just left her – eh? Quick work.'

He wore a soiled suit of blue flannel with a pair of dirty cricketing shoes; a dingy grey moustache drooped from his lip, and daylight could be seen in two places between the rim and the crown of his hat.

'Hallo! what are you doing here?' asked the ex-second-mate of the *Nan-Shan*, shaking hands hurriedly.

'Standing by for a job – chance worth taking – got a quiet hint,' explained the man with the broken hat, in jerky, apathetic wheezes.

The second shook his fist again at the *Nan-Shan*. 'There's a fellow there that ain't fit to have the command of a scow,' he declared, quivering with passion, while the other looked about listlessly.

'Is there?'

But he caught sight on the quay of a heavy seaman's chest, painted brown under a fringed sailcloth cover, and lashed with new manila line. He eyed it with awakened interest.

'I would talk and raise trouble if it wasn't for that damned Siamese flag. Nobody to go to – or I would make it hot for him. The fraud! Told his chief engineer – that's another fraud for you – I had lost my nerve. The greatest lot of ignorant fools that ever sailed the seas. No! You can't think . . . '

'Got your money all right?' enquired his seedy acquaintance suddenly.

'Yes. Paid me off on board,' raged the second mate. ' "Get your breakfast on shore," says he.'

'Mean skunk!' commented the tall man vaguely, and passed his tongue on his lips. 'What about having a drink of some sort?'

'He struck me,' hissed the second mate.

'No! Struck! You don't say?' The man in blue began to bustle about sympathetically. 'Can't possibly talk here. I want to know all about it. Struck – eh? Let's get a fellow to carry your chest. I know a quiet place where they have some bottled beer . . . '

Mr Jukes, who had been scanning the shore through a pair of glasses, informed the chief engineer afterwards that 'our late second mate hasn't been long in finding a friend. A chap looking uncommonly like a bummer. I saw them walk away together from the quay.'

The hammering and banging of the needful repairs did not disturb Captain MacWhirr. The steward found in the letter he wrote, in a tidy chart-room, passages of such absorbing interest that twice he was nearly caught in the act. But Mrs MacWhirr, in the drawing-room of the forty-pound house, stifled a yawn – perhaps out of self-respect – for she was alone.

She reclined in a plush-bottomed and gilt hammock-chair near a tiled fireplace, with Japanese fans on the mantel and a glow of coals in the grate. Lifting her hands, she glanced wearily here and there into the many pages. It was not her fault they were so prosy, so completely uninteresting – from 'My darling wife' at the beginning, to 'Your loving husband' at the end. She couldn't be really expected to understand all these ship affairs. She was glad, of course, to hear from him, but she had never asked herself why, precisely.

' . . . They are called typhoons . . . The mate did not seem to like it . . . Not in books . . . Couldn't think of letting it go on . . . '

The paper rustled sharply. ' . . . A calm that lasted over twenty minutes,' she read perfunctorily; and the next words her thoughtless eyes caught, on the top of another page, were: 'see you and the children again . . . ' She had a movement of impatience. He was always thinking of coming home. He had never had such a good salary before. What was the matter now!

It did not occur to her to turn back overleaf to look. She would have found it recorded there that between 4 and 6 a.m. on December 25th, Captain MacWhirr did actually think that his ship could not possibly live another hour in such a sea, and that he would never see his wife and children again. Nobody was to know this (his letters got mislaid so quickly) – nobody whatever but the steward, who had been greatly impressed by that disclosure. So much so, that he tried to give the cook some idea of the 'narrow squeak we all had' by saying solemnly, 'The old man himself had a dam' poor opinion of our chance.'

'How do you know?' asked contemptuously the cook, an old soldier, 'He hasn't told you, maybe?'

'Well, he did give me a hint to that effect,' the steward brazened it out.

'Get along with you! He will be coming to tell *me* next,' jeered the old cook over his shoulder.

Mrs MacWhirr glanced farther, on the alert. ' . . . Do what's fair . . . Miserable objects . . . Only three, with a broken leg each, and one . . . Thought had better keep the matter quiet . . . hope to have done the fair thing . . . '

She let fall her hands. No: there was nothing more about coming home. Must have been merely expressing a pious wish. Mrs MacWhirr's mind was set at ease, and a black marble clock, priced by the local jeweller at £3 18s. 6d., had a discreet stealthy tick.

The door flew open, and a girl, in the long-legged, short-frocked period of existence, flung into the room. A lot of colourless, rather lanky hair was scattered over her shoulders. Seeing her mother, she stood still, and directed her pale prying eyes upon the letter.

'From father,' murmured Mrs MacWhirr. 'What have you done with your ribbon?'

The girl put her hands up to her head and pouted.

'He's well,' continued Mrs MacWhirr languidly. 'At least I think so. He never says.' She had a little laugh. The girl's face expressed a wandering indifference, and Mrs MacWhirr surveyed her with fond pride.

'Go and get your hat,' she said after a while. 'I am going out to do some shopping. There is a sale at Linom's.'

'Oh, how jolly!' uttered the child impressively, in unexpectedly grave vibrating tones, and bounded out of the room.

It was a fine afternoon, with a grey sky and dry sidewalks. Outside the draper's Mrs MacWhirr smiled upon a woman in a black mantle of generous proportions, armoured in jet and crowned with flowers blooming falsely above a bilious matronly countenance. They broke into a swift little babble of greetings and exclamations both together, very hurried, as if the street were ready to yawn open and swallow all that pleasure before it could be expressed.

Behind them the high glass doors were kept on the swing. People couldn't pass, men stood aside waiting patiently, and Lydia was absorbed in poking the end of her parasol between the stone flags. Mrs MacWhirr talked rapidly.

'Thank you very much. He's not coming home yet. Of course it's very sad to have him away, but it's such a comfort to know he keeps so well.' Mrs MacWhirr drew breath. 'The climate there agrees with him,' she added beamingly, as if poor MacWhirr had been away touring in China for the sake of his health.

Neither was the chief engineer coming home yet. Mr Rout knew too well the value of a good billet.

'Solomon says wonders will never cease,' cried Mrs Rout joyously at the old lady in her armchair by the fire. Mr Rout's mother moved slightly, her withered hands lying in black half-mittens on her lap.

The eyes of the engineer's wife fairly danced on the paper. 'That captain of the ship he is in – a rather simple man, you remember, mother? – has done something rather clever, Solomon says.'

'Yes, my dear,' said the old woman meekly, sitting with bowed silvery head, and that air of inward stillness characteristic of very old people who seem lost in watching the last flickers of life. 'I think I remember.'

Solomon Rout, Old Sol, Father Sol, The Chief, 'Rout, good man' – Mr Rout, the condescending and paternal friend of youth, had been the baby of her many children – all dead by this time. And she remembered him best as a boy of ten – long before he went away to serve his apprenticeship in some great engineering works in the North. She had seen so little of him since, she had gone through so many years, that she had now to retrace her steps very far back to recognise him plainly in the mist of time. Sometimes it seemed that her daughter-in-law was talking of some strange man.

Mrs Rout junior was disappointed. 'H'm. H'm.' She turned the page. 'How provoking! He doesn't say what it is. Says I couldn't understand how much there was in it. Fancy! What could it be so very clever? What a wretched man not to tell us!'

She read on without further remark soberly, and at last sat looking into the fire. The chief wrote just a word or two of the typhoon; but something had moved him to express an increased longing for the companionship of the jolly woman. 'If it hadn't been that mother must be looked after, I would send you your passage-money today. You could set up a small house out here. I would have a chance to see you sometimes then. We are not growing younger . . . '

'He's well, mother,' sighed Mrs Rout, rousing herself.

'He always was a strong healthy boy,' said the old woman placidly.

But Mr Jukes' account was really animated and very full. His friend in the Western Ocean trade imparted it freely to the other officers of his liner. 'A chap I know writes to me about an extraordinary affair that happened on board his ship in that typhoon – you know – that we read of in the papers two months ago. It's the funniest thing! Just see for yourself what he says. I'll show you his letter.'

There were phrases in it calculated to give the impression of light-hearted, indomitable resolution. Jukes had written them in good faith, for he felt thus when he wrote. He described with lurid effect the scenes in the 'tween-deck. ' . . . It struck me in a flash that those confounded Chinamen couldn't tell we weren't a desperate kind of robbers. 'Tisn't good to part the Chinaman from his money if he is the stronger party. We need have been desperate indeed to go thieving in such weather, but what could these beggars know of us? So, without thinking of it twice, I got the hands away in a jiffy. Our work was done – that the old man had set his heart on. We cleared out without staying to enquire how they felt. I am convinced that if they had not been so unmercifully shaken, and afraid – each individual one of them – to stand up, we would have been torn to pieces. Oh! It was pretty complete, I can tell you; and you may run to and fro across the Pond to the end of time before you find yourself with such a job on your hands.'

After this he alluded professionally to the damage done to the ship, and went on thus: 'It was when the weather quieted down that the situation became confoundedly delicate. It wasn't made any better by us having been lately transferred to the Siamese flag; though the skipper can't see that it makes any difference – "as long as *we* are on board," he says. There are feelings that this man simply hasn't got – and there's an end of it. You might just as well try to make a bedpost understand. But apart from this it is an infernally lonely state for a ship to be going about the China seas with no proper consuls, not even a gunboat of her own anywhere, nor a body to go to in case of some trouble.

'My notion was to keep these Johnnies under hatches for another fifteen hours or so; as we weren't much farther than that from Fu-chau. We would find there, most likely, some sort of a man-of-war, and once under her guns we were safe enough; for surely any skipper of a man-of-war – English, French or Dutch – would see white men through as far as a row on board goes. We could get rid of them and their money afterwards by delivering them to their Mandarin or Taotai, or whatever they call these chaps in goggles you see being carried about in sedan-chairs through their stinking streets.

'The old man wouldn't see it somehow. He wanted to keep the matter quiet. He got that notion into his head, and a steam windlass couldn't drag it out of him. He wanted as little fuss made as possible, for the sake of the ship's name and for the sake of the owners – "for the sake of all concerned," says he, looking at me very hard. It made me angry hot. Of course you couldn't keep a thing like that quiet; but the chests had been secured in the usual manner and were safe enough for any earthly gale, while this had been an altogether fiendish business I couldn't give you even an idea of.

'Meantime, I could hardly keep on my feet. None of us had a spell of any sort for nearly thirty hours, and there the old man sat rubbing his chin, rubbing the top of his head, and so bothered he didn't even think of pulling his long boots off.

' "I hope, sir," says I, "you won't be letting them out on deck before we make ready for them in some shape or other." Not, mind you, that I felt very sanguine about controlling these beggars if they meant to take charge. A trouble with a cargo of Chinamen is no child's play. I was dam' tired too. "I wish," said I, "you would let us throw the whole lot of these dollars down to them and leave them to fight it out amongst themselves, while we get a rest."

' "Now you talk wild, Jukes," says he, looking up in his slow way that makes you ache all over, somehow. "We must plan out something that would be fair to all parties."

'I had no end of work on hand, as you may imagine, so I set the hands going, and then I thought I would turn in a bit. I hadn't been asleep in my bunk ten minutes when in rushes the steward and begins to pull at my leg.

' "For God's sake, Mr Jukes, come out! Come on deck quick, sir. Oh, do come out!"

'The fellow scared all the sense out of me. I didn't know what had happened: another hurricane – or what. Could hear no wind.

' "The Captain's letting them out. Oh, he is letting them out! Jump on deck, sir, and save us. The chief engineer has just run below for his revolver."

'That's what I understood the fool to say. However, Father Rout swears he went in there only to get a clean pocket-handkerchief. Anyhow, I made one jump into my trousers and flew on deck aft. There was certainly a good deal of noise going on forward of the bridge. Four of the hands with the boss'en were at work abaft. I passed up to them some of the rifles all the ships on the China coast carry in the cabin, and led them on the bridge. On the way I ran against Old Sol, looking startled and sucking at an unlighted cigar.

' "Come along," I shouted to him.

'We charged, the seven of us, up to the chart-room. All was over. There stood the old man with his sea-boots still drawn up to the hips and in shirt-sleeves – got warm thinking it out, I suppose. Bun-hin's dandy clerk at his elbow, as dirty as a sweep, was still green in the face. I could see directly I was in for something.

' "What the devil are these monkey tricks, Mr Jukes?" asks the old man, as angry as ever he could be. I tell you frankly it made me lose my tongue. "For God's sake, Mr Jukes," says he, "do take away these rifles from the men. Somebody's sure to get hurt before long if you don't. Damme, if this ship isn't worse than Bedlam! Look sharp now. I want you up here to help me and Bun-hin's Chinaman to count that money. You wouldn't mind lending a hand too, Mr Rout, now you are here. The more of us the better."

'He had settled it all in his mind while I was having a snooze. Had we been an English ship, or only going to land our cargo of coolies in an English port, like Hong Kong, for instance, there would have been no end of enquiries and bother, claims for damages and so on. But these Chinamen know their officials better than we do.

'The hatches had been taken off already, and they were all on deck after a night and a day down below. It made you feel queer to see so many gaunt, wild faces together. The beggars stared about at the sky, at the sea, at the ship, as though they had expected the whole thing to have been blown to pieces. And no wonder! They had had a doing that would have shaken the soul out of a white man. But then they say a Chinaman has no soul. He has, though, something about him that is deuced tough. There was a fellow (amongst others of the badly hurt) who had had his eye all but knocked out. It stood out of his head the size of half a hen's egg. This would have laid out a white man on his back for a month: and yet there was that chap elbowing here and there in the crowd and talking to the others as if nothing had been the matter. They made a great hubbub amongst themselves, and whenever the old man showed his bald head on the foreside of the bridge, they would all leave off jawing and look at him from below.

'It seems that after he had done his thinking he made that Bun-hin's fellow go down and explain to them the only way they could get their money back. He told me afterwards that, all the coolies having worked in the same place and for the same length of time, he reckoned he would be doing the fair thing by them as near as possible if he shared all the cash we had picked up equally among the lot. You couldn't tell one man's dollars from another's, he said, and if you asked each man how much money he brought on board he was afraid they would lie, and he would find himself a long way short. I think he was right there. As to giving up the money to any Chinese official he could scare up in Fu-chau, he said he might just as well put the lot in his own pocket at once for all the good it would be to them. I suppose they thought so too.

'We finished the distribution before dark. It was rather a sight: the sea running high, the ship a wreck to look at, these Chinamen staggering up on the bridge one by one for their share, and the old man still booted, and in his shirt-sleeves, busy paying out at the chart-room door, perspiring like anything, and now and then coming down sharp on myself or Father Rout

about one thing or another not quite to his mind. He took the share of
those who were disabled himself to them on the No. 2 hatch. There were
three dollars left over, and these went to the three most damaged coolies,
one to each. We turned-to afterwards, and shovelled out on deck heaps of
wet rags, all sorts of fragments of things without shape, and that you
couldn't give a name to, and let them settle the ownership themselves.

'This certainly is coming as near as can be to keeping the thing quiet for
the benefit of all concerned. What's your opinion, you pampered mail-boat
swell? The old chief says that this was plainly the only thing that could be
done. The skipper remarked to me the other day, "There are things you find
nothing about in books." I think that he got out of it very well for such a
stupid man.'

1901

FALK

A Reminiscence

Several of us, all more or less connected with the sea, were dining in a small river-hostelry not more than thirty miles from London, and less than twenty from that shallow and dangerous puddle to which our coasting men give the grandiose name of 'German Ocean'. And through the wide windows we had a view of the Thames; an enfilading view down the Lower Hope Reach. But the dinner was execrable, and all the feast was for the eyes.

That flavour of salt-water which for so many of us had been the very water of life permeated our talk. He who hath known the bitterness of the Ocean shall have its taste for ever in his mouth. But one or two of us, pampered by the life of the land, complained of hunger. It was impossible to swallow any of that stuff. And indeed there was a strange mustiness in everything. The wooden dining-room stuck out over the mud of the shore like a lacustrine dwelling; the planks of the floor seemed rotten; a decrepit old waiter tottered pathetically to and fro before an antediluvian and worm-eaten sideboard; the chipped plates might have been disinterred from some kitchen midden near an inhabited lake; and the chops recalled times more ancient still. They brought forcibly to one's mind the night of ages when the primeval man, evolving the first rudiments of cookery from his dim consciousness, scorched lumps of flesh at a fire of sticks in the company of other good fellows; then, gorged and happy, sat him back among the gnawed bones to tell his artless tales of experience – the tales of hunger and hunt – and of women, perhaps!

But luckily the wine happened to be as old as the waiter. So, comparatively empty, but upon the whole fairly happy, we sat back and told our artless tales. We talked of the sea and all its works. The sea never changes, and its works for all the talk of men are wrapped in mystery. But we agreed that the times were changed. And we talked of old ships, of sea-accidents, of breakdowns, dismastings; and of a man who brought his ship safe to Liverpool all the way from the River Plate under a jury rudder. We talked of wrecks, of short rations and of heroism – or at least of what the newspapers would have called heroism at sea – a manifestation of virtues quite different from the heroism of primitive times. And now and then falling silent all together we gazed at the sights of the river.

A P.&O. boat passed bound down. 'One gets jolly good dinners on board these ships,' remarked one of our band. A man with sharp eyes read out the name on her bows: *Arcadia*. 'What a beautiful model of a ship!' murmured some of us. She was followed by a small cargo-steamer, and the flag they hauled down aboard while we were looking showed her to be a Norwegian. She made an awful lot of smoke; and before it had quite blown away, a high-sided, short, wooden barque, in ballast and towed by a paddle-tug, appeared in front of the windows. All her hands were forward busy setting up the headgear; and aft a woman in a red hood, quite alone with the man at the wheel, paced the length of the poop back and forth, with the grey wool of some knitting work in her hands.

'German I should think,' muttered one. 'The skipper has his wife on board,' remarked another; and the light of the crimson sunset all ablaze behind the London smoke, throwing a glow of Bengal light upon the barque's spars, faded away from the Hope Reach.

Then one of us, who had not spoken before, a man of over fifty, that had commanded ships for a quarter of a century, looking after the barque now gliding far away, all black on the lustre of the river, said: This reminds me of an absurd episode in my life, now many years ago, when I got first the command of an iron barque, loading then in a certain Eastern seaport. It was also the capital of an Eastern kingdom, lying up a river as might be London lies up this old Thames of ours. No more need be said of the place; for this sort of thing might have happened anywhere where there are ships, skippers, tugboats, and orphan nieces of indescribable splendour. And the absurdity of the episode concerns only me, my enemy Falk, and my friend Hermann.

There seemed to be something like peculiar emphasis on the words 'my friend Hermann', which caused one of us (for we had just been speaking of heroism at sea) to say idly and nonchalantly: 'And was this Hermann a hero?'

Not at all, said our grizzled friend. No hero at all. He was a Schiff-führer: Ship-conductor. That's how they call a Master Mariner in Germany. I prefer our way. The alliteration is good, and there is something in the nomenclature that gives to us as a body the sense of corporate existence: Apprentice, Mate, Master, in the ancient and honourable craft of the sea. As to my friend Hermann, he might have been a consummate master of the honourable craft, but he was called officially Schiff-führer, and had the simple, heavy appearance of a well-to-do farmer, combined with the good-natured shrewdness of a small shopkeeper. With his shaven chin, round limbs, and heavy eyelids he did not look like a toiler, and even less like an adventurer of the sea. Still, he toiled upon the seas, in his own way, much as a shopkeeper works behind his counter. And his ship was the means by which he maintained his growing family.

She was a heavy, strong, blunt-bowed affair, awakening the ideas of primitive solidity, like the wooden plough of our forefathers. And there were, about her, other suggestions of a rustic and homely nature. The extraordinary timber projections which I have seen in no other vessel made her square stern resemble the tail end of a miller's wagon. But the four stern ports of her cabin, glazed with six little greenish panes each, and framed in wooden sashes painted brown, might have been the windows of a cottage in the country. The tiny white curtains and the greenery of flowerpots behind the glass completed the resemblance. On one or two occasions when passing under her stern I had detected from my boat a round arm in the act of tilting a watering-pot, and the bowed sleek head of a maiden whom I shall always call Hermann's niece, because as a matter of fact I've never heard her name, for all my intimacy with the family.

This, however, sprang up later on. Meantime in common with the rest of the shipping in that Eastern port, I was left in no doubt as to Hermann's notions of hygienic clothing. Evidently he believed in wearing good stout flannel next his skin. On most days little frocks and pinafores could be seen drying in the mizzen rigging of his ship, or a tiny row of socks fluttering on the signal halyards; but once a fortnight the family washing was exhibited in force. It covered the poop entirely. The afternoon breeze would incite to a weird and flabby activity all that crowded mass of clothing, with its vague suggestions of drowned, mutilated and flattened humanity. Trunks without heads waved at you arms without hands; legs without feet kicked fantastically with collapsible flourishes; and there were long white garments that, taking the wind fairly through their neck openings edged with lace, became for a moment violently distended as by the passage of obese and invisible bodies. On these days you could make out that ship at a great distance by the multicoloured grotesque riot going on abaft her mizzen-mast.

She had her berth just ahead of me, and her name was *Diana* – Diana not of Ephesus but of Bremen. This was proclaimed in white letters a foot long spaced widely across the stern (somewhat like the lettering of a shop-sign) under the cottage windows. This ridiculously unsuitable name struck one as an impertinence towards the memory of the most charming of goddesses; for, apart from the fact that the old craft was physically incapable of engaging in any sort of chase, there was a gang of four children belonging to her. They peeped over the rail at passing boats and occasionally dropped various objects into them. Thus, sometime before I knew Hermann to speak to, I received on my hat a horrid rag-doll belonging to Hermann's eldest daughter. However, these youngsters were upon the whole well behaved. They had fair heads, round eyes, round little knobby noses, and they resembled their father a good deal.

This *Diana* of Bremen was a most innocent old ship, and seemed to know nothing of the wicked sea, as there are on shore households that know nothing of the corrupt world. And the sentiments she suggested were unexceptionable and mainly of a domestic order. She was a home. All these dear children had learned to walk on her roomy quarterdeck. In such thoughts there is something pretty, even touching. Their teeth, I should judge, they had cut on the ends of her running gear. I have many times observed the baby Hermann (Nicholas) engaged in gnawing the whipping of the fore-royal brace. Nicholas' favourite place of residence was under the main fife-rail. Directly he was let loose he would crawl off there, and the first seaman who came along would bring him, carefully held aloft in tarry hands, back to the cabin door. I fancy there must have been a standing order to that effect. In the course of these transportations the baby, who was the only peppery person in the ship, tried to smite these stalwart young German sailors on the face.

Mrs Hermann, an engaging, stout housewife, wore on board baggy blue dresses with white dots. When, as happened once or twice, I caught her at an elegant little wash-tub rubbing hard on white collars, baby's socks, and Hermann's summer neckties, she would blush in girlish confusion, and raising her wet hands greet me from afar with many friendly nods. Her sleeves would be rolled up to the elbows, and the gold hoop of her wedding ring glittered among the soapsuds. Her voice was pleasant, she had a serene brow, smooth bands of very fair hair, and a good-humoured expression of the eyes. She was motherly and moderately talkative. When this simple matron smiled, youthful dimples broke out on her fresh broad cheeks. Hermann's niece on the other hand, an orphan and very silent, I never saw attempt a smile. This, however, was not gloom on her part but the restraint of youthful gravity.

They had carried her about with them for the last three years, to help with the children and be company for Mrs Hermann, as Hermann mentioned once to me. It had been very necessary while they were all little, he had added in a vexed manner. It was her arm and her sleek head that I had glimpsed one morning, through the stern-windows of the cabin, hovering over the pots of fuchsias and mignonette; but the first time I beheld her full length I surrendered to her proportions. They fix her in my mind, as great beauty, great intelligence, quickness of wit or kindness of heart might have made some other woman equally memorable.

With her it was form and size. It was her physical personality that had this imposing charm. She might have been witty, intelligent, and kind to an exceptional degree. I don't know, and this is not to the point. All I know is that she was built on a magnificent scale. Built is the only word. She was constructed, she was erected, as it were, with a regal lavishness. It staggered you to see this reckless expenditure of material upon a chit of a girl. She was youthful and also perfectly mature, as though she had been some fortunate immortal. She was heavy too, perhaps, but that's nothing. It only added to that notion of permanence. She was barely nineteen. But such shoulders! Such round arms! Such a shadowing forth of mighty limbs when with three long strides she pounced across the deck upon the overturned Nicholas – it's perfectly indescribable! She seemed a good, quiet girl, vigilant as to Lena's needs, Gustav's tumbles, the state of Carl's dear little nose – conscientious, hardworking, and all that. But what magnificent hair she had! Abundant, long, thick, of a tawny colour. It had the sheen of precious metals. She wore it plaited tightly into one single tress hanging girlishly down her back; and its end reached down to her waist. The massiveness of it surprised you. On my word it reminded one of a club. Her face was big, comely, of an unruffled expression. She had a good complexion, and her blue eyes were so pale that she appeared to look at the world with the empty white candour of a statue. You could not call her good-looking. It was something much more impressive. The simplicity of her apparel, the opulence of her form, her imposing stature, and the extraordinary sense of vigorous life that seemed to emanate from her like a perfume exhaled by a flower, made her beautiful with a beauty of a rustic and olympian order. To watch her reaching up to the clothes-line, with both arms raised high above her head, caused you to fall a-musing in a strain of pagan piety. Excellent Mrs Hermann's baggy cotton gowns had some sort of rudimentary frills at neck and bottom, but this girl's print frocks hadn't even a wrinkle; nothing but a few straight folds in the skirt falling to her feet, and these, when she stood still, had a severe and statuesque quality. She was inclined naturally to be still whether sitting or standing. However, I don't mean to say she was statuesque. She was too generously alive; but she could have stood for an allegoric statue of the Earth. I don't mean the worn-out earth of our possession, but a young Earth, a virginal planet undisturbed by the vision of a future teeming with the monstrous forms of life and death, clamorous with the cruel battles of hunger and thought.

The worthy Hermann himself was not very entertaining, though his English was fairly comprehensible. Mrs Hermann, who always let off one speech at least at me in an hospitable, cordial tone (and in Platt-Deutsch I suppose) I could not understand. As to their niece, however satisfactory to look upon (and she inspired you somehow with a hopeful view as to the prospects of mankind) she was a modest and silent presence, mostly engaged in sewing, only now and then, as I observed, falling over that work into a state of maidenly meditation. Her aunt sat opposite her, sewing also, with her feet propped on a wooden footstool. On the other side of the deck Hermann and I would get a couple of chairs out of the cabin and settle down to a smoking match, accompanied at long intervals by the pacific exchange of a few words. I came nearly every evening. Hermann I would find in his shirt sleeves. As soon as he returned from the shore on board his ship he commenced operations by taking off his coat; then he put on his head an embroidered round cap with a tassel, and changed his boots for a pair of cloth slippers. Afterwards he smoked at the cabin-door, looking at his children with an air of civic virtue, till they got caught one after another and put to bed in various staterooms. Lastly, we would drink some beer in the cabin, which was furnished with a wooden table on cross legs, and with black straight-backed chairs – more like a farm kitchen than a ship's cuddy. The sea and all nautical affairs seemed very far removed from the hospitality of this exemplary family.

And I liked this because I had a rather worrying time on board my own ship. I had been appointed ex-officio by the British Consul to take charge of her after a man who had died suddenly, leaving for the guidance of his successor some suspiciously unreceipted bills, a few dry-dock estimates hinting at bribery, and a quantity of vouchers for three years' extravagant expenditure; all these mixed up together in a dusty old violin-case lined with ruby velvet. I found besides a large account-book, which, when opened hopefully, turned out to my infinite consternation to be filled with verses – page after page of rhymed doggerel of a jovial and improper character, written in the neatest minute hand I ever did see. In the same fiddle-case a photograph of my predecessor, taken lately in Saigon, represented in front of a garden view, and in company of a female in strange draperies, an elderly, squat, rugged man of stern aspect in a clumsy suit of black broadcloth, and with the hair brushed forward above the temples in a manner reminding one of a boar's tusks. Of a fiddle, however, the only trace on board was the case, its empty husk as it were; but of the two last freights the ship had indubitably earned of late, there were not even the husks left. It was impossible to say where all that money had gone to. It wasn't on board. It had not been remitted home; for a letter from the owners, preserved in a desk evidently by the merest accident, complained mildly enough that they had not been favoured by a scratch of the pen for the last eighteen months. There were next to no stores on board, not an inch of spare rope or a yard of canvas The ship had been run bare, and I foresaw no end of difficulties before I could get her ready for sea.

As I was young then – not thirty yet – I took myself and my troubles very seriously. The old mate, who had acted as chief mourner at the captain's funeral, was not particularly pleased at my coming. But the fact is the fellow was not legally qualified for command, and the Consul was bound, if at all possible, to put a properly certificated man on board. As to the second mate, all I can say his name was Tottersen, or something like that. His practice was to wear on his head, in that tropical climate, a mangy fur cap. He was, without exception, the stupidest man I had ever seen on board ship. And he looked it too. He looked so confoundedly stupid that it was a matter of surprise for me when he answered to his name.

I drew no great comfort from their company, to say the least of it; while the prospect of making a long sea passage with those two fellows was depressing. And my other thoughts in solitude could not be of a gay complexion. The crew was sickly, the cargo was coming very slow; I foresaw I would have lots of trouble with the charterers, and doubted whether they would advance me enough money for the ship's expenses. Their attitude towards me was unfriendly. Altogether I was not getting on. I would discover at odd times (generally about midnight) that I was totally inexperienced, greatly ignorant of business, and hopelessly unfit for any sort of command; and when the steward had to be taken to the hospital ill with choleraic symptoms I felt bereaved of the only decent person at the after end of the ship. He was fully expected to recover, but in the meantime had to be replaced by some sort of servant. And on the recommendation of a certain Schomberg, the proprietor of the smaller of the two hotels in the place, I engaged a Chinaman. Schomberg, a brawny, hairy Alsatian, and an awful gossip, assured me that it was all right. 'First-class boy that. Came in the *suite* of his Excellency Tseng the Commissioner – you know. His Excellency Tseng lodged with me here for three weeks.'

He mouthed the Chinese Excellency at me with great unction, though the specimen of the '*suite*' did not seem very promising. At the time, however, I did not know what an untrustworthy humbug Schomberg was. The 'boy' might have been forty or a hundred and forty for all you could tell – one of those Chinamen of the death's-head type of face and completely inscrutable. Before the end of the third day he had revealed himself as a confirmed opium-smoker, a gambler, a most audacious thief, and a first-class sprinter. When he departed at the top of his speed with thirty-two golden sovereigns of my own hard-earned savings it was the last straw. I had reserved that money in case my difficulties came to the worst. Now it was gone I felt as poor and naked as a fakir. I clung to my ship, for all the bother she caused me, but what I could not bear were the long lonely evenings in her cuddy, where the atmosphere, made smelly by a leaky lamp, was agitated by the snoring of the mate. That fellow shut himself up in his stuffy cabin punctually at eight, and made gross and revolting noises like a waterlogged trombone. It was odious not to be able to worry oneself in comfort on board one's own ship. Everything in this world, I reflected, even the command of a nice little barque, may be made a delusion and a snare for the unwary spirit of pride in man.

From such reflections I was glad to make my escape on board that Bremen *Diana*. There apparently no whisper of the world's iniquities had ever penetrated. And yet she lived upon the wide sea: and the sea tragic and comic, the sea with its horrors and its peculiar scandals, the sea peopled by men and ruled by iron necessity is indubitably a part of the world. But that patriarchal old tub, like some saintly retreat, echoed nothing of it. She was world-proof. Her venerable innocence apparently had put a restraint on the roaring lusts of the sea. And yet I have known the sea too long to believe in its respect for decency. An elemental force is ruthlessly frank. It may, of course, have been Hermann's skilful seamanship, but to me it looked as if the allied oceans had refrained from smashing these high bulwarks, unshipping the lumpy rudder, frightening the children, and generally opening this family's eyes out of sheer reticence. It looked like reticence. The ruthless disclosure was, in the end, left for a man to make; a man strong and elemental enough and driven to unveil some secrets of the sea by the power of a simple and elemental desire.

This, however, occurred much later, and meantime I took sanctuary in that serene old ship early every evening. The only person on board that seemed to be in trouble was little Lena, and in due course I perceived that the health of the rag-doll was more than delicate. This object led a sort of 'in extremis' existence in a wooden box placed against the starboard mooring-bitts, tended and nursed with the greatest sympathy and care by all the children, who greatly enjoyed pulling long faces and moving with hushed footsteps. Only the baby – Nicholas – looked on with a cold, ruffianly leer, as if he had belonged to another tribe altogether. Lena perpetually sorrowed over the box, and all of them were in deadly earnest. It was wonderful the way these children would work up their compassion for that bedraggled thing I wouldn't have touched with a pair of tongs. I suppose they were exercising and developing their racial sentimentalism by the means of that dummy. I was only surprised that Mrs Hermann let Lena cherish and hug that bundle of rags to that extent, it was so disreputably and completely unclean. But Mrs Hermann would raise her fine womanly eyes from her needlework to look on with amused sympathy, and did not seem to see it, somehow, that this object of affection was a disgrace to the ship's purity. Purity, not cleanliness, is the word. It was pushed so far that I seemed to detect in this too a sentimental excess, as if dirt had been removed in very love. It is impossible to give you an idea of such a meticulous neatness. It was as if every morning that ship had been arduously explored with – with toothbrushes. Her very bowsprit three times a week had its toilette made with a cake of soap and a piece of soft flannel. Arrayed – I *must* say arrayed – arrayed artlessly in dazzling white paint as to wood and dark green as to ironwork the simple-minded distribution of these colours evoked the images of simple-minded peace, of arcadian felicity; and the childish comedy of disease and sorrow struck me sometimes as an abominably real blot upon that ideal state.

I enjoyed it greatly, and on my part I brought a little mild excitement into it. Our intimacy arose from the pursuit of that thief. It was in the evening, and Hermann, who, contrary to his habits, had stayed on shore late that day, was extricating himself backwards out of a little gharry on the river bank, opposite his ship, when the hunt passed. Realising the situation as though he had eyes in his shoulder-blades, he joined us with a leap and took the lead. The Chinaman fled silent like a rapid shadow on the dust of an extremely oriental road. I followed. A long way in the rear my mate whooped like a savage. A young moon threw a bashful light on a plain like a monstrous waste ground: the architectural mass of a Buddhist temple far away projected itself in dead black on the sky. We lost the thief of course; but in my disappointment I had to admire Hermann's presence of mind. The velocity that stodgy man developed in the interests of a complete stranger earned my warm gratitude – there was something truly cordial in his exertions.

He seemed as vexed as myself at our failure, and would hardly listen to my thanks. He said it was 'nothings', and invited me on the spot to come on board his ship and drink a glass of beer with him. We poked sceptically for a while amongst the bushes, peered without conviction into a ditch or two. There was not a sound: patches of slime glimmered feebly amongst the reeds. Slowly we trudged back, drooping under the thin sickle of the moon, and I heard him mutter to himself, 'Himmel! Zwei und dreissig Pfund!' He was impressed by the figure of my loss. For a long time we had ceased to hear the mate's whoops and yells.

Then he said to me, 'Everybody has his troubles,' and as we went on remarked that he would never have known anything of mine hadn't he by an extraordinary chance been detained on shore by Captain Falk. He didn't like to stay late ashore – he added with a sigh. The something doleful in his tone I put down to his sympathy with my misfortune, of course.

On board the *Diana* Mrs Hermann's fine eyes expressed much interest and commiseration. We had found the two women sewing face to face under the open skylight in the strong glare of the lamp. Hermann walked in first, starting in the very doorway to pull off his coat, and encouraging me with loud, hospitable ejaculations: 'Come in! This way! Come in, captain!' At once, coat in hand, he began to tell his wife all about it. Mrs Hermann put the palms of her plump hands together; I smiled and bowed with a heavy heart: the niece got up from her sewing to bring Hermann's slippers and his embroidered calotte, which he assumed pontifically, talking (about me) all the time. Billows of white stuff lay between the chairs on the cabin floor; I caught the words 'Zwei und dreissig Pfund' repeated several times, and presently came the beer, which seemed delicious to my throat, parched with running and the emotions of the chase.

I didn't get away till well past midnight, long after the women had retired. Hermann had been trading in the East for three years or more, carrying freights of rice and timber mostly. His ship was well known in all the ports from Vladivostok to Singapore. She was his own property. The profits had been moderate, but the trade answered well enough while the children were small yet. In another year or so he hoped he would be able to sell the old *Diana* to a firm in Japan for a fair price. He intended to return home, to Bremen, by mail boat, second class, with Mrs Hermann and the children. He told me all this stolidly, with slow puffs at his pipe. I was sorry when knocking the ashes out he began to rub his eyes. I would have sat with him till morning. What had I to hurry on board my own ship for? To face the broken rifled drawer in my stateroom. Ugh! The very thought made me feel unwell.

I became their daily guest, as you know. I think that Mrs Hermann from the first looked upon me as a romantic person. I did not, of course, tear my hair *coram populo* over my loss, and she took it for lordly indifference. Afterwards, I dare say, I did tell them some of my adventures – such as they were – and they marvelled greatly at the extent of my experience. Hermann would translate what he thought the most striking passages. Getting upon his legs, and as if delivering a lecture on a phenomenon, he addressed himself, with gestures, to the two women, who would let their sewing sink slowly on their laps. Meantime I sat before a glass of Hermann's beer, trying to look modest. Mrs Hermann would glance at me quickly, emit slight 'Ach!'s The girl never made a sound. Never. But she too would sometimes raise her pale eyes to look at me in her unseeing, gentle way. Her glance was by no means stupid; it beamed out soft and diffuse as the moon beams upon a landscape – quite differently from the scrutinising inspection of the stars. You were drowned in it, and imagined yourself to appear blurred. And yet this same glance when turned upon Christian Falk must have been as efficient as the searchlight of a battleship.

Falk was the other assiduous visitor on board, but from his behaviour he might have been coming to see the quarterdeck capstan. He certainly used to stare at it a good deal when keeping us company outside the cabin door, with one muscular arm thrown over the back of the chair, and his big shapely legs, in very tight white trousers, extended far out and ending in a pair of black shoes as roomy as punts. On arrival he would shake Hermann's hand with a mutter, bow to the women, and take up his careless and misanthropic attitude by our side. He departed abruptly, with a jump, going through the performance of grunts, handshakes, bow, as if in a panic. Sometimes, with a sort of discreet and convulsive effort, he approached the women and exchanged a few low words with them, half a dozen at most. On these occasions Hermann's usual stare became positively glassy and Mrs Hermann's kind countenance would colour up. The girl herself never turned a hair.

Falk was a Dane or perhaps a Norwegian, I can't tell now. At all events he was a Scandinavian of some sort, and a bloated monopolist to boot. It is possible he was unacquainted with the word, but he had a clear perception of the thing itself. His tariff of charges for towing ships in and out was the most brutally inconsiderate document of the sort I had ever seen. He was the commander and owner of the only tugboat on the river, a very trim white craft of 150 tons or more, as elegantly neat as a yacht, with a round wheelhouse rising like a glazed turret high above her sharp bows, and with one slender varnished pole mast forward. I dare say there are yet a few shipmasters afloat who remember Falk and his tug very well. He extracted his pound and a half of flesh from each of us merchant-skippers with an inflexible sort of indifference which made him detested and even feared. Schomberg used to remark: 'I won't talk about the fellow. I don't think he has six drinks from year's end to year's end in my place. But my advice is, gentlemen, don't you have anything to do with him, if you can help it.'

This advice, apart from unavoidable business relations, was easy to follow because Falk intruded upon no one. It seems absurd to compare a tugboat skipper to a centaur: but he reminded me somehow of an engraving in a little book I had as a boy, which represented centaurs at a stream, and there was one especially, in the foreground, prancing bow and arrows in hand, with regular severe features and an immense curled wavy beard, flowing down his breast. Falk's face reminded me of that centaur. Besides, he was a composite creature. Not a man-horse, it is true, but a man-boat. He lived on board his tug, which was always dashing up and down the river from early morn till dewy eve. In the last rays of the setting sun, you could pick out far away down the reach his beard borne high up on the white structure, foaming up stream to anchor for the night. There was the white-clad man's body, and the rich brown patch of the hair, and nothing below the waist but the 'thwart-ship white lines of the bridge-screens, that led the eye to the sharp white lines of the bows cleaving the muddy water of the river.

Separated from his boat, to me at least he seemed incomplete. The tug herself without his head and torso on the bridge looked mutilated as it were. But he left her very seldom. All the time I remained in harbour I saw him only twice on shore. On the first occasion it was at my charterers, where he came in misanthropically to get paid for towing out a French barque the day before. The second time I could hardly believe my eyes, for I beheld him reclining under his beard in a cane-bottomed chair in the billiard-room of Schomberg's hotel.

It was very funny to see Schomberg ignoring him pointedly. The artificiality of it contrasted strongly with Falk's natural unconcern. The big Alsatian talked loudly with his other customers, going from one little table to the other, and passing Falk's place of repose with his eyes fixed straight ahead. Falk sat there with an untouched glass at his elbow. He must have known by sight and name every white man in the room, but he never addressed a word to anybody. He acknowledged my presence by a drop of his eyelids, and that was all. Sprawling there in the chair, he would, now and again, draw the palms of both his hands down his face, giving at the same time a slight, almost imperceptible, shudder.

It was a habit he had, and of course I was perfectly familiar with it, since you could not remain an hour in his company without being made to wonder at such a movement breaking some long period of stillness. It was a passionate and inexplicable gesture. He used to make it at all sorts of times; as likely as not after he had been listening to little Lena's chatter about the suffering doll, for instance. The Hermann children always besieged him about his legs closely, though, in a gentle way, he shrank from them a little. He seemed, however, to feel a great affection for the whole family. For Hermann himself especially. He sought his company. In this case, for instance, he must have been waiting for him, because as soon as he appeared Falk rose hastily, and they went out together. Then Schomberg expounded in my hearing to three or four people his theory that Falk was after Captain Hermann's niece, and asserted confidently that nothing would come of it. It was the same last year when Captain Hermann was loading here, he said.

Naturally, I did not believe Schomberg, but I own that for a time I observed closely what went on. All I discovered was some impatience on Hermann's part. At the sight of Falk, stepping over the gangway, the excellent man would begin to mumble and chew between his teeth something that sounded like German swearwords. However, as we said, I'm not familiar with the language, and Hermann's soft, round-eyed countenance remained unchanged. Staring stolidly ahead he greeted him with, 'Wie geht's,' or in English, 'How are you?' with a throaty enunciation. The girl would look up for an instant and move her lips slightly: Mrs Hermann let her hands rest on her lap to talk volubly to him for a minute or so in her pleasant voice before she went on with her sewing again. Falk would throw himself into a chair, stretch his big legs, as like as not draw his hands down his face passionately. As to myself, he was not pointedly impertinent: it was rather as though he could not be bothered with such trifles as my existence; and the truth is that being a monopolist he was under no necessity to be amiable. He was sure to get his own extortionate terms out of me for towage whether he frowned or smiled. As a matter of fact, he did neither: but before many days elapsed he managed to astonish me not a little and to set Schomberg's tongue clacking more than ever.

It came about in this way. There was a shallow bar at the mouth of the river which ought to have been kept down, but the authorities of the State were piously busy gilding afresh the great Buddhist Pagoda just then, and I suppose had no money to spare for dredging operations. I don't know how it may be now, but at the time I speak of that sandbank was a great nuisance to the shipping. One of its consequences was that vessels of a certain draught of water, like Hermann's or mine, could not complete their loading in the river. After taking in as much as possible of their cargo, they had to go outside to fill up. The whole procedure was an unmitigated bore. When you thought you had as much on board as your ship could carry safely over the bar, you went and gave notice to your agents. They, in their turn, notified Falk that so-and-so was ready to go out. Then Falk (ostensibly when it fitted in with his other work, but, if the truth were known, simply when his arbitrary spirit moved him), after ascertaining carefully in the office that there was enough money to meet his bill, would come along unsympathetically, glaring at you with his yellow eyes from the bridge, and would drag you out dishevelled as to rigging, lumbered as to the decks, with unfeeling haste, as if to execution. And he would force you, too, to take the end of his own wire hawser, for the use of which there was of course an extra charge. To your shouted remonstrances against this extortion this towering trunk with one hand on the engine-room telegraph only shook its bearded head above the splash, the racket and the clouds of smoke, in which the tug, backing and filling in the smother of churning paddle-wheels behaved like a ferocious and impatient creature. He had her manned by the cheekiest gang of lascars I ever did see, whom he allowed to bawl at you insolently, and, once fast, he plucked you out of your berth as if he did not care what he smashed. Eighteen miles down the river you had to go behind him, and then three more along the coast to where a group of uninhabited rocky islets enclosed a sheltered anchorage. There you would have to lie at single anchor with your naked spars showing to seaward over these barren fragments of land scattered upon a very intensely blue sea. There was nothing to look at besides but a bare coast, the muddy edge of the brown plain with the sinuosities of the river you had left, traced in dull green, and the Great Pagoda uprising lonely and massive with shining curves and pinnacles like the gorgeous and stony efflorescence of tropical rocks. You had nothing to do but to wait fretfully for the balance of your cargo, which was sent out of the river with the greatest irregularity. And it was open to you to console yourself with the thought that, after all, this stage of bother meant that your departure from these shores was indeed approaching at last.

We both had to go through that stage, Hermann and I, and there was a sort of tacit emulation between the ships as to which should be ready first.

We kept on neck and neck almost to the finish, when I won the race by going personally to give notice in the forenoon; whereas Hermann, who was very slow in making up his mind to go ashore, did not get to the agents' office till late in the day. They told him there that my ship was first on turn for next morning, and I believe he told them he was in no hurry. It suited him better to go the day after.

That evening, on board the *Diana*, he sat with his plump knees well apart, staring and puffing at the curved mouthpiece of his pipe. Presently he spoke with some impatience to his niece about putting the children to bed. Mrs Hermann, who was talking to Falk, stopped short and looked at her husband uneasily, but the girl got up at once and drove the children before her into the cabin. In a little while Mrs Hermann had to leave us to quell what, from the sounds inside, must have been a dangerous mutiny. At this Hermann grumbled to himself. For half an hour longer Falk left alone with us fidgeted on his chair, sighed lightly, then at last, after drawing his hands down his face, got up, and as if renouncing the hope of making himself understood (he hadn't opened his mouth once) he said in English: 'Well . . . Good-night, Captain Hermann.' He stopped for a moment before my chair and looked down fixedly; I may even say he glared: and he went so far as to make a deep noise in his throat. There was in all this something so marked that for the first time in our limited intercourse of nods and grunts he excited in me something like interest. But next moment he disappointed me – for he strode away hastily without a nod even.

His manner was usually odd, it is true, and I certainly did not pay much attention to it; but that sort of obscure intention, which seemed to lurk in his nonchalance like a wary old carp in a pond, had never before come so near the surface. He had distinctly aroused my expectations. I would have been unable to say what it was I expected, but at all events I did not expect the absurd developments he sprung upon me no later than the break of the very next day.

I remember only that there was, on that evening, enough point in his behaviour to make me, after he had fled, wonder audibly what he might mean. To this Hermann, crossing his legs with a swing and settling himself viciously away from me in his chair, said: 'That fellow don't know himself what he means.'

There might have been some insight in such a remark. I said nothing, and, still averted, he added: 'When I was here last year he was just the same.' An eruption of tobacco smoke enveloped his head as if his temper had exploded like gunpowder.

I had half a mind to ask him point blank whether he, at least, didn't know why Falk, a notoriously unsociable man, had taken to visiting his ship with such assiduity. After all, I reflected suddenly, it was a most remarkable thing. I wonder now what Hermann would have said. As it turned out he didn't let me ask. Forgetting all about Falk apparently, he started a monologue on his plans for the future: the selling of the ship, the going home; and falling into a reflective and calculating mood he mumbled between regular jets of smoke about the expense. The necessity of disbursing passage-money for all his tribe seemed to disturb him in a manner that was the more striking because otherwise he gave no signs of a miserly disposition. And yet he fussed over the prospect of that voyage home in a mail-boat like a sedentary grocer who has made up his mind to see the world. He was racially thrifty I suppose, and for him there must have been a great novelty in finding himself obliged to pay for travelling – for sea travelling which was the normal state of life for the family – from the very cradle for most of them. I could see he grudged prospectively every single shilling which must be spent so absurdly. It was rather funny. He would become doleful over it, and then again, with a fretful sigh, he would suppose there was nothing for it now but to take three second-class tickets – and there were the four children to pay for besides. A lot of money that to spend at once. A big lot of money.

I sat with him listening (not for the first time) to these heart-searchings till I grew thoroughly sleepy, and then I left him and turned in on board my ship. At daylight I was awakened by a yelping of shrill voices, accompanied by a great commotion in the water, and the short, bullying blasts of a steam-whistle. Falk with his tug had come for me.

I began to dress. It was remarkable that the answering noise on board my ship together with the patter of feet above my head ceased suddenly. But I heard more remote guttural cries which seemed to express surprise and annoyance. Then the voice of my mate reached me howling expostulations to somebody at a distance. Other voices joined, apparently indignant; a chorus of something that sounded like abuse replied. Now and then the steam-whistle screeched.

Altogether that unnecessary uproar was distracting, but down there in my cabin I took it calmly. In another moment, I thought, I should be going down that wretched river, and in another week at the most I should be totally quit of the odious place and all the odious people in it.

Greatly cheered by the idea, I seized the hairbrushes and looking at myself in the glass began to use them. Suddenly a hush fell upon the noise outside, and I heard (the ports of my cabin were thrown open) – I heard a deep calm voice, not on board my ship, however, hailing resolutely in English, but with a strong foreign twang, 'Go ahead!'

There may be tides in the affairs of men which taken at the flood . . . and so on. Personally I am still on the look-out for that important turn. I am, however, afraid that most of us are fated to flounder for ever in the dead water of a pool whose shores are arid indeed. But I know that there are often in men's affairs unexpectedly – even irrationally – illuminating moments when an otherwise insignificant sound, perhaps only some perfectly commonplace gesture, suffices to reveal to us all the unreason, all the fatuous unreason, of our complacency. 'Go ahead' are not particularly striking words even when pronounced with a foreign accent; yet they petrified me in the very act of smiling at myself in the glass. And then, refusing to believe my ears, but already boiling with indignation, I ran out of the cabin and up on deck.

It was incredibly true. It was perfectly true. I had no eyes for anything but the *Diana*. It was she that was being taken away. She was already out of her berth and shooting athwart the river. 'The way this lunatic plucked that ship out is a caution,' said the awed voice of my mate close to my ear. 'Hey! Hallo! Falk! Hermann! What's this infernal trick?' I yelled in a fury.

Nobody heard me. Falk certainly could not hear me. His tug was turning at full speed away under the other bank. The wire hawser between her and the *Diana*, stretched as taut as a harpstring, vibrated alarmingly.

The high black craft careened over to the awful strain. A loud crack came out of her, followed by the tearing and splintering of wood. 'There!' said the awed voice in my ear. 'He's carried away their towing chock.' And then, with enthusiasm, 'Oh! Look! Look, sir! Look at them Dutchmen skipping out of the way on the forecastle. I hope to goodness he'll break a few of their shins before he's done with 'em.'

I yelled my vain protests. The rays of the rising sun coursing level along the plain warmed my back, but I was hot enough with rage. I could not have believed that a simple towing operation could suggest so plainly the idea of abduction, of rape. Falk was simply running off with the *Diana*.

The white tug careered out into the middle of the river. The red floats of her paddle-wheels revolving with mad rapidity tore up the whole reach into foam. The *Diana* in mid-stream waltzed round with as much grace as an old barn, and flew after her ravisher. Through the ragged fog of smoke driving headlong upon the water I had a glimpse of Falk's square motionless shoulders under a white hat as big as a cart-wheel, of his red face, his yellow staring eyes, his great beard. Instead of keeping a look-out ahead, he was deliberately turning his back on the river to glare at his tow. The tall heavy craft, never so used before in her life, seemed to have lost her senses; she took a wild sheer against her helm, and for a moment came straight at us, menacing and clumsy, like a runaway mountain. She piled up a streaming, hissing, boiling wave half-way up her blunt stem, my crew let out one great howl – and then we held our breaths. It was a near thing. But Falk had her! He had her in his clutch. I fancied I could hear the steel hawser ping as it surged across the *Diana*'s forecastle, with the hands on board of her bolting away from it in all directions. It was a near thing. Hermann, with his hair rumpled, in a snuffy flannel shirt and a pair of mustard-coloured trousers, had rushed to help with the wheel. I saw his terrified round face; I saw his very teeth uncovered by a sort of ghastly fixed grin; and in a great leaping tumult of water between the two ships the *Diana* whisked past so close that I could have flung a hairbrush at his head, for, it seems, I had kept them in my hands all the time. Meanwhile Mrs Hermann sat placidly on the skylight, with a woollen shawl on her shoulders. The excellent woman in response to my indignant gesticulations fluttered a handkerchief, nodding and smiling in the kindest way imaginable. The boys, only half-dressed, were jumping about the poop in great glee, displaying their gaudy braces; and Lena in a short scarlet petticoat, with peaked elbows and thin bare arms, nursed the rag-doll with devotion. The whole family passed before my sight as if dragged across a scene of unparalleled violence. The last I saw was Hermann's niece with the baby Hermann in her arms standing apart from the others. Magnificent in her close-fitting print frock, she displayed something so commanding in the manifest perfection of her figure that the sun seemed to be rising for her alone. The flood of light brought out the opulence of her form and the vigour of her youth in a glorifying way. She went by perfectly motionless and as if lost in meditation; only the hem of her skirt stirred in the draught; the sun rays broke on her sleek tawny hair; that bald-headed ruffian, Nicholas, was whacking her on the shoulder. I saw his tiny fat arm rise and fall in a workmanlike manner. And then the four cottage windows of the *Diana* came into view retreating swiftly down the river. The sashes were up, and one of the white calico curtains fluttered straight out like a streamer above the agitated water of the wake.

To be thus tricked out of one's turn was an unheard-of occurrence. In my agent's office, where I went to complain at once, they protested with apologies they couldn't understand how the mistake arose: but Schomberg, when I dropped in later to get some tiffin, though surprised to see me, was perfectly ready with an explanation. I found him seated at the end of a long narrow table, facing his wife – a scraggy little woman, with long ringlets and a blue tooth, who smiled abroad stupidly and looked frightened when you spoke to her. Between them a waggling punkah fanned twenty vacant cane-bottomed chairs and two rows of shiny plates. Three Chinamen in white jackets loafed with napkins in their hands around that desolation. Schomberg's pet *table-d'hôte* was not much of a success that day. He was feeding himself furiously and seemed to overflow with bitterness.

He began by ordering in a brutal voice the chops to be brought back for me, and turning in his chair: 'Mistake they told you? Not a bit of it! Don't you believe it for a moment, captain! Falk isn't a man to make mistakes unless on purpose.' His firm conviction was that Falk had been trying all along to curry favour on the cheap with Hermann. 'On the cheap – mind you! It doesn't cost him a cent to put that insult upon you, and Captain Hermann gets in a day ahead of your ship. Time's money! Eh? You are very friendly with Captain Hermann I believe, but a man is bound to be pleased at any little advantage he may get. Captain Hermann is a good businessman, and there's no such thing as a friend in business. Is there?' He leaned forward and began to cast stealthy glances as usual. 'But Falk is, and always was, a miserable fellow. I would despise him.'

I muttered, grumpily, that I had no particular respect for Falk.

'I would despise him,' he insisted, with an appearance of anxiety which would have amused me if I had not been fathoms deep in discontent. To a young man fairly conscientious and as well-meaning as only the young man can be, the current ill-usage of life comes with a peculiar cruelty. Youth that is fresh enough to believe in guilt, in innocence, and in itself, will always doubt whether it have not perchance deserved its fate. Sombre of mind and without appetite, I struggled with the chop while Mrs Schomberg sat with her everlasting stupid grin and Schomberg's talk gathered way like a slide of rubbish.

'Let me tell you. It's all about that girl. I don't know what Captain Hermann expects, but if he asked me I could tell him something about Falk. He's a miserable fellow. That man is a perfect slave. That's what I call him. A slave. Last year I started this *table d'hôte*, and sent cards out – you know. You think he had one meal in the house? Give the thing a trial? Not once. He has got hold now of a Madras cook – a blamed fraud that I hunted out of my cookhouse with a rattan. He was not fit to cook for white men. No, not for the white men's dogs either; but, see, any damned native that can boil a pot of rice is good enough for Mr Falk. Rice and a little fish he buys for a few cents from the fishing-boats outside is what he lives on. You would hardly credit it – eh? A white man, too . . .'

He wiped his lips, using the napkin with indignation, and looking at me. It flashed through my mind in the midst of my depression that if all the meat in the town was like these *table-d'hôte* chops, Falk wasn't so far wrong. I was on the point of saying this, but Schomberg's stare was intimidating. 'He's a vegetarian, perhaps,' I murmured instead.

'He's a miser. A miserable miser,' affirmed the hotel-keeper with great force. 'The meat here is not so good as at home – of course. And dear too. But look at me. I only charge a dollar for the tiffin, and one dollar and fifty cents for the dinner. Show me anything cheaper. Why am I doing it? There's little profit in this game. Falk wouldn't look at it. I do it for the sake of a lot of young white fellows here that hadn't a place where they could get a decent meal and eat it decently in good company. There's first-rate company always at my table.'

The convinced way he surveyed the empty chairs made me feel as if I had intruded upon a tiffin of ghostly Presences.

'A white man should eat like a white man, dash it all,' he burst out impetuously. 'Ought to eat meat, must eat meat. I manage to get meat for my patrons all the year round. Don't I? I am not catering for a dam' lot of coolies: Have another chop, captain . . . No? You, boy – take away!'

He threw himself back and waited grimly for the curry. The half-closed jalousies darkened the room pervaded by the smell of fresh whitewash: a swarm of flies buzzed and settled in turns, and poor Mrs Schomberg's smile seemed to express the quintessence of all the imbecility that had ever spoken, had ever breathed, had ever been fed on infamous buffalo meat within these bare walls. Schomberg did not open his lips till he was ready to thrust therein a spoonful of greasy rice. He rolled his eyes ridiculously before he swallowed the hot stuff, and only then broke out afresh.

'It is the most degrading thing. They take the dish up to the wheelhouse for him with a cover on it, and he shuts both the doors before he begins to eat. Fact! Must be ashamed of himself. Ask the engineer. He can't do without an engineer – don't you see – and as no respectable man can be expected to put up with such a table, he allows them fifteen dollars a month extra mess money. I assure you it is so! You just ask Mr Ferdinand da Costa. That's the engineer he has now. You may have seen him about my place, a delicate dark young man, with very fine eyes and a little moustache. He arrived here a year ago from Calcutta. Between you and me, I guess the money-lenders there must have been after him. He rushes here for a meal every chance he can get, for just please tell me what satisfaction is that for a well-educated young fellow to feed all alone in his cabin – like a wild beast? That's what Falk expects his engineers to put up with for fifteen dollars extra. And the rows on board every time a little smell of cooking gets about the deck! You wouldn't believe! The other day da Costa got the cook to fry a steak for him – a turtle steak it was too, not beef at all – and the fat caught or something. Young da Costa himself was telling me of it here in this room. "Mr Schomberg" – says he – "if I had let a cylinder cover blow off through the skylight by my negligence Captain Falk couldn't have been more savage. He frightened the cook so that he won't put anything on the fire for me now." Poor da Costa had tears in his eyes. Only try to put yourself in his place, captain: a sensitive, gentlemanly young fellow. Is he expected to eat his food raw? But that's your Falk all over. Ask anyone you like. I suppose the fifteen dollars extra he has to give keep on rankling – in there.'

And Schomberg tapped his manly breast. I sat half stunned by his irrelevant babble. Suddenly he gripped my forearm in an impressive and cautious manner, as if to lead me into a very cavern of confidence.

'It's nothing but enviousness,' he said in a lowered tone, which had a stimulating effect upon my wearied hearing. 'I don't suppose there is one person in this town that he isn't envious of. I tell you he's dangerous. Even I myself am not safe from him. I know for certain he tried to poison . . .'

'Oh, come now,' I cried, revolted.

'But I know for certain. The people themselves came and told me of it. He went about saying everywhere I was a worse pest to this town than the cholera. He had been talking against me ever since I opened this hotel. And he poisoned Captain Hermann's mind too. Last time the *Diana* was loading here Captain Hermann used to come in every day for a drink or a cigar. This time he hasn't been here twice in a week. How do you account for that?'

He squeezed my arm till he extorted from me some sort of mumble.

'He makes ten times the money I do. I've another hotel to fight against, and there is no other tug on the river. I am not in his way, am I? He wouldn't be fit to run an hotel if he tried. But that's just his nature. He can't bear to think I am making a living. I only hope it makes him properly wretched. He's like that in everything. He would like to keep a decent table well enough. But no – for the sake of a few cents. Can't do it. It's too much for him. That's what I call being a slave to it. But he's mean enough to kick up a row when his nose gets tickled a bit. See that? That just paints him. Miserly and envious. You can't account for it any other way. Can you? I have been studying him these three years.'

He was anxious I should assent to his theory. And indeed on thinking it over it would have been plausible enough if there hadn't been always the essential falseness of irresponsibility in Schomberg's chatter. However, I was not disposed to investigate the psychology of Falk. I was engaged just then in eating despondently a piece of stale Dutch cheese, being too much crushed to care what I swallowed myself, let alone bothering my head about Falk's ideas of gastronomy. I could expect from their study no clue to his conduct in matters of business, which seemed to me totally unrestrained by morality or even by the commonest sort of decency. How insignificant and contemptible I must appear, for the fellow to dare treat me like this – I reflected suddenly, writhing in silent agony. And I consigned Falk and all his peculiarities to the devil with so much mental fervour as to forget Schomberg's existence, till he grabbed my arm urgently. 'Well, you may think and think till every hair of your head falls off, captain; but you can't explain it in any other way.'

For the sake of peace and quietness I admitted hurriedly that I couldn't; persuaded that now he would leave off. But the only result was to make his moist face shine with the pride of cunning. He removed his hand for a moment to scare a black mass of flies off the sugar-basin, and caught hold of my arm again.

'To be sure. And in the same way everybody is aware he would like to get married. Only he can't. Let me quote you an instance. Well, two years ago a Miss Vanlo, a very ladylike girl, came from home to keep house for her brother, Fred, who had an engineering shop for small repairs by the water side. Suddenly Falk takes to going up to their bungalow after dinner and sitting for hours in the verandah saying nothing. The poor girl couldn't tell for the life of her what to do with such a man, so she would keep on playing the piano and singing to him evening after evening till she was ready to drop. And it wasn't as if she had been a strong young woman either. She was thirty, and the climate had been playing the deuce with her. Then – don't you know – Fred had to sit up with them for propriety, and during whole weeks on end never got a single chance to get to bed before midnight. That was not pleasant for a tired man – was it? And besides Fred had worries then because his shop didn't pay and he was dropping money fast. He just longed to get away from here and try his luck somewhere else, but for the sake of his sister he hung on and on till he ran himself into debt over his ears – I can tell you. I, myself, could show a handful of his chits for meals and drinks in my drawer. I could never find out tho' where he found all the money at last. Can't be but he must have got something out of that brother of his, a coal merchant in Port Said. Anyhow he paid everybody before he left, but the girl nearly broke her heart. Disappointment, of course, and at her age, don't you know ... Mrs

Schomberg here was very friendly with her, and she could tell you. Awful despair. Fainting fits. It was a scandal. A notorious scandal. To that extent that old Mr Siegers – not your present charterer, but Mr Siegers the father, the old gentleman who retired from business on a fortune and got buried at sea going home, *he* had to interview Falk in his private office. He was a man who could speak like a Dutch Uncle, and, besides, Messrs Siegers had been helping Falk with a good bit of money from the start. In fact you may say they made him as far as that goes. It so happened that just at the time he turned up here, their firm was chartering a lot of sailing-ships every year, and it suited their business that there should be good towing facilities on the river. See? . . . Well – there's always an ear at the keyhole – isn't there? In fact,' he lowered his tone confidentially, 'in this case it was a good friend of mine; a man you can see here any evening; only they conversed rather low. Anyhow my friend's certain that Falk was trying to make all sorts of excuses, and old Mr Siegers was coughing a lot. And yet Falk wanted all the time to be married too. Why! It's notorious the man has been longing for years to make a home for himself. Only he can't face the expense. When it comes to putting his hand in his pocket – it chokes him off. That's the truth and no other. I've always said so, and everybody agrees with me by this time. What do you think of that – eh?'

He appealed confidently to my indignation, but having a mind to annoy him I remarked, 'that it seemed to me very pitiful – if true'.

He bounced in his chair as if I had run a pin into him. I don't know what he might have said, only at that moment we heard through the half-open door of the billiard-room the footsteps of two men entering from the verandah, a murmur of two voices; at the sharp tapping of a coin on a table Mrs Schomberg half rose irresolutely. 'Sit still,' he hissed at her, and then, in an hospitable, jovial tone, contrasting amazingly with the angry glance that had made his wife sink in her chair, he cried very loud: 'Tiffin still going on in here, gentlemen.'

There was no answer, but the voices dropped suddenly. The head Chinaman went out. We heard the clink of ice in the glasses, pouring sounds, the shuffling of feet, the scraping of chairs. Schomberg, after wondering in a low mutter who the devil could be there at this time of the day, got up napkin in hand to peep through the doorway cautiously. He retreated rapidly on tiptoe, and whispering behind his hand informed me that it was Falk, Falk himself who was in there, and, what's more, he had Captain Hermann with him.

The return of the tug from the outer Roads was unexpected but possible, for Falk had taken away the *Diana* at half-past five, and it was now two o'clock. Schomberg wished me to observe that neither of these men would spend a dollar on a tiffin, which they must have wanted. But by the time I was ready to leave the dining-room Falk had gone. I heard the last of his big boots on the planks of the verandah. Hermann was sitting quite alone in the large, wooden room with the two lifeless billiard tables shrouded in striped covers, mopping his face diligently. He wore his best go-ashore clothes, a stiff collar, black coat, large white waistcoat, grey trousers. A white cotton sunshade with a cane handle reposed between his legs, his side whiskers were neatly brushed, his chin had been freshly shaved; and he only distantly resembled the dishevelled and terrified man in a snuffy night shirt and ignoble old trousers I had seen in the morning hanging on to the wheel of the *Diana*.

He gave a start at my entrance, and addressed me at once in some confusion, but with genuine eagerness. He was anxious to make it clear he had nothing to do with what he called the 'tam' pizness' of the morning. It was most inconvenient. He had reckoned upon another day up in town to settle his bills and sign certain papers. There were also some few stores to come, and sundry pieces of 'my ironwork', as he called it quaintly, landed for repairs, had been left behind. Now he would have to hire a native boat to take all this out to the ship. It would cost five or six dollars perhaps. He had had no warning from Falk. Nothing . . . He hit the table with his dumpy fist . . . Der verfluchte Kerl came in the morning like a 'tam' ropper', making a great noise, and took him away. His mate was not prepared, his ship was moored fast – he protested it was shameful to come upon a man in that way. Shameful! Yet such was the power Falk had on the river that when I suggested in a chilling tone that he might have simply refused to have his ship moved, Hermann was quite startled at the idea. I never realised so well before that this is an age of steam. The exclusive possession of a marine boiler had given Falk the whip hand of us all. Hermann recovering, put it to me appealingly that I knew very well how unsafe it was to contradict that fellow. At this I only smiled distantly.

'Der Kerl!' he cried. He was sorry he had not refused. He was indeed. The damage! The damage! What for all that damage! There was no occasion for damage. Did I know how much damage he had done? It gave me a certain satisfaction to tell him that I had heard his old wagon of a ship crack fore and aft as she went by. 'You passed close enough to me,' I added significantly.

He threw both his hands up to heaven at the recollection. One of them grasped by the middle the white parasol, and he resembled curiously a caricature of a shopkeeping citizen in one of his own German comic papers. 'Ach! That was dangerous,' he cried. I was amused. But directly he added with an appearance of simplicity, 'The side of your iron ship would have been crushed in like – like this matchbox.'

'Would it?' I growled, much less amused now; but by the time I had decided that this remark was not meant for a dig at me he had worked himself into a high state of resentfulness against Falk. The inconvenience, the damage, the expense! Gottferdam! Devil take the fellow. Behind the bar Schomberg with a cigar in his teeth, pretended to be writing with a pencil on a large sheet of paper; and as Hermann's excitement increased it made me comfortingly aware of my own calmness and superiority. But it occurred to me while I listened to his revilings, that after all the good man had come up in the tug. There perhaps – since he must come to town – he had no option. But evidently he had had a drink with Falk, either accepted or offered. How was that? So I checked him by saying loftily that I hoped he would make Falk pay for every penny of the damage.

'That's it! That's it! Go for him,' called out Schomberg from the bar, flinging his pencil down and rubbing his hands.

We ignored his noise. But Hermann's excitement suddenly went off the boil as when you remove a saucepan from the fire. I urged on his consideration that he had done now with Falk and Falk's confounded tug. He, Hermann, would not, perhaps, turn up again in this part of the world for years to come, since he was going to sell the *Diana* at the end of this very trip ('Go home passenger in a mail boat,' he murmured mechanically). He was therefore safe from Falk's malice. All he had to do was to race off to his consignees and stop payment of the towage bill before Falk had the time to get in and lift the money.

Nothing could have been less in the spirit of my advice than the thoughtful way in which he set about to make his parasol stay propped against the edge of the table.

While I watched his concentrated efforts with astonishment he threw at me one or two perplexed, half-shy glances. Then he sat down. 'That's all very well,' he said reflectively.

It cannot be doubted that the man had been thrown off his balance by being hauled out of the harbour against his wish. His stolidity had been profoundly stirred, else he would never have made up his mind to ask me unexpectedly whether I had not remarked that Falk had been casting eyes upon his niece. 'No more than myself,' I answered with literal truth. The girl was of the sort one necessarily casts eyes at in a sense. She made no noise, but she filled most satisfactorily a good bit of space.

'But you, captain, are not the same kind of man,' observed Hermann.

I was not, I am happy to say, in a position to deny this. 'What about the lady?' I could not help asking. At this he gazed for a time into my face, earnestly, and made as if to change the subject. I heard him beginning to mutter something unexpected, about his children growing old enough to require schooling. He would have to leave them ashore with their grandmother when he took up that new command he expected to get in Germany.

This constant harping on his domestic arrangements was funny. I suppose it must have been like the prospect of a complete alteration in his life. An epoch. He was going, too, to part with the *Diana*! He had served in her for years. He had inherited her. From an uncle, if I remember rightly. And the future loomed big before him, occupying his thought exclusively with all its aspects as on the eve of a venturesome enterprise. He sat there frowning and biting his lip, and suddenly he began to fume and fret.

I discovered to my momentary amusement that he seemed to imagine I could, should or ought, have caused Falk in some way to pronounce himself. Such a hope was incomprehensible, but funny. Then the contact with all this foolishness irritated me. I said crossly that I had seen no symptoms, but if there were any – since he, Hermann, was so sure – then it was still worse. What pleasure Falk found in humbugging people in just that way I couldn't say. It was, however, my solemn duty to warn him. It had lately, I said, come to my knowledge that there was a man (not a very long time ago either) who had been taken in just like this.

All this passed in undertones, and at this point Schomberg, exasperated at our secrecy, went out of the room slamming the door with a crash that positively lifted us in our chairs. This, or else what I had said, huffed my Hermann. He supposed, with a contemptuous toss of his head towards the door which trembled yet, that I had got hold of some of that man's silly tales. It looked, indeed, as though his mind had been thoroughly poisoned against Schomberg. 'His tales were – they were,' he repeated, seeking for the word – 'trash.' They were trash, he reiterated and moreover I was young yet . . .

This horrid aspersion (I regret I am no longer exposed to that sort of insult) made me huffy too. I felt ready in my own mind to back up every assertion of Schomberg's and on any subject. In a moment, devil only knows why, Hermann and I were looking at each other most inimically. He caught up his hat without more ado and I gave myself the pleasure of calling after him: 'Take my advice and make Falk pay for breaking up your ship. You aren't likely to get anything else out of him.'

When I got on board my ship later on, the old mate, who was very full of the events of the morning, remarked: 'I saw the tug coming back from the outer Roads just before two p.m.' (He never by any chance used the words morning or afternoon. Always p.m. or a.m., log-book style.) 'Smart work that. Man's always in a state of hurry. He's a regular chucker-out, ain't he, sir? There's a few pubs I know of in the East End of London that would be all the better for one of his sort around the bar.' He chuckled at his joke. 'A regular chucker-out. Now he has fired out that Dutchman head over heels, I suppose our turn's coming tomorrow morning.'

We were all on deck at break of day (even the sick – poor devils – had crawled out) ready to cast off in the twinkling of an eye. Nothing came. Falk did not come. At last, when I began to think that probably something had gone wrong in his engine-room, we perceived the tug going by, full pelt, down the river, as if we hadn't existed. For a moment I entertained the wild notion that he was going to turn round in the next reach. Afterwards I watched his smoke appear above the plain, now here, now there, according to the windings of the river. It disappeared. Then without a word I went down to breakfast. I just simply went down to breakfast.

Not one of us uttered a sound till the mate, after imbibing – by means of suction out of a saucer – his second cup of tea, exclaimed: 'Where the devil is the man gone to?'

'Courting!' I shouted, with such a fiendish laugh that the old chap didn't venture to open his lips any more.

I started to the office perfectly calm. Calm with excessive rage. Evidently they knew all about it already, and they treated me to a show of consternation. The manager, a soft-footed, immensely obese man, breathing short, got up to meet me, while all round the room the young clerks, bending over the papers on their desks, cast upward glances in my direction. The fat man, without waiting for my complaint, wheezing heavily and in a tone as if he himself were incredulous, conveyed to me the news that Falk – Captain Falk – had declined – had absolutely declined – to tow my ship – to have anything to do with my ship – this day or any other day. Never!

I did my best to preserve a cool appearance, but, all the same, I must have shown how much taken aback I was. We were talking in the middle of the room. Suddenly behind my back some ass blew his nose with great force, and at the same time another quill-driver jumped up and went out on the landing hastily. It occurred to me I was cutting a foolish figure there. I demanded angrily to see the principal in his private room.

The skin of Mr Siegers' head showed dead white between the iron-grey streaks of hair lying plastered crosswise from ear to ear over the top of his skull in the manner of a bandage. His narrow sunken face was of a uniform and permanent terracotta colour, like a piece of pottery. He was sickly, thin, and short, with wrists like a boy of ten. But from that debile body there issued a bullying voice, tremendously loud, harsh and resonant, as if produced by some powerful mechanical contrivance in the nature of a fog-horn. I do not know what he did with it in the private life of his home, but in the larger sphere of business it presented the advantage of overcoming arguments without the slightest mental effort, by the mere volume of sound. We had had several passages of arms. It took me all I knew to guard the interests of my owners – whom, *nota bene*, I had never seen – while Siegers (who had made their acquaintance some years before, during a business tour in Australia) pretended to the knowledge of their innermost minds, and, in the character of 'our very good friends', threw them perpetually at my head.

He looked at me with a jaundiced eye (there was no love lost between us), and declared at once that it was strange, very strange. His pronunciation of English was so extravagant that I can't even attempt to reproduce it. For instance, he said 'Fferie strantch'. Combined with the bellowing intonation it made the language of one's childhood sound weirdly startling, and even if considered purely as a kind of unmeaning noise it filled you with astonishment at first. 'They had,' he continued, 'been acquainted with Captain Falk for very many years, and never had any reason . . .'

'That's why I come to you, of course,' I interrupted. 'I've the right to know the meaning of this infernal nonsense.' In the half-light of the room, which was greenish, because of the tree-tops screening the window, I saw him writhe his meagre shoulders. It came into my head, as disconnected ideas will come at all sorts of times into one's head, that this, most likely, was the very room where, if the tale were true, Falk had been lectured by Mr Siegers, the father. Mr Siegers' (the son's) overwhelming voice, in brassy blasts, as though he had been trying to articulate his words through a trombone, was expressing his great regret at conduct characterised by a very marked want of discretion . . . As I lived I was being lectured too! His deafening gibberish was difficult to follow, but it was *my* conduct – mine! – that . . . Damn! I wasn't going to stand this.

'What on earth are you driving at?' I asked in a passion. I put my hat on my head (he never offered a seat to anybody), and as he seemed for the moment struck dumb by my irreverence, I turned my back on him and marched out. His vocal arrangements blared after me a few threats of coming down on the ship for the demurrage of the lighters, and all the other expenses consequent upon the delays arising from my frivolity.

Once outside in the sunshine my head swam. It was no longer a question of mere delay. I perceived myself involved in hopeless and humiliating absurdities that were leading me to something very like a disaster. 'Let us be calm,' I muttered to myself, and ran into the shade of a leprous wall. From that short side-street I could see the broad main thoroughfare, ruinous and gay, running away, away between stretches of decaying masonry, bamboo fences, ranges of arcades of brick and plaster, hovels of lath and mud, lofty temple gates of carved timber, huts of rotten mats – an immensely wide thoroughfare, loosely packed as far as the eye could reach with a barefooted and brown multitude paddling ankle deep in the dust. For a moment I felt myself about to go out of my mind with worry and desperation.

Some allowance must be made for the feelings of a young man new to responsibility. I thought of my crew. Half of them were ill, and I really began to think that some of them would end by dying on board if I couldn't get them out to sea soon. Obviously I should have to take my ship down the river, either working under canvas or dredging with the anchor down; operations which, in common with many modern sailors, I only knew theoretically. And I almost shrank from undertaking them shorthanded and without local knowledge of the river bed, which is so necessary for the confident handling of the ship. There were no pilots, no beacons, no buoys of any sort; but there was a very devil of a current for anybody to see, no end of shoal places, and at least two obviously awkward turns of the channel between me and the sea. But how dangerous these turns were I could not tell. I didn't even know what my ship was capable of! I had never handled her in my life. A misunderstanding between a man and his ship, in a difficult river with no room to make it up, is bound to end in trouble for the man. On the other hand, it must be owned I had not much reason to count upon a general run of good luck. And suppose I had the misfortune to pile her up high and dry on some beastly shoal? That would have been the final undoing of that voyage. It was plain that if Falk refused to tow me out he would also refuse to pull me off. This meant – what? A day lost at the very best; but more likely a whole fortnight of frizzling on some pestilential mudflat, of desperate work, of discharging cargo; more than likely it meant borrowing money at an exorbitant rate of interest – from the

Siegers' gang too at that. They were a power in the port. And that elderly seaman of mine, Gambril, had looked pretty ghastly when I went forward to dose him with quinine that morning. *He* would certainly die – not to speak of two or three others that seemed nearly as bad, and of the rest of them just ready to catch any tropical disease going. Horror, ruin and everlasting remorse. And no help. None. I had fallen amongst a lot of unfriendly lunatics!

At any rate, if I must take my ship down myself it was my duty to procure if possible some local knowledge. But that was not easy. The only person I could think of for that service was a certain Johnson, formerly captain of a country ship, but now spliced to a country wife and gone utterly to the bad. I had only heard of him in the vaguest way, as living concealed in the thick of two hundred thousand natives, and only emerging into the light of day for the purpose of hunting up some brandy. I had a notion that if I could lay my hands on him I would sober him on board my ship and use him for a pilot. Better than nothing. Once a sailor always a sailor – and he had known the river for years. But in our Consulate (where I arrived dripping after a sharp walk) they could tell me nothing. The excellent young men on the staff, though willing to help me, belonged to a sphere of the white colony for which that sort of Johnson does not exist. Their suggestion was that I should hunt the man up myself with the help of the Consulate's constable – an ex-sergeant-major of a regiment of Hussars.

This man, whose usual duty apparently consisted in sitting behind a little table in an outer room of Consular offices, when ordered to assist me in my search for Johnson displayed lots of energy and a marvellous amount of local knowledge of a sort. But he did not conceal an immense and sceptical contempt for the whole business. We explored together on that afternoon an infinity of infamous grog shops, gambling dens, opium dens. We walked up narrow lanes where our gharry – a tiny box of a thing on wheels, attached to a jibbing Burmah pony – could by no means have passed. The constable seemed to be on terms of scornful intimacy with Maltese, with Eurasians, with Chinamen, with Klings, and with the sweepers attached to a temple, with whom he talked at the gate. We interviewed also through a grating in a mud wall closing a blind alley an immensely corpulent Italian, who, the ex-sergeant-major remarked to me perfunctorily, had 'killed another man last year'. Thereupon he addressed him as 'Antonio' and 'Old Buck', though that bloated carcase, apparently more than half filling the sort of cell wherein it sat, recalled rather a fat pig in a stye. Familiar and never unbending, the sergeant chucked – absolutely chucked – under the chin a horribly wrinkled and shrivelled old hag propped on a stick, who had volunteered some sort of information: and with the same stolid face he kept up an animated conversation with the groups of swathed brown women, who sat smoking cheroots on the doorsteps of a long range of clay hovels. We got out of the gharry and clambered into dwellings airy like packing crates, or descended into places sinister like cellars. We got in, we drove on, we got out again for the sole purpose, as it seemed, of looking behind a heap of rubble.

The sun declined; my companion was curt and sardonic in his answers, but it appears we were just missing Johnson all along. At last our conveyance stopped once more with a jerk, and the driver jumping down opened the door.

A black mudhole blocked the lane. A mound of garbage crowned with the dead body of a dog arrested us not. An empty Australian beef tin bounded cheerily before the toe of my boot. Suddenly we clambered through a gap in a prickly fence . . .

It was a very clean native compound: and the big native woman, with bare brown legs as thick as bedposts, pursuing on all fours a silver dollar that came rolling out from somewhere, was Mrs Johnson herself. 'Your man's at home,' said the ex-sergeant, and stepped aside in complete and marked indifference to anything that might follow. Johnson – at home – stood with his back to a native house built on posts and with its walls made of mats. In his left hand he held a banana. Out of the right he dealt another dollar into space. The woman captured this one on the wing, and there and then plumped down on the ground to look at us with greater comfort.

'My man' was sallow of face, grizzled, unshaven, muddy on elbows and back; where the seams of his serge coat yawned you could see his white nakedness. The vestiges of a paper collar encircled his neck. He looked at us with a grave, swaying surprise. 'Where do you come from?' he asked. My heart sank. How could I have been stupid enough to waste energy and time for this?

But having already gone so far I approached a little nearer and declared the purpose of my visit. He would have to come at once with me, sleep on board my ship, and tomorrow, with the first of the ebb, he would give me his assistance in getting my ship down to the sea, without steam. A six-hundred-ton barque, drawing nine feet aft. I proposed to give him eighteen dollars for his local knowledge; and all the time I was speaking he kept on considering attentively the various aspects of the banana, holding first one side up to his eye, then the other.

'You've forgotten to apologise,' he said at last with extreme precision. 'Not being a gentleman yourself, you don't know apparently when you intrude upon a gentleman. I am one. I wish you to understand that when I am in funds I don't work, and now . . .'

I would have pronounced him perfectly sober had he not paused in great concern to try and brush a hole off the knee of his trousers.

'I have money – and friends. Every gentleman has. Perhaps you would like to know my friend? His name is Falk. You could borrow some money. Try to remember. F–A–L–K. Falk.' Abruptly his tone changed. 'A noble heart,' he said muzzily.

'Has Falk been giving you some money?' I asked, appalled by the detailed finish of the dark plot.

'Lent me, my good man, not given me,' he corrected suavely. 'Met me taking the air last evening, and being as usual anxious to oblige – Hadn't you better go to the devil out of my compound?'

And upon this, without other warning, he let fly with the banana, which missed my head and took the constable just under the left eye. He rushed at the miserable Johnson, stammering with fury. They fell . . . But why dwell on the wretchedness, the breathlessness, the degradation, the senselessness, the weariness, the ridicule and humiliation and – and – the perspiration, of these moments? I dragged the ex-hussar off. He was like a wild beast. It seems he had been greatly annoyed at losing his free afternoon on my account. The garden of his bungalow required his personal attention, and at the slight blow of the banana the brute in him had broken loose. We left Johnson on his back still black in the face, but beginning to kick feebly. Meantime, the big woman had remained sitting on the ground, apparently paralysed with extreme terror.

For half an hour we jolted inside our rolling box, side by side, in profound silence. The ex-sergeant was busy staunching the blood of a long scratch on his cheek. 'I hope you're satisfied,' he said suddenly. 'That's what comes of all that tomfool business. If you hadn't quarrelled with that tugboat skipper over some girl or other, all this wouldn't have happened.'

'You heard *that* story?' I said.

'Of course I heard. And I shouldn't wonder if the Consul-General himself doesn't come to hear of it. How am I to go before him tomorrow with that thing on my cheek – I want to know. It's *you* who ought to have got this!'

After that, till the gharry stopped and he jumped out without leave-taking, he swore to himself steadily, horribly; muttering great, purposeful, trooper oaths, to which the worst a sailor can do is like the prattle of a child. For my part I had just the strength to crawl into Schomberg's coffee-room, where I wrote at a little table a note to the mate instructing him to get everything ready for dropping down the river next day. I couldn't face my ship. Well! she had a clever sort of skipper and no mistake – poor thing! What a horrid mess! I took my head between my hands. At times the obviousness of my innocence would reduce me to despair. What had I done? If I had done something to bring about the situation I should at least have learned not to do it again. But I felt guiltless to the point of imbecility. The room was empty yet; only Schomberg prowled round me goggle-eyed and with a sort of awed respectful curiosity. No doubt he had set the story going himself; but he was a good-hearted chap, and I am really persuaded he participated in all my troubles. He did what he could for me. He ranged aside the heavy matchstand, set a chair straight, pushed a spittoon slightly with his foot – as you show small attentions to a friend under a great sorrow – sighed, and at last, unable to hold his tongue: 'Well! I warned you, captain. That's what comes of running your head against Mr Falk. Man'll stick at nothing.'

I sat without stirring, and after surveying me with a sort of commiseration in his eyes, he burst out in a hoarse whisper: 'But for a fine lump of a girl, she's a fine lump of a girl.' He made a loud smacking noise with his thick lips. 'The finest lump of a girl that I ever . . . ' he was going on with great unction, but for some reason or other broke off. I fancied myself throwing something at his head. 'I don't blame you, captain. Hang me if I do,' he said with a patronising air.

'Thank you,' I said resignedly. It was no use fighting against this false fate. I don't know even if I was sure myself where the truth of the matter began. The conviction that it would end disastrously had been driven into me by all the successive shocks my sense of security had received. I began to ascribe an extraordinary potency to agents in themselves powerless. It was as if Schomberg's baseless gossip had the power to bring about the thing itself or the abstract enmity of Falk could put my ship ashore.

I have already explained how fatal this last would have been. For my further action, my youth, my inexperience, my very real concern for the health of my crew must be my excuse. The action itself, when it came, was purely impulsive. It was set in movement quite undiplomatically and simply by Falk's appearance in the doorway of the coffee-room.

The room was full by then and buzzing with voices. I had been looked at with curiosity by everyone, but how am I to describe the sensation produced by the appearance of Falk himself blocking the doorway? The tension of expectation could be measured by the profundity of the silence that fell upon the very click of the billiard balls. As to Schomberg, he looked extremely frightened; he hated mortally any sort of row (*fracas* he called it) in his establishment. *Fracas* was bad for business, he affirmed; but, in truth, this specimen of portly, middle-aged manhood was of a timid disposition. I don't know what, considering my presence in the place, they all hoped would come of it. A sort of stag fight, perhaps. Or they may have supposed Falk had come in only to annihilate me completely. As a matter of fact, Falk had come in because Hermann had asked him to enquire after the precious white cotton parasol which, in the worry and excitement of the previous day, he had forgotten at the table where we had held our little discussion.

It was this that gave me my opportunity. I don't think I would have gone to seek Falk out. No. I don't think so. There are limits. But there was an opportunity and I seized it – I have already tried to explain why. Now I will merely state that, in my opinion, to get his sickly crew into the sea air and secure a quick despatch for his ship a skipper would be justified in going to any length, short of absolute crime. He should put his pride in his pocket; he may accept confidences; he must explain his innocence as if it were a sin; he may take advantage of misconceptions, of desires and of weaknesses; he ought to conceal his horror and other emotions, and, if the fate of a human being, and that human being a magnificent young girl, is strangely involved – why, he should contemplate that fate (whatever it might seem to be) without turning a hair. And all these things I have done: the explaining, the listening, the pretending – even to the discretion – and nobody, not even Hermann's niece, I believe, need throw stones at me now. Schomberg at all events needn't, since from first to last, I am happy to say, there was not the slightest '*fracas*'.

Overcoming a nervous contraction of the windpipe, I had managed to exclaim 'Captain Falk!' His start of surprise was perfectly genuine, but afterwards he neither smiled nor scowled. He simply waited. Then, when I had said, 'I must have a talk with you,' and had pointed to a chair at my table, he moved up to me, though he didn't sit down. Schomberg, however, with a long tumbler in his hand, was making towards us prudently, and I discovered then the only sign of weakness in Falk. He had for Schomberg a repulsion resembling that sort of physical fear some people experience at the sight of a toad. Perhaps to a man so essentially and silently concentrated upon himself (though he could talk well enough, as I was to find out presently) the other's irrepressible loquacity, embracing every human being within range of the tongue, might have appeared unnatural, disgusting, and monstrous. He suddenly gave signs of restiveness – positively like a horse about to rear, and, muttering hurriedly as if in great pain, 'No. I can't stand that fellow,' seemed ready to bolt. This weakness of his gave me the advantage at the very start. 'Verandah,' I suggested, as if rendering him a service, and walked him out by the arm. We stumbled over a few chairs; we had the feeling of open space before us, and felt the fresh breath of the river – fresh, but tainted. The Chinese theatres across the water made, in the sparsely twinkling masses of gloom an Eastern town presents at night, blazing centres of light, and of a distant and howling uproar. I felt him become suddenly tractable again like an animal, like a good-tempered horse when the object that scares him is removed. Yes. I felt in the darkness there how tractable he was, without my conviction of his inflexibility – tenacity, rather, perhaps – being in the least weakened. His very arm abandoning itself to my grasp was as hard as marble – like a limb of iron. But I heard a tumultuous scuffling of boot-soles within. The unspeakable idiots inside were crowding to the windows, climbing over each other's backs behind the blinds, billiard cues and all. Somebody broke a window-pane, and with the sound of falling glass, so suggestive of riot and devastation, Schomberg reeled out after us in a state of funk which had prevented his parting with his brandy and soda. He must have trembled like an aspen leaf. The piece of ice in the long tumbler he held in his hand tinkled with an effect of chattering teeth. 'I beg you, gentlemen,' he expostulated thickly. 'Come! Really, now, I must insist . . .'

How proud I am of my presence of mind! 'Hallo,' I said instantly in a loud and naïve tone, 'somebody's breaking your windows, Schomberg. Would you please tell one of your boys to bring out here a pack of cards and a couple of lights? And two long drinks. Will you?'

To receive an order soothed him at once. It was business. 'Certainly,' he said in an immensely relieved tone. The night was rainy, with wandering gusts of wind, and while we waited for the candles Falk said, as if to justify his panic, 'I don't interfere in anybody's business. I don't give any occasion for talk. I am a respectable man. But this fellow is always making out something wrong, and can never rest till he gets somebody to believe him.'

This was the first of my knowledge of Falk. This desire of respectability, of being like everybody else, was the only recognition he vouchsafed to the organisation of mankind. For the rest he might have been the member of a herd, not of a society. Self-preservation was his only concern. Not selfishness, but mere self-preservation. Selfishness presupposes consciousness, choice, the presence of other men; but his instinct acted as though he were the last of mankind nursing that law like the only spark of a sacred fire. I don't mean to say that living naked in a cavern would have satisfied him. Obviously he was the creature of the conditions to which he was born. No doubt self-preservation meant also the preservation of these conditions. But essentially it meant something much more simple, natural, and powerful. How shall I express it? It meant the preservation of the five senses of his body – let us say – taking it in its narrowest as well as in its widest meaning. I think you will admit before long the justice of this judgement. However, as we stood there together in the dark verandah I had judged nothing as yet – and I had no desire to judge – which is an idle practice anyhow. The light was long in coming.

'Of course,' I said in a tone of mutual understanding, 'it isn't exactly a game of cards I want with you.'

I saw him draw his hands down his face – the vague stir of the passionate and meaningless gesture; but he waited in silent patience. It was only when the lights had been brought out that he opened his lips. I understood his mumble to mean that 'he didn't know any game'.

'Like this, Schomberg and all the other fools will have to keep off,' I said tearing open the pack. 'Have you heard that we are universally supposed to be quarrelling about a girl? You know who – of course. I am really ashamed to ask, but is it possible that you do me the honour to think me dangerous?'

As I said these words I felt how absurd it was and also I felt flattered – for, really, what else could it be? His answer, spoken in his usual dispassionate undertone, made it clear that it was so, but not precisely as flattering as I supposed. He thought me dangerous with Hermann, more than with the girl herself; but, as to quarrelling, I saw at once how inappropriate the word was. We had no quarrel. Natural forces are not quarrelsome. You can't quarrel with the wind that inconveniences and humiliates you by blowing off your hat in a street full of people. He had no quarrel with me. Neither would a boulder, falling on my head, have had. He fell upon me in accordance with the law by which he was moved – not of gravitation, like a detached stone, but of self-preservation. Of course this is giving it a rather wide interpretation. Strictly speaking, he had existed and could have existed without being married. Yet he told me that he had found it more and more difficult to live alone. Yes. He told me this in his low, careless voice, to such a pitch of confidence had we arrived at the end of half an hour.

It took me just about that time to convince him that I had never dreamed of marrying Hermann's niece. Could any necessity have been more extravagant?

And the difficulty was the greater because he was so hard hit that he couldn't imagine anybody being able to remain in a state of indifference. Any man with eyes in his head, he seemed to think, could not help coveting so much bodily magnificence. This profound belief was conveyed by the manner he listened sitting sideways to the table and playing absently with a few cards I had dealt to him at random. And the more I saw into him the more I saw of him. The wind swayed the lights so that his sunburnt face, whiskered to the eyes, seemed to successively flicker crimson at me and to go out. I saw the extraordinary breadth of the high cheek-bones, the perpendicular style of the features, the massive forehead, steep like a cliff, denuded at the top, largely uncovered at the temples. The fact is I had never before seen him without his hat; but now, as if my fervour had made him hot, he had taken it off and laid it gently on the floor. Something peculiar in the shape and setting of his yellow eyes gave them the provoking silent intensity which characterised his glance. But the face was thin, furrowed, worn; I discovered that through the bush of his hair, as you may detect the gnarled shape of a tree trunk lost in a dense undergrowth. These overgrown cheeks were sunken. It was an anchorite's bony head fitted with a Capuchin's beard and adjusted to a herculean body. I don't mean athletic. Hercules, I take it, was not an athlete. He was a strong man, susceptible to female charms, and not afraid of dirt. And thus with Falk, who was a strong man. He was extremely strong, just as the girl (since I must think of them together) was magnificently attractive by the masterful power of flesh and blood, expressed in shape, in size, in attitude – that is, by a straight appeal to the senses. His mind meantime, preoccupied with respectability, quailed before Schomberg's tongue and seemed absolutely impervious to my protestations; and I went so far as to protest that I would just as soon think of marrying my mother's (dear old lady!) faithful female cook as Hermann's niece. Sooner, I protested, in my desperation, much sooner; but it did not appear that he saw anything out-rageous in the proposition, and in his sceptical immobility he seemed to nurse the argument that at all events the cook was very, very far away. It must be said that, just before, I had gone wrong by appealing to the evidence of my manner whenever I called on board the *Diana*. I had never attempted to approach the girl, or to speak to her, or even to look at her in any marked way. Nothing could be clearer. But, as his own idea of – let us say – courting, seemed to consist precisely in sitting silently for hours in the vicinity of the beloved object, that line of argument inspired him with distrust. Staring down his extended legs he let out a grunt – as much as to say, 'That's all very fine, but you can't throw dust in *my* eyes.'

At last I was exasperated into saying, 'Why don't you put the matter at rest by talking to Hermann?' and I added sneeringly: 'You don't expect me perhaps to speak for you?'

To this he said, very loud for him, 'Would you?'

And for the first time he lifted his head to look at me with wonder and incredulity. He lifted his head so sharply that there could be no mistake. I had touched a spring. I saw the whole extent of my opportunity, and could hardly believe in it.

'Why. Speak to . . . Well, of course,' I proceeded very slowly, watching him with great attention, for, on my word, I feared a joke. 'Not, perhaps, to the young lady herself. I can't speak German, you know. But . . .'

He interrupted me with the earnest assurance that Hermann had the highest opinion of me; and at once I felt the need for the greatest possible diplomacy at this juncture. So I demurred just enough to draw him on. Falk sat up, but except for a very noticeable enlargement of the pupils, till the irises of his eyes were reduced to two narrow yellow rings, his face, I should judge, was incapable of expressing excitement. 'Oh, yes! Hermann did have the greatest . . .'

'Take up your cards. Here's Schomberg peeping at us through the blind!' I said.

We went through the motions of what might have been a game of écarté. Presently the intolerable scandalmonger withdrew, probably to inform the people in the billiard-room that we two were gambling on the verandah like mad.

We were not gambling, but it was a game; a game in which I felt I held the winning cards. The stake, roughly speaking, was the success of the voyage – for me; and he, I apprehended, had nothing to lose. Our intimacy matured rapidly, and before many words had been exchanged I perceived that the excellent Hermann had been making use of me. That simple and astute Teuton had been, it seems, holding me up to Falk in the light of a rival. I was young enough to be shocked at so much duplicity. 'Did he tell you that in so many words?' I asked with indignation.

Hermann had not. He had given hints only; and of course it had not taken very much to alarm Falk; but, instead of declaring himself, he had taken steps to remove the family from under my influence. He was perfectly straightforward about it – as straightforward as a tile falling on your head. There was no duplicity in that man; and when I congratulated him on the perfection of his arrangements – even to the bribing of the wretched Johnson against me – he had a genuine movement of protest. Never bribed. He knew the man wouldn't work as long as he had a few cents in his pocket to get drunk on, and, naturally (he said – 'naturally') he let him have a dollar or two. He was himself a sailor, he said, and anticipated the view another sailor, like myself, was bound to take. On the other hand, he was sure that I should have to come to grief. He hadn't been knocking about for the last seven years up and down that river for nothing. It would have been no disgrace to me – but he asserted confidently I would have had my ship very awkwardly ashore at a spot two miles below the Great Pagoda . . .

And with all that he had no ill-will. That was evident. This was a crisis in which his only object had been to gain time – I fancy. And presently he mentioned that he had written for some jewellery, real good jewellery – had written to Hong Kong for it. It would arrive in a day or two.

'Well, then,' I said cheerily, 'everything is all right. All you've got to do is to present it to the lady together with your heart, and live happy ever after.'

Upon the whole he seemed to accept that view as far as the girl was concerned, but his eyelids drooped. There was still something in the way. For one thing Hermann disliked him so much. As to me, on the contrary, it seemed as though he could not praise me enough. Mrs Hermann too. He didn't know why they disliked him so. It made everything most difficult.

I listened impassive, feeling more and more diplomatic. His speech was not transparently clear. He was one of those men who seem to live, feel, suffer in a sort of mental twilight. But as to being fascinated by the girl and possessed by the desire of home life with her – it was as clear as daylight. So much being at stake, he was afraid of putting it to the hazard of the declaration. Besides, there was something else. And with Hermann being so set against him . . .

'I see,' I said thoughtfully, while my heart beat fast with the excitement of my diplomacy. 'I don't mind sounding Hermann. In fact, to show you how mistaken you were, I am ready to do all I can for you in that way.'

A light sigh escaped him. He drew his hands down his face, and it emerged, bony, unchanged of expression, as if all the tissues had been ossified. All the passion was in those big brown hands. He was satisfied. Then there was that other matter. If there were anybody on earth it was I who could persuade Hermann to take a reasonable view! I had a knowledge of the world and lots of experience. Hermann admitted this himself. And then I was a sailor too. Falk thought that a sailor would be able to understand certain things best . . .

He talked as if the Hermanns had been living all their life in a rural hamlet, and I alone had been capable, with my practice in life, of a large and indulgent view of certain occurrences. That was what my diplomacy was leading me to. I began suddenly to dislike it.

'I say, Falk,' I asked quite brusquely, 'you haven't already a wife put away somewhere?' The pain and disgust of his denial were very striking.

Couldn't I understand that he was as respectable as any white man hereabouts; earning his living honestly. He was suffering from my suspicion, and the low undertone of his voice made his protestations sound very pathetic. For a moment he shamed me, but, my diplomacy notwithstanding, I seemed to develop a conscience, as if in very truth it were in my power to decide the success of this matrimonial enterprise. By pretending hard enough we come to believe anything – anything to our advantage. And I had been pretending very hard, because I meant yet to be towed safely down the river. But, through conscience or stupidity, I couldn't help alluding to the Vanlo affair. 'You acted rather badly there. Didn't you?' was what I ventured actually to say – for the logic of our conduct is always at the mercy of obscure and unforeseen impulses.

His dilated pupils swerved from my face, glancing at the window with a sort of scared fury. We heard behind the blinds the continuous and sudden clicking of ivory, a jovial murmur of many voices, and Schomberg's deep manly laugh.

'That confounded old woman of a hotel-keeper then would never, never let it rest!' Falk exclaimed. Well, yes! It had happened two years ago. When it came to the point he owned he couldn't make up his mind to trust Fred Vanlo – no sailor, a bit of a fool too. He could not trust him, but, to stop his row, he had lent him enough money to pay all his debts before he left. I was greatly surprised to hear this. Then Falk could not be such a miser after all. So much the better for the girl. For a time he sat silent; then he picked up a card, and while looking at it he said: 'You need not think of anything bad. It was an accident. I've been unfortunate once.'

'Then in heaven's name say nothing about it.'

As soon as these words were out of my mouth I fancied I had said something immoral. He shook his head negatively. It had to be told. He considered it proper that the relations of the lady should know. No doubt – I thought to myself – had Miss Vanlo not been thirty and damaged by the climate he would have found it possible to entrust Fred Vanlo with this confidence. And then the figure of Hermann's niece appeared before my mind's eye, with the wealth of her opulent form, her rich youth, her lavish strength. With that powerful and immaculate vitality, her girlish form must have shouted aloud of life to that man, whereas poor Miss Vanlo could only sing sentimental songs to the strumming of a piano.

'And that Hermann hates me, I know it!' he cried in his undertone, with a sudden recrudescence of anxiety. 'I must tell them. It is proper that they should know. You would say so yourself.'

He then murmured an utterly mysterious allusion to the necessity for peculiar domestic arrangements. Though my curiosity was excited I did not want to hear any of his confidences. I feared he might give me a piece of information that would make my assumed role of matchmaker odious – however unreal it was. I was aware that he could have the girl for the asking; and keeping down a desire to laugh in his face, I expressed a confident belief in my ability to argue away Hermann's dislike for him. 'I am sure I can make it all right,' I said. He looked very pleased.

And when we rose not a word had been said about towage! Not a word! The game was won and the honour was safe. Oh! blessed white cotton umbrella! We shook hands, and I was holding myself with difficulty from breaking into a step dance of joy when he came back, striding all the length of the verandah, and said doubtfully: 'I say, captain, I have your word? You – you – won't turn round?'

Heavens! The fright he gave me. Behind his tone of doubt there was something desperate and menacing. The infatuated ass. But I was equal to the situation.

'My dear Falk,' I said, beginning to lie with a glibness and effrontery that amazed me even at the time – 'confidence for confidence.' (He had made no confidences.) 'I will tell you that I am already engaged to an extremely charming girl at home, and so you understand . . . '

He caught my hand and wrung it in a crushing grip.

'Pardon me. I feel it every day more difficult to live alone . . . '

'On rice and fish,' I interrupted smartly, giggling with the sheer nervousness of a danger escaped.

He dropped my hand as if it had become suddenly red hot. A moment of profound silence ensued, as though something extraordinary had happened.

'I promise you to obtain Hermann's consent,' I faltered out at last, and it seemed to me that he could not help seeing through that humbugging promise. 'If there's anything else to get over I shall endeavour to stand by you,' I conceded further, feeling somehow defeated and overborne; 'but you must do your best yourself.'

'I have been unfortunate once,' he muttered unemotionally, and turning his back on me he went away, thumping slowly the plank floor as if his feet had been shod with iron.

Next morning, however, he was lively enough as man-boat, a combination of splashing and shouting; of the insolent commotion below with the steady overbearing glare of the silent head-piece above. He turned us out most unnecessarily at an ungodly hour, but it was nearly eleven in the morning before he brought me up a cable's length from Hermann's ship. And he did it very badly too, in a hurry, and nearly contriving to miss altogether the patch of good holding ground, because, forsooth, he had caught sight of Hermann's niece on the poop. And so did I; and probably as soon as he had seen her himself. I saw the modest, sleek glory of the tawny head, and the full, grey shape of the girlish print frock she filled so perfectly, so satisfactorily, with the seduction of unfaltering curves – a very nymph of *Diana* the Huntress. And *Diana* the ship sat, high-walled and as solid as an institution, on the smooth level of the water, the most uninspiring and respectable craft upon the seas, useful and ugly, devoted to the support of domestic virtues like any grocer's shop on shore. At once Falk steamed away; for there was some work for him to do. He would return in the evening.

He ranged close by us, passing out dead slow, without a hail. The beat of the paddle-wheels reverberating amongst the stony islets, as if from the ruined walls of a vast arena, filled the anchorage confusedly with the clapping sounds of a mighty and leisurely applause. Abreast of Hermann's ship he stopped the engines; and a profound silence reigned over the rocks, the shore and the sea, for the time it took him to raise his hat aloft before the nymph of the grey print frock. I had snatched up my binoculars, and I can answer for it she didn't stir a limb, standing by the rail shapely and erect, with one of her hands grasping a rope at the height of her head, while the way of the tug carried slowly past her the lingering and profound homage of the man.

There was for me an enormous significance in the scene, the sense of having witnessed a solemn declaration. The die was cast. After such a manifestation he couldn't back out. And I reflected that it was nothing whatever to me now. With a rush of black smoke belching suddenly out of the funnel, and a mad swirl of paddle-wheels provoking a burst of weird and precipitated clapping, the tug shot out of the desolate arena. The rocky islets lay on the sea like the heaps of a cyclopean ruin on a plain; the centipedes and scorpions lurked under the stones; there was not a single blade of grass in sight anywhere, not a single lizard sunning himself on a boulder by the shore. When I looked again at Hermann's ship the girl had disappeared. I could not detect the smallest dot of a bird on the immense sky, and the flatness of the land continued the flatness of the sea to the naked line of the horizon.

This is the setting now inseparably connected with my knowledge of Falk's misfortune. My diplomacy had brought me there, and now I had only to wait the time for taking up the role of an ambassador. My diplomacy was a success; my ship was safe; old Gambril would probably live; a feeble sound of a tapping hammer came intermittently from the *Diana*. During the afternoon I looked at times at the old homely ship, the faithful nurse of Hermann's progeny, or yawned towards the distant temple of Buddha, like a lonely hillock on the plain, where shaven priests cherish the thoughts of that Annihilation which is the worthy reward of us all. Unfortunate! He had been unfortunate once. Well, that was not so bad as life goes. And what the devil could be the nature of that misfortune? I remembered that I had known a man before who had declared himself to have fallen, years ago, a victim to misfortune; but this misfortune, whose effects appeared permanent (he looked desperately hard up) when considered dispassionately, seemed indistinguishable from a breach of trust. Could it be something of that nature? Apart, however, from the utter improbability that he would offer to talk of it even to his future uncle-in-law I had a strange feeling that Falk's physique unfitted him for that sort of delinquency. As the person of Hermann's niece exhaled the profound physical charm of feminine form, so her adorer's big frame embodied to my senses the hard, straight masculinity that would conceivably kill but would not condescend to cheat. The thing was obvious. I might just as well have suspected the girl of a curvature of the spine. And I perceived that the sun was about to set.

The smoke of Falk's tug hove in sight, far away at the mouth of the river. It was time for me to assume the character of an ambassador, and the negotiation would not be difficult except in the matter of keeping my countenance. It was all too extravagantly nonsensical, and I conceived that it would be best to compose for myself a grave demeanour. I practised this in my boat as I went along, but the bashfulness that came secretly upon me the moment I stepped on the deck of the *Diana* is inexplicable. As soon as we had exchanged greetings Hermann asked me eagerly if I knew whether Falk had found his white parasol.

'He's going to bring it to you himself directly,' I said with great solemnity. 'Meantime I am charged with an important message for which he begs your favourable consideration. He is in love with your niece . . . '

'*Ach So!*' he hissed with an animosity that made my assumed gravity change into the most genuine concern. What meant this tone? And I hurried on.

'He wishes, with your consent of course, to ask her to marry him at once – before you leave here, that is. He would speak to his Consul.'

Hermann sat down and smoked violently. Five minutes passed in that furious meditation, and then, taking the long pipe out of his mouth, he burst into a hot diatribe against Falk – against his cupidity, his stupidity (a fellow that can hardly be got to say 'yes' or 'no' to the simplest question) – against his outrageous treatment of the shipping in port (because he saw they were at his mercy) – and against his manner of walking, which to his (Hermann's) mind showed a conceit positively unbearable. The damage to the old *Diana* was not forgotten, of course, and there was nothing of any nature said or done by Falk (even to the last offer of refreshment in the hotel) that did not seem to have been a cause of offence. 'Had the cheek' to drag him (Hermann) into that coffee-room; as though a drink from him could make up for forty-seven dollars and fifty cents of damage in the cost of wood alone – not counting two days' work for the carpenter. Of course he would not stand in the girl's way. He was going home to Germany. There were plenty of poor girls walking about in Germany.

'He's very much in love,' was all I found to say.

'Yes,' he cried. 'And it is time, too, after making himself and me talked about ashore the last voyage I was here, and then now again; coming on board every evening unsettling the girl's mind, and saying nothing. What sort of conduct is that?'

The seven thousand dollars the fellow was always talking about did not, in his opinion, justify such behaviour. Moreover, nobody had seen them. He (Hermann) seriously doubted if there were seven thousand cents, and the tug, no doubt, was mortgaged up to the top of the funnel to the firm of Siegers. But let that pass. He wouldn't stand in the girl's way. Her head was so turned that she had become no good to them of late. Quite unable even to put the children to bed without her aunt. It was bad for the children; they got unruly; and yesterday he had actually had to give Gustav a thrashing.

For that, too, Falk was made responsible apparently. And looking at my Hermann's heavy, puffy, good-natured face, I knew he would not exert himself till greatly exasperated, and, therefore, would thrash very hard, and being fat would resent the necessity. How Falk had managed to turn the girl's head was more difficult to understand. I supposed Hermann would know. And then hadn't there been Miss Vanlo? It could not be his silvery tongue, or the subtle seduction of his manner; he had no more of what is called 'manner' than an animal – which, however, on the other hand, is never, and can never be called vulgar. Therefore it must have been his bodily appearance, exhibiting a virility of nature as exaggerated as his beard, and resembling a sort of constant ruthlessness. It was seen in the very manner he lolled in the chair. He meant no offence, but his intercourse was characterised by that sort of frank disregard of susceptibilities a man of seven foot six, living in a world of dwarfs, would naturally assume, without in the least wishing to be unkind. But amongst men of his own stature, or nearly, this frank use of his advantages, in such matters as the awful towage bills for instance, caused much impotent gnashing of teeth. When attentively considered it seemed appalling at times. He was a strange beast. But maybe women liked it. Seen in that light he was well worth taming, and I suppose every woman at the bottom of her heart considers herself as a tamer of strange beasts. But Hermann arose with precipitation to carry the news to his wife. I had barely the time, as he made for the cabin door, to grab him by the seat of his inexpressibles. I begged him to wait till Falk in person had spoken with him. There remained some small matter to talk over, as I understood.

He sat down again at once, full of suspicion.

'What matter?' he said surlily. 'I have had enough of his nonsense. There's no matter at all, as he knows very well; the girl has nothing in the world. She came to us in one thin dress when my brother died, and I have a growing family.'

'It can't be anything of that kind,' I opined. 'He's desperately enamoured of your niece. I don't know why he did not say so before. Upon my word, I believe it is because he was afraid to lose, perhaps, the felicity of sitting near her on your quarterdeck.'

I intimated my conviction that his love was so great as to be in a sense cowardly. The effects of a great passion are unaccountable. It has been known to make a man timid. But Hermann looked at me as if I had foolishly raved; and the twilight was dying out rapidly.

'You don't believe in passion, do you, Hermann?' I said cheerily. 'The passion of fear will make a cornered rat courageous. Falk's in a corner. He will take her off your hands in one thin frock just as she came to you. And after ten years' service it isn't a bad bargain,' I added.

Far from taking offence, he resumed his air of civic virtue. The sudden night came upon him while he stared placidly along the deck, bringing in contact with his thick lips, and taking away again after a jet of smoke, the curved mouthpiece fitted to the stem of his pipe. The night came upon him and buried in haste his whiskers, his globular eyes, his puffy pale face, his fat knees and the vast flat slippers on his fatherly feet. Only his short arms in respectable white shirt-sleeves remained very visible, propped up like the flippers of a seal reposing on the strand.

'Falk wouldn't settle anything about repairs. Told me to find out first how much wood I should require and he would see,' he remarked; and after he had spat peacefully in the dusk we heard over the water the beat of the tug's floats. There is, on a calm night, nothing more suggestive of fierce and headlong haste than the rapid sound made by the paddle-wheels of a boat threshing her way through a quiet sea; and the approach of Falk towards his fate seemed to be urged by an impatient and passionate desire. The engines must have been driven to the very utmost of their revolutions. We heard them slow down at last, and, vaguely, the white hull of the tug appeared moving against the black islets, whilst a slow and rhythmical clapping as of thousands of hands rose on all sides. It ceased all at once, just before Falk brought her up. A single brusque splash was followed by the long-drawn rumbling of iron links running through the hawse pipe. Then a solemn silence fell upon the Roadstead.

'He will soon be here,' I murmured, and after that we waited for him without a word. Meantime, raising my eyes, I beheld the glitter of a lofty sky above the *Diana*'s mastheads. The multitude of stars gathered into clusters, in rows, in lines, in masses, in groups, shone all together, unanimously – and the few isolated ones, blazing by themselves in the midst of dark patches, seemed to be of a superior kind and of an inextinguishable nature. But long striding footsteps were heard hastening along the deck; the high bulwarks of the *Diana* made a deeper darkness. We rose from our chairs quickly, and Falk, appearing before us, all in white, stood still.

Nobody spoke at first, as though we had been covered with confusion. His arrival was fiery, but his white bulk, of indefinite shape and without features, made him loom up like a man of snow.

'The captain here has been telling me . . . ' Hermann began in a homely and amicable voice; and Falk had a low, nervous laugh. His cool, negligent undertone had no inflexions, but the strength of a powerful emotion made him ramble in his speech. He had always desired a home. It was difficult to live alone, though he was not answerable. He was domestic; there had been difficulties; but since he had seen Hermann's niece he found that it had become at last impossible to live by himself. 'I mean – impossible,' he repeated with no sort of emphasis and only with the slightest of pauses, but the word fell into my mind with the force of a new idea.

'I have not said anything to her yet,' Hermann observed quietly. And Falk dismissed this by a, 'That's all right. Certainly. Very proper.' There was a necessity for perfect frankness – in marrying, especially. Hermann seemed attentive, but he seized the first opportunity to ask us into the cabin. 'And by the by, Falk,' he said innocently, as we passed in, 'the timber came to no less than forty-seven dollars and fifty cents.'

Falk, uncovering his head, lingered in the passage. 'Some other time,' he said; and Hermann nudged me angrily – I don't know why. The girl alone in the cabin sat sewing at some distance from the table. Falk stopped short in the doorway. Without a word, without a sign, without the slightest inclination of his bony head, by the silent intensity of his look alone, he seemed to lay his herculean frame at her feet. Her hands sank slowly on her lap, and raising her clear eyes, she let her soft, beaming glance enfold him from head to foot like a slow and pale caress. He was very hot when he sat down; she, with bowed head, went on with her sewing; her neck was very white under the light of the lamp; but Falk, hiding his face in the palms of his hands, shuddered faintly. He drew them down, even to his beard, and his uncovered eyes astonished me by their tense and irrational expression – as though he had just swallowed a heavy gulp of alcohol. It passed away while he was binding us to secrecy. Not that he cared, but he did not like to be spoken about; and I looked at the girl's marvellous, at her wonderful, at her regal hair, plaited tight into that one astonishing and maidenly tress. Whenever she moved her well-shaped head it would stir stiffly to and fro on her back. The thin cotton sleeve fitted the irreproachable roundness of her arm like a skin; and her very dress, stretched on her bust, seemed to palpitate like a living tissue with the strength of vitality animating her body. How good her complexion was, the outline of her soft cheek and the small convoluted conch of her rosy ear! To pull her needle she kept the little finger apart from the others; it seemed a waste of power to see her sewing – eternally sewing – with that industrious and precise movement of her arm, going on eternally upon all the oceans, under all the skies, in innumerable harbours. And suddenly I heard Falk's voice declare that he could not marry a woman unless she knew of something in his life that had happened ten years ago. It was an accident. An unfortunate accident. It would affect the domestic arrangements of their home, but, once told, it need not be alluded to again for the rest of their lives. 'I should want my wife to feel for me,' he said. 'It has made me unhappy.' And how could he keep the knowledge of it to himself – he asked us – perhaps through years and years of companionship? What sort of companionship would that be? He had thought it over. A wife must know. Then why not at once? He counted on Hermann's kindness for presenting the affair in the best possible light. And Hermann's countenance, mystified before, became very sour. He stole an inquisitive glance at me. I shook my head blankly. Some people thought, Falk went on, that such an experience changed a man for the rest of his life. He couldn't say. It was hard, awful, and not to be forgotten, but he did not think himself a worse man than before. Only he talked in his sleep now, he believed . . . At last I began to think he had accidentally killed someone; perhaps a friend – his own father maybe; when he went on to say that probably we were aware he never touched meat. Throughout he spoke English, of course, on my account.

He swayed forward heavily.

The girl, with her hands raised before her pale eyes, was threading her needle. He glanced at her, and his mighty trunk overshadowed the table, bringing nearer to us the breadth of his shoulders, the thickness of his neck, and that incongruous, anchorite head, burnt in the desert, hollowed and lean as if by excesses of vigils and fasting. His beard flowed imposingly downwards, out of sight, between the two brown hands gripping the edge of the table, and his persistent glance, made sombre by the wide dilations of the pupils, fascinated.

'Imagine to yourselves,' he said in his ordinary voice, 'that I have eaten man.'

I could only ejaculate a faint 'Ah!' of complete enlightenment. But Hermann, dazed by the excessive shock, actually murmured, 'Himmel! What for?'

'It was my terrible misfortune to do so,' said Falk in a measured undertone. The girl, unconscious, sewed on. Mrs Hermann was absent in one of the staterooms, sitting up with Lena, who was feverish; but Hermann suddenly put both his hands up with a jerk. The embroidered calotte fell, and, in the twinkling of an eye, he had rumpled his hair all ends up in a most extravagant manner. In this state he strove to speak; with every effort his eyes seemed to start further out of their sockets; his head looked like a mop. He choked, gasped, swallowed, and managed to shriek out the one word, 'Beast!'

From that moment till Falk went out of the cabin the girl, with her hands folded on the work lying in her lap, never took her eyes off him. His own, in the blindness of his heart, darted all over the cabin, only seeking to avoid the sight of Hermann's raving. It was ridiculous, and was made almost terrible by the stillness of every other person present. It was contemptible, and was made appalling by the man's overmastering horror of this awful sincerity, coming to him suddenly, with the confession of such a fact. He walked with great strides; he gasped. He wanted to know from Falk how dared he to come and tell him this? Did he think himself a proper person to be sitting in this cabin where his wife and children lived? Tell his niece! Expected him to tell his niece! His own brother's daughter! Shameless! Did I ever hear tell of such impudence? – he appealed to me. 'This man here ought to have gone and hidden himself out of sight instead of . . .'

'But it's a great misfortune for me. But it's a great misfortune for me,' Falk would ejaculate from time to time.

However, Hermann kept on running frequently against the corners of the table. At last he lost a slipper, and crossing his arms on his breast, walked up with one stocking foot very close to Falk, in order to ask him whether he did think there was anywhere on earth a woman abandoned enough to mate with such a monster. 'Did he? Did he? Did he?' I tried to restrain him. He tore himself out of my hands; he found his slipper, and, endeavouring to put it on, stormed standing on one leg – and Falk, with a face unmoved and averted eyes, grasped all his mighty beard in one vast palm.

'Was it right then for me to die myself?' he asked thoughtfully. I laid my hand on his shoulder.

'Go away,' I whispered imperiously, without any clear reason for this advice, except that I wished to put an end to Hermann's odious noise. 'Go away.'

He looked searchingly for a moment at Hermann before he made a move. I left the cabin, too, to see him out of the ship. But he hung about the quarterdeck.

'It is my misfortune,' he said in a steady voice.

'You were stupid to blurt it out in such a manner. After all, we don't hear such confidences everyday.'

'What does the man mean?' he mused in deep undertones. 'Somebody had to die – but why me?'

He remained still for a time in the dark – silent; almost invisible. All at once he pinned my elbows to my sides. I felt utterly powerless in his grip, and his voice, whispering in my ear, vibrated.

'It's worse than hunger. Captain, do you know what that means? And I could kill then – or be killed. I wish the crowbar had smashed my skull ten years ago. And I've got to live now. Without her. Do you understand? Perhaps many years. But how? What can be done? If I had allowed myself to look at her once I would have carried her off before that man in my hands – like this.'

I felt myself snatched off the deck, then suddenly dropped – and I staggered backwards, feeling bewildered and bruised. What a man! All was still; he was gone. I heard Hermann's voice declaiming in the cabin, and I went in.

I could not at first make out a single word, but Mrs Hermann, who, attracted by the noise, had come in some time before, with an expression of surprise and mild disapproval depicted broadly on her face, was giving now all the signs of profound, helpless agitation. Her husband shot a string of guttural words at her, and instantly putting out one hand to the bulkhead as if to save herself from falling, she clutched the loose bosom of her dress with the other. He harangued the two women extraordinarily, with much of his shirt hanging out of his waistbelt, stamping his foot, turning from one to the other, sometimes throwing both his arms together, straight up above his rumpled hair, and keeping them in that position while he uttered a passage of loud denunciation; at others folding them tight across his breast – and then he hissed with indignation, elevating his shoulders and protruding his head. The girl was crying.

She had not changed her attitude. From her steady eyes that, following Falk in his retreat, had remained fixed wistfully on the cabin door, the tears fell rapid, thick, on her hands, on the work in her lap, warm and gentle like a shower in spring. She wept without grimacing, without noise – very touching, very quiet, with something more of pity than of pain in her face, as one weeps in compassion rather than in grief – and Hermann, before her, declaimed. I caught several times the word 'Mensch', man; and also 'Fressen', which last I looked up afterwards in my dictionary. It means 'Devour'. Hermann seemed to be requesting an answer of some sort from her; his whole body swayed. She remained mute and perfectly still; at last his agitation gained her; she put the palms of her hands together, her full lips parted, no sound came. His voice scolded shrilly, his arms went like a windmill – suddenly he shook a thick fist at her. She burst out into loud sobs. He seemed stupefied.

Mrs Hermann rushed forward babbling rapidly. The two women fell on each other's necks, and, with an arm round her niece's waist, she led her away. Her own eyes were simply streaming, her face was flooded. She shook her head back at me negatively, I wonder why to this day. The girl's head dropped heavily on her shoulder. They disappeared together.

Then Hermann sat down and stared at the cabin floor.

'We don't know all the circumstances,' I ventured to break the silence. He retorted tartly that he didn't want to know of any. According to his ideas no circumstances could excuse a crime – and certainly not such a crime. This was the opinion generally received. The duty of a human being was to starve. Falk therefore was a beast, an animal; base, low, vile, despicable, shameless, and deceitful. He had been deceiving him since last year. He was, however, inclined to think that Falk must have gone mad quite recently; for no sane person, without necessity, uselessly, for no earthly reason, and regardless of another's self-respect and peace of mind, would own to having devoured human flesh. 'Why tell?' he cried. 'Who was asking him?' It showed Falk's brutality because after all he had selfishly caused him (Hermann) much pain. He would have preferred not to know that such an unclean creature had been in the habit of caressing his children. He hoped I would say nothing of all this ashore, though. He wouldn't like it to get about that he had been intimate with an eater of men – a common cannibal. As to the scene he had made (which I judged quite unnecessary) he was not going to inconvenience and restrain himself for a fellow that went about courting and upsetting girls' heads, while he knew all the time that no decent housewifely girl could think of marrying him. At least he (Hermann) could not conceive how any girl could. 'Fancy Lena! . . . No, it was impossible. The thoughts that would come into their heads every time they sat down to a meal. Horrible! Horrible!'

'You are too squeamish, Hermann,' I said.

He seemed to think it was eminently proper to be squeamish if the word meant disgust at Falk's conduct; and turning up his eyes sentimentally he drew my attention to the horrible fate of the victims – the victims of that Falk. I said that I knew nothing about them. He seemed surprised. Could not anybody imagine without knowing? He – for instance – felt he would like to avenge them. But what if – said I – there had not been any? They might have died as it were, naturally – of starvation. He shuddered. But to be eaten – after death! To be devoured! He gave another deep shudder, and asked suddenly, 'Do you think it is true?'

His indignation and his personality together would have been enough to spoil the reality of the most authentic thing. When I looked at him I doubted the story – but the remembrance of Falk's words, looks, gestures, invested it not only with an air of reality but with the absolute truth of primitive passion.

'It is true just as much as you are able to make it; and exactly in the way you like to make it. For my part, when I hear you clamouring about it, I don't believe it is true at all.'

And I left him pondering. The men in my boat, lying at the foot of *Diana*'s side-ladder, told me that the captain of the tug had gone away in his gig some time ago.

I let my fellows pull an easy stroke; because of the heavy dew the clear sparkle of the stars seemed to fall on me cold and wetting. There was a sense of lurking gruesome horror somewhere in my mind, and it was mingled with clear and grotesque images. Schomberg's gastronomic tittle-tattle was responsible for these; and I half hoped I should never see Falk again. But the first thing my anchor-watchman told me was that the captain of the tug was on board. He had sent his boat away and was now waiting for me in the cuddy.

He was lying full length on the stern settee, his face buried in the cushions. I had expected to see it discomposed, contorted, despairing. It was nothing of the kind; it was just as I had seen it twenty times, steady and glaring from the bridge of the tug. It was immovably set and hungry, dominated like the whole man by the singleness of one instinct.

He wanted to live. He had always wanted to live. So we all do – but in us the instinct serves a complex conception, and in him this instinct existed alone. There is in such simple development a gigantic force, and like the pathos of a child's naïve and uncontrolled desire. He wanted that girl, and the utmost that can be said for him was that he wanted that particular girl alone. I think I saw then the obscure beginning, the seed germinating in the soil of an unconscious need, the first shoot of that tree bearing now for a mature mankind the flower and the fruit, the infinite gradation in shades and in flavour of our discriminating love. He was a child. He was as frank as a child too. He was hungry for the girl, terribly hungry, as he had been terribly hungry for food.

Don't be shocked if I declare that in my belief it was the same need, the same pain, the same torture. We are in his case allowed to contemplate the foundation of all the emotions – that one joy which is to live, and the one sadness at the root of the innumerable torments. It was made plain by the way he talked. He had never suffered so. It was gnawing, it was fire; it was there, like this! And after pointing below his breastbone, he made a hard wringing motion with his hands. And I assure you that, seen as I saw it with my bodily eyes, it was anything but laughable. And again, as he was presently to tell me (alluding to an early incident of the disastrous voyage when some damaged meat had been flung overboard), he said that a time soon came when his heart ached (that was the expression he used), and he was ready to tear his hair out at the thought of all that rotten beef thrown away.

I had heard all this; I witnessed his physical struggles, seeing the working of the rack and hearing the true voice of pain. I witnessed it all patiently, because the moment I came into the cuddy he had called upon me to stand by him – and this, it seems, I had diplomatically promised.

His agitation was impressive and alarming in the little cabin, like the floundering of a great whale driven into a shallow cove in a coast. He stood up;

he flung himself down headlong; he tried to tear the cushion with his teeth; and again hugging it fiercely to his face he let himself fall on the couch. The whole ship seemed to feel the shock of his despair; and I contemplated with wonder the lofty forehead, the noble touch of time on the uncovered temples, the unchanged hungry character of the face – so strangely ascetic and so incapable of portraying emotion.

What should he do? He had lived by being near her. He had sat – in the evening – I knew? – all his life! She sewed. Her head was bent – so. Her head – like this – and her arms. Ah! Had I seen? Like this.

He dropped on a stool, bowed his powerful neck whose nape was red, and with his hands stitched the air, ludicrous, sublimely imbecile and comprehensible.

And now he couldn't have her? No! That was too much. After thinking too that . . . What had he done? What was my advice? Take her by force? No? Mustn't he? Who was there then to kill him? For the first time I saw one of his features move: a fighting teeth-baring curl of the lip . . . 'Not Hermann, perhaps.' He lost himself in thought as though he had fallen out of the world.

I may note that the idea of suicide apparently did not enter his head for a single moment. It occurred to me to ask: 'Where was it that this shipwreck of yours took place?'

'Down south,' he said vaguely with a start.

'You are not down south now,' I said. 'Violence won't do. They would take her away from you in no time. And what was the name of the ship?'

'*Borgmester Dahl*,' he said. 'It was no shipwreck.'

He seemed to be waking up by degrees from that trance, and waking up calmed.

'Not a shipwreck? What was it?'

'Breakdown,' he answered, looking more like himself every moment. By this only I learned that it was a steamer. I had till then supposed they had been starving in boats or on a raft – or perhaps on a barren rock.

'She did not sink then?' I asked in surprise. He nodded. 'We sighted the southern ice,' he pronounced dreamily.

'And you alone survived?'

He sat down. 'Yes. It was a terrible misfortune for me. Everything went wrong. All the men went wrong. I survived.'

Remembering the things one reads of it was difficult to realise the true meaning of his answers. I ought to have seen at once – but I did not; so difficult is it for our minds, remembering so much, instructed so much, informed of so much, to get in touch with the real actuality at our elbow. And with my head full of preconceived notions as to how a case of 'cannibalism and suffering at sea' should be managed I said – 'You were then so lucky in the drawing of lots?'

'Drawing of lots?' he said. 'What lots? Do you think I would have allowed my life to go for the drawing of lots?'

Not if he could help it, I perceived, no matter what other life went.

'It was a great misfortune. Terrible. Awful,' he said. 'Many heads went wrong, but the best men would live.'

'The toughest, you mean,' I said. He considered the word. Perhaps it was strange to him, though his English was so good.

'Yes,' he asserted at last. 'The best. It was everybody for himself at last and the ship open to all.'

Thus from question to question I got the whole story. I fancy it was the only way I could that night have stood by him. Outwardly at least he was himself again; the first sign of it was the return of that incongruous trick he had of drawing both his hands down his face – and it had its meaning now, with that slight shudder of the frame and the passionate anguish of these hands uncovering a hungry immovable face, the wide pupils of the intent, silent, fascinating eyes.

It was an iron steamer of a most respectable origin. The burgomaster of Falk's native town had built her. She was the first steamer ever launched there. The burgomaster's daughter had christened her. Country people drove in carts from miles around to see her. He told me all this. He got the berth as, what we should call, a chief mate. He seemed to think it had been a feather in his cap; and, in his own corner of the world, this lover of life was of good parentage.

The burgomaster had advanced ideas in the ship-owning line. At that time not everyone would have known enough to think of despatching a cargo steamer to the Pacific. But he loaded her with pitch-pine deals and sent her off to hunt for her luck. Wellington was to be the first port, I fancy. It doesn't matter, because in latitude 44° south and somewhere half-way between Good Hope and New Zealand the tail-shaft broke and the propeller dropped off.

They were steaming then with a fresh gale on the quarter and all their canvas set, to help the engines. But by itself the sail power was not enough to keep way on her. When the propeller went the ship broached-to at once, and the masts got whipped overboard.

The disadvantage of being dismasted consisted in this, that they had nothing to hoist flags on to make themselves visible at a distance. In the course of the first few days several ships failed to sight them; and the gale was drifting them out of the usual track. The voyage had been, from the first, neither very successful nor very harmonious. There had been quarrels on board. The captain was a clever, melancholic man, who had no unusual grip on his crew. The ship had been amply provisioned for the passage, but, somehow or other, several barrels of meat were found spoiled on opening, and had been thrown overboard soon after leaving home, as a sanitary measure. Afterwards the crew of the *Borgmester Dahl* thought of that rotten carrion with tears of regret, covetousness and despair.

She drove south. To begin with, there had been an appearance of organisation, but soon the bonds of discipline became relaxed. A sombre idleness succeeded. They looked with sullen eyes at the horizon. The gales increased: she lay in the trough, the seas made a clean breach over her. On one frightful night, when they expected their hulk to turn over with them every moment, a heavy sea broke on board, deluged the store-rooms and spoiled the best part of the remaining provisions. It seems the hatch had not been properly secured. This instance of neglect is characteristic of utter discouragement. Falk tried to inspire some energy into his captain, but failed. From that time he retired more into himself, always trying to do his utmost in the situation. It grew worse. Gale succeeded gale, with black mountains of water hurling themselves on the *Borgmester Dahl*. Some of the men never left their bunks; many became quarrelsome. The chief-engineer, an old man, refused to speak at all to anybody. Others shut themselves up in their berths to cry. On calm days the inert steamer rolled on a leaden sea under a murky sky, or showed, in sunshine, the squalor of sea waifs, the dried white salt, the rust, the jagged broken places. Then the gales came again. They kept body and soul together on short rations. Once, an English ship, scudding in a storm, tried to stand by them, heaving-to pluckily under their lee. The seas swept her decks; the men in oilskins clinging to her rigging looked at them, and they made desperate signs over their shattered bulwarks. Suddenly her main-topsail went, yard and all, in a terrific squall; she had to bear up under bare poles and disappeared.

Other ships had spoken them before, but at first they had refused to be taken off, expecting the assistance of some steamer. There were very few steamers in those latitudes then; and when they desired to leave this dead and drifting carcase, no ship came in sight. They had drifted south out of men's knowledge. They failed to attract the attention of a lonely whaler: and very soon the edge of the polar ice-cap rose from the sea and closed the southern horizon like a wall. One morning they were alarmed by finding themselves floating amongst detached pieces of ice. But the fear of sinking passed away like their vigour, like their hopes; the shocks of the floes knocking against the ship's side could not rouse them from their apathy: and the *Borgmester Dahl* drifted out again, unharmed, into open water. They hardly noticed the change.

The funnel had gone overboard in one of the heavy rolls; two of their three boats had disappeared, washed away in bad weather, and the davits swung to and fro, unsecured, with chafed ropes' ends waggling to the roll. Nothing was done on board, and Falk told me how he had often listened to the water washing about the dark engine-room where the engines, stilled for ever, were decaying slowly into a mass of rust, as the stilled heart decays within the lifeless body. At first, after the loss of the motive power, the tiller had been thoroughly secured by lashings. But in course of time these had rotted, chafed, rusted, parting one by one: and the rudder, freed, banged heavily to and fro night and day, sending dull shocks through the whole frame of the vessel. This was dangerous. Nobody cared enough to lift a little finger. He told me that even now sometimes waking up at night, he fancied he could hear the dull vibrating thuds. The pintles carried away, and it dropped off at last.

The final catastrophe came with the sending off of their one remaining boat. It was Falk who had managed to preserve her intact, and now it was agreed that some of the hands should sail away into the track of the shipping to procure assistance. She was provisioned with all the food they could spare for the six who were to go. They waited for a fine day. It was long in coming. At last one morning they lowered her into the water.

Directly, in that demoralised crowd, trouble broke out. Two men who had no business there had jumped into the boat under the pretence of unhooking the tackles, while some sort of squabble arose on the deck amongst these weak, tottering spectres of a ship's company. The captain, who had been for days living secluded and unapproachable in the chart-room, came to the rail. He ordered the two men to come up on board and menaced them with his revolver. They pretended to obey, but suddenly cutting the boat's painter, gave a shove against the ship's side and made ready to hoist the sail.

'Shoot, sir! Shoot them down!' cried Falk – 'and I will jump overboard to regain the boat.' But the captain, after taking aim with an irresolute arm, turned suddenly away.

A howl of rage arose. Falk dashed into his cabin for his own pistol. When he returned it was too late. Two more men had leaped into the water, but the fellows in the boat beat them off with the oars, hoisted the boat's lug and sailed away. They were never heard of again.

Consternation and despair possessed the remaining ship's company, till the apathy of utter hopelessness reasserted its sway. That day a fireman committed suicide, running up on deck with his throat cut from ear to ear, to the horror of all hands. He was thrown overboard. The captain had locked himself in the chart-room, and Falk, knocking vainly for admittance, heard him reciting over and over again the names of his wife and children, not as if calling upon them or commending them to God, but in a mechanical voice like an exercise of memory. Next day the doors of the chart-room were swinging open to the roll of the ship, and the captain had disappeared. He must during the night have jumped into the sea. Falk locked both the doors and kept the keys.

The organised life of the ship had come to an end. The solidarity of the men had gone. They became indifferent to each other. It was Falk who took in hand the distribution of such food as remained. They boiled their boots for soup to eke out the rations, which only made their hunger more intolerable. Sometimes whispers of hate were heard passing between the languid skeletons that drifted endlessly to and fro, north and south, east and west, upon that carcase of a ship.

And in this lies the grotesque horror of this sombre story. The last extremity of sailors, overtaking a small boat or a frail craft, seems easier to bear, because of the direct danger of the seas. The confined space, the close contact, the imminent menace of the waves, seem to draw men together, in spite of madness, suffering and despair. But there was a ship – safe, convenient, roomy: a ship with beds, bedding, knives, forks, comfortable cabins, glass and china, and a complete cook's galley, pervaded, ruled and possessed by the pitiless spectre of starvation. The lamp oil had been drunk, the wicks cut up for food, the candles eaten. At night she floated dark in all her recesses and full of fears. One day Falk came upon a man gnawing a splinter of pine wood. Suddenly he threw the piece of wood away, tottered to the rail, and fell over. Falk, too late to prevent the act, saw him claw the ship's side desperately before he went down. Next day another man did the same thing, after uttering horrible imprecations. But this one somehow managed to get hold of the broken rudder chains and hung on there, silently. Falk set about trying to save him, and all the time the man, holding with both hands, looked at him anxiously with his sunken eyes. Then, just as Falk was ready to put his hand on him, the man let go his hold and sank like a stone. Falk reflected on these sights. His heart revolted against the horror of death, and he said to himself that he would struggle for every precious minute of his life.

One afternoon – as the survivors lay about on the after deck – the carpenter, a tall man with a black beard, spoke of the last sacrifice. There was nothing eatable left on board. Nobody said a word to this; but that company separated quickly, these listless feeble spectres slunk off one by one to hide in fear of each other. Falk and the carpenter remained on deck together. Falk liked the big carpenter. He had been the best man of the lot, helpful and ready as long as there was anything to do, the longest hopeful, and had preserved to the last some vigour and decision of mind.

They did not speak to each other. Henceforth no voices were to be heard conversing sadly on board that ship. After a time the carpenter tottered away forward; but later on Falk, going to drink at the freshwater pump, had the inspiration to turn his head. The carpenter had stolen upon him from behind, and, summoning all his strength, was aiming with a crowbar a blow at the back of his skull.

Dodging just in time, Falk made his escape and ran into his cabin. While he was loading his revolver there, he heard the sound of heavy blows struck upon the bridge. The locks of the chart-room doors were slight, they flew open, and the carpenter, possessing himself of the captain's revolver, fired a shot of defiance.

Falk was about to go on deck and have it out at once, when he remarked that one of the ports of his cabin commanded the approaches to the fresh water-pump. Instead of going out he remained in and secured the door. 'The best man shall survive,' he said to himself – and the other, he reasoned, must at sometime or other come there to drink. These starving men would drink often to cheat the pangs of their hunger. But the carpenter too must have noticed the position of the port. They were the two best men in the ship, and the game was with them. All the rest of the day Falk saw no one and heard no sound. At night he strained his eyes. It was dark – he heard a rustling noise once, but he was certain that no one could have come near the pump. It was to the left of his deck port, and he could not have failed to see a man, for the night was clear and starry. He saw nothing; towards morning another faint noise made him suspicious. Deliberately and quietly he unlocked his door. He had not slept, and had not given way to the horror of the situation. He wanted to live.

But during the night the carpenter, without at all trying to approach the pump, had managed to creep quietly along the starboard bulwark, and, unseen, had crouched down right under Falk's deck port. When daylight came he rose up suddenly, looked in, and putting his arm through the round brass-framed opening, fired at Falk within a foot. He missed – and Falk, instead of attempting to seize the arm holding the weapon, opened his door unexpectedly, and with the muzzle of his long revolver nearly touching the other's side, shot him dead.

The best man had survived. Both of them had at the beginning just strength enough to stand on their feet, and both had displayed pitiless resolution, endurance, cunning and courage – all the qualities of classic heroism. At once Falk threw overboard the captain's revolver. He was a born monopolist. Then after the report of the two shots, followed by a profound silence, there crept out into the cold, cruel dawn of Antarctic regions, from various hiding-places, over the deck of that dismantled corpse of a ship floating on a grey sea ruled by iron necessity and with a heart of ice – there crept into view one by one, cautious, slow, eager, glaring, and unclean, a band of hungry and livid skeletons. Falk faced them, the possessor of the only firearm on board, and the second best man – the carpenter – was lying dead between him and them.

'He was eaten, of course,' I said.

He bent his head slowly, shuddered a little, drawing his hands over his face, and said, 'I had never any quarrel with that man. But there were our lives between him and me.'

Why continue the story of that ship, that story before which, with its freshwater pump like a spring of death, its man with the weapon, the sea ruled by iron necessity, its spectral band swayed by terror and hope, its mute and unhearing heaven? – the fable of the *Flying Dutchman* with its convention of crime and its sentimental retribution fades like a graceful wreath, like a wisp of white mist. What is there to say that every one of us cannot guess for himself? I believe Falk began by going through the ship, revolver in hand, to annex all the matches. Those starving wretches had plenty of matches! He had no mind to have the ship set on fire under his feet, either from hate or from despair. He lived in the open, camping on the bridge, commanding all the after deck and the only approach to the pump. He lived! Some of the others lived too – concealed, anxious, coming out one by one from their hiding-places at the seductive sound of a shot. And he was not selfish. They shared, but only three of them all were alive when a whaler, returning from her cruising-ground, nearly ran over the waterlogged hull of the *Borgmester Dahl*, which, it seems, in the end had in some way sprung a leak in both her holds, but being loaded with deals could not sink.

'They all died,' Falk said. 'These three too, afterwards. But I would not die. All died, all! under this terrible misfortune. But was I, too, to throw away my life? Could I? Tell me, captain? I was alone there, quite alone, just like the others. Each man was alone. Was I to give up my revolver? Who to? Or was I to throw it into the sea? What would have been the good? Only the best man would survive. It was a great, terrible, and cruel misfortune.'

He had survived! I saw him before me as though preserved for a witness to the mighty truth of an unerring and eternal principle. Great beads of perspiration stood on his forehead. And suddenly it struck the table with a heavy blow, as he fell forward throwing his hands out.

'And this is worse,' he cried. 'This is a worse pain! This is more terrible.'

He made my heart thump with the profound conviction of his cry. And after he had left me alone I called up before my mental eye the image of the girl weeping silently, abundantly, patiently, and as if irresistibly. I thought of her tawny hair. I thought how, if unplaited, it would have covered her all round as low as the hips, like the hair of a siren. And she had bewitched him. Fancy a man who would guard his own life with the inflexibility of a pitiless and immovable fate, being brought to lament that once a crowbar had missed his skull! The sirens sing and lure to death, but this one had been weeping silently as if for the pity of his life. She was the tender and voiceless siren of this appalling navigator. He evidently wanted to live his whole conception of life. Nothing else would do. And she too was a servant of that life that, in the midst of death, cries aloud to our senses. She was eminently fitted to interpret for him its feminine side. And in her own way, and with her own profusion of sensuous charms, she also seemed to illustrate the eternal truth of an unerring principle. I don't know though what sort of principle Hermann illustrated when he turned up early on board my ship with a most perplexed air. It struck me, however, that he too would do his best to survive. He seemed greatly calmed on the subject of Falk, but still very full of it.

'What is it you said I was last night? You know,' he asked after some preliminary talk. 'Too – too – I don't know. A very funny word.'

'Squeamish?' I suggested.

'Yes. What does it mean?'

'That you exaggerate things – to yourself. Without enquiry, and so on.'

He seemed to turn it over in his mind. We went on talking. This Falk was the plague of his life. Upsetting everybody like this! Mrs Hermann was rather unwell this morning. His niece was crying still. There was nobody to look after the children. He struck his umbrella on the deck. She would be like that for months. Fancy carrying all the way home, second class, a perfectly useless girl who is crying all the time. It was bad for Lena too, he observed;

but on what grounds I could not guess. Perhaps of the bad example. That child was already sorrowing and crying enough over the rag doll. Nicholas was really the least sentimental person of the family.

'Why does she weep?' I asked.

'From pity,' cried Hermann.

It was impossible to make out women. Mrs Hermann was the only one he pretended to understand. She was very, very upset and doubtful.

'Doubtful about what?' I asked.

He averted his eyes and did not answer this. It was impossible to make them out. For instance, his niece was weeping for Falk. Now he (Hermann) would like to wring his neck – but then . . . He supposed he had too tender a heart. 'Frankly,' he asked at last, 'what do you think of what we heard last night, captain?'

'In all these tales,' I observed, 'there is always a good deal of exaggeration.'

And not letting him recover from his surprise I assured him that I knew all the details. He begged me not to repeat them. His heart was too tender. They made him feel unwell. Then, looking at his feet and speaking very slowly, he supposed that he need not see much of them after they were married. For, indeed, he could not bear the sight of Falk. On the other hand it was ridiculous to take home a girl with her head turned. A girl that weeps all the time and is of no help to her aunt.

'Now you will be able to do with one cabin only on your passage home,' I said.

'Yes, I had thought of that,' he said brightly, almost. 'Yes! Himself, his wife, four children – one cabin might do. Whereas if his niece went . . .'

'And what does Mrs Hermann say to it?' I enquired.

Mrs Hermann did not know whether a man of that sort could make a girl happy – she had been greatly deceived in Captain Falk. She had been very upset last night.

Those good people did not seem to be able to retain an impression for a whole twelve hours. I assured him on my own personal knowledge that Falk possessed in himself all the qualities to make his niece's future prosperous. He said he was glad to hear this, and that he would tell his wife. Then the object of the visit came out. He wished me to help him to resume relations with Falk. His niece, he said, had expressed the hope I would do so in my kindness. He was evidently anxious that I should, for though he seemed to have forgotten nine-tenths of his last night's opinions and the whole of his indignation, yet he evidently feared to be sent to the right-about. 'You told me he was very much in love,' he concluded slyly, and leered in a sort of bucolic way.

As soon as he had left my ship I called Falk on board by signal – the tug still lying at the anchorage. He took the news with calm gravity, as though he had all along expected the stars to fight for him in their courses.

I saw them once more together, and only once – on the quarterdeck of the

Diana. Hermann sat smoking with a shirt-sleeved elbow hooked over the back of his chair. Mrs Hermann was sewing alone. As Falk stepped over the gangway, Hermann's niece, with a slight swish of the skirt and a swift friendly nod to me, glided past my chair.

They met in sunshine abreast of the mainmast. He held her hands and looked down at them, and she looked up at him with her candid and unseeing glance. It seemed to me they had come together as if attracted, drawn and guided to each other by a mysterious influence. They were a complete couple. In her grey frock, palpitating with life, generous of form, olympian and simple, she was indeed the siren to fascinate that dark navigator, this ruthless lover of the five senses. From afar I seemed to feel the masculine strength with which he grasped those hands she had extended to him with a womanly swiftness. Lena, a little pale, nursing her beloved lump of dirty rags, ran towards her big friend; and then in the drowsy silence of the good old ship Mrs Hermann's voice rang out so changed that it made me spin round in my chair to see what was the matter.

'Lena, come here!' she screamed. And this good-natured matron gave me a wavering glance, dark and full of fearsome distrust. The child ran back, surprised, to her knee. But the two, standing before each other in sunlight with clasped hands, had heard nothing, had seen nothing and no one. Three feet away from them in the shade a seaman sat on a spar, very busy splicing a strop, and dipping his fingers into a tar-pot, as if utterly unaware of their existence.

When I returned in command of another ship, some five years afterwards, Mr and Mrs Falk had left the place. I should not wonder if Schomberg's tongue had succeeded at last in scaring Falk away for good; and, indubitably, there was a tale still going about the town of a certain Falk, owner of a tug, who had won his wife at cards from the captain of an English ship.

1901

HEART OF DARKNESS

The *Nellie*, a cruising yawl, swung to her anchor without a flutter of the sails, and was at rest. The flood had made, the wind was nearly calm, and being bound down the river, the only thing for it was to come to and wait for the turn of the tide.

The sea-reach of the Thames stretched before us like the beginning of an interminable waterway. In the offing the sea and the sky were welded together without a joint, and in the luminous space the tanned sails of the barges drifting up with the tide seemed to stand still in red clusters of canvas sharply peaked, with gleams of varnished sprits. A haze rested on the low shores that ran out to sea in vanishing flatness. The air was dark above Gravesend, and farther back still seemed condensed into a mournful gloom, brooding motionless over the biggest, and the greatest, town on earth.

The Director of Companies was our captain and our host. We four affectionately watched his back as he stood in the bows looking to seaward. On the whole river there was nothing that looked half so nautical. He resembled a pilot, which to a seaman is trustworthiness personified. It was difficult to realise his work was not out there in the luminous estuary, but behind him, within the brooding gloom.

Between us there was, as I have already said somewhere, the bond of the sea. Besides holding our hearts together through long periods of separation, it had the effect of making us tolerant of each other's yarns – and even convictions. The Lawyer – the best of old fellows – had, because of his many years and many virtues, the only cushion on deck, and was lying on the only rug. The Accountant had brought out already a box of dominoes, and was toying architecturally with the bones. Marlow sat cross-legged right aft, leaning against the mizzen-mast. He had sunken cheeks, a yellow complexion, a straight back, an ascetic aspect, and, with his arms dropped, the palms of hands outwards, resembled an idol. The Director, satisfied the anchor had good hold, made his way aft and sat down amongst us. We exchanged a few words lazily. Afterwards there was silence on board the yacht. For some reason or other we did not begin that game of dominoes. We felt meditative, and fit for nothing but placid staring. The day was ending in a serenity of still and exquisite brilliance. The water shone pacifically; the sky, without a speck, was a benign immensity of unstained light; the very mist on the Essex marshes was like a gauzy and radiant fabric, hung from the wooded rises inland, and draping the low shores in diaphanous folds. Only the gloom to the west, brooding over the upper reaches, became more sombre every minute, as if angered by the approach of the sun.

And at last, in its curved and imperceptible fall, the sun sank low, and from glowing white changed to a dull red without rays and without heat, as if about to go out suddenly, stricken to death by the touch of that gloom brooding over a crowd of men.

Forthwith a change came over the waters, and the serenity became less brilliant but more profound. The old river in its broad reach rested unruffled at the decline of day, after ages of good service done to the race that peopled its banks, spread out in the tranquil dignity of a waterway leading to the uttermost ends of the earth. We looked at the venerable stream not in the vivid flush of a short day that comes and departs for ever, but in the august light of abiding memories. And indeed nothing is easier for a man who has, as the phrase goes, 'followed the sea' with reverence and affection than to evoke the great spirit of the past upon the lower reaches of the Thames. The tidal current runs to and fro in its unceasing service, crowded with memories of men and ships it had borne to the rest of home or to the battles of the sea. It had known and served all the men of whom the nation is proud, from Sir Francis Drake to Sir John Franklin, knights all, titled and untitled – the great knights-errant of the sea. It had borne all the ships whose names are like jewels flashing in the night of time, from the *Golden Hind* returning with her round flanks full of treasure, to be visited by the Queen's Highness and thus pass out of the gigantic tale, to the *Erebus* and *Terror*, bound on other conquests – and that never returned. It had known the ships and the men. They had sailed from Deptford, from Greenwich, from Erith – the adventurers and the settlers; kings' ships and the ships of men on 'Change; captains, admirals, the dark 'interlopers' of the Eastern trade, and the commissioned 'generals' of East India fleets. Hunters for gold or pursuers of fame, they all had gone out on that stream, bearing the sword, and often the torch, messengers of the might within the land, bearers of a spark from the sacred fire. What greatness had not floated on the ebb of that river into the mystery of an unknown earth! . . . The dreams of men, the seed of commonwealths, the germs of empires.

The sun set; the dusk fell on the stream, and lights began to appear along the shore. The Chapman lighthouse, a three-legged thing erect on a mudflat, shone strongly. Lights of ships moved in the fairway – a great stir of lights going up and going down. And farther west on the upper reaches the place of the monstrous town was still marked ominously on the sky, a brooding gloom in sunshine, a lurid glare under the stars.

'And this also,' said Marlow suddenly, 'has been one of the dark places of the earth.'

He was the only man of us who still 'followed the sea.' The worst that could be said of him was that he did not represent his class. He was a seaman, but he was a wanderer too, while most seaman lead, if one may so express it, a sedentary life. Their minds are of the stay-at-home order, and their home is always with them – the ship; and so is their country – the sea. One ship is very much like another, and the sea is always the same. In the immutability of their surroundings the foreign shores, the foreign faces, the changing immensity of life, glide past, veiled not by a sense of mystery but by a slightly disdainful ignorance; for there is nothing mysterious to a seaman unless it be the sea itself, which is the mistress of his existence and as inscrutable as Destiny. For the rest, after his hours of work, a casual stroll or a casual spree on shore suffices to unfold for him the secret of a whole continent, and generally he finds the secret not worth knowing. The yarns of seamen have a direct simplicity, the whole meaning of which lies within the shell of a cracked nut. But Marlow was not typical (if his propensity to spin yarns be excepted), and to him the meaning of an episode was not inside like a kernel but outside, enveloping the tale which brought it out only as a glow brings out a haze, in the likeness of one of these misty halos that sometimes are made visible by the spectral illumination of moonshine.

His remark did not seem at all surprising. It was just like Marlow. It was accepted in silence. No one took the trouble to grunt even; and presently he said, very slow – 'I was thinking of very old times, when the Romans first came here, nineteen hundred years ago – the other day . . . Light came out of this river since – you say Knights? Yes; but it is like a running blaze on a plain, like a flash of lightning in the clouds. We live in the flicker – may it last as long as the old earth keeps rolling! But darkness was here yesterday. Imagine the feelings of a commander of a fine – what d'ye call 'em? – trireme in the Mediterranean, ordered suddenly to the north; run overland across the Gauls in a hurry; put in charge of one of these craft the legionaries – a wonderful lot of handy men they must have been too – used to build, apparently by the hundred, in a month or two, if we may believe what we read. Imagine him here – the very end of the world, a sea the colour of lead, a sky the colour of smoke, a kind of ship about as rigid as a concertina – and going up this river with stores, or orders, or what you like. Sandbanks, marshes, forests, savages – precious little to eat fit for a civilised man, nothing but Thames water to drink. No Falernian wine here, no going ashore. Here and there a military camp lost in a wilderness, like a needle in a bundle of hay – cold, fog, tempests, disease, exile, and death – death skulking in the air, in the water, in the bush. They must have been dying like flies here. Oh yes – he did it. Did it very well, too, no doubt, and without thinking much about it either, except afterwards to brag of what he had gone through in his time, perhaps. They were men enough to face the darkness. And perhaps he was cheered by keeping his eye on a chance of promotion to the fleet at Ravenna by and by, if he had good friends in Rome and survived the awful climate. Or think of a decent young citizen in a toga – perhaps too much dice, you know – coming out here in the train of some prefect, or tax-gatherer, or trader, even, to mend his fortunes. Land in a swamp, march through the woods, and in some inland post feel the savagery, the utter savagery, had closed round him – all that mysterious life of the wilderness that stirs in the forest, in the jungles, in the hearts of wild men. There's no initiation either into such mysteries. He has to live in the midst of the incomprehensible, which is also detestable. And it has a fascination, too, that goes to work upon him. The fascination of the abomination – you know, Imagine the growing regrets, the longing to escape, the powerless disgust, the surrender, the hate.'

He paused.

'Mind,' he began again, lifting one arm from the elbow, the palm of the hand outwards, so that, with his legs folded before him, he had the pose of a Buddha preaching in European clothes and without a lotus-flower – 'Mind, none of us would feel exactly like this. What saves us is efficiency – the devotion to efficiency. But these chaps were not much account, really. They were no colonists; their administration was merely a squeeze, and nothing more, I suspect. They were conquerors, and for that you want only brute force – nothing to boast of, when you have it, since your strength is just an accident arising from the weakness of others. They grabbed what they could get for the sake of what was to be got. It was just robbery with violence, aggravated murder on a great scale, and men going at it blind – as is very proper for those who tackle a darkness. The conquest of the earth, which mostly means the taking it away from those who have a different complexion or slightly flatter noses than ourselves, is not a pretty thing when you look into it too much. What redeems it is the idea only. An idea at the back of it; not a sentimental pretence but an idea; and an unselfish belief in the idea – something you can set up, and bow down before, and offer a sacrifice to . . . '

He broke off. Flames glided in the river, small green flames, red flames, white flames, pursuing, overtaking, joining, crossing each other – then separating slowly or hastily. The traffic of the great city went on in the deepening night upon the sleepless river. We looked on, waiting patiently – there was nothing else to do till the end of the flood; but it was only after a long silence, when he said, in a hesitating voice, 'I suppose you fellows remember I did once turn freshwater sailor for a bit,' that we knew we were fated, before the ebb began to run, to hear about one of Marlow's inconclusive experiences.

'I don't want to bother you much with what happened to me personally,' he began, showing in this remark the weakness of many tellers of tales who seem so often unaware of what their audience would best like to hear; 'yet to understand the effect of it on me you ought to know how I got out there, what I saw, how I went up that river to the place where I first met the poor chap. It was the farthest point of navigation and the culminating point of my experience. It seemed somehow to throw a kind of light on everything about me – and into my thoughts. It was sombre enough too – and pitiful – not extraordinary in any way – not very clear either. No, not very clear. And yet it seemed to throw a kind of light.

'I had then, as you remember, just returned to London after a lot of Indian Ocean, Pacific, China Seas – a regular dose of the East – six years or so; and I was loafing about, hindering you fellows in your work and invading your homes, just as though I had got a heavenly mission to civilise you. It was very fine for a time, but after a bit I did get tired of resting. Then I began to look for a ship – I should think the hardest work on earth. But the ships wouldn't even look at me. And I got tired of that game too.

'Now when I was a little chap I had a passion for maps. I would look for hours at South America, or Africa, or Australia, and lose myself in all the glories of exploration. At that time there were many blank spaces on the earth, and when I saw one that looked particularly inviting on a map (but they all look that) I would put my finger on it and say, When I grow up I will go there. The North Pole was one of these places, I remember. Well, I haven't been there yet, and shall not try now. The glamour's off. Other places were scattered about the Equator, and in every sort of latitude all over the two hemispheres. I have been in some of them, and . . . well, we won't talk about that. But there was one yet – the biggest, the most blank, so to speak – that I had a hankering after.

'True, by this time it was not a blank space any more. It had got filled since my boyhood with rivers and lakes and names. It had ceased to be a blank space of delightful mystery – a white patch for a boy to dream gloriously over. It had become a place of darkness. But there was in it one river especially, a mighty big river, that you could see on the map, resembling an immense snake uncoiled, with its head in the sea, its body at rest curving afar over a vast country, and its tail lost in the depths of the land. And as I looked at the map of it in a shop-window, it fascinated me as a snake would a bird – a silly little bird. Then I remembered there was a big concern, a Company for trade on that river. Dash it all! I thought to myself, they can't trade without using some kind of craft on that lot of fresh water – steamboats! Why shouldn't I try to get charge of one. I went on along Fleet Street, but could not shake off the idea. The snake had charmed me.

'You understand it was a Continental concern, that Trading society; but I have a lot of relations living on the Continent, because it's cheap and not so nasty as it looks, they say.

'I am sorry to own I began to worry them. This was already a fresh departure for me. I was not used to get things that way, you know. I always went my own road and on my own legs where I had a mind to go. I wouldn't have believed it of myself; but, then – you see – I felt somehow I must get there by hook or by crook. So I worried them. The men said "My dear fellow," and did nothing. Then – would you believe it? – I tried the women. I, Charlie Marlow, set the women to work – to get a job. Heavens! Well, you see, the notion drove me. I had an aunt, a dear enthusiastic soul. She wrote: "It will be delightful. I am ready to do anything, anything for you. It is a glorious idea. I know the wife of a very high personage in the Administration, and also a man who has lots of influence with," etc., etc. She was determined to make no end of fuss to get me appointed skipper of a river steamboat, if such was my fancy.

'I got my appointment – of course; and I got it very quick. It appears the Company had received news that one of their captains had been killed in a scuffle with the natives. This was my chance, and it made me the more anxious to go. It was only months and months afterwards, when I made the attempt to recover what was left of the body, that I heard the original quarrel arose from a misunderstanding about some hens. Yes, two black hens. Fresleven – that was the fellow's name, a Dane – thought himself wronged somehow in the bargain, so he went ashore and started to hammer the chief of the village with a stick. Oh, it didn't surprise me in the least to hear this, and at the same time to be told that Fresleven was the gentlest, quietest creature that ever walked on two legs. No doubt he was; but he had been a couple of years already out there engaged in the noble cause, you know, and he probably felt the need at last of asserting his self-respect in some way. Therefore he whacked the old nigger mercilessly, while a big crowd of his people watched him, thunderstruck, till some man – I was told the chief's son – in desperation at hearing the old chap yell, made a tentative jab with a spear at the white man – and of course it went quite easy between the shoulder-blades. Then the whole population cleared into the forest, expecting all kinds of calamities to happen, while, on the other hand, the steamer Fresleven commanded left also in a bad panic, in charge of the engineer, I believe. Afterwards nobody seemed to trouble much about Fresleven's remains, till I got out and stepped into his shoes. I couldn't let it rest, though; but when an opportunity offered at last to meet my predecessor, the grass growing through his ribs was tall enough to hide his bones. They were all there. The supernatural being had not been touched after he fell. And the village was deserted, the huts gaped black, rotting, all askew within the fallen enclosures. A calamity had come to it, sure enough. The people had vanished. Mad terror had scattered them, men, women, and children, through the bush, and they had never returned. What became of the hens I don't know either. I should think the cause of progress got them, anyhow. However, through this glorious affair I got my appointment, before I had fairly begun to hope for it.

'I flew around like mad to get ready, and before forty-eight hours I was crossing the Channel to show myself to my employers, and sign the contract. In a very few hours I arrived in a city that always makes me think of a whited sepulchre. Prejudice no doubt. I had no difficulty in finding the Company's offices. It was the biggest thing in the town, and everybody I met was full of it. They were going to run an over-sea empire, and make no end of coin by trade.

'A narrow and deserted street in deep shadow, high houses, innumerable windows with venetian blinds, a dead silence, grass sprouting between the stones, imposing carriage archways right and left, immense double doors standing ponderously ajar. I slipped through one of these cracks, went up a swept and ungarnished staircase, as arid as a desert, and opened the first door I came to. Two women, one fat and the other slim, sat on straw-bottomed chairs, knitting black wool. The slim one got up and walked straight at me – still knitting with downcast eyes – and only just as I began to think of getting out of her way, as you would for a somnambulist, stood still, and looked up. Her dress was as plain as an umbrella-cover, and she turned round without a word and preceded me into a waiting-room. I gave my name, and looked about. Deal table in the middle, plain chairs all round the walls, on one end a large shining map, marked with all the colours of a rainbow. There was a vast amount of red – good to see at any time, because one knows that some real work is done in there, a deuce of a lot of blue, a little green, smears of orange, and, on the East Coast, a purple patch, to show where the jolly pioneers of progress drink the jolly lager-beer. However, I wasn't going into any of these. I was going into the yellow. Dead in the centre. And the river was there – fascinating – deadly – like a snake. Ough! A door opened, a white-haired secretarial head, but wearing a compassionate expression, appeared and a skinny forefinger beckoned me into the sanctuary. Its light was dim, and a heavy writing-desk squatted in the middle. From behind that structure came out an impression of pale plumpness in a frock-coat. The great man himself. He was five feet six, I should judge, and had his grip on the handle-end of ever so many millions. He shook hands, I fancy, murmured vaguely, was satisfied with my French. *Bon voyage*.

'In about forty-five seconds I found myself again in the waiting-room with the compassionate secretary, who, full of desolation and sympathy, made me sign some document. I believe I undertook amongst other things not to disclose any trade secrets. Well, I am not going to.

'I began to feel slightly uneasy. You know I am not used to such ceremonies, and there was something ominous in the atmosphere. It was just as though I had been let into some conspiracy – I don't know – something not quite right; and I was glad to get out. In the outer room the two women knitted black wool feverishly. People were arriving, and the younger one was walking back and forth introducing them. The old one sat on her chair. Her flat cloth slippers were propped up on a footwarmer, and a cat reposed on her lap. She wore a starched white affair on her head, had a wart on one cheek, and silver-rimmed spectacles hung on the tip of her nose. She glanced at me above the glasses. The swift and indifferent placidity of that look troubled me. Two youths with foolish and cheery countenances were being piloted over, and she threw at them the same quick glance of unconcerned wisdom. She seemed to know all about them and about me too. An eerie feeling came over me. She seemed uncanny and fateful. Often far away there I thought of these two, guarding the door of Darkness, knitting black wool as for a warm pall, one introducing, introducing continuously to the unknown, the other scrutinising the cheery and foolish faces with unconcerned old eyes. *Ave!* Old knitter of black wool. *Morituri te salutant.* Not many of those she looked at ever saw her again – not half, by a long way.

'There was yet a visit to the doctor. "A simple formality," assured me the secretary, with an air of taking an immense part in all my sorrows. Accordingly a young chap wearing his hat over the left eyebrow, some clerk I suppose – there must have been clerks in the business, though the house was as still as a house in a city of the dead – came from somewhere upstairs, and led me forth. He was shabby and careless, with ink-stains on the sleeves of his jacket, and his cravat was large and billowy, under a chin shaped like the toe of an old boot. It was a little too early for the doctor, so I proposed a drink, and thereupon he developed a vein of joviality. As we sat over our vermouths he glorified the Company's business, and by and by I expressed casually my surprise at him not going out there. He became very cool and collected all at once. "I am not such a fool as I look, quoth Plato to his disciples," he said sententiously, emptied his glass with great resolution, and we rose.

'The old doctor felt my pulse, evidently thinking of something else the while, "Good, good for there," he mumbled, and then with a certain eagerness asked me whether I would let him measure my head. Rather surprised, I said Yes, when he produced a thing like calipers and got the dimensions back and front and every way, taking notes carefully. He was an unshaven little man in a threadbare coat like a gaberdine, with his feet in slippers, and I thought him a harmless fool. "I always ask leave, in the interests of science, to measure the crania of those going out there," he said. "And when they come back too?" I asked. "Oh, I never see them," he remarked; "and, moreover, the changes take place inside, you know." He smiled, as if at some quiet joke. "So you are going out there. Famous. Interesting too." He gave me a searching glance, and made another note. "Ever any madness in your family?" he asked, in a matter-of-fact tone. I felt very annoyed. "Is that question in the interests of science too?" "It would be," he said, without taking notice of my irritation, "interesting for science to watch the mental changes of individuals, on the spot, but . . . " "Are you an alienist?" I interrupted. "Every doctor should be – a little," answered that original, imperturbably. "I have a little theory which you Messieurs who go out there must help me to prove. This is my share in the advantages my country shall reap from the possession of such a magnificent dependency. The mere wealth I leave to others. Pardon my questions, but you are the first Englishman coming under my observation . . ." I hastened to assure him I was not in the least typical. "If I were," said I, "I wouldn't be talking like this with you." "What you say is rather profound, and probably erroneous," he said, with a laugh. "Avoid irritation more than exposure to the sun. Adieu. How do you English say, eh? Goodbye. Ah! Goodbye. Adieu. In the tropics one must before everything keep calm." . . . He lifted a warning forefinger . . . "*Du calme, du calme. Adieu.*"

'One thing more remained to do – say goodbye to my excellent aunt. I found her triumphant. I had a cup of tea – the last decent cup of tea for many days – and in a room that most soothingly looked just as you would expect a lady's drawing-room to look, we had a long quiet chat by the fireside. In the course of these confidences it became quite plain to me I had been represented to the wife of the high dignitary, and goodness knows to how many more people besides, as an exceptional and gifted creature – a piece of good fortune for the Company – a man you don't get hold of everyday. Good heavens! and I was going to take charge of a twopenny-halfpenny river-steamboat with a penny whistle attached! It appeared, however, I was also one of the Workers, with a capital – you know. Something like an emissary of light, something like a lower sort of apostle. There had been a lot of such rot let loose in print and talk just about that time, and the excellent woman, living right in the rush of all that humbug, got carried off her feet. She talked about "weaning those ignorant millions from their horrid ways," till, upon my word, she made me quite uncomfortable. I ventured to hint that the Company was run for profit.

' "You forget, dear Charlie, that the labourer is worthy of his hire," she said, brightly. It's queer how out of touch with truth women are. They live in a world of their own, and there had never been anything like it, and never can be. It is too beautiful altogether, and if they were to set it up it would go to pieces before the first sunset. Some confounded fact we men have been living contentedly with ever since the day of creation would start up and knock the whole thing over.

'After this I got embraced, told to wear flannel, be sure to write often, and so on – and I left. In the street I don't know why – a queer feeling came to me that I was an impostor: Odd thing that I, who used to clear out for any part of the world at twenty-four hours' notice, with less thought than most men give to the crossing of a street, had a moment – I won't say of hesitation, but of startled pause, before this commonplace affair. The best way I can explain it to you is by saying that, for a second or two, I felt as though, instead of going to the centre of a continent, I were about to set off for the centre of the earth.

'I left in a French steamer, and she called in every blamed port they have out there, for, as far as I could see, the sole purpose of landing soldiers and custom-house officers. I watched the coast. Watching a coast as it slips by the ship is like thinking about an enigma. There it is before you – smiling, frowning, inviting, grand, mean, insipid, or savage, and always mute with an air of whispering, Come and find out. This one was almost featureless, as if still in the making, with an aspect of monotonous grimness. The edge of a colossal jungle, so dark-green as to be almost black, fringed with white surf, ran straight, like a ruled line, far, far away along a blue sea whose glitter was blurred by a creeping mist. The sun was fierce, the land seemed to glisten and drip with steam. Here and there greyish-whitish specks showed up clustered inside the white surf, with a flag flying above them perhaps. Settlements some centuries old, and still no bigger than pin-heads on the untouched expanse of their background. We pounded along, stopped, landed soldiers; went on, landed custom-house clerks to levy toll in what looked like a God-forsaken wilderness, with a tin shed and a flag-pole lost in it; landed more soldiers – to take care of the custom-house clerks, presumably. Some, I heard, got drowned in the surf; but whether they did or not, nobody seemed particularly to care. They were just flung out there, and on we went. Every day the coast looked the same, as though we had not moved; but we passed various places = trading places – with names like Gran' Bassam, Little Popo; names that seemed to belong to some sordid farce acted in front of a sinister backcloth. The idleness of a passenger, my isolation amongst all these men with whom I had no point of contact, the oily and languid sea, the uniform sombreness of the coast, seemed to keep me away from the truth of things, within the toil of a mournful and senseless delusion. The voice of the surf heard now and then was a positive pleasure, like the speech of a brother. It was something natural, that had its reason, that had a meaning. Now and then a boat from the shore gave one a momentary contact with reality. It was paddled by black fellows. You could see from afar the white of their eyeballs glistening. They shouted, sang; their bodies streamed with perspiration; they had faces like grotesque masks – these chaps; but they had bone, muscle, a wild vitality, an intense energy of movement, that was as natural and true as the surf along their coast. They wanted no excuse for being there. They were a great comfort to look at. For a time I would feel I belonged still to a world of straightforward facts; but the feeling would not last long. Something would turn up to scare it away. Once, I remember, we came upon a man-of-war anchored off the coast. There wasn't even a shed there, and she was shelling the bush. It appears the French had one of their wars going on thereabouts. Her ensign dropped limp like a rag; the muzzles of the long six-inch guns stuck out all over the low hull; the greasy, slimy swell swung her up lazily and let her down, swaying her thin masts. In the empty immensity of earth, sky, and water, there she was, incomprehensible, firing into a continent. Pop, would go one of the six-inch guns; a small flame would dart and vanish, a little white smoke would disappear, a tiny projectile would give a feeble screech – and nothing happened. Nothing could happen. There was a touch of insanity in the proceeding, a sense of lugubrious drollery in the sight; and it was not dissipated by somebody on board assuring me earnestly there was a camp of natives – he called them enemies! – hidden out of sight somewhere.

'We gave her her letters (I heard the men in that lonely ship were dying of fever at the rate of three a-day) and went on. We called at some more places with farcical names, where the merry dance of death and trade goes on in a still and earthy atmosphere as of an overheated catacomb; all along the formless coast bordered by dangerous surf, as if Nature herself had tried to ward off intruders; in and out of rivers, streams of death in life, whose banks were rotting into mud, whose waters, thickened into slime, invaded the contorted mangroves, that seemed to writhe at us in the extremity of an impotent despair. Nowhere did we stop long enough to get a particularised impression, but the general sense of vague and oppressive wonder grew upon me. It was like a weary pilgrimage amongst hints for nightmares.

'It was upward of thirty days before I saw the mouth of the big river. We anchored off the seat of the government. But my work would not begin till some two hundred miles farther on. So as soon as I could I made a start for a place thirty miles higher up.

'I had my passage on a little seagoing steamer. Her captain was a Swede, and knowing me for a seaman, invited me on the bridge. He was a young man, lean, fair, and morose, with lanky hair and a shuffling gait. As we left the miserable little wharf, he tossed his head contemptuously at the shore. "Been living there?" he asked. I said, "Yes." "Fine lot these government chaps – are they not?" he went on, speaking English with great precision and considerable bitterness. "It is funny what some people will do for a few francs a-month. I wonder what becomes of that kind when it goes up country?" I said to him I expected to see that soon. "So–o–o!" he exclaimed. He shuffled athwart, keeping one eye ahead vigilantly. "Don't be too sure," he continued. "The other day I took up a man who hanged himself on the road. He was a Swede, too." "Hanged himself! Why, in God's name?" I cried. He kept on looking out watchfully. "Who knows? The sun too much for him, or the country perhaps."

'At last we opened a reach. A rocky cliff appeared, mounds of turned-up earth by the shore, houses on a hill, others with iron roofs, amongst a waste of excavations, or hanging to the declivity. A continuous noise of the rapids above hovered over this scene of inhabited devastation. A lot of people, mostly black and naked, moved about like ants. A jetty projected into the river. A blinding sunlight drowned all this at times in a sudden recrudescence of glare. "There's your Company's station," said the Swede, pointing to three wooden barrack-like structures on the rocky slope. "I will send your things up. Four boxes did you say? So. Farewell."

'I came upon a boiler wallowing in the grass, then found a path leading up the hill. It turned aside for the boulders, and also for an undersized railway-truck lying there on its back with its wheels in the air. One was off. The thing looked as dead as the carcass of some animal. I came upon more pieces of decaying machinery, a stack of rusty rails. To the left a clump of trees made a shady spot, where dark things seemed to stir feebly. I blinked, the path was steep. A horn tooted to the right, and I saw the black people run. A heavy and dull detonation shook the ground, a puff of smoke came out of the cliff, and that was all. No change appeared on the face of the rock. They were building a railway. The cliff was not in the way or anything; but this objectless blasting was all the work going on.

'A slight clinking behind me made me turn my head. Six black men advanced in a file, toiling up the path. They walked erect and slow, balancing small baskets full of earth on their heads, and the clink kept time with their footsteps. Black rags were wound round their loins, and the short ends behind waggled to and fro like tails. I could see every rib, the joints of their limbs were like knots in a rope; each had an iron collar on his neck, and all were connected together with a chain whose bights swung between them, rhythmically clinking. Another report from the cliff made me think suddenly of that ship of war I had seen firing into a continent. It was the same kind of ominous voice; but these men could by no stretch of imagination be called enemies. They were called criminals, and the outraged law, like the bursting shells, had come to them, an insoluble mystery from the sea. All their meagre breasts panted together, the violently dilated nostrils quivered, the eyes stared stonily uphill. They passed me within six inches, without a glance, with that complete, deathlike indifference of unhappy savages. Behind this raw matter one of the reclaimed, the product of the new forces at work, strolled despondently, carrying a rifle by its middle. He had a uniform jacket with one button off, and seeing a white man on the path, hoisted his weapon to his shoulder with alacrity. This was simple prudence, white men being so much alike at a distance that he could not tell who I might be. He was speedily reassured, and with a large, white, rascally grin, and a glance at his charge, seemed to take me into partnership in his exalted trust. After all, I also was a part of the great cause of these high and just proceedings.

'Instead of going up, I turned and descended to the left. My idea was to let that chain-gang get out of sight before I climbed the hill. You know I am not particularly tender; I've had to strike and to fend off. I've had to resist and to attack sometimes – that's only one way of resisting – without counting the exact cost, according to the demands of such sort of life as I had blundered into. I've seen the devil of violence, and the devil of greed, and the devil of hot desire; but by all the stars! these were strong, lusty, red-eyed devils, that swayed and drove men – men, I tell you. But as I stood on this hillside, I foresaw that in the blinding sunshine of that land I would become acquainted with a flabby, pretending, weak-eyed devil of a rapacious and pitiless folly. How insidious he could be, too, I was only to find out several months later and a thousand miles farther. For a moment I stood appalled, as though by a warning. Finally I descended the hill, obliquely, towards the trees I had seen.

'I avoided a vast artificial hole somebody had been digging on the slope, the purpose of which I found it impossible to divine. It wasn't a quarry or a sandpit, anyhow. It was just a hole. It might have been connected with the philanthropic desire of giving the criminals something to do. I don't know. Then I nearly fell into a very narrow ravine, almost no more than a scar in the hillside. I discovered that a lot of imported drainage-pipes for the settlement had been tumbled in there. There wasn't one that was not broken. It was a wanton smash-up. At last I got under the trees. My purpose was to stroll into the shade for a moment; but no sooner within than it seemed to me I had stepped into the gloomy circle of some Inferno. The rapids were near, and an uninterrupted, uniform, headlong, rushing noise filled the mournful stillness of the grove, where not a breath stirred, not a leaf moved, with a mysterious sound – as though the tearing pace of the launched earth had suddenly become audible.

'Black shapes crouched, lay, sat between the trees, leaning against the trunks, clinging to the earth, half coming out, half effaced within the dim light, in all the attitudes of pain, abandonment, and despair. Another mine on the cliff went off, followed by a slight shudder of the soil under my feet. The work was going on. The work! And this was the place where some of the helpers had withdrawn to die.

'They were dying slowly – it was very clear. They were not enemies, they were not criminals, they were nothing earthly now – nothing but black shadows of disease and starvation, lying confusedly in the greenish gloom. Brought from all the recesses of the coast in all the legality of time contracts, lost in uncongenial surroundings, fed on unfamiliar food, they sickened, became inefficient, and were then allowed to crawl away and rest. These moribund shapes were free as air – and nearly as thin. I began to distinguish the gleam of the eyes under the trees. Then, glancing down, I saw a face near my hand. The black bones reclined at full length with one shoulder against the tree, and slowly the eyelids rose and the sunken eyes looked up at me, enormous and vacant, a kind of blind, white flicker in the depths of the orbs, which died out slowly. The man seemed young – almost a boy – but you know with them it's hard to tell. I found nothing else to do but to offer him one of my good Swede's ship's biscuits I had in my pocket. The fingers closed slowly on it and held – there was no other movement and no other glance. He had tied a bit of white worsted round his neck – Why? Where did he get it? Was it a badge – an ornament – a charm – a propitiatory act? Was there any idea at all connected with it? It looked startling round his black neck, this bit of white thread from beyond the seas.

'Near the same tree two more bundles of acute angles sat with their legs drawn up. One, with his chin propped on his knees, stared at nothing, in an intolerable and appalling manner: his brother phantom rested its forehead, as if overcome with a great weariness; and all about others were scattered in every pose of contorted collapse, as in some picture of a massacre or a pestilence. While I stood horror-struck, one of these creatures rose to his hands and knees, and went off on all-fours towards the river to drink. He lapped out of his hand, then sat up in the sunlight, crossing his shins in front of him and after a time let his woolly head fall on his breastbone.

'I didn't want any more loitering in the shade, and I made haste towards the station. When near the buildings I met a white man, in such an unexpected elegance of get-up that in the first moment I took him for a sort of vision. I saw a high starched collar, white cuffs, a light alpaca jacket, snowy trousers, a clear necktie, and varnished boots. No hat. Hair parted, brushed, oiled, under a green-lined parasol held in a big white hand. He was amazing, and had a penholder behind his ear.

'I shook hands with this miracle, and I learned he was the Company's chief accountant, and that all the bookkeeping was done at this station. He had come out for a moment, he said, "to get a breath of fresh air." The expression sounded wonderfully odd, with its suggestion of sedentary desk-life.

I wouldn't have mentioned the fellow to you at all, only it was from his lips that I first heard the name of the man who is so indissolubly connected with the memories of that time. Moreover, I respected the fellow. Yes; I respected his collars, his vast cuffs, his brushed hair. His appearance was certainly that of a hairdresser's dummy; but in the great demoralisation of the land he kept up his appearance. That's backbone. His starched collars and got-up shirt-fronts were achievements of character. He had been out nearly three years; and, later, I could not help asking him how he managed to sport such linen. He had just the faintest blush, and said modestly, "I've been teaching one of the native women about the station. It was difficult. She had a distaste for the work." Thus this man had verily accomplished something. And he was devoted to his books, which were in apple-pie order.

'Everything else in the station was in a muddle – heads, things, buildings. Strings of dusty niggers with splay feet arrived and departed; a stream of manufactured goods, rubbishy cottons, beads, and brass-wire set into the depths of darkness, and in return came a precious trickle of ivory.

'I had to wait in the station for ten days – an eternity. I lived in a hut in the yard, but to be out of the chaos I would sometimes get into the accountant's office. It was built of horizontal planks, and so badly put together that, as he bent over his high desk, he was barred from neck to heels with narrow strips of sunlight. There was no need to open the big shutter to see. It was hot there too; big flies buzzed fiendishly, and did not sting, but stabbed. I sat generally on the floor, while, of faultless appearance (and even slightly scented), perching on a high stool, he wrote, he wrote. Sometimes he stood up for exercise. When a truckle-bed with a sick man (some invalided agent from up-country) was put in there, he exhibited a gentle annoyance. "The groans of this sick person," he said, "distract my attention. And without that it is extremely difficult to guard against clerical errors in this climate."

'One day he remarked, without lifting his head, "In the interior you will no doubt meet Mr Kurtz." On my asking who Mr Kurtz was, he said he was a first-class agent; and seeing my disappointment at this information, he added slowly, laying down his pen, "He is a very remarkable person." Further questions elicited from him that Mr Kurtz was at present in charge of a trading post, a very important one, in the true ivory-country, at "the very bottom of there. Sends in as much ivory as all the others put together . . ." He began to write again. The sick man was too ill to groan. The flies buzzed in a great peace.

'Suddenly there was a growing murmur of voices and a great tramping of feet. A caravan had come in. A violent babble of uncouth sounds burst out on the other side of the planks. All the carriers were speaking together, and in the midst of the uproar the lamentable voice of the chief agent was heard "giving it up" tearfully for the twentieth time that day . . . He rose slowly. "What a frightful row," he said. He crossed the room gently to look at the sick man, and returning, said to me, "He does not hear." "What! Dead?"

I asked, startled. "No, not yet," he answered, with great composure. Then, alluding with a toss of the head to the tumult in the station-yard, "When one has got to make correct entries, one comes to hate those savages – hate them to the death." He remained thoughtful for a moment. "When you see Mr Kurtz," he went on, "tell him from me that everything here" – he glanced at the desk – " is very satisfactory. I don't like to write to him – with those messengers of ours you never know who may get hold of your letter – at that Central Station." He stared at me for a moment with his mild, bulging eyes. "Oh, he will go far, very far," he began again. "He will be a somebody in the Administration before long. They, above – the Council in Europe, you know – mean him to be."

'He turned to his work. The noise outside had ceased, and presently in going out I stopped at the door. In the steady buzz of flies the homeward-bound agent was lying flushed and insensible; the other, bent over his books, was making correct entries of perfectly correct transactions; and fifty feet below the doorstep I could see the still treetops of the grove of death.

'Next day I left that station at last, with a caravan of sixty men, for a two-hundred-mile tramp.

'No use telling you much about that. Paths, paths, everywhere; a stamped-in network of paths spreading over the empty land, through long grass, through burnt grass, through thickets, down and up chilly ravines, up and down stony hills ablaze with heat; and a solitude, a solitude, nobody, not a hut. The population had cleared out a long time ago. Well, if a lot of mysterious niggers armed with all kinds of fearful weapons suddenly took to travelling on the road between Deal and Gravesend, catching the yokels right and left to carry heavy loads for them, I fancy every farm and cottage thereabouts would get empty very soon. Only here the dwellings were gone too. Still I passed through several abandoned villages. There's something pathetically childish in the ruins of grass walls. Day after day, with the stamp and shuffle of sixty pair of bare feet behind me, each pair under a 60-lb load. Camp, cook, sleep, strike camp, march. Now and then a carrier dead in harness, at rest in the long grass near the path, with an empty water-gourd and his long staff lying by his side. A great silence around and above. Perhaps on some quiet night the tremor of far-off drums, sinking, swelling, a tremor vast, faint; a sound weird, appealing, suggestive, and wild – and perhaps with as profound a meaning as the sound of bells in a Christian country. Once a white man in an unbuttoned uniform, camping on the path with an armed escort of lank Zanzibaris, very hospitable and festive – not to say drunk. Was looking after the upkeep of the road, he declared. Can't say I saw any road or any upkeep, unless the body of a middle-aged Negro, with a bullet-hole in the forehead, upon which I absolutely stumbled three miles farther on, may be considered as a permanent improvement. I had a white companion too, not a bad chap, but rather too fleshy and with the exasperating habit of fainting on the hot hillsides, miles away from the least bit of shade and water.

Annoying, you know, to hold your own coat like a parasol over a man's head while he is coming-to. I couldn't help asking him once what he meant by coming there at all. "To make money, of course. What do you think?" he said, scornfully. Then he got fever, and had to be carried in a hammock slung under a pole. As he weighed sixteen stone I had no end of rows with the carriers. They jibbed, ran away, sneaked off with their loads in the night – quite a mutiny. So, one evening, I made a speech in English with gestures, not one of which was lost to the sixty pairs of eyes before me, and the next morning I started the hammock off in front all right. An hour afterwards I came upon the whole concern wrecked in a bush – man, hammock, groans, blankets, horrors. The heavy pole had skinned his poor nose. He was very anxious for me to kill somebody, but there wasn't the shadow of a carrier near. I remembered the old doctor – "It would be interesting for science to watch the mental changes of individuals, on the spot." I felt I was becoming scientifically interesting. However, all that is to no purpose. On the fifteenth day I came in sight of the big river again, and hobbled into the Central Station. It was on a backwater surrounded by scrub and forest, with a pretty border of smelly mud on one side, and on the three others enclosed by a crazy fence of rushes. A neglected gap was all the gate it had, and the first glance at the place was enough to let you see the flabby devil was running that show. White men with long staves in their hands appeared languidly from amongst the buildings, strolling up to take a look at me, and then retired out of sight somewhere. One of them, a stout, excitable chap with black moustaches, informed me with great volubility and many digressions, as soon as I told him who I was, that my steamer was at the bottom of the river. I was thunderstruck. What, how, why? Oh, it was "all right." The "manager himself" was there. All quite correct. "Everybody had behaved splendidly! splendidly!" – "You must," he said in agitation, "go and see the general manager at once. He is waiting!"

'I did not see the real significance of that wreck at once. I fancy I see it now, but I am not sure – not at all. Certainly the affair was too stupid – when I think of it – to be altogether natural. Still . . . But at the moment it presented itself simply as a confounded nuisance. The steamer was sunk. They had started two days before in a sudden hurry up the river with the manager on board, in charge of some volunteer skipper, and before they had been out three hours they tore the bottom out of her on stones, and she sank near the south bank. I asked myself what I was to do there, now my boat was lost. As a matter of fact, I had plenty to do in fishing my command out of the river. I had to set about it the very next day. That, and the repairs when I brought the pieces to the station, took some months.

'My first interview with the manager was curious. He did not ask me to sit down after my twenty-mile walk that morning. He was commonplace in complexion, in feature, in manners, and in voice. He was of middle size and of ordinary build. His eyes, of the usual blue, were perhaps remarkably cold, and he certainly could make his glance fall on one as trenchant and heavy as an axe. But even at these times the rest of his person seemed to disclaim the intention. Otherwise there was only an indefinable, faint expression of his lips, something stealthy – a smile – not a smile – I remember it, but I can't explain. It was unconscious, this smile was, though just after he had said something it got intensified for an instant. It came at the end of his speeches like a seal applied on the words to make the meaning of the commonest phrase appear absolutely inscrutable. He was a common trader, from his youth up employed in these parts – nothing more. He was obeyed, yet he inspired neither love nor fear, nor even respect. He inspired uneasiness. That was it! Uneasiness. Not a definite mistrust – just uneasiness – nothing more. You have no idea how effective such a . . . a . . . faculty can be. He had no genius for organising, for initiative, or for order even. That was evident in such things as the deplorable state of the station. He had no learning, and no intelligence. His position had come to him – why? Perhaps because he was never ill . . . He had served three terms of three years out there . . . Because triumphant health in the general rout of constitutions is a kind of power in itself. When he went home on leave he rioted on a large scale – pompously. Jack ashore – with a difference – in externals only. This one could gather from his casual talk. He originated nothing, he could keep the routine going – that's all. But he was great. He was great by this little thing that it was impossible to tell what could control such a man. He never gave that secret away. Perhaps there was nothing within him. Such a suspicion made one pause – for out there there were no external checks. Once when various tropical diseases had laid low almost every "agent" in the station, he was heard to say, "Men who come out here should have no entrails." He sealed the utterance with that smile of his, as though it had been a door opening into a darkness he had in his keeping. You fancied you had seen things – but the seal was on. When annoyed at meal-times by the constant quarrels of the white men about precedence, he ordered an immense round table to be made, for which a special house had to be built. This was the station's mess-room. Where he sat was the first place – the rest were nowhere. One felt this to be his unalterable conviction. He was neither civil nor uncivil. He was quiet. He allowed his "boy" – an overfed young Negro from the coast – to treat the white men, under his very eyes, with provoking insolence.

'He began to speak as soon as he saw me. I had been very long on the road. He could not wait. Had to start without me. The up-river stations had to be relieved. There had been so many delays already that he did not know who was dead and who was alive, and how they got on – and so on, and so on. He paid no attention to my explanations, and, playing with a stick of sealing-wax, repeated several times that the situation was "very grave, very grave." There were rumours that a very important station was in jeopardy, and its chief, Mr Kurtz, was ill. Hoped it was not true. Mr Kurtz was . . . I felt weary and irritable. Hang Kurtz, I thought. I interrupted him by saying I had heard of

Mr Kurtz on the coast. "Ah! So they talk of him down there," he murmured to himself. Then he began again, assuring me Mr Kurtz was the best agent he had, an exceptional man, of the greatest importance to the Company; therefore I could understand his anxiety. He was, he said, "very, very uneasy." Certainly he fidgeted on his chair a good deal, exclaimed, "Ah, Mr Kurtz!" broke the stick of sealing-wax and seemed dumfounded by the accident. Next thing he wanted to know "how long it would take to" . . . I interrupted him again. Being hungry, you know, and kept on my feet too, I was getting savage. "How could I tell?" I said. "I hadn't even seen the wreck yet – some months, no doubt." All this talk seemed to me so futile. "Some months," he said. "Well let us say three months before we can make a start. Yes. That ought to do the affair." I flung out of his hut (he lived all alone in a clay hut with a sort of verandah) muttering to myself my opinion of him. He was a chattering idiot. Afterwards I took it back when it was borne in upon me startlingly with what extreme nicety he had estimated the time requisite for the "affair".

'I went to work the next day, turning, so to speak, my back on that station. In that way only it seemed to me I could keep my hold on the redeeming facts of life. Still, one must look about sometimes; and then I saw this station, these men strolling aimlessly about in the sunshine of the yard. I asked myself sometimes what it all meant. They wandered here and there with their absurd long staves in their hands, like a lot of faithless pilgrims bewitched inside a rotten fence. The word "ivory" rang in the air, was whispered, was sighed. You would think they were praying to it. A taint of imbecile rapacity blew through it all, like a whiff from some corpse. By Jove! I've never seen anything so unreal in my life. And outside, the silent wilderness surrounding this cleared speck on the earth struck me as something great and invincible, like evil or truth, waiting patiently for the passing away of this fantastic invasion.

'Oh, these months! Well, never mind. Various things happened. One evening a grass shed full of calico, cotton prints, beads, and I don't know what else, burst into a blaze so suddenly that you would have thought the earth had opened to let an avenging fire consume all that trash. I was smoking my pipe quietly by my dismantled steamer, and saw them all cutting capers in the light, with their arms lifted high, when the stout man with moustaches came tearing down to the river, a tin pail in his hand, assured me that everybody was "behaving splendidly, splendidly," dipped about a quart of water and tore back again. I noticed there was a hole in the bottom of his pail.

'I strolled up. There was no hurry. You see the thing had gone off like a box of matches. It had been hopeless from the very first. The flame had leaped high, driven everybody back, lighted up everything – and collapsed. The shed was already a heap of embers glowing fiercely. A nigger was being beaten near by. They said he had caused the fire in some way; be that as it may, he was screeching most horribly. I saw him, later, for several days, sitting in a bit of shade looking very sick and trying to recover himself:

afterwards he arose and went out – and the wilderness without a sound took him into its bosom again. As I approached the glow from the dark I found myself at the back of two men, talking. I heard the name of Kurtz pronounced, then the words, "take advantage of this unfortunate accident". One of the men was the manager. I wished him a good-evening. "Did you ever see anything like it – eh? it is incredible," he said, and walked off. The other man remained. He was a first-class agent, young, gentlemanly, a bit reserved, with a forked little beard and a hooked nose. He was stand-offish with the other agents, and they on their side said he was the manager's spy upon them. As to me, I had hardly ever spoken to him before. We got into talk, and by and by we strolled away from the hissing ruins. Then he asked me to his room, which was in the main building of the station. He struck a match, and I perceived that this young aristocrat had not only a silver-mounted dressing-case but also a whole candle all to himself. Just at that time the manager was the only man supposed to have any right to candles. Native mats covered the clay walls; a collection of spears, assegais, shields, knives was hung up in trophies. The business entrusted to this fellow was the making of bricks – so I had been informed; but there wasn't a fragment of a brick anywhere in the station, and he had been there more than a year – waiting. It seems he could not make bricks without something, I don't know what – straw maybe. Anyways, it could not be found there, and as it was not likely to be sent from Europe, it did not appear clear to me what he was waiting for. An act of special creation perhaps. However, they were all waiting – all the sixteen or twenty pilgrims of them – for something; and upon my word it did not seem an uncongenial occupation, from the way they took it, though the only thing that ever came to them was disease – as far as I could see. They beguiled the time by backbiting and intriguing against each other in a foolish kind of way. There was an air of plotting about that station, but nothing came of it, of course. It was as unreal as everything else – as the philanthropic pretence of the whole concern, as their talk, as their government, as their show of work. The only real feeling was a desire to get appointed to a trading-post where ivory was to be had, so that they could earn percentages. They intrigued and slandered and hated each other only on that account – but as to effectually lifting a little finger – oh, no. By heavens! there is something after all in the world allowing one man to steal a horse while another must not look at a halter. Steal a horse straight out. Very well. He has done it. Perhaps he can ride. But there is a way of looking at a halter that would provoke the most charitable of saints into a kick.

'I had no idea why he wanted to be sociable, but as we chatted in there it suddenly occurred to me the fellow was trying to get at something – in fact, pumping me. He alluded constantly to Europe, to the people I was supposed to know there – putting leading questions as to my acquaintances in the sepulchral city, and so on. His little eyes glittered like mica discs – with curiosity – though he tried to keep up a bit of superciliousness. At first I was astonished, but very soon I became awfully curious to see what he would find out from me. I couldn't possibly imagine what I had in me to make it worth his while. It was very pretty to see how he baffled himself, for in truth my body was full only of chills, and my head had nothing in it but that wretched steamboat business. It was evident he took me for a perfectly shameless prevaricator. At last he got angry, and, to conceal a movement of furious annoyance, he yawned. I rose. Then I noticed a small sketch in oils, on a panel, representing a woman, draped and blindfolded, carrying a lighted torch. The background was sombre – almost black. The movement of the woman was stately, and the effect of the torchlight on the face was sinister.

'It arrested me, and he stood by civilly, holding an empty half-pint champagne bottle (medical comforts) with the candle stuck in it. To my question he said Mr Kurtz had painted this – in this very station more than a year ago – while waiting for means to go to his trading-post. "Tell me, pray," said I, "who is this Mr Kurtz?"

' "The chief of the Inner Station," he answered in a short tone, looking away. "Much obliged," I said, laughing. "And you are the brickmaker of the Central Station. Everyone knows that." He was silent for a while. "He is a prodigy," he said at last. "He is an emissary of pity, and science, and progress, and devil knows what else. We want," he began to declaim suddenly, "for the guidance of the cause entrusted to us by Europe, so to speak, higher intelligence, wide sympathies, a singleness of purpose." "Who says that?" I asked. "Lots of them," he replied. "Some even write that; and so *he* comes here, a special being, as you ought to know." "Why ought I to know?" I interrupted, really surprised. He paid no attention. "Yes. Today he is chief of the best station, next year he will be assistant-manager, two years more and . . . but I dare say you know what he will be in two years' time. You are of the new gang – the gang of virtue. The same people who sent him specially also recommended you. Oh, don't say no. I've my own eyes to trust." Light dawned upon me. My dear aunt's influential acquaintances were producing an unexpected effect upon that young man. I nearly burst into a laugh. "Do you read the Company's confidential correspondence?" I asked. He hadn't a word to say. It was great fun. "When Mr Kurtz," I continued severely, "is General Manager, you won't have the opportunity."

'He blew the candle out suddenly, and we went outside. The moon had risen. Black figures strolled about listlessly, pouring water on the glow, whence proceeded a sound of hissing; steam ascended in the moonlight, the beaten nigger groaned somewhere. "What a row the brute makes!" said the indefatigable man with the moustaches, appearing near us. "Serve him right. Transgression – punishment – bang! Pitiless, pitiless. That's the only way. This will prevent all conflagrations for the future. I was just telling the manager . . . " He noticed my companion, and became crestfallen all at once. "Not in bed yet," he said, with a kind of servile heartiness; "it's so natural. Ha! Danger – agitation." He vanished. I went on to the riverside, and the other followed me. I heard a scathing murmur at my ear, "Heap of muffs – go to." The pilgrims could be seen in knots gesticulating, discussing. Several had still their staves in their hands. I verily believe they took these sticks to bed with them. Beyond the fence the forest stood up spectrally in the moonlight, and through the dim stir, through the faint sounds of that lamentable courtyard, the silence of the land went home to one's very heart – its mystery, its greatness, the amazing reality of its concealed life. The hurt nigger moaned feebly somewhere near by, and then fetched a deep sigh that made me mend my pace away from there. I felt a hand introducing itself under my arm. "My dear sir," said the fellow, "I don't want to be misunderstood, and especially by you, who will see Mr Kurtz long before I can have that pleasure. I wouldn't like him to get a false idea of my disposition . . ."

'I let him run on, this papier-mâché Mephistopheles, and it seemed to me that if I tried I could poke my forefinger through him, and would find nothing inside but a little loose dirt, maybe. He, don't you see, had been planning to be assistant-manager by and by under the present man, and I could see that the coming of that Kurtz had upset them both not a little. He talked precipitately, and I did not try to stop him. I had my shoulders against the wreck of my steamer, hauled up on the slope like a carcass of some big river animal. The smell of mud, of primeval mud, by Jove! was in my nostrils, the high stillness of primeval forest was before my eyes; there were shiny patches on the black creek. The moon had spread over everything a thin layer of silver – over the rank grass, over the mud, upon the wall of matted vegetation standing higher than the wall of a temple, over the great river I could see through a sombre gap glittering, glittering, as it flowed broadly by without a murmur. All this was great, expectant, mute, while the man jabbered about himself. I wondered whether the stillness on the face of the immensity looking at us two were meant as an appeal or as a menace. What were we who had strayed in here? Could we handle that dumb thing, or would it handle us? I felt how big how confoundedly big, was that thing that couldn't talk, and perhaps was deaf as well. What was in there? I could see a little ivory coming out from there, and I had heard Mr Kurtz was in there. I had heard enough about it too – God knows! Yet somehow it didn't bring any image with it – no more than if I had been told an angel or a fiend was in there. I believed it in the same way one of you might believe there are inhabitants in the planet Mars. I knew once a Scotch sailmaker who was certain, dead sure, there were people in Mars. If you asked him for some idea how they looked and behaved, he would get shy and mutter something about "walking on all-fours". If you as much as smiled, he would – though a man of sixty – offer to fight you. I would not have gone so far as to fight for Kurtz, but I went for him near enough to a lie. You know I hate, detest, and can't bear a lie, not because I am straighter than the rest of us, but simply because it appals me. There is a taint of death, a flavour of mortality in lies – which is exactly what I hate and detest in the world – what I want to forget. It makes me miserable and sick, like biting something rotten would do. Temperament, I suppose. Well, I went near enough to it by letting the young fool there believe anything he liked to imagine as to my influence in Europe. I became in an instant as much of a pretence as the rest of the bewitched pilgrims. This simply because I had a notion it somehow would be of help to that Kurtz whom at the time I did not see – you understand. He was just a word for me. I did not see the man in the name any more than you do. Do you see him? Do you see the story? Do you see anything? It seems to me I am trying to tell you a dream – making a vain attempt, because no relation of a dream can convey the dream-sensation, that commingling of absurdity, surprise, and bewilderment in a tremor of struggling revolt, that notion of being captured by the incredible which is of the very essence of dreams. . . '

He was silent for a while.

' . . . No, it is impossible; it is impossible to convey the life-sensation of any given epoch of one's existence – that which makes its truth, its meaning – its subtle and penetrating essence. It is impossible. We live, as we dream – alone . . . '

He paused again as if reflecting, then added – 'Of course in this you fellows see more than I could then. You see me, whom you know. . . '

It had become so pitch dark that we listeners could hardly see one another. For a long time already he, sitting apart, had been no more to us than a voice. There was not a word from anybody. The others might have been asleep, but I was awake. I listened, I listened on the watch for the sentence, for the word, that would give me the clue to the faint uneasiness inspired by this narrative that seemed to shape itself without human lips in the heavy night-air of the river.

' . . . Yes – I let him run on,' Marlow began again, 'and think what he pleased about the powers that were behind me. I did! And there was nothing behind me! There was nothing but that wretched, old, mangled steamboat I was leaning against, while he talked fluently about "the necessity for every man to get on". "And when one comes out here, you conceive, it is not to gaze at the moon." Mr Kurtz was a "universal genius", but even a genius would find it easier to work with "adequate tools – intelligent men". He did not make bricks – why, there was a physical impossibility in the way – as I was well aware; and if he did secretarial work for the manager, it was because "no sensible man rejects wantonly the confidence of his superiors." Did I see it? I saw it. What more did I want? What I really wanted was rivets, by heaven! Rivets. To get on with the work – to stop the hole. Rivets I wanted. There were cases of them down at the coast – cases – piled up – burst – split! You kicked a loose rivet at every second step in that station yard on the hillside. Rivets had rolled into the grove of death. You could fill your pockets with rivets for the trouble of stooping down – and there wasn't one rivet to be found where it was wanted. We had plates that would do, but nothing to fasten them with. And every week the messenger, a lone Negro, letter-bag on shoulder and staff in hand, left our station for the coast. And several times a week a coast caravan came in with trade goods – ghastly glazed calico that made you shudder only to look at it, glass beads value about a penny a quart, confounded spotted cotton handkerchiefs. And no rivets. Three carriers could have brought all that was wanted to set that steamboat afloat.

'He was becoming confidential now, but I fancy my unresponsive attitude must have exasperated him at last, for he judged it necessary to inform me he feared neither God nor devil, let alone any mere man. I said I could see that very well, but what I wanted was a certain quantity of rivets – and rivets were what really Mr Kurtz wanted, if he had only known it. Now letters went to the coast every week. . . . "My dear sir," he cried, "I write from dictation." I demanded rivets. There was a way – for an intelligent man. He changed his manner; became very cold, and suddenly began to talk about a hippopotamus; wondered whether sleeping on board the steamer (I stuck to my salvage night and day) I wasn't disturbed. There was an old hippo that had the bad habit of getting out on the bank and roaming at night over the station grounds. The pilgrims used to turn out in a body and empty every rifle they could lay hands on at him. Some even had sat up o' nights for him. All this energy was wasted, though. "That animal has a charmed life," he said; "but you can say this only of brutes in this country. No man – you apprehend me? – no man here bears a charmed life." He stood there for a moment in the moonlight with his delicate hooked nose set a little askew, and his mica eyes glittering without a wink, then, with a curt Good-night, he strode off. I could see he was disturbed and considerably puzzled, which made me feel more hopeful than I had been for days. It was a great comfort to turn from that chap to my influential friend, the battered, twisted, ruined, tin-pot steamboat. I clambered on board. She rang under my feet like an empty Huntley & Palmer biscuit-tin kicked along a gutter; she was nothing like so solid in make, and rather less pretty in shape, but I had expended enough hard work on her to make me love her. No influential friend would have served me better. She had given me a chance to come out a bit – to find out what I could do. No, I don't like work. I had rather laze about and think of all the fine things that can be done. I don't like work – no man does – but I like what is in the work – the chance to find yourself. Your own reality – for yourself, not for others – what no other man can ever know. They can only see the mere show, and never can tell what it really means.

'I was not surprised to see somebody sitting aft, on the deck, with his legs dangling over the mud. You see I rather chummed with the few mechanics there were in that station, whom the other pilgrims naturally despised – on account of their imperfect manners, I suppose. This was the foreman – a boiler-maker by trade – a good worker. He was a lank, bony, yellow-faced man, with big intense eyes. His aspect was worried, and his head was as bald as the palm of my hand; but his hair in falling seemed to have stuck to his chin, and had prospered in the new locality, for his beard hung down to his waist.

He was a widower with six young children (he had left them in charge of a sister of his to come out there), and the passion of his life was pigeon-flying. He was an enthusiast and a connoisseur. He would rave about pigeons. After work hours he used sometimes to come over from his hut for a talk about his children and his pigeons; at work, when he had to crawl in the mud under the bottom of the steamboat, he would tie up that beard of his in a kind of white serviette he brought for the purpose. It had loops to go over his ears. In the evening he could be seen squatted on the bank rinsing that wrapper in the creek with great care, then spreading it solemnly on a bush to dry.

'I slapped him on the back and shouted "We shall have rivets!" He scrambled to his feet exclaiming "No! Rivets!" as though he couldn't believe his ears. Then in a low voice, "You . . . eh?" I don't know why we behaved like lunatics. I put my finger to the side of my nose and nodded mysteriously. "Good for you!" he cried, snapped his fingers above his head, lifting one foot. I tried a jig. We capered on the iron deck. A frightful clatter came out of that hulk, and the virgin forest on the other bank of the creek sent it back in a thundering roll upon the sleeping station. It must have made some of the pilgrims sit up in their hovels. A dark figure obscured the lighted doorway of the manager's hut, vanished, then, a second or so after, the doorway itself vanished too. We stopped, and the silence driven away by the stamping of our feet flowed back again from the recesses of the land. The great wall of vegetation, an exuberant and entangled mass of trunks, branches, leaves, boughs, festoons, motionless in the moonlight, was like a rioting invasion of soundless life, a rolling wave of plants, piled up, crested, ready to topple over the creek, to sweep every little man of us out of his little existence. And it moved not. A deadened burst of mighty splashes and snorts reached us from afar, as though an ichthyosaurus had been taking a bath of glitter in the great river. "After all," said the boiler-maker in a reasonable tone, "why shouldn't we get the rivets?" Why not, indeed! I did not know of any reason why we shouldn't. "They'll come in three weeks," I said confidently.

'But they didn't. Instead of rivets there came an invasion, an infliction, a visitation. It came in sections during the next three weeks, each section headed by a donkey carrying a white man in new clothes and tan shoes, bowing from that elevation right and left to the impressed pilgrims. A quarrelsome band of footsore sulky niggers trod on the heels of the donkey; a lot of tents, camp-stools, tin boxes, white cases, brown bales would be shot down in the courtyard, and the air of mystery would deepen a little over the muddle of the station. Five such instalments came, with their absurd air of disorderly flight with the loot of innumerable outfit shops and provision stores, that, one would think, they were lugging, after a raid, into the wilderness for equitable division. It was an inextricable mess of things decent in themselves but that human folly made look like the spoils of thieving.

'This devoted band called itself the Eldorado Exploring Expedition, and I believe they were sworn to secrecy. Their talk, however, was the talk of sordid buccaneers: it was reckless without hardihood, greedy without audacity, and cruel without courage; there was not an atom of foresight or of serious intention in the whole batch of them, and they did not seem aware these things are wanted for the work of the world. To tear treasure out of the bowels of the land was their desire, with no more moral purpose at the back of it than there is in burglars breaking into a safe. Who paid the expenses of the noble enterprise I don't know; but the uncle of our manager was leader of that lot.

'In exterior he resembled a butcher in a poor neighbourhood, and his eyes had a look of sleepy cunning. He carried his fat paunch with ostentation on his short legs, and during the time his gang infested the station spoke to no one but his nephew. You could see these two roaming about all day long with their heads close together in an everlasting confab.

'I had given up worrying myself about the rivets. One's capacity for that kind of folly is more limited than you would suppose. I said Hang! – and let things slide. I had plenty of time for meditation, and now and then I would give some thought to Kurtz. I wasn't very interested in him. No. Still, I was curious to see whether this man, who had come out equipped with moral ideas of some sort, would climb to the top after all, and how he would set about his work when there.'

2

'One evening as I was lying flat on the deck of my steamboat, I heard voices approaching – and there were the nephew and the uncle strolling along the bank. I laid my head on my arm again, and had nearly lost myself in a doze, when somebody said in my ear, as it were: "I am as harmless as a little child, but I don't like to be dictated to. Am I the manager – or am I not? I was ordered to send him there. It's incredible." . . . I became aware that the two were standing on the shore alongside the forepart of the steamboat, just below my head. I did not move; it did not occur to me to move: I was sleepy. "It *is* unpleasant," grunted the uncle. "He has asked the Administration to be sent there," said the other, "with the idea of showing what he could do; and I was instructed accordingly. Look at the influence that man must have. Is it not frightful?" They both agreed it was frightful, then made several bizarre remarks: "Make rain and fine weather – one man – the Council – by the nose" – bits of absurd sentences that got the better of my drowsiness, so that I had pretty near the whole of my wits about me when the uncle said, "The climate may do away with this difficulty for you. Is he alone there?" "Yes," answered the manager; "he sent his assistant down the river with a note to me in these terms: 'Clear this poor devil out of the country, and don't bother sending more of that sort. I had rather be alone than have the kind of men you can dispose of with me.' It was more than a year ago. Can you imagine such impudence!" "Anything since then?" asked the other, hoarsely. "Ivory," jerked the nephew; "lots of it – prime sort – lots – most annoying, from him." "And with that?" questioned the heavy rumble. "Invoice," was the reply fired out, so to speak. Then silence. They had been talking about Kurtz.

'I was broad awake by this time, but, lying perfectly at ease, remained still, having no inducement to change my position. "How did that ivory come all this way?" growled the elder man, who seemed very vexed. The other explained that it had come with a fleet of canoes in charge of an English half-caste clerk Kurtz had with him; that Kurtz had apparently intended to return himself, the station being by that time bare of goods and stores, but after coming three hundred miles, had suddenly decided to go back, which he started to do alone in a small dugout with four paddlers, leaving the half-caste to continue down the river with the ivory. The two fellows there seemed astounded at anybody attempting such a thing. They were at a loss for an adequate motive. As to me, I seemed to see Kurtz for the first time. It was a distinct glimpse: the dugout, four paddling savages, and the lone white man turning his back suddenly on the headquarters, on relief, on thoughts of home – perhaps; setting his face towards the depths of the wilderness, towards his empty and desolate station. I did not know the motive. Perhaps he was just simply a fine fellow who stuck to his work for its own sake. His name, you understand, had not been pronounced once. He was "that man". The half-caste, who, as far as I could see, had conducted a difficult trip with great prudence and pluck, was invariably alluded to as "that scoundrel". The "scoundrel" had reported that the "man" had been very ill – had recovered imperfectly . . . The two below me moved away then a few paces, and strolled back and forth at some little distance. I heard: "Military post – doctor – two hundred miles – quite alone now – unavoidable delays – nine months – no news – strange rumours." They approached again, just as the manager was saying, "No one, as far as I know, unless a species of wandering trader – a pestilential fellow, snapping ivory from the natives." Who was it they were talking about now? I gathered in snatches that this was some man supposed to be in Kurtz's district, and of whom the manager did not approve. "We will not be free from unfair competition till one of these fellows is hanged for an example," he said. "Certainly," grunted the other; "get him hanged! Why not? Anything – anything can be done in this country. That's what I say; nobody here, you understand, *here*, can endanger your position. And why? You stand the climate – you outlast them all. The danger is in Europe; but there before I left I took care to – " They moved off and whispered, then their voices rose again. "The extraordinary series of delays is not my fault. I did my possible." The fat man sighed, "Very sad." "And the pestiferous absurdity of his talk," continued the other; "he bothered me enough when he was here. 'Each station should be like a beacon on the road towards better things, a centre for trade of course, but also for humanising, improving, instructing.' Conceive you – that ass! And he wants to be manager! No, it's – " Here he got choked by excessive indignation, and I lifted my head the least bit. I was surprised to see how near they were – right under me. I could have spat upon their hats. They were looking on the ground, absorbed in thought. The manager was switching his leg with a slender twig; – his sagacious relative lifted his head. "You have been well since you came out this time?" he asked. The other gave a start. "Who? I? Oh! Like a charm – like a charm. But the rest – oh, my goodness! All sick. They die so quick, too, that I haven't the time to send them out of the country – it's incredible!" "H'm. Just so," grunted the uncle. "Ah! my boy, trust to this – I say, trust to this." I saw him extend his short flipper of an arm for a gesture that took in the forest, the creek, the mud, the river – seemed to beckon with a dishonouring flourish before the sunlit face of the land a treacherous appeal to the lurking death, to the hidden evil, to the profound darkness of its heart. It was so startling that I leaped to my feet and looked back at the edge of the forest, as though I had expected an answer of some sort to that black display of confidence. You know the foolish notions that come to one sometimes. The high stillness confronted these two figures with its ominous patience, waiting for the passing away of a fantastic invasion.

'They swore aloud together – out of sheer fright, I believe – then pretending not to know anything of my existence, turned back to the station. The sun was low; and leaning forward side by side, they seemed to be tugging painfully uphill their two ridiculous shadows of unequal length, that trailed behind them slowly over the tall grass without bending a single blade.

'In a few days the Eldorado Expedition went into the patient wilderness, that closed upon it as the sea closes over a diver. Long afterwards the news came that all the donkeys were dead. I know nothing as to the fate of the less valuable animals. They, no doubt, like the rest of us, found what they deserved. I did not inquire. I was then rather excited at the prospect of meeting Kurtz very soon. When I say very soon I mean it comparatively. It was just two months from the day we left the creek when we came to the bank below Kurtz's station.

'Going up that river was like travelling back to the earliest beginnings of the world, when vegetation rioted on the earth and the big trees were kings. An empty stream, a great silence, an impenetrable forest. The air was warm, thick, heavy, sluggish. There was no joy in the brilliance of sunshine. The long stretches of the waterway ran on, deserted, into the gloom of overshadowed distances. On silvery sandbanks hippos and alligators sunned themselves side by side. The broadening waters flowed through a mob of wooded islands; you lost your way on that river as you would in a desert, and butted all day long against shoals, trying to find the channel, till you thought yourself bewitched and cut off for ever from everything you had known once –somewhere – far away – in another existence perhaps. There were moments when one's past came back to one, as it will sometimes when you have not a moment to spare to yourself; but it came in the shape of an unrestful and noisy dream, remembered with wonder amongst the overwhelming realities of this strange world of plants, and water, and silence. And this stillness of life did not in the least resemble a peace. It was the stillness of an implacable force brooding over an inscrutable intention. It looked at you with a vengeful aspect. I got used to it afterwards; I did not see it any more; I had no time. I had to keep guessing at the channel; I had to discern, mostly by inspiration, the signs of hidden banks; I watched for sunken stones; I was learning to clap my teeth smartly before my heart flew out, when I shaved by a fluke some infernal sly old snag that would have ripped the life out of the tin-pot steamboat and drowned all the pilgrims; I had to keep a look-out for the signs of dead wood we could cut up in the night for next day's steaming. When you have to attend to things of that sort, to the mere incidents of the surface, the reality – the reality, I tell you – fades. The inner truth is hidden – luckily, luckily. But I felt it all the same; I felt often its mysterious stillness watching me at my monkey tricks, just as it watches you fellows performing on your respective tight-ropes for – what is it? half a crown a tumble – '

'Try to be civil, Marlow,' growled a voice, and I knew there was at least one listener awake besides myself.

'I beg your pardon. I forgot the heartache which makes up the rest of the price. And indeed what does the price matter, if the trick be well done? You do your tricks very well. And I didn't do badly either, since I managed not to sink that steamboat on my first trip. It's a wonder to me yet. Imagine a blindfolded man set to drive a van over a bad road. I sweated and shivered over that business considerably, I can tell you. After all, for a seaman, to scrape the bottom of the thing that's supposed to float all the time under his care is the unpardonable sin. No one may know of it, but you never forget the thump – eh? A blow on the very heart. You remember it, you dream of it, you wake up at night and think of it – years after – and go hot and cold all over. I don't pretend to say that steamboat floated all the time. More than once she had to wade for a bit, with twenty cannibals splashing around and pushing. We had enlisted some of these chaps on the way for a crew. Fine fellows – cannibals – in their place. They were men one could work with, and I am grateful to them. And, after all, they did not eat each other before my face: they had brought along a provision of hippo-meat which went rotten, and made the mystery of the wilderness stink in my nostrils. Phoo! I can sniff it now. I had the manager on board and three or four pilgrims with their staves – all complete. Sometimes we came upon a station close by the bank, clinging to the skirts of the unknown, and the white men rushing out of a tumbledown hovel, with great gestures of joy and surprise and welcome, seemed very strange – had the appearance of being held there captive by a spell. The word ivory would ring in the air for a while – and on we went again into the silence, along empty reaches, round the still bends, between the high walls of our winding way, reverberating in hollow claps the ponderous beat of the stern-wheel. Trees, trees, millions of trees, massive, immense, running up high; and at their foot, hugging the bank against the stream, crept the little begrimed steamboat, like a sluggish beetle crawling on the floor of a lofty portico. It made you feel very small, very lost, and yet it was not altogether depressing, that feeling. After all, if you were small, the grimy beetle crawled on – which was just what you wanted it to do. Where the pilgrims imagined it crawled to I don't know. To some place where they expected to get something, I bet! For me it crawled towards Kurtz – exclusively; but when the steam-pipes started leaking we crawled very slow. The reaches opened before us and closed behind, as if the forest had stepped leisurely across the water to bar the way for our return. We penetrated deeper and deeper into the heart of darkness. It was very quiet there. At night sometimes the roll of drums behind the curtain of trees would run up the river and remain sustained faintly, as if hovering in the air high over our heads, till the first break of day. Whether it meant war, peace, or prayer we could not tell. The dawns were heralded by the descent of a chill stillness; the woodcutters slept, their fires burned low; the snapping of a twig would make you start. We were wanderers on a prehistoric earth, on an earth that wore the aspect of an unknown planet. We could have fancied ourselves the first of men taking possession of an accursed inheritance, to be subdued at the cost of profound anguish and of excessive toil. But suddenly, as we struggled round a bend, there would be a glimpse of rush walls, of peaked grass-roofs, a burst of yells, a whirl of black limbs, a mass of hands clapping, of feet stamping, of bodies swaying, of eyes rolling, under the droop of heavy and motionless foliage. The steamer toiled along slowly on the edge of a black and incomprehensible frenzy. The prehistoric man was cursing us, praying to us, welcoming us – who could tell? We were cut off from the comprehension of our surroundings; we glided past like phantoms, wondering and secretly appalled, as sane men would be before an enthusiastic outbreak in a madhouse. We could not understand because we were too far and could not remember, because we were travelling in the night of first ages, of those ages that are gone, leaving hardly a sign – and no memories.

'The earth seemed unearthly. We are accustomed to look upon the shackled form of a conquered monster, but there – there you could look at a thing monstrous and free. It was unearthly, and the men were – No, they were not inhuman. Well, you know, that was the worst of it – this suspicion of their not being inhuman. It would come slowly to one. They howled and leaped, and spun, and made horrid faces; but what thrilled you was just the thought of their humanity – like yours – the thought of your remote kinship with this wild and passionate uproar. Ugly. Yes, it was ugly enough; but if you were man enough you would admit to yourself that there was in you just the faintest trace of a response to the terrible frankness of that noise, a dim suspicion of there being a meaning in it which you – you so remote from the night of first ages – could comprehend. And why not? The mind of man is capable of anything – because everything is in it, all the past as well as all the future. What was there after all? Joy, fear, sorrow, devotion, valour, rage – who can tell? – but truth – truth stripped of its cloak of time. Let the fool gape and shudder – the man knows, and can look on without a wink. But he must at least be as much of a man as these on the shore. He must meet that truth with his own true stuff – with his own inborn strength. Principles? Principles won't do. Acquisitions, clothes, pretty rags – rags that would fly off at the first good shake. No; you want a deliberate belief. An appeal to me in this fiendish row – is there? Very well; I hear; I admit, but I have a voice too, and for good or evil mine is the speech that cannot be silenced. Of course, a fool, what with sheer fright and fine sentiments, is always safe. Who's that grunting? You wonder I didn't go ashore for a howl and a dance? Well, no – I didn't. Fine sentiments, you say? Fine sentiments, be hanged! I had no time. I had to mess about with white-lead and strips of woollen blanket helping to put bandages on those leaky steam-pipes – I tell you. I had to watch the steering, and circumvent those snags, and get the tin-pot along by hook or by crook. There was surface-truth enough in these things to save a wiser man. And between whiles I had to look after the savage who was fireman. He was an improved specimen; he could fire up a vertical boiler. He was there below me, and, upon my word, to look at him was as edifying as seeing a dog in a parody of breeches and a feather hat, walking on his hind-legs. A few months of training had done for that really fine chap. He squinted at the steam-gauge and at the water-gauge with an evident effort of intrepidity – and he had filed teeth too, the poor devil, and the wool of his pate shaved into queer patterns, and three ornamental scars on each of his cheeks. He ought to have been clapping his hands and stamping his feet on the bank, instead of which he was hard at work, a thrall to strange witchcraft, full of improving knowledge. He was useful because he had been instructed; and what he knew was this – that should the water in that transparent thing disappear, the evil spirit inside the boiler would get angry through the greatness of his thirst and take a terrible vengeance. So he sweated and fired up and watched the glass fearfully (with an impromptu charm, made of rags, tied to his arm, and a piece of polished bone, as big as a watch, stuck flatways through his lower lip), while the wooded banks slipped past us slowly, the short noise was left behind, the interminable miles of silence – and we crept on, towards Kurtz. But the snags were thick, the water was treacherous and shallow, the boiler seemed indeed to have a sulky devil in it, and thus neither that fireman nor I had any time to peer into our creepy thoughts.

'Some fifty miles below the Inner Station we came upon a hut of reeds, an inclined and melancholy pole, with the unrecognisable tatters of what had been a flag of some sort flying from it, and a neatly stacked woodpile. This was unexpected. We came to the bank, and on the stack of firewood found a flat piece of board with some faded pencil-writing on it. When deciphered it said:

"Wood for you. Hurry up. Approach cautiously." There was a signature, but it was illegible – not Kurtz – a much longer word. Hurry up. Where? Up the river? "Approach cautiously." We had not done so. But the warning could not have been meant for the place where it could be only found after approach. Something was wrong above. But what – and how much? That was the question. We commented adversely upon the imbecility of that telegraphic style. The bush around said nothing, and would not let us look very far, either. A torn curtain of red twill hung in the doorway of the hut, and flapped sadly in our faces. The dwelling was dismantled; but we could see a white man had lived there not very long ago. There remained a rude table – a plank on two posts; a heap of rubbish reposed in a dark corner, and by the door I picked up a book. It had lost its covers, and the pages had been thumbed into a state of extremely dirty softness; but the back had been lovingly stitched afresh with white cotton thread, which looked clean yet. It was an extraordinary find. Its title was, *An Inquiry into some Points of Seamanship*, by a man Tower, Towson – some such name – Master in His Majesty's Navy. The matter looked dreary reading enough, with illustrative diagrams and repulsive tables of figures, and the copy was sixty years old. I handled this amazing antiquity with the greatest possible tenderness, lest it should dissolve in my hands. Within, Towson or Towser was inquiring earnestly into the breaking strain of ships' chains and tackle, and other such matters. Not a very enthralling book; but at the first glance you could see there a singleness of intention, an honest concern for the right way of going to work, which made these humble pages, thought out so many years ago, luminous with another than a professional light. The simple old sailor, with his talk of chains and purchases, made me forget the jungle and the pilgrims in a delicious sensation of having come upon something unmistakably real. Such a book being there was wonderful enough; but still more astounding were the notes pencilled in the margin, and plainly referring to the text. I couldn't believe my eyes! They were in cipher! Yes, it looked like cipher. Fancy a man lugging with him a book of that description into this nowhere and studying it – and making notes – in cipher at that! It was an extravagant mystery.

'I had been dimly aware for some time of a worrying noise, and when I lifted my eyes I saw the woodpile was gone, and the manager, aided by all the pilgrims; was shouting at me from the riverside. I slipped the book into my pocket. I assure you to leave off reading was like tearing myself away from the shelter of an old and solid friendship.

'I started the lame engine ahead. "It must be this miserable trader – this intruder," exclaimed the manager, looking back malevolently at the place we had left. "He must be English," I said. "It will not save him from getting into trouble if he is not careful," muttered the manager darkly. I observed with assumed innocence that no man was safe from trouble in this world.

'The current was more rapid now, the steamer seemed at her last gasp, the stern-wheel flopped languidly, and I caught myself listening on tiptoe for the next beat of the float, for in sober truth I expected the wretched thing to give up every moment. It was like watching the last flickers of a life. But still we crawled. Sometimes I would pick out a tree a little way ahead to measure our progress towards Kurtz by, but I lost it invariably before we got abreast. To keep the eyes so long on one thing was too much for human patience. The manager displayed a beautiful resignation. I fretted and fumed and took to arguing with myself whether or no I would talk openly with Kurtz; but before I could come to any conclusion it occurred to me that my speech or my silence, indeed any action of mine, would be a mere futility. What did it matter what anyone knew or ignored? What did it matter who was manager? One gets sometimes such a flash of insight. The essentials of this affair lay deep under the surface, beyond my reach, and beyond my power of meddling.

'Towards the evening of the second day we judged ourselves about eight miles from Kurtz's station. I wanted to push on; but the manager looked grave, and told me the navigation up there was so dangerous that it would be advisable, the sun being very low already, to wait where we were till next morning. Moreover, he pointed out that if the warning to approach cautiously were to be followed, we must approach in daylight – not at dusk, or in the dark. This was sensible enough. Eight miles meant nearly three hours' steaming for us, and I could also see suspicious ripples at the upper end of the reach. Nevertheless, I was annoyed beyond expression at the delay, and most unreasonably too, since one night more could not matter much after so many months. As we had plenty of wood, and caution was the word, I brought up in the middle of the stream. The reach was narrow, straight, with high sides like a railway cutting. The dusk came gliding into it long before the sun had set. The current ran smooth and swift, but a dumb immobility sat on the banks. The living trees, lashed together by the creepers and every living bush of the undergrowth, might have been changed into stone, even to the slenderest twig, to the lightest leaf. It was not sleep – it seemed unnatural, like a state of trance. Not the faintest sound of any kind could be heard. You looked on amazed, and began to suspect yourself of being deaf – then the night came suddenly, and struck you blind as well. About three in the morning some large fish leaped, and the loud splash made me jump as though a gun had been fired. When the sun rose there was a white fog, very warm and clammy, and more blinding than the night. It did not shift or drive; it was just there, standing all round you like something solid. At eight or nine, perhaps, it lifted as a shutter lifts. We had a glimpse of the towering multitude of trees, of the immense matted jungle, with the blazing little ball of the sun hanging over it – all perfectly still – and then the white shutter came down again, smoothly, as if sliding in greased grooves. I ordered the chain, which we had begun to heave in, to be paid out again. Before it stopped running with a muffled rattle, a cry, a very loud cry, as of infinite desolation, soared slowly in the opaque air. It ceased. A complaining clamour, modulated in savage discords, filled our ears. The sheer unexpectedness of it made my hair stir under my cap. I don't know how it struck the others: to me it seemed as though the mist itself had screamed, so suddenly, and apparently from all sides at once, did this tumultuous and mournful uproar arise. It culminated in a hurried outbreak of almost intolerably excessive shrieking, which stopped short, leaving us stiffened in a variety of silly attitudes, and obstinately listening to the nearly as appalling and excessive silence. "Good God! What is the meaning – ?" stammered at my elbow one of the pilgrims – a little fat man, with sandy hair and red whiskers, who wore side-spring boots, and pink pyjamas tucked into his socks. Two others remained open-mouthed a whole minute, then dashed into the little cabin, to rush out incontinently and stand darting scared glances, with Winchesters at "ready" in their hands. What we could see was just the steamer we were on, her outlines blurred as though she had been on the point of dissolving, and a misty strip of water, perhaps two feet broad, around her – and that was all. The rest of the world was nowhere, as far as our eyes and ears were concerned. Just nowhere. Gone, disappeared; swept off without leaving a whisper or a shadow behind.

'I went forward, and ordered the chain to be hauled in short, so as to be ready to trip the anchor and move the steamboat at once if necessary. "Will they attack?" whispered an awed voice. "We will be all butchered in this fog," murmured another. The faces twitched with the strain, the hands trembled slightly, the eyes forgot to wink. It was very curious to see the contrast of expressions of the white men and of the black fellows of our crew, who were as much strangers to that part of the river as we, though their homes were only eight hundred miles away. The whites, of course greatly discomposed, had besides a curious look of being painfully shocked by such an outrageous row. The others had an alert, naturally interested expression; but their faces were essentially quiet, even those of the one or two who grinned as they hauled at the chain. Several exchanged short, grunting phrases, which seemed to settle the matter to their satisfaction. Their headman, a young, broad-chested black, severely draped in dark-blue fringed cloths, with fierce nostrils and his hair all done up artfully in oily ringlets, stood near me. "Aha!" I said, just for good fellowship's sake. "Catch 'im," he snapped, with a bloodshot widening of his eyes and a flash of sharp teeth – "catch 'im. Give 'im to us." "To you, eh?" I asked; "what would you do with them?" "Eat 'im!" he said, curtly, and, leaning his elbow on the rail, looked out into the fog in a dignified and profoundly pensive attitude. I would no doubt have been properly horrified, had it not occurred to me that he and his chaps must be very hungry: that they must have been growing increasingly hungry for at least this month past. They had been engaged for six months (I don't think a single one of them had any clear idea of time, as we at the end of countless ages have. They still belonged to the beginnings of time – had no inherited experience to teach them as it were), and of course, as long as there was a piece of paper written over in accordance with some farcical law or other made down the river, it didn't enter anybody's head to trouble how they would live. Certainly they had brought with them some rotten hippo-meat, which couldn't have lasted very long, anyway, even if the pilgrims hadn't, in the midst of a shocking hullabaloo, thrown a considerable quantity of it overboard. It looked like a high-handed proceeding; but it was really a case of legitimate self-defence. You can't breathe dead hippo waking, sleeping, and eating, and at the same time keep your precarious grip on existence. Besides that, they had given them every week three pieces of brass wire, each about nine inches long; and the theory was they were to buy their provisions with that currency in riverside villages. You can see how *that* worked. There were either no villages, or the people were hostile, or the director, who like the rest of us fed out of tins, with an occasional old he-goat thrown in, didn't want to stop the steamer for some more or less recondite reason. So, unless they swallowed the wire itself, or made loops of it to snare the fishes with, I don't see what good their extravagant salary could be to them. I must say it was paid with a regularity worthy of a large and honourable trading company. For the rest, the only thing to eat – though it didn't look eatable in the least – I saw in their possession was a few lumps of some stuff like half-cooked dough, of a dirty lavender colour, they kept wrapped in leaves, and now and then swallowed a piece of, but so small that it seemed done more for the looks of the thing than for any serious purpose of sustenance. Why in the name of all the gnawing devils of hunger they didn't go for us – they were thirty to five – and have a good tuck in for once, amazes me now when I think of it. They were big powerful men, with not much capacity to weigh the consequences, with courage, with strength, even yet, though their skins were no longer glossy and their muscles no longer hard. And I saw that something restraining, one of those human secrets that baffle probability, had come into play there. I looked at them with a swift quickening of interest – not because it occurred to me I might be eaten by them before very long, though I own to you that just then I perceived – in a new light, as it were – how unwholesome the pilgrims looked, and I hoped, yes, I positively hoped, that my aspect was not so – what shall I say? – so – unappetising: a touch of fantastic vanity which fitted well with the dream-sensation that pervaded all my days at that time. Perhaps I had a little fever too. One can't live with one's finger everlastingly on one's pulse. I had often "a little fever", or a little touch of other things – the playful paw-strokes of the wilderness, the preliminary trifling before the more serious onslaught which came in due course. Yes; I looked at them as you would on any human being, with a curiosity of their impulses, motives, capacities, weaknesses, when brought to the test of an inexorable physical necessity. Restraint! What possible restraint? Was it superstition, disgust, patience, fear – or some kind of primitive honour? No fear can stand up to hunger, no patience can wear it out, disgust simply does not exist where hunger is; and as to superstition, beliefs, and what you may call principles, they are less than chaff in a breeze. Don't you know the devilry of lingering starvation, its exasperating torment, its black thoughts, its sombre and brooding ferocity? Well, I do. It takes a man all his inborn strength to fight hunger properly. It's really easier to face bereavement, dishonour, and the perdition of one's soul – than this kind of prolonged hunger. Sad, but true. And these chaps too had no earthly reason for any kind of scruple. Restraint! I would just as soon have expected restraint from a hyena prowling amongst the corpses of a battlefield. But there was the fact facing me – the fact dazzling, to be seen, like the foam on the depths of the sea, like a ripple on an unfathomable enigma, a mystery greater – when I thought of it – than the curious, inexplicable note of desperate grief in this savage clamour that had swept by us on the river-bank, behind the blind whiteness of the fog.

'Two pilgrims were quarrelling in hurried whispers as to which bank. "Left." "No, no; how can you? Right, right, of course." "It is very serious," said the manager's voice behind me; "I would be desolated if anything should happen to Mr Kurtz before we came up." I looked at him, and had not the slightest doubt he was sincere. He was just the kind of man who would wish to preserve appearances. That was his restraint. But when he muttered something about going on at once, I did not even take the trouble to answer him. I knew, and he knew, that it was impossible. Were we to let go our hold of the bottom, we would be absolutely in the air – in space. We wouldn't be able to tell where we were going to – whether up or down stream, or across – till we fetched against one bank or the other – and then we wouldn't know at first which it was. Of course I made no move. I had no mind for a smash-up. You couldn't imagine a more deadly place for a shipwreck. Whether drowned at once or not, we were sure to perish speedily in one way or another. "I authorise you to take all the risks," he said, after a short silence. "I refuse to take any," I said shortly; which was just the answer he expected, though its tone might have surprised him. "Well, I must defer to your judgement. You are captain," he said, with marked civility. I turned my shoulder to him in sign of my appreciation, and looked into the fog. How long would it last? It was the most hopeless look-out. The approach to this Kurtz grubbing for ivory in the wretched bush was beset by as many dangers as though he had been an enchanted princess sleeping in a fabulous castle. "Will they attack, do you think?" asked the manager, in a confidential tone.

'I did not think they would attack, for several obvious reasons. The thick fog was one. If they left the bank in their canoes they would get lost in it, as we would be if we attempted to move. Still, I had also judged the jungle of both banks quite impenetrable – and yet eyes were in it, eyes that had seen us. The riverside bushes were certainly very thick; but the undergrowth behind was evidently penetrable. However, during the short lift I had seen no canoes anywhere in the reach – certainly not abreast of the steamer. But what made the idea of attack inconceivable to me was the nature of the noise – of the cries we had heard. They had not the fierce character boding of immediate hostile intention. Unexpected, wild, and violent as they had been, they had given me an irresistible impression of sorrow. The glimpse of the steamboat had for some reason filled those savages with unrestrained grief. The danger, if any, I expounded, was from our proximity to a great human passion let loose. Even extreme grief may ultimately vent itself in violence – but more generally takes the form of apathy . . .

'You should have seen the pilgrims stare! They had no heart to grin, or even to revile me; but I believe they thought me gone mad – with fright, maybe. I delivered a regular lecture. My dear boys, it was no good bothering. Keep a look-out? Well, you may guess I watched the fog for the signs of lifting as a cat watches a mouse; but for anything else our eyes were of no more use to us than if we had been buried miles deep in a heap of cotton-wool. It felt like it too – choking, warm, stifling. Besides, all I said, though it sounded extravagant, was absolutely true to fact. What we afterwards alluded to as an attack was really an attempt at repulse. The action was very far from being aggressive – it was not even defensive, in the usual sense: it was undertaken under the stress of desperation, and in its essence was purely protective.

'It developed itself, I should say, two hours after the fog lifted, and its commencement was at a spot, roughly speaking, about a mile and a half below Kurtz's station. We had just floundered and flopped round a bend, when I saw an islet, a mere grassy hummock of bright green, in the middle of the stream. It was the only thing of the kind; but as we opened the reach more, I perceived it was the head of a long sandbank, or rather of a chain of shallow patches stretching down the middle of the river. They were discoloured, just awash, and the whole lot was seen just under the water, exactly as a man's backbone is seen running down the middle of his back under the skin. Now, as far as I did see, I could go to the right or to the left of this. I didn't know either channel, of course. The banks looked pretty well alike, the depth appeared the same; but as I had been informed the station was on the west side, I naturally headed for the western passage.

'No sooner had we fairly entered it than I became aware it was much narrower than I had supposed. To the left of us there was the long un-interrupted shoal, and to the right a high, steep bank heavily overgrown with bushes. Above the bush the trees stood in serried ranks. The twigs overhung the current thickly, and from distance to distance a large limb of some tree projected rigidly over the stream. It was then well on in the afternoon, the face of the forest was gloomy, and a broad strip of shadow had already fallen on the water. In this shadow we steamed up – very slowly, as you may imagine. I sheered her well inshore – the water being deepest near the bank, as the sounding-pole informed me.

'One of my hungry and forbearing friends was sounding in the bows just below me. This steamboat was exactly like a decked scow. On the deck there were two little teak-wood houses, with doors and windows. The boiler was in the fore-end, and the machinery right astern. Over the whole there was a light roof, supported on stanchions. The funnel projected through that roof, and in front of the funnel a small cabin built of light planks served for a pilot-house. It contained a couch, two camp-stools, a loaded Martini-Henry leaning in one corner, a tiny table, and the steering-wheel. It had a wide door in front and a broad shutter at each side. All these were always thrown open, of course. I spent my days perched up there on the extreme fore-end of that roof, before the door. At night I slept, or tried to, on the couch. An athletic black belonging to some coast tribe, and educated by my poor predecessor, was the helmsman. He sported a pair of brass earrings, wore a blue cloth wrapper from the waist to the ankles, and thought all the world of himself. He was the most unstable kind of fool I had ever seen. He steered with no end of a swagger while you were by; but if he lost sight of you, he became instantly the prey of an abject funk, and would let that cripple of a steamboat get the upper hand of him in a minute.

'I was looking down at the sounding-pole, and feeling much annoyed to see at each try a little more of it stick out of that river, when I saw my poleman give up the business suddenly, and stretch himself flat on the deck, without even taking the trouble to haul his pole in. He kept hold on it though, and it trailed in the water. At the same time the fireman, whom I could also see below me, sat down abruptly before his furnace and ducked his head. I was amazed. Then I had to look at the river mighty quick, because there was a snag in the fairway. Sticks, little sticks, were flying about – thick: they were whizzing before my nose, dropping below me, striking behind me against my pilot-house. All this time the river, the shore, the woods, were very quiet – perfectly quiet. I could only hear the heavy splashing thump of the stern-wheel and the patter of these things. We cleared the snag clumsily. Arrows, by Jove! We were being shot at! I stepped in quickly to close the shutter on the land-side. That fool-helmsman, his hands on the spokes, was lifting his knees high, stamping his feet, champing his mouth, like a reined-in horse. Confound him! And we were staggering within ten feet of the bank. I had to lean right out to swing the heavy shutter, and I saw a face amongst the leaves on the level with my own, looking at me very fierce and steady; and then suddenly, as though a veil had been removed from my eyes, I made out, deep in the tangled gloom, naked breasts, arms, legs, glaring eyes – the bush was swarming with human limbs in movement, glistening, of bronze colour. The twigs shook, swayed, and rustled, the arrows flew out of them, and then the shutter came to. "Steer her straight," I said to the helmsman. He held his head rigid, face forward; but his eyes rolled, he kept on, lifting and setting down his feet gently, his mouth foamed a little. "Keep quiet!" I said in a fury. I might just as well have ordered a tree not to sway in the wind. I darted out. Below me there was a great scuffle of feet on the iron deck; confused exclamations; a voice screamed, "Can you turn back?" I caught sight of a V-shaped ripple on the water ahead. What? Another snag! A fusillade burst out under my feet. The pilgrims had opened with their

Winchesters, and were simply squirting lead into that bush. A deuce of a lot of smoke came up and drove slowly forward. I swore at it. Now I couldn't see the ripple or the snag either. I stood in the doorway, peering, and the arrows came in swarms. They might have been poisoned, but they looked as though they wouldn't kill a cat. The bush began to howl. Our woodcutters raised a warlike whoop; the report of a rifle just at my back deafened me. I glanced over my shoulder, and the pilot-house was yet full of noise and smoke when I made a dash at the wheel. The fool-nigger had dropped everything, to throw the shutter open and let off that Martini-Henry. He stood before the wide opening, glaring, and I yelled at him to come back, while I straightened the sudden twist out of that steamboat. There was no room to turn even if I had wanted to, the snag was somewhere very near ahead in that confounded smoke, there was no time to lose, so I just crowded her into the bank – right into the bank, where I knew the water was deep.

'We tore slowly along the overhanging bushes in a whirl of broken twigs and flying leaves. The fusillade below stopped short, as I had foreseen it would when the squirts got empty. I threw my head back to a glinting whizz that traversed the pilot-house, in at one shutter-hole and out at the other. Looking past that mad helmsman, who was shaking the empty rifle and yelling at the shore, I saw vague forms of men running bent double, leaping, gliding, distinct, incomplete, evanescent. Something big appeared in the air before the shutter, the rifle went overboard, and the man stepped back swiftly, looked at me over his shoulder in an extraordinary, profound, familiar manner, and fell upon my feet. The side of his head hit the wheel twice, and the end of what appeared a long cane clattered round and knocked over a little camp-stool. It looked as though after wrenching that thing from somebody ashore he had lost his balance in the effort. The thin smoke had blown away, we were clear of the snag, and looking ahead I could see that in another hundred yards or so I would be free to sheer off, away from the bank; but my feet felt so very warm and wet that I had to look down. The man had rolled on his back and stared straight up at me; both his hands clutched that cane. It was the shaft of a spear that, either thrown or lunged through the opening, had caught him in the side just below the ribs; the blade had gone in out of sight, after making a frightful gash; my shoes were full; a pool of blood lay very still, gleaming dark-red under the wheel; his eyes shone with an amazing lustre. The fusillade burst out again. He looked at me anxiously, gripping the spear like something precious, with an air of being afraid I would try to take it away from him. I had to make an effort to free my eyes from his gaze and attend to the steering. With one hand I felt above my head for the line of the steam whistle, and jerked out screech after screech hurriedly. The tumult of angry and warlike yells was checked instantly, and then from the depths of the woods went out such a tremulous and prolonged wail of mournful fear and utter despair as may be imagined to follow the flight of the last hope from the earth. There was a great commotion in the bush; the shower of arrows stopped, a few dropping shots rang out sharply – then silence, in which the languid beat of the stern-wheel came plainly to my ears. I put the helm hard a-starboard at the moment when the pilgrim in pink pyjamas, very hot and agitated, appeared in the doorway. "The manager sends me – " he began in an official tone, and stopped short. "Good God!" he said, glaring at the wounded man.

'We two whites stood over him, and his lustrous and inquiring glance enveloped us both. I declare it looked as though he would presently put to us some question in an understandable language; but he died without uttering a sound, without moving a limb, without twitching a muscle. Only in the very last moment, as though in response to some sign we could not see, to some whisper we could not hear, he frowned heavily, and that frown gave to his black death-mask an inconceivably sombre, brooding, and menacing expression. The lustre of inquiring glance faded swiftly into vacant glassiness. "Can you steer?" I asked the agent eagerly. He looked very dubious; but I made a grab at his arm, and he understood at once I meant him to steer whether or no. To tell you the truth, I was morbidly anxious to change my shoes and socks. "He is dead," murmured the fellow, immensely impressed. "No doubt about it," said I, tugging like mad at the shoe-laces. "And by the way, I suppose Mr Kurtz is dead as well by this time."

'For the moment that was the dominant thought. There was a sense of extreme disappointment, as though I had found out I had been striving after something altogether without a substance. I couldn't have been more disgusted if I had travelled all this way for the sole purpose of talking with Mr Kurtz. Talking with . . . I flung one shoe overboard, and became aware that that was exactly what I had been looking forward to – a talk with Kurtz. I made the strange discovery that I had never imagined him as doing, you know, but as discoursing. I didn't say to myself, "Now I will never see him," or "Now I will never shake him by the hand," but, "Now I will never hear him." The man presented himself as a voice. Not of course that I did not connect him with some sort of action. Hadn't I been told in all the tones of jealousy and admiration that he had collected, bartered, swindled, or stolen more ivory than all the other agents together? That was not the point. The point was in his being a gifted creature, and that of all his gifts the one that stood out pre-eminently, that carried with it a sense of real presence, was his ability to talk, his words – the gift of expression, the bewildering, the illuminating, the most exalted and the most contemptible, the pulsating stream of light, or the deceitful flow from the heart of an impenetrable darkness.

'The other shoe went flying unto the devil-god of that river. I thought, By Jove! It's all over. We are too late; he has vanished – the gift has vanished, by means of some spear, arrow, or club. I will never hear that chap speak after all – and my sorrow had a startling extravagance of emotion, even such as I had noticed in the howling sorrow of these savages in the bush. I couldn't have felt more of lonely desolation somehow, had I been robbed of a belief or had missed my destiny in life . . . Why do you sigh in this beastly way, somebody? Absurd? Well, absurd. Good Lord! mustn't a man ever – Here, give me some tobacco' . . .

There was a pause of profound stillness, then a match flared, and Marlow's lean face appeared, worn, hollow, with downward folds and dropped eyelids, with an aspect of concentrated attention; and as he took vigorous draws at his pipe, it seemed to retreat and advance out of the night in the regular flicker of the tiny flame. The match went out.

'Absurd!' he cried. 'This is the worst of trying to tell . . . Here you all are, each moored with two good addresses, like a hulk with two anchors, a butcher round one corner, a policeman round another, excellent appetites, and temperature normal – you hear – normal from year's end to year's end. And you say, Absurd! Absurd be – exploded! Absurd! My dear boys, what can you expect from a man who out of sheer nervousness had just flung overboard a pair of new shoes! Now I think of it, it is amazing I did not shed tears. I am, upon the whole, proud of my fortitude. I was cut to the quick at the idea of having lost the inestimable privilege of listening to the gifted Kurtz. Of course I was wrong. The privilege was waiting for me. Oh yes, I heard more than enough. And I was right, too. A voice. He was very little more than a voice. And I heard – him – it – this voice – other voices – all of them were so little more than voices – and the memory of that time itself lingers around me, impalpable, like a dying vibration of one immense jabber, silly, atrocious, sordid, savage, or simply mean, without any kind of sense. Voices, voices – even the girl herself – now – '

He was silent for a long time.

'I laid the ghost of his gifts at last with a lie,' he began suddenly. 'Girl! What? Did I mention a girl? Oh, she is out of it – completely. They – the women I mean – are out of it – should be out of it. We must help them to stay in that beautiful world of their own, lest ours gets worse. Oh, she had to be out of it. You should have heard the disinterred body of Mr Kurtz saying, "My Intended." You would have perceived directly then how completely she was out of it. And the lofty frontal bone of Mr Kurtz! They say the hair goes on growing sometimes, but this – ah – specimen, was impressively bald. The wilderness had patted him on the head, and, behold, it was like a ball – an ivory ball; it had caressed him, and – lo! – he had withered; it had taken him, loved him, embraced him, got into his veins, consumed his flesh, and sealed his soul to its own by the inconceivable ceremonies of some devilish initiation. He was its spoiled and pampered favourite. Ivory? I should think so. Heaps of it, stacks of it. The old mud shanty was bursting with it. You would think there was not a single tusk left either above or below the ground in the whole country. "Mostly fossil," the manager had remarked disparagingly. It was no more fossil than I am; but they call it fossil when it is dug up. It appears these niggers do bury the tusks sometimes – but evidently they couldn't bury this parcel deep enough to save the gifted Mr Kurtz from his fate. We filled the steamboat with it, and had to pile a lot on the deck. Thus he could see and enjoy as long as he could see, because the appreciation of this favour had remained with him to the last. You should have heard him say, "My ivory." Oh yes, I heard him. "My Intended, my ivory, my station, my river, my –" everything belonged to him. It made me hold my breath in expectation of hearing the wilderness burst into a prodigious peal of laughter that would shake the fixed stars in their places. Everything belonged to him – but that was a trifle. The thing was to know what he belonged to, how many powers of darkness claimed him for their own. That was the reflection that made you creepy all over. It was impossible – it was not good for one either – trying to imagine. He had taken a high seat amongst the devils of the land – I mean literally. You can't understand. How could you? – with solid pavement under your feet, surrounded by kind neighbours ready to cheer you or to fall on you, stepping delicately between the butcher and the policeman, in the holy terror of scandal and gallows and lunatic asylums – how can you imagine what particular region of the first ages a man's untrammelled feet may take him into by the way of solitude – utter solitude without a policeman – by the way of silence – utter silence, where no warning voice of a kind neighbour can be heard whispering of public opinion? These little things make all the great difference. When they are gone you must fall back upon your own innate strength, upon your own capacity for faithfulness. Of course you may be too much of a fool to go wrong – too dull even to know you are being assaulted by the powers of darkness. I take it, no fool ever made a bargain for his soul with the devil: the fool is too much of a fool, or the devil too much of a devil – I don't know which. Or you may be such a thunderingly exalted creature as to be altogether deaf and blind to anything but heavenly sights and sounds. Then the earth for you is only a standing place – and whether to be like this is your loss or your gain I won't pretend to say. But most of us are neither one nor the other. The earth for us is a place to live in, where we must put up with sights, with sounds, with smells, too, by Jove! – breathe dead hippo, so to speak, and not be contaminated. And there, don't you see? your strength comes in, the faith in your ability for the digging of unostentatious holes to bury the stuff in – your power of devotion, not to yourself, but to an obscure, back-breaking business. And that's difficult enough. Mind, I am not trying to excuse or even explain – I am trying to account to myself for – for – Mr Kurtz – for the shade of Mr Kurtz. This initiated wraith from the back of Nowhere honoured me with its amazing confidence before it vanished altogether. This was because it could speak English to me. The original Kurtz had been educated partly in England, and – as he was good enough to say himself – his sympathies were in the right place. His mother was half-English, his father was half-French. All Europe contributed to the making of Kurtz; and by and by I learned that, most appropriately, the International Society for the Suppression of Savage Customs had entrusted him with the making of a report, for its future guidance. And he had written it too. I've seen it. I've read it. It was eloquent, vibrating with eloquence, but too highly strung, I think. Seventeen pages of close writing he had found time for! But this must have been before his – let us say – nerves, went wrong, and caused him to preside at certain midnight dances ending with unspeakable rites, which – as far as I reluctantly gathered from what I heard at various times – were offered up to him – do you understand? – to Mr Kurtz himself. But it was a beautiful piece of writing. The opening paragraph, however, in the light of later information, strikes me now as ominous. He began with the argument that we whites, from the point of development we had arrived at, "must necessarily appear to them [savages] in the nature of supernatural beings – we approach them with the might as of a deity," and so on, and so on. "By the simple exercise of our will we can exert a power for good practically unbounded," etc., etc. From that point he soared and took me with him. The peroration was magnificent, though difficult to remember, you know. It gave me the notion of an exotic Immensity ruled by an august Benevolence. It made me tingle with enthusiasm. This was the unbounded power of eloquence – of words – of burning noble words. There were no practical hints to interrupt the magic current of phrases, unless a kind of note at the foot of the last page, scrawled evidently much later, in an unsteady hand, may be regarded as the exposition of a method. It was very simple, and at the end of that moving appeal to every altruistic sentiment it blazed at you, luminous and terrifying, like a flash of lighting in a serene sky: "Exterminate all the brutes!" The curious part was that he had apparently forgotten all about that valuable postscriptum, because, later on, when he in a sense came to himself, he repeatedly entreated me to take good care of "my pamphlet" (he called it), as it was sure to have in the future a good influence upon his career. I had full information about all these things, and, besides, as it turned out, I was to have the care of his memory. I've done enough for it to give me the indisputable right to lay it, if I choose, for an everlasting rest in the dustbin of progress, amongst all the sweepings and, figuratively speaking, all the dead cats of civilisation. But then, you see, I can't choose. He won't be forgotten. Whatever he was, he was not common. He had the power to charm or frighten rudimentary souls into an aggravated witch-dance in his honour; he could also fill the small souls of the pilgrims with bitter misgivings: he had one devoted friend at least, and he had conquered one soul in the world that was neither rudimentary nor tainted with self-seeking. No; I can't forget him, though I am not prepared to affirm the fellow was exactly worth the life we lost in getting to him. I missed my late helmsman awfully – I missed him even while his body was still lying in the pilot-house. Perhaps you will think it passing strange, this regret for a savage who was no more account than a grain of sand in a black Sahara. Well, don't you see, he had done something, he had steered; for months I had him at my back – a help – an instrument. It was a kind of partnership. He steered for me – I had to look after him, I worried about his deficiencies, and thus a subtle bond had been created, of which I only became aware when it was suddenly broken. And the intimate profundity of that look he gave me when he received his hurt remains to this day in my memory – like a claim of distant kinship affirmed in a supreme moment.

'Poor fool! If he had only left that shutter alone. He had no restraint, no restraint – just like Kurtz – a tree swayed by the wind. As soon as I had put on a dry pair of slippers, I dragged him out, after first jerking the spear out of his side, which operation I confess I performed with my eyes shut tight. His heels leaped together over the little doorstep; his shoulders were pressed to my breast; I hugged him from behind desperately. Oh! he was heavy, heavy; heavier than any man on earth, I should imagine. Then without more ado I tipped him overboard. The current snatched him as though he had been a wisp of grass, and I saw the body roll over twice before I lost sight of it for ever. All the pilgrims and the manager were then congregated on the awning-deck about the pilot-house, chattering at each other like a flock of excited magpies, and there was a scandalised murmur at my heartless promptitude. What they wanted to keep that body hanging about for I can't guess. Embalm it, maybe. But I had also heard another, and a very ominous, murmur on the deck below. My friends the woodcutters were likewise scandalised, and with a better show of reason – though I admit that the reason itself was quite inadmissible. Oh, quite! I had made up my mind that if my late helmsman was to be eaten, the fishes alone should have him. He had been a very second-rate helmsman while alive, but now he was dead he might have become a first-class temptation, and possibly cause some startling trouble. Besides, I was anxious to take the wheel, the man in pink pyjamas showing himself a hopeless duffer at the business.

'This I did directly the simple funeral was over. We were going half-speed, keeping right in the middle of the stream, and I listened to the talk about me. They had given up Kurtz, they had given up the station; Kurtz was dead, and the station had been burnt – and so on – and so on. The red-haired pilgrim was beside himself with the thought that at least this poor Kurtz had been properly revenged. "Say! We must have made a glorious slaughter of them in the bush. Eh? What do you think? Say?" He positively danced, the bloodthirsty little gingery beggar. And he had nearly fainted when he saw the wounded man! I could not help saying, "You made a glorious lot of smoke, anyhow." I had seen, from the way the tops of the bushes rustled and flew, that almost all the shots had gone too high. You can't hit anything unless you take aim and fire from the shoulder; but these chaps fired from the hip with their eyes shut. The retreat, I maintained – and I was right – was caused by the screeching of the steam-whistle. Upon this they forgot Kurtz, and began to howl at me with indignant protests.

'The manager stood by the wheel murmuring confidentially about the necessity of getting well away down the river before dark at all events, when I saw in the distance a clearing on the riverside and the outlines of some sort of building. "What's this?" I asked. He clapped his hands in wonder. "The station!" he cried. I edged in at once, still going half-speed.

'Through my glasses I saw the slope of a hill interspersed with rare trees and perfectly free from undergrowth. A long decaying building on the summit was half buried in the high grass; the large holes in the peaked roof gaped black from afar; the jungle and the woods made a background. There was no enclosure or fence of any kind; but there had been one apparently, for near the house half a dozen slim posts remained in a row, roughly trimmed, and with their upper ends ornamented with round carved balls. The rails, or whatever there had been between, had disappeared. Of course the forest surrounded all that. The river-bank was clear, and on the water-side I saw a white man under a hat like a cart-wheel beckoning persistently with his whole arm. Examining the edge of the forest above and below, I was almost certain I could see movements – human forms gliding here and there. I steamed past prudently, then stopped the engines and let her drift down. The man on the shore began to shout, urging us to land. "We have been attacked," screamed the manager. "I know – I know. It's all right," yelled back the other, as cheerful as you please. "Come along. It's all right. I am glad."

'His aspect reminded me of something I had seen – something funny I had seen somewhere. As I manoeuvred to get alongside, I was asking myself, "What does this fellow look like?" Suddenly I got it. He looked like a harlequin. His clothes had been made of some stuff that was brown holland probably, but it was covered with patches all over, with bright patches, blue, red, and yellow – patches on the back, patches on the front, patches on elbows, on knees; coloured binding round his jacket, scarlet edging at the bottom of his trousers; and the sunshine made him look extremely gay and wonderfully neat withal, because you could see how beautifully all this patching had been done. A beardless, boyish face, very fair, no features to speak of, nose peeling, little blue eyes, smiles and frowns chasing each other over that open countenance like sunshine and shadow on a wind-swept plain. "Look out, captain!" he cried; "there's a snag lodged in here last night." What! Another snag? I confess I swore shamefully. I had nearly holed my cripple, to finish off that charming trip. The harlequin on the bank turned his little pug-nose up to me. "You English?" he asked, all smiles. "Are you?" I shouted from the wheel. The smiles vanished, and he shook his head as if sorry for my disappointment. Then he brightened up. "Never mind!" he cried encouragingly. "Are we in time?" I asked. "He is up there," he replied, with a toss of the head up the hill, and becoming gloomy all of a sudden. His face was like the autumn sky, overcast one moment and bright the next.

'When the manager, escorted by the pilgrims, all of them armed to the teeth, had gone to the house this chap came on board. "I say, I don't like this. These natives are in the bush," I said. He assured me earnestly it was all right. "They are simple people," he added; "well, I am glad you came. It took me all my time to keep them off." "But you said it was all right," I cried. "Oh, they meant no harm," he said; and as I stared he corrected himself, "Not exactly." Then vivaciously, "My faith, your pilot-house wants a clean up!" In the next breath he advised me to keep enough steam on the boiler to blow the whistle in case of any trouble. "One good screech will do more for you than all your rifles. They are simple people," he repeated. He rattled away at such a rate he quite overwhelmed me. He seemed to be trying to make up for lots of silence, and actually hinted, laughing, that such was the case. "Don't you talk with Mr Kurtz?" I said. "You don't talk with that man – you listen to him," he exclaimed with severe exaltation. "But now – " He waved his arm, and in the twinkling of an eye was in the uttermost depths of despondency. In a moment he came up again with a jump, possessed himself of both my hands, shook them continuously, while he gabbled: "Brother sailor . . . honour . . . pleasure . . . delight . . . introduce myself . . . Russian . . . son of an arch-priest . . . Government of Tambov . . . What? Tobacco! English tobacco; the excellent English tobacco! Now, that's brotherly. Smoke? Where's a sailor that does not smoke?"

'The pipe soothed him, and gradually I made out he had run away from school, had gone to sea in a Russian ship; ran away again; served some time in English ships; was now reconciled with the arch-priest. He made a point of that. "But when one is young one must see things, gather experience, ideas; enlarge the mind." "Here!" I interrupted. "You can never tell! Here I met Mr Kurtz," he said, youthfully solemn and reproachful. I held my tongue after that. It appears he had persuaded a Dutch trading-house on the coast to fit him out with stores and goods, and had started for the interior with a light heart, and no more idea of what would happen to him than a baby. He had been wandering about that river for nearly two years alone, cut off from everybody and everything. "I am not so young as I look. I am twenty-five," he said. "At first old Van Shuyten would tell me to go to the devil," he narrated with keen enjoyment; "but I stuck to him, and talked and talked, till at last he got afraid I would talk the hind-leg off his favourite dog, so he gave me some cheap things and a few guns, and told me he hoped he would never see my face again. Good old Dutchman, Van Shuyten. I've sent him one small lot of ivory a year ago, so that he can't call me a little thief when I get back. I hope he got it. And for the rest I don't care. I had some wood stacked for you. That was my old house. Did you see?"

'I gave him Towson's book. He made as though he would kiss me, but restrained himself. "The only book I had left, and I thought I had lost it," he said, looking at it ecstatically. "So many accidents happen to a man going about alone, you know. Canoes get upset sometimes – and sometimes you've got to clear out so quick when the people get angry." He thumbed the pages. "You made notes in Russian?" I asked. He nodded. "I thought they were written in cipher," I said. He laughed, then became serious. "I had lots of trouble to keep these people off," he said. "Did they want to kill you?" I asked. "Oh no!" he cried, and checked himself. "Why did they attack us?" I pursued.

He hesitated, then said shamefacedly, "They don't want him to go." "Don't they?" I said, curiously. He nodded a nod full of mystery and wisdom. "I tell you," he cried, "this man has enlarged my mind." He opened his arms wide, staring at me with his little blue eyes that were perfectly round.'

3

'I looked at him, lost in astonishment. There he was before me, in motley, as though he had absconded from a troupe of mimes, enthusiastic, fabulous. His very existence was improbable, inexplicable, and altogether bewildering. He was an insoluble problem. It was inconceivable how he had existed, how he had succeeded in getting so far, how he had managed to remain – why he did not instantly disappear. "I went a little farther," he said, "then still a little farther – till I had gone so far that I don't know how I'll ever get back. Never mind. Plenty time. I can manage. You take Kurtz away quick – quick – I tell you." The glamour of youth enveloped his particoloured rags, his destitution, his loneliness, the essential desolation of his futile wanderings. For months – for years – his life hadn't been worth a day's purchase; and there he was gallantly, thoughtlessly alive, to all appearance indestructible solely by the virtue of his few years and of his unreflecting audacity. I was seduced into something like admiration – like envy. Glamour urged him on, glamour kept him unscathed. He surely wanted nothing from the wilderness but space to breathe in and to push on through. His need was to exist, and to move onwards at the greatest possible risk, and with a maximum of privation. If the absolutely pure, uncalculating, unpractical spirit of adventure had ever ruled a human being, it ruled this be-patched youth. I almost envied him the possession of this modest and clear flame. It seemed to have consumed all thought of self so completely, that, even while he was talking to you, you forgot that it was he – the man before your eyes – who had gone through these things. I did not envy him his devotion to Kurtz, though. He had not meditated over it. It came to him, and he accepted it with a sort of eager fatalism. I must say that to me it appeared about the most dangerous thing in every way he had come upon so far.

'They had come together unavoidably, like two ships becalmed near each other, and lay rubbing sides at last. I suppose Kurtz wanted an audience, because on a certain occasion, when encamped in the forest, they had talked all night, or more probably Kurtz had talked. "We talked of everything," he said, quite transported at the recollection. "I forgot there was such a thing as sleep. The night did not seem to last an hour. Everything! Everything! . . . Of love too." "Ah, he talked to you of love!" I said, much amused. "It isn't what you think," he cried, almost passionately. "It was in general. He made me see things – things."

'He threw his arms up. We were on deck at the time, and the headman of my woodcutters, lounging near by, turned upon him his heavy and glittering eyes. I looked around, and I don't know why, but I assure you that never, never before, did this land, this river, this jungle, the very arch of this blazing sky, appear to me so hopeless and so dark, so impenetrable to human thought, so pitiless to human weakness. "And, ever since, you have been with him, of course?" I said.

'On the contrary. It appears their intercourse had been very much broken by various causes. He had, as he informed me proudly, managed to nurse Kurtz through two illnesses (he alluded to it as you would to some risky feat), but as a rule Kurtz wandered alone, far in the depths of the forest. "Very often coming to this station, I had to wait days and days before he would turn up," he said. "Ah, it was worth waiting for! – sometimes." "What was he doing? exploring or what?" I asked. "Oh yes, of course;" he had discovered lots of villages, a lake too – he did not know exactly in what direction; it was dangerous to inquire too much – but mostly his expeditions had been for ivory. "But he had no goods to trade with by that time," I objected. "There's a good lot of cartridges left even yet," he answered, looking away. "To speak plainly, he raided the country," I said. He nodded. "Not alone, surely!" He muttered something about the villages round that lake. "Kurtz got the tribe to follow him, did he?" I suggested. He fidgeted a little. "They adored him," he said. The tone of these words was so extraordinary that I looked at him searchingly. It was curious to see his mingled eagerness and reluctance to speak of Kurtz. The man filled his life, occupied his thoughts, swayed his emotions. "What can you expect?" he burst out; "he came to them with thunder and lightning, you know – and they had never seen anything like it – and very terrible. He could be very terrible. You can't judge Mr Kurtz as you would an ordinary man. No, no, no! Now – just to give you an idea – I don't mind telling you, he wanted to shoot me too one day – but I don't judge him." "Shoot you!" I cried. "What for?" "Well, I had a small lot of ivory the chief of that village near my house gave me. You see I used to shoot game for them. Well, he wanted it, and wouldn't hear reason. He declared he would shoot me unless I gave him the ivory and then cleared out of the country, because he could do so, and had a fancy for it, and there was nothing on earth to prevent him killing whom he jolly well pleased. And it was true too. I gave him the ivory. What did I care! But I didn't clear out. No, no. I couldn't leave him. I had to be careful, of course; till we got friendly again for a time. He had his second illness then. Afterwards I had to keep out of the way; but I didn't mind. He was living for the most part in those villages on the lake. When he came down to the river, sometimes he would take to me, and sometimes it was better for me to be careful. This man suffered too much. He hated all this, and somehow he couldn't get away. When I had a chance I begged him to try and leave while there was time; I offered to go back with him. And he would say yes, and then he would remain; go off on another ivory hunt; disappear for weeks; forget himself amongst these people – forget himself – you know." "Why! he's mad," I said. He protested indignantly. Mr Kurtz couldn't be mad. If I had heard him talk, only two days ago, I wouldn't dare hint at such a thing . . . I had taken up my binoculars while we talked, and was looking at the shore, sweeping the limit of the forest at each side and at the back of the house. The consciousness of there being people in that bush, so silent, so quiet – as silent and quiet as the ruined house on the hill – made me uneasy. There was no sign on the face of nature of this amazing tale that was not so much told as suggested to me in desolate exclamations, completed by shrugs, in interrupted phrases, in hints ending in deep sighs. The woods were unmoved, like a mask – heavy, like the closed door of a prison – they looked with their air of hidden knowledge, of patient expectation, of unapproachable silence. The Russian was explaining to me that it was only lately that Mr Kurtz had come down to the river, bringing along with him all the fighting men of that lake tribe. He had been absent for several months – getting himself adored, I suppose – and had come down unexpectedly, with the intention to all appearance of making a raid either across the river or down stream. Evidently the appetite for more ivory had got the better of the – what shall I say? – less material aspirations. However he had got much worse suddenly. "I heard he was lying helpless, and so I came up – took my chance," said the Russian. "Oh, he is bad, very bad." I directed my glass to the house. There were no signs of life, but there was the ruined roof, the long mud wall peeping above the grass, with three little square window-holes, no two of the same size; all this brought within reach of my hand, as it were. And then I made a brusque movement, and one of the remaining posts of that vanished fence leaped up in the field of my glass. You remember I told you I had been struck at the distance by certain attempts at ornamentation, rather remarkable in the ruinous aspect of the place. Now I had suddenly a nearer view, and its first result was to make me throw my head back as if before a blow. Then I went carefully from post to post with my glass, and I saw my mistake. These round knobs were not ornamental but symbolic; they were expressive and puzzling, striking and disturbing – food for thought and also for the vultures if there had been any looking down from the sky; but at all events for such ants as were industrious enough to ascend the pole. They would have been even more impressive, those heads on the stakes, if their faces had not been turned to the house. Only one, the first I had made out, was facing my way. I was not so shocked as you may think. The start back I had given was really nothing but a movement of surprise. I had expected to see a knob of wood there, you know. I returned deliberately to the first I had seen – and there it was, black, dried, sunken, with closed eyelids – a head that seemed to sleep at the top of that pole, and, with the shrunken dry lips showing a narrow white line of the teeth, was smiling too, smiling continuously at some endless and jocose dream of that eternal slumber.

'I am not disclosing any trade secrets. In fact the manager said afterwards that Mr Kurtz's methods had ruined the district. I have no opinion on that point, but I want you clearly to understand that there was nothing exactly profitable in these heads being there. They only showed that Mr Kurtz lacked restraint in the gratification of his various lusts, that there was something wanting in him – some small matter which, when the pressing need arose, could not be found under his magnificent eloquence. Whether he knew of this deficiency himself I can't say. I think the knowledge came to him at last – only at the very last. But the wilderness had found him out early, and had taken on him a terrible vengeance for the fantastic invasion. I think it had whispered to him things about himself which he did not know, things of which he had no conception till he took counsel with this great solitude – and the whisper had proved irresistibly fascinating. It echoed loudly within him because he was hollow at the core . . . I put down the glass, and the head that had appeared near enough to be spoken to seemed at once to have leaped away from me into inaccessible distance.

'The admirer of Mr Kurtz was a bit crestfallen. In a hurried, indistinct voice he began to assure me he had not dared to take these – say, symbols – down. He was not afraid of the natives; they would not stir till Mr Kurtz gave the word. His ascendancy was extraordinary. The camps of these people surrounded the place, and the chiefs came every day to see him. They would crawl . . . "I don't want to know anything of the ceremonies used when approaching Mr Kurtz," I shouted. Curious, this feeling that came over me that such details would be more intolerable than those heads drying on the stakes under Mr Kurtz's windows. After all, that was only a savage sight, while I seemed at one bound to have been transported into some lightless region of subtle horrors, where pure, uncomplicated savagery was a positive relief, being something that had a right to exist – obviously – in the sunshine. The young man looked at me with surprise. I suppose it did not occur to him that Mr Kurtz was no idol of mine. He forgot I hadn't heard any of these splendid monologues on, what was it? on love, justice, conduct of life – or what not. If it had come to crawling before Mr Kurtz, he crawled as much as the veriest savage of them all. I had no idea of the conditions, he said: these heads were the heads of rebels. I shocked him excessively by laughing. Rebels! What would be the next definition I was to hear? There had been enemies, criminals, workers – and these were rebels. Those rebellious heads looked very subdued to me on their sticks. "You don't know how such a life tries a man like Kurtz," cried Kurtz's last disciple. "Well, and you?" I said. "I! I! I am a simple man. I have no great thoughts. I want nothing from anybody. How can you compare me to . . .?" His feelings were too much for speech, and suddenly he broke down. "I don't understand," he groaned. "I've been doing my best to keep him alive, and that's enough. I had no hand in all this.

I have no abilities. There hasn't been a drop of medicine or a mouthful of invalid food for months here. He was shamefully abandoned. A man like this, with such ideas. Shamefully! Shamefully! I – I – haven't slept for the last ten nights. . . ."

'His voice lost itself in the calm of the evening. The long shadows of the forest had slipped down hill while we talked, had gone far beyond the ruined hovel, beyond the symbolic row of stakes. All this was in the gloom, while we down there were yet in the sunshine, and the stretch of the river abreast of the clearing glittered in a still and dazzling splendour, with a murky and overshadowed bend above and below. Not a living soul was seen on the shore. The bushes did not rustle.

'Suddenly round the corner of the house a group of men appeared, as though they had come up from the ground. They waded waist-deep in the grass, in a compact body, bearing an improvised stretcher in their midst. Instantly, in the emptiness of the landscape, a cry arose whose shrillness pierced the still air like a sharp arrow flying straight to the very heart of the land; and, as if by enchantment, streams of human beings – of naked human beings – with spears in their hands, with bows, with shields, with wild glances and savage movements, were poured into the clearing by the dark-faced and pensive forest. The bushes shook, the grass swayed for a time, and then everything stood still in attentive immobility.

' "Now, if he does not say the right thing to them we are all done for," said the Russian at my elbow. The knot of men with the stretcher had stopped too, half-way to the steamer, as if petrified. I saw the man on the stretcher sit up, lank and with an uplifted arm, above the shoulders of the bearers. "Let us hope that the man who can talk so well of love in general will find some particular reason to spare us this time," I said. I resented bitterly the absurd danger of our situation, as if to be at the mercy of that atrocious phantom had been a dishonouring necessity. I could not hear a sound, but through my glasses I saw the thin arm extended commandingly, the lower jaw moving, the eyes of that apparition shining darkly far in its bony head that nodded with grotesque jerks. Kurtz – Kurtz – that means short in German – don't it? Well, the name was as true as everything else in his life – and death. He looked at least seven feet long. His covering had fallen off, and his body emerged from it pitiful and appalling as from a winding-sheet. I could see the cage of his ribs all astir, the bones of his arm waving. It was as though an animated image of death carved out of old ivory had been shaking its hand with menaces at a motionless crowd of men made of dark and glittering bronze. I saw him open his mouth wide – it gave him a weirdly voracious aspect, as though he had wanted to swallow all the air, all the earth, all the men before him. A deep voice reached me faintly. He must have been shouting. He fell back suddenly. The stretcher shook as the bearers staggered forward again, and almost at the same time I noticed that the crowd of savages was vanishing without any perceptible movement of retreat, as if the forest that had ejected these beings so suddenly had drawn them in again as the breath is drawn in a long aspiration.

'Some of the pilgrims behind the stretcher carried his arms – two shotguns, a heavy rifle, and a light revolver-carbine – the thunderbolts of that pitiful Jupiter. The manager bent over him murmuring as he walked beside his head. They laid him down in one of the little cabins – just a room for a bed-place and a camp-stool or two, you know. We had brought his belated correspondence, and a lot of torn envelopes and open letters littered his bed. His hand roamed feebly amongst these papers. I was struck by the fire of his eyes and the composed languor of his expression. It was not so much the exhaustion of disease. He did not seem in pain. This shadow looked satiated and calm, as though for the moment it had had its fill of all the emotions.

'He rustled one of the letters, and looking straight in my face said, "I am glad." Somebody had been writing to him about me. These special recommendations were turning up again. The volume of tone he emitted without effort, almost without the trouble of moving his lips, amazed me. A voice! a voice! It was grave, profound, vibrating, while the man did not seem capable of a whisper. However, he had enough strength in him – factitious no doubt – to very nearly make an end of us, as you shall hear directly.

'The manager appeared silently in the doorway; I stepped out at once and he drew the curtain after me. The Russian, eyed curiously by the pilgrims, was staring at the shore. I followed the direction of his glance.

'Dark human shapes could be made out in the distance, flitting indistinctly against the gloomy border of the forest, and near the river two bronze figures, leaning on tall spears, stood in the sunlight under fantastic head-dresses of spotted skins, warlike and still in statuesque repose. And from right to left along the lighted shore moved a wild and gorgeous apparition of a woman.

'She walked with measured steps, draped in striped and fringed cloths, treading the earth proudly, with a slight jingle and flash of barbarous ornaments. She carried her head high; her hair was done in the shape of a helmet; she had brass leggings to the knee, brass wire gauntlets to the elbow, a crimson spot on her tawny cheek, innumerable necklaces of glass beads on her neck; bizarre things, charms, gifts of witch-men, that hung about her, glittered and trembled at every step. She must have had the value of several elephant tusks upon her. She was savage and superb, wild-eyed and magnificent; there was something ominous and stately in her deliberate progress. And in the hush that had fallen suddenly upon the whole sorrowful land, the immense wilderness, the colossal body of the fecund and mysterious life seemed to look at her, pensive, as though it had been looking at the image of its own tenebrous and passionate soul.

'She came abreast of the steamer, stood still, and faced us. Her long shadow fell to the water's edge. Her face had a tragic and fierce aspect of wild sorrow and of dumb pain mingled with the fear of some struggling, half-shaped resolve. She stood looking at us without a stir, and like the wilderness itself, with an air of brooding over an inscrutable purpose. A whole minute passed, and then she made a step forward. There was a low jingle, a glint of yellow metal, a sway of fringed draperies, and she stopped as if her heart had failed her. The young fellow by my side growled. The pilgrims murmured at my back. She looked at us all as if her life had depended upon the unswerving steadiness of her glance. Suddenly she opened her bared arms and threw them up rigid above her head, as though in an uncontrollable desire to touch the sky, and at the same time the swift shadows darted out on the earth, swept around on the river, gathering the steamer into a shadowy embrace. A formidable silence hung over the scene.

'She turned away slowly, walked on, following the bank, and passed into the bushes to the left. Once only her eyes gleamed back at us in the dusk of the thickets before she disappeared.

' "If she had offered to come aboard I really think I would have tried to shoot her," said the man of patches, nervously. "I had been risking my life every day for the last fortnight to keep her out of the house. She got in one day and kicked up a row about those miserable rags I picked up in the storeroom to mend my clothes with. I wasn't decent. At least it must have been that, for she talked like a fury to Kurtz for an hour, pointing at me now and then. I don't understand the dialect of this tribe. Luckily for me, I fancy Kurtz felt too ill that day to care, or there would have been mischief. I don't understand . . . No – it's too much for me. Ah, well, it's all over now."

'At this moment I heard Kurtz's deep voice behind the curtain: "Save me! – save the ivory, you mean. Don't tell me. Save *me*! Why, I've had to save you. You are interrupting my plans now. Sick! Sick! Not so sick as you would like to believe. Never mind. I'll carry my ideas out yet – I will return. I'll show you what can be done. You with your little peddling notions – you are interfering with me. I will return. I . . . "

'The manager came out. He did me the honour to take me under the arm and lead me aside. "He is very low, very low," he said. He considered it necessary to sigh, but neglected to be consistently sorrowful. "We have done all we could for him – haven't we? But there is no disguising the fact, Mr Kurtz has done more harm than good to the Company. He did not see the time was not ripe for vigorous action. Cautiously, cautiously – that's my principle. We must be cautious yet. The district is closed to us for a time. Deplorable! Upon the whole, the trade will suffer. I don't deny there is a remarkable quantity of ivory – mostly fossil. We must save it, at all events – but look how precarious the position is – and why? Because the method is unsound." "Do you," said I, looking at the shore, "call it 'unsound method'?" "Without doubt," he exclaimed, hotly. "Don't you?" . . . "No method at all," I murmured after a while. "Exactly," he exulted. "I anticipated this. Shows a complete want of judgement. It is my duty to point it out in the proper quarter." "Oh," said I, "that fellow – what's his name? – the brickmaker, will make a readable report for you." He appeared confounded for a moment. It seemed to me I had never breathed an atmosphere so vile, and I turned mentally to Kurtz for relief – positively for relief. "Nevertheless I think Mr Kurtz is a remarkable man," I said with emphasis. He started, dropped on me a cold heavy glance, said very quietly, "He *was*," and turned his back on me. My hour of favour was over; I found myself lumped along with Kurtz as a partisan of methods for which the time was not ripe: I was unsound! Ah! but it was something to have at least a choice of nightmares.

'I had turned to the wilderness really, not to Mr Kurtz, who, I was ready to admit, was as good as buried. And for a moment it seemed to me as if I also were buried in a vast grave full of unspeakable secrets. I felt an intolerable weight oppressing my breast, the smell of the damp earth, the unseen presence of victorious corruption, the darkness of an impenetrable night . . . The Russian tapped me on the shoulder. I heard him mumbling and stammering something about "brother seaman – couldn't conceal – knowledge of matters that would affect Mr Kurtz's reputation." I waited. For him evidently Mr Kurtz was not in his grave; I suspect that for him Mr Kurtz was one of the immortals. "Well!" said I at last, "speak out. As it happens, I am Mr Kurtz's friend – in a way."

'He stated with a good deal of formality that, had we not been "of the same profession", he would have kept the matter to himself without regard to consequences. "He suspected there was an active ill-will towards him on the part of these white men that – " "You are right," I said, remembering a certain conversation I had overheard. "The manager thinks you ought to be hanged." He showed a concern at this intelligence which amused me at first. "I had better get out of the way quietly," he said, earnestly. "I can do no more for Kurtz now, and they would soon find some excuse. What's to stop them? There's a military post three hundred miles from here." "Well, upon my word," said I, "perhaps you had better go if you have any friends amongst the savages near by." "Plenty," he said. "They are simple people – and I want nothing, you know." He stood biting his lip, then: "I don't want any harm to happen to these whites here, but of course I was thinking of Mr Kurtz's reputation – but you are a brother seaman and – " "All right," said I, after a time. "Mr Kurtz's reputation is safe with me." I did not know how truly I spoke.

'He informed me, lowering his voice, that it was Kurtz who had ordered the attack to be made on the steamer. "He hated sometimes the idea of being taken away – and then again . . . But I don't understand these matters. I am a simple man. He thought it would scare you away – that you would give it up, thinking him dead. I could not stop him. Oh, I had an awful time of it this last month." "Very well," I said. "He is all right now." "Ye–e–es," he muttered, not very convinced apparently. "Thanks," said I; "I shall keep my eyes open." "But quiet – eh?" he urged, anxiously. "It would be awful for his reputation if anybody here – " I promised a complete discretion with great gravity. "I have a canoe and three black fellows waiting not very far. I am off. Could you give me a few Martini-Henry cartridges?" I could, and did, with proper secrecy. He helped himself, with a wink at me, to a handful of my tobacco. "Between sailors – you know – good English tobacco." At the door of the pilot-house he turned round – "I say, haven't you a pair of shoes you could spare?" He raised one leg. "Look." The soles were tied with knotted strings sandal-wise under his bare feet. I rooted out an old pair, at which he looked with admiration before tucking it under his left arm. One of his pockets (bright red) was bulging with cartridges, from the other (dark blue) peeped "Towson's Inquiry," etc., etc. He seemed to think himself excellently well equipped for a renewed encounter with the wilderness. "Ah! I'll never, never meet such a man again. You ought to have heard him recite poetry – his own too it was, he told me. Poetry!" He rolled his eyes at the recollection of these delights. "Oh, he enlarged my mind!" "Goodbye," said I. He shook hands and vanished in the night. Sometimes I ask myself whether I had ever really seen him – whether it was possible to meet such a phenomenon! . . .

'When I woke up shortly after midnight his warning came to my mind with its hint of danger that seemed, in the starred darkness, real enough to make me get up for the purpose of having a look round. On the hill a big fire burned, illuminating fitfully a crooked corner of the station-house. One of the agents with a picket of a few of our blacks, armed for the purpose, was keeping guard over the ivory; but deep within the forest, red gleams that wavered, that seemed to sink and rise from the ground amongst confused columnar shapes of intense blackness, showed the exact position of the camp where Mr Kurtz's adorers were keeping their uneasy vigil. The monotonous beating of a big drum filled the air with muffled shocks and a lingering vibration. A steady droning sound of many men chanting each to himself some weird incantation came out from the black, flat wall of the woods as the humming of bees comes out of a hive, and had a strange narcotic effect upon my half-awake senses. I believe I dozed off leaning over the rail, till an abrupt burst of yells, an overwhelming outbreak of a pent-up and mysterious frenzy, woke me up in a bewildered wonder. It was cut short all at once, and the low droning went on with an effect of audible and soothing silence. I glanced casually into the little cabin. A light was burning within, but Mr Kurtz was not there.

'I think I would have raised an outcry if I had believed my eyes. But I didn't believe them at first – the thing seemed so impossible. The fact is I was completely unnerved by a sheer blank fright, pure abstract terror, unconnected with any distinct shape of physical danger. What made this emotion so over-powering was – how shall I define it? – the moral shock I received, as if something altogether monstrous, intolerable to thought and odious to the soul, had been thrust upon me unexpectedly. This lasted of course the merest fraction of a second, and then the usual sense of commonplace, deadly danger, the possibility of a sudden onslaught and massacre, or something of the kind, which I saw impending, was positively welcome and composing. It pacified me, in fact, so much, that I did not raise an alarm.

'There was an agent buttoned up inside an ulster and sleeping on a chair on deck within three feet of me. The yells had not awakened him; he snored very slightly; I left him to his slumbers and leaped ashore. I did not betray Mr Kurtz – it was ordered I should never betray him – it was written I should be loyal to the nightmare of my choice. I was anxious to deal with this shadow by myself alone – and to this day I don't know why I was so jealous of sharing with anyone the peculiar blackness of that experience.

'As soon as I got on the bank I saw a trail – a broad trail through the grass. I remember the exultation with which I said to myself, "He can't walk – he is crawling on all-fours – I've got him." The grass was wet with dew. I strode rapidly with clenched fists. I fancy I had some vague notion of falling upon him and giving him a drubbing. I don't know. I had some imbecile thoughts. The knitting old woman with the cat obtruded herself upon my memory as a most improper person to be sitting at the other end of such an affair. I saw a row of pilgrims squirting lead in the air out of Winchesters held to the hip. I thought I would never get back to the steamer, and imagined myself living alone and unarmed in the woods to an advanced age. Such silly things – you know. And I remember I confounded the beat of the drum with the beating of my heart, and was pleased at its calm regularity.

'I kept to the track though – then stopped to listen. The night was very clear; a dark blue space, sparkling with dew and starlight, in which black things stood very still. I thought I could see a kind of motion ahead of me. I was strangely cocksure of everything that night. I actually left the track and ran in a wide semicircle (I verily believe chuckling to myself) so as to get in front of that stir, of that motion I had seen – if indeed I had seen anything. I was circumventing Kurtz as though it had been a boyish game.

'I came upon him, and, if he had not heard me coming, I would have fallen over him too, but he got up in time. He rose, unsteady, long, pale, indistinct, like a vapour exhaled by the earth, and swayed slightly, misty and silent before me; while at my back the fires loomed between the trees, and the murmur of many voices issued from the forest. I had cut him off cleverly; but when actually confronting him I seemed to come to my senses, I saw the danger in its right proportion. It was by no means over yet. Suppose he began to shout? Though he could hardly stand, there was still plenty of vigour in his voice. "Go away – hide yourself," he said, in that profound tone. It was very awful. I glanced back. We were within thirty yards from the nearest fire. A black figure stood up, strode on long black legs, waving long black arms, across the glow. It had horns – antelope horns, I think – on its head. Some sorcerer, some witch-man, no doubt: it looked fiend-like enough. "Do you know what you are doing?" I whispered. "Perfectly," he answered, raising his voice for that single word: it sounded to me far off and yet loud, like a hail through a speaking-trumpet. If he makes a row we are lost, I thought to myself. This clearly was not a case for fisticuffs, even apart from the very natural aversion I had to beat that Shadow – this wandering and tormented thing. "You will be lost," I said –"utterly lost." One gets sometimes such a flash of inspiration, you know. I did say the right thing, though indeed he could not have been more irretrievably lost than he was at this very moment, when the foundations of our intimacy were being laid – to endure – to endure – even to the end – even beyond.

' "I had immense plans," he muttered irresolutely. "Yes," said I; "but if you try to shout I'll smash your head with – " There was not a stick or a stone near. "I will throttle you for good," I corrected myself. "I was on the threshold of great things," he pleaded, in a voice of longing, with a wistfulness of tone that made my blood run cold. "And now for this stupid scoundrel – " "Your success in Europe is assured in any case," I affirmed, steadily. I did not want to have the throttling of him, you understand – and indeed it would have been very little use for any practical purpose. I tried to break the spell – the heavy, mute spell of the wilderness – that seemed to draw him to its pitiless breast by the awakening of forgotten and brutal instincts, by the memory of gratified and monstrous passions. This alone, I was convinced, had driven him out to the edge of the forest, to the bush, towards the gleam of fires, the throb of drums, the drone of weird incantations; this alone had beguiled his unlawful soul beyond the bounds of permitted aspirations. And, don't you see, the terror of the position was not in being knocked on the head – though I had a very lively sense of that danger too – but in this, that I had to deal with a being to whom I could not appeal in the name of anything high or low. I had, even like the niggers, to invoke him – himself – his own exalted and incredible degradation. There was nothing either above or below him, and I knew it. He had kicked himself loose of the earth. Confound the man! he had kicked the very earth to pieces. He was alone, and I before him did not know whether I stood on the ground or floated in the air. I've been telling you what we said – repeating the phrases we pronounced – but what's the good? They were common everyday words – the familiar, vague sounds exchanged on every waking day of life. But what of that? They had behind them, to my mind, the terrific suggestiveness of words heard in dreams, of phrases spoken in nightmares. Soul! If anybody had ever struggled with a soul, I am the man. And I wasn't arguing with a lunatic either. Believe me or not, his intelligence was perfectly clear – concentrated, it is true, upon himself with horrible intensity, yet clear; and therein was my only chance – barring, of course, the killing him there and then, which wasn't so good, on account of unavoidable noise. But his soul was mad. Being alone in the wilderness, it had looked within itself, and, by heavens! I tell you, it had gone mad. I had – for my sins, I suppose – to go through the ordeal of looking into it myself. No eloquence could have been so withering to one's belief in mankind as his final burst of sincerity. He struggled with himself too. I saw it – I heard it. I saw the inconceivable mystery of a soul that knew no restraint, no faith, and no fear, yet struggling blindly with itself. I kept my head pretty well; but when I had him at last stretched on the couch, I wiped my forehead, while my legs shook under me as though I had carried half a ton on my back down that hill. And yet I had only supported him, his bony arm clasped round my neck – and he was not much heavier than a child.

'When next day we left at noon, the crowd, of whose presence behind the curtain of trees I had been acutely conscious all the time, flowed out of the woods again, filled the clearing, covered the slope with a mass of naked, breathing, quivering, bronze bodies. I steamed up a bit, then swung down-stream, and two thousand eyes followed the evolutions of the splashing, thumping, fierce river-demon beating the water with its terrible tail and breathing black smoke into the air. In front of the first rank, along the river, three men, plastered with bright red earth from head to foot, strutted to and fro restlessly. When we came abreast again, they faced the river, stamped their feet, nodded their horned heads, swayed their scarlet bodies; they shook towards the fierce river-demon a bunch of black feathers, a mangy skin with a pendent tail – something that looked like a dried gourd; they shouted periodically together strings of amazing words that resembled no sounds of human language; and the deep murmurs of the crowd, interrupted suddenly, were like the responses of some satanic litany.

'We had carried Kurtz into the pilot-house: there was more air there. Lying on the couch, he stared through the open shutter. There was an eddy in the mass of human bodies, and the woman with helmeted head and tawny cheeks rushed out to the very brink of the stream. She put out her hands, shouted something, and all that wild mob took up the shout in a roaring chorus of articulated, rapid, breathless utterance.

' "Do you understand this?" I asked.

'He kept on looking out past me with fiery, longing eyes, with a mingled expression of wistfulness and hate. He made no answer, but I saw a smile, a smile of indefinable meaning, appear on his colourless lips that a moment after twitched convulsively. "Do I not?" he said slowly, gasping, as if the words had been torn out of him by a supernatural power.

'I pulled the string of the whistle, and I did this because I saw the pilgrims on deck getting out their rifles with an air of anticipating a jolly lark. At the sudden screech there was a movement of abject terror through that wedged mass of bodies. "Don't! don't you frighten them away," cried someone on deck disconsolately. I pulled the string time after time. They broke and ran, they leaped, they crouched, they swerved, they dodged the flying terror of the sound. The three red chaps had fallen flat, face down on the shore, as though they had been shot dead. Only the barbarous and superb woman did not so much as flinch, and stretched tragically her bare arms after us over the sombre and glittering river.

'And then that imbecile crowd down on the deck started their little fun, and I could see nothing more for smoke.

'The brown current ran swiftly out of the heart of darkness, bearing us down towards the sea with twice the speed of our upward progress; and Kurtz's life was running swiftly too, ebbing, ebbing out of his heart into the sea of inexorable time. The manager was very placid, he had no vital anxieties now, he took us both in with a comprehensive and satisfied glance: the "affair" had come off as well as could be wished. I saw the time approaching when I would be left alone of the party of "unsound method". The pilgrims looked upon me with disfavour. I was, so to speak, numbered with the dead. It is strange how I accepted this unforeseen partnership, this choice of nightmares forced upon me in the tenebrous land invaded by these mean and greedy phantoms.

'Kurtz discoursed. A voice! a voice! It rang deep to the very last. It survived his strength to hide in the magnificent folds of eloquence the barren darkness of his heart. Oh, he struggled! he struggled! The wastes of his weary brain were haunted by shadowy images now – images of wealth and fame revolving obsequiously round his inextinguishable gift of noble and lofty expression. My Intended, my station, my career, my ideas – these were the subjects for the occasional utterances of elevated sentiments. The shade of the original Kurtz frequented the bedside of the hollow sham, whose fate it was to be buried presently in the mould of primeval earth. But both the diabolic love and the unearthly hate of the mysteries it had penetrated fought for the possession of that soul satiated with primitive emotions, avid of lying fame, of sham distinction, of all the appearances of success and power.

'Sometimes he was contemptibly childish. He desired to have kings meet him at railway-stations on his return from some ghastly Nowhere, where he intended to accomplish great things. "You show them you have in you something that is really profitable, and then there will be no limits to the recognition of your ability," he would say. "Of course you must take care of the motives – right motives – always." The long reaches that were like one and the same reach, monotonous bends that were exactly alike, slipped past the steamer with their multitude of secular trees looking patiently after this grimy fragment of another world, the forerunner of change, of conquest, of trade, of massacres, of blessings. I looked ahead – piloting. "Close the shutter," said Kurtz suddenly one day; "I can't bear to look at this." I did so. There was a silence. "Oh, but I will wring your heart yet!" he cried at the invisible wilderness.

'We broke down – as I had expected – and had to lie up for repairs at the head of an island. This delay was the first thing that shook Kurtz's confidence. One morning he gave me a packet of papers and a photograph – the lot tied together with a shoestring. "Keep this for me," he said. "This noxious fool" (meaning the manager) "is capable of prying into my boxes when I am not looking." In the afternoon I saw him. He was lying on his back with closed eyes, and I withdrew quietly, but I heard him mutter, "Live rightly, die, die . . ." I listened. There was nothing more. Was he rehearsing some speech in his sleep, or was it a fragment of a phrase from some newspaper article? He had been writing for the papers and meant to do so again, "for the furthering of my ideas. It's a duty."

'His was an impenetrable darkness. I looked at him as you peer down at a man who is lying at the bottom of a precipice where the sun never shines. But I had not much time to give him, because I was helping the engine-driver to take to pieces the leaky cylinders, to straighten a bent connecting-rod, and in other such matters. I lived in an infernal mess of rust, filings, nuts, bolts, spanners, hammers, ratchet-drills – things I abominate, because I don't get on with them. I tended the little forge we fortunately had aboard; I toiled wearily in a wretched scrap-heap – unless I had the shakes too bad to stand.

'One evening coming in with a candle I was startled to hear him say a little tremulously, "I am lying here in the dark waiting for death." The light was within a foot of his eyes. I forced myself to murmur, "Oh, nonsense!" and stood over him as if transfixed.

'Anything approaching the change that came over his features I have never seen before, and hope never to see again. Oh, I wasn't touched. I was fascinated. It was as though a veil had been rent. I saw on that ivory face the expression of sombre pride, of ruthless power, of craven terror – of an intense and hopeless despair. Did he live his life again in every detail of desire, temptation, and surrender during that supreme moment of complete knowledge? He cried in a whisper at some image, at some vision – he cried out twice, a cry that was no more than a breath – ' "The horror! The horror!"'

"I blew the candle out and left the cabin. The pilgrims were dining in the mess-room, and I took my place opposite the manager, who lifted his eyes to give me a questioning glance, which I successfully ignored. He leaned back, serene, with that peculiar smile of his sealing the unexpressed depths of his meanness. A continuous shower of small flies streamed upon the lamp, upon the cloth, upon our hands and faces. Suddenly the manager's boy put his insolent black head in the doorway, and said in a tone of scathing contempt – ' "Mistah Kurtz – he dead."'

'All the pilgrims rushed out to see. I remained, and went on with my dinner. I believe I was considered brutally callous. However, I did not eat much. There was a lamp in there – light, don't you know – and outside it was so beastly, beastly dark. I went no more near the remarkable man who had pronounced a judgement upon the adventures of his soul on this earth. The voice was gone. What else had been there? But I am of course aware that next day the pilgrims buried something in a muddy hole.

'And then they very nearly buried me.

'However, as you see, I did not go to join Kurtz there and then. I did not. I remained to dream the nightmare out to the end, and to show my loyalty to Kurtz once more. Destiny. My destiny! Droll thing life is – that mysterious arrangement of merciless logic for a futile purpose. The most you can hope from it is some knowledge of yourself – that comes too late – a crop of inextinguishable regrets. I have wrestled with death. It is the most unexciting contest you can imagine. It takes place in an impalpable greyness, with nothing underfoot, with nothing around, without spectators, without clamour, without glory, without the great desire of victory, without the great fear of defeat, in a sickly atmosphere of tepid scepticism, without much belief in your own right, and still less in that of your adversary. If such is the form of ultimate wisdom, then life is a greater riddle than some of us think it to be. I was within a hair's-breadth of the last opportunity for pronouncement, and I found with humiliation that probably I would have nothing to say. This is the reason why I affirm that Kurtz was a remarkable man. He had something to say. He said it. Since I had peeped over the edge myself, I understand better the meaning of his stare, that could not see the flame of the candle, but was wide enough to embrace the whole universe, piercing enough to penetrate all the hearts that beat in the darkness. He had summed up – he had judged. "The horror!" He was a remarkable man. After all, this was the expression of some sort of belief; it had candour, it had conviction, it had a vibrating note of revolt in its whisper, it had the appalling face of a glimpsed truth – the strange commingling of desire and hate. And it is not my own extremity I remember best – a vision of greyness without form filled with physical pain, and a careless contempt for the evanescence of all things – even of this pain itself. No! It is his extremity that I seem to have lived through. True, he had made that last stride, he had stepped over the edge, while I had been permitted to draw back my hesitating foot. And perhaps in this is the whole difference; perhaps all wisdom, and all truth, and all sincerity, are just compressed into that inappreciable moment of time in which we step over the threshold of the invisible. Perhaps! I like to think my summing-up would not have been a word of careless contempt. Better his cry – much better. It was an affirmation, a moral victory paid for by innumerable defeats, by abominable terrors, by abominable satisfactions. But it was a victory! That is why I have remained loyal to Kurtz to the last, and even beyond, when a long time after I heard once more, not his own voice, but the echo of his magnificent eloquence thrown to me from a soul as translucently pure as a cliff of crystal.

'No, they did not bury me, though there is a period of time which I remember mistily, with a shuddering wonder, like a passage through some inconceivable world that had no hope in it and no desire. I found myself back in the sepulchral city resenting the sight of people hurrying through the streets to filch a little money from each other, to devour their infamous cookery, to gulp their unwholesome beer, to dream their insignificant and silly dreams. They trespassed upon my thoughts. They were intruders whose knowledge of life was to me an irritating pretence, because I felt so sure they could not possibly know the things I knew. Their bearing, which was simply the bearing of commonplace individuals going about their business in the assurance of perfect safety, was offensive to me like the outrageous flauntings of folly in the face of a danger it is unable to comprehend. I had no particular desire to enlighten them, but I had some difficulty in restraining myself from laughing in their faces, so full of stupid importance. I dare say I was not very well at that time. I tottered about the streets – there were various affairs to settle – grinning bitterly at perfectly respectable persons. I admit my behaviour was inexcusable, but then my temperature was seldom normal in these days. My dear aunt's endeavours to "nurse up my strength" seemed altogether beside the mark. It was not my strength that wanted nursing, it was my imagination that wanted soothing. I kept the bundle of papers given me by Kurtz, not knowing exactly what to do with it. His mother had died lately, watched over, as I was told, by his Intended. A clean-shaved man, with an official manner and wearing gold-rimmed spectacles, called on me one day and made inquiries, at first circuitous, afterwards suavely pressing, about what he was pleased to denominate certain "documents". I was not surprised, because I had had two rows with the manager on the subject out there. I had refused to give up the smallest scrap out of that package, and I took the same attitude with the spectacled man. He became darkly menacing at last, and with much heat argued that the Company had the right to every bit of information about its "territories". And, said he, "Mr Kurtz's knowledge of unexplored regions must have been necessarily extensive and peculiar – owing to his great abilities and to the deplorable circumstances in which he had been placed: therefore – " I assured him Mr Kurtz's knowledge, however extensive, did not bear upon the problems of commerce or administration. He invoked then the name of science. "It would be an incalculable loss if," etc., etc. I offered him the report on the "Suppression of Savage Customs," with the postscriptum torn off. He took it up eagerly, but ended by sniffing at it with an air of contempt. "This is not what we had a right to expect," he remarked. "Expect nothing else," I said. "There are only private letters." He withdrew upon some threat of legal proceedings, and I saw him no more; but another fellow, calling himself Kurtz's cousin, appeared two days later and was anxious to hear all the details about his dear relative's last moments. Incidentally he gave me to understand that Kurtz had been essentially a great musician. "There was the making of an immense success," said the man, who was an organist, I believe, with lank grey hair flowing over a greasy coat-collar. I had no reason to doubt his statement; and to this day I am unable to say what was Kurtz's profession, whether he ever had any – which was the greatest of his talents. I had taken him for a painter who wrote for the papers, or else for a journalist who could paint – but even the cousin (who took snuff during the interview) could not tell me what he had been – exactly. He was a universal genius – on that point I agreed with the old chap, who thereupon blew his nose noisily into a large cotton handkerchief and withdrew in senile agitation, bearing off some family letters and memoranda without importance. Ultimately a journalist anxious to know something of the fate of his "dear colleague" turned up. This visitor informed me Kurtz's proper sphere ought to have been politics "on the popular side". He had furry straight eyebrows, bristly hair cropped short, an eyeglass on a broad ribbon, and, becoming expansive, confessed his opinion that Kurtz really couldn't write a bit – "but heavens! how that man could talk! He electrified large meetings. He had faith – don't you see? – he had the faith. He could get himself to believe anything – anything. He would have been a splendid leader of an extreme party." "What party?" I asked. "Any party," answered the other. "He was an – an – extremist." Did I not think so? I assented. Did I know, he asked, with a sudden flash of curiosity, "what it was that had induced him to go out there?" "Yes," said I, and forthwith handed him the famous Report for publication, if he thought fit. He glanced through it hurriedly, mumbling all the time, judged "it would do", and took himself off with this plunder.

'Thus I was left at last with a slim packet of letters and the girl's portrait. She struck me as beautiful – I mean she had a beautiful expression. I know that the sunlight can be made to lie too, yet one felt that no manipulation of light and pose could have conveyed the delicate shade of truthfulness upon those features. She seemed ready to listen without mental reservation, without suspicion, without a thought for herself. I concluded I would go and give her back her portrait and those letters myself. Curiosity? Yes; and also some other feeling perhaps. All that had been Kurtz's had passed out of my hands: his soul, his body, his station, his plans, his ivory, his career. There remained only his memory and his Intended – and I wanted to give that up too to the past, in a way – to surrender personally all that remained of him with me to that oblivion which is the last word of our common fate. I don't defend myself. I had no clear perception of what it was I really wanted. Perhaps it was an impulse of unconscious loyalty, or the fulfilment of one of these ironic necessities that lurk in the facts of human existence. I don't know. I can't tell. But I went.

'I thought his memory was like the other memories of the dead that accumulate in every man's life – a vague impress on the brain of shadows that had fallen on it in their swift and final passage; but before the high and ponderous door, between the tall houses of a street as still and decorous as a well-kept alley in a cemetery, I had a vision of him on the stretcher, opening his mouth voraciously, as if to devour all the earth with all its mankind. He lived then before me; he lived as much as he had ever lived – a shadow insatiable of splendid appearances, of frightful realities; a shadow darker than the shadow of the night, and draped nobly in the folds of a gorgeous eloquence. The vision seemed to enter the house with me – the stretcher, the phantom-bearers, the wild crowd of obedient worshippers, the gloom of the forests, the glitter of the reach between the murky bends, the beat of the drum, regular and muffled like the beating of a heart – the heart of a conquering darkness. It was a moment of triumph for the wilderness, an invading and vengeful rush which, it seemed to me, I would have to keep back alone for the salvation of another soul. And the memory of what I had heard him say afar there, with the horned shapes stirring at my back, in the glow of fires, within the patient woods, those broken phrases came back to me, were heard again in their ominous and terrifying simplicity. I remembered his abject pleading, his abject threats, the colossal scale of his vile desires, the meanness, the torment, the tempestuous anguish of his soul. And later on I seemed to see his collected languid manner, when he said one day, "This lot of ivory now is really mine. The Company did not pay for it. I collected it myself at a very great personal risk. I am afraid they will try to claim it as theirs though. H'm. It is a difficult case. What do you think I ought to do – resist? Eh? I want no more than justice" . . . He wanted no more than justice – no more than justice. I rang the bell before a mahogany door on the first floor, and while I waited he seemed to stare at me out of the glassy panel – stare with that wide and immense stare embracing, condemning, loathing all the universe. I seemed to hear the whispered cry, "The horror! The horror!"

'The dusk was falling. I had to wait in a lofty drawing-room with three long windows from floor to ceiling that were like three luminous and bedraped columns. The bent gilt legs and backs of the furniture shone in indistinct curves. The tall marble fireplace had a cold and monumental whiteness. A grand piano stood massively in a corner, with dark gleams on the flat surfaces like a sombre and polished sarcophagus. A high door opened – closed. I rose.

'She came forward, all in black, with a pale head, floating towards me in the dusk. She was in mourning. It was more than a year since his death, more than a year since the news came; she seemed as though she would remember and mourn for ever. She took both my hands in hers and murmured, "I had heard you were coming." I noticed she was not very young – I mean not girlish. She had a mature capacity for fidelity, for belief, for suffering. The room seemed to have grown darker, as if all the sad light of the cloudy evening had taken refuge on her forehead. This fair hair, this pale visage, this pure brow, seemed surrounded by an ashy halo from which the dark eyes looked out at me. Their glance was guileless, profound, confident, and trustful. She carried her sorrowful head as though she were proud of that sorrow, as though she would say, I – I alone know how to mourn for him as he deserves. But while we were still shaking hands, such a look of awful desolation came upon her face that I perceived she was one of those creatures that are not the playthings of Time. For her he had died only yesterday. And, by Jove! the impression was so powerful that for me too he seemed to have died only yesterday – nay, this very minute. I saw her and him in the same instant of time – his death and her sorrow – I saw her sorrow in the very moment of his death. Do you understand? I saw them together – I heard them together. She had said, with a deep catch of the breath, "I have survived"; while my strained ears seemed to hear distinctly, mingled with her tone of despairing regret, the summing-up whisper of his eternal condemnation. I asked myself what I was doing there, with a sensation of panic in my heart as though I had blundered into a place of cruel and absurd mysteries not fit for a human being to behold. She motioned me to a chair. We sat down. I laid the packet gently on the little table, and she put her hand over it . . . "You knew him well," she murmured, after a moment of mourning silence.

' "Intimacy grows quick out there," I said. "I knew him as well as it is possible for one man to know another."

' "And you admired him," she said. "It was impossible to know him and not to admire him. Was it?"

' "He was a remarkable man," I said, unsteadily. Then before the appealing fixity of her gaze, that seemed to watch for more words on my lips, I went on, "It was impossible not to – "

' "Love him," she finished eagerly, silencing me into an appalled dumbness. "How true! how true! But when you think that no one knew him so well as I! I had all his noble confidence. I knew him best."

' "You knew him best," I repeated. And perhaps she did. But with every word spoken the room was growing darker, and only her forehead, smooth and white, remained illumined by the inextinguishable light of belief and love.

' "You were his friend," she went on. "His friend," she repeated, a little louder. "You must have been if he had given you this, and sent you to me. I feel I can speak to you – and oh! I must speak. I want you – you who have heard his last words – to know I have been worthy of him . . . It is not pride . . . Yes! I am proud to know I understood him better than anyone on earth – he told me so himself. And since his mother died I have had no one – no one – to – to – "

'I listened. The darkness deepened. I was not even sure whether he had given me the right bundle. I rather suspect he wanted me to take care of another batch of his papers which, after his death, I saw the manager examining under the lamp. And the girl talked, easing her pain in the certitude of my sympathy; she talked as thirsty men drink. I had heard that her engagement with Kurtz had been disapproved by her people. He wasn't rich enough or something. And indeed I don't know whether he had not been a pauper all his life. He had given me some reason to infer that it was his impatience of comparative poverty that drove him out there.

' ". . . Who was not his friend who had heard him speak once?" she was saying. "He drew men towards him by what was best in them." She looked at me with intensity. "It is the gift of the great," she went on, and the sound of her low voice seemed to have the accompaniment of all the other sounds, full of mystery, desolation, and sorrow, I had ever heard – the ripple of the river, the soughing of the trees swayed by the wind, the murmurs of the crowds, the faint ring of incomprehensible words cried from afar, the whisper of a voice speaking from beyond the threshold of an eternal darkness. "But you have heard him! You know!" she cried.

' "Yes, I know," I said with something like despair in my heart, but bowing my head before the faith that was in her, before that great and saving illusion that shone with an unearthly glow in the darkness, in the triumphant darkness from which I could not have defended her – from which I could not even defend myself.

' "What a loss to me – to us!" – she corrected herself with beautiful generosity; then added in a murmur, "To the world." By the last gleams of twilight I could see the glitter of her eyes, full of tears – of tears that would not fall.

' "I have been very happy – very fortunate – very proud," she went on. "Too fortunate. Too happy for a little while. And now I am unhappy for – for life."

'She stood up; her fair hair seemed to catch all the remaining light in a glimmer of gold. I rose too.

' "And of all this," she went on, mournfully, "of all his promise, and of all his greatness, of his generous mind, of his noble heart, nothing remains – nothing but a memory. You and I – ' "We shall always remember him," I said hastily.

' "No!" she cried. "It is impossible that all this should be lost – that such a life should be sacrificed to leave nothing – but sorrow. You know what vast plans he had. I knew of them too – I could not perhaps understand – but others knew of them. Something must remain. His words, at least, have not died."

' "His words will remain," I said.

' "And his example," she whispered to herself. "Men looked up to him – his goodness shone in every act. His example – "

' "True," I said; "his example too. Yes, his example. I forgot that."

' "But I do not. I cannot – I cannot believe – not yet. I cannot believe that I shall never see him again, that nobody will see him again, never, never, never."

'She put out her arms as if after a retreating figure, stretching them black and with clasped pale hands across the fading and narrow sheen of the window. Never see him! I saw him clearly enough then. I shall see this eloquent phantom as long as I live, and I shall see her too, a tragic and familiar Shade, resembling in this gesture another one, tragic also, and bedecked with powerless charms, stretching bare brown arms over the glitter of the infernal stream, the stream of darkness. She said suddenly very low, "He died as he lived."

' "His end," said I, with dull anger stirring in me; "was in every way worthy of his life."

' "And I was not with him," she murmured. My anger subsided before a feeling of infinite pity.

' "Everything that could be done – " I mumbled.

' "Ah, but I believed in him more than anyone on earth – more than his own mother, more than – himself. He needed me! Me! I would have treasured every sigh, every word, every sign, every glance."

'I felt like a chill grip on my chest. "Don't," I said, in a muffled voice.

' "Forgive me. I – I – have mourned so long in silence – in silence . . . You were with him – to the last? I think of his loneliness. Nobody near to understand him as I would have understood. Perhaps no one to hear . . . "

' "To the very end," I said, shakily. "I heard his very last words . . . " I stopped in a fright.

' "Repeat them," she murmured in a heart-broken tone. "I want – I want – something – something – to – to live with."

'I was on the point of crying at her, "Don't you hear them?" The dusk was repeating them in a persistent whisper all around us, in a whisper that seemed to swell menacingly like the first whisper of a rising wind. "The horror! the horror!"

' "His last word – to live with," she insisted. "Don't you understand I loved him – I loved him – I loved him!"

'I pulled myself together and spoke slowly.

' "The last word he pronounced was – your name."

'I heard a light sigh and then my heart stood still, stopped dead short by an exulting and terrible cry, by the cry of inconceivable triumph and of unspeakable pain. "I knew it – I was sure!" . . . She knew. She was sure. I heard her weeping; she had hidden her face in her hands. It seemed to me that the house would collapse before I could escape, that the heavens would fall upon my head. But nothing happened. The heavens do not fall for such a trifle. Would they have fallen, I wonder, if I had rendered Kurtz that justice which was his due? Hadn't he said he wanted only justice? But I couldn't. I could not tell her. It would have been too dark – too dark altogether . . . '

Marlow ceased, and sat apart, indistinct and silent, in the pose of a meditating Buddha. Nobody moved for a time. 'We have lost the first of the ebb,' said the Director, suddenly. I raised my head. The offing was barred by a black bank of clouds, and the tranquil waterway leading to the uttermost ends of the earth flowed sombre under an overcast sky – seemed to lead into the heart of an immense darkness.

1902

THE END OF THE TETHER

For a long time after the course of the steamer *Sofala* had been altered for the land, the low swampy coast had retained its appearance of a mere smudge of darkness beyond a belt of glitter. The sunrays fell violently upon the calm sea – seemed to shatter themselves upon an adamantine surface into sparkling dust, into a dazzling vapour of light that blinded the eye and wearied the brain with its unsteady brightness.

Captain Whalley did not look at it. When his Serang, approaching the roomy cane armchair which he filled capably, had informed him in a low voice that the course was to be altered, he had risen at once and had remained on his feet, face forward, while the head of his ship swung through a quarter of a circle. He had not uttered a single word, not even the word to steady the helm. It was the Serang, an elderly, alert, little Malay, with a very dark skin, who murmured the order to the helmsman. And then slowly Captain Whalley sat down again in the armchair on the bridge and fixed his eyes on the deck between his feet.

He could not hope to see anything new upon this lane of the sea. He had been on these coasts for the last three years. From Low Cape to Malantan the distance was fifty miles, six hours' steaming for the old ship with the tide, or seven against. Then you steered straight for the land, and by and by three palms would appear on the sky, tall and slim, and with their dishevelled heads in a bunch, as if in confidential criticism of the dark mangroves. The *Sofala* would be headed towards the sombre strip of the coast, which at a given moment, as the ship closed with it obliquely, would show several clean shining fractures – the brimful estuary of a river. Then on through a brown liquid, three parts water and one part black earth, on and on between the low shores, three parts black earth and one part brackish water, the *Sofala* would plough her way upstream, as she had done once every month for these seven years or more, long before he was aware of her existence, long before he had ever thought of having anything to do with her and her invariable voyages. The old ship ought to have known the road better than her men, who had not been kept so long at it without a change; better than the faithful Serang, whom he had brought over from his last ship to keep the captain's watch; better than he himself, who had been her captain for the last three years only. She could always be depended upon to make her courses. Her compasses were never out. She was no trouble at all to take about, as if her great age had given her knowledge, wisdom, and steadiness. She made her landfalls to a degree of the bearing, and almost to a minute of her allowed time. At any moment, as he sat on the bridge without looking up, or lay sleepless in his bed, simply by reckoning the days and the hours he could tell where he was – the precise spot of the beat. He knew it well too, this monotonous huckster's round, up and down the Straits; he knew its order and its sights and its people. Malacca to begin with, in at daylight and out at dusk, to cross over with a rigid phosphorescent wake this highway of the Far East. Darkness and gleams on the water, clear stars on a black sky, perhaps the lights of a home steamer keeping her unswerving course in the middle, or maybe the elusive shadow of a native craft with her mat sails flitting by silently – and low land on the other side in sight at daylight. At noon the three palms of the next place of call, up a sluggish river. The only white man residing there was a retired young sailor, with whom he had become friendly in the course of many voyages. Sixty miles farther on there was another place of call, a deep bay with only a couple of houses on the beach. And so on, in and out, picking up coastwise cargo here and there, and finishing with a hundred miles' steady steaming through the maze of an archipelago of small islands up to a large native town at the end of the beat. There was a three days' rest for the old ship before he started her again in inverse order, seeing the same shores from another bearing, hearing the same voices in the same places, back again to the *Sofala*'s port of registry on the great highway to the East, where he would take up a berth nearly opposite the big stone pile of the harbour office till it was time to start again on the old round of sixteen hundred miles and thirty days. Not a very enterprising life, this, for Captain Whalley, Henry Whalley, otherwise Daredevil Harry Whalley, of the *Condor*, a famous clipper in her day. No. Not a very enterprising life for a man who had served famous firms, who had sailed famous ships (more than one or two of them his own); who had made famous passages, had been the pioneer of new routes and new trades; who had steered across the unsurveyed tracts of the South Seas, and had seen the sun rise on uncharted islands. Fifty years at sea, and forty out in the East ('a pretty thorough apprenticeship,' he used to remark smilingly), had made him honourably known to a generation of shipowners and merchants in all the ports from Bombay clear over to where the East merges into the West upon the coast of the two Americas. His fame remained writ, not very large but plain enough, on the Admiralty charts. Was there not somewhere between Australia and China a Whalley Island and a Condor Reef? On that dangerous coral formation the celebrated clipper had hung stranded for three days, her captain and crew throwing her cargo overboard with one hand and with the other, as it were, keeping off her a flotilla of savage war-canoes. At that time neither the island nor the reef had any official existence. Later the officers of her Majesty's steam-vessel *Fusilier*, despatched to make a survey of the route, recognised in the adoption of these two names the enterprise of the man and the solidity of the ship. Besides, as anyone who cares may see, the *General Directory* vol. ii. p. 410, begins the description of the 'Malotu or Whalley

Passage' with the words: 'This advantageous route, first, discovered in 1850 by Captain Whalley in the ship *Condor*,' etc., and ends by recommending it warmly to sailing vessels leaving the China ports for the south in the months from December to April inclusive.

This was the clearest gain he had out of life. Nothing could rob him of this kind of fame. The piercing of the Isthmus of Suez, like the breaking of a dam, had let in upon the East a flood of new ships, new men, new methods of trade. It had changed the face of the Eastern seas and the very spirit of their life; so that his early experiences meant nothing whatever to the new generation of seamen.

In those bygone days he had handled many thousands of pounds of his employers' money and of his own; he had attended faithfully, as by law a shipmaster is expected to do, to the conflicting interests of owners, charterers, and underwriters. He had never lost a ship or consented to a shady transaction; and he had lasted well, outlasting in the end the conditions that had gone to the making of his name. He had buried his wife (in the Gulf of Petchili), had married off his daughter to the man of her unlucky choice, and had lost more than an ample competence in the crash of the notorious Travancore and Deccan Banking Corporation, whose downfall had shaken the East like an earthquake. And he was sixty-seven years old.

2

His age sat lightly enough on him; and of his ruin he was not ashamed. He had not been alone to believe in the stability of the Banking Corporation. Men whose judgement in matters of finance was as expert as his seamanship had commended the prudence of his investments, and had themselves lost much money in the great failure. The only difference between him and them was that he had lost his all. And yet not his all. There had remained to him from his lost fortune a very pretty little barque, *Fair Maid*, which he had bought to occupy his leisure of a retired sailor – 'to play with,' as he expressed it himself.

He had formally declared himself tired of the sea the year preceding his daughter's marriage. But after the young couple had gone to settle in Melbourne he found out that he could not make himself happy on shore. He was too much of a merchant sea-captain for mere yachting to satisfy him. He wanted the illusion of affairs; and his acquisition of the *Fair Maid* preserved the continuity of his life. He introduced her to his acquaintances in various ports as 'my last command'. When he grew too old to be trusted with a ship, he would lay her up and go ashore to be buried, leaving directions in his will to have the barque towed out and scuttled decently in deep water on the day of the funeral. His daughter would not grudge him the satisfaction of knowing that no stranger would handle his last command after him. With the fortune he was able to leave her, the value of a five-hundred-ton barque was neither here nor there. All this would be said with a jocular twinkle in his eye: the vigorous old man had too much vitality for the sentimentalism of regret; and a little wistfully withal, because he was at home in life, taking a genuine pleasure in its feelings and its possessions; in the dignity of his reputation and his wealth, in his love for his daughter, and in his satisfaction with the ship – the plaything of his lonely leisure.

He had the cabin arranged in accordance with his simple ideal of comfort at sea. A big bookcase (he was a great reader) occupied one side of his stateroom; the portrait of his late wife, a flat bituminous oil-painting representing the profile and one long black ringlet of a young woman, faced his bed-place. Three chronometers ticked him to sleep and greeted him on waking with the tiny competition of their beats. He rose at five every day. The officer of the morning watch, drinking his early cup of coffee aft by the wheel, would hear through the wide orifice of the copper ventilators all the splashings, blowings, and splutterings of his captain's toilet. These noises would be followed by a sustained deep murmur of the Lord's Prayer recited in a loud earnest voice. Five minutes afterwards the head and shoulders of Captain Whalley emerged out of the companion-hatchway. Invariably he paused for a while on the stairs, looking all round at the horizon; upwards at the trim of the sails; inhaling deep draughts of the fresh air. Only then he would step out on the poop, acknowledging the hand raised to the peak of the cap with a majestic and benign 'Good-morning to you.' He walked the deck till eight scrupulously. Sometimes, not above twice a year, he had to use a thick cudgel-like stick on account of a stiffness in the hip – a slight touch of rheumatism, he supposed. Otherwise he knew nothing of the ills of the flesh. At the ringing of the breakfast bell he went below to feed his canaries, wind up the chronometers, and take the head of the table. From there he had before his eyes the big carbon photographs of his daughter, her husband, and two fat-legged babies – his grandchildren – set in black frames into the maple-wood bulkheads of the cuddy. After breakfast he dusted the glass over these portraits himself with a cloth, and brushed the oil painting of his wife with a plummet kept suspended from a small brass hook by the side of the heavy gold frame. Then with the door of his stateroom shut, he would sit down on the couch under the portrait to read a chapter out of a thick pocket Bible – her Bible. But on some days he only sat there for half an hour with his finger between the leaves and the closed book resting on his knees. Perhaps he had remembered suddenly how fond of boat-sailing she used to be.

She had been a real shipmate and a true woman too. It was like an article of faith with him that there never had been, and never could be, a brighter, cheerier home anywhere afloat or ashore than his home under the poop-deck of the *Condor*, with the big main cabin all white and gold, garlanded as if for a perpetual festival with an unfading wreath. She had decorated the centre of every panel with a cluster of home flowers. It took her a twelvemonth to go round the cuddy with this labour of love. To him it had remained a marvel of painting, the highest achievement of taste and skill; and as to old Swinburne, his mate, every time he came down to his meals he stood transfixed with admiration before the progress of the work. You could almost smell these roses, he declared, sniffing the faint flavour of turpentine which at that time pervaded the saloon, and (as he confessed afterwards) made him somewhat less hearty than usual in tackling his food. But there was nothing of the sort to interfere with his enjoyment of her singing. 'Mrs Whalley is a regular out-and-out nightingale, sir,' he would pronounce with a judicial air after listening profoundly over the skylight to the very end of the piece. In fine weather, in the second dog-watch, the two men could hear her trills and roulades going on to the accompaniment of the piano in the cabin. On the very day they got engaged he had written to London for the instrument; but they had been married for over a year before it reached them, coming out round the Cape. The big case made part of the first direct general cargo landed in Hong Kong harbour – an event that to the men who walked the busy quays of today seemed as hazily remote as the dark ages of history. But Captain Whalley could in a half-hour of solitude live again all his life, with its romance, its idyll, and its sorrow. He had to close her eyes himself. She went away from under the ensign like a sailor's wife, a sailor herself at heart. He had read the service over her, out of her own prayer-book, without a break in his voice. When he raised his eyes he could see old Swinburne facing him with his cap pressed to his breast, and his rugged, weather-beaten, impassive face streaming with drops of water like a lump of chipped red granite in a shower. It was all very well for that old sea-dog to cry. He had to read on to the end; but after the splash he did not remember much of what happened for the next few days. An elderly sailor of the crew, deft at needlework, put together a mourning frock for the child out of one of her black skirts.

He was not likely to forget; but you cannot dam up life like a sluggish stream. It will break out and flow over a man's troubles, it will close upon a sorrow like the sea upon a dead body, no matter how much love has gone to the bottom. And the world is not bad. People had been very kind to him; especially Mrs Gardner, the wife of the senior partner in Gardner, Patteson & Co., the owners of the *Condor*. It was she who volunteered to look after the little one, and in due course took her to England (something of a journey in those days, even by the overland mail route) with her own girls to finish her education. It was ten years before he saw her again. As a little child she had never been frightened of bad weather; she would beg to be taken up on deck in the bosom of his oilskin coat to watch the big seas hurling themselves upon the *Condor*. The swirl and crash of the waves seemed to fill her small soul with a breathless delight. 'A good boy spoiled,' he used to say of her in joke. He had named her Ivy because of the sound of the word, and obscurely fascinated by a vague association of ideas. She had twined herself tightly round his heart, and he intended her to cling close to her father as to a tower of strength; forgetting, while she was little, that in the nature of things she would probably elect to cling to someone else. But he loved life well enough for even that event to give him a certain satisfaction, apart from his more intimate feeling of loss.

After he had purchased the *Fair Maid* to occupy his loneliness, he hastened to accept a rather unprofitable freight to Australia simply for the opportunity of seeing his daughter in her own home. What made him dissatisfied there was not to see that she clung now to somebody else, but that the prop she had selected seemed on closer examination 'a rather poor stick' – even in the matter of health. He disliked his son-in-law's studied civility perhaps more than his method of handling the sum of money he had given Ivy at her marriage. But of his apprehensions he said nothing. Only on the day of his departure, with the hall-door open all ready, holding her hands and looking steadily into her eyes, he had said, 'You know, my dear, all I have is for you and the chicks. Mind you write to me openly.' She had answered him by an almost imperceptible movement of her head. She resembled her mother in the colour of her eyes, and in character – and also in this, that she understood him without many words.

Sure enough she had to write; and some of these letters made Captain Whalley lift his white eyebrows. For the rest he considered he was reaping the true reward of his life by being thus able to produce on demand whatever was needed. He had not enjoyed himself so much in a way since his wife had died. Characteristically enough his son-in-law's punctuality in failure caused him at a distance to feel a sort of kindness towards the man. The fellow was so perpetually being jammed on a lee shore that to charge it all to his reckless navigation would be manifestly unfair. No, no! He knew well what that meant. It was bad luck. His own had been simply marvellous, but he had seen in his life too many good men – seamen and others – go under with the sheer weight of bad luck not to recognise the fatal signs. For all that, he was cogitating on the best way of tying up very strictly every penny he had to leave, when with a preliminary rumble of rumours (whose first sound reached him in Shanghai as it happened), the shock of the big failure came; and, after passing through the phases of stupor, of incredulity, of indignation, he had to accept the fact that he had nothing to speak of to leave.

Upon that, as if he had only waited for this catastrophe, the unlucky man, away there in Melbourne, gave up his unprofitable game, and sat down – in an invalid's bath-chair at that too. 'He will never walk again,' wrote the wife. For the first time in his life Captain Whalley was a bit staggered.

The *Fair Maid* had to go to work in bitter earnest now. It was no longer a matter of preserving alive the memory of Daredevil Harry Whalley in the

Eastern Seas, or of keeping an old man in pocket-money and clothes, with, perhaps, a bill for a few hundred first-class cigars thrown in at the end of the year. He would have to buckle-to and keep her going hard on a scant allowance of gilt for the gingerbread scrolls at her stem and stern.

This necessity opened his eyes to the fundamental changes of the world. Of his past only the familiar names remained, here and there, but the things and the men, as he had known them, were gone. The name of Gardner, Patteson & Co. was still displayed on the walls of warehouses by the water-side, on the brass plates and window-panes in the business quarters of more than one Eastern port, but there was no longer a Gardner or a Patteson in the firm. There was no longer for Captain Whalley an armchair and a welcome in the private office, with a bit of business ready to be put in the way of an old friend, for the sake of bygone services. The husbands of the Gardner girls sat behind the desks in that room where, long after he had left the employ, he had kept his right of entrance in the old man's time. Their ships now had yellow funnels with black tops, and a timetable of appointed routes like a confounded service of tramways. The winds of December and June were all one to them; their captains (excellent young men he doubted not) were, to be sure, familiar with Whalley Island, because of late years the Government had established a white fixed light on the north end (with a red danger sector over the Condor Reef), but most of them would have been extremely surprised to hear that a flesh-and-blood Whalley still existed – an old man going about the world trying to pick up a cargo here and there for his little barque.

And everywhere it was the same. Departed the men who would have nodded appreciatively at the mention of his name, and would have thought themselves bound in honour to do something for Daredevil Harry Whalley. Departed the opportunities which he would have known how to seize; and gone with them the white-winged flock of clippers that lived in the boisterous uncertain life of the winds, skimming big fortunes out of the foam of the sea. In a world that pared down the profits to an irreducible minimum, in a world that was able to count its disengaged tonnage twice over every day, and in which lean charters were snapped up by cable three months in advance, there were no chances of fortune for an individual wandering haphazard with a little barque – hardly indeed any room to exist.

He found it more difficult from year to year. He suffered greatly from the smallness of remittances he was able to send his daughter. Meantime he had given up good cigars, and even in the matter of inferior cheroots limited himself to six a day. He never told her of his difficulties, and she never enlarged upon her struggle to live. Their confidence in each other needed no explanations, and their perfect understanding endured without protestations of gratitude or regret. He would have been shocked if she had taken it into her head to thank him in so many words, but he found it perfectly natural that she should tell him she needed two hundred pounds.

He had come in with the *Fair Maid* in ballast to look for a freight in the

Sofala's port of registry, and her letter met him there. Its tenor was that it was no use mincing matters. Her only resource was in opening a boarding-house, for which the prospects, she judged, were good. Good enough, at any rate, to make her tell him frankly that with two hundred pounds she could make a start. He had torn the envelope open, hastily, on deck, where it was handed to him by the ship-chandler's runner, who had brought his mail at the moment of anchoring. For the second time in his life he was appalled, and remained stock-still at the cabin door with the paper trembling between his fingers. Open a boarding-house! Two hundred pounds for a start! The only resource! And he did not know where to lay his hands on two hundred pence.

All that night Captain Whalley walked the poop of his anchored ship, as though he had been about to close with the land in thick weather, and uncertain of his position after a run of many grey days without a sight of sun, moon, or stars. The black night twinkled with the guiding lights of seamen and the steady straight lines of lights on shore; and all around the *Fair Maid* the riding lights of ships cast trembling trails upon the water of the roadstead. Captain Whalley saw not a gleam anywhere till the dawn broke and he found out that his clothing was soaked through with the heavy dew.

His ship was awake. He stopped short, stroked his wet beard, and descended the poop ladder backwards, with tired feet. At the sight of him the chief officer, lounging about sleepily on the quarterdeck, remained open-mouthed in the middle of a great early-morning yawn.

'Good-morning to you,' pronounced Captain Whalley solemnly, passing into the cabin. But he checked himself in the doorway, and without looking back, 'By the bye,' he said, 'there should be an empty wooden case put away in the lazarette. It has not been broken up – has it?'

The mate shut his mouth, and then asked as if dazed, 'What empty case, sir?'

'A big flat packing-case belonging to that painting in my room. Let it be taken up on deck and tell the carpenter to look it over. I may want to use it before long.'

The chief officer did not stir a limb till he had heard the door of the captain's stateroom slam within the cuddy. Then he beckoned aft the second mate with his forefinger to tell him that there was something 'in the wind'.

When the bell rang Captain Whalley's authoritative voice boomed out through a closed door, 'Sit down and don't wait for me.' And his impressed officers took their places, exchanging looks and whispers across the table. What! No breakfast? And after apparently knocking about all night on deck, too! Clearly, there was something in the wind. In the skylight above their heads, bowed earnestly over the plates, three wire cages rocked and rattled to the restless jumping of the hungry canaries; and they could detect the sounds of their 'old man's' deliberate movements within his stateroom. Captain Whalley was methodically winding up the chronometers, dusting the portrait of his late wife, getting a clean white shirt out of the drawers, making himself ready in his punctilious unhurried manner to go ashore. He could not have swallowed a single mouthful of food that morning. He had made up his mind to sell the *Fair Maid*.

3

Just at that time the Japanese were casting far and wide for ships of European build, and he had no difficulty in finding a purchaser, a speculator who drove a hard bargain, but paid cash down for the *Fair Maid*, with a view to a profitable resale. Thus it came about that Captain Whalley found himself on a certain afternoon descending the steps of one of the most important post-offices of the East with a slip of bluish paper in his hand. This was the receipt of a registered letter enclosing a draft for two hundred pounds, and addressed to Melbourne. Captain Whalley pushed the paper into his waistcoat-pocket, took his stick from under his arm, and walked down the street.

It was a recently opened and untidy thoroughfare with rudimentary sidewalks and a soft layer of dust cushioning the whole width of the road. One end touched the slummy street of Chinese shops near the harbour, the other drove straight on, without houses, for a couple of miles, through patches of jungle-like vegetation, to the yard gates of the new Consolidated Docks Company. The crude frontages of the new Government buildings alternated with the blank fencing of vacant plots, and the view of the sky seemed to give an added spaciousness to the broad vista. It was empty and shunned by natives after business hours, as though they had expected to see one of the tigers from the neighbourhood of the New Waterworks on the hill coming at a loping canter down the middle to get a Chinese shopkeeper for supper. Captain Whalley was not dwarfed by the solitude of the grandly planned street. He had too fine a presence for that. He was only a lonely figure walking purposefully, with a great white beard like a pilgrim, and with a thick stick that resembled a weapon. On one side the new Courts of Justice had a low and unadorned portico of squat columns half concealed by a few old trees left in the approach. On the other the pavilion wings of the new Colonial Treasury came out to the line of the street. But Captain Whalley, who had now no ship and no home, remembered in passing that on that very site when he first came out from England there had stood a fishing village, a few mat huts erected on piles between a muddy tidal creek and a miry pathway that went writhing into a tangled wilderness without any docks or waterworks.

No ship – no home. And his poor Ivy away there had no home either. A boarding-house is no sort of home though it may get you a living. His feelings were horribly rasped by the idea of the boarding-house. In his rank of life he had that truly aristocratic temperament characterised by a scorn of vulgar gentility and by prejudiced views as to the derogatory nature of certain occupations. For his own part he had always preferred sailing merchant ships (which is a straightforward occupation) to buying and selling merchandise, of which the essence is to get the better of somebody in a bargain – an undignified trial of wits at best. His father had been Colonel Whalley (retired) of the H.E.I. Company's service, with very slender means besides his pension, but with distinguished connections. He could remember as a boy how frequently waiters at the inns, country tradesmen and small people of that sort, used to 'My lord' the old warrior on the strength of his appearance.

Captain Whalley himself (he would have entered the Navy if his father had not died before he was fourteen) had something of a grand air which would have suited an old and glorious admiral; but he became lost like a straw in the eddy of a brook amongst the swarm of brown and yellow humanity filling a thoroughfare, that by contrast with the vast and empty avenue he had left seemed as narrow as a lane and absolutely riotous with life. The walls of the houses were blue; the shops of the Chinamen yawned like cavernous lairs; heaps of nondescript merchandise overflowed the gloom of the long range of arcades, and the fiery serenity of sunset took the middle of the street from end to end with a glow like the reflection of a fire. It fell on the bright colours and the dark faces of the barefooted crowd, on the pallid yellow backs of the half-naked jostling coolies, on the accoutrements of a tall Sikh trooper with a parted beard and fierce moustaches on sentry before the gate of the police compound. Looming very big above the heads in a red haze of dust, the tightly packed car of the cable tramway navigated cautiously up the human stream, with the incessant blare of its horn, in the manner of a steamer groping in a fog.

Captain Whalley emerged like a diver on the other side, and in the desert shade between the walls of closed warehouses removed his hat to cool his brow. A certain disrepute attached to the calling of a landlady of a boarding-house. These women were said to be rapacious, unscrupulous, untruthful; and though he contemned no class of his fellow-creatures – God forbid! – these were suspicions to which it was unseemly that a Whalley should lay herself open. He had not expostulated with her, however. He was confident she shared his feelings; he was sorry for her; he trusted her judgement; he considered it a merciful dispensation that he could help her once more – but in his aristocratic heart of hearts he would have found it more easy to reconcile himself to the idea of her turning seamstress. Vaguely he remembered reading years ago a touching piece called the 'Song of the Shirt'. It was all very well making songs about poor women. The granddaughter of Colonel Whalley, the landlady of a boarding-house! Pooh! He replaced his hat, dived into two pockets, and stopping a moment to apply a flaring match to the end of a cheap cheroot, blew an embittered cloud of smoke at a world that could hold such surprises.

Of one thing he was certain – that she was the own child of a clever mother. Now he had got over the wrench of parting with his ship, he perceived clearly that such a step had been unavoidable. Perhaps he had been growing aware of it all along with an unconfessed knowledge. But she, far away there, must have had an intuitive perception of it, with the pluck to face that truth and the courage to speak out – all the qualities which had made her mother a woman of such excellent counsel.

It would have had to come to that in the end! It was fortunate she had forced his hand. In another year or two it would have been an utterly barren sale. To keep the ship going he had been involving himself deeper every year. He was defenceless before the insidious work of adversity, to whose more open assaults he could present a firm front; like a cliff that stands unmoved the open battering of the sea, with a lofty ignorance of the treacherous backwash undermining its base. As it was, every liability satisfied, her request answered, and owing no man a penny, there remained to him from the proceeds a sum of five hundred pounds put away safely. In addition he had upon his person some forty odd dollars – enough to pay his hotel bill, providing he did not linger too long in the modest bedroom where he had taken refuge.

Scantily furnished, and with a waxed floor, it opened into one of the side-verandahs. The straggling building of bricks, as airy as a birdcage, resounded with the incessant flapping of rattan screens worried by the wind between the whitewashed square pillars of the sea-front. The rooms were lofty, a ripple of sunshine flowed over the ceilings; and the periodical invasions of tourists from some passenger steamer in the harbour flitted through the wind-swept dusk of the apartments with the tumult of their unfamiliar voices and impermanent presences, like relays of migratory shades condemned to speed headlong round the earth without leaving a trace. The babble of their irruptions ebbed out as suddenly as it had arisen; the draughty corridors and the long chairs of the verandahs knew their sightseeing hurry or their prostrate repose no more; and Captain Whalley, substantial and dignified, left well-nigh alone in the vast hotel by each light-hearted scurry, felt more and more like a stranded tourist with no aim in view, like a forlorn traveller without a home. In the solitude of his room he smoked thoughtfully, gazing at the two sea-chests which held all that he could call his own in this world. A thick roll of charts in a sheath of sailcloth leaned in a corner; the flat packing-case containing the portrait in oils and the three carbon photographs had been pushed under the bed. He was tired of discussing terms, of assisting at surveys, of all the routine of the business. What to the other parties was merely the sale of a ship was to him a momentous event involving a radically new view of existence. He knew that after this ship there would be no other; and the hopes of his youth, the exercise of his abilities, every feeling and achievement of his manhood, had been indissolubly connected with ships. He had served ships; he had owned ships; and even the years of his actual retirement from the sea had been made bearable by the idea that he had only to stretch out his hand full of money to get a ship. He had been at liberty to feel as though he were the owner of all the ships in the world. The selling of this one was weary work; but when she passed from him at last, when he signed the last receipt, it was as though all the ships had gone out of the world together, leaving him on the shore of inaccessible oceans with seven hundred pounds in his hands.

Striding firmly, without haste, along the quay, Captain Whalley averted his glances from the familiar roadstead. Two generations of seamen born since his first day at sea stood between him and all these ships at the anchorage. His own was sold, and he had been asking himself, What next?

From the feeling of loneliness, of inward emptiness – and of loss too, as if his very soul had been taken out of him forcibly – there had sprung at first a desire to start right off and join his daughter. 'Here are the last pence,' he would say to her; 'take them, my dear. And here's your old father: you must take him too.'

His soul recoiled, as if afraid of what lay hidden at the bottom of this impulse. Give up! Never! When one is thoroughly weary all sorts of nonsense come into one's head. A pretty gift it would have been for a poor woman – this seven hundred pounds with the encumbrance of a hale old fellow more than likely to last for years and years to come. Was he not as fit to die in harness as any of the youngsters in charge of these anchored ships out yonder? He was as solid now as ever he had been. But as to who would give him work to do, that was another matter. Were he, with his appearance and antecedents, to go about looking for a junior's berth, people, he was afraid, would not take him seriously; or else if he succeeded in impressing them, he would maybe obtain their pity, which would be like stripping yourself naked to be kicked. He was not anxious to give himself away for less than nothing. He had no use for anybody's pity. On the other hand, a command – the only thing he could try for with due regard for common decency – was not likely to be lying in wait for him at the corner of the next street. Commands don't go a-begging nowadays. Ever since he had come ashore to carry out the business of the sale he had kept his ears open, but had heard no hint of one being vacant in the port. And even if there had been one, his successful past itself stood in his way. He had been his own employer too long. The only credential he could produce was the testimony of his whole life. What better recommendation could anyone require? But vaguely he felt that the unique document would be looked upon as an archaic curiosity of the Eastern waters, a screed traced in obsolete words – in a half-forgotten language.

Revolving these thoughts, he strolled on near the railings of the quay, broad-chested, without a stoop, as though his big shoulders had never felt the burden of the loads that must be carried between the cradle and the grave. No single betraying fold or line of care disfigured the reposeful modelling of his face. It was full and untanned; and the upper part emerged, massively quiet, out of the downward flow of silvery hair, with the striking delicacy of its clear complexion and the powerful width of the forehead. The first cast of his glance fell on you candid and swift, like a boy's; but because of the ragged snowy thatch of the eyebrows the affability of his attention acquired the character of a keen and searching scrutiny. With age he had put on flesh a little, had increased his girth like an old tree presenting no symptoms of decay; and even the opulent, lustrous ripple of white hairs upon his chest seemed an attribute of unquenchable vitality and vigour.

Once rather proud of his great bodily strength, and even of his personal appearance, conscious of his worth, and firm in his rectitude, there had remained to him, like the heritage of departed prosperity, the tranquil bearing of a man who had proved himself fit in every sort of way for the life of his choice. He strode on squarely under the projecting brim of an ancient Panama hat. It had a low crown, a crease through its whole diameter, a narrow black ribbon. Imperishable and a little discoloured, this headgear made it easy to pick him out from afar on thronged wharves and in the busy streets. He had never adopted the comparatively modern fashion of pipeclayed cork helmets. He disliked the form; and he hoped he could manage to keep a cool head to the end of his life without all these contrivances for hygienic ventilation. His hair was cropped close, his linen always of immaculate whiteness; a suit of thin grey flannel, worn threadbare but scrupulously brushed, floated about his burly limbs, adding to his bulk by the looseness of its cut. The years had mellowed the good-humoured, imperturbable audacity of his prime into a temper carelessly serene; and the leisurely tapping of his iron-shod stick accompanied his footfalls with a self-confident sound on the flagstones. It was impossible to connect such a fine presence and this unruffled aspect with the belittling troubles of poverty; the man's whole existence appeared to pass before you, facile and large, in the freedom of means as ample as the clothing of his body.

The irrational dread of having to break into his five hundred pounds for personal expenses in the hotel disturbed the steady poise of his mind. There was no time to lose. The bill was running up. He nourished the hope that this five hundred would perhaps be the means, if everything else failed, of obtaining some work which, keeping his body and soul together (not a matter of great outlay), would enable him to be of use to his daughter. To his mind it was her own money which he employed, as it were, in backing her father and solely for her benefit. Once at work, he would help her with the greater part of his earnings; he was good for many year yet, and this boarding-house business, he argued to himself, whatever the prospects, could not be much of a gold-mine from the first start. But what work? He was ready to lay hold of anything in an honest way so that it came quickly to his hand; because the five hundred pounds must be preserved intact for eventual use. That was the great point. With the entire five hundred one felt a substance at one's back; but it seemed to him that should he let it dwindle to four-fifty or even four-eighty, all the efficiency would be gone out of the money, as though there were some magic power in the round figure. But what sort of work?

Confronted by that haunting question as by an uneasy ghost, for whom he had no exorcising formula, Captain Whalley stopped short on the apex of a small bridge spanning steeply the bed of a canalised creek with granite shores. Moored between the square blocks a seagoing Malay prau floated half hidden under the arch of masonry, with her spars lowered down, without a sound of life on board, and covered from stem to stern with a ridge of palm-leaf mats. He had left behind him the overheated pavements bordered by the stone frontages that, like the sheer face of cliffs, followed the sweep of the quays; and an unconfined spaciousness of orderly and sylvan aspect opened before him its wide plots of rolled grass, like pieces of green carpet smoothly pegged out, its long ranges of trees lined up in colossal porticos of dark shafts roofed with a vault of branches.

Some of these avenues ended at the sea. It was a terraced shore; and beyond, upon the level expanse, profound and glistening like the gaze of a dark-blue eye, an oblique band of stippled purple lengthened itself indefinitely through the gap between a couple of verdant twin islets. The masts and spars of a few ships far away, hull down in the outer roads, sprang straight from the water in a fine maze of rosy lines pencilled on the clear shadow of the eastern board. Captain Whalley gave them a long glance. The ship, once his own, was anchored out there. It was staggering to think that it was open to him no longer to take a boat at the jetty and get himself pulled off to her when the evening came. To no ship. Perhaps never more. Before the sale was concluded, and till the purchase-money had been paid, he had spent daily some time on board the *Fair Maid*. The money had been paid this very morning, and now, all at once, there was positively no ship that he could go on board of when he liked; no ship that would need his presence in order to do her work – to live. It seemed an incredible state of affairs, something too bizarre to last. And the sea was full of craft of all sorts. There was that prau lying so still swathed in her shroud of sewn palm-leaves – she too had her indispensable man. They lived through each other, this Malay he had never seen, and this high-sterned thing of no size that seemed to be resting after a long journey. And of all the ships in sight, near and far, each was provided with a man, the man without whom the finest ship is a dead thing, a floating and purposeless log.

After his one glance at the roadstead he went on, since there was nothing to turn back for, and the time must be got through somehow. The avenues of big trees ran straight over the Esplanade, cutting each other at diverse angles, columnar below and luxuriant above. The interlaced boughs high up there seemed to slumber; not a leaf stirred overhead: and the reedy cast-iron lamp-posts in the middle of the road, gilt like sceptres, diminished in a long perspective, with their globes of white porcelain atop, resembling a barbarous decoration of ostriches' eggs displayed in a row. The flaming sky kindled a tiny crimson spark upon the glistening surface of each glassy shell.

With his chin sunk a little, his hands behind his back, and the end of his stick marking the gravel with a faint wavering line at his heels, Captain Whalley reflected that if a ship without a man was like a body without a soul, a sailor without a ship was of not much more account in this world than an aimless log adrift upon the sea. The log might be sound enough by itself, tough of fibre, and hard to destroy – but what of that! And a sudden sense of irremediable idleness weighted his feet like a great fatigue.

A succession of open carriages came bowling along the newly opened sea-road. You could see across the wide grass-plots the discs of vibration made by the spokes. The bright domes of the parasols swayed lightly outwards like full-blown blossoms on the rim of a vase; and the quiet sheet of dark-blue water, crossed by a bar of purple, made a background for the spinning wheels and the high action of the horses, whilst the turbaned heads of the Indian servants elevated above the line of the sea horizon glided rapidly on the paler blue of the sky. In an open space near the little bridge each turn-out trotted smartly in a wide curve away from the sunset; then pulling up sharp, entered the main alley in a long slow-moving file with the great red stillness of the sky at the back. The trunks of mighty trees stood all touched with red on the same side, the air seemed aflame under the high foliage, the very ground under the hoofs of the horses was red. The wheels turned solemnly; one after another the sunshades drooped, folding their colours like gorgeous flowers shutting their petals at the end of the day. In the whole half-mile of human beings no voice uttered a distinct word, only a faint thudding noise went on mingled with slight jingling sounds, and the motionless heads and shoulders of men and women sitting in couples emerged stolidly above the lowered hoods – as if wooden. But one carriage and pair coming late did not join the line.

It fled along in a noiseless roll; but on entering the avenue one of the dark bays snorted, arching his neck and shying against the steel-tipped pole; a flake of foam fell from the bit upon the point of a satiny shoulder, and the dusky face of the coachman leaned forward at once over the hands taking a fresh grip of the reins. It was a long dark-green landau, having a dignified and buoyant motion between the sharply curved C-springs, and a sort of strictly official majesty in its supreme elegance. It seemed more roomy than is usual, its horses seemed slightly bigger, the appointments a shade more perfect, the servants perched somewhat higher on the box. The dresses of three women – two young and pretty, and one, handsome, large, of mature age – seemed to fill completely the shallow body of the carriage. The fourth face was that of a man, heavy lidded, distinguished and sallow, with a sombre, thick, iron-grey imperial and moustaches, which somehow had the air of solid appendages. His Excellency.

The rapid motion of that one equipage made all the others appear utterly inferior, blighted, and reduced to crawl painfully at a snail's pace. The landau distanced the whole file in a sort of sustained rush; the features of the occupants whirling out of sight left behind an impression of fixed stares and impassive vacancy; and after it had vanished in full flight as it were, notwithstanding the long line of vehicles hugging the curb at a walk, the whole lofty vista of the avenue seemed to lie open and emptied of life in the enlarged impression of an august solitude.

Captain Whalley had lifted his head to look, and his mind, disturbed in its meditation, turned with wonder (as men's minds will do) to matters of no importance. It struck him that it was to this port, where he had just sold his last ship, that he had come with the very first he had ever owned, and with his head full of a plan for opening a new trade with a distant part of the Archipelago. The then governor had given him no end of encouragement. No Excellency he – this Mr Denham – this governor with his jacket off; a man who tended night and day, so to speak, the growing prosperity of the settlement with the self-forgetful devotion of a nurse for a child she loves; a lone bachelor who lived as in a camp with the few servants and his three dogs in what was called then the Government Bungalow: a low-roofed structure on the half-cleared slope of a hill, with a new flagstaff in front and a police orderly on the verandah. He remembered toiling up that hill under a heavy sun for his audience; the unfurnished aspect of the cool shaded room; the long table covered at one end with piles of papers, and with two guns, a brass telescope, a small bottle of oil with a feather stuck in the neck at the other – and the flattering attention given to him by the man in power. It was an undertaking full of risk he had come to expound, but a twenty minutes' talk in the Government Bungalow on the hill had made it go smoothly from the start. And as he was retiring Mr Denham, already seated before the papers, called out after him, 'Next month the *Dido* starts for a cruise that way, and I shall request her captain officially to give you a look in and see how you get on.' The *Dido* was one of the smart frigates on the China station – and five-and-thirty years make a big slice of time. Five-and thirty years ago an enterprise like his had for the colony enough importance to be looked after by a Queen's ship. A big slice of time. Individuals were of some account then. Men like himself; men, too, like poor Evans, for instance, with his red face, his coal-black whiskers, and his restless eyes, who had set up the first patent slip for repairing small ships, on the edge of the forest, in a lonely bay three miles up the coast. Mr Denham had encouraged that enterprise too, and yet somehow poor Evans had ended by dying at home deucedly hard up. His son, they said, was squeezing oil out of coconuts for a living on some God-forsaken islet of the Indian Ocean; but it was from that patent slip in a lonely wooded bay that had sprung the workshops of the Consolidated Docks Company, with its three graving basins carved out of solid rock, its wharves, its jetties, its electric-light plant, its steam-power houses – with its gigantic sheer-legs, fit to lift the heaviest weight ever carried afloat, and whose head could be seen like the top of a queer white monument peeping over bushy points of land and sandy promontories, as you approached the New Harbour from the west.

There had been a time when men counted: there were not so many carriages in the colony then, though Mr Denham, he fancied, had a buggy. And Captain Whalley seemed to be swept out of the great avenue by the swirl of a mental backwash. He remembered muddy shores, a harbour without quays, the one solitary wooden pier (but that was a public work) jutting out crookedly, the first coal-sheds erected on Monkey Point, that caught fire mysteriously and smouldered for days, so that amazed ships came into a roadstead full of sulphurous fog, and the sun hung blood-red at midday. He remembered the things, the faces, and something more besides – like the faint flavour of a cup quaffed to the bottom, like a subtle sparkle of the air that was not to be found in the atmosphere of today.

In this evocation, swift and full of detail like a flash of magnesium light into the niches of a dark memorial hall, Captain Whalley contemplated things once important, the efforts of small men, the growth of a great place, but now robbed of all consequence by the greatness of accomplished facts, by hopes greater still; and they gave him for a moment such an almost physical grip upon time, such a comprehension of our unchangeable feelings, that he stopped short, struck the ground with his stick, and ejaculated mentally, 'What the devil am I doing here!' He seemed lost in a sort of surprise; but he heard his name called out in wheezy tones once, twice – and turned on his heels slowly.

He beheld then, waddling towards him autocratically, a man of an old-fashioned and gouty aspect, with hair as white as his own, but with shaved, florid cheeks, wearing a necktie – almost a neckcloth – whose stiff ends projected far beyond his chin; with round legs, round arms, a round body, a round face – generally producing the effect of his short figure having been distended by means of an air-pump as much as the seams of his clothing would stand. This was the Master-Attendant of the port. A master-attendant is a superior sort of harbour-master; a person, out in the East, of some consequence in his sphere; a Government official, a magistrate for the waters of the port, and possessed of vast but ill-defined disciplinary authority over seamen of all classes. This particular Master-Attendant was reported to consider it miserably inadequate, on the ground that it did not include the power of life and death. This was a jocular exaggeration. Captain Eliott was fairly satisfied with his position, and nursed no inconsiderable sense of such power as he had. His conceited and tyrannical disposition did not allow him to let it dwindle in his hands for want of use. The uproarious, choleric frankness of his comments on people's character and conduct caused him to be feared at bottom; though in conversation many pretended not to mind him in the least, others would only smile sourly at the mention of his name, and there were even some who dared to pronounce him 'a meddlesome old ruffian'. But for almost all of them one of Captain Eliott's outbreaks was nearly as distasteful to face as a chance of annihilation.

5

As soon as he had come up quite close he said, mouthing in a growl – 'What's this I hear, Whalley? Is it true you're selling the *Fair Maid*?'

Captain Whalley, looking away, said the thing was done – money had been paid that morning; and the other expressed at once his approbation of such an extremely sensible proceeding. He had got out of his trap to stretch his legs, he explained, on his way home to dinner. Sir Frederick looked well at the end of his time. Didn't he?

Captain Whalley could not say; had only noticed the carriage going past.

The Master-Attendant, plunging his hands into the pockets of an alpaca jacket inappropriately short and tight for a man of his age and appearance, strutted with a slight limp, and with his head reaching only to the shoulder of Captain Whalley, who walked easily, staring straight before him. They had been good comrades years ago, almost intimates. At the time when Whalley commanded the renowned *Condor*, Eliott had charge of the nearly as famous *Ringdove* for the same owners; and when the appointment of Master-Attendant was created, Whalley would have been the only other serious candidate. But Captain Whalley, then in the prime of life, was resolved to serve no one but his own auspicious Fortune. Far away, tending his hot irons, he was glad to hear the other had been successful. There was a worldly suppleness in bluff Ned Eliott that would serve him well in that sort of official appointment. And they were so dissimilar at bottom that as they came slowly to the end of the avenue before the Cathedral, it had never come into Whalley's head that he might have been in that man's place – provided for to the end of his days.

The sacred edifice, standing in solemn isolation amongst the converging avenues of enormous trees, as if to put grave thoughts of heaven into the hours of ease, presented a closed Gothic portal to the light and glory of the west. The glass of the rosace above the ogive glowed like fiery coal in the deep carvings of a wheel of stone. The two men faced about.

'I'll tell you what they ought to do next, Whalley,' growled Captain Eliott suddenly.

'Well?'

'They ought to send a real live lord out here when Sir Frederick's time is up. Eh?'

Captain Whalley perfunctorily did not see why a lord of the right sort should not do as well as anyone else. But this was not the other's point of view.

'No, no. Place runs itself. Nothing can stop it now. Good enough for a lord,' he growled in short sentences. 'Look at the changes in our own time. We need a lord here now. They have got a lord in Bombay.'

He dined once or twice every year at the Government House – a many-windowed, arcaded palace upon a hill laid out in roads and gardens. And lately he had been taking about a duke in his Master-Attendant's steam-launch to visit the harbour improvements. Before that he had 'most obligingly' gone out in person to pick out a good berth for the ducal yacht. Afterwards he had an invitation to lunch on board. The duchess herself lunched with them. A big woman with a red face. Complexion quite sunburnt. He should think ruined. Very gracious manners. They were going on to Japan . . .

He ejaculated these details for Captain Whalley's edification, pausing to blow out his cheeks as if with a pent-up sense of importance, and repeatedly protruding his thick lips till the blunt crimson end of his nose seemed to dip into the milk of his moustache. The place ran itself; it was fit for any lord; it gave no trouble except in its Marine department – in its Marine department, he repeated twice, and after a heavy snort began to relate how the other day her Majesty's Consul-General in French Cochin-China had cabled to him – in his official capacity – asking for a qualified man to be sent over to take charge of a Glasgow ship whose master had died in Saigon.

'I sent word of it to the officers' quarters in the Sailors' Home,' he continued, while the limp in his gait seemed to grow more accentuated with the increasing irritation of his voice. 'Place's full of them. Twice as many men as there are berths going in the local trade. All hungry for an easy job. Twice as many – and – What d'you think, Whalley? . . . '

He stopped short; his hands clenched and thrust deeply downwards, seemed ready to burst the pockets of his jacket. A slight sigh escaped Captain Whalley.

'Hey? You would think they would be falling over each other. Not a bit of it. Frightened to go home. Nice and warm out here to lie about a verandah waiting for a job. I sit and wait in my office. Nobody. What did they suppose? That I was going to sit there like a dummy with the Consul-General's cable before me? Not likely. So I looked up a list of them I keep by me and sent word for Hamilton – the worst loafer of them all – and just made him go. Threatened to instruct the steward of the Sailors' Home to have him turned out neck and crop. He did not think the berth was good enough – if – you – please. "I've your little record by me," said I. "You came ashore here eighteen months ago, and you haven't done six months' work since. You are in debt for your board now at the Home, and I suppose you reckon the Marine Office will pay in the end. Eh? So it shall; but if you don't take this chance, away you go to England, assisted passage, by the first homeward steamer that comes along. You are no better than a pauper. We don't want any white paupers here." I scared him. But look at the trouble all this gave me.'

'You would not have had any trouble,' Captain Whalley said almost involuntarily, 'if you had sent for me.'

Captain Eliott was immensely amused; he shook with laughter as he walked. But suddenly he stopped laughing. A vague recollection had crossed his mind. Hadn't he heard it said at the time of the Travancore and Deccan smash that poor Whalley had been cleaned out completely. 'Fellow's hard up, by heavens!' he thought; and at once he cast a sidelong upward glance at his companion. But Captain Whalley was smiling austerely straight before him, with a carriage of the head inconceivable in a penniless man – and he became reassured. Impossible. Could not have lost everything. That ship had been only a hobby of his. And the reflection that a man who had confessed to receiving that very morning a presumably large sum of money was not likely to spring upon him a demand for a small loan put him entirely at his ease again. There had come a long pause in their talk, however, and not knowing how to begin again, he growled out soberly, 'We old fellows ought to take a rest now.'

'The best thing for some of us would be to die at the oar,' Captain Whalley said negligently.

'Come, now. Aren't you a bit tired by this time of the whole show?' muttered the other sullenly.

'Are you?'

Captain Eliott was. Infernally tired. He only hung on to his berth so long in order to get his pension on the highest scale before he went home. It would be no better than poverty, anyhow; still, it was the only thing between him and the workhouse. And he had a family. Three girls, as Whalley knew. He gave 'Harry, old boy', to understand that these three girls were a source of the greatest anxiety and worry to him. Enough to drive a man distracted.

'Why? What have they been doing now?' asked Captain Whalley with a sort of amused absent-mindedness.

'Doing! Doing nothing. That's just it. Lawn-tennis and silly novels from morning to night . . .'

If one of them at least had been a boy! But all three! And, as ill-luck would have it, there did not seem to be any decent young fellows left in the world. When he looked around in the club he saw only a lot of conceited popinjays too selfish to think of making a good woman happy. Extreme indigence stared him in the face with all that crowd to keep at home. He had cherished the idea of building himself a little house in the country – in Surrey – to end his days in, but he was afraid it was out of the question . . . and his staring eyes rolled upwards with such a pathetic anxiety that Captain Whalley charitably nodded down at him, restraining a sort of sickening desire to laugh.

'You must know what it is yourself, Harry. Girls are the very devil for worry and anxiety.'

'Ay! But mine is doing well,' Captain Whalley pronounced slowly, staring to the end of the avenue.

The Master-Attendant was glad to hear this. Uncommonly glad. He remembered her well. A pretty girl she was.

Captain Whalley, stepping out carelessly, assented as if in a dream.

'She was pretty.'

The procession of carriages was breaking up.

One after another they left the file to go off at a trot, animating the vast avenue with their scattered life and movement; but soon the aspect of dignified solitude returned and took possession of the straight wide road. A syce in white stood at the head of a Burmah pony harnessed to a varnished two-wheel cart; and the whole thing waiting by the curb seemed no bigger than a child's toy forgotten under the soaring trees. Captain Eliott waddled up to it and made as if to clamber in, but refrained; and keeping one hand resting easily on the shaft, he changed the conversation from his pension, his daughters, and his poverty back again to the only other topic in the world – the Marine Office, the men and the ships of the port.

He proceeded to give instances of what was expected of him; and his thick voice drowsed in the still air like the obstinate droning of an enormous bumble-bee. Captain Whalley did not know what was the force or the weakness that prevented him from saying good-night and walking away. It was as though he had been too tired to make the effort. How queer. More queer than any of Ned's instances. Or was it that overpowering sense of idleness alone that made him stand there and listen to these stories? Nothing very real had ever troubled Ned Eliott; and gradually he seemed to detect deep in, as if wrapped up in the gross wheezy rumble, something of the clear hearty voice of the young captain of the *Ringdove*. He wondered if he too had changed to the same extent; and it seemed to him that the voice of his old chum had not changed so very much – that the man was the same. Not a bad fellow the pleasant, jolly Ned Eliott, friendly, well up to his business – and always a bit of a humbug. He remembered how he used to amuse his poor wife. She could read him like an open book. When the *Condor* and the *Ringdove* happened to be in port together, she would frequently ask him to bring Captain Eliott to dinner. They had not met often since those old days. Not once in five years, perhaps. He regarded from under his white eyebrows this man he could not bring himself to take into his confidence at this juncture; and the other went on with his intimate outpourings, and as remote from his hearer as though he had been talking on a hilltop a mile away.

He was in a bit of a quandary now as to the steamer *Sofala*. Ultimately every hitch in the port came into his hands to undo. They would miss him when he was gone in another eighteen months, and most likely some retired naval officer had been pitch-forked into the appointment – a man that would understand nothing and care less. That steamer was a coasting craft having a steady trade connection as far north as Tenasserim; but the trouble was she could get no captain to take her on her regular trip. Nobody would go in her. He really had no power, of course, to order a man to take a job. It was all very well to stretch a point on the demand of a consul-general, but . . .

'What's the matter with the ship?' Captain Whalley interrupted in measured tones.

'Nothing's the matter. Sound old steamer. Her owner has been in my office this afternoon tearing his hair.'

'Is he a white man?' asked Whalley in an interested voice.

'He calls himself a white man,' answered the Master-Attendant scornfully; 'but if so, it's just skin-deep and no more. I told him that to his face too.'

'But who is he, then?'

'He's the chief engineer of her. See *that*, Harry?'

'I see,' Captain Whalley said thoughtfully. 'The engineer. I see.'

How the fellow came to be a shipowner at the same time was quite a tale. He came out third in a home ship nearly fifteen years ago, Captain Eliott remembered, and got paid off after a bad sort of row both with his skipper and his chief. Anyway, they seemed jolly glad to get rid of him at all costs. Clearly a mutinous sort of chap. Well, he remained out here, a perfect nuisance, everlastingly shipped and unshipped, unable to keep a berth very long; pretty nigh went through every engine-room afloat belonging to the colony. Then suddenly, 'What do you think happened, Harry?'

Captain Whalley, who seemed lost in a mental effort as of doing a sum in his head, gave a slight start. He really couldn't imagine. The Master-Attendant's voice vibrated dully with hoarse emphasis. The man actually had the luck to win the second great prize in the Manilla lottery. All these engineers and officers of ships took tickets in that gamble. It seemed to be a perfect mania with them all.

Everybody expected now that he would take himself off home with his money, and go to the devil in his own way. Not at all. The *Sofala*, judged too small and not quite modern enough for the sort of trade she was in, could be got for a moderate price from her owners, who had ordered a new steamer from Europe. He rushed in and bought her. This man had never given any signs of that sort of mental intoxication the mere fact of getting hold of a large sum of money may produce – not till he got a ship of his own; but then he went off his balance all at once: came bouncing into the Marine Office on some transfer business, with his hat hanging over his left eye and switching a little cane in his hand, and told each one of the clerks separately that 'Nobody could put him out now. It was his turn. There was no one over him on earth, and there never would be either.' He swaggered and strutted between the desks, talking at the top of his voice, and trembling like a leaf all the while, so that the current business of the office was suspended for the time he was in there, and everybody in the big room stood open-mouthed looking at his antics. Afterwards he could be seen during the hottest hours of the day with his face as red as fire rushing along up and down the quays to look at his ship from different points of view: he seemed inclined to stop every stranger he came across just to let them know 'that there would be no longer anyone over him; he had bought a ship; nobody on earth could put him out of his engine-room now.'

Good bargain as she was, the price of the *Sofala* took up pretty near all the lottery-money. He had left himself no capital to work with. That did not matter so much, for these were the halcyon days of steam coasting trade, before some of the home shipping firms had thought of establishing local fleets to feed their main lines. These, when once organised, took the biggest slices out of that cake, of course; and by and by a squad of confounded German tramps turned up east of Suez Canal and swept up all the crumbs. They prowled on the cheap to and fro along the coast and between the islands, like a lot of sharks in the water ready to snap up anything you let drop. And then the high old times were over for good; for years the *Sofala* had made no more, he judged, than a fair living. Captain Eliott looked upon it as his duty in every way to assist an English ship to hold her own; and it stood to reason that if for want of a captain the *Sofala* began to miss her trips she would very soon lose her trade. There was the quandary. The man was too impracticable. 'Too much of a beggar on horseback from the first,' he explained. 'Seemed to grow worse as the time went on. In the last three years he's run through eleven skippers; he had tried every single man here, outside of the regular lines. I had warned him before that this would not do. And now, of course, no one will look at the *Sofala*. I had one or two men up at my office and talked to them; but, as they said to me, what was the good of taking the berth to lead a regular dog's life for a month and then get the sack at the end of the first trip? The fellow, of course, told me it was all nonsense; there had been a plot hatching for years against him. And now it has come. All the horrid sailors in the port had conspired to bring him to his knees, because he was an engineer.'

Captain Eliott emitted a throaty chuckle.

'And the fact is, that if he misses a couple more trips he need never trouble himself to start again. He won't find any cargo in his old trade. There's too much competition nowadays for people to keep their stuff lying about for a ship that does not turn up when she's expected. It's a bad look-out for him. He swears he will shut himself on board and starve to death in his cabin rather than sell her – even if he could find a buyer. And that's not likely in the least. Not even the Japs would give her insured value for her. It isn't like selling sailing-ships. Steamers *do* get out of date, besides getting old.'

'He must have laid by a good bit of money though,' observed Captain Whalley quietly.

The Harbour-Master puffed out his purple cheeks to an amazing size.

'Not a stiver, Harry. Not – a – single sti–ver.'

He waited; but as Captain Whalley, stroking his beard slowly, looked down on the ground without a word, he tapped him on the forearm, tiptoed, and said in a hoarse whisper – 'The Manilla lottery has been eating him up.'

He frowned a little, nodding in tiny affirmative jerks. They all were going in for it; a third of the wages paid to ships' officers ('in my port,' he snorted) went to Manilla. It was a mania. That fellow Massy had been bitten by it like the rest of them from the first; but after winning once he seemed to have persuaded himself he had only to try again to get another big prize. He had taken dozens and scores of tickets for every drawing since. What with this vice, and his ignorance of affairs, ever since he had improvidently bought that steamer he had been more or less short of money.

This, in Captain Eliott's opinion, gave an opening for a sensible sailor-man with a few pounds to step in and save that fool from the consequences of his folly. It was his craze to quarrel with his captains. He had had some really good men too, who would have been too glad to stay if he would only let them. But no. He seemed to think he was no owner unless he was kicking somebody out in the morning and having a row with the new man in the evening. What was wanted for him was a master with a couple of hundred or so to take an interest in the ship on proper conditions. You don't discharge a man for no fault, only because of the fun of telling him to pack up his traps and go ashore, when you know that in that case you are bound to buy back his share. On the other hand, a fellow with an interest in the ship is not likely to throw up his job in a huff about a trifle. He had told Massy that. He had said: ' "This won't do, Mr Massy. We are getting very sick of you here in the Marine Office. What you must do now is to try whether you could get a sailor to join you as partner. That seems to be the only way." And that was sound advice, Harry.'

Captain Whalley, leaning on his stick, was perfectly still all over, and his hand, arrested in the act of stroking, grasped his whole beard. And what did the fellow say to that?

The fellow had the audacity to fly out at the Master-Attendant. He had received the advice in a most impudent manner. 'I didn't come here to be laughed at,' he had shrieked. 'I appeal to you as an Englishman and a shipowner brought to the verge of ruin by an illegal conspiracy of your beggarly sailors, and all you condescend to do for me is to tell me to go and get a partner!' . . . The fellow had presumed to stamp with rage on the floor of the private office. Where was he going to get a partner? Was he being taken for a fool? Not a single one of that contemptible lot ashore at the

'Home' had twopence in his pocket to bless himself with. The very native curs in the bazaar knew that much . . . 'And it's true enough, Harry,' rumbled Captain Eliott judicially. 'They are much more likely one and all to owe money to the Chinamen in Denham Road for the clothes on their backs. "Well," said I, "you make too much noise over it for my taste, Mr Massy. Good-morning." He banged the door after him; he dared to bang my door, confound his cheek!'

The head of the Marine department was out of breath with indignation; then recollecting himself as it were, 'I'll end by being late to dinner – yarning with you here . . . wife doesn't like it.'

He clambered ponderously into the trap; leaned out sideways, and only then wondered wheezily what on earth Captain Whalley could have been doing with himself of late. They had had no sight of each other for years and years till the other day when he had seen him unexpectedly in the office.

What on earth . . .

Captain Whalley seemed to be smiling to himself in his white beard.

'The earth is big,' he said vaguely.

The other, as if to test the statement, stared all round from his driving-seat. The Esplanade was very quiet; only from afar, from very far, a long way from the sea-shore, across the stretches of grass, through the long ranges of trees, came faintly the toot – toot – toot of the cable car beginning to roll before the empty peristyle of the Public Library on its three-mile journey to the New Harbour Docks.

'Doesn't seem to be so much room on it,' growled the Master-Attendant, 'since these Germans came along shouldering us at every turn. It was not so in our time.'

He fell into deep thought, breathing stertorously, as though he had been taking a nap open-eyed. Perhaps he too, on his side, had detected in the silent pilgrim-like figure, standing there by the wheel, like an arrested wayfarer, the buried lineaments of the features belonging to the young captain of the *Condor*. Good fellow – Harry Whalley – never very talkative. You never knew what he was up to – a bit too offhand with people of consequence, and apt to take a wrong view of a fellow's actions. Fact was he had a too good opinion of himself. He would have liked to tell him to get in and drive him home to dinner. But one never knew. Wife would not like it.

'And it's funny to think, Harry,' he went on in a big, subdued drone, 'that of all the people on it there seems only you and I left to remember this part of the world as it used to be . . .'

He was ready to indulge in the sweetness of a sentimental mood had it not struck him suddenly that Captain Whalley, unstirring and without a word, seemed to be awaiting something – perhaps expecting . . . He gathered the reins at once and burst out in bluff, hearty growls – 'Ha! My dear boy. The men we have known – the ships we've sailed – ay! and the things we've done . . .'

The pony plunged – the syce skipped out of the way. Captain Whalley raised his arm.

'Goodbye.'

6

The sun had set. And when, after drilling a deep hole with his stick, he moved from that spot the night had massed its army of shadows under the trees. They filled the eastern ends of the avenue as if only waiting the signal for a general advance upon the open spaces of the world; they were gathering low between the deep stone-faced banks of the canal. The Malay prau, half-concealed under the arch of the bridge, had not altered its position a quarter of an inch. For a long time Captain Whalley stared down over the parapet, till at last the floating immobility of that beshrouded thing seemed to grow upon him into something inexplicable and alarming. The twilight abandoned the zenith; its reflected gleams left the world below, and the water of the canal seemed to turn into pitch. Captain Whalley crossed it.

The turning to the right, which was his way to his hotel, was only a very few steps farther. He stopped again (all the houses of the sea-front were shut up, the quayside was deserted, but for one or two figures of natives walking in the distance) and began to reckon the amount of his bill. So many days in the hotel at so many dollars a day. To count the days he used his fingers: plunging one hand into his pocket, he jingled a few silver coins. All right for three days more; and then, unless something turned up, he must break into the five hundred – Ivy's money – invested in her father. It seemed to him that the first meal coming out of that reserve would choke him – for certain. Reason was of no use. It was a matter of feeling. His feelings had never played him false.

He did not turn to the right. He walked on, as if there still had been a ship in the roadstead to which he could get himself pulled off in the evening. Far away, beyond the houses, on the slope of an indigo promontory closing the view of the quays, the slim column of a factory-chimney smoked quietly straight up into the clear air. A Chinaman, curled down in the stem of one of the half-dozen sampans floating off the end of the jetty, caught sight of a beckoning hand. He jumped up, rolled his pigtail round his head swiftly, tucked in two rapid movements his wide dark trousers high up his yellow thighs, and by a single, noiseless, finlike stir of the oars, sheered the sampan alongside the steps with the ease and precision of a swimming fish.

'*Sofala*,' articulated Captain Whalley from above; and the Chinaman, a new emigrant probably, stared upwards with a tense attention as if waiting to see the queer word fall visibly from the white man's lips. 'Sofala,' Captain Whalley repeated; and suddenly his heart failed him. He paused. The shores, the islets, the high ground, the low points, were dark: the horizon had grown sombre; and across the eastern sweep of the shore the white obelisk, marking the landing-place of the telegraph-cable, stood like a pale ghost on the beach before the dark spread of uneven roofs, intermingled with palms, of the native town. Captain Whalley began again.

'Sofala. Savee So-fa-la, John?'

This time the Chinaman made out that bizarre sound, and grunted his assent uncouthly, low down in his bare throat. With the first yellow twinkle of a star that appeared like the head of a pin stabbed deep into the smooth, pale, shimmering fabric of the sky, the edge of a keen chill seemed to cleave through the warm air of the earth. At the moment of stepping into the sampan to go and try for the command of the Sofala Captain Whalley shivered a little.

When on his return he landed on the quay again, Venus, like a choice jewel set low on the hem of the sky, cast a faint gold trail behind him upon the roadstead, as level as a floor made of one dark and polished stone. The lofty vaults of the avenues were black – all black overhead – and the porcelain globes on the lamp-posts resembled egg-shaped pearls, gigantic and luminous, displayed in a row whose farther end seemed to sink in the distance, down to the level of his knees. He put his hands behind his back. He would now consider calmly the discretion of it before saying the final word tomorrow. His feet scrunched the gravel loudly – the discretion of it. It would have been easier to appraise had there been a workable alternative. The honesty of it was indubitable: he meant well by the fellow; and periodically his shadow leaped up intense by his side on the trunks of the trees, to lengthen itself, oblique and dim, far over the grass – repeating his stride.

The discretion of it. Was there a choice? He seemed already to have lost something of himself; to have given up to a hungry spectre something of his truth and dignity in order to live. But his life was necessary. Let poverty do its worst in exacting its toll of humiliation. It was certain that Ned Eliott had rendered him, without knowing it, a service for which it would have been impossible to ask. He hoped Ned would not think there had been something underhand in his action. He supposed that now when he heard of it he would understand – or perhaps he would only think Whalley an eccentric old fool. What would have been the good of telling him – any more than of blurting the whole tale to that man Massy? Five hundred pounds ready to invest. Let him make the best of that. Let him wonder. You want a captain – I want a ship. That's enough. B–r–r–r. What a disagreeable impression that empty, dark, echoing steamer had made upon him . . .

A laid-up steamer was a dead thing and no mistake; a sailing-ship somehow seems always ready to spring into life with the breath of the incorruptible heaven; but a steamer, thought Captain Whalley, with her fires out, without the warm whiffs from below meeting you on her decks, without the hiss of steam, the clangs of iron in her breast – lies there as cold and still and pulseless as a corpse.

In the solitude of the avenue, all black above and lighted below, Captain Whalley, considering the discretion of his course, met, as it were incidentally, the thought of death. He pushed it aside with dislike and contempt. He almost laughed at it; and in the unquenchable vitality of his age only thought with a kind of exultation how little he needed to keep body and soul together. Not a bad investment for the poor woman this solid carcass of her father. And for the rest – in case of anything – the agreement should be clear: the whole five hundred to be paid back to her integrally within three months. Integrally. Every penny. He was not to lose any of her money whatever else had to go – a little dignity – some of his self-respect. He had never before allowed anybody to remain under any sort of false impression as to himself. Well, let that go – for her sake. After all, he had never *said* anything misleading – and Captain Whalley felt himself corrupt to the marrow of his bones. He laughed a little with the intimate scorn of his worldly prudence. Clearly, with a fellow of that sort, and in the peculiar relation they were to stand to each other, it would not have done to blurt out everything. He did not like the fellow. He did not like his spells of fawning loquacity and bursts of resentfulness. In the end – a poor devil. He would not have liked to stand in his shoes. Men were not evil, after all. He did not like his sleek hair, his queer way of standing at right angles, with his nose in the air, and glancing along his shoulder at you. No. On the whole, men were not bad – they were only silly or unhappy.

Captain Whalley had finished considering the discretion of that step – and there was the whole long night before him. In the full light his long beard would glisten like a silver breastplate covering his heart; in the spaces between the lamps his burly figure passed less distinct, loomed very big, wandering, and mysterious. No; there was not much real harm in men: and all the time a shadow marched with him, slanting on his left hand – which in the East is a presage of evil.

*   *   *

'Can you make out the clump of palms yet, Serang?' asked Captain Whalley from his chair on the bridge of the *Sofala* approaching the bar of Batu Beru.

'No, Tuan. By and by see.' The old Malay, in a blue dungaree suit, planted on his bony dark feet under the bridge awning, put his hands behind his back and stared ahead out of the innumerable wrinkles at the corners of his eyes.

Captain Whalley sat still, without lifting his head to look for himself. Three years – thirty-six times. He had made these palms thirty-six times from the southward. They would come into view at the proper time. Thank

God, the old ship made her courses and distances trip after trip, as correct as clockwork. At last he murmured again – 'In sight yet?'

'The sun makes a very great glare, Tuan.'

'Watch well, Serang.'

'Ya, Tuan.'

A white man had ascended the ladder from the deck noiselessly, and had listened quietly to this short colloquy. Then he stepped out on the bridge and began to walk from end to end, holding up the long cherrywood stem of a pipe. His black hair lay plastered in long lanky wisps across the bald summit of his head; he had a furrowed brow, a yellow complexion, and a thick shapeless nose. A scanty growth of whisker did not conceal the contour of his jaw. His aspect was of brooding care; and sucking at a curved black mouthpiece, he presented such a heavy overhanging profile that even the Serang could not help reflecting sometimes upon the extreme unloveliness of some white men.

Captain Whalley seemed to brace himself up in his chair, but gave no recognition whatever to his presence. The other puffed jets of smoke; then suddenly – 'I could never understand that new mania of yours of having this Malay here for your shadow, partner.'

Captain Whalley got up from the chair in all his imposing stature and walked across to the binnacle, holding such an unswerving course that the other had to back away hurriedly, and remained as if intimidated, with the pipe trembling in his hand. 'Walk over me now,' he muttered in a sort of astounded and discomfited whisper. Then slowly and distinctly he said – 'I – am – not – dirt.' And then added defiantly, 'As you seem to think.'

The Serang jerked out – 'See the palms now, Tuan.'

Captain Whalley strode forward to the rail; but his eyes, instead of going straight to the point, with the assured keen glance of a sailor, wandered irresolutely in space, as though he, the discoverer of new routes, had lost his way upon this narrow sea.

Another white man, the mate, came up on the bridge. He was tall, young, lean, with a moustache like a trooper, and something malicious in the eye. He took up a position beside the engineer. Captain Whalley, with his back to them, inquired – 'What's on the log?'

'Eighty-five,' answered the mate quickly, and nudged the engineer with his elbow.

Captain Whalley's muscular hands squeezed the iron rail with an extraordinary force; his eyes glared with an enormous effort; he knitted his eyebrows, the perspiration fell from under his hat – and in a faint voice he murmured, 'Steady her, Serang – when she is on the proper bearing.'

The silent Malay stepped back, waited a little, and lifted his arm warningly to the helmsman. The wheel revolved rapidly to meet the swing of the ship. Again the mate nudged the engineer. But Massy turned upon him.

'Mr Sterne,' he said violently, 'let me tell you – as a shipowner – that you are no better than a confounded fool.'

Sterne went down smirking and apparently not at all disconcerted, but the engineer Massy remained on the bridge, moving about with uneasy self-assertion. Everybody on board was his inferior – everyone without exception. He paid their wages and found them their food. They ate more of his bread and pocketed more of his money than they were worth; and they had no care in the world, while he alone had to meet all the difficulties of shipowning. When he contemplated his position in all its menacing entirety, it seemed to him that he had been for years the prey of a band of parasites; and for years he had scowled at everybody connected with the *Sofala* except, perhaps, at the Chinese firemen who served to get her along. Their use was manifest: they were an indispensable part of the machinery of which he was the master.

When he passed along his decks he shouldered those he came across brutally; but the Malay deck hands had learned to dodge out of his way. He had to bring himself to tolerate them because of the necessary manual labour of the ship which must be done. He had to struggle and plan and scheme to keep the *Sofala* afloat – and what did he get for it? Not even enough respect. They could not have given him enough of that if all their thoughts and all their actions had been directed to that end. The vanity of possession, the vainglory of power, had passed away by this time, and there remained only the material embarrassments, the fear of losing that position which had turned out not worth having, and an anxiety of thought which no abject subservience of men could repay.

He walked up and down. The bridge was his own after all. He had paid for it; and with the stem of the pipe in his hand he would stop short at times as if to listen with a profound and concentrated attention to the deadened beat of the engines (his own engines) and the slight grinding of the steering chains upon the continuous low wash of water alongside. But for these sounds, the ship might have been lying as still as if moored to a bank, and as silent as if abandoned by every living soul; only the coast, the low coast of mud and mangroves with the three palms in a bunch at the back, grew slowly more distinct in its long straight line, without a single feature to arrest attention. The native passengers of the *Sofala* lay about on mats under the awnings; the smoke of her funnel seemed the only sign of her life and connected with her gliding motion in a mysterious manner.

Captain Whalley on his feet, with a pair of binoculars in his hand and the little Malay Serang at his elbow, like an old giant attended by a wizened pigmy, was taking her over the shallow water of the bar.

This submarine ridge of mud, scoured by the stream out of the soft bottom of the river and heaped up far out on the hard bottom of the sea, was difficult to get over. The alluvial coast having no distinguishing marks, the bearings of the crossing-place had to be taken from the shape of the mountains inland. The guidance of a form flattened and uneven at the top like a grinder tooth, and of another smooth, saddle-backed summit, had to be searched for within the great unclouded glare that seemed to shift and float like a dry fiery mist, filling the air, ascending from the water, shrouding the distances, scorching to the eye. In this veil of light the near edge of the shore alone stood out almost coal-black with an opaque and motionless solidity. Thirty miles away the serrated range of the interior stretched across the horizon, its outlines and shades of blue, faint and tremulous like a background painted on airy gossamer on the quivering fabric of an impalpable curtain let down to the plain of alluvial soil; and the openings of the estuary appeared, shining white, like bits of silver let into the square pieces snipped clean and sharp out of the body of the land bordered with mangroves.

On the forepart of the bridge the giant and the pigmy muttered to each other frequently in quiet tones. Behind them Massy stood sideways with an expression of disdain and suspense on his face. His globular eyes were perfectly motionless, and he seemed to have forgotten the long pipe he held in his hand.

On the fore-deck below the bridge, steeply roofed with the white slopes of the awnings, a young lascar seaman had clambered outside the rail. He adjusted quickly a broad band of sail canvas under his armpits, and throwing his chest against it, leaned out far over the water. The sleeve of his thin cotton shirt, cut off close to the shoulder, bared his brown arm of full rounded form and with a satiny skin like a woman's. He swung it rigidly with the rotary and menacing action of a slinger: the 14-lb weight hurtled circling in the air, then suddenly flew ahead as far as the curve of the bow. The wet thin line swished like scratched silk running through the dark fingers of the man, and the plunge of the lead close to the ship's side made a vanishing silvery scar upon the golden glitter; then after an interval the voice of the young Malay uplifted and long-drawn declared the depth of the water in his own language.

'Tiga stengah,' he cried after each splash and pause, gathering the line busily for another cast. Tiga stengah, which means three fathom and a half. For a mile or so from seaward there was a uniform depth of water right up to the bar. 'Half-three. Half-three. Half-three,' – and his modulated cry, returned leisurely and monotonous, like the repeated call of a bird, seemed to float away in sunshine and disappear in the spacious silence of the empty sea and of a lifeless shore lying open, north and south, east and west, without the stir of a single cloud-shadow or the whisper of any other voice.

The owner-engineer of the *Sofala* remained very still behind the two seamen of different race, creed, and colour; the European with the time-defying vigour of his old frame, the little Malay, old too, but slight and shrunken like a withered brown leaf blown by a chance wind under the mighty shadow of the other. Very busy looking forward at the land, they had not a glance to spare; and Massy, glaring at them from behind, seemed to resent their attention to their duty like a personal slight upon himself.

This was unreasonable; but he had lived in his own world of unreasonable resentments for many years. At last, passing his moist palm over the rare lanky wisps of coarse hair on the top of his yellow head, he began to talk slowly.

'A leadsman, you want! I suppose that's your correct mail-boat style. Haven't you enough judgement to tell where you are by looking at the land? Why, before I had been a twelvemonth in the trade I was up to that trick – and I am only an engineer. I can point to you from here where the bar is, and I could tell you besides that you are likely as not to stick her in the mud in about five minutes from now; only you would call it interfering, I suppose. And there's that written agreement of ours, that says I mustn't interfere.'

His voice stopped. Captain Whalley, without relaxing the set severity of his features, moved his lips to ask in a quick mumble – 'How near, Serang?'

'Very near now, Tuan,' the Malay muttered rapidly.

'Dead slow,' said the Captain aloud in a firm tone.

The Serang snatched at the handle of the telegraph. A gong clanged down below. Massy with a scornful snigger walked off and put his head down the engine-room skylight.

'You may expect some rare fooling with the engines, Jack,' he bellowed. The space into which he stared was deep and full of gloom; and the grey gleams of steel down there seemed cool after the intense glare of the sea around the ship. The air, however, came up clammy and hot on his face. A short hoot on which it would have been impossible to put any sort of interpretation came from the bottom cavernously. This was the way in which the second engineer answered his chief.

He was a middle-aged man with an inattentive manner, and apparently wrapped up in such a taciturn concern for his engines that he seemed to have lost the use of speech. When addressed directly his only answer would be a grunt or a hoot, according to the distance. For all the years he had been in the *Sofala* he had never been known to exchange as much as a frank Good-morning with any of his shipmates. He did not seem aware that men came and went in the world; he did not seem to see them at all. Indeed he never recognised his shipmates on shore. At table (the four white men of the *Sofala* messed together) he sat looking into his plate dispassionately, but at the end of the meal would jump up and bolt down below as if a sudden thought had impelled him to rush and see whether somebody had not stolen the engines while he dined. In port at the end of the trip he went ashore regularly, but no one knew where he spent his evenings or in what manner. The local coasting fleet had preserved a wild and incoherent tale of his infatuation for the wife of a sergeant in an Irish infantry regiment. The regiment, however, had done its turn of garrison duty there ages before, and was gone somewhere to the other side of the earth, out of men's knowledge. Twice or perhaps three times in the course of the year he would take too much to drink. On these occasions he returned on board at an earlier hour than usual; ran across the deck balancing himself with his spread arms like a tightrope walker; and locking the door of his cabin, he would converse and argue with himself the livelong night in an amazing variety of tones; storm, sneer and whine with an inexhaustible persistence. Massy in his berth next door, raising himself on his elbow, would discover that his second had remembered the name of every white man that had passed through the *Sofala* for years and years back. He remembered the names of men that had died, that had gone home, that had gone to America: he remembered in his cups the names of men whose connection with the ship had been so short that Massy had almost forgotten its circumstances and could barely recall their faces. The inebriated voice on the other side of the bulkhead commented upon them all with an extraordinary and ingenious venom of scandalous inventions. It seems they had all offended him in some way, and in return he had found them all out. He muttered darkly; he laughed sardonically; he crushed them one after another; but of his chief, Massy, he babbled with an envious and naïve admiration. Clever scoundrel! Don't meet the likes of him every day. Just look at him. Ha! Great! Ship of his own. Wouldn't catch *him* going wrong. No fear – the beast! And Massy, after listening with a gratified smile to these artless tributes to his greatness, would begin to shout, thumping at the bulkhead with both fists – 'Shut up, you lunatic! Won't you let me go to sleep, you fool!'

But a half smile of pride lingered on his lips; outside the solitary lascar told off for night duty in harbour, perhaps a youth fresh from a forest village, would stand motionless in the shadows of the deck listening to the endless drunken gabble. His heart would be thumping with breathless awe of white men: the arbitrary and obstinate men who pursue inflexibly their incomprehensible purposes – beings with weird intonations in the voice, moved by unaccountable feelings, actuated by inscrutable motives.

8

For a while after his second's answering hoot Massy hung over the engine-room gloomily. Captain Whalley, who, by the power of five hundred pounds, had kept his command for three years, might have been suspected of never having seen that coast before. He seemed unable to put down his glasses, as though they had been glued under his contracted eyebrows. This settled frown gave to his face an air of invincible and just severity; but his raised elbow trembled slightly, and the perspiration poured from under his hat as if a second sun had suddenly blazed up at the zenith by the side of the ardent still globe already there, in whose blinding white heat the earth whirled and shone like a mote of dust.

From time to time, still holding up his glasses, he raised his other hand to wipe his streaming face. The drops rolled down his cheeks, fell like rain upon the white hairs of his beard, and brusquely, as if guided by an uncontrollable and anxious impulse, his arm reached out to the stand of the engine-room telegraph.

The gong clanged down below. The balanced vibration of the dead-slow speed ceased together with every sound and tremor in the ship, as if the great stillness that reigned upon the coast had stolen in through her sides of iron and taken possession of her innermost recesses. The illusion of perfect immobility seemed to fall upon her from the luminous blue dome without a stain arching over a flat sea without a stir. The faint breeze she had made for herself expired, as if all at once the air had become too thick to budge; even the slight hiss of the water on her stem died out. The narrow, long hull, carrying its way without a ripple, seemed to approach the shoal water of the bar by stealth. The plunge of the lead with the mournful, mechanical cry of the lascar came at longer and longer intervals; and the men on her bridge seemed to hold their breath, The Malay at the helm looked fixedly at the compass card, the Captain and the Serang stared at the coast.

Massy had left the skylight, and, walking flatfooted, had returned softly to the very spot on the bridge he had occupied before. A slow, lingering grin exposed his set of big white teeth: they gleamed evenly in the shade of the awning like the keyboard of a piano in a dusky room.

At last, pretending to talk to himself in excessive astonishment, he said not very loud – 'Stop the engines now. What next, I wonder?'

He waited, stooping from the shoulders, his head bowed, his glance oblique. Then raising his voice a shade – 'If I dared make an absurd remark I would say that you haven't the stomach to . . .'

But a yelling spirit of excitement, like some frantic soul wandering unsuspected in the vast stillness of the coast, had seized upon the body of the lascar at the lead. The languid monotony of his singsong changed to a swift, sharp clamour. The weight flew after a single whirr, the line whistled, splash followed splash in haste. The water had shoaled, and the man, instead of the drowsy tale of fathoms, was calling out the soundings in feet.

'Fifteen feet. Fifteen, fifteen! Fourteen, fourteen . . .'

Captain Whalley lowered the arm holding the glasses. It descended slowly as if by its own weight; no other part of his towering body stirred; and the swift cries with their eager warning note passed him by as though he had been deaf.

Massy, very still, and turning an attentive ear, had fastened his eyes upon the silvery, close-cropped back of the steady old head. The ship herself seemed to be arrested but for the gradual decrease of depth under her keel.

'Thirteen feet . . . Thirteen! Twelve!' cried the leadsman anxiously below the bridge. And suddenly the barefooted Serang stepped away noiselessly to steal a glance over the side.

Narrow of shoulder, in a suit of faded blue cotton, an old grey felt hat rammed down on his head, with a hollow in the nape of his dark neck, and with his slender limbs, he appeared from the back no bigger than a boy of fourteen. There was a childlike impulsiveness in the curiosity with which he watched the spread of the voluminous, yellowish convolutions rolling up from below to the surface of the blue water like massive clouds driving slowly upwards on the unfathomable sky. He was not startled at the sight in the least. It was not doubt, but the certitude that the keel of the *Sofala* must be stirring the mud now, which made him peep over the side.

His peering eyes, set aslant in a face of the Chinese type, a little old face, immovable, as if carved in old brown oak, had informed him long before that the ship was not headed at the bar properly. Paid off from the *Fair Maid*, together with the rest of the crew, after the completion of the sale, he had hung, in his faded blue suit and floppy grey hat, about the doors of the Harbour Office, till one day, seeing Captain Whalley coming along to get a crew for the *Sofala*, he had put himself quietly in the way, with his bare feet in the dust and an upward mute glance. The eyes of his old commander had fallen on him favourably – it must have been an auspicious day – and in less than half an hour the white men in the 'Ofiss' had written his name on a document as Serang of the fire-ship *Sofala*. Since that time he had repeatedly looked at that estuary, upon that coast, from this bridge and from this side of the bar. The record of the visual world fell through his eyes upon his unspeculating mind as on a sensitised plate through the lens of a camera. His knowledge was absolute and precise; nevertheless, had he been asked his opinion, and especially if questioned in the downright, alarming manner of white men, he would have displayed the hesitation of ignorance. He was certain of his facts – but such a certitude counted for little against the doubt what answer would be pleasing. Fifty years ago, in a jungle village, and before he was a day old, his father (who died without ever seeing a white face) had had his nativity cast by a man of skill and wisdom in astrology, because in the arrangement of the stars may be read the last word of human destiny. His destiny had been to thrive by the favour of various white men on the sea. He had swept the decks of ships, had tended their helms, had minded their stores, had risen at last to be a Serang; and his placid mind had remained as incapable of penetrating the simplest motives of those he served as they themselves were incapable of detecting through the crust of the earth the secret nature of its heart, which may be fire or may be stone. But he had no doubt whatever that the *Sofala* was out of the proper track for crossing the bar at Batu Beru.

It was a slight error. The ship could not have been more than twice her own length too far to the northward; and a white man at a loss for a cause (since it was impossible to suspect Captain Whalley of blundering ignorance, of want of skill, or of neglect) would have been inclined to doubt the testimony of his senses. It was some such feeling that kept Massy motionless, with his teeth laid bare by an anxious grin. Not so the Serang. He was not troubled by any intellectual mistrust of his senses. If his captain chose to stir the mud it was well. He had known in his life white men indulge in outbreaks equally strange. He was only genuinely interested to see what would come of it. At last, apparently satisfied, he stepped back from the rail.

He had made no sound: Captain Whalley, however, seemed to have observed the movements of his Serang. Holding his head rigidly, he asked with a mere stir of his lips – 'Going ahead still, Serang?'

'Still going a little, Tuan,' answered the Malay. Then added casually, 'She is over.'

The lead confirmed his words; the depth of water increased at every cast, and the soul of excitement departed suddenly from the lascar swung in the canvas belt over the *Sofala*'s side. Captain Whalley ordered the lead in, set the engines ahead without haste, and averting his eyes from the coast directed the Serang to keep a course for the middle of the entrance.

Massy brought the palm of his hand with a loud smack against his thigh.

'You grazed on the bar. Just look astern and see if you didn't. Look at the track she left. You can see it plainly. Upon my soul, I thought you would! What made you do that? What on earth made you do that? I believe you are trying to scare me.'

He talked slowly, as it were circumspectly, keeping his prominent black eyes on his captain. There was also a slight plaintive note in his rising choler, for, primarily, it was the clear sense of a wrong suffered undeservedly that made him hate the man who, for a beggarly five hundred pounds, claimed a sixth part of the profits under the three years' agreement. Whenever his resentment got the better of the awe the person of Captain Whalley inspired he would positively whimper with fury.

'You don't know what to invent to plague my life out of me. I would not have thought that a man of your sort would condescend . . .'

He paused, half hopefully, half timidly, whenever Captain Whalley made the slightest movement in the deck-chair, as though expecting to be conciliated by a soft speech or else rushed upon and hunted off the bridge.

'I am puzzled,' he went on again, with the watchful unsmiling baring of his big teeth. 'I don't know what to think. I do believe you are trying to frighten me. You very nearly planted her on the bar for at least twelve hours, besides getting the engines choked with mud. Ships can't afford to lose twelve hours on a trip nowadays – as you ought to know very well, and do know very well to be sure, only . . .'

His slow volubility, the sideways cranings of his neck, the black glances out of the very corners of his eyes, left Captain Whalley unmoved. He looked at the deck with a severe frown. Massy waited for some little time, then began to threaten plaintively.

'You think you've got me bound hand and foot in that agreement. You think you can torment me in any way you please. Ah! But remember it has another six weeks to run yet. There's time for me to dismiss you before the three years are out. You will do yet something that will give me the chance to dismiss you, and make you wait a twelvemonth for your money before you can take yourself off and pull out your five hundred, and leave me without a penny to get the new boilers for her. You gloat over that idea – don't you? I do believe you sit here gloating. It's as if I had sold my soul for five hundred pounds to be everlastingly damned in the end . . . '

He paused, without apparent exasperation, then continued evenly – ' . . . With the boilers worn out and the survey hanging over my head, Captain Whalley – Captain Whalley, I say, what do you do with your money? You must have stacks of money somewhere – a man like you must. It stands to reason. I am not a fool, you know, Captain Whalley – partner.'

Again he paused, as though he had done for good. He passed his tongue over his lips, gave a backward glance at the Serang conning the ship with quiet whispers and slight signs of the hand. The wash of the propeller sent a swift ripple, crested with dark froth, upon a long flat spit of black slime. The *Sofala* had entered the river; the trail she had stirred up over the bar was a mile astern of her now, out of sight, had disappeared utterly; and the smooth, empty sea along the coast was left behind in the glittering desolation of sunshine. On each side of her, low down, the growth of sombre twisted mangroves covered the semi-liquid banks; and Massy continued in his old tone, with an abrupt start, as if his speech had been ground out of him, like the tune of a music-box, by turning a handle.

'Though if anybody ever got the best of me, it is you. I don't mind saying this. I've said it – there! What more can you want? Isn't that enough for your pride, Captain Whalley. You got over me from the first. It's all of a piece, when I look back at it. You allowed me to insert that clause about intemperance without saying anything, only looking very sick when I made a point of it going in black on white. How could I tell what was wrong about you? There's generally something wrong somewhere. And, lo and behold! when you come on board it turns out that you've been in the habit of drinking nothing but water for years and years.'

His dogmatic reproachful whine stopped. He brooded profoundly, after the manner of crafty and unintelligent men. It seemed inconceivable that Captain Whalley should not laugh at the expression of disgust that overspread the heavy, yellow countenance. But Captain Whalley never raised his eyes – sitting in his armchair, outraged, dignified, and motionless.

'Much good it was to me,' Massy remonstrated monotonously, 'to insert a clause of dismissal for intemperance against a man who drinks nothing but water. And you looked so upset, too, when I read my draft in the lawyer's office that morning, Captain Whalley – you looked so crestfallen, that I made sure I had gone home on your weak spot. A shipowner can't be too careful as to the sort of skipper he gets. You must have been laughing at me in your sleeve all the blessed time . . . Eh? What are you going to say?'

Captain Whalley had only shuffled his feet slightly. A dull animosity became apparent in Massy's sideways stare.

'But recollect that there are other grounds of dismissal. There's habitual carelessness, amounting to incompetence – there's gross and persistent neglect of duty. I am not quite as big a fool as you try to make me out to be. You have been careless of late – leaving everything to that Serang. Why! I've seen you letting that old fool of a Malay take bearings for you, as if you were too big to attend to your work yourself. And what do you call that silly touch-and-go manner in which you took the ship over the bar just now? You expect me to put up with that.'

Leaning on his elbow against the ladder abaft the bridge, Sterne, the mate, tried to hear, blinking the while from the distance at the second engineer, who had come up for a moment, and stood in the engine-room companion. Wiping his hands on a bunch of cotton waste, he looked about with indifference to the right and left at the river-banks slipping astern of the *Sofala* steadily.

Massy turned full at the chair. The character of his whine became again threatening.

'Take care. I may yet dismiss you and freeze your money for a year. I may . . .'

But before the silent, rigid immobility of the man whose money had come in the nick of time to save him from utter ruin, his voice died out in his throat.

'Not that I want you to go,' he resumed after a silence, and in an absurdly insinuating tone. 'I want nothing better than to be friends and renew the agreement, if you will consent to find another couple of hundred to help with the new boilers, Captain Whalley. I've told you before. She must have new boilers; you know it as well as I do. Have you thought this over?'

He waited. The slender stem of the pipe with its bulky lump of a bowl at the end hung down from his thick lips. It had gone out. Suddenly he took it from between his teeth and wrung his hands slightly.

'Don't you believe me?' He thrust the pipe bowl into the pocket of his shiny black jacket.

'It's like dealing with the devil,' he said. 'Why don't you speak? At first you were so high and mighty with me I hardly dared to creep about my own deck. Now I can't get a word from you. You don't seem to see me at all. What does it mean? Upon my soul, you terrify me with this deaf and dumb trick. What's going on in that head of yours? What are you plotting against me there so hard that you can't say a word? You will never make me believe that you – you – don't know where to lay your hands on a couple of hundred. You have made me curse the day I was born . . .'

'Mr Massy,' said Captain Whalley suddenly, without stirring.

The engineer started violently.

'If that is so I can only beg you to forgive me.'

'Starboard,' muttered the Serang to the helmsman; and the *Sofala* began to swing round the bend into the second reach.

'Ough!' Massy shuddered. 'You make my blood run cold. What made you come here? What made you come aboard that evening all of a sudden, with your high talk and your money – tempting me? I always wondered what was your motive? You fastened yourself on me to have easy times and grow fat on my life blood, I tell you. Was that it? I believe you are the greatest miser in the world, or else why . . .'

'No. I am only poor,' interrupted Captain Whalley stonily.

'Steady,' murmured the Serang. Massy turned away with his chin on his shoulder.

'I don't believe it,' he said in his dogmatic tone. Captain Whalley made no movement. 'There you sit like a gorged vulture – exactly like a vulture.'

He embraced the middle of the reach and both the banks in one blank unseeing circular glance, and left the bridge slowly.

9

On turning to descend Massy perceived the head of Sterne the mate loitering, with his sly confident smile, his red moustaches and blinking eyes, at the foot of the ladder.

Sterne had been a junior in one of the larger shipping concerns before joining the *Sofala*. He had thrown up his berth, he said, 'on general principles'. The promotion in the employ was very slow, he complained, and he thought it was time for him to try and get on a bit in the world. It seemed as though nobody would ever die or leave the firm; they all stuck fast in their berths till they got mildewed; he was tired of waiting; and he feared that when a vacancy did occur the best servants were by no means sure of being treated fairly. Besides, the captain he had to serve under – Captain Provost – was an unaccountable sort of man and had taken a dislike to him for some reason or other. For doing rather more than his bare duty as likely as not. When he had done anything wrong he could take a talking to, like a man; but he expected to be treated like a man too, and not to be addressed invariably as though he were a dog. He had asked Captain Provost plump and plain to tell him where he was at fault, and Captain Provost, in a most scornful way, had told him that he was a perfect officer, and that if he disliked the way he was being spoken to there was the gangway – he could take himself off ashore at once. But everybody knew what sort of man Captain Provost was. It was no use appealing to the office. Captain Provost had too much influence in the employ. All the same, they had to give him a good character. He made bold to say there was nothing in the world against him, and, as he had happened to hear that the mate of the *Sofala* had been taken to the hospital that morning with a sunstroke, he thought there would be no harm in seeing whether he would not do . . .

He had come to Captain Whalley freshly shaved, red-faced, thin-flanked, throwing out his lean chest; and had recited his little tale with an open and manly assurance. Now and then his eyelids quivered slightly, his hand would steal up to the end of the flaming moustache; his eyebrows were straight, furry, of a chestnut colour, and the directness of his gaze seemed to tremble on the verge of impudence. Captain Whalley had engaged him temporarily; then, the other man having been ordered home by the doctors, he had remained for the next trip, and then the next. He had now attained permanency, and the performance of his duties was marked by an air of serious, single-minded application. Directly he was spoken to, he began to smile attentively, with a great deference expressed in his whole attitude; but there was in the rapid winking which went on all the time something quizzical, as though he had possessed the secret of some universal joke cheating all creation and impenetrable to other mortals.

Grave and smiling he watched Massy come down step by step; when the chief engineer had reached the deck he swung about, and they found themselves face to face. Matched as to height and utterly dissimilar, they confronted each other as if there had been something between them – something else than the bright strip of sunlight that, falling through the wide lacing of two awnings, cut crosswise the narrow planking of the deck and separated their feet as it were a stream; something profound and subtle and incalculable, like an unexpressed understanding, a secret mistrust, or some sort of fear.

At last Sterne, blinking his deep-set eyes and sticking forward his scraped, clean-cut chin, as crimson as the rest of his face, murmured – 'You've seen? He grazed! You've seen?'

Massy, contemptuous, and without raising his yellow, fleshy countenance, replied in the same pitch – 'Maybe. But if it had been you we would have been stuck fast in the mud.'

'Pardon me, Mr Massy. I beg to deny it. Of course a shipowner may say what he jolly well pleases on his own deck. That's all right; but I beg to . . .'

'Get out of my way!'

The other had a slight start, the impulse of suppressed indignation perhaps, but held his ground. Massy's downward glance wandered right and left, as though the deck all round Sterne had been bestrewn with eggs that must not be broken, and he had looked irritably for places where he could set his feet in flight. In the end he too did not move, though there was plenty of room to pass on.

'I heard you say up there,' went on the mate – 'and a very just remark it was too – that there's always something wrong . . . '

'Eavesdropping is what's wrong with *you*, Mr Sterne.'

'Now, if you would only listen to me for a moment, Mr Massy, sir, I could . . .'

'You are a sneak,' interrupted Massy in a great hurry, and even managed to get so far as to repeat, 'a common sneak,' before the mate had broken in argumentatively – "Now, sir, what is it you want? You want . . .'

'I want – I want,' stammered Massy, infuriated and astonished –'I want? How do you know that I want anything? How dare you? . . . What do you mean? . . . What are you after – you . . . '

'Promotion.' Sterne silenced him with candid bravado. The engineer's round soft cheeks quivered still, but he said quietly enough – 'You are only worrying my head off,' and Sterne met him with a confident little smile.

'A chap in business I know (well up in the world he is now) used to tell me that this was the proper way. "Always push on to the front," he would say. "Keep yourself well before your boss. Interfere whenever you get a chance. Show him what you know. Worry him into seeing you." That was his advice. Now I know no other boss than you here. You are the owner, and no one else counts for *that* much in my eyes. See, Mr Massy? I want to get on. I make no secret of it that I am one of the sort that means to get on. These are the men to make use of, sir. You haven't arrived at the top of the tree sir, without finding that out – I dare say.'

'Worry your boss in order to get on,' repeated Massy, as if awestruck by the irreverent originality of the idea. 'I shouldn't wonder if this was just what the Blue Anchor people kicked you out of their employ for. Is that what you call getting on? You shall get on in the same way here if you aren't careful – I can promise you.'

At this Sterne hung his head, thoughtful, perplexed, winking hard at the deck. All his attempts to enter into confidential relations with his owner had led of late to nothing better than these dark threats of dismissal; and a threat of dismissal would check him at once into a hesitating silence as though he were not sure that the proper time for defying it had come. On this occasion he seemed to have lost his tongue for a moment, and Massy, getting in motion, heavily passed him by with an abortive attempt at shouldering. Sterne defeated it by stepping aside. He turned then swiftly, opening his mouth very wide as if to shout something after the engineer, but seemed to think better of it.

Always – as he was ready to confess – on the look-out for an opening to get on, it had become an instinct with him to watch the conduct of his immediate superiors for something 'that one could lay hold of'. It was his belief that no skipper in the world would keep his command for a day if only the owners could be 'made to know'. This romantic and naïve theory had led him into trouble more than once, but he remained incorrigible; and his character was so instinctively disloyal that whenever he joined a ship the intention of ousting his commander out of the berth and taking his place was always present at the back of his head, as a matter of course. It filled the leisure of his waking hours with the reveries of careful plans and compromising discoveries – the dreams of his sleep with images of lucky turns and favourable accidents. Skippers had been known to sicken and die at sea, than which nothing could be better to give a smart mate a chance of showing what he's made of. They also would tumble overboard sometimes: he had heard of one or two such cases. Others again . . . But, as it were constitutionally, he was faithful to the belief that the conduct of no single one of them would stand the test of careful watching by a man who 'knew what's what' and who kept his eyes 'skinned pretty well' all the time.

After he had gained a permanent footing on board the *Sofala* he allowed his perennial hope to rise high. To begin with, it was a great advantage to have an old man for captain: the sort of man besides who in the nature of things was likely to give up the job before long from one cause or another. Sterne was greatly chagrined, however, to notice that he did not seem anyway near being past his work yet. Still, these old men go to pieces all at once sometimes. Then there was the owner-engineer close at hand to be impressed by his zeal and steadiness. Sterne never for a moment doubted the obvious nature of his own merits (he was really an excellent officer); only, nowadays, professional merit alone does not take a man along fast enough. A chap must have some push in him, and must keep his wits at work too to help him forward. He made up his mind to inherit the charge of this steamer if it was to be done at all; not indeed estimating the command of the *Sofala* as a very great catch, but for the reason that, out East especially, to make a start is everything, and one command leads to another.

He began by promising himself to behave with great circumspection; Massy's sombre and fantastic humours intimidated him as being outside one's usual sea experience; but he was quite intelligent enough to realise almost from the first that he was there in the presence of an exceptional situation. His peculiar prying imagination penetrated it quickly; the feeling that there was in it an element which eluded his grasp exasperated his impatience to get on. And so one trip came to an end, then another, and he had begun his third before he saw an opening by which he could step in with any sort of effect. It had all been very queer and very obscure; something had been going on near him, as if separated by a chasm from the common life and the working routine of the ship, which was exactly like the life and the routine of any other coasting steamer of that class.

Then one day he made his discovery.

It came to him after all these weeks of watchful observation and puzzled surmises, suddenly, like the long-sought solution of a riddle that suggests itself to the mind in a flash. Not with the same authority, however. Great heavens! Could it be that? And after remaining thunderstruck for a few seconds he tried to shake it off with self-contumely, as though it had been the product of an unhealthy bias towards the Incredible, the Inexplicable, the Unheard-of – the Mad!

This – the illuminating moment – had occurred the trip before, on the return passage. They had just left a place of call on the mainland called Pangu; they were steaming straight out of a bay. To the east a massive headland closed the view, with the tilted edges of the rocky strata showing through its ragged clothing of rank bushes and thorny creepers. The wind had begun to sing in the rigging; the sea along the coast, green and as if swollen a little above the line of the horizon, seemed to pour itself over, time after time, with a slow and thundering fall, into the shadow of the leeward cape; and across the wide opening the nearest of a group of small islands stood enveloped in the hazy yellow light of a breezy sunrise; still farther out the hummocky tops of other islets peeped out motionless above the water of the channels between, scoured tumultuously by the breeze.

The usual track of the *Sofala* both going and returning on every trip led her for a few miles along this reef-infested region. She followed a broad lane of water, dropping astern, one after another, these crumbs of the earth's crust resembling a squadron of dismasted hulks run in disorder upon a foul ground of rocks and shoals. Some of these fragments of land appeared, indeed, no bigger than a stranded ship; others, quite flat, lay awash like anchored rafts, like ponderous, black rafts of stone; several, heavily timbered and round at the base, emerged in squat domes of deep green foliage that shuddered darkly all over to the flying touch of cloud shadows driven by the sudden gusts of the squally season. The thunderstorms of the coast broke frequently over that cluster; it turned then shadowy in its whole extent; it turned more dark, and as if more still in the play of fire; as if more impenetrably silent in the peals of thunder; its blurred shapes vanished – dissolving utterly at times in the thick rain – to reappear clear-cut and black in the stormy light against the grey sheet of the cloud – scattered on the slaty round table of the sea. Unscathed by storms, resisting the work of years, unfretted by the strife of the world, there it lay unchanged as on that day, four hundred years ago, when first beheld by Western eyes from the deck of a high-pooped caravel.

It was one of these secluded spots that may be found on the busy sea, as on land you come sometimes upon the clustered houses of a hamlet untouched by men's restlessness, untouched by their need, by their thought, and as if forgotten by time itself. The lives of uncounted generations had passed it by, and the multitudes of seafowl, urging their way from all the points of the horizon to sleep on the outer rocks of the group, unrolled the converging evolutions of their flight in long sombre streamers upon the glow of the sky. The palpitating cloud of their wings soared and stooped over the pinnacles of the rocks, over the rocks slender like spires, squat like martello towers; over the pyramidal heaps like fallen ruins, over the lines of bald boulders showing like a wall of stones battered to pieces and scorched by lightning – with the sleepy, clear glimmer of water in every breach. The noise of their continuous and violent screaming filled the air.

This great noise would meet the *Sofala* coming up from Batu Beru; it would meet her on quiet evenings, a pitiless and savage clamour enfeebled by distance, the clamour of seabirds settling to rest, and struggling for a footing at the end of the day. No one noticed it especially on board; it was the voice of their ship's unerring landfall, ending the steady stretch of a hundred miles. She had made good her course, she had run her distance till the punctual islets began to emerge one by one, the points of rocks, the hummocks of earth . . . and the cloud of birds hovered – the restless cloud emitting a strident and cruel uproar, the sound of the familiar scene, the living part of the broken land beneath, of the outspread sea, and of the high sky without a flaw.

But when the *Sofala* happened to close with the land after sunset she would find everything very still there under the mantle of the night. All would be still, dumb, almost invisible – but for the blotting out of the low constellations occulted in turns behind the vague masses of the islets whose true outlines eluded the eye amongst the dark spaces of the heaven: and the ship's three lights, resembling three stars – the red and the green with the white above – her three lights, like three companion stars wandering on the earth, held their unswerving course for the passage at the southern end of the group. Sometimes there were human eyes open to watch them come nearer, travelling smoothly in the sombre void; the eyes of a naked fisherman in his canoe floating over a reef. He thought drowsily: 'Ha! The fire-ship that once in every moon goes in and comes out of Pangu Bay.' More he did not know of her. And just as he had detected the faint rhythm of the propeller beating the calm water a mile and a half away, the time would come for the *Sofala* to alter her course, the lights would swing off him their triple beam – and disappear.

A few miserable, half-naked families, a sort of outcast tribe of long-haired, lean, and wild-eyed people, strove for their living in this lonely wilderness of islets, lying like an abandoned outwork of the land at the gates of the bay. Within the knots and loops of the rocks the water rested more transparent than crystal under their crooked and leaky canoes, scooped out of the trunk of a tree: the forms of the bottom undulated slightly to the dip of a paddle; and the men seemed to hang in the air, they seemed to hang enclosed within the fibres of a dark, sodden log, fishing patiently in a strange, unsteady, pellucid, green air above the shoals.

Their bodies stalked brown and emaciated as if dried up in the sunshine; their lives ran out silently; the homes where they were born, went to rest, and died – flimsy sheds of rushes and coarse grass eked out with a few ragged mats – were hidden out of sight from the open sea. No glow of their household fires ever kindled for a seaman a red spark upon the blind night of the group: and the calms of the coast, the flaming long calms of the equator, the unbreathing, concentrated calms like the deep introspection of a passionate nature, brooded awfully for days and weeks together over the unchangeable inheritance of their children; till at last the stones, hot like live embers, scorched the naked sole, till the water clung warm, and sickly, and as if thickened, about the legs of lean men with girded loins, wading thigh-deep in the pale blaze of the shallows. And it would happen now and then that the *Sofala*, through some delay in one of the ports of call, would heave in sight making for Pangu Bay as late as noonday.

Only a blurring cloud at first, the thin mist of her smoke would arise mysteriously from an empty point on the clear line of sea and sky. The taciturn fishermen within the reefs would extend their lean arms towards the offing; and the brown figures stooping on the tiny beaches, the brown figures of men, women, and children grubbing in the sand in search of turtles' eggs, would rise up, crooked elbow aloft and hand over the eyes, to watch this monthly apparition glide straight on, swerve off – and go by. Their ears caught the panting of that ship; their eyes followed her till she passed between the two capes of the mainland going at full speed as though she hoped to make her way unchecked into the very bosom of the earth.

On such days the luminous sea would give no sign of the dangers lurking on both sides of her path. Everything remained still, crushed by the overwhelming power of the light; and the whole group, opaque in the sunshine – the rocks resembling pinnacles, the rocks resembling spires, the rocks resembling ruins; the forms of islets resembling beehives, resembling molehills; the islets recalling the shapes of haystacks, the contours of ivy-clad towers – would stand reflected together upside down in the unwrinkled water, like carved toys of ebony disposed on the silvered plate-glass of a mirror.

The first touch of blowing weather would envelop the whole at once in the spume of the windward breakers, as if in a sudden cloudlike burst of steam; and the clear water seemed fairly to boil in all the passages. The provoked sea outlined exactly in a design of angry foam the wide base of the group; the submerged level of broken waste and refuse left over from the building of the coast near by, projecting its dangerous spurs, all awash, far into the channel, and bristling with wicked long spits often a mile long: with deadly spits made of froth and stones.

And even nothing more than a brisk breeze – as on that morning, the voyage before, when the *Sofala* left Pangu Bay early, and Mr Sterne's discovery was to blossom out like a flower of incredible and evil aspect from the tiny seed of instinctive suspicion – even such a breeze had enough strength to tear the placid mask from the face of the sea. To Sterne, gazing with indifference, it had been like a revelation to behold for the first time the dangers marked by the hissing livid patches on the water as distinctly as on the engraved paper of a chart. It came into his mind that this was the sort of day most favourable for a stranger attempting the passage: a clear day, just windy enough for the sea to break on every ledge, buoying, as it were, the channel plainly to the sight;

whereas during a calm you had nothing to depend on but the compass and the practised judgement of your eye. And yet the successive captains of the *Sofala* had had to take her through at night more than once. Nowadays you could not afford to throw away six or seven hours of a steamer's time. That you couldn't. But then use is everything, and with proper care . . . The channel was broad and safe enough; the main point was to hit upon the entrance correctly in the dark – for if a man got himself involved in that stretch of broken water over yonder he would never get out with a whole ship – if he ever got out at all.

This was Sterne's last train of thought independent of the great discovery. He had just seen to the securing of the anchor, and had remained forward idling away a moment or two. The captain was in charge on the bridge. With a slight yawn he had turned away from his survey of the sea and had leaned his shoulders against the fish davit.

These, properly speaking, were the very last moments of ease he was to know on board the *Sofala*. All the instants that came after were to be pregnant with purpose and intolerable with perplexity. No more idle, random thoughts; the discovery would put them on the rack, till sometimes he wished to goodness he had been fool enough not to make it at all. And yet, if his chance to get on rested on the discovery of 'something wrong', he could not have hoped for a greater stroke of luck.

10

The knowledge was too disturbing, really. There was 'something wrong' with a vengeance, and the moral certitude of it was at first simply frightful to contemplate. Sterne had been looking aft in a mood so idle, that for once he was thinking no harm of anyone. His captain on the bridge presented himself naturally to his sight. How insignificant, how casual was the thought that had started the train of discovery – like an accidental spark that suffices to ignite the charge of a tremendous mine!

Caught under by the breeze, the awnings of the foredeck bellied upwards and collapsed slowly, and above their heavy flapping the grey stuff of Captain Whalley's roomy coat fluttered incessantly around his arms and trunk. He faced the wind in full light, with his great silvery beard blown forcibly against his chest; the eyebrows overhung heavily the shadows whence his glance appeared to be staring ahead piercingly. Sterne could just detect the twin gleam of the whites shifting under the shaggy arches of the brow. At short range these eyes, for all the man's affable manner, seemed to look you through and through. Sterne never could defend himself from that feeling when he had occasion to speak with his captain. He did not like it. What a big heavy man he appeared up there, with that little shrimp of a Serang in close attendance – as was usual in this extraordinary steamer! Confounded absurd custom that. He resented it. Surely the old fellow could have looked after his ship without that loafing native at his elbow. Sterne wriggled his shoulders with disgust. What was it? Indolence or what?

That old skipper must have been growing lazy for years. They all grew lazy out East here (Sterne was very conscious of his own unimpaired activity); they got slack all over. But he towered very erect on the bridge; and quite low by his side, as you see a small child looking over the edge of a table, the battered soft hat and the brown face of the Serang peeped over the white canvas screen of the rail.

No doubt the Malay was standing back, nearer to the wheel; but the great disparity of size in close association amused Sterne like the observation of a bizarre fact in nature. There were as queer fish out of the sea as any in it.

He saw Captain Whalley turn his head quickly to speak to his Serang; the wind whipped the whole white mass of the beard sideways. He would be directing the chap to look at the compass for him, or what not. Of course. Too much trouble to step over and see for himself. Sterne's scorn for that bodily indolence which overtaxes white men in the East increased on reflection. Some of them would be utterly lost if they hadn't all these natives at their beck and call; they grew perfectly shameless about it too. He was not of that sort, thank God! It wasn't in him to make himself dependent for his work on any shrivelled-up little Malay like that. As if one could ever trust a silly native for anything in the world! But that fine old man thought differently, it seems. There they were together, never far apart; a pair of them, recalling to the mind an old whale attended by a little pilot-fish.

The fancifulness of the comparison made him smile. A whale with an inseparable pilot-fish! That's what the old man looked like; for it could not be said he looked like a shark, though Mr Massy had called him that very name. But Mr Massy did not mind what he said in his savage fits. Sterne smiled to himself – and gradually the ideas evoked by the sound, by the imagined shape of the word pilot-fish; the ideas of aid, of guidance needed and received, came uppermost in his mind: the word pilot awakened the idea of trust, of dependence, the idea of the welcome, clear-eyed help brought to the seaman groping for the land in the dark: groping blindly in fogs: feeling his way in the thick weather of the gales that, filling the air with a salt mist blown up from the sea, contract the range of sight on all sides to a shrunken horizon that seems within reach of the hand.

A pilot sees better than a stranger, because his local knowledge, like a sharper vision, completes the shapes of things hurriedly glimpsed; penetrates the veils of mist spread over the land by the storms of the sea; defines with certitude the outlines of a coast lying under the pall of fog, the forms of landmarks half buried in a starless night as in a shallow grave. He recognises because he already knows. It is not to his far-reaching eye but to his more extensive knowledge that the pilot looks for certitude; for this certitude of the ship's position on which may depend a man's good fame and the peace of his conscience, the justification of the trust deposited in his hands, with his own life too, which is seldom wholly his to throw away, and the humble lives of others rooted in distant affections, perhaps, and made as weighty as the lives of kings by the burden of the awaiting mystery. The pilot's knowledge brings relief and certitude to the commander of a ship; the Serang, however, in his fanciful suggestion of a pilot-fish attending a whale, could not in any way be credited with a superior knowledge. Why should he have it? These two men had come on that run together – the white and the brown – on the same day: and of course a white man would learn more in a week than the best native would in a month. He was made to stick to the skipper as though he were of some use – as the pilot-fish, they say, is to the whale. But how – it was very marked – how? A pilot-fish – a pilot – a . . . But if not superior knowledge then . . .

Sterne's discovery was made. It was repugnant to his imagination, shocking to his ideas of honesty, shocking to his conception of mankind. This enormity affected one's outlook on what was possible in this world: it was as if for instance the sun had turned blue, throwing a new and sinister light on men and nature. Really in the first moment he had felt sickish, as though he had got a blow below the belt: for a second the very colour of the sea seemed changed – appeared queer to his wandering eye; and he had a passing, unsteady sensation in all his limbs as though the earth had started turning the other way.

A very natural incredulity succeeding this sense of upheaval brought a measure of relief. He had gasped; it was over. But afterwards during all that day sudden paroxysms of wonder would come over him in the midst of his occupations. He would stop and shake his head. The revolt of his incredulity had passed away almost as quick as the first emotion of discovery, and for the next twenty-four hours he had no sleep. That would never do. At meal-times (he took the foot of the table set up for the white men on the bridge) he could not help losing himself in a fascinated contemplation of Captain Whalley opposite. He watched the deliberate upward movements of the arm; the old man put his food to his lips as though he never expected to find any taste in his daily bread, as though he did not know anything about it. He fed himself like a somnambulist. 'It's an awful sight,' thought Sterne; and he watched the long period of mournful, silent immobility, with a big brown hand lying loosely closed by the side of the plate, till he noticed the two engineers to the right and left looking at him in astonishment. He would close his mouth in a hurry then, and lowering his eyes, wink rapidly at his plate. It was awful to see the old chap sitting there; it was even awful to think that with three words he could blow him up sky-high. All he had to do was to raise his voice and pronounce a single short sentence, and yet that simple act seemed as impossible to attempt as moving the sun out of its place in the sky. The old chap could eat in his terrific mechanical way; but Sterne, from mental excitement, could not – not that evening, at any rate.

He had had ample time since to get accustomed to the strain of the meal-hours. He would never have believed it. But then use is everything; only the very potency of his success prevented anything resembling elation. He felt like a man who, in his legitimate search for a loaded gun to help him on his way through the world, chances to come upon a torpedo – upon a live torpedo with a shattering charge in its head and a pressure of many atmospheres in its tail. It is the sort of weapon to make its possessor careworn and nervous. He had no mind to be blown up himself; and he could not get rid of the notion that the explosion was bound to damage him too in some way.

This vague apprehension had restrained him at first. He was able now to eat and sleep with that fearful weapon by his side, with the conviction of its power always in his mind. It had not been arrived at by any reflective process; but once the idea had entered his head, the conviction had followed overwhelmingly in a multitude of observed little facts to which before he had given only a languid attention. The abrupt and faltering intonations of the deep voice; the taciturnity put on like an armour; the deliberate, as if guarded, movements; the long immobilities, as if the man he watched had been afraid to disturb the very air: every familiar gesture, every word uttered in his hearing, every sigh overheard, had acquired a special significance, a confirmatory import.

Every day that passed over the *Sofala* appeared to Sterne simply crammed full with proofs – with incontrovertible proofs. At night, when off duty, he would steal out of his cabin in pyjamas (for more proofs) and stand a full hour, perhaps, on his bare feet below the bridge, as absolutely motionless as the awning stanchion in its deck socket near by. On the stretches of easy navigation it is not usual for a coasting captain to remain on deck all the time of his watch. The Serang keeps it for him as a matter of custom; in open water, on a straight course, he is usually trusted to look after the ship by himself. But this old man seemed incapable of remaining quietly down below. No doubt he could not sleep. And no wonder. This was also a proof. Suddenly in the silence of the ship panting upon the still, dark sea, Sterne would hear a low voice above him exclaiming nervously – 'Serang!'

'Tuan!'

'You are watching the compass well?'

'Yes, I am watching, Tuan.'

'The ship is making her course?'

'She is, Tuan. Very straight.'

'It is well; and remember, Serang, that the order is, that you are to mind the helmsmen and keep a look-out with care, the same as if I were not on deck.'

Then, when the Serang had made his answer, the low tones on the bridge would cease, and everything round Sterne seemed to become more still and more profoundly silent. Slightly chilled and with his back aching a little from long immobility, he would steal away to his room on the port side of the deck. He had long since parted with the last vestige of incredulity; of the original emotions, set into a tumult by the discovery, some trace of the first awe alone remained. Not the awe of the man himself – he could blow him up sky-high with six words – rather it was an awestruck indignation at the reckless perversity of avarice (what else could it be?), at the mad and sombre resolution that for the sake of a few dollars more seemed to set at nought the common rule of conscience and pretended to struggle against the very decree of Providence.

You could not find another man like this one in the whole round world – thank God. There was something devilishly dauntless in the character of such a deception which made you pause.

Other considerations occurring to his prudence had kept him tongue-tied from day to day. It seemed to him now that it would yet have been easier to speak out in the first hour of discovery. He almost regretted not having made a row at once. But then the very monstrosity of the disclosure . . . Why! he could hardly face it himself, let alone pointing it out to somebody else. Moreover, with a desperado of that sort one never knew. The object was not to get him out (that was as well as done already), but to step into his place. Bizarre as the thought seemed he might have shown fight. A fellow up to working such a fraud would have enough cheek for anything; a fellow that, as it were, stood up against God Almighty Himself. He was a horrid marvel – that's what he was: he was perfectly capable of brazening out the affair scandalously till he got him (Sterne) kicked out of the ship and everlastingly damaged his prospects in this part of the East. Yet if you want to get on something must be risked. At times Sterne thought he had been unduly timid of taking action in the past; and what was worse, it had come to this, that in the present he did not seem to know what action to take.

Massy's savage moroseness was too disconcerting. It was an incalculable factor of the situation. You could not tell what there was behind that insulting ferocity. How could one trust such a temper? It did not put Sterne in bodily fear for himself, but it frightened him exceedingly as to his prospects.

Though of course inclined to credit himself with exceptional powers of observation, he had by now lived too long with his discovery. He had gone on looking at nothing else, till at last one day it occurred to him that the thing was so obvious that no one could miss seeing it. There were four white men in all on board the *Sofala*. Jack, the second engineer, was too dull to notice anything that took place out of his engine-room. Remained Massy – the owner – the interested person – nearly going mad with worry. Sterne had heard and seen more than enough on board to know what ailed him; but his exasperation seemed to make him deaf to cautious overtures. If he had only known it, there was the very thing he wanted. But how could you bargain with a man of that sort? It was like going into a tiger's den with a piece of raw meat in your hand. He was as likely as not to rend you for your pains. In fact, he was always threatening to do that very thing; and the urgency of the case, combined with the impossibility of handling it with safety, made Sterne in his watches below toss and mutter open-eyed in his bunk, for hours, as though he had been burning with fever.

Occurrences like the crossing of the bar just now were extremely alarming to his prospects. He did not want to be left behind by some swift catastrophe. Massy being on the bridge, the old man had to brace himself up, and make a show, he supposed. But it was getting very bad with him, very bad indeed, now. Even Massy had been emboldened to find fault this time; Sterne, listening at the foot of the ladder, had heard the other's whimpering and artless denunciations. Luckily the beast was very stupid and could not see the why of all this. However, small blame to him; it took a clever man to hit upon the cause. Nevertheless, it was high time to do something. The old man's game could not be kept up for many days more.

'I may yet lose my life at this fooling – let alone my chance,' Sterne mumbled angrily to himself, after the stooping back of the chief engineer had disappeared round the corner of the skylight. Yes, no doubt – he thought; but to blurt out his knowledge would not advance his prospects. On the contrary, it would blast them utterly as likely as not. He dreaded another failure. He had a vague consciousness of not being much liked by his fellows in this part of the world; inexplicably enough, for he had done nothing to them. Envy, he supposed. People were always down on a clever chap who made no bones about his determination to get on. To do your duty and count on the gratitude of that brute Massy would be sheer folly. He was a bad lot. Unmanly! A vicious man! Bad! Bad! A brute! A brute without a spark of anything human about him; without so much as simple curiosity even, or else surely he would have responded in some way to all these hints he had been given . . . Such insensibility was almost mysterious. Massy's state of exasperation seemed to Sterne to have made him stupid beyond the ordinary silliness of shipowners.

Sterne, meditating on the embarrassments of that stupidity, forgot himself completely. His stony, unwinking stare was fixed on the planks of the deck.

The slight quiver agitating the whole fabric of the ship was more perceptible in the silent river, shaded and still like a forest path. The *Sofala*, gliding with an even motion, had passed beyond the coast-belt of mud and mangroves. The shores rose higher, in firm sloping banks, and the forest of big trees came down to the brink. Where the earth had been crumbled by the floods it showed a steep brown cut, denuding a mass of roots intertwined as if wrestling underground; and in the air, the interlaced boughs, bound and loaded with creepers, carried on the struggle for life, mingled their foliage in one solid wall of leaves, with here and there the shape of an enormous dark pillar soaring, or a ragged opening, as if torn by the flight of a cannonball, disclosing the impenetrable gloom within, the secular inviolable shade of the virgin forest. The thump of the engines reverberated regularly like the strokes of a metronome beating the measure of the vast silence, the shadow of the western wall had fallen across the river, and the smoke pouring backwards from the funnel eddied down behind the ship, spread a thin dusky veil over the sombre water, which, checked by the flood-tide, seemed to lie stagnant in the whole straight length of the reaches.

Sterne's body, as if rooted on the spot, trembled slightly from top to toe with the internal vibration of the ship; from under his feet came sometimes a sudden clang of iron, the noisy burst of a shout below; to the right the leaves of the tree-tops caught the rays of the low sun, and seemed to shine with a golden green light of their own shimmering around the highest boughs which stood out black against a smooth blue sky that seemed to droop over the bed of the river like the roof of a tent. The passengers for Batu Beru, kneeling on the planks, were engaged in rolling their bedding of mats busily; they tied up bundles, they snapped the locks of wooden chests. A pockmarked pedlar of small wares threw his head back to drain into his throat the last drops out of an earthenware bottle before putting it away in a roll of blankets. Knots of travelling traders standing about the deck conversed in low tones; the followers of a small Rajah from down the coast, broad-faced simple young fellows in white drawers and round white cotton caps with their coloured sarongs twisted across their bronze shoulders, squatted on their hams on the hatch, chewing betel with bright red mouths as if they had been tasting blood. Their spears, lying piled up together within the circle of their bare toes, resembled a casual bundle of dry bamboos; a thin, livid Chinaman, with a bulky package wrapped up in leaves already thrust under his arm, gazed ahead eagerly; a wandering Kling rubbed his teeth with a bit of wood, pouring over the side a bright stream of water out of his lips; the fat Rajah dozed in a shabby deck-chair – and at the turn of every bend the two walls of leaves reappeared running parallel along the banks, with their impenetrable solidity fading at the top to a vaporous mistiness of countless slender twigs growing free, of young delicate branches shooting from the topmost limbs of hoary trunks, of feathery heads of climbers like delicate silver sprays standing up without a quiver. There was not a sign of a clearing anywhere; not a trace of human habitation, except when in one place, on the bare end of a low point under an isolated group of slender tree-ferns, the jagged, tangled remnants of an old hut on piles appeared with that peculiar aspect of ruined bamboo walls that look as if smashed with a club. Farther on, half hidden under the drooping bushes, a canoe containing a man and a woman together with a dozen green cocoanuts in a heap, rocked helplessly after the *Solala* had passed, like a navigating contrivance of venturesome insects, of travelling ants; while two glassy folds of water streaming away from each bow of the steamer across the whole width of the river ran with her upstream smoothly, fretting their outer ends into a brown whispering tumble of froth against the miry foot of each bank.

'I must,' thought Sterne, 'bring that brute Massy to his bearings. It's getting too absurd in the end. Here's the old man up there buried in his chair – he may just as well be in his grave for all the use he'll ever be in the world – and the Serang's in charge. Because that's what he is. In charge. In the place that's mine by rights. I must bring that savage brute to his bearings. I'll do it at once, too . . . '

When the mate made an abrupt start, a little brown half-naked boy, with large black eyes, and the string of a written charm round his neck, became panic-struck at once. He dropped the banana he had been munching, and ran to the knee of a grave dark Arab in flowing robes, sitting like a Biblical figure, incongruously, on a yellow tin trunk corded with a rope of twisted rattan. The father, unmoved, put out his hand to pat the little shaven poll protectingly.

I I

Sterne crossed the deck upon the track of the chief engineer. Jack, the second, retreating backwards down the engine-room ladder, and still wiping his hands, treated him to an incomprehensible grin of white teeth out of his grimy hard face; Massy was nowhere to be seen. Sterne scratched at the door softly, then, putting his lips to the rose of the ventilator, said – 'I must speak to you, Mr Massy. Just give me a minute or two.'

'I am busy. Go away from my door.'

'But pray, Mr Massy . . . '

'You go away. D'you hear? Take yourself off altogether – to the other end of the ship – quite away . . . ' The voice inside dropped low. 'To the devil.'

Sterne paused: then very quietly – 'It's rather pressing. When do you think you will be at liberty, sir?'

The answer to this was an exasperated 'Never'; and at once Sterne, with a very firm expression of face, turned the handle.

Mr Massy's stateroom – a narrow, one-berth cabin – smelt strongly of soap, and presented to view a swept, dusted, unadorned neatness, not so much bare as barren, not so much severe as starved and lacking in humanity, like the ward of a public hospital, or rather (owing to the small size) like the clean retreat of a desperately poor but exemplary person. Not a single photograph frame ornamented the bulkheads; not a single article of clothing, not as much as a spare cap, hung from the brass hooks. All the inside was painted in one plain tint of pale blue; two big sea-chests in sailcloth covers and with iron padlocks fitted exactly in the space under the bunk. One glance was enough to embrace all the strip of scrubbed planks within the four unconcealed corners. The absence of the usual settee was striking; the teak-wood top of the washing-stand seemed hermetically closed, and so was the lid of the writing-desk, which protruded from the partition at the foot of the bed-place, containing a mattress as thin as a pancake under a threadbare blanket with a faded red stripe, and a folded mosquito-net against the nights spent in harbour. There was not a scrap of paper anywhere in sight, no boots on the floor, no litter of any sort, not a speck of dust anywhere; no traces of pipe-ash even, which, in a heavy smoker, was morally revolting, like a manifestation of extreme hypocrisy; and the bottom of the old wooden armchair (the only seat there), polished with much use, shone as if its shabbiness had been waxed. The screen of leaves on the bank, passing as if unrolled endlessly in the round opening of the port, sent a wavering network of light and shade into the place.

Sterne, holding the door open with one hand, had thrust in his head and shoulders. At this amazing intrusion Massy, who was doing absolutely nothing, jumped up speechless.

'Don't call names,' murmured Sterne hurriedly. 'I won't be called names. I think of nothing but your good, Mr Massy.'

A pause as of extreme astonishment followed. They both seemed to have lost their tongues. Then the mate went on with discreet glibness.

'You simply couldn't conceive what's going on on board your ship. It wouldn't enter your head for a moment. You are too good – too – too upright, Mr Massy, to suspect anybody of such a. . . It's enough to make your hair stand on end.'

He watched for the effect: Massy seemed dazed, uncomprehending. He only passed the palm of his hand on the coal-black wisps plastered across the top of his head. In a tone suddenly changed to confidential audacity Sterne hastened on.

'Remember that there's only six weeks left to run. . .' The other was looking at him stonily . . . 'So anyhow you shall require a captain for the ship before long.'

Then only, as if that suggestion had scarified his flesh in the manner of red-hot iron, Massy gave a start and seemed ready to shriek. He contained himself by a great effort.

'Require – a – captain,' he repeated with scathing slowness. 'Who requires a captain? You dare tell me that I need any of you humbugging sailors to run my ship. You and your likes have been fattening on me for years. It would have hurt me less to throw my money overboard. Pam–pe–red us–e–less f–f–f–frauds. The old ship knows as much as the best of you.' He snapped his teeth audibly and growled through them. 'The silly law requires a captain.'

Sterne had taken heart of grace meantime.

'And the silly insurance people too, as well,' he said lightly. 'But never mind that. What I want to ask is: Why shouldn't *I* do, sir? I don't say but you could take a steamer about the world as well as any of us sailors. I don't pretend to tell *you* that it is a very great trick . . .' He emitted a short, hollow guffaw, familiarly . . . 'I didn't make the law – but there it is; and I am an active young fellow; I quite hold with your ideas; I know your ways by this time, Mr Massy. I wouldn't try to give myself airs like that – that – er – lazy specimen of an old man up there.'

He put a marked emphasis on the last sentence, to lead Massy away from the track in case . . . but he did not doubt of now holding his success. The chief engineer seemed nonplussed, like a slow man invited to catch hold of a whirligig of some sort.

'What you want, sir, is a chap with no nonsense about him, who would be content to be your sailing-master. Quite right too. Well, I am fit for the work as much as that Serang. Because that's what it amounts to. Do you know, sir, that a dam' Malay like a monkey is in charge of your ship – and no one else? Just listen to his feet pit-patting above us on the bridge – real officer in charge. He's taking her up the river while the great man is wallowing in the chair – perhaps asleep; and if he is, that would not make it much worse either – take my word for it.'

He tried to thrust himself farther in. Massy, with lowered forehead, one hand grasping the back of the armchair, did not budge.

'You think, sir, that the man has got you tight in his agreement . . .' Massy raised a heavy snarling face at this . . . 'Well, sir, one can't help hearing of it on board. It's no secret. And it has been the talk on shore for years; fellows have been making bets about it. No, sir! It's *you* who have got him at your mercy. You will say that you can't dismiss him for indolence. Difficult to prove in court, and so on. Why, yes. But if you say the word, sir, I can tell you something about his indolence that will give you the clear right to fire him out on the spot and put me in charge for the rest of this very trip – yes, sir, before we leave Batu Beru – and make him pay a dollar a day for his keep till we get back, if you like. Now, what do you think of that? Come, sir. Say the word. It's really well worth your while, and I am quite ready to take your bare word. A definite statement from you would be as good as a bond.'

His eyes began to shine. He insisted. A simple statement – and he thought to himself that he would manage somehow to stick in his berth as long as it suited him. He would make himself indispensable; the ship had a bad name in her port; it would be easy to scare the fellows off. Massy would have to keep him.

'A definite statement from me would be enough,' Massy repeated slowly.

'Yes, sir. It would.' Sterne stuck out his chin cheerily and blinked at close quarters with that unconscious impudence which had the power to enrage Massy beyond anything.

The engineer spoke very distinctly.

'Listen well to me, then, Mr Sterne: I wouldn't – d'ye hear? – I wouldn't promise you the value of twopence for anything *you* can tell me.'

He struck Sterne's arm away with a smart blow, and catching hold of the handle pulled the door to. The terrific slam darkened the cabin instantaneously to his eyes as if after the flash of an explosion. At once he dropped into the chair. 'Oh no! You don't!' he whispered faintly.

The ship had in that place to shave the bank so close that the gigantic wall of leaves came gliding like a shutter against the port; the darkness of the primeval forest seemed to flow into that bare cabin with the odour of rotting leaves, of sodden soil – the strong muddy smell of the living earth steaming uncovered after the passing of a deluge. The bushes swished loudly alongside; above there was a series of crackling sounds, with a sharp rain of small broken branches falling on the bridge; a creeper with a great rustle snapped on the head of a boat davit, and a long, luxuriant green twig actually whipped in and out of the open port, leaving behind a few torn leaves that remained suddenly at rest on Mr Massy's blanket. Then, the ship sheering out in the stream, the light began to return, but did not augment beyond a subdued clearness: for the sun was very low already, and the river, wending its sinuous course through a multitude of secular trees as if at the bottom of a precipitous gorge, had been already invaded by a deepening gloom – the swift precursor of the night.

'Oh no, you don't!' murmured the engineer again. His lips trembled almost imperceptibly; his hands too, a little: and to calm himself he opened the writing-desk, spread out a sheet of thin greyish paper covered with a mass of printed figures and began to scan them attentively for the twentieth time this trip at least.

With his elbows propped, his head between his hands, he seemed to lose himself in the study of an abstruse problem in mathematics. It was the list of the winning numbers from the last drawing of the great lottery which had been the one inspiring fact of so many years of his existence. The conception of a life deprived of that periodical sheet of paper had slipped away from him entirely, as another man, according to his nature, would not have been able to conceive a world without fresh air, without activity, or without affection. A great pile of flimsy sheets had been growing for years in his desk, while the *Sofala*, driven by the faithful Jack, wore out her boilers in tramping up and down the Straits, from cape to cape, from river to river, from bay to bay; accumulating by that hard labour of an overworked, starved ship the blackened mass of these documents. Massy kept them under lock and key like a treasure. There was in them, as in the experience of life, the fascination of hope, the excitement of a half-penetrated mystery, the longing of a half-satisfied desire.

For days together, on a trip, he would shut himself up in his berth with them: the thump of the toiling engines pulsated in his ear; and he would weary his brain poring over the rows of disconnected figures, bewildering by their senseless sequence, resembling the hazards of destiny itself. He nourished a conviction that there must be some logic lurking somewhere in the results of chance. He thought he had seen its very form. His head swam; his limbs ached; he puffed at his pipe mechanically; a contemplative stupor would soothe the fretfulness of his temper, like the passive bodily quietude procured by a drug, while the intellect remains tensely on the stretch. Nine, nine, nought, four, two. He made a note. The next winning number of the great prize was forty-seven thousand and five. These numbers of course would have to be avoided in the future when writing to Manilla for the tickets. He mumbled, pencil in hand . . . 'and five. Hm . . . hm.' He wetted his finger: the papers rustled. Ha! But what's this? Three years ago, in the September drawing, it was number nine, nought, four, two that took the first prize. Most remarkable. There was a hint there of a definite rule! He was afraid of missing some recondite principle in the overwhelming wealth of his material. What could it be? and for half an hour he would remain dead still, bent low over the desk, without twitching a muscle. At his back the whole berth would be thick with a heavy body of smoke, as if a bomb had burst in there, unnoticed, unheard.

At last he would lock up the desk with the decision of unshaken confidence, jump up and go out. He would walk swiftly back and forth on that part of the foredeck which was kept clear of the lumber and of the bodies of the native passengers. They were a great nuisance, but they were also a source of profit that could not be disdained. He needed every penny of profit the *Sofala* could make. Little enough it was, in all conscience! The incertitude of chance gave him no concern, since he had somehow arrived at the conviction that, in the course of years, every number was bound to have his winning turn. It was simply a matter of time and of taking as many tickets as he could afford for every drawing. He generally took rather more; all the earnings of the ship went that way, and also the wages he allowed himself as chief engineer. It was the wages he paid to others that he begrudged with a reasoned and at the same time a passionate regret. He scowled at the lascars with their deck brooms, at the quartermasters rubbing the brass rails with greasy rags; he was eager to shake his fist and roar abuse in bad Malay at the poor carpenter – a timid, sickly, opium-fuddled Chinaman, in loose blue drawers for all costume, who invariably dropped his tools and fled below, with streaming tail and shaking all over, before the fury of that 'devil'. But it was when he raised up his eyes to the bridge where one of these sailor frauds was always planted by law in charge of his ship that he felt almost dizzy with rage. He abominated them all; it was an old feud, from the time he first went to sea, an unlicked cub with a great opinion of himself, in the engine-room. The slights that had been put upon him. The persecutions he had suffered at the hands of skippers – of absolute nobodies in a steamship after all. And now that he had risen to be a shipowner they were still a plague to him: he had absolutely to pay away precious money to the conceited useless loafers. As if a fully qualified engineer – who was the owner as well – were not fit to be trusted with the whole charge of a ship. Well! he made it pretty warm for them; but it was a poor consolation. He had come in time to hate the ship too for the repairs she required, for the coal-bills he had to pay, for the poor beggarly freights she earned. He would clench his hand as he walked and hit the rail a sudden blow, viciously, as though she could be made to feel pain. And yet he could not do without her; he needed her; he must hang on to her tooth and nail to keep his head above water till the expected flood of fortune came sweeping up and landed him safely on the high shore of his ambition.

It was now to do nothing, nothing whatever, and have plenty of money to do it on. He had tasted of power, the highest form of it his limited experience was aware of – the power of shipowning. What a deception! Vanity of vanities! He wondered at his folly. He had thrown away the substance for the shadow. Of the gratification of wealth he did not know enough to excite his imagination with any visions of luxury. How could he – the child of a drunken boiler-maker – going straight from the workshop into the engine-room of a north-country collier! But the notion of the absolute idleness of wealth he could very well conceive. He revelled in it, to forget his present troubles; he imagined himself walking about the streets of Hull (he knew their gutters well as a boy) with his pockets full of sovereigns. He would buy himself a house; his married sisters, their husbands, his old workshop chums, would render him infinite homage. There would be nothing to think of. His word would be law. He had been out of work for a long time before he won his prize, and he remembered how Carlo Mariani (commonly known as Paunchy Charley), the Maltese hotel-keeper at the slummy end of Denham Street, had cringed joyfully before him in the evening, when the news had come. Poor Charley, though he made his living by ministering to various abject vices, gave credit for their food to many a piece of white wreckage. He was naïvely overjoyed at the idea of his old bills being paid, and he reckoned confidently on a spell of festivities in the cavernous grog-shop downstairs. Massy remembered the curious, respectful looks of the 'trashy' white men in the place. His heart had swelled within him. Massy had left Charley's infamous den directly he had realised the possibilities open to him, with his nose in the air. Afterwards the memory of these adulations was a great sadness.

This was the true power of money – and no trouble with it, nor any thinking required either. He thought with difficulty and felt vividly; to his blunt brain the problems offered by any ordered scheme of life seemed in their cruel toughness to have been put in his way by the obvious malevolence of men. As a shipowner everyone had conspired to make him a nobody. How could he have been such a fool as to purchase that accursed ship? He had been abominably swindled; there was no end to this swindling; and as the difficulties of his improvident ambition gathered thicker round him, he really came to hate everybody he had ever come in contact with. A temper naturally irritable and an amazing sensitiveness to the claims of his own personality had ended by making of life for him a sort of inferno – a place where his lost soul had been given up to the torment of savage brooding.

But he had never hated anyone so much as that old man who turned up one evening to save him from an utter disaster – from the conspiracy of the wretched sailors. He seemed to have fallen on board from the sky. His footsteps echoed on the empty steamer, and the strange deep-toned voice on deck repeating interrogatively the words, 'Mr Massy, Mr Massy there?' had been startling like a wonder. And coming up from the depths of the cold engine-room, where he had been pottering dismally with a candle amongst the enormous shadows, thrown on all sides by the skeleton limbs of machinery,

Massy had been struck dumb by astonishment in the presence of that imposing old man with a beard like a silver plate, towering in the dusk rendered lurid by the expiring flames of sunset.

'Want to see me on business? What business? I am doing no business. Can't you see that this ship is laid up?' Massy had turned at bay before the pursuing irony of his disaster. Afterwards he could not believe his ears. What was that old fellow getting at? Things don't happen that way. It was a dream. He would presently wake up and find the man vanished like a shape of mist. The gravity, the dignity, the firm and courteous tone of that athletic old stranger impressed Massy. He was almost afraid. But it was no dream. Five hundreds pounds are no dream. At once he became suspicious. What did it mean? Of course it was an offer to catch hold of for dear life. But what could there be behind?

Before they had parted, after appointing a meeting in a solicitor's office early on the morrow, Massy was asking himself, What is his motive? He spent the night in hammering out the clauses of the agreement – a unique instrument of its sort whose tenor got bruited abroad somehow and became the talk and wonder of the port.

Massy's object had been to secure for himself as many ways as possible of getting rid of his partner without being called upon at once to pay back his share. Captain Whalley's efforts were directed to making the money secure. Was it not Ivy's money – a part of her fortune whose only other asset was the time-defying body of her old father? Sure of his forbearance in the strength of his love for her, he accepted, with stately serenity, Massy's stupidly cunning paragraphs against his incompetence, his dishonesty, his drunkenness, for the sake of other stringent stipulations. At the end of three years he was at liberty to withdraw from the partnership, taking his money with him. Provision was made for forming a fund to pay him off. But if he left the *Sofala* before the term, from whatever cause (barring death), Massy was to have a whole year for paying. 'Illness?' the lawyer had suggested: a young man fresh from Europe and not overburdened with business, who was rather amused. Massy began to whine unctuously, 'How could he be expected? . . .'

'Let that go,' Captain Whalley had said with a superb confidence in his body. 'Acts of God,' he added. In the midst of life we are in death, but he trusted his Maker with a still greater fearlessness – his Maker who knew his thoughts, his human affections, and his motives. His Creator knew what use he was making of his health – how much he wanted it . . . 'I trust my first illness will be my last. I've never been ill that I can remember,' he had remarked. 'Let it go.'

But at this early stage he had already awakened Massy's hostility by refusing to make it six hundred instead of five. 'I cannot do that,' was all he had said, simply, but with so much decision that Massy desisted at once from pressing the point, but had thought to himself, 'Can't! Old curmudgeon.

Won't! He must have lots of money, but he would like to get hold of a soft berth and the sixth part of my profits for nothing if he only could.'

And during these years Massy's dislike grew under the restraint of something resembling fear.

The simplicity of that man appeared dangerous. Of late he had changed, however, had appeared less formidable and with a lessened vigour of life, as though he had received a secret wound. But still he remained incomprehensible in his simplicity, fearlessness, and rectitude. And when Massy learned that he meant to leave him at the end of the time, to leave him confronted with the problem of the boilers, his dislike blazed up secretly into hate.

It had made him so clear-eyed that for a long time now Mr Sterne could have told him nothing he did not know. He had much ado in trying to terrorise that mean sneak into silence; he wanted to deal alone with the situation; and – incredible as it might have appeared to Mr Sterne – he had not yet given up the desire and the hope of inducing that hated old man to stay. Why! there was nothing else to do, unless he were to abandon his chances of fortune. But now, suddenly, since the crossing of the bar at Batu Beru things seemed to be coming rapidly to a point. It disquieted him so much that the study of the winning numbers failed to soothe his agitation: and the twilight in the cabin deepened, very sombre.

He put the list away, muttering once more, 'Oh no, my boy, you don't. Not if I know it.' He did not mean the blinking, eavesdropping humbug to force his action. He took his head again into his hands; his immobility confined in the darkness of this shut-up little place seemed to make him a thing apart infinitely removed from the stir and the sounds of the deck.

He heard them: the passengers were beginning to jabber excitedly; somebody dragged a heavy box past his door. He heard Captain Whalley's voice above – 'Stations, Mr Sterne.' And the answer from somewhere on deck forward – 'Ay, ay, sir,'

'We shall moor head up stream this time; the ebb has made.'

'Head up stream, sir.'

'You will see to it, Mr Sterne.'

The answer was covered by the autocratic clang of the engine-room gong. The propeller went on beating slowly: one, two, three; one, two, three – with pauses as if hesitating on the turn. The gong clanged time after time, and the water churned this way and that by the blades was making a great noisy commotion alongside. Mr Massy did not move. A shore-light on the other bank, a quarter of a mile across the river, drifted, no bigger than a tiny star, passing slowly athwart the circle of the port. Voices from Mr Van Wyk's jetty answered the hails from the ship; ropes were thrown and missed and thrown again; the swaying flame of a torch carried in a large sampan coming to fetch away in state the Rajah from down the coast cast a sudden ruddy glare into his cabin, over his very person. Mr Massy did not move. After a few last ponderous turns the engines stopped, and the prolonged clanging of the gong signified that the captain had done with them. A great number of boats and canoes of all sizes boarded the off-side of the *Sofala*. Then after a time the tumult of splashing, of cries, of shuffling feet, of packages dropped with a thump, the noise of the native passengers going away, subsided slowly. On the shore, a voice, cultivated, slightly authoritative, spoke very close alongside – 'Brought any mail for me this time?'

'Yes, Mr Van Wyk.' This was from Sterne, answering over the rail in a tone of respectful cordiality. 'Shall I bring it up to you?'

But the voice asked again – 'Where's the captain?'

'Still on the bridge, I believe. He hasn't left his chair. Shall I . . .'

The voice interrupted negligently – 'I will come on board.'

'Mr Van Wyk,' Sterne suddenly broke out with an eager effort, 'will you do me the favour . . .'

The mate walked away quickly towards the gangway. A silence fell. Mr Massy in the dark did not move.

He did not move even when he heard slow shuffling footsteps pass his cabin lazily. He contented himself to bellow out through the closed door – 'You – Jack!'

The footsteps came back without haste; the door-handle rattled, and the second engineer appeared in the opening, shadowy in the sheen of the skylight at his back, with his face apparently as black as the rest of his figure.

'We have been very long coming up this time,' Mr Massy growled, without changing his attitude.

'What do you expect with half the boiler tubes plugged up for leaks.' The second defended himself loquaciously.

'None of your lip,' said Massy.

'None of your rotten boilers – I say,' retorted his faithful subordinate without animation, huskily. 'Go down there and carry a head of steam on them yourself – if you dare. I don't.'

'You aren't worth your salt then,' Massy said. The other made a faint noise which resembled a laugh but might have been a snarl.

'Better go slow than stop the ship altogether,' he admonished his admired superior. Mr Massy moved at last. He turned in his chair, and grinding his teeth – 'Dam' you and the ship! I wish she were at the bottom of the sea. Then you would have to starve.'

The trusty second engineer closed the door gently.

Massy listened. Instead of passing on to the bathroom where he should have gone to clean himself, the second entered his cabin, which was next door. Mr Massy jumped up and waited. Suddenly he heard the lock snap in there. He rushed out and gave a violent kick to the door.

'I believe you are locking yourself up to get drunk,' he shouted.

A muffled answer came after a while.

'My own time.'

'If you take to boozing on the trip I'll fire you out,' Massy cried.

An obstinate silence followed that threat. Massy moved away perplexed. On the bank two figures appeared, approaching the gangway. He heard a voice tinged with contempt – 'I would rather doubt your word. But I shall certainly speak to him of this.'

The other voice, Sterne's, said with a sort of regretful formality – 'Thanks. That's all I want. I must do my duty.'

Mr Massy was surprised. A short, dapper figure leaped lightly on the deck and nearly bounded into him where he stood beyond the circle of light from the gangway lamp. When it had passed towards the bridge, after exchanging a hurried 'Good-evening,' Massy said surlily to Sterne, who followed with slow steps – 'What is it you're making up to Mr Van Wyk for, now?'

'Far from it, Mr Massy. I am not good enough for Mr Van Wyk. Neither are you, sir, in his opinion, I am afraid. Captain Whalley is, it seems. He's gone to ask him to dine up at the house this evening.'

Then he murmured to himself darkly – 'I hope he will like it.'

12

Mr Van Wyk, the white man of Batu Beru, an ex-naval officer who, for reasons best known to himself, had thrown away the promise of a brilliant career to become the pioneer of tobacco-planting on that remote part of the coast, had learned to like Captain Whalley. The appearance of the new skipper had attracted his attention. Nothing more unlike all the diverse types he had seen succeeding each other on the bridge of the *Sofala* could be imagined.

At that time Batu Beru was not what it has become since: the centre of a prosperous tobacco-growing district, a tropically suburban-looking little settlement of bungalows in one long street shaded with two rows of trees, embowered by the flowering and trim luxuriance of the gardens, with a three-mile-long carriage-road for the afternoon drives and a first-class Resident with a fat, cheery wife to lead the society of married estate-managers and unmarried young fellows in the service of the big companies.

All this prosperity was not yet; and Mr Van Wyk prospered alone on the left bank on his deep clearing carved out of the forest, which came down above and below to the water's edge. His lonely bungalow faced across the river the houses of the Sultàn: a restless and melancholy old ruler who had done with love and war, for whom life no longer held any savour (except of evil forebodings) and time never had any value. He was afraid of death, and hoped he would die before the white men were ready to take his country from him. He crossed the river frequently (with never less than ten boats crammed full of people), in the wistful hope of extracting some information on the subject from his own white man. There was a certain chair on the verandah he always took: the dignitaries of the court squatted on the rugs and skins between the furniture: the inferior people remained below on the grass-plot between the house and the river in rows three or four deep all along the front. Not seldom the visit began at daybreak. Mr Van Wyk tolerated these inroads. He would nod out of his bedroom window, toothbrush or razor in hand, or pass through the throng of courtiers in his bathing robe. He appeared and disappeared humming a tune, polished his nails with attention, rubbed his shaved face with eau-de-Cologne, drank his early tea, went out to see his coolies at work: returned, looked through some papers on his desk, read a page or two in a book or sat before his cottage piano leaning back on the stool, his arms extended, fingers on the keys, his body swaying slightly from side to side. When absolutely forced to speak he gave evasive vaguely soothing answers out of pure compassion: the same feeling perhaps made him so lavishly hospitable with the aerated drinks that more than once he left himself without soda-water for a whole week. That old man had granted him as much land as he cared to have cleared: it was neither more nor less than a fortune.

Whether it was fortune or seclusion from his kind that Mr Van Wyk sought, he could not have pitched upon a better place. Even the mail-boats of the subsidised company calling on the veriest clusters of palm-thatched hovels along the coast steamed past the mouth of Batu Beru river far away in the offing. The contract was old: perhaps in a few years' time, when it had expired, Batu Beru would be included in the service; meantime all Mr Van Wyk's mail was addressed to Malacca, whence his agent sent it across once a month by the *Sofala* . It followed that whenever Massy had run short of money (through taking too many lottery tickets), or got into a difficulty about a skipper, Mr Van Wyk was deprived of his letters and newspapers. In so far he had a personal interest in the fortunes of the *Sofala*. Though he considered himself a hermit (and for no passing whim evidently, since he had stood eight years of it already), he liked to know what went on in the world.

Handy on the verandah upon a walnut *étagère* (it had come last year by the *Sofala* – everything came by the *Sofala*) there lay, piled up under bronze weights, a pile of *The Times* weekly edition, the large sheets of the *Rotterdam Courant*, the *Graphic* in its world-wide green wrappers, an illustrated Dutch publication without a cover, the numbers of a German magazine with covers of the 'Bismarck malade' colour. There were also parcels of new music – though the piano (it had come years ago by the *Sofala*) in the damp atmosphere of the forests was generally out of tune. It was vexing to be cut off from everything for sixty days at a stretch sometimes, without any means of knowing what was the matter. And when the *Sofala* reappeared Mr Van Wyk would descend the steps of the verandah and stroll over the grass-plot in front of his house, down to the water-side, with a frown on his white brow.

'You've been laid up after an accident, I presume.'

He addressed the bridge, but before anybody could answer Massy was sure to have already scrambled ashore over the rail and pushed in, squeezing the palms of his hands together, bowing his sleek head as if gummed all over the top with black threads and tapes. And he would be so enraged at the necessity of having to offer such an explanation that his moaning would be positively pitiful while all the time he tried to compose his big lips into a smile.

'No, Mr Van Wyk. You would not believe it. I couldn't get one of those wretches to take the ship out. Not a single one of the lazy beasts could be induced, and the law, you know, Mr Van Wyk . . .'

He moaned at great length apologetically; the words conspiracy, plot, envy, came out prominently, whined with greater energy. Mr Van Wyk, examining with a faint grimace his polished fingernails, would say, 'H'm. Very unfortunate,' and turn his back on him.

Fastidious, clever, slightly sceptical, accustomed to the best society (he had held a much-envied shore appointment at the Ministry of Marine for a year preceding his retreat from his profession and from Europe), he possessed a latent warmth of feeling and a capacity for sympathy which were concealed by a sort of haughty, arbitrary indifference of manner arising from his early training; and by a something an enemy might have called foppish, in his aspect – like a distorted echo of past elegancies. He managed to keep an almost military discipline amongst the coolies of the estate he had dragged into the light of day out of the tangle and shadows of the jungle; and the white shirt he put on every evening with its stiff glossy front and high collar looked as if he had meant to preserve the decent ceremony of evening-dress, but had wound a thick crimson sash above his hips as a concession to the wilderness, once his adversary, now his vanquished companion. Moreover, it was a hygienic precaution. Worn wide open in front, a short jacket of some airy silken stuff floated from his shoulders. His fluffy, fair hair, thin at the top, curled slightly at the sides; a carefully arranged moustache, an ungarnished forehead, the gleam of low patent shoes peeping under the wide bottom of trousers cut straight from the same stuff as the gossamer coat, completed a figure recalling, with its sash, a pirate chief of romance, and at the same time the elegance of a slightly bald dandy indulging, in seclusion, a taste for unorthodox costume.

It was his evening get-up. The proper time for the *Sofala* to arrive at Batu Beru was an hour before sunset, and he looked picturesque, and somehow quite correct too, walking at the water's edge on the background of grass slope crowned with a low long bungalow with an immensely steep roof of palm thatch, and clad to the eaves in flowering creepers. While the *Sofala* was being made fast he strolled in the shade of the few trees left near the landing-place, waiting till he could go on board. Her white men were not of his kind. The old Sultan (though his wistful invasions were a nuisance) was really much more acceptable to his fastidious taste. But still they were white; the periodical visits of the ship made a break in the well-filled sameness of the days without disturbing his privacy. Moreover, they were necessary from a business point of view; and through a strain of preciseness in his nature he was irritated when she failed to appear at the appointed time.

The cause of the irregularity was too absurd, and Massy, in his opinion, was a contemptible idiot. The first time the *Sofala* reappeared under the new agreement swinging out of the bend below, after he had almost given up all hope of ever seeing her again, he felt so angry that he did not go down at once to the landing-place. His servants had come running to him with the news, and he had dragged a chair close against the front rail of the verandah, spread his elbows out, rested his chin on his hands, and went on glaring at her fixedly while she was being made fast opposite his house. He could make out easily all the white faces on board. Who on earth was that kind of patriarch they had got there on the bridge now?

At last he sprang up and walked down the gravel path. It was a fact that the very gravel for his paths had been imported by the *Sofala*. Exasperated out of his quiet superciliousness, without looking at anyone right or left, he accosted Massy straightway in so determined a manner that the engineer, taken aback, began to stammer unintelligibly. Nothing could be heard but the words: 'Mr Van Wyk . . . Indeed, Mr Van Wyk . . . For the future, Mr Van Wyk' – and by the suffusion of blood Massy's vast bilious face acquired an unnatural orange tint, out of which the disconcerted coal-black eyes shone in an extraordinary manner.

'Nonsense. I am tired of this. I wonder you have the impudence to come alongside my jetty as if I had it made for your convenience alone.'

Massy tried to protest earnestly. Mr Van Wyk was very angry. He had a good mind to ask that German firm – those people in Malacca – what was their name? – boats with green funnels. They would be only too glad of the opening to put one of their small steamers on the run. Yes; Schnitzler, Jacob Schnitzler, would in a moment. Yes. He had decided to write without delay.

In his agitation Massy caught up his falling pipe.

'You don't mean it, sir!' he shrieked.

'You shouldn't mismanage your business in this ridiculous manner.'

Mr Van Wyk turned on his heel. The other three whites on the bridge had not stirred during the scene. Massy walked hastily from side to side, puffed out his cheeks, suffocated.

'Stuck-up Dutchman!'

And he moaned out feverishly a long tale of griefs. The efforts he had made for all these years to please that man. This was the return you got for it, eh? Pretty. Write to Schnitzler – let in the green-funnel boats – get an old Hamburg Jew to ruin him. No, really he could laugh . . . He laughed sobbingly . . . Ha! ha! ha! And make him carry the letters in his own ship presumably.

He stumbled across a grating and swore. He would not hesitate to fling the Dutchman's correspondence overboard – the whole confounded bundle.

He had never, never made any charge for that accommodation. But Captain Whalley, his new partner, would not let him probably; besides, it would be only putting off the evil day. For his own part he would make a hole in the water rather than look on tamely at the green funnels overrunning his trade.

He raved aloud. The China boys hung back with the dishes at the foot of the ladder. He yelled from the bridge down at the deck, 'Aren't we going to have any chow this evening at all?' then turned violently to Captain Whalley, who waited, grave and patient, at the head of the table, smoothing his beard in silence now and then with a forbearing gesture.

'You don't seem to care what happens to me. Don't you see that this affects your interests as much as mine? It's no joking matter.'

He took the foot of the table growling between his teeth.

'Unless you have a few thousands put away somewhere. I haven't.'

Mr Van Wyk dined in his thoroughly lit-up bungalow, putting a point of splendour in the night of his clearing above the dark bank of the river. Afterwards he sat down to his piano, and in a pause he became aware of slow footsteps passing on the path along the front. A plank or two creaked under a heavy tread; he swung half round on the music-stool, listening with his fingertips at rest on the keyboard. His little terrier barked violently, backing in from the verandah. A deep voice apologised gravely for 'this intrusion'. He walked out quickly.

At the head of the steps the patriarchal figure, who was the new captain of the *Sofala* apparently (he had seen a round dozen of them, but not one of that sort), towered without advancing. The little dog barked unceasingly, till a flick of Mr Van Wyk's handkerchief made him spring aside into silence. Captain Whalley, opening the matter, was met by a punctiliously polite but determined opposition.

They carried on their discussion standing where they had come face to face. Mr Van Wyk observed his visitor with attention. Then at last, as if forced out of his reserve – 'I am surprised that you should intercede for such a confounded fool.'

This outbreak was almost complimentary, as if its meaning had been, 'That such a man as you should intercede! 'Captain Whalley let it pass by without flinching. One would have thought he had heard nothing. He simply went on to state that he was personally interested in putting things straight between them. Personally . . .

But Mr Van Wyk, really carried away by his disgust with Massy, became very incisive – 'Indeed – if I am to be frank with you – his whole character does not seem to me particularly estimable or trustworthy . . . '

Captain Whalley, always straight, seemed to grow an inch taller and broader, as if the girth of his chest had suddenly expanded under his beard.

'My dear sir, you don't think I came here to discuss a man with whom I am – I am – h'm – closely associated.'

A sort of solemn silence lasted for a moment. He was not used to asking favours, but the importance he attached to this affair had made him willing to try . . . Mr Van Wyk, favourably impressed, and suddenly mollified by a desire to laugh, interrupted – 'That's all right if you make it a personal matter; but you can do no less than sit down and smoke a cigar with me.'

A slight pause, then Captain Whalley stepped forward heavily. As to the regularity of the service, for the future he made himself responsible for it; and his name was Whalley – perhaps to a sailor (he was speaking to a sailor, was he not?) not altogether unfamiliar. There was a lighthouse now, on an island. Maybe Mr Van Wyk himself . . .

'Oh yes. Oh indeed.' Mr Van Wyk caught on at once. He indicated a chair. How very interesting. For his own part he had seen some service in the last Acheen War, but had never been so far East. Whalley Island? Of course. Now that was very interesting. What changes his guest must have seen since.

'I can look further back even – on a whole half-century.'

Captain Whalley expanded a bit. The flavour of a good cigar (it was a weakness) had gone straight to his heart, also the civility of that young man. There was something in that accidental contact of which he had been starved in his years of struggle.

The front wall retreating made a square recess furnished like a room. A lamp with a milky glass shade, suspended below the slope of the high roof at the end of a slender brass chain, threw a bright round of light upon a little table bearing an open book and an ivory paper-knife. And, in the translucent shadows beyond, other tables could be seen, a number of easy-chairs of various shapes, with a great profusion of skin rugs strewn on the teak-wood planking all over the verandah. The flowering creepers scented the air. Their foliage clipped out between the uprights made as if several frames of thick unstirring leaves reflecting the lamplight in a green glow. Through the opening at his elbow Captain Whalley could see the gangway lantern of the *Sofala* burning dim by the shore, the shadowy masses of the town beyond the open lustrous darkness of the river, and, as if hung along the straight edge of the projecting eaves, a narrow black strip of the night sky full of stars – resplendent. The famous cigar in hand he had a moment of complacency.

'A trifle. Somebody must lead the way. I just showed that the thing could be done; but you men brought up to the use of steam cannot conceive the vast importance of my bit of venturesomeness to the Eastern trade of the time. Why, that new route reduced the average time of a southern passage by eleven days for more than half the year. Eleven days! It's on record. But the remarkable thing – speaking to a sailor – I should say was . . . '

He talked well, without egotism, professionally. The powerful voice, produced without effort, filled the bungalow even into the empty rooms with a deep and limpid resonance, seemed to make a stillness outside; and Mr Van Wyk was surprised by the serene quality of its tone, like the perfection of manly gentleness. Nursing one small foot, in a silk sock and a patent leather shoe, on his knee, he was immensely entertained. It was as if nobody could talk like this now, and the overshadowed eyes, the flowing white beard, the big frame, the serenity, the whole temper of the man, were an amazing survival from the prehistoric times of the world coming up to him out of the sea.

Captain Whalley had been also the pioneer of the early trade in the Gulf of Pe-tchi-li. He even found occasion to mention that he had buried his 'dear wife' there six-and-twenty years ago. Mr Van Wyk, impassive, could not help speculating in his mind swiftly as to the sort of woman that would mate with such a man. Did they make an adventurous and well-matched pair? No. Very possibly she had been small, frail, no doubt very feminine – or most likely commonplace with domestic instincts, utterly insignificant. But Captain Whalley was no garrulous bore, and shaking his head as if to dissipate the momentary gloom that had settled on his handsome old face, he alluded conversationally to Mr Van Wyk's solitude.

Mr Van Wyk affirmed that sometimes he had more company than he wanted. He mentioned smilingly some of the peculiarities of his intercourse with 'My Sultan'. He made his visits in force. Those people damaged his grass-plot in front (it was not easy to obtain some approach to a lawn in the tropics), and the other day had broken down some rare bushes he had planted over there. And Captain Whalley remembered immediately that, in 'forty-seven, the then Sultan, 'this man's grandfather', had been notorious as a great protector of the piratical fleets of praus from farther East. They had a safe refuge in the river at Batu Beru. He financed more especially a Balinini chief called Haji Daman. Captain Whalley, nodding significantly his bushy white eyebrows, had very good reason to know something of that. The world had progressed since that time.

Mr Van Wyk demurred with unexpected acrimony. Progressed in what? he wanted to know.

Why, in knowledge of truth, in decency, in justice, in order – in honesty too, since men harmed each other mostly from ignorance. It was, Captain Whalley concluded quaintly, more pleasant to live in.

Mr Van Wyk whimsically would not admit that Mr Massy, for instance, was more pleasant naturally than the Balinini pirates.

The river had not gained much by the change. They were in their way every bit as honest. Massy was less ferocious than Haji Daman no doubt, but . . .

'And what about you, my good sir?' Captain Whalley laughed a deep soft laugh. '*You* are an improvement, surely.'

He continued in a vein of pleasantry. A good cigar was better than a knock on the head – the sort of welcome he would have found on this river forty or fifty years ago. Then leaning forward slightly, he became earnestly serious. It seems as if, outside their own sea-gypsy tribes, these rovers had hated all mankind with an incomprehensible, bloodthirsty hatred. Meantime their depredations had been stopped, and what was the consequence? The new generation was orderly, peaceable, settled in prosperous villages. He could speak from personal knowledge. And even the few survivors of that time – old men now – had changed so much, that it would have been unkind to remember against them that they had ever slit a throat in their lives. He had one especially in his mind's eye: a dignified, venerable headman of a certain large coast village about sixty miles sou'west of Tampasuk. It did one's heart good to see him, to hear that man speak. He might have been a ferocious savage once. What men wanted was to be checked by superior intelligence, by superior knowledge, by superior force too – yes, by force held in trust from God and sanctified by its use in accordance with His declared will. Captain Whalley believed a disposition for good existed in every man, even if the world were not a very happy place as a whole. In the wisdom of men he had not so much confidence. The disposition had to be helped up pretty sharply sometimes, he admitted. They might be silly, wrong-headed, unhappy; but naturally evil – no. There was at bottom a complete harmlessness at least . . .

'Is there?' Mr Van Wyk snapped acrimoniously.

Captain Whalley laughed at the interjection, in the good humour of large, tolerating certitude. He could look back at half a century, he pointed out. The smoke oozed placidly through the white hairs hiding his kindly lips.

'At all events,' he resumed after a pause, 'I am glad that they've had no time to do you much harm as yet.'

This allusion to his comparative youthfulness did not offend Mr Van Wyk, who got up and wriggled his shoulders with an enigmatic half-smile. They walked out together amicably into the starry night towards the riverside. Their footsteps resounded unequally on the dark path. At the shore end of the gangway the lantern, hung low to the handrail, threw a vivid light on the white legs and the big black feet of Mr Massy waiting about anxiously. From the waist upwards he remained shadowy, with a row of buttons gleaming up to the vague outline of his chin.

'You may thank Captain Whalley for this,' Mr Van Wyk said curtly to him before turning away.

The lamps on the verandah flung three long squares of light between the uprights far over the grass. A bat flitted before his face like a circling flake of velvety blackness. Along the jasmine hedge the night air seemed heavy with the fall of perfumed dew; flower-beds bordered the path; the clipped bushes uprose in dark rounded clumps here and there before the house; the dense foliage of creepers filtered the sheen of the lamplight within in a soft glow all along the front; and everything near and far stood still in a great immobility, in a great sweetness.

Mr Van Wyk (a few years before he had had occasion to imagine himself treated more badly than anybody alive had ever been by a woman) felt for Captain Whalley's optimistic views the disdain of a man who had once been credulous himself. His disgust with the world (the woman for a time had filled it for him completely) had taken the form of activity in retirement, because, though capable of great depth of feeling, he was energetic and essentially practical. But there was in that uncommon old sailor, drifting on the outskirts of his busy solitude, something that fascinated his scepticism. His very simplicity (amusing enough) was like a delicate refinement of an upright character. The striking dignity of manner could be nothing else, in a man reduced to such a humble position, but the expression of something essentially noble in the character. With all his trust in mankind he was no fool; the serenity of his temper at the end of so many years, since it could not obviously have been appeased by success, wore an air of profound wisdom. Mr Van Wyk was amused at it sometimes. Even the very physical traits of the old captain of the *Sofala*, his powerful frame, his reposeful mien, his intelligent, handsome face, the big limbs, the benign courtesy, the touch of rugged severity in the shaggy eyebrows, made up a seductive personality. Mr Van Wyk disliked littleness of every kind, but there was nothing small about that man, and in the exemplary regularity of many trips an intimacy had grown up between them, a warm feeling at bottom under a kindly stateliness of forms agreeable to his fastidiousness.

They kept their respective opinions on all worldly matters. His other convictions Captain Whalley never intruded. The difference of their ages was like another bond between them. Once, when twitted with the un-charitableness of his youth, Mr Van Wyk, running his eye over the vast proportions of his interlocutor, retorted in friendly banter – 'Oh. You'll come to my way of thinking yet. You'll have plenty of time. Don't call yourself old: you look good for a round hundred.'

But he could not help his stinging incisiveness, and though moderating it by an almost affectionate smile, he added – 'And by then you will probably consent to die from sheer disgust.'

Captain Whalley, smiling too, shook his head. 'God forbid!'

He thought that perhaps on the whole he deserved something better than to die in such sentiments. The time of course would have to come, and he trusted to his Maker to provide a manner of going out of which he need not be ashamed. For the rest he hoped he would live to a hundred if need be: other men had been known; it would be no miracle. He expected no miracles.

The pronounced, argumentative tone caused Mr Van Wyk to raise his head and look at him steadily. Captain Whalley was gazing fixedly with a rapt expression, as though he had seen his Creator's favourable decree written in mysterious characters on the wall. He kept perfectly motionless for a few seconds, then got his vast bulk on to his feet so impetuously that Mr Van Wyk was startled.

He struck first a heavy blow on his inflated chest: and, throwing out horizontally a big arm that remained steady, extended in the air like the limb of a tree on a windless day – 'Not a pain or an ache there. Can you see this shake in the least?'

His voice was low, in an awing, confident contrast with the headlong emphasis of his movements. He sat down abruptly.

'This isn't to boast of it, you know. I am nothing,' he said in his effortless strong voice, that seemed to come out as naturally as a river flows. He picked up the stump of the cigar he had laid aside, and added peacefully, with a slight nod, 'As it happens, my life is necessary; it isn't my own, it isn't – God knows.'

He did not say much for the rest of the evening, but several times Mr Van Wyk detected a faint smile of assurance flitting under the heavy moustache.

Later on Captain Whalley would now and then consent to dine 'at the house'. He could even be induced to drink a glass of wine. 'Don't think I am afraid of it, my good sir,' he explained. 'There was a very good reason why I should give it up.'

On another occasion, leaning back at ease, he remarked, 'You have treated me most – most humanely, my dear Mr Van Wyk; from the very first.'

'You'll admit there was some merit,' Mr Van Wyk hinted slily. 'An associate of that excellent Massy . . . Well, well, my dear captain, I won't say a word against him.'

'It would be no use your saying anything against him,' Captain Whalley affirmed a little moodily. 'As I've told you before, my life – my work, is necessary, not for myself alone. I can't choose.' . . . He paused, turned the glass before him right round . . . 'I have an only child – a daughter.'

The ample downward sweep of his arm over the table seemed to suggest a small girl at a vast distance. 'I hope to see her once more before I die. Meantime it's enough to know that she has me sound and solid, thank God. You can't understand how one feels. Bone of my bone, flesh of my flesh; the very image of my poor wife. Well, she . . .'

Again he paused, then pronounced stoically the words, 'She has a hard struggle.'

And his head fell on his breast, his eyebrows remained knitted, as by an effort of meditation. But generally his mind seemed steeped in the serenity of boundless trust in a higher power. Mr Van Wyk wondered sometimes how much of it was due to the splendid vitality of the man, to the bodily vigour which seems to impart something of its force to the soul. But he had learned to like him very much.

13

This was the reason why Mr Sterne's confidential communication, delivered hurriedly on the shore alongside the dark silent ship, had disturbed his equanimity. It was the most incomprehensible and unexpected thing that could happen; and the perturbation of his spirit was so great that, forgetting all about his letters, he ran rapidly up the bridge ladder.

The portable table was being put together for dinner to the left of the wheel by two pig-tailed 'boys', who as usual snarled at each other over the job, while another, a doleful, burly, very yellow Chinaman, resembling Mr Massy, waited apathetically with the cloth over his arm and a pile of thick dinner-plates against his chest. A common cabin lamp with its globe missing, brought up from below, had been hooked to the wooden framework of the awning; the side-screens had been lowered all round; Captain Whalley filling the depths of the wicker-chair seemed to sit benumbed in a canvas tent crudely lighted, and used for the storing of nautical objects; a shabby steering-wheel, a battered brass binnacle on a stout mahogany stand, two dingy life-buoys, an old cork fender lying in a corner, dilapidated deck-lockers with loops of thin rope instead of door-handles.

He shook off the appearance of numbness to return Mr Van Wyk's unusually brisk greeting, but relapsed directly afterwards. To accept a pressing invitation to dinner 'up at the house' cost him another very visible physical effort. Mr Van Wyk, perplexed, folded his arms, and leaning back against the rail, with his little, black, shiny feet well out, examined him covertly.

'I've noticed of late that you are not quite yourself, old friend.'

He put an affectionate gentleness into the last two words. The real intimacy of their intercourse had never been so vividly expressed before.

'Tut, tut, tut!'

The wicker-chair creaked heavily.

'Irritable,' commented Mr Van Wyk to himself; and aloud, 'I'll expect to see you in half an hour then,' he said negligently, moving off.

'In half an hour,' Captain Whalley's rigid silvery head repeated behind him as if out of a trance.

Amidships, below, two voices, close against the engine-room, could be heard answering each other – one angry and slow, the other alert.

'I tell you the beast has locked himself in to get drunk.'

'Can't help it now, Mr Massy. After all, a man has a right to shut himself up in his cabin in his own time.'

'Not to get drunk.'

'I heard him swear that the worry with the boilers was enough to drive any man to drink,' Sterne said maliciously.

Massy hissed out something about bursting the door in. Mr Van Wyk, to avoid them, crossed in the dark to the other side of the deserted deck. The planking of the little wharf rattled faintly under his hasty feet.

'Mr Van Wyk! Mr Van Wyk!'

He walked on: somebody was running on the path. 'You've forgotten to get your mail.'

Sterne, holding a bundle of papers in his hand, caught up with him.

'Oh, thanks.'

But, as the other continued at his elbow, Mr Van Wyk stopped short.

The overhanging eaves, descending low upon the lighted front of the bungalow, threw their black straight-edged shadow into the great body of the night on that side. Everything was very still. A tinkle of cutlery and a slight jingle of glasses were heard. Mr Van Wyk's servants were laying the table for two on the verandah.

'I am afraid you give me no credit whatever for my good intentions in the matter I've spoken to you about,' said Sterne.

'I simply don't understand you.'

'Captain Whalley is a very audacious man, but he will understand that his game is up. That's all that anybody need ever know of it from me. Believe me, I am very considerate in this, but duty is duty. I don't want to make a fuss. All I ask you, as his friend, is to tell him from me that the game's up. That will be sufficient.'

Mr Van Wyk felt a loathsome dismay at this queer privilege of friendship. He would not demean himself by asking for the slightest explanation; to drive the other away with contumely he did not think prudent – as yet, at any rate. So much assurance staggered him. Who could tell what there could be in it? he thought. His regard for Captain Whalley had the tenacity of a disinterested sentiment, and his practical instinct coming to his aid, he concealed his scorn.

'I gather, then, that this is something grave.'

'Very grave,' Sterne assented solemnly, delighted at having produced an effect at last. He was ready to add some effusive protestations of regret at the 'unavoidable necessity', but Mr Van Wyk cut him short – very civilly, however.

Once on the verandah Mr Van Wyk put his hands in his pockets, and, straddling his legs, stared down at a black panther skin lying on the floor before a rocking-chair. 'It looks as if the fellow had not the pluck to play his own precious game openly,' he thought.

This was true enough. In the face of Massy's last rebuff Sterne dared not declare his knowledge. His object was simply to get charge of the steamer and keep it for some time. Massy would never forgive him for forcing himself on; but if Captain Whalley left the ship of his own accord, the command would devolve upon him for the rest of the trip; so he hit upon the brilliant idea of scaring the old man away. A vague menace, a mere hint, would be enough in such a brazen case; and, with a strange admixture of compassion, he thought that Batu Beru was a very good place for throwing up the sponge. The skipper could go ashore quietly, and stay with that Dutchman of his. Weren't these two as thick as thieves together? And on reflection he seemed to see that there was a way to work the whole thing through that great friend of the old man's. This was another brilliant idea. He had an inborn preference for circuitous methods. In this particular case he desired to remain in the background as much as possible, to avoid exasperating Massy needlessly. No fuss! Let it all happen naturally.

Mr Van Wyk all through the dinner was conscious of a sense of isolation that invades sometimes the closeness of human intercourse. Captain Whalley failed lamentably and obviously in his attempts to eat something. He seemed overcome by a strange absent-mindedness. His hand would hover irresolutely, as if left without guidance by a preoccupied mind. Mr Van Wyk had heard him coming up from a long way off in the profound stillness of the riverside, and had noticed the irresolute character of the footfalls. The toe of his boot had struck the bottom stair as though he had come along mooning with his head in the air right up to the steps of the verandah. Had the captain of the *Sofala* been another sort of man he would have suspected the work of age there. But one glance at him was enough. Time – after, indeed, marking him for its own – had given him up to his usefulness, in which his simple faith would see a proof of Divine mercy. 'How could I contrive to warn him?' Mr Van Wyk wondered, as if Captain Whalley had been miles and miles away, out of sight and earshot of all evil. He was sickened by an immense disgust of Sterne. To even mention his threat to a man like Whalley would be positively indecent. There was something more vile and insulting in its hint than in a definite charge of crime – the debasing taint of blackmailing. 'What could anyone bring against him?' he asked himself. This was a limpid personality. 'And for what object?' The Power that man trusted had thought fit to leave him nothing on earth that envy could lay hold of, except a bare crust of bread.

'Won't you try some of this?' he asked, pushing a dish slightly. Suddenly it occurred to Mr Van Wyk that Sterne might possibly be coveting the command of the *Sofala*. His cynicism was quite startled by what looked like a proof that no man may count himself safe from his kind unless in the very abyss of misery. An intrigue of that sort was hardly worth troubling about, he judged; but still, with such a fool as Massy to deal with, Whalley ought to and must be warned.

At this moment Captain Whalley, bolt upright, the deep cavities of the eyes overhung by a bushy frown, and one large brown hand resting on each side of his empty plate, spoke across the table-cloth abruptly – 'Mr Van Wyk, you've always treated me with the most humane consideration.'

'My dear captain, you make too much of the simple fact that I am not a savage.' Mr Van Wyk, utterly revolted by the thought of Sterne's obscure attempt, raised his voice incisively, as if the mate had been hiding somewhere within earshot. 'Any consideration I have been able to show was no more than the rightful due of a character I've learned to regard by this time with an esteem that nothing can shake.'

A slight ring of glass made him lift his eyes from the slice of pineapple he was cutting into small pieces on his plate. In changing his position Captain Whalley had contrived to upset an empty tumbler.

Without looking that way, leaning sideways on his elbow, his other hand shading his brow, he groped shadily for it, then desisted. Van Wyk stared blankly, as if something momentous had happened all at once. He did not know why he should feel so startled; but he forgot Sterne utterly for the moment.

'Why, what's the matter?'

And Captain Whalley, half-averted, in a deadened, agitated voice, muttered – 'Esteem!'

'And I may add something more,' Mr Van Wyk, very steady-eyed, pronounced slowly.

'Hold! Enough!' Captain Whalley did not change his attitude or raise his voice. 'Say no more! I can make you no return. I am too poor even for that now. Your esteem is worth having. You are not a man that would stoop to deceive the poorest sort of devil on earth, or make a ship unseaworthy every time he takes her to sea.'

Mr Van Wyk, leaning forward, his face gone pink all over, with the starched table-napkin over his knees, was inclined to mistrust his senses, his power of comprehension, the sanity of his guest.

'Where? Why? In the name of God! – what's this? What ship? I don't understand who . . . '

'Then, in the name of God, it is I! A ship's unseaworthy when her captain can't see. I am going blind.'

Mr Van Wyk made a slight movement, and sat very still afterwards for a few seconds; then, with the thought of Sterne's 'The game's up,' he ducked under the table to pick up the napkin which had slipped off his knees. This was the game that was up. And at the same time the muffled voice of Captain Whalley passed over him – 'I've deceived them all. Nobody knows.'

He emerged flushed to the eyes. Captain Whalley, motionless under the full blaze of the lamp, shaded his face with his hand.

'And you had that courage?'

'Call it by what name you like. But you are a humane man – a – a – gentleman, Mr Van Wyk. You may have asked me what I had done with my conscience.'

He seemed to muse, profoundly silent, very still in his mournful pose.

'I began to tamper with it in my pride. You begin to see a lot of things when you are going blind. I could not be frank with an old chum even. I was not frank with Massy – no, not altogether. I knew he took me for a wealthy sailor fool, and I let him. I wanted to keep up my importance – because there was poor Ivy away there – my daughter. What did I want to trade on his misery for? I did trade on it – for her. And now, what mercy could I expect from him? He would trade on mine if he knew it. He would hunt the old fraud out, and stick to the money for a year. Ivy's money. And I haven't kept a penny for myself. How am I going to live for a year. A year! In a year there will be no sun in the sky for her father.'

His deep voice came out, awfully veiled, as though he had been over-whelmed by the earth of a landslide and talking of the thoughts that haunt the dead in their graves. A cold shudder ran down Mr Van Wyk's back.

'And how long is it since you have . . . ?' he began.

'It was a long time before I could bring myself to believe in this – this – visitation.' Captain Whalley spoke with gloomy patience from under his hand.

He had not thought he had deserved it. He had begun by deceiving himself from day to day, from week to week. He had the Serang at hand there – an old servant. It came on gradually, and when he could no longer deceive himself . . .

His voice died out almost.

'Rather than give her up I set myself to deceive you all.'

'It's incredible,' whispered Mr Van Wyk. Captain Whalley's appalling murmur flowed on.

'Not even the sign of God's anger could make me forget her. How could I forsake my child, feeling my vigour all the time – the blood warm within me? Warm as yours. It seems to me that, like the blinded Samson, I would find the strength to shake down a temple upon my head. She's a struggling woman – my own child that we used to pray over together, my poor wife and I. Do you remember that day I as well as told you that I believed God would let me live to a hundred for her sake? What sin is there in loving your child? Do you see it? I was ready for her sake to live for ever. I half believed I would. I've been praying for death since. Ha! Presumptuous man – you wanted to live . . .'

A tremendous, shuddering upheaval of that big frame, shaken by a gasping sob, set the glasses jingling all over the table, seemed to make the whole house tremble to the roof-tree. And Mr Van Wyk whose feeling of outraged love had been translated into a form of struggle with nature, understood very well that, for that man whose whole life had been conditioned by action, there could exist no other expression for all the emotions; that, to voluntarily cease venturing, doing, enduring, for his child's sake, would have been exactly like plucking his warm love for her out of his living heart. Something too monstrous, too impossible, even to conceive.

Captain Whalley had not changed his attitude, that seemed to express something of shame, sorrow, and defiance.

'I have even deceived you. If it had not been for that word "esteem". These are not the words for me. I would have lied to you. Haven't I lied to you? Weren't you going to trust your property on board this very trip?'

'I have a floating yearly policy,' Mr Van Wyk said almost unwittingly, and was amazed at the sudden cropping up of a commercial detail.

'The ship is unseaworthy, I tell you. The policy would be invalid if it were known . . .'

'We shall share the guilt, then.'

'Nothing could make mine less,' said Captain Whalley.

He had not dared to consult a doctor; the man would have perhaps asked who he was, what he was doing; Massy might have heard something. He had lived on without any help, human or divine. The very prayers stuck in his throat. What was there to pray for? and death seemed as far as ever. Once he got into his cabin he dared not come out again; when he sat down he dared not get up; he dared not raise his eyes to anybody's face; he felt reluctant to look upon the sea or up to the sky. The world was fading before his great fear of giving himself away. The old ship was his last friend; he was not afraid of her; he knew every inch of her deck; but at her too he hardly dared to look, for fear of finding he could see less than the day before. A great incertitude enveloped him. The horizon was gone; the sky mingled darkly with the sea. Who was this figure standing over yonder? what was this thing lying down there? And a frightful doubt of the reality of what he could see made even the remnant of sight that remained to him an added torment, a pitfall always open for his miserable pretence. He was afraid to stumble inexcusably over something – to say a fatal Yes or No to a question. The hand of God was upon him, but it could not tear him away from his child. And, as if in a nightmare of humiliation, every featureless man seemed an enemy.

He let his hand fall heavily on the table. Mr Van Wyk, arms down, chin on breast, with a gleam of white teeth pressing on the lower lip, meditated on Sterne's 'The game's up.'

'The Serang of course does not know.'

'Nobody,' said Captain Whalley, with assurance.

'Ah, yes. Nobody. Very well. Can you keep it up to the end of the trip? That is the last under the agreement with Massy.'

Captain Whalley got up and stood erect, very stately, with the great white beard lying like a silver breastplate over the awful secret of his heart. Yes; that was the only hope there was for him of ever seeing her again, of securing the money, the last he could do for her, before he crept away somewhere – useless, a burden, a reproach to himself. His voice faltered.

'Think of it! Never see her any more: the only human being besides myself now on earth that can remember my wife. She's just like her mother. Lucky the poor woman is where there are no tears shed over those they loved on earth and that remain to pray not to be led into temptation – because, I suppose, the blessed know the secret of grace in God's dealings with His created children.'

He swayed a little, said with austere dignity – 'I don't. I know only the child He has given me.'

And he began to walk. Mr Van Wyk, jumping up, saw the full meaning of the rigid head, the hesitating feet, the vaguely extended hand. His heart was beating fast; he moved a chair aside, and instinctively advanced as if to offer his arm. But Captain Whalley passed him by, making for the stairs quite straight.

'He could not see me at all out of his line,' Van Wyk thought, with a sort of awe. Then going to the head of the stairs, he asked a little tremulously – 'What is it like – like a mist – like . . .'

Captain Whalley, half-way down, stopped, and turned round undismayed to answer.

'It is as if the light were ebbing out of the world. Have you ever watched the ebbing sea on an open stretch of sands withdrawing farther and farther away from you? It is like this – only there will be no flood to follow. Never. It is as if the sun were growing smaller, the stars going out one by one. There can't be many left that I can see by this. But I haven't had the courage to look of late . . .' He must have been able to make out Mr Van Wyk, because he checked him by an authoritative gesture and a stoical – 'I can get about alone yet.'

It was as if he had taken his line, and would accept no help from men, after having been cast out, like a presumptuous Titan, from his heaven. Mr Van Wyk, arrested, seemed to count the footsteps right out of earshot. He walked between the tables, tapping smartly with his heels, took up a paper-knife, dropped it after a vague glance along the blade; then happening upon the piano, struck a few chords, standing up before the keyboard with an attentive poise of the head like a piano-tuner; closing it, he pivoted on his heels brusquely, avoided the little terrier sleeping trustfully on crossed forepaws, came upon the stairs next, and, as though he had lost his balance on the top step, ran down headlong out of the house. His servants, beginning to clear the table, heard him mutter to himself (evil words no doubt) down there, and then after a pause go away with a strolling gait in the direction of the wharf.

The bulwarks of the *Sofala* lying alongside the bank made a low, black wall on the undulating contour of the shore. Two masts and a funnel uprose from behind it with a great rake, as if about to fall: a solid, square elevation in the middle bore the ghostly shapes of white boats, the curves of davits, lines of rail and stanchions, all confused and mingling darkly everywhere; but low down, amidships, a single lighted port stared out on the night, perfectly round, like a small, full moon, whose yellow beam caught a patch of wet mud, the edge of trodden grass, two turns of heavy cable wound round the foot of a thick wooden post in the ground.

Mr Van Wyk, peering alongside, heard a muzzy boastful voice apparently jeering at a person called Prendergast. It mouthed abuse thickly, choked; then pronounced very distinctly the word 'Murphy,' and chuckled. Glass tinkled tremulously. All these sounds came from the lighted port. Mr Van Wyk hesitated, stooped; it was impossible to look through unless he went down into the mud.

'Sterne,' he said, half aloud.

The drunken voice within said gladly – 'Sterne – of course. Look at him blink. Look at him! Sterne, Whalley, Massy. Massy, Whalley, Sterne. But Massy's the best. You can't come over him. He would just love to see you starve.'

Mr Van Wyk moved away, made out farther forward a shadowy head stuck out from under the awnings as if on the watch, and spoke quietly in Malay, 'Is the mate asleep?'

'No. Here, at your service.'

In a moment Sterne appeared, walking as noiselessly as a cat on the wharf.

'It's so jolly dark, and I had no idea you would be down tonight.'

'What's this horrible raving?' asked Mr Van Wyk, as if to explain the cause of a shudder that ran over him audibly.

'Jack's broken out on a drunk. That's our second. It's his way. He will be right enough by tomorrow afternoon, only Mr Massy will keep on worrying up and down the deck. We had better get away.'

He muttered suggestively of a talk 'up at the house'. He had long desired to effect an entrance there, but Mr Van Wyk nonchalantly demurred: it would not, he feared, be quite prudent, perhaps; and the opaque black shadow under one of the two big trees left at the landing-place swallowed them up, impenetrably dense by the side of the wide river, that seemed to spin into threads of glitter the light of a few big stars dropped here and there upon its outspread and flowing stillness.

'The situation is grave beyond doubt,' Mr Van Wyk said. Ghost-like in their white clothes they could not distinguish each other's features, and their feet made no sound on the soft earth. A sort of purring was heard. Mr Sterne felt gratified by such a beginning.

'I thought, Mr Van Wyk, a gentleman of your sort would see at once how awkwardly I was situated.'

'Yes, very. Obviously his health is bad. Perhaps he's breaking up. I see, and he himself is well aware – I assume I am speaking to a man of sense – he is well aware that his legs are giving out.'

'His legs – Ah!' Mr Sterne was disconcerted, and then turned sulky. 'You may call it his legs if you like; what I want to know is whether he intends to clear out quietly. That's a good one, too! His legs! Pooh!'

'Why, yes. Only look at the way he walks,' Mr Van Wyk took him up in a perfectly cool and undoubting tone. 'The question, however, is whether your sense of duty does not carry you too far from your true interest. After all, I too could do something to serve you. You know who I am.'

'Everybody along the Straits has heard of you, sir.'

Mr Van Wyk presumed that this meant something favourable. Sterne had a soft laugh at this pleasantry. He should think so! To the opening statement, that the partnership agreement was to expire at the end of this very trip, he gave an attentive assent. He was aware. One heard of nothing else on board all the blessed day long. As to Massy, it was no secret that he was in a jolly deep hole with these worn-out boilers. He would have to borrow somewhere a couple of hundred first of all to pay off the captain; and then he would have to raise money on mortgage upon the ship for the new boilers – that is, if he could find a lender at all. At best it meant loss of time, a break in the trade, short earnings for the year – and there was always the danger of having his connection filched away from him by the Germans. It was whispered about that he had already tried two firms. Neither would have anything to do with him. Ship too old, and the man too well known in the place . . . Mr Sterne's final rapid winking remained buried in the deep darkness sibilating with his whispers.

'Supposing, then, he got the loan,' Mr Van Wyk resumed in a deliberate undertone, 'on your own showing he's more than likely to get a mortgagee's man thrust upon him as captain. For my part, I know that I would make that very stipulation myself if I had to find the money. And as a matter of fact I am thinking of doing so. It would be worth my while in many ways. Do you see how this would bear on the case under discussion?'

'Thank you, sir. I am sure you couldn't get anybody that would care more for your interests.'

'Well, it suits my interest that Captain Whalley should finish his time. I shall probably take a passage with you down the Straits. If that can be done, I'll be on the spot when all these changes take place, and in a position to look after *your* interests.'

'Mr Van Wyk, I want nothing better. I am sure I am infinitely . . . '

'I take it, then, that this may be done without any trouble.'

'Well, sir, what risk there is can't be helped; but (speaking to you as my employer now) the thing is more safe than it looks. If anybody had told me of it I wouldn't have believed it, but I have been looking on myself. That old Serang has been trained up to the game. There's nothing the matter with his – his – limbs, sir. He's got used to do things on his own in a remarkable way. And let me tell you, sir, that Captain Whalley, poor man, is by no means useless. Fact. Let me explain to you, sir. He stiffens up that old monkey of a Malay, who knows well enough what to do. Why, he must have kept captain's watches in all sorts of country ships off and on for the last five-and-twenty years. These natives, sir, as long as they have a white man close at the back, will go on doing the right thing most surprisingly well – even if left quite to themselves . . . Only the white man must be of the sort to put starch into them, and the captain is the one for that. Why, sir, he has drilled him so well that now he needs hardly speak at all. I have seen that little wrinkled ape made to take the ship out of Pangu Bay on a blowy morning and on all through the islands; take her out first-rate, sir, dodging under the old man's elbow, and in such quiet style that you could not have told for the life of you which of the two was doing the work up there. That's where our poor friend would be still of use to the ship even if – if – he could no longer lift a foot, sir. Providing the Serang does not know that there's anything wrong.'

'He doesn't.'

'Naturally not. Quite beyond his apprehension. They aren't capable of finding out anything about us, sir.'

'You seem to be a shrewd man,' said Mr Van Wyk in a choked mutter, as though he were feeling sick.

'You'll find me a good enough servant, sir.'

Mr Sterne hoped now for a handshake at least, but unexpectedly, with a 'What's this? Better not to be seen together,' Mr Van Wyk's white shape wavered, and instantly seemed to melt away in the black air under the roof of boughs. The mate was startled. Yes. There was that faint thumping clatter.

He stole out silently from under the shade. The lighted port-hole shone from afar. His head swam with the intoxication of sudden success. What a thing it was to have a gentleman to deal with! He crept aboard, and there was something weird in the shadowy stretch of empty decks, echoing with shouts and blows proceeding from a darker part amidships. Massy was raging before the door of the berth: the drunken voice within flowed on undisturbed in the violent racket of kicks.

'Shut up! Put your light out and turn in, you confounded swilling pig – you! D'you hear me, you beast?'

The kicking stopped, and in the pause the muzzy oracular voice announced from within – 'Ah! Massy, now – that's another thing. Massy's deep.'

'Who's that aft there? You, Sterne? He'll drink himself into a fit of horrors.' The chief engineer appeared vague and big at the corner of the engine-room skylight.

'He will be good enough for duty tomorrow. I would let him be, Mr Massy.'

Sterne slipped away into his berth, and at once had to sit down. His head swam with exultation. He got into his bunk as if in a dream. A feeling of profound peace, of pacific joy, came over him. On deck all was quiet.

Mr Massy, with his ear against the door of Jack's cabin, listened critically to a deep stertorous breathing within. This was a dead-drunk sleep. The bout was over: tranquillised on that score, he too went in, and with slow wriggles got out of his old tweed jacket. It was a garment with many pockets, which he used to put on at odd times of the day, being subject to sudden chilly fits, and when he felt warmed he would take it off and hang it about anywhere all over the ship. It would be seen swinging on belaying-pins, thrown over the heads of winches, suspended on people's very door-handles for that matter. Was he not the owner? But his favourite place was a hook on a wooden awning stanchion on the bridge, almost against the binnacle. He had even in the early days more than one tussle on that point with Captain Whalley, who desired the bridge to be kept tidy. He had been overawed then. Of late, though, he had been able to defy his partner with impunity. Captain Whalley never seemed to notice anything now. As to the Malays, in their awe of that scowling man not one of the crew would dream of laying a hand on the thing, no matter where or what it swung from.

With an unexpectedness which made Mr Massy jump and drop the coat at his feet, there came from the next berth the crash and thud of a headlong, jingling, clattering fall. The faithful Jack must have dropped to sleep suddenly as he sat at his revels, and now had gone over chair and all, breaking, as it seemed by the sound, every single glass and bottle in the place. After the terrific smash all was still for a time in there, as though he had killed himself on the spot. Mr Massy held his breath. At last a sleepy uneasy groaning sigh was exhaled slowly on the other side of the bulkhead.

'I hope to goodness he's too drunk to wake up now,' muttered Mr Massy.

The sound of a softly knowing laugh nearly drove him to despair. He swore violently under his breath. The fool would keep him awake all night now for certain. He cursed his luck. He wanted to forget his maddening troubles in sleep sometimes. He could detect no movements. Without apparently making the slightest attempt to get up, Jack went on sniggering to himself where he lay; then began to speak, where he had left off as it were – 'Massy! I love the dirty rascal. He would like to see his poor old Jack starve – but just you look where he has climbed to.' . . . He hiccoughed in a superior, leisurely manner . . . 'Ship-owning it with the best. A lottery ticket you want. Ha! ha! I will give you lottery tickets, my boy. Let the old ship sink and the old chum starve – that's right. He don't go wrong – Massy don't. Not he. He's a genius – that man is. That's the way to win your money. Ship and chum must go.'

'The silly fool has taken it to heart,' muttered Massy to himself. And, listening with a softened expression of face for any slight sign of returning drowsiness, he was discouraged profoundly by a burst of laughter full of joyful irony.

'Would like to see her at the bottom of the sea! Oh, you clever, clever devil! Wish her sunk, eh? I should think you would, my boy; the damned old thing and all your troubles with her. Rake in the insurance money – turn your back on your old chum – all's well – gentleman again.'

A grim stillness had come over Massy's face. Only his big black eyes rolled uneasily. The raving fool. And yet it was all true. Yes. Lottery tickets, too. All true. What? Beginning again? He wished he wouldn't . . .

But it was even so. The imaginative drunkard on the other side of the bulkhead shook off the deathlike stillness that after his last words had fallen on the dark ship moored to a silent shore.

'Don't you dare to say anything against George Massy, Esquire. When he's tired of waiting he will do away with her. Look out! Down she goes – chum and all. He'll know how to . . .'

The voice hesitated, weary, dreamy, lost, as if dying away in a vast open space.

'. . . find a trick that will work. He's up to it – never fear . . .'

He must have been very drunk, for at last the heavy sleep gripped him with the suddenness of a magic spell, and the last word lengthened itself into an interminable, noisy, indrawn snore. And then even the snoring stopped, and all was still.

But it seemed as though Mr Massy had suddenly come to doubt the efficacy of sleep as against a man's troubles; or perhaps he had found the relief he needed in the stillness of a calm contemplation that may contain the vivid thoughts of wealth, of a stroke of luck, of long idleness, and may bring before you the imagined form of every desire; for, turning about and throwing his arms over the edge of his bunk, he stood there with his feet on his favourite old coat, looking out through the round port into the night over the river. Sometimes a breath of wind would enter and touch his face, a cool breath charged with the damp, fresh feel from a vast body of water. A glimmer here and there was all he could see of it; and once he might after all suppose he had dozed off, since there appeared before his vision, unexpectedly and connected with no dream, a row of flaming and gigantic figures – three nought seven one two – making up a number such as you may see on a lottery ticket. And then all at once the port was no longer black: it was pearly grey, framing a shore crowded with houses, thatched roof beyond thatched roof, walls of mats and bamboo, gables of carved teak timber. Rows of dwellings raised on a forest of piles lined the steely band of the river, brimful and still, with the tide on the turn. This was Batu Beru – and the day had come.

Mr Massy shook himself, put on the tweed coat, and, shivering nervously as if from some great shock, made a note of the number. A fortunate, rare hint that. Yes; but to pursue fortune one wanted money – ready cash.

Then he went out and prepared to descend into the engine-room. Several small jobs had to be seen to, and Jack was lying dead drunk on the floor of his cabin with the door locked at that. His gorge rose at the thought of work. Ay! But if you wanted to do nothing you had to get first a good bit of money. A ship won't save you. True, all true. He was tired of waiting for some chance that would rid him at last of that ship that had turned out a curse on his life.

14

The deep, interminable hoot of the steam-whistle had, in its grave, vibrating note, something intolerable, which sent a slight shudder down Mr Van Wyk's back. It was the early afternoon; the *Sofala* was leaving Batu Beru for Pangu, the next place of call. She swung in the stream, scantily attended by a few canoes, and, gliding on the broad river, became lost to view from the Van Wyk bungalow.

Its owner had not gone this time to see her off. Generally he came down to the wharf, exchanged a few words with the bridge while she cast off, and waved his hand to Captain Whalley at the last moment. This day he did not even go as far as the balustrade of the verandah. 'He couldn't see me if I did,' he said to himself. 'I wonder whether he can make out the house at all.' And this thought somehow made him feel more alone than he had ever felt for all these years. What was it? Six or seven? Seven. A long time.

He sat on the verandah with a closed book on his knee, and, as it were, looked out upon his solitude, as if the fact of Captain Whalley's blindness had opened his eyes to his own. There were many sorts of heartaches and troubles, and there was no place where they could not find a man out.

And he felt ashamed, as though he had for six years behaved like a peevish boy.

His thought followed the *Sofala* on her way. On the spur of the moment he had acted impulsively, turning to the thing most pressing. And what else could he have done? Later on he should see. It seemed necessary that he should come out into the world, for a time at least. He had money – something could be arranged; he would grudge no time, no trouble, no loss of his solitude. It weighed on him now – and Captain Whalley appeared to him as he had sat shading his eyes, as if, being deceived in the trust of his faith, he were beyond all the good and evil that can be wrought by the hands of men.

Mr Van Wyk's thoughts followed the *Sofala* down the river, winding about through the belt of the coast forest, between the buttressed shafts of the big trees, through the mangrove strip, and over the bar. The ship crossed it easily in broad daylight, piloted, as it happened, by Mr Sterne, who took the watch from four to six, and then went below to hug himself with delight at the prospect of being virtually employed by a rich man – like Mr Van Wyk. He could not see how any hitch could occur now. He did not seem able to get over the feeling of being 'fixed up at last'. From six to eight, in the course of duty, the Serang looked alone after the ship. She had a clear road before her now till about three in the morning, when she would close with the Pangu group. At eight Mr Sterne came out cheerily to take charge again till midnight. At ten he was still chirruping and humming to himself on the bridge, and about that time Mr Van Wyk's thought abandoned the *Sofala*. Mr Van Wyk had fallen asleep at last.

Massy, blocking the engine-room companion, jerked himself into his tweed jacket surlily, while the second waited with a scowl.

'Oh. You came out! You sot! Well, what have you got to say for yourself?'

He had been in charge of the engines till then. A sombre fury darkened his mind: a hot anger against the ship, against the facts of life, against the men for their cheating, against himself too – because of an inward tremor in his heart.

An incomprehensible growl answered him.

'What? Can't you open your mouth now? You yelp out your infernal rot loud enough when you are drunk. What do you mean by abusing people in that way? – you old useless boozer, you!'

'Can't help it. Don't remember anything about it. You shouldn't listen.'

'You dare to tell me! What do you mean by going on a drunk like this?'

'Don't ask me. Sick of the dam' boilers – you would be. Sick of life.'

'I wish you were dead, then. You've made me sick of you. Don't you remember the uproar you made last night? You miserable old soaker!'

'No; I don't. Don't want to. Drink is drink.'

'I wonder what prevents me from kicking you out. What do you want here?'

'Relieve you. You've been long enough down there, George.'

'Don't you George me – you tippling old rascal, you! If I were to die tomorrow you would starve. Remember that. Say Mr Massy.'

'Mr Massy,' repeated the other stolidly.

Dishevelled, with dull bloodshot eyes, a snuffy, grimy shirt, greasy trousers, naked feet thrust into ragged slippers, he bolted in head down directly Massy had made way for him.

The chief engineer looked around. The deck was empty as far as the taffrail. All the native passengers had left in Batu Beru this time, and no others had joined. The dial of the patent log tinkled periodically in the dark at the end of the ship. It was a dead calm, and, under the clouded sky, through the still air that seemed to cling warm, with a seaweed smell, to her slim hull, on a sea of sombre grey and unwrinkled, the ship moved on an even keel, as if floating detached in empty space. But Mr Massy slapped his forehead, tottered a little, and caught hold of a belaying-pin at the foot of the mast.

'I shall go mad,' he muttered, walking across the deck unsteadily. A shovel was scraping loose coal down below – a fire-door clanged. Sterne on the bridge began whistling a new tune.

Captain Whalley, sitting on the couch, awake and fully dressed, heard the door of his cabin open. He did not move in the least, waiting to recognise the voice, with an appalling strain of prudence.

A bulkhead lamp blazed on the white paint, the crimson plush, the brown varnish of mahogany tops. The white wood packing-case under the bed-place had remained unopened for three years now, as though Captain Whalley had felt that, after the *Fair Maid* was gone, there could be no abiding-place on earth for his affections. His hands rested on his knees; his handsome head with big eyebrows presented a rigid profile to the doorway. The expected voice spoke out at last.

'Once more, then. What am I to call you?'

Ha! Massy. Again. The weariness of it crushed his heart – and the pain of shame was almost more than he could bear without crying out.

'Well. Is it to be "partner" still?'

'You don't know what you ask.'

'I know what I want . . . '

Massy stepped in and closed the door.

' . . . And I am going to have a try for it with you once more.'

His whine was half persuasive, half menacing.

'For it's no manner of use to tell me that you are poor. You don't spend anything on yourself, that's true enough; but there's another name for that. You think you are going to have what you want out of me for three years, and then cast me off without hearing what I think of you. You think I would have submitted to your airs if I had known you had only a beggarly five hundred pounds in the world. You ought to have told me.'

'Perhaps,' said Captain Whalley, bowing his head. 'And yet it has saved you.' . . . Massy laughed scornfully . . . 'I have told you often enough since.'

'And I don't believe you now. When I think how I let you lord it over my ship! Do you remember how you used to bullyrag me about my coat and *your* bridge? It was in his way. *His* bridge! "And I won't be a party to this – and I couldn't think of doing that." Honest man! And now it all comes out. "I am poor, and I can't. I have only this five hundred in the world." '

He contemplated the immobility of Captain Whalley, that seemed to present an unconquerable obstacle in his path. His face took a mournful cast.

'You are a hard man.'

'Enough,' said Captain Whalley, turning upon him. 'You shall get nothing from me, because I have nothing of mine to give away now.'

'Tell that to the marines!'

Mr Massy, going out, looked back once; then the door closed, and Captain Whalley, alone, sat as still as before. He had nothing of his own – even his own past of honour, of truth, of just pride, was gone. All his spotless life had fallen into the abyss. He had said his last goodbye to it. But what belonged to *her*, that he meant to save. Only a little money. He would take it to her in his own hands – this last gift of a man that had lasted too long. And an immense and fierce impulse, the very passion of paternity, flamed up with all the unquenched vigour of his worthless life in a desire to see her face.

Just across the deck Massy had gone straight to his cabin, struck a light, and hunted up the note of the dreamed number whose figures had flamed up also with the fierceness of another passion. He must contrive somehow not to miss a drawing. That number meant something. But what expedient could he contrive to keep himself going?

'Wretched miser!' he mumbled.

If Mr Sterne could at no time have told him anything new about his partner, he could have told Mr Sterne that another use could be made of a man's affliction than just to kick him out, and thus defer the term of a difficult payment for a year. To keep the secret of the affliction and induce him to stay was a better move. If without means, he would be anxious to remain; and that settled the question of refunding him his share. He did not know exactly how much Captain Whalley was disabled; but if it so happened that he put the ship ashore somewhere for good and all, it was not the owner's fault – was it? He was not obliged to know that there was anything wrong. But probably nobody would raise such a point, and the ship was fully insured. He had had enough self-restraint to pay up the premiums. But this was not all. He could not believe Captain Whalley to be so confoundedly destitute as not to have some more money put away somewhere. If he, Massy, could get hold of it, that would pay for the boilers, and everything went on as before. And if she got lost in the end, so much the better. He hated her: he loathed the troubles that took his mind off the chances of fortune. He wished her at the bottom of the sea, and the insurance money in his pocket. And as, baffled, he left Captain Whalley's cabin, he enveloped in the same hatred the ship with the worn-out boilers and the man with the dimmed eyes.

And our conduct after all is so much a matter of outside suggestion, that had it not been for his Jack's drunken gabble he would have there and then had it out with this miserable man, who would neither help, nor stay, nor yet lose the ship. The old fraud! He longed to kick him out. But he restrained himself. Time enough for that – when he liked. There was a fearful new thought put into his head. Wasn't he up to it after all? How that beast Jack had raved! 'Find a safe trick to get rid of her.' Well, Jack was not so far wrong. A very clever trick had occurred to him. Ay! But what of the risk?

A feeling of pride – the pride of superiority to common prejudices – crept into his breast, made his heart beat fast, his mouth turn dry. Not everybody would dare; but he was Massy, and he was up to it!

Six bells were struck on deck. Eleven! He drank a glass of water, and sat down for ten minutes or so to calm himself. Then he got out of his chest a small bull's-eye lantern of his own and lit it.

Almost opposite his berth, across the narrow passage under the bridge, there was, in the iron deck-structure covering the stokehold fiddle and the boiler-space, a storeroom with iron sides, iron roof, iron-plated floor, too, on account of the heat below. All sorts of rubbish was shot there: it had a mound of scrap-iron in a corner; rows of empty oil-cans; sacks of cotton-waste, with a heap of charcoal, a deck-forge, fragments of an old hencoop, winch-covers all in rags, remnants of lamps; and a brown felt hat, discarded by a man dead now (of a fever on the Brazil coast), who had been once mate of the *Sofala*, had remained for years jammed forcibly behind a length of burst copper pipe, flung at sometime or other out of the engine-room. A complete and impervious blackness pervaded that Capharnaum of forgotten things. A small shaft of light from Mr Massy's bull's-eye fell slanting right through it.

His coat was unbuttoned; he shot the bolt of the door (there was no other opening), and, squatting before the scrap-heap, began to pack his pockets with pieces of iron. He packed them carefully, as if the rusty nuts, the broken bolts, the links of cargo chain, had been so much gold he had that one chance to carry away. He packed his side-pockets till they bulged, the breast-pocket, the pockets inside. He turned over the pieces. Some he rejected. A small mist of powdered rust began to rise about his busy hands. Mr Massy knew something of the scientific basis of his clever trick. If you want to deflect the magnetic needle of a ship's compass, soft iron is the best; likewise many small pieces in the pockets of a jacket would have more effect than a few large ones, because in that way you obtain a greater amount of surface for weight in your iron, and it's surface that tells.

He slipped out swiftly – two strides sufficed – and in his cabin he perceived that his hands were all red – red with rust. It disconcerted him, as though he had found them covered with blood: he looked himself over hastily. Why, his trousers too! He had been rubbing his rusty palms on his legs.

He tore off the waistband button in his haste, brushed his coat, washed his hands. Then the air of guilt left him, and he sat down to wait.

He sat bolt upright and weighted with iron in his chair. He had a hard, lumpy bulk against each hip, felt the scrappy iron in his pockets touch his ribs at every breath, the downward drag of all these pounds hanging upon his shoulders. He looked very dull too, sitting idle there, and his yellow face, with motionless black eyes, had something passive and sad in its quietness.

When he heard eight bells struck above his head, he rose and made ready to go out. His movements seemed aimless, his lower lip had dropped a little, his eyes roamed about the cabin, and the tremendous tension of his will had robbed them of every vestige of intelligence.

With the last stroke of the bell the Serang appeared noiselessly on the bridge to relieve the mate. Sterne overflowed with good nature, since he had nothing more to desire.

'Got your eyes well open yet, Serang? It's middling dark; I'll wait till you get your sight properly.'

The old Malay murmured, looked up with his worn eyes, sidled away into the light of the binnacle, and, clasping his hands behind his back, fixed his eyes on the compass-card.

'You'll have to keep a good look-out ahead for land, about half-past three. It's fairly clear, though. You have looked in on the captain as you came along – eh? He knows the time? Well, then, I am off.'

At the foot of the ladder he stood aside for the captain. He watched him go up with an even, certain tread, and remained thoughtful for a moment. 'It's funny,' he said to himself, 'but you can never tell whether that man has seen you or not. He might have heard me breathe this time.'

He was a wonderful man when all was said and done. They said he had had a name in his day. Mr Sterne could well believe it; and he concluded serenely that Captain Whalley must be able to see people more or less – as himself just now, for instance – but not being certain of anybody, had to keep up that unnoticing silence of manner for fear of giving himself away. Mr Sterne was a shrewd guesser.

This necessity of every moment brought home to Captain Whalley's heart the humiliation of his falsehood. He had drifted into it from paternal love, from incredulity, from boundless trust in divine justice meted out to men's feelings on this earth. He would give his poor Ivy the benefit of another month's work; perhaps the affliction was only temporary. Surely God would not rob his child of his power to help, and cast him naked into a night without end. He had caught at every hope; and when the evidence of his misfortune was stronger than hope, he tried not to believe the manifest thing.

In vain. In the steadily darkening universe a sinister clearness fell upon his ideas. In the illuminating moments of suffering he saw life, men, all things, the whole earth with all her burden of created nature, as he had never seen them before.

Sometimes he was seized with a sudden vertigo and an overwhelming terror; and then the image of his daughter appeared. Her, too, he had never seen so clearly before. Was it possible that he should ever be unable to do anything whatever for her? Nothing. And not see her any more? Never.

Why? The punishment was too great for a little presumption, for a little pride. And at last he came to cling to his deception with a fierce determination to carry it out to the end, to save her money intact, and behold her once more with his own eyes. Afterwards – what? The idea of suicide was revolting to the vigour of his manhood. He had prayed for death till the prayers had stuck in his throat. All the days of his life he had prayed, for daily bread, and not to be led into temptation, in a childlike humility of spirit. Did words mean anything? Whence did the gift of speech come? The violent beating of his heart reverberated in his head – seemed to shake his brain to pieces.

He sat down heavily in the deck-chair to keep the pretence of his watch. The night was dark. All the nights were dark now.

'Serang,' he said, half aloud.

'Ada, Tuan. I am here.'

'There are clouds on the sky?'

'There are, Tuan.'

'Let her be steered straight. North.'

'She is going north, Tuan.'

The Serang stepped back. Captain Whalley recognised Massy's footfalls on the bridge.

The engineer walked over to port and returned, passing behind the chair several times. Captain Whalley detected an unusual character as of prudent care in this prowling. The near presence of that man brought with it always a recrudescence of moral suffering for Captain Whalley. It was not remorse. After all, he had done nothing but good to the poor devil. There was also a sense of danger – the necessity of a greater care.

Massy stopped and said – 'So you still say you must go?'

'I must indeed.'

'And you couldn't at least leave the money for a term of years?'

'Impossible.'

'Can't trust it with me without your care, eh?

Captain Whalley remained silent. Massy sighed deeply over the back of the chair.

'It would just do to save me,' he said in a tremulous voice.

'I've saved you once.'

The chief engineer took off his coat with careful movements, and proceeded to feel for the brass hook screwed into the wooden stanchion. For this purpose he placed himself right in front of the binnacle, thus hiding completely the compass-card from the quartermaster at the wheel. 'Tuan!' the lascar at last murmured softly, meaning to let the white man know that he could not see to steer.

Mr Massy had accomplished his purpose. The coat was hanging from the nail, within six inches of the binnacle. And directly he had stepped aside the quartermaster, a middle-aged, pock-marked, Sumatra Malay, almost as dark as a Negro, perceived with amazement that in that short time, in this smooth water, with no wind at all, the ship had gone swinging far out of her course. He had never known her get away like this before. With a slight grunt of astonishment he turned the wheel hastily to bring her head back north, which was the course. The grinding of the steering-chains, the chiding murmurs of the Serang, who had come over to the wheel, made a slight stir, which attracted Captain Whalley's anxious attention. He said, 'Take better care.' Then everything settled to the usual quiet on the bridge. Mr Massy had disappeared.

But the iron in the pockets of the coat had done its work; and the *Sofala*, heading north by the compass made untrue by this simple device, was no longer making a safe course for Pangu Bay.

The hiss of water parted by her stem, the throb of her engines, all the sounds of her faithful and laborious life, went on uninterrupted in the great calm of the sea joining on all sides the motionless layer of cloud over the sky. A gentle stillness as vast as the world seemed to wait upon her path, enveloping her lovingly in a supreme caress. Mr Massy thought there could be no better night for an arranged shipwreck.

Run up high and dry on one of the reefs east of Pangu – wait for daylight – hole in the bottom – out boats – Pangu Bay same evening. That's about it. As soon as she touched he would hasten on the bridge, get hold of the coat (nobody would notice in the dark), and shake it upside down over the side, or even fling it into the sea. A detail. Who could guess? Coat been seen hanging there from that hook hundreds of times. Nevertheless, when he sat down on the lower step of the bridge-ladder his knees knocked together a little. The waiting part was the worst of it. At times he would begin to pant quickly, as though he had been running, and then breathe largely, swelling with the intimate sense of a mastered fate. Now and then he would hear the shuffle of the Serang's bare feet up there: quiet, low voices would exchange a few words, and lapse almost at once into silence . . .

'Tell me directly you see any land, Serang.'

'Yes, Tuan. Not yet.'

'No, not yet,' Captain Whalley would agree.

The ship had been the best friend of his decline. He had sent all the money he had made by and in the *Sofala* to his daughter. His thought lingered on the name. How often he and his wife had talked over the cot of the child in the big stern-cabin of the *Condor*; she would grow up, she would marry, she would love them, they would live near her and look at her happiness – it would go on without end. Well, his wife was dead, to the child he had given all he had to give; he wished he could come near her, see her, see her face once, live in the sound of her voice, that could make the darkness of the living grave ready for him supportable. He had been starved of love too long. He imagined her tenderness.

The Serang had been peering forward, and now and then glancing at the chair. He fidgeted restlessly, and suddenly burst out close to Captain Whalley – 'Tuan, do you see anything of the land?'

The alarmed voice brought Captain Whalley to his feet at once. He! See! And at the question, the curse of his blindness seemed to fall on him with a hundredfold force.

'What's the time?' he cried.

'Half-past three, Tuan.'

'We are close. You *must* see. Look, I say. Look.'

Mr Massy, awakened by the sudden sound of talking from a short doze on the lowest step, wondered why he was there. Ah! A faintness came over him. It is one thing to sow the seed of an accident and another to see the monstrous fruit hanging over your head ready to fall in the sound of agitated voices. 'There's no danger,' he muttered thickly to himself.

The horror of incertitude had seized upon Captain Whalley, the miserable mistrust of men, of things – of the very earth. He had steered that very course thirty-six times by the same compass – if anything was certain in this world it was its absolute, unerring correctness. Then what had happened? Did the Serang lie? Why lie? Why? Was he going blind too?

'Is there a mist? Look low on the water. Low down, I say.'

'Tuan, there's no mist. See for yourself.'

Captain Whalley steadied the trembling of his limbs by an effort. Should he stop the engines at once and give himself away? A gust of irresolution swayed all sorts of bizarre notions in his mind. The unusual had come, and he was not fit to deal with it. In this passage of inexpressible anguish he saw her face – the face of a young girl – with an amazing strength of illusion. No, he must not give himself away after having gone so far for her sake.

'You steered the course? You made it? Speak the truth.'

'Ya, Tuan. On the course now. Look.'

Captain Whalley strode to the binnacle, which to him made such a dim spot of light in an infinity of shapeless shadow. By bending his face right down to the glass he had been able before . . .

Having to stoop so low, he put out, instinctively, his arm to where he knew there was a stanchion to steady himself against. His hand closed on something that was not wood but cloth. The slight pull adding to the weight, the loop broke, and Mr Massy's coat falling, struck the deck heavily with a dull thump, accompanied by a lot of clicks.

'What's this?'

Captain Whalley fell on his knees, with groping hands extended in a frank gesture of blindness. They trembled, these hands feeling for the truth. He saw it. Iron near the compass. Wrong course. Wreck her! His ship. Oh no. Not that.

'Jump and stop her!' he roared out in a voice not his own.

He ran himself – hands forward, a blind man, and while the clanging of the gong echoed still all over the ship, she seemed to butt full tilt into the side of a mountain.

It was low water along the north side of the strait. Mr Massy had not reckoned on that. Instead of running aground for half her length, the *Sofala* butted the sheer ridge of a stone reef which would have been awash at high water. This made the shock absolutely terrific. Everybody in the ship that was standing was thrown down headlong: the shaken rigging made a great rattling to the very trucks. All the lights went out; several chain-guys, snapping, clattered against the funnel; there were crashes, pings of parted wire-rope, splintering sounds, loud cracks; the masthead lamp flew over the bows, and all the doors about the deck began to bang heavily. Then, after having hit, she rebounded, hit the second time the very same spot like a battering-ram. This completed the havoc; the funnel, with all the guys gone, fell over with a hollow sound of thunder, smashing the wheel to bits, crushing the frame of the awnings, breaking the lockers, filling the bridge with a mass of broken wood. Captain Whalley picked himself up and stood knee-deep in wreckage, torn, bleeding, knowing the nature of the danger he had escaped mostly by the sound, and holding Mr Massy's coat in his arms.

By this time Sterne (he had been flung out of his bunk) had set the engines astern. They worked for a few turns, then a voice bawled out, 'Get out of the damned engine-room, Jack!' – and they stopped; but the ship had gone clear of the reef and lay still, with a heavy cloud of steam issuing from the broken deck-pipes, and vanishing in wispy shapes into the night. Notwithstanding the suddenness of the disaster there was no shouting, as if the very violence of the shock had half-stunned the shadowy lot of people swaying here and there about her decks. The voice of the Serang pronounced distinctly above the confused murmurs – 'No bottom.' He had heaved the lead.

Mr Sterne cried out next in a strained pitch – 'Where the devil has she got to? Where are we?'

Captain Whalley replied in a calm bass – 'Amongst the reefs to the eastward.'

'You know it, sir? Then she will never get out again.'

'She will be gone in five minutes. Boats, Sterne. Even one will save you all in this calm.'

The Chinaman stokers went in a disorderly rush for the port boats. Nobody tried to check them. The Malays, after a moment of confusion, became quiet, and Mr Sterne showed a good countenance. Captain Whalley had not moved. His thoughts were darker than this night in which he had lost his first ship.

'He made me lose a ship.'

Another tall figure standing before him amongst the litter of the smash on the bridge whispered insanely – 'Say nothing of it.'

Massy stumbled closer. Captain Whalley heard the chattering of his teeth. 'I have the coat.'

'Throw it down and come along,' urged the chattering voice. 'B–b–b–b–boat!'

'You will get five years for this.'

Mr Massy had lost his voice. His speech was a mere dry rustling in his throat.
'Have mercy!'

'Had you any when you made me lose my ship? Mr Massy, you shall get five years for this!'

'I wanted money! Money! My own money! I will give you some money. Take half of it. You love money yourself.'

'There's a justice . . . '

Massy made an awful effort, and in a strange, half-choked utterance – 'You blind devil! It's you that drove me to it.'

Captain Whalley, hugging the coat to his breast, made no sound. The light had ebbed for ever from the world – let everything go. But this man should not escape scot-free.

Sterne's voice commanded – 'Lower away!'

The blocks rattled.

'Now then,' he cried, 'over with you. This way. You, Jack, here. Mr Massy! Mr Massy! Captain! Quick, sir! Let's get – '

'I shall go to prison for trying to cheat the insurance, but you'll get exposed; you, honest man, who has been cheating me. You are poor. Aren't you? You've nothing but the five hundred pounds. Well, you have nothing at all now. The ship's lost, and the insurance won't be paid.'

Captain Whalley did not move. True! Ivy's money! Gone in this wreck. Again he had a flash of insight. He was indeed at the end of his tether.

Urgent voices cried out together alongside. Massy did not seem able to tear himself away from the bridge. He chattered and hissed despairingly – 'Give it up to me! Give it up!'

'No,' said Captain Whalley; 'I could not give it up. You had better go. Don't wait, man, if you want to live. She's settling down by the head fast. No; I shall keep it, but I shall stay on board.'

Massy did not seem to understand; but the love of life, awakened suddenly, drove him away from the bridge.

Captain Whalley laid the coat down, and stumbled amongst the heaps of wreckage to the side.

'Is Mr Massy with you?' he called out into the night.

Sterne from the boat shouted – 'Yes; we've got him. Come along, sir. It's madness to stay longer.'

Captain Whalley felt along the rail carefully, and, without a word, cast off the painter. They were expecting him still down there. They were waiting, till a voice suddenly exclaimed – 'We are adrift! Shove off!'

'Captain Whalley! Leap! . . . pull up a little . . . leap! You can swim.'

In that old heart, in that vigorous body, there was, that nothing should be wanting, a horror of death that apparently could not be overcome by the horror of blindness. But after all, for Ivy he had carried his point, walking in his darkness to the very verge of a crime. God had not listened to his prayers. The light had finished ebbing out of the world; not a glimmer. It was a dark waste; but it was unseemly that a Whalley who had gone so far to carry a point should continue to live. He must pay the price.

'Leap as far as you can, sir; we will pick you up.'

They did not hear him answer. But their shouting seemed to remind him of something. He groped his way back, and sought for Mr Massy's coat. He could swim indeed; people sucked down by the whirlpool of a sinking ship do come up sometimes to the surface, and it was unseemly that a Whalley, who had made up his mind to die, should be beguiled by chance into a struggle. He would put all these pieces of iron into his own pockets.

They, looking from the boat, saw the *Sofala*, a black mass upon a black sea, lying still at an appalling cant. No sound came from her. Then, with a great bizarre shuffling noise, as if the boilers had broken through the bulkheads, and with a faint muffled detonation, where the ship had been there appeared for a moment something standing upright and narrow, like a rock out of the sea. Then that too disappeared.

When the *Sofala* failed to come back to Batu Beru at the proper time, Mr Van Wyk understood at once that he would never see her any more. But he did not know what had happened till some weeks afterwards, when, in a native craft lent him by his Sultan, he had made his way to the *Sofala*'s port of registry, where already her existence and the official inquiry into her loss were beginning to be forgotten.

It had not been a very remarkable or interesting case, except for the fact that the captain had gone down with his sinking ship. It was the only life lost; and Mr Van Wyk would not have been able to learn any details had it not been for Sterne, whom he met one day on the quay near the bridge over the creek, almost on the very spot where Captain Whalley, to preserve his daughter's five hundred pounds intact, had turned to get a sampan which would take him on board the *Sofala*.

From afar Mr Van Wyk saw Sterne blink straight at him and raise his hand to his hat. They drew into the shade of a building (it was a bank), and the mate related how the boats with the crew got into Pangu Bay about six hours after the accident, and how they had lived for a fortnight in a state of destitution before they found an opportunity to get away from that beastly place. The inquiry had exonerated everybody from all blame. The loss of the ship was put down to an unusual set of the current. Indeed, it could not have been anything else: there was no other way to account for the ship being set seven miles to the eastward of her position during the middle watch.

'A piece of bad luck for me, sir.' Sterne passed his tongue on his lips and glanced aside. 'I lost the advantage of being employed by you, sir. I can never be sorry enough. But here it is: one man's poison, another man's meat. This could not have been handier for Mr Massy if he had arranged that shipwreck himself. The most timely total loss I've ever heard of.'

'What became of that Massy?' asked Mr Van Wyk.

'He, sir? Ha! Ha! He would keep on telling me that he meant to buy another ship; but as soon as he had the money in his pocket he cleared out for Manilla by mail-boat early in the morning. I gave him chase right aboard, and he told me then he was going to make his fortune dead sure in Manilla. I could go to the devil for all he cared. And yet he as good as promised to give me the command if I didn't talk too much.'

'You never said anything . . . ' Mr Van Wyk began.

'Not I, sir. Why should I? I mean to get on, but the dead aren't in my way,' said Sterne. His eyelids were beating rapidly, then drooped for an instant. 'Besides, sir, it would have been an awkward business. You made me hold my tongue just a bit too long.'

'Do you know how it was that Captain Whalley remained on board? Did he really refuse to leave? Come now! Or was it perhaps an accidental . . . ?'

'Nothing!' Sterne interrupted with energy. 'I tell you I yelled for him to leap overboard. He simply *must* have cast off the painter of the boat himself. We all yelled to him – that is, Jack and I. He wouldn't even answer us. The ship was as silent as a grave to the last. Then the boilers fetched away, and down she went. Accident! Not it! The game was up, sir, I tell you.'

This was all that Sterne had to say.

Mr Van Wyk had been of course made the guest of the club for a fortnight, and it was there that he met the lawyer in whose office had been signed the agreement between Massy and Captain Whalley.

'Extraordinary old man,' he said. 'He came into my office from nowhere in particular as you may say, with his five hundred pounds to invest, and that engineer fellow following him anxiously. And now he is gone out a little inexplicably, just as he came. I could never understand him quite. There was no mystery at all about that Massy, eh? I wonder whether Whalley refused to leave the ship. It would have been foolish. He was blameless, as the court found.'

Mr Van Wyk had known him well, he said, and he could not believe in suicide. Such an act would not have been in character with what he knew of the man.

'It is my opinion too,' the lawyer agreed. The general theory was that the captain had remained too long on board trying to save something of importance. Perhaps the chart which would clear him, or else something of value in his cabin. The painter of the boat had come adrift of itself, it was supposed. However, strange to say, some little time before that voyage poor Whalley had called in his office and had left with him a sealed envelope addressed to his daughter, to be forwarded to her in case of his death. Still it was nothing very unusual, especially in a man of his age. Mr Van Wyk shook his head. Captain Whalley looked good for a hundred years.

'Perfectly true,' assented the lawyer. 'The old fellow looked as though he had come into the world full-grown and with that long beard. I could never, somehow, imagine him either younger or older – don't you know. There was a sense of physical power about that man too. And perhaps that was the secret of that something peculiar in his person which struck everybody who came in contact with him. He looked indestructible by any ordinary means that put an end to the rest of us. His deliberate, stately courtesy of manner was full of significance. It was as though he were certain of having plenty of time for everything. Yes, there was something indestructible about him; and the way he talked sometimes you might have thought he believed it himself. When he called on me last with that letter he wanted me to take charge of, he was not depressed at all. Perhaps a shade more deliberate in his talk and manner. Not depressed in the least. Had he a presentiment, I wonder? Perhaps! Still it seems a miserable end for such a striking figure.'

'On yes! It was a miserable end,' Mr Van Wyk said, with so much fervour that the lawyer looked up at him curiously; and afterwards, after parting with, him, he remarked to an acquaintance – 'Queer person that Dutch tobacco-planter from Batu Beru. Know anything of him?'

'Heaps of money,' answered the bank manager. 'I hear he's going home by the next mail to form a company to take over his estates. Another tobacco district thrown open. He's wise, I think. These good times won't last for ever.'

In the southern hemisphere Captain Whalley's daughter had no presentiment of evil when she opened the envelope addressed to her in the lawyer's handwriting. She had received it in the afternoon; all the boarders had gone out, her boys were at school, her husband sat upstairs in his big armchair with a book, thin-faced, wrapped up in rugs to the waist. The house was still, and the greyness of a cloudy day lay against the panes of the windows.

In a shabby dining-room, where a faint cold smell of dishes lingered all the year round, sitting at the end of a long table surrounded by many chairs pushed in with their backs close against the edge of the perpetually laid table-cloth, she read the opening sentences: 'Most profound regret – painful duty – your father is no more – in accordance with his instructions – fatal casualty – consolation – no blame attached to his memory . . .'

Her face was thin, her temples a little sunk under the smooth bands of black hair, her lips remained resolutely compressed, while her dark eyes grew larger, till at last, with a low cry, she stood up, and instantly stooped to pick up another envelope which had slipped off her knees on to the floor.

She tore it open, snatched out the enclosure . . .

'My dearest child,' it said, 'I am writing this while I am able yet to write legibly. I am trying hard to save for you all the money that is left; I have only kept it to serve you better. It is yours. It shall not be lost; it shall not be touched. There's five hundred pounds. Of what I have earned I have kept nothing back till now. For the future, if I live, I must keep back some – a little – to bring me to you. I must come to you. I must see you once more.

'It is hard to believe that you will ever look on these lines. God seems to have forgotten me. I want to see you – and yet death would be a greater favour. If you ever read these words, I charge you to begin by thanking a God merciful at last, for I shall be dead then, and it will be well. My dear, I am at the end of my tether.'

The next paragraph began with the words: 'My sight is going . . .'

She read no more that day. The hand holding up the paper to her eyes fell slowly, and her slender figure in a plain black dress walked rigidly to the window. Her eyes were dry: no cry of sorrow or whisper of thanks went up to heaven from her lips. Life had been too hard, for all the efforts of his love. It had silenced her emotions. But for the first time in all these years its sting had departed, the carking care of poverty, the meanness of a hard struggle for bread. Even the image of her husband and of her children seemed to glide away from her into the grey twilight; it was her father's face alone that she saw, as though he had come to see her, always quiet and big, as she had seen him last, but with something more august and tender in his aspect.

She slipped his folded letter between the two buttons of her plain black bodice, and leaning her forehead against a window-pane remained there till dusk, perfectly motionless, giving him all the time she could spare. Gone! Was it possible?

My God, was it possible? The blow had come softened by the spaces of the earth, by the years of absence. There had been whole days when she had not thought of him at all – had no time. But she had loved him, she felt she had loved him after all.

AN ANARCHIST

(A Desperate Tale)

That year I spent the best two months of the dry season on one of the estates – in fact, on the principal cattle estate – of a famous meat-extract manufacturing company.

BOS. Bos. You have seen the three magic letters on the advertisement pages of magazines and newspapers, in the windows of provision merchants, and on calendars for next year you receive by post in the month of November. They scatter pamphlets also, written in a sickly enthusiastic style and in several languages, giving statistics of slaughter and bloodshed enough to make a Turk turn faint. The 'art' illustrating that 'literature' represents in vivid and shining colours a large and enraged black bull stamping upon a yellow snake writhing in emerald-green grass, with a cobalt-blue sky for a background. It is atrocious and it is an allegory. The snake symbolises disease, weakness – perhaps mere hunger, which last is the chronic disease of the majority of mankind. Of course everybody knows the BOS Ltd, with its unrivalled products: Vinobos, Jellybos, and the latest unequalled perfection, Tribos, whose nourishment is offered to you not only highly concentrated, but already half digested. Such apparently is the love that limited company bears to its fellow-men – even as the love of the father and mother penguin for their hungry fledglings.

Of course the capital of a country must be productively employed. I have nothing to say against the company. But being myself animated by feelings of affection towards my fellow-men, I am saddened by the modern system of advertising. Whatever evidence it offers of enterprise, ingenuity, impudence, and resource in certain individuals, it proves to my mind the wide prevalence of that form of mental degradation which is called gullibility.

In various parts of the civilised and uncivilised world I have had to swallow BOS with more or less benefit to myself, though without great pleasure. Prepared with hot water and abundantly peppered to bring out the taste, this extract is not really unpalatable. But I have never swallowed its advertisements. Perhaps they have not gone far enough. As far as I can remember they make no promise of everlasting youth to the users of BOS, nor yet have they claimed the power of raising the dead for their estimable products. Why this austere reserve, I wonder! But I don't think they would have had me even on these terms. Whatever form of mental degradation I may (being but human) be suffering from, it is not the popular form. I am not gullible.

I have been at some pains to bring out distinctly this statement about myself in view of the story which follows. I have checked the facts as far as possible. I have turned up the files of French newspapers, and I also talked with the officer who commands the military guard on the Ile Royale, when in the course of my travels I reached Cayenne. I believe the story to be in the main true. It is the sort of story that no man, I think, would ever invent about himself, for it is neither grandiose nor flattering, nor yet funny enough to gratify a perverted vanity.

It concerns the engineer of the steam-launch belonging to the Marañon cattle estate of BOS Co. Ltd. This estate is also an island – an island as big as a small province, lying in the estuary of a great South American river. It is wild and not beautiful, but the grass growing on its low plains seems to possess exceptionally nourishing and flavouring qualities. It resounds with the lowing of innumerable herds – a deep and distressing sound under the open sky, rising like a monstrous protest of prisoners condemned to death. On the mainland, across twenty miles of discoloured muddy water, there stands a city whose name, let us say, is Horta.

But the most interesting characteristic of this island (which seems like a sort of penal settlement for condemned cattle) consists in its being the only known habitat of an extremely rare and gorgeous butterfly. The species is even more rare than it is beautiful, which is not saying little. I have already alluded to my travels. I travelled at that time, but strictly for myself and with a moderation unknown in our days of round-the-world tickets. I even travelled with a purpose. As a matter of fact, I am – 'Ha, ha, ha! – a desperate butterfly-slayer. Ha, ha, ha!'

This was the tone in which Mr Harry Gee, the manager of the cattle station, alluded to my pursuits. He seemed to consider me the greatest absurdity in the world. On the other hand, the BOS Co. Ltd, represented to him the acme of the nineteenth century's achievement. I believe that he slept in his leggings and spurs. His days he spent in the saddle flying over the plains, followed by a train of half-wild horsemen, who called him Don Enrique, and who had no definite idea of the BOS Co. Ltd, which paid their wages. He was an excellent manager, but I don't see why, when we met at meals, he should have thumped me on the back, with loud derisive enquiries: 'How's the deadly sport today? Butterflies going strong? Ha, ha, ha!' – especially as he charged me two dollars *per diem* for the hospitality of the BOS Co. Ltd (capital £1,500,000, fully paid up), in whose balance-sheet for that year those monies are no doubt included. 'I don't think I can make it anything less in justice to my company,' he had remarked, with extreme gravity, when I was arranging with him the terms of my stay on the island.

His chaff would have been harmless enough if intimacy of intercourse in the absence of all friendly feeling were not a thing detestable in itself. Moreover, his facetiousness was not very amusing. It consisted in the wearisome repetition of descriptive phrases applied to people with a burst of laughter. 'Desperate butterfly-slayer. Ha, ha, ha!' was one sample of his peculiar wit which he himself enjoyed so much. And in the same vein of exquisite humour he called my attention to the engineer of the steam-launch, one day, as we strolled on the path by the side of the creek.

The man's head and shoulders emerged above the deck, over which were scattered various tools of his trade and a few pieces of machinery. He was doing some repairs to the engines. At the sound of our footsteps he raised anxiously a grimy face with a pointed chin and a tiny fair moustache. What could be seen of his delicate features under the black smudges appeared to me wasted and livid in the greenish shade of the enormous tree spreading its foliage over the launch moored close to the bank.

To my great surprise, Harry Gee addressed him as 'Crocodile', in that half-jeering, half-bullying tone which is characteristic of self-satisfaction in his delectable kind: 'How does the work get on, Crocodile?'

I should have said before that the amiable Harry had picked up French of a sort somewhere in some colony or other – and that he pronounced it with a disagreeable forced precision as though he meant to guy the language. The man in the launch answered him quickly in a pleasant voice. His eyes had a liquid softness and his teeth flashed dazzlingly white between his thin, drooping lips.

The manager turned to me, very cheerful and loud, explaining: 'I call him Crocodile because he lives half in, half out of the creek. Amphibious – see? There's nothing else amphibious living on the island except crocodiles; so he must belong to the species eh? But in reality he's nothing less than *un citoyen anarchiste de Barcelone*.'

'A citizen anarchist from Barcelona?' I repeated, stupidly, looking down at the man.

He had turned to his work in the engine-well of the launch and presented his bowed back to us. In that attitude I heard him protest, very audibly: 'I do not even know Spanish.'

'Hey? What? You dare to deny you come from over there?' the accomplished manager was down on him truculently.

At this the man straightened himself up, dropping a spanner he had been using, and faced us; but he trembled in all his limbs.

'I deny nothing, nothing, nothing!' he said, excitedly.

He picked up the spanner and went to work again without paying any further attention to us. After looking at him for a minute or so, we went away.

'Is he really an anarchist?' I asked, when out of earshot.

'I don't care a hang what he is,' answered the humorous official of the BOS Co. 'I gave him the name because it suited me to label him in that way. It's good for the company.'

'For the company!' I exclaimed, stopping short.

'Aha!' he triumphed, tilting up his hairless pug face and straddling his thin, long legs. 'That surprises you. I am bound to do my best for my company. They have enormous expenses. Why – our agent in Horta tells me they spend fifty thousand pounds every year in advertising all over the world! One can't be too economical in working the show. Well, just you listen. When I took charge here the estate had no steam-launch. I asked for one, and kept on asking by every mail till I got it; but the man they sent out with it chucked his job at the end of two months, leaving the launch moored at the pontoon in Horta. Got a better screw at a sawmill up the river – blast him! And ever since it has been the same thing. Any Scotch or Yankee vagabond that likes to call himself a mechanic out here gets eighteen pounds a month, and the next you know he's cleared out, after smashing something as likely as not. I give you my word that some of the objects I've had for engine-drivers couldn't tell the boiler from the funnel. But this fellow understands his trade, and I don't mean him to clear out. See?'

And he struck me lightly on the chest for emphasis. Disregarding his peculiarities of manner, I wanted to know what all this had to do with the man being an anarchist.

'Come!' jeered the manager. 'If you saw suddenly a barefooted, unkempt chap slinking amongst the bushes on the sea face of the island, and at the same time observed less than a mile from the beach, a small schooner full of niggers hauling off in a hurry, you wouldn't think the man fell there from the sky, would you? And it could be nothing else but either that or Cayenne. I've got my wits about me. Directly I sighted this queer game I said to myself – "Escaped Convict". I was as certain of it as I am of seeing you standing here this minute. So I spurred on straight at him. He stood his ground for a bit on a sand hillock crying out: "*Monsieur! Monsieur! Arrêtez!*" then at the last moment broke and ran for life. Says I to myself, "I'll tame you before I'm done with you." So without a single word I kept on, heading him off here and there. I rounded him up towards the shore, and at last I had him corralled on a spit, his heels in the water and nothing but sea and sky at his back, with my horse pawing the sand and shaking his head within a yard of him.

'He folded his arms on his breast then and stuck his chin up in a sort of desperate way; but I wasn't to be impressed by the beggar's posturing.

'Says I, "You're a runaway convict."

'When he heard French, his chin went down and his face changed.

' "I deny nothing," says he, panting yet, for I had kept him skipping about in front of my horse pretty smartly. I asked him what he was doing there. He had got his breath by then, and explained that he had meant to make his way to a farm which he understood (from the schooner's people, I suppose) was to be found in the neighbourhood. At that I laughed aloud and he got uneasy. Had he been deceived? Was there no farm within walking distance?

'I laughed more and more. He was on foot, and of course the first bunch of cattle he came across would have stamped him to rags under their hoofs. A dismounted man caught on the feeding-grounds hasn't got the ghost of a chance.

' "My coming upon you like this has certainly saved your life," I said. He remarked that perhaps it was so; but that for his part he had imagined I had wanted to kill him under the hoofs of my horse. I assured him that nothing would have been easier had I meant it. And then we came to a sort of dead stop. For the life of me I didn't know what to do with this convict, unless I chucked him into the sea. It occurred to me to ask him what he had been transported for. He hung his head.

' "What is it?" says I. "Theft, murder, rape, or what?" I wanted to hear what he would have to say for himself, though of course I expected it would be some sort of lie. But all he said was – ' "Make it what you like. I deny nothing. It is no good denying anything."

'I looked him over carefully and a thought struck me.

' "They've got anarchists there, too," I said. 'Perhaps you're one of them."

' "I deny nothing whatever, monsieur," he repeats.

'This answer made me think that perhaps he was not an anarchist. I believe those damned lunatics are rather proud of themselves. If he had been one, he would have probably confessed straight out.

' "What were you before you became a convict?"

' "Ouvrier," he says. "And a good workman, too."

'At that I began to think he must be an anarchist, after all. That's the class they come mostly from, isn't it? I hate the cowardly bomb-throwing brutes. I almost made up my mind to turn my horse short round and leave him to starve or drown where he was, whichever he liked best. As to crossing the island to bother me again, the cattle would see to that. I don't know what induced me to ask – ' "What sort of workman?"

'I didn't care a hang whether he answered me or not. But when he said at once, "Mécanicien, monsieur," I nearly jumped out of the saddle with excitement. The launch had been lying disabled and idle in the creek for three weeks. My duty to the company was clear. He noticed my start, too, and there we were for a minute or so staring at each other as if bewitched.

' "Get up on my horse behind me," I told him. "You shall put my steam-launch to rights." '

These are the words in which the worthy manager of the Marañon estate related to me the coming of the supposed anarchist. He meant to keep him – out of a sense of duty to the company – and the name he had given him would prevent the fellow from obtaining employment anywhere in Horta. The *vaqueros* of the estate, when they went on leave, spread it all over the town. They did not know what an anarchist was, nor yet what Barcelona meant. They called him Anarchisto de Barcelona, as if it were his Christian name and surname. But the people in town had been reading in their papers about the anarchists in Europe and were very much impressed. Over the jocular addition of 'de Barcelona' Mr Harry Gee chuckled with immense satisfaction. 'That breed is particularly murderous, isn't it? It makes the sawmills crowd still more afraid of having anything to do with him – see?' he exulted, candidly. 'I hold him by that name better than if I had him chained up by the leg to the deck of the steam-launch.

'And mark,' he added, after a pause, 'he does not deny it. I am not wronging him in any way. He is a convict of some sort, anyhow.'

'But I suppose you pay him some wages, don't you?' I asked.

'Wages! What does he want with money here? He gets his food from my kitchen and his clothing from the store. Of course I'll give him something at the end of the year, but you don't think I'd employ a convict and give him the same money I would give an honest man? I am looking after the interests of my company first and last.'

I admitted that, for a company spending fifty thousand pounds every year in advertising, the strictest economy was obviously necessary. The manager of the Marañon Estancia grunted approvingly.

'And I'll tell you what,' he continued: 'if I were certain he's an anarchist and he had the cheek to ask me for money, I would give him the toe of my boot. However, let him have the benefit of the doubt. I am perfectly willing to take it that he has done nothing worse than to stick a knife into somebody – with extenuating circumstances – French fashion, don't you know. But that subversive sanguinary rot of doing away with all law and order in the world makes my blood boil. It's simply cutting the ground from under the feet of every decent, respectable, hard-working person. I tell you that the consciences of people who have them, like you or I, must be protected in some way; or else the first low scoundrel that came along would in every respect be just as good as myself. Wouldn't he, now? And that's absurd!'

He glared at me. I nodded slightly and murmured that doubtless there was much subtle truth in his view.

The principal truth discoverable in the views of Paul the engineer was that a little thing may bring about the undoing of a man.

'*Il ne faut pas beaucoup pour perdre un homme,*' he said to me, thoughtfully, one evening.

I report this reflection in French, since the man was of Paris, not of Barcelona at all. At the Marañon he lived apart from the station, in a small shed with a metal roof and straw walls, which he called *mon atelier*. He had a work-bench there. They had given him several horse-blankets and a saddle – not that he ever had occasion to ride, but because no other bedding was used by the working-hands, who were all *vaqueros* – cattlemen. And on this horseman's gear, like a son of the plains, he used to sleep amongst the tools of his trade, in a litter of rusty scrap-iron, with a portable forge at his head, under the work-bench sustaining his grimy mosquito-net.

Now and then I would bring him a few candle ends saved from the scant supply of the manager's house. He was very thankful for these. He did not like to lie awake in the dark, he confessed. He complained that sleep fled from him. '*Le sommeil me fuit,*' he declared, with his habitual air of subdued stoicism, which made him sympathetic and touching. I made it clear to him that I did not attach undue importance to the fact of his having been a convict.

Thus it came about that one evening he was led to talk about himself. As one of the bits of candle on the edge of the bench burned down to the end, he hastened to light another.

He had done his military service in a provincial garrison and returned to Paris to follow his trade. It was a well-paid one. He told me with some pride that in a short time he was earning no less than ten francs a day. He was thinking of setting up for himself by and by and of getting married.

Here he sighed deeply and paused. Then with a return to his stoical note: 'It seems I did not know enough about myself.'

On his twenty-fifth birthday two of his friends in the repairing shop where he worked proposed to stand him a dinner. He was immensely touched by this attention.

'I was a steady man,' he remarked, 'but I am not less sociable than any other body.'

The entertainment came off in a little café on the Boulevard de la Chapelle. At dinner they drank some special wine. It was excellent. Everything was excellent; and the world – in his own words – seemed a very good place to live in. He had good prospects, some little money laid by, and the affection of two excellent friends. He offered to pay for all the drinks after dinner, which was only proper on his part.

They drank more wine; they drank liqueurs, cognac, beer, then more liqueurs and more cognac. Two strangers sitting at the next table looked at him, he said, with so much friendliness, that he invited them to join the party.

He had never drunk so much in his life. His elation was extreme, and so pleasurable that whenever it flagged he hastened to order more drinks.

'It seemed to me,' he said, in his quiet tone and looking on the ground in the gloomy shed full of shadows, 'that I was on the point of just attaining a great and wonderful felicity. Another drink, I felt, would do it. The others were holding out well with me, glass for glass.'

But an extraordinary thing happened. At something the strangers said his elation fell. Gloomy ideas – *des idées noires* – rushed into his head. All the world outside the café appeared to him as a dismal, evil place where a multitude of poor wretches had to work and slave to the sole end that a few individuals should ride in carriages and live riotously in palaces. He became ashamed of his happiness. The pity of mankind's cruel lot wrung his heart. In a voice choked with sorrow he tried to express these sentiments. He thinks he wept and swore in turns.

The two new acquaintants hastened to applaud his humane indignation. Yes. The amount of injustice in the world was indeed scandalous. There was only one way of dealing with the rotten state of society. Demolish the whole *sacrée boutique*. Blow up the whole iniquitous show.

Their heads hovered over the table. They whispered to him eloquently; I don't think they quite expected the result. He was extremely drunk – mad drunk. With a howl of rage he leaped suddenly upon the table. Kicking over the bottles and glasses, he yelled: '*Vive l'anarchie!* Death to the capitalists!' He yelled this again and again. All round him broken glass was falling, chairs were being swung in the air, people were taking each other by the throat. The police dashed in. He hit, bit, scratched and struggled, till something crashed down upon his head . . .

He came to himself in a police cell, locked up on a charge of assault, seditious cries, and anarchist propaganda.

He looked at me fixedly with his liquid, shining eyes, that seemed very big in the dim light.

'That was bad. But even then I might have got off somehow, perhaps,' he said, slowly.

I doubt it. But whatever chance he had was done away with by a young socialist lawyer who volunteered to undertake his defence. In vain he assured him that he was no anarchist; that he was a quiet, respectable mechanic, only too anxious to work ten hours per day at his trade. He was represented at the trial as the victim of society and his drunken shoutings as the expression of infinite suffering. The young lawyer had his way to make, and this case was just what he wanted for a start. The speech for the defence was pronounced magnificent.

The poor fellow paused, swallowed, and brought out the statement: 'I got the maximum penalty applicable to a first offence.'

I made an appropriate murmur. He hung his head and folded his arms.

'When they let me out of prison,' he began, gently, 'I made tracks, of course, for my old workshop. My *patron* had a particular liking for me before; but when he saw me he turned green with fright and showed me the door with a shaking hand.'

While he stood in the street, uneasy and disconcerted, he was accosted by a middle-aged man who introduced himself as an engineer's fitter, too. 'I know who you are,' he said. 'I have attended your trial. You are a good comrade and your ideas are sound. But the devil of it is that you won't be able to get work anywhere now. These bourgeois'll conspire to starve you. That's their way. Expect no mercy from the rich.'

To be spoken to so kindly in the street had comforted him very much. His seemed to be the sort of nature needing support and sympathy. The idea of not being able to find work had knocked him over completely. If his *patron*, who knew him so well for a quiet, orderly, competent workman, would have nothing to do with him now – then surely nobody else would. That was clear. The police, keeping their eye on him, would hasten to warn every employer inclined to give him a chance. He felt suddenly very helpless, alarmed and idle; and he followed the middle-aged man to the *estaminet* round the corner where he met some other good companions. They assured him that he would not be allowed to starve, work or no work. They had drinks all round to the discomfiture of all employers of labour and to the destruction of society.

He sat biting his lower lip.

'That is, monsieur, how I became a *compagnon*,' he said. The hand he passed over his forehead was trembling. 'All the same, there's something wrong in a world where a man can get lost for a glass more or less.'

He never looked up, though I could see he was getting excited under his dejection. He slapped the bench with his open palm.

'No!' he cried. 'It was an impossible existence! Watched by the police, watched by the comrades, I did not belong to myself any more! Why, I could not even go to draw a few francs from my savings-bank without a comrade hanging about the door to see that I didn't bolt! And most of them were neither more nor less than housebreakers. The intelligent, I mean. They robbed the rich; they were only getting back their own, they said. When I had had some drink I believed them. There were also the fools and the mad. *Des exaltés – quoi!* When I was drunk I loved them. When I got more drink I was angry with the world. That was the best time. I found refuge from misery in rage. But one can't be always drunk – *n'est-ce pas, monsieur?* And when I was sober I was afraid to break away. They would have stuck me like a pig.'

He folded his arms again and raised his sharp chin with a bitter smile.

'By and by they told me it was time to go to work. The work was to rob a bank. Afterwards a bomb would be thrown to wreck the place. My beginner's part would be to keep watch in a street at the back and to take care of a black bag with the bomb inside till it was wanted. After the meeting at which the affair was arranged a trusty comrade did not leave me an inch. I had not dared to protest; I was afraid of being done away with quietly in that room; only, as we were walking together, I wondered whether it would not be better for me to throw myself suddenly into the Seine. But while I was turning it over in my mind we had crossed the bridge, and afterwards I had not the opportunity.'

In the light of the candle end, with his sharp features, fluffy little moustache, and oval face, he looked at times delicately and gaily young, and then appeared quite old, decrepit, full of sorrow, pressing his folded arms to his breast.

As he remained silent I felt bound to ask: 'Well! And how did it end?'

'Deportation to Cayenne,' he answered.

He seemed to think that somebody had given the plot away. As he was keeping watch in the back street, bag in hand, he was set upon by the police. 'These imbeciles,' had knocked him down without noticing what he had in his hand. He wondered how the bomb failed to explode as he fell. But it didn't explode.

'I tried to tell my story in court,' he continued. 'The president was amused. There were in the audience some idiots who laughed.'

I expressed the hope that some of his companions had been caught, too. He shuddered slightly before he told me that there were two – Simon, called also Biscuit, the middle-aged fitter who spoke to him in the street, and a fellow of the name of Mafile, one of the sympathetic strangers who had applauded his sentiments and consoled his humanitarian sorrows when he got drunk in the café.

'Yes,' he went on, with an effort, 'I had the advantage of their company over there on St Joseph's Island, amongst some eighty or ninety other convicts. We were all classed as dangerous.'

St Joseph's Island is the prettiest of the Iles de Salut. It is rocky and green, with shallow ravines, bushes, thickets, groves of mango-trees, and many feathery palms. Six warders armed with revolvers and carbines are in charge of the convicts kept there.

An eight-oared galley keeps up the communication in the daytime, across a channel a quarter of a mile wide, with the Ile Royale, where there is a military post. She makes the first trip at six in the morning. At four in the afternoon her service is over, and she is then hauled up into a little dock on the Ile Royale and a sentry put over her and a few smaller boats. From that time till next morning the island of St Joseph remains cut off from the rest of the world, with the warders patrolling in turn the path from the warders' house to the convict huts, and a multitude of sharks patrolling the waters all round.

Under these circumstances the convicts planned a mutiny. Such a thing had never been known in the penitentiary's history before. But their plan was not without some possibility of success. The warders were to be taken by surprise and murdered during the night. Their arms would enable the convicts to shoot down the people in the galley as she came alongside in the morning. The galley once in their possession, other boats were to be captured, and the whole company was to row away up the coast.

At dusk the two warders on duty mustered the convicts as usual. Then they proceeded to inspect the huts to ascertain that everything was in order. In the second they entered they were set upon and absolutely smothered under the numbers of their assailants. The twilight faded rapidly. It was a new moon; and a heavy black squall gathering over the coast increased the profound darkness of the night. The convicts assembled in the open space, deliberating upon the next step to be taken, argued amongst themselves in low voices.

'You took part in all this?' I asked.

'No. I knew what was going to be done, of course. But why should I kill these warders? I had nothing against them. But I was afraid of the others. Whatever happened, I could not escape from them. I sat alone on the stump of a tree with my head in my hands, sick at heart at the thought of a freedom that could be nothing but a mockery to me. Suddenly I was startled to perceive the shape of a man on the path near by. He stood perfectly still, then his form became effaced in the night. It must have been the chief warder coming to see what had become of his two men. No one noticed him. The convicts kept on quarrelling over their plans. The leaders could not get themselves obeyed. The fierce whispering of that dark mass of men was very horrible.

'At last they divided into two parties and moved off. When they had passed me I rose, weary and hopeless. The path to the warders' house was dark and silent, but on each side the bushes rustled slightly. Presently I saw a faint thread of light before me. The chief warder, followed by his three men, was approaching cautiously. But he had failed to close his dark lantern properly. The convicts had seen that faint gleam, too. There was an awful savage yell, a turmoil on the dark path, shots fired, blows, groans: and with the sound of smashed bushes, the shouts of the pursuers and the screams of the pursued, the man-hunt, the warder-hunt, passed by me into the interior of the island. I was alone. And I assure you, monsieur, I was indifferent to everything. After standing still for a while, I walked on along the path till I kicked something hard. I stooped and picked up a warder's revolver. I felt with my fingers that it was loaded in five chambers. In the gusts of wind I heard the convicts calling to each other far away, and then a roll of thunder would cover the soughing and rustling of the trees. Suddenly, a big light ran across my path very low along the ground. And it showed a woman's skirt with the edge of an apron.

'I knew that the person who carried it must be the wife of the head warder. They had forgotten all about her, it seems. A shot rang out in the interior of the island, and she cried out to herself as she ran. She passed on. I followed, and presently I saw her again. She was pulling at the cord of the big bell which hangs at the end of the landing-pier, with one hand, and with the other she was swinging the heavy lantern to and fro. This is the agreed signal for the Ile Royale should assistance be required at night. The wind carried the sound away from our island and the light she swung was hidden on the shore side by the few trees that grow near the warders' house.

'I came up quite close to her from behind. She went on without stopping, without looking aside, as though she had been all alone on the island. A brave woman, monsieur. I put the revolver inside the breast of my blue blouse and waited. A flash of lightning and a clap of thunder destroyed both the sound and the light of the signal for an instant, but she never faltered, pulling at the cord and swinging the lantern as regularly as a machine. She was a comely woman of thirty – no more. I thought to myself, "All that's no good on a night like this." And I made up my mind that if a body of my fellow-convicts came down to the pier – which was sure to happen soon – I would shoot her through the head before I shot myself. I knew the "comrades" well. This idea of mine gave me quite an interest in life, monsieur; and at once, instead of remaining stupidly exposed on the pier, I retreated a little way and crouched behind a bush. I did not intend to let myself be pounced upon unawares and be prevented perhaps from rendering a supreme service to at least one human creature before I died myself.

'But we must believe the signal was seen, for the galley from Ile Royale came over in an astonishingly short time. The woman kept right on till the light of her lantern flashed upon the officer in command and the bayonets of the soldiers in the boat. Then she sat down and began to cry.

'She didn't need me any more. I did not budge. Some soldiers were only in their shirt-sleeves, others without boots, just as the call to arms had found them. They passed by my bush at the double. The galley had been sent away for more; and the woman sat all alone crying at the end of the pier, with the lantern standing on the ground near her.

'Then suddenly I saw in the light at the end of the pier the red pantaloons of two more men. I was overcome with astonishment. They, too, started off at a run. Their tunics flapped unbuttoned and they were bareheaded. One of them panted out to the other, "Straight on, straight on!"

'Where on earth did they spring from, I wondered. Slowly I walked down the short pier. I saw the woman's form shaken by sobs and heard her moaning more and more distinctly, "Oh, my man! my poor man! my poor man!" I stole on quietly. She could neither hear nor see anything. She had thrown her apron over her head and was rocking herself to and fro in her grief. But I remarked a small boat fastened to the end of the pier.

'Those two men – they looked like *sous-officiers* – must have come in it, after being too late, I suppose, for the galley. It is incredible that they should have thus broken the regulations from a sense of duty. And it was a stupid thing to do. I could not believe my eyes in the very moment I was stepping into that boat.

'I pulled along the shore slowly. A black cloud hung over the Iles de Salut. I heard firing, shouts. Another hunt had begun – the convict-hunt. The oars were too long to pull comfortably. I managed them with difficulty, though the boat herself was light. But when I got round to the other side of the island the squall broke in rain and wind. I was unable to make head against it. I let the boat drift ashore and secured her.

'I knew the spot. There was a tumbledown old hovel standing near the water. Cowering in there I heard through the noises of the wind and the falling downpour some people tearing through the bushes. They came out on the strand. Soldiers perhaps. A flash of lightning threw everything near me into violent relief. Two convicts!

'And directly an amazed voice exclaimed, "It's a miracle!" It was the voice of Simon, otherwise Biscuit.

'And another voice growled, "What's a miracle?"

' "Why, there's a boat lying here!"

' "You must be mad, Simon! But there is, after all . . . A boat."

'They seemed awed into complete silence. The other man was Mafile. He spoke again, cautiously.

' "It is fastened up. There must be somebody here."

'I spoke to them from within the hovel: "I am here."

'They came in then, and soon gave me to understand that the boat was theirs, not mine. "There are two of us," said Mafile, "against you alone."

'I got out into the open to keep clear of them for fear of getting a treacherous blow on the head. I could have shot them both where they stood. But I said nothing. I kept down the laughter rising in my throat. I made myself very humble and begged to be allowed to go. They consulted in low tones about my fate, while with my hand on the revolver in the bosom of my blouse I had their lives in my power. I let them live. I meant them to pull that boat. I represented to them with abject humility that I understood the management of a boat, and that, being three to pull, we could get a rest in turns. That decided them at last. It was time. A little more and I would have gone into screaming fits at the drollness of it.'

At this point his excitement broke out. He jumped off the bench and gesticulated. The great shadows of his arms darting over roof and walls made the shed appear too small to contain his agitation.

'I deny nothing,' he burst out. 'I was elated, monsieur. I tasted a sort of felicity. But I kept very quiet. I took my turns at pulling all through the night. We made for the open sea, putting our trust in a passing ship. It was a foolhardy action. I persuaded them to it. When the sun rose the immensity of water was calm, and the Iles de Salut appeared only like dark specks from the top of each swell. I was steering then. Mafile, who was pulling bow, let out an oath and said, "We must rest."

'The time to laugh had come at last. And I took my fill of it, I can tell you. I held my sides and rolled in my seat, they had such startled faces. "What's got into him, the animal?" cries Mafile.

'And Simon, who was nearest to me, says over his shoulder to him, "Devil take me if I don't think he's gone mad!"

'Then I produced the revolver. Aha! In a moment they both got the stoniest eyes you can imagine. Ha, ha! They were frightened. But they pulled. Oh, yes, they pulled all day, sometimes looking wild and sometimes looking faint. I lost nothing of it because I had to keep my eyes on them all the time, or else – crack! – they would have been on top of me in a second. I rested my revolver hand on my knee all ready and steered with the other. Their faces began to blister. Sky and sea seemed on fire round us and the sea steamed in the sun. The boat made a sizzling sound as she went through the water. Sometimes Mafile foamed at the mouth and sometimes he groaned. But he pulled. He dared not stop. His eyes became bloodshot all over, and he had bitten his lower lip to pieces. Simon was as hoarse as a crow.

' "Comrade – " he begins.

' "There are no comrades here. I am your *patron*."

' "*Patron*, then," he says, "in the name of humanity let us rest."

'I let them. There was a little rainwater washing about the bottom of the boat. I permitted them to snatch some of it in the hollow of their palms. But as I gave the command *"En route"* I caught them exchanging significant glances. They thought I would have to go to sleep sometime! Aha! But I did not want to go to sleep. I was more awake than ever. It is they who went to sleep as they pulled, tumbling off the thwarts head over heels suddenly, one after another. I let them lie. All the stars were out. It was a quiet world. The sun rose. Another day. *Allez! En route!*

'They pulled badly. Their eyes rolled about and their tongues hung out. In the middle of the forenoon Mafile croaks out: "Let us make a rush at him, Simon. I would just as soon be shot at once as to die of thirst, hunger, and fatigue at the oar."

'But while he spoke he pulled; and Simon kept on pulling too. It made me smile. Ah! They loved their life, these two, in this evil world of theirs, just as I used to love my life, too, before they spoiled it for me with their phrases. I let them go on to the point of exhaustion, and only then I pointed at the sails of a ship on the horizon.

'Aha! You should have seen them revive and buckle to their work! For I kept them at it to pull right across that ship's path. They were changed. The sort of pity I had felt for them left me. They looked more like themselves every minute. They looked at me with the glances I remembered so well. They were happy. They smiled.

' "Well," says Simon, "the energy of that youngster has saved our lives. If he hadn't made us, we could never have pulled so far out into the track of ships. Comrade, I forgive you. I admire you."

'And Mafile growls from forward: "We owe you a famous debt of gratitude, comrade. You are cut out for a chief."

'Comrade, monsieur! Ah, what a good word! And they, such men as these two, had made it accursed. I looked at them. I remembered their lies, their promises, their menaces, and all my days of misery. Why could they not have left me alone after I came out of prison? I looked at them and thought that while they lived I could never be free. Never. Neither I nor others like me with warm hearts and weak heads. For I know I have not a strong head, monsieur. A black rage came upon me the rage of extreme intoxication – but not against the injustice of society. Oh, no!

' "I must be free!" I cried, furiously.

' "*Vive la liberté!*" yells that ruffian Mafile. "*Mort aux bourgeois* who send us to Cayenne! They shall soon know that we are free."

'The sky, the sea, the whole horizon, seemed to turn red, blood red all round the boat. My temples were beating so loud that I wondered they did not hear. How is it that they did not? How is it they did not understand?

'I heard Simon ask, "Have we not pulled far enough out now?"

' "Yes. Far enough," I said. I was sorry for him; it was the other I hated. He hauled in his oar with a loud sigh, and as he was raising his hand to wipe his forehead with the air of a man who has done his work, I pulled the trigger of my revolver and shot him like this off the knee, right through the heart.

'He tumbled down, with his head hanging over the side of the boat. I did not give him a second glance. The other cried out piercingly. Only one shriek of horror. Then all was still.

'He slipped off the thwart on to his knees and raised his clasped hands before his face in an attitude of supplication. "Mercy," he whispered, faintly. "Mercy for me! – comrade."

' "Ah, comrade," I said, in a low tone. "Yes, comrade, of course. Well, then, shout *Vive l'anarchie.*"

'He flung up his arms, his face up to the sky and his mouth wide open in a great yell of despair. "*Vive l'anarchie! Vive –* "

'He collapsed all in a heap, with a bullet through his head.

'I flung them both overboard. I threw away the revolver, too. Then I sat down quietly. I was free at last! At last. I did not even look towards the ship; I did not care; indeed, I think I must have gone to sleep, because all of a sudden there were shouts and I found the ship almost on top of me. They hauled me on board and secured the boat astern. They were all blacks, except the captain, who was a mulatto. He alone knew a few words of French. I could not find out where they were going nor who they were. They gave me something to eat every day; but I did not like the way they used to discuss me in their language. Perhaps they were deliberating about throwing me overboard in order to keep possession of the boat. How do I know? As we were passing this island I asked whether it was inhabited. I understood from the mulatto that there was a house on it. A farm, I fancied, they meant. So I asked them to put me ashore on the beach and keep the boat for their trouble. This, I imagine, was just what they wanted. The rest you know.'

After pronouncing these words he lost suddenly all control over himself. He paced to and fro rapidly, till at last he broke into a run; his arms went like a windmill and his ejaculations became very much like raving. The burden of them was that he 'denied nothing, nothing!' I could only let him go on, and sat out of his way, repeating, '*Calmez vous, Calmez vous,*' at intervals, till his agitation exhausted itself.

I must confess, too, that I remained there long after he had crawled under his mosquito-net. He had entreated me not to leave him; so, as one sits up with a nervous child, I sat up with him – in the name of humanity – till he fell asleep.

On the whole, my idea is that he was much more of an anarchist than he confessed to me or to himself; and that, the special features of his case apart, he was very much like many other anarchists. Warm heart and weak head – that is the word of the riddle; and it is a fact that the bitterest contradictions and the deadliest conflicts of the world are carried on in every individual breast capable of feeling and passion.

From personal enquiry I can vouch that the story of the convict mutiny was in every particular as stated by him.

When I got back to Horta from Cayenne and saw the 'Anarchist' again, he did not look well. He was more worn, still more frail, and very livid indeed under the grimy smudges of his calling. Evidently the meat of the company's main herd (in its unconcentrated form) did not agree with him at all.

It was on the pontoon in Horta that we met; and I tried to induce him to leave the launch moored where she was and follow me to Europe there and then. It would have been delightful to think of the excellent manager's surprise and disgust at the poor fellow's escape. But he refused with unconquerable obstinacy!

'Surely you don't mean to live always here!' I cried. He shook his head.

'I shall die here,' he said. Then added moodily, 'Away from *them*.'

Sometimes I think of him lying open-eyed on his horseman's gear in the low shed full of tools and scraps of iron – the anarchist slave of the Marañon estate, waiting with resignation for that sleep which 'fled' from him, as he used to say, in such an unaccountable manner

1906

THE INFORMER

(An Ironic Tale)

Mr X came to me, preceded by a letter of introduction from a good friend of mine in Paris, specifically to see my collection of Chinese bronzes and porcelain.

My friend in Paris is a collector, too. He collects neither porcelain, nor bronzes, nor pictures, nor medals, nor stamps, nor anything that could be profitably dispersed under an auctioneer's hammer. He would reject, with genuine surprise, the name of a collector. Nevertheless, that's what he is by temperament. He collects acquaintances. It is delicate work. He brings to it the patience, the passion, the determination of a true collector of curiosities. His collection does not contain any royal personages. I don't think he considers them sufficiently rare and interesting; but, with that exception, he has met with and talked to everyone worth knowing on any conceivable ground. He observes them, listens to them, penetrates them, measures them, and puts the memory away in the galleries of his mind. He has schemed, plotted, and travelled all over Europe in order to add to his collection of distinguished personal acquaintances.

As he is wealthy, well connected, and unprejudiced, his collection is pretty complete, including objects (or should I say subjects?) whose value is unappreciated by the vulgar, and often unknown to popular fame. Of those specimens my friend is naturally the most proud.

He wrote to me of X: 'He is the greatest rebel (*révolté*) of modern times. The world knows him as a revolutionary writer whose savage irony has laid bare the rottenness of the most respectable institutions. He has scalped every venerated head, and has mangled at the stake of his wit every received opinion and every recognised principle of conduct and policy. Who does not remember his flaming red revolutionary pamphlets? Their sudden swarmings used to overwhelm the powers of every Continental police like a plague of crimson gadflies. But this extreme writer has been also the active inspirer of secret societies, the mysterious unknown Number One of desperate conspiracies suspected and unsuspected, matured or baffled. And the world at large has never had an inkling of that fact! This accounts for him going about amongst us to this day, a veteran of many subterranean campaigns, standing aside now, safe within his reputation of merely the greatest destructive publicist that ever lived.'

Thus wrote my friend, adding that Mr X was an enlightened connoisseur of bronzes and china, and asking me to show him my collection.

X turned up in due course. My treasures are disposed in three large rooms without carpets and curtains. There is no other furniture than the *étagères* and the glass cases whose contents shall be worth a fortune to my heirs. I allow no fires to be lighted, for fear of accidents, and a fireproof door separates them from the rest of the house.

It was a bitter cold day. We kept on our overcoats and hats. Middle-sized and spare, his eyes alert in a long, Roman-nosed countenance, X walked on his neat little feet, with short steps, and looked at my collection intelligently. I hope I looked at him intelligently, too. A snow-white moustache and imperial made his nutbrown complexion appear darker than it really was. In his fur coat and shiny tall hat that terrible man looked fashionable. I believe he belonged to a noble family, and could have called himself Vicomte X de la Z if he chose. We talked nothing but bronzes and porcelain. He was remarkably appreciative. We parted on cordial terms.

Where he was staying I don't know. I imagine he must have been a lonely man. Anarchists, I suppose, have no families – not, at any rate, as we understand that social relation. Organisation into families may answer to a need of human nature, but in the last instance it is based on law, and therefore must be something odious and impossible to an anarchist. But, indeed, I don't understand anarchists. Does a man of that – of that – persuasion still remain an anarchist when alone, quite alone and going to bed, for instance? Does he lay his head on the pillow, pull his bedclothes over him, and go to sleep with the necessity of the *chambardement général*, as the French slang has it, of the general blow-up, always present to his mind? And if so how can he? I am sure that if such a faith (or such a fanaticism) once mastered my thoughts I would never be able to compose myself sufficiently to sleep or eat or perform any of the routine acts of daily life. I would want no wife, no children; I could have no friends, it seems to me; and as to collecting bronzes or china, that, I should say, would be quite out of the question. But I don't know. All I know is that Mr X took his meals in a very good restaurant which I frequented also.

With his head uncovered, the silver topknot of his brushed-up hair completed the character of his physiognomy, all bony ridges and sunken hollows, clothed in a perfect impassiveness of expression. His meagre brown hands emerging from large white cuffs came and went breaking bread, pouring wine, and so on, with quiet mechanical precision. His head and body above the tablecloth had a rigid immobility. This firebrand, this great agitator, exhibited the least possible amount of warmth and animation. His voice was rasping, cold, and monotonous in a low key. He could not be called a talkative personality; but with his detached calm manner he appeared as ready to keep the conversation going as to drop it at any moment.

And his conversation was by no means commonplace. To me, I own, there was some excitement in talking quietly across a dinner-table with a man whose venomous pen-stabs had sapped the vitality of at least one monarchy.

That much was a matter of public knowledge. But I knew more. I knew of him – from my friend – as a certainty what the guardians of social order in Europe had at most only suspected, or dimly guessed at.

He had had what I may call his underground life. And as I sat, evening after evening, facing him at dinner, a curiosity in that direction would naturally arise in my mind. I am a quiet and peaceable product of civilisation, and know no passion other than the passion for collecting things which are rare, and must remain exquisite even if approaching to the monstrous. Some Chinese bronzes are monstrously precious. And here (out of my friend's collection), here I had before me a kind of rare monster. It is true that this monster was polished and in a sense even exquisite. His beautiful unruffled manner was that. But then he was not of bronze. He was not even Chinese, which would have enabled one to contemplate him calmly across the gulf of racial difference. He was alive and European; he had the manner of good society, wore a coat and hat like mine, and had pretty near the same taste in cooking. It was too frightful to think of.

One evening he remarked, casually, in the course of conversation, 'There's no amendment to be got out of mankind except by terror and violence.'

You can imagine the effect of such a phrase out of such a man's mouth upon a person like myself, whose whole scheme of life had been based upon a suave and delicate discrimination of social and artistic values. Just imagine! Upon me, to whom all sorts and forms of violence appeared as unreal as the giants, ogres, and seven-headed hydras whose activities affect, fantastically, the course of legends and fairy-tales!

I seemed suddenly to hear above the festive bustle and clatter of the brilliant restaurant the mutter of a hungry and seditious multitude.

I suppose I am impressionable and imaginative. I had a disturbing vision of darkness, full of lean jaws and wild eyes, amongst the hundred electric lights of the place. But somehow this vision made me angry, too. The sight of that man, so calm, breaking bits of white bread, exasperated me. And I had the audacity to ask him how it was that the starving proletariat of Europe to whom he had been preaching revolt and violence had not been made indignant by his openly luxurious life. 'At all this,' I said, pointedly, with a glance round the room and at the bottle of champagne we generally shared between us at dinner.

He remained unmoved.

'Do I feed on their toil and their heart's blood? Am I a speculator or a capitalist? Did I steal my fortune from a starving people? No! They know this very well. And they envy me nothing. The miserable mass of the people is generous to its leaders. What I have acquired has come to me through my writings; not from the millions of pamphlets distributed gratis to the hungry and the oppressed, but from the hundreds of thousands of copies sold to the well-fed bourgeois. You know that my writings were at one time the rage, the fashion – the thing to read with wonder and horror, to turn your eyes up at my pathos . . . or else, to laugh in ecstasies at my wit.'

'Yes,' I admitted. 'I remember, of course; and I confess frankly that I could never understand that infatuation.'

'Don't you know yet,' he said, 'that an idle and selfish class loves to see mischief being made, even if it is made at its own expense? Its own life being all a matter of pose and gesture, it is unable to realise the power and the danger of a real movement and of words that have no sham meaning. It is all fun and sentiment. It is sufficient, for instance, to point out the attitude of the old French aristocracy towards the philosophers whose words were preparing the Great Revolution. Even in England, where you have some common-sense, a demagogue has only to shout loud enough and long enough to find some backing in the very class he is shouting at. You, too, like to see mischief being made. The demagogue carries the amateurs of emotion with him. Amateurism in this, that, and the other thing is a delightfully easy way of killing time, and feeding one's own vanity – the silly vanity of being abreast with the ideas of the day after tomorrow. Just as good and otherwise harmless people will join you in ecstasies over your collection without having the slightest notion in what its marvellousness really consists.'

I hung my head. It was a crushing illustration of the sad truth he advanced. The world is full of such people. And that instance of the French aristocracy before the Revolution was extremely telling, too. I could not traverse his statement, though its cynicism – always a distasteful trait – took off much of its value to my mind. However, I admit I was impressed. I felt the need to say something which would not be in the nature of assent and yet would not invite discussion.

'You don't mean to say,' I observed, airily, 'that extreme revolutionists have ever been actively assisted by the infatuation of such people?'

'I did not mean exactly that by what I said just now. I generalised. But since you ask me, I may tell you that such help has been given to revolutionary activities, more or less consciously, in various countries. And even in this country.'

'Impossible!' I protested with firmness. 'We don't play with fire to that extent.'

'And yet you can better afford it than others, perhaps. But let me observe that most women, if not always ready to play with fire, are generally eager to play with a loose spark or so.'

'Is this a joke?' I asked, smiling.

'If it is, I am not aware of it,' he said, woodenly. 'I was thinking of an instance. Oh! mild enough in a way . . .'

I became all expectation at this. I had tried many times to approach him on his underground side, so to speak. The very word had been pronounced between us. But he had always met me with his impenetrable calm.

'And at the same time,' Mr X continued, 'it will give you a notion of the difficulties that may arise in what you are pleased to call underground work.

It is sometimes difficult to deal with them. Of course there is no hierarchy amongst the affiliated. No rigid system.'

My surprise was great, but short-lived. Clearly, amongst extreme anarchists there could be no hierarchy; nothing in the nature of a law of precedence. The idea of anarchy ruling among anarchists was comforting, too. It could not possibly make for efficiency.

Mr X startled me by asking, abruptly, 'You know Hermione Street?'

I nodded doubtful assent. Hermione Street has been, within the last three years, improved out of any man's knowledge. The name exists still, but not one brick or stone of the old Hermione Street is left now.

It was the old street he meant, for he said: 'There was a row of two-storeyed brick houses on the left, with their backs against the wing of a great public building – you remember. Would it surprise you very much to hear that one of these houses was for a time the centre of anarchist propaganda and of what you would call underground action?'

'Not at all,' I declared. Hermione Street had never been particularly respectable, as I remembered it.

'The house was the property of a distinguished government official,' he added, sipping his champagne.

'Oh, indeed!' I said, this time not believing a word

'Of course he was not living there,' Mr X continued. 'But from ten till four he sat next door to it, the dear man, in his well-appointed private room in the wing of the public building I've mentioned. To be strictly accurate, I must explain that the house in Hermione Street did not really belong to him. It belonged to his grown-up children – a daughter and a son. The girl, a fine figure, was by no means vulgarly pretty. To more personal charm than mere youth could account for, she added the seductive appearance of enthusiasm, of independence, of courageous thought. I suppose she put on these appearances as she put on her picturesque dresses and for the same reason: to assert her individuality at any cost. You know, women would go to any length almost for such a purpose. She went to a great length. She had acquired all the appropriate gestures of revolutionary convictions – the gestures of pity, of anger, of indignation against the anti-humanitarian vices of the social class to which she belonged herself. All this sat on her striking personality as well as her slightly original costumes. Very slightly original; just enough to mark a protest against the philistinism of the overfed taskmasters of the poor. Just enough, and no more. It would not have done to go too far in that direction – you understand. But she was of age, and nothing stood in the way of her offering her house to the revolutionary workers.'

'You don't mean it!' I cried.

'I assure you,' he affirmed, 'that she made that very practical gesture. How else could they have got hold of it? The cause is not rich. And, moreover, there would have been difficulties with any ordinary house-agent, who would have wanted references and so on. The group she came in contact with while exploring the poor quarters of the town (you know the gesture of charity and personal service which was so fashionable some years ago) accepted with gratitude. The first advantage was that Hermione Street is, as you know, well away from the suspect part of the town specially watched by the police.

'The ground floor consisted of a little Italian restaurant, of the flyblown sort. There was no difficulty in buying the proprietor out. A woman and a man belonging to the group took it on. The man had been a cook. The comrades could get their meals there, unnoticed amongst the other customers. This was another advantage. The first floor was occupied by a shabby Variety Artists' Agency – an agency for performers in inferior music-halls, you know. A fellow called Bomm, I remember. He was not disturbed. It was rather favourable than otherwise to have a lot of foreign-looking people, jugglers, acrobats, singers of both sexes, and so on, going in and out all day long. The police paid no attention to new faces, you see. The top floor happened, most conveniently, to stand empty then.'

X interrupted himself to attack impassively, with measured movements, a *bombe glacée* which the waiter had just set down on the table. He swallowed carefully a few spoonfuls of the iced sweet, and asked me, 'Did you ever hear of Stone's Dried Soup?'

'Hear of what?'

'It was,' X pursued, evenly, 'a comestible article once rather prominently advertised in the dailies, but which never, somehow, gained the favour of the public. The enterprise fizzled out, as you say here. Parcels of their stock could be picked up at auctions at considerably less than a penny a pound. The group bought some of it, and an agency for Stone's Dried Soup was started on the top floor. A perfectly respectable business. The stuff, a yellow powder of extremely unappetising aspect, was put up in large square tins, of which six went to a case. If anybody ever came to give an order, it was, of course, executed. But the advantage of the powder was this, that things could be concealed in it very conveniently. Now and then a special case got put on a van and sent off to be exported abroad under the very nose of the policeman on duty at the corner. You understand?'

'I think I do,' I said, with an expressive nod at the remnants of the *bombe* melting slowly in the dish.

'Exactly. But the cases were useful in another way, too. In the basement, or in the cellar at the back, rather, two printing-presses were established. A lot of revolutionary literature of the most inflammatory kind was got away from the house in Stone's Dried Soup cases. The brother of our anarchist young lady found some occupation there. He wrote articles, helped to set up type and pull off the sheets, and generally assisted the man in charge, a very able young fellow called Sevrin.

'The guiding spirit of that group was a fanatic of social revolution. He is dead now. He was an engraver and etcher of genius. You must have seen his work. It is much sought after by certain amateurs now. He began by being revolutionary in his art, and ended by becoming a revolutionist, after his wife and child had died in want and misery. He used to say that the bourgeois, the smug, overfed lot, had killed them. That was his real belief. He still worked at his art and led a double life. He was tall, gaunt, and swarthy, with a long, brown beard and deep-set eyes. You must have seen him. His name was Horne.'

At this I was really startled. Of course years ago I used to meet Horne about. He looked like a powerful, rough gypsy, in an old top hat, with a red muffler round his throat and buttoned up in a long, shabby overcoat. He talked of his art with exaltation, and gave one the impression of being strung up to the verge of insanity. A small group of connoisseurs appreciated his work. Who would have thought that this man . . . Amazing! And yet it was not, after all, so difficult to believe.

'As you see,' X went on, 'this group was in a position to pursue its work of propaganda, and the other kind of work, too, under very advantageous conditions. They were all resolute, experienced men of a superior stamp. And yet we became struck at length by the fact that plans prepared in Hermione Street almost invariably failed.'

'Who were "we"?' I asked, pointedly.

'Some of us in Brussels – at the centre,' he said, hastily. 'Whatever vigorous action originated in Hermione Street seemed doomed to failure. Something always happened to baffle the best-planned manifestations in every part of Europe. It was a time of general activity. You must not imagine that all our failures are of a loud sort, with arrests and trials. That is not so. Often the police work quietly, almost secretly, defeating our combinations by clever counter-plotting. No arrests, no noise, no alarming of the public mind and inflaming the passions. It is a wise procedure. But at that time the police were too uniformly successful from the Mediterranean to the Baltic. It was annoying and began to look dangerous. At last we came to the conclusion that there must be some untrustworthy elements amongst the London groups. And I came over to see what could be done quietly.

'My first step was to call upon our young Lady Amateur of anarchism at her private house. She received me in a flattering way. I judged that she knew nothing of the chemical and other operations going on at the top of the house in Hermione Street. The printing of anarchist literature was the only "activity" she seemed to be aware of there. She was displaying very strikingly the usual signs of severe enthusiasm, and had already written many sentimental articles with ferocious conclusions. I could see she was enjoying herself hugely, with all the gestures and grimaces of deadly earnestness. They suited her big-eyed, broad-browed face and the good carriage of her shapely head, crowned by a magnificent lot of brown hair done in an unusual and becoming style. Her brother was in the room, too, a serious youth, with arched eyebrows and wearing a red necktie, who struck me as being absolutely in the dark about everything in the world, including himself. By and by a tall young man came in.

He was clean-shaved with a strong bluish jaw and something of the air of a taciturn actor or of a fanatical priest: the type with thick black eyebrows – you know. But he was very presentable indeed. He shook hands at once vigorously with each of us. The young lady came up to me and murmured sweetly, "Comrade Sevrin."

'I had never seen him before. He had little to say to us, but sat down by the side of the girl, and they fell at once into earnest conversation. She leaned forward in her deep armchair, and took her nicely rounded chin in her beautiful white hand. He looked attentively into her eyes. It was the attitude of love-making, serious, intense, as if on the brink of the grave. I suppose she felt it necessary to round and complete her assumption of advanced ideas, of revolutionary lawlessness, by making believe to be in love with an anarchist. And this one, I repeat, was extremely presentable, notwithstanding his fanatical black-browed aspect. After a few stolen glances in their direction, I had no doubt that he was in earnest. As to the lady, her gestures were unapproachable, better than the very thing itself in the blended suggestion of dignity, sweetness, condescension, fascination, surrender, and reserve. She interpreted her conception of what that precise sort of love-making should be with consummate art. And so far, she, too, no doubt, was in earnest. Gestures – but so perfect!

'After I had been left alone with our Lady Amateur I informed her guardedly of the object of my visit. I hinted at our suspicions. I wanted to hear what she would have to say, and half expected some perhaps unconscious revelation. All she said was, "That's serious," looking delightfully concerned and grave. But there was a sparkle in her eyes which meant plainly, "How exciting!" After all, she knew little of anything except of words. Still, she undertook to put me in communication with Horne, who was not easy to find unless in Hermione Street, where I did not wish to show myself just then.

'I met Horne. This was another kind of a fanatic altogether. I exposed to him the conclusion we in Brussels had arrived at, and pointed out the significant series of failures. To this he answered with irrelevant exaltation: "I have something in hand that shall strike terror into the heart of these gorged brutes."

'And then I learned that, by excavating in one of the cellars of the house, he and some companions had made their way into the vaults under the great public building I have mentioned before. The blowing up of a whole wing was a certainty as soon as the materials were ready.

'I was not so appalled at the stupidity of that move as I might have been had not the usefulness of our centre in Hermione Street become already very problematical. In fact, in my opinion it was much more of a police trap by this time than anything else.

'What was necessary now was to discover what, or rather who, was wrong, and I managed at last to get that idea into Horne's head. He glared, perplexed, his nostrils working as if he were sniffing treachery in the air.

'And here comes a piece of work which will no doubt strike you as a sort of theatrical expedient. And yet what else could have been done? The problem was to find out the untrustworthy member of the group. But no suspicion could be fastened on one more than another. To set a watch upon them all was not very practicable. Besides, that proceeding often fails. In any case, it takes time, and the danger was pressing. I felt certain that the premises in Hermione Street would be ultimately raided, though the police had evidently such confidence in the informer that the house, for the time being, was not even watched. Horne was positive on that point. Under the circumstances it was an unfavourable symptom. Something had to be done quickly.

'I decided to organise a raid myself upon the group. Do you understand? A raid of other trusty comrades personating the police. A conspiracy within a conspiracy. You see the object of it, of course. When apparently about to be arrested I hoped the informer would betray himself in some way or other; either by some unguarded act or simply by his unconcerned demeanour, for instance. Of course there was the risk of complete failure and the no lesser risk of some fatal accident in the course of resistance, perhaps, or in the efforts at escape. For, as you will easily see, the Hermione Street group had to be actually and completely taken unawares, as I was sure they would be by the real police before very long. The informer was amongst them, and Horne alone could be let into the secret of my plan.

'I will not enter into the detail of my preparations. It was not very easy to arrange, but it was done very well, with a really convincing effect. The sham police invaded the restaurant, whose shutters were immediately put up. The surprise was perfect. Most of the Hermione Street party were found in the second cellar, enlarging the hole communicating with the vaults of the great public building. At the first alarm, several comrades bolted through impulsively into the aforesaid vault, where, of course, had this been a genuine raid, they would have been hopelessly trapped. We did not bother about them for the moment. They were harmless enough. The top floor caused considerable anxiety to Horne and myself. There, surrounded by tins of Stone's Dried Soup, a comrade, nicknamed the Professor (he was an ex-science student), was engaged in perfecting some new detonators. He was an abstracted, self-confident, sallow little man, armed with large round spectacles, and we were afraid that under a mistaken impression he would blow himself up and wreck the house about our ears. I rushed upstairs and found him already at the door, on the alert, listening, as he said, to "suspicious noises down below". Before I had quite finished explaining to him what was going on he shrugged his shoulders disdainfully and turned away to his balances and test-tubes. His was the true spirit of an extreme revolutionist. Explosives were his faith, his hope, his weapon, and his shield. He perished a couple of years afterwards in a secret laboratory through the premature explosion of one of his improved detonators.

'Hurrying down again, I found an impressive scene in the gloom of the big cellar. The man who personated the inspector (he was no stranger to the part) was speaking harshly, and giving bogus orders to his bogus subordinates for the removal of his prisoners. Evidently nothing enlightening had happened so far. Horne, saturnine and swarthy, waited with folded arms, and his patient, moody expectation had an air of stoicism well in keeping with the situation. I detected in the shadows one of the Hermione Street group surreptitiously chewing up and swallowing a small piece of paper. Some compromising scrap, I suppose; perhaps just a note of a few names and addresses. He was a true and faithful "companion". But the fund of secret malice which lurks at the bottom of our sympathies caused me to feel amused at that perfectly uncalled for performance.

'In every other respect the risky experiment, the theatrical *coup*, if you like to call it so, seemed to have failed. The deception could not be kept up much longer; the explanation would bring about a very embarrassing and even grave situation. The man who had eaten the paper would be furious. The fellows who had bolted away would be angry, too.

'To add to my vexation, the door communicating with the other cellar, where the printing-presses were, flew open, and our young lady revolutionist appeared, a black silhouette in a close-fitting dress and a large hat, with the blaze of gas flaring in there at her back. Over her shoulder I perceived the arched eyebrows and the red necktie of her brother.

'The last people in the world I wanted to see then! They had gone that evening to some amateur concert for the delectation of the poor people, you know; but she had insisted on leaving early, on purpose to call in Hermione Street on the way home, under the pretext of having some work to do. Her usual task was to correct the proofs of the Italian and French editions of the *Alarm Bell* and the *Firebrand* . . . '

'Heavens!' I murmured. I had been shown once a few copies of these publications. Nothing, in my opinion, could have been less fit for the eyes of a young lady. They were the most advanced things of the sort; advanced, I mean, beyond all bounds of reason and decency. One of them preached the dissolution of all social and domestic ties; the other advocated systematic murder. To think of a young girl calmly tracking printers' errors all along the sort of abominable sentences I remembered was intolerable to my sentiment of womanhood. Mr X, after giving me a glance, pursued steadily.

'I think, however, that she came mostly to exercise her fascinations upon Sevrin, and to receive his homage in her queenly and condescending way. She was aware of both – her power and his homage – and enjoyed them with, I dare say, complete innocence. We have no ground in expediency or morals to quarrel with her on that account. Charm in woman and exceptional intelligence in man are a law unto themselves. Is it not so?'

I refrained from expressing my abhorrence of that licentious doctrine because of my curiosity.

'But what happened then?' I hastened to ask.

X went on crumbling slowly a small piece of bread with a careless left hand. 'What happened, in effect,' he confessed, 'is that she saved the situation.'

'She gave you an opportunity to end your rather sinister farce,' I suggested.

'Yes,' he said, preserving his impassive bearing. 'The farce was bound to end soon. And it ended in a very few minutes. And it ended well. Had she not come in, it might have ended badly. Her brother, of course, did not count. They had slipped into the house quietly some time before. The printing-cellar had an entrance of its own. Not finding anyone there, she sat down to her proofs, expecting Sevrin to return to his work at any moment. He did not do so. She grew impatient, heard through the door the sounds of a disturbance in the other cellar and naturally came in to see what was the matter.

'Sevrin had been with us. At first he had seemed to me the most amazed of the whole raided lot. He appeared for an instant as if paralysed with astonishment. He stood rooted to the spot. He never moved a limb. A solitary gas-jet flared near his head; all the other lights had been put out at the first alarm. And presently, from my dark corner, I observed on his shaven actor's face an expression of puzzled, vexed watchfulness. He knitted his heavy eyebrows. The corners of his mouth dropped scornfully. He was angry. Most likely he had seen through the game, and I regretted I had not taken him from the first into my complete confidence.

'But with the appearance of the girl he became obviously alarmed. It was plain. I could see it grow. The change of his expression was swift and startling. And I did not know why. The reason never occurred to me. I was merely astonished at the extreme alteration of the man's face. Of course he had not been aware of her presence in the other cellar; but that did not explain the shock her advent had given him. For a moment he seemed to have been reduced to imbecility. He opened his mouth as if to shout, or perhaps only to gasp. At any rate, it was somebody else who shouted. This somebody else was the heroic comrade whom I had detected swallowing a piece of paper. With laudable presence of mind he let out a warning yell.

' "It's the police! Back! Back! Run back, and bolt the door behind you."

'It was an excellent hint; but instead of retreating the girl continued to advance, followed by her long-faced brother in his knickerbocker suit, in which he had been singing comic songs for the entertainment of a joyless proletariat. She advanced not as if she had failed to understand – the word "police" has an unmistakable sound – but rather as if she could not help herself. She did not advance with the free gait and expanding presence of a distinguished amateur anarchist amongst poor, struggling professionals, but with slightly raised shoulders, and her elbows pressed close to her body, as if trying to shrink within herself. Her eyes were fixed immovably upon Sevrin. Sevrin the man, I fancy; not Sevrin the anarchist. But she advanced. And that was natural. For all their assumption of independence, girls of that class are used to the feeling of being specially protected, as, in fact, they are. This feeling accounts for nine-tenths of their audacious gestures. Her face had gone completely colourless. Ghastly. Fancy having it brought home to her so brutally that she was the sort of person who must run away from the police! I believe she was pale with indignation, mostly, though there was, of course, also the concern for her intact personality, a vague dread of some sort of rudeness. And, naturally, she turned to a man, to the man on whom she had a claim of fascination and homage – the man who could not conceivably fail her at any juncture.'

'But,' I cried, amazed at this analysis, 'if it had been serious, real, I mean – as she thought it was – what could she expect him to do for her?'

X never moved a muscle of his face.

'Goodness knows. I imagine that this charming, generous, and independent creature had never known in her life a single genuine thought; I mean a single thought detached from small human vanities, or whose source was not in some conventional perception. All I know is that after advancing a few steps she extended her hand towards the motionless Sevrin. And that at least was no gesture. It was a natural movement. As to what she expected him to do, who can tell? The impossible. But whatever she expected, it could not have come up, I am safe to say, to what he had made up his mind to do, even before that entreating hand had appealed to him so directly. It had not been necessary. From the moment he had seen her enter that cellar, he had made up his mind to sacrifice his future usefulness, to throw off the impenetrable, solidly fastened mask it had been his pride to wear – '

'What do you mean?' I interrupted, puzzled. 'Was it Sevrin, then, who was – '

'He was. The most persistent, the most dangerous, the craftiest, the most systematic of informers. A genius amongst betrayers. Fortunately for us, he was unique. The man was a fanatic, I have told you. Fortunately, again, for us, he had fallen in love with the accomplished and innocent gestures of that girl. An actor in desperate earnest himself, he must have believed in the absolute value of conventional signs. As to the grossness of the trap into which he fell, the explanation must be that two sentiments of such absorbing magnitude cannot exist simultaneously in one heart. The danger of that other and unconscious comedian robbed him of his vision, of his perspicacity, of his judgement. Indeed, it did at first rob him of his self-possession. But he regained that through the necessity – as it appeared to him imperiously – to do something at once. To do what? Why, to get her out of the house as quickly as possible. He was desperately anxious to do that. I have told you he was terrified. It could not be about himself. He had been surprised and annoyed at a move quite unforeseen and premature. I may even say he had been furious. He was accustomed to arrange the last scene of his betrayals with a deep, subtle art which left his revolutionist reputation untouched. But it seems clear to me that at the same time he had resolved to make the best of it, to keep his mask resolutely on. It was only with the discovery of her being in the house that everything – the forced calm, the restraint of his fanaticism, the mask – all came off together in a kind of panic. Why panic, do you ask? The answer is very simple. He remembered – or, I dare say, he had never forgotten – the Professor alone at the top of the house, pursuing his researches, surrounded by tins upon tins of Stone's Dried Soup. There was enough in some few of them to bury us all where we stood under a heap of bricks. Sevrin, of course, was aware of that. And we must believe, also, that he knew the exact character of the man. He had gauged so many such characters! Or perhaps he only gave the Professor credit for what he himself was capable of. But, in any case, the effect was produced. And suddenly he raised his voice in authority.

' "Get the lady away at once."

'It turned out that he was as hoarse as a crow; result, no doubt, of the intense emotion. It passed off in a moment. But these fateful words issued forth from his contracted throat in a discordant, ridiculous croak. They required no answer. The thing was done. However, the man personating the inspector judged it expedient to say roughly: "She shall go soon enough, together with the rest of you."

'These were the last words belonging to the comedy part of this affair.

'Oblivious of everything and everybody, Sevrin strode towards him and seized the lapels of his coat. Under his thin bluish cheeks one could see his jaws working with passion.

' "You have men posted outside. Get the lady taken home at once. Do you hear? Now. Before you try to get hold of the man upstairs."

' "Oh! There is a man upstairs," scoffed the other, openly. "Well, he shall be brought down in time to see the end of this."

'But Sevrin, beside himself, took no heed of the tone.

' "Who's the imbecile meddler who sent you blundering here? Didn't you understand your instructions? Don't you know anything? It's incredible. Here – "

'He dropped the lapels of the coat and, plunging his hand into his breast, jerked feverishly at something under his shirt. At last he produced a small square pocket of soft leather, which must have been hanging like a scapulary from his neck by the tape whose broken ends dangled from his fist.

' "Look inside," he spluttered, flinging it in the other's face. And instantly he turned round towards the girl. She stood just behind him, perfectly still and silent. Her set, white face gave an illusion of placidity. Only her staring eyes seemed bigger and darker.

'He spoke rapidly, with nervous assurance. I heard him distinctly promise her to make everything as clear as daylight presently. But that was all I caught. He stood close to her, never attempting to touch her even with the tip of his little finger – and she stared at him stupidly. For a moment, however, her eyelids descended slowly, pathetically, and then, with the long black eyelashes lying on her white cheeks, she looked ready to fall down in a swoon. But she never even swayed where she stood. He urged her loudly to follow him at once, and walked towards the door at the bottom of the cellar stairs without looking behind him. And, as a matter of fact, she did move after him a pace or two. But, of course, he was not allowed to reach the door. There were angry exclamations, a short, fierce scuffle. Flung away violently, he came flying backwards upon her, and fell. She threw out her arms in a gesture of dismay and stepped aside, just clear of his head, which struck the ground heavily near her shoe.

'He grunted with the shock. By the time he had picked himself up, slowly, dazedly, he was awake to the reality of things. The man into whose hands he had thrust the leather case had extracted therefrom a narrow strip of bluish paper. He held it up above his head, and, as after the scuffle an expectant uneasy stillness reigned once more, he threw it down disdainfully with the words, "I think, comrades, that this proof was hardly necessary".'

'Quick as thought, the girl stooped after the fluttering slip. Holding it spread out in both hands, she looked at it; then, without raising her eyes, opened her fingers slowly and let it fall.

'I examined that curious document afterwards. It was signed by a very high personage, and stamped and countersigned by other high officials in various countries of Europe. In his trade – or shall I say, in his mission? – that sort of talisman might have been necessary, no doubt. Even to the police itself – all but the heads – he had been known only as Sevrin the noted anarchist.

'He hung his head, biting his lower lip. A change had come over him, a sort of thoughtful, absorbed calmness. Nevertheless, he panted. His sides worked visibly, and his nostrils expanded and collapsed in weird contrast with his sombre aspect of a fanatical monk in a meditative attitude, but with something, too, in his face of an actor intent upon the terrible exigencies of his part. Before him Horne declaimed, haggard and bearded, like an inspired denunciatory prophet from a wilderness. Two fanatics. They were made to understand each other. Does this surprise you? I suppose you think that such people would be foaming at the mouth and snarling at each other?'

I protested hastily that I was not surprised in the least; that I thought nothing of the kind; that anarchists in general were simply inconceivable to me mentally, morally, logically, sentimentally, and even physically. X received this declaration with his usual woodenness and went on.

'Horne had burst out into eloquence. While pouring out scornful invective, he let tears escape from his eyes and roll down his black beard unheeded. Sevrin panted quicker and quicker. When he opened his mouth to speak, everyone hung on his words.

' "Don't be a fool, Horne," he began. "You know very well that I have done this for none of the reasons you are throwing at me." And in a moment he became outwardly as steady as a rock under the other's lurid stare. "I have been thwarting, deceiving, and betraying you – from conviction."

'He turned his back on Horne, and addressing the girl, repeated the words: "From conviction."

'It's extraordinary how cold she looked. I suppose she could not think of any appropriate gesture. There can have been few precedents indeed for such a situation.

' "Clear as daylight," he added. "Do you understand what that means? From conviction."

'And still she did not stir. She did not know what to do. But the luckless wretch was about to give her the opportunity for a beautiful and correct gesture.

' "I have felt in me the power to make you share this conviction," he protested, ardently. He had forgotten himself; he made a step towards her – perhaps he stumbled. To me he seemed to be stooping low as if to touch the hem of her garment. And then the appropriate gesture came. She snatched her skirt away from his polluting contact and averted her head with an upward tilt. It was magnificently done, this gesture of conventionally unstained honour, of an unblemished high-minded amateur.

'Nothing could have been better. And he seemed to think so, too, for once more he turned away. But this time he faced no one. He was again panting frightfully, while he fumbled hurriedly in his waistcoat pocket, and then raised his hand to his lips. There was something furtive in this movement, but directly afterwards his bearing changed. His laboured breathing gave him a resemblance to a man who had just run a desperate race; but a curious air of detachment, of sudden and profound indifference, replaced the strain of the striving effort. The race was over. I did not want to see what would happen next. I was only too well aware. I tucked the young lady's arm under mine without a word, and made my way with her to the stairs.

'Her brother walked behind us. Half-way up the short flight she seemed unable to lift her feet high enough for the steps, and we had to pull and push to get her to the top. In the passage she dragged herself along, hanging on my arm, helplessly bent like an old woman. We issued into an empty street through a half-open door, staggering like besotted revellers. At the corner we stopped a four-wheeler, and the ancient driver looked round from his box with morose scorn at our efforts to get her in. Twice during the drive I felt her collapse on my shoulder in a half-faint. Facing us, the youth in knickerbockers remained as mute as a fish, and, till he jumped out with the latch-key, sat more still than I would have believed it possible.

'At the door of their drawing-room she left my arm and walked in first, catching at the chairs and tables. She unpinned her hat, then, exhausted with the effort, her cloak still hanging from her shoulders, flung herself into a deep armchair, sideways, her face half buried in a cushion. The good brother appeared silently before her with a glass of water. She motioned it away. He drank it himself and walked off to a distant corner – behind the grand piano, somewhere. All was still in this room where I had seen, for the first time, Sevrin, the anti-anarchist, captivated and spellbound by the consummate and hereditary grimaces that in a certain sphere of life take the place of feelings with an excellent effect. I suppose her thoughts were busy with the same memory. Her shoulders shook violently. A pure attack of nerves. When it quieted down she affected firmness, "What is done to a man of that sort? What will they do to him?"

' "Nothing. They can do nothing to him," I assured her, with perfect truth. I was pretty certain he had died in less than twenty minutes from the moment his hand had gone to his lips. For if his fanatical anti-anarchism went even as far as carrying poison in his pocket, only to rob his adversaries of legitimate vengeance, I knew he would take care to provide something that would not fail him when required.

'She drew an angry breath. There were red spots on her cheeks and a feverish brilliance in her eyes.

' "Has ever anyone been exposed to such a terrible experience? To think that he had held my hand! That man!" Her face twitched, she gulped down a pathetic sob. "If I ever felt sure of anything, it was of Sevrin's high-minded motives."

'Then she began to weep quietly, which was good for her. Then through her flood of tears, half resentful, "What was it he said to me? – 'From conviction!' It seemed a vile mockery. What could he mean by it?"

' "That, my dear young lady," I said, gently, "is more than I or anybody else can ever explain to you." '

Mr X flicked a crumb off the front of his coat.

'And that was strictly true as to her. Though Horne, for instance, understood very well; and so did I, especially after we had been to Sevrin's lodging in a dismal back street of an intensely respectable quarter. Horne was known there as a friend, and we had no difficulty in being admitted, the slatternly maid merely remarking, as she let us in, that "Mr Sevrin had not been home that night." We forced open a couple of drawers in the way of duty, and found a little useful information. The most interesting part was his diary; for this man, engaged in such deadly work, had the weakness to keep a record of the most damnatory kind. There were his acts and also his thoughts laid bare to us. But the dead don't mind that. They don't mind anything.

' "From conviction." Yes. A vague but ardent humanitarianism had urged him in his first youth into the bitterest extremity of negation and revolt. Afterwards his optimism flinched. He doubted and became lost. You have heard of converted atheists. These turn often into dangerous fanatics, but the soul remains the same. After he had got acquainted with the girl, there are to be met in that diary of his very queer politico-amorous rhapsodies. He took her sovereign grimaces with deadly seriousness. He longed to convert her. But all this cannot interest you. For the rest, I don't know if you remember – it is a good many years ago now – the journalistic sensation of the "Hermione Street Mystery"; the finding of a man's body in the cellar of an empty house; the inquest; some arrests; many surmises – then silence – the usual end for many obscure martyrs and confessors. The fact is, he was not enough of an optimist. You must be a savage, tyrannical, pitiless, thick-and-thin optimist, like Horne, for instance, to make a good social rebel of the extreme type.'

He rose from the table. A waiter hurried up with his overcoat; another held his hat in readiness.

'But what became of the young lady?' I asked.

'Do you really want to know?' he said, buttoning himself in his fur coat carefully. 'I confess to the small malice of sending her Sevrin's diary. She went into retirement; then she went to Florence; then she went into retreat in a convent. I can't tell where she will go next. What does it matter? Gestures! Gestures! Mere gestures of her class.'

He fitted on his glossy high hat with extreme precision, and casting a rapid glance round the room, full of well-dressed people, innocently dining, muttered between his teeth: 'And nothing else! That is why their kind is fated to perish.'

I never met Mr X again after that evening. I took to dining at my club. On my next visit to Paris I found my friend all impatience to hear of the effect produced on me by this rare item of his collection. I told him all the story, and he beamed on me with the pride of his distinguished specimen.

'Isn't X well worth knowing?' he bubbled over in great delight. 'He's unique, amazing, absolutely terrific.'

His enthusiasm grated upon my finer feelings. I told him curtly that the man's cynicism was simply abominable.

'Oh, abominable! abominable!' assented my friend, effusively. 'And then, you know, he likes to have his little joke sometimes,' he added in a confidential tone.

I fail to understand the connection of this last remark. I have been utterly unable to discover where in all this the joke comes in.

1906

IL CONDE

(A Pathetic Tale)

Vedi Napoli e poi mori.

The first time we got into conversation was in the National Museum in Naples, in the rooms on the ground floor containing the famous collection of bronzes from Herculaneum and Pompeii: that marvellous legacy of antique art whose delicate perfection has been preserved for us by the catastrophic fury of a volcano.

He addressed me first, over the celebrated Resting Hermes which we had been looking at side by side. He said the right things about that wholly admirable piece. Nothing profound. His taste was natural rather than cultivated. He had obviously seen many fine things in his life and appreciated them: but he had no jargon of a dilettante or the connoisseur. A hateful tribe. He spoke like a fairly intelligent man of the world, a perfectly unaffected gentleman.

We had known each other by sight for some few days past. Staying in the same hotel – good, but not extravagantly up to date – I had noticed him in the vestibule going in and out. I judged he was an old and valued client. The bow of the hotel-keeper was cordial in its deference, and he acknowledged it with familiar courtesy. For the servants he was *Il Conde*. There was some squabble over a man's parasol – yellow silk with white lining sort of thing – the waiters had discovered abandoned outside the dining-room door. Our gold-laced door-keeper recognised it and I heard him directing one of the lift boys to run after *Il Conde* with it. Perhaps he was the only count staying in the hotel, or perhaps he had the distinction of being *the* count *par excellence*, conferred upon him because of his tried fidelity to the house.

Having conversed at the Museo – and by the by he had expressed his dislike of the busts and statues of Roman emperors in the gallery of marbles: their faces were too vigorous, too pronounced for him – having conversed already in the morning I did not think I was intruding when in the evening, finding the dining-room very full, I proposed to share his little table. Judging by the quiet urbanity of his consent he did not think so either. His smile was very attractive.

He dined in an evening waistcoat and a 'smoking' (he called it so) with a black tie. All this of very good cut, not new – just as these things should be. He was, morning or evening, very correct in his dress. I have no doubt that his whole existence had been correct, well ordered and conventional, undisturbed by startling events. His white hair brushed upwards off a lofty forehead gave him the air of an idealist, of an imaginative man. His white moustache, heavy but carefully trimmed and arranged, was not unpleasantly tinted a golden yellow in the middle. The faint scent of some very good perfume, and of good cigars (that last an odour quite remarkable to come upon in Italy) reached me across the table. It was in his eyes that his age showed most. They were a little weary with creased eyelids. He must have been sixty or a couple of years more. And he was communicative. I would not go so far as to call it garrulous – but distinctly communicative.

He had tried various climates, of Abbazia, of the Riviera, of other places, too, he told me; but the only one which suited him was the climate of the Gulf of Naples. The ancient Romans, who, he pointed out to me, were men expert in the art of living, knew very well what they were doing when they built their villas on these shores, in Baiae, in Vico, in Capri. They came down to this seaside in search of health, bringing with them their trains of mimes and flute-players to amuse their leisure. He thought it extremely probable that the Romans of the higher classes were specially predisposed to painful rheumatic affections.

This was the only personal opinion I heard him express. It was based on no special erudition. He knew no more of the Romans than an average informed man of the world is expected to know. He argued from personal experience. He had suffered himself from a painful and dangerous rheumatic affection till he found relief in this particular spot of Southern Europe.

This was three years ago, and ever since he had taken up his quarters on the shores of the gulf, either in one of the hotels in Sorrento or hiring a small villa in Capri. He had a piano, a few books; picked up transient acquaintances of a day, week, or month in the stream of travellers from all Europe. One can imagine him going out for his walks in the streets and lanes, becoming known to beggars, shopkeepers, children, country people; talking amiably over the walls to the *contadini* – and coming back to his rooms or his villa to sit before the piano, with his white hair brushed up and his thick orderly moustache, 'to make a little music for myself'. And, of course, for a change there was Naples near by – life, movement, animation, opera. A little amusement, as he said, is necessary for health. Mimes and flute-players, in fact. Only unlike the magnates of ancient Rome, he had no affairs of the city to call him away from these moderate delights. He had no affairs at all. Probably he had never had any grave affairs to attend to in his life. It was a kindly existence, with its joys and sorrows regulated by the course of Nature – marriages, births, deaths – ruled by the prescribed usages of good society and protected by the State.

He was a widower; but in the months of July and August he ventured to cross the Alps for six weeks on a visit to his married daughter. He told me her name. It was that of a very aristocratic family. She had a castle – in Bohemia, I think. This is as near as I ever came to ascertaining his nationality. His own name, strangely enough, he never mentioned. Perhaps he thought I had seen it on the published list. Truth to say, I never looked. At any rate, he was a good European – he spoke four languages to my certain knowledge – and a man of fortune. Not of great fortune evidently and appropriately. I imagine that to be extremely rich would have appeared to him improper, *outré* – too blatant altogether. And obviously, too, the fortune was not of his making. The making of a fortune cannot be achieved without some roughness. It is a matter of temperament. His nature was too kindly for strife. In the course of conversation he mentioned his estate quite by the way, in reference to that painful and alarming rheumatic affection. One year, staying incautiously beyond the Alps as late as the middle of September, he had been laid up for three months in that lonely country house with no one but his valet and the caretaking couple to attend to him. Because, as he expressed it, he 'kept no establishment there'. He had only gone for a couple of days to confer with his land agent. He promised himself never to be so imprudent in the future. The first weeks of September would find him on the shores of his beloved gulf.

Sometimes in travelling one comes upon such lonely men, whose only business is to wait for the unavoidable. Deaths and marriages have made a solitude round them, and one really cannot blame their endeavours to make the waiting as easy as possible. As he remarked to me, 'At my time of life freedom from physical pain is a very important matter.'

It must not be imagined that he was a wearisome hypochondriac. He was really much too well-bred to be a nuisance. He had an eye for the small weaknesses of humanity. But it was a good-natured eye. He made a restful, easy, pleasant companion for the hours between dinner and bedtime. We spent three evenings together, and then I had to leave Naples in a hurry to look after a friend who had fallen seriously ill in Taormina. Having nothing to do, *Il Conde* came to see me off at the station. I was somewhat upset, and his idleness was always ready to take a kindly form. He was by no means an indolent man.

He went along the train peering into the carriages for a good seat for me, and then remained talking cheerily from below. He declared he would miss me that evening very much and announced his intention of going after dinner to listen to the band in the public garden, the Villa Nazionale. He would amuse himself by hearing excellent music and looking at the best society. There would be a lot of people, as usual.

I seem to see him yet – his raised face with a friendly smile under the thick moustaches, and his kind, fatigued eyes. As the train began to move, he addressed me in two languages: first in French, saying, '*Bon voyage*'; then, in his very good, somewhat emphatic English, encouragingly, because he could see my concern: 'All will – be well – yet!'

My friend's illness having taken a decidedly favourable turn, I returned to Naples on the tenth day. I cannot say I had given much thought to *Il Conde* during my absence, but entering the dining-room I looked for him in his habitual place. I had an idea he might have gone back to Sorrento to his piano and his books and his fishing. He was great friends with all the boatmen, and fished a good deal with lines from a boat. But I made out his white head in the

crowd of heads, and even from a distance noticed something unusual in his
attitude. Instead of sitting erect, gazing all round with alert urbanity, he
drooped over his plate. I stood opposite him for some time before he looked
up, a little wildly, if such a strong word can be used in connection with his
correct appearance.

'Ah, my dear sir! Is it you?' he greeted me. 'I hope all is well.'

He was very nice about my friend. Indeed, he was always nice, with the
niceness of people whose hearts are genuinely humane. But this time it cost
him an effort. His attempts at general conversation broke down into dullness.
It occurred to me he might have been indisposed. But before I could frame the
enquiry he muttered: 'You find me here very sad.'

'I am sorry for that,' I said. 'You haven't had bad news, I hope?'

It was very kind of me to take an interest. No. It was not that. No bad
news, thank God. And he became very still as if holding his breath. Then,
leaning forward a little, and in an odd tone of awed embarrassment, he took
me into his confidence.

'The truth is that I have had a very – a very – how shall I say? – abominable
adventure happen to me.'

The energy of the epithet was sufficiently startling in that man of moderate
feelings and toned-down vocabulary. The word unpleasant I should have
thought would have fitted amply the worst experience likely to befall a man of
his stamp. And an adventure, too. Incredible! But it is in human nature to
believe the worst; and I confess I eyed him stealthily, wondering what he had
been up to. In a moment, however, my unworthy suspicions vanished. There
was a fundamental refinement of nature about the man which made me
dismiss all idea of some more or less disreputable scrape.

'It is very serious. Very serious.' He went on, nervously. 'I will tell you
after dinner, if you will allow me.'

I expressed my perfect acquiescence by a little bow, nothing more. I wished
him to understand that I was not likely to hold him to that offer, if he thought
better of it later on. We talked of indifferent things, but with a sense of
difficulty quite unlike our former easy, gossipy intercourse. The hand raising
a piece of bread to his lips, I noticed, trembled slightly. This symptom, in
regard of my reading of the man, was no less than startling.

In the smoking-room he did not hang back at all. Directly we had taken
our usual seats he leaned sideways over the arm of his chair and looked
straight into my eyes earnestly.

'You remember,' he began, 'that day you went away? I told you then I
would go to the Villa Nazionale to hear some music in the evening.'

I remembered. His handsome old face, so fresh for his age, unmarked by
any trying experience, appeared haggard for an instant. It was like the passing
of a shadow. Returning his steadfast gaze, I took a sip of my black coffee. He
was systematically minute in his narrative, simply in order, I think, not to let
his excitement get the better of him.

After leaving the railway station, he had an ice, and read the paper in a café. Then he went back to the hotel, dressed for dinner, and dined with a good appetite. After dinner he lingered in the hall (there were chairs and tables there) smoking his cigar; talked to the little girl of the Primo Tenore of the San Carlo theatre, and exchanged a few words with that 'amiable lady', the wife of the Primo Tenore. There was no performance that evening, and these people were going to the Villa also. They went out of the hotel. Very well.

At the moment of following their example – it was half-past nine already – he remembered he had a rather large sum of money in his pocket-book. He entered, therefore, the office and deposited the greater part of it with the bookkeeper of the hotel. This done, he took a *carozella* and drove to the seashore. He got out of the cab and entered the Villa on foot from the Largo di Vittoria end.

He stared at me very hard. And I understood then how really impressionable he was. Every small fact and event of that evening stood out in his memory as if endowed with mystic significance. If he did not mention to me the colour of the pony which drew the *carozella*, and the aspect of the man who drove, it was a mere oversight arising from his agitation, which he repressed manfully.

He had then entered the Villa Nazionale from the Largo di Vittoria end. The Villa Nazionale is a public pleasure-ground laid out in grass plots, bushes, and flower-beds between the houses of the Riviera di Chiaja and the waters of the bay. Alleys of trees, more or less parallel, stretch its whole length – which is considerable. On the Riviera di Chiaja side the electric tramcars run close to the railings. Between the garden and the sea is the fashionable drive, a broad road bordered by a low wall, beyond which the Mediterranean splashes with gentle murmurs when the weather is fine.

As life goes on late at night in Naples, the broad drive was all astir with a brilliant swarm of carriage lamps moving in pairs, some creeping slowly, others running rapidly under the thin, motionless line of electric lamps defining the shore. And a brilliant swarm of stars hung above the land humming with voices, piled up with houses, glittering with lights – and over the silent flat shadows of the sea.

The gardens themselves are not very well lit. Our friend went forward in the warm gloom, his eyes fixed upon a distant luminous region extending nearly across the whole width of the Villa, as if the air had glowed there with its own cold, bluish, and dazzling light. This magic spot, behind the black trunks of trees and masses of inky foliage, breathed out sweet sounds mingled with bursts of brassy roar, sudden clashes of metal, and grave, vibrating thuds.

As he walked on, all these noises combined together into a piece of elaborate music whose harmonious phrases came persuasively through a great disorderly murmur of voices and shuffling of feet on the gravel of that open space. An enormous crowd immersed in the electric light, as if in a bath of some radiant and tenuous fluid shed upon their heads by luminous globes, drifted in its hundreds round the band. Hundreds more sat on chairs in more or less concentric circles, receiving unflinchingly the great waves of sonority that ebbed out into the darkness. The Count penetrated the throng, drifted with it in tranquil enjoyment, listening and looking at the faces. All people of good society: mothers with their daughters, parents and children, young men and young women all talking, smiling, nodding to each other. Very many pretty faces, and very many pretty toilettes. There was, of course, a quantity of diverse types: showy old fellows with white moustaches, fat men, thin men, officers in uniform; but what predominated, he told me, was the South Italian type of young man, with a colourless, clear complexion, red lips, jet-black little moustache and liquid black eyes so wonderfully effective in leering or scowling.

Withdrawing from the throng, the Count shared a little table in front of the café with a young man of just such a type. Our friend had some lemonade. The young man was sitting moodily before an empty glass. He looked up once, and then looked down again. He also tilted his hat forward. Like this – The Count made the gesture of a man pulling his hat down over his brow, and went on: 'I think to myself: he is sad; something is wrong with him; young men have their troubles. I take no notice of him, of course. I pay for my lemonade, and go away.'

Strolling about in the neighbourhood of the band, the Count thinks he saw twice that young man wandering alone in the crowd. Once their eyes met. It must have been the same young man, but there were so many there of that type that he could not be certain. Moreover, he was not very much concerned except in so far that he had been struck by the marked, peevish discontent of that face.

Presently, tired of the feeling of confinement one experiences in a crowd, the Count edged away from the band. An alley, very sombre by contrast, presented itself invitingly with its promise of solitude and coolness. He entered it, walking slowly on till the sound of the orchestra became distinctly deadened. Then he walked back and turned about once more. He did this several times before he noticed that there was somebody occupying one of the benches.

The spot being midway between two lamp-posts the light was faint.

The man lolled back in the corner of the seat, his legs stretched out, his arms folded and his head drooping on his breast. He never stirred, as though he had fallen asleep there, but when the Count passed by next time he had changed his attitude. He sat leaning forward. His elbows were propped on his knees, and his hands were rolling a cigarette. He never looked up from that occupation.

The Count continued his stroll away from the band. He returned slowly, he said. I can imagine him enjoying to the full, but with his usual tranquillity, the balminess of this southern night and the sounds of music softened delightfully by the distance.

Presently, he approached for the third time the man on the garden seat, still leaning forward with his elbows on his knees. It was a dejected pose. In the semi-obscurity of the alley his high shirt collar and his cuffs made small patches of vivid whiteness. The Count said that he had noticed him getting up brusquely as if to walk away, but almost before he was aware of it the man stood before him asking in a low, gentle tone whether the *signore* would have the kindness to oblige him with a light.

The Count answered this request by a polite 'Certainly', and dropped his hands with the intention of exploring both pockets of his trousers for the matches.

'I dropped my hands,' he said, 'but I never put them in my pockets. I felt a pressure there – '

He put the tip of his finger on a spot close under his breastbone, the very spot of the human body where a Japanese gentleman begins the operations of the hara-kiri, which is a form of suicide following upon dishonour, upon an intolerable outrage to the delicacy of one's feelings.

'I glance down,' the Count continued in an awestruck voice, 'and what do I see? A knife! A long knife – '

'You don't mean to say,' I exclaimed, amazed, 'that you have been held up like this in the Villa at half-past ten o'clock, within a stone's throw of a thousand people!'

He nodded several times, staring at me with all his might.

'The clarinet,' he declared, solemnly, 'was finishing his solo, and I assure you I could hear every note. Then the band crashed *fortissimo*, and that creature rolled its eyes and gnashed its teeth hissing at me with the greatest ferocity, "Be silent! No noise or – "

I could not get over my astonishment.

'What sort of knife was it?' I asked, stupidly.

'A long blade. A stiletto – perhaps a kitchen knife. A long narrow blade. It gleamed. And his eyes gleamed. His white teeth, too. I could see them. He was very ferocious. I thought to myself: "If I hit him he will kill me." How could I fight with him? He had the knife and I had nothing. I am nearly seventy, you know, and that was a young man. I seemed even to recognise him. The moody young man of the café. The young man I met in the crowd. But I could not tell. There are so many like him in this country.'

The distress of that moment was reflected in his face. I should think that physically he must have been paralysed by surprise. His thoughts, however, remained extremely active. They ranged over every alarming possibility. The idea of setting up a vigorous shouting for help occurred to him, too. But he did nothing of the kind, and the reason why he refrained gave me a good opinion of his mental self-possession. He saw in a flash that nothing prevented the other from shouting, too.

'That young man might in an instant have thrown away his knife and pretended I was the aggressor. Why not? He might have said I attacked him.

Why not? It was one incredible story against another! He might have said anything – bring some dishonouring charge against me – what do I know? By his dress he was no common robber. He seemed to belong to the better classes. What could I say? He was an Italian – I am a foreigner. Of course, I have my passport, and there is our consul – but to be arrested, dragged at night to the police office like a criminal.'

He shuddered. It was in his character to shrink from scandal, much more than from mere death. And certainly for many people this would have always remained – considering certain peculiarities of Neapolitan manners – a deucedly queer story. The Count was no fool. His belief in the respectable placidity of life having received this rude shock, he thought that now anything might happen. But also a notion came into his head that this young man was perhaps merely an infuriated lunatic.

This was for me the first hint of his attitude towards this adventure. In his exaggerated delicacy of sentiment he felt that nobody's self-esteem need be affected by what a madman may choose to do to one. It became apparent, however, that the Count was to be denied that consolation. He enlarged upon the abominably savage way in which that young man rolled his glistening eyes and gnashed his white teeth. The band was going now through a slow movement of solemn braying by all the trombones, with deliberately repeated bangs of the big drum.

'But what did you do?' I asked, greatly excited.

'Nothing,' answered the Count. 'I let my hands hang down very still. I told him quietly I did not intend making a noise. He snarled like a dog, then said in an ordinary voice: "*Vostro portofolio.*"

'So I naturally,' continued the Count – and from this point acted the whole thing in pantomime. Holding me with his eyes, he went through all the motions of reaching into his inside breast pocket, taking out a pocket-book, and handing it over. But that young man, still bearing steadily on the knife, refused to touch it.

He directed the Count to take the money out himself, received it into his left hand, motioned the pocketbook to be returned to the pocket, all this being done to the sweet thrilling of flutes and clarinets sustained by the emotional drone of the hautboys. And the 'young man', as the Count called him, said: 'This seems very little.'

'It was, indeed, only 340 or 360 lire,' the Count pursued. 'I had left my money in the hotel, as you know. I told him this was all I had on me. He shook his head impatiently and said: "*Vostro orologio.*" '

The Count gave me the dumb show of pulling out his watch, detaching it. But, as it happened, the valuable gold half-chronometer he possessed had been left at a watchmaker's for cleaning. He wore that evening (on a leather guard) the Waterbury fifty-franc thing he used to take with him on his fishing expeditions. Perceiving the nature of this booty, the well-dressed robber made a contemptuous clicking sound with his tongue like this, 'Tse-Ah!' and waved it away hastily. Then, as the Count was returning the disdained object to his pocket, he demanded, with a threateningly increased pressure of the knife on the epigastrum by way of reminder: '*Vostri anelli.*'

'One of the rings,' went on the Count, 'was given me many years ago by my wife; the other is the signet ring of my father. I said, "No. *That* you shall not have!"'

Here the Count reproduced the gesture corresponding to that declaration by clapping one hand upon the other, and pressing both thus against his chest. It was touching in its resignation. 'That you shall not have,' he repeated, firmly, and closed his eyes, fully expecting – I don't know whether I am right in recording that such an unpleasant word had passed his lips – fully expecting to feel himself being – I really hesitate to say – being disembowelled by the push of the long, sharp blade resting murderously against the pit of his stomach – the very seat, in all human beings, of anguishing sensations.

Great waves of harmony went on flowing from the band.

Suddenly the Count felt the nightmarish pressure removed from the sensitive spot. He opened his eyes. He was alone. He had heard nothing. It is probable that 'the young man' had departed, with light steps, some time before, but the sense of the horrid pressure had lingered even after the knife had gone. A feeling of weakness came over him. He had just time to stagger to the garden seat. He felt as though he had held his breath for a long time. He sat all in a heap, panting with the shock of the reaction.

The band was executing, with immense bravura, the complicated finale. It ended with a tremendous crash. He heard it unreal and remote, as if his ears had been stopped, and then the hard clapping of a thousand, more or less, pairs of hands, like a sudden hail-shower passing away. The profound silence which succeeded recalled him to himself.

A tramcar resembling a long glass box wherein people sat with their heads strongly lighted, ran along swiftly within sixty yards of the spot where he had been robbed. Then another rustled by, and yet another going the other way. The audience about the band had broken up, and were entering the alley in small conversing groups. The Count sat up straight and tried to think calmly of what had happened to him. The vileness of it took his breath away again. As far as I can make it out he was disgusted with himself. I do not mean to say with his behaviour. Indeed, if his pantomimic rendering of it for my information was to be trusted, it was simply perfect. No, it was not that. He was not ashamed. He was shocked at being the selected victim, not of robbery so much as of contempt. His tranquillity had been wantonly desecrated. His lifelong, kindly nicety of outlook had been defaced.

Nevertheless, at that stage, before the iron had time to sink deep, he was able to argue himself into comparative equanimity. As his agitation calmed down somewhat, he became aware that he was frightfully hungry. Yes, hungry. The sheer emotion had made him simply ravenous. He left the seat and, after walking for some time, found himself outside the gardens and before an arrested tramcar, without knowing very well how he came there. He got in as if in a dream, by a sort of instinct. Fortunately he found in his trouser pocket a copper to satisfy the conductor. Then the car stopped, and as everybody was getting out he got out too. He recognised the Piazza San Ferdinando, but apparently it did not occur to him to take a cab and drive to the hotel. He remained in distress on the piazza like a lost dog, thinking vaguely of the best way of getting something to eat at once.

Suddenly he remembered his twenty-franc piece. He explained to me that he had that piece of French gold for something like three years. He used to carry it about with him as a sort of reserve in case of accident. Anybody is liable to have his pocket picked – a quite different thing from a brazen and insulting robbery.

The monumental arch of the Galleria Umberto faced him at the top of a noble flight of stairs. He climbed these without loss of time, and directed his steps towards the Café Umberto. All the tables outside were occupied by a lot of people who were drinking. But as he wanted something to eat, he went inside into the café, which is divided into aisles by square pillars set all round with long looking-glasses. The Count sat down on a red plush bench against one of these pillars, waiting for his risotto. And his mind reverted to his abominable adventure.

He thought of the moody, well-dressed young man, with whom he had exchanged glances in the crowd around the bandstand, and who, he felt confident, was the robber. Would he recognise him again? Doubtless. But he did not want ever to see him again. The best thing was to forget this humiliating episode.

The Count looked round anxiously for the coming of his risotto, and, behold! to the left against the wall – there sat the young man. He was alone at a table, with a bottle of some sort of wine or syrup and a carafe of iced water before him. The smooth olive cheeks, the red lips, the little jet-black moustache turned up gallantly, the fine black eyes a little heavy and shaded by long eyelashes, that peculiar expression of cruel discontent to be seen only in the busts of some Roman emperors – it was he, no doubt at all. But that was a type. The Count looked away hastily. The young officer over there reading a paper was like that, too. Same type. Two young men farther away playing draughts also resembled – The Count lowered his head with the fear in his heart of being everlastingly haunted by the vision of that young man. He began to eat his risotto. Presently he heard the young man on his left call the waiter in a bad-tempered tone.

At the call, not only his own waiter, but two other idle waiters belonging to a quite different row of tables, rushed towards him with obsequious alacrity, which is not the general characteristic of the waiters in the Café Umberto. The young man muttered something and one of the waiters walking rapidly to the nearest door called out into the Galleria: 'Pasquale! O! Pasquale!'

Everybody knows Pasquale, the shabby old fellow who, shuffling between the tables, offers for sale cigars, cigarettes, picture postcards, and matches to the clients of the café. He is in many respects an engaging scoundrel. The Count saw the grey-haired, unshaven ruffian enter the café, the glass case hanging from his neck by a leather strap, and, at a word from the waiter, make his shuffling way with a sudden spurt to the young man's table. The young man was in need of a cigar with which Pasquale served him fawningly. The old pedlar was going out, when the Count, on a sudden impulse, beckoned to him.

Pasquale approached, the smile of deferential recognition combining oddly with the cynical searching expression of his eyes. Leaning his case on the table, he lifted the glass lid without a word. The Count took a box of cigarettes and urged by a fearful curiosity, asked as casually as he could – 'Tell me, Pasquale, who is that young *signore* sitting over there?'

The other bent over his box confidentially.

'That, *Signor Conde,*' he said, beginning to rearrange his wares busily and without looking up, 'that is a young *cavaliere* of a very good family from Bari. He studies in the university here, and is the chief, *capo*, of an association of young men – of very nice young men.'

He paused, and then, with mingled discretion and pride of knowledge, murmured the explanatory word 'Camorra' and shut down the lid. 'A very powerful Camorra,' he breathed out. 'The professors themselves respect it greatly . . . *una lira e cinquanta centesimi, Signor Conde.*'

Our friend paid with the gold piece. While Pasquale was making up the change, he observed that the young man, of whom he had heard so much in a few words, was watching the transaction covertly. After the old vagabond had withdrawn with a bow, the Count settled with the waiter and sat still. A numbness, he told me, had come over him.

The young man paid, too, got up, and crossed over, apparently for the purpose of looking at himself in the mirror set in the pillar nearest to the Count's seat. He was dressed all in black with a dark green bow tie. The Count looked round, and was startled by meeting a vicious glance out of the corners of the other's eyes. The young *cavaliere* from Bari (according to Pasquale; but Pasquale is, of course, an accomplished liar) went on arranging his tie, settling his hat before the glass, and meantime he spoke just loud enough to be heard by the Count. He spoke through his teeth with the most insulting venom of contempt and gazing straight into the mirror.

'Ah! So you had some gold on you – you old liar – you old *birba* – you *furfante*! But you are not done with me yet.'

The fiendishness of his expression vanished like lightning, and he lounged out of the café with a moody, impassive face.

The poor Count, after telling me this last episode, fell back trembling in his chair. His forehead broke into perspiration. There was a wanton insolence in the spirit of this outrage which appalled even me. What it was to the Count's delicacy I won't attempt to guess. I am sure that if he had not been too refined to do such a blatantly vulgar thing as dying from apoplexy in a café, he would have had a fatal stroke there and then. All irony apart, my difficulty was to keep him from seeing the full extent of my commiseration. He shrank from every excessive sentiment, and my commiseration was practically unbounded. It did not surprise me to hear that he had been in bed a week. He had got up to make his arrangements for leaving Southern Italy for good and all.

And the man was convinced that he could not live through a whole year in any other climate!

No argument of mine had any effect. It was not timidity, though he did say to me once: 'You do not know what a Camorra is, my dear sir. I am a marked man.' He was not afraid of what could be done to him. His delicate conception of his dignity was defiled by a degrading experience. He couldn't stand that. No Japanese gentleman, outraged in his exaggerated sense of honour, could have gone about his preparations for hara-kiri with greater resolution. To go home really amounted to suicide for the poor Count.

There is a saying of Neapolitan patriotism, intended for the information of foreigners, I presume: 'See Naples and then die.' *Vedi Napoli e poi mori*. It is a saying of excessive vanity, and everything excessive was abhorrent to the nice moderation of the poor Count. Yet, as I was seeing him off at the railway station, I thought he was behaving with singular fidelity to its conceited spirit. *Vedi Napoli!* . . . He had seen it! He had seen it with startling thoroughness – and now he was going to his grave. He was going to it by the *train de luxe* of the International Sleeping Car Company, *via* Trieste and Vienna. As the four long, sombre coaches pulled out of the station I raised my hat with the solemn feeling of paying the last tribute of respect to a funeral *cortège*. *Il Conde*'s profile, much aged already, glided away from me in stony immobility, behind the lighted pane of glass – *Vedi Napoli e poi mori!*

1906

THE SECRET SHARER

On my right hand there were lines of fishing-stakes resembling a mysterious system of half-submerged bamboo fences, incomprehensible in its division of the domain of tropical fishes, and crazy of aspect as if abandoned forever by some nomad tribe of fishermen now gone to the other end of the ocean; for there was no sign of human habitation as far as the eye could reach. To the left a group of barren islets, suggesting ruins of stone walls, towers, and blockhouses, had its foundations set in a blue sea that itself looked solid, so still and stable did it lie below my feet; even the track of light from the westering sun shone smoothly, without that animated glitter which tells of an imperceptible ripple. And when I turned my head to take a parting glance at the tug which had just left us anchored outside the bar, I saw the straight line of the flat shore joined to the stable sea, edge to edge, with a perfect and unmarked closeness, in one levelled floor half brown, half blue under the enormous dome of the sky. Corresponding in their insignificance to the islets of the sea, two small clumps of trees, one on each side of the only fault in the impeccable joint, marked the mouth of the river Meinam we had just left on the first preparatory stage of our homeward journey; and, far back on the inland level, a larger and loftier mass, the grove surrounding the great Paknam pagoda, was the only thing on which the eye could rest from the vain task of exploring the monotonous sweep of the horizon. Here and there gleams as of a few scattered pieces of silver marked the windings of the great river; and on the nearest of them, just within the bar, the tug steaming right into the land became lost to my sight, hull and funnel and masts, as though the impassive earth had swallowed her up without an effort, without a tremor. My eye followed the light cloud of her smoke, now here, now there, above the plain, according to the devious curves of the stream, but always fainter and farther away, till I lost it at last behind the mitre-shaped hill of the great pagoda. And then I was left alone with my ship, anchored at the head of the Gulf of Siam.

She floated at the starting-point of a long journey, very still in an immense stillness, the shadows of her spars flung far to the eastward by the setting sun. At that moment I was alone on her decks. There was not a sound in her – and around us nothing moved, nothing lived, not a canoe on the water, not a bird in the air, not a cloud in the sky. In this breathless pause at the threshold of a long passage we seemed to be measuring our fitness for a long and arduous enterprise, the appointed task of both our existences to be carried out, far from all human eyes, with only sky and sea for spectators and for judges.

There must have been some glare in the air to interfere with one's sight, because it was only just before the sun left us that my roaming eyes made out beyond the highest ridge of the principal islet of the group something which did away with the solemnity of perfect solitude. The tide of darkness flowed on swiftly; and with tropical suddenness a swarm of stars came out above the shadowy earth, while I lingered yet, my hand resting lightly on my ship's rail as if on the shoulder of a trusted friend. But, with all that multitude of celestial bodies staring down at one, the comfort of quiet communion with her was gone for good. And there were also disturbing sounds by this time – voices, footsteps forward; the steward flitted along the maindeck, a busily ministering spirit; a handbell tinkled urgently under the poop-deck . . .

I found my two officers waiting for me near the supper table, in the lighted cuddy. We sat down at once, and as I helped the chief mate, I said: 'Are you aware that there is a ship anchored inside the islands? I saw her mastheads above the ridge as the sun went down.'

He raised sharply his simple face, overcharged by a terrible growth of whisker, and emitted his usual ejaculations: 'Bless my soul, sir! You don't say so!'

My second mate was a round-cheeked, silent young man, grave beyond his years, I thought; but as our eyes happened to meet I detected a slight quiver on his lips. I looked down at once. It was not my part to encourage sneering on board my ship. It must be said, too, that I knew very little of my officers. In consequence of certain events of no particular significance, except to myself, I had been appointed to the command only a fortnight before. Neither did I know much of the hands forward. All these people had been together for eighteen months or so, and my position was that of the only stranger on board. I mention this because it has some bearing on what is to follow. But what I felt most was my being a stranger to the ship; and if all the truth must be told, I was somewhat of a stranger to myself. The youngest man on board (barring the second mate), and untried as yet by a position of the fullest responsibility, I was willing to take the adequacy of the others for granted. They had simply to be equal to their tasks; but I wondered how far I should turn out faithful to that ideal conception of one's own personality every man sets up for himself secretly.

Meantime the chief mate, with an almost visible effect of collaboration on the part of his round eyes and frightful whiskers, was trying to evolve a theory of the anchored ship. His dominant trait was to take all things into earnest consideration. He was of a painstaking turn of mind. As he used to say, he 'liked to account to himself' for practically everything that came in his way, down to a miserable scorpion he had found in his cabin a week before. The why and the wherefore of that scorpion – how it got on board and came to select his room rather than the pantry (which was a dark place and more what a scorpion would be partial to), and how on earth it managed to drown itself in the inkwell of his writing-desk – had exercised him infinitely. The ship within the islands was much more easily accounted for; and just as we were about to rise from table he made his pronouncement. She was, he doubted not, a ship from home lately arrived. Probably she drew too much water to cross the bar except at the top of spring tides. Therefore she went into that natural harbour to wait for a few days in preference to remaining in an open roadstead.

'That's so,' confirmed the second mate, suddenly, in his slightly hoarse voice. 'She draws over twenty feet. She's the Liverpool ship *Sephora* with a cargo of coal. Hundred and twenty-three days from Cardiff.'

We looked at him in surprise.

'The tugboat skipper told me when he came on board for your letters, sir,' explained the young man. 'He expects to take her up the river the day after tomorrow.'

After thus overwhelming us with the extent of his information he slipped out of the cabin. The mate observed regretfully that he 'could not account for that young fellow's whims'. What prevented him telling us all about it at once, he wanted to know.

I detained him as he was making a move. For the last two days the crew had had plenty of hard work, and the night before they had had very little sleep. I felt painfully that I – a stranger – was doing something unusual when I directed him to let all hands turn in without setting an anchor-watch. I proposed to keep on deck myself till one o'clock or thereabouts. I would get the second mate to relieve me at that hour.

'He will turn out the cook and the steward at four,' I concluded, 'and then give you a call. Of course at the slightest sign of any sort of wind we'll have the hands up and make a start at once.'

He concealed his astonishment. 'Very well, sir.' Outside the cuddy he put his head in the second mate's door to inform him of my unheard-of caprice to take a five hours' anchor-watch on myself. I heard the other raise his voice incredulously – 'What? The captain himself?' Then a few more murmurs, a door closed, then another. A few moments later I went on deck.

My strangeness, which had made me sleepless, had prompted that unconventional arrangement, as if I had expected in those solitary hours of the night to get on terms with the ship of which I knew nothing, manned by men of whom I knew very little more. Fast alongside a wharf, littered like any ship in port with a tangle of unrelated things, invaded by unrelated shore people, I had hardly seen her yet properly. Now, as she lay cleared for sea, the stretch of her maindeck seemed to me very fine under the stars. Very fine, very roomy for her size, and very inviting. I descended the poop and paced the waist, my mind picturing to myself the coming passage through the Malay Archipelago, down the Indian Ocean, and up the Atlantic. All its phases were familiar enough to me, every characteristic, all the alternatives which were likely to face me on the high seas – everything! . . . except the novel responsibility of command. But I took heart from the reasonable thought that the ship was like other ships, the men like other men, and that the sea was not likely to keep any special surprises expressly for my discomfiture.

Arrived at that comforting conclusion, I bethought myself of a cigar and went below to get it. All was still down there. Everybody at the after end of the ship was sleeping profoundly. I came out again on the quarterdeck, agreeably at ease in my sleeping-suit on that warm breathless night, barefooted, a glowing cigar in my teeth, and, going forward, I was met by the profound silence of the fore end of the ship. Only as I passed the door of the forecastle I heard a deep, quiet, trustful sigh of some sleeper inside. And suddenly I rejoiced in the great security of the sea as compared with the unrest of the land, in my choice of that untempted life presenting no disquieting problems, invested with an elementary moral beauty by the absolute straightforwardness of its appeal and by the singleness of its purpose.

The riding-light in the fore-rigging burned with a clear, untroubled, as if symbolic, flame, confident and bright in the mysterious shades of the night. Passing on my way aft along the other side of the ship, I observed that the rope side-ladder, put over, no doubt, for the master of the tug when he came to fetch away our letters, had not been hauled in as it should have been. I became annoyed at this, for exactitude in small matters is the very soul of discipline. Then I reflected that I had myself peremptorily dismissed my officers from duty, and by my own act had prevented the anchor-watch being formally set and things properly attended to. I asked myself whether it was wise ever to interfere with the established routine of duties even from the kindest of motives. My action might have made me appear eccentric. Goodness only knew how that absurdly whiskered mate would 'account' for my conduct, and what the whole ship thought of that informality of their new captain. I was vexed with myself.

Not from compunction certainly, but, as it were mechanically, I proceeded to get the ladder in myself. Now a side-ladder of that sort is a light affair and comes in easily, yet my vigorous tug, which should have brought it flying on board, merely recoiled upon my body in a totally unexpected jerk. What the devil! . . . I was so astounded by the immovableness of that ladder that I remained stock-still, trying to account for it to myself like that imbecile mate of mine. In the end, of course, I put my head over the rail.

The side of the ship made an opaque belt of shadow on the darkling glassy shimmer of the sea. But I saw at once something elongated and pale floating very close to the ladder. Before I could form a guess a faint flash of phosphorescent light, which seemed to issue suddenly from the naked body of a man, flickered in the sleeping water with the elusive, silent play of summer lightning in a night sky. With a gasp I saw revealed to my stare a pair of feet, the long legs, a broad livid back immersed right up to the neck in a greenish cadaverous glow. One hand, awash, clutched the bottom rung of the ladder. He was complete but for the head. A headless corpse! The cigar dropped out of my gaping mouth with a tiny plop and a short hiss quite audible in the absolute stillness of all things under heaven. At that I suppose he raised up his face, a dimly pale oval in the shadow of the ship's side. But even then I could only barely make out down there the shape of his black-haired head. However, it was enough for the horrid, frost-bound sensation which had gripped me about the chest to pass off. The moment of vain exclamations was past, too. I only climbed on the spare spar and leaned over the rail as far as I could, to bring my eyes nearer to that mystery floating alongside.

As he hung by the ladder, like a resting swimmer, the sea-lightning played about his limbs at every stir; and he appeared in it ghastly, silvery, fish-like. He remained as mute as a fish, too. He made no motion to get out of the water, either. It was inconceivable that he should not attempt to come on board, and strangely troubling to suspect that perhaps he did not want to. And my first words were prompted by just that troubled incertitude.

'What's the matter?' I asked in my ordinary tone, speaking down to the face upturned exactly under mine.

'Cramp,' it answered, no louder. Then slightly anxious, 'I say, no need to call anyone.'

'I was not going to,' I said.

'Are you alone on deck?'

'Yes.'

I had somehow the impression that he was on the point of letting go the ladder to swim away beyond my ken – mysterious as he came. But, for the moment, this being appearing as if he had risen from the bottom of the sea (it was certainly the nearest land to the ship) wanted only to know the time. I told him. And he, down there, tentatively: 'I suppose your captain's turned in?'

'I am sure he isn't,' I said.

He seemed to struggle with himself, for I heard something like the low, bitter murmur of doubt. 'What's the good?' His next words came out with a hesitating effort.

'Look here, my man. Could you call him out quietly?'

I thought the time had come to declare myself.

'*I* am the captain.'

I heard a 'By Jove!' whispered at the level of the water. The phosphorescence flashed in the swirl of the water all about his limbs, his other hand seized the ladder.

'My name's Leggatt.'

The voice was calm and resolute. A good voice. The self-possession of that man had somehow induced a corresponding state in myself. It was very quietly that I remarked: 'You must be a good swimmer.'

'Yes. I've been in the water practically since nine o'clock. The question for me now is whether I am to let go this ladder and go on swimming till I sink from exhaustion, or – to come on board here.'

I felt this was no mere formula of desperate speech, but a real alternative in the view of a strong soul. I should have gathered from this that he was young;

indeed, it is only the young who are ever confronted by such clear issues. But at the time it was pure intuition on my part. A mysterious communication was established already between us two – in the face of that silent, darkened tropical sea. I was young, too; young enough to make no comment. The man in the water began suddenly to climb up the ladder, and I hastened away from the rail to fetch some clothes.

Before entering the cabin I stood still, listening in the lobby at the foot of the stairs. A faint snore came through the closed door of the chief mate's room. The second mate's door was on the hook, but the darkness in there was absolutely soundless. He, too, was young and could sleep like a stone. Remained the steward, but he was not likely to wake up before he was called. I got a sleeping-suit out of my room and, coming back on deck, saw the naked man from the sea sitting on the main-hatch, glimmering white in the darkness, his elbows on his knees and his head in his hands. In a moment he had concealed his damp body in a sleeping-suit of the same grey-stripe pattern as the one I was wearing and followed me like my double on the poop. Together we moved right aft, barefooted, silent.

'What is it?' I asked in a deadened voice, taking the lighted lamp out of the binnacle, and raising it to his face.

'An ugly business.'

He had rather regular features; a good mouth; light eyes under somewhat heavy, dark eyebrows; a smooth, square forehead; no growth on his cheeks; a small, brown moustache, and a well-shaped, round chin. His expression was concentrated, meditative, under the inspecting light of the lamp I held up to his face; such as a man thinking hard in solitude might wear. My sleeping-suit was just right for his size. A well-knit young fellow of twenty-five at most. He caught his lower lip with the edge of white, even teeth.

'Yes,' I said, replacing the lamp in the binnacle. The warm, heavy tropical night closed upon his head again.

'There's a ship over there,' he murmured.

'Yes, I know. The *Sephora*. Did you know of us?'

'Hadn't the slightest idea. I am the mate of her – ' He paused and corrected himself. 'I should say I *was*.'

'Aha! Something wrong?'

'Yes. Very wrong indeed. I've killed a man.'

'What do you mean? Just now?'

'No, on the passage. Weeks ago. Thirty-nine south. When I say a man – '

'Fit of temper,' I suggested, confidently.

The shadowy, dark head, like mine, seemed to nod imperceptibly above the ghostly grey of my sleeping-suit. It was, in the night, as though I had been faced by my own reflection in the depths of a sombre and immense mirror.

'A pretty thing to have to own up to for a *Conway* boy,' murmured my double, distinctly.

'You're a *Conway* boy?'

'I am,' he said, as if startled. Then, slowly . . . 'Perhaps you too –'

It was so; but being a couple of years older I had left before he joined. After a quick interchange of dates a silence fell; and I thought suddenly of my absurd mate with his terrific whiskers and the 'Bless my soul – you don't say so' type of intellect.

My double gave me an inkling of his thoughts by saying: 'My father's a parson in Norfolk. Do you see me before a judge and jury on that charge? For myself I can't see the necessity. There are fellows that an angel from heaven – And I am not that. He was one of those creatures that are just simmering all the time with a silly sort of wickedness. Miserable devils that have no business to live at all. He wouldn't do his duty and wouldn't let anybody else do theirs. But what's the good of talking! You know well enough the sort of ill-conditioned snarling cur –'

He appealed to me as if our experiences had been as identical as our clothes. And I knew well enough the pestiferous danger of such a character where there are no means of legal repression. And I knew well enough also that my double there was no homicidal ruffian. I did not think of asking him for details, and he told me the story roughly in brusque, disconnected sentences. I needed no more. I saw it all going on as though I were myself inside that other sleeping-suit.

'It happened while we were setting a reefed foresail, at dusk. Reefed foresail! You understand the sort of weather. The only sail we had left to keep the ship running; so you may guess what it had been like for days. Anxious sort of job, that. He gave me some of his cursed insolence at the sheet. I tell you I was overdone with this terrific weather that seemed to have no end to it. Terrific, I tell you – and a deep ship. I believe the fellow himself was half crazed with funk. It was no time for gentlemanly reproof, so I turned round and felled him like an ox. He up and at me. We closed just as an awful sea made for the ship. All hands saw it coming and took to the rigging, but I had him by the throat, and went on shaking him like a rat, the men above us yelling, "Look out! look out!" Then a crash as if the sky had fallen on my head. They say that for over ten minutes hardly anything was to be seen of the ship – just the three masts and a bit of the forecastle head and of the poop all awash driving along in a smother of foam. It was a miracle that they found us, jammed together behind the forebits. It's clear that I meant business, because I was holding him by the throat still when they picked us up. He was black in the face. It was too much for them. It seems they rushed us aft together, gripped as we were, screaming "Murder!" like a lot of lunatics, and broke into the cuddy. And the ship running for her life, touch and go all the time, any minute her last in a sea fit to turn your hair grey only a-looking at it. I understand that the skipper, too, started raving like the rest of them. The man had been deprived of sleep for more than a week, and to have this sprung on him at the height of a furious gale nearly drove him out of his mind. I wonder they didn't fling me overboard after getting the carcass of their precious shipmate out of my fingers. They had rather a job to separate us, I've been told. A sufficiently fierce story to make an old judge and a respectable jury sit up a bit. The first thing I heard when I came to myself was the maddening howling of that endless gale, and on that the voice of the old man. He was hanging on to my bunk, staring into my face out of his sou'wester.

' "Mr Leggatt, you have killed a man. You can act no longer as chief mate of this ship." '

His care to subdue his voice made it sound monotonous. He rested a hand on the end of the skylight to steady himself with, and all that time did not stir a limb, so far as I could see. 'Nice little tale for a quiet tea-party,' he concluded in the same tone.

One of my hands, too, rested on the end of the skylight; neither did I stir a limb, so far as I knew. We stood less than a foot from each other. It occurred to me that if old 'Bless my soul – you don't say so' were to put his head up the companion and catch sight of us, he would think he was seeing double, or imagine himself come upon a scene of weird witchcraft; the strange captain having a quiet confabulation by the wheel with his own grey ghost. I became very much concerned to prevent anything of the sort. I heard the other's soothing undertone.

'My father's a parson in Norfolk,' it said. Evidently he had forgotten he had told me this important fact before. Truly a nice little tale.

'You had better slip down into my stateroom now,' I said, moving off stealthily. My double followed my movements; our bare feet made no sound; I let him in, closed the door with care, and, after giving a call to the second mate, returned on deck for my relief.

'Not much sign of any wind yet,' I remarked when he approached.

'No, sir. Not much,' he assented, sleepily, in his hoarse voice, with just enough deference, no more, and barely suppressing a yawn.

'Well, that's all you have to look out for. You have got your orders.'

'Yes, sir.'

I paced a turn or two on the poop and saw him take up his position face forward with his elbow in the ratlines of the mizzen-rigging before I went below. The mate's faint snoring was still going on peacefully. The cuddy lamp was burning over the table on which stood a vase with flowers, a polite attention from the ship's provision merchant – the last flowers we should see for the next three months at the very least. Two bunches of bananas hung from the beam symmetrically, one on each side of the rudder-casing. Everything was as before in the ship – except that two of her captain's sleeping-suits were simultaneously in use, one motionless in the cuddy, the other keeping very still in the captain's stateroom.

It must be explained here that my cabin had the form of the capital letter L, the door being within the angle and opening into the short part of the letter. A couch was to the left, the bed-place to the right; my writing-desk and the chronometers' table faced the door. But anyone opening it, unless he stepped right inside, had no view of what I call the long (or vertical) part of the letter. It contained some lockers surmounted by a bookcase; and a few clothes, a thick jacket or two, caps, oilskin coat, and suchlike, hung on hooks. There was at the bottom of that part a door opening into my bathroom, which could be entered also directly from the saloon. But that way was never used.

The mysterious arrival had discovered the advantage of this particular shape. Entering my room, lighted strongly by a big bulkhead lamp swung on gimbals above my writing-desk, I did not see him anywhere till he stepped out quietly from behind the coats hung in the recessed part.

'I heard somebody moving about, and went in there at once,' he whispered.

I, too, spoke under my breath.

'Nobody is likely to come in here without knocking and getting permission.'

He nodded. His face was thin and the sunburn faded, as though he had been ill. And no wonder. He had been, I heard presently, kept under arrest in his cabin for nearly nine weeks. But there was nothing sickly in his eyes or in his expression. He was not a bit like me, really; yet, as we stood leaning over my bed-place, whispering side by side, with our dark heads together and our backs to the door, anybody bold enough to open it stealthily would have been treated to the uncanny sight of a double captain busy talking in whispers with his other self.

'But all this doesn't tell me how you came to hang on to our side-ladder,' I enquired, in the hardly audible murmurs we used, after he had told me something more of the proceedings on board the *Sephora* once the bad weather was over.

'When we sighted Java Head I had had time to think all those matters out several times over. I had six weeks of doing nothing else, and with only an hour or so every evening for a tramp on the quarterdeck.'

He whispered, his arms folded on the side of my bed-place, staring through the open port. And I could imagine perfectly the manner of this thinking out – a stubborn if not a steadfast operation; something of which I should have been perfectly incapable.

'I reckoned it would be dark before we closed with the land,' he continued, so low that I had to strain my hearing, near as we were to each other, shoulder touching shoulder almost. 'So I asked to speak to the old man. He always seemed very sick when he came to see me – as if he could not look me in the face. You know, that foresail saved the ship. She was too deep to have run long under bare poles. And it was I that managed to set it for him. Anyway, he came. When I had him in my cabin – he stood by the door looking at me as if I had the halter round my neck already – I asked him right away to leave my cabin door unlocked at night while the ship was going through Sunda Straits. There would be the Java coast within two or three miles, off Angier Point. I wanted nothing more. I've had a prize for swimming – my second year in the *Conway*.'

'I can believe it,' I breathed out.

'God only knows why they locked me in every night. To see some of their faces you'd have thought they were afraid I'd go about at night strangling people. Am I a murdering brute? Do I look it? By Jove! if I had been he wouldn't have trusted himself like that into my room. You'll say I might have chucked him aside and bolted out, there and then – it was dark already. Well, no. And for the same reason I wouldn't think of trying to smash the door. There would have been a rush to stop me at the noise, and I did not mean to get into a confounded scrimmage. Somebody else might have got killed – for I would not have broken out only to get chucked back, and I did not want any more of that work. He refused, looking more sick than ever. He was afraid of the men, and also of that old second mate of his who had been sailing with him for years – a grey-headed old humbug; and his steward, too, had been with him devil knows how long – seventeen years or more – a dogmatic sort of loafer who hated me like poison, just because I was the chief mate. No chief mate ever made more than one voyage in the *Sephora*, you know. Those two old chaps ran the ship. Devil only knows what the skipper wasn't afraid of (all his nerve went to pieces altogether in that hellish spell of bad weather we had) – of what the law would do to him – of his wife, perhaps. Oh, yes! she's on board. Though I don't think she would have meddled. She would have been only too glad to have me out of the ship in any way. The "brand of Cain" business, don't you see. That's all right. I was ready enough to go off wandering on the face of the earth – and that was price enough to pay for an Abel of that sort. Anyhow, he wouldn't listen to me. "This thing must take its course. I represent the law here." He was shaking like a leaf. "So you won't?" "No!" "Then I hope you will be able to sleep on that," I said, and turned my back on him. "I wonder that *you* can," cries he, and locks the door.

'Well, after that, I couldn't. Not very well. That was three weeks ago. We have had a slow passage through the Java Sea; drifted about Carimata for ten days. When we anchored here they thought, I suppose, it was all right. The nearest land (and that's five miles) is the ship's destination; the consul would soon set about catching me; and there would have been no object in bolting to these islets there. I don't suppose there's a drop of water on them. I don't know how it was, but tonight that steward, after bringing me my supper, went out to let me eat it, and left the door unlocked. And I ate it – all there was, too. After I had finished I strolled out on the quarterdeck. I don't know that I meant to do anything. A breath of fresh air was all I wanted, I believe. Then a sudden temptation came over me. I kicked off my slippers and was in the water before I had made up my mind fairly. Somebody heard the splash and they raised an awful hullabaloo. "He's gone! Lower the boats! He's committed suicide! No, he's swimming." Certainly I was swimming. It's not so easy for a swimmer like me to commit suicide by drowning. I landed on the nearest islet before the boat left the ship's side. I heard them pulling about in the dark, hailing, and so on, but after a bit they gave up. Everything quieted down and the anchorage became as still as death. I sat down on a stone and began to think. I felt certain they would start searching for me at daylight. There was no place to hide on those stony things – and if there had been, what would have been the good? But now I was clear of that ship, I was not going back. So after a while I took off all my clothes, tied them up in a bundle with a stone inside, and dropped them in the deep water on the outer side of that islet. That was suicide enough for me. Let them think what they liked, but I didn't mean to drown myself. I meant to swim till I sank – but that's not the same thing. I struck out for another of these little islands, and it was from that one that I first saw your riding-light. Something to swim for. I went on easily, and on the way I came upon a flat rock a foot or two above water. In the daytime, I dare say, you might make it out with a glass from your poop. I scrambled up on it and rested myself for a bit. Then I made another start. That last spell must have been over a mile.'

His whisper was getting fainter and fainter, and all the time he stared straight out through the porthole, in which there was not even a star to be seen. I had not interrupted him. There was something that made comment impossible in his narrative, or perhaps in himself; a sort of feeling, a quality, which I can't find a name for. And when he ceased, all I found was a futile whisper: 'So you swam for our light?'

'Yes – straight for it. It was something to swim for. I couldn't see any stars low down because the coast was in the way, and I couldn't see the land, either. The water was like glass. One might have been swimming in a confounded thousand-feet-deep cistern with no place for scrambling out anywhere; but what I didn't like was the notion of swimming round and round like a crazed bullock before I gave out; and as I didn't mean to go back . . . No. Do you see me being hauled back, stark naked, off one of these little islands by the scruff of the neck and fighting like a wild beast? Somebody would have got killed for certain, and I did not want any of that. So I went on. Then your ladder – '

'Why didn't you hail the ship?' I asked, a little louder.

He touched my shoulder lightly. Lazy footsteps came right over our heads and stopped. The second mate had crossed from the other side of the poop and might have been hanging over the rail, for all we knew.

'He couldn't hear us talking – could he?' My double breathed into my very ear, anxiously.

His anxiety was an answer, a sufficient answer, to the question I had put to him. An answer containing all the difficulty of that situation. I closed the porthole quietly, to make sure. A louder word might have been overheard.

'Who's that?' he whispered then.

'My second mate. But I don't know much more of the fellow than you do.'

And I told him a little about myself. I had been appointed to take charge while I least expected anything of the sort, not quite a fortnight ago. I didn't know either the ship or the people. Hadn't had the time in port to look about me or size anybody up. And as to the crew, all they knew was that I was appointed to take the ship home. For the rest, I was almost as much of a stranger on board as himself, I said. And at the moment I felt it most acutely. I felt that it would take very little to make me a suspect person in the eyes of the ship's company.

He had turned about meantime; and we, the two strangers in the ship, faced each other in identical attitudes.

'Your ladder – ' he murmured, after a silence. 'Who'd have thought of finding a ladder hanging over at night in a ship anchored out here! I felt just then a very unpleasant faintness. After the life I've been leading for nine weeks, anybody would have got out of condition. I wasn't capable of swimming round as far as your rudder-chains. And, lo and behold! there was a ladder to get hold of. After I gripped it I said to myself, 'What's the good?' When I saw a man's head looking over I thought I would swim away presently and leave him shouting – in whatever language it was. I didn't mind being looked at. I – I liked it. And then you speaking to me so quietly – as if you had expected me – made me hold on a little longer. It had been a confounded lonely time – I don't mean while swimming. I was glad to talk a little to somebody that didn't belong to the *Sephora*. As to asking for the captain, that was a mere impulse. It could have been no use, with all the ship knowing about me and the other people pretty certain to be round here in the morning. I don't know – I wanted to be seen, to talk with somebody, before I went on. I don't know what I would have said . . . "Fine night, isn't it?" or something of the sort.'

'Do you think they will be round here presently?' I asked with some incredulity.

'Quite likely,' he said, faintly.

He looked extremely haggard all of a sudden. His head rolled on his shoulders.

'H'm. We shall see then. Meantime get into that bed,' I whispered. 'Want help? There.'

It was a rather high bed-place with a set of drawers underneath. This amazing swimmer really needed the lift I gave him by seizing his leg. He tumbled in, rolled over on his back, and flung one arm across his eyes. And then, with his face nearly hidden, he must have looked exactly as I used to look in that bed. I gazed upon my other self for a while before drawing across carefully the two green serge curtains which ran on a brass rod. I thought for a moment of pinning them together for greater safety, but I sat down on the couch, and once there I felt unwilling to rise and hunt for a pin. I would do it in a moment. I was extremely tired, in a peculiarly intimate way, by the strain of stealthiness, by the effort of whispering and the general secrecy of this excitement. It was three o'clock by now and I had been on my feet since nine, but I was not sleepy; I could not have gone to sleep. I sat there, fagged out, looking at the curtains, trying to clear my mind of the confused sensation of being in two places at once, and greatly bothered by an exasperating knocking in my head. It was a relief to discover suddenly that it was not in my head at all, but on the outside of the door. Before I could collect myself the words 'Come in' were out of my mouth, and the steward entered with a tray, bringing in my morning coffee. I had slept, after all, and I was so frightened that I shouted, 'This way! I am here, steward,' as though he had been miles away. He put down the tray on the table next the couch and only then said, very quietly, 'I can see you are here, sir.' I felt him give me a keen look, but I dared not meet his eyes just then. He must have wondered why I had drawn the curtains of my bed before going to sleep on the couch. He went out, hooking the door open as usual.

I heard the crew washing decks above me. I knew I would have been told at once if there had been any wind. Calm, I thought, and I was doubly vexed. Indeed, I felt dual more than ever. The steward reappeared suddenly in the doorway. I jumped up from the couch so quickly that he gave a start.

'What do you want here?'

'Close your port, sir – they are washing decks.'

'It is closed,' I said, reddening.

'Very well, sir.' But he did not move from the doorway and returned my stare in an extraordinary, equivocal manner for a time. Then his eyes wavered, all his expression changed, and in a voice unusually gentle, almost coaxingly: 'May I come in to take the empty cup away, sir?'

'Of course!' I turned my back on him while he popped in and out. Then I unhooked and closed the door and even pushed the bolt. This sort of thing could not go on very long. The cabin was as hot as an oven, too. I took a peep at my double, and discovered that he had not moved, his arm was still over his eyes; but his chest heaved; his hair was wet; his chin glistened with perspiration. I reached over him and opened the port.

'I must show myself on deck,' I reflected.

Of course, theoretically, I could do what I liked, with no one to say nay to me within the whole circle of the horizon; but to lock my cabin door and take the key away I did not dare. Directly I put my head out of the companion I saw the group of my two officers, the second mate barefooted, the chief mate in long india-rubber boots, near the break of the poop, and the steward half-way down the poop-ladder talking to them eagerly. He happened to catch sight of me and dived, the second ran down on the main-deck shouting some order or other, and the chief mate came to meet me, touching his cap.

There was a sort of curiosity in his eye that I did not like. I don't know whether the steward had told them that I was 'queer' only, or downright drunk, but I know the man meant to have a good look at me. I watched him coming with a smile which, as he got into point-blank range, took effect and froze his very whiskers. I did not give him time to open his lips.

'Square the yards by lifts and braces before the hands go to breakfast.'

It was the first particular order I had given on board that ship; and I stayed on deck to see it executed, too. I had felt the need of asserting myself without loss of time. That sneering young cub got taken down a peg or two on that occasion, and I also seized the opportunity of having a good look at the face of every foremast man as they filed past me to go to the after braces. At breakfast time, eating nothing myself, I presided with such frigid dignity that the two mates were only too glad to escape from the cabin as soon as decency permitted; and all the time the dual working of my mind distracted me almost to the point of insanity. I was constantly watching myself, my secret self, as dependent on my actions as my own personality, sleeping in that bed, behind that door which faced me as I sat at the head of the table. It was very much like being mad, only it was worse because one was aware of it.

I had to shake him for a solid minute, but when at last he opened his eyes it was in the full possession of his senses, with an enquiring look.

'All's well so far,' I whispered. 'Now you must vanish into the bathroom.'

He did so, as noiseless as a ghost, and I then rang for the steward, and facing him boldly, directed him to tidy up my stateroom while I was having my bath – 'and be quick about it'. As my tone admitted of no excuses, he said, 'Yes, sir,' and ran off to fetch his dustpan and brushes. I took a bath and did most of my dressing, splashing, and whistling softly for the steward's edification, while the secret sharer of my life stood drawn up bolt upright in that little space, his face looking very sunken in daylight, his eyelids lowered under the stern, dark line of his eyebrows drawn together by a slight frown.

When I left him there to go back to my room the steward was finishing dusting. I sent for the mate and engaged him in some insignificant conversation. It was, as it were, trifling with the terrific character of his whiskers; but my object was to give him an opportunity for a good look at my cabin. And then I could at last shut, with a clear conscience, the door of my stateroom and get my double back into the recessed part. There was nothing else for it. He had to sit still on a small folding stool, half smothered by the heavy coats hanging there. We listened to the steward going into the bathroom out of the saloon filling the water-bottles there, scrubbing the bath, setting things to rights, whisk, bang, clatter – out again into the saloon – turn the key – click. Such was my scheme for keeping my second self invisible. Nothing better could be contrived under the circumstances. And there we sat; I at my writing-desk ready to appear busy with some papers, he behind me, out of sight of the door. It would not have been prudent to talk in daytime; and I could not have stood the excitement of that queer sense of whispering to myself. Now and then, glancing over my shoulder, I saw him far back there, sitting rigidly on the low stool, his bare feet close together, his arms folded, his head hanging on his breast – and perfectly still. Anybody would have taken him for me.

I was fascinated by it myself. Every moment I had to glance over my shoulder. I was looking at him when a voice outside the door said: 'Beg pardon, sir.'

'Well!' . . . I kept my eyes on him, and so, when the voice outside the door announced, 'There's a ship's boat coming our way, sir,' I saw him give a start – the first movement he had made for hours. But he did not raise his bowed head.

'All right. Get the ladder over.'

I hesitated. Should I whisper something to him? But what? His immobility seemed never to have been disturbed. What could I tell him he did not know already? . . . Finally I went on deck.

2

The skipper of the *Sephora* had a thin red whisker all round his face, and the sort of complexion that goes with hair of that colour; also the particular, rather smeary shade of blue in the eyes. He was not exactly a showy figure; his shoulders were high, his stature but middling – one leg slightly more bandy than the other. He shook hands, looking vaguely around. A spiritless tenacity was his main characteristic, I judged. I behaved with a politeness which seemed to disconcert him. Perhaps he was shy. He mumbled to me as if he were ashamed of what he was saying; gave his name (it was something like Archbold – but at this distance of years I am hardly sure), his ship's name, and a few other particulars of that sort, in the manner of a criminal making a reluctant and doleful confession. He had had terrible weather on the passage out – terrible – terrible – wife aboard, too.

By this time we were seated in the cabin and the steward brought in a tray with a bottle and glasses. 'Thanks! No.' Never took liquor. Would have some water, though. He drank two tumblerfuls. Terrible thirsty work. Ever since daylight had been exploring the islands round his ship.

'What was that for – fun?' I asked, with an appearance of polite interest.

'No!' He sighed. 'Painful duty.'

As he persisted in his mumbling and I wanted my double to hear every word, I hit upon the notion of informing him that I regretted to say I was hard of hearing.

'Such a young man, too!' he nodded, keeping his smeary blue, unintelligent eyes fastened upon me. What was the cause of it – some disease? he enquired, without the least sympathy and as if he thought that, if so, I'd got no more than I deserved.

'Yes; disease,' I admitted in a cheerful tone which seemed to shock him. But my point was gained, because he had to raise his voice to give me his tale. It is not worth while to record that version. It was just over two months since all this had happened, and he had thought so much about it that he seemed completely muddled as to its bearings, but still immensely impressed.

'What would you think of such a thing happening on board your own ship? I've had the *Sephora* for these fifteen years. I am a well-known shipmaster.'

He was densely distressed – and perhaps I should have sympathised with him if I had been able to detach my mental vision from the unsuspected sharer of my cabin as though he were my second self. There he was on the other side of the bulkhead, four or five feet from us, no more, as we sat in the saloon. I looked politely at Captain Archbold (if that was his name), but it was the other I saw, in a grey sleeping-suit, seated on a low stool, his bare feet close together, his arms folded, and every word said between us falling into the ears of his dark head bowed on his chest.

'I have been at sea now, man and boy, for seven-and-thirty years, and I've never heard of such a thing happening in an English ship. And that it should be my ship. Wife on board, too.'

I was hardly listening to him.

'Don't you think,' I said, 'that the heavy sea which, you told me, came aboard just then might have killed the man? I have seen the sheer weight of a sea kill a man very neatly, by simply breaking his neck.'

'Good God!' he uttered, impressively, fixing his smeary blue eyes on me. 'The sea! No man killed by the sea ever looked like that.' He seemed positively scandalised at my suggestion. And as I gazed at him, certainly not prepared for anything original on his part, he advanced his head close to mine and thrust his tongue out at me so suddenly that I couldn't help starting back.

After scoring over my calmness in this graphic way he nodded wisely. If I had seen the sight, he assured me, I would never forget it as long as I lived. The weather was too bad to give the corpse a proper sea burial. So next day at dawn they took it up on the poop, covering its face with a bit of bunting; he read a short prayer, and then, just as it was, in its oilskins and long boots, they launched it amongst those mountainous seas that seemed ready every moment to swallow up the ship herself and the terrified lives on board of her.

'That reefed foresail saved you,' I threw in.

'Under God – it did,' he exclaimed fervently. 'It was by a special mercy, I firmly believe, that it stood some of those hurricane squalls.'

'It was the setting of that sail which – ' I began.

'God's own hand in it,' he interrupted me. 'Nothing less could have done it. I don't mind telling you that I hardly dared give the order. It seemed impossible that we could touch anything without losing it, and then our last hope would have been gone.'

The terror of that gale was on him yet. I let him go on for a bit, then said, casually – as if returning to a minor subject: 'You were very anxious to give up your mate to the shore people, I believe?'

He was. To the law. His obscure tenacity on that point had in it something incomprehensible and a little awful; something, as it were, mystical, quite apart from his anxiety that he should not be suspected of 'countenancing any doings of that sort'. Seven-and-thirty virtuous years at sea, of which over twenty of immaculate command, and the last fifteen in the *Sephora*, seemed to have laid him under some pitiless obligation.

'And you know,' he went on, groping shamefacedly amongst his feelings, 'I did not engage that young fellow. His people had some interest with my owners. I was in a way forced to take him on. He looked very smart, very gentlemanly, and all that. But do you know – I never liked him, somehow. I am a plain man. You see, he wasn't exactly the sort for the chief mate of a ship like the *Sephora*.'

I had become so connected in thoughts and impressions with the secret sharer of my cabin that I felt as if I, personally, were being given to understand that I, too, was not the sort that would have done for the chief mate of a ship like the *Sephora*. I had no doubt of it in my mind.

'Not at all the style of man. You understand,' he insisted, superfluously, looking hard at me.

I smiled urbanely. He seemed at a loss for a while.

'I suppose I must report a suicide.'

'Beg pardon?'

'Suicide! That's what I'll have to write to my owners directly I get in.'

'Unless you manage to recover him before tomorrow,' I assented, dispassionately . . . 'I mean, alive.'

He mumbled something which I really did not catch, and I turned my ear to him in a puzzled manner.

He fairly bawled: 'The land – I say, the mainland is at least seven miles off my anchorage.'

'About that.'

My lack of excitement, of curiosity, of surprise, of any sort of pronounced interest, began to arouse his distrust. But except for the felicitous pretence of deafness I had not tried to pretend anything. I had felt utterly incapable of playing the part of ignorance properly, and therefore was afraid to try. It is also certain that he had brought some ready-made suspicions with him, and that he viewed my politeness as a strange and unnatural phenomenon. And yet how else could I have received him? Not heartily! That was impossible for psychological reasons, which I need not state here. My only object was to keep off his enquiries. Surlily? Yes, but surliness might have provoked a point-blank question. From its novelty to him and from its nature, punctilious courtesy was the manner best calculated to restrain the man. But there was the danger of his breaking through my defence bluntly. I could not, I think have met him by a direct lie, also for psychological (not moral) reasons. If he had only known how afraid I was of his putting my feeling of identity with the other to the test! But, strangely enough (I thought of it only afterward), I believe that he was not a little disconcerted by the reverse side of that weird situation, by something in me that reminded him of the man he was seeking – suggested a mysterious similitude to the young fellow he had distrusted and disliked from the first.

However that might have been, the silence was not very prolonged. He took another oblique step.

'I reckon I had no more than a two-mile pull to your ship. Not a bit more.'

'And quite enough, too, in this awful heat,' I said.

Another pause full of mistrust followed. Necessity, they say, is mother of invention, but fear, too, is not barren of ingenious suggestions. And I was afraid he would ask me point-blank for news of my other self.

'Nice little saloon, isn't it?' I remarked, as if noticing for the first time the way his eyes roamed from one closed door to the other. 'And very well fitted out, too. Here, for instance,' I continued, reaching over the back of my seat negligently and flinging the door open, 'is my bathroom.'

He made an eager movement, but hardly gave it a glance. I got up, shut the door of the bathroom, and invited him to have a look round, as if I were very proud of my accommodation. He had to rise and be shown round, but he went through the business without any raptures whatever.

'And now we'll have a look at my stateroom,' I declared, in a voice as loud as I dared to make it, crossing the cabin to the starboard side with purposely heavy steps.

He followed me in and gazed around. My intelligent double had vanished. I played my part.

'Very convenient – isn't it?'

'Very nice. Very comf...' He didn't finish, and went out brusquely as if to escape from some unrighteous wiles of mine. But it was not to be. I had been too frightened not to feel vengeful; I felt I had him on the run, and I meant to keep him on the run. My polite insistence must have had something menacing in it, because he gave in suddenly. And I did not let him off a single item: mate's room, pantry, storerooms, the very sail-locker which was also under the poop – he had to look into them all. When at last I showed him out on the quarterdeck he drew a long, spiritless sigh, and mumbled dismally that he must really be going back to his ship now. I desired my mate, who had joined us, to see to the captain's boat.

The man of whiskers gave a blast on the whistle which he used to wear hanging round his neck, and yelled, '*Sephora* away!' My double down there in my cabin must have heard, and certainly could not feel more relieved than I. Four fellows came running out from somewhere forward and went over the side, while my own men, appearing on deck too, lined the rail. I escorted my visitor to the gangway ceremoniously, and nearly overdid it. He was a tenacious beast. On the very ladder he lingered, and in that unique, guiltily conscientious manner of sticking to the point: 'I say . . . you . . . you don't think that –'

I covered his voice loudly: 'Certainly not . . . I am delighted. Goodbye.'

I had an idea of what he meant to say, and just saved myself by the privilege of defective hearing. He was too shaken generally to insist, but my mate, close witness of that parting, looked mystified and his face took on a thoughtful cast. As I did not want to appear as if I wished to avoid all communication with my officers, he had the opportunity to address me.

'Seems a very nice man. His boat's crew told our chaps a very extraordinary story, if what I am told by the steward is true. I suppose you had it from the captain, sir?'

'Yes. I had a story from the captain.'

'A very horrible affair – isn't it, sir?'

'It is.'

'Beats all these tales we hear about murders in Yankee ships.'

'I don't think it beats them. I don't think it resembles them in the least.'

'Bless my soul – you don't say so! But of course I've no acquaintance whatever with American ships, not I, so I couldn't go against your knowledge. It's horrible enough for me . . . But the queerest part is that those fellows seemed to have some idea the man was hidden aboard here. They had really. Did you ever hear of such a thing?'

'Preposterous – isn't it?'

We were walking to and fro athwart the quarterdeck. No one of the crew forward could be seen (the day was Sunday), and the mate pursued: 'There was some little dispute about it. Our chaps took offence. "As if we would harbour a thing like that," they said. "Wouldn't you like to look for him in our coal-hole?" Quite a tiff. But they made it up in the end. I suppose he did drown himself. Don't you, sir?'

'I don't suppose anything.'

'You have no doubt in the matter, sir?'

'None whatever.'

I left him suddenly. I felt I was producing a bad impression, but with my double down there it was most trying to be on deck. And it was almost as trying to be below. Altogether a nerve-trying situation. But on the whole I felt less torn in two when I was with him. There was no one in the whole ship whom I dared take into my confidence. Since the hands had got to know his story, it would have been impossible to pass him off for anyone else, and an accidental discovery was to be dreaded now more than ever . . .

The steward being engaged in laying the table for dinner, we could talk only with our eyes when I first went down. Later in the afternoon we had a cautious try at whispering. The Sunday quietness of the ship was against us; the stillness of air and water around her was against us; the elements, the men were against us – everything was against us in our secret partnership; time itself – for this could not go on forever. The very trust in Providence was, I suppose, denied to his guilt. Shall I confess that this thought cast me down very much? And as to the chapter of accidents which counts for so much in the book of success, I could only hope that it was closed. For what favourable accident could be expected?

'Did you hear everything?' were my first words as soon as we took up our position side by side, leaning over my bed-place.

He had. And the proof of it was his earnest whisper, 'The man told you he hardly dared to give the order.'

I understood the reference to be to that saving foresail.

'Yes. He was afraid of it being lost in the setting.'

'I assure you he never gave the order. He may think he did, but he never gave it. He stood there with me on the break of the poop after the maintopsail blew away, and whimpered about our last hope – positively whimpered about it and nothing else – and the night coming on! To hear one's skipper go on like that in such weather was enough to drive any fellow out of his mind. It worked me up into a sort of desperation. I just took it into my own hands and went away from him, boiling, and – But what's the use telling you? *You* know! . . . Do you think that if I had not been pretty fierce with them I should have got the men to do anything? Not it! The bo's'n perhaps? Perhaps! It wasn't a heavy sea – it was a sea gone mad! I suppose the end of the world will be something like that; and a man may have the heart to see it coming once and be done with it – but to have to face it day after day I don't blame anybody. I was precious little better than the rest. Only – I was an officer of that old coal-waggon, anyhow – '

'I quite understand,' I conveyed that sincere assurance into his ear. He was out of breath with whispering; I could hear him pant slightly. It was all very simple. The same strung-up force which had given twenty-four men a chance, at least, for their lives, had, in a sort of recoil, crushed an unworthy mutinous existence.

But I had no leisure to weigh the merits of the matter – footsteps in the saloon, a heavy knock. 'There's enough wind to get under way with, sir.' Here was the call of a new claim upon my thoughts and even upon my feelings.

'Turn the hands up,' I cried through the door. 'I'll be on deck directly.'

I was going out to make the acquaintance of my ship. Before I left the cabin our eyes met – the eyes of the only two strangers on board. I pointed to the recessed part where the little camp-stool awaited him and laid my finger on my lips. He made a gesture – somewhat vague – a little mysterious, accompanied by a faint smile, as if of regret.

This is not the place to enlarge upon the sensations of a man who feels for the first time a ship move under his feet to his own independent word. In my case they were not unalloyed. I was not wholly alone with my command; for there was that stranger in my cabin. Or rather, I was not completely and wholly with her. Part of me was absent. That mental feeling of being in two places at once affected me physically as if the mood of secrecy had penetrated my very soul. Before an hour had elapsed since the ship had begun to move, having occasion to ask the mate (he stood by my side) to take a compass bearing of the Pagoda, I caught myself reaching up to his ear in whispers. I say I caught myself, but enough had escaped to startle the man. I can't describe it otherwise than by saying that he shied. A grave, preoccupied manner, as though he were in possession of some perplexing intelligence, did not leave him henceforth. A little later I moved away from the rail to look at the compass with such a stealthy gait that the helmsman noticed it – and I could not help noticing the unusual roundness of his eyes. These are trifling instances, though it's to no commander's advantage to be suspected of ludicrous eccentricities. But I was also more seriously affected. There are to a seaman certain words, gestures, that should in given conditions come as naturally, as instinctively as the winking of a menaced eye. A certain order should spring on to his lips without thinking; a certain sign should get itself made, so to speak, without reflection. But all unconscious alertness had abandoned me. I had to make an effort of will to recall myself back (from the cabin) to the conditions of the moment. I felt that I was appearing an irresolute commander to those people who were watching me more or less critically.

And, besides, there were the scares. On the second day out, for instance, coming off the deck in the afternoon (I had straw slippers on my bare feet) I stopped at the open pantry door and spoke to the steward. He was doing something there with his back to me. At the sound of my voice he nearly jumped out of his skin, as the saying is, and incidentally broke a cup.

'What on earth's the matter with you?' I asked, astonished.

He was extremely confused. 'Beg your pardon, sir. I made sure you were in your cabin.'

'You see I wasn't.'

'No, sir. I could have sworn I had heard you moving in there not a moment ago. It's most extraordinary . . . very sorry, sir.'

I passed on with an inward shudder. I was so identified with my secret double that I did not even mention the fact in those scanty, fearful whispers we exchanged. I suppose he had made some slight noise of some kind or other. It would have been miraculous if he hadn't at one time or another. And yet, haggard as he appeared, he looked always perfectly self-controlled, more than calm – almost invulnerable. On my suggestion he remained almost entirely in the bathroom, which, upon the whole, was the safest place. There could be really no shadow of an excuse for anyone ever wanting to go in there, once the steward had done with it. It was a very tiny place. Sometimes he reclined on the floor, his legs bent, his head sustained on one elbow. At others I would find him on the camp-stool, sitting in his grey sleeping-suit and with his cropped dark hair like a patient, unmoved convict. At night I would smuggle him into my bed-place, and we would whisper together, with the regular footfalls of the officer of the watch passing and repassing over our heads. It was an infinitely miserable time. It was lucky that some tins of fine preserves were stowed in a locker in my stateroom; hard bread I could always get hold of; and so he lived on stewed chicken, pâté de foie gras, asparagus, cooked oysters, sardines – on all sorts of abominable sham delicacies out of tins. My early morning coffee he always drank; and it was all I dared do for him in that respect.

Every day there was the horrible manoeuvring to go through so that my room and then the bathroom should be done in the usual way. I came to hate the sight of the steward, to abhor the voice of that harmless man. I felt that it was he who would bring on the disaster of discovery. It hung like a sword over our heads.

The fourth day out, I think (we were then working down the east side of the Gulf of Siam, tack for tack, in light winds and smooth water) – the fourth day, I say, of this miserable juggling with the unavoidable, as we sat at our evening meal, that man, whose slightest movement I dreaded, after putting down the dishes ran up on deck busily. This could not be dangerous. Presently he came down again; and then it appeared that he had remembered a coat of mine which I had thrown over a rail to dry after having been wetted in a shower which had passed over the ship in the afternoon. Sitting stolidly at the head of the table I became terrified at the sight of the garment on his arm. Of course he made for my door. There was no time to lose.

'Steward,' I thundered. My nerves were so shaken that I could not govern my voice and conceal my agitation. This was the sort of thing that made my terrifically whiskered mate tap his forehead with his forefinger. I had detected him using that gesture while talking on deck with a confidential air to the carpenter. It was too far to hear a word, but I had no doubt that this pantomime could only refer to the strange new captain.

'Yes, sir,' the pale-faced steward turned resignedly to me. It was this maddening course of being shouted at, checked without rhyme or reason, arbitrarily chased out of my cabin, suddenly called into it, sent flying out of his pantry on incomprehensible errands, that accounted for the growing wretchedness of his expression.

'Where are you going with that coat?'

'To your room, sir.'

'Is there another shower coming?'

'I'm sure I don't know, sir. Shall I go up again and see, sir?'

'No! never mind.'

My object was attained, as of course my other self in there would have heard everything that passed. During this interlude my two officers never raised their eyes off their respective plates; but the lip of that confounded cub, the second mate, quivered visibly.

I expected the steward to hook my coat on and come out at once. He was very slow about it; but I dominated my nervousness sufficiently not to shout after him. Suddenly I became aware (it could be heard plainly enough) that the fellow for some reason or other was opening the door of the bathroom. It was the end. The place was literally not big enough to swing a cat in. My voice died in my throat and I went stony all over. I expected to hear a yell of surprise and terror, and made a movement, but had not the strength to get on my legs. Everything remained still. Had my second self taken the poor wretch by the throat? I don't know what I would have done next moment if

I had not seen the steward come out of my room, close the door, and then stand quietly by the sideboard.

'Saved,' I thought. 'But, no! Lost! Gone! He was gone!'

I laid my knife and fork down and leaned back in my chair. My head swam. After a while, when sufficiently recovered to speak in a steady voice, I instructed my mate to put the ship round at eight o'clock himself.

'I won't come on deck,' I went on. 'I think I'll turn in, and unless the wind shifts I don't want to be disturbed before midnight. I feel a bit seedy.'

'You did look middling bad a little while ago,' the chief mate remarked without showing any great concern.

They both went out, and I stared at the steward clearing the table. There was nothing to be read on that wretched man's face. But why did he avoid my eyes, I asked myself. Then I thought I should like to hear the sound of his voice.

'Steward!'

'Sir!' Startled as usual.

'Where did you hang up that coat?'

'In the bathroom, sir.' The usual anxious tone. 'It's not quite dry yet, sir.'

For some time longer I sat in the cuddy. Had my double vanished as he had come? But of his coming there was an explanation, whereas his disappearance would be inexplicable . . . I went slowly into my dark room, shut the door, lighted the lamp, and for a time dared not turn round. When at last I did I saw him standing bolt-upright in the narrow recessed part. It would not be true to say I had a shock, but an irresistible doubt of his bodily existence flitted through my mind. Can it be, I asked myself, that he is not visible to other eyes than mine? It was like being haunted. Motionless, with a grave face, he raised his hands slightly at me in a gesture which meant clearly, 'Heavens! what a narrow escape!' Narrow indeed. I think I had come creeping quietly as near insanity as any man who has not actually gone over the border. That gesture restrained me, so to speak.

The mate with the terrific whiskers was now putting the ship on the other tack. In the moment of profound silence which follows upon the hands going to their stations I heard on the poop his raised voice: 'Hard alee!' and the distant shout of the order repeated on the maindeck. The sails, in that light breeze, made but a faint fluttering noise. It ceased. The ship was coming round slowly; I held my breath in the renewed stillness of expectation; one wouldn't have thought that there was a single living soul on her decks. A sudden brisk shout, 'Mainsail haul!' broke the spell, and in the noisy cries and rush overhead of the men running away with the main-brace we two, down in my cabin, came together in our usual position by the bed-place.

He did not wait for my question. 'I heard him fumbling here and just managed to squat myself down in the bath,' he whispered to me. 'The fellow only opened the door and put his arm in to hang the coat up. All the same – '

'I never thought of that,' I whispered back, even more appalled than before at the closeness of the shave, and marvelling at that something unyielding in his character which was carrying him through so finely. There was no agitation in his whisper. Whoever was being driven distracted, it was not he. He was sane. And the proof of his sanity was continued when he took up the whispering again.

'It would never do for me to come to life again.'

It was something that a ghost might have said. But what he was alluding to was his old captain's reluctant admission of the theory of suicide. It would obviously serve his turn – if I had understood at all the view which seemed to govern the unalterable purpose of his action.

'You must maroon me as soon as ever you can get amongst these islands off the Cambodje shore,' he went on.

'Maroon you! We are not living in a boy's adventure tale,' I protested. His scornful whispering took me up.

'We aren't indeed! There's nothing of a boy's tale in this. But there's nothing else for it. I want no more. You don't suppose I am afraid of what can be done to me? Prison or gallows or whatever they may please. But you don't see me coming back to explain such things to an old fellow in a wig and twelve respectable tradesmen, do you? What can they know whether I am guilty or not – or of *what* I am guilty, either? That's my affair. What does the Bible say? "Driven off the face of the earth." Very well. I am off the face of the earth now. As I came at night so I shall go.'

'Impossible!' I murmured. 'You can't.'

'Can't? . . . Not naked like a soul on the Day of Judgment. I shall freeze on to this sleeping-suit. The Last Day is not yet – and . . . you have understood thoroughly. Didn't you?'

I felt suddenly ashamed of myself. I may say truly that I understood – and my hesitation in letting that man swim away from my ship's side had been a mere sham sentiment, a sort of cowardice.

'It can't be done now till next night,' I breathed out. 'The ship is on the offshore tack and the wind may fail us.'

'As long as I know that you understand,' he whispered. 'But of course you do. It's a great satisfaction to have got somebody to understand. You seem to have been there on purpose.' And in the same whisper, as if we two whenever we talked had to say things to each other which were not fit for the world to hear, he added, 'It's very wonderful.'

We remained side by side talking in our secret way – but sometimes silent or just exchanging a whispered word or two at long intervals. And as usual he stared through the port. A breath of wind came now and again into our faces. The ship might have been moored in dock, so gently and on an even keel she slipped through the water, that did not murmur even at our passage, shadowy and silent like a phantom sea.

At midnight I went on deck, and to my mate's great surprise put the ship round on the other tack. His terrible whiskers flitted round me in silent criticism. I certainly should not have done it if it had been only a question of getting out of that sleepy gulf as quickly as possible. I believe he told the second mate, who relieved him, that it was a great want of judgement. The other only yawned. That intolerable cub shuffled about so sleepily and lolled against the rails in such a slack, improper fashion that I came down on him sharply.

'Aren't you properly awake yet?'

'Yes, sir! I am awake.'

'Well, then, be good enough to hold yourself as if you were. And keep a look-out. If there's any current we'll be closing with some islands before daylight.'

The east side of the gulf is fringed with islands, some solitary, others in groups. On the blue background of the high coast they seem to float on silvery patches of calm water, arid and grey, or dark green and rounded like clumps of evergreen bushes, with the larger ones, a mile or two long, showing the outlines of ridges, ribs of grey rock under the dank mantle of matted leafage. Unknown to trade, to travel, almost to geography, the manner of life they harbour is an unsolved secret. There must be villages – settlements of fishermen at least – on the largest of them, and some communication with the world is probably kept up by native craft. But all that forenoon, as we headed for them, fanned along by the faintest of breezes, I saw no sign of man or canoe in the field of the telescope I kept on pointing at the scattered group.

At noon I gave no orders for a change of course, and the mate's whiskers became much concerned and seemed to be offering themselves unduly to my notice.

At last I said: 'I am going to stand right in. Quite in – as far as I can take her.'

The stare of extreme surprise imparted an air of ferocity also to his eyes, and he looked truly terrific for a moment.

'We're not doing well in the middle of the gulf,' I continued, casually. 'I am going to look for the land breezes tonight.'

'Bless my soul! Do you mean, sir, in the dark amongst the lot of all them islands and reefs and shoals?'

'Well – if there are any regular land breezes at all on this coast one must get close inshore to find them, mustn't one?'

'Bless my soul!' he exclaimed again under his breath. All that afternoon he wore a dreamy, contemplative appearance which in him was a mark of perplexity. After dinner I went into my stateroom as if I meant to take some rest. There we two bent our dark heads over a half-unrolled chart lying on my bed.

'There,' I said. 'It's got to be Koh-ring. I've been looking at it ever since sunrise. It has got two hills and a low point. It must be inhabited. And on the coast opposite there is what looks like the mouth of a biggish river – with some town, no doubt, not far up. It's the best chance for you that I can see.'

'Anything. Koh-ring let it be.'

He looked thoughtfully at the chart as if surveying chances and distances from a lofty height – and following with his eyes his own figure wandering on the blank land of Cochin-China, and then passing off that piece of paper clean out of sight into uncharted regions. And it was as if the ship had two captains to plan her course for her. I had been so worried and restless running up and down that I had not had the patience to dress that day. I had remained in my sleeping-suit, with straw slippers and a soft floppy hat. The closeness of the heat in the gulf had been most oppressive, and the crew were used to see me wandering in that airy attire.

'She will clear the south point as she heads now,' I whispered into his ear. 'Goodness only knows when, though, but certainly after dark. I'll edge her in to half a mile, as far as I may be able to judge in the dark – '

'Be careful,' he murmured, warningly – and I realised suddenly that all my future, the only future for which I was fit, would perhaps go irretrievably to pieces in any mishap to my first command.

I could not stop a moment longer in the room. I motioned him to get out of sight and made my way on the poop. That unplayful cub had the watch. I walked up and down for a while thinking things out, then beckoned him over.

'Send a couple of hands to open the two quarterdeck ports,' I said, mildly.

He actually had the impudence, or else so forgot himself in his wonder at such an incomprehensible order, as to repeat: 'Open the quarterdeck ports! What for, sir?'

'The only reason you need concern yourself about is because I tell you to do so. Have them open wide and fastened properly.'

He reddened and went off, but I believe made some jeering remark to the carpenter as to the sensible practice of ventilating a ship's quarterdeck. I know he popped into the mate's cabin to impart the fact to him because the whiskers came on deck, as it were by chance, and stole glances at me from below – for signs of lunacy or drunkenness, I suppose.

A little before supper, feeling more restless than ever, I rejoined, for a moment, my second self. And to find him sitting so quietly was surprising, like something against nature, inhuman.

I developed my plan in a hurried whisper.

'I shall stand in as close as I dare and then put her round. I shall presently find means to smuggle you out of here into the sail-locker, which communicates with the lobby. But there is an opening, a sort of square for hauling the sails out, which gives straight on the quarterdeck and which is never closed in fine weather, so as to give air to the sails. When the ship's way is deadened in stays and all the hands are aft at the main-braces you shall have a clear road to slip out and get overboard through the open quarterdeck port. I've had them both fastened up. Use a rope's end to lower yourself into the water so as to avoid a splash – you know. It could be heard and cause some beastly complication.'

He kept silent for a while, then whispered, 'I understand.'

'I won't be there to see you go,' I began with an effort. 'The rest . . . I only hope I have understood, too.'

'You have. From first to last' – and for the first time there seemed to be a faltering, something strained in his whisper. He caught hold of my arm, but the ringing of the supper bell made me start. He didn't, though; he only released his grip.

After supper I didn't come below again till well past eight o'clock. The faint, steady breeze was loaded with dew; and the wet, darkened sails held all there was of propelling power in it. The night, clear and starry, sparkled darkly, and the opaque, lightless patches shifting slowly against the low stars were the drifting islets. On the port bow there was a big one more distant and shadowily imposing by the great space of sky it eclipsed.

On opening the door I had a back view of my very own self looking at a chart. He had come out of the recess and was standing near the table.

'Quite dark enough,' I whispered.

He stepped back and leaned against my bed with a level, quiet glance. I sat on the couch. We had nothing to say to each other. Over our heads the officer of the watch moved here and there. Then I heard him move quickly. I knew what that meant. He was making for the companion; and presently his voice was outside my door.

'We are drawing in pretty fast, sir. Land looks rather close.'

'Very well,' I answered. 'I am coming on deck directly.'

I waited till he was gone out of the cuddy, then rose. My double moved too. The time had come to exchange our last whispers, for neither of us was ever to hear each other's natural voice.

'Look here!' I opened a drawer and took out three sovereigns. 'Take this, anyhow. I've got six and I'd give you the lot, only I must keep a little money to buy some fruit and vegetables for the crew from native boats as we go through Sunda Straits.'

He shook his head.

'Take it,' I urged him, whispering desperately. 'No one can tell what – '

He smiled and slapped meaningly the only pocket of the sleeping-jacket. It was not safe, certainly. But I produced a large old silk handkerchief of mine, and tying the three pieces of gold in a corner, pressed it on him. He was touched, I suppose, because he took it at last and tied it quickly round his waist under the jacket, on his bare skin.

Our eyes met; several seconds elapsed, till, our glances still mingled, I extended my hand and turned the lamp out. Then I passed through the cuddy, leaving the door of my room wide open. . . . 'Steward!'

He was still lingering in the pantry in the greatness of his zeal, giving a rub-up to a plated cruet stand the last thing before going to bed. Being careful not to wake up the mate, whose room was opposite, I spoke in an undertone.

He looked round anxiously. 'Sir!'

'Can you get me a little hot water from the galley?'

'I am afraid, sir, the galley fire's been out for some time now.'

'Go and see.'

He fled up the stairs.

'Now,' I whispered, loudly, into the saloon – too loudly, perhaps, but I was afraid I couldn't make a sound. He was by my side in an instant – the double captain slipped past the stairs – through a tiny dark passage . . . a sliding door. We were in the sail-locker, scrambling on our knees over the sails. A sudden thought struck me. I saw myself wandering barefooted, bareheaded, the sun beating on my dark poll. I snatched off my floppy hat and tried hurriedly in the dark to ram it on my other self. He dodged and fended off silently. I wonder what he thought had come to me before he understood and suddenly desisted. Our hands met gropingly, lingered united in a steady, motionless clasp for a second . . . No word was breathed by either of us when they separated.

I was standing quietly by the pantry door when the steward returned.

'Sorry, sir. Kettle barely warm. Shall I light the spirit-lamp?'

'Never mind.'

I came out on deck slowly. It was now a matter of conscience to shave the land as close as possible – for now he must go overboard whenever the ship was put in stays. Must! There could be no going back for him. After a moment I walked over to leeward and my heart flew into my mouth at the nearness of the land on the bow. Under any other circumstances I would not have held on a minute longer. The second mate had followed me anxiously.

I looked on till I felt I could command my voice.

'She will weather,' I said then in a quiet tone.

'Are you going to try that, sir?' he stammered out incredulously.

I took no notice of him and raised my tone just enough to be heard by the helmsman.

'Keep her good full.'

'Good full, sir.'

The wind fanned my cheek, the sails slept, the world was silent. The strain of watching the dark loom of the land grow bigger and denser was too much for me. I had shut my eyes – because the ship must go closer. She must! The stillness was intolerable. Were we standing still?

When I opened my eyes the second view started my heart with a thump. The black southern hill of Koh-ring seemed to hang right over the ship like a towering fragment of the everlasting night. On that enormous mass of blackness there was not a gleam to be seen, not a sound to be heard. It was gliding irresistibly toward us and yet seemed already within reach of the hand. I saw the vague figures of the watch grouped in the waist, gazing in awed silence.

'Are you going on, sir,' enquired an unsteady voice at my elbow.

I ignored it. I had to go on.

'Keep her full. Don't check her way. That won't do now,' I said, warningly.

'I can't see the sails very well,' the helmsman answered me, in strange, quavering tones.

Was she close enough? Already she was, I won't say in the shadow of the land, but in the very blackness of it, already swallowed up as it were, gone too close to be recalled, gone from me altogether.

'Give the mate a call,' I said to the young man who stood at my elbow as still as death. 'And turn all hands up.'

My tone had a borrowed loudness reverberated from the height of the land. Several voices cried out together: 'We are all on deck, sir.'

Then stillness again, with the great shadow gliding closer, towering higher, without a light, without a sound. Such a hush had fallen on the ship that she might have been a bark of the dead floating in slowly under the very gate of Erebus.

'My God! Where are we?'

It was the mate moaning at my elbow. He was thunderstruck, and as it were deprived of the moral support of his whiskers. He clapped his hands and absolutely cried out, 'Lost!'

'Be quiet,' I said, sternly.

He lowered his tone, but I saw the shadowy gesture of his despair. 'What are we doing here?'

'Looking for the land wind.'

He made as if to tear his hair, and addressed me recklessly.

'She will never get out. You have done it, sir. I knew it'd end in something like this. She will never weather, and you are too close now to stay. She'll drift ashore before she's round. O my God!'

I caught his arm as he was raising it to batter his poor devoted head, and shook it violently.

'She's ashore already,' he wailed, trying to tear himself away.

'Is she? . . . Keep good full there!'

'Good full, sir,' cried the helmsman in a frightened, thin, childlike voice.

I hadn't let go the mate's arm and went on shaking it. 'Ready about, do you hear? You go forward' – shake – 'and stop there' – shake – 'and hold your noise' – shake – 'and see these head-sheets properly overhauled' – shake, shake – shake.

And all the time I dared not look toward the land lest my heart should fail me. I released my grip at last and he ran forward as if fleeing for dear life.

I wondered what my double there in the sail-locker thought of this commotion. He was able to hear everything – and perhaps he was able to understand why, on my conscience, it had to be thus close – no less. My first order 'Hard alee!' re-echoed ominously under the towering shadow of Koh-ring as if I had shouted in a mountain gorge. And then I watched the land intently. In that smooth water and light wind it was impossible to feel the ship coming-to. No! I could not feel her. And my second self was making now ready to slip out and lower himself overboard. Perhaps he was gone already . . . ?

The great black mass brooding over our very mastheads began to pivot away from the ship's side silently. And now I forgot the secret stranger ready to depart, and remembered only that I was a total stranger to the ship. I did not know her. Would she do it? How was she to be handled?

I swung the mainyard and waited helplessly. She was perhaps stopped, and her very fate hung in the balance, with the black mass of Koh-ring like the gate of the everlasting night towering over her taffrail. What would she do now? Had she way on her yet? I stepped to the side swiftly, and on the shadowy water I could see nothing except a faint phosphorescent flash revealing the glassy smoothness of the sleeping surface. It was impossible to tell – and I had not learned yet the feel of my ship. Was she moving? What I needed was something easily seen, a piece of paper, which I could throw overboard and watch. I had nothing on me. To run down for it I didn't dare. There was no time. All at once my strained, yearning stare distinguished a white object floating within a yard of the ship's side. White on the black water. A phosphorescent flash passed under it. What was that thing? . . . I recognised my own floppy hat. It must have fallen off his head . . . and he didn't bother. Now I had what I wanted – the saving mark for my eyes. But I hardly thought of my other self, now gone from the ship, to be hidden forever from all friendly faces, to be a fugitive and a vagabond on the earth, with no brand of the curse on his sane forehead to stay a slaying hand . . . too proud to explain.

And I watched the hat – the expression of my sudden pity for his mere flesh. It had been meant to save his homeless head from the dangers of the sun. And now – behold – it was saving the ship, by serving me for a mark to help out the ignorance of my strangeness. Ha! It was drifting forward, warning me just in time that the ship had gathered sternway.

'Shift the helm,' I said in a low voice to the seaman standing still like a statue.

The man's eyes glistened wildly in the binnacle light as he jumped round to the other side and spun round the wheel.

I walked to the break of the poop. On the overshadowed deck all hands stood by the forebraces waiting for my order. The stars ahead seemed to be gliding from right to left. And all was so still in the world that I heard the quiet remark 'She's round,' passed in a tone of intense relief between two seamen.

'Let go and haul.'

The foreyards ran round with a great noise, amidst cheery cries. And now the frightful whiskers made themselves heard giving various orders. Already the ship was drawing ahead. And I was alone with her. Nothing! no one in the world should stand now between us, throwing a shadow on the way of silent knowledge and mute affection, the perfect communion of a seaman with his first command.

Walking to the taffrail, I was in time to make out, on the very edge of a
darkness thrown by a towering black mass like the very gateway of Erebus –
yes, I was in time to catch an evanescent glimpse of my white hat left behind
to mark the spot where the secret sharer of my cabin and of my thoughts, as
though he were my second self, had lowered himself into the water to take his
punishment: a free man, a proud swimmer striking out for a new destiny.

1910

PRINCE ROMAN

'Events which happened seventy years ago are perhaps rather too far off to be dragged aptly into a mere conversation. Of course the year 1831 is for us an historical date, one of these fatal years when in the presence of the world's passive indignation and eloquent sympathies we had once more to murmur "*Vae Victis*" and count the cost in sorrow. Not that we were ever very good at calculating, either in prosperity or in adversity. That's a lesson we could never learn, to the great exasperation of our enemies who have bestowed upon us the epithet of Incorrigible . . . '

The speaker was of Polish nationality, that nationality not so much alive as surviving, which persists in thinking, breathing, speaking, hoping and suffering in its grave, railed in by a million of bayonets and triple-sealed with the seals of three great empires.

The conversation was about aristocracy. How did this, nowadays discredited, subject come up? It is some years ago now and the precise recollection has faded. But I remember that it was not considered practically as an ingredient in the social mixture; and I verily believe that we arrived at that subject through some exchange of ideas about patriotism – a somewhat discredited sentiment, because the delicacy of our humanitarians regards it as a relic of barbarism. Yet neither the great Florentine painter who closed his eyes in death thinking of his city, nor St Francis blessing with his last breath the town of Assisi were barbarians. It requires a certain greatness of soul to interpret patriotism worthily – or else a sincerity of feeling denied to the vulgar refinement of modern thought which cannot understand the august simplicity of a sentiment proceeding from the very nature of things and men.

The aristocracy we were talking about was the very highest, the great families of Europe, not impoverished, not converted, not liberalised, the most distinctive and specialised class of all classes, for which even ambition itself does not exist among the usual incentives to activity and regulators of conduct.

The undisputed right of leadership having passed away from them we judged that their great fortunes, their cosmopolitanism, brought about by wide alliances, their elevated station, in which there is so little to gain and so much to lose, must make their position difficult in times of political commotion or national upheaval. No longer born to command – which is the very essence of aristocracy – it becomes difficult for them to do ought else but hold aloof from the great movements of popular passion.

We had reached that conclusion when the remark about far off events was made and the date of 1831 mentioned. And the speaker continued:

'I don't mean to say that I knew Prince Roman at that remote time. I begin to feel pretty ancient, but I am not so ancient as that. In fact Prince Roman was married the very year my father was born. It was in 1828; the nineteenth century was young yet and the Prince was even younger than the century, but I don't know exactly by how much. In any case his was an early marriage. It was an ideal alliance from every point of view. The girl was young and beautiful, an orphan heiress of a great name and of a great fortune. The Prince, then an officer in the Guards and distinguished amongst his fellows by something reserved and reflective in his character, had fallen headlong in love with her beauty, her charm and the serious qualities of her mind and heart. He was a rather silent young man; but his glances, his bearing, his whole person expressed his absolute devotion to the woman of his choice, a devotion which she returned in her own frank and fascinating manner.

'The flame of this pure young passion promised to burn for ever; and for a season it lit up the dry, cynical atmosphere of the great world of St Petersburg. The Emperor Nicholas himself, the grandfather of the present man, the one who died from the Crimean war, the last perhaps of the autocrats with a mystical belief in the divine character of his mission, showed some interest in this pair of married lovers. It is true that Nicholas kept a watchful eye on all the doings of the great Polish nobles. The young people leading a life appropriate to their station were obviously wrapped up in each other; and society, fascinated by the sincerity of a feeling moving serenely among the artificialities of its anxious and fastidious agitation, watched them with benevolent indulgence and an amused tenderness.

'The marriage was the social event of 1828 in the capital. Just forty years afterwards I was staying in the country house of my mother's brother in our southern provinces.

'It was the dead of winter. The great lawn in front was as pure and smooth as an Alpine snowfield, a white and feathery level sparkling under the sun as if sprinkled with diamond-dust, declining gently to the lake – a long, sinuous piece of frozen water looking bluish and more solid than the earth. A cold brilliant sun glided low above an undulating horizon of great folds of snow in which the villages of Ukrainian peasants remained out of sight, like clusters of boats hidden in the hollows of a running sea. And everything was very still.

'I don't know now how I had managed to escape at eleven o'clock in the morning from the schoolroom. I was a boy of eight, the little girl, my cousin, a few months younger than myself, though hereditarily more quick-tempered, was less adventurous. So I had escaped alone; and presently I found myself in the great stone-paved hall, warmed by a monumental stove of white tiles, a much more pleasant locality than the schoolroom which for some reason or other, perhaps hygienic, was always kept at a low temperature.

'We children were aware that there was a guest staying in the house. He had arrived the night before just as we were being driven off to bed. We broke back through the line of beaters to rush and flatten our noses against the dark window panes; but we were too late to see him alight. We had only watched in a ruddy glare the big travelling carriage on sleigh-runners harnessed with six horses, a black mass against the snow, going off to the stables, preceded by a horseman carrying a blazing ball of tow and resin in an iron basket at the end of a long stick swung from his saddle bow. Two stable boys had been sent out early in the afternoon along the snow-tracks to meet the expected guest at dusk and light his way with these road torches. At that time, you must remember, there was not a single mile of railways in our southern provinces. My little cousin and I had no knowledge of trains and engines, except from picture-books, as of things rather vague, extremely remote, and not particularly interesting unless to grown-ups who travelled abroad.

'Our notion of princes, perhaps a little more precise, was mainly literary and had a glamour reflected from the light of fairy tales, in which princes always appear young, charming, heroic and fortunate. Yet, as well as any other children, we could draw a firm line between the real and the ideal. We knew that princes were historical personages. And there was some glamour in that fact too. But what had driven me to roam cautiously over the house like an escaped prisoner, was the hope of snatching an interview with a special friend of mine, the head forester, who generally came to make his report at that time of the day. I yearned for news of a certain wolf. You know, in a country where wolves are to be found, every winter almost brings forward an individual eminent by the audacity of his misdeeds, by his more perfect wolfishness, so to speak. I wanted to hear some new thrilling tale of that wolf – perhaps the dramatic story of his death . . .

'But there was no one in the hall.

'Deceived in my hopes I became suddenly very much depressed. Unable to slip back in triumph to my studies I elected to stroll spiritlessly into the billiard-room where certainly I had no business. There was no one there either, and I felt very lost and desolate under its high ceiling, all alone with the massive English billiard-table which seemed, in heavy, rectilinear silence, to disapprove of that small boy's intrusion.

'As I began to think of retreat I heard footsteps in the adjoining drawing-room; and, before I could turn tail and flee, my uncle and his guest appeared in the doorway. To run away after having been seen would have been highly improper, so I stood my ground. My uncle looked surprised to see me; the guest by his side was a spare man, of average stature, buttoned up in a black frock coat and holding himself very erect with a stiffly soldier-like carriage. From the folds of a soft white cambric neckcloth peeped the points of a collar close against each shaven cheek. A few wisps of thin grey hair were brushed smoothly across the top of his bald head. His face, which must have been beautiful in its day, had preserved in age the harmonious simplicity of its lines. What amazed me was its even, almost deathlike pallor. He seemed to me to be prodigiously old; a faint smile, a mere momentary alteration in the set of his thin lips acknowledged my blushing confusion; and I became greatly interested to see him reach into the inside breastpocket of his coat. He extracted therefrom a lead pencil and a block of detachable pages, which he handed to my uncle with an almost imperceptible bow.

'I was very much astonished, but my uncle received it as a matter of course. He wrote something at which the other glanced and nodded slightly. A thin wrinkled hand – the hand was older than the face – patted my cheek and then rested on my head lightly. An unringing voice, a voice as colourless as the face itself, issued from his sunken lips, while the eyes, dark and still, looked down at me kindly.

' "And how old is this shy little boy?"

'Before I could answer my uncle wrote down my age on the pad. I was deeply impressed. What was this ceremony? Was this personage too great to be spoken to? Again he glanced at the pad, and again gave a nod, and again that impersonal, mechanical voice was heard – "He resembles his grandfather."

'I remembered my paternal grandfather. He had died not long before. He, too, was prodigiously old. And to me it seemed perfectly natural that two such ancient and venerable persons should have known each other in the dim ages of creation before my birth. But my uncle obviously had not been aware of the fact. So obviously that the mechanical voice explained.

' "Yes, yes. Comrades in '31. He was one of those who knew. Old times, my dear sir, old times . . . "

'He made a gesture as if to put aside an importunate ghost. And now they were both looking down at me. I wondered whether anything was expected from me. To my round, questioning eyes my uncle remarked, "He's completely deaf." And the unrelated, inexpressive voice said – "Give me your hand."

'Acutely conscious of inky fingers I put it out timidly. I had never seen a deaf person before and was rather startled. He pressed it firmly and then gave me a final pat on the head.

'My uncle addressed me weightily.

' "You have shaken hands with Prince Roman S—. It's something for you to remember when you grow up."

'I was impressed by his tone. I had enough historical information to know vaguely that the Princes S— counted amongst the sovereign princes of Ruthenia till the union of all Ruthenian lands to the kingdom of Poland, when they became great Polish magnates, sometime at the beginning of the fifteenth century. But what concerned me most was the failure of the fairytale glamour. It was shocking to discover a prince who was deaf, bald, meagre, and so prodigiously old. It never occurred to me that this imposing and disappointing man had been young, rich, beautiful. I could not know that he had been happy in the felicity of an ideal marriage uniting two young hearts, two great names and two great fortunes; happy with a happiness which, as in fairy tales, seemed destined to last forever . . .

'But it did not last forever. It was fated not to last very long even by the measure of the days allotted to men's passage on this earth, where enduring happiness is only found in the conclusion of fairy tales. A daughter was born to them and shortly afterwards the health of the young princess began to fail. For a time she bore up with smiling intrepidity, sustained by the feeling that now her existence was necessary for the happiness of two lives. But at last the husband, thoroughly alarmed by the rapid changes in her appearance, obtained an unlimited leave and took her away from the capital, to his parents in the country.

'The old prince and princess were extremely frightened at the state of their beloved daughter-in-law. Preparations were at once made for a journey abroad. But it seemed as if it were already too late; and the invalid herself opposed the project with gentle obstinacy. Thin and pale in the great armchair, where the insidious and obscure nervous malady made her appear smaller and more frail every day without effacing the smile of her eyes or the charming grace of her wasted face, she clung to her native land and wished to breathe her native air. Nowhere else could she expect to get well so quickly, nowhere else would it be so easy for her to die.

'She died before her little girl was two years old. The grief of the husband was terrible and the more alarming to his parents because perfectly silent and dry-eyed. After the funeral, while the immense bareheaded crowd of peasants surrounding the private chapel in the grounds was dispersing, the Prince, waving away his friends and relations, remained alone to watch the masons of the estate closing the family vault. When the last stone was in position he uttered a groan, the first sound of pain which had escaped from him for days, and walking away with lowered head shut himself up again in his apartments.

'His father and mother feared for his reason. His outward tranquillity was appalling to them. They had nothing to trust to but that very youth which made his despair so self-absorbed and so intense. Old Prince John, fretful and anxious, repeated, "Poor Roman should be roused somehow. He's so young." But they could find nothing to rouse him with. And the old princess, wiping her eyes, wished in her heart he were young enough to come and cry at her knee.

'In time Prince Roman making an effort would join now and again the family circle. But it was as if his heart and his mind had been buried in the family vault with the wife he had lost. He took to wandering in the woods with a gun, watched over secretly by one of the keepers, who would report in the evening that "His Serenity has never fired a shot all day". Sometimes walking to the stables in the morning he would order in subdued tones a horse to be saddled, wait switching his boot till it was led up to him, then mount without a word and ride out of the gates at a walking pace. He would be gone all day. People saw him on the roads looking neither to the right nor to the left, white-faced, sitting rigidly in the saddle like a horseman of stone on a living mount.

'The peasants working in the fields, the great unhedged fields, looked after him from the distance; and sometimes some sympathetic old woman on the threshold of a low, thatched hut, was moved to make the sign of the cross in the air behind his back; as though he were one of themselves, a simple village soul struck by a sore affliction.

'He rode looking straight ahead, seeing no one, as if the earth were empty and all mankind buried in that grave which had opened so suddenly in his path to swallow up his happiness. What were men to him with their sorrows, joys, labours and passions, from which she who had been all the world to him had been cut off so early?

'They did not exist; and he would have felt as completely lonely and abandoned as a man in the toils of a cruel nightmare if it had not been for this countryside where he had been born and had spent his happy boyish years. He knew it well – every slight rise crowned with trees amongst the ploughed fields, every dell concealing a village. The dammed streams made a chain of lakes set in the green meadows. Far away to the north the great Lithuanian forest faced the sun, no higher than a hedge; and to the south, the way to the plains, the vast brown spaces of the earth touched the blue sky.

'And this familiar landscape associated with the days without thought and without sorrow, this land the charm of which he felt without even looking at it, soothed his pain, like the presence of an old friend who sits silent and disregarded by one in some dark hour of life.

'One afternoon, it happened that the Prince, after turning his horse's head for home, remarked a low dense cloud of dark dust cutting off slantwise a part of the view. He reined in on a knoll and peered. There were slender gleams of steel here and there in that cloud, and it contained moving forms which revealed themselves at last as a long line of peasant carts full of soldiers, moving slowly in double file under the escort of mounted Cossacks.

'It was like an immense reptile creeping over the fields; its head dipped out of sight in a slight hollow and its tail went on writhing and growing shorter as though the monster were eating its way slowly into the very heart of the land.

'The Prince directed his way through a village lying a little off the track. The roadside inn, with its stable, byre and barn under one enormous thatched roof, resembled a deformed, hunchbacked, ragged giant, sprawling amongst the small huts of the peasants. The innkeeper, a portly, dignified Jew, clad in a black satin coat reaching down to his heels and girt with a red sash, stood at the door stroking his long silvery beard.

'He watched the Prince approach and bowed gravely from the waist, not expecting to be noticed even, since it was well known that their young lord had no eyes for anything or anybody in his grief. It was quite a shock for him when the Prince pulled up and asked: "What's all this, Yankel?"

' "That is, please your Serenity, that is a convoy of footsoldiers; they are hurrying down to the south."

'He glanced right and left cautiously, but as there was no one near but some children playing in the dust of the village street, he came up close to the stirrup.

' "Doesn't your Serenity know? It has begun already down there. All the landowners great and small are out in arms, and even the common people have risen. Only yesterday the saddler from Grodek" (it was a tiny market-town near by) "went through here with his two apprentices on his way to join. He left even his cart with me. I gave him a guide through our neighbourhood. You know, your Serenity, our people they travel a lot and they see all that's going on, and they know all the roads."

'He tried to keep down his excitement, for the Jew Yankel, innkeeper and tenant of all the mills on the estate, was a Polish patriot.

'And in a still lower voice: "I was already a married man when the French and all the other nations passed this way with Napoleon. Tse! Tse! That was a great harvest for death, Nu! Perhaps this time God will help."

'The Prince nodded. "Perhaps – " and falling into deep meditation he let his horse take him home.

'That night he wrote a letter and early in the morning sent a mounted express to the post town. During the day he came out of his taciturnity, to the great joy of the family circle, and conversed with his father of recent events – the revolt in Warsaw, the flight of the Grand Duke Constantine, the first slight successes of the Polish army (at that time there was a Polish army), the risings in the provinces. Old Prince John, moved and uneasy, speaking from a purely aristocratic point of view, mistrusted the popular origins of the movement, regretted its democratic tendencies, and did not believe in the possibility of success.

'He was sad, inwardly agitated.

' "I am judging all this calmly. There are secular principles of legitimity and order which have been violated in this reckless enterprise for the sake of most subversive illusions. Though of course the patriotic impulses of the heart . . . "

'Prince Roman had listened in a thoughtful attitude. He took advantage of the pause to tell his father quietly that he had sent that morning a letter to St Petersburg resigning his commission in the Guards.

'The old prince remained silent. He thought that he ought to have been consulted. His son was also ordnance officer to the Emperor and he knew that the Tzar would never forget this appearance of defection in a Polish noble. In a discontented tone he pointed out to his son that as it was he had an unlimited leave. The right thing would have been to keep quiet. They had too much tact at court to recall a man of his name. Or at worst some distant mission might have been asked for – to the Caucasus for instance – away from this unhappy struggle which was wrong in principle and therefore destined to fail.

' "Presently you shall find yourself without any interest in life and with no occupation. And you shall need something to occupy you, my poor boy. You have acted rashly, I fear."

'Prince Roman murmured, ' "I thought it better."

'His father faltered under his steady gaze.

' "Well, well – perhaps! But as ordnance officer to the Emperor and in favour with all the Imperial family . . . "

' "Those people had never been heard of when our house was already illustrious," the young man let fall disdainfully.

'This was the sort of remark to which the old prince was sensible. "Well – perhaps it is better," he conceded at last.

'The father and son parted affectionately for the night. The next day Prince Roman seemed to have fallen back into the depths of his indifference. He rode out as usual. He remembered that the day before he had seen a reptile-like convoy of soldiery bristling with bayonets crawling over the face of that land which was his. The woman he loved had been his too. Death had robbed him of her. Her loss had been to him a moral shock. It had opened his heart to a greater sorrow, his mind to a vaster thought, his eyes to all the past, and to the existence of another love fraught with pain but as mysteriously imperative as that lost one to which he had entrusted his happiness.

'That evening he retired earlier than usual and rang for his personal servant.

' "Go and see if there is light yet in the quarters of the Master-of-the Horse. If he is still up ask him to come and speak to me."

'While the servant was absent on this errand the Prince tore up hastily some papers, locked the drawers of his desk, and hung a medallion containing the miniature of his wife round his neck against his breast.

'The man the Prince was expecting belonged to that past which the death of his love had called to life. He was of a family of small nobles who for generations had been adherents, servants and friends of the Princes S—. He remembered the times before the last partition, and had taken part in the struggles of the last hour. He was a typical old Pole of that class, with a great capacity for emotion, for blind enthusiasm; with martial instincts and simple beliefs; and even with the old-time habit of larding his speech with Latin words. And his kindly shrewd eyes, his ruddy face, his lofty brow and his thick, grey, pendent moustache were also very typical of his kind

' "Listen, Master Francis," the Prince said familiarly and without preliminaries. "Listen, old friend. I am going to vanish from here quietly. I go where something louder than my grief and yet something with a voice very like it calls me. I confide in you alone. You will say what's necessary when the time comes."

'The old man understood. His extended hands trembled exceedingly. But as soon as he found his voice he thanked God aloud for letting him live long enough to see the descendant of the illustrious family in its youngest generation give an example, *coram gentibus*, of the love of his country and of valour in the field. He doubted not of his dear Prince attaining a place in council and in war worthy of his high birth; he saw already that *in fulgore* of family glory *affulget patride serenitas*. At the end of the speech he burst into tears and fell into the Prince's arms.

'The Prince quieted the old man, and when he had him seated in an armchair and comparatively composed he said: "Don't misunderstand me, Master Francis. You know how I loved my wife. A loss like that opens one's eyes to unsuspected truths. There is no question here of leadership and glory. I mean to go alone and to fight obscurely in the ranks. I am going to offer my country what is mine to offer, that is my life, as simply as the saddler from Grodek who went through yesterday with his apprentices . . ."

'The old man cried out at this. That could never be. He could not allow it. But he had to give way before the arguments and the express will of the Prince.

' "Ha! If you say that it is a matter of feeling and conscience – so be it. But you cannot go utterly alone. Alas! that I am too old to be of any use. *Cripit verba dolor*, my dear Prince, at the thought that I am over seventy and of no more account in the world than a cripple in the church porch. It seems that to sit at home and pray to God for the nation and for you is all I am fit for. But there is my son, my youngest boy, Peter. He will make a worthy companion for you. And as it happens he's staying with me here. There has not been for ages a Prince S— hazarding his life without a companion of our name to ride by his side. You must have by you somebody who knows who you are if only to let your parents and your old servant hear what is happening to you. And when does your Princely Mightiness mean to start?"

' "In an hour," said the Prince; and the old man hurried off to warn his son.

'Prince Roman took up a candlestick and walked quietly along a dark corridor in the silent house. The head-nurse said afterwards that waking up suddenly she saw the Prince looking at his child, one hand shading the light from its eyes. He stood and gazed at her for some time, and then putting the candlestick on the floor bent over the cot and kissed lightly the little girl, who did not wake. He went out noiselessly taking the light away with him. She saw his face perfectly well, but she could read nothing of his purpose in it. It was pale but perfectly calm, and after he turned away from the cot he never looked back at it once.

'The only other trusted person, besides the old man and his son Peter, was the Jew Yankel. When he asked the Prince where precisely he wanted to be guided the Prince answered, "To the nearest party." A grandson of the Jew, a lanky youth, conducted the two young men by little known paths, across woods and morasses, and led them in sight of the few fires of a small detachment camped in a hollow. Some invisible horses neighed, a voice in the dark cried "Who goes there?" . . . and the young Jew departed hurriedly, explaining that he must make haste home to be in time for keeping the Sabbath.

'Thus, humbly and in accord with the simplicity of the vision of duty he saw when death had removed the brilliant bandage of happiness from his eyes, did Prince Roman bring his offering to his country. His companion made himself known as the son of the Master-of-the-Horse to the Princes S— and declared him to be a relation, a distant cousin from the same parts as himself and, as people presumed, of the same name. In truth no one enquired much. Two more young men, clearly of the right sort, had joined. Nothing more natural.

'Prince Roman did not remain long in the south. One day while scouting with several others, they were ambushed near the entrance of a village by some Russian infantry. The first discharge laid low a good many and the rest scattered in all directions. The Russians, too, did not stay, being afraid of a return in force. After some time, the peasants coming to view the scene extricated Prince Roman from under his dead horse. He was unhurt but his faithful companion had been one of the first to fall. The Prince helped the peasants to bury him and the other dead.

'Then alone, not certain where to find the body of partisans which was constantly moving about in all directions, he resolved to try and join the main Polish army facing the Russians on the borders of Lithuania. Disguised in peasant clothes, in case of meeting some marauding Cossacks, he wandered a couple of weeks before he came upon a village occupied by a regiment of Polish cavalry on outpost duty.

'On a bench, before a peasant hut of a better sort, sat an elderly officer whom he took for the Colonel. The Prince approached respectfully, told his story shortly and stated his desire to enlist; and when asked his name by the officer, who had been looking him over carefully, he gave on the spur of the moment the name of his dead companion.

'The elderly officer thought to himself: Here's the son of some peasant proprietor of the liberated class. He liked his appearance. "And can you read and write, my good fellow?" he asked.

' "Yes, your honour, I can," said the Prince.

' "Good. Come along inside the hut, the regimental adjutant is there. He will enter your name and administer the oath to you."

The adjutant stared very hard at the newcomer but said nothing. When all the forms had been gone through and the recruit gone out, he turned to his superior officer.

' "Do you know who that is?"

' "Who? That Peter? A likely chap."

' "That's Prince Roman S—."

' "Nonsense."

'But the adjutant was positive. He had seen the Prince several times, about two years before, in the Castle in Warsaw. He had even spoken to him once at a reception of officers held by the Grand Duke. "He's changed. He seems much older, but I am certain of my man. I have a good memory for faces."

'The two officers looked at each other in silence. "He's sure to be recognised sooner or later," murmured the adjutant.

'The Colonel shrugged his shoulders. "It's no affair of ours – if he has a fancy to serve in the ranks. As to being recognised it's not so likely. All our officers and men come from the other end of Poland."

'He meditated gravely for a while, then smiled. "He told me he could read and write. There's nothing to prevent me making him a sergeant at the first opportunity. He's sure to shape all right."

'Prince Roman as a non-commissioned officer surpassed the Colonel's expectations. Before long Sergeant Peter became famous for his resourcefulness and courage. It was not the reckless courage of a desperate man; it was a self-possessed, as if conscientious, valour which nothing could dismay; a boundless but equable devotion, unaffected by time, by reverses, by the discouragement of endless retreats, by the bitterness of waning hopes and the horrors of pestilence added to the toils and perils of war. It was in this year that the cholera made its first appearance in Europe. It devastated the camps of both armies, affecting the firmest minds with the terror of a mysterious death stalking silently between the piled-up arms and around the bivouac fires.

'A sudden shriek would wake up the harassed soldiers and they would see in the glow of embers one of themselves writhe on the ground like a worm trodden on by an invisible foot. And before the dawn broke he would be stiff and cold. Parties so visited have been known to rise like one man, abandon the fire and run off into the night in mute panic. Or a comrade talking to you on the march would stammer suddenly in the middle of a sentence, roll affrighted eyes, and fall down with distorted face and blue lips, breaking the ranks with the convulsions of his agony. Men were struck in the saddle, on sentry duty, in the firing line, carrying orders, serving the guns. I have been told that in a battalion forming under fire with perfect steadiness for the assault of a village, three cases occurred within five minutes at the head of the column; and the attack could not be delivered because the leading companies scattered all over the fields like chaff before the wind.

'Sergeant Peter, young as he was, had a great influence over his men. It was said that the number of desertions in the squadron in which he served was less than in any other in the whole of that cavalry division. Such was supposed to be the compelling example of one man's quiet intrepidity in facing every form of danger and terror.

'However that may be, he was liked and trusted generally. When the end came and the remnants of that army corps, hard pressed on all sides, were preparing to cross the Prussian frontier, Sergeant Peter had enough influence to rally round him a score of troopers. He managed to escape with them at night from the hemmed-in army. He led this band through two hundred miles of country covered by numerous Russian detachments and ravaged by the cholera. But this was not to avoid captivity, to go into hiding and try to save themselves. No. He led them into a fortress which was still occupied by the Poles, and where the last stand of the vanquished revolution was to be made.

'This looks like mere fanaticism. But fanaticism is human. Man has adored ferocious divinities. There is ferocity in every passion, even in love itself. The religion of undying hope resembles the mad cult of despair, of death, of annihilation. The difference lies in the moral motive springing from the secret needs and the unexpressed aspiration of the believers. It is only to vain men that all is vanity; and all is deception only to those who have never been sincere with themselves.

'It was in the fortress that my grandfather found himself together with Sergeant Peter. My grandfather was a neighbour of the S— family in the country, but he did not know Prince Roman, who, however, knew his name perfectly well. The Prince introduced himself one night as they both sat on the ramparts, leaning against a gun carriage.

'The service he wished to ask for was, in case of his being killed, to have the intelligence conveyed to his parents.

'They talked in low tones, the other servants of the piece lying about near them. My grandfather gave the required promise, and then asked frankly – for he was greatly interested by the disclosure so unexpectedly made: "But tell me, Prince, why this bequest. Have you any evil forebodings as to yourself?"

' "Not in the least; I was thinking of my people. They have no idea where I am," answered Prince Roman. "I'll engage to do as much for you, if you like. It's certain that half of us at least shall be killed before the end, so there's an even chance of one of us surviving the other."

'My grandfather told him where, as he supposed, his wife and children were then. From that moment till the end of the siege the two were much together. On the day of the great assault my grandfather received a severe wound. The town was taken. Next day the citadel itself, its hospital full of dead and dying, its magazines empty, its defenders having burnt their last cartridge, opened its gates.

'During all the campaign the Prince, exposing his person conscientiously on every occasion, had not received a scratch. No one had recognised him, or at any rate had betrayed his identity. Till then, as long as he did his duty, it had mattered nothing who he was.

'Now, however, the position was changed. As ex-guardsman and as late ordnance officer to the Emperor, this rebel ran a serious risk of being given special attention in the shape of a firing squad at ten paces. For more than a month he remained lost in the miserable crowd of prisoners packed in the casemates of the citadel, with just enough food to keep body and soul together but otherwise allowed to die from wounds, privation and disease at the rate of forty or so a day.

'The position of the fortress being central, new parties, captured in the open in the course of a thorough pacification, were being sent in frequently.

Amongst such newcomers there happened to be a young man, a personal friend of the Prince from his schooldays. He recognised him, and in the extremity of his dismay cried aloud, "My God! Roman, you here!"

'It is said that years of life embittered by remorse paid for this momentary lack of self-control. All this happened in the main quadrangle of the citadel. The warning gesture of the Prince came too late. An officer of the gendarmes on guard had heard the exclamation. The incident appeared to him worth inquiring into. The investigation which followed was not very arduous because the Prince, asked categorically for his real name, owned up at once.

'The intelligence of the Prince S— being found amongst the prisoners was sent to St Petersburg. His parents were already there living in sorrow, incertitude and apprehension. The capital of the Empire was the safest place to reside in for a noble whose son had disappeared so mysteriously from home in a time of rebellion. The old people had not heard from him, or of him, for months. They took care not to contradict the rumours of suicide from despair circulating in the great world, which remembered the interesting love-match, the charming and frank happiness brought to an end by death. But they hoped secretly that their son survived, and that he had been able to cross the frontier with that part of the army which had surrendered to the Prussians.

'The news of his captivity was a crushing blow. Directly, nothing could be done for him. But the greatness of their name, of their position, their relations and connections in the highest spheres, enabled his parents to act indirectly; and they moved heaven and earth, as the saying is, to save their son from the "consequences of his madness", as poor Prince John did not hesitate to express himself. Great personages were approached by society leaders, high dignitaries were interviewed, powerful officials were induced to take an interest in that affair. The help of every possible secret influence was enlisted. Some private secretaries got heavy bribes. The mistress of a certain senator obtained a large sum of money.

'But, as I have said, in such a glaring case no direct appeal could be made and no open steps taken. All that could be done was to incline by private representation the mind of the President of the Military Commission to the side of clemency. He ended by being impressed by the hints and suggestions, some of them from very high quarters, which he received from St Petersburg. And, after all, the gratitude of such great nobles as the Princes S— was something worth having from a worldly point of view. He was a good Russian, but he was also a good-natured man. Moreover, the hate of Poles was not at that time a cardinal article of patriotic creed as it became some thirty years later. He felt well disposed at first sight towards that young man, bronzed, thin-faced, worn out by months of hard campaigning, the hardships of the siege and the rigours of captivity.

'The Commission was composed of three officers. It sat in the citadel in a bare, vaulted room behind a long black table. Some clerks occupied the two ends, and, besides the gendarmes who brought in the Prince, there was no one else there.

'Within those four sinister walls shutting out from him all the sights and sounds of liberty, all hopes of the future, all consoling illusions – alone in the face of his enemies erected for judges – who can tell how much love of life there was in Prince Roman? How much remained of that sense of duty, revealed to him in sorrow? How much of his awakened love for his native country? That country which demands to be loved as no other country has ever been loved, with the mournful affection one bears to the unforgotten dead and with the unextinguishable fire of a hopeless passion which only a living, breathing, warm ideal can kindle in our breasts for our pride, for our weariness, for our exultation, for our undoing.

'There is something monstrous in the thought of such an exaction till it stands before us embodied in the shape of a fidelity without fear and without reproach. Nearing the supreme moment of his life the Prince could only have had the feeling that it was about to end. He answered the questions put to him clearly, concisely . . . with the most profound indifference. After all those tense months of action to talk was a weariness to him. But he concealed it, lest his foes should suspect in his manner the apathy of discouragement or the numbness of a crushed spirit. The details of his conduct could have no importance one way or another; with his thoughts these men had nothing to do. He preserved a scrupulously courteous tone. He had refused the permission to sit down.

'What happened at this preliminary examination is only known from the presiding officer. Pursuing the only possible course in that glaringly bad case he tried from the first to bring to the Prince's mind the line of defence he wished him to take. He absolutely framed his questions so as to put the right answers in the culprit's mouth, going so far as to suggest the very words – how, distracted by excessive grief after his young wife's death, rendered irresponsible for his conduct by his despair, in a moment of blind recklessness, without realising the highly reprehensible nature of the act, nor yet its danger and its dishonour, he went off to join the nearest rebels on a sudden impulse. And that now, penitently . . .

'But Prince Roman was silent. The military judges looked at him hopefully. In silence he reached for a pen and wrote on a sheet of paper he found under his hand: "I joined the national rising from conviction."

'He pushed the paper across the table. The president took it up, showed it in turn to his two colleagues sitting to the right and left, then looking fixedly at Prince Roman let it fall from his hand. And the silence remained unbroken till he spoke to the gendarmes ordering them to remove the prisoner.

'Such was the written testimony of Prince Roman in the supreme moment of his life. I have heard that the princes of the S— family, in all its branches, adopted the last two words, "from conviction", for the device under the armorial bearings of their house. I don't know whether the report is true.

My uncle could not tell me. He remarked only that, naturally, it was not to be seen on Prince Roman's own seal.

'He was condemned for life to Siberian mines. Emperor Nicholas, who always took personal cognisance of all sentences on Polish nobility, wrote with his own hand in the margin: "The authorities are severely warned to take care that this convict walks in chains like any other criminal every step of the way."

'It was a sentence of deferred death. Very few survived entombment in these mines for more than three years. Yet as he was reported as still alive at the end of that time he was allowed, on a petition of his parents and by way of exceptional grace, to serve as common soldier in the Caucasus. All communication with him was forbidden. He had no civil rights. For all practical purposes except that of suffering he was a dead man. The little child he had been so careful not to wake up when he kissed her in her cot, inherited all the fortune after Prince John's death. Her existence saved those immense estates from confiscation.

'It was twenty-five years before Prince Roman, stone deaf, his health broken, was permitted to return to Poland. His daughter, married splendidly to a Polish-Austrian *grand seigneur* and moving in the cosmopolitan sphere of the highest European aristocracy, lived mostly abroad in Nice and Vienna. He, settling down on one of her estates, not the one with the palatial residence but another where there was a modest little house, saw very little of her.

'But Prince Roman did not shut himself up as if his work were done. There was hardly anything done in the private and public life of the neighbourhood in which Prince Roman's advice and assistance were not called upon, and never in vain. It was well said that his days did not belong to himself but to his fellow citizens. And especially he was the particular friend of all returned exiles, helping them with purse and advice, arranging their affairs and finding them means of livelihood.

'I heard from my uncle many tales of his devoted activity, in which he was always guided by a simple wisdom, a high sense of honour and the most scrupulous conception of private and public probity. He remains a living figure for me because of that meeting in a billiard-room, when, in my anxiety to hear about a particularly wolfish wolf, I came in momentary contact with a man who was pre-eminently a man amongst all men capable of feeling deeply, of believing steadily, of loving ardently.

'I remember to this day the grasp of Prince Roman's bony, wrinkled hand closing on my small inky paw, and my uncle's half-serious, half-amused way of looking down at his trespassing nephew.

'They moved on and forgot that little boy. But I did not move; I gazed after them, not so much disappointed as disconcerted by this Prince so utterly unlike a prince in a fairy tale. They moved very slowly across the room. Before reaching the other door the Prince stopped; and I heard him – I seem to hear him now – saying: "I wish you would write to Vienna about filling up that post. He's a most deserving fellow – and your recommendation would be decisive."

'My uncle's face turned to him expressed genuine wonder. It said as plainly as any speech could say: what better recommendation than a father's can be needed? The Prince was quick at reading expressions. Again he spoke with the toneless accent of a man who has not heard his own voice for years, for whom the soundless world is like an abode of silent shades.

'And to this day I remember the very words.

' "I ask you because, you see, my daughter and my son-in-law don't believe me to be a good judge of men. They think that I let myself be guided too much by mere sentiment."

1911

THE SHADOW-LINE

A Confession

Worthy of my undying regard

To
BORYS AND ALL OTHERS
who like himself have crossed
in early youth the shadow-line
of their generation
WITH LOVE

Author's Note

This story, which I admit to be in its brevity a fairly complex piece of work, was not intended to touch on the supernatural. Yet more than one critic has been inclined to take it in that way, seeing in it an attempt on my part to give the fullest scope to my imagination by taking it beyond the confines of the world of living, suffering humanity. But as a matter of fact my imagination is not made of stuff so elastic as all that. I believe that if I attempted to put the strain of the supernatural on it it would fail deplorably and exhibit an unlovely gap. But I could never have attempted such a thing, because all my moral and intellectual being is penetrated by an invincible conviction that whatever falls under the dominion of our senses must be in nature and, however exceptional, cannot differ in its essence from all the other effects of the visible and tangible world of which we are a self-conscious part. The world of the living contains enough marvels and mysteries as it is; marvels and mysteries acting upon our emotions and intelligence in ways so inexplicable that it would almost justify the conception of life as an enchanted state. No, I am too firm in my consciousness of the marvellous to be ever fascinated by the mere supernatural, which (take it any way you like) is but a manufactured article, the fabrication of minds insensitive to the intimate delicacies of our relation to the dead and to the living, in their countless multitudes; a desecration of our tenderest memories; an outrage on our dignity.

Whatever my native modesty may be it will never condescend so low as to seek help for my imagination within those vain imaginings common to all ages and that in themselves are enough to fill all lovers of mankind with unutterable sadness. As to the effect of a mental or moral shock on a common mind, it is quite a legitimate subject for study and description. Mr Burns' moral being receives a severe shock in his relations with his late captain, and this in his diseased state turns into a mere superstitious fancy compounded of fear and animosity. This fact is one of the elements of the story, but there is nothing supernatural in it, nothing so to speak from beyond the confines of this world which in all conscience holds enough mystery and terror in itself.

Perhaps if I had published this tale, which I have had for a long time in my mind, under the title of 'First Command' no suggestion of the supernatural would have been found in it by any impartial reader, critical or otherwise. I will not consider here the origins of the feeling in which its actual title, 'The Shadow-Line', occurred to my mind. Primarily the aim of this piece of writing was the presentation of certain facts which certainly were associated with the change from youth, carefree and fervent, to the more self-conscious and more poignant period of maturer life. Nobody can doubt that before the supreme trial of a whole generation I had an acute consciousness of the minute and insignificant character of my own obscure experience. There could be no question here of any parallelism. That notion never entered my head. But there was a feeling of identity, though with an enormous difference of scale – as of one single drop measured against the bitter and stormy immensity of an ocean. And this was very natural too. For when we begin to meditate on the meaning of our own past it seems to fill all the world in its profundity and its magnitude. This book was written in the last three months of the year 1916. Of all the subjects of which a writer of tales is more or less conscious within himself this is the only one I found it possible to attempt at the time. The depth and the nature of the mood with which I approached it is best expressed perhaps in the dedication which strikes me now as a most disproportionate thing – as but another instance of the overwhelming greatness of our own emotion to ourselves.

This much having been said, I may pass on now to a few remarks about the mere material of the story. As to locality it belongs to that part of the Eastern Seas from which I have carried away into my writing life the greatest number of suggestions. From my statement that I thought of this story for a long time under the title of 'First Command' the reader may guess that it is concerned with my personal experience. And as a matter of fact it *is* personal experience seen in perspective with the eye of the mind and coloured by that affection one can't help feeling for such events of one's life as one has no reason to be ashamed of. And that affection is as intense (I appeal here to universal experience) as the shame, and almost the anguish with which one remembers some unfortunate occurrences, down to mere mistakes in speech, that have been perpetrated by one in the past. The effect of perspective in memory is to make things loom large because the essentials stand out isolated from their surroundings of insignificant daily facts which have naturally faded out of one's mind. I remember that period of my sea-life with pleasure because begun inauspiciously it turned out in the end a success from a personal point of view, leaving a tangible proof in the terms of the letter the owners of the ship wrote to me two years afterwards when I resigned my command in order to come home. This resignation marked the beginning of another phase of my seaman's life, its terminal phase, if I may say so, which in its own way has coloured another portion of my writings. I didn't know then how near its end my sea-life was, and therefore I felt no sorrow except at parting with the ship. I was sorry also to break my connection with the firm who owned her and who were pleased to receive with friendly kindness and give their confidence to a man who had entered their service in an accidental manner and in very adverse circumstances. Without disparaging the earnestness of my purpose I suspect now that luck had no small part in the success of the trust reposed in me.

And one cannot help remembering with pleasure the time when one's best efforts were seconded by a run of luck.

The words '*Worthy of my undying regard*' selected by me for the motto on the title page are quoted from the text of the book itself; and, though one of my critics surmised that they applied to the ship, it is evident from the place where they stand that they refer to the men of that ship's company: complete strangers to their new captain and who yet stood by him so well during those twenty days that seemed to have been passed on the brink of a slow and agonising destruction. And *that* is the greatest memory of all! For surely it is a great thing to have commanded a handful of men worthy of one's undying regard.

JOSEPH CONRAD
1920

– D'autre fois, calme plat, grand miroir
De mon désespoir.

BAUDELAIRE

Chapter 1

Only the young have such moments. I don't mean the very young. No. The very young have, properly speaking, no moments. It is the privilege of early youth to live in advance of its days in all the beautiful continuity of hope which knows no pauses and no introspection.

One closes behind one the little gate of mere boyishness – and enters an enchanted garden. Its very shades glow with promise. Every turn of the path has its seduction. And it isn't because it is an undiscovered country. One knows well enough that all mankind had streamed that way. It is the charm of universal experience from which one expects an uncommon or personal sensation – a bit of one's own.

One goes on recognising the landmarks of the predecessors, excited, amused, taking the hard luck and the good luck together – the kicks and the halfpence, as the saying is – the picturesque common lot that holds so many possibilities for the deserving or perhaps for the lucky. Yes. One goes on. And the time, too, goes on – till one perceives ahead a shadow-line warning one that the region of early youth, too, must be left behind.

This is the period of life in which such moments of which I have spoken are likely to come. What moments? Why, the moments of boredom, of weariness, of dissatisfaction. Rash moments. I mean moments when the still young are inclined to commit rash actions, such as getting married suddenly or else throwing up a job for no reason.

This is not a marriage story. It wasn't so bad as that with me. My action, rash as it was, had more the character of divorce – almost of desertion. For no reason on which a sensible person could put a finger I threw up my job – chucked my berth – left the ship of which the worst that could be said was that she was a steamship and therefore, perhaps, not entitled to that blind loyalty which . . . However, it's no use trying to put a gloss on what even at the time I myself half suspected to be a caprice.

It was in an Eastern port. She was an Eastern ship, inasmuch as then she belonged to that port. She traded among dark islands on a blue reef-scarred sea, with the Red Ensign over the taffrail and at her masthead a house-flag, also red, but with a green border and with a white crescent in it. For an Arab owned her, and a Syed at that. Hence the green border on the flag. He was the head of a great House of Straits Arabs, but as loyal a subject of the complex British Empire as you could find east of the Suez Canal. World politics did not trouble him at all, but he had a great occult power amongst his own people.

It was all one to us who owned the ship. He had to employ white men in the shipping part of his business, and many of those he so employed had never set eyes on him from the first to the last day. I myself saw him but once, quite accidentally on a wharf – an old, dark little man, blind in one eye, in a snowy robe and yellow slippers. He was having his hand severely kissed by a crowd of Malay pilgrims to whom he had done some favour, in the way of food and money. His alms-giving, I have heard, was most extensive, covering almost the whole Archipelago. For isn't it said that 'The charitable man is the friend of Allah'?

Excellent (and picturesque) Arab owner, about whom one needed not to trouble one's head, a most excellent Scottish ship – for she was that from the keel up – excellent sea-boat, easy to keep clean, most handy in every way, and if it had not been for her internal propulsion, worthy of any man's love, I cherish to this day a profound respect for her memory. As to the kind of trade she was engaged in and the character of my shipmates, I could not have been happier if I had had the life and the men made to my order by a benevolent Enchanter.

And suddenly I left all this. I left it in that, to us, inconsequential manner in which a bird flies away from a comfortable branch. It was as though all unknowing I had heard a whisper or seen something. Well – perhaps! One day I was perfectly right and the next everything was gone – glamour, flavour, interest, contentment – everything. It was one of these moments, you know. The green sickness of late youth descended on me and carried me off. Carried me off that ship, I mean.

We were only four white men on board, with a large crew of Kalashes and two Malay petty officers. The Captain stared hard as if wondering what ailed me. But he was a sailor, and he, too, had been young at one time. Presently a smile came to lurk under his thick iron-grey moustache, and he observed that, of course, if I felt I must go he couldn't keep me by main force. And it was arranged that I should be paid off the next morning. As I was going out of the chart-room he added suddenly, in a peculiar wistful tone, that he hoped I would find what I was so anxious to go and look for. A soft, cryptic utterance which seemed to reach deeper than any diamond-hard tool could have done. I do believe he understood my case.

But the second engineer attacked me differently. He was a sturdy young Scot, with a smooth face and light eyes. His honest red countenance emerged out of the engine-room companion and then the whole robust man, with shirt sleeves turned up, wiping slowly the massive forearms with a lump of cotton-waste. And his light eyes expressed bitter distaste, as though our friendship had turned to ashes. He said weightily: 'Oh! Aye! I've been thinking it was about time for you to run away home and get married to some silly girl.'

It was tacitly understood in the port that John Nieven was a fierce misogynist; and the absurd character of the sally convinced me that he meant to be nasty – very nasty – had meant to say the most crushing thing he could think of. My laugh sounded deprecatory. Nobody but a friend could be so angry as that. I became a little crestfallen. Our chief engineer also took a characteristic view of my action, but in a kindlier spirit.

He was young, too, but very thin, and with a mist of fluffy brown beard all round his haggard face. All day long, at sea or in harbour, he could be seen walking hastily up and down the after-deck, wearing an intense, spiritually rapt expression, which was caused by a perpetual consciousness of unpleasant physical sensations in his internal economy. For he was a confirmed dyspeptic. His view of my case was very simple. He said it was nothing but deranged liver. Of course! He suggested I should stay for another trip and meantime dose myself with a certain patent medicine in which his own belief was absolute. 'I'll tell you what I'll do. I'll buy you two bottles, out of my own pocket. There. I can't say fairer than that, can I?'

I believe he would have perpetrated the atrocity (or generosity) at the merest sign of weakening on my part. By that time, however, I was more discontented, disgusted, and dogged than ever. The past eighteen months, so full of new and varied experience, appeared a dreary, prosaic waste of days. I felt – how shall I express it? – that there was no truth to be got out of them.

What truth? I should have been hard put to it to explain. Probably, if pressed, I would have burst into tears simply. I was young enough for that.

Next day the Captain and I transacted our business in the harbour office. It was a lofty, big, cool, white room, where the screened light of day glowed serenely. Everybody in it – the officials, the public – were in white. Only the heavy polished desks gleamed darkly in a central avenue, and some papers lying on them were blue. Enormous punkahs sent from on high a gentle draught through that immaculate interior and upon our perspiring heads.

The official behind the desk we approached grinned amiably and kept it up till, in answer to his perfunctory question, 'Sign off and on again?' my Captain answered, 'No! Signing off for good.' And then his grin vanished in sudden solemnity. He did not look at me again till he handed me my papers with a sorrowful expression, as if they had been my passports for Hades.

While I was putting them away he murmured some question to the Captain, and I heard the latter answer good-humouredly: 'No. He leaves us to go home.'

'Oh!' the other exclaimed, nodding mournfully over my sad condition.

I didn't know him outside the official building, but he leaned forward over the desk to shake hands with me, compassionately, as one would with some poor devil going out to be hanged; and I am afraid I performed my part ungraciously, in the hardened manner of an impenitent criminal.

No homeward-bound mail-boat was due for three or four days. Being now a man without a ship, and having for a time broken my connection with the sea – become, in fact, a mere potential passenger – it would have been more appropriate perhaps if I had gone to stay at an hotel. There it was, too, within a stone's throw of the harbour office, low, but somehow palatial, displaying its white, pillared pavilions surrounded by trim grass plots. I would have felt a passenger indeed in there! I gave it a hostile glance and directed my steps towards the Officers' Sailors' Home.

I walked in the sunshine, disregarding it, and in the shade of the big trees on the esplanade without enjoying it. The heat of the tropical East descended through the leafy boughs, enveloping my thinly-clad body, clinging to my rebellious discontent, as if to rob it of its freedom.

The Officers' Home was a large bungalow with a wide verandah and a curiously suburban-looking little garden of bushes and a few trees between it and the street. That institution partook somewhat of the character of a residential club, but with a slightly Governmental flavour about it, because it was administered by the Harbour Office. Its manager was officially styled Chief Steward. He was an unhappy, wizened little man, who if put into a jockey's rig would have looked the part to perfection. But it was obvious that at sometime or other in his life, in some capacity or other, he had been connected with the sea. Possibly in the comprehensive capacity of a failure.

I should have thought his employment a very easy one, but he used to affirm for some reason or other that his job would be the death of him someday. It was rather mysterious. Perhaps everything naturally was too much trouble for him. He certainly seemed to hate having people in the house.

On entering it I thought he must be feeling pleased. It was as still as a tomb. I could see no one in the living rooms; and the verandah, too, was empty, except for a man at the far end dozing prone in a long chair. At the noise of my footsteps he opened one horribly fish-like eye. He was a stranger to me. I retreated from there, and, crossing the dining-room – a very bare apartment with a motionless punkah hanging over the centre table – I knocked at a door labelled in black letters: 'Chief Steward'.

The answer to my knock being a vexed and doleful plaint: 'Oh, dear! Oh, dear! What is it now?' I went in at once.

It was a strange room to find in the tropics. Twilight and stuffiness reigned in there. The fellow had hung enormously ample, dusty, cheap lace curtains over his windows, which were shut. Piles of cardboard boxes, such as milliners and dressmakers use in Europe, cumbered the corners; and by some means he had procured for himself the sort of furniture that might have come out of a respectable parlour in the East End of London – a horsehair sofa, armchairs of the same. I glimpsed grimy antimacassars scattered over that horrid upholstery, which was awe-inspiring, insomuch that one could not guess what mysterious accident, need, or fancy had collected it there. Its owner had taken off his tunic, and in white trousers and a thin short-sleeved singlet prowled behind the chair-backs nursing his meagre elbows.

An exclamation of dismay escaped him when he heard that I had come for a stay; but he could not deny that there were plenty of vacant rooms.

'Very well. Can you give me the one I had before?'

He emitted a faint moan from behind a pile of cardboard boxes on the table, which might have contained gloves or handkerchiefs or neckties. I wonder what the fellow did keep in them? There was a smell of decaying coral, or Oriental dust, of zoological specimens in that den of his. I could only see the top of his head and his unhappy eyes levelled at me over the barrier.

'It's only for a couple of days,' I said, intending to cheer him up.

'Perhaps you would like to pay in advance?' he suggested eagerly.

'Certainly not!' I burst out directly I could speak. 'Never heard of such a thing! This is the most infernal cheek . . . '

He had seized his head in both hands – a gesture of despair which checked my indignation.

'Oh, dear! Oh, dear! Don't fly out like this. I am asking everybody.'

'I don't believe it,' I said bluntly.

'Well, I am going to. And if you gentlemen all agreed to pay in advance I could make Hamilton pay up too. He's always turning up ashore dead broke, and even when he has some money he won't settle his bills. I don't know what to do with him. He swears at me and tells me I can't chuck a white man out into the street here. So if you only would . . . '

I was amazed. Incredulous too. I suspected the fellow of gratuitous impertinence. I told him with marked emphasis that I would see him and Hamilton hanged first, and requested him to conduct me to my room with no more of his nonsense. He produced then a key from somewhere and led the way out of his lair, giving me a vicious sidelong look in passing.

'Anyone I know staying here?' I asked him before he left my room.

He had recovered his usual pained impatient tone, and said that Captain Giles was there, back from a Solo Sea trip. Two other guests were staying also. He paused. And, of course, Hamilton, he added.

'Oh, yes! Hamilton,' I said, and the miserable creature took himself off with a final groan.

His impudence still rankled when I came into the dining-room at tiffin time. He was there on duty overlooking the Chinamen servants. The tiffin was laid on one end only of the long table, and the punkah was stirring the hot air lazily – mostly above a barren waste of polished wood.

We were four around the cloth. The dozing stranger from the chair was one. Both his eyes were partly opened now, but they did not seem to see anything. He was supine. The dignified person next him, with short side whiskers and a carefully scraped chin, was, of course, Hamilton. I have never seen anyone so full of dignity for the station in life Providence had been pleased to place him in. I had been told that he regarded me as a rank outsider. He raised not only his eyes, but his eyebrows as well, at the sound I made pulling back my chair.

Captain Giles was at the head of the table. I exchanged a few words of greeting with him and sat down on his left. Stout and pale, with a great shiny dome of a bald forehead and prominent brown eyes, he might have been anything but a seaman. You would not have been surprised to learn that he was an architect. To me (I know how absurd it is) to me he looked like a churchwarden. He had the appearance of a man from whom you would expect sound advice, moral sentiments, with perhaps a platitude or two thrown in on occasion, not from a desire to dazzle, but from honest conviction.

Though very well known and appreciated in the shipping world, he had no regular employment. He did not want it. He had his own peculiar position. He was an expert. An expert in – how shall I say it? – in intricate navigation. He was supposed to know more about remote and imperfectly charted parts of the Archipelago than any man living. His brain must have been a perfect warehouse of reefs, positions, bearings, images of headlands, shapes of obscure coasts, aspects of innumerable islands, desert and otherwise. Any ship, for instance, bound on a trip to Palawan or somewhere that way would have Captain Giles on board, either in temporary command or 'to assist the master'. It was said that he had a retaining fee from a wealthy firm of Chinese steamship owners, in view of such services. Besides, he was always ready to relieve any man who wished to take a spell ashore for a time. No owner was ever known to object to an arrangement of that sort. For it seemed to be the established opinion at the port that Captain Giles was as good as the best, if not a little better. But in Hamilton's view he was an 'outsider'. I believe that for Hamilton the generalisation 'outsider' covered the whole lot of us; though I suppose that he made some distinctions in his mind.

I didn't try to make conversation with Captain Giles, whom I had not seen more than twice in my life. But, of course, he knew who I was. After a while, inclining his big shiny head my way, he addressed me first in his friendly fashion. He presumed from seeing me there, he said, that I had come ashore for a couple of days' leave.

He was a low-voiced man. I spoke a little louder, saying that: No – I had left the ship for good.

'A free man for a bit,' was his comment.

'I suppose I may call myself that – since eleven o'clock,' I said.

Hamilton had stopped eating at the sound of our voices. He laid down his knife and fork gently, got up, and muttering something about 'this infernal heat cutting one's appetite', went out of the room. Almost immediately we heard him leave the house down the verandah steps.

On this Captain Giles remarked easily that the fellow had no doubt gone off to look after my old job. The Chief Steward, who had been leaning against the wall, brought his face of an unhappy goat nearer to the table and addressed us dolefully. His object was to unburden himself of his eternal grievance against Hamilton. The man kept him in hot water with the Harbour Office as to the state of his accounts. He wished to goodness he would get my job, though in truth what would it be? Temporary relief at best.

I said: 'You needn't worry. He won't get my job. My successor is on board already.'

He was surprised, and I believe his face fell a little at the news. Captain Giles gave a soft laugh. We got up and went out on the verandah, leaving the supine stranger to be dealt with by the Chinamen. The last thing I saw they had put a plate with a slice of pineapple on it before him and stood back to watch what would happen. But the experiment seemed a failure. He sat insensible.

It was imparted to me in a low voice by Captain Giles that this was an officer of some Rajah's yacht which had come into our port to be dry-docked. Must have been 'seeing life' last night, he added, wrinkling his nose in an intimate, confidential way which pleased me vastly. For Captain Giles had prestige. He was credited with wonderful adventures and with some mysterious tragedy in his life. And no man had a word to say against him. He continued: 'I remember him first coming ashore here some years ago. Seems only the other day. He was a nice boy. Oh! these nice boys!'

I could not help laughing aloud. He looked startled, then joined in the laugh. 'No! No! I didn't mean that,' he cried. 'What I meant is that some of them do go soft mighty quick out here.'

Jocularly I suggested the beastly heat as the first cause. But Captain Giles disclosed himself possessed of a deeper philosophy. Things out East were made easy for white men. That was all right. The difficulty was to go on keeping white, and some of these nice boys did not know how. He gave me a searching look, and in a benevolent, heavy-uncle manner asked point blank: 'Why did you throw up your berth?'

I became angry all of a sudden; for you can understand how exasperating such a question was to a man who didn't know. I said to myself that I ought to shut up that moralist; and to him aloud I said with challenging politeness: 'Why . . . ? Do you disapprove?'

He was too disconcerted to do more than mutter confusedly: 'I! . . . In a general way . . . ' and then gave me up. But he retired in good order, under the cover of a heavily humorous remark that he, too, was getting soft, and that this was his time for taking his little siesta – when he was on shore. 'Very bad habit. Very bad habit.'

The simplicity of the man would have disarmed a touchiness even more youthful than mine. So when next day at tiffin he bent his head towards me and said that he had met my late Captain last evening, adding in an undertone: 'He's very sorry you left. He had never had a mate that suited him so well,' I answered him earnestly, without any affectation, that I certainly hadn't been so comfortable in any ship or with any commander in all my seagoing days.

'Well – then,' he murmured.

'Haven't you heard, Captain Giles, that I intend to go home?'

'Yes,' he said benevolently. 'I have heard that sort of thing so often before.'

'What of that?' I cried. I thought he was the most dull, unimaginative man I had ever met. I don't know what more I would have said, but the much-belated Hamilton came in just then and took his usual seat. So I dropped into a mumble.

'Anyhow, you shall see it done this time.'

Hamilton, beautifully shaved, gave Captain Giles a curt nod, but didn't even condescend to raise his eyebrows at me; and when he spoke it was only to tell the Chief Steward that the food on his plate wasn't fit to be set before a gentleman. The individual addressed seemed much too unhappy to groan. He only cast his eyes up to the punkah and that was all.

Captain Giles and I got up from the table, and the stranger next to Hamilton followed our example, manoeuvring himself to his feet with difficulty. He, poor fellow, not because he was hungry but I verily believe only to recover his self-respect, had tried to put some of that unworthy food into his mouth. But after dropping his fork twice and generally making a failure of it, he had sat still with an air of intense mortification combined with a ghastly glazed stare. Both Giles and I had avoided looking his way at table.

On the verandah he stopped short on purpose to address to us anxiously a long remark which I failed to understand completely. It sounded like some horrible unknown language. But when Captain Giles, after only an instant for reflection, answered him with homely friendliness, 'Aye, to be sure. You are right there,' he appeared very much gratified indeed, and went away (pretty straight too) to seek a distant long chair.

'What was he trying to say?' I asked with disgust.

'I don't know. Mustn't be down too much on a fellow. He's feeling pretty wretched, you may be sure; and tomorrow he'll feel worse yet.'

Judging by the man's appearance it seemed impossible. I wondered what sort of complicated debauch had reduced him to that unspeakable condition. Captain Giles' benevolence was spoiled by a curious air of complacency which I disliked. I said with a little laugh: 'Well, he will have you to look after him.'

He made a deprecatory gesture, sat down, and took up a paper. I did the same. The papers were old and uninteresting, filled up mostly with dreary stereotyped descriptions of Queen Victoria's first jubilee celebrations. Probably we should have quickly fallen into a tropical afternoon doze if it had not been for Hamilton's voice raised in the dining-room. He was finishing his tiffin there. The big double doors stood wide open permanently, and he could not have had any idea how near to the doorway our chairs were placed. He was heard in a loud, supercilious tone answering some statement ventured by the Chief Steward.

'I am not going to be rushed into anything. They will be glad enough to get a gentleman I imagine. There is no hurry.'

A loud whispering from the steward succeeded and then again Hamilton was heard with even intenser scorn.

'What? That young ass who fancies himself for having been chief mate with Kent so long? . . . Preposterous.'

Giles and I looked at each other. Kent being the name of my late commander, Captain Giles' whisper, 'He's talking of you,' seemed to me sheer waste of breath. The Chief Steward must have stuck to his point whatever it was, because Hamilton was heard again more supercilious, if possible, and also very emphatic: 'Rubbish, my good man! One doesn't *compete* with a rank outsider like that. There's plenty of time.'

Then there was pushing of chairs, footsteps in the next room, and plaintive expostulations from the Steward, who was pursuing Hamilton, even out of doors through the main entrance.

'That's a very insulting sort of man,' remarked Captain Giles – superfluously, I thought. 'Very insulting. You haven't offended him in some way, have you?'

'Never spoke to him in my life,' I said grumpily. 'Can't imagine what he means by competing. He has been trying for my job after I left – and didn't get it. But that isn't exactly competition.'

Captain Giles balanced his big, benevolent head thoughtfully. 'He didn't get it,' he repeated very slowly. 'No, not likely either, with Kent. Kent is no end sorry you left him. He gives you the name of a good seaman too.'

I flung away the paper I was still holding. I sat up, I slapped the table with my open palm. I wanted to know why he would keep harping on that, my absolutely private affair. It was exasperating, really.

Captain Giles silenced me by the perfect equanimity of his gaze. 'Nothing to be annoyed about,' he murmured reasonably, with an evident desire to soothe the childish irritation he had aroused. And he was really a man of an appearance so inoffensive that I tried to explain myself as much as I could. I told him that I did not want to hear any more about what was past and gone. It had been very nice while it lasted, but now it was done with I preferred not to talk about it or even think about it. I had made up my mind to go home.

He listened to the whole tirade in a particular, lending-the-ear attitude, as if trying to detect a false note in it somewhere; then straightened himself up and appeared to ponder sagaciously over the matter.

'Yes. You told me you meant to go home. Anything in view there?'

Instead of telling him that it was none of his business I said sullenly: 'Nothing that I know of.'

I had indeed considered that rather blank side of the situation I had created for myself by leaving suddenly my very satisfactory employment. And I was not very pleased with it. I had it on the tip of my tongue to say that common sense had nothing to do with my action, and that therefore it didn't deserve the interest Captain Giles seemed to be taking in it. But he was puffing at a short wooden pipe now, and looked so guileless, dense, and commonplace, that it seemed hardly worth while to puzzle him either with truth or sarcasm.

He blew a cloud of smoke, then surprised me by a very abrupt: 'Paid your passage money yet?'

Overcome by the shameless pertinacity of a man to whom it was rather difficult to be rude, I replied with exaggerated meekness that I had not done so yet. I thought there would be plenty of time to do that tomorrow.

And I was about to turn away, withdrawing my privacy from his fatuous, objectless attempts to test what sort of stuff it was made of, when he laid down his pipe in an extremely significant manner, you know, as if a critical moment had come, and leaned sideways over the table between us.

'Oh! You haven't yet!' He dropped his voice mysteriously. 'Well, then I think you ought to know that there's something going on here.'

I had never in my life felt more detached from all earthly goings on. Freed from the sea for a time, I preserved the sailor's consciousness of complete independence from all land affairs. How could they concern me? I gazed at Captain Giles' animation with scorn rather than with curiosity.

To his obviously preparatory question whether our Steward had spoken to me that day I said he hadn't. And what's more he would have had precious little encouragement if he had tried to. I didn't want the fellow to speak to me at all.

Unrebuked by my petulance, Captain Giles, with an air of immense sagacity, began to tell me a minute tale about a Harbour Office peon. It was absolutely pointless. A peon was seen walking that morning on the verandah with a letter in his hand. It was in an official envelope. As the habit of these fellows is, he had shown it to the first white man he came across. That man was our friend in the armchair. He, as I knew, was not in a state to interest himself in any sublunary matters. He could only wave the peon away. The peon then wandered on along the verandah and came upon Captain Giles, who was there by an extraordinary chance . . .

At this point he stopped with a profound look. The letter, he continued, was addressed to the Chief Steward. Now what could Captain Ellis, the Master Attendant, want to write to the Steward for? The fellow went every morning, anyhow, to the Harbour Office with his report, for orders or what not. He hadn't been back more than an hour before there was an office peon chasing him with a note. Now what was that for?

And he began to speculate. It was not for this – and it could not be for that. As to that other thing it was unthinkable.

The fatuousness of all this made me stare. If the man had not been somehow a sympathetic personality I would have resented it like an insult. As it was, I felt only sorry for him. Something remarkably earnest in his gaze prevented me from laughing in his face. Neither did I yawn at him. I just stared.

His tone became a shade more mysterious. Directly the fellow (meaning the Steward) got that note he rushed for his hat and bolted out of the house. But it wasn't because the note called him to the Harbour Office. He didn't go there. He was not absent long enough for that. He came darting back in no time, flung his hat away, and raced about the dining-room moaning and slapping his forehead. All these exciting facts and manifestations had been observed by Captain Giles. He had, it seems, been meditating upon them ever since.

I began to pity him profoundly. And in a tone which I tried to make as little sarcastic as possible I said that I was glad he had found something to occupy his morning hours.

With his disarming simplicity he made me observe, as if it were a matter of some consequence, how strange it was that he should have spent the morning indoors at all. He generally was out before tiffin, visiting various offices, seeing his friends in the harbour, and so on. He had felt out of sorts somewhat on rising. Nothing much. Just enough to make him feel lazy.

All this with a sustained, holding stare which, in conjunction with the general inanity of the discourse, conveyed the impression of mild, dreary lunacy. And when he hitched his chair a little and dropped his voice to the low note of mystery, it flashed upon me that high professional reputation was not necessarily a guarantee of sound mind.

It never occurred to me then that I didn't know in what soundness of mind exactly consisted and what a delicate and, upon the whole, unimportant matter it was. With some idea of not hurting his feelings I blinked at him in an interested manner. But when he proceeded to ask me mysteriously whether I remembered what had passed just now between that Steward of ours and 'that man Hamilton', I only grunted sour assent and turned away my head.

'Aye. But do you remember every word?' he insisted tactfully.

'I don't know. It's none of my business,' I snapped out, consigning, moreover, the Steward and Hamilton aloud to eternal perdition.

I meant to be very energetic and final, but Captain Giles continued to gaze at me thoughtfully. Nothing could stop him. He went on to point out that my personality was involved in that conversation. When I tried to preserve the semblance of unconcern he became positively cruel. I heard what the man had said? Yes? What did I think of it then? – he wanted to know.

Captain Giles' appearance excluding the suspicion of mere sly malice, I came to the conclusion that he was simply the most tactless idiot on earth. I almost despised myself for the weakness of attempting to enlighten his common understanding. I started to explain that I did not think anything whatever. Hamilton was not worth a thought. What such an offensive loafer . . . – 'Aye! that he is,' interjected Captain Giles – . . . thought or said was below any decent man's contempt, and I did not propose to take the slightest notice of it.

This attitude seemed to me so simple and obvious that I was really astonished at Giles giving no sign of assent. Such perfect stupidity was almost interesting.

'What would you like me to do?' I asked, laughing. 'I can't start a row with him because of the opinion he has formed of me. Of course, I've heard of the contemptuous way he alludes to me. But he doesn't intrude his contempt on my notice. He has never expressed it in my hearing. For even just now he didn't know we could hear him. I should only make myself ridiculous.'

That hopeless Giles went on puffing at his pipe moodily. All at once his face cleared, and he spoke.

'You missed my point.'

'Have I? I am very glad to hear it,' I said.

With increasing animation he stated again that I had missed his point. Entirely. And in a tone of growing self-conscious complacency he told me that few things escaped his attention, and he was rather used to think them out, and generally from his experience of life and men arrived at the right conclusion.

This bit of self-praise, of course, fitted excellently the laborious inanity of the whole conversation. The whole thing strengthened in me that obscure feeling of life being but a waste of days, which, half-unconsciously, had driven me out of a comfortable berth, away from men I liked, to flee from the menace of emptiness . . . and to find inanity at the first turn. Here was a man of recognised character and achievement disclosed as an absurd and dreary chatterer. And it was probably like this everywhere – from east to west, from the bottom to the top of the social scale.

A great discouragement fell on me. A spiritual drowsiness. Giles' voice was going on complacently; the very voice of the universal hollow conceit. And I was no longer angry with it. There was nothing original, nothing new, startling, informing to expect from the world: no opportunities to find out something about oneself, no wisdom to acquire, no fun to enjoy. Everything was stupid and overrated, even as Captain Giles was. So be it.

The name of Hamilton suddenly caught my ear and roused me up.

'I thought we had done with him,' I said, with the greatest possible distaste.

'Yes. But considering what we happened to hear just now I think you ought to do it.'

'Ought to do it?' I sat up bewildered. 'Do what?'

Captain Giles confronted me very much surprised.

'Why! Do what I have been advising you to try. You go and ask the Steward what was there in that letter from the Harbour Office. Ask him straight out.'

I remained speechless for a time. Here was something unexpected and original enough to be altogether incomprehensible. I murmured, astounded, 'But I thought it was Hamilton that you . . .'

'Exactly. Don't you let him. You do what I tell you. You tackle that Steward. You'll make him jump, I bet,' insisted Captain Giles, waving his smouldering pipe impressively at me. Then he took three rapid puffs at it.

His aspect of triumphant acuteness was indescribable. Yet the man remained a strangely sympathetic creature. Benevolence radiated from him ridiculously, mildly, impressively. It was irritating, too. But I pointed out coldly, as one who deals with the incomprehensible, that I didn't see any reason to expose myself to a snub from the fellow. He was a very unsatisfactory steward and a miserable wretch besides, but I would just as soon think of tweaking his nose.

'Tweaking his nose,' said Captain Giles in a scandalised tone. 'Much use it would be to you.'

That remark was so irrelevant that one could make no answer to it. But the sense of the absurdity was beginning at last to exercise its well-known fascination. I felt I must not let the man talk to me any more. I got up, observing curtly that he was too much for me – that I couldn't make him out.

Before I had time to move away he spoke again in a changed tone of obstinacy and puffing nervously at his pipe.

'Well – he's a – no account cuss – anyhow. You just ask him. That's all.'

That new manner impressed me – or rather made me pause. But sanity asserting its sway at once, I left the verandah after giving him a mirthless smile. In a few strides I found myself in the dining-room, now cleared and empty. But during that short time various thoughts occurred to me, such as: that Giles had been making fun of me, expecting some amusement at my expense; that I probably looked silly and gullible; that I knew very little of life . . .

The door facing me across the dining-room flew open, to my extreme surprise. It was the door inscribed with the word 'Steward' and the man himself ran out of his stuffy Philistinish lair, in his absurd hunted-animal manner, making for the garden door.

To this day I don't know what made me call after him: 'I say! Wait a minute.' Perhaps it was the sidelong glance he gave me; or possibly I was yet under the influence of Captain Giles' mysterious earnestness. Well, it was an impulse of some sort; an effect of that force somewhere within our lives which shapes them this way or that. For if these words had not escaped from my lips (my will had nothing to do with that) my existence would, to be sure, have been still a seaman's existence, but directed on now to me utterly inconceivable lines.

No. My will had nothing to do with it. Indeed, no sooner had I made that fateful noise than I became extremely sorry for it. Had the man stopped and faced me I would have had to retire in disorder. For I had no notion to carry out Captain Giles' idiotic joke, either at my own expense or at the expense of the Steward.

But here the old human instinct of the chase came into play. He pretended to be deaf, and I, without thinking a second about it, dashed along my own side of the dining table and cut him off at the very door.

'Why can't you answer when you are spoken to?' I asked roughly.

He leaned against the side of the door. He looked extremely wretched. Human nature is, I fear, not very nice right through. There are ugly spots in it. I found myself growing angry, and that, I believe, only because my quarry looked so woebegone. Miserable beggar!

I went for him without more ado. 'I understand there was an official communication to the Home from the Harbour Office this morning. Is that so?'

Instead of telling me to mind my own business, as he might have done, he began to whine with an undertone of impudence. He couldn't see me anywhere this morning. He couldn't be expected to run all over the town after me.

'Who wants you to?' I cried. And then my eyes became opened to the inwardness of things and speeches, the triviality of which had been so baffling and tiresome.

I told him I wanted to know what was in that letter. My sternness of tone and behaviour was only half assumed. Curiosity can be a very fierce sentiment – at times.

He took refuge in a silly, muttering sulkiness. It was nothing to me, he mumbled. I had told him I was going home. And since I was going home he didn't see why he should . . .

That was the line of his argument, and it was irrelevant enough to be almost insulting. Insulting to one's intelligence, I mean.

In that twilight region between youth and maturity, in which I had my being then, one is peculiarly sensitive to that kind of insult. I am afraid my behaviour to the Steward became very rough indeed. But it wasn't in him to face out anything or anybody. Drug habit or solitary tippling, perhaps. And when I forgot myself so far as to swear at him he broke down and began to shriek.

I don't mean to say that he made a great outcry. It was a cynical shrieking confession, only faint – piteously faint. It wasn't very coherent either, but sufficiently so to strike me dumb at first. I turned my eyes from him in righteous indignation, and perceived Captain Giles in the verandah doorway surveying quietly the scene, his own handiwork, if I may express it in that way. His smouldering black pipe was very noticeable in his big, paternal fist. So, too, was the glitter of his heavy gold watch-chain across the breast of his white tunic. He exhaled an atmosphere of virtuous sagacity thick enough for any innocent soul to fly to confidently. I flew to him.

'You would never believe it,' I cried. 'It was a notification that a master is wanted for some ship. There's a command apparently going about and this fellow puts the thing in his pocket.'

The Steward screamed out in accents of loud despair, 'You will be the death of me!'

The mighty slap he gave his wretched forehead was very loud, too. But when I turned to look at him he was no longer there. He had rushed away somewhere out of sight. This sudden disappearance made me laugh.

This was the end of the incident – for me. Captain Giles, however, staring at the place where the Steward had been, began to haul at his gorgeous gold chain till at last the watch came up from the deep pocket like solid truth from a well. Solemnly he lowered it down again and only then said: 'Just three o'clock. You will be in time – if you don't lose any, that is.'

'In time for what?' I asked.

'Good Lord! For the Harbour Office. This must be looked into.'

Strictly speaking, he was right. But I've never had much taste for investigation, for showing people up and all that, no doubt, ethically meritorious kind of work. And my view of the episode was purely ethical. If anyone had to be the death of the Steward I didn't see why it shouldn't be Captain Giles himself, a man of age and standing, and a permanent resident. Whereas I, in comparison, felt myself a mere bird of passage in that port. In fact, it might have been said that I had already broken off my connection. I muttered that I didn't think – it was nothing to me . . .

'Nothing?' repeated Captain Giles, giving some signs of quiet, deliberate indignation. 'Kent warned me you were a peculiar young fellow. You will tell me next that a command is nothing to you – and after all the trouble I've taken, too!'

'The trouble!' I murmured, uncomprehending. What trouble? All I could remember was being mystified and bored by his conversation for a solid hour after tiffin. And he called that taking a lot of trouble.

He was looking at me with a self-complacency which would have been odious in any other man. All at once, as if a page of a book had been turned over disclosing a word which made plain all that had gone before, I perceived that this matter had also another than an ethical aspect.

And still I did not move. Captain Giles lost his patience a little. With an angry puff at his pipe he turned his back on my hesitation.

But it was not hesitation on my part. I had been, if I may express myself so, put out of gear mentally. But as soon as I had convinced myself that this stale, unprofitable world of my discontent contained such a thing as a command to be seized, I recovered my powers of locomotion.

It's a good step from the Officers' Home to the Harbour Office; but with the magic word 'Command' in my head I found myself suddenly on the quay as if transported there in the twinkling of an eye, before a portal of dressed white stone above a flight of shallow white steps.

All this seemed to glide towards me swiftly. The whole great roadstead to the right was just a mere flicker of blue, and the dim cool hall swallowed me up out of the heat and glare of which I had not been aware till the very moment I passed in from it.

The broad inner staircase insinuated itself under my feet somehow. Command is a strong magic. The first human beings I perceived distinctly since I had parted with the indignant back of Captain Giles were the crew of the harbour steam-launch lounging on the spacious landing about the curtained archway of the shipping office.

It was there that my buoyancy abandoned me. The atmosphere of official-dom would kill anything that breathes the air of human endeavour, would extinguish hope and fear alike in the supremacy of paper and ink. I passed heavily under the curtain which the Malay coxswain of the harbour launch raised for me. There was nobody in the office except the clerks, writing in two industrious rows. But the head shipping-master hopped down from his elevation and hurried along on the thick mats to meet me in the broad central passage.

He had a Scottish name, but his complexion was of a rich olive hue, his short beard was jet black, and his eyes, also black, had a languishing expression. He asked confidentially: 'You want to see Him?'

All lightness of spirit and body having departed from me at the touch of officialdom, I looked at the scribe without animation and asked in my turn wearily: 'What do you think? Is it any use?'

'My goodness! He has asked for you twice today.'

This emphatic He was the supreme authority, the Marine Superintendent, the Harbour-Master – a very great person in the eyes of every single quill-driver in the room. But that was nothing to the opinion he had of his own greatness.

Captain Ellis looked upon himself as a sort of divine (pagan) emanation, the deputy-Neptune for the circumambient seas. If he did not actually rule the waves, he pretended to rule the fate of the mortals whose lives were cast upon the waters.

This uplifting illusion made him inquisitorial and peremptory. And as his temperament was choleric there were fellows who were actually afraid of him. He was redoubtable, not in virtue of his office, but because of his unwarrantable assumptions. I had never had anything to do with him before.

I said: 'Oh! He has asked for me twice. Then perhaps I had better go in.'

'You must! You must!'

The shipping-master led the way with a mincing gait round the whole system of desks to a tall and important-looking door, which he opened with a deferential action of the arm.

He stepped right in (but without letting go of the handle) and, after gazing reverently down the room for a while, beckoned me in by a silent jerk of the head. Then he slipped out at once and shut the door after me most delicately.

Three lofty windows gave on the harbour. There was nothing in them but the dark-blue sparkling sea and the paler luminous blue of the sky. My eye caught in the depths and distances of these blue tones the white speck of some big ship just arrived and about to anchor in the outer roadstead. A ship from home – after perhaps ninety days at sea. There is something touching about a ship coming in from sea and folding her white wings for a rest.

The next thing I saw was the topknot of silver hair surmounting Captain Ellis's smooth red face, which would have been apoplectic if it hadn't had such a fresh appearance.

Our deputy-Neptune had no beard on his chin, and there was no trident to be seen standing in a corner anywhere, like an umbrella. But his hand was holding a pen – the official pen, far mightier than the sword in making or marring the fortune of simple toiling men. He was looking over his shoulder at my advance.

When I had come well within range he saluted me by a nerve-shattering: 'Where have you been all this time?'

As it was no concern of his I did not take the slightest notice of the shot. I said simply that I had heard there was a master needed for some vessel, and being a sailing-ship man I thought I would apply . . .

He interrupted me. 'Why! Hang it! *You* are the right man for that job – if there had been twenty others after it. But no fear of that. They are all afraid to catch hold. That's what's the matter.'

He was very irritated. I said innocently: 'Are they, sir. I wonder why?'

'Why!' he fumed. 'Afraid of the sails. Afraid of a white crew. Too much trouble. Too much work. Too long out here. Easy life and deck-chairs more their mark. Here I sit with the Consul-General's cable before me, and the only man fit for the job not to be found anywhere. I began to think you were funking it too . . .'

'I haven't been long getting to the office,' I remarked calmly.

'You have a good name out here, though,' he growled savagely without looking at me.

'I am very glad to hear it from you, sir,' I said.

'Yes. But you are not on the spot when you are wanted. You know you weren't. That steward of yours wouldn't dare to neglect a message from this office. Where the devil did you hide yourself for the best part of the day?'

I only smiled kindly down on him, and he seemed to recollect himself, and asked me to take a seat. He explained that the master of a British ship having died in Bankok the Consul-General had cabled to him a request for a competent man to be sent out to take command.

Apparently, in his mind, I was the man from the first, though for the looks of the thing the notification addressed to the Sailors' Home was general. An agreement had already been prepared. He gave it to me to read, and when I handed it back to him with the remark that I accepted its terms, the deputy-Neptune signed it, stamped it with his own exalted hand, folded it in four (it was a sheet of blue foolscap), and presented it to me – a gift of extraordinary potency, for, as I put it in my pocket, my head swam a little.

'This is your appointment to the command,' he said with a certain gravity. 'An official appointment binding the owners to conditions which you have accepted. Now – when will you be ready to go?'

I said I would be ready that very day if necessary. He caught me at my word with great readiness. The steamer *Melita* was leaving for Bankok that evening about seven. He would request her captain officially to give me a passage and wait for me till ten o'clock.

Then he rose from his office chair, and I got up too. My head swam, there was no doubt about it, and I felt a heaviness of limbs as if they had grown bigger since I had sat down on that chair. I made my bow.

A subtle change in Captain Ellis's manner became perceptible as though he had laid aside the trident of deputy-Neptune. In reality, it was only his official pen that he had dropped on getting up.

Chapter 2

He shook hands with me: 'Well, there you are, on your own, appointed officially under my responsibility.'

He was actually walking with me to the door. What a distance off it seemed! I moved like a man in bonds. But we reached it at last. I opened it with the sensation of dealing with mere dream-stuff, and then at the last moment the fellowship of seamen asserted itself, stronger than the difference of age and station. It asserted itself in Captain Ellis's voice.

'Goodbye – and good luck to you,' he said so heartily that I could only give him a grateful glance. Then I turned and went out, never to see him again in my life. I had not made three steps into the outer office when I heard behind my back a gruff, loud, authoritative voice, the voice of our deputy-Neptune.

It was addressing the head shipping-master, who, having let me in, had, apparently, remained hovering in the middle distance ever since.

'Mr R., let the harbour launch have steam up to take the captain here on board the *Melita* at half-past nine tonight.'

I was amazed at the startled assent of R.'s 'Yes, sir.' He ran before me out on the landing. My new dignity sat yet so lightly on me that I was not aware that it was I, the Captain, the object of this last graciousness. It seemed as if all of a sudden a pair of wings had grown on my shoulders. I merely skimmed along the polished floor.

But R. was impressed.

'I say!' he exclaimed on the landing, while the Malay crew of the steam-launch standing by looked stonily at the man for whom they were going to be kept on duty so late, away from their gambling, from their girls, or their pure domestic joys. 'I say! His own launch. What have you done to him?'

His stare was full of respectful curiosity. I was quite confounded.

'Was it for me? I hadn't the slightest notion,' I stammered out.

He nodded many times. 'Yes. And the last person who had it before you was a Duke. So, there!'

I think he expected me to faint on the spot. But I was in too much of a hurry for emotional displays. My feelings were already in such a whirl that this staggering information did not seem to make the slightest difference. It fell into the seething cauldron of my brain, and I carried it off with me after a short but effusive passage of leave-taking with R.

The favour of the great throws an aureole round the fortunate object of its selection. That excellent man enquired whether he could do anything for me.

He had known me only by sight, and he was well aware he would never see me again; I was, in common with the other seamen of the port, merely a subject for official writing, filling up of forms with all the artificial superiority of a man of pen and ink to the men who grapple with realities outside the consecrated walls of official buildings. What ghosts we must have been to him! Mere symbols to juggle with in books and heavy registers, without brains and muscles and perplexities; something hardly useful and decidedly inferior.

And he – the office hours being over – wanted to know if he could be of any use to me!

I ought, properly speaking – I ought to have been moved to tears. But I did not even think of it. It was only another miraculous manifestation of that day of miracles. I parted from him as if he had been a mere symbol. I floated down the staircase. I floated out of the official and imposing portal. I went on floating along.

I use that word rather than the word 'flew', because I have a distinct impression that, though uplifted by my aroused youth, my movements were deliberate enough. To that mixed white, brown, and yellow portion of mankind, out abroad on their own affairs, I presented the appearance of a man walking rather sedately. And nothing in the way of abstraction could have equalled my deep detachment from the forms and colours of this world. It was, as it were, absolute.

And yet, suddenly, I recognised Hamilton. I recognised him without effort, without a shock, without a start. There he was, strolling towards the Harbour Office with his stiff, arrogant dignity. His red face made him noticeable at a distance. It flamed, over there, on the shady side of the street.

He had perceived me too. Something (unconscious exuberance of spirits, perhaps) moved me to wave my hand to him elaborately. This lapse from good taste happened before I was aware that I was capable of it.

The impact of my impudence stopped him short, much as a bullet might have done. I verily believe he staggered, though as far as I could see he didn't actually fall. I had gone past in a moment and did not turn my head. I had forgotten his existence.

The next ten minutes might have been ten seconds or ten centuries for all my consciousness had to do with it. People might have been falling dead around me, houses crumbling, guns firing, I wouldn't have known. I was thinking: 'By Jove! I have got it.' *It* being the command. It had come about in a way utterly unforeseen in my modest day-dreams.

I perceived that my imagination had been running in conventional channels and that my hopes had always been drab stuff. I had envisaged a command as a result of a slow course of promotion in the employ of some highly respectable firm. The reward of faithful service. Well, faithful service was all right. One would naturally give that for one's own sake, for the sake of the ship, for the love of the life of one's choice; not for the sake of the reward.

There is something distasteful in the notion of a reward.

And now here I had my command, absolutely in my pocket, in a way undeniable indeed, but most unexpected; beyond my imaginings, outside all reasonable expectations, and even notwithstanding the existence of some sort of obscure intrigue to keep it away from me. It is true that the intrigue was feeble, but it helped the feeling of wonder – as if I had been specially destined for that ship I did not know, by some power higher than the prosaic agencies of the commercial world.

A strange sense of exultation began to creep into me. If I had worked for that command ten years or more there would have been nothing of the kind. I was a little frightened.

'Let us be calm,' I said to myself.

Outside the door of the Officers' Home the wretched Steward seemed to be waiting for me. There was a broad flight of a few steps, and he ran to and fro on the top of it as if chained there. A distressed cur. He looked as though his throat were too dry for him to bark.

I regret to say I stopped before going in. There had been a revolution in my moral nature. He waited open-mouthed, breathless, while I looked at him for half a minute.

'And you thought you could keep me out of it,' I said scathingly.

'You said you were going home,' he squeaked miserably. 'You said so. You said so.'

'I wonder what Captain Ellis will have to say to that excuse,' I uttered slowly with a sinister meaning.

His lower jaw had been trembling all the time and his voice was like the bleating of a sick goat. 'You have given me away? You have done for me?'

Neither his distress nor yet the sheer absurdity of it was able to disarm me. It was the first instance of harm being attempted to be done to me – at any rate, the first I had ever found out. And I was still young enough, still too much on this side of the shadow-line, not to be surprised and indignant at such things.

I gazed at him inflexibly. Let the beggar suffer. He slapped his forehead and I passed in, pursued, into the dining-room, by his screech: 'I always said you'd be the death of me.'

This clamour not only overtook me, but went ahead, as it were, on to the verandah and brought out Captain Giles.

He stood before me in the doorway in all the commonplace solidity of his wisdom. The gold chain glittered on his breast. He clutched a smouldering pipe.

I extended my hand to him warmly and he seemed surprised, but did respond heartily enough in the end, with a faint smile of superior knowledge which cut my thanks short as if with a knife. I don't think that more than one word came out. And even for that one, judging by the temperature of my face, I had blushed as if for a bad action. Assuming a detached tone, I wondered how on earth he had managed to spot the little underhand game that had been going on.

He murmured complacently that there were but few things done in the town that he could not see the inside of. And as to this house, he had been using it off and on for nearly ten years. Nothing that went on in it could escape his great experience. It had been no trouble to him. No trouble at all.

Then in his quiet, thick tone he wanted to know if I had complained formally of the Steward's action.

I said that I hadn't – though, indeed, it was not for want of opportunity. Captain Ellis had gone for me bald-headed in a most ridiculous fashion for being out of the way when wanted.

'Funny old gentleman,' interjected Captain Giles. 'What did you say to that?'

'I said simply that I came along the very moment I heard of his message. Nothing more. I didn't want to hurt the Steward. I would scorn to harm such an object. No. I made no complaint, but I believe he thinks I've done so. Let him think. He's got a fright that he won't forget in a hurry, for Captain Ellis would kick him out into the middle of Asia . . . '

'Wait a moment,' said Captain Giles, leaving me suddenly. I sat down feeling very tired, mostly in my head. Before I could start a train of thought he stood again before me, murmuring the excuse that he had to go and put the fellow's mind at ease.

I looked up with surprise. But in reality I was indifferent. He explained that he had found the Steward lying face downwards on the horsehair sofa. He was all right now.

'He would not have died of fright,' I said contemptuously.

'No. But he might have taken an overdose out of one of those little bottles he keeps in his room,' Captain Giles argued seriously. 'The confounded fool has tried to poison himself once – a couple of years ago.'

'Really,' I said without emotion. 'He doesn't seem very fit to live, anyhow.'

'As to that, it may be said of a good many.'

'Don't exaggerate like this!' I protested, laughing irritably. 'But I wonder what this part of the world would do if you were to leave off looking after it, Captain Giles? Here you have got me a command and saved the Steward's life in one afternoon. Though why you should have taken all that interest in either of us is more than I can understand.'

Captain Giles remained silent for a minute. Then gravely: 'He's not a bad steward really. He can find a good cook, at any rate. And, what's more, he can keep him when found. I remember the cooks we had here before his time . . . '

I must have made a movement of impatience, because he interrupted himself with an apology for keeping me yarning there, while no doubt I needed all my time to get ready.

What I really needed was to be alone for a bit. I seized this opening hastily. My bedroom was a quiet refuge in an apparently uninhabited wing of the building. Having absolutely nothing to do (for I had not unpacked my things), I sat down on the bed and abandoned myself to the influences of the hour. To the unexpected influences . . .

And first I wondered at my state of mind. Why was I not more surprised? Why? Here I was, invested with a command in the twinkling of an eye, not in the common course of human affairs, but more as if by enchantment. I ought to have been lost in astonishment. But I wasn't. I was very much like people in fairy tales. Nothing ever astonishes them. When a fully appointed gala coach is produced out of a pumpkin to take her to a ball Cinderella does not exclaim. She gets in quietly and drives away to her high fortune.

Captain Ellis (a fierce sort of fairy) had produced a command out of a drawer almost as unexpectedly as in a fairy tale. But a command is an abstract idea, and it seemed a sort of 'lesser marvel' till it flashed upon me that it involved the concrete existence of a ship.

A ship! My ship! She was mine, more absolutely mine for possession and care than anything in the world; an object of responsibility and devotion. She was there waiting for me, spellbound, unable to move, to live, to get out into the world (till I came), like an enchanted princess. Her call had come to me as if from the clouds. I had never suspected her existence. I didn't know how she looked, I had barely heard her name, and yet we were indissolubly united for a certain portion of our future, to sink or swim together!

A sudden passion of anxious impatience rushed through my veins and gave me such a sense of the intensity of existence as I have never felt before or since. I discovered how much of a seaman I was, in heart, in mind, and, as it were, physically – a man exclusively of sea and ships; the sea the only world that counted, and the ships the test of manliness, of temperament, of courage and fidelity – and of love.

I had an exquisite moment. It was unique also. Jumping up from my seat, I paced up and down my room for a long time. But when I came into the dining-room I behaved with sufficient composure. I only couldn't eat anything at dinner.

Having declared my intention not to drive but to walk down to the quay, I must render the wretched Steward justice that he bestirred himself to find me some coolies for the luggage. They departed, carrying all my worldly possessions (except a little money I had in my pocket) slung from a long pole. Captain Giles volunteered to walk down with me.

We followed the sombre, shaded alley across the Esplanade. It was moderately cool there under the trees. Captain Giles remarked, with a sudden laugh: 'I know who's jolly thankful at having seen the last of you.'

I guessed that he meant the Steward. The fellow had borne himself to me in a sulkily frightened manner at the last. I expressed my wonder that he should have tried to do me a bad turn for no reason at all.

'Don't you see that what he wanted was to get rid of our friend Hamilton by dodging him in front of you for that job? That would have removed him for good, see?'

'Heavens!' I exclaimed, feeling humiliated somehow. 'Can it be possible? What a fool he must be! That overbearing, impudent loafer! Why! He couldn't . . . And yet he's nearly done it, I believe; for the Harbour Office was bound to send somebody.'

'Aye. A fool like our Steward can be dangerous sometimes,' declared Captain Giles sententiously. 'Just because he is a fool,' he added, imparting further instruction in his complacent low tones. 'For,' he continued in the manner of a set demonstration, 'no sensible person would risk being kicked out of the only berth between himself and starvation just to get rid of a simple annoyance – a small worry. Would he now?'

'Well, no,' I conceded, restraining a desire to laugh at that something mysteriously earnest in delivering the conclusions of his wisdom as though they were the product of prohibited operations. 'But that fellow looks as if he were rather crazy. He must be.'

'As to that, I believe everybody in the world is a little mad,' he announced quietly.

'You make no exceptions?' I enquired, just to hear his answer.

He kept silent for a little while, then got home in an effective manner.

'Why! Kent says that even of you.'

'Does he?' I retorted, extremely embittered all at once against my former captain. 'There's nothing of that in the written character from him which I've got in my pocket. Has he given you any instances of my lunacy?'

Captain Giles explained in a conciliating tone that it had been only a friendly remark in reference to my abrupt leaving of the ship for no apparent reason.

I muttered grumpily: 'Oh! leaving his ship,' and mended my pace. He kept up by my side in the deep gloom of the avenue as if it were his conscientious duty to see me out of the colony as an undesirable character. He panted a little, which was rather pathetic in a way. But I was not moved. On the contrary. His discomfort gave me a sort of malicious pleasure.

Presently I relented, slowed down, and said: 'What I really wanted was to get a fresh grip. I felt it was time. Is that so very mad?'

He made no answer. We were issuing from the avenue. On the bridge over the canal a dark, irresolute figure seemed to be awaiting something or somebody.

It was a Malay policeman, barefooted, in his blue uniform. The silver band on his little round cap shone dimly in the light of the street lamp. He peered in our direction timidly.

Before we could come up to him he turned about and walked in front of us in the direction of the jetty. The distance was some hundred yards; and then I found my coolies squatting on their heels. They had kept the pole on their shoulders, and all my worldly goods, still tied to the pole, were resting on the ground between them. As far as the eye could reach along the quay there was not another soul abroad except the police peon, who saluted us.

It seems he had detained the coolies as suspicious characters, and had forbidden them the jetty. But at a sign from me he took off the embargo with alacrity. The two patient fellows, rising together with a faint grunt, trotted off along the planks, and I prepared to take my leave of Captain Giles, who stood there with an air as though his mission were drawing to a close. It could not be denied that he had done it all. And while I hesitated about an appropriate sentence he made himself heard: 'I expect you'll have your hands pretty full of tangled-up business.'

I asked him what made him think so; and he answered that it was his general experience of the world. Ship a long time away from her port, owners inaccessible by cable, and the only man who could explain matters dead and buried.

'And you yourself new to the business in a way,' he concluded in a sort of unanswerable tone.

'Don't insist,' I said. 'I know it only too well. I only wish you could impart to me some small portion of your experience before I go. As it can't be done in ten minutes I had better not begin to ask you. There's that harbour launch waiting for me too. But I won't feel really at peace till I have that ship of mine out in the Indian Ocean.'

He remarked casually that from Bankok to the Indian Ocean was a pretty long step. And this murmur, like a dim flash from a dark lantern, showed me for a moment the broad belt of islands and reefs between that unknown ship, which was mine, and the freedom of the great waters of the globe.

But I felt no apprehension. I was familiar enough with the Archipelago by that time. Extreme patience and extreme care would see me through the region of broken land, of faint airs and of dead water to where I would feel at last my command swing on the great swell and list over to the great breath of regular winds, that would give her the feeling of a large, more intense life. The road would be long. All roads are long that lead towards one's heart's desire. But this road my mind's eye could see on a chart, professionally, with all its complications and difficulties, yet simple enough in a way. One is a seaman or one is not. And I had no doubt of being one.

The only part I was a stranger to was the Gulf of Siam. And I mentioned this to Captain Giles. Not that I was concerned very much. It belonged to the same region the nature of which I knew, into whose very soul I seemed to have looked during the last months of that existence with which I had broken now, suddenly, as one parts with some enchanting company.

'The gulf . . . Ay! A funny piece of water – that,' said Captain Giles.

Funny, in this connection, was a vague word. The whole thing sounded like an opinion uttered by a cautious person mindful of actions for slander.

I didn't enquire as to the nature of that funniness. There was really no time. But at the very last he volunteered a warning.

'Whatever you do keep to the east side of it. The west side is dangerous at this time of the year. Don't let anything tempt you over. You'll find nothing but trouble there.'

Though I could hardly imagine what could tempt me to involve my ship amongst the currents and reefs of the Malay shore, I thanked him for the advice.

He gripped my extended arm warmly, and the end of our acquaintance came suddenly in the words: 'Good-night.'

That was all he said: 'Good-night.' Nothing more. I don't know what I intended to say, but surprise made me swallow it, whatever it was. I choked slightly, and then exclaimed with a sort of nervous haste: 'Oh! Good-night, Captain Giles, good-night.'

His movements were always deliberate, but his back had receded some distance along the deserted quay before I collected myself enough to follow his example and made a half turn in the direction of the jetty.

Only my movements were not deliberate. I hurried down to the steps and leaped into the launch. Before I had fairly landed in her stern-sheets the slim little craft darted away from the jetty with a sudden swirl of her propeller and the hard rapid puffing of the exhaust in her vaguely gleaming brass funnel amidships.

The misty churning at her stern was the only sound in the world. The shore lay plunged in the silence of the deepest slumber. I watched the town recede still and soundless in the hot night, till the abrupt hail, 'Steam-launch, ahoy!' made me spin round face forward. We were close to a white, ghostly steamer. Lights shone on her decks, in her port-holes. And the same voice shouted from her: 'Is that our passenger?'

'It is,' I yelled.

Her crew had been obviously on the jump. I could hear them running about. The modern spirit of haste was loudly vocal in the orders to 'Heave away on the cable' – to 'Lower the side-ladder', and in urgent requests to me to 'Come along, sir! We have been delayed three hours for you . . . Our time is seven o'clock, you know!'

I stepped on the deck. I said 'No! I don't know.' The spirit of modern hurry was embodied in a thin, long-armed, long-legged man, with a closely-clipped grey beard. His meagre hand was hot and dry. He declared feverishly: 'I am hanged if I would have waited another five minutes – harbour-master or no harbour-master.'

'That's your own business,' I said. 'I didn't ask you to wait for me.'

'I hope you don't expect any supper,' he burst out. 'This isn't a boarding-house afloat. You are the first passenger I ever had in my life and I hope to goodness you will be the last.'

I made no answer to this hospitable communication; and, indeed, he didn't wait for any, bolting away on to his bridge to get his ship under way.

For the four days he had me on board he did not depart from that half-hostile attitude. His ship having been delayed three hours on my account he couldn't forgive me for not being a more distinguished person. He was not exactly outspoken about it, but that feeling of annoyed wonder was peeping out perpetually in his talk.

He was absurd.

He was also a man of much experience, which he liked to trot out; but no greater contrast with Captain Giles could have been imagined. He would have amused me if I had wanted to be amused. But I did not want to be amused. I was like a lover looking forward to a meeting. Human hostility was nothing to me. I thought of my unknown ship. It was amusement enough, torment enough, occupation enough.

He perceived my state, for his wits were sufficiently sharp for that, and he poked sly fun at my preoccupation in the manner some nasty, cynical old men assume towards the dreams and illusions of youth. I, on my side, refrained from questioning him as to the appearance of my ship, though I knew that being in Bankok every month or so he must have known her by sight. I was not going to expose the ship, my ship! to some slighting reference.

He was the first really unsympathetic man I had ever come in contact with. My education was far from being finished, though I didn't know it. No! I didn't know it.

All I knew was that he disliked me and had some contempt for my person. Why? Apparently because his ship had been delayed three hours on my account. Who was I to have such a thing done for me? Such a thing had never been done for him. It was a sort of jealous indignation.

My expectation, mingled with fear, was wrought to its highest pitch. How slow had been the days of the passage and how soon they were over. One morning, early, we crossed the bar, and while the sun was rising splendidly over the flat spaces of the land we steamed up the innumerable bends, passed under the shadow of the great gilt pagoda, and reached the outskirts of the town.

There it was, spread largely on both banks, the Oriental capital which had as yet suffered no white conqueror; an expanse of brown houses of bamboo, of mats, of leaves, of a vegetable-matter style of architecture, sprung out of the brown soil on the banks of the muddy river. It was amazing to think that in those miles of human habitations there was not probably half a dozen pounds of nails. Some of those houses of sticks and grass, like the nests of an aquatic race, clung to the low shores. Others seemed to grow out of the water; others again floated in long anchored rows in the very middle of the stream. Here and there in the distance, above the crowded mob of low, brown roof ridges, towered great piles of masonry, King's Palace, temples, gorgeous and dilapidated, crumbling under the vertical sunlight, tremendous, overpowering, almost palpable, which seemed to enter one's breast with the breath of one's nostrils and soak into one's limbs through every pore of one's skin.

The ridiculous victim of jealousy had for some reason or other to stop his engines just then. The steamer drifted slowly up with the tide. Oblivious of my new surroundings I walked the deck, in anxious, deadened abstraction, a commingling of romantic reverie with a very practical survey of my qualifications. For the time was approaching for me to behold my command and to prove my worth in the ultimate test of my profession.

Suddenly I heard myself called by that imbecile. He was beckoning me to come up on his bridge.

I didn't care very much for that, but as it seemed that he had something particular to say I went up the ladder.

He laid his hand on my shoulder and gave me a slight turn, pointing with his other arm at the same time.

'There! That's your ship, Captain,' he said.

I felt a thump in my breast – only one, as if my heart had then ceased to beat. There were ten or more ships moored along the bank, and the one he meant was partly hidden from my sight by her next astern. He said: 'We'll drift abreast her in a moment.'

What was his tone? Mocking? Threatening? Or only indifferent? I could not tell. I suspected some malice in this unexpected manifestation of interest.

He left me, and I leaned over the rail of the bridge looking over the side. I dared not raise my eyes. Yet it had to be done – and, indeed, I could not have helped myself. I believe I trembled.

But directly my eyes had rested on my ship all my fear vanished. It went off swiftly, like a bad dream. Only that a dream leaves no shame behind it, and that I felt a momentary shame at my unworthy suspicions.

Yes, there she was. Her hull, her rigging filled my eye with a great content. That feeling of life-emptiness which had made me so restless for the last few months lost its bitter plausibility, its evil influence, dissolved in a flow of joyous emotion.

At the first glance I saw that she was a high-class vessel, a harmonious creature in the lines of her fine body, in the proportioned tallness of her spars. Whatever her age and her history, she had preserved the stamp of her origin. She was one of those craft that, in virtue of their design and complete finish, will never look old. Amongst her companions moored to the bank, and all bigger than herself, she looked like a creature of high breed – an Arab steed in a string of carthorses.

A voice behind me said in a nasty equivocal tone: 'I hope you are satisfied with her, Captain.' I did not even turn my head. It was the master of the steamer, and whatever he meant, whatever he thought of her, I knew that, like some rare women, she was one of those creatures whose mere existence is enough to awaken an unselfish delight. One feels that it is good to be in the world in which she has her being.

That illusion of life and character which charms one in men's finest handiwork radiated from her. An enormous baulk of teak-wood timber swung over her hatchway; lifeless matter, looking heavier and bigger than anything aboard of her. When they started lowering it the surge of the tackle sent a quiver through her from water-line to the trucks up the fine nerves of her rigging, as though she had shuddered at the weight. It seemed cruel to load her so . . .

Half an hour later, putting my foot on her deck for the first time, I received the feeling of deep physical satisfaction. Nothing could equal the fullness of that moment, the ideal completeness of that emotional experience which had come to me without the preliminary toil and disenchantments of an obscure career.

My rapid glance ran over her, enveloped, appropriated the form concreting the abstract sentiment of my command. A lot of details perceptible to a seaman struck my eye vividly in that instant. For the rest, I saw her disengaged from the material conditions of her being. The shore to which she was moored was as if it did not exist. What were to me all the countries of the globe? In all the parts of the world washed by navigable waters our relation to each other would be the same – and more intimate than there are words to express in the language. Apart from that, every scene and episode would be a mere passing show. The very gang of yellow coolies busy about the main hatch was less substantial than the stuff dreams are made of. For who on earth would dream of Chinamen? . . .

I went aft, ascended the poop, where, under the awning, gleamed the brasses of the yacht-like fittings, the polished surfaces of the rails, the glass of the skylights. Right aft two seamen, busy cleaning the steering gear, with the reflected ripples of light running playfully up their bent backs, went on with their work, unaware of me and of the almost affectionate glance I threw at them in passing towards the companion-way of the cabin.

The doors stood wide open, the slide was pushed right back. The half-turn of the staircase cut off the view of the lobby. A low humming ascended from below, but it stopped abruptly at the sound of my descending footsteps.

Chapter 3

The first thing I saw down there was the upper part of a man's body projecting backwards, as it were, from one of the doors at the foot of the stairs. His eyes looked at me very wide and still. In one hand he held a dinner plate, in the other a cloth.

'I am your new captain,' I said quietly.

In a moment, in the twinkling of an eye, he had got rid of the plate and the cloth and jumped to open the cabin door. As soon as I passed into the saloon he vanished, but only to reappear instantly, buttoning up a jacket he had put on with the swiftness of a 'quick-change' artist.

'Where's the chief mate?' I asked.

'In the hold, I think, sir. I saw him go down the after-hatch ten minutes ago.'

'Tell him I am on board.'

The mahogany table under the skylight shone in the twilight like a dark pool of water. The sideboard, surmounted by a wide looking-glass in an ormolu frame, had a marble top. It bore a pair of silver-plated lamps and some other pieces – obviously a harbour display. The saloon itself was panelled in two kinds of wood in the excellent, simple taste prevailing when the ship was built.

I sat down in the armchair at the head of the table – the captain's chair, with a small tell-tale compass swung above it – a mute reminder of unremitting vigilance.

A succession of men had sat in that chair. I became aware of that thought suddenly, vividly, as though each had left a little of himself between the four walls of these ornate bulkheads; as if a sort of composite soul, the soul of command, had whispered suddenly to mine of long days at sea and of anxious moments.

'You, too!' it seemed to say, 'you, too, shall taste of that peace and that unrest in a searching intimacy with your own self – obscure as we were and as supreme in the face of all the winds and all the seas, in an immensity that receives no impress, preserves no memories, and keeps no reckoning of lives.'

Deep within the tarnished ormolu frame, in the hot half-light sifted through the awning, I saw my own face propped between my hands. And I stared back at myself with the perfect detachment of distance, rather with curiosity than with any other feeling, except of some sympathy for this latest representative of what for all intents and purposes was a dynasty; continuous not in blood, indeed, but in its experience, in its training, in its conception of duty, and in the blessed simplicity of its traditional point of view of life.

It struck me that this quietly staring man whom I was watching, both as if he were myself and somebody else, was not exactly a lonely figure. He had his place in a line of men whom he did not know, of whom he had never heard; but who were fashioned by the same influences, whose souls in relation to their humble life's work had no secrets for him.

Suddenly I perceived that there was another man in the saloon, standing a little on one side and looking intently at me. The chief mate. His long, red moustache determined the character of his physiognomy, which struck me as pugnacious in (strange to say) a ghastly sort of way.

How long had he been there looking at me, appraising me in my unguarded day-dreaming state? I would have been more disconcerted if, having the clock set in the top of the mirror-frame right in front of me, I had not noticed that its long hand had hardly moved at all.

I could not have been in that cabin more than two minutes altogether. Say three . . . So he could not have been watching me more than a mere fraction of a minute, luckily. Still, I regretted the occurrence.

But I showed nothing of it as I rose leisurely (it had to be leisurely) and greeted him with perfect friendliness.

There was something reluctant and at the same time attentive in his bearing. His name was Burns. We left the cabin and went round the ship together. His face in the full light of day appeared very worn, meagre, even haggard. Somehow I had a delicacy as to looking too often at him; his eyes, on the contrary, remained fairly glued on my face. They were greenish and had an expectant expression.

He answered all my questions readily enough, but my ear seemed to catch a tone of unwillingness. The second officer, with three or four hands, was busy forward. The mate mentioned his name and I nodded to him in passing. He was very young. He struck me as rather a cub.

When we returned below I sat down on one end of a deep, semicircular, or, rather, semi-oval settee, upholstered in red plush. It extended right across the whole after-end of the cabin. Mr Burns, motioned to sit down, dropped into one of the swivel-chairs round the table, and kept his eyes on me as persistently as ever, and with that strange air as if all this were make-believe and he expected me to get up, burst into a laugh, slap him on the back, and vanish from the cabin.

There was an odd stress in the situation which began to make me uncomfortable. I tried to react against this vague feeling.

'It's only my inexperience,' I thought.

In the face of that man, several years, I judged, older than myself, I became aware of what I had left already behind me – my youth. And that was indeed poor comfort. Youth is a fine thing, a mighty power – as long as one does not think of it. I felt I was becoming self-conscious. Almost against my will I assumed a moody gravity. I said: 'I see you have kept her in very good order, Mr Burns.'

Directly I had uttered these words I asked myself angrily why the deuce did I want to say that? Mr Burns in answer had only blinked at me. What on earth did he mean?

I fell back on a question which had been in my thoughts for a long time – the most natural question on the lips of any seaman whatever joining a ship. I voiced it (confound this self-consciousness) in a *dégagé* cheerful tone: 'I suppose she can travel – what?'

Now a question like this might have been answered normally, either in accents of apologetic sorrow or with a visibly suppressed pride, in a 'I don't want to boast, but you shall see' sort of tone. There are sailors, too, who would have been roughly outspoken: 'Lazy brute,' or openly delighted: 'She's a flyer.' Two ways, if four manners.

But Mr Burns found another way, a way of his own which had, at all events, the merit of saving his breath, if no other.

Again he did not say anything. He only frowned. And it was an angry frown. I waited. Nothing more came.

'What's the matter? . . . Can't you tell after being nearly two years in the ship?' I addressed him sharply.

He looked as startled for a moment as though he had discovered my presence only that very moment. But this passed off almost at once. He put on an air of indifference. But I suppose he thought it better to say something. He said that a ship needed, just like a man, the chance to show the best she could do, and that this ship had never had a chance since he had been on board of her. Not that he could remember. The last captain . . . He paused.

'Has he been so very unlucky?' I asked with frank incredulity. Mr Burns turned his eyes away from me. No, the late captain was not an unlucky man. One couldn't say that. But he had not seemed to want to make use of his luck.

Mr Burns – man of enigmatic moods – made this statement with an inanimate face and staring wilfully at the rudder casing. The statement itself was obscurely suggestive. I asked quietly: 'Where did he die?'

'In this saloon. Just where you are sitting now,' answered Mr Burns.

I repressed a silly impulse to jump up; but upon the whole I was relieved to hear that he had not died in the bed which was now to be mine. I pointed out to the chief mate that what I really wanted to know was where he had buried his late captain.

Mr Burns said that it was at the entrance to the gulf. A roomy grave; a sufficient answer. But the mate, overcoming visibly something within him – something like a curious reluctance to believe in my advent (as an irrevocable fact, at any rate), did not stop at that – though, indeed, he may have wished to do so.

As a compromise with his feelings, I believe, he addressed himself persistently to the rudder-casing, so that to me he had the appearance of a man talking in solitude, a little unconsciously, however.

His tale was that at seven bells in the forenoon watch he had all hands mustered on the quarterdeck and told them that they had better go down to say goodbye to the captain.

Those words, as if grudged to an intruding personage, were enough for me to evoke vividly that strange ceremony: the barefooted, bareheaded seamen crowding shyly into that cabin, a small mob pressed against that sideboard, uncomfortable rather than moved, shirts open on sunburnt chests, weather-beaten faces, and all staring at the dying man with the same grave and expectant expression.

'Was he conscious?' I asked.

'He didn't speak, but he moved his eyes to look at them,' said the mate.

After waiting a moment Mr Burns motioned the crew to leave the cabin, but he detained the two eldest men to stay with the captain while he went on deck with his sextant to 'take the sun'. It was getting towards noon and he was anxious to obtain a good observation for latitude. When he returned below to put his sextant away he found that the two men had retreated out into the lobby. Through the open door he had a view of the captain lying easy against the pillows. He had 'passed away' while Mr Burns was taking his observation. As near noon as possible. He had hardly changed his position.

Mr Burns sighed, glanced at me inquisitively, as much as to say, 'Aren't you going yet?' and then turned his thoughts from his new captain back to the old, who, being dead, had no authority, was not in anybody's way, and was much easier to deal with.

Mr Burns dealt with him at some length. He was a peculiar man – of sixty-five about – iron grey, hard-faced, obstinate, and uncommunicative. He used to keep the ship loafing at sea for inscrutable reasons. Would come on deck at night sometimes, take some sail off her, God only knows why or wherefore, then go below, shut himself up in his cabin, and play on the violin for hours – till daybreak perhaps. In fact, he spent most of his time day or night playing the violin. That was when the fit took him. Very loud, too.

It came to this, that Mr Burns mustered his courage one day and remonstrated earnestly with the captain. Neither he nor the second mate could get a wink of sleep in their watches below for the noise . . . And how could they be expected to keep awake while on duty? he pleaded. The answer of that stern man was that if he and the second mate didn't like the noise, they were welcome to pack up their traps and walk over the side. When this alternative was offered the ship happened to be six hundred miles from the nearest land.

Mr Burns at this point looked at me with an air of curiosity. I began to think that my predecessor was a remarkably peculiar old man.

But I had to hear stranger things yet. It came out that this stern, grim, wind-tanned, rough, sea-salted, taciturn sailor of sixty-five was not only an artist, but a lover as well. In Haiphong, when they got there after a course of most unprofitable peregrinations (during which the ship was nearly lost twice), he got himself, in Mr Burns' own words, 'mixed up' with some woman. Mr Burns had had no personal knowledge of that affair, but positive evidence of it existed in the shape of a photograph taken in Haiphong. Mr Burns found it in one of the drawers in the captain's room.

In due course I, too, saw that amazing human document (I even threw it overboard later). There he sat, with his hands reposing on his knees, bald, squat, grey, bristly, recalling a wild boar somehow; and by his side towered an awful, mature, white female with rapacious nostrils and a cheaply ill-omened stare in her enormous eyes. She was disguised in some semi-oriental, vulgar, fancy costume. She resembled a low-class medium or one of those women who tell fortunes by cards for half a crown. And yet she was striking. A professional sorceress from the slums. It was incomprehensible. There was something awful in the thought that she was the last reflection of the world of passion for the fierce soul which seemed to look at one out of the sardonically savage face of that old seaman. However, I noticed that she was holding some musical instrument – guitar or mandoline – in her hand. Perhaps that was the secret of her sortilege.

For Mr Burns that photograph explained why the unloaded ship was kept sweltering at anchor for three weeks in a pestilential hot harbour without air. They lay there and gasped. The captain, appearing now and then on short visits, mumbled to Mr Burns unlikely tales about some letters he was waiting for.

Suddenly, after vanishing for a week, he came on board in the middle of the night and took the ship out to sea with the first break of dawn. Daylight showed him looking wild and ill. The mere getting clear of the land took two days, and somehow or other they bumped slightly on a reef. However, no leak developed, and the captain, growling, 'No matter,' informed Mr Burns that he had made up his mind to take the ship to Hong Kong and dry-dock her there.

At this Mr Burns was plunged into despair. For indeed, to beat up to Hong Kong against a fierce monsoon, with a ship not sufficiently ballasted and with her supply of water not completed, was an insane project.

But the captain growled peremptorily, 'Stick her at it,' and Mr Burns, dismayed and enraged, stuck her at it, and kept her at it, blowing away sails, straining the spars, exhausting the crew – nearly maddened by the absolute conviction that the attempt was impossible and was bound to end in some catastrophe.

Meantime the captain, shut up in his cabin and wedged in a corner of his settee against the crazy bounding of the ship, played the violin – or, at any rate, made continuous noise on it.

When he appeared on deck he would not speak and not always answer when spoken to. It was obvious that he was ill in some mysterious manner, and beginning to break up.

As the days went by the sounds of the violin became less and less loud, till at last only a feeble scratching would meet Mr Burns' ear as he stood in the saloon listening outside the door of the captain's stateroom.

One afternoon in perfect desperation he burst into that room and made such a scene, tearing his hair and shouting such horrid imprecations that he cowed the contemptuous spirit of the sick man. The water-tanks were low, they had not gained fifty miles in a fortnight. She would never reach Hong Kong.

It was like fighting desperately towards destruction for the ship and the men. This was evident without argument. Mr Burns, losing all restraint, put his face close to his captain's and fairly yelled: 'You, sir, are going out of the world. But I can't wait till you are dead before I put the helm up. You must do it yourself. You must do it now!'

The man on the couch snarled in contempt: 'So I am going out of the world – am I?'

'Yes, sir – you haven't many days left in it,' said Mr Burns, calming down. 'One can see it by your face.'

'My face, eh? . . . Well, put the helm up and be damned to you.'

Burns flew on deck, got the ship before the wind, then came down again, composed but resolute.

'I've shaped a course for Pulo Condor, sir,' he said. 'When we make it, if you are still with us, you'll tell me into what port you wish me to take the ship and I'll do it.'

The old man gave him a look of savage spite, and said these atrocious words in deadly, slow tones: 'If I had my wish, neither the ship nor any of you would ever reach a port. And I hope you won't.'

Mr Burns was profoundly shocked. I believe he was positively frightened at the time. It seems, however, that he managed to produce such an effective laugh that it was the old man's turn to be frightened. He shrank within himself and turned his back on him.

'And his head was not gone then,' Mr Burns assured me excitedly. 'He meant every word of it.'

Such was practically the late captain's last speech. No connected sentence passed his lips afterwards. That night he used the last of his strength to throw his fiddle over the side. No one had actually seen him in the act, but after his death Mr Burns couldn't find the thing anywhere. The empty case was very much in evidence, but the fiddle was clearly not in the ship. And where else could it have gone to but overboard?

'Threw his violin overboard!' I exclaimed.

'He did,' cried Mr Burns excitedly. 'And it's my belief he would have tried to take the ship down with him if it had been in human power. He never meant her to see home again. He wouldn't write to his owners, he never wrote to his old wife either – he wasn't going to. He had made up his mind to cut adrift from everything. That's what it was. He didn't care for business, or freights, or for making a passage – or anything. He meant to have gone wandering about the world till he lost her with all hands.'

Mr Burns looked like a man who had escaped great danger. For a little he would have exclaimed: 'If it hadn't been for me!' And the transparent innocence of his indignant eyes was underlined quaintly by the arrogant pair of moustaches which he proceeded to twist, and as if extend, horizontally.

I might have smiled if I had not been busy with my own sensations, which were not those of Mr Burns. I was already the man in command. My sensations could not be like those of any other man on board. In that community I stood, like a king in his country, in a class all by myself. I mean an hereditary king, not a mere elected head of a state. I was brought there to rule by an agency as remote from the people and as inscrutable almost to them as the Grace of God.

And like a member of a dynasty, feeling a semi-mystical bond with the dead, I was profoundly shocked by my immediate predecessor.

That man had been in all essentials but his age just such another man as myself. Yet the end of his life was a complete act of treason, the betrayal of a tradition which seemed to me as imperative as any guide on earth could be. It appeared that even at sea a man could become the victim of evil spirits. I felt on my face the breath of unknown powers that shape our destinies.

Not to let the silence last too long I asked Mr Burns if he had written to his captain's wife. He shook his head. He had written to nobody.

In a moment he became sombre. He never thought of writing. It took him all his time to watch incessantly the loading of the ship by a rascally Chinese stevedore. In this Mr Burns gave me the first glimpse of the real chief mate's soul which dwelt uneasily in his body.

He mused, then hastened on with gloomy force.

'Yes! The captain died as near noon as possible. I looked through his papers in the afternoon. I read the service over him at sunset and then I stuck the ship's head north and brought her in here. I – brought – her – in.'

He struck the table with his fist.

'She would hardly have come in by herself,' I observed. 'But why didn't you make for Singapore instead?'

His eyes wavered. 'The nearest port,' he muttered sullenly.

I had framed the question in perfect innocence, but this answer (the difference in distance was insignificant) and his manner offered me a clue to the simple truth. He took the ship to a port where he expected to be confirmed in his temporary command from lack of a qualified master to put over his head; whereas Singapore, he surmised justly, would be full of qualified men. But his naïve reasoning forgot to take into account the telegraph cable reposing on the bottom of the very Gulf up which he had turned that ship which he imagined himself to have saved from destruction. Hence the bitter flavour of our interview. I tasted it more and more distinctly – and it was less and less to my taste.

'Look here, Mr Burns,' I began, very firmly. 'You may as well understand that I did not run after this command. It was pushed in my way. I've accepted it. I am here to take the ship home first of all, and you may be sure that I shall see to it that every one of you on board here does his duty to that end. This is all I have to say – for the present.'

He was on his feet by this time, but instead of taking his dismissal he remained with trembling, indignant lips, and looking at me hard as though, really, after this, there was nothing for me to do in common decency but to vanish from his outraged sight. Like all very simple emotional states this was moving. I felt sorry for him – almost sympathetic, till (seeing that I did not vanish) he spoke in a tone of forced restraint.

'If I hadn't a wife and a child at home you may be sure, sir, I would have asked you to let me go the very minute you came on board.'

I answered him with a matter-of-course calmness as though some remote third person were in question.

'And I, Mr Burns, would not have let you go. You have signed the ship's articles as chief officer, and till they are terminated at the final port of discharge I shall expect you to attend to your duty and give me the benefit of your experience to the best of your ability.'

Stony incredulity lingered in his eyes; but it broke down before my friendly attitude. With a slight upward toss of his arms (I got to know that gesture well afterwards) he bolted out of the cabin.

We might have saved ourselves that little passage of harmless sparring. Before many days had elapsed it was Mr Burns who was pleading with me anxiously not to leave him behind; while I could only return him but doubtful answers. The whole thing took on a somewhat tragic complexion.

And this horrible problem was only an extraneous episode, a mere complication in the general problem of how to get that ship – which was mine with her appurtenances and her men, with her body and her spirit now slumbering in that pestilential river – how to get her out to sea.

Mr Burns, while still acting captain, had hastened to sign a charter-party which in an ideal world without guile would have been an excellent document. Directly I ran my eye over it I foresaw trouble ahead unless the people of the other part were quite exceptionally fair-minded and open to argument.

Mr Burns, to whom I imparted my fears, chose to take great umbrage at them. He looked at me with that usual incredulous stare, and said bitterly: 'I suppose, sir, you want to make out I've acted like a fool?'

I told him, with my systematic kindliness which always seemed to augment his surprise, that I did not want to make out anything. I would leave that to the future.

And, sure enough, the future brought in a lot of trouble. There were days when I used to remember Captain Giles with nothing short of abhorrence. His confounded acuteness had let me in for this job; while his prophecy that I 'would have my hands full' coming true, made it appear as if done on purpose to play an evil joke on my young innocence.

Yes. I had my hands full of complications which were most valuable as 'experience'. People have a great opinion of the advantages of experience. But in that connection experience means always something disagreeable as opposed to the charm and innocence of illusions.

I must say I was losing mine rapidly. But on these instructive complications I must not enlarge more than to say that they could all be resumed in the one word: delay.

A mankind which has invented the proverb, 'Time is money,' will understand my vexation. The word 'Delay' entered the secret chamber of my brain, resounded there like a tolling bell which maddens the ear, affected all my senses, took on a black colouring, a bitter taste, a deadly meaning.

'I am really sorry to see you worried like this. Indeed, I am . . .'

It was the only humane speech I used to hear at that time. And it came from a doctor, appropriately enough.

A doctor is humane by definition. But that man was so in reality. His speech was not professional. I was not ill. But other people were, and that was the reason of his visiting the ship.

He was the doctor of our Legation and, of course, of the Consulate too. He looked after the ship's health, which generally was poor, and trembling, as it were, on the verge of a break-up. Yes. The men ailed. And thus time was not only money, but life as well.

I had never seen such a steady ship's company. As the doctor remarked to me: 'You seem to have a most respectable lot of seamen.' Not only were they consistently sober, but they did not even want to go ashore. Care was taken to expose them as little as possible to the sun. They were employed on light work under the awnings. And the humane doctor commended me.

'Your arrangements appear to me to be very judicious, my dear captain.'

It is difficult to express how much that pronouncement comforted me. The doctor's round full face framed in a light-coloured whisker was the perfection of a dignified amenity. He was the only human being in the world who seemed to take the slightest interest in me. He would generally sit in the cabin for half an hour or so at every visit.

I said to him one day: 'I suppose the only thing now is to take care of them as you are doing, till I can get the ship to sea?'

He inclined his head, shutting his eyes under the large spectacles, and murmured: 'The sea . . . undoubtedly.'

The first member of the crew fairly knocked over was the steward – the first man to whom I had spoken on board. He was taken ashore (with choleraic symptoms) and died there at the end of a week. Then, while I was still under the startling impression of this first home-thrust of the climate, Mr Burns gave up and went to bed in a raging fever without saying a word to anybody.

I believe he had partly fretted himself into that illness; the climate did the rest with the swiftness of an invisible monster ambushed in the air, in the water, in the mud of the river-bank. Mr Burns was a predestined victim.

I discovered him lying on his back, glaring sullenly and radiating heat on one like a small furnace. He would hardly answer my questions, and only grumbled: couldn't a man take an afternoon off duty with a bad headache – for once?

That evening, as I sat in the saloon after dinner, I could hear him muttering continuously in his room. Ransome, who was clearing the table, said to me: 'I am afraid, sir, I won't be able to give the mate all the attention he's likely to need. I will have to be forward in the galley a great part of my time.'

Ransome was the cook. The mate had pointed him out to me the first day, standing on the deck, his arms crossed on his broad chest, gazing on the river.

Even at a distance his well-proportioned figure, something thoroughly sailor-like in his poise, made him noticeable. On nearer view the intelligent, quiet eyes, a well-bred face, the disciplined independence of his manner made up an attractive personality. When, in addition, Mr Burns told me that he was the best seaman in the ship, I expressed my surprise that in his earliest prime and of such appearance he should sign on as cook on board a ship.

'It's his heart,' Mr Burns had said. 'There's something wrong with it. He mustn't exert himself too much or he may drop dead suddenly.'

And he was the only one the climate had not touched – perhaps because, carrying a deadly enemy in his breast, he had schooled himself into a systematic control of feelings and movements. When one was in the secret this was apparent in his manner. After the poor steward died, and as he could not be replaced by a white man in this Oriental port, Ransome had volunteered to do the double work.

'I can do it all right, sir, as long as I go about it quietly,' he had assured me.

But obviously he couldn't be expected to take up sick-nursing in addition. Moreover, the doctor peremptorily ordered Mr Burns ashore.

With a seaman on each side holding him up under the arms, the mate went over the gangway more sullen than ever. We built him up with pillows in the gharry, and he made an effort to say brokenly: 'Now – you've got – what you wanted – got me out of – the ship.'

'You were never more mistaken in your life, Mr Burns,' I said quietly, duly smiling at him; and the trap drove off to a sort of sanatorium, a pavilion of bricks which the doctor had in the grounds of his residence.

I visited Mr Burns regularly. After the first few days, when he didn't know anybody, he received me as if I had come either to gloat over a crushed enemy or else to curry favour with a deeply-wronged person. It was either one or the other, just as it happened according to his fantastic sick-room moods. Whichever it was, he managed to convey it to me even during the period when he appeared almost too weak to talk. I treated him to my invariable kindliness.

Then one day, suddenly, a surge of downright panic burst through all this craziness.

If I left him behind in this deadly place he would die. He felt it, he was certain of it. But I wouldn't have the heart to leave him ashore. He had a wife and child in Sydney.

He produced his wasted forearms from under the sheet which covered him and clasped his fleshless claws. He would die! He would die here . . .

He absolutely managed to sit up, but only for a moment, and when he fell back I really thought that he would die there and then. I called to the Bengali dispenser, and hastened away from the room.

Next day he upset me thoroughly by renewing his entreaties. I returned an evasive answer, and left him the picture of ghastly despair. The day after I went in with reluctance, and he attacked me at once in a much stronger voice and with an abundance of argument which was quite startling. He presented his case with a sort of crazy vigour, and asked me finally how would I like to have a man's death on my conscience? He wanted me to promise that I would not sail without him.

I said that I really must consult the doctor first. He cried out at that. The doctor! Never! That would be a death sentence.

The effort had exhausted him. He closed his eyes, but went on rambling in a low voice. I had hated him from the start. The late captain had hated him too. Had wished him dead. Had wished all hands dead . . .

'What do you want to stand in with that wicked corpse for, sir? He'll have you too,' he ended, blinking his glazed eyes vacantly.

'Mr Burns,' I cried, very much discomposed, 'what on earth are you talking about?'

He seemed to come to himself, though he was too weak to start.

'I don't know,' he said languidly. 'But don't ask that doctor, sir. You and I are sailors. Don't ask him, sir. Someday perhaps you will have a wife and child yourself.'

And again he pleaded for the promise that I would not leave him behind. I had the firmness of mind not to give it to him. Afterwards this sternness seemed criminal; for my mind was made up. That prostrated man, with hardly strength enough to breathe and ravaged by a passion of fear, was irresistible. And, besides, he had happened to hit on the right words. He and I were sailors. That was a claim, for I had no other family. As to the wife-and-child (someday) argument, it had no force. It sounded merely bizarre.

I could imagine no claim that would be stronger and more absorbing than the claim of that ship, of these men snared in the river by silly commercial complications, as if in some poisonous trap.

However, I had nearly fought my way out. Out to sea. The sea – which was pure, safe, and friendly. Three days more.

That thought sustained and carried me on my way back to the ship. In the saloon the doctor's voice greeted me, and his large form followed his voice, issuing out of the starboard spare cabin where the ship's medicine chest was kept securely lashed in the bed-place.

Finding that I was not on board he had gone in there, he said, to inspect the supply of drugs, bandages, and so on. Everything was completed and in order.

I thanked him; I had just been thinking of asking him to do that very thing, as in a couple of days, as he knew, we were going to sea, where all our troubles of every sort would be over at last.

He listened gravely and made no answer. But when I opened to him my mind as to Mr Burns, he sat down by my side, and, laying his hand on my knee amicably, begged me to think what it was I was exposing myself to.

The man was just strong enough to bear being moved and no more. But he couldn't stand a return of the fever. I had before me a passage of sixty days perhaps, beginning with intricate navigation and ending probably with a lot of bad weather. Could I run the risk of having to go through it single-handed, with no chief officer and with a second quite a youth? . . .

He might have added that it was my first command too. He did probably think of that fact, for he checked himself. It was very present to my mind.

He advised me earnestly to cable to Singapore for a chief officer, even if I had to delay my sailing for a week.

'Not a day,' I said. The very thought gave me the shivers. The hands seemed fairly fit, all of them, and this was the time to get them away. Once at sea I was not afraid of facing anything. The sea was now the only remedy for all my troubles.

The doctor's glasses were directed at me like two lamps searching the genuineness of my resolution. He opened his lips as if to argue further, but shut them again without saying anything. I had a vision of poor Burns so vivid in his exhaustion, helplessness, and anguish, that it moved me more than the reality I had come away from only an hour before. It was purged from the drawbacks of his personality, and I could not resist it.

'Look here,' I said. 'Unless you tell me officially that the man must not be moved I'll make arrangements to have him brought on board tomorrow, and shall take the ship out of the river next morning, even if I have to anchor outside the bar for a couple of days to get her ready for sea.'

'Oh! I'll make all the arrangements myself,' said the doctor at once. 'I spoke as I did only as a friend – as a well-wisher, and that sort of thing.'

He rose in his dignified simplicity and gave me a warm handshake, rather solemnly, I thought. But he was as good as his word. When Mr Burns appeared at the gangway carried on a stretcher, the doctor himself walked by its side. The programme had been altered in so far that this transportation had been left to the last moment, on the very morning of our departure.

It was barely an hour after sunrise. The doctor waved his big arm to me from the shore and walked back at once to his trap, which had followed him empty to the riverside. Mr Burns, carried across the quarterdeck, had the appearance of being absolutely lifeless. Ransome went down to settle him in his cabin. I had to remain on deck to look after the ship, for the tug had got hold of our tow-rope already.

The splash of our shore-fasts falling in the water produced a complete change of feeling in me. It was like the imperfect relief of awakening from a nightmare. But when the ship's head swung down the river away from that town, Oriental and squalid, I missed the expected elation of that striven-for moment. What there was, undoubtedly, was a relaxation of tension which translated itself into a sense of weariness after an inglorious fight.

About midday we anchored a mile outside the bar. The afternoon was busy for all hands. Watching the work from the poop, where I remained all the time, I detected in it some of the languor of the six weeks spent in the steaming heat of the river. The first breeze would blow that away. Now the calm was complete. I judged that the second officer – a callow youth with an unpromising face – was not, to put it mildly, of that invaluable stuff from which a commander's right hand is made. But I was glad to catch along the main deck a few smiles on those seamen's faces at which I had hardly had time to have a good look as yet. Having thrown off the mortal coil of shore affairs, I felt myself familiar with them and yet a little strange, like a long-lost wanderer among his kin.

Ransome flitted continually to and fro between the galley and the cabin. It was a pleasure to look at him. The man positively had grace. He alone of all the crew had not had a day's illness in port. But with the knowledge of that uneasy heart within his breast I could detect the restraint he put on the natural sailor-like agility of his movements. It was as though he had something very fragile or very explosive to carry about his person and was all the time aware of it.

I had occasion to address him once or twice. He answered me in his pleasant quiet voice and with a faint, slightly wistful smile. Mr Burns appeared to be resting. He seemed fairly comfortable.

After sunset I came out on deck again to meet only a still void. The thin, featureless crust of the coast could not be distinguished. The darkness had risen around the ship like a mysterious emanation from the dumb and lonely waters. I leaned on the rail and turned my ear to the shadows of the night. Not a sound. My command might have been a planet flying vertiginously on its appointed path in a space of infinite silence. I clung to the rail as if my sense of balance were leaving me for good. How absurd. I hailed nervously.

'On deck there!'

The immediate answer, 'Yes, sir,' broke the spell. The anchor-watch man ran up the poop ladder smartly. I told him to report at once the slightest sign of a breeze coming.

Going below I looked in on Mr Burns. In fact, I could not avoid seeing him, for his door stood open. The man was so wasted that, in that white cabin, under a white sheet, and with his diminished head sunk in the white pillow, his red moustaches captured one's eyes exclusively, like something artificial – a pair of moustaches from a shop exhibited there in the harsh light of the bulkhead-lamp without a shade.

While I stared with a sort of wonder he asserted himself by opening his eyes and even moving them in my direction. A minute stir.

'Dead calm, Mr Burns,' I said resignedly.

In an unexpectedly distinct voice Mr Burns began a rambling speech. Its tone was very strange, not as if affected by his illness, but as if of a different nature. It sounded unearthly. As to the matter, I seemed to make out that it was the fault of the 'old man' – the late captain – ambushed down there under the sea with some evil intention. It was a weird story.

I listened to the end; then stepping into the cabin I laid my hand on the mate's forehead. It was cool. He was light-headed only from extreme weakness. Suddenly he seemed to become aware of me, and in his own voice – of course, very feeble – he asked regretfully: 'Is there no chance at all to get under way, sir?'

'What's the good of letting go our hold of the ground only to drift, Mr Burns?' I answered.

He sighed, and I left him to his immobility. His hold on life was as slender as his hold on sanity. I was oppressed by my lonely responsibilities. I went into my cabin to seek relief in a few hours' sleep, but almost before I closed my eyes the man on deck came down reporting a light breeze. Enough to get under way with, he said.

And it was no more than just enough. I ordered the windlass manned, the sails loosed, and the topsails set. But by the time I had cast the ship I could hardly feel any breath of wind. Nevertheless, I trimmed the yards and put everything on her. I was not going to give up the attempt.

Chapter 4

With her anchor at the bow and clothed in canvas to her very trucks, my command seemed to stand as motionless as a model ship set on the gleams and shadows of polished marble. It was impossible to distinguish land from water in the enigmatical tranquillity of the immense forces of the world. A sudden impatience possessed me.

'Won't she answer the helm at all?' I said irritably to the man whose strong brown hands grasping the spokes of the wheel stood out lighted on the darkness; like a symbol of mankind's claim to the direction of its own fate.

He answered me: 'Yes, sir. She's coming-to slowly.'

'Let her head come up to south.'

'Aye, aye, sir.'

I paced the poop. There was not a sound but that of my footsteps, till the man spoke again.

'She is at south now, sir.'

I felt a slight tightness of the chest before I gave out the first course of my first command to the silent night, heavy with dew and sparkling with stars. There was a finality in the act committing me to the endless vigilance of my lonely task.

'Steady her head at that,' I said at last. 'The course is south.'

'South, sir,' echoed the man.

I sent below the second mate and his watch and remained in charge, walking the deck through the chill, somnolent hours that precede the dawn.

Slight puffs came and went, and whenever they were strong enough to wake up the black water the murmur alongside ran through my very heart in a delicate crescendo of delight and died away swiftly. I was bitterly tired. The very stars seemed weary of waiting for daybreak. It came at last with a mother-of-pearl sheen at the zenith, such as I had never seen before in the tropics, unglowing, almost grey, with a strange reminder of high latitudes.

The voice of the look-out man hailed from forward: 'Land on the port bow, sir.'

'All right.'

Leaning on the rail I never even raised my eyes. The motion of the ship was imperceptible. Presently Ransome brought me the cup of morning coffee. After I had drunk it I looked ahead, and in the still streak of very bright pale orange light I saw the land profiled flatly as if cut out of black paper and seeming to float on the water as light as cork. But the rising sun turned it into mere dark vapour, a doubtful, massive shadow trembling in the hot glare.

The watch finished washing decks. I went below and stopped at Mr Burns' door (he could not bear to have it shut), but hesitated to speak to him till he moved his eyes. I gave him the news.

'Sighted Cape Liant at daylight. About fifteen miles.'

He moved his lips then, but I heard no sound till I put my ear down, and caught the peevish comment: 'This is crawling . . . No luck.'

'Better luck than standing still, anyhow,' I pointed out resignedly, and left him to whatever thoughts or fancies haunted his hopeless prostration.

Later that morning, when relieved by my second officer, I threw myself on my couch and for some three hours or so I really found oblivion. It was so perfect that on waking up I wondered where I was. Then came the immense relief of the thought: on board my ship! At sea! At sea!

Through the port-holes I beheld an unruffled, sun-smitten horizon. The horizon of a windless day. But its spaciousness alone was enough to give me a sense of a fortunate escape, a momentary exultation of freedom.

I stepped out into the saloon with my heart lighter than it had been for days. Ransome was at the sideboard preparing to lay the table for the first sea dinner of the passage. He turned his head, and something in his eyes checked my modest elation.

Instinctively I asked: 'What is it now?' not expecting in the least the answer I got. It was given with that sort of contained serenity which was characteristic of the man.

'I am afraid we haven't left all sickness behind us, sir.'

'We haven't! What's the matter?'

He told me then that two of our men had been taken bad with fever in the night. One of them was burning and the other was shivering, but he thought that it was pretty much the same thing. I thought so too. I felt shocked by the news. 'One burning, the other shivering, you say? No. We haven't left the sickness behind. Do they look very ill?'

'Middling bad, sir.' Ransome's eyes gazed steadily into mine. We exchanged smiles. Ransome's a little wistful, as usual, mine no doubt grim enough, to correspond with my secret exasperation.

I asked: 'Was there any wind at all this morning?'

'Can hardly say that, sir. We've moved all the time though. The land ahead seems a little nearer.'

That was it. A little nearer. Whereas if we had only had a little more wind, only a very little more, we might, we should, have been abreast of Liant by this time and increasing our distance from that contaminated shore. And it was not only the distance. It seemed to me that a stronger breeze would have blown away the infection which clung to the ship. It obviously did cling to the ship. Two men. One burning, one shivering. I felt a distinct reluctance to go and look at them. What was the good? Poison is poison. Tropical fever is tropical fever. But that it should have stretched its claw after us over the sea seemed to me an extraordinary and unfair licence. I could hardly believe that it could be anything worse than the last desperate pluck of the evil from which we were escaping into the clean breath of the sea. If only that breath had been a little stronger. However, there was the quinine against the fever. I went into the spare cabin where the medicine chest was kept to prepare two doses. I opened it full of faith as a man opens a miraculous shrine. The upper part was inhabited by a collection of bottles, all square-shouldered and as like each other as peas. Under that orderly array there were two drawers, stuffed as full of things as one could imagine – paper packages, bandages, cardboard boxes officially labelled. The lower of the two, in one of its compartments, contained our provision of quinine.

There were five bottles, all round and all of a size. One was about a third full. The other four remained still wrapped up in paper and sealed. But I did not expect to see an envelope lying on top of them. A square envelope, belonging, in fact, to the ship's stationery.

It lay so that I could see it was not closed down, and on picking it up and turning it over I perceived that it was addressed to myself. It contained a half-sheet of notepaper, which I unfolded with a queer sense of dealing with the uncanny, but without any excitement as people meet and do extraordinary things in a dream.

'My dear Captain,' it began, but I ran to the signature. The writer was the doctor. The date was that of the day on which, returning from my visit to Mr Burns in the hospital, I had found the excellent doctor waiting for me in the cabin; and when he told me that he had been putting in time inspecting the medicine chest for me. How bizarre! While expecting me to come in at any moment he had been amusing himself by writing me a letter, and then as I came in had hastened to stuff it into the medicine-chest drawer. A rather incredible proceeding. I turned to the text in wonder.

In a large, hurried, but legible hand the good, sympathetic man for some reason, either of kindness or more likely impelled by the irresistible desire to express his opinion, with which he didn't want to damp my hopes before, was warning me not to put my trust in the beneficial effects of a change from land to sea. 'I didn't want to add to your worries by discouraging your hopes,' he wrote. 'I am afraid that, medically speaking, the end of your troubles is not yet.' In short, he expected me to have to fight a probable return of tropical illness. Fortunately I had a good provision of quinine. I should put my trust in that, and administer it steadily, when the ship's health would certainly improve.

I crumpled up the letter and rammed it into my pocket. Ransome carried off two big doses to the men forward. As to myself, I did not go on deck as yet. I went instead to the door of Mr Burns' room, and gave him that news, too.

It was impossible to say the effect it had on him. At first I thought that he was speechless. His head lay sunk in the pillow. He moved his lips enough, however, to assure me that he was getting much stronger; a statement shockingly untrue on the face of it.

That afternoon I took my watch as a matter of course. A great over-heated stillness enveloped the ship and seemed to hold her motionless in a flaming ambience composed in two shades of blue. Faint, hot puffs eddied nervelessly from her sails. And yet she moved. She must have. For, as the sun was setting, we had drawn abreast of Cape Liant and dropped it behind us: an ominous retreating shadow in the last gleams of twilight.

In the evening, under the crude glare of his lamp, Mr Burns seemed to have come more to the surface of his bedding. It was as if a depressing hand had been lifted off him. He answered my few words by a comparatively long, connected speech. He asserted himself strongly. If he escaped being smothered by this stagnant heat, he said, he was confident that in a very few days he would be able to come up on deck and help me.

While he was speaking I trembled lest this effort of energy should leave him lifeless before my eyes. But I cannot deny that there was something comforting in his willingness. I made a suitable reply, but pointed out to him that the only thing that could really help us was wind – a fair wind.

He rolled his head impatiently on the pillow. And it was not comforting in the least to hear him begin to mutter crazily about the late captain, that old man buried in latitude 8° 20', right in our way – ambushed at the entrance of the Gulf.

'Are you still thinking of your late captain, Mr Burns?' I said. 'I imagine the dead feel no animosity against the living. They care nothing for them.'

'You don't know that one,' he breathed out feebly.

'No. I didn't know him, and he didn't know me. And so he can't have any grievance against me, anyway.'

'Yes. But there's all the rest of us on board,' he insisted.

I felt the inexpungible strength of common sense being insidiously menaced by this gruesome, by this insane delusion. And I said: 'You mustn't talk so much. You will tire yourself.'

'And there is the ship herself,' he persisted in a whisper.

'Now, not a word more,' I said, stepping in and laying my hand on his cool forehead. It proved to me that this atrocious absurdity was rooted in the man himself and not in the disease, which, apparently, had emptied him of every power, mental and physical, except that one fixed idea.

I avoided giving Mr Burns any opening for conversation for the next few days. I merely used to throw him a hasty, cheery word when passing his door. I believe that if he had had the strength he would have called out after me more than once. But he hadn't the strength. Ransome, however, observed to me one afternoon that the mate 'seemed to be picking up wonderfully'.

'Did he talk any nonsense to you of late?' I asked casually.

'No, sir.' Ransome was startled by the direct question; but, after a pause, he added equably: 'He told me this morning, sir, that he was sorry he had to bury our late captain right in the ship's way, as one may say, out of the Gulf.'

'Isn't this nonsense enough for you?' I asked, looking confidently at the intelligent, quiet face on which the secret uneasiness in the man's breast had thrown a transparent veil of care.

Ransome didn't know. He had not given a thought to the matter. And with a faint smile he flitted away from me on his never-ending duties, with his usual guarded activity.

Two more days passed. We had advanced a little way – a very little way – into the larger space of the Gulf of Siam. Seizing eagerly upon the elation of the first command thrown into my lap, by the agency of Captain Giles, I had yet an uneasy feeling that such luck as this has got perhaps to be paid for in some way. I had held, professionally, a review of my chances. I was competent enough for that. At least, I thought so. I had a general sense of my preparedness which only a man pursuing a calling he loves can know. That feeling seemed to me the most natural thing in the world. As natural as breathing. I imagined I could not have lived without it.

I don't know what I expected. Perhaps nothing else than that special intensity of existence which is the quintessence of youthful aspirations. Whatever I expected I did not expect to be beset by hurricanes. I knew better than that. In the Gulf of Siam there are no hurricanes. But neither did I expect to find myself bound hand and foot to the hopeless extent which was revealed to me as the days went on.

Not that the evil spell held us always motionless. Mysterious currents drifted us here and there, with a stealthy power made manifest by the changing vistas of the islands fringing the east shore of the Gulf. And there were winds too, fitful and deceitful. They raised hopes only to dash them into the bitterest disappointment, promises of advance ending in lost ground, expiring in sighs, dying into dumb stillness in which the currents had it all their own way – their own inimical way.

The Island of Koh-ring, a great, black, upheaved ridge amongst a lot of tiny islets, lying upon the glassy water like a triton amongst minnows, seemed to be the centre of the fatal circle. It seemed impossible to get away from it. Day after day it remained in sight. More than once, in a favourable breeze, I would take its bearing in the fast ebbing twilight, thinking that it was for the last time. Vain hope. A night of fitful airs would undo the gains of temporary favour, and the rising sun would throw out the black relief of Koh-ring, looking more barren, inhospitable, and grim than ever.

'It's like being bewitched, upon my word,' I said once to Mr Burns, from my usual position in the doorway.

He was sitting up in his bed-place. He was progressing towards the world of living men, if he could hardly have been said to have rejoined it yet. He nodded to me his frail and bony head in a wisely mysterious assent.

'Oh, yes, I know what you mean,' I said. 'But you cannot expect me to believe that a dead man has the power to put out of joint the meteorology of this part of the world. Though indeed it seems to have gone utterly wrong. The land and sea breezes have got broken up into small pieces. We cannot depend upon them for five minutes together.'

'It won't be very long now before I can come up on deck,' muttered Mr Burns, 'and then we shall see.'

Whether he meant this for a promise to grapple with supernatural evil I couldn't tell. At any rate, it wasn't the kind of assistance I needed. On the other hand, I had been living on deck practically night and day so as to take advantage of every chance to get my ship a little more to the southward. The mate, I could see, was extremely weak yet, and not quite rid of his delusion, which to me appeared but a symptom of his disease. At all events, the hopefulness of an invalid was not to be discouraged. I said: 'You will be most welcome there, I am sure, Mr Burns. If you go on improving at this rate you'll be presently one of the healthiest men in the ship.'

This pleased him, but his extreme emaciation converted his self-satisfied smile into a ghastly exhibition of long teeth under the red moustache.

'Aren't the fellows improving, sir?' he asked soberly, with an extremely sensible expression of anxiety on his face.

I answered him only with a vague gesture and went away from the door. The fact was that disease played with us capriciously very much as the winds did. It would go from one man to another with a lighter or heavier touch, which always left its mark behind, staggering some, knocking others over for a time, leaving this one, returning to another, so that all of them had now an invalidish aspect and a hunted, apprehensive look in their eyes; while Ransome and I, the only two completely untouched, went amongst them assiduously distributing quinine. It was a double fight. The adverse weather held us in front and the disease pressed on our rear. I must say that the men were very good. The constant toil of trimming the yards they faced willingly. But all spring was out of their limbs, and as I looked at them from the poop I could not keep from my mind the dreadful impression that they were moving in poisoned air.

Down below, in his cabin, Mr Burns had advanced so far as not only to be able to sit up, but even to draw up his legs. Clasping them with bony arms, like an animated skeleton, he emitted deep, impatient sighs.

'The great thing to do, sir,' he would tell me on every occasion, when I gave him the chance, 'the great thing is to get the ship past 8° 20' of latitude. Once she's past that we're all right.'

At first I used only to smile at him, though, God knows, I had not much heart left for smiles. But at last I lost my patience.

'Oh, yes. The latitude 8° 20'. That's where you buried your late captain, isn't it?' Then with severity: 'Don't you think, Mr Burns, it's about time you dropped all that nonsense?'

He rolled at me his deep-sunken eyes in a glance of invincible obstinacy. But for the rest, he only muttered, just loud enough for me to hear, something about 'Not surprised . . . find . . . play us some beastly trick yet . . .'

Such passages as this were not exactly wholesome for my resolution. The stress of adversity was beginning to tell on me. At the same time I felt a contempt for that obscure weakness of my soul. I said to myself disdainfully that it should take much more than that to affect in the smallest degree my fortitude.

I didn't know then how soon and from what unexpected direction it would be attacked.

It was the very next day. The sun had risen clear of the southern shoulder of Koh-ring, which still hung, like an evil attendant, on our port quarter. It was intensely hateful to my sight. During the night we had been heading all round the compass, trimming the yards again and again, to what I fear must have been for the most part imaginary puffs of air. Then just about sunrise we got for an hour an inexplicable, steady breeze, right in our teeth. There was no sense in it. It fitted neither with the season of the year, nor with the secular experience of seamen as recorded in books, nor with the aspect of the sky. Only purposeful malevolence could account for it. It sent us travelling at a great pace away from our proper course; and if we had been out on pleasure sailing bent it would have been a delightful breeze, with the awakened sparkle of the sea, with the sense of motion and a feeling of unwonted freshness. Then all at once, as if disdaining to carry farther the sorry jest, it dropped and died out completely in less than five minutes. The ship's head swung where it listed; the stilled sea took on the polish of a steel plate in the calm.

I went below, not because I meant to take some rest, but simply because I couldn't bear to look at it just then. The indefatigable Ransome was busy in the saloon. It had become a regular practice with him to give me an informal health report in the morning. He turned away from the sideboard with his usual pleasant, quiet gaze. No shadow rested on his intelligent forehead.

'There are a good many of them middling bad this morning, sir,' he said in a calm tone.

'What? All knocked out?'

'Only two actually in their bunks, sir, but . . .'

'It's last night that has done for them. We have had to pull and haul all the blessed time.'

'I heard, sir. I had a mind to come out and help, only, you know . . .'

'Certainly not. You mustn't . . . The fellows lie at night about the decks, too. It isn't good for them.'

Ransome assented. But men couldn't be looked after like children. Moreover, one could hardly blame them for trying for such coolness and such air as there was to be found on deck. He himself, of course, knew better.

He was, indeed, a reasonable man. Yet it would have been hard to say that the others were not. The last few days had been for us like the ordeal of the fiery furnace. One really couldn't quarrel with their common, imprudent humanity making the best of the moments of relief, when the night brought in the illusion of coolness and the starlight twinkled through the heavy, dew-laden air. Moreover, most of them were so weakened that hardly anything could be done without everybody that could totter mustering on the braces. No, it was no use remonstrating with them. But I fully believed that quinine was of very great use indeed.

I believed in it. I pinned my faith to it. It would save the men, the ship, break the spell by its medicinal virtue, make time of no account, the weather but a passing worry, and, like a magic powder working against mysterious malefices, secure the first passage of my first command against the evil powers of calms and pestilence. I looked upon it as more precious than gold, and unlike gold, of which there hardly ever seems to be enough anywhere, the ship had a sufficient store of it. I went in to get it with the purpose of weighing out doses. I stretched my hand with the feeling of a man reaching for an unfailing panacea, took up a fresh bottle and unrolled the wrapper, noticing as I did so that the ends, both top and bottom, had come unsealed . . .

But why record all the swift steps of the appalling discovery? You have guessed the truth already. There was the wrapper, the bottle, and the white powder inside, some sort of powder! But it wasn't quinine. One look at it was quite enough. I remember that at the very moment of picking up the bottle, before I even dealt with the wrapper, the weight of the object I had in my hand gave me an instant of premonition. Quinine is as light as feathers; and my nerves must have been exasperated into an extraordinary sensibility. I let the bottle smash itself on the floor. The stuff, whatever it was, felt gritty under the sole of my shoe. I snatched up the next bottle and then the next. The weight alone told the tale. One after another they fell, breaking at my feet, not because I threw them down in my dismay, but slipping through my fingers as if this disclosure were too much for my strength.

It is a fact that the very greatness of a mental shock helps one to bear up against it, by producing a sort of temporary insensibility. I came out of the stateroom stunned, as if something heavy had dropped on my head. From the other side of the saloon, across the table, Ransome, with a duster in his hand, stared open-mouthed. I don't think that I looked wild. It is quite possible that I appeared to be in a hurry because I was instinctively hastening up on deck.

An example this of training become instinct. The difficulties, the dangers, the problems of a ship at sea must be met on deck.

To this fact, as it were of nature, I responded instinctively; which may be taken as a proof that for a moment I must have been robbed of my reason.

I was certainly off my balance, a prey to impulse, for at the bottom of the stairs I turned and flung myself at the doorway of Mr Burns' cabin. The wildness of his aspect checked my mental disorder. He was sitting up in his bunk, his body looking immensely long, his head drooping a little sideways, with affected complacency. He flourished, in his trembling hand, on the end of a forearm no thicker than a stout walking-stick, a shining pair of scissors which he tried before my very eyes to jab at his throat.

I was to a certain extent horrified; but it was rather a secondary sort of effect, not really strong enough to make me yell at him in some such manner as: 'Stop!' . . . 'Heavens!' 'What are you doing?'

In reality he was simply overtaxing his returning strength in a shaky attempt to clip off the thick growth of his red beard. A large towel was spread over his lap, and a shower of stiff hairs, like bits of copper wire, was descending on it at every snip of the scissors.

He turned to me his face grotesque beyond the fantasies of mad dreams, one cheek all bushy as if with a swollen flame, the other denuded and sunken, with the untouched long moustache on that side asserting itself, lonely and fierce. And while he stared thunderstruck, with the gaping scissors on his fingers, I shouted my discovery at him fiendishly, in six words, without comment.

Chapter 5

I heard the clatter of the scissors escaping from his hand, noted the perilous heave of his whole person over the edge of the bunk after them, and then, returning to my first purpose, pursued my course on to the deck. The sparkle of the sea filled my eyes. It was gorgeous and barren, monotonous and without hope under the empty curve of the sky. The sails hung motionless and slack, the very folds of their sagging surfaces moved no more than carved granite. The impetuosity of my advent made the man at the helm start slightly. A block aloft squeaked incomprehensibly, for what on earth could have made it do so? It was a whistling note like a bird's. For a long, long time I faced an empty world, steeped in an infinity of silence, through which the sunshine poured and flowed for some mysterious purpose. Then I heard Ransome's voice at my elbow.

'I have put Mr Burns back to bed, sir.'

'You have.'

'Well, sir, he got out, all of a sudden, but when he let go of the edge of his bunk he fell down. He isn't light-headed, though, it seems to me.'

'No,' I said dully, without looking at Ransome. He waited for a moment, then, cautiously as if not to give offence: 'I don't think we need lose much of that stuff, sir,' he said, 'I can sweep it up, every bit of it almost, and then we could sift the glass out. I will go about it at once. It will not make the breakfast late, not ten minutes.'

'Oh, yes,' I said bitterly. 'Let the breakfast wait, sweep up every bit of it, and then throw the damned lot overboard!'

The profound silence returned, and when I looked over my shoulder Ransome – the intelligent, serene Ransome – had vanished from my side. The intense loneliness of the sea acted like poison on my brain. When I turned my eyes to the ship, I had a morbid vision of her as a floating grave. Who hasn't heard of ships found drifting, haphazard, with their crews all dead? I looked at the seaman at the helm, I had an impulse to speak to him, and, indeed, his face took on an expectant cast as if he had guessed my intention. But in the end I went below, thinking I would be alone with the greatness of my trouble for a little while. But through his open door Mr Burns saw me come down, and addressed me grumpily: 'Well, sir?'

I went in. 'It isn't well at all,' I said.

Mr Burns, re-established in his bed-place, was concealing his hirsute cheek in the palm of his hand.

'That confounded fellow has taken away the scissors from me,' were the next words he said.

The tension I was suffering from was so great that it was perhaps just as well that Mr Burns had started on this grievance. He seemed very sore about it and grumbled, 'Does he think I am mad, or what?'

'I don't think so, Mr Burns,' I said. I looked upon him at that moment as a model of self-possession. I even conceived on that account a sort of admiration for that man, who had (apart from the intense materiality of what was left of his beard) come as near to being a disembodied spirit as any man can do and live. I noticed the preternatural sharpness of the ridge of his nose, the deep cavities of his temples, and I envied him. He was so reduced that he would probably die very soon. Enviable man! So near extinction – while I had to bear within me a tumult of suffering vitality, doubt, confusion, self-reproach, and an indefinite reluctance to meet the horrid logic of the situation. I could not help muttering: 'I feel as if I were going mad myself.'

Mr Burns glared spectrally, but otherwise wonderfully composed.

'I always thought he would play us some deadly trick,' he said, with a peculiar emphasis on the *he*.

It gave me a mental shock, but I had neither the mind, nor the heart, nor the spirit to argue with him. My form of sickness was indifference. The creeping paralysis of a hopeless outlook. So I only gazed at him. Mr Burns broke into further speech.

'Eh? What? No! You won't believe it? Well, how do you account for this? How do you think it could have happened?'

'Happened?' I repeated dully. 'Why, yes, how in the name of the infernal powers did this thing happen?'

Indeed, on thinking it out, it seemed incomprehensible that it should just be like this: the bottles emptied, refilled, rewrapped, and replaced. A sort of plot, a sinister attempt to deceive, a thing resembling sly vengeance – but for what? – or else a fiendish joke. But Mr Burns was in possession of a theory. It was simple, and he uttered it solemnly in a hollow voice.

'I suppose they have given him about fifteen pounds in Haiphong for that little lot.'

'Mr Burns!' I cried.

He nodded grotesquely over his raised legs, like two broomsticks in the pyjamas, with enormous bare feet at the end.

'Why not? The stuff is pretty expensive in this part of the world, and they were very short of it in Tonkin. And what did he care? You have not known him. I have, and I have defied him. He feared neither God, nor devil, nor man, nor wind, nor sea, nor his own conscience. And I believe he hated everybody and everything. But I think he was afraid to die. I believe I am the only man who ever stood up to him. I faced him in that cabin where you live now, when he was sick, and I cowed him then. He thought I was going to twist his neck for him. If he had had his way we would have been beating up against the north-east monsoon, as long as he lived and afterwards too, for ages and ages. Acting the Flying Dutchman in the China Sea! Ha! Ha!'

'But why should he replace the bottles like this?' . . . I began.

'Why shouldn't he? Why should he want to throw the bottles away? They fit the drawer. They belong to the medicine chest.'

'And they were wrapped up,' I cried.

'Well, the wrappers were there. Did it from habit, I suppose, and as to refilling, there is always a lot of stuff they send in paper parcels that burst after a time. And then, who can tell? I suppose you didn't taste it, sir? But, of course, you are sure . . .'

'No,' I said. 'I didn't taste it. It is all overboard now.'

Behind me, a soft, cultivated voice said: 'I have tasted it. It seemed a mixture of all sorts, sweetish, saltish, very horrible.'

Ransome, stepping out of the pantry, had been listening for some time, as it was very excusable in him to do.

'A dirty trick,' said Mr Burns. 'I always said he would.'

The magnitude of my indignation was unbounded. And the kind, sympathetic doctor too. The only sympathetic man I ever knew . . . instead of writing that warning letter, the very refinement of sympathy, why didn't the man make a proper inspection? But, as a matter of fact, it was hardly fair to blame the doctor. The fittings were in order and the medicine chest is an officially arranged affair. There was nothing really to arouse the slightest suspicion. The person I could never forgive was myself. Nothing should ever be taken for granted. The seed of everlasting remorse was sown in my breast.

'I feel it's all my fault,' I exclaimed, 'mine, and nobody else's. That's how I feel. I shall never forgive myself.'

'That's very foolish, sir,' said Mr Burns fiercely.

And after this effort he fell back exhausted on his bed. He closed his eyes, he panted; this affair, this abominable surprise had shaken him up, too. As I turned away I perceived Ransome looking at me blankly. He appreciated what it meant, but he managed to produce his pleasant, wistful smile. Then he stepped back into his pantry, and I rushed up on deck again to see whether there was any wind, any breath under the sky, any stir of the air, any sign of hope. The deadly stillness met me again. Nothing was changed except that there was a different man at the wheel. He looked ill. His whole figure drooped, and he seemed rather to cling to the spokes than hold them with a controlling grip. I said to him: 'You are not fit to be here.'

'I can manage, sir,' he said feebly.

As a matter of fact, there was nothing for him to do. The ship had no steerage way. She lay with her head to the westward, the everlasting Koh-ring visible over the stern, with a few small islets, black spots in the great blaze, swimming before my troubled eyes. And but for those bits of land there was no speck on the sky, no speck on the water, no shape of vapour, no wisp of smoke, no sail, no boat, no stir of humanity, no sign of life, nothing!

The first question was, what to do? What could one do? The first thing to do obviously was to tell the men. I did it that very day. I wasn't going to let the knowledge simply get about. I would face them. They were assembled on the quarterdeck for the purpose. Just before I stepped out to speak to them I discovered that life could hold terrible moments. No confessed criminal had ever been so oppressed by his sense of guilt. This is why, perhaps, my face was set hard and my voice curt and unemotional while I made my declaration that I could do nothing more for the sick, in the way of drugs. As to such care as could be given them they knew they had had it.

I would have held them justified in tearing me limb from limb. The silence which followed upon my words was almost harder to bear than the angriest uproar. I was crushed by the infinite depth of its reproach. But, as a matter of fact, I was mistaken. In a voice which I had great difficulty in keeping firm, I went on: 'I suppose, men, you have understood what I said, and you know what it means.'

A voice or two were heard: 'Yes, sir . . . We understand.'

They had kept silent simply because they thought that they were not called upon to say anything; and when I told them that I intended to run into Singapore and that the best chance for the ship and the men was in the efforts all of us, sick and well, must make to get her along out of this, I received the encouragement of a low, assenting murmur and of a louder voice exclaiming: 'Surely there is a way out of this blamed hole.'

Here is an extract from the notes I wrote at the time.

> We have lost Koh-ring at last. For many days now I don't think I have been two hours below altogether. I remain on deck, of course, night and day, and the nights and the days wheel over us in succession, whether long or short, who can say? All sense of time is lost in the monotony of expectation, of hope, and of desire – which is only one: Get the ship to the southward! Get the ship to the southward! The effect is curiously mechanical; the sun climbs and descends, the night swings over our heads as if somebody below the horizon were turning a crank. It is the pettiest, the most aimless! ... and all through that miserable performance I go on, tramping, tramping the deck. How many miles have I walked on the poop of that ship! A stubborn pilgrimage of sheer restlessness, diversified by short excursions below to look upon Mr Burns. I don't know whether it is an illusion, but he seems to become more substantial from day to day. He doesn't say much, for, indeed, the situation doesn't lend itself to idle remarks. I notice this even with the men as I watch them moving or sitting about the decks. They don't talk to each other. It strikes me that if there exist an invisible ear catching the whispers of the earth, it will find this ship the most silent spot on it ...
>
> No, Mr Burns has not much to say to me. He sits in his bunk with his beard gone, his moustaches flaming, and with an air of silent determination on his chalky physiognomy. Ransome tells me he devours all the food that is given him to the last scrap, but that, apparently, he sleeps very little. Even at night, when I go below to fill my pipe, I notice that, though dozing flat on his back, he still looks very determined. From the side glance he gives me when awake it seems as though he were annoyed at being interrupted in some arduous mental operation; and as I emerge on deck the ordered arrangement of the stars meets my eye, unclouded, infinitely wearisome. There they are: stars, sun, sea, light, darkness, space, great waters; the formidable Work of the Seven Days, into which mankind seems to have blundered unbidden. Or else decoyed. Even as I have been decoyed into this awful, this death-haunted command ...

The only spot of light in the ship at night was that of the compass-lamps, lighting up the faces of the succeeding helmsmen; for the rest we were lost in the darkness, I walking the poop and the men lying about the decks. They were all so reduced by sickness that no watches could be kept. Those who were able to walk remained all the time on duty, lying about in the shadows of the main deck, till my voice raised for an order would bring them to their enfeebled feet, a tottering little group, moving patiently about the ship, with hardly a murmur, a whisper amongst them all. And every time I had to raise my voice it was with a pang of remorse and pity.

Then about four o'clock in the morning a light would gleam forward in the galley. The unfailing Ransome with the uneasy heart, immune, serene, and active, was getting ready the early coffee for the men. Presently he would bring me a cup up on the poop, and it was then that I allowed myself to drop into my deck-chair for a couple of hours of real sleep. No doubt I must have been snatching short dozes when leaning against the rail for a moment in sheer exhaustion; but, honestly, I was not aware of them, except in the painful form of convulsive starts that seemed to come on me even while I walked. From about five, however, until after seven I would sleep openly under the fading stars.

I would say to the helmsman: 'Call me at need,' and drop into that chair and close my eyes, feeling that there was no more sleep for me on earth. And then I would know nothing till, sometime between seven and eight, I would feel a touch on my shoulder and look up at Ransome's face, with its faint, wistful smile and friendly, grey eyes, as though he were tenderly amused at my slumbers. Occasionally the second mate would come up and relieve me at early coffee time. But it didn't really matter. Generally it was a dead calm, or else faint airs so changing and fugitive that it really wasn't worth while to touch a brace for them. If the air steadied at all the seaman at the helm could be trusted for a warning shout: 'Ship's all aback, sir!' which like a trumpet-call would make me spring a foot above the deck. Those were the words which it seemed to me would have made me spring up from eternal sleep. But this was not often. I have never met since such breathless sunrises. And if the second mate happened to be there (he had generally one day in three free of fever) I would find him sitting on the skylight half-senseless, as it were, and with an idiotic gaze fastened on some object near by – a rope, a cleat, a belaying pin, a ringbolt.

That young man was rather troublesome. He remained cubbish in his sufferings. He seemed to have become completely imbecile; and when the return of fever drove him to his cabin below the next thing would be that we would miss him from there. The first time it happened Ransome and I were very much alarmed. We started a quiet search and ultimately Ransome discovered him curled up in the sail-locker, which opened into the lobby by a sliding-door. When remonstrated with, he muttered sulkily, 'It's cool in there.' That wasn't true. It was only dark there.

The fundamental defects of his face were not improved by its uniform livid hue. It was not so with many of the men. The wastage of ill-health seemed to idealise the general character of the features, bringing out the unsuspected nobility of some, the strength of others, and in one case revealing an essentially comic aspect. He was a short, gingery, active man with a nose and chin of the Punch type, and whom his shipmates called 'Frenchy'. I don't know why. He may have been a Frenchman, but I never heard him utter a single word in French.

To see him coming aft to the wheel comforted one. The blue dungaree trousers turned up the calf, one leg a little higher than the other, the clean check shirt, the white canvas cap, evidently made by himself, made up a whole of peculiar smartness, and the persistent jauntiness of his gait, even, poor fellow, when he couldn't help tottering, told of his invincible spirit. There was also a man called Gambril. He was the only grizzled person in the ship. His face was of an austere type. But if I remember all their faces, wasting tragically before my eyes, most of their names have vanished from my memory.

The words that passed between us were few and puerile in regard of the situation. I had to force myself to look them in the face. I expected to meet reproachful glances. There were none. The expression of suffering in their eyes was indeed hard enough to bear. But that they couldn't help. For the rest, I ask myself whether it was the temper of their souls or the sympathy of their imagination that made them so wonderful, so worthy of my undying regard.

For myself, neither was my soul highly tempered, nor my imagination properly under control. There were moments when I felt, not only that I would go mad, but that I had gone mad already; so that I dared not open my lips for fear of betraying myself by some insane shriek. Luckily I had only orders to give, and an order has a steadying influence upon him who has to give it. Moreover, the seaman, the officer of the watch, in me was sufficiently sane. I was like a mad carpenter making a box. Were he ever so convinced that he was King of Jerusalem, the box he would make would be a sane box. What I feared was a shrill note escaping me involuntarily and upsetting my balance. Luckily, again, there was no necessity to raise one's voice. The brooding stillness of the world seemed sensitive to the slightest sound like a whispering gallery. The conversational tone would almost carry a word from one end of the ship to the other. The terrible thing was that the only voice that I ever heard was my own. At night especially it reverberated very lonely amongst the planes of the unstirring sails.

Mr Burns, still keeping to his bed with that air of secret determination, was moved to grumble at many things. Our interviews were short five-minute affairs, but fairly frequent. I was everlastingly diving down below to get a light, though I did not consume much tobacco at that time. The pipe was always going out; for in truth my mind was not composed enough to enable me to get a decent smoke. Likewise, for most of the time during the twenty-four hours I could have struck matches on deck and held them aloft till the flame burnt my fingers. But I always used to run below. It was a change. It was the only break in the incessant strain; and, of course, Mr Burns through the open door could see me come in and go out every time.

With his knees gathered up under his chin and staring with his greenish eyes over them, he was a weird figure, and with my knowledge of the crazy notion in his head, not a very attractive one for me. Still, I had to speak to him now and then, and one day he complained that the ship was very silent.

For hours and hours, he said, he was lying there, not hearing a sound, till he did not know what to do with himself.

'When Ransome happens to be forward in his galley everything's so still that one might think everybody in the ship was dead,' he grumbled. 'The only voice I do hear sometimes is yours, sir, and that isn't enough to cheer me up. What's the matter with the men? Isn't there one left that can sing out at the ropes?'

'Not one, Mr Burns,' I said. 'There is no breath to spare on board this ship for that. Are you aware that there are times when I can't muster more than three hands to do anything?'

He asked swiftly but fearfully: 'Nobody dead yet, sir?'

'No.'

'It wouldn't do,' Mr Burns declared forcibly. 'Mustn't let him. If he gets hold of one he will get them all.'

I cried out angrily at this. I believe I even swore at the disturbing effect of these words. They attacked all the self-possession that was left to me. In my endless vigil in the face of the enemy I had been haunted by gruesome images enough. I had had visions of a ship drifting in calms and swinging in light airs, with all her crew dying slowly about her decks. Such things had been known to happen.

Mr Burns met my outburst by a mysterious silence.

'Look here,' I said. 'You don't believe yourself what you say. You can't. It's impossible. It isn't the sort of thing I have a right to expect from you. My position's bad enough without being worried with your silly fancies.'

He remained unmoved. On account of the way in which the light fell on his head I could not be sure whether he had smiled faintly or not. I changed my tone.

'Listen,' I said. 'It's getting so desperate that I had thought for a moment, since we can't make our way south, whether I wouldn't try to steer west and make an attempt to reach the mail-boat track. We could always get some quinine from her, at least. What do you think?'

He cried out: 'No, no, no. Don't do that, sir. You mustn't for a moment give up facing that old ruffian. If you do he will get the upper hand of us.'

I left him. He was impossible. It was like a case of possession. His protest, however, was essentially quite sound. As a matter of fact, my notion of heading out west on the chance of sighting a problematical steamer could not bear calm examination. On the side where we were we had enough wind, at least from time to time, to struggle on towards the south. Enough, at least, to keep hope alive. But suppose that I had used those capricious gusts of wind to sail away to the westward, into some region where there was not a breath of air for days on end, what then? Perhaps my appalling vision of a ship floating with a dead crew would become a reality for the discovery weeks afterwards by some horror-stricken mariners.

That afternoon Ransome brought me up a cup of tea, and while waiting there, tray in hand, he remarked in the exactly right tone of sympathy: 'You are holding out well, sir.'

'Yes,' I said. 'You and I seem to have been forgotten.'

'Forgotten, sir?'

'Yes, by the fever-devil who has got on board this ship,' I said.

Ransome gave me one of his attractive, intelligent, quick glances and went away with the tray. It occurred to me that I had been talking somewhat in Mr Burns' manner. It annoyed me. Yet often in darker moments I forgot myself into an attitude towards our troubles more fit for a contest against a living enemy.

Yes. The fever-devil had not laid his hand yet either on Ransome or on me. But he might at any time. It was one of those thoughts one had to fight down, keep at arm's length at any cost. It was unbearable to contemplate the possibility of Ransome, the housekeeper of the ship, being laid low. And what would happen to my command if I got knocked over, with Mr Burns too weak to stand without holding on to his bed-place and the second mate reduced to a state of permanent imbecility? It was impossible to imagine, or, rather, it was only too easy to imagine.

I was alone on the poop. The ship having no steerage way, I had sent the helmsman away to sit down or lie down somewhere in the shade. The men's strength was so reduced that all unnecessary calls on it had to be avoided. It was the austere Gambril with the grizzly beard. He went away readily enough, but he was so weakened by repeated bouts of fever, poor fellow, that in order to get down the poop ladder he had to turn sideways and hang on with both hands to the brass rail. It was just simply heartbreaking to watch. Yet he was neither very much worse nor much better than most of the half-dozen miserable victims I could muster up on deck.

It was a terribly lifeless afternoon. For several days in succession low clouds had appeared in the distance, white masses with dark convolutions resting on the water, motionless, almost solid, and yet all the time changing their aspects subtly. Towards evening they vanished as a rule. But this day they awaited the setting sun, which glowed and smouldered sulkily amongst them before it sank down. The punctual and wearisome stars reappeared over our mastheads, but the air remained stagnant and oppressive.

The unfailing Ransome lighted the binnacle lamps and glided, all shadowy, up to me.

'Will you go down and try to eat something, sir?' he suggested.

His low voice startled me. I had been standing looking out over the rail, saying nothing, feeling nothing, not even the weariness of my limbs, overcome by the evil spell.

'Ransome,' I asked abruptly, 'how long have I been on deck? I am losing the notion of time.'

'Fourteen days, sir,' he said. 'It was a fortnight last Monday since we left the anchorage.'

His equable voice sounded mournful somehow. He waited a bit, then added: 'It's the first time that it looks as if we were to have some rain.'

I noticed then the broad shadow on the horizon extinguishing the low stars completely, while those overhead, when I looked up, seemed to shine down on us through a veil of smoke.

How it got there, how it had crept up so high, I couldn't say. It had an ominous appearance. The air did not stir. At a renewed invitation from Ransome I did go down into the cabin to – in his words – 'try to eat something'. I don't know that the trial was very successful. I suppose at that period I did exist on food in the usual way; but the memory is now that in those days life was sustained on invincible anguish, as a sort of infernal stimulant exciting and consuming at the same time.

It's the only period of my life in which I attempted to keep a diary. No, not the only one. Years later, in conditions of moral isolation, I did put down on paper the thoughts and events of a score of days. But this was the first time. I don't remember how it came about or how the pocket-book and the pencil came into my hands. It's inconceivable that I should have looked for them on purpose. I suppose they saved me from the crazy trick of talking to myself.

Strangely enough, in both cases I took to that sort of thing in circumstances in which I did not expect, in colloquial phrase, 'to come out of it'. Neither could I expect the record to outlast me. This shows that it was purely a personal need for intimate relief and not a call of egotism.

Here I must give another sample of it, a few detached lines, now looking very ghostly to my own eyes, out of the part scribbled that very evening –

There is something going on in the sky like a decomposition, like a corruption of the air, which remains as still as ever. After all, mere clouds, which may or may not hold wind or rain. Strange that it should trouble me so. I feel as if all my sins had found me out. But I suppose the trouble is that the ship is still lying motionless, not under command; and that I have nothing to do to keep my imagination from running wild amongst the disastrous images of the worst that may befall us. What's going to happen? Probably nothing. Or anything. It may be a furious squall coming, butt-end foremost. And on deck there are five men with the vitality and the strength of, say, two. We may have all our sails blown away. Every stitch of canvas has been on her since we broke ground at the mouth of the Meinam, fifteen days ago . . . or fifteen centuries. It seems to me that all my life before that momentous day is infinitely remote, a fading memory of light-hearted youth, something on the other side of a shadow. Yes, sails may very well be blown away. And that would be like a death sentence on the men. We haven't strength enough on board to bend another suit; incredible thought, but it is true. Or we may even get dismasted. Ships have been dismasted in squalls simply because they weren't handled quick enough, and we have no power to whirl the yards around. It's like being bound hand

and foot preparatory to having one's throat cut. And what appals me most of all is that I shrink from going on deck to face it. It's due to the ship, it's due to the men who are there on deck – some of them, ready to put out the last remnant of their strength at a word from me. And I am shrinking from it. From the mere vision. My first command. Now I understand that strange sense of insecurity in my past. I always suspected that I might be no good. And here is proof positive. I am shirking it. I am no good.

At that moment, or, perhaps, the moment after, I became aware of Ransome standing in the cabin. Something in his expression startled me. It had a meaning which I could not make out. I exclaimed: 'Somebody's dead!'

It was his turn then to look startled.

'Dead? Not that I know of, sir. I have been in the forecastle only ten minutes ago and there was no dead man there then.'

'You did give me a scare,' I said.

His voice was extremely pleasant to listen to. He explained that he had come down below to close Mr Burns' port in case it should come on to rain. He did not know that I was in the cabin, he added.

'How does it look outside?' I asked him.

'Very black indeed, sir. There is something in it for certain.'

'In what quarter?'

'All round, sir.'

I repeated idly: 'All round. For certain,' with my elbows on the table.

Ransome lingered in the cabin as if he had something to do there, but hesitated about doing it. I said suddenly: 'You think I ought to be on deck?'

He answered at once but without any particular emphasis or accent: 'I do, sir.'

I got to my feet briskly, and he made way for me to go out. As I passed through the lobby I heard Mr Burns' voice saying: 'Shut the door of my room, will you, steward?' And Ransome's rather surprised: 'Certainly, sir.'

I thought that all my feelings had been dulled into complete indifference. But I found it as trying as ever to be on deck. The impenetrable blackness beset the ship so close that it seemed that by thrusting one's hand over the side one could touch some unearthly substance. There was in it an effect of inconceivable terror and of inexpressible mystery. The few stars overhead shed a dim light upon the ship alone, with no gleams of any kind upon the water, in detached shafts piercing an atmosphere which had turned to soot. It was something I had never seen before, giving no hint of the direction from which any change would come, the closing in of a menace from all sides.

There was still no man at the helm. The immobility of all things was perfect. If the air had turned black, the sea, for all I knew, might have turned solid. It was no good looking in any direction, watching for any sign, speculating upon the nearness of the moment. When the time came the blackness would overwhelm silently the bit of starlight falling upon the ship, and the end of all things would come without a sigh, stir, or murmur of any kind, and all our hearts would cease to beat, like run-down clocks.

It was impossible to shake off that sense of finality. The quietness that came over me was like a foretaste of annihilation. It gave me a sort of comfort, as though my soul had become suddenly reconciled to an eternity of blind stillness.

The seaman's instinct alone survived whole in my moral dissolution. I descended the ladder to the quarterdeck. The starlight seemed to die out before reaching that spot, but when I asked quietly: 'Are you there, men?' my eyes made out shadowy forms starting up around me, very few, very indistinct; and a voice spoke: 'All here, sir.' Another amended anxiously: 'All that are any good for anything, sir.'

Both voices were very quiet and unringing; without any special character of readiness or discouragement. Very matter-of-fact voices.

'We must try to haul this mainsail close up,' I said.

The shadows swayed away from me without a word. Those men were the ghosts of themselves, and their weight on a rope could be no more than the weight of a bunch of ghosts. Indeed, if ever a sail was hauled up by sheer spiritual strength it must have been that sail, for, properly speaking, there was not muscle enough for the task in the whole ship, let alone the miserable lot of us on deck. Of course, I took the lead in the work myself. They wandered feebly after me from rope to rope, stumbling and panting. They toiled like Titans. We were an hour at it at least, and all the time the black universe made no sound. When the last leech-line was made fast, my eyes, accustomed to the darkness, made out the shapes of exhausted men drooping over the rails, collapsed on hatches. One hung over the after-capstan, sobbing for breath; and I stood amongst them like a tower of strength, impervious to disease and feeling only the sickness of my soul. I waited for some time, fighting against the weight of my sins, against my sense of unworthiness, and then I said: 'Now, men, we'll go aft and square the mainyard. That's about all we can do for the ship; and for the rest she must take her chance.'

Chapter 6

As we all went up it occurred to me that there ought to be a man at the helm. I raised my voice not much above a whisper, and, noiselessly, an uncomplaining spirit in a fever-wasted body appeared in the light aft, the head with hollow eyes illuminated against the blackness which had swallowed up our world – and the universe. The bared forearm extended over the upper spokes seemed to shine with a light of its own.

I murmured to that luminous appearance: 'Keep the helm right amidships.'

It answered in a tone of patient suffering: 'Right amidships, sir.'

Then I descended to the quarterdeck. It was impossible to tell whence the blow would come. To look round the ship was to look into a bottomless, black pit. The eye lost itself in inconceivable depths.

I wanted to ascertain whether the ropes had been picked up off the deck. One could only do that by feeling with one's feet. In my cautious progress I came against a man in whom I recognised Ransome. He possessed an unimpaired physical solidity which was manifest to me at the contact. He was leaning against the quarterdeck capstan and kept silent. It was like a revelation. He was the collapsed figure sobbing for breath I had noticed before we went on the poop.

'You have been helping with the mainsail!' I exclaimed in a low tone.

'Yes, sir,' sounded his quiet voice.

'Man! What were you thinking of? You mustn't do that sort of thing.'

After a pause he assented. 'I suppose I mustn't.' Then after another short silence he added: 'I am all right now,' quickly, between the tell-tale gasps.

I could neither hear nor see anybody else; but when I spoke up, answering sad murmurs filled the quarterdeck, and its shadows seemed to shift here and there. I ordered all the halyards laid down on deck clear for running.

'I'll see to that, sir,' volunteered Ransome in his natural, pleasant tone, which comforted one and aroused one's compassion too, somehow.

That man ought to have been in his bed, resting, and my plain duty was to send him there. But perhaps he would not have obeyed me. I had not the strength of mind to try. All I said was: 'Go about it quietly, Ransome.'

Returning on the poop I approached Gambril. His face, set with hollow shadows in the light, looked awful, finally silenced. I asked him how he felt, but hardly expected an answer. Therefore I was astonished at his comparative loquacity.

'Them shakes leaves me as weak as a kitten, sir,' he said, preserving finely that air of unconsciousness as to anything but his business a helmsman should never lose. 'And before I can pick up my strength that there hot fit comes along and knocks me over again.'

He sighed. There was no complaint in his tone, but the bare words were enough to give me a horrible pang of self-reproach. It held me dumb for a time. When the tormenting sensation had passed off I asked: 'Do you feel strong enough to prevent the rudder taking charge if she gets sternway on her? It wouldn't do to get something smashed about the steering-gear now. We've enough difficulties to cope with as it is.'

He answered with just a shade of weariness that he was strong enough to hang on. He could promise me that she shouldn't take the wheel out of his hands. More he couldn't say.

At that moment Ransome appeared quite close to me, stepping out of the darkness into visibility suddenly, as if just created with his composed face and pleasant voice.

Every rope on deck, he said, was laid down clear for running, as far as one could make certain by feeling. It was impossible to see anything. Frenchy had stationed himself forward. He said he had a jump or two left in him yet.

Here a faint smile altered for an instant the clear, firm design of Ransome's lips. With his serious clear, grey eyes, his serene temperament, he was a priceless man altogether. Soul as firm as the muscles of his body.

He was the only man on board (except me, but I had to preserve my liberty of movement) who had a sufficiency of muscular strength to trust to. For a moment I thought I had better ask him to take the wheel. But the dreadful knowledge of the enemy he had to carry about him made me hesitate. In my ignorance of physiology it occurred to me that he might die suddenly, from excitement, at a critical moment.

While this gruesome fear restrained the ready words on the tip of my tongue, Ransome stepped back two paces and vanished from my sight.

At once an uneasiness possessed me, as if some support had been withdrawn. I moved forward too, outside the circle of light, into the darkness that stood in front of me like a wall. In one stride I penetrated it. Such must have been the darkness before creation. It had closed behind me. I knew I was invisible to the man at the helm. Neither could I see anything. He was alone, I was alone, every man was alone where he stood. And every form was gone too, spar, sail, fittings, rails; everything was blotted out in the dreadful smoothness of that absolute night.

A flash of lightning would have been a relief – I mean physically. I would have prayed for it if it hadn't been for my shrinking apprehension of the thunder. In the tension of silence I was suffering from it seemed to me that the first crash must turn me into dust.

And thunder was, most likely, what would happen next. Stiff all over and hardly breathing, I waited with a horribly strained expectation. Nothing happened. It was maddening. But a dull, growing ache in the lower part of my face made me aware that I had been grinding my teeth madly enough, for God knows how long.

It's extraordinary I should not have heard myself doing it; but I hadn't. By an effort which absorbed all my faculties I managed to keep my jaw still. It required much attention, and while thus engaged I became bothered by curious, irregular sounds of faint tapping on the deck. They could be heard single, in pairs, in groups. While I wondered at this mysterious devilry, I received a slight blow under the left eye and felt an enormous tear run down my cheek. Raindrops. Enormous. Forerunners of something. Tap. Tap. Tap . . .

I turned about, and, addressing Gambril earnestly, entreated him to 'hang on to the wheel'. But I could hardly speak from emotion. The fatal moment had come. I held my breath. The tapping had stopped as unexpectedly as it had begun, and there was a renewed moment of intolerable suspense; something like an additional turn of the racking screw. I don't suppose I would have ever screamed, but I remember my conviction that there was nothing else for it but to scream.

Suddenly – how am I to convey it? Well, suddenly the darkness turned into water. This is the only suitable figure. A heavy shower, a downpour, comes along, making a noise. You hear its approach on the sea, in the air too, I verily believe. But this was different. With no preliminary whisper or rustle, without a splash, and even without the ghost of impact, I became instantaneously soaked to the skin. Not a very difficult matter, since I was wearing only my sleeping-suit. My hair got full of water in an instant, water streamed on my skin, it filled my nose, my ears, my eyes. In a fraction of a second I swallowed quite a lot of it.

As to Gambril, he was fairly choked. He coughed pitifully, the broken cough of a sick man; and I beheld him as one sees a fish in an aquarium by the light of an electric bulb, an elusive, phosphorescent shape. Only he did not glide away. But something else happened. Both binnacle lamps went out. I suppose the water forced itself into them, though I wouldn't have thought that possible, for they fitted into the cowl perfectly.

The last gleam of light in the universe had gone, pursued by a low exclamation of dismay from Gambril. I groped for him and seized his arm. How startlingly wasted it was.

'Never mind,' I said. 'You don't want the light. All you need to do is to keep the wind, when it comes, at the back of your head. You understand?'

'Aye, aye, sir . . . But I should like to have a light,' he added nervously.

All that time the ship lay as steady as a rock. The noise of the water pouring off the sails and spars, flowing over the break of the poop, had stopped short. The poop scuppers gurgled and sobbed for a little while longer, and then perfect silence, joined to perfect immobility, proclaimed the yet unbroken spell of our helplessness, poised on the edge of some violent issue, lurking in the dark.

I started forward restlessly. I did not need my sight to pace the poop of my ill-starred first command with perfect assurance. Every square foot of her decks was impressed indelibly on my brain, to the very grain and knots of the planks. Yet, all of a sudden, I fell clean over something, landing full length on my hands and face.

It was something big and alive. Not a dog – more like a sheep, rather. But there were no animals in the ship. How could an animal . . . It was an added and fantastic horror which I could not resist. The hair of my head stirred even as I picked myself up, awfully scared; not as a man is scared while his judgement, his reason still try to resist, but completely, boundlessly, and, as it were, innocently scared – like a little child.

I could see It – that Thing! The darkness, of which so much had just turned into water, had thinned down a little. There It was! But I did not hit upon the notion of Mr Burns issuing out of the companion on all fours till he attempted to stand up, and even then the idea of a bear crossed my mind first.

He growled like one when I seized him round the body. He had buttoned himself up into an enormous winter overcoat of some woolly material, the weight of which was too much for his reduced state. I could hardly feel the incredibly thin lath of his body, lost within the thick stuff, but his growl had depth and substance: Confounded dumb ship with a craven, tiptoeing crowd. Why couldn't they stamp and go with a brace? Wasn't there one God-forsaken lubber in the lot fit to raise a yell on a rope?

'Skulking's no good, sir,' he attacked me directly. 'You can't slink past the old murderous ruffian. It isn't the way. You must go for him boldly – as I did. Boldness is what you want. Show him that you don't care for any of his damned tricks. Kick up a jolly old row.'

'Good God, Mr Burns,' I said angrily. 'What on earth are you up to? What do you mean by coming up on deck in this state?'

'Just that! Boldness. The only way to scare the old bullying rascal.'

I pushed him, still growling, against the rail. 'Hold on to it,' I said roughly. I did not know what to do with him. I left him in a hurry, to go to Gambril, who had called faintly that he believed there was some wind aloft. Indeed, my own ears had caught a feeble flutter of wet canvas, high up overhead, the jingle of a slack chain sheet . . .

These were eerie, disturbing, alarming sounds in the dead stillness of the air around me. All the instances I had heard of topmasts being whipped out of a ship while there was not wind enough on her deck to blow out a match rushed into my memory.

'I can't see the upper sails, sir,' declared Gambril shakily.

'Don't move the helm. You'll be all right,' I said confidently.

The poor man's nerve was gone. I was not in much better case. It was the moment of breaking strain and was relieved by the abrupt sensation of the ship moving forward as if of herself under my feet. I heard plainly the soughing of the wind aloft, the low cracks of the upper spars taking the strain, long before I could feel the least draught on my face turned aft, anxious and sightless like the face of a blind man.

Suddenly a louder sounding note filled our ears, the darkness started streaming against our bodies, chilling them exceedingly. Both of us, Gambril and I, shivered violently in our clinging, soaked garments of thin cotton. I said to him: 'You are all right now, my man. All you've got to do is to keep the wind at the back of your head. Surely you are up to that. A child could steer this ship in smooth water.'

He muttered: 'Aye! A healthy child.' And I felt ashamed of having been passed over by the fever which had been preying on every man's strength but mine, in order that my remorse might be the more bitter, the feeling of unworthiness more poignant, and the sense of responsibility heavier to bear.

The ship had gathered great way on her almost at once on the calm water. I felt her slipping through it with no other noise but a mysterious rustle alongside. Otherwise she had no motion at all, neither lift nor roll. It was a disheartening steadiness which had lasted for eighteen days now; for never, never had we had wind enough in that time to raise the slightest run of the sea. The breeze freshened suddenly. I thought it was high time to get Mr Burns off the deck. He worried me. I looked upon him as a lunatic who would be very likely to start roaming over the ship and break a limb or fall overboard.

I was truly glad to find he had remained holding on where I had left him, sensibly enough. He was, however, muttering to himself ominously.

This was discouraging. I remarked in a matter-of-fact tone: 'We have never had so much wind as this since we left the roads.'

'There's some heart in it too,' he growled judiciously. It was a remark of a perfectly sane seaman. But he added immediately: 'It was about time I should come on deck. I've been nursing my strength for this – just for this. Do you see it, sir?'

I said I did, and proceeded to hint that it would be advisable for him to go below now and take a rest.

His answer was an indignant: 'Go below! Not if I know it, sir.'

Very cheerful! He was a horrible nuisance. And all at once he started to argue. I could feel his crazy excitement in the dark.

'You don't know how to go about it, sir. How could you? All this whispering and tiptoeing is no good. You can't hope to slink past a cunning, wide-awake, evil brute like he was. You never heard him talk. Enough to make your hair stand on end. No! No! He wasn't mad. He was no more mad than I am. He was just downright wicked. Wicked so as to frighten most people. I will tell you what he was. He was nothing less than a thief and a murderer at heart. And do you think he's any different now because he's dead? Not he! His carcass lies a hundred fathom under, but he's just the same . . . in latitude 8° 20' North.'

He snorted defiantly. I noted with weary resignation that the breeze had got lighter while he raved. He was at it again.

'I ought to have thrown the beggar out of the ship over the rail like a dog. It was only on account of the men . . . Fancy having to read the Burial Service over a brute like that! . . . "Our departed brother" . . . I could have laughed. That was what he couldn't bear. I suppose I am the only man that ever stood up to laugh at him. When he got sick it used to scare that . . . brother . . . Brother . . . Departed . . . Sooner call a shark brother.'

The breeze had let go so suddenly that the way of the ship brought the wet sails heavily against the masts. The spell of deadly stillness had caught us up again. There seemed to be no escape.

'Hallo!' exclaimed Mr Burns in a startled voice. 'Calm again!'

I addressed him as though he had been sane.

'This is the sort of thing we've been having for seventeen days, Mr Burns,'

I said with intense bitterness. 'A puff, then a calm, and in a moment, you'll see, she'll be swinging on her heel with her head away from her course to the devil somewhere.'

He caught at the word. 'The old dodging Devil,' he screamed piercingly, and burst into such a loud laugh as I had never heard before. It was a provoking, mocking peal, with a hair-raising, screeching over-note of defiance. I stepped back utterly confounded.

Instantly there was a stir on the quarterdeck, murmurs of dismay. A distressed voice cried out in the dark below us: 'Who's that gone crazy, now?'

Perhaps they thought it was their captain! Rush is not the word that could be applied to the utmost speed the poor fellows were up to; but in an amazing short time every man in the ship able to walk upright had found his way on to that poop.

I shouted to them: 'It's the mate. Lay hold of him a couple of you . . .'

I expected this performance to end in a ghastly sort of fight. But Mr Burns cut his derisive screeching dead short and turned upon them fiercely, yelling: 'Aha! Dog-gone ye! You've found your tongues – have ye? I thought you were dumb. Well, then – laugh! Laugh – I tell you. Now then – all together. One, two, three – laugh!'

A moment of silence ensued, of silence so profound that you could have heard a pin drop on the deck. Then Ransome's unperturbed voice uttered pleasantly the words: 'I think he has fainted, sir – ' The little motionless knot of men stirred, with low murmurs of relief. 'I've got him under the arms. Get hold of his legs, someone.'

Yes. It was a relief. He was silenced for a time – for a time. I could not have stood another peal of that insane screeching. I was sure of it; and just then Gambril, the austere Gambril, treated us to another vocal performance. He began to sing out for relief. His voice wailed pitifully in the darkness: 'Come aft, somebody! I can't stand this. Here she'll be off again directly and I can't . . .'

I dashed aft myself meeting on my way a hard gust of wind whose approach Gambril's ear had detected from afar and which filled the sails on the main in a series of muffled reports mingled with the low plaint of the spars. I was just in time to seize the wheel while Frenchy, who had followed me, caught up the collapsing Gambril. He hauled him out of the way, admonished him to lie still where he was, and then stepped up to relieve me, asking calmly: 'How am I to steer her, sir.'

'Dead before it, for the present. I'll get you a light in a moment.'

But going forward I met Ransome bringing up the spare binnacle lamp. That man noticed everything, attended to everything, shed comfort around him as he moved. As he passed me he remarked in a soothing tone that the stars were coming out. They were. The breeze was sweeping clear the sooty sky, breaking through the indolent silence of the sea.

The barrier of awful stillness which had encompassed us for so many days as though we had been accursed was broken. I felt that. I let myself fall on to the skylight seat. A faint white ridge of foam, thin, very thin, broke alongside. The first for ages – for ages. I could have cheered, if it hadn't been for the sense of guilt which clung to all my thoughts secretly. Ransome stood before me.

'What about the mate,' I asked anxiously. 'Still unconscious?'

'Well, sir – it's funny.' Ransome was evidently puzzled. 'He hasn't spoken a word, and his eyes are shut. But it looks to me more like sound sleep than anything else.'

I accepted this view as the least troublesome of any, or at any rate, least disturbing. Dead faint or deep slumber, Mr Burns had to be left to himself for the present. Ransome remarked suddenly: 'I believe you want a coat, sir.'

'I believe I do,' I sighed out.

But I did not move. What I felt I wanted were new limbs. My arms and legs seemed utterly useless, fairly worn out. They didn't even ache. But I stood up all the same to put on the coat when Ransome brought it up. And when he suggested that he had better now 'take Gambril forward', I said: 'All right. I'll help you to get him down on the main deck.'

I found that I was quite able to help, too. We raised Gambril up between us. He tried to help himself along like a man, but all the time he was enquiring piteously: 'You won't let me go when we come to the ladder? You won't let me go when we come to the ladder?'

The breeze kept on freshening and blew true, true to a hair. At daylight by careful manipulation of the helm we got the foreyards to run square by themselves (the water keeping smooth) and then went about hauling the ropes tight. Of the four men I had had with me at night, I could see now only two. I didn't enquire as to the others. They had given in. For a time only I hoped.

Our various tasks forward occupied us for hours, the two men with me moved so slowly and had to rest so often. One of them remarked that 'every blamed thing in the ship felt about a hundred times heavier than its proper weight'. This was the only complaint uttered. I don't know what we should have done without Ransome. He worked with us, silent too, with a little smile frozen on his lips. From time to time I murmured to him: 'Go steady' – 'Take it easy, Ransome' – and received a quick glance in reply.

When we had done all we could do to make things safe, he disappeared into his galley. Some time afterwards, going forward for a look round, I caught sight of him through the open door. He sat upright on the locker in front of the stove, with his head leaning back against the bulkhead. His eyes were closed; his capable hands held open the front of his thin cotton shirt baring tragically his powerful chest, which heaved in painful and laboured gasps. He didn't hear me.

I retreated quietly and went straight on to the poop to relieve Frenchy, who by that time was beginning to look very sick. He gave me the course with great formality and tried to go off with a jaunty step, but reeled widely twice before getting out of my sight.

And then I remained all alone aft, steering my ship, which ran before the wind with a buoyant lift now and then, and even rolling a little. Presently Ransome appeared before me with a tray. The sight of food made me ravenous all at once. He took the wheel while I sat down on the after grating to eat my breakfast.

'This breeze seems to have done for our crowd,' he murmured. 'It just laid them low – all hands.'

'Yes,' I said. 'I suppose you and I are the only two fit men in the ship.'

'Frenchy says there's still a jump left in him. I don't know. It can't be much,' continued Ransome with his wistful smile. 'Good little man that. But suppose, sir, that this wind flies round when we are close to the land – what are we going to do with her?'

'If the wind shifts round heavily after we close in with the land she will either run ashore or get dismasted or both. We won't be able to do anything with her. She's running away with us now. All we can do is to steer her. She's a ship without a crew.'

'Yes. All laid low,' repeated Ransome quietly. 'I do give them a look-in forward every now and then, but it's precious little I can do for them.'

'I, and the ship, and everyone on board of her, are very much indebted to you, Ransome,' I said warmly.

He made as though he had not heard me, and steered in silence till I was ready to relieve him. He surrendered the wheel, picked up the tray, and for a parting shot informed me that Mr Burns was awake and seemed to have a mind to come up on deck.

'I don't know how to prevent him, sir. I can't very well stop down below all the time.'

It was clear that he couldn't. And sure enough Mr Burns came on deck dragging himself painfully aft in his enormous overcoat. I beheld him with a natural dread. To have him around and raving about the wiles of a dead man while I had to steer a wildly rushing ship full of dying men was a rather dreadful prospect.

But his first remarks were quite sensible in meaning and tone. Apparently he had no recollection of the night scene. And if he had he didn't betray himself once. Neither did he talk very much. He sat on the skylight looking desperately ill at first, but that strong breeze, before which the last remnant of my crew had wilted down, seemed to blow a fresh stock of vigour into his frame with every gust. One could almost see the process.

By way of sanity test I alluded on purpose to the late captain. I was delighted to find that Mr Burns did not display undue interest in the subject. He ran over the old tale of that savage ruffian's iniquities with a certain vindictive gusto and then concluded unexpectedly: 'I do believe, sir, that his brain began to go a year or more before he died.'

A wonderful recovery. I could hardly spare it as much admiration as it deserved, for I had to give all my mind to the steering.

In comparison with the hopeless languor of the preceding days this was dizzy speed. Two ridges of foam streamed from the ship's bows; the wind sang in a strenuous note which under other circumstances would have expressed to me all the joy of life. Whenever the hauled-up mainsail started trying to slat and bang itself to pieces in its gear, Mr Burns would look at me apprehensively.

'What would you have me do, Mr Burns? We can neither furl it nor set it. I only wish the old thing would thrash itself to pieces and be done with it. This beastly racket confuses me.'

Mr Burns wrung his hands, and cried out suddenly: 'How will you get the ship into harbour, sir, without men to handle her?'

And I couldn't tell him.

Well – it did get done about forty hours afterwards. By the exorcising virtue of Mr Burns' awful laugh, the malicious spectre had been laid, the evil spell broken, the curse removed. We were now in the hands of a kind and energetic Providence. It was rushing us on . . .

I shall never forget the last night, dark, windy, and starry. I steered. Mr Burns, after having obtained from me a solemn promise to give him a kick if anything happened, went frankly to sleep on the deck close to the binnacle. Convalescents need sleep. Ransome, his back propped against the mizzenmast and a blanket over his legs, remained perfectly still, but I don't suppose he closed his eyes for a moment. That embodiment of jauntiness, Frenchy, still under the delusion that there was 'a jump' left in him, had insisted on joining us; but mindful of discipline, had laid himself down as far on the forepart of the poop as he could get, alongside the bucket-rack.

And I steered, too tired for anxiety, too tired for connected thought. I had moments of grim exultation and then my heart would sink awfully at the thought of that forecastle at the other end of the dark deck, full of fever-stricken men – some of them dying. By my fault. But never mind. Remorse must wait. I had to steer.

In the small hours the breeze weakened, then failed altogether. About five it returned, gentle enough, enabling us to head for the roadstead. Daybreak found Mr Burns sitting wedged up with coils of rope on the stern-grating, and from the depths of his overcoat steering the ship with very white bony hands; while Ransome and I rushed along the decks letting go all the sheets and halliards by the run. We dashed next up on to the forecastle head. The perspiration of labour and sheer nervousness simply poured off our heads as we toiled to get the anchors cock-billed. I dared not look at Ransome as we worked side by side. We exchanged curt words; I could hear him panting close to me and I avoided turning my eyes his way for fear of seeing him fall down and expire in the act of putting out his strength – for what? Indeed for some distinct ideal.

The consummate seaman in him was aroused. He needed no directions. He knew what to do. Every effort, every movement was an act of consistent heroism. It was not for me to look at a man thus inspired.

At last all was ready, and I heard him say, 'Hadn't I better go down and open the compressors now, sir?'

'Yes. Do,' I said. And even then I did not glance his way. After a time his voice came up from the main-deck: 'When you like, sir. All clear on the windlass here.'

I made a sign to Mr Burns to put the helm down and then I let both anchors go one after another, leaving the ship to take as much cable as she wanted. She took the best part of them both before she brought up. The loose sails coming aback ceased their maddening racket above my head. A perfect stillness reigned in the ship. And while I stood forward feeling a little giddy in that sudden peace, I caught faintly a moan or two and the incoherent mutterings of the sick in the forecastle.

As we had a signal for medical assistance flying on the mizzen it is a fact that before the ship was fairly at rest three steam-launches from various men-of-war arrived alongside; and at least five naval surgeons clambered on board. They stood in a knot gazing up and down the empty main deck, then looked aloft – where not a man could be seen either.

I went towards them – a solitary figure in a blue-and-grey-striped sleeping-suit and a pipe-clayed cork helmet on its head. Their disgust was extreme. They had expected surgical cases. Each one had brought his carving tools with him. But they soon got over their little disappointment. In less than five minutes one of the steam-launches was rushing shorewards to order a big boat and some hospital people for the removal of the crew. The big steam-pinnace went off to her ship to bring over a few bluejackets to furl my sails for me.

One of the surgeons had remained on board. He came out of the forecastle looking impenetrable, and noticed my enquiring gaze.

'There's nobody dead in there, if that's what you want to know,' he said deliberately. Then added in a tone of wonder: 'The whole crew!'

'And very bad?'

'And very bad,' he repeated. His eyes were roaming all over the ship. 'Heavens! What's that?'

'That,' I said, glancing aft, 'is Mr Burns, my chief officer.'

Mr Burns with his moribund head nodding on the stalk of his lean neck was a sight for anyone to exclaim at. The surgeon asked: 'Is he going to the hospital too?'

'Oh, no,' I said jocosely. 'Mr Burns can't go on shore till the mainmast goes. I am very proud of him. He's my only convalescent.'

'You look . . . ' began the doctor staring at me. But I interrupted him angrily: 'I am not ill.'

'No . . . You look queer.'

'Well, you see, I have been seventeen days on deck.'

'Seventeen! . . . But you must have slept.'

'I suppose I must have. I don't know. But I'm certain that I didn't sleep for the last forty hours.'

'Phew! . . . You will be going ashore presently, I suppose?'

'As soon as ever I can. There's no end of business waiting for me there.'

The surgeon released my hand, which he had taken while we talked, pulled out his pocket book, wrote in it rapidly, tore out the page, and offered it to me.

'I strongly advise you to get this prescription made up for yourself ashore. Unless I am much mistaken you will need it this evening.'

'What is it then?' I asked with suspicion.

'Sleeping draught,' answered the surgeon curtly; and moving with an air of interest towards Mr Burns he engaged him in conversation.

As I went below to dress to go ashore, Ransome followed me. He begged my pardon; he wished, too, to be sent ashore and paid off.

I looked at him in surprise. He was waiting for my answer with an air of anxiety.

'You don't mean to leave the ship!' I cried out.

'I do really, sir. I want to go and be quiet somewhere. Anywhere. The hospital will do.'

'But, Ransome,' I said, 'I hate the idea of parting with you.'

'I must go,' he broke in. 'I have a right!' He gasped and a look of almost savage determination passed over his face. For an instant he was another being. And I saw under the worth and the comeliness of the man the humble reality of things. Life was a boon to him – this precarious hard life – and he was thoroughly alarmed about himself.

'Of course I shall pay you off if you wish it,' I hastened to say. 'Only I must ask you to remain on board till this afternoon. I can't leave Mr Burns absolutely by himself in the ship for hours.'

He softened at once and assured me with a smile and in his natural pleasant voice that he understood that very well.

When I returned on deck everything was ready for the removal of the men. It was the last ordeal of that episode which had been maturing and tempering my character – though I did not know it.

It was awful. They passed under my eyes one after another – each of them an embodied reproach of the bitterest kind, till I felt a sort of revolt wake up in me. Poor Frenchy had gone suddenly under. He was carried past me insensible, his comic face horribly flushed and as if swollen, breathing stertorously. He looked more like Mr Punch than ever; a disgracefully intoxicated Mr Punch.

The austere Gambril, on the contrary, had improved temporarily. He insisted on walking on his own feet to the rail – of course with assistance on each side of him. But he gave way to a sudden panic at the moment of being swung over the side and began to wail pitifully: 'Don't let them drop me, sir.

Don't let them drop me, sir!' While I kept on shouting to him in most soothing accents: 'All right, Gambril. They won't! They won't!'

It was no doubt very ridiculous. The bluejackets on our deck were grinning quietly, while even Ransome himself (much to the fore in lending a hand) had to enlarge his wistful smile for a fleeting moment.

I left for the shore in the steam-pinnace, and on looking back beheld Mr Burns actually standing up by the taffrail, still in his enormous woolly overcoat. The bright sunlight brought out his weirdness amazingly. He looked like a frightful and elaborate scarecrow set up on the poop of a death-stricken ship, to keep the seabirds from the corpses.

Our story had got about already in town and everybody on shore was most kind. The marine office let me off the port dues, and as there happened to be a shipwrecked crew staying in the Home I had no difficulty in obtaining as many men as I wanted. But when I enquired if I could see Captain Ellis for a moment, I was told in accents of pity for my ignorance that our deputy-Neptune had retired and gone home on a pension about three weeks after I left the port. So I suppose that my appointment was the last act, outside the daily routine, of his official life.

It is strange how on coming ashore I was struck by the springy step, the lively eyes, the strong vitality of everyone I met. It impressed me enormously. And amongst those I met there was Captain Giles of course. It would have been very extraordinary if I had not met him. A prolonged stroll in the business part of the town was the regular employment of all his mornings when he was ashore.

I caught the glitter of the gold watch-chain across his chest ever so far away. He radiated benevolence.

'What is it I hear?' he queried with a 'kind uncle' smile, after shaking hands. 'Twenty-one days from Bankok?'

'Is this all you've heard?' I said. 'You must come to tiffin with me. I want you to know exactly what you have let me in for.'

He hesitated for almost a minute.

'Well – I will,' he decided condescendingly at last.

We turned into the hotel. I found to my surprise that I could eat quite a lot. Then over the cleared table-cloth I unfolded to Captain Giles all the story since I took command in all its professional and emotional aspects, while he smoked patiently the big cigar I had given him.

Then he observed sagely: 'You must feel jolly well tired by this time.'

'No,' I said. 'Not tired. But I'll tell you, Captain Giles, how I feel. I feel old. And I must be. All of you on shore look to me just a lot of skittish youngsters that have never known a care in the world.'

He didn't smile. He looked insufferably exemplary. He declared: 'That will pass. But you do look older – it's a fact.'

'Aha!' I said.

'No! No! The truth is that one must not make too much of anything in life, good or bad.'

'Live at half-speed,' I murmured perversely. 'Not everybody can do that.'

'You'll be glad enough presently if you can keep going even at that rate,' he retorted with his air of conscious virtue. 'And there's another thing: a man should stand up to his bad luck, to his mistakes, to his conscience, and all that sort of thing. Why – what else would you have to fight against?'

I kept silent. I don't know what he saw in my face, but he asked abruptly: 'Why – you aren't faint-hearted?'

'God only knows, Captain Giles,' was my sincere answer.

'That's all right,' he said calmly. 'You will learn soon how not to be faint-hearted. A man has got to learn everything – and that's what so many of those youngsters don't understand.'

'Well I am no longer a youngster.'

'No,' he conceded. 'Are you leaving soon?'

'I am going on board directly,' I said. 'I shall pick up one of my anchors and heave in to half-cable on the other as soon as my new crew comes on board and I shall be off at daylight tomorrow.'

'You will?' grunted Captain Giles approvingly. 'That's the way. You'll do.'

'What did you expect? That I would want to take a week ashore for a rest?' I said, irritated by his tone. 'There's no rest for me till she's out in the Indian Ocean and not much of it even then.'

He puffed at the cigar moodily, as if transformed.

'Yes, that's what it amounts to,' he said in a musing tone. It was as if a ponderous curtain had rolled up disclosing an unexpected Captain Giles. But it was only for a moment, merely the time to let him add: 'Precious little rest in life for anybody. Better not think of it.'

We rose, left the hotel, and parted from each other in the street with a warm handshake, just as he began to interest me for the first time in our intercourse.

The first thing I saw when I got back to the ship was Ransome on the quarterdeck sitting quietly on his neatly lashed sea-chest.

I beckoned him to follow me into the saloon where I sat down to write a letter of recommendation for him to a man I knew on shore.

When finished I pushed it across the table. 'It may be of some good to you when you leave the hospital.'

He took it, put it in his pocket. His eyes were looking away from me – nowhere. His face was anxiously set.

'How are you feeling now?' I asked.

'I don't feel bad now, sir,' he answered stiffly. 'But I am afraid of its coming on . . . ' The wistful smile came back on his lips for a moment. 'I – I am in a blue funk about my heart, sir.'

I approached him with extended hand. His eyes, not looking at me, had a strained expression. He was like a man listening for a warning call.

'Won't you shake hands, Ransome?' I said gently.

He exclaimed, flushed up dusky red, gave my hand a hard wrench – and next moment, left alone in the cabin, I listened to him going up the companion stairs cautiously, step by step, in mortal fear of starting into sudden anger our common enemy it was his hard fate to carry consciously within his faithful breast.

1915

THE TALE

Outside the large single window the crepuscular light was dying out slowly in a great square gleam without colour, framed rigidly in the gathering shades of the room.

It was a long room. The irresistible tide of the night ran into the most distant part of it, where the whispering of a man's voice, passionately interrupted and passionately renewed, seemed to plead against the answering murmurs of infinite sadness.

At last no answering murmur came. His movement when he rose slowly from his knees by the side of the deep, shadowy couch holding the shadowy suggestion of a reclining woman revealed him tall under the low ceiling, and sombre all over except for the crude discord of the white collar under the shape of his head and the faint, minute spark of a brass button here and there on his uniform.

He stood over her a moment masculine and mysterious in his immobility before he sat down on a chair near by. He could see only the faint oval of her upturned face and, extended on her black dress, her pale hands, a moment before abandoned to his kisses and now as if too weary to move.

He dared not make a sound, shrinking as a man would do from the prosaic necessities of existence. As usual, it was the woman who had the courage. Her voice was heard first – almost conventional – while her being vibrated yet with conflicting emotions.

'Tell me something,' she said.

The darkness hid his surprise and then his smile. Had he not just said to her everything worth saying in the world – and that not for the first time!

'What am I to tell you?' he asked, in a voice creditably steady. He was beginning to feel grateful to her for that something final in her tone which had eased the strain.

'Why not tell me a tale?'

'A tale!' He was really amazed.

'Yes. Why not?'

These words came with a slight petulance, the hint of a loved woman's capricious will, which is capricious only because it feels itself to be a law, embarrassing sometimes and always difficult to elude.

'Why not?' he repeated, with a slightly mocking accent, as though he had been asked to give her the moon. But now he was feeling a little angry with her for that feminine mobility that slips out of an emotion as easily as out of a splendid gown.

He heard her say a little unsteadily, with a sort of fluttering intonation which made him think suddenly of a butterfly's flight: 'You used to tell – your – your simple and – and professional – tales very well at one time. Or well enough to interest me. You had a – a sort of art – in the days – the days before the war.'

'Really?' he said, with involuntary gloom. 'But now, you see, the war is going on,' he continued in such a dead, equable tone that she felt a slight chill fall over her shoulders. And yet she persisted. For there's nothing more unswerving in the world than a woman's caprice.

'It could be a tale not of this world,' she explained.

'You want a tale of the other, the better world?' he asked, with matter-of-fact surprise. 'You must evoke for that task those who have already gone there.'

'No. I don't mean that. I mean another – some other – world. In the universe – not in heaven.'

'I am relieved. But you forget that I have only a five days' leave.'

'Yes. And I've also taken a five days' leave from – from my duties.'

'I like that word.'

'What word?'

'Duty.'

'It is horrible sometimes.'

'Oh, that's because you think it's narrow. But it isn't. It contains infinities, and – and so – '

'What is this jargon?'

He disregarded the interjected scorn. 'An infinity of absolution, for instance,' he continued. 'But as to this "another world" – who's going to look for it and for the tale that is in it?'

'You,' she said, with a strange, almost rough, sweetness of assertion.

He made a shadowy movement of assent in his chair, the irony of which not even the gathered darkness could render mysterious.

'As you will. In that world, then, there was once upon a time a Commanding Officer and a Northman. Put in the capitals, please, because they had no other names. It was a world of seas and continents and islands – '

'Like the earth,' she murmured, bitterly.

'Yes. What else could you expect from sending a man made of our common, tormented clay on a voyage of discovery? What else could he find? What else could you understand or care for, or feel the existence of even? There was comedy in it and slaughter.'

'Always like the earth,' she murmured.

'Always. And since I could find in the universe only what was deeply rooted in the fibres of my being there was love in it too. But we won't talk of that.'

'No. We won't,' she said, in a neutral tone which concealed perfectly her relief – or her disappointment. Then after a pause she added: 'It's going to be a comic story.'

'Well – ' he paused too. 'Yes. In a way. In a very grim way. It will be human, and, as you know, comedy is but a matter of the visual angle. And it won't be a noisy story. All the long guns in it will be dumb – as dumb as so many telescopes.'

'Ah, there are guns in it, then! And may I ask – where?'

'Afloat. You remember that the world of which we speak had its seas. A war was going on in it. It was a funny world and terribly in earnest. Its war was being carried on over the land, over the water, under the water, up in the air, and even under the ground. And many young men in it, mostly in wardrooms and messrooms, used to say to each other – pardon the unparliamentary word – they used to say, "It's a damned bad war, but it's better than no war at all." Sounds flippant, doesn't it?'

He heard a nervous, impatient sigh in the depths of the couch while he went on without a pause: 'And yet there is more in it than meets the eye. I mean more wisdom. Flippancy, like comedy, is but a matter of visual first-impression. That world was not very wise. But there was in it a certain amount of common working sagacity. That, however, was mostly worked by the neutrals in diverse ways, public and private, which had to be watched; watched by acute minds and also by actual sharp eyes. They had to be very sharp indeed, too, I assure you.'

'I can imagine,' she murmured, appreciatively.

'What is there that you can't imagine?' he pronounced, soberly. 'You have the world in you. But let us go back to our Commanding Officer, who, of course, commanded a ship of a sort. My tales if often professional (as you remarked just now) have never been technical. So I'll just tell you that the ship was of a very ornamental sort once, with lots of grace and elegance and luxury about her. Yes, once! She was like a pretty woman who had suddenly put on a suit of sackcloth and stuck revolvers in her belt. But she floated lightly, she moved nimbly, she was quite good enough.'

'That was the opinion of the Commanding Officer?' said the voice from the couch.

'It was. He used to be sent out with her along certain coasts to see – what he could see. Just that. And sometimes he had some preliminary information to help him, and sometimes he had not. And it was all one, really. It was about as useful as information trying to convey the locality and intentions of a cloud, of a phantom taking shape here and there and impossible to seize, would have been.

'It was in the early days of the war. What at first used to amaze the Commanding Officer was the unchanged face of the waters, with its familiar expression, neither more friendly nor more hostile. On fine days the sun strikes sparks upon the blue; here and there a peaceful smudge of smoke hangs in the distance, and it is impossible to believe that the familiar clear horizon traces the limit of one great circular ambush.

'Yes, it is impossible to believe, till someday you see a ship, not your own ship (that isn't so impressive), but some ship in company, blow up all of a sudden and plop under almost before you know what has happened to her. Then you begin to believe. Henceforth you go out for the work to see – what you can see, and you keep on at it with the conviction that someday you will die from something you have not seen. One envies the soldiers at the end of the day, wiping the sweat and blood from their faces, counting the dead fallen to their hands, looking at the devastated fields, the torn earth that seems to suffer and bleed with them. One does, really. The final brutality of it – the taste of primitive passion – the ferocious frankness of the blow struck with one's hand – the direct call and the straight response. Well, the sea gave you nothing of that, and seemed to pretend that there was nothing the matter with the world.'

She interrupted, stirring a little.

'Oh, yes. Sincerity – frankness – passion – three words of your gospel. Don't I know them!'

'Think! Isn't it ours – believed in common?' he asked, anxiously, yet without expecting an answer, and went on at once. 'Such were the feelings of the Commanding Officer. When the night came trailing over the sea, hiding what looked like the hypocrisy of an old friend, it was a relief. The night blinds you frankly – and there are circumstances when the sunlight may grow as odious to one as falsehood itself. Night is all right.

'At night the Commanding Officer could let his thoughts get away – I won't tell you where. Somewhere where there was no choice but between truth and death. But thick weather, though it blinded one, brought no such relief. Mist is deceitful, the dead luminosity of the fog is irritating. It seems that you *ought* to see.

'One gloomy, nasty day the ship was steaming along her beat in sight of a rocky, dangerous coast that stood out intensely black like an Indian-ink drawing on grey paper. Presently the Second in Command spoke to his chief. He thought he saw something on the water, to seaward. Small wreckage, perhaps.

' "But there shouldn't be any wreckage here, sir," he remarked.

' "No," said the Commanding Officer. "The last reported submarined ships were sunk a long way to the westward. But one never knows. There may have been others since then not reported nor seen. Gone with all hands."

'That was how it began. The ship's course was altered to pass the object close; for it was necessary to have a good look at what one could see. Close, but without touching; for it was not advisable to come in contact with objects of any form whatever floating casually about. Close, but without stopping or even diminishing speed; for in those times it was not prudent to linger on any particular spot, even for a moment. I may tell you at once that the object was not dangerous in itself. No use in describing it. It may have been nothing more remarkable than, say, a barrel of a certain shape and colour. But it was significant.

'The smooth bow-wave hove it up as if for a closer inspection, and then the ship, brought again to her course, turned her back on it with indifference, while twenty pairs of eyes on her deck stared in all directions trying to see – what they could see.

'The Commanding Officer and his Second in Command discussed the object with understanding. It appeared to them to be not so much a proof of the sagacity as of the activity of certain neutrals. This activity had in many cases taken the form of replenishing the stores of certain submarines at sea. This was generally believed, if not absolutely known. But the very nature of things in those early days pointed that way. The object, looked at closely and turned away from with apparent indifference, put it beyond doubt that something of the sort had been done somewhere in the neighbourhood.

'The object in itself was more than suspect. But the fact of its being left in evidence roused other suspicions. Was it the result of some deep and devilish purpose? As to that all speculation soon appeared to be a vain thing. Finally the two officers came to the conclusion that it was left there most likely by accident, complicated possibly by some unforeseen necessity; such, perhaps, as the sudden need to get away quickly from the spot, or something of that kind.

'Their discussion had been carried on in curt, weighty phrases, separated by long, thoughtful silences. And all the time their eyes roamed about the horizon in an everlasting, almost mechanical effort of vigilance. The younger man summed up grimly: "Well, it's evidence. That's what this is. Evidence of what we were pretty certain of before. And plain, too."

' "And much good it will do to us," retorted the Commanding Officer. "The parties are miles away; the submarine, devil only knows where, ready to kill; and the noble neutral slipping away to the eastward, ready to lie!"

'The Second in Command laughed a little at the tone. But he guessed that the neutral wouldn't even have to lie very much. Fellows like that, unless caught in the very act, felt themselves pretty safe. They could afford to chuckle. That fellow was probably chuckling to himself. It's very possible he had been before at the game and didn't care a rap for the bit of evidence left behind. It was a game in which practice made one bold and successful too.

'And again he laughed faintly. But his Commanding Officer was in revolt against the murderous stealthiness of methods and the atrocious callousness of complicities that seemed to taint the very source of men's deep emotions and noblest activities; to corrupt their imagination which builds up the final conceptions of life and death. He suffered – '

The voice from the sofa interrupted the narrator.

'How well I can understand that in him!'

He bent forward slightly.

'Yes. I too. Everything should be open in love and war. Open as the day, since both are the call of an ideal which it is so easy, so terribly easy, to degrade in the name of Victory.'

He paused: then went on: 'I don't know that the Commanding Officer delved so deep as that into his feelings. But he did suffer from them – a sort of disenchanted sadness. It is possible, even, that he suspected himself of folly. Man is various. But he had no time for much introspection, because from the south-west a wall of fog had advanced upon his ship. Great convolutions of vapours flew over, swirling about masts and funnel, which looked as if they were beginning to melt. Then they vanished.

'The ship was stopped, all sounds ceased, and the very fog became motionless, growing denser and as if solid in its amazing dumb immobility. The men at their stations lost sight of each other. Footsteps sounded stealthy; rare voices, impersonal and remote, died out without resonance. A blind white stillness took possession of the world.

'It looked, too, as if it would last for days. I don't mean to say that the fog did not vary a little in its density. Now and then it would thin out mysteriously, revealing to the men a more or less ghostly presentment of their ship. Several times the shadow of the coast itself swam darkly before their eyes through the fluctuating opaque brightness of the great white cloud clinging to the water.

'Taking advantage of these moments, the ship had been moved cautiously nearer the shore. It was useless to remain out in such thick weather. Her officers knew every nook and cranny of the coast along their beat. They thought that she would be much better in a certain cove. It wasn't a large place, just ample room for a ship to swing at her anchor. She would have an easier time of it till the fog lifted up.

'Slowly, with infinite caution and patience, they crept closer and closer, seeing no more of the cliffs than an evanescent dark loom with a narrow border of angry foam at its foot. At the moment of anchoring the fog was so thick that for all they could see they might have been a thousand miles out in the open sea. Yet the shelter of the land could be felt. There was a peculiar quality in the stillness of the air. Very faint, very elusive, the wash of the ripple against the encircling land reached their ears, with mysterious sudden pauses.

'The anchor dropped, the leads were laid in. The Commanding Officer went below into his cabin. But he had not been there very long when a voice outside his door requested his presence on deck. He thought to himself: "What is it now?" He felt some impatience at being called out again to face the wearisome fog.

'He found that it had thinned again a little and had taken on a gloomy hue from the dark cliffs which had no form, no outline, but asserted themselves as a curtain of shadows all round the ship, except in one bright spot, which was the entrance from the open sea. Several officers were looking that way from the bridge. The Second in Command met him with the breathlessly whispered information that there was another ship in the cove.

'She had been made out by several pairs of eyes only a couple of minutes before. She was lying at anchor very near the entrance – a mere vague blot on the fog's brightness. And the Commanding Officer by staring in the direction pointed out to him by eager hands ended by distinguishing it at last himself. Indubitably a vessel of some sort.

' "It's a wonder we didn't run slap into her when coming in," observed the Second in Command.

' "Send a boat on board before she vanishes," said the Commanding Officer. He surmised that this was a coaster. It could hardly be anything else. But another thought came into his head suddenly. "It is a wonder," he said to his Second in Command, who had rejoined him after sending the boat away.

'By that time both of them had been struck by the fact that the ship so suddenly discovered had not manifested her presence by ringing her bell.

' "We came in very quietly, that's true," concluded the younger officer. "But they must have heard our leadsmen at least. We couldn't have passed her more than fifty yards off. The closest shave! They may even have made us out, since they were aware of something coming in. And the strange thing is that we never heard a sound from her. The fellows on board must have been holding their breath."

' "Aye," said the Commanding Officer, thoughtfully.

'In due course the boarding-boat returned, appearing suddenly alongside, as though she had burrowed her way under the fog. The officer in charge came up to make his report, but the Commanding Officer didn't give him time to begin.

'He cried from a distance: "Coaster, isn't she?"

' "No, sir. A stranger – a neutral," was the answer.

' "No. Really! Well, tell us all about it. What is she doing here?"

'The young man stated then that he had been told a long and complicated story of engine troubles. But it was plausible enough from a strictly professional point of view and it had the usual features: disablement, dangerous drifting along the shore, weather more or less thick for days, fear of a gale, ultimately a resolve to go in and anchor anywhere on the coast, and so on. Fairly plausible.

' "Engines still disabled?" enquired the Commanding Officer.

' "No, sir. She has steam on them."

'The Commanding Officer took his Second aside. "By Jove!" he said, "you were right! They were holding their breaths as we passed them. They were."

'But the Second in Command had his doubts now.

' "A fog like this does muffle small sounds, sir," he remarked. "And what could his object be, after all?"

' "To sneak out unnoticed," answered the Commanding Officer.

' "Then why didn't he? He might have done it, you know. Not exactly unnoticed, perhaps. I don't suppose he could have slipped his cable without making some noise. Still, in a minute or so he would have been lost to view – clean gone before we had made him out fairly. Yet he didn't."

'They looked at each other. The Commanding Officer shook his head. Such suspicions as the one which had entered his head are not defended easily. He did not even state it openly. The boarding officer finished his report. The cargo of the ship was of a harmless and useful character. She was bound to an English port. Papers and everything in perfect order. Nothing suspicious to be detected anywhere.

'Then passing to the men, he reported the crew on deck as the usual lot. Engineers of the well-known type, and very full of their achievement in repairing the engines. The mate surly. The master rather a fine specimen of a Northman, civil enough, but appeared to have been drinking. Seemed to be recovering from a regular bout of it.

' "I told him I couldn't give him permission to proceed. He said he wouldn't dare to move his ship her own length out in such weather as this, permission or no permission. I left a man on board though."

' "Quite right."

'The Commanding Officer, after communing with his suspicions for a time, called his Second aside.

' "What if she were the very ship which had been feeding some infernal submarine or other?" he said in an undertone.

'The other started. Then, with conviction: "She would get off scot-free. You couldn't prove it, sir."

' "I want to look into it myself."

' "From the report we've heard I am afraid you couldn't even make a case for reasonable suspicion, sir."

' "I'll go on board all the same."

'He had made up his mind. Curiosity is the great motive power of hatred and love. What did he expect to find? He could not have told anybody – not even himself.

'What he really expected to find there was the atmosphere, the atmosphere of gratuitous treachery, which in his view nothing could excuse; for he thought that even a passion of unrighteousness for its own sake could not excuse that. But could he detect it? Sniff it? Taste it? Receive some mysterious communication which would turn his invincible suspicions into a certitude strong enough to provoke action with all its risks?

'The master met him on the after-deck, loomed up in the fog amongst the blurred shapes of the usual ships' fittings. He was a robust Northman, bearded, and in the force of his age. A round leather cap fitted his head closely. His hands were rammed deep into the pockets of his short leather jacket. He kept them there while he explained that at sea he lived in the chart-room, and led the way there, striding carelessly. Just before reaching the door under the bridge he staggered a little, recovered himself, flung it open, and stood aside, leaning his shoulder as if involuntarily against the side of the house, and staring vaguely into the fog-filled space. But he followed the Commanding Officer at once, flung the door to, snapped on the electric light, and hastened to thrust his hands back into his pockets, as though afraid of being seized by them either in friendship or in hostility.

'The place was stuffy and hot. The usual chart-rack overhead was full, and the chart on the table was kept unrolled by an empty cup standing on a saucer half-full of some spilt dark liquid. A slightly nibbled biscuit reposed on the chronometer-case. There were two settees, and one of them had been made up into a bed with a pillow and some blankets, which were now very much tumbled. The Northman let himself fall on it, his hands still in his pockets.

' "Well, here I am," he said, with a curious air of being surprised at the sound of his own voice.

'The Commanding Officer from the other settee observed the handsome flushed face. Drops of fog hung on the yellow beard and moustaches of the Northman. The much darker eyebrows ran together in a puzzled frown, and suddenly he jumped up.

' "What I mean is that I don't know where I am. I really don't," he burst out, with extreme earnestness. "Hang it all! I got turned around somehow. The fog has been after me for a week. More than a week. And then my engines broke down. I will tell you how it was."

'He burst out into loquacity. It was not hurried, but it was insistent. It was not continuous for all that. It was broken by the most queer, thoughtful pauses. Each of these pauses lasted no more than a couple of seconds, and each had the profundity of an endless meditation. When he began again nothing betrayed in him the slightest consciousness of these intervals. There was the same fixed glance, the same unchanged earnestness of tone. He didn't know. Indeed, more than one of these pauses occurred in the middle of a sentence.

'The Commanding Officer listened to the tale. It struck him as more plausible than simple truth is in the habit of being. But that, perhaps, was prejudice. All the time the Northman was speaking the Commanding Officer had been aware of an inward voice, a grave murmur in the depth of his very own self, telling another tale, as if on purpose to keep alive in him his indignation and his anger with that baseness of greed or of mere outlook which lies often at the root of simple ideas.

'It was the story that had been already told to the boarding officer an hour or so before. The Commanding Officer nodded slightly at the Northman from time to time. The latter came to an end and turned his eyes away. He added, as an afterthought: "Wasn't it enough to drive a man out of his mind with worry? And it's my first voyage to this part, too. And the ship's my own. Your officer has seen the papers. She isn't much, as you can see for yourself. Just an old cargo-boat. Bare living for my family."

'He raised a big arm to point at a row of photographs plastering the bulkhead. The movement was ponderous, as if the arm had been made of lead.

'The Commanding Officer said, carelessly: "You will be making a fortune yet for your family with this old ship."

' "Yes, if I don't lose her," said the Northman, gloomily.

' "I mean – out of this war," added the Commanding Officer.

'The Northman stared at him in a curiously unseeing and at the same time interested manner, as only eyes of a particular blue shade can stare.

' "And you wouldn't be angry at it," he said, "would you? You are too much of a gentleman. We didn't bring this on you. And suppose we sat down and cried. What good would that be? Let those cry who made the trouble," he concluded, with energy. "Time's money, you say. Well – *this* time *is* money. Oh! isn't it!"

'The Commanding Officer tried to keep under the feeling of immense disgust. He said to himself that it was unreasonable. Men were like that – moral cannibals feeding on each other's misfortunes. He said aloud: "You have made it perfectly plain how it is that you are here. Your log-book confirms you very minutely. Of course, a log-book may be cooked. Nothing easier."

'The Northman never moved a muscle. He was gazing at the floor; he seemed not to have heard. He raised his head after a while.

' "But you can't suspect me of anything," he muttered, negligently.

'The Commanding Officer thought: "Why should he say this?"

'Immediately afterwards the man before him added: "My cargo is for an English port."

'His voice had turned husky for the moment. The Commanding Officer reflected: "That's true. There can be nothing. I can't suspect him. Yet why was he lying with steam up in this fog – and then, hearing us come in, why didn't he give some sign of life? Why? Could it be anything else but a guilty conscience? He could tell by the leadsmen that this was a man-of-war."

'Yes – why? The Commanding Officer went on thinking: "Suppose I ask him and then watch his face. He will betray himself in some way. It's perfectly plain that the fellow *has* been drinking. Yes, he has been drinking; but he will have a lie ready all the same." The Commanding Officer was one of those men who are made morally and almost physically uncomfortable by the mere thought of having to beat down a lie. He shrank from the act in scorn and disgust, which was invincible because more temperamental than moral.

'So he went out on deck instead and had the crew mustered formally for his inspection. He found them very much what the report of the boarding officer had led him to expect. And from their answers to his questions he could discover no flaw in the log-book story.

'He dismissed them. His impression of them was – a picked lot; have been promised a fistful of money each if this came off; all slightly anxious, but not frightened. Not a single one of them likely to give the show away. They don't feel in danger of their life. They know England and English ways too well!

'He felt alarmed at catching himself thinking as if his vaguest suspicions were turning into a certitude. For, indeed, there was no shadow of reason for his interference. There was nothing to give away.

'He returned to the chart-room. The Northman had lingered behind there; and something subtly different in his bearing, more bold in his blue, glassy stare, induced the Commanding Officer to conclude that the fellow had snatched at the opportunity to take another swig at the bottle he must have had concealed somewhere.

'He noticed, too, that the Northman on meeting his eyes put on an elaborately surprised expression. At least, it seemed elaborated. Nothing could be trusted. And the Englishman felt himself with astonishing conviction faced by an enormous lie, solid like a wall, with no way round to get at the truth, whose ugly murderous face he seemed to see peeping over at him with a cynical grin.

' "I dare say," he began, suddenly, "you are wondering at my proceedings, though I am not detaining you, am I? You wouldn't dare to move in thick fog?"

' "I don't know where I am," the Northman ejaculated, earnestly. "I really don't."

'He looked around as if the very chart-room fittings were strange to him. The Commanding Officer asked him whether he had not seen any unusual objects floating about while he was at sea.

' "Objects! What objects? We were groping blind in the fog for days."

' "We had a few clear intervals," said the Commanding Officer. "And I'll tell you what we have seen and the conclusion I've come to about it."

'He told him in a few words. He heard the sound of a sharp breath indrawn through closed teeth. The Northman with his hand on the table stood absolutely motionless and dumb. He stood as if thunderstruck. Then he produced a fatuous smile.

'Or at least so it appeared to the Commanding Officer. Was this significant, or of no meaning whatever? He didn't know, he couldn't tell. All the truth had departed out of the world as if drawn in, absorbed in this monstrous villainy this man was – or was not – guilty of.

' "Shooting's too good for people that conceive neutrality in this pretty way," remarked the Commanding Officer, after a silence.

' "Yes, yes, yes," the Northman assented, hurriedly – then added an unexpected and dreamy-voiced, "Perhaps."

'Was he pretending to be drunk, or only trying to appear sober? His glance was straight, but it was somewhat glazed. His lips outlined themselves firmly under his yellow moustache. But they twitched. Did they twitch? And why was he drooping like this in his attitude?

' "There's no perhaps about it," pronounced the Commanding Officer sternly.

'The Northman had straightened himself. And unexpectedly he looked stern too.

' "No. But what about the tempters? Better kill that lot off. There's about four, five, six million of them," he said, grimly; but in a moment changed into a whining key. "But I had better hold my tongue. You have some suspicions."

' "No, I've no suspicions," declared the Commanding Officer.

never faltered. At that moment he had the certitude. The air of the room was thick with guilt and falsehood braving the discovery, defying the right, common decency, all humanity of feeling, every scruple of conduct.

'The Northman drew a long breath. "Well, we know that you English are gentlemen. But let us speak the truth. Why should we love you so very much? You haven't done anything to be loved. We don't love the other people, of course. They haven't done anything for that either. A fellow comes along with a bag of gold . . . I haven't been in Rotterdam my last voyage for nothing."

' "You may be able to tell something interesting, then, to our people when you come into port," interjected the Officer.

' "I might. But you keep some people in your pay at Rotterdam. Let them report. I am a neutral – am I not? . . . Have you ever seen a poor man on one side and a bag of gold on the other? Of course, I couldn't be tempted. I haven't the nerve for it. Really I haven't. It's nothing to me. I am just talking openly for once."

' "Yes. And I am listening to you," said the Commanding Officer quietly.

'The Northman leaned forward over the table. "Now that I know you have no suspicions, I talk. You don't know what a poor man is. I do. I am poor myself. This old ship, she isn't much, and she is mortgaged, too. Bare living, no more. Of course, I wouldn't have the nerve. But a man who has nerve! See. The stuff he takes aboard looks like any other cargo – packages, barrels, tins, copper tubes – what not. He doesn't see it work. It isn't real to him. But he sees the gold. That's real. Of course, nothing could induce me. I suffer from an internal disease. I would either go crazy from anxiety – or – or – take to drink or something. The risk is too great. Why – ruin!"

' "It should be death." The Commanding Officer got up, after this curt declaration, which the other received with a hard stare oddly combined with an uncertain smile. The Officer's gorge rose at the atmosphere of murderous complicity which surrounded him, denser, more impenetrable, more acrid than the fog outside.

' "It's nothing to me," murmured the Northman, swaying visibly.

' "Of course not," assented the Commanding Officer, with a great effort to keep his voice calm and low. The certitude was strong within him. "But I am going to clear all you fellows off this coast at once. And I will begin with you. You must leave in half an hour."

'By that time the Officer was walking along the deck with the Northman at his elbow.

' "What! In this fog?" the latter cried out, huskily.

' "Yes, you will have to go in this fog."

' "But I don't know where I am. I really don't."

'The Commanding Officer turned round. A sort of fury possessed him. The eyes of the two men met. Those of the Northman expressed a profound amazement.

' "Oh, you don't know how to get out." The Commanding Officer spoke with composure, but his heart was beating with anger and dread. "I will give you your course. Steer south-by-east-half-east for about four miles and then you will be clear to haul to the eastward for your port. The weather will clear up before very long."

' "Must I? What could induce me? I haven't the nerve."

' "And yet you must go. Unless you want to – "

' "I don't want to," panted the Northman. "I've enough of it."

'The Commanding Officer got over the side. The Northman remained still as if rooted to the deck. Before his boat reached his ship the Commanding Officer heard the steamer beginning to pick up her anchor. Then, shadowy in the fog, she steamed out on the given course.

' "Yes," he said to his officers, "I let him go." '

The narrator bent forward towards the couch, where no movement betrayed the presence of a living person.

'Listen,' he said, forcibly. 'That course would lead the Northman straight on a deadly ledge of rock. And the Commanding Officer gave it to him. He steamed out – ran on it – and went down. So he had spoken the truth. He did not know where he was. But it proves nothing. Nothing either way. It may have been the only truth in all his story. And yet . . . He seems to have been driven out by a menacing stare – nothing more.'

He abandoned all pretence.

'Yes, I gave that course to him. It seemed to me a supreme test. I believe – no, I don't believe. I don't know. At the time I was certain. They all went down; and I don't know whether I have done stern retribution – or murder; whether I have added to the corpses that litter the bed of the unreadable sea the bodies of men completely innocent or basely guilty. I don't know. I shall never know.'

He rose. The woman on the couch got up and threw her arms round his neck. Her eyes put two gleams in the deep shadow of the room. She knew his passion for truth, his horror of deceit, his humanity.

'Oh, my poor, poor – '

'I shall never know,' he repeated, sternly, disengaged himself, pressed her hands to his lips, and went out.

1917